KING
RAVEN

OTHER BOOKS BY STEPHEN R. LAWHEAD

The Skin Map
Patrick, Son of Ireland

THE CELTIC CRUSADES:
The Iron Lance
The Black Rood
The Mystic Rose
Byzantium

THE SONG OF ALBION:
The Paradise War
The Silver Hand
The Endless Knot

THE PENDRAGON CYCLE:
Taliesin
Merlin
Arthur
Pendragon
Grail
Avalon
Empyrion I: The Search for Fierra
Empyrion II: The Siege of Dome
Dream Thief

THE DRAGON KING TRILOGY:
In the Hall of the Dragon King
The Warlords of Nin
The Sword and the Flame

KING RAVEN

The Complete Trilogy: Hood, Scarlet, and Tuck

STEPHEN R. LAWHEAD

THOMAS NELSON

Since 1798

NASHVILLE   DALLAS   MEXICO CITY   RIO DE JANEIRO

Published in Nashville, Tennessee, by Thomas Nelson. Thomas Nelson is a registered trademark of Thomas Nelson, Inc.

Thomas Nelson, Inc., titles may be purchased in bulk for educational, business, fund-raising, or sales promotional use. For information, please e-mail SpecialMarkets@ThomasNelson.com.

Map illustration created by Mary Hooper.

ISBN: 978-1-40168-538-6

Printed in the United States of America
11 12 13 14 15 QG 5 4 3 2 1

✄ CONTENTS ✄

Pronunciation Guide

Many of the old Celtic words and names are strange to modern eyes, but they are not as difficult to pronounce as they might seem at first glance. A little effort—and the following rough guide—will help you enjoy the sound of these ancient words.

Consonants — As in English, but with the following exceptions:

c:	hard — as in *c*at (never soft, as in *c*ent)
ch:	hard — as in Ba*ch* (never soft, as in *ch*urch)
dd:	a hard *th* sound, as in *th*en
f:	a hard *v* sound, as in o*f*
ff:	a soft *f* sound, as in o*ff*
g:	hard — as in *g*irl (never soft, as in *G*eorge)
ll:	a Gaelic distinctive, sounded as *tl* or *hl* on the sides of the tongue
r:	rolled or slightly trilled, especially at the beginning of a word
rh:	breathed out as if *h-r* and heavy on the *h* sound
s:	soft — as in *s*in (never hard, as in hi*s*); when followed by a vowel it takes on the *sh* sound
th:	soft — as in *th*istle (never hard, as in *th*en)

Vowels — As in English, but generally with the lightness of short vowel sounds

a:	short, as in c*a*n
á:	slightly softer than above, as in *a*we;
e:	usually short, as in m*e*t
é:	long *a* sound, as in h*e*y
i:	usually short, as in p*i*n
í:	long *e* sound, as in s*ee*
o:	usually short, as in h*o*t

ó:	long *o* sound, as in w*oe*
ô:	long *o* sound, as in g*o*
u:	usually sounded as a short *i*, as in p*i*n;
ú:	long *u* sound as in s*ue*
ù:	short *u* sound as in m*u*ck
w:	sounded as a long *u*, as in h*ue*; before vowels often becomes a soft consonant as in the name G*w*en
y:	usually short, as in p*i*n; sometimes *u* as in p*u*n; when long, sounded *e* as in s*ee*; rarely, *y* as in wh*y*)

The careful reader will have noted that there is very little difference between *i*, *u*, and *y*—they are almost identical to non-Celts and modern readers.

Most Celtic words are stressed on the next to the last syllable. For example, the personal name Gofannon is stressed go-FAN-non, and the place name Penderwydd is stressed pen-DER-width, and so on.

KING RAVEN

TRILOGY

England and
The March

1080 – 1100 AD

RHI BRAN'S WORLD

Cymru

Lloegr

to Lundein

Wintan Caestir
(Caer Wintod)

King's Road

to Lundein

Caer
Gloiu

Hereford

King's Road

the March

the March

Coed Cadw

Saint
Dyfrig

Glascwm

Elfael
Cadarn

Caer
Rhodl

Alanelli

the
March

Gwynedd

Cymru

Mor Hafren

St. George's Channel

KING RAVEN: BOOK I

This book is dedicated to
the Schloss Mittersill Community
with heartfelt thanks and gratitude
for their understanding,
encouragement, and support.

⊰ PROLOGUE ⊱

The pig was young and wary, a yearling boar timidly testing the wind for strange scents as it ventured out into the honey-coloured light of a fast-fading day. Bran ap Brychan, Prince of Elfael, had spent the entire day stalking the greenwood for a suitable prize, and he meant to have this one.

Eight years old and the king's sole heir, he knew well enough that he would never be allowed to go out into the forest alone. So rather than seek permission, he had simply taken his bow and four arrows early that morning and stolen from the caer unnoticed. This hunt, like the young boar, was dedicated to his mother, the queen.

She loved the hunt and gloried in the wild beauty and visceral excitement of the chase. Even when she did not ride herself, she would ready a welcome for the hunters with a saddle cup and music, leading the women in song. "Don't be afraid," she told Bran when, as a toddling boy, he had been dazzled and a little frightened by the noise and revelry. "We belong to the land. Look, Bran!" She lifted a slender hand toward the hills and the forest rising like a living rampart beyond. "All that you see is the work of our Lord's hand. We rejoice in his provision."

Stricken with a wasting fever, Queen Rhian had been sick most of the summer, and in his childish imaginings, Bran had determined that if he could present her with a stag or a boar that he had brought down all by himself, she would laugh and sing as she always did, and she would feel better. She would be well again.

All it would take was a little more patience and . . .

Still as stone, he waited in the deepening shadow. The young boar stepped nearer, its small pointed ears erect and proud. It took another step and stopped to sample the tender shoots of a mallow plant. Bran, an arrow already nocked to the string, pressed the bow forward, feeling the tension in his shoulder and back just the way Iwan said he should. "Do not aim the arrow," the older youth had instructed him. "Just *think* it to the mark. Send it on your thought, and if your thought is true, so, too, will fly the arrow."

Pressing the bow to the limit of his strength, he took a steadying breath and released the string, feeling the sharp tingle on his fingertips. The arrow blazed across the distance, striking the young pig low in the chest behind the front legs. Startled, it flicked its tail rigid, and turned to bolt into the wood . . . but two steps later its legs tangled; it stumbled and went down. The stricken creature squealed once and tried to rise, then subsided, dead where it fell.

Bran loosed a wild whoop of triumph. The prize was his!

He ran to the pig and put his hand on the animal's sleek, slightly speckled haunch, feeling the warmth there. "I am sorry, my friend, and I thank you," he murmured as Iwan had taught him. "I need your life to live."

It was only when he tried to shoulder his kill that Bran realised his great mistake. The dead weight of the animal was more than he could lift by himself. With a sinking heart, he stood gazing at his glorious prize as tears came to his eyes. It was all for nothing if he could not carry the trophy home in triumph.

Sinking down on the ground beside the warm carcass, Bran put his head in his hands. He could not carry it, and he would not leave it. What was he going to do?

As he sat contemplating his predicament, the sounds of the forest grew loud in his ears: the chatter of a squirrel in a treetop, the busy click and hum of insects, the rustle of leaves, the hushed flutter of wings above him, and then . . .

"Bran!"

Bran started at the voice. He glanced around hopefully.

"Here!" he called. "Here! I need help!"

"Go back!" The voice seemed to come from above. He raised his eyes to see a huge black bird watching him from a branch directly over his head.

It was only an old raven. "Shoo!"

"Go back!" said the bird. "Go back!"

"I won't," shouted Bran. He reached for a stick on the path, picked it up, drew back, and threw it at the bothersome bird. "Shut up!"

The stick struck the raven's perch, and the bird flew off with a cry that sounded to Bran like laughter. "Ha, ha, haw! Ha, ha, haw!"

"Stupid bird," he muttered. Turning again to the young pig beside him, he remembered what he had seen other hunters do with small game. Releasing the string on his bow, he gathered the creature's short legs and tied the hooves together with the cord. Then, passing the stave through the bound hooves and gripping the stout length of oak in either hand, he tried to lift it. The carcass was still too heavy for him, so he began to drag his prize through the forest, using the bow.

It was slow going, even on the well-worn path, with frequent stops to rub the sweat from his eyes and catch his breath. All the while, the day dwindled around him.

No matter. He would not give up. Clutching the bow stave in his hands, he struggled on, step by step, tugging the young boar along the trail, reaching the edge of the forest as the last gleam of twilight faded across the valley to the west.

"Bran!"

The shout made him jump. It was not a raven this time, but a voice he knew. He turned and looked down the slope toward the valley to see Iwan coming toward him, long legs paring the distance with swift strides.

"Here!" Bran called, waving his aching arms overhead. "Here I am!"

"In the name of all the saints and angels," the young man said when he came near enough to speak, "what do you think you are doing out here?"

"Hunting," replied Bran. Indicating his kill with a hunter's pride, he said, "It strayed in front of my arrow, see?"

"I see," replied Iwan. Giving the pig a cursory glance, he turned and started away again. "We have to go. It's late, and everyone is looking for you."

Bran made no move to follow.

Looking back, Iwan said, "Leave it, Bran! They are searching for you. We must hurry."

"No," Bran said. "Not without the boar." He stooped once more to the carcass, seized the bow stave, and started tugging again.

Iwan returned, took him roughly by the arm, and pulled him away. "Leave the stupid thing!"

"It is for my mother!" the boy shouted, the tears starting hot and quick. As the tears began to fall, he bent his head and repeated more softly, "Please, it is for my mother."

"Weeping Judas!" Iwan relented with an exasperated sigh. "Come then. We will carry it together."

Iwan took one end of the bow stave, Bran took the other, and between them they lifted the carcass off the ground. The wood bent but did not break, and they started away again—Bran stumbling ever and again in a forlorn effort to keep pace with his long-legged friend.

Night was upon them, the caer but a brooding black eminence on its mound in the centre of the valley, when a party of mounted searchers appeared. "He was hunting," Iwan informed them. "A hunter does not leave his prize."

The riders accepted this, and the young boar was quickly secured behind the saddle of one of the horses; Bran and Iwan were taken up behind other riders, and the party rode for the caer. The moment they arrived, Bran slid from the horse and ran to his mother's chamber behind the hall. "Hurry," he called. "Bring the boar!"

Queen Rhian's chamber was lit with candles, and two women stood over her bed when Bran burst in. He ran to her bedside and knelt down. "Mam! See what I brought you!"

She opened her eyes, and recognition came to her. "There you are, my dearling. They said they could not find you."

"I went hunting," he announced. "For you."

"For me," she whispered. "A fine thing, that. What did you find?"

"Look!" he said proudly as Iwan strode into the room with the pig slung over his shoulders.

"Oh, Bran," she said, the ghost of a smile touching her dry lips. "Kiss me, my brave hunter."

He bent his face to hers and felt the heat of her dry lips on his. "Go now. I will sleep a little," she told him, "and I will dream of your triumph."

She closed her eyes then, and Bran was led from the room. But she had smiled, and that was worth all the world to him.

Queen Rhian did not waken in the morning. By the next evening she was dead, and Bran never saw his mother smile again. And although he continued to hone his skill with the bow, he lost all interest in the hunt.

5

PART ONE

DAY OF
THE WOLF

CHAPTER I

"Bran!" The shout rattled through the stone-flagged yard. "Bran! Get your sorry tail out here! We're leaving!"

Red-faced with exasperation, King Brychan ap Tewdwr climbed stiffly into the saddle, narrowed eyes scanning the ranks of mounted men awaiting his command. His feckless son was not amongst them. Turning to the warrior on the horse beside him, he demanded, "Iwan, where is that boy?"

"I have not seen him, lord," replied the king's champion. "Neither this morning nor at the table last night."

"Curse his impudence!" growled the king, snatching the reins from the hand of his groom. "The one time I need him beside me and he flits off to bed that slut of his. I will not suffer this insolence, and I will not wait."

"If it please you, lord, I will send one of the men to fetch him."

"No! It does not bloody please me!" roared Brychan. "He can stay behind, and the devil take him!"

Turning in the saddle, he called for the gate to be opened. The heavy timber doors of the fortress groaned and swung wide. Raising his hand, he gave the signal.

"Ride out!" Iwan cried, his voice loud in the early morning calm.

King Brychan, Lord of Elfael, departed with the thirty-five Cymry of his mounted warband at his back. The warriors, riding in twos and threes, descended the rounded slope of the hill and fanned out across the shallow, cup-shaped valley, fording the stream that cut across the meadow and following the cattle trail as it rose to meet the dark, bristling rampart of the forest known to the folk of the valley as *Coed Cadw*, the Guarding Wood.

At the edge of the forest, Brychan and his escort joined the road. Ancient, deep-rutted, overgrown, and sunken low between its high earthen banks, the bare dirt track bent its way south and east over the rough hills and through the broad expanse of dense primeval forest until descending into the broad Wye Vale, where it ran along the wide, green waters of the easy-flowing river. Farther on, the road passed through the two principal towns of the region: Hereford, an English market town, and Caer Gloiu, the ancient Roman settlement in the wide, marshy lowland estuary of Mor Hafren. In four days, this same road would bring them to Lundein, where the Lord of Elfael would face the most difficult trial of his long and arduous reign.

"There was a time," Brychan observed bitterly, "when the last warrior to reach the meeting place was put to death by his comrades as punishment for his lack of zeal. It was deemed the first fatality of the battle."

"Allow me to fetch the prince for you," Iwan offered. "He could catch up before the day is out."

"I will not hear it." Brychan dismissed the suggestion with a sharp chop of his hand. "We've wasted too much breath on that worthless whelp. I will deal with him when we return," he said, adding under his breath, "and he will wish to heaven he had never been born."

With an effort, the aging king pushed all thoughts of his profligate son aside and settled into a sullen silence that lasted well into the day. Upon reaching the Vale of Wye, the travellers descended the broad slope into the valley and proceeded along the river. The road was good here, and the water wide, slow flowing, and shallow. Around midday, they stopped on the moss-grown banks to water the horses and take some food for themselves before moving on.

Iwan had given the signal to remount, and they were just pulling the heads of the horses away from the water when a jingling clop was heard on the road. A moment later four riders appeared, coming into view around the base of a high-sided bluff.

One look at the long, pallid faces beneath their burnished warcaps, and the king's stomach tightened. "Ffreinc!" grumbled Brychan, putting his hand to his sword. They were Norman *marchogi*, and the British king and his subjects despised them utterly.

"To arms, men," called Iwan. "Be on your guard."

Upon seeing the British warband, the Norman riders halted in the road. They wore conical helmets and, despite the heat of the day, heavy mail shirts over padded leather jerkins that reached down below their knees. Their shins were covered with polished steel greaves, and leather gauntlets protected their hands, wrists, and forearms. Each carried a sword on his hip and a short spear tucked into a saddle pouch. A narrow shield shaped like an elongated raindrop, painted blue, was slung upon each of their backs.

"Mount up!" Iwan commanded, swinging into the saddle.

Brychan, at the head of his troops, called a greeting in his own tongue, twisting his lips into an unaccustomed smile of welcome. When his greeting was not returned, he tried English—the hated but necessary language used when dealing with the backward folk of the southlands. One of the riders seemed to understand. He made a curt reply in French and then turned and spurred his horse back the way he had come; his three companions remained in place, regarding the British warriors with wary contempt.

Seeing his grudging attempt at welcome rebuffed, Lord Brychan raised his reins and urged his mount forward. "Ride on, men," he ordered, "and keep your eyes on the filthy devils."

At the British approach, the three knights closed ranks, blocking the road. Unwilling to suffer an insult, however slight, Brychan commanded them to move aside. The Norman knights made no reply but remained planted firmly in the centre of the road.

Brychan was on the point of ordering his warband to draw their swords and ride over the arrogant fools when Iwan spoke up, saying, "My lord, our business in Lundein will put an end to this unseemly harassment. Let us endure this last slight with good grace and heap shame on the heads of these cowardly swine."

"You would surrender the road to them?"

"I would, my lord," replied the champion evenly. "We do not want the report of a fight to mar our petition in Lundein."

Brychan stared dark thunder at the Ffreinc soldiers.

"My lord?" said Iwan. "I think it is best."

"Oh, very well," huffed the king at last. Turning to the warriors behind him, he called, "To keep the peace, we will go around."

As the Britons prepared to yield the road, the first Norman rider returned, and with him another man on a pale grey mount with a high leather saddle. This one wore a blue cloak fastened at the throat with a large silver brooch. "You there!" he called in English. "What are you doing?"

Brychan halted and turned in the saddle. "Do you speak to me?"

"I do speak to you," the man insisted. "Who are you, and where are you going?"

"The man you address is Rhi Brychan, Lord and King of Elfael," replied Iwan, speaking up quickly. "We are about business of our own which takes us to Lundein. We seek no quarrel and would pass by in peace."

"Elfael?" wondered the man in the blue cloak. Unlike the others, he carried no weapons, and his gauntlets were white leather. "You are British."

"That we are," replied Iwan.

"What is your business in Lundein?"

"It is our affair alone," replied Brychan irritably. "We ask only to journey on without dispute."

"Stay where you are," replied the blue-cloaked man. "I will summon my lord and seek his disposition in the matter."

The man put spurs to his mount and disappeared around the bend in the road. The Britons waited, growing irritated and uneasy in the hot sun.

The blue-cloaked man reappeared some moments later, and with him was another, also wearing blue, but with a spotless white linen shirt and trousers of fine velvet. Younger than the others, he wore his fair hair long to his shoulders, like a woman's; with his sparse, pale beard curling along the soft line of his jaw, he appeared little more than a youngster preening in his father's clothes. Like the others with him, he carried a shield on his shoulder and a long sword on his hip. His horse was black, and it was larger than any plough horse Brychan had ever seen.

"You claim to be Rhi Brychan, Lord of Elfael?" the newcomer asked in a voice so thickly accented the Britons could barely make out what he said.

"I make no claim, sir," replied Brychan with terse courtesy, the English thick on his tongue. "It is a very fact."

"Why do you ride to Lundein with your warband?" inquired the pasty-faced youth. "Can it be that you intend to make war on King William?"

"On no account, sir," replied Iwan, answering to spare his lord the indignity of this rude interrogation. "We go to swear fealty to the king of the Ffreinc."

At this, the two blue-cloaked figures leaned near and put their heads together in consultation. "It is too late. William will not see you."

"Who are *you* to speak for the king?" demanded Iwan.

"I say again, this affair does not concern you," added Brychan.

"You are wrong. It has become my concern," replied the young man in blue. "I am Count Falkes de Braose, and I have been given the commot of Elfael." He thrust his hand into his shirt and brought out a square of parchment. "This I have received in grant from the hand of King William himself."

"Liar!" roared Brychan, drawing his sword. All thirty-five of his warband likewise unsheathed their blades.

"You have a choice," the Norman lord informed them imperiously. "Give over your weapons and swear fealty to me . . ."

"Or?" sneered Brychan, glaring contempt at the five Ffreinc warriors before him.

"Or die like the very dogs you are," replied the young man simply.

"Hie! Up!" shouted the British king, slapping the rump of his horse with the flat of his sword. The horse bolted forward. "Take them!"

Iwan lofted his sword and circled it twice around his head to signal the warriors, and the entire warband spurred their horses to attack. The Normans held their ground for two or three heartbeats and then turned as one and fled back along the road, disappearing around the bend at the base of the bluff.

King Brychan was first to reach the place. He rounded the bend at a gallop, flying headlong into an armed warhost of more than three hundred Norman marchogi, both footmen and knights, waiting with weapons at the ready.

Throwing the reins to the side, the king wheeled his mount and headed for the riverbank. "Ambush! Ambush!" he cried to those thundering up behind him. "It's a trap!"

The oncoming Cymry, seeing their king flee for the water with a score of marchogi behind him, raced to cut them off. They reached the enemy flank and careered into it at full gallop, spears couched.

Horses reared and plunged as they went over; riders fell and were trampled. The British charge punched a hole in the Norman flank and carried them deep into the ranks. Using spears and swords, they proceeded to cut a swathe through the dense thicket of enemy troops.

Iwan, leading the charge, sliced the air with his spear, thrusting again and again, carving a crimson pathway through horseflesh and manflesh alike. With deadly efficiency, he took the fight to the better-armed and better-protected marchogi and soon outdistanced his own comrades.

Twisting in the saddle, he saw that the attack had bogged down behind him. The Norman knights, having absorbed the initial shock of the charge, were now surrounding the smaller Cymry force. It was time to break off lest the warband become engulfed.

With a flick of the reins, Iwan started back over the bodies of those he had cut down. He had almost reached the main force of struggling Cymry when two massive Norman knights astride huge destriers closed the path before him. Swords raised, they swooped down on him.

Iwan thrust his spear at the one on the right, only to have the shaft splintered by the one on the left. Throwing the ragged end into the

15

Norman's face, he drew his sword and, pulling back hard on the reins, turned his mount and slipped aside as the two closed within striking distance. One of the knights lunged at him, swinging wildly. Iwan felt the blade tip rake his upper back, then he was away.

King Brychan, meanwhile, reached the river and turned to face his attackers—four marchogi coming in hard behind levelled spears. Lashing out with his sword, Brychan struck at the first rider, catching him a rattling blow along the top of the shield. He then swung on the second, slashing at the man's exposed leg. The warrior gave out a yelp and threw his shield into Brychan's face. The king smashed it aside with the pommel of his sword. The shield swung away and down, revealing the point of a spear.

Brychan heaved himself back to avoid the thrust, but the spear caught him in the lower gut, just below his wide belt. The blade burned as it pierced his body. He loosed a savage roar and hacked wildly with his sword. The shaft of the spear sheared away, taking a few of the soldier's fingers with it.

Raising his blade again, the king turned to meet the next attacker . . . but too late. Even as his elbow swung up, an enemy blade thrust in. He felt a cold sting, and pain rippled up his arm. His hand lost its grip. The sword spun from his fingers as he swayed in the saddle, recoiling from the blow.

Iwan, fighting free of the clash, raced to his lord's aid. He saw the king's blade fall to the water as Brychan reeled and then slumped. The champion slashed the arm of one attacker and opened the side of another as he sped by. Then his way was blocked by a sudden swirl of Norman attackers. Hacking with wild and determined energy, he tried to force his way through by dint of strength alone, but the enemy riders closed ranks against him.

His sword became a gleaming flash around him as he struck out again and again. He dropped one knight, whose misjudged thrust went wide, and wounded another, who desperately reined his horse away and out of range of the champion's lethal blade.

As he turned to take the third attacker, Iwan glimpsed his king struggling to keep his saddle. He saw Brychan lurch forward and topple from his horse into the water.

The king struggled to his knees and beheld his champion fighting to reach him a short distance away. "Ride!" he shouted. "Flee! You must warn the people!"

Rhi Brychan made one last attempt to rise, got his feet under him and took an unsteady step, then collapsed. The last thing Iwan saw was the body of his king floating facedown in the turgid, bloodstained waters of the Wye.

"A kiss before I go," Bran murmured, taking a handful of thick dark hair and pressing a curled lock to his lips. "Just one."

"No!" replied Mérian, pushing him away. "Away with you."

"A kiss first," he insisted, inhaling the rosewater fragrance of her hair and skin.

"If my father finds you here, he will flay us both," she said, still resisting. "Go now—before someone sees you."

"A kiss only, I swear," Bran whispered, sliding close.

She regarded the young man beside her doubtfully. Certainly, there was not another in all the valleys like him. In looks, grace, and raw seductive appeal, he knew no equal. With his black hair, high handsome brow, and a ready smile that was, as always, a little lopsided and deceptively shy—the mere sight of Bran ap Brychan caused female hearts young and old to flutter when he passed.

Add to this a supple wit and a free-ranging, unfettered charm, and the Prince of Elfael was easily the most ardently discussed bachelor amongst the marriageable young women of the region. The fact that he also stood next in line to the kingship was not lost on any of them. More than one lovesick young lady sighed herself to sleep at night in the fervent hope of winning Bran ap Brychan's heart for her own— causing more than one determined father to vow to nail that wastrel's head to the nearest doorpost if he ever caught him within a Roman mile of his virgin daughter's bed.

Yet and yet, there was a flightiness to his winsome ways, a fickle inconstancy to even his most solemn affirmations, a lack of fidelity in his ardour. He possessed a waggish capriciousness that most often showed itself in a sly refusal to take seriously the genuine concerns of life. Bran flitted from one thing to the next as the whim took him, never remaining long enough to reap the all-too-inevitable conse- quences of his flings and frolics.

Lithe and long-limbed, habitually clothed in the darkest hues, which gave him an appearance of austerity—an impression completely overthrown by the puckish glint in his clear dark eyes and the sudden, unpredictable, and utterly provocative smile—he nevertheless gorged on an endless glut of indulgence, forever helping himself to the best of everything his noble position could offer. King Brychan's rake of a son was unashamedly pleased with himself.

"A kiss, my love, and I will take wings," Bran whispered, pressing himself closer still.

Feeling both appalled and excited by the danger Bran always brought with him, Mérian closed her eyes and brushed his cheek with her lips. "There!" she said firmly, pushing him away. "Now off with you."

"Ah, Mérian," he said, placing his head on her warm breast, "how can I go, when to leave you is to leave my heart behind?"

"You promised!" she hissed in exasperation, stiff arms forcing him away again.

There came the sound of a shuffling footstep outside the kitchen door.

"Hurry!" Suddenly terrified, she grabbed him by the sleeve and pulled him to his feet. "It might be my father."

"Let him come. I am not afraid. We will have this out once and for all."

"Bran, no!" she pleaded. "If you have any thought for me at all, do not let anyone find you here."

"Very well," Bran replied. "I go."

He leaned close and stole a lingering kiss, then leapt to the window frame, pushed open the shutter, and prepared to jump. "Until tonight, my love," he said over his shoulder, then dropped to the ground in the yard outside.

Mérian rushed to the window and pulled the heavy wooden shutter closed, then turned and began busying herself, stirring up the embers on the hearth as the sleep-numbed cook shambled into the large, dark room.

Bran leaned back against the side of the house and listened to the voices drifting down from the room above—to the cook's mumbled question and Mérian's explanation of what she was doing in the kitchen before break of day. He smiled to himself. True, he had not yet succeeded in winning his way into Mérian's bed; Lord Cadwgan's fetching daughter was proving a match worthy of his wiles. Even so, before summer was gone he would succeed. Of that he was certain.

Oh, but the season of warmth and light was everywhere in full retreat. Already the soft greens and yellows of summer were fading into autumn drab. Soon, all too soon, the fair, bright days would give way to the endless grey of clouds and mist and icy, wind-lashed rain.

That was a concern for another time; now he must be on his way. Drawing the hood of his cloak over his head, Bran darted across the

21

yard, scaled the wall at its lowest span, and ran to his horse, which was tethered behind a hawthorn thicket next to the wall.

With the wind at his back and a little luck, he would reach Caer Cadarn well before his father departed for Lundein.

The day was breaking fair, and the track was dry, so he pushed his mount hard: pelting down the broad hillsides, splashing across the streams, and flying up the steep, wheel-rutted trails. Luck was not with him, however, for he had just glimpsed the pale shimmer of the caer's whitewashed wooden palisade in the distance when his horse pulled up lame. The unfortunate beast jolted to a halt and refused to go farther.

No amount of coaxing could persuade the animal to move. Sliding from the saddle, Bran examined the left foreleg. The shoe had torn away—probably lost amidst the rocks of the last streambed—and the hoof was split. There was blood on the fetlock. Bran lowered the leg with a sigh and, retrieving the reins, began leading his limping mount along the track.

His father would be waiting now, and he would be angry. But then, he thought, when was Lord Brychan *not* angry?

For the last many years—indeed, ever since Bran could remember—his father had nursed one continual simmering rage. It forever seethed just beneath the surface and was only too likely to boil over at the slightest provocation. And then, God help whoever or whatever was nearby. Objects were hurled against walls; dogs were kicked, and servants too; everyone within shouting distance received the ready lash of their surly lord's tongue.

Bran arrived at the caer far later than he had intended, slinking through the wide-open gate. Like a smith opening the forge furnace door, he braced himself for the heat of his father's angry blast. But the yard was empty of all save Gwrgi, the lord's half-blind staghound, who came snuffling up to put his wet muzzle in Bran's palm. "Everyone gone?" Bran asked, looking around. The old dog licked the back of his hand.

Just then his father's steward stepped from the hall. A dour and disapproving stilt of a man, he loomed over all the comings and goings of the caer like a damp cloud and was never happy unless he could make someone else as miserable as himself. "You are too late," he informed Bran, ripe satisfaction dripping from his thin lips.

"I can see that, Maelgwnt," said Bran. "How long ago did they leave?"

"You won't catch them," replied the steward, "if that's what you're thinking. Sometimes I wonder if you *think* at all."

"Get me a horse," ordered Bran.

"Why?" Maelgwnt asked, eyeing the mount standing inside the gate. "Have you ruined another one?"

"Just get me a horse. I don't have time to argue."

"Of course, sire, right away," sniffed the steward. "As soon as you tell me where to find one."

"What do you mean?" demanded Bran.

"There are none."

With a grunt of impatience, Bran hurried to the stable at the far end of the long, rectangular yard. He found one of the grooms mucking out the stalls. "Quick, Cefn, I need a horse."

"Lord Bran," said the young servant, "I'm sorry. There are none left."

"They've taken them *all*?"

"The whole warband was summoned," the groom explained. "They needed every horse but the mares."

Bran knew which horses he meant. There were four broodmares to which five colts had been born in early spring. The foals were of an age to wean but had not yet been removed from their mothers.

"Bring me the black," Bran commanded. "She will have to do."

"What about Hathr?" inquired the groom.

"Hathr threw a shoe and split a hoof. He'll need looking after for a few days, and I must join my father on the road before the day is out."

"Lord Brychan said we were not to use—"

"I *need* a horse, Cefn," said Bran, cutting off his objection. "Saddle the black—and hurry. I must ride hard if I am to catch them."

While the groom set about preparing the mare, Bran hurried to the kitchen to find something to eat. The cook and her two young helpers were busy shelling peas and protested the intrusion. With smiles and winks and murmured endearments, however, Bran cajoled, and old Mairead succumbed to his charm as she always did. "You'll be king one day," she chided, "and is this how you will fare? Snatching meals from the hearth and running off who-knows-where all day?"

"I'm going to Lundein, Mairead. It is a far journey. Would you have your future king starve on the way, or go a-begging like a leper?"

"Lord have mercy!" clucked the cook, setting aside her chore. "Never let it be said anyone went hungry from my hearth."

She ladled some fresh milk into a bowl, into which she broke chunks of hard brown bread, then sat him down on a stool. While he ate, she cut a few slices of new summer sausage and gave him two green apples, which he stuffed into the pouch at his belt. Bran spooned down the milk and bread and then, throwing the elderly servant a kiss, bounded from the kitchen and back across the yard to the stable, where Cefn was just tightening the saddle cinch on his horse.

"A world of thanks to you, Cefn. You have saved my life."

"Olwen is the best broodmare we have—see you don't push her too hard," called the groom as the prince clattered out into the yard. Bran gave him a breezy wave, and the groom added under his breath, "And may our Lord Brychan have mercy on you."

Out on the trail once more, Bran felt certain he could win his way back into his father's good graces. It might take a day or two, but once the king saw how dutifully the prince was prepared to conduct himself in Lundein, Brychan would not fail to restore his son to favour. First, however, Bran set himself to think up a plausible tale to help excuse his apparent absence.

Thus, he put his mind to spinning a story which, if not entirely believable, would at least be entertaining enough to lighten the king's foul mood. This task occupied him as he rode easily along the path through the forest. He had just started up the long, meandering track leading to the high and thickly forested ridge that formed the western boundary of the broad Wye Vale and was thinking that with any luck at all, he might still catch his father and the warband before dusk. This thought dissolved instantly upon seeing a lone rider lurching toward him on a hobbling horse.

He was still some distance away, but Bran could see that the man was hunched forward in the saddle as if to urge his labouring mount to greater speed. *Probably drunk, rotten sot,* thought Bran, *and doesn't realise his horse is dead on its feet.* Well, he would stop the empty-headed lout and see if he could find out how far ahead his father might be.

Closer, something about the man seemed familiar.

As the rider drew nearer, Bran grew increasingly certain he knew the man, and he was not wrong.

It was Iwan.

25

Bernard de Neufmarché stormed down the narrow corridor leading from the main hall to his private chambers deep in the protecting stone wall of the fortress. His red velvet cloak was grey with the dust of travel, his back throbbed with the dull, persistent ache of fatigue, and his mind was a spinning maelstrom of dark thoughts as black as his mood. *Seven years lost!* he fumed. *Ruined, wasted, and lost!*

He had been patient, prudent, biding his time, watching and waiting for precisely the right moment to strike. And now, in one precipitous act, unprovoked and unforeseen, the red-haired brigand of a king, William, had allied himself with that milksop Baron de Braose and his mewling nephew, Count Falkes. That was bad enough. To make a disastrous business worse, the irresponsible king had also reversed the long-held royal policy of his father and allowed de Braose to launch an invasion into the interior of Wales.

Royal let to plunder Wales was the very development Neufmarché had been waiting for, but now it had been ruined by the greedy, grasping de Braose mob. Their ill-conceived thrashing around the countryside would put the wily Britons on their guard, and any advancement on Bernard's part would now be met with stiff-necked resistance and accomplished only at considerable expense of troops and blood.

So be it!

Waiting had brought him nothing, and he would wait no longer.

At the door to his rooms, he shouted for his chamberlain. "Remey!" he cried. "My writing instruments! At once!"

Flinging open the door, he strode to the hearth, snatched up a reed from the bundle, and thrust it into the small, sputtering fire. He then carried the burning rush to the candletree atop the square oak table that occupied the centre of the room and began lighting the candles. As the shadows shrank beneath the lambent light, the baron dashed wine from a jar into his silver cup, raised it to his lips, and drank a deep, thirsty draught. He then shouted for his chamberlain again and collapsed into his chair.

"Seven years, by the Virgin!" he muttered. He drank again and cried, "Remey!" This time his summons was answered by the quick slap of soft boots on the flagstone threshold.

"Sire," said the servant, bustling into the room with his arms full of writing utensils—rolls of parchment, an inkhorn, a bundle of quills, sealing wax, and a knife. "I did not expect you to return so soon. I trust everything went well?"

"No," growled the baron irritably, "it did not go well. It went very badly. While I was paying court to the king, de Braose and his snivelling nephew were sending an army through my lands to snatch Elfael and who knows what all else from under my nose."

Remey sighed in commiseration. An aging lackey with the face of a ferret and a long, narrow head perpetually covered by a shapeless cap of thick grey felt, he had been in the service of the Neufmarché clan since he was a boy at Le Neuf-March-en-Lions in Beauvais. He knew

28

well his master's moods and appetites and was usually able to antici-
pate them with ease. But today he had been caught napping, and this
annoyed him almost as much as the king had annoyed the baron.

"The de Braose are unscrupulous, as we all know," Remey observed,
arranging the items he had brought on the table before the baron.

"Cut me a pen," the baron ordered. Taking up a roll of parchment,
he sliced off a suitable square with his dagger and smoothed the prepared skin on the table before him.

Remey, meanwhile, selected a fine long goose quill and expertly
pared the tip on an angle and split it with the pen knife. "See if this
will suffice," he said, offering the prepared writing instrument to
his master.

Bernard pulled the stopper from the inkhorn and dipped the pen.
He made a few preliminary swirls on the parchment and said, "It will
do. Now bring me my dinner. None of that broth, mind. I've ridden
all day, and I'm hungry. I want meat and bread—some of that pie, too.
And more wine."

"At once, my lord," replied the servant, leaving his master to his work.

By the time Remey returned, accompanied this time by two kitchen
servants bearing trays of food and drink, Neufmarché was leaning back
in his chair studying the document he had just composed. "Listen to
this," said the baron, and holding the parchment before his eyes, he
began to read what he had written.

Remey held his head to one side as his master read. It was a letter
to the baron's father in Beauvais requesting a transfer of men and
equipment to aid in the conquest of new territories in Britain.

". . . the resulting acquisitions will enlarge our holdings at least
threefold," Bernard read, "with good land, much of which is valley
lowlands possessing tillable soil suitable for a variety of crops, while
the rest is mature forest which, besides timber, will provide excellent

hunting . . ." Here the baron broke off. "What do you think, Remey? Is it enough?"

"I should think so. Lord Geoffrey was out here two years ago and is well aware of the desirability of the Welsh lands. I have no doubt he will send the required aid."

"I concur," decided Bernard. Bending once more to the parchment, he finished the letter and signed his name. Then, rolling the parchment quickly, he tied the bundle and sealed it, pressing his heavy gold ring into the soft puddle of brown wax dripped from the stick in Remey's hands. "There," he said, setting the bundle aside, "now bring me that tray and fill my cup. When you've done that, go find Ormand."

"Of course, sire," replied the chamberlain, gesturing for the two kitchen servants to place the trays of food before the baron while he refilled the silver cup from a flagon. "I believe I saw young Ormand in the hall only a short while ago."

"Good," said Bernard, spearing one of the hard-crusted pies from the tray with his knife. "Tell him to prepare to ride out at first light. This letter must reach Beauvais before the month is out."

The baron bit into the cold pie and chewed thoughtfully. He ate a little more and then took another long draught of wine, wiped his mouth with the back of his hand, and said, "Now then, go find my wife and tell her I have returned."

"I have already spoken to my lady's maidservant, sire," replied Remey, starting for the door. "I will inform Ormand that you wish to see him."

Baron Neufmarché was left alone to eat his meal in peace. As the food and wine soothed his agitated soul, he began to look more favourably on the conquest to come. *Perhaps,* he thought, *I have been over-hasty.* Perhaps, in the heat of temper, he had allowed his anger to cloud his perception. He might have lost Elfael, true enough, but Buellt was the real prize, and it would be his; and beyond Buellt lay the ripe, fertile heartland of Dyfed and Ceredigion. It was all good land—wild, for the most part, and undeveloped—just waiting for a man with the boldness of vision, determination, and ambition to make it prosper and produce. Bernard de Neufmarché, Baron of the Shires of Gloucester and Hereford, imagined himself just that man.

Yes, the more he thought about it, the more he was certain he was right; despite the king's outrageous behaviour, things were working out for the best after all. Under the proper circumstances, Elfael, that small and undistinguished commot in the centre of the Welsh hill country, could ensnare the rash invaders in difficulties for years to come. In fact, with the timely application of a few simple principles of subterfuge, the baron could ensure that little Elfael would become the grasping de Braose family's downfall.

The baron was basking in the warmth of this self-congratulatory humour when he heard the latch on his door rattle. The soft cough with which his visitor announced herself indicated that his wife had joined him. His momentary feeling of pleasure dimmed and faded.

"You have returned earlier than expected, my lord," she said, her voice falling soft and low in the quiet of the room.

Bernard took his time answering. Setting aside his cup, he turned his head and looked at her. Pale and wan, she appeared even more wraithlike than when he had last seen her, only a few days ago. Her eyes were large, dark-rimmed circles in the ashen skin of her thin face, and her long lank hair hung straight, making her seem all the more frail and delicate.

"You are looking well, my lady," he lied, smiling. He rose stiffly and offered her his chair.

"Thank you, my lord," she replied. "But sit; you are at meat. I will not disturb you. I only wished to acknowledge your return." She bowed slightly from the waist and turned to leave.

"Agnes, stay," he said and noticed the tremor that coursed through her body.

"I have had my dinner and was just about to go to prayers," she informed her husband. "But very well, I will sit with you awhile. If that is what you wish."

Bernard removed his chair and placed it at the side of the table. "Only if it is no trouble," he said.

"Far from it," she insisted. "It is a very pleasure in itself."

He seated her and then pulled another chair to his place. "Wine?" he asked, lifting the flagon.

"I think not, thank you." Head erect, shoulders level, slender back straight as a lance shaft, she perched lightly on the edge of her chair—as if she feared it might suddenly take wing beneath her negligible weight.

"If you change your mind . . ." The baron refilled his cup and resumed his seat. His wife was suffering, to be sure, and that was real enough. Even so, he could not help feeling that she brought it on herself with her perverse unwillingness to adapt in the slightest measure to the demands of her new home and its all-too-often inhospitable climate. She refused to dress more warmly or eat more heartily—as conditions warranted. Thus, she lurched from one vague illness to another, enduring febrile distempers, agues, fluxes, and other mysterious maladies, all with the resigned patience of an expiring saint.

"Remey said you summoned Ormand."

"Yes, I am sending him to Beauvais with a letter for the duke," he replied, swirling the wine in his cup. "The conquest of Wales has begun, and I will not be left out of it. I am requesting troopsmen-at-arms and as many knights as he can spare."

"A letter? For your father?" she asked, the light leaping up in her eyes for the first time since she had entered the room. "Do not bother Ormand with such a task—I will take the letter for you."

"No," replied Bernard. "The journey is too arduous for you. It is out of the question."

"Nonsense," she countered. "The journey would do me a world of good—the sea air and warmer weather would be just the elixir to restore me."

"I need you here," said the baron. "There is going to be a campaign in the spring, and there is much to make ready." He raised the silver cup to his lips, repeating, "It is out of the question. I am sorry."

Lady Agnes sat in silence for a moment, studying her hands in her lap. "This campaign is important to you, I suppose?" she wondered.

"Important? What a question, woman! Of course, it is of the highest importance. A successful outcome will extend our holdings into the very heart of Wales," the baron said, growing excited at the thought. "Our estates will increase threefold . . . fivefold—and our revenues likewise! I'd call that *important*, wouldn't you?" he sneered.

"Then," Agnes suggested lightly, "I would think it equally important to ensure that success by securing the necessary troops."

"Of course," answered Bernard irritably. "It goes without saying—which is why I wrote the letter."

His wife lifted her thin shoulders in a shrug of studied indifference. "As you say."

He let the matter rest there for a moment, but something in her tone suggested she knew more than she had said.

"Why?" he asked, his suspicion getting the better of him at last.

"Oh," she said, turning her eyes to the fire once more, "no reason."

"Come now, my dear. Let us have it out. You have a thought in this matter, I can tell, and I will hear it."

"You flatter me, I'm sure, husband," she replied. "I am content."

"But I am not!" he said, anger edging into his tone. "What is in your mind?"

"Do not raise your voice to me, sire!" she snapped. "I assure you it is not seemly."

"Very well!" he said, his voice loud in the chamber. He glared at her for a moment and then tried again. "But see here, it is folly to quarrel. Consider that I am overtired from a long journey—it is that making me sharp, nothing more. Therefore, let us be done with this foolishness." He coaxed her with a smile. "Now tell me, my dear, what is in your mind?"

"Since you ask," she said, "it occurs to me that if the campaign is as gravely important as you contend, then I would not entrust such an undertaking to a mere equerry."

"Why not? Ormand is entirely trustworthy."

"That is as may be," she allowed primly, "but if you really need the troops, then why place so much weight on a mere letter in the hand of an insignificant menial?"

"And what would you do?"

"I'd send a suitable emissary instead."

"An emissary."

"Yes," she agreed, "and what better emissary than the sole and beloved daughter-in-law of the duke himself?" She paused, allowing her words to take effect. "Duke Geoffrey can easily refuse a letter in Ormand's hand," she concluded, "as you and I know only too well. But refuse me? Never."

Bernard considered this for a moment, tapping the silver base of his cup with a finger. What she suggested was not entirely without merit. He could already see certain advantages. If she went, she might obtain not only troops, but money as well. And it was true that the old duke could never deny his daughter-in-law anything. He might fume and fret for a few days, but he would succumb to her wishes in the end.

HOOD

"Very well," decided the baron abruptly, "you shall go. Ormand will accompany you—and your maidservants, of course—but you will bear the letter yourself and read it to the duke when you judge him in a favourable mood to grant our request."

Lady Agnes smiled and inclined her head in acquiescence to his desires. "As always, my husband, your counsel is impeccable."

Bran stirred his mount to speed. "Iwan!" he cried. At the sound of his name, the king's champion raised himself in the saddle, and Bran saw blood oozing down the warrior's padded leather tunic.

"Bran!" the warrior gasped. "Bran, thank God. Listen—"

"Iwan, what has happened? Where are the others?"

"We were attacked at Wye ford," he said. "Ffreinc—three hundred or more . . . sixty, maybe seventy knights, the rest footmen."

Lurching sideways, he seized the young prince by the arm. "Bran, you must ride . . . ," he began, but his eyes rolled up into his head; he slumped and toppled from the saddle.

Bran, holding tight to his arm, tried to lower his longtime friend more gently to the ground. Iwan landed hard nonetheless and sprawled between the horses. Bran slid off the mare and eased the wounded man onto his back. "Iwan! Iwan!" he said, trying to rouse him. "My father, the warband—where are the others?"

"Dead," moaned Iwan. "All . . . all of them dead."

Bran quickly retrieved a waterskin from its place behind his saddle.

"Here," he said, holding the skin to the warrior's mouth, "drink a little. It will restore you."

The battlechief sucked down a long, thirsty draught and then shoved the skin away. "You must raise the alarm," he said, some vigour returning to his voice. He clutched at Bran and held him fast. "You must ride and warn the people. Warn everyone. The king is dead, and the Ffreinc are coming."

"How much time do we have?" asked Bran.

"Enough, pray God," said the battlechief. "Less if you stay. Go now."

Bran hesitated, unable to decide what should be done.

"Now!" Iwan said, pushing the prince away. "There is but time to hide the women and children."

"We will go together. I will help you."

"Go!" snarled Iwan. "Leave me!"

"Not like this."

Ignoring the wounded man's curses, Bran helped him to his feet and back into the saddle. Then, taking up the reins of Iwan's horse, he led them both back the way he had come. Owing to the battlechief's wound, they travelled more slowly than Bran would have wished, eventually reaching the western edge of the forest, where he paused to allow the horses and wounded man to rest. "Is there much pain?" he asked.

"Not so much," Iwan said, pressing a hand to his chest. "Ah, a little . . ."

"We'll wait here awhile." Bran dismounted, walked a few paces ahead, and crouched beside the road, scanning the valley for any sign of the enemy invaders.

The broad, undulating lowlands of Elfael spread before him, shimmering gently in the blue haze of an early autumn day. Secluded, green, fertile, a region of gentle, wooded hills seamed through with clear-running streams and brooks, it lay pleasantly between the high, bare stone crags of mountains to the north and east and the high moorland wastes to the south. Not the largest cantref beyond the Marches, in Bran's estimation it tendered in charm what it lacked in size.

In the near distance, the king's fortress on its high mound, white-washed walls gleaming in the sunlight, stood sentinel at the gateway to Elfael, which seemed to drowse in the heavy, honeyed light. So quiet, so peaceful—the likelihood of anything disturbing such a deep and luxurious serenity seemed impossibly remote, a mere cloud shadow passing over a sun-bright meadow, a little dimming of the light before the sun blazed forth again. Caer Cadarn had been his family's home for eight generations, and he had never imagined anything could ever change that.

Bran satisfied himself that all was calm—at least for the moment—then returned to his mount and swung into the saddle once more.

"See anything?" asked Iwan. Hollow-eyed, his face was pale and dripping with sweat.

"No Ffreinc," Bran replied, "yet."

They started down into the valley at a trot. Bran did not stop at the hill fort but rode straight to Llanelli, the tiny monastery that occupied the heel of the valley and stood halfway between the fortress and Glascwm, the chief town of the neighbouring cantref—and the only settlement of any size in the entire region. Although merely an outpost of the larger abbey of Saint Dyfrig at Glascwm, the Llanelli monastery served the people of Elfael well. The monks, Bran had decided, not only would know best how to raise an alarm to warn the people, but also would be able to help Iwan.

The gates of the monastery were open, so they rode through and halted in the bare-earth yard outside the little timber and mud-daubed church. "Brother Ffreol! Brother Ffreol!" Bran shouted; he leapt from the saddle and ran to the door of the church. A lone priest was kneeling before the altar. An elderly man, he turned as Bran burst in upon his prayers.

"Lord Bran," said the old man, rising shakily to his feet. "God be good to you."

"Where is Brother Ffreol?"

"I am sure I cannot say," replied the aging monk. "He might be anywhere. Why all this shouting?"

Without reply, Bran seized the bell rope. The bell pealed wildly in response to his frantic pulling, and soon monks were hurrying to the church from every direction. First through the door was Brother Cefan, a local lad only slightly older than Bran himself. "Lord Bran, what is wrong?"

"Where is Ffreol?" demanded Bran, still tugging on the bell rope. "I need him."

"He was in the scriptorium a short while ago," replied the youth. "I don't know where he is now."

"Find him!" ordered Bran. "Hurry!"

The young brother darted back through the door, colliding with Bishop Asaph, a dour, humourless drone of advancing age and, as Bran had always considered, middling ability. "You there!" he shouted, striding into the church. "Stop that! You hear? Release that rope at once!"

Bran dropped the rope and spun around.

"Oh, it's you, Bran," said the bishop, his features arranging themselves in a frown of weary disapproval. "I might have guessed. What, pray, is the meaning of this spirited summons?"

"No time to waste, bishop," said Bran. Rushing up, he snatched the churchman by the sleeve of his robe and pulled him out of the church and into the yard, where twenty or so of the monastery's inhabitants were quickly gathering.

"Calm yourself," said Bishop Asaph, shaking himself free of Bran's grasp. "We're all here, so explain this commotion if you can."

"The Ffreinc are coming," said Bran. "Three hundred marchogi—they are on their way here now." Pointing to the battlechief sitting slumped in the saddle, he said, "Iwan fought them, and he's wounded. He needs help at once."

"Marchogi!" gasped the gathered monks, glancing fearfully at one another.

"But why tell *us*?" wondered the bishop. "Your father should be the one to—"

"The king is dead," Bran said. "They murdered him—and the rest of the warband with him. Everyone is dead. We have no protection."

"I do not understand," sputtered the bishop. "What do you mean? Everyone?"

Fear snaked through the gathered monks. "The warband dead! We are lost!"

Brother Ffreol appeared, pushing his way through the crowd. "Bran, I saw you ride in. There is trouble. What has happened?"

"The Ffreinc are coming!" he said, turning to meet the priest and pull him close. "Three hundred marchogi. They're on their way to Elfael now."

"Will Rhi Brychan fight them?"

"He already did," said Bran. "There was a battle on the road. My father and his men have been killed. Iwan alone escaped to warn us. He is injured—here," he said, moving to the wounded champion, "help me get him down."

Together with a few of the other brothers, they eased the warrior down from his horse and laid him on the ground. While Brother Galen, the monastery physician, began examining the wounds, Bran said, "We must raise the alarm. There is still time for everyone to flee."

"Leave that with me. I will see to it," replied Ffreol. "You must ride to Caer Cadarn and gather everything you care to save. Go now— and may God go with you."

"Wait a moment," said the bishop, raising his hand to stop them from hurrying off. Turning to Bran, he said, "Why would the Ffreinc come here? Your father has arranged to swear a treaty of peace with William the Red."

"And he was on his way to do just that!" snapped Bran, growing angry at the perfunctory insinuation that he was lying. "Am I the Red King's counsellor now that I should be privy to a Ffreinc rogue's thoughts?" He glared at the suspicious bishop.

"Calm yourself, my son," said Asaph stiffly. "There is no need to mock. I was only asking."

"They will arrive in force," Bran said, climbing into the saddle once more. "I will save what I can from the caer and return here for Iwan."

42

"And then?" wondered Asaph.

"We will flee while there is still time!"

The bishop shook his head. "No, Bran. You must ride to Lundein instead. You must finish what your father intended."

"No," replied Bran. "It is impossible. I cannot go to Lundein— and even if I did, the king would never listen to me."

"The king *will* listen," the bishop insisted. "William is not un- reasonable. You must talk to him. You must tell him what has hap- pened and seek redress."

"Red William will not see me!"

"Bran," said Brother Ffreol. He came to stand at the young man's stir- rup and placed his hand on his leg as if to restrain him. "Bishop Asaph is right. You will be king now. William will certainly see you. And when he does, you must swear the treaty your father meant to undertake."

Bran opened his mouth to object, but Bishop Asaph stopped him, saying, "A grave mistake has been made, and the king must provide remedy. You must obtain justice for your people."

"Mistake!" cried Bran. "My father has been killed, and his war-band slaughtered!"

"Not by William," the bishop pointed out. "When the king hears what has happened, he will punish the man who did this and make reparations."

Bran rejected the advice out of hand. The course they urged was childish and dangerous. Before he could begin to explain the utter folly of their plan, Asaph turned to the brothers who stood looking on and commanded them to take the alarm to the countryside and town. "The people are not to oppose the Ffreinc by force," instructed the bishop sternly. "This is a holy decree, tell them. Enough blood has been shed already—and that needlessly. We must not give the enemy cause to attack. God willing, this occupation will be brief. But until it ends, we will all endure it as best we can."

The bishop sent his messengers away, saying, "Go now, and with all speed. Tell everyone you meet to spread the word—each to his neighbour. No one is to be overlooked."

The monks hurried off, deserting the monastery on the run. Bran watched them go, grave misgivings mounting by the moment. "Now then," said Bishop Asaph, turning once more to Bran, "you must reach Lundein as quickly as possible. The sooner this error can be remedied, the less damage will result and the better for everyone. You must leave at once."

"This is madness," Bran told him. "We'll all be killed."

"It is the only way," Ffreol asserted. "You must do it for the sake of Elfael and the throne."

Bran stared incredulously at the two churchmen. Every instinct told him to run, to fly.

43

"I will go with you," offered Ffreol. "Whatever I can do to aid you in this, trust it will be done."

"Good," said the bishop, satisfied with this arrangement. "Now go, both of you, and may God lend you his own wisdom and the swiftness of very angels."

44

Racing up the ramp, Bran flew through the gates of Caer Cadarn. He leapt from the saddle, shouting before his feet touched the ground. The disagreeable Maelgwnt drifted into the yard. "What now?" he asked. "Foundered another horse? Two in one day—what will your father say, I wonder?"

"My father is dead," Bran said, his tone lashing, "and all who rode with him, save Iwan."

The steward's eyes narrowed as he tried to work out the likelihood of Bran's wild assertion. "If that is a jest, it is a poor one—even for you."

"It is God's own truth!" Bran snarled. Clutching the startled man by the arm, he turned him around and marched swiftly toward the king's hall. "They were attacked by a Ffreinc warhost that is on its way here now," he explained. "They will come here first. Take the strong-box and silver to the monastery—the servants, too. Leave no one behind. The marchogi will take the fortress and everything in it for their own."

"What about the livestock?" asked Maelgwnt.

"To the monastery," replied Bran, dashing for the door. "Use your head, man! Anything worth saving—take it to Llanelli. The monks will keep it safe for us."

He ran through the hall to the armoury beyond: a square, thick-walled room with long slits for windows. As he expected, the best weapons were gone; the warband had taken all but a few rusty, bent-bladed swords and some well-worn spears. He selected the most serviceable of these and then turned to the rack of longbows hanging on the far wall.

For some reason—probably for decorum's sake in Lundein—his father had left all the warbows behind. He picked one up, tried it, and slung it over his shoulder. He tucked a red-rusted sword into his belt, grabbed up a sheaf of arrows and several of the least blunt spears, and then raced to the stables. Dumping the weapons on the floor, Bran commanded Cefn to saddle another of the mares. "When you're finished, bring it to the yard. Brother Ffreol is on his way here by foot; I want to leave the moment he arrives."

Cefn, wan and distraught, made no move to obey. "Is it true?"

"The massacre?" Bran asked. "Yes, it's true. Ffreol and I ride now to Lundein to see the Red King, swear allegiance, and secure the return of our lands. As soon as I leave, run and find Maelgwnt—do everything he says. We're moving everything to the monastery. Never fear, you will be safe there. Understand?"

Cefn nodded.

"Good. Hurry now. There is not much time."

Bran returned to the kitchen to find the old cook comforting her young helpers. They were huddled beneath her ample arms like chicks beneath the wings of a hen, and she held them, patting their shoulders and stroking their heads. "Mairead, I need provisions," Bran said, striding quickly into the room. "Brother Ffreol and I are riding to Lundein at once."

"Bran! Oh, Bran!" wailed the woman. "Rhi Brychan is dead!"

"He is," Bran replied, pulling the two whimpering girls from her grasp.

"And all who rode with him?"

"Gone," he confirmed. "And we will mourn them properly when we have rid ourselves of these scabby Ffreinc thieves. But you must listen to me now. As soon as I am gone, Maelgwnt will take everyone to Llanelli. Stay there until I return. The Ffreinc will not harm you if you remain at the monastery with the monks. Do you hear me?"

The woman nodded, her eyes filled with unshed tears. Bran turned her and pushed her gently away. "Off with you now! Hurry and bring the food to the yard."

Next, Bran dashed to his father's chamber and to the small wooden casket where the king kept his ready money. The real treasure was kept in the strongbox that Maelgwnt would see hidden at the monastery—two hundred marks in English silver. The smaller casket contained but a few marks used for buying at the market, paying for favours, bestowing largesse on the tenants, and other occasional uses.

There were four bags of coins in all—more than enough to see them safely to Lundein and back. Bran scooped up the little leather bags, stuffed them into his shirt, then ran back out to the yard, where Brother Ffreol was just coming through the gate, leading Iwan on horseback behind him.

"Iwan, what are you doing here?" Bran asked, running to meet them. "You should stay at the monastery where they can tend you."

"Save your breath," advised Ffreol. "I've already tried to dissuade him, but he refuses to heed a word I say."

47

"I am going with you," the battlechief declared flatly. "That is the end of it."

"You are wounded," Bran pointed out needlessly.

"Not so badly that I cannot sit in a saddle," answered the big man. "I want to see the look in the Red King's eye when we stand before him and demand justice. And," he added, "if a witness to this outrage is required, then you will have one."

Bran opened his mouth to object once more, but Ffreol said, "Let him be. If he feels that way about it, nothing we say will discourage him, and stubborn as he is, he'd only follow us anyway."

Glancing toward the stable, Bran muttered, "What is keeping Cefn?" He shouted for the groom to hurry; when that brought no response, he started for the stable to see what was taking so long.

Brother Ffreol held him back, saying, "Calm yourself, Bran. You've been running all day. Rest when you can. We will be on our way soon enough."

"Not soon enough for me," he cried, racing off to the stable to help Cefn finish saddling the horses. They were leading two mares into the yard when Mairead appeared with her two kitchen helpers, each carrying a cloth sack bulging with provisions. While the priest blessed the women and prayed over them, Bran and Cefn arranged the tuck bags behind the saddles and strapped them down, secreting the money in the folds. "Come, Ffreol," Bran said, taking the reins from the groom and mounting the saddle, "if they catch us here, all is lost."

". . . and may the Lord make his face to shine upon you and give you his peace through all things whatsoever may befall you," intoned the priest, bestowing a kiss on the bowed head of each woman in turn. "Amen. Now off with you! Help Maelgwnt, and then all of you hie to Llanelli as soon as you can."

The sun was already low in the west by the time the three riders crossed the stream and started up the long rising slope toward the edge of the forest; their shadows stretched long on the road, going before them like spindly, misshapen ghosts. They rode in silence until entering the shady margin of the trees.

Coed Cadw, the Guarding Wood, was a dense tangle of ancient trees: oak, elm, lime, plane—all the titans of the wood. Growing amongst and beneath these giants were younger, smaller trees and thickets of hazel and beech. The road itself was lined with blackberry brambles that formed a hedge wall along either side so thick and lush that three paces off the road in any direction and a person could no longer be seen from the path.

"Is it wise, do you think," asked the priest, "to keep to the road? The marchogi are certain to be on it too."

"I do not doubt it," replied Bran, "but going any other way would take far too long. If we keep our wits about us, we will hear them long before they hear us, and we can easily get off the road and out of sight."

Iwan, his face tight with pain, said nothing. Brother Ffreol accepted Bran's assurances, and they rode on.

"Do you think we should have seen the Ffreinc by now?" asked the monk after a while. "If they had been in a hurry to reach Elfael, we would certainly have met them. They probably stopped to make camp for the night. God be praised."

"You praise God for that?"

"I do," admitted the monk. "It means the Cymry have at least one night to hide their valuables and get to safety."

"One night," mocked Bran. "As much as all that!"

"Wars have turned on less," the priest pointed out. "If the Conqueror's arrow had flown but a finger's breadth to the right of Harold's eye, the Ffreinc would not be here now."

"Yes, well, it seems to me that if God really wanted praising, he'd

49

have prevented the filthy Ffreinc and their foul marchogi from coming here in the first place."

"Do you have the mind of God now that you know all things good and ill for each and every one of his creatures?"

"It does not take the mind of God," replied Bran carelessly, "to know that anytime a Norman stands at your gate it is for ill and never good. That is a doctrine more worthy than any Bishop Asaph ever professed."

"Jesu forgive you," sighed the priest. "Such irreverence."

"Irreverent or not, it is true."

They fell silent and rode on. As the sun sank lower, the shadows on the trail gathered, deepening beneath the trees and brushwood; the sounds became hushed and furtive as the forest drew in upon itself for the night.

The road began to rise more steeply toward the spine of the ridge, and Bran slowed the pace. In a little while the gloom had spread so that the gap between trees was as dark as the black boles themselves, and the road shone as a ghost-pale ribbon stretching dimly away into the deepening night.

"I think we should stop," suggested Brother Ffreol. "It will soon be too dark to see. We could rest and eat something. Also, I want to tend Iwan's wound."

Bran was of a mind to ride all night, but one look at the wounded warrior argued otherwise, so he gave in and allowed the monk to have his way. They picketed the horses and made camp at the base of an oak just out of sight of the road, ate a few mouthfuls of bread and a little hard cheese, and then settled down to sleep beneath the tree's protecting limbs. Wrapped in his cloak, Bran slept uneasily, rising again as it became light enough to tell tree from shadow.

He roused Ffreol and then went to Iwan, who came awake at his touch. "How do you feel?" he asked, kneeling beside the champion.

"Never better," Iwan said as he tried to sit up. The pain hit him hard and slammed him back once more. He grimaced and blew air through his mouth, panting like a winded hound. "Perhaps I will try that again," he said through clenched teeth, "more slowly this time."

"Wait a moment," said Ffreol, putting out his hand. "Let me see your binding." He pulled open the big man's shirt and looked at the bandage wrapped around his upper chest. "It is clean still. There is little blood," he announced, greatly reassured.

"Then it is time we made a start."

"When we have prayed," said the monk.

"Oh, very well," sighed Bran. "Just get on with it."

The priest gathered his robe around him, and folding his hands, he closed his eyes and began to pray for the speedy and sure success of their mission. Bran followed the sound of his voice more than the words and imagined that he heard a low, rhythmic drumming marking out the cadence. He listened for a while before realising that he was not imagining the sound. "Quiet!" he hissed. "Someone's coming."

Ffreol helped Iwan to his feet, and the two disappeared into the underbrush; Bran darted to the horses and threw his cloak over their heads to keep them quiet, then stood and held the cloak in place so the animals would not shake it off. Brother Ffreol, flat on the ground, watched the narrow slice of road that he could see from beneath his bush. "Ffreinc!" he whispered a few moments later. "Scores of them." He paused, then added, "Hundreds."

Bran, holding the horses' heads, heard the creak and rattle of wagon wheels, followed by the dull, hollow clop of hundreds of hooves and the tramp of leather-shod feet—a pulsing beat that seemed to go on and on and on.

At long last, the sound gradually faded and the bird-fretted silence of the forest returned. "I believe they have gone," said Ffreol softly.

He rose and brushed off his robe. Bran stood listening for a moment longer, and when no one else appeared on the road, he uncovered the horses' heads. Working quickly and quietly, he saddled the horses and then led the animals through the forest, within sight of the road. When, after walking a fair distance, no more marchogi appeared, he allowed them to leave the forest path and return to the road. The three travellers took to the saddle once more and bolted for Lundein.

By midmorning Bran, Iwan, and Brother Ffreol had begun the long, sloping ascent of the ridge overlooking the Vale of Wye. Upon reaching the top, they paused and looked down into the broad valley and the glittering sweep of the lazy green river. In the distance they could see the dark flecks of birds circling and swooping in the cloudless sky. Bran saw them, and his stomach tightened with apprehension.

As the men approached the river ford, the strident calls of carrion feeders filled the air—ravens, rooks, and crows for the most part, but there were others. Hawks, buzzards, and even an owl or two wheeled in tight circles above the trees.

Bran stopped at the water's edge. The soft ground of the riverbank was raggedly churned and chewed, as if a herd of giant boar had undertaken to plough the water marge with their tusks. There were no corpses to be seen, but here and there flies buzzed in thick black clouds over congealing puddles where blood had collected in a horse's hoofprint. The air was heavy and rank with the sickly sweet stench of death.

Bran dismounted and walked back toward the road, where most of the fighting had taken place. He looked down and saw that in the place where he stood the earth took on a deeper, ruddy hue where a warrior's lifeblood had stained the ground on which he died.

"This is where it happened," mused Brother Ffreol with quiet reverence. "This is where the warriors of Elfael were overthrown."

"Aye," confirmed Iwan, his face grim and grey with fatigue and pain. "This is where we were ambushed and massacred." He lifted his hand and pointed to the wide bend of the river. "Rhi Brychan fell there," he said. "By the time I reached him, his body had been washed away."

Bran, mouth pressed into a thin white line, stared at the water and said nothing. Once he might have felt a twinge of regret at his father's passing, but not now. Years of accumulated grievances had long ago removed his father from his affections. Sorrow alone could not surmount the rancour and bitterness, nor span the aching distance between them. He whispered a cold farewell and turned once more to the battleground.

Images of chaos sprang into his mind—a desperate battle between woefully outnumbered and lightly armed Britons and heavy, hulking, mail-clad Ffreinc knights. He saw the blood haze hang like a mist in the air above the slaughter and heard the echoed clash of steel on steel, of blade on wood and bone, the fast-fading shouts and screams of men and horses as they died.

Looking toward the wood to the north, he saw the birds flocking to their feeding frenzy. Squawking, shrieking, they fought and fluttered, battering wings against one another in their greed. Grabbing up stones from the riverbank, he ran to the place, throwing rocks into the midst of the feathered scavengers as he ran.

Reluctant to leave the mound on which they fed, the scolding birds fluttered up and settled again as the angry stones sailed past.

Stooping once more, he took up another handful of rocks and, screaming at the top of his lungs, let fly. One of the missiles struck a greedy
red-beaked crow and snapped its neck. The wounded bird flopped,
beating its wings in a last frantic effort to rise; Bran threw again and
the bird lay still.

The hillock was covered with brush and branches cut from the
thickets and trees along the riverbank. Pulling a stick from the pile,
Bran began beating at the flesh eaters; they hopped and dodged, reluctant to give ground. Bran, screaming like a demon, lashed with the
branch, driving the scavengers away. They fled with angry reluctance,
crying their outrage to the sky as Bran pulled brushwood from the
stack to lay bare a massed heap of corpses.

The stick in his hand fell away, and Bran staggered backward, overwhelmed by the calamity that had taken the lives of his kinsmen and
friends. The birds had feasted well. There were gaping hollows where
eyes had been; flesh had been stripped from faces; ragged holes had
been wrested in rib cages to expose the soft viscera. Human no longer,
they were merely so much rotting meat.

No! These were men he knew. They were friends, riding companions, fellow hunters, drinking mates—some of them from times before
he could remember. They had taught him trail craft, had given him his
first lessons with blunted wooden weapons made for him with their
own hands. They had picked him up when he fell from his horse, corrected his aim when he practised with the bow, and along the way,
taught him much of what he knew of life. To see them now with their
empty eyes and livid, blackening faces, their ruined bodies beginning
to bloat, was more than he could bear.

As he gazed in mute horror at the confused tangle of slashed and
bloodied limbs and torsos, something deep inside himself gave way—
as if a ligament or sinew suddenly snapped under the strain of a load

too heavy to bear. His soul spun into a void of bloodred rage. His vision narrowed, and it seemed as if his surroundings had taken on a keener, harder edge but were now viewed from a long way off. It seemed to Bran that he gazed at the world through a red-tinged tunnel.

There was another hill nearby—also crudely covered with brush and lopped-off tree branches. Bran ran to it, uncovered it, and without realising what he was doing, climbed up onto the tangled jumble of bodies. He sank to his knees and grasped the arms of the corpses with his hands, tugging on them as if urging their sleeping owners to wake again and rise. "Get up!" he shouted. "Open your eyes!" He saw a face he recognised; seizing the corpse's arm, he jerked on it, crying, "Evan, wake up!" He saw another: "Geronwy! The Ffreinc are here!" He began calling the names of those he remembered, "Bryn! Ifan! Oryg! Gerallt! Idris! Madog! Get up, all of you!"

"Bran!" Brother Ffreol, shocked and alarmed, ran to pull him away. "Bran! For the love of God, come down from there!"

Stumbling up over the dead, the monk reached out and snagged Bran by the sleeve and hauled him down, dragging the prince back to solid ground and back to himself once more.

Bran heard Ffreol's voice and felt the monk's hands on him, and awareness came flooding back. The blood-tinged veil through which he viewed the world dimmed and faded, and he was himself once more. He felt weak and hollow, like a man who has slaved all night in his sleep and awakened exhausted.

"What were you doing up there?" demanded Brother Ffreol.

Bran shook his head. "I thought . . . I—" Suddenly, his stomach heaved; he pitched forward on hands and knees and retched.

Ffreol stood with him until he finished. When Bran could stand again, the priest turned to the death mound and sank to his knees in the soft earth. Bran knelt beside him, and Iwan painfully dismounted and knelt beside his horse as Brother Ffreol spread his arms, palms upward in abject supplication.

Closing his eyes and turning his face to heaven, the priest said, "Merciful Father, our hearts are pierced with the sharp arrow of grief. Our words fail; our souls quail; our spirits recoil before the injustice of this hateful iniquity. We are undone.

"God and Creator, gather the souls of our kinsmen to your Great Hall, forgive their sins and remember only their virtues, and bind them to yourself with the strong bands of fellowship.

"For ourselves, Mighty Father, I pray you keep us from the sin of hatred, keep us from the sin of vengeance, keep us from the sin of despair, but protect us from the wicked schemes of our enemies. Walk with us now on this uncertain road. Send angels to go before us, angels to go behind, angels on either side, angels above and below—guarding, shielding, encompassing." He paused for a moment and then added, "May the Holy One give us the courage of righteousness and grant us strength for this day and through all things whatsoever shall befall us. Amen."

Bran, kneeling beside him, stared at the ground and tried to add his "Amen," but the word clotted and died in his throat. After a moment, he raised his head and gazed for the last time on the heap of corpses before turning his face away.

Then, while Bran bathed in the river to wash the stink of death and gore from his hands and clothes, Ffreol and Iwan covered the bodies once more with fresh-cut branches of hazel and holly, the better to keep the birds away. Bran finished, and the three grief-sick men remounted and rode on as the cacophony of carrion feeders renewed behind them. Just after midday they crossed the border into England and a short while later approached the English town of Hereford. The town was full of Ffreinc now, so they moved on

57

quickly without stopping. From Hereford, the road was wide and well used, if deeply rutted. They encountered few people and spoke to none, pretending to be deep in conversation with one another whenever they saw anyone approaching, all the while remaining watchful and wary.

Beyond Hereford, the land sloped gently down toward the lowlands and the wide Lundein estuary still some way beyond the distant horizon of rumpled, cultivated hills. As daylight began to fail, they took refuge in a beech grove beside the road near the next ford; while Bran watered the horses, Ffreol prepared a meal from the provisions in their tuck bags. They ate in silence, and Bran listened to the rooks flocking to the woods for the night. The sound of their coarse calls renewed the horror of the day. He saw the broken bodies of his friends once more. With an effort, he concentrated on the fire, holding the hateful images at bay.

"It will take time," Ffreol said, the sound of his voice a distant buzz in Bran's ears, "but the memory will fade, believe me." At the sound of his voice, Bran struggled back from the brink. "The memory of this black day will fade," Ffreol was saying as he broke twigs and fed them to the fire. "It will vanish like a bad taste in your mouth. One day it will be gone, and you will be left with only the sweetness."

"There was little sweetness," sniffed Bran. "My father, the king, was not an easy man."

"I was talking about the others—your friends in the warband."

Bran acknowledged the remark with a grunt.

"But you are right," Ffreol continued; he snapped another twig. "Brychan was not an easy man. God be praised, you have the chance to do something about that. You can be a better king than your father."

"No." Bran picked up the dried husk of a beechnut and tossed it into the fire as if consigning his own fragile future to the flames.

He cared little enough for the throne and all its attendant difficulties. What difference did it make who was king anyway? "That's over now. Finished."

"You *will* be king," declared Iwan, stirring himself from his bleak reverie. "The kingdom will be restored. Never doubt it."

But Bran did doubt it. For most of his life he had maintained a keen disinterest in all things having to do with kingship. He had never imagined himself occupying his father's throne at Caer Cadarn or leading a host of men into battle. Those things, like the other chores of nobility, were the sole occupation of his father. Bran always had other pursuits. So far as Bran could tell, to reign was merely to invite a perpetual round of frustration and aggravation that lasted from the moment one took the crown until it was laid aside. Only a power-crazed thug like his father would solicit such travail. Any way he looked at it, sovreignty exacted a heavy price, which Bran had seen firsthand and which, now that it came to it, he found himself unwilling to pay.

"You will be king," Iwan asserted again. "On my life, you will."

Bran, reluctant to disappoint the injured champion with a facile denial, held his tongue. The three were silent again for a time, watching the flames and listening to the sounds of the wood around them as its various denizens prepared for night. Finally, Bran asked, "What if they will not see us in Lundein?"

"Oh, William the Red will see us, make no mistake." Iwan raised his head and regarded Bran over the fluttering fire. "You are a subject lord come to swear fealty. He will see you and be glad of it. He will welcome you as one king welcomes another."

"I am not the king," Bran pointed out.

"You are heir to the throne," replied the champion. "It is the same thing."

Ffreol said, "When we return to Elfael, we will observe the proper

59

rites and ceremonies. But this will be the first duty of your reign—to place Elfael under the protection of the English throne and—"

"And all of us become boot-licking slaves of the stinking Ffreinc," Bran said, his tone bitter and biting. "What is the stupid bloody point?"

"We keep our land!" Iwan retorted. "We keep our lives."

"If God and King William allow!" sneered Bran.

"Nay, Bran," said Ffreol. "We will pay tribute, yes, and count it a price worth paying to live our lives as we choose."

"Pay tribute to the very brutes that would plunder us if we didn't," growled Bran. "That stinks to high heaven."

"Does it stink worse than death?" asked Iwan. Bran, shamed by the taunt, merely glared.

"It is unjust," granted Ffreol, trying to soothe, "but that is ever the way of things."

"Did you think it would be different?" asked Iwan angrily. "Saints and angels, Bran, it was never going to be easy."

"It could at least be fair," muttered Bran.

"Fair or not, you must do all you can to protect our lands and the lives of our people," Ffreol told him. "To protect those least able to protect themselves. That much, at least, has not changed. That was ever the sole purpose and duty of kingship. Since the beginning of time it has not changed."

Bran accepted this observation without further comment. He stared gloomily into the fire, wishing he had followed his first impulse to leave Elfael and all its troubles as far behind as possible.

After a time, Iwan asked about Lundein. Ffreol had been to the city several times on church business in years past, and he described for Bran and Iwan what they might expect to find when they arrived. As he talked, night deepened around them, and they continued to feed the fire until they grew too tired to keep their eyes open. They then wrapped themselves in their cloaks and fell asleep in the quiet grove.

Rising again at dawn, the travellers shook the leaves and dew from their cloaks, watered the horses, and continued on. The day passed much like the one before, except that the settlements became more numerous and the English presence in the land became more marked, until Bran was convinced that they had left Britain far behind and entered an alien country, where the houses were small and dark and crabbed, where grim-faced people dressed in curious garb made up of coarse dun-coloured cloth stood and stared at passing travellers with suspicion in their dull peasant eyes. Despite the sunlight streaming down from a clear blue sky, the land seemed dismal and unhappy. Even the animals, in their woven willow enclosures, appeared bedraggled and morose.

Nor was the aspect to improve. The farther south they went, the more abject the countryside appeared. Settlements of all kinds became more numerous—how the English loved their villages—but these were not wholesome places. Clustered together in what Bran considered suffocating proximity anywhere the earth offered a flat space and a little running water, the close-set hovels sprouted like noxious mushrooms on earth stripped of all trees and greenery—which the mud-dwellers used to make humpbacked houses, barns, and byres for their livestock, which they kept in muck-filled pens beside their low, smoky dwellings.

Thus, a traveller could always smell an English town long before he reached it, and Bran could only shake his head in wonder at the thought of abiding in perpetual fug and stench. In his opinion, the people lived no better than the pigs they slopped, slaughtered, and fed upon.

As the sun began to lower, the three riders crested the top of a broad hill and looked down into the Vale of Hafren and the gleaming arc of the Hafren River. A smudgy brown haze in the valley betrayed their destination for the night: the town of Gleawancaester, which began life in ancient times as a simple outpost of the Roman Legio Augusta XX. Owing to its pride of place by the river and the proximity of iron mines, the town begun by legionary veterans had grown slowly over the centuries until the arrival of the English, who transformed it into a market centre for the region.

The road into the vale widened as it neared the city, which to Bran's eyes was worse than any he had seen so far—if only because it was larger than any other they had yet passed. Squatting hard by the river, with twisting, narrow streets of crowded hovels clustered around a huge central market square of beaten earth, Gleawancaester—Caer Gloiu of the Britons—had long ago outgrown the stout stone walls of the Roman garrison, which could still be seen in the lower courses of the city's recently refurbished fortress.

Like the town's other defences—a wall and gate, still unfinished— a new bridge of timber and stone bore testimony to Ffreinc occupation. Norman bridges were wide and strong, built to withstand heavy traffic and ensure that the steady stream of horses, cattle, and merchant wagons flowed unimpeded into and out of the markets.

Bran noticed the increase in activity as they approached the bridge. Here and there, tall, clean-shaven Ffreinc moved amongst the shorter, swarthier English residents. The sight of these horse-faced foreigners with their long, straight-cut hair and pale, sun-starved flesh walking about with such toplofty arrogance made the gorge rise in his throat. He forcibly turned his face away to keep from being sick.

Before crossing the bridge, they dismounted to stretch their legs and water the horses at a wooden trough set up next to a riverside well. As they were waiting, Bran noticed two barefoot, ragged little

62

girls walking together, carrying a basket of eggs between them—no doubt bound for the market. They fell in with the traffic moving across the bridge. Two men in short cloaks and tunics loitered at the rail, and as the girls passed by, one of the men, grinning at his companion, stuck out his foot, tripping the nearest girl. She fell sprawling onto the bridge planks; the basket overturned, spilling the eggs.

Bran, watching this confrontation develop, immediately started toward the child. When, as the second girl bent to retrieve the basket, the man kicked it from her grasp, scattering eggs every which way, Bran was already on the bridge.

Iwan, glancing up from the trough, took in the girls, Bran, and the two thugs and shouted for Bran to come back.

"Where is he going?" wondered Ffreol, looking around.

"To make trouble," muttered Iwan.

The two little girls, tearful now, tried in vain to gather up the few unbroken eggs, only to have them kicked from their hands or trodden on by passersby—much to the delight of the louts on the bridge. The toughs were so intent on their merriment that they failed to notice the slender Welshman bearing down on them until Bran, lurching forward as if slipping on a broken egg, stumbled up to the man who had tripped the girl. The fellow made to shove Bran away, whereupon Bran seized his arm, spun him around, and pushed him over the rail. His surprised yelp was cut short as the dun-coloured water closed over his head. "Oops!" said Bran. "How clumsy of me."

"Mon Dieu!" objected the other, backing away.

Bran turned on him and drew him close. "What is that you say?" he asked. "You wish to join him?"

"Bran! Leave him alone!" shouted Ffreol as he pulled Bran off the man. "He can't understand you. Let him go!"

63

The oaf spared a quick glance at his friend, sputtering and floundering in the river below, then fled down the street. "I think he understood well enough," observed Bran.

"Come away," said Ffreol.

"Not yet," said Bran. Taking the purse at his belt, he untied it and withdrew two silver pennies. Turning to the older of the two girls, he wiped the remains of an eggshell from her cheek. "Give those to your mother," he said, pressing the coins into the girl's grubby fist. Closing her hand upon the coins, he repeated, "For your mother."

Brother Ffreol picked up the empty basket and handed it to the younger girl; he spoke a quick word in English, and the two scampered away. "Now unless you have any other battles you wish to fight in front of God and everybody," he said, taking Bran by the arm, "let us get out of here before you draw a crowd."

"Well done," said Iwan, his grin wide and sunny as Bran and Ffreol returned to the trough.

"We are strangers here," Ffreol remonstrated. "What, in the holy name of Peter, were you thinking?"

"Only that heads can be as easily broken as eggs," Bran replied, "and that justice ought sometimes to protect those least able to protect themselves." He glowered dark defiance at the priest. "Or has that changed?"

Ffreol drew breath to object but thought better of it. Turning away abruptly, he announced, "We have ridden far enough for one day. We will spend the night here."

"We will not!" objected Iwan, curling his lip in a sneer. "I'd rather sleep in a sty than stay in this stinking place. It is crawling with vermin."

"There is an abbey here, and we will be welcome," the priest pointed out.

"An abbey filled with Ffreinc, no doubt," Bran grumbled. "You can stay there if you want. I'll not set foot in the place."

"I agree," said Iwan, his voice dulled with pain. He sat on the edge of the trough, hunched over his wound as if protecting it.

The monk fell silent, and they mounted their horses and continued on. They crossed the bridge and passed through the untidy sprawl of muddy streets and low-roofed hovels. Smoke from cooking fires filled the streets, and all the people Bran saw were either hurrying home with a bundle of firewood on their backs or carrying food to be prepared—a freshly killed chicken to be roasted, a scrap of bacon, a few leeks, a turnip or two. Seeing the food reminded Bran that he had eaten very little in the last few days, and his hunger came upon him with the force of a kick. He scented the aroma of roasting meat on the evening air, and his mouth began to water. He was on the point of suggesting to Brother Ffreol that they should return to the centre of town and see if there might be an inn near the market square, when the monk suddenly announced, "I know just the place!" He urged his horse to a trot and proceeded toward the old south gate. "This way!"

The priest led his reluctant companions out through the gate and up the curving road as it ascended the steep riverbank. Shortly, they came to a stand of trees growing atop the bluff above the river, overlooking the town. "Here it is—just as I remembered!"

Bran took one look at an odd eight-sided timber structure with a high, steeply pitched roof and a low door with a curiously curved lintel and said, "A barn? You've brought us to a barn?"

"Not a barn," the monk assured him, sliding from the saddle. "It is an old cell."

"A priest's cell," Bran said, regarding the edifice doubtfully. There was no cross atop the structure, no window, no outward markings of any kind to indicate its function. "Are you sure?"

"The blessed Saint Ennion once lived here," Ffreol explained, moving toward the door. "A long time ago."

Bran shrugged. "Who lives here now?"

"A friend." Taking hold of a braided cord that passed through one doorpost, the monk gave the cord a strong tug. A bell sounded from somewhere inside. Ffreol, smiling in anticipation of a glad welcome, pulled the cord again and said, "You'll see."

Ffreol waited a moment, and when no one answered, he gave the braided cord a more determined pull. The bell sounded once more—a clean, clear peal in the soft evening air. Bran looked around, taking in the old oratory and its surroundings.

The cell stood at the head of a small grove of beech trees. The ground was covered with thick grass through which an earthen pathway led down the hillside into the town. In an earlier time, it occupied the grove as a woodland shrine overlooking the river. Now it surveyed the squalid prospect of a busy market town with its herds and carts and the slow-moving boats bearing iron ore to be loaded onto ships waiting at the larger docks downriver.

When a third pull on the bell rope brought no response, Ffreol turned and scratched his head. "He must be away."

"Can we not just let ourselves in?" asked Bran.

"Perhaps," allowed Ffreol. Putting his hand to the leather strap that served for a latch, he pulled, and the door opened inward. He pushed it farther and stuck in his head. "Pax vobiscum!" he shouted and waited for an answer. "There is no one here. We will wait inside."

Iwan, wincing with pain, was helped to dismount and taken inside to rest. Bran gathered up the reins of the horses and led them into the grove behind the cell; the animals were quickly unsaddled and tethered beneath the trees so they could graze. He found a leather bucket and hauled water from a stoup beside the cell. When he had finished watering the horses and settled them for the night, he joined the others in the oratory; by this time, Ffreol had a small fire going in the hearth that occupied one corner of the single large room.

It was, Bran thought, an odd dwelling—half house, half church. There was a sleeping place and a stone-lined hearth, but also an altar with a large wooden cross and a single wax candle. A solitary narrow window opened in the wall high above the altar, and a chain of sausages hung from an iron hook beside the hearth directly above a low three-legged stool. Next to the stool was a pair of leather shoes with thick wooden soles—the kind worn by those who work the mines. Crumbs of bread freckled both the altar and the hearthstones, and the smell of boiled onions mingled with incense.

Ffreol approached the altar, knelt, and said a prayer of blessing for the keeper of the cell. "I hope nothing has happened to old Faganus," he said when he finished.

"Saints and sinners are we all," said a gruff voice from the open doorway. "Old Faganus is long dead and buried."

Startled, Bran turned quickly, his hand reaching for his knife. A quick lash of a stout oak staff caught him on the arm. "Easy, son," advised the owner of the staff. "I will behave if you will."

Into the cell stepped a very short, very fat man. The crown of his head came only to Bran's armpit, and his bulk filled the doorway in which he stood. Dressed in the threadbare brown robes of a mendicant priest, he balanced his generous girth on two absurdly thin, bandy legs; his shoulders sloped and his back was slightly bent, giving him a stooped, almost dwarfish appearance; however, his thick-muscled arms and chest looked as if he could crush ale casks in his brawny embrace.

He carried a slender staff of unworked oak in one hand and held a brace of hares by a leather strap with the other. His tonsure was out-grown and in need of reshaving; his bare feet were filthy and caked with river mud, some of which had found its way to his full, fleshy jowls. He regarded his three intruders with bold and unflinching dark eyes, as ready to wallop them as welcome them.

"God be good to you," said Ffreol from the altar. "Are you priest here now?"

"Who might you be?" demanded the rotund cleric. He was one of the order of begging brothers which the Ffreinc called *fréres* and the English called friars. They were all but unknown amongst the Cymry.

"We might be the King of England and his barons," replied Iwan, rising painfully. "My friend asked you a question."

Quick as a flick of a whip, the oak staff swung out, catching Iwan on the meaty part of the shoulder. He started forward, but the priest thumped him with the knob end of the staff in the centre of the chest. The champion crumpled as if struck by lightning. He fell to his knees, gasping for breath.

"It was only a wee tap, was it not?" the priest said in amazement, turning wide eyes to Bran and Ffreol. "I swear on Sweet Mary's wedding veil, it was only a tap."

"He was wounded in a battle several days ago," Bran said. Kneeling beside the injured warrior, he helped raise him to his feet.

"Oh my soul, I didn't mean to hurt the big 'un," he sighed. To Ffreol, he said, "Aye, I am priest here now. Who are you?"

"I am Brother Ffreol of Llanelli in Elfael."

"Never heard of it," declared the brown-robed priest.

"It is in Cymru," Bran offered in a snide tone, "which you sons of Saecsens call Wales."

"Careful, boy," snipped the priest. "Come over high-handed with me, and I'll give you a thump to remind you of your manners. Don't think I won't."

"Go on, then," Bran taunted, thrusting forward. "I'll have that stick of yours so far up your—"

"Peace!" cried Ffreol, rushing forward to place himself between Bran and the brown priest. "We mean no harm. Pray, forgive my quick-tempered friends. We have suffered a grave calamity in the last days, and I fear it has clouded our better judgement." This last was said with a glare of disapproval at Bran and Iwan. "Please forgive us."

"Very well, since you ask," the priest granted with a sudden smile. "I forgive you." Laying his staff aside, he said, "So now! We know whence you came, but we still lack names for you all. Do they have proper names in Elfael? Or are they in such short supply that you must hoard them and keep them to yourselves?"

"Allow me to present Bran ap Brychan, prince and heir of Elfael," said Ffreol, drawing himself upright. "And this is Iwan ap Iestyn, champion and battlechief."

"Hail and welcome, friends," replied the little friar, raising his hands in declamation. "The blessings of a warm hearth beneath a dry roof are yours tonight. May it be so always."

Now it was Bran's turn to be amazed. "How is it that you speak Cymry?"

The brown priest gave him a wink. "And here was I, thinking you hotheaded sons of the valleys were as stupid as stumps." He chuckled and shook his head. "It took you long enough. Indeed, sire, I speak the tongue of the blessed."

"But you're English," Bran pointed out.

"Aye, English as the sky is blue," said the friar, "but I was carried off as a boy to Powys, was I not? I was put to work in a copper mine up there and slaved away until I was old enough and bold enough to escape. Almost froze to death, I did, for it was a full harsh winter, but the brothers at Llandewi took me in, did they not? And that is where I found my vocation and took my vows." He smiled a winsome, toothy grin and bowed, his round belly almost touching his knees. "I am Brother Aethelfrith," he declared proudly. "Thirty years in God's service." To Iwan, he said, "I'm sorry if I smacked you too hard."

"No harm done, Brother Eathel . . . Aelith . . . ," Iwan stuttered, trying to get his British tongue around the Saxon name.

"Aethelfrith," the priest repeated. "It means 'nobility and peace', or some such nonsense." He grinned at his guests. "Here now, what have you brought me?"

"Brought you?" asked Bran. "We haven't brought you anything."

"Everyone who seeks shelter here brings me something," explained the priest.

"We didn't know we were coming," said Bran.

"Yet here you are." The fat priest stuck out his hand.

"Perhaps a coin might suffice?" said Ffreol. "We would be grateful for a meal and a bed."

"Aye, a coin is acceptable," allowed Aethelfrith doubtfully. "Two is better, of course. Three, now! For three pennies I sing a psalm and say a prayer for all of you—*and* we will have wine with our dinner."

"Three it is!" agreed Ffreol.

The brown priest turned to Bran expectantly and held out his hand.

Bran, irked by the friar's brash insistence, frowned. "You want the money now?"

"Oh, aye."

With a pained sigh, Bran turned his back on the priest and drew the purse from his belt. Opening the drawstring, he shook out a handful of coins, looking for any clipped coins amongst the whole. He found two half pennies and was looking for a third when Aethelfrith appeared beside him and said, "Splendid! I'll take those."

Before Bran could stop him, the priest had snatched up three bright new pennies. "Here, boyo!" he said, handing Bran the two fat hares on the strap. "You get these coneys skinned and cleaned and ready to roast when I get back."

"Wait!" said Bran, trying to snatch back the coins. "Give those back!"

"Hurry now," said Aethelfrith, darting away with surprising speed on his ludicrous bowed legs. "It will be dark soon, and I mean to have a feast tonight."

Bran followed him to the door. "Are you certain you're a priest?" Bran called after him, but the only reply he heard was a bark of cheerful laughter.

Resigned to his task, Bran went out and found a nearby stone and set to work skinning and gutting the hares. Ffreol soon joined him and sat down to watch. "Strange fellow," he observed after a time.

"Most thieves are more honest."

Brother Ffreol chuckled. "He is a good hand with that staff."

"When his victim is unarmed, perhaps," allowed Bran dully. He stripped the fur from one plump animal. "If I'd had a sword in my hand . . ."

"Be of good cheer," said Ffreol. "This is a fortuitous meeting. I feel it. We now have a friend in this place, and that is well worth a coin or two."

"Three," corrected Bran. "And all of them new."

Ffreol nodded and then said, "He will repay that debt a thousand times over—ten thousand."

Something in his friend's tone made Bran glance up sharply. "Why do you say that?"

Ffreol offered a small, reticent smile and shrugged. "It is nothing—a feeling only."

Bran resumed his chore, and Ffreol watched him work. The two sat in companionable silence as evening enfolded them in a gentle twilight. The hares were gutted and washed by the time Friar Aethelfrith returned with a bag on his back and a small cask under each arm. "I did not know if you preferred wine or ale," he announced, "so I bought both."

Handing one of the casks to Bran, he gave the other to Ffreol and then, opening the bag, drew out a fine loaf of fresh-baked bread and a great hunk of pale yellow cheese. "Three moons if a day since I had fresh bread," he confided. "Three threes of moons since I had a drink of wine." Offering Bran another of his preposterous bows, he said, "A blessing on the Lord of the Feast. May his days never cease and his tribe increase!"

Bran smiled in spite of himself and declared, "Bring the jars and let the banquet begin!"

They returned to the oratory, where Iwan, reclining beside the hearth, had built up the fire to a bright, crackling blaze. While Aethelfrith scurried around readying their supper, Ffreol found wooden cups and poured out the ale. Their host paused long enough to suck down a cup and then returned to his preparations, spitting the fat hares and placing them at the fireside for Iwan to tend. He then brought a wooden trencher with broken bread and bite-sized chunks of cheese, and four long fire-forks, which he passed to his guests.

They sat around the hearth and toasted bread and cheese and drank to each other's health while waiting for the meat to cook.

73

Slowly, the cares of the last days began to release their hold on Bran and his companions.

"A toast!" said Iwan at one point, raising his cup. "I drink to our good host, Aethleth—" He stumbled at the hurdle of the name once more. He tried again, but the effort proved beyond him. Casting an eye over the plump priest, he said, "Fat little bag of vittles that he is, I will call him Tuck."

"*Friar* Tuck to you, boyo!" retorted the priest with a laugh. Cocking his head to one side, he said, "And it is Iwan, is it not? What is that in couth speech?" He tapped his chin with a stubby finger. "It's *John*, I think. Yes, John. So, overgrown infant that he is, I will call him Little John." He raised his cup, sloshing ale over the rim, "So, now! I lift my cup to Little John and to his friends. May you always have ale enough to wet your tongues, wit enough to know friend from foe, and strength enough for every fight."

Ffreol, moved as much by the camaraderie around the hearth as by the contents of his cup, raised his voice in solemn, priestly declamation, saying, "I am not lying when I say that I have feasted in the halls of kings, but rarely have I supped with a nobler company than sits beneath this humble roof tonight." Lofting his cup, he said, "God's blessing on us. Brothers all!"

The sun was high and warm by the time the men were ready to depart Aethelfrith's oratory. Bran and Iwan bade the priest farewell, and Brother Ffreol bestowed a blessing, saying, "May the grace and peace of Christ be upon you, and the shielding of all the saints be around you, and nine holy angels aid and uphold you through all things." He then raised himself to the saddle, saying, "Do not drink all the wine, brother. Save some for our return. God willing, we will join you again on our way home."

"Then you had better hurry about your business," Aethelfrith called. "That wine will not last long."

Bran, eager to be away, slapped the reins and trotted out onto the road. Ffreol and Iwan followed close behind, and the three resumed their journey to Lundein. The horses were just finding their stride when they heard a familiar voice piping, "Wait! Wait!"

Turning around in the saddle, Bran saw the bandy-legged friar running after them. Thinking they had forgotten something, he pulled up.

"I'm coming with you," Aethelfrith declared.

Bran regarded the man's disgraceful robe, bare feet, ragged tonsure, and untidy beard. He glanced at Ffreol and shook his head.

"Your offer is thoughtful, to be sure," replied Brother Ffreol, "but we would not burden you with our affairs."

"Maybe not," he allowed, "but God wants me to go."

"God wants you to go," Iwan scoffed lightly. "You speak for God now, do you?"

"No," the priest allowed, "but I know he wants me to go."

"And how, pray, do you know this?"

Aethelfrith offered a diffident smile. "He told me."

"Well," replied the battlechief lightly, "until he tells *me*, I say you stay here and guard the wine cask."

Ffreol lifted a hand in farewell, and the three started off again, but after only a few dozen paces, Bran looked around again to see the plump priest hurrying after them, robes lifted high, his bowed legs churning. "Go back!" he called, not bothering to stop.

"I cannot," replied Aethelfrith. "It is not your voice I heed, but God's. I am compelled to come with you."

"I think we should take him," Brother Ffreol said.

"He is too slow afoot," Bran pointed out. "He could never keep pace."

"True," agreed Ffreol as the priest came puffing up. Reaching down his hand, he said, "You can ride with me, Tuck." Aethelfrith took the offered hand and began wriggling labouriously up onto the back of the horse.

"What?" said Iwan. Indicating Bran and himself, he said, "Are we not to have a say in this?"

"Say whatever you like," Aethelfrith replied. "I am certain God is willing to listen."

Iwan grumbled, but Bran laughed. "Stung you," he chuckled, "eh, Little John?"

For five days they journeyed on, following the road as it bent its way south and east over the broad lowland hills from whose tops could be seen a land of green and golden fields strewn with the smudgy brown blots of innumerable settlements. They travelled more slowly with four; owing to the extra weight, they had to stop and rest the horses more frequently. But what he cost them in time, Tuck made up in songs and rhymes and stories about the saints—and this made the journey more enjoyable.

The countryside became ever more densely populated—roads, lanes, and trackways seamed the valleys, and the cross-topped steeples of churches adorned every hilltop. Over all hung the odour of the dung heap, pungent and heavy in the sultry air. By the time the sprawl of Lundein appeared beyond the wide gleaming sweep of the Thames, Bran was heartily sick of England and already longing to return to Elfael. Ordinarily, he would not have endured such a misery in silence, but the sight of the city brought the reason for their sojourn fresh to mind, and his soul sank beneath the weight of an infinitely greater grief. He merely bit his lip and passed through the wretched realm, his gaze level, his face hard.

On its way into the city, the road widened to resemble a broad, bare, wheel-rutted expanse hemmed in on each side by row upon row of houses, many flanked by narrow yards out of which merchants and craftsmen pursued their various trades. Carters, carpenters, and wheelwrights bartered with customers ankle deep in wood shavings; blacksmiths hammered glowing rods on anvils to produce andirons, fire grates, ploughshares, door bands and hinges, chains, and horseshoes; corders sat in their doorways, winding jute into hanks that rose in mounded coils at their feet; potters ferried planks lined with sun-dried pitchers, jars, and bowls to their nearby kilns. Everywhere Bran looked, people seemed to be intensely busy, but he saw no place that looked at all friendly to strangers.

They rode on and soon came to a low house fronting the river. Several dozen barrels were lined up outside the entrance beside the road. Some of the barrels were topped with boards, behind which a young woman with hair the colour of spun gold and a bright red kerchief across her bare shoulders dispensed jars of ale to a small gathering of thirsty travellers. Without a second thought, Bran turned aside, dismounted, and walked to the board.

"Pax vobiscum," he said, dusting off his Latin.

She gave him a nod and patted the board with her hand—a sign he took to mean she wanted to see his money first. As Bran dug out his purse and searched for a suitable coin, the others joined him.

"Allow me," said Aethelfrith, pushing up beside him. He brought out an English penny. "Coin of the realm," he said, holding the small silver disc between thumb and forefinger. "And for this we should eat like kings as well, should we not?" He handed the money to the alewife. "Four jars, good woman," he said in English. "And fill them full to overflowing."

"There is food, too?" asked Bran as the woman poured out three large jars from a nearby pitcher.

"Inside the house," replied the cleric. Following Bran's gaze, he added, "but we'll not be going in there."

"Why not? It seems a good enough place." He could smell the aroma of roast pork and onions on the light evening breeze.

"Oh, aye, a good enough place to practise iniquity, perhaps, or lose your purse—if not your life." He shook his head at the implied depravity. "But we have a bed waiting for us where we will not be set upon by anything more onerous than a psalm."

"You know of such a place?" asked Ffreol.

"There is a monastery just across the river," Friar Aethelfrith informed them. "The Abbey of Saint Mary the Virgin. I have stayed there before. They will give us a bowl and bed for the night."

Aethelfrith's silver penny held good for four more jars and half a loaf of bread, sliced and smeared with pork drippings, which only served to rouse their appetites. Halfway through the second jar, Bran had begun to feel as if Lundein might not be as bad as his first impression had led him to believe. He became more certain when he caught the young alewife watching him; she offered him a saucy smile and gave a little toss of her head, indicating that he should follow. With a nod and a wink, she disappeared around the back of the house, with Bran a few steps behind her. As Bran came near, she lifted her skirt a little and extended her leg to reveal a shapely ankle.

"It is a lovely river, is it not?" observed Aethelfrith, falling into step beside him.

"It is not the river I am looking at," said Bran. "Go back and finish your ale, and I will join you when I've finished here."

"Oh," replied the friar, "I think you've had enough already." Waving to the young woman, he took Bran by the arm and steered him back the way they had come. "Evening is upon us," he observed. "We'll be going on."

"I'm hungry," said Bran. Glancing back at the alewife, he saw that she had gone inside. "We should eat something."

"Aye, we will," agreed Tuck, "but not here." They rejoined the others, and Bran returned to his jar, avoiding the stern glance of Brother Ffreol. "Drink up, my friends," ordered Tuck. "It is time we were moving along."

With a last look toward the inn, Bran drained his cup and reluctantly followed the others back to their mounts and climbed back into the saddle. "How many times have you been to Lundein?" he asked as they continued their slow plod into the city.

"Oh, a fair few," Aethelfrith replied. "Four or five times, I think, though the last time was when old King William was on the throne." He paused to consider. "Seven years ago, perhaps."

At King's Bridge they stopped in the road. Bran had never seen a bridge so wide and long, and despite the crowds now hurrying to their homes on the other side of the river, he was not certain he wanted to venture out too far. He was on the point of dismounting to lead his horse across when Aethelfrith saw his hesitation. "Five hundred men on horseback cross this bridge every day," he called, "and oxcarts by the score. It will yet bear a few more."

"I was merely admiring the handiwork," Bran told him. He gave his mount a slap and started across. Indeed, it was ingeniously constructed with beams of good solid oak and iron spikes; it neither swayed nor creaked as they crossed. All the same, he was happy to reach the far side, where Aethelfrith, now afoot, began leading them up one narrow, shadowed street and down another until the three Welshmen had lost all sense of direction.

"I know it is here somewhere," said Aethelfrith. They paused at a small crossroads to consider where to look next. The twisting streets were filling up with smoke from the hearth fires of the houses round about.

"Night is upon us," Ffreol pointed out. "If we cannot find it in the daylight, we will fare no better in the dark."

"We are near," insisted the fat little priest. "I remember this place, do I not?"

Just then a bell rang out—a clear, distinct tone in the still evening air.

"Ah!" cried Aethelfrith. "That will be the call to vespers. This way!" Following the sound of the bell, they soon arrived at a gate in a stone wall. "Here!" he said, hurrying to the gate. "This is the place—I told you I would remember."

"So you did," replied Bran. "How could we have doubted?"

The mendicant priest pulled a small rope that passed through a hole in the wooden door. Another bell tinkled softly, and presently the door swung open. A thin, round-shouldered priest dressed in a long robe of undyed wool stepped out to greet them. One glance at the two priests in their robes, and he said, "Welcome, brothers! Peace and welcome."

A quick word with the porter, and their lodgings for the night were arranged. They ate soup with the brothers in the refectory, and while Ffreol and Aethelfrith attended the night vigil with the resident monks, Bran and Iwan went to the cell provided for them and fell asleep on fleece-covered straw mats. Upon arising with the bell the next morning, Bran saw that Ffreol and Aethelfrith were already at prayer; he pulled on his boots, brushed the straw from his cloak, and went out into the abbey yard to wait until the holy office was finished.

While he waited, he rehearsed in his mind what they should say to William the Red. Now that the fateful day had dawned, Bran found himself lost for words and dwarfed by the awful knowledge of how much depended upon his ability to persuade the English king of the injustice being perpetrated on his people. His heart sank lower and lower as he contemplated the dreary future before him: an impoverished lackey to a Ffreinc bounder whose reputation for profligate spending was exceeded only by his whoring and drinking.

When at last Ffreol and Aethelfrith emerged from the chapel, Bran had decided he would swear an oath to the devil himself if it would keep the vile invaders from Elfael.

The travellers took their leave and, passing beyond the monastery gates, entered the streets of the city to make their way to the White Tower, as the king's stronghold was known.

Bran could see the pale stone structure rising above the rooftops of the low, mean houses sheltering in the shadows of the fortress walls. At the gates, Brother Ffreol declared Bran's nobility and announced their intent to the porter, who directed them into the yard and showed them where to tie their horses. They were then met by a liveried servant, who conducted them into the fortress itself and to a large anteroom lined with benches on which a score or more men—mostly Ffreinc, but some English—were already waiting; others were standing in clumps and knots the length of the room. The thought of having to wait his turn until all had been seen cast Bran into a dismal mood.

They settled in a far corner of the room. Every now and then a courtier would appear, summon one or more petitioners, and take them away. For good or ill, those summoned never returned to the anteroom, so the mood remained one of hopeful, if somewhat desperate, optimism. "I have heard of people waiting twenty days or more to speak to the king," Friar Aethelfrith confided as he cast his glance around the room at the men lining the benches.

"We will not bide that long," Bran declared, but he sank a little further into gloom at the thought. Some of those in the room did indeed look as if they might have taken up more or less permanent residence there; they brought out food from well-stocked tuck bags, some slept, and others whiled away the time playing at dice. Morning passed, and the day slowly crept away.

It was after midday, and Bran's stomach had begun reminding him that he had eaten nothing but soup and hard bread since the day before, when the door at the end of the great vestibule opened and a courtier in yellow leggings and a short tunic and mantle of bright green entered, passing slowly along the benches and eyeing the petitioners who looked up hopefully. At his approach, Bran stood. "We want to see the king," he said in his best Latin.

"Yes," replied the man, "and what is the nature of your business here?"

"We want to see the king."

"To be sure." The court official glanced at those attending Bran and said, "You four are together?"

"We are," replied Bran.

"The question is *why* would you see the king?"

"We have come to seek redress for a crime committed in the king's name," Bran explained.

The official's glance sharpened. "What sort of crime?"

"The slaughter of our lord and his warband and the seizure of our lands," volunteered Brother Ffreol, taking his place beside Bran.

"Indeed!" The courtier became grave. "When did this happen?"

"Not more than ten days ago," replied Bran.

The courtier regarded the men before him and made up his mind. "Come."

"We will see the king now?"

"You will follow me."

The official led them through the wooden door and into the next room, which, although smaller than the anteroom they had just left, was whitewashed and strewn with fresh straw; at one end was a fireplace, and opposite the hearth was an enormous tapestry hung from an iron rod. The hand-worked cloth depicted the risen Christ on his heavenly throne, holding an orb and sceptre. The centre of the room was altogether taken up by a stout table at which sat three men in highbacked chairs. The two men at each end of the table wore robes of deep brown and skullcaps of white linen. The man in the centre was dressed in a robe of black satin trimmed with fox fur; his skullcap was red silk and almost the same colour as his long, flowing locks. He also wore a thick gold chain around his neck, attached to which were a

cross and a polished crystal lens. Before the men were piles of parchments and pots containing goose quills and ink, and all three were
writing on squares of parchment before them; the scratch of their
pens was the only sound in the room.

"Yes?" said one of the men as the four approached the table. He
did not raise his eyes from his writing. "What is it?"

"Murder and the unlawful seizure of lands," intoned the courtier.

"This is not a matter for the royal court," replied the man dismissively, dipping his pen. "You must take it up with the Court of the
Assizor."

"I thought perhaps this particular case might interest you, my lord
bishop," the courtier said.

"Interesting or not, we do not adjudicate criminal cases," sighed
the man. "You must place the matter before the assizes."

Before the courtier could make a reply, Bran said, "We appeal to
the king's justice because the crime was committed in the king's name."

At this the man in the red skullcap glanced up; interest quickened
eyes keen and rapacious as a hawk's. "In the king's name, did you say?"

"Yes," replied Bran. "Truly."

The man's eyes narrowed. "You are Welsh."

"British, yes."

"What is your name?"

"Here stands before you Bran ap Brychan, prince and heir to the
throne of Elfael," said Iwan, speaking up to save his future king the
embarrassment of having to affirm his own nobility.

"I see." The man in the red silk cap leaned back in his chair. The
gold cross on his chest had rubies to mark the places where nails had
been driven into the saviour's hands and feet. He raised the crystal lens
and held it before a sharp blue eye. "Tell me what happened."

"Forgive me, sir, are you the king?" asked Bran.

"My lord, we have no time for such as this. They are—," began the man in the white skullcap. His objection was silenced by a flick of his superior's hand.

"King William has been called away to Normandie," explained the man in the red skullcap. "I am Cardinal Ranulf of Bayeux, Chief Justiciar of England. I am authorised to deal with all domestic matters in the king's absence. You may speak to me as you would speak to His Majesty." Offering a mirthless smile, the cardinal said, "Pray, continue. I would hear more of this alleged crime."

Bran nodded and licked his lips. "Nine days ago, my father, Lord Brychan of Elfael, set off for Lundein to swear allegiance to King William. He was ambushed on the road by Ffreinc marchogi, who killed him and all who were with him, save one. My father and the warband of Elfael were massacred and their bodies left to rot beside the road."

"My sympathies," said Ranulf. "May I ask how you know the men who committed this crime were, as you call them, Ffreinc marchogi?"

Bran put out a hand to Iwan. "This man survived and witnessed all that took place. He is the only one to escape with his life."

"Is this true?" wondered the cardinal.

"It is, my lord, every word," affirmed Iwan. "The leader of this force is a man named Falkes de Braose. He claims to have received Elfael by a grant from King William."

Ranulf of Bayeux raised the long white quill and held it lengthwise between his hands as if studying it for imperfections. "It is true that His Majesty has recently issued a number of such grants," the cardinal told them. Turning to his assistant on the left, he said, "Bring me the de Braose grant."

Without a word the man in the chair beside him rose and crossed the room, disappearing through a door behind the tapestry.

"There would seem to be some confusion here," allowed the cardinal when his man had gone, "but we will soon find the cause." Regarding the three before him, he added, "We keep good records. It is the Norman way."

Friar Aethelfrith stifled a hoot of contempt for the man's insinuation. Instead, he beamed beatifically and loosed a soft fart.

A moment later the cardinal's assistant returned bearing a square of parchment bound by a red satin riband. This he untied and placed before his superior, who took it up and began to read aloud very quickly, skipping over unimportant parts. "Be it known . . . this day . . . by the power and enfranchisement . . . Ah!" he said. "Here it is."

He then read out the pertinent passage for the petitioners. "Granted to William de Braose, Baron, Lord of the Rape of Bramber, in recognition for his support and enduring loyalty, the lands comprising the Welsh commot Elfael so called, entitled free and clear for himself and his heirs in perpetuity, in exchange for the sum of two hundred marks."

"We were sold for two hundred marks?" wondered Iwan.

"A token sum," replied the cardinal dryly. "It is customary."

"The Norman way, no doubt," put in Aethelfrith.

"But it is Count Falkes de Braose who has taken the land," Bran pointed out, "not the baron."

"Baron William de Braose is his uncle, I believe," said the cardinal. "But, yes, that is undoubtedly where the confusion has arisen. There is no provision for Falkes to assume control of the land, as he is not a direct heir. The baron himself must occupy the land or forfeit his claim. Therefore, as Chief Justiciar, I will allow this grant to be rescinded."

"I do thank you, my lord," said Bran, sweet relief surging through him. "I am much obliged."

The cardinal raised his hand. "Please, hear me out. I will allow the grant to be revoked for a payment to the crown of six hundred marks."

"Six hundred!" gasped Bran. "It was given to de Braose for two hundred."

"In recognition of his loyalty and support during the rebellion of the Barons," intoned the cardinal. "Yes. For you it will be six hundred *and* fealty sworn to King William."

"That is robbery!" snapped Bran.

The cardinal's eyes snapped quick fire. "It is a bargain, boy." He stared at Bran for a moment and then pulled the parchment to himself, adding, "In any case, that is my decision. The matter will be held in abeyance until such time as the money is paid." He gestured to his assistant, who began writing an addendum to the grant.

Bran stared at the churchman and felt the despair melt away in a sudden surge of white-hot rage. His vision became blood-tinged and hard. He saw the bland face and shrewd eyes, the man's flaming red hair, and it was all he could do to keep from seizing the imperious cleric, pulling him bodily across the table, and beating the superior smirk off that smug face with his fists.

Rigid as a stump, hands clenched in rage, he stared at the courtiers as his grip on reality slipped away. In a blood-tinted vision, he saw a tub of oil at his feet, and before anyone could stop him, he snatched up the tub and emptied it over the table, drenching the cardinal, his clerks, and their stacks of parchment. As the irate courtiers spluttered, Bran calmly withdrew an oil-soaked parchment from the pile; he held it to a torch in a wall sconce and set it ablaze. He blew on it to strengthen the flame, then tossed it back onto the table. The oil flared, igniting the table, parchments, and men in a single conflagration. The clerks pawed at the flames with their hands and succeeded only in spreading them. The cardinal, gripped with terror, cried out like a child as tongues of fire leapt to his hair and turned the rich fox fur trim into a collar of living flame. Bran glimpsed himself standing gaunt and grim as the howling clerics fled the room, each oil-soaked footprint alighting behind them as they ran. He saw Ranulf of Bayeux's face bubble and crack like the skin of a pig on a spit, and as the cardinal fought for his last breath—

"Abeyance, my lord," said Ffreol. "Forgive me, but does that mean Baron de Braose keeps the land?"

At the sound of Ffreol's voice, Bran came to himself once more. He felt drained and somewhat light-headed. Without awaiting the cardinal's reply, he turned on his heel and strode from the chamber.

"Until the money is paid, yes," Cardinal Ranulf replied to Ffreol. He reached for a small bronze bell to summon the porter. "Do not bother to return here until you have the silver in hand." He rang the bell to end the audience, saying, "God grant you a good day and pleasant journey home."

"And a pleasant journey home," minced Aethelfrith in rude parody of Cardinal Ranulf. "Bring me my staff, and I will give that bloated toad a pleasant journey hence!"

Bran, scowling darkly, said nothing and walked on through the gates, leaving the White Tower without a backward glance. The unfairness, the monstrous injustice of the cardinal's demand sent waves of anger surging through him. Into his mind flashed the memory of a time years ago when a similar injustice had driven him down and defeated him: Bran had been out with some of the men; as they rode along the top of a ridgeway, they spied in the valley below a band of Irish raiders herding stolen cattle across the cantref. Outnumbered and lightly armed, Bran had let the raiders pass unchallenged and then hurried back to the caer to tell his father. They met the king in the yard, along with the rest of the warriors of the warband. "You let them go—and yet dare to show your face to me?" growled the king when Bran told him what had happened.

"We would have been slaughtered outright," Bran explained, backing away. "There were too many of them."

"You worthless little coward!" the king shouted. The warriors gathered in the yard looked on as the king drew back his hand and let fly, catching Bran on the side of the head. The blow sent the boy spinning to the ground. "Better to die in battle than live as a coward!" the king roared. "Get up!"

"Lose ten good men for the sake of a few cows?" countered Bran, climbing to his feet. "Only a fool would think that was better."

"You snivelling brat!" roared Brychan, lashing out again. Bran stood to the blow this time, which only enraged his father the more. The king struck him again and yet again—until Bran, unable to bear the abuse any longer, turned and fled the yard, sobbing with pain and frustration.

The bruises from that encounter lasted a long time, the humiliation longer still. Any ambition Bran might have held for the crown died that day; the throne of Elfael could crumble to dust for all he cared.

They did not stay in Lundein again that night but fled the city sprawl as if pursued by demons. The moon rose nearly full and the sky remained clear, so they rode on through the night, stopping only a little before dawn to rest the horses and sleep. Bran had little to say the next day or the day after. They reached the oratory, and Brother Aethelfrith prevailed upon them to spend the night under his roof, and for the sake of wounded Iwan, Bran agreed. While the friar scurried about to prepare a meal for his guests, Bran and Ffreol took care of the horses and settled them for the night.

"It isn't fair," muttered Bran, securing the tether line to the slender trunk of a beech tree. He turned to Ffreol and exclaimed, "I still don't see how the king could sell us like that. Who gave him the right?"

"Red William?" replied the monk, raising his eyebrows at the sudden outburst from the all-but-silent Bran.

"Aye, Red William. He has no authority over Cymru."

"The Ffreinc claim that kingship descends from God," Ffreol pointed out. "William avows divine right for his actions."

"What has England to do with us?" Bran demanded. "Why can't they leave us alone?"

"Answer that," replied the monk sagely, "and you answer the riddle of the ages. Throughout the long history of our race, no tribe or nation has ever been able to simply leave us alone."

That night Bran sat in the corner by the hearth, sipping wine in sombre silence, brooding over the unfairness of the Ffreinc king, the inequity of a world where the whims of one fickle man could doom so many, and the seemingly limitless injustices—large and small—of life in general. And why was everyone looking to him to put it right? *For the sake of Elfael and the throne,* Ffreol had said. Well, the throne of Elfael had done nothing for him—save provide him with a distant and disapproving father. Remove the throne of Elfael— take away Elfael itself and all her people. Would the world be so different? Would the world even notice the loss? Besides, if God in his wisdom had bestowed his blessing on King William, favouring the Ffreinc ascendancy with divine approval, who were any of them to disagree?

When heaven joined battle against you, who could stand?

Early the next morning, the three thanked Friar Aethelfrith for his help, bade him farewell, and resumed the homeward journey. They rode through that day and the next, and it was not until late on the third day that they came in sight of the great, rumpled swath of forest that formed the border between England and Cymru. The dark mood that had dogged them since Lundein began to lift at last. Once amongst the sheltering trees of Coed Cadw, the oppression of England and its rapacious king dwindled to mere annoyance. The forest had weathered the ravages of men and their petty concerns from the beginning of time and would prevail. What was one red-haired Ffreinc tyrant against that?

"It is only money, after all," observed Ffreol, optimism making him expansive. "We have only to pay them and Elfael is safe once more."

"If silver is what the Red King wants," said Iwan, joining in, "silver is what he will get. We will buy back our land from the greedy Ffreinc bastards."

Bran said, "There are two hundred marks in my father's strongbox. That is a start."

"And a good one," declared Iwan. All three fell silent for a moment. "How will we get the rest?" Iwan asked at last, voicing the thought all three shared.

"We will go to the people and tell them what is required," said Bran. "We will raise it."

"That may not be so easy," cautioned Brother Ffreol. "If you could somehow empty every silver coin from every pocket, purse, and crock in Elfael, you might get another hundred marks at most."

To his dismay, Bran realised that was only too true. Lord Brychan was the wealthiest man in three cantrefs, and he had never possessed more than three hundred marks all at once in the best of times.

Six hundred marks. Cardinal Ranulf might as well have asked for the moon or a hatful of stars. He was just as likely to get one as the other.

Unwilling to succumb to despair again so soon, Bran gave the mare a slap and picked up the pace. Soon he was racing through the darkening wood, speeding along the road, feeling the cool evening air on his face. After a time, his mount began to tire, so at the next fording place, Bran reined up. He slid from the saddle and led the horse a little way along the stream, where the animal could drink. He cupped a few handfuls of water to his mouth and drew his wet hands over the back of his neck. The water cooled his temper somewhat. It would be dark soon, he noticed; already the shadows were thickening, and the forest was growing hushed with the coming of night.

Bran was still kneeling at the stream, gazing at the darkening forest, when Ffreol and Iwan arrived. They dismounted and led their horses to the water. "A fine chase," said Ffreol. "I have not ridden like that since I was a boy." Squatting down beside Bran, he put a hand to the young man's shoulder and said, "We'll find a way to raise the money, Bran, never fear."

Bran nodded.

"It will be dark soon," Iwan pointed out. "We will not reach Caer Cadarn tonight."

"We'll lay up at the next good place we find," said Bran.

He started to climb into the saddle, but Ffreol said, "It is vespers. Come, both of you, join me, and we will continue after prayers."

They knelt beside the ford then, and Ffreol raised his hands, saying:

I am bending my knee
In the eye of the Father who created me,
In the eye of the Son who befriended me,
In the eye of the Spirit who walks with me,
In companionship and affection.
Through thine own Anointed One, O God,
Bestow upon us fullness in our need . . .

Brother Ffreol's voice flowed out over the stream and along the water. Bran listened, and his mind began to wander. Iwan's hissed warning brought him back with a start. "Listen!" The champion held up his hand for silence. "Did you hear that?"

"I heard nothing but the sound of my own voice," replied the priest. He closed his eyes and resumed his prayer. "Grant us this night your peace—"

There came a shout behind them. *"Arrêt!"*

The three rose and turned as one to see four Ffreinc marchogi on the road behind them. Weapons drawn, the soldiers advanced, walking warily, their expressions grave in the dim light.

"Ride!" shouted Iwan, darting to his horse. "Hie!"

The cry died in his throat, for even as the three prepared to flee, five more marchogi stepped from the surrounding wood. Their blades glimmered dimly in the dusky light. Even so, Iwan, wounded as he was, would have challenged them and taken his chances, but Ffreol prevented him. "Iwan! No! They'll kill you."

"They mean to kill us anyway," replied the warrior carelessly. "We must fight."

"No!" Ffreol put out a restraining hand and pulled him back. "Let me talk to them."

Before Iwan could protest, the monk stepped forward. Stretching out empty hands, he walked a few paces to meet the advancing knights. "Pax vobiscum!" he called. Continuing in Latin, he said, "Peace to you this night. Please, put up your swords. You have nothing to fear from us."

One of the Ffreinc made a reply that neither Bran nor Iwan understood. The priest repeated himself, speaking more slowly; he stepped closer, holding out his hands to show that he had no weapons. The knight who had spoken moved to intercept him. The point of his sword flicked the air. Ffreol took another step, then stopped and looked down.

"Ffreol?" called Bran.

The monk made no answer but half turned as he glanced back toward Bran and Iwan. Even in the failing light, Bran could see that blood covered the front of the monk's robe.

Ffreol himself appeared confused by this. He looked down again, and then his hands found the gaping rent in his throat. He clutched at the wound, and blood spilled over his fingers. "Pax vobiscum," he spluttered, then crashed to his knees in the road.

"You filthy scum!" screamed Bran. Leaping to the saddle, he drew his sword and spurred his horse forward to put himself between the wounded priest and the Ffreinc attackers. He was instantly surrounded. Bran made but one sweeping slash with his blade before he was hauled kicking from the saddle.

Fighting free of the hands that gripped him, he struggled to where Brother Ffreol lay on his side. The monk reached out a hand and brought Bran's face close to his lips. "God keep you," he whispered, his voice a fading whisper.

"Ffreol!" cried Bran. "No!"

The priest gave out a little sigh and laid his head upon the road. Bran fell upon the body. Clutching the priest's face between his hands, he shouted, "Ffreol! Ffreol!" But his friend and confessor was dead. Then Bran felt the hands of his captors on him; they hauled him to his feet and dragged him away.

Jerking his head around, he saw Iwan thrashing wildly with his sword as the marchogi swarmed around him. "Here!" Bran shouted. "To me! To me!"

That was all he could get out before he was flung to the ground and pinned there with a boot on his neck, his face shoved into the dirt. He tried to wrestle free but received a sharp kick in the ribs, and then the air was driven from his lungs by a knee in his back.

With a last desperate effort, he twisted on the ground, seized the leg of the marchogi, and pulled him down. Grasping the soldier's helmet, Bran yanked it off and began pummelling the startled soldier with it. In his mind, it was not a nameless Ffreinc soldier he bludgeoned senseless, but ruthless King William himself.

In the frenzy of the fight, Bran felt the handle of the soldier's knife, drew it, and raised his arm to plunge the point into the knight's throat. As the blade slashed down, however, the marchogi fell on him, pulling him away, cheating him of the kill. Screaming and writhing in their grasp, kicking and clawing like an animal caught in a net, Bran tried to fight free. Then one of the knights raised the butt of a spear, and the night exploded in a shower of stars and pain as blow after blow rained down upon him.

CHAPTER 10

"You are Welsh, yes? A Briton?"

Bruised, bloodied, and bound at the wrists by a rope that looped around his neck, Bran was dragged roughly forward and forced to his knees before a man standing in the wavering pool of light from a hand-held torch. Dressed in a long tunic of yellow linen with a short blue cloak and boots of soft brown leather, he carried neither sword nor spear, and the others deferred to him. Bran took him to be their lord.

"Are you a Briton?" He spoke English with the curious flattened nasal tone of the Ffreinc. "Answer me!" He nodded to one of the soldiers, who gave Bran a quick kick in the ribs.

The pain of the blow roused Bran. He lifted his head to gaze with loathing at his inquisitor.

"I think you are Welsh, yes?" the Ffreinc noble said.

Unwilling to dignify the word, Bran merely nodded.

"What were you doing on the road?" asked the man.

"Travelling," mumbled Bran. His voice sounded strange and loud in his ears; his head throbbed from the knocks he had taken.

"At night?"

"My friends and I—we had business in Lundein. We were on our way home." He raised accusing eyes to his Ffreinc interrogator. "The man your soldiers killed was a priest, you bloody—" Bran lunged forward, but the soldier holding the rope yanked him back. He was forced down on his knees once more. "You will all rot in hell."

"Perhaps," admitted the man. "We think he was a spy."

"He was a man of God, you murdering bastard!"

"And the other one?"

"What about the other one?" asked Bran. "Did you kill him, too?"

"He has eluded capture."

That was something at least. "Let me go," Bran said. "You have no right to hold me. I've done nothing."

"It is for my lord to hold or release you as he sees fit," said the Ffreinc nobleman. "I am his seneschal."

"Who is your lord? I demand to speak to him."

"Speak to him you shall, Welshman," replied the seneschal. "You are coming with us." Turning to the marchogi holding the torches, he said, *"Liez-le."*

Bran spent the rest of the night tied to a tree, nursing a battered skull and a consuming hatred of the Ffreinc. His friend, Brother Ffreol, cut down like a dog in the road and himself taken captive . . . This, added to the gross injustice of Cardinal Ranulf's demands, overthrew the balance of Bran's mind—a balance already made precarious by the loss of his father and the warband.

He passed in and out of consciousness, his dreams merging with reality until he could no longer tell one from the other. In his mind he walked a dark forest pathway, longbow in hand and a quiver of arrows on his hip. Over and over again, he heard the sound of hoofbeats, and a Ffreinc knight would thunder out of the darkness, brandishing a sword. As the knight closed on him, blade held high, Bran would slowly raise the bow and send an arrow into his attacker's heart. The shock of the impact lifted the rider from the saddle and pinned him to a tree. The horse would gallop past, and Bran would walk on. This same event repeated itself throughout the long night as Bran moved through his dream, leaving an endless string of corpses dangling in the forest.

Sometime before morning, the moon set, and Bran heard an owl cry in the treetop above him. He came awake then and found himself bound fast to a stout elm tree, but uncertain how he had come to be there. Groggily, like a man emerging from a drunken stupor, he looked around. There were Ffreinc soldiers sleeping on the ground nearby. He saw their inert bodies, and his first thought was that he had killed them.

But no, they breathed still. They were alive, and he was a captive. His head beat with a steady throb; his ribs burned where he had been kicked. There was a nasty metallic taste in his mouth, as if he had been sucking on rusty iron. His shirt was wet where he had sweat through it, and the night air was cold where the cloth clung to his skin. He ached from head to heel.

When the owl called again, memory came flooding back in a confused rush of images: an enemy soldier writhing and moaning, his face a battered, bloody pulp; mailed soldiers swarming out of the shadows; the body of his friend Ffreol crumpled in the road, grasping at words as life fled through a slit in his throat; a blade glinting swift and sharp in the moonlight; Iwan, horse rearing, sword sweeping a wide, lethal arc as he galloped away; a Ffreinc helmet, greasy with blood, lifted high against a pale summer moon . . .

So it was true. Not *all* of it was a dream. He could still tell the difference. That was some small comfort at least. He told himself he had to keep his wits about him if he was to survive, and on that thought, he closed his eyes and called upon Saint Michael to help him in his time of need.

The Ffreinc marchogi broke camp abruptly. Bran was tied to his own horse as the troops made directly for Caer Cadarn. The invaders moved slowly, burdened as they were with ox-drawn wagons full of weapons, tools, and provisions. Alongside the men-at-arms were others—smiths and builders. A few of the invaders had women and children with them. They were not raiders, Bran concluded, but armed settlers. They were coming to Elfael, and they meant to stay.

Once free of the forest, the long, slow cavalcade passed through an apparently empty land. No one worked the fields; no one was seen on the road or even around the few farms and settlements scattered amongst the distant hillsides. Bran took this to mean that the monks had been able to raise the alarm and spread the word; the people had fled to the monastery at Llanelli.

At their approach to the caer, the Ffreinc seneschal rode ahead to inform his lord of their arrival. By the time they started up the ramp, the gates were open. Everything in the caer appeared to be in good order—nothing out of place, no signs of destruction or pillage. It appeared as though the new residents had simply replaced the old, continuing the steady march of life in the caer without missing a step.

The marchogi threw Bran, still bound, into the tiny root cellar beneath the kitchen, and there he languished through the rest of the day. The cool, damp dark complemented his misery, and he embraced it, mourning his losses and cursing the infinite cruelty of fate. He cursed the Ffreinc, and cursed his father, too.

Why, oh why, had Rhi Brychan held out so long? If he had sworn fealty to Red William when peace was first offered—as Cadwgan, in the neighbouring cantref of Eiwas, and other British kings had long since done—then at least the throne of Elfael would still be free, and his father, the warband, and Brother Ffreol would still be alive. True, Elfael would be subject to the Ffreinc and much the poorer for it, but they would still have their land and their lives.

Why had Rhi Brychan refused the Conqueror's repeated offers of peace?

Stubbornness, Bran decided. Pure, mean, pigheaded stubbornness and spite.

Bran's mother had always been able to moderate her husband's harsher views, even as she lightened his darker moods. Queen Rhian had provided the levity and love that Bran remembered in his early years. With her death, that necessary balance and influence ceased, never to be replaced by another. At first, young Bran had done what he could to imitate his mother's engaging ways—to be the one to brighten the king's dour disposition. He learned riddles and songs and made up amusing stories to tell, but of course it was not the same. Without his queen, the king had grown increasingly severe. Always a demanding man, Brychan had become a bitter, exacting, dissatisfied tyrant, finding fault with everyone and everything. Nothing was ever good enough. Certainly, nothing Bran ever did was good enough. Young Bran, striving to please and yearning for the approving touch of a father's hand, only ever saw that hand raised in anger.

Thus, he learned at an early age that since he could never please his father, he might as well please himself. That is the course he had pursued ever since—much to his father's annoyance and eventual despair.

So now the king was dead. From the day the Conqueror seized the throne of the English overlords, Brychan had resisted. Having to suffer the English was bad enough; their centuries-long presence in Britain was, to him, still a fresh wound into which salt was rubbed almost daily. Brychan, like his Celtic fathers, reckoned time not in years or decades, but in whole generations. If he looked back to a time when Britain and the Britons were the sole masters of their island realm, he also looked forward to a day when the Cymry would be free again. Thus, when William, Duke of Normandie, settled his bulk on Harold's throne that fateful Christmas day, Rhi Brychan vowed he would die before swearing allegiance to any Ffreinc usurper.

At long last, thought Bran, that oft-repeated boast had been challenged—and the challenge made good. Brychan was dead, his warriors with him, and the pale high-handed foreigners ran rampant through the land.

How now, Father? Bran reflected bitterly. *Is this what you hoped to achieve? The vile enemy sits on your throne, and your heir squats in the pit. Are you proud of your legacy?*

It was not until the following morning that Bran was finally released and marched to his father's great hall. He was brought to stand before a slender young man, not much older than himself, who, despite the mild summer day, sat hunched by the hearth, warming his white hands at the flames as if it were the dead of winter.

Dressed in a spotless blue tunic and yellow mantle, the thin-faced fellow observed Bran's scuffed and battered appearance with a grimace of disgust. "You will answer me—if you can, Briton," said the young man. His Latin, though heavily accented, could at least be understood. "What is your name?"

The sight of the fair-haired interloper sitting in the chair Rhi Brychan used for a throne offended Bran in a way he would not have thought possible. When he failed to reply quickly enough, the young man who, apparently, was lord and leader of the invaders rose from his seat, drew back his arm, and gave Bran a sharp, backhanded slap across the mouth.

Hatred leapt up hot and quick. Bran swallowed it down with an effort. "I am called Gwrgi," he answered, taking the first name that came to mind.

"Where is your home?"

"Ty Gwyn," Bran lied. "In Brycheiniog."

"You are a nobleman, I think," decided the Norman lord. His downy beard and soft dark eyes gave him a look of mild innocence—like a lamb or a yearling calf.

"No," replied Bran, his denial firm. "I am not a nobleman."

"Yes," asserted his inquisitor, "I think you are." He reached out and took hold of Bran's sleeve, rubbing the cloth between his fingers as if to appraise its worth. "A prince, perhaps, or at least a knight."

"I am a merchant," Bran replied with dull insistence.

"I think," the Ffreinc lord concluded, "you are not." He gave his narrow head a decisive shake, making his curls bounce. "All noblemen claim to be commoners when captured. You would be foolish to do otherwise."

When Bran said nothing, the Norman drew back his hand and let fly again, catching Bran on the cheek, just below the eye. The heavy gold ring on the young man's finger tore the flesh; blood welled up and trickled down the side of his face. "I am not a nobleman," muttered Bran through clenched teeth. "I am a merchant."

"A pity," sniffed the young lord, turning away. "Noblemen we ransom—beggars, thieves, and spies we kill." He nodded to his attending soldiers. "Take him away."

"No! Wait!" shouted Bran. "Ransom! You want money? Silver? I can get it."

The Ffreinc lord spoke a word to his men. They halted, still holding Bran tightly between them. "How much?" inquired the young lord.

103

"A little," replied Bran. "Enough."

The Norman gathered his blue cloak around his shoulders and studied his captive for a moment. "I think you are lying, Welshman." The word was a slur in his mouth. "But no matter. We can always kill you later."

He turned away and resumed his place by the fire. "I am Count Falkes de Braose," he announced, settling himself in the chair once more. "I am lord of this place now, so mind your tongue, and we shall yet come to a satisfactory agreement."

Bran, determined to appear pliant and dutiful, answered respectfully. "That is my fervent hope, Count de Braose."

"Good. Then let us arrange your ransom," replied the count. "The amount you must pay will depend on your answers to my questions."

"I understand," Bran said, trying to sound agreeable. "I will answer as well as I can."

"Where were you and that priest going when my men found you on the road?"

"We were returning from Lundein," replied Bran. "Brother Ffreol had business with the monastery there, and I was hoping to buy some cloth to sell in the markets hereabouts."

"This business of yours compelled you to ride at night. Why?"

"We had been away a long time," answered Bran, "and Brother Ffreol was anxious to get home. He had an important message for his bishop, or so he said."

"I think you were spies," de Braose announced.

Bran shook his head. "No."

"What about the other one? Was he a merchant, too?"

"Iwan?" said Bran. "Iwan is a friend. He rode with us to provide protection."

"A task at which he failed miserably," observed the count. "He escaped, but we will find him—and when we do, he will be made to pay for his crimes."

Bran took this to mean he had injured or killed at least one of the marchogi in the skirmish on the road.

"Only a coward would kill a priest," observed Bran. "Since you require men to pay for their crimes, why not begin with your own?"

The count leaned forward dangerously. "If you wish to keep your tongue, you will speak with more respect." He sat back and smoothed his tunic with his long fingers. "Now then, you knew my men were attacked by your people on that same road some days ago?"

"I was in Lundein, as I said," Bran replied. "I heard nothing of it."

"No?" wondered the count, holding his head to one side. "I can tell you the attack was crushed utterly. The lord of this place and his pitifully few warriors were wiped out."

"Three hundred against thirty," Bran replied, bitterness sharpening his tone. "It would not have been difficult."

"Careful," chided the count. "Are you certain you knew nothing of this battle?"

"Not a word," Bran told him, trying to sound both sincere and disinterested. "But I know how many men the King of Elfael had at his command."

"And you say you know nothing of the priest's business?"

"No. He did not tell me—why would he? I am no priest," Bran remarked. "Churchmen can be very secretive when it suits them."

"Could it have something to do with the money the priest was carrying?" inquired the count. He gestured to a nearby table and the four bags of coins lying there. Bran glanced at the table; the thieving Ffreinc had, of course, searched the horses and found the money Bran had hidden amongst the provisions.

"It is possible," allowed Bran. "I did not think priests carry so much money otherwise."

"No," agreed de Braose, "they do not." He frowned, apparently deciding there was nothing more to be learned. "Very well," he said at last, "about the ransom. It will be fifty marks."

Bran felt bitter laughter rising in his throat. Cardinal Ranulf wanted six hundred; what was fifty more?

"Fifty marks," he repeated. Determined not to allow the enemy the pleasure of seeing him squirm, Bran shrugged and adopted a thoughtful air. "A heavy price for one who is neither lord nor landholder."

De Braose regarded him with an appraising look. "You think it too high. What value would you place on your life?"

"I could get ten marks," Bran told him, trying to make himself sound reasonable. "Maybe twelve."

"Twenty-five."

"Fifteen, maybe," Bran offered reluctantly. "But it would take time."

"How much time?"

"Four days," said Bran, pursing his lips in close calculation. "Five would be better."

"You have one," the Norman lord decided. "And the ransom will be twenty marks."

"Twenty, then," agreed Bran reluctantly. "But I will need a horse."

De Braose shook his head slowly. "You will go afoot."

"If I am not to have a horse, I will certainly need more time," said Bran. He would have the money before the morning was out but did not want the Ffreinc to know that.

"Either you can find the ransom or you cannot," concluded de Braose, making up his mind. "You have one day—no more. And you must swear on the cross that you will return here with the money."

"Then I am free to go?" asked Bran, surprised that it should be so easy.

"Swear it," said de Braose.

Bran looked his enemy in the eye and said, "I do swear on the cross of Christ that I will return with money enough to purchase my ransom." He glanced at the two knights standing by the door. "I can go now?"

De Braose inclined his long head. "Yes, and I urge you to make haste. Bring the money to me before sunset. If you fail, you will be caught and your life will be forfeit, do you understand me?"

"Of course." Bran turned on his heel and strode away. It was all he could do to refrain from breaking into a run the moment he left the hall. To maintain the pretence, he calmly crossed the yard under the gaze of the marchogi and strode from the caer. He suspected that his new overlords watched him from the fortress, so he continued his purposeful, unbroken stride until the trees along the river at the valley bottom took him from sight—then he ran all the way to Llanelli to tell Bishop Asaph the grievous news about Brother Ffreol.

"Where is everyone?" shouted Bran, dashing through the gate and into the tidy spare yard of the Llanelli monastery. He had expected the yard to be full to overflowing with familiar faces of cowering, frightened Cymry seeking refuge from the invaders.

"Lord Bran! Thank God you are safe," replied Brother Eilbeg, the porter, hurrying after him.

Bran turned on him. "What happened to those I sent here?" he demanded.

"They've been taken to Saint Dyfrig's. Bishop Asaph thought they would be better cared for at the abbey until it is safe to return."

"Where is the bishop?"

"At prayer, sire," replied the monk. He looked through the door behind Bran, as if hoping to see someone else, then asked, "Where is Brother Ffreol?"

Bran made no answer but sped to the chapel, where he found Bishop Asaph on his knees before the altar, hands outstretched. "My lord," said Bran abruptly, "I have news."

The bishop concluded his prayer and turned to see who it was that interrupted his communion. One quick glance at Bran's bruised face told him there had been more trouble. "How bad is it?" asked the bishop, grasping the edge of the altar to pull himself to his feet.

"As bad as can be," Bran replied. "Brother Ffreol is dead. Iwan escaped, but they are searching for him to kill him."

The bishop's shoulders dropped, and he sagged against the near wall. He put a hand out to steady himself and paused a long moment, eyes closed, his lips moving in a silent prayer. Bran waited, and when the bishop had composed himself, he quickly explained how they had been caught on the road by marchogi who had killed the good brother without provocation.

"And you?" asked Asaph. "You fought free?"

Bran shook his head. "They took me captive and brought me to the caer. I was released to raise ransom for myself."

The bishop shook his head sadly. He gazed at Bran as if trying to fathom the depths of such outrageous events. "Cut down in the road, you say? For no reason?"

"No reason at all," confirmed Bran. "They are murderous Ffreinc bastards—that is all the reason they need."

"Did he suffer at all?"

"No," replied Bran with a quick shake of his head. "His death was quick. There was little pain."

Asaph gazed back at him with damp, doleful eyes and fingered the knotted ends of his cincture. "And yet they let you simply walk away?"

"The count thinks I am a nobleman."

Asaph's wizened face creased in a frown of incomprehension. "But you *are* a nobleman."

"I told him otherwise—although he refused to believe me."

"What will you do now?"

"I agreed to give him twenty marks in exchange for my freedom. I am honour-bound to bring him the money; otherwise he would never have let me go."

"We must go to Ffreol," murmured the bishop, starting for the chapel door. "We must go find his body and—"

"Did you hear me?" demanded Bran. Gripping the bishop's shoulder tightly, he spun the old man around. "I said I need the money."

"The ransom, yes—how much do you need?"

"Twenty marks in silver," repeated Bran quickly. "The strongbox—my father's treasure box—where is it? There should be more than enough to pay—" The sudden expression of anxiety on the bishop's face stopped him. The bishop looked away.

"The strongbox, Asaph," Bran said, his voice low and tense. "Where is it?"

"Count de Braose has taken it," the bishop replied.

"What!" cried Bran. "You were supposed to hide it from them!"

"They came here, the count and some of his men—they asked if we had any treasure," replied the churchman. "They wanted it. I had to give it to them."

"Fool!" shouted Bran. "In the name of all that is holy, why?"

"Bran, I could not lie," answered Asaph, growing indignant. "Lying is a venal sin. Love in the heart, truth on the lips—that is our rule."

"You just *gave* it to them?" Bran glared at the sanctimonious cleric, anger flicking like a whip from his gaze. "You've just killed me; do you know that?"

"I hardly think—"

"Listen to me, you old goat," spat Bran. "I must pay de Braose the ransom by sunset today, or I will be hunted down and executed. Where am I going to find that money now?"

The bishop, unrepentant, raised a finger heavenward. "God will provide."

"He already did!" snarled Bran. "The money was here, and you let them take it!" He growled with frustration and stalked to the open doorway of the chapel, then turned back suddenly. "I need a horse."

"That will be difficult."

"I do not care how difficult it is. Unless you want to see me dead this time tomorrow, you will find a horse at once. Do you understand me?"

"Where will you go?"

"North," answered Bran decisively. "Ffreol would still be alive and I would be safe there now if we had not listened to you."

The bishop bent his head, accepting the reproach.

Bran said, "My mother's kinsmen are in Gwynedd. When I tell them what has happened here, they will take me in. But I need a horse and supplies to travel."

"Saint Ernin's abbey serves the northern cantrefs," observed the bishop. "If you need help, you can call on them."

"Just get me that horse," commanded Bran, taking the cleric roughly by the arm and steering him toward the door.

"I will see what I can find." The bishop left, shaking his head and murmuring, "Poor Ffreol. We must go and claim his body so that he can be buried here amongst his brothers."

Bran walked alongside him, urging the elderly churchman to a quicker pace. "Yes, yes," he agreed. "You must claim the body, by all means. But first the horse—otherwise you will be digging *two* graves this time tomorrow."

The bishop nodded and hurried away. Bran watched him for a moment and then walked to the small guest lodge beside the gate; he looked around the near-empty cell. In one corner was a bed made of rushes overspread with a sheepskin. He crossed to the bed, lay down, and, overcome by the accumulated exertions of the last days, closed his eyes and sank into a blessedly dreamless sleep.

It was late when he woke again; the sun was well down, and the shadows stretched long across the empty yard. The bishop, he soon learned, had sent three monks in search of a horse; none of the three had yet returned. The bishop himself had taken a party with an oxcart to retrieve the body of Brother Ffreol. There was nothing to do, so he returned to the guest lodge to stew over the stupidity of churchmen and rue his rotten luck. He sprawled on the bench outside the chapter house, listening to the intermittent bell as it tolled the offices. Little by little, the once-bright day faded to a dull yellow haze.

He dozed and awoke to yet another bell. Presently the monks began appearing; in twos and threes they entered the yard, hurrying from their various chores. "That bell—what was it?" Bran asked one of the brothers as he passed.

"It is only vespers, sire," replied the priest respectfully.

Bran's heart sank at the word: *vespers*. Eventide prayer—the day gone, and he was still within shouting distance of the caer. He slumped back against the mud-daubed wall and stuck his feet out in front of him. Asaph was worse than useless, and he felt a ripe fool for trusting him. If he had known the silly old man had given his father's treasure to de Braose—simply handed it over, by Job's bones—he could have lit out for the northern border the moment the count set him free.

He was on the point of fleeing Llanelli when an errant breeze brought a savoury aroma from the cookhouse, and he suddenly remembered how hungry he was. An instant later he was on his feet and moving toward the refectory. He would eat and then go.

Nothing was easier than cadging a meal from Brother Bedo, the kitchener. A cheerful, red-faced lump with watery eyes and a permanent stoop from bending over his pots and steaming cauldrons, no creature that begged a crust was ever turned away from his door.

"Lord Bran, bless me, it's you," he said, pulling Bran into the room and sitting him down on a three-legged stool at the table. "I heard what happened to you on the road—a sorry business, a full sorry business indeed, God's truth. Brother Ffreol was one of our best, you know. He would have been bishop one day, he would—if not abbot also."

"He was my confessor," volunteered Bran. "He was a friend and a good man."

"I don't suppose it could have been helped?" asked the kitchener, placing a wooden trencher of roast meat and bread on the table before Bran.

"There was nothing to be done," Bran said. "Even if he'd had a hundred warriors at his back, it would not have made the slightest difference."

"Ah, so, well . . ." Bedo poured out a jar of thin ale into a small leather cup. "Bless him—and bless you, too, that you were there to comfort him at his dying breath."

Bran accepted the monk's words without comment. There had been precious little comforting in Ffreol's last moments. The chaos of that terrible night rose before him once more, and Bran's eyesight dimmed with tears. He finished his meal without further talk, then thanked the brother and went out, already planning the route he would take through the valley, away from the caer and Count de Braose's ransom demand.

The moon had risen above the far hills when Bran slipped through the gate. He had walked only a few dozen paces when he heard someone calling after him. "Lord Bran! Wait!" He looked around to see three dusty, footsore monks leading a swaybacked plough horse.

"What is that?" asked Bran, regarding the animal doubtfully.

"My lord," the monk said, "it is the best we could find. Anyone with a seemly mount has sent it away, and the Ffreinc have already taken the rest." The monk regarded the horse wearily. "It may not be much, but trust me, it is this or nothing."

"Worse than nothing," Bran grumbled. Snatching the halter rope from the monk's hands, he clambered up onto the beast's bony back. "Tell the bishop I have gone. I will send word from Gwynedd." With that, he departed on his pathetic mount.

Bran had never ridden a beast as slow and stumble-footed as the one he now sat atop. The creature plodded along in the dying moonlight, head down, nose almost touching the ground. Despite Bran's most ardent insistence, piteous begging, and harrowing threats, the animal refused to assume a pace swifter than a hoof-dragging amble.

Thus, night was all but spent by the time Bran came in sight of Caer Rhodl, the fortress of Mérian's father, King Cadwgan, rising up out of the mists of the morning that would be. Tethering the plough horse to a rowan bush in a gully beside the track, Bran ran the rest of the way on foot. He scaled the low wall at his customary place and dropped into the empty yard. The caer was silent. The watchmen, as usual, were asleep.

Quick and silent as a shadow, Bran darted across the dark expanse of yard to the far corner of the house. Mérian's room was at the back, its single small window opening onto the kitchen herb garden. He crept along the side of the house until he came to her window and then, pressing his ear to the rough wooden shutter, paused to listen. Hearing nothing, he pulled on the shutter; it swung open easily, and he paused again. When nothing stirred inside, he whispered, "Mérian . . . ," and waited, then whispered again, slightly louder. "Mérian! Be quick!"

This time his call was answered by the sound of a hushed footfall and the rustle of clothing. In a moment, Mérian's face appeared in the window, pale in the dim light. "You should not have come," she said. "I won't let you in—not tonight."

"There was a battle," he told her. "My father has been killed—the entire warband with him. The Ffreinc have taken Elfael."

"Oh, Bran!" she gasped. "How did it happen?"

"They have a grant from King William. They are taking everything."

"But this is terrible," she said. "Are you hurt?"

"I was not in the battle," he said. "But they are searching for me."

"What are you going to do?"

"I'm leaving for Gwynedd—now, at once. I have kinsmen there. But I need a horse."

"You want me to give you a horse?" Mérian shook her head. "I cannot. I dare not. My father would scream the roof down."

"I will pay him," said Bran. "Or find a way to return it. Please, Mérian."

"Is there not some other way?"

He raised a hand and squeezed her arm. "Please, Mérian, you're the only one who can help me now." He gazed at her in the glowing light of a rising sun and, in spite of himself, felt his desire quicken. On a sudden inspiration, he said, "I love you, Mérian. Come with me. We will go together, you and I—far away from all of this."

"Bran, think what you're saying!" She pulled free. "I cannot just run away, nor can you." Leaning forward as far as the small window would allow, she clutched at him. "Listen to me, Bran. You must go back. It is the people of Elfael who will need you now and in the days to come. You will be king. You must think of your people."

"The Ffreinc will kill me!" protested Bran.

"Shh!" she said, placing her fingertips to his lips. "Someone will hear you."

"I failed to pay the ransom," Bran explained, speaking more softly. "If I go back to Elfael empty-handed, they'll kill me—they mean to kill me anyway, I think. The only reason I'm still alive is because they want the money first."

"Come," she said, making up her mind. "We must go to my father. You must tell him what you have told me. He will know what to do."

"Your father hates me." Bran rejected the idea outright. "No. I am not going back. Elfael is lost. I have to get away now while I still have a chance." He raised a hand to stroke her cheek. "Come with me, Mérian. We can be together."

"Bran, listen. Be reasonable. Let my father help you."

"Will he give twenty marks to free me?" Mérian bit her lip doubtfully. "No?" sneered Bran. "I thought not. He'd sooner see my head on a pike."

"He will go with you and talk to them. He stands in good stead with Baron Neufmarché. The Ffreinc will listen to him. He will help you."

"I'm leaving, Mérian." Bran backed away from the window. "It was a mistake to come here . . ."

"Just wait there," she said and disappeared suddenly. She was back an instant later. "Here, take this," she said. Reaching out, she dropped a small leather bag into his hand. It chinked as he caught it. "It is not much," she said, "but it is all I have."

"I need a weapon," he said, tucking the bag away. "Can you get me a sword? Or a spear? Both would be best."

"Let me see." She darted away again and was gone longer this time. Bran waited. The sky brightened. The rising sun bathed his back with its warming rays. It would be daylight before he could start out, and that would mean finding a way north that avoided as much of Elfael as possible. He was pondering this when Mérian returned to the window.

"I couldn't get a sword," she said, "but I found this. It belongs to my brother." She pushed the polished ash-wood shaft of a longbow out to him, followed by a sheaf of arrows.

Bran took the weapons, thanked her coolly, and stepped away from the window. "Farewell, Mérian," he said, raising a hand in parting.

"Please don't go." Reaching out, she strained after him, brushing his fingertips with her own. "Think of your people, Bran," she said, her voice pleading. "They need you. How can you help them in Gwynedd?"

"I love you, Mérian," he said, still backing away. "Remember me."

"Bran, no!" she called. "Wait!"

But he was already running for his life.

CHAPTER 12

By the time Bran reached the stream separating the
two cantrefs, the sun was burning through the mist that swathed
the forest to the east and collected in the hollows of the lowlands.
Astride his slow horse, he cursed his luck. He had considered simply taking a horse from Cadwgan's stable but could not think how
to do so without waking one of the stable hands. And even if he
had been able to achieve that, adding the wrath of Lord Cadwgan
to his woes was not a prospect to be warmly embraced. The last
thing he needed just now was an irate king's search party hot on his
heels.

Despite his slow pace, he rode easily along the valley bottom
through fields glistening with early morning dew. The crops were ripe,
and soon the harvest season would be upon them. Long before the
first scythe touched a barley stalk, however, Bran would be far away
beyond the forest and mountain fastness to the north, enjoying the
warmth and safety of a kinsman's hearth.

There were, Bran considered as he clopped along, two ways to

Gwynedd through the Cymraic heartland. Elfael straddled both, and neither was very good.

The first and most direct way was straight across Elfael to Coed Cadw and then through dense woodland all the way to the mountains. They were not high mountains, but they were rough, broken crags of shattered stone, and difficult to cross—all the more so for a man alone and without adequate supplies. The second route was less direct; it meant skirting the southern border of Elfael and working patiently through the intricate interlacing of low hills and hidden valleys to the west before turning north along the coast.

This second route was slower and passed uncomfortably close to Caer Cadarn before bending away to the west. There was a risk that he might be seen. Still, it kept him out of the treacherous mountain pathways and made best use of his mount's limited value as a steady plodder.

Bran did not relish the idea of passing so close to the unfriendly Ffreinc, but it could not be helped. He considered laying up somewhere and waiting until nightfall; however, the idea of trying to remain hidden under de Braose's nose and then thrashing around the countryside in the dark lacked the allure of ready flight. The day was new, he reckoned, and he would pass Caer Cadarn at the nearest point while it was still early morning and the invaders would most likely be otherwise occupied. Perhaps they were not even looking for him yet.

He reached the boundary stream but did not cross. Instead, he turned his slow steed west and, in the interest of keeping well out of sight of Caer Cadarn, followed the narrow waterway as it snaked through the gorsy lowlands that formed the border between Elfael and Brycheiniog to the south. In time, the stream would swing around to the northwest, entering Maelienydd, a region of rough hills and cramped valleys that he hoped to cross as quickly as possible. Then he would head for Arwstli, angling north all the while toward Powys—and so work his way cantref by cantref to Gwynedd and a glad welcome amongst his mother's people.

Bran was thinking about how distraught and outraged his kinsmen would be upon learning the news of his father's cruel murder and the loss of Elfael when the distant echo of a scream brought him up short. He tried telling himself he had imagined it only and was halfway down the path toward believing that when the terrified shriek came again: a woman's voice, carried on the breeze and, though faint, clearly signifying terrible distress. Bran halted, listened again, and then turned his mount in the direction of the cry.

He crossed the stream into the far southwestern toe of Elfael. Over the nearest hill, he saw the first threads of black smoke rising in the clear morning air. He crested the hill and looked over into the valley on the other side, where he saw the settlement called Nant Cwm, a fair-sized holding comprised of a large house and a yard with several barns and a few outbuildings. Even from a distance, he could see that it was under attack; smoke was spewing from the door of the barn and from the roof of the house. There were five saddled horses in the yard between the house and barn, but no riders. Then, as Bran watched, a man burst from the front door of the house, almost flying. He ran a few steps, his feet tangled, then fell sprawling on his side. Right behind him came his attackers—two Ffreinc men-at-arms with drawn swords. Two more marchogi emerged from the house, dragging a woman between them.

Bran saw the hated Ffreinc, and his anger flared white hot in an instant. Snatching up the bow Mérian had given him, he grabbed the sheaf of arrows, and before he knew his feet had touched ground, he was racing down the hill toward the settlement.

In the yard, the farmer cried out, throwing his hands before him—

121

clearly pleading for his life. The two Ffreinc standing over him raised their swords. The woman screamed again, struggling in the grasp of her captors. The farmer shouted again and tried to rise. Bran saw the swords glint hard and bright in the sun as they slashed and fell. The farmer writhed in a vain attempt to avoid the blows. The fierce blades slashed again, and the man lay still.

At the farmer's death, Bran's vision hardened to a single, piercing beam, and the world flashed crimson. He bit his lip to keep from crying out his rage as he flew toward the fight. As soon as he judged he was within the longbow's range, he squatted down and opened the cloth bundle.

There were but six arrows. Every arrow would have to count. Bran nocked the first onto the string, pulled the feathered shaft close to his cheek, and took aim—his target the nearer of the two soldiers struggling with the farmer's wife.

Just as he was about to let fly, the farmhouse door opened and out of the burning building ran a young boy of, perhaps, six or seven summers.

One of the marchogi shouted, and from around the far side of the house another Ffreinc soldier appeared with a sword in one hand and the leash of an enormous hunting dog in the other. This was the commander—a knight with a round steel helmet and a long hauberk of ringed mail. The knight saw the boy escaping across the yard and gave a shout. When the child failed to stop, he loosed the hound.

With staggering speed, the snarling, slavvering beast ran down the boy. The mother screamed as the hound, fully as big as her son, closed on the fleeing child.

The hound leapt, and the terrified boy stumbled. Bran let fly in the same instant.

The arrow whirred as it streaked home, burying itself in the hound's slender neck, even as the beast's jaws snatched at the child's unprotected throat. The dog crumpled and rolled to the side, teeth still gnashing, forelegs raking the air.

As the whimpering boy climbed to his feet, the Ffreinc men-at-arms searched the surrounding hills for the source of the unexpected arrow. The knight who had released the dog was the first to spot Bran crouching on the hill above the settlement. He shouted a command to his marchogi, pointing toward the hillside with his sword.

He was still pointing when an arrow—like a weird, feathered flower—sprouted in the middle of his mail-clad stomach.

The sword spun from his hand, and the knight crashed to his knees, clutching the shaft of the arrow. He gave out a roar of pain and outrage, and the two soldiers standing over the dead farmer leapt to life. They charged at a run, blades high, across the yard and up the hill.

Bran, working with uncanny calm, placed another arrow on the string, took his time to pull, hold, and aim. When he let fly, the missile sang to its mark. The first warrior was struck and spun completely around by the force of the arrow. The second ran on a few more steps, then halted abruptly, jerked to his full height by the slender oak shaft that slammed into his chest.

Next, Bran turned his attention to the two marchogi holding the woman. No one was struggling now; all three were staring in flatfooted disbelief at the lone archer crouching on the hillside.

By the time Bran had another arrow on the string and was taking aim, the two had released the woman and were running for the horses. One of the marchogi had the presence of mind to try to cut off any possible pursuit; he gathered the reins of the riderless horses, leapt into the saddle, and fled the slaughter ground.

Bran raced down to the farmyard, pausing at the foot of the hill to release another arrow. He drew and loosed at the nearest of the two fleeing riders. The arrow flew straight and true, sizzling through the air to sink its sharp metal head deep between the shoulders of the Ffreinc warrior, who arched his back and flung his arms wide as if to embrace the sky. The galloping horse ran on a few more steps, and the warrior slumped sideways and plunged heavily to the ground.

Bran's last arrow streaked toward the sole remaining soldier as he gained the low rise at the far end of the yard. Lashing his mount hard, the rider swerved at the last instant as the missile ripped by, slashing through the tall grass. The fleeing warrior sped on and did not look back.

Bran hurried to the farmwife, who was on her knees, clutching her wailing son. "You must get away from here!" he told her, urgency making him sharp. "They might come back in force." The woman just stared at him. "You must go!" he insisted. "Do you understand?"

She nodded and, still holding tight to her child, turned her tearful gaze back to the yard where her husband lay. Bran saw the look and relented. He allowed her a moment and then took her gently by the shoulder and turned her to face him. "They will come back," he said, softening his tone. "You must get away while you can."

"I have no place to go," cried the woman, turning again to the twisted, bloody body of her dead husband. "Oh, Gyredd!" Her face crumpled, and she began to weep.

"Lady, you will mourn him in good time," Bran said, "but later, when you are safe. You must think of your child now and do what is best for him."

Taking the crying boy into his arms, he walked quickly to the horse on the hill, urging the woman to hurry. Its rider slain, the animal had stopped running and was now grazing contentedly. If he considered taking the good horse for himself and giving the plough horse to the farmwife, one look at the woman struggling valiantly to bear up under the calamity that had befallen her abolished any such thought.

Here was a woman with a boy so much like himself at that age they could have been brothers.

"Here is what you will do," Bran said, speaking slowly. "You will take the lad and ride to the abbey. The monks at Saint Dyfrig's will take care of you until it is safe to return, or until you find somewhere else to go."

He helped her onto the horse, holding the boy as she climbed into the saddle. "Go now," he commanded, lifting the child and placing him in the saddle in front of his mother. "Tell them what happened here, and they will take care of you."

Putting his hand to the bridle, Bran ran the horse to the top of the rise where he could get a clear view of the countryside around. There were no marchogi to be seen, so he pointed the woman in the direction of the monastery. "Take good care of your mother, lad," he told the boy, then gave the horse a slap on the rump to send them off. "Do not stop until you reach the abbey," he called. "I will see to things here."

"God bless you," said the woman, turning in the saddle as the horse jolted into motion.

Bran watched until they were well away and then hurried back to the farm. He dragged the dead farmer to the grassy hillside, then fetched a wooden shovel from the barn; the fire had been hastily set, and the flames had already burned down to smouldering ash, leaving the barn intact. Working quickly, he dug a shallow grave in the green grass at the foot of the hill, then rolled the body into the long depression and began piling the soft earth over the corpse.

He left the shovel at the head of the grave to mark the place and then ran to retrieve his arrows. Pulling them from the bodies was a grim task, but they were too valuable to waste, and he had no way to replace them. Despite his care, one of them broke when he tried to worry it free from the rib cage of the dead soldier, and the one that

125

had missed its target could not be found. In the end, he had to settle for recovering but four of the six.

He wiped the iron heads on the grass, bundled them up again, and then hurried to retrieve his shamble-footed mount. Grabbing a handful of mane, he swung up onto the swaybacked creature once more and, with much kicking and cursing, clopped away.

He did not get far.

Upon reaching the top of the hill, he glanced back toward the settlement. At that moment, five marchogi on horseback crested the rise beyond Nant Cwm. The riders paused, as if searching out a direction to follow. Bran halted and sat very still, hoping they would not see him. This hope, like all the others he had conceived since the Ffreinc arrived, died as it was born.

Even as he watched, one of the riders raised an arm and pointed in his direction. Bran did not wait to see more. He slapped the reins hard across the withers of his plough horse mount and kicked back hard with his heels. The startled animal responded with a gratifying burst of speed that carried him over the crest of the hill and out of sight of the riders.

Once over the hilltop, the nag slowed and stopped, and Bran swiftly scanned the descent for his best chance of escape. The slope fell away steeply to the stream he had been following. On the other side the land opened onto a meadow grazing land—flat and bereft of any rock or tree big enough to hide behind. Away to the northeast rose the thick dark line of Coed Cadw.

He turned his face to the north, kicked his mount to life once more, and rode for the strong, protecting wall of the forest.

CHAPTER 13

The ancient woodland rampart rose before him in vast dark folds, like a great bristling pelt covering the deep, rocky roots of Yr Wyddfa, the Region of Snows in the north. His rickety mount trotted along at a pace resembling a canter, and still some distance away from the nearest trees, Bran despaired of reaching them before his galloping pursuers overtook him.

Midway between himself and the forest, a course of rock jutted up out of the mounded earth, forming a narrow spine of stone that ran all the way to the forest. Tiring quickly now, his slow-footed animal resumed its customary amble. Bran slung the bow across his chest and, gripping his clutch of arrows, slid off the beast's back and sent it on. As it sauntered away without him, he bounded to the rocky outcrop and ducked behind it.

He knew the marchogi would not follow a riderless horse, and the lazy animal would not wander far, but he hoped the slight misdirection would distract them at least long enough to allow him to reach the shelter of the forest. Once amongst the trees, he had no doubt at all that he could elude pursuit without difficulty. The forest was a place he knew well.

Crouching low to keep his head below the jagged line of rock, Bran worked his way quickly up the rising slope toward the tree line, pausing now and again to scan the open ground behind him. He saw no sign of the marchogi and took heart. Perhaps they had given up the chase and returned to pillage the farm instead.

The last few hundred paces rose up a steep embankment, at the top of which lay the forest edge. Bran paused and gathered himself for the last mad scramble. Gulping air, he tried to calm his racing heart as, with a final glance behind him, he ran to the escarpment. It took longer than he thought to reach it, but clambering over the grey lichen-covered rocks on hands and knees, he eventually gained the top, pulling himself up the last rise with his hands and gripping the arrow bundle with his teeth.

The trees lay just ahead. He put his head down and staggered on. He had taken but a half-dozen steps when a Ffreinc rider appeared from the edge of the forest and stepped directly into his path. Bran did not have time even to raise his bow before the warrior was on him. Sword drawn, the soldier spoke a command that Bran could not understand and indicated that Bran was to turn around and start back the way he had come.

Instead, Bran ran toward him, dove under the belly of the horse, and, legs churning, continued running. The rider gave a shout and put spurs to his mount. Bran flew to the forest.

This first rider cried after him, and his shout was answered by another. A second rider appeared, racing along the margin of the forest to cut off Bran's flight before he could reach the wood.

Desperation lent him speed. He gained the entrance to the dark refuge of Coed Cadw as two more riders joined the chase. The rippling thud of the horses' hooves thrummed on the turf, punctuated by gusting blasts of air through the galloping animals' nostrils. On the riders came, whooping and shouting as they converged on his trail, readying their spears as if he were a deer for the kill.

They were loud, and they were overconfident. And they had not enough wit to know to quit the saddle before entering the wood. Realising this, Bran stopped dead on the trail and turned to face his attacker. The oncoming rider gave out a wild shriek of triumph and heaved his lance. Bran saw the spearhead spin as the lance left the rider's hand. He gave a simple feint to the side, and the spear sliced the air where his head had been. The rider cursed and came on, drawing his sword.

Whirling around, Bran retrieved the spear and, turning back, knelt and planted the butt of the shaft in the ground as the charger sped forward—too fast to elude the trap. Unable to stop, the hapless animal ran onto the blade. With a scream of agony, the horse plunged on a few more strides before it became tangled in the undergrowth and went down in a heap of flailing hooves and thrashing legs. The rider was thrown over the neck of his mount and landed on hands and knees. Bran rushed to the stunned knight, ripped the knife from his belt, and with a shriek like the cry of a banshee, plunged the blade into the exposed flesh of the man's neck, between his helmet and mail shirt. The knight struggled to his knees, clawing at the blade, as Bran ran for the shelter of the trees.

A few strides into the wood, the main trail split into several smaller paths, fanning out into the tangle of trees and undergrowth. Bran chose one that passed between two close-grown trees—wide enough to admit him, but narrow enough to hinder a rider. His feet were already on the path, and he was through the gap when the second rider reached the place.

129

He heard a frustrated shout behind him and the tormented whinny of a horse. Bran glanced back to see that the rider had halted because his mount was tangled in the branches of a low-lying bramble thicket, and the warrior was having difficulty extricating himself.

Unslinging his bow, Bran shook the arrows from the bundle and snatched one from the ground. He pressed the bow forward, took aim, and let fly. The missile sped through the trees and took the rider in the chest just below the collarbone. The force of the impact slammed the warrior backward in the saddle, but he kept his seat. Bran sent a second arrow after the first. It flew wide of the mark by a mere hairsbreadth.

He had two arrows left. He bent down to snatch them up, and as he straightened, he glimpsed a blur of movement out of the corner of his eye.

The spear sped through the air. Bran tried to leap aside, but the steel-tipped length of ash was expertly thrown, and the blade caught him midstride, striking high on the right shoulder. The force of the throw knocked him off his feet and sent him sprawling forward.

Bran fell hard and heard something snap beneath him. He had landed on the arrows, breaking one of the slender shafts in the fall. One arrow left. Gasping for breath, he rolled onto his side, and the spear came free.

The rider drove in fast behind his throw, sword drawn and raised high, ready to part Bran's head from his shoulders. Bran, crouching in the path, picked up the bow and the last arrow; he nocked the shaft to the string, pressing the longbow forward in the same swift motion.

The wound in his shoulder erupted with a ferocious agony. Bran gasped aloud, his body convulsed, and his fingers released their grip on the string. The arrow scudded off along the trail, to no effect. He threw down the bow, picked up the Ffreinc lance that had wounded him, and stumbled from the path, pushing deeper into the wood.

The coarse shouts of his attackers grew louder and more urgent as they ordered their pursuit. The branches were now too close grown and tangled, the trail too narrow for men on horseback. Bran sensed the marchogi were dismounting; they would continue the chase on foot.

Using their momentary inattention, he turned off the trail and dove into the undergrowth. Moving as quickly and quietly as possible, he slipped through the crowded ranks of slender young hazel and beech trees, scrambling over the fallen trunks of far older elms until he came to another, wider path.

He paused to listen.

The voices of his pursuers reached him from the trail he had left behind. Soon they would realise their quarry was no longer on the path they pursued; when that happened, they would spread out and begin a slower, more careful search.

He put his hand to his injured shoulder and probed the wound with his fingers. The ache was fierce and fiery, and blood was trickling down his back in a sticky rivulet. It would be best to find some way to bind the wound lest one of the pursuers see the blood and pick up his trail that way. Luckily, he thought with grim satisfaction, the marchogi no longer had a dog with them.

As if in answer to this thought, there came a sound that turned his bowels to water: the hoarse baying of a hound on scent. It was still some way off, but once the animal reached the trailhead, the hunt would be all but finished.

Turning away, Bran lurched on, following the path as it twisted and turned, pressing ever deeper into the wood. He ran, listening to the cry of the hound grow louder by degrees, keenly alert for something, anything, that might throw the beast off his scent.

Then, all at once the sound ended. The forest went quiet.

Bran stopped.

His shoulder was aflame, and cold sweat beaded on his brow. He waited, drawing air deep into his lungs, trying to steady his racing heart.

Suddenly, the hound gave out a long, rising howl that was followed instantly by a shout from one of the soldiers. The dog had found his trail again.

Bran staggered forward once more. He knew he could not long elude his pursuers now—a few moments, more or less, and the chase would end.

And then, just ahead, he spied a low opening in the brush and, beneath it, dark, well-churned earth: the telltale sign of a run used by wild pigs. He dove for it and scrambled forward on hands and knees, dragging the spear with him. His pursuers were still on the trail he had just quit.

He drove himself on, wriggling through the undergrowth, around rocks and over roots. Low-hanging branches tore at him, snagging his clothing and skin.

The hound reached the end of the pig run and hesitated. At first the marchogi assumed the dog had been distracted by the scent of the pigs. There was a shout and a yelp as they dragged the dog away from the entrance to the run and moved on down the trail.

Bran gathered himself for another push. Pulling himself up by the shaft of the spear, he lurched ahead—four heartbeats later, the hound loosed another rising howl, and the chase resumed behind him.

Gritting his teeth against the pain, Bran ran on.

Above the crashing and thrashing in the wood behind him, he heard something else: the liquid murmur of falling water. Bran followed the sound and in a moment came to a small, boulder-strewn clearing. A swift-flowing stream cut through its centre, coursing around the base of the huge, round moss-covered stones.

Bran picked his way amongst the rocks, only to find that the path ended in a sheer drop. The stream plunged into a pool beneath the stony ledge on which Bran was standing. The waters gathered in the pool and then flowed away into the hidden heart of Coed Cadw.

Bran gazed at the pool and realised that, like the path, his flight had ended, too.

With his back to the waterfall, he turned to make his last stand. His breath came in shaky gasps. Sweat flowed down his face and neck. The shaft of the spear was slick with his blood. He wiped his hands on his clothes and tightened his grip on the spear as the marchogi approached, their voices loud in the silence of the forest.

They reached the clearing all at once—the hound and three men—bursting into the glade in a blind rush. Two soldiers held spears, and the third grasped the leash of the hound. The dog saw Bran and began straining at its lead, snarling with slavering fury and clawing the air to reach him.

The soldiers hesitated, uncertain where they were. Bran saw the cast of their eyes as they took in the rocks, the waterfall, and then . . . himself, standing perfectly still on a stone above the fall.

The dog handler shouted to the others; the knight on his left raised his spear and drew back his arm. Bran readied himself to dodge the throw.

There came a shout, and a fourth man entered the rock-filled hollow behind the others; he wielded a sword, and the front of his hauberk was stained with blood from the arrow wound beneath his collarbone. He made a motion with his hand, and the marchogi under his command spread out.

Bran tightened his grip on the spear and braced himself for the attack.

The man with the sword raised his hand, but before he could give the signal, there was a sharp snap, like that of a slap in the face. The

133

hound, suddenly and unexpectedly free of its broken leash, bounded toward Bran, its jaws agape.

Bran turned to meet the hound. One of the soldiers, seeing Bran move, launched his spear.

Both dog and spear reached Bran at the same time. Bran jerked his body to the side. The spear sailed harmlessly by, but the jaws of the hound closed on his arm. Bran dropped his spear and threw his free arm around the neck of the dog, trying to strangle the animal as its teeth ripped into the skin and tendons of his arm.

Two more spears were already in the air. The first found its mark, passing through the dog and striking Bran. The hound gave out a yelp, and Bran felt a wicked sting in the centre of his chest.

Wounded, his vision suddenly blurred with the pain, Bran fought to keep his balance on the rock ledge. Too late he saw the glint in the air of a spear streaking toward him. Thrown high, it missed his throat but sliced through the soft part of his cheek as it grazed along his jaw.

The jolt rocked him backward.

He teetered on the ledge for an instant, and then, still clasping the dying dog like a shield before his body, he plunged over the waterfall and into the pool below.

The last thing he saw was the face of one of his attackers peering cautiously over the edge of the fall. Then Bran closed his eyes and let the stream bear him away.

PART TWO

IN COED CADW

Mérian took the news of Bran's death hard—much harder than she herself might have predicted had she ever dreamed such a possibility could occur. True, she heartily resented Bran ap Brychan for running away and deserting his people in their time of need; she might have forgiven him all else, if not for that. On the other hand, she knew him to be a selfish, reckless, manipulating rascal. Thus, though utterly irritated and angry with him, she had not been at all surprised by his decision to flee. She told herself that she would never see him again.

Even so, never in her most resentful disposition did she conceive—much less *wish*—that any harm would come to him. That he had been caught and killed trying to escape filled her with morbid anguish. The news—reported by her father's steward and overheard by her as he related the latest marketplace gossip to the cook and scullery girls—hit her like a blow to the stomach. Unable to breathe, she sagged against the doorpost and stifled a cry with her fist.

Sometime later, when summoned to her father's chamber, where she was informed, she was able to bear up without betraying the true depth of her feelings. Shocked, horrified, mournful, and leaden with sorrow, Mérian moved through the first awful day feeling as if the ground she trod was no longer solid beneath her feet—as if the very earth was fragile, delicate, and thin as the shell of a robin's egg, and as if any moment the crust on which she stood might shatter and she would instantly plunge from the world of light and air into the utter, perpetual, suffocating darkness of the tomb.

Soon, everyone in King Cadwgan's court was talking of nothing else but Bran's sad, but really only-too-predictable, demise. That was harder still for Mérian. She put on a brave face. She tried to appear as if the news of Bran and the misfortune that had befallen Elfael meant little to her, or rather that it meant merely as much as bad news from other places ever meant to anyone not directly concerned—as if, lamentable though it surely was, the fate of the wayward son of a neighbouring king ultimately was nothing to do with her.

"Yes," she would agree, "isn't it awful? Those poor people—what will they do?"

She told herself time and again that Bran had been an unreliable friend at best; that his apparent interest in her was nothing more than carnal, which was entirely true; and that his sad death had, at the very least, delivered her from a life of profound and perpetual unhappiness. These things and more she told herself—spoke them aloud, even. But no matter how often she rehearsed the reasons she should be relieved to be free of Bran ap Brychan, she could not make herself believe them. Nor, for all the truth of her assertions, could she make herself feel less wretched.

She kept a tight rein on herself when others were nearby. She neither wept nor sobbed; not one sorrowing sigh escaped her lips. Her features remained composed, thoughtful perhaps, but not distraught, less yet grief-stricken. Anyone observing Mérian might have thought her distracted or concerned. Knowing that nothing good could come of any overt display of emotion where Bran was concerned, she swallowed her grief and behaved as if the news of Bran's death was a thing of negligible significance amidst the more troubling news of the murder of Brychan ap Tewdwr and all his warband and the unwarranted Ffreinc advance into neighbouring Elfael. Here, if only here, she and her stern father agreed: the Ffreinc had no right to kill a sitting king and seize his cantref.

"It is a bad business," King Cadwgan told her, shaking his grey head. "Very bad. It should not have happened, and William Rufus should answer. But Brychan had been warned more than once to make his peace. I urged him to go to Lundein long ago—*years* ago! We all did! Would he listen? He was a hell-bent, bloody-minded fool—"

"Father!" Mérian objected. "It is beneath you to speak ill of the dead, and bad luck besides."

"Beneath me?" wondered Cadwgan. "Daughter, it is kindness itself! I knew the man, and of times would have called him my friend. You know that. On Saint Becuma's knees, I swear that man could be so maddeningly pigheaded—and mean with it! If there was ever a man with a colder heart, I don't want to know him." He raised an admonishing finger to his daughter. "Mark my words, girl, now that Brychan and his reprobate son are gone, we will soon count it a blessing in disguise."

"Father!" she protested once more, her voice quivering slightly. "You should not say such things."

"If I speak my mind, it is not out of malice. You know me better than that, I hope. Though we may not like it, that is God's own truth. Brychan's son was a rogue, and his death saved a hangman's fee."

"I will not stay and listen to this," declared Mérian as she turned quickly and hurried away.

"What did I say?" called her father after her. "If anyone has cause to mourn Bran ap Brychan's death, it is the hangman who was cheated out of his pay!"

Mérian's mother was more sympathetic but no more comforting. "I know it is hard to accept," said Queen Anora, threading her embroidery needle, "when someone you know has died. He was such a handsome boy—if only he had been better brought up, he might have made a good king. Alas, his mother died so young. Rhian was a beauty, and kindness itself—if a little flighty, so they say. Still, it's a pity she was not there to raise him." She sighed, then went back to her needle. "You can thank God you were not allowed to receive him in company."

"I know, Mother," said Mérian glumly, turning her face away. "How well I know."

"Soon you will forget all about him." She offered her daughter a hopeful smile. "Time will heal, and the hurt will pass. Mark my words, the pain will pass."

Mérian knew her parents were right, though she would not have expressed her opinions quite so harshly. Even so, she could not make her heart believe the things they said: it went on aching, and nothing anyone said soothed the pain. In the end, Mérian determined to keep her thoughts, like her grief, to herself.

Each day, she went about her chores as if the raw wound of sorrow was already skinning over. She attended her weaving with care and patience. She helped the women prepare the animal skins that would become furs to adorn winter cloaks and tunics. She stood barefoot in the warm sun and raked the newly harvested beans over the drying floor. She twirled the spindle between her deft fingers to spin new-carded wool into thread, watching the skein grow as she wound it round and round. Though she laboured with diligence, she did not feel the thread pass through her fingertips, nor the rake in her hands; she did not smell the strong curing salts she rubbed into the skins; her fingers gathered the wool of their own accord without her guidance.

Each day, she completed her duties with her usual care—as if the thought of Bran hunted down and speared to death like some poor, fear-crazed animal was not the sole occupation of her thoughts, as if the anguish at his passing was not continually churning in her gentle heart.

And if, each night, she cried silently in her bed, each morning she rose fresh faced and resolved not to allow any of these secret feelings to manifest themselves in word or deed. In this she made good.

As the weeks passed, she thought less about Bran and his miserable death and more about the fate of his leaderless people. Of course, they were not—as Garran, her elder brother, so helpfully pointed out—leaderless. "They have a new king now—William Rufus," he told her. "And his subject lord, Count de Braose, is their ruler."

"De Braose is a vile murderer," Mérian snapped.

"That may be," Garran granted with irritating magnanimity, "but he has been given the commot by the king. And," he delighted in pointing out, "the crown is divinely appointed by God. The king is justice, and his word is law."

"The king is himself a usurper," she countered.

"As were most of those before him," replied her brother, smug in his argument. "Facts are facts, dear sister. The Saxon stole the land from us, and now the Ffreinc have stolen it from them. We possess what we hold by King William's sufferance. He is our sovereign lord now, and it is no good wishing otherwise, so you had best make peace with how things are."

"*You* make peace with how things are," she answered haughtily. "I will remain true to our own kind."

"Then you will continue to live in the past," Garran scoffed. "The old ways are over for us. Times are changing, Mérian. The Ffreinc are showing us the way to peace and prosperity."

"They are showing us the way to *hell!*" she shouted, storming from his presence.

That young Prince Bran had died needlessly was bad enough. That he had been killed trying to flee was shameful, yes, but anyone might have done the same in his place. What she found impossible to comprehend or accept was her brother's implied assertion that their Norman overlords were somehow justified in their crime by the innate superiority of their customs or character, or whatever it was her brother found so enamouring.

The Ffreinc are brutes and they are wrong, she insisted to herself. *And that King William of theirs is the biggest brute of all!*

After that last exchange, she refused to talk to anyone further regarding the tragedy that had befallen Bran and Elfael. She kept her thoughts to herself and buried her feelings deep in the fastness of her heart.

Baron de Neufmarché, along with twenty men-at-arms, accompanied his wife to the ship waiting at Hamtun docks. Although he had used the ship *Le Cygne* in the past and knew both the captain and pilot by name, he nevertheless inspected the vessel bow to stern before allowing his wife to board. He supervised the loading of men, horses, provisions, and weapons—his wife would travel with Ormand, his seneschal, and a guard of seven men. Inside a small casket made of elm wood, Lady Agnes carried the letter he had written to his father and the gift of a gold buckle received from the Conqueror himself in recognition of the baron's loyalty during the season of northern discontent in the years following the invasion.

Once Agnes was established in her quarters beneath the ship's main deck, the baron bade his wife farewell. "The tide is on the rise. Godspeed, lady wife," he said. Raising her hand to his lips, he kissed her cold fingers and added, "I wish you a mild and pleasant winter, and a glad Christmas."

"It may be that I can return before the snow," she ventured, hope lending a lightness to her voice. "We could observe Christmas together."

"No"—Bernard shook his head firmly—"it is far too dangerous. Winter gales make the sea treacherous. If anything should happen to you, I could not forgive myself." He smiled. "Enjoy your sojourn at home—it is brief enough. Time will pass swiftly, and we will celebrate the success of your undertaking with the addition of a new estate."

"*Très bien,*" replied Lady Agnes. "Have a care for yourself, my husband." She leaned close and put her lips against his cheek. "Until we meet again, *adieu, mon chéri.*"

The pilot called down from the deck above that the tide was beginning to run. The baron kissed his wife once more and returned to the wharf. A short time later, the tide had risen sufficiently to put out to sea. The captain called for a crewman to cast off; the ropes were loosed, and the ship pushed on poles away from the dock. Once in the centre of the river, the vessel was caught by the current, turned, and headed out into the estuary and the unprotected sea beyond.

Bernard watched all this from the wooden dock. Only when the ship raised sail and cleared the headland at the wide river mouth did he return to his waiting horse and give the order to start for home. The journey took two days, and by the time he reached his westernmost castle at Hereford, he had decided to make a sortie into Welsh territory, into the cantref of Brycheiniog, to see what he could learn of the land he meant to possess.

Bran no longer knew how long he had been dragging his wounded body through the underbrush. Whole days passed in blinding flashes of pain and shuddering sickness. He could feel his strength departing, his lucid times growing fewer and further apart. He could no longer count on his senses to steer him aright; he heard the voices of people who were not there, and often what he saw before him was, on nearer examination, mere phantasm.

Following his plunge into the pool, he had been swept downstream a fair distance. The current carried him along high-sided banks overhung with leafless branches and great moss-covered limbs, deeper and ever deeper into the forest until finally washing him into the shallows of a green pool surrounded by the wrecks of enormous trees, the boles of which had toppled and fallen over one another like the colossal pillars of a desolated temple.

The warm, shallow water revived him, and he opened his eyes to find himself surrounded by half-sunk, waterlogged trunks and broken boughs. Green slime formed a thick sludge on the surface of the pool, and the air was rank with the stench of fetid stagnant water and decay, and black with shifting clouds of mayflies. Bran struggled upright and, on hands and knees, hauled himself over a sunken log and into the soft, soggy embrace of a peat bog, where he collapsed, a quivering, pain-wracked lump.

Evening was fast upon him when he had finally roused himself that first day and, aching in every joint and muscle, gathered his feet beneath him and climbed up on unsteady legs. Following a deer trail, he lurched like a half-drowned creature from the swamp and staggered into the haven of the greenwood. His chief concern that first night was finding shelter where he could rest and bind his wounds.

He did not know how badly he was injured—only that he was alive and grateful to be so. Once he found shelter, he would remove his tunic and see what he could do to bandage himself. After he had rested and regained his strength, he would make his way to the nearest habitation

145

and secure the aid of his fellow Cymry to continue his flight to safe haven in the north.

As twilight cast a purple gloom over the forest at the end of that first day, Bran found a great oak with a hollowed-out cavity down in the earth beneath the roots. The place had been used by a bear or badger; the earthy musk of the creature still lingered in the cavity. But the hole was dry and warm, and Bran fell asleep the moment he lay down his head.

He woke with a burning thirst, and light-headed from hunger. His wounds throbbed, and his muscles were stiff. There was nothing for his hunger, but he could hear the soft burble of a brook nearby, and easing himself upright, he made his unsteady way to the moss-carpeted bank. He knelt and, with some difficulty because of the cut that ran along the side of his face, stretching from cheekbone to ear, cupped water to his mouth. The inside of his cheek was as raw as sliced meat, and his tongue traced an undulating line like a thick, blood-soaked string.

The cold water made the inside of his mouth sting and brought tears to his eyes, but he quenched his thirst as best he could and then carefully removed his tunic and mantle to better assess his injuries. He could not see the cut in his upper back, but by reaching around cautiously, he was able to feel that it had stopped bleeding. The deep rent in his chest was easier to examine. Caked with dried blood that he gently washed away, the cut was ragged and ratty, the skin puckered along the edges. The wound ached with a persistent throb; the bones had been nicked when the blade forced his ribs apart, but he did not think any had been broken.

Lastly, he examined the bite on his arm. The limb was tender— the hound's teeth had broken the skin, nothing worse—the flesh swollen and sore, but the ragged half circle of raised red puncture wounds did not seem to be festering. He bathed his arm in the brook

146

and washed the dried blood from his chest and stomach. He tried to bathe the spear cut on his upper back but succeeded only in dribbling water over his shoulders and making himself cold. He drew on his clothes and contemplated the choices before him.

So far as he could see, he had but two courses: return to Elfael and try to find someone to take him in, or continue on to Gwynedd and hope to find help somewhere along the way before he reached the mountains.

The land to the north was rough and inhospitable to a man alone. Even if he had the great good fortune of making it through the forest unaided, the chances of finding help were remote. Elfael, on the other hand, was very nearly deserted; most of his countrymen had fled, and the Ffreinc were seeking his blood. It came to him that he could do no better than try to take his own advice and go to Saint Dyfrig's to seek sanctuary with the monks.

The decision was easily made, and he gathered what strength he could muster and set out. With any luck, he allowed himself to think, day's end would find him behind friendly walls, resting in the guest lodge.

Bran's luck had so far proved as irksomely elusive as the trail. It served him no better now. The forest pathways crossed one another in bewildering profusion, each one leading on to others—over and under fallen trunks, down steep grades into rills and narrow defiles, up sharp-angled ridges and scrub-covered hillsides. Hunger had long since become a constant, gnawing pain in his stomach. He could drink from the streams and brooks he encountered, but nourishing food was scarce. There were mushrooms in extravagant overabundance, but most, he knew, were poisonous, and he did not trust himself to recognise the good ones. Finding nothing else, he chewed hazel twigs just to have something in his mouth.

Hungry, pain-riddled, he allowed his mind to wander.

He imagined himself received into the safety of the abbey and wel-

147

comed to a dinner of roast lamb, braised leeks, and oat bread and ale. This comforting dream awakened a ferocious appetite that refused to subside—even when he tried to appease it with sour blackberries gobbled by the purple handful from a bramble bush. In his haste, he bit the inside of his cheek, breaking open the wound afresh and driving him to his knees in agony. He lay for a long time on the ground, rocking back and forth in misery until he became aware that he was being watched.

"What?" asked a voice somewhere above him. "What?"

Raising his eyes, Bran saw a big black rook on a branch directly over his head. The bird regarded him with a shiny bead of an eye. "What?"

He dimly remembered a story about a starving prophet fed by crows. "Bring me bread."

"What?" asked the bird, stretching its wings.

"Bread," Bran said, his voice a breathless groan. "Bring me some bread."

The rook cocked its head to one side. "What?"

"Stupid bird." Angered by the rook's refusal to aid in his revival, Bran dragged himself to his feet once more. The bird started at the movement; it flew off shrieking, its cry of "Die! Die!" echoing through the wood.

Bran looked around and realised with a sinking heart that he had dreamed most of the day away. He moved on then, dejected and afraid to trust his increasingly unreliable judgement. The wounds to his chest and back throbbed with every step and were hot to the touch. As daylight deteriorated around him, his steps slowed to an exhausted shuffle; hunger burned like a flame in his gut, and it hurt his chest to breathe. The long day ended, leaving him worse off than when it had begun, and night closed over him like a fist. He closed his eyes beneath the limbs of a sheltering elm and spent an uncomfortable night on the ground.

When he rose again the next morning, he was just as weary as when he lay down. Climbing to his feet on that second day, he felt fear circling him like a preying beast. He remembered thinking that if he did not find a trail out of the wood, this day might be his last. That was when he had decided to follow the next stream he found, thinking that it would eventually lead to the river that ran through the middle of Elfael.

This he did, and at first it seemed his determination would be rewarded, for the forest thinned and he glimpsed open sky ahead. Closer, he saw sunlight on green grass and imagined the valley spreading beyond. He limped toward the place and, as he passed the last trees, stepped out into a wide meadow—at the centre of which was a shimmering pool. Dragonflies flitted around the water's edge, and larks soared high above. The stream he had been following emptied itself into the pool and, so far as he could tell, did not emerge again.

It had taken him the better part of two days to reach another dead end, and now, as he gazed around him, he knew his strength was gone. Hope crushed to a cold cinder, Bran staggered stiff legged through the long grass to stand gazing down into the water, too tired to do anything but stand.

After a time, he lowered himself painfully down to kneel at the water's edge, drank a few mouthfuls, then sat down beside the pool. He would rest a little before moving on. He fell back in the grass and closed his eyes, giving way to the fatigue that paralysed him. When he woke again, it was dark. The moon was high above a line of clouds moving in from the northwest. Exhausted still, he closed his eyes and went back to sleep.

It rained before morning, but Bran did not rise. And that was how the old woman found him the next day.

She hobbled from the forest on her stout legs and stood for a long time contemplating the wreck of him. "Dost thou ever seek half measures?" she asked, glancing skyward. "Whether 'tis meet or ill, I know not. But heavy was the hand that broke this reed."

She paused, as if listening. "Oh, aye," she muttered. "Aye and ever aye. Your servant obeys."

With that she removed the moth-eaten rag that was her cloak and placed it over the wounded man. Then she retreated to the forest the way she had come. It was midday before she returned, leading two ragged men pulling a handcart. She directed them to the place where she had found the unconscious young man; he was where she left him, still covered by her cloak.

"We could dig a grave," suggested one of the men upon observing the wounded stranger's pale, bloodless flesh. "I do believe 'twould be a mercy."

"Nay, nay," she said. "Take him to my hearth."

"He needs more than hearth care," observed the man, scratching a bristly jaw. "This 'un needs holy unction."

"Go to, Cynvar," the old woman replied. "If thou wouldst but stir thyself to action—and yon stump with thee"—she indicated the second man still standing beside the cart—"methinks we mayest yet hold death's angel at bay."

"You know best, *budolion*," replied the man. He motioned to his fellow, and the two lifted the stranger into the cart. The movement caused the wounded man to moan softly, but he did not waken.

"Gently, gently," chided the old woman. "I have work enough without thee breaking his bones."

She laid a wrinkled hand against the pale young stranger's wounded cheek and then touched two fingers to his cold brow. "Peace, beloved," she crooned. "In my grasp I hold thee, and I will not let thee go."

Turning to the men once more, she said, "Grows the grass beneath thy feet? About thy business, lads! Be quick."

Count Falkes de Braose anticipated the arrival of his cousin with all the fret and ferment of a maid awaiting a suitor. He could not remain seated for more than a few moments at a time before he leapt to his feet and ran to inspect some detail he had already seen and approved twice over. Ill at ease in his own skin, he started at every stray sound, and each new apprehension caused his heart to sink: What if Earl Philip arrived late? What if he met trouble on the way? What if he did not arrive at all?

He fussed over the furnishings of his new stronghold: Were they adequate? Were they too spare? Would he be considered niggardly—or worse yet, a spendthrift? He worried about the preparation of the feast: Was the fare sumptuous enough? Was the wine palatable? Was the meat well seasoned? Was the bread too hard, the soup too thin, the ale too sweet or too sour? How many men would come with Philip? How long would they stay?

When these and all the other worries overwhelmed him, he grew resentful of the torment. What cause did Philip have to be angry with him? After all, he had taken Elfael with but a bare handful of casualties. Most of the footmen had not even used their weapons. His first campaign, and it was an absolute triumph! What more could anyone ask?

By the time Philip, Earl of Gloucester, arrived with his retinue late in the day, Falkes was limp with nervous exhaustion. "Cousin!" boomed Philip, striding across the pennon-festooned yard of Caer Cadarn. He was a tall, long-legged man, with dark hair and an expanding bald spot that he kept hidden beneath a cap trimmed in marten fur. His riding gauntlets were trimmed in the same fur, as were the tops of his boots. "It is good to see you, I do declare it! How long has it been? Three years? Four?"

"Welcome!" uttered Falkes in a strangled cry. He loped across the yard with unsteady strides. "I pray you had an uneventful journey— peaceful, that is."

"It was. God's grace, it was," answered Philip, pulling his kinsman into a rough embrace. "But you now—are you well?" He cast a quizzical eye over his younger cousin. "You seem pale and fevered."

"It is nothing—an ague born of anticipation—it will pass." Falkes turned and flapped a hand in the vague direction of the hall. "Valroix Palace it is not," he apologised, "but consider it yours for as long as you desire to stay."

Philip cast a dubious glance at the crude timber structure. "Well, so long as it keeps the rain off, I am satisfied."

"Then come, let us share the welcome cup, and you can tell me how things stand at court." Falkes started across the yard, then remembered himself and stopped. "How is Uncle? Is he well? It is a shame he could not accompany you. I should like to properly thank him for entrusting the settlement of his newest commot to me."

"Father is well, and he is pleased, never fear," replied Philip de Braose. Removing his gauntlets, he tucked them in his belt. "He would have liked nothing better than to accompany me, but the king has come to rely on him so that he will not abide the baron to remain out of sight for more than a day or two before calling him to attendance. Nevertheless, the baron has instructed me to bring him a full account of your deeds and acquisitions."

"*Bien sûr!* You shall have it," said Falkes, nervousness making his voice a little too loud. Turning to the knights and men-at-arms in Philip's company, he called, "Messires, you are most welcome here. Quarters have been arranged, and a feast has been prepared for your arrival. But first, it would please me if you would join me in raising a cup of wine."

He then led his guests into the great hall, the walls of which had been newly washed until they gleamed as white as the Seven Maidens. Fresh green rushes had been strewn over the sand-scoured wooden floor, permeating the enormous room with a clean scent of mown hay. A great heap of logs was blazing on the hearth at one end of the room, where, on an iron spit, half an ox was slowly roasting, the juices sizzling in a pan snugged in the glowing coals.

Several board-and-trestle tables had been erected, draped in cloths, and decked with fir branches. As the men settled on the long benches, the steward and his serving boys filled an assortment of vessels with wine drawn from a tun brought from Aquitaine. When each of the guests was in possession of a cup, their host raised his chalice and called, "My friends, let us drink to King William and his continued good health! Long may he reign!"

"King William!" they all cried and downed the first of many such cups that night. With the men thus fortified, the celebration soon turned into a revel, and Count Falkes's anxiety slowly gave way to a pleasant, wine-induced contentment. Cousin Philip seemed happy with his efforts and would certainly return to his uncle with a good report. As the evening wore on, Falkes became more and more the jovial host, urging his guests to eat and drink their fill; and when they had done so, he invited his own men, and some of their wives, to join the festivities. Those who knew how to play music brought their instruments, and there was singing and dancing, which filled the hall and lasted far into the night.

Accordingly, it was not until late the next day that Falkes and Philip found opportunity to sit down together. "You have done well, Cousin," Philip asserted. "Father always said that Elfael was a plum ripe for the plucking."

"How right he was," agreed Falkes readily. "I hope you will tell him how grateful I am for his confidence. I look forward to an early demonstration of my loyalty and thanks."

"Rest assured I will tell him. Know you, he has charged me to convey a secret—all being well."

"I hope you think it so," said Falkes.

"It could not be better," replied Philip. "Therefore, I am eager to inform you that the baron intends to make Elfael his staging ground for the conquest of the territories."

"Which territories?" wondered Falkes.

"Selyf, Maelienydd, and Buellt."

"Three commots!" Falkes exclaimed. "That is . . . ambitious."

Falkes had no idea his uncle entertained such far-reaching plans. But then, with the endorsement of the king, what was to prevent Baron de Braose from laying claim to the whole of Wales?

"Ambitious, to be sure," avowed Philip pleasantly. "My father is intent, and he is determined. Moreover, he has the fortune to make it possible."

"I would never doubt it."

"Good," replied Philip, as if a knotty issue had been decided. "To this end, the baron requires you to undertake a survey of the land to be completed before spring."

"Before spring—," repeated Falkes, struggling to keep up. "But we have only just begun to establish—"

"Zut!" said Philip, brushing aside his objection before it could be spoken aloud. "The baron will send his own men to perform the survey. You need only aid them with an appropriate guard to ensure their safety while they work."

"I see." The pale count nodded thoughtfully. "And what is this survey to determine?"

"The baron requires three castles to be built—one on the border to the north, one south, and one west—on sites best suited for controlling the territories beyond each of those borders. This the surveyors will determine."

"Three castles," mused Falkes, stroking his thin, silky beard. The cost of such an undertaking would be staggering. He hoped he would not be expected to help pay for the project.

Philip, seeing the shadow of apprehension flit across his cousin's face, quickly explained. "You will appreciate," he continued, "that the building will be funded out of the baron's own treasury."

Falkes breathed easier for the reassurance. "What about the people of Elfael?" he wondered.

"What about them?"

"I assume they will be required to supply ready labour."

"Of course—we must have workers in sufficient number."

"They may resist."

"I don't see how they can," declared Philip. "You said the king and his son have already been removed, along with their men-at-arms. If you were to encounter any meaningful resistance, you would certainly have done so by now. Whatever opposition we meet from here on will be easily overcome."

Despite his cousin's effortless assurance, Falkes remained sceptical.

He had no clear idea how many of the original inhabitants remained in Elfael. Most seemed to have fled, but it was difficult to determine their numbers, for even in the best of times they rarely stayed in one place, preferring to wander here and there as the whim took them, much like the cattle they raised and which formed their chief livelihood. Be that as it may, those few who remained in the scattered farms and steadings were certain to have something to say about invaders taking their property, even if it was mostly grazing land.

"You can tell your father, my uncle, that he will find everything in good order by next spring, God willing. In the meantime, I will await the arrival of the surveyors—and what is more, I will accompany them personally to see that all is carried out according to the baron's wishes."

They talked of the work to be done, the materials to be obtained, the number of men who would be needed, and so on. In all that followed, Count Falkes paid most stringent attention—especially when it came to the labourers who would be required.

It was common practise amongst the Ffreinc to entice the local population of conquered lands to help with construction work; for a little pay, parcels of land, or promises of preferential dealings, an ample workforce could often be gathered from the immediate area. The custom had been applied to rousing effect amongst the Saxons. This is how the Conqueror and his barons had accomplished so much so quickly in the subjugation and domination of England. There was no reason why the same practise should not also work in Wales.

The prospect of ready silver went a long way toward slaking any lingering thirst for rebellion. Often those who shouted the loudest about rising up against the invaders were the same ones who profited most handily from the invasion. God knows, Baron de Braose's renowned treasury had won more battles than his soldiers and could be relied upon to do so again. And as everyone knew, the Welsh, for

all their prideful bluster, were just as greedy for gain as the most grasping, lack-land Saxon.

It was with this in mind that the two kinsmen rode out the following day to view the commot. Philip wanted to get a better idea of
the region and see firsthand the land that had so quickly fallen under
their control.

The day began well, with a high, bright sky and a fresh breeze
pushing low clouds out of the west. Autumn was advancing; everywhere the land was slumping down toward its winter rest. The leaves
on the trees had turned and were flying from the branches like golden
birds across a pale blue sky. Away in the distance, always in the distance, defining the boundary of the commot, towered the green-black
wall of the forest, looming like a line of clouds, dark and turbulent,
heralding the advance of a coming storm.

The two noblemen, each accompanied by a knight and three men-
at-arms, rode easily together through the valley and across the rolling
hills. They passed by the little monastery at Llanelli and paused to
examine the setting of the place and the construction of the various
buildings before riding on. They also visited one of Elfael's few far-flung
settlements, cradled amongst the branching valleys. This one, huddled
in the wind shadow of the area's highest hill, consisted of a house and
barn, a granary, and a coop for chickens. It, like so many others, was
abandoned. The people had gone—where, Falkes had no idea.

After visiting a few of the dwellings, they returned to their
horses. "A piss-poor place," observed Earl Philip, climbing back into
the saddle. "I would not allow one of my dogs to live here." He
shook his head. "Are they all like this?"

"More or less," replied Falkes. "They are mostly herdsmen, from
what I can tell. They follow their cattle, and these holdings are often
abandoned for months at a time."

"What about the farms, the crops?" wondered Philip, taking up the reins.

"There are few enough of those," answered Falkes, turning his horse back onto the trackway. "Most of the open land is used for grazing."

"That will change," decided Philip. "This soil is rich—look at the grass, lush and thick as it is! You could grow an abundance of grain here—enough to feed an army."

"Which is precisely what will be needed," replied Falkes, urging his mount forward. He thought about the baron's plans to subdue the next commots. "Two or three armies."

They rode to the top of the hill above the settlement and looked out over the empty valley with its narrow stream snaking through the deep green grass, rippling in the wind. In his mind's eye, Earl Philip could see farms and villages springing up throughout the territory. There would be mills—for wood and wool and grain—and storehouses, barns, and granaries. There would be dwellings for the farmers, the workers, the craftsmen: tanners, chandlers, wainwrights, ironsmiths, weavers, bakers, dyers, carpenters, butchers, fullers, leatherers, and all the rest.

There would be churches, too, one for each village and town, and perhaps a monastery or two as well. Maybe, in time, an abbey.

"A good place," mused Falkes.

"Yes." His cousin smiled and nodded. "And it is a good thing we have come." He let his gaze sweep over the hilltops and up to the blue vault of heaven and felt the warm sun on his face. "Elfael is a rough gem, but with work it will polish well."

"To be sure," agreed Falkes. "God willing."

"Oh, God has already willed it," Philip assured him. "As sure as William is king, there is no doubt about that." He paused, then added, "None whatsoever."

CHAPTER 17

The day following the feast of Saint Edmund—three weeks after Earl Philip's visit—and the weather had turned raw. The wind was rising out of the north, gusting sharply, pushing low, dirty clouds over the hills. Count Falkes's thin frame was aching with the chill, and he longed to turn around and ride back to the scorching, great fire he kept blazing in the hearth, but the baron's men were still disputing over the map they were making, and he did not want to appear irresolute or less than fully supportive of his uncle's grand enterprise.

There were four of them—an architect, a surveyor, and two apprentices—and although Falkes could not be sure, he suspected that in addition to their charting activities, they were also spies. The questions they asked and the interest they took in his affairs put the count on his guard; he knew only too well that he enjoyed his present position through the sufferance of Baron de Braose. Not a day went by that he did not ponder how to further advance his uncle's good opinion of him and his abilities, for as Elfael had been given, so Elfael could be taken away. Without it, he would become again what he had been: one more impoverished nobleman desperate to win the favour of his betters.

Fate had reached down and plucked him from the heaving ranks of desperate nobility. Against every expectation, he had been singled out for advancement and granted this chance to make good. Spoil this, and Falkes knew another opportunity would never come his way. For him, it was Elfael . . . or nothing.

Thus, he must ever and always remain vigilant and ruthless in his dealings with the Welsh under his rule, nor could he afford to show any weakness to his countrymen, however insignificant, that might give the baron cause to send him back to Normandie in disgrace.

Although his cousin Philip heartily assured him that his uncle, the baron, applauded his accomplishments, Falkes reckoned he would not be secure in his position as Lord of Elfael until the de Braose banner flew unopposed over the surrounding commots. So despite the bone-cracking cold, a most miserable Falkes remained with his visitors, sitting on his horse and shivering in the damp wind.

The surveying party had arrived the day before when the first wains rolled down into the shallow bowl of the valley. Bumping across the stream that was now a swift-running torrent, the high-sided, wooden-wheeled vehicles toiled up the slope and came to a stop at the foot of the mound on which the fortress stood. The wagons, five in all, were full of tools and supplies for the men who would oversee the construction of the three castles Baron de Braose had commissioned. Building work would not begin until the spring, but the baron was anxious to waste not a single day; he wanted everything to be ready when the masons and their teams of apprentices arrived with the thaw.

By the time the wildflowers brushed the hilltops with gold, the foundations of each defensive tower would be established. When the stars of the equinox shone over the sites, the ditches would be man deep and the walls shoulder high. By midsummer, the central mound would belly to the sky, and stone curtains twice the height of the workmen would crown the hillcrests. And when the time came for the master mason to call his men to pack their tools and load the wains to return to their families in Wintancaester, Oxenforde, and Gleawancaester, the walls and keep, bailey, donjon, and ditch would be half-finished.

For now, however, the wagons and animals would remain in sight of Caer Cadarn, where their drivers would camp in the lee of the fortress to shelter from the perpetual wind and icy rain that roared down out of the northwest. All winter long, Count Falkes's men-at-arms would be kept busy hunting for the table, while the footmen and servants foraged for wood to keep the fires ablaze in hearth and fire ring of caer and camp.

It was not at all a convivial country, Falkes decided, for although winter had yet to arrive in force, the count had never been so cold in all his life. Curse the baron's impatience! If only the invasion of Elfael could have waited until the spring. As it was, Falkes and his men had come so late to Wales that they had not had time to adequately prepare for the season of snow and ice. Falkes found he had seriously underestimated the severity of the British weather; his clothes—he wore two or three tunics and mantles at a time, along with his heaviest cloak—were too thin and made of the wrong stuff. His fingers and toes suffered perpetual chilblains. He stamped his way around the fortress, clapping his hands and flapping his arms across his chest to keep warm. By night, he took to his bed after supper and burrowed deep under the fleeces and skins and cloaks that served him for bed-clothes in his dank, wind-fretted chamber.

Just this morning he had awakened in his bed, aghast to find that frost had formed on the bedclothes overnight; he swore an oath that he would not sleep another night in that room. If it meant he had to bed down with the servants and dogs beside the hearth in the great hall, so be it. The only time his hands and feet were ever warm was when he sat in his chair before the hearth, with arms and legs outstretched toward the fire—a position he could maintain only for a few moments altogether; but those were moments of pure bliss in what looked to be a long, grinding, bitter winter—more ordeal than season.

It was not until the light was beginning to fail and the surveyor could no longer read the chart he was making that the builders decided to stop for the day and return to Caer Cadarn. The count was the first to turn his horse and head for home. As the work party came in sight of the fortress, the skies opened and rain began hammering down in driving sheets. Falkes lashed his mount to speed and covered the remaining distance at a gallop. He raced up the long ramp, through the gates, and into the yard to find a half dozen unfamiliar horses tethered to the rail outside the stable.

"Who has come?" he asked, throwing the reins of his mount to the head stabler.

"It is Baron Neufmarché of Hereford," replied the groom. "He arrived only a short while ago."

Neufmarché here? Mon Dieu! This is a worry, thought the count. *What could he possibly want with me?*

Dashing back across the rain-scoured yard, a very wet Falkes de Braose entered the great hall. There, standing before a gloriously radiant hearth, was his uncle's compatriot and chief rival, accompanied by five of his men: knights every one. "Baron Neufmarché!" called Falkes. He shrugged off his sodden cloak and tossed it to a waiting servant. "This is an unexpected pleasure," he brayed, trying to sound far more gracious than he felt at the moment. Striding quickly forward, he rubbed the warmth back into his long hands. "Welcome! Welcome, messires, to you all!"

"My dear Count de Braose," replied the baron with a polite bow of courtesy. "Pray forgive our intrusion—we were on our way north, but this vile weather has driven us to shelter. I hope we do not trespass on your hospitality."

"Please," replied Falkes, oozing cordiality, "I am honoured." He glanced around to see the cups in the hands of his guests. "I see my servants have seen to your refreshment. *Bon.*"

"Yes, your seneschal is most obliging," the baron assured him. Taking up a spare cup, already poured, he handed it to the count. "Here, drink and warm yourself by the fire. You have had an inclement ride."

Feeling uncomfortably like a guest in his own house, Falkes neverthe-less thanked the baron and accepted the cup. Withdrawing a poker from the fire, he plunged it into the wine; the hot iron sizzled and sputtered. The count then raised his steaming cup and said, "To King William!" Several cups later, when a meal had been prepared and they all sat down together, the count at last discovered the errand that brought the baron to his door, and it had nothing to do with seeking shelter from the rain.

"I have long wished to visit the Earl of Rhuddland," the baron informed him, spearing a piece of roast beef with his knife. "I confess I may have waited too far into the autumn, but affairs at court kept me in Lundien longer than I anticipated." He lifted a shoulder. *"C'est la vie."*

Count Falkes allowed himself a sly, secret smile; he knew Baron Neufmarché had been summoned by King William to attend him in Lundein and kept waiting several days before finally being sent away. William the Red had still not completely forgiven the contrary noble-men who had upheld his brother Robert's claim to the throne, legiti-mate though it undoubtedly was. When the dust of revolt had settled, William had tacitly pardoned those he considered rebels, returning them to rank and favour—although he could not resist harassing them in small ways just to prove the point.

The delay Neufmarché complained of had allowed the count's uncle to make good the de Braose clan's first foray into Wales without interference from the lords of neighbouring territories. While Neufmarché was idling in Lundien, Count Falkes had, with uncommon swiftness and ease, conquered Elfael. The whole campaign had been closely planned to avoid extraneous entanglements from the likes of rival lords such as Neufmarché, for if Baron de Braose had had to beg Neufmarché for permission to cross his lands that lay between Norman England and the Welsh provinces, Falkes was fairly certain they would all be waiting still.

"You have done well," the baron said, gazing around the hall approvingly, "and in a very short time. I take it the Welsh gave you no trouble?"

"Very little," affirmed Falkes. "There is a monastery nearby, with a few monks and some women and children in hiding. The rest seem to have scattered to the hills. I expect we won't see them until the spring." He cut into a plump roast fowl on the wooden trencher before him. "By then we will be well fortified hereabouts, and opposition will be futile." He sliced into the succulent breast of the bird, raised a bite on his knife, and nibbled daintily.

Neufmarché caught the veiled reference to increased fortification. *No one builds fortresses to hold down a few monks and some women and children*, he thought and guessed the rest. "They are a strange people," he observed, and several of his knights grunted their agreement. "Sly and secretive."

"*Bien sûr*," Falkes replied. He chewed thoughtfully and asked, trying to sound casual, "Do you plan to make a foray yourself?"

The bluntness of the question caught the baron off guard. "Me? I have no plans," he lied. "But now that you mention it, the thought has crossed my mind." He raised his cup to give himself time to think and then continued, "I confess, your example gives me heart. If I imagined that acquiring land would be so easy, I might give it some serious consideration." He paused as if entertaining the possibility of an attack in Wales for the very first time. "Busy as I am ruling the estates under my command, I'm not at all certain a campaign just now would be wise."

"You would know better than I," Falkes conceded. "This is my first experience ruling an estate of any size. No doubt I have much to learn."

"You are too modest," Neufmarché replied with a wide, expansive smile. "From what I have seen, you learn very quickly." He drained his cup and held it aloft. A servant appeared and refilled it at once. "I drink to your every success!"

"And I to yours, *mon ami*," said Count Falkes de Braose. "And I to yours."

The next morning, the baron departed with an invitation for Falkes to visit him whenever he passed through his lands in Herefordshire. "I will look forward to it with keenest pleasure," said the count as he waved his visitors away. He then hurried to his chamber, where he drafted a hasty letter to his uncle, informing him of the progress with the ongoing survey of the building sites—as well as his adversary's unannounced visit. Falkes sealed the letter and dispatched a messenger the moment his guests were out of sight.

Angharad stirred the simmering contents of the cauldron with a long wooden spoon and listened to the slow *plip, plip, plip* of the rain falling from the rim of stone onto the wet leaves at the entrance to the cave. She took up the bound sprig of a plant she had gathered during the summer and with a deft motion rolled the dry leaves back and forth between her palms, crumbling the herb into the broth. The aroma of her potion was growing ever more pungent in the close air of the cave.

Every now and then she would cast a glance toward the fleece-wrapped bundle lying on a bed of pine boughs and covered with moss and deer pelts. Sometimes the man inside the bundle would moan softly, but for the most part his sleep was as silent as the dead. Her skill with healing unguents and potions extended to that small mercy if nothing more.

When the infusion was ready, she lifted the cauldron from the fire and carried it to a nearby rock, where it was left to cool. Then, taking up an armful of twigs from the heap just inside the cave entrance, she returned to her place by the fire.

"One for the Great King on his throne so white," she said, tossing a twig onto the embers. She waited until the small branch flared into flame, then reached for another, saying, "Two for the Son the King begat."

This curious ritual continued for some time—taking up a twig and consigning it to the flames with a little verse spoken in a child's rhythmic singsong—and the simple chant reached the young man in his pain-fretted sleep.

> Three for the Errant Goose both swift and wild.
> Four for Pangur Ban the cat.
> Five for the Martyrs undefiled—
> Aye, five for the Martyrs undefiled.

She paused and cupped a hand above the fire for a moment, allowing the smoke to gather, then turned her palm, releasing a little white cloud. As the smoke floated up and dispersed, she continued her verse.

> Six for the Virgins who watch and wait.
> Seven for the Bards in halls of oak.
> Eight for the patches on Padraig's cloak.
> Nine for the lepers at the gate.
> Ten for the rays of Love's pure light—
> Aye, ten for the rays of Love's pure light.

Though the young man did not wake, the softly droning words and the simple rhythm seemed to soothe him. His breathing slowed and deepened, and his stiff muscles eased.

Angharad heard the change in his breathing and smiled to herself. She went to test the heat of the potion in the cauldron; it was still hot but no longer bubbling. Picking up the big copper kettle, she carried it

168

to where Bran lay, drew her three-legged stool near, and began gently pulling away the fleeces that covered him.

His flesh was dull and waxen, his wounds livid and angry. The right side of his face was roundly swollen, the skin discoloured. The teeth marks on his arm where the hound had fastened its jaws were puncture wounds, deep but clean—as was the slash between his shoulder blades. Painful as any of these wounds might have been, none were life-threatening. Rather, it was the ragged gash in the centre of his chest that worried her most. The iron blade had not pricked a lung, nor pierced the watery sac of the heart; but the lance head had driven cloth from his tunic and hair from the hound deep into the cut. These things, in her experience, could make even insignificant injuries fester and turn sour, bringing on fever, delirium, and finally death.

She sighed as she placed her fingertips on the bulbous swelling. The flesh was hot beneath her gentle fingertips, oozing watery blood and yellow pus. He had been wandering a few days before she had found him, and the wounds had already begun to go rancid. Therefore, she had taken great pains to prepare the proper infusion with which to wash the wound and had gathered the instruments to enlarge it so she could carefully dig out any scraps of foreign matter.

Angharad had expected him to come to her injured. She had foreseen the fight and knew the outcome, but the wounds he had suffered would tax her skill sorely. He was a strong one, his strength green and potent; even so, he would need all of it, and more besides, if he was to survive.

Bending to the cauldron, she took up a bit of clean cloth from a neat stack she had prepared; she folded the cloth and soaked it in the hot liquid and then gently, gently applied it to the gash in his chest. The heat caused him to moan in his sleep, but he did not wake. She let the cloth remain and, taking up another, soaked it and placed it on the side of his face.

169

When the second cloth had been carefully arranged, she returned to the first, removed it, placed it back in the cauldron, and began again.

So it went.

All through the night, the old woman remained hunched on her little stool, moving with slow purpose from one wound to the next, removing the cloth, dipping it, and replacing it. When the potion in the cauldron cooled, she returned it to the embers of her fire and brought it back to the boil. Heat was needed to draw out the poison of the wounds.

While she worked, she sang—an old song in the Elder Tongue, something she had learned from her own banfáith many, many years ago—the tale of Bran the Blesséd and his journey to Tir na' Nog. It was a song about a champion who, after a long sojourn in the Otherworld, had returned to perform the Hero Feat for his people: a tale full of hope, longing, and triumph—fitting, she thought, for the man beneath her care.

As dawn seeped into the rainy sky to the east, Angharad finished. She set aside the cauldron and rose slowly, arching her back to ease the ache there. Then she knelt once more and, taking up a handful of dried moss, placed it gently over the young man's wounds before covering him with the sheepskins. Later that day, she would begin the purification procedure all over again, and the next day, too, and perhaps the next. But for now, it was enough.

She rose and returned the cauldron to the edge of the fire ring, and settling herself once more on the three-legged stool, she pulled her cloak around her shoulders and closed her eyes on the day.

Bran did not know how long he had been lying in the dark, listening to the rain: a day, perhaps many days. Try as he might, he could not remember ever hearing such a sound before. He could vaguely remember what rain was and what it looked like, but so far as he could recall, this was the first time he had ever heard it patter down on earth and rocks and drip from the canopy of leaves to the sodden forest pathways below.

Unable to move, he was content to lie with his eyes closed, listening to the oddly musical sound. He did not want to open his eyes for fear of what he might see. Flitting through his shattered memory were weird and worrisome images: a snarling dog that snapped at his throat; a body floating in a pool; a black-shadowed hole in the ground that was both stronghold and tomb; and a hideous, decrepit old woman bearing a steaming cauldron. It was a nightmare, he told himself: the dreams of a pain-haunted man and nothing more.

He knew he was badly injured. He did not know how this had come to be nor even how he knew it to be true. Nevertheless, he accepted this fact without question. Then again, perhaps it was part of the same nightmare as the old crone—who could say?

However it was, the woman seemed to be intimately connected with another curious image that kept spinning through his mind: that of himself, wrapped in soft white fleece and lying full-length on a bed of pine boughs and moss covered by deerskins. Now and then, the image changed, taking on the quality of a dream—a peculiar reverie made familiar through repetition. In this dream he hovered in the air like a hawk, gazing down upon his own body from some place high above. At first he did not know who this hapless fellow in the rude bed might be. The young man's face was round and oddly misshapen, one side purple black and bloated beyond all recognition. His skin was dull and lustreless and of an awful waxy colour; no breath stirred the unfortunate's lungs. The poor wretch was dead, Bran concluded.

And that is when the old woman had first appeared. A hag with a

171

bent back and a face like a dried apple, she limped to the dead man's bed, carrying the gurgling pot fresh from the fire. She leaned low and peered into the fellow's face, shaking her head slowly as she carefully positioned the cauldron and settled herself cross-legged on the ground beside him. Then, rocking back and forth, she began to sing. Bran thought he had heard the song before but could not say where. And then, abruptly, the dream ended—always at the same place. The injured man and the old woman simply vanished in a blinding white haze, and most upsetting, Bran found himself waking in the dark and occupying the injured man's place.

This distressing transformation did not upset him as much as it might have because of the overwhelming sympathy Bran felt for the unfortunate fellow. Not only did he feel sorry for the young man, but he felt as if they might have been friends in the past. At the same time, he resented the repulsive old woman's intrusions. If not for her, Bran imagined he and the wounded man would have been free to leave that dark place and roam at will in the fields of light.

He knew about these far-off fields because he had seen them, caught fleeting glimpses of them in his other dreams. In these dreams he was often flying, soaring above an endless landscape of softly rounded hills over which the most wonderful, delicate, crystalline rays of sunlight played in ever-shifting colours—as if the soft summer breeze had become somehow visible as it drifted over the tall grass in richly variegated hues to delight the eye. Nor was this all, for accompanying the blithe colours was a soft flutelike music, buoyant as goose down on the breeze, far-off as the remembered echo of a whisper. Soft and sweet and low, it gradually modulated from one note to the next in fine harmony.

The first time he saw the fields of light, the sight made his heart ache with yearning; he wanted nothing more than to go there, to explore that wondrous place, but something prevented him. Once, in his dream, he had made a determined rush toward the glorious fields, and it appeared he would at last succeed in reaching them. But the old woman suddenly arose before him—it was Angharad; he knew her by the quick glance of her dark eye—except that she was no longer the hideous hag who dwelt in the darksome hole. Gone were her bent back and filthy tangles of stringy hair; gone her withered limbs, gone her coarse-woven, shapeless dress.

The woman before him was beauty made flesh. Her tresses were long and golden hued, her skin flawless, soft, and supple; her gown was woven of glistening white samite and trimmed in ermine; the slippers on her feet were scarlet silk, beaded with tiny pearls. She gazed upon him with large, dark eyes that held a look of mild disapproval. He moved to step past her, but she simply raised her hand.

"Where do you go, *mo croi?*" she asked, her voice falling like gentle laughter on his ear.

He opened his mouth to frame a reply but could make no sound.

"Come," she said, smiling, "return with me now. It is not yet time for you to leave."

Reaching out, she touched him lightly on the arm, turning him to lead him away. He resisted, still staring at the wonderful fields beyond.

"Dearest heart," she said, pressing luscious lips to his ear, "yon meadow will remain, but you cannot. Come, return you must. We have work to do."

So she led him back from the edge of the field, back to the warm darkness and the slow *plip, plip, plip* of the falling rain. Sometime later—he could not say how long—Bran heard singing. It was the voice from his dream, and this time he opened his eyes to dim shadows moving gently on the rock walls of his primitive chamber.

Slowly, he turned his head toward the sound, and there she was.

Although it was dark as a dovecote inside the cave, he could see her lumpen, ungainly form as she stood silhouetted by the fitful, flickering flames. She was as hideous as the hag of his recent nightmares, but as he knew now, she was no dream. She, like the hole in the ground where he lay, was only too real.

"Who are you?" asked Bran. His head throbbed with the effort of forming the words, and his voice cracked, barely a whisper. The old woman did not turn or look around but continued stirring the foul-smelling brew.

It was some time before Bran could work up the strength to ask again, with slightly more breath, "Woman, who are you?"

At this, the crone dropped her stirring stick and turned her wrinkled face to peer at him over a hunched shoulder, regarding him with a sharp, black, birdlike eye. Her manner put Bran in mind of a crow examining a possible meal or a bright bauble to steal away to a treetop nest.

"Can you speak?" asked Bran. Each word sent a peal of agony crashing through his head, and he winced. The side of his face felt as stiff and unyielding as a plank of oak.

"Aye, speak and sing," she replied, and her voice was far less unpleasant than her appearance suggested. "The question is, methinks, can thee?"

Bran opened his mouth, but a reply seemed too much effort. He simply shook his head—and instantly wished he had not moved at all, for even this slight motion sent towering waves of pain and nausea surging through his gut. He closed his eyes and waited for the unpleasantness to pass and the world to right itself once more.

"I thought not," the old woman told him. "Thou best not speak until I bid thee."

She turned from him then, and he watched her as she rose slowly and, bending from her wide hips, removed the pot from the flames and set it on a nearby rock to cool. She then came to his bed, where she sat for some time, gazing at him with that direct, unsettling glance. At length, she said, "Thou art hungry. Some broth have I made thee."

Bran, unable to make a coherent reply, merely blinked his eyes in silent assent. She busied herself by the fire, returning a short time later with a wooden bowl. Taking up a spoon made from a stag's horn, she dipped it into the bowl and brought it to Bran's mouth, parting his lips with a gentle yet insistent pressure.

Barely able to open his mouth, he allowed some of the lukewarm liquid to slide over his teeth and down his throat. It had a dusky, herb-rich flavour that reminded him of a greenwood glen in deep autumn.

She lifted the spoon once more, and he sucked down the broth. "There, and may it well become you," she said soothingly. "Thou mayest yet make good your return to Tir na' Nog."

An inexplicable sense of pride and accomplishment flushed his cheeks, and he suddenly found himself eager to please her with this trifling display of infant skill. The broth, although thin and clear, was strangely filling, and Bran found that after only a few more sips from the spoon, he could hold no more. The food settled his stomach, and exhausted with the small effort expended, he closed his eyes and slept.

When he woke again, it was brighter in the cave, and he was hungry again. As before, the old woman was there to serve him some of the herbal broth. He ate gratefully, but without trying to speak, and then slept after his meal.

Life proceeded like this for many days: he would wake to find his guardian beside him, ready to feed him his broth, whereupon, after only a few sips from the stag horn spoon, he would be overcome by the urge to sleep. Upon waking, he would find himself better refreshed than before, and what is more, Bran not only found that he was eating more each time, but also suspected that the intervals between sleeping and eating were shorter.

The comforting routine was interrupted one day when Bran awoke to find himself alone in the cave. He moved his head to look around, but the hag was nowhere to be seen. The pit-pat drip of water that had accompanied his waking moments for the last many days was gone. Alone and unobserved, he decided to stand up.

Slowly, cautiously, he levered himself onto the elbow of his good arm. His shoulders were stiff, and his chest ached; even the tiniest movement set off a crippling surge of agony that left him panting. At each attack he would pause, eyes squeezed shut, clutching his chest, until the waves of pain receded and he could see straight again.

On the ground near his bed was a shallow iron basin full of water; guarding against any sudden moves, he stretched out his hand and was able to hook two fingers over the rim and pull the heavy vessel closer. When the water stopped sloshing around the basin, he leaned over it and looked in. The face staring back at him was woefully misshapen; the right side was puffy and discoloured, and a jagged black line ran from the lower lip to the earlobe. The flesh along this lightning-strike line was pinched and puckered beneath a rough beard, which had been unevenly shaved to keep the hair away from the wound.

Angry at what he saw reflected in the water, he gave the basin a shove and instantly regretted it. The violent movement caused another upwelling of pain, greater than any before. He could not bear it and fell back, tears streaming down the sides of his face. He moaned, and that started him coughing, which opened the wound in his chest. The next thing he knew, he was coughing up blood.

The stuff came bubbling up his throat, thick and sweet, and spilled over his chin. He gagged and hacked, spitting blood in a fine red mist over himself. Each cough brought forth another, and he could not catch his breath. Just when he thought he would choke to death on his own blood, the old woman appeared beside him.

"What hast thou done?" she asked, kneeling beside him.

Unable to reply, he wheezed and spluttered, blood welling up over his teeth. With a quick motion, Angharad tore aside the sheepskin covering and placed a gentle hand on his chest. "Peace!" she whispered, like a mother to a distraught and unquiet child.

> Power of moon have I over thee,
> Power of sun have I over thee,
> Power of stars have I over thee,
> Power of rain have I over thee,
> Power of wind have I over thee,
> Power of heaven have I over thee,
> Power of heaven have I over thee in the power
>   of God to heal thee.

She moved her hand over his chest, her fingertips softly brushing the injured flesh. "Closed for thee thy wound, and stanched thy blood. As Christ bled upon the cross, so closeth he thy wound for thee," she intoned, her voice a caress.

> A part of this hurt on the high mountains,
> A part of this hurt on the grass-deep meadow,
> A part of this hurt on the heathered moors,
> A part of this hurt on the great surging sea
>   that has best means to bear it.
> This hurt on the great surging sea, she herself
>   has the best means to bear it for
>   thee . . . away . . . away . . . away.

Under Angharad's warm touch, the pain subsided. His lungs eased their laboured pumping, and his breathing calmed. Bran lay back, his chin and chest glistening with gore, and mouthed the words, *Thank you.*

Taking a bit of rag, she soaked it in the basin and began washing him clean, working patiently and slowly. She hummed as she worked, and Bran felt himself relaxing under her gentle ministrations. "Now wilt thou sleep," the old woman told him when she finished.

Eyelids heavy, he closed his eyes and sank into the soft, dark, timeless place where his dreams kindled and flared with strange visions of impossible feats, of people he knew but had never met, of things past—or perhaps yet to come—when the king and queen gave life and love to the people, when bards lauded the deeds of heroes, when the land bestowed its gifts in abundance, when God looked with favour upon his children and hearts were glad. Over all he dreamed that night, there loomed the shape of a strange bird with a long beak and a face as smooth and hard and black as charred bone.

Spring could not come soon enough for Falkes de Braose. The count ached for an end to the roof-rattling, teeth-chattering cold of the most inhospitable winter he had ever known—and it had only just begun! As he shivered in his chair, wrapped in cloaks and robes—a very hillock of dun-coloured wool—he consoled himself with the thought that when winter came next year, he would be firmly ensconced in his own private chamber in a newly built stone keep. In blissful dreams he conjured snug, wood-panelled rooms hung with heavy tapestries to keep out the searching fingers of the frigid wind, and a down-filled bed set before a blazing hearth all his own. He would never again suffer the dank drear of the great hall, with its drafts and smoke and freezing damp.

He would not abide another winter swaddled like a grotesquely oversized worm waiting for spring so it could shrug off its cocoon. Next winter, a ready supply of fuel would be laid in; he would determine how much was required and then treble the amount. This daily struggle to squeeze inadequate warmth from wet timber was slow insanity, and the count vowed never to endure it again. This time next year, he would laugh at the rain and cheerfully thumb his nose at each snowflake as it floated to the ground.

Meanwhile, he waited in perpetual dudgeon for the spring thaw, studying the plans drawn by the master architect for the baron's new borderland castles: one facing the yet-to-be-conquered northwestern territories, one to anchor the centre and the lands to the south, and one to defend the backs of the other two from any attacks arising from the east. The castles were, with only slight variations, all the same, but Falkes studied each sheaf of drawings with painstaking care, trying to think of improvements to the designs that he could suggest and that might win his uncle's approval. So far, he had come up with only one: increasing the size of the cistern that captured rainwater for use in times of emergency. As this detail was not likely to impress his uncle, he kept at his scrutiny and dreamed of warmer climes.

Five days after the feast of Saint Benedict, a messenger arrived with a letter from the baron. "Good news, I hope," said Falkes to the courier, taking receipt of the wrapped parchment. "Will you stay?"

"My lord baron requires an answer without delay," replied the man, shaking rainwater from his cloak and boots.

"Does he indeed?" Falkes, his interest sufficiently piqued, waved the courier away to the cookhouse. Alone again, he broke the seal, unrolled the small scrap of parchment, and settled back in his chair, holding the crabbed script before his eyes. He read the letter through to the end and then scanned it again to make sure he had not missed anything.

The message was simple enough: his uncle, eager to strengthen his grasp on Elfael so that he could begin his long-anticipated invasion into fresh territories, desired the construction of his new castles to begin without further delay. The baron was sending masons and skilled workers at once. Further, many of these would be bringing their families, eliminating the need to return home when the building season ended, thus allowing them to work longer before winter brought a halt to their labours. Therefore, Baron de Braose wanted his nephew to put every available resource of time and energy into building a town and establishing a market so that the workers and their families would have a place to live while the construction continued.

"A town!" spluttered Falkes. "He wants an entire town raised before next winter!"

The baron concluded his letter saying that he knew he could rely on his nephew to carry out his command with utmost zeal and purpose, and that when the baron arrived on Saint Michael's Day to inspect the work, he trusted he would find all ready and in good order.

Falkes was still sitting in his chair with a stunned expression on his long face when the messenger returned. "My lord?" asked the man, approaching uncertainly.

Falkes stirred and glanced up. "Yes? Oh, it is you. Did you find something to eat?"

"Thank you, sire, I have had a good meal."

"Well," replied Falkes absently, "I am glad to hear it. I suppose you want to get back, so I . . ." His voice trailed off as he sat gazing into the flames on the hearth.

"Ahem," coughed the messenger after a moment. "If you please, sire, what reply am I to make to the baron?"

Raising the letter to his eyes once more, Falkes took a deep breath and said, "You may tell the baron that his nephew is eager to carry out his wishes and will press ahead with all speed. Tell him . . ." His voice grew small at the thought of the enormity of the task before him.

"Pardon?" asked the messenger. "You were saying?"

"Yes, yes," resumed the count irritably. "Tell the baron his nephew wishes him success in all his undertakings. No, tell him . . . Tell the

baron nothing. Wait but a little, and I will compose a proper reply."
He flicked his long fingers at the messenger. "You may go see to your
mount."

Bowing quickly, the messenger departed. Falkes went to his table,
took up his pen, and wrote a coolly compliant answer to his uncle's
demand on the same parchment, then rolled and resealed it and called
for a servant to take the letter to the waiting messenger. He heard the
clatter of iron-shod hooves in the courtyard a short time later and,
closing his eyes, leaned his head against the back of his chair.

An entire town to raise in one summer. Impossible! It could not
be done. Was his uncle insane? The baron himself, with all his men
and money, could surely not accomplish such a thing.

He slumped farther into his chair and pulled the woollen cloaks
more tightly under his chin as hopelessness wrapped its dark tendrils
around him. Three castles to erect, and now a complete town as well.
His own dream of a warm chamber in a newly enlarged fortress receded
at an alarming pace.

By the Blesséd Virgin, a town!

So lost in his despair was he that it was not until the next day that
Falkes found a way out of the dilemma: it did not have to be a *whole*
town. That would come, in time and in good order. For now, the
undertaking could be something much more modest—a market square,
a meeting hall, a few houses, and, of course, a church. Constructing
even that much would be difficult enough—where was he to find the
labourers? Why, a church alone would require as many men as he had
ready to hand; where would he find the rest?

The church alone . . . , he thought, and the thought brought him
upright in his chair. *Yes! Of course!* Why, the answer was staring him full
in the face.

He rose and, leaving the warmth of his hall behind, rushed out into the snow-covered yard, calling for his seneschal. "Orval! Orval!" he cried. "Bring me Bishop Asaph!"

The summons came while the bishop was conducting an audit of food supplies with the kitchener. It was turning into a hard winter, and this year's harvest had been poor; the monastery was still sheltering a dozen or so people who, for one reason or another, could not escape to Saint Dyfrig's. Thus, the bishop was concerned about the stock of food on hand and wanted to know how long it would last.

Together with Brother Brocmal, he was examining the monastery's modest storerooms, making an exact accounting, when the riders arrived to fetch him. "Bishop Asaph!" called the porter, running across the yard. "The Ffreinc—the Ffreinc have come for you!"

"Calm yourself, brother," Asaph said. "Deliver your charge with some measure of decorum, if you please."

The porter gulped down a mouthful of air. "Three riders in de Braose livery have come," he said. "They have a horse for you and say you are to accompany them to Caer Cadarn."

"I see. Well, go back and tell them I am busy just now but will attend them as soon as I have finished."

"They said I was to bring you at once," countered the porter. "If you refused, they said they would come and drag you away by your ears!"

"Did they indeed!" exclaimed the bishop. "Well, I will save them the trouble." Handing the tally scroll to the kitchener, he said, "Continue with the accounting, Brother Brocmal, while I deal with our impatient guests."

"Of course, bishop," replied Brother Brocmal.

Asaph returned with the porter and found three marchogi on

horseback waiting with a saddled fourth horse. "Pax vobiscum," said the bishop, "I am Father Asaph. How may I be of assistance?" He spoke his best Latin, slowly, so they would understand.

"Count de Braose wants you," said the foremost rider.

"So I have been given to understand," replied the bishop, who explained that he was in the midst of a necessary undertaking and would come as soon as he was finished.

"No," said the horseman. "He wants you now."

"Now," explained the bishop, still smiling, "is not convenient. I will come when my duties allow."

"He doesn't care if it is convenient," replied the soldier. "We have orders to bring you without delay."

He nodded to his two companions, who began dismounting. "Oh, very well," said Asaph, moving quickly to the waiting horse. "The sooner gone, the sooner finished."

With the help of the porter, the bishop mounted the saddle and took up the reins. "Well? Are you coming?" he asked in a voice thick with sarcasm. "Apparently, it does not do to keep the count waiting."

Without another word, the marchogi turned their mounts and rode from the yard out into a dazzling, sun-bright day. The soldiers led the way across the snow-covered valley, and the bishop followed at an unhurried pace, letting his mind wander as it would. He was still trying to get the measure of these new overlords, and each encounter taught him a new lesson in how to deal with the Ffreinc invaders.

Strictly speaking, they were not Ffreinc, or Franks, at all; they were Normans. There was a difference—not that any of the Britons he knew cared for such fine distinctions. To the people of the valleys beyond the March, the tall strangers were invaders from France—that was all they knew, or needed to know. To the Britons, be they Ffreinc,

Angevin, or Norman, they were merely the latest in a long line of would-be conquerors.

Before the Normans, there were the English, and before the English, the Danes, and the Saxons before them. And each invader had carved out dominions for themselves and had gradually been gathered in and woven into the many-coloured mantle that was the Island of the Mighty.

These Normans were, from what he knew of them, ambitious and industrious, capable of great acts of piety and even greater brutality. They built churches wherever they went and filled them on holy days with devout worshippers, who nevertheless lived like hellions the rest of the time. It was said of the Ffreinc that they would blithely burn a village, slaughter all the men, and hang all the women and children, and then hurry off to church lest they miss a Mass.

Be that as it may, the Normans were Christian at least—which was more than could be said for the Danes or English when they had first arrived on Britain's fair shores. That being the case, the Church had decided that the Normans were to be treated as brothers in Christ—albeit as one would treat a domineering, wildly violent, and unpredictable older brother.

There was, so far as Bishop Asaph could see, no other alternative. Had he not urged King Brychan—if once, then a thousand times over the years—to acknowledge the Conqueror, swear fealty, pay his taxes, and do what he could to allow his people to live in peace? *"What?"* Asaph could hear the king cry in outrage. *"Am I to kneel and kiss the rosy rump of that usurping knave? And me a king in my own country? Let me be roasted alive before I stoop to pucker!"*

Well, he had sown his patch and reaped his reward, God save him—and his feckless son, too. Now that was a very shame. Profligate, recklessly licentious, and dissolute the prince may have been—no mistake

185

about it, he was all that and more—yet he had qualities his father lacked, hidden though they might have been. Were they hidden so deeply as to never be recovered? That was the question he had often asked himself.

Alas, the question was moot, and would so forever remain. With Bran's death, the old era passed and a new had begun. Like it or not, the Ffreinc were a fact of life, and they were here to stay. The path was as clear as the choice before him: his only hope of guiding his scattered flock through the storms ahead was to curry favour with the ruling powers. Bishop Asaph intended to get along with them however he could and hope—and pray—for the best.

It was in this frame of mind that Llanelli's deferential senior cleric entered the fortress where Count Falkes de Braose sat blowing on numb fingers in his damp, smoke-filled hall, beside a sputtering fire of green wood.

"Ah, Bishop Asaph," said the count, glancing around as the church-man was led into the hall. "It is good to see you again. I trust you are well?" Falkes sniffed and drew a sleeve under his runny nose.

"Yes," answered the bishop stiffly, "well enough."

"I, on the other hand, seem destined to endure no end of suffer-ing," opined the count, "what with one thing and another—and this vile weather on top of it all."

"And yet despite your sufferings, you remain alive to complain," observed the bishop, his voice taking on the chill of the room. In Falkes's presence he felt anew the loss of Brother Ffreol and the death of Bran—not to mention the massacre at Wye Ford. Ffreol's death had been an accident—that was what he had been told. The slaughter of the king and warband was, regrettably, a consequence of war he would have to accept. Bran's death was, in his mind, without justifica-tion. That the prince had been killed trying to escape without paying the ransom was, he considered, beside the point. Whatever anyone thought of the young man, he was Elfael's rightful king and should have been accorded due respect and courtesy.

"Mind your tongue, priest, if you value it at all," threatened de Braose, who promptly sneezed. "I am in no mood for your insolence."

Duly chastised, Asaph folded his hands and said, "I was told you required my assistance. How may I be of service?"

Waving a long hand toward the empty chair on the other side of the fireplace, de Boase said, "Sit down and I will tell you." When the churchman had taken his seat, the count declared, "It has been determined that Elfael needs a town."

"A town," the bishop repeated. "As it happens, I have long advocated a similar plan."

"Have you indeed?" sniffed Falkes. "Well then. We agree. It is to be a market town." He went on to explain what would be required and when.

The cleric listened, misgiving mounting with every breath. When the count paused to sneeze once more, the bishop spoke up. "Pray, excuse me, my lord, but who do you expect to build this town?"

"Your people, of course," confirmed the count, stretching his hands toward the fire. "Who else?"

"But this is impossible!" declared Asaph. "We cannot build you an entire town in a single summer."

The count's eyes narrowed dangerously. "It will profit both of us."

"Be that as it may, it cannot be done," objected the churchman. "Even if we possessed a ready supply of tools and material, who would do the building?"

"Be at ease," said the count. "You are growing distraught over nothing. Have I not already said that we will use as much existing building work as possible? We will begin with that and add only what is necessary. It does not have to be a city, mind—a small market village will do."

STEPHEN R.
LAWHEAD

"What *existing* buildings do you mean?"

"I mean," replied the count with exaggerated patience, "those buildings already established—the church and outbuildings and whatnot."

"But . . . but . . . ," cried the bishop in a strangled voice. "That is my monastery you are talking about!"

"*Oui*," agreed the count placidly. "We will begin there. Those structures can easily be converted to other uses. We need only raise a few houses, a grange hall, smithery, and such like. Your monastery serves . . . what? A paltry handful of monks? My town will become a centre of commerce and prosperity for the whole valley. Where is the difficulty?"

"The difficulty, Count de Braose," replied the bishop, fighting to keep his voice level, "is that I will no longer have a monastery."

"Your monastery is no longer required," stated the count. "We need a market town, not a monkery."

"There has been a monastery in this valley for eleven generations," Asaph pointed out. He raised his hands and shook his head vehemently. "No. I will not preside over its destruction. It is out of the question."

The churchman's outright and obstinate refusal irritated de Braose; he felt the warmth of anger rising in him, and his voice grew hushed. "*Au contraire*, bishop," he said, "it *is* the question. See here, we must have a town, and quickly. People are coming to settle in the valley; we need a town."

He paused, gathered his nerves, and then continued in a more conciliatory tone, "The labourers will be drawn from the residents of the valley, and the materials will be supplied from the woods and stone fields of Elfael. I have already undertaken the requisition of the necessary tools and equipment, as well as oxen and wagons for transport. Anything else that you require will be likewise supplied.

All that remains," he said in conclusion, "is for you to supply the men. They will be ready to work as soon as the last snow has melted. Is that clear?"

"Which *men* do you imagine I command?" demanded the bishop in his anger at being thrown out of his beloved monastery. "There are no men," he snapped, "only a paltry handful of monks."

"The Welsh," said Falkes. "The people of Elfael, your country-men—that is who I mean."

"The men of Elfael are gone," scoffed the bishop. "The best were slaughtered on their way to Lundein," he said pointedly, "and the rest fled. The only ones left are those who had nowhere else to go, and if they have any sense at all, they will stay far away from this valley."

The count glared from beneath his brows. "Courtesy, priest," warned de Braose. "Sarcasm ill becomes you."

"Count de Braose," appealed the bishop, "every able-bodied man gathered his family and his flocks and fled the valley the moment you and your soldiers arrived. There *are* no men."

"Then you must find some," said Falkes, growing weary of the bishop's unwillingness to see things from his point of view. "I do not care where you find them, but find them you will."

"And if I decline to aid you in this?"

"Then," replied Falkes, his voice falling to a whisper, "you will quickly learn how I repay disloyalty. I assure you it can be extremely unpleasant."

Bishop Asaph stared in disbelief. "You would threaten a priest of Christ?"

The young count shrugged.

"And this . . . after I delivered the king's treasury to you? This is how I am to be repaid? We agreed that the church would not be harmed. You gave me your word."

"Your church will be in a town," said the count. "Where is the harm?"

"We are under the authority of Rome," Asaph pointed out. "You hold no power over us."

"I hold a royal grant for this commot. Any interference in the establishment of my rule will be reckoned treason, which is punishable by death." He spread his hands as if to indicate that the matter was beyond his immediate control. "But we need not dwell on such unhappy things. You have plenty of time to make the right decision."

"You cannot do this," blurted the bishop. "In the name of God, you cannot."

"Oh, I think you will find that I can," replied Falkes. "One way or another there will be a town in this valley. You can help me, or you and your precious monks will perish. The choice, my dear bishop, is yours."

Winter laid siege to the forest and set up encampment on the hilltops and valleys throughout Elfael. The tiny, branch-framed patch of sky that could be seen from the mouth of the cave was often obscured, cast over with heavy, snow-laden clouds. Bran, warm beneath layered furs and skins, would sometimes wake in the night and listen to the gale as it shrieked through the naked trees outside, beating the bare branches together and sending the snow drifting high and deep over the forest trails and trackways.

The cave, however fierce the storm outside, remained dry and surprisingly comfortable. Bran spent his days dozing and planning his eventual departure; when he grew strong enough to leave this place, he would resume his flight to the north. Having no other plan, that was as good as any. For now, however, he remained content to sleep and eat and recover his strength. Sometimes he would wake to find himself alone, but Angharad always returned by day's end—often with a fat hare or two slung over her shoulder, and once with half a small deer, which she hung from an iron hook set in the rock at the entrance to the cave. In the evenings, she cooked their simple meals and tended his wounds while the pot bubbled on the fire.

And at night, each night of that long winter, the cave was transformed. No longer a rock-bound hole in a cliff face, it became a shining gateway into another world. For each night after they had eaten, Angharad sang.

The first time it took Bran by surprise. Without any hint or warning of what was to come, the old woman disappeared into the dark interior of the cave and returned bearing a harp. Finely made of walnut and elm wood, with pegs of oak, the curve of its shapely prow was polished smooth by years of handling.

Bran watched as she carefully brushed away the dust with the hem of her mantle, tightened the strings, and tuned the instrument. Then, settled on her stool, her head bent near as if in close communion with an old friend, a frown of concentration on her puckered face, Angharad had begun to play—and Bran's bemusement turned to astonished delight.

The music those gnarled old fingers coaxed from the harp strings that night was pure enchantment, woven tapestries of melody, wonder made audible. And when she opened her mouth to sing, Bran felt himself lifted out of himself and transported to places he never knew existed. Like the ancient harp cradled in her lap, Angharad's voice took on a beauty and quality far surpassing the rude instrument. At once agile and sure and gentle, the old woman's singing voice possessed a fluid, supple strength—now soaring like the wind over the far-off mountains, now a bird in flight, now a cresting wave rolling upon the shore.

And was it not strange that when Angharad sang, she herself was subtly changed? No longer the gray hag in a tattered robe, she assumed a more noble, almost regal aspect, a dignity her shabby surroundings ordinarily denied, or at least obscured from view. Well-accustomed to her presence now, Bran was no longer repulsed by her appearance; in the same way, he no longer noticed her odd, archaic way of speaking with her thee and thou and wouldst and goest, and all the rest. Neither her aspect nor her speech seemed remarkable; he accepted both the same way he recognized her healing skill: they seemed natural to her, and most naturally her.

In fact, as Bran soon came to appreciate, with a harp in her weathered hands, Angharad became more herself.

Extraordinary as it was to Bran, that first night's performance was merely the seeding of a disused well, or the clearing of a brush-filled spring to let fresh new waters flow. Thereafter, as night after night she took her place on the stool and cradled the harp to her bosom, Angharad's voice, like fine gold, began to take on added luster through use. A voice so rare, Bran mused, must come from somewhere else, from some other time or place, from some other world—perhaps from the very world Angharad's songs described.

The world Angharad sang into being was the Elder World, the realm of princely warriors and their noble lovers. She sang of long-forgotten heroes, kings, and conquerors; of warrior queens and ladies of such beauty that nations rose and fell at the fleeting glance of a limpid eye; of dangerous deeds and queer enchantments; of men and women of ancient renown at whose names the heart rose and the blood raced faster.

She sang of Arianrhod, Pryderi, Llew, Danu, and Carridwen, and all their glorious adventures; of Pwyll and Rhiannon, and their impossible love; of Taliesin, Arthur Pendragon, and wise Myrddin Embries, whose fame made Britain the Island of the Mighty. She sang of the Cauldron of Rebirth, the Isle of the Everliving, and the making of many-splendoured Albion.

One night, Bran realised that he had not heard such tales since he was a child. This, he thought, was why the songs touched him so deeply. Not since the death of his mother had anyone sung to him. This is why he listened to them all with the same awed attention. Caught up in the stories, he lived them as they took life within him; he became Bladudd, the blighted prince who sojourned seven years in unjust servitude; he became the lowly swineherd Tucmal, who challenged the giant champion Ogygia to mortal combat; he flew with doomed Yspilladan on his beautiful wings of swan feathers and wax; he spent a lonely lifetime in hopeless pining for the love of beautiful, inconstant Blodeuwedd; he was a warrior standing shoulder to shoulder with brave Meldryn Mawr to fight against dread Lord Nudd and his demon horde in a land of ice and snow . . . All these and many more did Bran become.

After each night's song, Angharad laid aside the harp and sat for a time, gazing into the fire as if into a window through which she could see the very things she sang about. After a time, her body would give a little shake, and she would come to herself again, like one emerging from a spell. Sometimes the sense of what he had heard eluded him— she could tell by the frown that knitted his brow and tugged at the corner of his mouth that he had not understood. So, wrapping her arms around her knees as she sat on her three-legged stool, she would gaze into the fire and talk about the story and its inner meaning—the spirit of the song, Angharad called it.

As Bran's knowledge grew, so did his appreciation of the stories themselves. He began to behold possibilities and portents, glimmerings of distant hope, flashes of miracle. The things he heard in Angharad's songs were more than mere fancy—the stuff itinerant minstrels plied— they were tokens of knowledge in another, deeper, rarer form. Perhaps they were even a form of power, but one long dormant. At the very least, these songs were markers along a sacred and ancient pathway that led deep into the heart of the land and its people—his land, his people—a spirit and life that would be crushed out of existence beneath the heavy, unfeeling rule of the coldhearted Ffreinc.

It snowed the day Bran finally regained his feet. Leaning heavily on the old woman, he shuffled with agonizing slowness to the mouth of the cave to stand and watch silent white flakes drift down from the close grey sky to cover the forest in a fine seamless garment of glistening white. He felt the cold air on his face and hands and drew it deep into his lungs, shivering with the icy tingle. The sensation made him cough; it still hurt, but the coughing no longer made him gasp with pain. He braved it for the chance to simply stand and watch the swirling flakes spin and dance as they floated to earth.

After being so long abed, with nothing to look at but the dull grey rock walls of the cave, Bran considered that he had rarely seen anything so beautiful. The dizzying sweep and curl and gyre of the falling flakes made him smile as he turned his light-dazzled eyes to the sky. The old woman seemed to approve of the pleasure he took in the sight; she bore him up with her sturdy peasant strength, watching the enjoyment flit across Bran's thin, haggard features.

When he grew tired, Angharad fetched him a staff. She returned with a sturdy length of hawthorn; placing it in his hands, she indicated that Bran should go and relieve himself. He hobbled gingerly out into the little clearing; the snow fell on him, the fat, wet flakes stinging sweetly as they alighted on his exposed skin, stuck, and instantly melted.

Although it felt odd standing in the snow within sight of the old woman at the mouth the cave, Bran was glad to be able to stand like a man on his own two feet once more and not have to squat on a pot like a child. He returned to the cave, shaking and sweating and tottering like an invalid no longer able to lift his feet, but beaming as if he had journeyed to the very edge of the earth and lived to tell the tale.

The old woman did not rush out to help him but waited at the cave mouth for each stumbling step to bring him back. When he entered the cave, she took his face between her rough hands and blew her warm breath upon him. "You can speak," she told him, "if you will."

Up until that moment, Bran did not feel he had anything to say, but now all the pent-up words came bubbling up in a confused and tangled rush, only to stick in his throat. He stood swaying on the staff, his tongue tingling with half-formed thoughts and questions, struggling to frame the words until she laid a sooty finger on his lips and said, "Time enough for all your questions anon, but sit down now and rest."

She did not lead him back to his bed as he expected, but sat him on her three-legged stool beside the fire ring. While he warmed himself, she made a meal for them—a stew with meat this time, a nice fat hare, along with some leeks and wild turnips and dried mushrooms gathered through the autumn and dried in the sun. When she had cut up everything and tossed it into the cauldron, she took a few handfuls of ground wheat, some salt, water, honey, dried berries, and dried herbs and began making up little cakes with dough left over from the last batches.

Bran sat and watched her deft fingers prepare the food, and his thoughts slowed and clarified. "What is your name?" he asked at last, and was surprised to hear a voice that sounded much like the one he knew as his own.

She smiled without glancing up and continued kneading the dough for a moment before answering. She shaped a small loaf and set it to warm and rise on a stone near the fire. Then, looking him full in the face, she replied, "I am Angharad."

"Are you a *gwrach*," he asked, "a sorceress?"

She bent to her work once more, and Bran thought she would not answer. "Please, I mean no disrespect," he said. "Only it seems to me that no one can do what you do without the aid of powerful magic." He paused, watching her mix the flour, and then asked again, "Truly, are you a sorceress?"

"I am as you see me," she replied. She shaped another small loaf and put it beside the first. "Different people see different things. What do you see?"

Embarrassed now to tell her what he really thought—that he saw a repulsive crone with bits of leaf and seeds in her hair; that he saw a grotesque hag with smoke-darkened skin in a filthy, grease-stained rag of a dress; that he saw a hunchbacked, shambling wreck of a human being—Bran swallowed his blunt observations and instead replied, "I see the woman who with great skill and wisdom has saved my life."

"I ask you now," she replied, rolling the dough between her calloused palms, "was it a life worth the saving?"

"I do hope you think so," he replied.

Angharad stopped her work. Her face grew still as she regarded him with an intensity like the lick of a naked flame over his skin. "It is my most fervent hope," she said, her voice solemn as a pledge. "What is more, all of Elfael joins me in that hope."

Bran, feeling suddenly very unworthy of such esteem, lowered his gaze to the fire and said no more that night.

Many more days passed, and Bran's strength slowly increased. Restless and frustrated by his inability to move about as he would like, he sat and moped by the fire, idly feeding twigs and bark and branches to the flames. He knew he was not well enough to leave yet, and even if he could have limped more than a few paces without exhausting himself, winter, with its blizzards and blasts, still raged. That did not hinder him from wishing he could go and making plans to leave.

Angharad, he knew, would not prevent him. She had said as much, and he had no reason to believe otherwise. Indeed, she seemed more than sympathetic to his plight, for she, too, nursed a low-smouldering hatred for the Ffreinc who had seized Elfael, killed the king, and wiped out the warband. Outlanders, she called them, whose presence was an offence under heaven, a stink in the nostrils of God.

While Bran shared this view, he could not see himself effecting any significant change in the situation. Even if he had been so inclined, as the matter stood, he was a man marked for death. If he was caught in Elfael again, Bran knew Count de Braose would not hesitate to finish what he had almost succeeded in accomplishing at the forest's edge.

The fear of that attack would come swarming out of the night to kindle in him an intense passion to escape, to flee to a safe haven in the north, to leave Elfael and never look back. Other times, he saw himself standing over the body of Count de Braose, his lance blade deep in his effete enemy's guts. Occasionally, Bran imagined there might be a way to unite those two conflicting ambitions. Perhaps he could fly away to safety, persuade his kinsmen in the north to join with him, and return to Elfael with a conquering warhost to drive the Ffreinc invaders from the land.

This last idea was late in coming. His impulse from the beginning had been escape, and it still claimed first place in his thoughts. The notion of staying to fight for his land and people had occurred to him in due course—seeded, no doubt, by the stories Angharad told, stories that filled his head with all kinds of new and unfamiliar thoughts.

One morning, Bran rose early to find his wizened guardian gone and himself alone. Feeling rested and able, he set himself the task of walking from the cave to the edge of the clearing. The day was clear and bright, the sun newly risen, the air crisp. He drew a deep breath and felt the tightness in his chest and side—as if inner cords still bound him. His shoulder ached with the cold, but he was used to it now, and it no longer bothered him. His legs felt strong enough, so he began to walk—slowly, with exaggerated care.

The ground sloped down from the mouth of the cave, and he saw the path trodden by Angharad on her errands and, judging by the other tracks in the well-trampled snow, a multitude of forest creatures as well. He hobbled across the open expanse and arrived in good order at the edge of the clearing.

Flushed with the exhilaration of this small achievement, he decided to press himself a little further. He entered the forest, walking with greater confidence along the well-packed snow track. It felt good to move and stretch. The downhill path was gentle, and soon he reached a small rill. The stream was covered by a thin layer of translucent ice; he could hear water running underneath.

The track turned and ran alongside the stream; without thinking, he followed. In a little while he came to a place where the ground dropped away steeply. The water entered a deep cutting carved into the slope and disappeared in a series of stony cascades. The path followed this ravine, but it was far too steep for Bran, so he turned and started back the way he had come. When he reached the place where the path joined the stream, he continued on, soon reaching another impasse. On his left hand, a rocky shelf jutted up, twice his height; on his right the stream flowed at the bottom of a rough defile, and dead ahead, the trunk of a fallen elm blocked the path like a gnarled, black, bark-covered wall.

He did not trust his ability to clamber over the fallen log—in his present condition, he did not dare risk it. He had no choice but to retrace his steps, so he turned around and started back to the cave. It was then he learned that he had walked farther than he intended, and also that he had seriously misjudged the slight uphill climb.

The rise was steep, and the snow slick underfoot. Twice he slipped and fell; he caught himself both times, but each fall was accompanied by a sharp tearing sensation—as if his wounds were being ripped open once more. The second time, he paused on his hands and knees in the snow and waited until the waves of pain subsided.

After that, he proceeded much more carefully, but the exertion soon taxed his rapidly tiring muscles; he was forced to stop to rest and catch his breath every few dozen paces. Despite the cold, he began to sweat. His tunic and mantle were soon soaked through, and his damp clothes grew clammy and froze, chilling him to the bone. By the time the cave came into sight, he was shaking with cold and gasping with pain.

Head down, wheezing like a wounded bear, Bran shuffled the last hundred paces to the cave, staggered in, and collapsed on his bed. He lay a long time, shivering, too weak to pull the fleeces over himself.

This was how Angharad found him sometime later when she returned with a double brace of woodcocks.

Bran sensed a movement and opened his eyes to see her bending over him, the birds dangling in her hand and her brow creased with concern. "You went out," she said simply.

"I did," he said, his voice husky with fatigue. He clenched his jaw tightly to keep his teeth from chattering.

"You should not have done so." Laying aside the birds, she straightened his limbs in his bed, then arranged the fleeces over him.

"I am sorry," he murmured, sinking gratefully beneath the coverings. He closed his eyes and shivered.

Angharad built up the fire again and set about preparing the woodcocks for their supper. Bran dozed on and off through the rest of the day; when he finally roused himself once more, it was dark outside. The cave was warm and filled with the aroma of roasting meat. He sat up stiffly and rubbed his chest; the wound was sore, and he felt a burning deep inside.

The old woman saw him struggle to rise and came to him. "You will stay abed," she told him.

"No," he said, far more forcefully than he felt. "I want to get up."

"You have overtired yourself and must rest now. Tonight you will stay abed."

"I won't argue," he said, accepting her judgement. "But will you still sing to me?"

Angharad smiled. "One would almost think you liked my singing," she replied.

That night after supper, Bran lay in his bed, aching and sore, skin flushed with fever, barely able to keep his eyes open. But he listened to that incomparable voice, and as before, the cave disappeared and he travelled to that Elder Realm, where Angharad's tales took life. That night he listened as, for the first time, she sang him a tale of King Raven.

Angharad settled herself beside Bran on her three-legged stool. She plucked a harp string and silenced it with the flat of her hand. Closing her eyes, she held her head to one side, as if listening to a voice he could not hear. He watched her shadow on the cave wall, gently wavering in the firelight as she cradled the harp to her breast and began to stroke the lowest string—softly, gently releasing a rich, sonorous note into the silence of the cave.

Angharad began to sing—a low whisper of exhaled breath that gathered force to become an inarticulate moan deep in her throat. The harp note pulsed quicker, and the moan became a cry. The cry became a word, and the word a name: *Rhi Bran.*

Bran heard it, and the small hairs on his arms stood up.

Again and again, Angharad invoked the name, and Bran felt his heart quicken. Rhi Bran. King Raven—his own name and his rightful title—but cast in a newer, fiercer, almost frightening light.

Angharad's fingers stroked a melody from the harp, her voice rose to meet it, and the tale of King Raven began. This is what she sang:

In the Elder Time, when the dew of Creation was still fresh on the ground, Bran Bendigedig awakened in this worlds-realm. A beautiful boy, he grew to be a handsome man, renowned amongst his people for his courage and valour. And his valour was such that it was exceeded only by his virtue, which was exceeded only by his wisdom, which was itself exceeded only by his honesty. Bran the Blesséd he was called, and no one who saw him doubted that if ever there was a man touched by the All Wise and granted every boon in abundance, it was he. Thus, he possessed all that was needful for a life of utter joy and delight, save one thing only. A single blessing eluded him, and that was contentment.

Bran Bendigedig's heart was restless, always seeking, never finding—for if it was known what would satisfy his unquiet heart, that knowledge was more completely hidden than a single drop of water in all the oceans of the world. And the knowledge of his lack grew to become a fire deep inside him that burned his bones and filled his mouth with the taste of ashes.

One day, when he could endure his discontent no longer, he put on his best boots, kissed his mother and father farewell, and began to walk. "I will not stop walking until I have found the thing which will quell my restless heart and fill this hunger in my soul."

Thus, he began a journey through many lands, through kingdoms and dominions of every kind. At the end of seven years, he reached a distant shore and gazed across a narrow sea, where he beheld the fairest island that he or anyone else had ever seen. Its white cliffs glowed in the dying sunlight like a wall of fine pale gold, and larks soared high above the green-topped hills, singing in the gentle evening air. He wanted nothing more than to go to the island without delay, but night was coming, and he knew he could not reach the far shore in time, so he settled down to spend the night on the strand, intending to cross over the narrow sea with the next morning's new light.

Unable to sleep, he lay on the beach all night long, listening to the fitful wash of the waves over the pebbles, feeling as if his heart would burst for restlessness. When the sun rose again, he rose with it and looked out at the many-splendoured island as it lay before him in the midst of the silver sea. Then, as the rising sun struck the white cliffs, setting them aglow with a light that dazzled the eyes, Bran struck out. Drawing himself up to full height, he grew until his head brushed the clouds, whereupon he waded out into the narrow sea, which reached only to the knot of his belt. He reached the opposite shore in nine great strides, emerging from the water at his normal height.

He spread his arms to the sun, and while he stood waiting for the bright rays to dry his clothes, he heard the most delightful music, and he turned to see a lady on a milk-white horse approaching a little way off. The music arose from a flute that she played as she cantered along the water's edge in the sweet, honeyed light of the rising sun. Her hair shone with the brightness of a flame, and her skin was firm and soft. Her limbs were fine and straight, her gown was yellow satin, edged in blue, and her eyes were green as new grass or apples in summer.

As she came near, she caught sight of Bran, standing alone on the strand, and she stopped playing. "I give you good greeting, sir," she said; her voice, so light and melodious, melted Bran in his innermost parts. "What is your name?"

"I am Bran Bendigedig," said he. "I am a stranger here."

"Yet you are welcome," said the lady. "I see that you are beguiled by the sight of this fair island."

"That I am," Bran confessed. "But no less than by the sight of you, my lady. If ever I boast of seeing a fairer face in all this wide world, may I die a liar's death. What is your name?"

"Would that you had asked me anything else," she told him sadly, "for I am under a strong *geas* never to reveal my name to anyone until the day of Albion's release."

"If that is all that prevents you, then take heart," Bran replied boldly, for the moment she spoke those first words in his ear, he knew beyond all doubt that the thing required to bring contentment to his restless heart was the name of the lady before him—just to know her name and, knowing it, to possess it and, possessing it, to hold her beside him forever. With her as his wife, his heart would find peace at last. "Only tell me who or what Albion might be," Bran said, "and I will achieve its release before the sun has run its course."

"Would that you had promised anything else," the lady told him. "Albion is the name of this place, and it is the fairest island known. Ten years ago a plague came to these shores, and it is this which now devastates the island. Every morning I come to the sea-strand in the time-between-times in the hope of finding someone who can break the wicked spell that holds Albion in thrall."

"Today your search has ended," replied Bran, his confidence undimmed. "Only tell me what to do, and it will be done."

"Though your spirit may be bold and your hand strong, Albion's release will take more than that. Many great men have tried, but none have succeeded, for the plague is no ordinary illness or disease. It is an evil enchantment, and it takes the form of a race of giants who by their mighty strength cause such havoc and devastation that my heart quails at the mere mention of them."

"Fear for nothing, noble lady," Bran said. "The All Wise in his boundless wisdom has granted me every good gift, and I can do wonderfully well whatever I put my hand to."

At this the lady smiled, and, oh, her smile was even more radiant than the sunlight on the shining cliffs. "The day you deliver Albion, I will give you my name—and more than that, if you only ask."

"Then rest assured," replied Bran, "that on that very day, I will return to ask for your hand and more—I will ask for your heart also." The lady bent her shapely neck in assent and then told him what he had to do to release Albion from the evil spell and break the geas that bound her.

Bran the Blesséd listened well to all she said; then, bidding her farewell, he started off. He came to a river that the lady had told him to expect, then followed it to the centre of the isle. For three days and nights he walked, stopping only now and then to drink from the pure waters of the river, for his heart burned within him at the thought of marrying the most beautiful woman in the world.

As the sun rose on the fourth day, he came to a great dark wood—the forest from which all other forests in the world had their beginning. He entered the forest, and just as the lady had told him, after walking three more days, he came to a glade where two roads crossed. He strode to the centre of the crossroads and sat down to wait. After a time, he heard the sound of someone approaching and looked up to see an old man with a white beard hobbling toward him. The man was bent low to the ground beneath heavy bundles of sticks he was carrying, so low that his beard swept the ground before him.

Seeing this man whom the lady had told him to expect, Bran

jumped up and hailed him. "You there! You see before you a man of purpose who would speak to you."

"And *you* see before *you* a man who was once a king in his own country," the man replied. "A little respect would become you."

"My lord, forgive me," replied Bran. "May I come near and speak to you?"

"You may approach—not that I could prevent you," answered the old man. Nevertheless, he motioned Bran to come near. "What is your name?" asked the old man.

"I am Bran Bendigedig," he answered. "I have come to seek the release of Albion from the plague that assails it."

"Too bad for you," said the bent-backed man, straining beneath his load of sticks. "Many good men have tried to break the spell; as many as have tried, that many have failed."

"It may be as you say," offered Bran, "but I doubt there are two men like me in all the world. If there is another, I have never heard of him." He explained how he had met the noble lady on the strand and had pledged himself to win her hand.

"I ween that you are a bold man, perhaps even a lucky one," said the aged noble. "But though you were an army of like-minded, hardy men, you would still fail. The enchantment that besets Albion cannot be broken except by one thing, and one thing alone."

"What is that thing?" asked Bran. "Tell me, and then stand back and watch what I will do."

"It is not for me to say," replied the former lord.

Pointing to the road that led deeper into the forest, the old man said, "Go down that road until you come to a great forest, and continue on until you come to a glade in the centre of the wood. You will know it by a mound that is in the centre of the glade. In the centre of the mound is a standing stone, and at the foot of the standing stone, you will find a fountain. Beside the fountain is a slab of white marble, and on the slab you will find a silver bowl attached by a chain so that it may not be stolen away. Dip a bowl of water from the fountain and dash it upon the marble slab. Then stand aside and wait. Be patient, and it will be revealed to you what to do."

Bran thanked the man and journeyed on along the forest road. In a little while, he began seeing signs of devastation of which the noble lady had warned him: houses burned; fields trampled flat; hills gouged out; streams diverted from their natural courses; whole trees uprooted, overturned, and thrust back into the hole with roots above and branches below. The mutilated bodies of dead animals lay everywhere on the ground, their limbs rent, their bodies torn asunder. Away to the east, a great fire burned a swathe through the high wooded hills, blotting out the sun and turning the sky black with smoke.

Bran looked upon this appalling destruction. *Who could do such a thing?* he wondered, and his heart moved within him with anger and sorrow for the ruined land.

He moved on, walking through desolation so bleak it made tears well up in his eyes to think what had been so cruelly destroyed. After two days, he came to the glade in the centre of the forest. There, as the old man had said, he saw an enormous mound, and from the centre of this mound rose a tall, slender standing stone. Bran ascended the mound and stood before the narrow stone; there at his feet he saw a clear-running fountain and, beside it, the marble slab with the silver bowl attached by a thick chain. Kneeling down, he dipped the silver bowl into the fountain, filled it, and then dashed the water over the pale stone.

Instantly, there came a peal of thunder loud enough to shake the ground, the wind blew with uncommon fury, and hail fell from the sky. So fiercely did it fall that Bran feared it would beat through his skin and flesh to crack his very bones. Clinging to the standing stone, he pressed himself hard against it for shelter, covered his head with his arms, and bore the assault as best he could.

In a short while the hail and wind abated, and the thunder echoed away. He heard then a grinding noise—like that of a millstone as it crushes the hard seeds of grain. He looked and saw a crevice open in the ground and a yellow vapour issuing from the gap like a foul breath. In the midst of the yellow fumes there appeared a woman—so old and withered that she looked as if she might be made of sticks wrapped in a dried leather sack.

Her hair—what little remained—was a tangled, ratty mass of leaves and twigs, moss and feathers, and bird droppings; her mouth was a slack gash in the lower part of her face, through which Bran could see but a single rotten tooth; her clothing was a filthy rag so threadbare it resembled cobwebs, and so small her withered dugs showed above one end and her spindly thighs below the other. Her face was more skull than visage, her eyes sunken deep in their sockets, where they gleamed like two shiny stones.

Bran took but a single brief look before turning away, swallowing his disgust as she advanced toward him.

"You there!" she called, her voice cracking like a dry husk. "Do you know what you have done? Do you have any idea?"

Half-shielding his eyes with his hand, Bran offered a sickly smile and answered, "I have done that which was required of me, nothing more."

"Oh, have you now?" queried the hag. "By heaven's lights, you will soon wish you had not done that."

"Woman," said Bran, "I am wishing that already!"

"Tell me your name and what it is that you want," said the woman, "and I will see if there is any help for you."

"I am Bran Bendigedig, and I have come to break the vile enchantment that ravages Albion."

"I did not ask *why* you have come," the old crone laughed. "I asked what it is that you want."

"I was born with an unquiet heart that has never been satisfied—not that it is any of your affair," Bran told her.

"Silence!" screeched the woman in a voice so loud that Bran clapped his hands over his ears lest he lose his hearing. "Respect is a valuable treasure that costs nothing. If you would keep your tongue, see that it learns some courtesy."

"Forgive me," Bran spluttered. "It was not my wish to offend you. If I spoke harshly just then, it was merely from impatience. You see, I have met a noble lady who is all my heart's desire, and I have set myself to win her if I can. To do that, I have vowed to rid Albion of the plague that even now wreaks such havoc on this fairest of islands."

The wretched hag put her face close to Bran's—so close that Bran could smell the stink she gave off and had to pinch his nostrils shut. She squinted her eyes with the intensity of her scrutiny. "Is that what you are about?" she asked at last.

"I am," replied Bran. "If you can help me, I will be in your debt. If not, only tell me someone who can, and I will trouble you no more."

"You ask my help," said the ancient woman, "and though you may not know it, you could not have asked a better creature under heaven, for help you shall receive—though it comes at a cost."

"It is ever the way of things," sighed Bran. "What is the price?"

"I will tell you how to break the wicked enchantment that binds Albion—and I hope you succeed, for unless you do, Albion is lost and will soon be a wasteland."

"And the price?" asked Bran, feeling the restlessness beginning to mount like a sneeze inside him.

"The price is this: that on the day Albion is released, you will take the place of the man the giants have killed."

"That is no burden to me," remarked Bran with relief. "I thought it would be more."

"There are some who think the cost too great." She shrugged her skinny shoulders, and Bran could almost hear them creak. "Nevertheless, that is the price. Do you agree?"

"I do," said Bran the Blesséd. "In truth, I would pay whatever you asked to break the curse and win my heart's desire."

"Done! Done!" crowed the old woman in triumph. "Then listen well, and do exactly as I say."

Laying her bony fingers on Bran's strong arm, the hag led him from the mound and into the ruined forest. They passed through death and devastation that would have made the very stones weep, and walked on until they came to a high hill that was topped by a magnificent white fortress. At the base of the hill flowed a river; once sparkling and clear, it now ran ruddy brown with the blood of the slaughtered.

Pointing to the fortress, the hag said, "Up there you will find the tribe of giants who have enthralled this fair island and whose presence is a very plague. Kill them all and the spell will be broken, and your triumph will be assured."

"If that is all," replied Bran grandly, "why did you not tell me sooner? It is as good as done." He made to start off at once.

The ancient crone prevented him, saying, "Wait! There is more. You should know also that the giants have slain the Lord of the Forest and taken possession of his cauldron, called the Cauldron of Rebirth on account of its miraculous virtue: that whatever living creature, man or animal it matters not, though he were dead and dismembered, mutilated, torn into a thousand pieces, and those pieces eaten, if any part of the corpse is put into the cauldron when it is on the boil, life will return, and the creature will emerge hale and whole once more."

Amazed, Bran exclaimed, "Truly, that is a wonder! Rest assured that I will stop at nothing to reclaim this remarkable vessel."

"Do so," promised the hag, "and your deepest desire will be granted."

Off he went, crossing the river of blood and ascending the high hill. As Bran drew closer, he saw that the white fortress was not, as he had assumed, built of choice marble, but of the skulls and bones of murdered beasts and humans, used like so much rubble to erect the high white walls, turrets, and towers. A sickening smell rose from the bones, which, though it made him gag, also raised Bran's fury against the giants.

Boldly he approached the gate, and boldly entered. There was neither guard nor porter to prevent him, so he strode across the courtyard and entered the hall. However much the courtyard stank, the odour inside the hall was that much worse.

From the hall, he could hear the sound of a great roister. He crept to the massive door, peered inside, and instantly wished he had not. He saw seven giants, the least of which was three times the height of any human man, and the greatest amongst them was three times the height of the smallest. Each giant was a gruesomely ugly brute with pale, blotchy skin; shaggy, long hair that hung down his broad back in nasty, tangled hanks; and a single large eyebrow across his thick, overhanging forehead. Each giant was more hideous than the last, with fat, fleshy lips and an enormous, long nose shaped like the beak of a malformed bird. Their necks were short and squat, their arms ridiculously long, and their legs thin through the shank and fat at the thigh. They all carried clubs of iron, which any two human men would have found a burden to lift.

Three long tables filled the hall, and on those tables was a feast of roast meat of every kind of creature under heaven, which the giants ate with ravenous abandon. While they ate—rending the carcasses with their hands, stuffing the meat down their stubby necks, spitting out the bones, and then washing it all down with great, greedy draughts of rendered lard and fat drawn from a score of vats around the hall—they laughed and sang in disagreeable voices and raised such a revel that Bran's head throbbed like a beaten drum with the noise.

The Blesséd Bran stood for a moment, gazing upon the carnage of the feast, and felt an implacable rage rise inside him. Then, across the hall, he spied an enormous kettle of burnished bronze and copper, silver and gold—so large it could easily hold sixteen human men at once; or three teams of oxen; or nine horses; or seven stags, three deer, and a fawn. A fire of oak logs blazed away beneath the prodigious vessel.

Seeing this, Bran thought, *The prize is within my grasp,* and taking a deep breath, he stepped boldly through the door. "Giants!" he called, "The feast is over! You have eaten your last corpse. I give you fair warning—doom is upon you!"

The giants were startled to hear this loud voice, and they were even more surprised when they saw the tiny man who made such a bold and foolish claim. They laughed in their beards and blew their noses at him. Two of them bared their horrible backsides, and the others mocked him with rude gestures. Up rose the chief of the monstrous clan, and he was the most repulsive brute of them all; taller than seven normal men, he was greasy with the blood of the meat he had been gorging.

Sneering, he opened his gate of a mouth and bellowed, "What you lack in size, you make up for in stupidity. I've eaten five of your race already today and will gladly count you amongst them. What is your name, little man?"

"Call me *Silidons*, for such I am," said Bran, hiding his true name behind a word that means "nobody." "You will have to kill me first, and I have never lost a fight I entered."

"Then you cannot have entered many. Today we will put you to the test." So saying, the giant lifted his massive hand and commanded two of his nearest fellows forward. "Seize him! Show this imbecile how we deal with anyone foolish enough to oppose us!"

The two giants rose and lumbered forth, their fleshy lips wide in distorted grins. Bran stepped forward, and as he did so, he grew in size to half again his height; another step doubled his size. Now the crown of his head came up to the giants' chests.

The giants saw this and were astonished but undaunted. "Is that the best you can do?" they laughed. Taking up their iron clubs, they swung at Bran, first one way and then the other. Bran leapt over the first and ducked under the second; then, leaping straight up into the air, he lashed out with his foot and caught one of the giants in the middle of the forehead. The great brute dropped his club and grabbed his head. Snatching up the enormous weapon,

Bran swung with all his might and crushed the skull of the giant, who gave out a throaty groan and lay still.

Seeing his comrade bested so easily infuriated the second attacker. Roaring with rage, he whirled his heavy club around his head and smashed it down, cracking the flagstones. Bran stepped neatly aside as the club struck the floor, then quickly climbed the broad shaft as if it were an iron mounting block. When the giant lifted the club, Bran leapt into the brute's face and drove both fists into the giant's eyes. The ghastly creature screamed and fell to his knees, clutching his eyes with both hands. Calmly, Bran picked up the club and swung hard. The brute pitched forward onto his face and rose no more.

Looking around, he called, "Who will be next?"

Crazed with fear and spitting with rage, the remaining giants rose as one and charged Bran, who ran to meet them, growing bigger with every step until he was a head taller than the tallest. Four blows were thrown, one after another, and four giants fell, leaving only the enormous chieftain still on his feet. Not only bigger, he was also quicker than the others, and before Bran could turn, he reached out and seized Bran by the throat. Drawing a deep breath, Bran willed his neck to become a column of white granite; with all his strength the giant chieftain could not break that thick column.

Meanwhile, Bran took hold of the giant's protruding ears. Grabbing one in each hand, he yanked hard, pulling the giant chieftain forward and driving the point of his granite chin right between the odious monster's bulging eyes. The giant's knees buckled, and he tumbled backwards like a toppled pine tree, striking his head on the stone floor and expiring before he could draw his next breath.

Triumphant, Bran strode to the hearth and plucked the still-bubbling cauldron from the flames. Grasping the miraculous pot in his strong arms of stone, Bran walked from the castle of bone, back to the world outside, where he once again met the ancient hag who was waiting for him.

The hag jumped up and scurried to meet him. "Truly, you are a mighty champion!" she cried. "From this day you are my husband."

Bran glanced at her askance. "Lady, if lady you be, I am no such thing," he declared. "You said I would achieve my greatest desire, and marriage to you is far from that. And even if I were so minded, I could not, for I am promised to another."

The wild-haired hag opened her gaping, toothless mouth and laughed in Bran's face. "O man of little understanding! Do you not know that whoever possesses the Cauldron of Rebirth is the Lord of the Forest? He is my husband, and I am his wife." Reaching out, she seized him with her scaly, clawlike hands and pressed her drooling lips close to his face.

Repulsed, Bran reared back and shook off her grip. He started to run away, but she pursued him with uncanny swiftness. Bran changed himself into a stag and bolted away at speed, but the hag became a wolf and raced after him. When Bran saw that he could not elude her that way, he changed into a rabbit; the hag changed into a fox and matched him stride for stride. When he saw that she was gaining on him, Bran changed into an otter, slid into the clear-running stream, and swam away. The hag, however, changed into a great salmon and caught him by the tail.

Bran felt the hag's teeth biting into him and leapt from the stream, dragging the salmon with him. Once out of the water, the salmon loosed its hold, and instantly Bran turned into a raven and flew away.

But the hag, now become an eagle, flew up, seized him in her strong talons, and pulled him from the sky. "You led me on a fine chase, but I have caught you, my proud raven!" she cackled with glee, resuming her former repulsive shape. "And now you must marry me."

Squirming and pecking at the bony fingers clasped tightly around him, Bran, still in the form of a raven, cried, "I never will! I have promised myself to another. Even now she is waiting for me on the shining shore."

"Bran, Bran," said the hag, "do you not know that I am that selfsame woman?" Smiling grotesquely, she told him all that had happened to him since meeting him that very morning on the strand where she went every day in the guise of a beautiful lady to search for a champion to become her mate. "It was myself you promised to take to wife," she concluded. "Now lie with me and do your duty as a husband."

Horrified, Bran cried out, "I never will!"

"Since you refuse," said the old woman, still clutching him between her hands, "you leave me no choice!" With that, she spat into her right hand and rubbed her spittle on Bran's sleek head, saying, "A raven you are, and a raven you shall remain—until the day you fulfil your vow to take me to wife."

The hag released Bran then, and he found that though he could still change his shape at will—now one creature, now another—he always assumed the form of a raven in the end. Thus, he took up his duties as Rhi Bran the Hud, Lord of the Forest, whom some call the Dark Enchanter of the Wood. And from that day to this, he abides as a great black raven still.

The last note faded into silence. Laying aside the harp, Angharad gazed at the rapt young man before her and said, "That is the song of King Raven. Dream on it, my son, and let it be a healing dream to you."

PART THREE

THE MAY DANCE

arm winds from the sea brought an early spring, and a wet one. From Saint David's Day to the Feast of Saint John, the sky remained a low, slate-grey expanse of dribbling rain that swelled the streams and rivers throughout the Marches. Then the skies finally cleared, and the land dried beneath a sun so bright and warm that the miserable Outlanders in their rusting mail almost forgot the hardships of the winter past.

The first wildflowers appeared, and with them wagons full of tools and building materials, rolling into the valley from Baron de Braose's extensive holdings in the south. The old dirt trackways were not yet firm enough, but Baron de Braose was eager to begin, so the first wagons to reach the valley churned the soft earth into deep, muddy trenches to swamp all those who would come after. From morning to night the balmy air was filled with the calls of the drivers, the crack of whips, and the bawling of the oxen as they struggled to haul the heavy-laden vehicles through the muck.

The Cymry also returned to the lower valleys from their winter sanctuaries in the high hills. Although most had fled the cantref, a few remained—farmers for the most part, who could not, like the sheep and cattle herders, simply take their property elsewhere—and a few of the more stubborn herdsmen who had contemplated their choices over the winter and concluded that they were unwilling to give up good grazing land to the Ffreinc. The farmers began readying their fields for sowing, and the herdsmen returned to the pastures. Following the age-old pattern of the clans from time past remembering—working through the season of sun and warmth, storing up for the season of rain and ice, when they took their ease in communal dwellings around a shared hearth—the people of the region silently reasserted their claim to the land of their ancestors. For the first time since the arrival of the Ffreinc, Elfael began to assume something of its former aspect.

Count Falkes de Braose considered the reappearance of the British a good sign. It meant, he thought, that the people had decided to accept life under his rule and would recognise him as their new overlord. He still intended to press them into helping build the town the baron required—and the castles, too, if needed—but beyond that he had no other plans for them. So long as they did what they were told, and with swift obedience, he and the local population would achieve a peaceable association. Of course, any opposition to his rule would be met with fierce retaliation—still, that was the way of the world, and only to be expected, no?

Anticipating a solid season of industry—a town to raise and border fortifications to be established—the count sent a messenger to the monastery to remind Bishop Asaph of his duty to supply British labourers to supplement the ranks of builders the baron would provide. He then busied himself with supervising the allotment of tools and materials for the various sites. Together with the architect and master mason, he inspected each of the sites to make sure that nothing had been overlooked and all was in readiness. He personally marked out the boundaries for the various towers and castle ditch enclosures, spending long days beneath the blue, cloud-crowded sky, and counted it work well done. He wanted to be ready when the baron's promised builders arrived. Time was short, and there was much to be done before the autumn storms brought an end to the year's labour.

Nothing would be allowed to impede the progress he meant to make. Only too aware that his future hung by the slender thread of his uncle, the baron's, good pleasure, Falkes agonised over his arrangements; he ate little and slept less, worrying himself into a state of near exhaustion over the details large and small.

On a sunny, windblown morning, the master mason approached Falkes on one of his visits to the building sites. "If it please you, sire, I would like to begin tomorrow," he said. Having supervised the raising of no fewer than seven castles in Normandie, Master Gernaud—with his red face beneath his battered straw hat and faded yellow sweat rag around his neck—was a solid veteran of the building trade. These were to be the first castles he had raised outside France.

"Nothing would please me more," the count replied. "Pray begin, Master Gernaud, and may God speed your work."

"We will soon have need of the rough labourers," the mason pointed out.

"It has been arranged," replied the count with confidence. "You shall have them."

Two days passed, however, and none of the required British volunteers appeared.

When, after a few more days, not a single British worker had come to any of the building sites, Falkes de Braose sent for Bishop Asaph and demanded to know why.

"Have you spoken to them?" asked Falkes, leaning on the back of his oversized chair. The hall was empty save for the count and his guest; every available hand—excepting his personal servants and a few soldiers required to keep the fortress in order—had been sent to help with the construction.

"I have done as you required," replied the churchman in a tone suggesting he could do no more than that.

"Did you tell them we must have the town established? Each day delayed is another day we must work in the winter cold."

"I told them," said Asaph.

"Then where are they?" queried Falkes, growing irate at the inconvenience perpetrated by the absent locals. "Why don't they come?"

"They are farmers, not quarrymen or masons. It is ploughing season, and the fields must be prepared for sowing. They dare not delay; otherwise there will be no harvest." He paused, plucked up his courage, and added, "Last year's harvest was very poor, as you know. And unless they are allowed to put in their crops, the people will starve. They are hungry enough already."

"What?" cried Falkes. "Do you suggest this is in any way my fault? They fled their holdings. The ignorant louts were in no danger, but they fled anyway. The blame lies with them."

"I merely state the fact that the farmers of Elfael were prevented from gathering in the harvest last year, and now there is precious little ready food in the valleys."

"They should have thought of that before they ran off and abandoned their fields!" Falkes cried, slapping the back of the chair with his long hands. "What of their cattle? Let them slaughter a few of those if they're hungry."

"The cattle are the only wealth they possess, lord count. They cannot slaughter them. Anyway, the herds must be built up through the summer if there is to be food enough to see them through the winter."

"This is not my concern!" Falkes insisted. "This problem is of their own making and will not be laid at *my* door."

"Count de Braose," said the bishop in a conciliatory tone, "they are simple folk, and they were afraid of your troops. Their king and warband had just been slain. They feared for their lives. What did you expect—that they would rush with glad hosannas to welcome you?"

"That tongue of yours will get you hanged yet, priest," warned de Braose, wagging a long finger in warning. "I would guard it if I were you."

"Will that help raise your castles?" asked Asaph. "I merely point out that if they ran away, it was for good reason. They are afraid, and nothing they have seen from you has changed that."

"I meant them no harm," insisted the count, growing petulant. "Nor do I mean them harm now. But the town *will* be raised, and the fortresses *will* be built. This commot *will* be settled and civilised, and that is the end of it." Crossing his arms over his narrow chest, Falkes thrust out his chin as if daring the churchman to disagree.

Bishop Asaph, squeezed between the rock of the count's demands and the hard place of his people's obstinate resistance to any such scheme, decided there was no harm in trying to mitigate the damage and ingratiate himself with the count. "I see you are determined," he said. "Might I offer a suggestion?"

"If you must," granted Falkes.

"It is only this. Why not wait until the fields have been sown and planted?" suggested the churchman. "Once the crops are in, the people will be more amenable to helping with the building. Grant them a reprieve until the sowing is finished. They will thank you for it, and it will demonstrate your fairness and good faith."

"*Dieu défend!* Delay the building? That I will *not* do!" cried Falkes. He took three quick strides and then turned on the bishop once more.

227

"Here now! I give you one more day to inform the people and assemble the required labourers—the two strongest men from each family or settlement. They will come to your monastery, where they will be met and assigned to one of the building sites." Glaring at the frowning cleric, he said, "Is that understood?"

"Of course," the bishop replied diffidently. "But what if they refuse to come? I can only relay your demands. I am not their lord—"

"But I am!" snapped Falkes. "And yours as well." When the bishop made no reply, he asked, "If they fail to comply, they will be punished."

"I will tell them."

"See that you do." Falkes dismissed the churchman then. As Asaph reached the door, the count added, "I will come to the monastery yard at dawn tomorrow. The workers will be ready."

228

The bishop nodded, departing without another word. Upon arriving at the monastery, he commanded the porter to sound the bell and convene the monks, who were quickly dispatched to the four corners of the cantref to carry the count's summons to the people.

When Count de Braose and his men arrived at the monastery the next morning, they found fifteen surly men and four quarrelsome boys standing in the mostly empty yard with their bishop. The count rode through the gate, took one look at the desultory crew, and cried, "What? Is this all? Where are the others?"

"There are no others," replied Bishop Asaph.

"I distinctly said *two* from every holding," complained the count. "I thought I made that clear."

"Some of the holdings are so small that there is only one man," explained the bishop. Indicating the sullen gathering, he said, "These represent every holding in Elfael." Looking at the unhappy faces around him, he asked the count, "Did you think there would be more?"

"There *must* be more!" roared Falkes de Braose. "Work is already falling behind for lack of labourers. We must have more."

"That is as it may be, but I have done as you commanded."

"It is not enough."

"Then perhaps you should have invaded a more populous cantref," snipped the cleric.

"Do not mock me," growled the count, turning away. He strode to his horse. "Find more workers. Bring them in. Bring everybody in— women too. Bring them all. I want them here tomorrow morning."

"My lord count," said the bishop, "I beg you to reconsider. The ploughing will soon be finished. That is of utmost concern, and it cannot wait."

"My *town* cannot wait!" shouted Falkes. Raising himself to the saddle, he said, "I will not be commanded by the likes of you. Have fifty workers here tomorrow morning, or one holding will burn."

"Count de Braose!" cried the bishop. "You cannot mean that, surely."

"I do most certainly mean exactly what I say. I have been too lenient with you people, but that leniency is about to end."

"But you must reconsider—"

"Must? Must?" the count sneered, stepping his horse close to the cleric, who shrank away. "Who are you to tell me what I *must* or *must not* do? Have the fifty, or lose a farm."

With that, the count wheeled his horse and rode from the yard. As the Ffreinc reached the gate, one of the boys picked up a stone and let fly, striking the count in the middle of the back. Falkes whirled around angrily but could not tell who had thrown the rock; all were standing with hands at their sides, staring with dour contempt, men as well as boys.

Unwilling to allow the insult to stand, Falkes rode back to confront them. "Who threw the stone?" he demanded. When no one answered, he called to the bishop. "Make them tell me!"

"They do not speak Latin," replied the churchman coolly. "They only speak Cymry and a little Saxon."

"Then you ask for me, priest!" said the count. "And be quick about it. I want an answer."

The bishop addressed the group, and there was a brief discussion. "It seems that no one saw anything, count," the cleric reported. "But they all vow to keep a close watch for such disgraceful behaviour in the future."

"Do they indeed? Well, for one, at least, there will be no future." Indicating a smirking lad standing off to one side, the count spoke a command in Ffreinc to his soldiers, and instantly two of the marchogi dismounted and rounded on the panic-stricken youth.

The elder Britons leapt forward to intervene but were prevented by the swiftly drawn swords of the remaining soldiers. After a momentary scuffle and much shouting, the offending youngster was marched to the centre of the yard, where he was made to stand while the count, drawing his sword, approached his quivering, bawling prisoner.

"Wait! Stop!" cried the bishop. "No, please! Don't kill him!" Asaph rushed forward to place himself between the count and his victim, but two of the soldiers caught him and dragged him back. "Please, spare the child. He will work for you all summer if you spare him. Do not kill him, I beg you."

Count de Braose tested the blade and then raised his arm and, with a fury born of frustration, yanked down the boy's trousers and struck the boy's exposed backside with the flat of his sword—once, twice, and again. Thin red welts appeared on the pale white skin, and the boy began to wail with impotent fury.

Satisfied with the punishment, the count sheathed his sword, then

raised his foot and placed his boot against the crying lad's wounded
rump and gave him a hard shove. The boy, his legs tangled in his
trousers, stumbled and fell on his chin in the dirt, where he lay, weeping hot tears of pain and humiliation.

The count turned from his victim, strode to his horse, and
mounted the saddle once more. "Tomorrow I want fifty men here,
ready to work," he announced. "Fifty, do you hear?" He paused as the
bishop translated his words. "Fifty workmen or, by heaven, a farm will
burn." His words were still ringing in the yard as he and his soldiers
rode out.

The next morning there were twenty-eight workers waiting when
the count's men arrived, and most of those were monks, as the entire
monastery—save aged Brother Clyro, who was too old to be of much
use at heavy labour—rallied to the cause. Bishop Asaph hastened to
explain the deficit and promised more workers the next day, but the
count was not of a mood to listen. Since the tally was short the
required number, the count ordered his soldiers to ride to the nearest
farm and put it to the torch. Later, the smoke from the burning darkened the sky to the west, and the following day, eighteen more Cymry—
ten men, six women, and two more boys—joined the labour force,
bringing the total to forty-six, only four shy of the number decreed by
the count.

Falkes de Braose and his men entered the yard to find the bishop
on his knees before a sulky and fearful gathering of native Cymry and
monks. The bishop pleaded with the count to rescind his order and
accept those who had come as sufficient fulfilment of his demand.
When that failed to sway the implacable overlord, Asaph stretched
himself out on the ground before the count and begged for one more
day to find workers to make up the number.

The count ignored his entreaties and ordered another holding to be burned. That night the monks offered prayers of deliverance all night long. The next morning four more workers appeared—two of them women with babes in arms—bringing up the total to the required fifty, and no more farms were destroyed.

232

CHAPTER *23* ⚖

With the onset of warmer weather, Bran felt more and more restless confined to the cave. Angharad observed his discontent and, on fine days, allowed him to sit outside on a rock in the sun; but she never let him venture too far, and he was rarely out of her sight for more than a moment or two at a time. Bran was still weaker than he knew, and his eagerness to resume his flight to the north made him prone to overtax himself. He mistook convalescence for indolence and resented it, seldom missing an opportunity to let Angharad know he felt himself a prisoner under her care. This was natural enough, she knew, but there was more.

Lately, Bran's sleep had grown fitful and erratic; several times as dawn light broke in the east, he had called out; when she rose and went to him, he was asleep still but sweating and breathing hard. The reason, Angharad suspected, was that the story was working on him. His acceptance of the tale that night had been complete. Weak from his wandering in the snow, his fatigue had left him in an unusually receptive condition—unusual, that is, for one so strong-willed and naturally contrary; he had been in that state of alert serenity the bards called the *trwyddo ennyd*, the seeding time, and which they recognised as a singular moment for learning. This condition of attentive repose allowed the song to sink deep into Bran's being, passing beneath his all-too-ready defences. Now it was under his skin, burrowing deep into his bones, seeping into his soul, changing him from the inside out, though he did not know it.

There would come a day when the meaning would break upon him; maybe sooner, maybe later, but it would come. And for this, as much as for the progress of his healing, Angharad watched him so that she would be there when it happened.

She also made plans.

One day, as Bran sat outside in a pool of warm sunlight, Angharad appeared with an ash-wood stave in her hand. She came to where he sat and said, "Stand up, Bran."

Yawning, he did so, and she placed the length of wood against his shoulder. "What is this?" he asked. "Measuring me for a druid staff?" In his restlessness, he had begun mocking her quaintly antiquated ways. The wise woman knew the source of his impatience and astutely ignored it.

"Nay, nay," she said, "you would have to spend seventeen years at least before you could hold one of those—and you would have had to begin before your seventh summer. This," she said, placing the stave in his hands, "is your next occupation."

"Herding sheep?"

"If that is your desire. I had something else in mind, but the choice is yours."

He looked at the slender length of wood. Almost as long as he was tall, it had a good heft and balance. "A bow?" he guessed. "You want me to make a bow?"

234

She smiled. "And here I was thinking you slow-witted. Yes, I want you to make a bow."

Bran examined the length of ash once more. He held it up and looked down its length. Here and there it bent slightly out of true—not so badly that it could not be worked—but that was not the problem. "No," he said at last, "it cannot be done."

The old woman looked at the stave and then at Bran. "Why not, Master Bran?"

"Do not call me that!" he said roughly. "I am a nobleman, remember, a prince—not a common tradesman."

"You ceased being a prince when you abandoned your people," she said. Though her voice was quiet, her manner was unforgiving, and Bran felt the now-familiar rush of shame. It was not the first time she had berated him for his plan to flee Elfael. Laying a hand on the stave, she said, "Tell me why the wood cannot be worked."

"It is too green," replied Bran, petulance making his voice low.

"Explain, please."

"If you knew anything about making a longbow, you would know that you cannot simply cut a branch and begin shaping. You must first season the wood, cure it—a year at least. Otherwise it will warp as it dries and will never bend properly." He made to hand the length of ash back to her. "You can make a druid staff out of it, perhaps, but not a bow."

"And what leads you to think I have not already seasoned this wood?"

"Have you?" Bran asked. "A year?"

"Not a year, no," she said.

"Well then—" He shrugged and again tried to give the stave back to her.

"Two years," she told him. "I kept it wrapped in leather so it would not dry too quickly."

"Two years," he repeated suspiciously. "I don't believe you." In truth, he *did* believe her; he simply did not care to consider the more far-reaching implications of her remark.

Angharad had turned away and was moving toward the cave. "Sit," she said. "I will bring you the tools."

Bran settled himself on the rock once more. He had made a bow only twice as a lad, but he had seen them made countless times. His father's warriors regularly filled their winter days, as well as the hall itself, with sawdust and wood shavings as they sat around the fire, regaling each other with their impossible boasts and lies. For battle, the longbow was the prime weapon of choice for all True Sons of Prydein—and a fair few of her fearless daughters, too. In skilled hands, a stout warbow was a formidable weapon—light, durable, easily made with materials ready to hand, and above all, devastatingly deadly.

Bran, like most every child who had grown up in the secluded valleys and rough hills of the west, had been taught the bowman's art from the time he could stand on his own two unsteady legs. As a boy he had often gone to sleep with raw, throbbing fingers and aching arms. At seven years, he had earned a permanent scar on his left wrist from the lash of the bowstring all summer. At eight, he had brought down a young boar all by himself—a gift for his dying mother. Although hunting had ceased to interest him after that, he had continued to practise with the warband, and by his thirteenth year, he could pull a man's bow and put a fowler's arrow through the eye of a crow perched on a standing stone three hundred paces away.

This was not a skill unique to himself; every warrior he knew could do the same—as well as any farmer worth his salt. The ability to direct an arrow with accuracy over implausible lengths was a common, but no less highly prized, facility, and one which made best use of another of the weapon's considerable qualities: it allowed a combatant to strike from a distance, silently if need be—a virtue unequalled by any other weapon Bran knew.

When Angharad shortly reappeared with an adz, a pumice stone, and several well-honed chisels and knives from her trove of unknown treasures somewhere deep in the cave, Bran set to work, tentatively at first, but with growing confidence as his hands remembered their craft. Soon he was toiling away happily, sitting on his rock in the warm sun, stripping the bark from the admittedly well-seasoned length of ash. As he worked, he listened to the birds in the greening trees round about and attuned his ears to the forest sounds. This became, as she had intended, his principal occupation. As the days passed, Angharad noticed that when he was working on the bow, Bran fretted less and was more content. On days when it rained, he sat in the cave entrance beneath the overhanging ledge and laboured there.

Slowly, the slender length of ash took form beneath his hands. He worked with deliberate care; there was no hurry, after all. He knew he was not yet fit enough for the journey across the mountains. It would be high summer when that day came, and by then the bow would be finished and ready to use.

Bran still planned on leaving. As soon as his wrinkled physician pronounced him hale and whole once more, he would wish her farewell and leave the forest and Elfael without looking back.

But one day, as he thought about his plan, something awakened inside him—a vague uneasiness, almost like a grinding in the pit of his stomach. It was a mildly disagreeable feeling, and he quickly turned his attention to something else. From that moment, however, the discomfort returned whenever his thoughts happened to touch on the point of his leaving. At first, he considered it a form of discontent— a daylight manifestation of the same restlessness he often experienced at night. Even so, the subtle anxiety was growing, and all too soon

Bran began experiencing a bitter, unpleasant taste in his mouth whenever he thought about any aspect of his future whatsoever.

Unwilling to confront the pain fermenting inside him, Bran pushed down the disagreeable feeling and ignored it. But there, deep in the inner core of his hidden heart, it festered and grew as he worked the wood—shaping it, smoothing it, slowly creating just the right curve along the belly and back so that it would bend uniformly along its length—and he forgot the blight that was spreading in his soul.

When at last he had the stave shaped just right, he brought it to Angharad, passing it to her with an absurdly inordinate sense of achievement. He could not stop grinning as she held the smooth ash-wood bow in her rough, square hands and tested the bend with her weight. "Well?" he asked, unable to contain himself any longer. "What do you think?"

"I think I was right to call you Master Bran," she replied. "You have a craftsman's aptitude for the tools."

"It *is* good, is it not?" he said, reaching out to stroke the smooth, tight-grained wood. "The stave was excellent."

"You worked it well," she told him, handing it back. "I cannot say when I've seen a finer bow."

"Ash is good," he allowed, "although yew is better." Glancing up, he caught Angharad's eye and added, "I don't blame you, mind. It is difficult to find a serviceable limb."

"Ah, well, just you finish this," she told him. "I want to see if you can hunt with it."

He caught the challenge in her words. "You think I could not bring down a stag? Or a boar even?"

"Maybe a small one," she allowed, teasing, "if it was also slow of foot and weakhearted."

"I do not hunt anymore," he told her. "But if I did, I'd bring back the biggest, swiftest, strongest stag you've ever seen—a genuine Lord of the Forest."

She regarded him with a curious, bird-bright eye. His use of the term tantalised. Could it be that her pupil was ready for the next step on his journey? "Finish the bow first, Master Bran," she said, "and then we'll see what we shall see."

Completing his work on the bow took longer than he expected. Obtaining the rawhide for the grip, slicing it thin, and braiding it so that it could be wound tightly around the centre of the stave was the work of several days. Making the bowstring proved an even more imposing task. Bran had never made a bowstring; those were always provided by one of the women of the caer.

Faced with this chore, he was not entirely certain which material was best, or where it might be found. He consulted Angharad. "They used hemp," he told her. "Also flax—I think. But I don't know where they got it."

"Hemp is easy enough to find. Given a little time, I could get flax, too. Which would you prefer?"

"Either," he said. "Whichever can be got soonest."

"You shall have it."

Two days later, Angharad presented him with a bound bundle of dried hemp stalks. "You will have to strip it and beat it to get the threads," she told him. "I can show you."

The next sunny day found them outside the cave, cutting off the leaves and small stems and then beating the long, fibrous stalks on a flat stone. Once the stalks began to break down, it was easy work to pull the loosened threads away. The long outer fibres were tough and hairy, but the inner ones were finer, and these Bran carefully collected into a tidy, coiled heap.

"Now they must be twisted," Bran told her. Selecting a few of the

239

STEPHEN R.
LAWHEAD

better strands, he tied them to a willow branch; while Angharad slowly, steadily turned the branch, Bran patiently wound the long threadlike fibres over one another, carefully adding in new ones as he went along to increase the length. The process was repeated until he had six long strings of twisted strands, which were then tightly and painstakingly braided together to make two bowstrings of three braided strands each.

Determining the length of the bowstring took some time, too. Bran had to string and unstring the bow a dozen times before he was happy with the bend and suppleness of the draw. When he finished, he proclaimed himself satisfied with the result and declared, "Now for the arrows."

Making arrows was not a chore he had ever undertaken either; but, like the other tasks, he had watched it done often enough to know the process. "Willow is easiest to work, but difficult to find in suitable lengths," he mused aloud before the fire while Angharad cooked their supper. "Beech and birch, also. Ash, alder, and hornbeam are sturdier. Oak is the most difficult to shape, but it is strongest of all. It is also heavier, so the arrows do not fly as far—good for hunting bigger animals, though," he added, "and for battle, of course."

"Each of those trees abounds in the forest," Angharad offered. "Tomorrow, we can go out together and find some branches."

"Very well," agreed Bran. It would be the first time he had been allowed to walk into the forest since the winter ramble that had sent him back to his sickbed. Even so, he did not want to appear too excited lest Angharad change her mind. "If you think I'm ready."

"Bran," she said gently, "you are not a prisoner here."

He nodded, adopting a diffident air, but inwardly he was very much a prisoner yearning for release.

The next day they walked a short distance into the wood to select suitable branches from various trees. "The arrow tips will be difficult to make," Bran offered, swinging the axe as they walked along. "If I could get back into the caer, I'd soon have all the arrowheads I needed—arrows, too."

"What about flint?"

The idea of a stone-tipped arrow was so old-fashioned, it made Bran chuckle. "I doubt if anyone alive in all of Britain still knows how to make an arrowhead of flint."

Now it was Angharad's turn to laugh. "There is one in the Island of the Mighty who remembers."

Bran stopped walking and stared after her. "Who *are* you, Angharad?"

When she did not answer, he hurried to catch her. "I mean it—who are you that you know all these things?"

"And I have already told you."

"Tell me again."

Angharad stopped, turned, and faced him. "Will you listen this time? And listening, will you believe?"

"I will try."

She shook her head. "No. You are not ready." She resumed her pace.

"Angharad!" bawled Bran in frustration. "Please! Anyway, what difference does it make whether I believe or not? Just tell me."

Angharad stopped again. "It makes a world of difference," she declared solemnly. "It matters so much that sometimes it takes my breath away. Greater than life or death; greater than this world and the world to come. There is no end to the amount of difference it can make."

She moved on, but Bran did not follow. "You speak in riddles! How am I to understand you when you talk like that?"

Angharad turned on him with a sudden fury that forced him back a step. "What did you do with your life, Master Bran?" she demanded accusingly. "More to the point, what will you do with your life now that you have it back?"

Bran started to protest but shut his mouth even as he drew breath to speak. It was futile to challenge her—better to keep quiet.

"Answer me that," she told him, "and then I will answer you."

Bran glared back at her. What reply could he make that she would not revile?

"Nothing to say?" inquired Angharad with sweet insincerity. "I thought not. Think long before you speak again."

Her words stung him like a slap, and they did more. They ripped open the hole into which he had pushed all the festering blackness in his soul—soon to come welling up with a vengeance.

Although spies had long ago confirmed his suspicions—three castles were being erected on the borders of Elfael—Baron Neufmarché wished to see the de Braose bastion-building venture for himself.

Now that warmer weather had come to the valleys, he thought it time to pay another visit to the count. Along the way, he could visit his British minions and see how the spring planting progressed. As overlord of a subject people, it never hurt to make an unannounced appearance now and then to better judge the mood and temper of those beneath his rule. Lord Cadwgan had given him little trouble during his reign, and for that the baron was shrewd enough to be grateful. But with the long-awaited expansion into Welsh territory begun, Neufmarché thought it would be best to see how things stood on the ground, reward loyalty and industry, and snuff out any sparks of discontent before they could catch fire.

With this in mind, the baron struck out one bright morning with a small entourage for Caer Rhodl, the stronghold of King Cadwgan.

Upon his arrival two days later, the Welsh king received him with polite, if subdued, courtesy. "My Lord Neufmarché," said Cadwgan, emerging from his hall. "I wonder that you did not send your steward ahead so I would know to expect you. Then you would have received a proper welcome."

"My thanks all the same, but I did not know I was coming here myself," lied the baron with a genial smile. "I was already on the road when I decided to make this stop. I expect no ceremony. Here, ride with me—I have it in mind to inspect the fields."

The king called for horses to be saddled so that he and his steward and a few warriors of his retinue could accompany the baron. Together, they rode out from the stronghold into the countryside. "Winter was hard hereabouts?" asked the baron amiably.

"Hard enough," replied the king. "Harder for those in the next cantref." He indicated Elfael to the north with a slight lift of his chin. "Aye," he continued, as if just considering it for the first time. "They lost the harvest, and that was bad enough, but now they have been prevented from planting."

"Truly?" wondered Baron Neufmarché with genuine curiosity. Any word of others' difficulties interested him. "Why is that, do you know?"

"It's that new count—that kinsman of de Braose! First, he runs them all off, and now that he has them back, he's herded them together and he's making them work on his accursed fortresses."

"He is building fortresses?" wondered the baron. He gazed at the king with an innocent expression.

"Aye, three of them," replied the king grimly. "That's what I hear," he concluded, "and I have no reason to believe otherwise."

"Very ambitious," granted Baron Neufmarché. "I would not think he needed such fortification to govern little Elfael."

"Nay, it's his uncle, the baron, who has eyes on the cantrefs to the north and west. He means to take as much as he can grab."

"So it would seem."

"Aye, and I know it. Greedy bastards," swore Cadwgan, "they cannot even rule the commot they've been given! What do they want with more land?" The king spat again and shook his head slowly—as if contemplating a ruin that could easily be avoided. "Mark my words, nothing good will come of this."

The baron sighed. "I fear you could be right."

Upon reaching the holding, the baron made a thorough inspection, asked many questions of the farmers—about the last harvest, the new planting, the adequacy of the spring rains—and walked out into one of the fields, where he bent down and rubbed dirt between his hands, as if testing the worth of the soil. At the end of his survey, he professed himself well pleased with the farmers' efforts and called to his seneschal to send the head of the settlement two casks of good dark ale as a token of his thanks and good wishes.

The baron and the king rode on to the next holding, where the herdsmen were grazing cattle. The baron asked how the cattle had fared during the winter and how it was going with the spring calving and whether they would see a good increase this year. He received a favourable reply in each case, and after concluding his enquiry, ordered two more casks of ale to be sent to the settlement.

Then, turning their horses, the party rode back to the caer, where King Cadwgan commanded his cooks to prepare a festive supper in honour of his overlord's unexpected, though not altogether unwelcome, visit. The baron had made Cadwgan feel like a knowledgeable confidant, a trusted advisor, and for that he ordered the best of what he had to offer: beeswax candles for the board, fine woven cloths to dress the table, silver plates on which to eat and silver cups for the wine he had

245

been saving for such an occasion, and choice slices from the haunch of
venison aging in the larder. Fresh straw was to be spread on the floor
and a fragrant fire of apple wood and heather lit in the hearth.

"You will put your feet beneath my board tonight," Cadwgan told
him, "and allow me to show you true Cymry hospitality."

"I would like nothing better," replied the baron, pleased with how
well his scheme was coming together.

The king ordered his steward to conduct the baron to a chamber
for his use and to prepare water for washing. "When you are ready,
come join me in the hall. I will have a jar waiting."

The baron dutifully obeyed his host and, after refreshing himself
in his room, returned a little while later to the hall, where he was
delighted to see that two beautiful young women had joined them.
They were standing on each side of the hearth, where a fire brightly
burned.

"Baron Neufmarché," announced the king, "I present my daughter, Mérian, and her cousin Essylt."

Mérian, slightly older of the two, tall and willowy with long, dark
hair, was wearing a simple gown of pale green linen; her cousin Essylt,
fair with a pleasant, plump face and a delicate mouth, was dressed in
a gown the colour of fresh butter. Both possessed an air of demure yet
guileless confidence.

Mérian regarded him with frank appraisal as she extended a small
wooden trencher with pieces of bread torn from a loaf. "Be welcome
here, Baron Neufmarché," she said in a voice so soft and low that it
sent a pang of longing through the baron's tough heart.

"May you want for nothing while you are here," said Essylt, stepping forward with a small dish of salt in her cupped hands.

"I am charmed, my ladies," professed the baron, speaking the complete truth for the first time that day. Taking a piece of bread from the

offered board, he dipped it in the salt and ate it. "Peace to this house tonight," he said, offering his hand.

"Your servant, Baron Neufmarché," replied the king's daughter. She accepted the baron's hand, performed a graceful curtsy, and bowed her head; her long, dark curls parted, slightly exposing the nape of a slender neck and the curve of a shapely shoulder.

"As I am yours," said the baron, delighted by the splendid young woman. Although he also accepted the courtesy of the young woman called Essylt, his eyes never left the dark-haired beauty before him.

"Father tells me you approve of the fieldwork," said Mérian, not waiting to be addressed.

"Indeed," replied the baron. "It is good work and well done."

"And the herds—they were also to your liking?"

"I have rarely seen better," answered the baron politely. "Your people know their cattle—as I have always said. I am pleased."

"Well then, I expect we shall see an increase in our taxes again this year," she said with a crisp smile.

"Here now!" objected her father quickly; he gave the forthright young woman a glance of fierce disapproval. To the baron, he said, "Please forgive my daughter. She is of a contrary mind and sometimes forgets her place."

"That is true," acknowledged Mérian lightly. "I do humbly beg your pardon." So saying, she offered another little bow, which, although performed with simple grace, was in no way deferential.

"Pardon granted," replied the baron lightly. Despite the glancing sting of her remark—which would certainly have earned a less winsome subject stiff punishment—the baron found it easy to forgive her and was glad for the opportunity to do so. Her direct, uncomplicated manner was refreshing; it put him in mind of a spirited young horse that has yet to be trained to the halter. He would, he considered, give much to be the man to bring her to saddle.

The two young women were sent to fetch the jars the king had ordered. They returned with overflowing cups, which they offered the king and his noble guest. The two made to retreat then, but the baron said, "Please, stay. Join us." To the king he said, "I find the company of ladies often a pleasant thing when taking my evening meal."

Queer as the request might be, Cadwgan was not about to offend his guest—there were matters he wished to negotiate before the night was finished—so he lauded the idea. "Of course! Of course, I was just about to suggest the same thing myself. Mérian, Essylt, you will stay. Mérian, fetch your mother and tell her we will all dine together tonight."

Mérian dipped her head in acquiescence to this odd suggestion, so neither her father nor his guest saw her large, dark eyes roll in derision.

The king then offered a health to the baron, ". . . and to King William, may God bless his soul!"

"Hear! Hear!" seconded the baron with far more zeal than he felt. In truth, he still nursed a grudge against the king for the humiliation suffered at Red William's hands when the baron had last been summoned to court.

Still, he drank heartily and asked after his subject lord's interest in hunting. The conversation grew warm and lively then. Queen Anora joined them after a while to say that dinner was ready and they all could be seated. The dining party moved to the board then, and Baron Bernard contrived to have Mérian sit beside him.

The party dined well, if not extravagantly, and the baron enjoyed himself far more than at any time in recent memory. The nearness of the enchanting creature next to him proved as stimulating as any cup of wine, and he availed himself of every opportunity to engage the young lady's attention by passing along news of royal affairs in

Lundein which, he imagined, would be of interest to her, as they were to every young lady he had ever known.

The meal ended all too soon. The baron, unable to think how to prolong it, bade his host a good night and retired to his chamber, where he lay awake a long time thinking about King Cadwgan's lovely dark-haired daughter.

Bran and Angharad spent the next days collecting branches suitable for arrows. The best of these were bundled and carried back to the clearing outside the cave, where Bran set to work, trimming off leaves and twigs, stripping bark, arranging the raw lengths in the sun, and turning them as they dried. He worked alone, with calm, purposeful intent. Outwardly placid, his heart was nevertheless in turmoil—unquiet, gnawing inwardly on itself with ravenous discontent—as if, starving, he hungered for something he could not name.

Meanwhile, Angharad dug chunks of flint from a nearby riverbank to make points for Bran's arrows. With a tidy heap of rocks before her, she settled herself cross-legged on the ground, a folded square of sheepskin on one knee. Then, taking up a piece of flint, she placed it on the pad of sheepskin and, using a small copper hammer, began tapping. From time to time, she would use an egg-shaped piece of sandstone to smooth the piece she was working on. Occasionally, she chose the front tooth of a cow to apply pressure along the worked edge to flake off a tiny bit of flint. With practised precision, Angharad shaped each small point.

Working in companionable silence, she and Bran bent to their respective tasks with only the sound of her slow, rhythmic *tap, tap, tap* between them. When Bran had fifteen shafts finished, and Angharad an equal number of flint tips, they began gathering feathers for the flights—goose and red kite and swan. The goose and swan they picked up at disused nests beside the river, which lay a half day's walk to the northwest of the cave; the red kite feathers they got from another nest, this one in a stately elm at the edge of a forest meadow.

Together they cut the feathers, stripped one side, trimmed them to length, and then bound the prepared flight to the end of the shaft with narrow strips of leather. Bran carefully notched the other end and slotted in one of Angharad's flint tips, which was securely bound with wet rawhide. The resulting arrow looked to Bran like something from an era beyond recall, but it was perfectly balanced and, he expected, would fly well enough.

With a few serviceable arrows to tuck into his belt, the next thing was to try the longbow. His first attempt to draw the bowstring sent crippling pain through his chest and shoulder. It was such a surprise that he let out a yelp and almost dropped the weapon. The arrow spun from the string and slid through the grass before striking the root of a tree.

He tried two more times before giving up, dejected and sore. "Why downcast, Master Bran?" Angharad chided when she found him slumped against the rock outside the cave a little later. "Did you expect to attain your former strength in one day?"

On his next attempt, he lengthened the string to make the bow easier to draw and tried again. This improved the outcome somewhat, but not by much—the arrow flew in an absurdly rounded arc to fall a few dozen paces away. A child might produce a similar effect, but it was progress. After a few more equally dismal attempts, his shoulder began to ache, so he put the bow away and went in search of more branches to make arrows.

This was to become his habit by day: working with the bow, slowly increasing his strength, struggling to reclaim his shattered skills until the ache in his shoulder or chest became too great to ignore, and then putting aside the bow to go off in search of arrow wood or dig in the cliff side for good flints. If he appeared to toil away happily enough by day, each evening he felt the change come over him with the drawing in of the night. Always, he sat at the fireside, staring at the flames: moody, peevish, petulant.

Angharad still sang to him, but Bran could no longer concentrate on the songs. Ever and again, he drifted in his mind to a dark and lonely place, invariably becoming lost in it and overwhelmed by sudden, palpable feelings of hopelessness and despair.

Finally, one night, as Angharad sang the tale of Rhonabwy's Dream, he raised his head and shouted, "Do you have to play that stupid harp all the time? And the singing! Why can't you just shut up for once?"

The old woman paused, the melody still ringing from the harp strings. She held her head to one side and regarded him intently, as if she had just heard the echo of a word long expected.

"And stop staring at me!" Bran snapped. "Just leave me to myself!"

"So," she said quietly, laying aside the harp, "we come to it at last."

Bran turned his face away. Her habit of simply accepting his outbursts was maddening.

Angharad gathered her ragged skirts and stood. She shuffled around the fire ring to stand before him. "The time has come, Master Bran. Follow me."

"No," he said stubbornly. "And stop calling me that!"

"I will call you by a better name when you have earned one."

"You ugly old crone!" he growled savagely. "You are nothing. I cannot stand another moment of your insane mumbling. I am leaving." He glared at her, fists clenched on his knees. "Tomorrow, I will go, and nothing you say can stop me."

"If that is your choice, I will not prevent you," she told him. Moving to the mouth of the cave, she paused and beckoned him. "Tonight, however, you will come with me. I have something to show you."

With that, she turned on her heel and went out into the night. She waited for a moment, and when he did not come, she called him again.

Reluctantly, and with much bitter complaining, Bran emerged from the cave. It was dark, and the pathways she walked could not be seen; yet somehow her feet unerringly found the way. Bran soon stopped grumbling and concentrated instead on keeping up with the old woman and avoiding the branches that reached out and slapped at him.

They walked for some time, and as Bran began to tire, much of the anger dissipated. "Where are we going?" he asked at last, sweating now, slightly winded. "Is it much farther? If it is, I need to rest."

"No," she told him, "just over the top of the next rise."

Sighing heavily, he moved on—trudging along, head down, hands loose, feet dragging. They mounted the long, rising incline of a ridge, at the crest of which the trees thinned around them. Once over the ridgetop, the ground sloped away sharply, and Bran found himself standing at the edge of the forest, looking down into a shallow, bowl-shaped valley barely discernible in the light of a pale half-moon just clearing the treetops to the southeast.

"So this is what you dragged me out here to see?" he asked. His eyes caught a gleam of light below, and then another.

As he looked down into the valley, he began seeing more lights—

tiny flecks, glints and shards of light, moving slowly over the surface of the ground in a weird, slow dance.

"What—," he began, stopped, and gaped again. "In the name of Saint Dafyd, what is that?"

"It is happening all over Elfael," Angharad said, indicating the night-dark land with a wide sweep of her arm. "It is the May Dance."

"The May Dance," repeated Bran without understanding.

"Your people are ploughing their fields."

"Ploughing! By night?" he said, turning toward her. "Why? And why so late in the season?"

"They are made to labour for Count de Braose all day," the old woman explained. "Night is the only time they have to put in the crops. So they toil by lantern light, planting the fields."

"But it is too late," Bran pointed out. "The crops will never mature to harvest before winter."

"That is likely," Angharad agreed, "but starvation is assured if they do nothing." She turned once more to the slowly swinging lights glimmering across the valley. "They dance with death," she said. "What else can they do?"

Bran stiffened at the words. He gazed at the moving lights and felt his anger rising.

"Why did you show me this?" he shouted suddenly.

"So that you will know."

"And what am I supposed to do about it?" he said. "Tell me that. What am I supposed to do?"

"Help them," Angharad said softly.

"No! Not me! I can do nothing!" he insisted. Turning away abruptly, he strode off, retreating back into the forest. "I am leaving tomorrow," he shouted over his shoulder, "and nothing you say can stop me!"

Angharad watched him for a moment; then, turning her face to the

255

sky, she murmured, "You see? You see how it is with him? Everything is a fight. A wild boar would be less headstrong—*and* more charming." She paused, as if listening to an unheard voice, then sighed. "Your servant obeys."

Retracing her steps, she made her way back to the cave.

Determined to make good his vow, Bran rose at dawn to bid Angharad farewell. A night's sleep had softened his mood, if not his resolve. He regretted shouting at her and sought to make amends. He said kindly, "I will be forever grateful to you for saving my life. I will never forget you."

"Nor I you, Master Bran."

He smiled at her use of the disdained name. Unable to put words to the volatile mix of emotions churning in his heart, he stood silent for a moment lest he say something he would regret, then turned to collect his bow and arrows. "Well, I will go now."

"If that is your choice."

Glancing around quickly, he said, "You know that I do not wish to leave this way."

"Oh, I believe you do," the old woman replied. "This *is* your way, and you are ever used to having your way in all things. Why should this leaving be different from any other?"

Her reproach annoyed him afresh, but he had promised himself that nothing she could say would change his mind or alter his course. "Why do you torment me this way?" he said in a tone heavy with resignation. "What do you want from me?"

"What do *I* want?" she threw back at him. "Only this—I want you to be the man you were born to be."

"How do you know what I was born to be?"

"You were born to be a king," Angharad replied simply. "You were born to lead your people. Beyond that, God only knows."

HOOD

"King!" raged Bran, lashing out with a fury that surprised even himself. "My father was the king. He was a heavy-handed tyrant who thought only of himself and how the world had wronged him. You want me to be like him?"

"Not like him," Angharad countered. "Better." She held the young man with her uncompromising gaze. "Hear me now, Bran ap Brychan. You are not your father. You could be twice the king he was—and ten times the man—if you so desired."

"And you hear *me*, Angharad!" said Bran, his voice rising with his temper. "I do not want to be king!"

The old woman's eyes searched his face. "What did he do to you, Master Bran, that you fear it so?"

"I am not afraid," he insisted. "It is just . . ." His voice faltered. How could he express a lifetime of hurt and humiliation, of need and neglect, in mere words?

"I don't want it. I never wanted it," he said, turning away from the old woman at last. "Find someone else."

"There is no one else, Master Bran," she said. "Without a king, the people will die. Elfael will die."

Bran uttered an inarticulate growl of frustration and, turning away again, strode quickly to the cave entrance. "Farewell, Angharad. I will remember you."

"Go your way, Master Bran. But if you think about me at all, remember only this: a raven you are, and a raven you will remain— until you fulfil your vow."

Bran stopped in the cave entrance and gave a bitter laugh. "I made no vow, Angharad," he said, her name a slur in his mouth. "Just you remember *that*."

With swift strides, his long legs carried him from the cave. Angry and determined to put as much distance as possible between himself

257

and Angharad's unreasonable expectations, he walked far into the forest before it occurred to him that he had not the slightest idea where he was going. As many times as he had been out gathering materials to make arrows, he had paid little heed to directions and pathways; and last night when Angharad led him to the valley overlook—from which he would certainly be able to find his way—it had been dark and the pathway unseen.

Already tired, he stopped walking and sat down on a fallen log to rest and think the matter through. The simplest solution, of course, would be to return to the cave and demand that Angharad lead him to the valley. That smacked too much of humiliation, and he rejected the idea outright. He would exhaust all other possibilities before confronting that disagreeable old hag again.

After trying to work out a direction from the sun, he rose from his perch and set off once more. This time, he walked more slowly and tried to spy out any familiar features that might guide him. Although he found no end of pathways—runs used by deer and wild pigs, and even an old charcoal burners' trackway—the trails were so intertwined and tangled, crossing over one another, circling back, and crossing again, that he only succeeded in disorienting himself further.

He moved with more deliberate care now, reading direction from the moss on the trees. Certainly, he thought, if he kept moving north, he would eventually reach the high, open heathlands, and beyond them the mountains. All he had to do was get clear of the trees.

Morning lengthened, and the day warmed beneath a fulsome sun, and Bran began to grow hungry. How had he forgotten to bring provisions? Despite months of thinking of nothing but escape, now that the day had come, he was appalled to discover how little he had actually prepared. He had no food, no water, no money, nor even any idea which way to go. He looked at the bow in his hand and marvelled that he had remembered to bring that.

Well, he could get something to eat at the first settlement—just as soon as he found a way out of this accursed forest. Shouldering his bow, he trudged on with a growing hunger in his belly to match his unquiet heart.

CHAPTER 26

It was bad enough having to stand by and watch as his beloved monastery was destroyed piecemeal, but the tacit enslavement of his people was more than he could bear. Elfael's men and women toiled like beasts of burden—digging the defensive ditches; building the earthen ramparts; carrying stone and timber to raise the baron's strongholds; and pulling down buildings, clearing rubble, and salvaging materials for the town. From dawn's first light to evening's last gleam, they drudged for the baron. Then, often as not, they went home to work their own fields by the light of the moon, when it shone, and by torchlight and bonfires when it did not.

The bishop pitied them. What choice did they have? To refuse to work meant the loss of another holding—a prospect no one could abide. So they worked and muttered strong curses under their breath for the Ffreinc outlanders.

This was not the way it was supposed to be. He and the count had an understanding, an agreement. The bishop had lived up to his part of the bargain: he had delivered the treasure of Elfael's king to Count de Braose in good faith, had offered no resistance and counselled the same amongst his flock; he had accepted Count de Braose as the new authority in Elfael and had trusted him to do right by the Cymry under his rule. But the Ffreinc did not deal fairly. They took what they wanted and behaved as they pleased, never giving a thought to the Cymry now languishing under their reign.

It could not continue. The scant rations left from the previous winter were dwindling rapidly, and in some places in the valley the Cymry were beginning to run out of food. Something must be done, and with both lord and heir dead, it fell to Bishop Asaph to do it.

Joining Brother Clyro in the chapel, he announced, "I have decided to speak to Count de Braose. I want you to remain in the chapel and uphold me before the Throne of Mercy."

"How would you have me pray, father?" asked old Brother Clyro. "That God would remove this oppression, or that God would turn the hearts of the oppressors toward peace?" A pedantic, unimaginative man, a scribe and a scholar, he could be counted on to carry out the bishop's instructions to the letter but, as ever, insisted on knowing the precise nature of those instructions.

"Pray for a softening of Count de Braose's heart," the bishop sighed, humouring him, "a turning from his ways, and for food to sustain the people through this ordeal."

"It will be done," replied Clyro with a nod.

Leaving the elderly cleric in the chapel, Bishop Asaph walked through the building site that had once been the monastery yard and struck off along the dirt road to the caer. The day had grown warm, and he was thirsty by the time he reached the fortress. The place was all but deserted, save for a crippled stable hand who, in the absence of the others who were aiding construction of the town, had been pressed into duty as a porter.

"Bishop Asaph to see Count de Braose," the cleric declared, presenting himself before the servant, who smelled of the stable. "It is a matter of highest importance. I demand audience with the count at once."

The porter's laugh as he limped across the yard was all the reply he received, and in the end, the bishop was made to wait in the yard until the count consented to receive him.

While he was waiting, however, another visitor arrived: a Norman lord, by the look of him. Astride a fine big horse and splendidly arrayed, with an escort of two retainers and three soldiers, he was, Asaph decided, most likely a count, or perhaps even a baron. Clearly a man of some importance.

Thus, it was with some surprise that the bishop heard himself hailed by the noble visitor. "You there!" the stranger called in a tone well suited to command. "Come here. I would speak to you."

The bishop dutifully obeyed. "Your servant, my lord."

"You are Welsh, yes?" asked the stranger in good, if slightly accented, Latin.

"I am of the Cymry, my lord," answered the bishop. "That is correct."

"And a priest?"

"I am Father Asaph, bishop of what is left of the monastery of Llanelli," replied the churchman. "Whom do I have the pleasure of addressing?"

"I am Bernard de Neufmarché, Baron of Gloucester and Hereford." Indicating that the bishop was to follow, the baron led the churchman aside, out of the hearing of his own men and the count's overcurious porter. "Tell me, how do the people hereabouts fare?"

The question was so unexpected that the bishop could only ask, "Which people?"

"*Your* people—the Welsh. How do they fare under the count's rule?"

"Poorly," answered the bishop without hesitation. "They fare poorly indeed, sire. They are forced to work for the count, building his strongholds, yet he does not feed them—nor do they have any food of their own." Asaph went on to explain about the meagre harvest of the previous year and how the count's ambitious building scheme had interfered with this year's planting. He concluded, saying, "That is why I have come—to make entreaty with the count to release grain from his stores to feed the people."

Baron Neufmarché listened to all the churchman had to say, nodding solemnly to himself. "Word of this has reached me," he confided. "With your permission, bishop, I will see what I can do."

"Truly?" wondered Asaph, greatly impressed. "But why should you do anything for us?"

Neufmarché merely leaned close and, in a lowered voice, said, "Because it pleases me. But see that it remains a secret between ourselves, understood?"

The bishop considered the baron's words for a moment, then agreed. "As you say," he replied. "I praise God for your kind intervention."

The baron rejoined his men, and they were conducted directly to the hall, leaving a bewildered bishop to stand in the yard. "Father of Light," he prayed, "something has just happened which passes all understanding—at least, *I* cannot make any sense of it. Yet, Strong Redeemer, I pray that the meaning will be for good, and not ill, for all of us who wait on the Lord's deliverance in this time of testing."

The bishop remained in a corner of the yard, lifting his voice in prayer. He was still praying when, a little later, Count Falkes's seneschal came looking for them. "My lord will deal with you now," Orval told him and started away again. "At once."

The bishop followed the seneschal to the door of the hall and was conducted inside, where the count was seated in his customary chair beside the hearth. Baron Neufmarché was also in attendance, standing a little to one side; the visiting baron appeared to pay no heed to the bishop as he continued talking quietly to his own men. "Pax vobiscum," said the bishop, raising his hand palm outward and making the sign of the cross.

"Yes? Yes?" said the count, as if irritated by his visitor's display of piety. "Get on with it. As you can see, I am busy. I have important guests."

"I will be brief," replied the bishop. "Simply put, the people are hungry. You cannot make them work all day without food, and if they have none of their own, then you must feed them."

Count de Braose stared at the cleric for a moment, his lip curling with displeasure. "My dear confused bishop," began the count after a moment, "your complaint is unfounded."

"I think not," objected the bishop. "It is the very truth."

The count lifted a long, languid hand and raised a finger. "In the first place," he said, "if your people have no food, it is their own fault—merely the natural consequence of abandoning their land and leaving good crops in the field. This was entirely without cause, as we have already established." Another finger joined the first. "Secondly, it is not—"

"I do beg your pardon," interrupted Neufmarché, stepping forward. Turning away from his knights, he addressed the count directly. "I could not help overhearing—but am I to understand that you make your subjects work for you, yet refuse to feed them?"

"It is a fact," declared the bishop. "He has enslaved the entire valley and provides nothing for the people."

"Enslaved," snorted the count. "You dare use that word? It is an unfortunate circumstance," corrected the count. Turning his attention to the baron, he said, "Do *you* undertake to feed all your subjects, baron?"

"No," replied the baron, "not all of them—only those who render me good service. The ox or horse that pulls plough or wagon is fed—it is the same for any man who labours on my behalf."

The count twitched with growing discomfort. "Well and good," he allowed, "but this is a predicament of their own making. A hard lesson it may be, but they will learn it all the same. I rule here now," the count said, facing the bishop once more, "and the sooner they accept this, the better."

"And who will you rule," asked the baron, "when your subjects have starved to death?" Advancing a few paces toward the bishop, the baron made a small bow of deference and said, "I am Baron Neufmarché, and I stand ready to supply grain, meat, and other provisions if it would aid you in this present difficulty."

"I thank you, and my people thank you, sire," said the bishop, careful not to let on that they had already spoken of the matter in private. "Our prayers for deliverance are answered."

"What?" objected the count. "Am I to have nothing to say about this?"

"Of course," allowed Neufmarché, "I would never intrude in the affairs of another lord in his realm. I merely make the offer as a gesture of goodwill. If you prefer to give them the grain out of your own stores, that is entirely your decision."

The bishop, hands folded as if in prayer, turned hopeful eyes to the count, awaiting his answer.

Falkes hesitated, tapping the arms of his chair with his long fingers. "It is true that the storehouses are nearly empty and that we shall have to bring in supplies very soon. Therefore," he said, making up his mind, "I accept your offer of goodwill, Neufmarché."

"Splendid!" cried the baron. "Let us consider this the first step along the road toward a peaceful and harmonious alliance. We are neighbours, after all, and we should look toward the satisfaction of our mutual interests. I will dispatch the supplies immediately upon my return to Hereford."

Seeing in Baron Neufmarché a resourceful new ally, and emboldened by his presence, the bishop plucked up his courage and announced, "There is yet one more matter I would bring before you, lord count."

Knowing himself the subject of the baron's scrutiny, Falkes sighed, "Go on, then."

"The two farms you burned—special provision must be made for the farmers and their families. They have lost everything. I want tools and supplies to be replaced at once so they can rebuild."

Hearing this, the baron swung toward the count, "You burned their farms?"

The count, aghast to find himself trapped between two accusers, rose abruptly from his chair as if it had suddenly become too hot. "I burned some barns, nothing more," blustered the count nervously. "The threat was merely an enticement to obedience. It would not have happened if they had complied with my request."

"Those families had little enough already, and that little has been taken from them. I demand redress," said Asaph, far more forcefully than he would have dared had it not been for the baron looking on.

"Oh, very well," said Count Falkes, a sickly smile spreading on his lips. He turned to the baron, who returned his gaze with stern disapproval. "They will be given tools and other supplies so they can rebuild."

Regarding the bishop, the baron said, "Are you satisfied?"

"When the tools and supplies have been delivered to the church," said the bishop, "I will consider the matter concluded."

"Well then," said Baron Neufmarché. He turned to an extremely agitated Count Falkes and offered a sop. "I think we can put this

unfortunate incident behind us and welcome a more salutary future."
He spoke as a parent coaxing a wayward child back into the warm
bosom of family fellowship.

The count was not slow to snatch a chance to regain a measure of
dignity. "Nothing would please me more, baron." To the bishop, he
said, "If there is nothing else, you are dismissed. Neufmarché and I
have business to discuss."

Asaph made a stiff bow and withdrew quietly, leaving the noblemen to their talk. Once outside, he departed Caer Cadarn in a rush to
bring the good news of the baron's kindness to the people.

By the end of his second day in the forest, Bran was footsore, weary, and voraciously hungry. Twice he had sighted deer, twice loosed an arrow and missed; his shoulder still pained him, and it would take many more days of practise before he recovered his easy mastery of the weapon. He had retrieved one arrow, but the other had been lost—along with any hope of a meal. And though the berries on the brambles and raspberry canes were still green and bitter, he was proud enough to refuse the growing impulse to return to the cave and beg Angharad's help. The notion smelled of weakness and surrender, and he rejected it outright.

So as the twilight shadows deepened in the leaf-bound glades, he drank his fill from a clear-running stream and prepared to spend another night in the forest. He found the disused den of a roe deer in a hollow beneath the roots of an ancient oak and crawled in. He lay back in the dry leaves and observed a spider enshroud a trapped cricket in a cocoon of silk and leave it dangling, suspended by a single strand above his head.

As Bran watched, he listened to the sounds of the woodland transforming itself for night as the birds flocked to roost and night's children began to awaken: mice and voles, badgers, foxes, bats—all with their particular voices—and it seemed to him then, as never before, that a forest was more than a place to hunt and gather timber, or else better avoided. More than a stand of moss-heavy trees; more than a sweet-water spring bubbling up from the roots of a distant mountain; more than a smooth-pebbled pool, gleaming, radiant as a jewel in a green hidden dell, or a flower-strewn meadow surrounded by a slender host of white swaying birches, or a badger delving in the dark earth beneath a rough-barked elm, or a fox kit eluding a diving hawk; more than a proud stag standing watch over his clan . . . More than these, the forest was itself a living thing, its life made up of all the smaller lives contained within its borders.

This realization proved so strong that it startled him, and he marvelled at its potency. It was, perhaps, the first time a thought like this had ever taken hold in Bran, and after the initial jolt passed, he found himself enjoying the unique freshness of the raw idea—divining the spirit of the Greene Wood, he called it. He turned it over and over in his mind, exploring its dimensions, delighting in its imaginative potential. It occurred to him that Angharad was largely responsible for this new way of thinking: that with her songs and stories and her old-fashioned, earthy ways, she had awakened in him a new kind of sight or understanding. Surely, Angharad had bewitched him, charmed him with some strange arboreal enchantment that made the forest seem a realm over which he might gain some small dominion. Angharad the Hudolion, the Enchantress of the Wood, had worked her wiles on him, and he was in her thrall. Rather than fear or dread, the conviction produced a sudden exultation. He felt, inexplicably, that he had passed some trial, gained some mastery, achieved some virtue. And although he could not yet put a name to the thing he had accomplished, he gloried in it all the same.

He lay back in the hollow of the great oak's roots as if embraced by strong encircling arms. It seemed to him that he was no longer a stranger in the forest, an intruder in a foreign realm . . . He *belonged* here. He could be at home here. In this place, he could move as freely as a king in his caer, a lord of a leaf and branch and living things—like the hero of the story: Rhi Bran.

He fell asleep with that thought still turning in his mind.

Deep in the night, he dreamed that he stood on the high crest of a craggy hill rising in the centre of the forest, the wind swirling around him. Suddenly, he felt the urge to fly, and stretching out his arms, he lifted them high. To his amazement, his arms sprouted long black feathers; the wind gusted, and he was lifted up and borne aloft, rising up and up into the clear blue Cymraic sky. Out over the forest he sailed; looking down, he saw the massed treetops far below—a thick, green, rough and rumpled skin, with the threads of streams seamed through it like veins. He saw the silvery glint of a lake and the bare domes of rock peaks. Away in the misty distance he saw the wide green sweep of the Vale of Elfael with its handful of farms and settlements scattered over a rolling, rumpled land that glowed like a gemstone beneath the light of an untroubled sun. Higher and still higher he soared, revelling in his flight, sailing over the vast extent of the greenwood.

From somewhere far below, there arose a cry—a wild, ragged wail, like that of a terrorised child who will not be comforted or consoled. The sound grew until it assaulted heaven with its insistence. Unable to ignore it, he sailed out over the valley to see what could cause such anguish. Scanning the ground far below, a movement on the margin of the forest caught his eye. He circled lower for a closer look: hunters.

They had dogs with them and were armed with lances and swords. That they should violate the sanctity of his realm angered Bran, and he determined to drive them away. He swooped down, ready to defend his woodland kingdom, only to realise, too late, that it was himself they were hunting.

He plummeted instantly to earth, landing on the path some little way ahead of the invading men. The sharp-sighted dogs saw him and howled to be released. As Bran gathered himself to flee, the hunters loosed the hounds.

Bran ran into the forest, found a dark nook beneath a rock, and crawled in to hide. But the dogs had got his scent, and they came running, baying for his blood . . .

Bran awakened with the sound of barking still echoing through the trees. A soft mist curled amongst the roots of the trees, and dew glistened on the lower leaves and on the grassy path.

The long rising note came again and, close behind, the very beast itself: a lean, long-legged grey hunting hound with clipped ears and a shaggy pelt, bounding with great, galloping strides through the morning fog.

Seizing his bow, Bran nocked an arrow and drew back the string. He was on the point of loosing the missile when a small boy appeared, racing after the dog. Barefoot, dirty-faced, with long, tangled dark hair, the lad appeared to be no more than six or seven years old. He saw Bran the same instant Bran saw him; the boy glimpsed the weapon in Bran's hands and halted just as Bran's fingers released the string.

In the same instant a voice cried, "Pull up!"

Distracted by the shout, Bran's aim faltered, and the arrow went wide; the hound leapt, colliding with Bran and carrying him to the ground. Bran crossed his arms over his neck to protect his throat . . . as the dog licked his face. It took a moment for Bran to understand that

272

he was not being attacked. Taking hold of the dog's iron-studded collar, he tried to free himself from the beast's eager attentions, but it stood on his chest, holding him to the ground. "Off!" cried Bran. "Get off!"

"Look at you now," said Angharad as she came to stand over him. "And is this not how I first found you?"

"I surrender," Bran told her. "Get him off."

The old woman gestured to the boy, who came running and pulled the dog away.

Bran rolled to his feet and brushed at the dog's muddy footprints. Angharad smiled and reached down to help him. "I thought you were away to the north country and the safety of a rich kinsman's hearth," she said, her smile brimming with merry mischief. "How is it that you are still forest bound?"

"You would know that better than I," replied Bran. Embarrassed to be so easily found, he nevertheless welcomed the sight of the old woman.

"Aye," she agreed, "I would. But we have had this discussion before, I think." She extended her hand, and Bran saw that she held a cloth bundle. "Your fast is over, Master Bran. Come, let us eat together one last time."

Bran, chastened by his luckless wandering through the forest, dutifully fell into step behind the old woman as she led her little party a short distance to a glade and there spread out a meal of cold meat, nuts, dried fruit, mushrooms, honey cakes, and eggs. The three of them ate quietly; Angharad divided the meat and shared it out between them. When the edge of his hunger had been blunted, Bran turned to the boy, who seemed curiously familiar to him, and asked, "What's your name?"

The boy raised big dark eyes to him but made no reply.

Thinking the boy had not understood him, Bran asked again, and this time the lad raised a dirty finger to his lips and shook his head.

"He is telling you he cannot speak," explained Angharad. "I call him Gwion Bach."

"He is a kinsman of yours?"

"Not mine," she replied lightly. "He belongs to the forest—one of many who live here. When I told him I was going to find you, he insisted on coming, too. I think he knows you."

Bran examined the boy more closely . . . the attack in the farm-yard—could it be the same boy? "One of many," he repeated after a moment. "And *are* there many?"

"More now that the Ffreinc have come," she answered, handing the boy a small boiled egg, which he peeled and popped into his mouth with a smack of his lips.

Bran considered this for a moment and then said, "You knew I would be here. You knew I would not be able to find my way out of the wood alone." He did not accuse her of laying a spell on him, but it was in his mind. "You knew, and still you let me go."

"It was your decision. I said I would not prevent you."

He smiled and shook his head. "I am a fool, Angharad, as we both know. But you could have told me the way out."

"Oh, aye," she agreed cheerfully, "but you did not ask." Growing suddenly serious, she regarded him with a look of unsettling direct-ness. "What is your desire, Bran?" Their meal finished, it was time, once more, for them to part. "What will you do?"

Bran regarded the old woman before him; wrinkled and stooped she might be, but shrewd as a den of weasels. In her mouth the ques-tion was more than it seemed. He hesitated, feeling that much depended on the answer.

What answer could he give? Despite his newfound appreciation of the forest, he knew the Ffreinc would kill him on sight. Seeking refuge amongst his mother's kinsmen was still a good plan. In the months he had been living with Angharad, no better scheme had come to him, nor did anything more useful occur to him now. "I will go to my people," he replied, and the words thudded to the ground like an admission of defeat.

"If that is what you wish," the old woman allowed as graciously as Bran could have hoped, "then follow me, and I will lead you to the place where you can find them."

Gathering up the remains of the meal, Angharad set off with Bran following and little Gwion Bach and the dog running along behind. They walked at an unhurried pace along barely discernible trails that Angharad read with ease. After a time, Bran noticed that the trees grew taller, the spaces between them narrower and more shadowed; the sun became a mere glimmer of shattered gold in the dense leaf canopy overhead; the trail became soft underfoot, thick with moss and damp leaves; the very air grew heavier and more redolent of earth and water and softly decaying wood. Here and there, he heard the tiny rustlings of creatures that lived in shady nooks. Everywhere—around this rock, on the other side of that holly bush, beyond the purple beech wall—he heard the sound of water: dripping off branches, trickling along unseen courses.

275

The morning passed, and they paused to rest and drink from a brook no wider than a man's foot. Angharad passed out handfuls of hazelnuts from the bag she carried. "A good day," observed Bran. He owed his life to the old woman who had saved him, and as much as he wanted to part on good terms, he also wanted her to understand why he had to leave. "A good day to begin a journey," he added.

"Aye," she replied, "it is that." Her answer, though agreeable, did not provide him the opening he sought, and he could think of no way to broach the subject. He fell silent, and they continued on a short while later, pressing ever deeper into the forest. The farther they went, the darker, wilder, and more ancient the woodland became. The smaller trees—beeches, birch, and hawthorn—gave way to the larger woodland lords: hornbeam, plane, and elm. The immense boles rose like pillars from the earth to uphold tremendous limbs, which formed a timber ceiling of intertwined branches. It would be possible, Bran imagined, to move through this part of the forest without ever setting foot on the ground.

Deeper they went, and deeper grew the shadows, and more silent the surrounding wood with a hush that was at once peaceful and slightly ominous—as if the woodland solitude was wary of trespass and imposed a guarded watch on strangers.

Bran's senses quickened. He imagined eyes on him, observing him, marking him as he passed. The impression grew with every step until he began darting glances right and left; the dense wood defied sight; the tangles of branch and vine were impenetrable.

Finally, the old woman stopped, and Bran caught the scent of smoke on the air. "Where are we?" he asked.

Extending a hand, she pointed to an enormous oak that had been struck by lightning during a storm long ago. Half-hollow now, the trunk had split and splayed outward to form a natural arch. The path on which they stood led through the centre of the blast-riven oak. "I am to go through there?"

A quick nod was the only answer he received.

Drawing himself up, he stepped to the fire-blackened arch, passing through the strange portal and into the unknown.

Stepping through the dark arch, Bran found himself holding his breath as if he were plunging into the sea, or leaping from a wall from which he could not see the ground below. On the other side of the oak arch was a hedge wall through which passed a narrow path. Two quick strides brought him through the hedge and into an enormous glade—a great wide greensward of a valley in the heart of the wood, bounded by a ring of towering trees that formed a stout palisade of solid oak around the mossy-banked clearing.

And there, spread out across the floor of the dell, was a camp with dwellings unlike any Bran had ever seen, made of brushwood and branches, the antlers of stags and hinds, woven grass, bark, bone, and hide. Some were little more than branches bent over a hollow in the ground. Others were more substantial shelters of such weird and fanciful construction that Bran was at once entranced and a little unsettled by the sight. He did not see the people who inhabited these queer dwellings, but having heard him coming a long way off, they saw him.

Moments before Bran emerged from the arch of the hedge wall

beyond the shattered oak, women whisked children out of sight, men disappeared behind trees and huts, and the settlement that only moments before had been astir with activity now appeared deserted.

"Is anybody here?" called Bran.

As if awaiting his signal, the menfolk emerged from hiding, some carrying sticks and tools for weapons. Seeing that he was alone, they approached. There were, Bran estimated quickly, perhaps thirty men and older boys, ragged, their clothes patched and worn—like those the farmers gave the stick-men in the fields to frighten the birds.

"Pax vobiscum," Bran called. When that brought no response, he repeated it in Cymry, *"Hedd a dy!"* The men continued advancing. Silent, wary as deer, they closed ranks, dark eyes watching the stranger who had appeared without warning in their midst.

"Sefyll!" called Angharad, taking her place beside Bran. Her appearance halted the advance.

One of the menfolk returned the greeting. "Hudolion!" He was joined by others, and suddenly everyone was calling, "Hudoles!" and "Hudolion!"

Ignoring Bran, they hurried to greet the old woman as she scrambled gingerly down the mossy bank into the shallow basin of the glade. The respect and adulation provoked by her appearance impressed Bran. Clearly, she had some place of honour in this rough outcast clan.

"Welcome, hudolion," called one of the men, advancing through the knot of people gathered around her. Tall and lean, there was something of the wolf about him; he wore a short red cloak folded over his shoulder in the manner of a Roman soldier of old. The others parted to let him through, and as he took his place before the old woman, he touched the back of a grimy hand to his forehead in the ancient sign of submission and salutation.

"Greetings, Siarles," she said. "Greetings, everyone." Lifting a hand to Bran, she said, "Do you not recognise Prince Bran ap Brychan when you see him?"

The man called Siarles stepped nearer for a closer look. He peered into Bran's face uncertainly, cool grey eyes moving over the young man's features. He then turned to those behind him. "Call the big 'un," he commanded, and a slender youth with a downy moustache raced away. "I do not," Siarles said, turning once more to Bran and Angharad, "but if it is as you say, then *he* will."

The youth ran to one of the larger huts and called to someone inside. A moment later, a large, well-muscled man stepped from the low entrance of the hut. As he straightened, Bran saw his face for the first time.

"Iwan?" cried Bran, rushing to meet him.

"Bran? Mary and Joseph in a manger, Bran!" A grin spread across his broad face; his thick moustache twitched with pleasure. Seizing Bran, he gathered him in a crushing embrace. "Bran ap Brychan," he said, "I never thought to see you again."

"If it had not been for Angharad, no one ever would," Bran confessed, gazing up into the face of his father's champion. "By heaven, it is good to see you."

Iwan raised his hand high and called out in a voice that resounded through the glade. "Hear me, everyone! Before you stands Bran ap Brychan, heir to the throne of Elfael! Make him welcome!"

Then, turning once more to Bran, the warrior clapped his hand to the young man's shoulder. "Humble it may be," Iwan said, "but my hearth will be all the merrier with you for company."

"I would be honoured," Bran told him.

"Come, we will share a cup," announced Iwan. "I am that anxious to hear how you fared all this time without me."

The former champion turned on his heel and started back to his

279

hut. Bran caught Angharad by the arm and whispered, "You did not tell them I was coming?"

"The choice, my son, was always yours alone," she replied.

"You knew this would happen," he insisted. "You must have known all along."

"You said you wanted to go to your people." Extending a gnarled hand to the bedraggled gathering before him, she said, "Here are your people, Bran."

How strange she was, this old woman standing before him—at once aged and ageless. The dark eyes gazing out at him from that wrinkled visage were as keen as blades, her mind sharper still. Bran was, he knew, at her mercy and always had been. "Who are you, Angharad?" he asked.

"You asked me once," she replied, "but you were not ready to receive the answer. Are you ready now?"

"I am—I mean, I think so."

"Then come," Angharad said. "It will not take long. Iwan will wait." She led him to a round moss- and bracken-covered hut in the centre of the settlement. The hide of a red ox served for a door, and here she paused, saying, "If you enter, Master Bran, you must leave your unbelief outside."

"I will," he told her. "So far as I am able, I will."

She regarded him without expression and then smiled. "I suppose that will have to do." To the others who had followed them, she said, "Go about your business. Siarles, tell Iwan we will join him soon. I would speak to Bran alone a moment." The people moved off reluctantly; Angharad gave Bran a little bow and, drawing aside the red oxhide, said, "Be welcome here, Prince of Elfael."

Bran stepped into the dim interior of the odd dwelling. Although dark, it was surprisingly ample and comfortable. Light filtered in through a single hole in the roof directly over the stone-lined fire pit in the centre of the room. The furnishings were spare. A single three-legged stool, a row of woven grass baskets along the curving wall, and a bed of reeds and fleeces were the only belongings in the room. These Bran took in with a single glance as he entered.

A second look revealed another item he did not see until his eyes had better adjusted to the dusky interior: a robe made entirely of feathers, all of them black. Drawn to the peculiar garment, he ran his hand over the glossy plumage. "What is this?"

"It is the Bird Spirit Cloak," replied the old woman. "Come, sit down." She indicated a place opposite her at the fire ring.

"They called you hudolion," Bran said, settling himself cross-legged on a grass mat. "Are you?" he asked. "Are you an enchantress?"

"I have been called many things," she replied simply. "Hag . . . Whore . . . Leper . . . Witch . . . I am each of these and none. Banfáith of Elfael . . . True Bard of Britain, these titles are also mine. Call me what you will, I am myself alone, the last of my kind."

In her words Bran heard the echo of a long-forgotten time, a time when Britain belonged to Britons alone, and when its sons and daughters walked beneath free skies.

The old woman exhaled gently and closed her eyes. She was silent for a long moment and then drew a deep breath. When she spoke again, her voice had changed, taking on the timbre and cadence of one of her songs. "Not for Angharad the friendly hearth, the silver-strung harp, or torc of gold," she said, almost singing the words. "In the forest she resides, living like the wild things—the nimble fox, elusive bear, or phantom wolf. Like these, her four-footed sisters, the forest is her shelter and her stronghold."

She exhaled again, and another long pause ensued. Bran, accustomed to the old woman's queer moods and eccentric ways, knew better than to interrupt her. He waited in silence for her to continue.

"Oh, beloved, yes, the greenwood is her caer, but it is not her home," she said after a moment. "Angharad was born to a more exalted position. She was born to bless the hall of a king with her song, to adorn and complete a noble sovereign with her strengthening presence. But the world has turned, the kings grown small, and the bards sing no more.

"Listen! Do not turn away. There was a time once, long ago, when the bards were lauded in the halls of kings, when rulers of the Cymry dispensed gold rings and jewelled armbands to the Chieftains of Song, when all men listened to the old tales, gloried in them, and so magnified their understanding; a time when lord and lady alike heeded the Head of Wisdom and sought the counsel of the Learned in all things.

"Alas! That time is gone. Everywhere kings quarrel amongst themselves, wasting their substance on trivialities and the meaningless pursuit of power, each one striving to rise at the expense of the other. They are maggots in manure, fighting for supremacy of the dung heap. Meanwhile, the enemy goes from strength to strength. The invader waxes mighty while the *Gwr Gwyr*, the True Men, melt away like mist on a sun-bright morning.

"The Day of the Wolf has dawned. The dire shape of its coming was seen and foretold, its arrival awaited with fear and dread. At long last it is here, and there are none who can turn it aside. Hear me, O Rhi Bran, the Red King stretches out his hand across the land, grasping, seizing, rending. He will not be satisfied until all lies under his dominion, or until he awakens from his sleep of death and acknowledges the law of love and justice laid down before the foundations of the world."

She spoke with eyes shut, her head weaving from side to side, as if listening to a melody Bran could not hear.

"I am Angharad, and here in the forest I watch and wait. For, as I live and breathe, the promise of my birth will yet be proved. By the grace of the Christ, my druid, I will yet compose a song to be sung before a king worthy of his praise." Then, slowly opening her eyes, she gazed at Bran directly. "Do you believe me when I say this?"

"I do believe," replied Bran without hesitation. More than anything else he had ever wanted, he ached for those words, somehow, to be true.

Bishop Asaph stood in the door of his old wooden chapel, watching the labourers break a hole in the wall of his former chapter house, which was to become the residence of Count de Braose's chief magistrate and tax collector—an ominous development, to be sure, but of a piece with the multitude of changes taking place throughout Elfael almost daily.

The monastery yard had slowly become the market square of the new town, and the various monastic buildings either converted to accommodate new uses or pulled down to make way for bigger, more serviceable buildings. One row of monks' cells was being removed to make way for a blacksmith forge and granary. The long, low wattle-and-daub refectory was to be a guildhall, and the modest scriptorium a town treasury. That there were no guilds in Elfael seemed not to matter; that no one paid taxes was, apparently, beside the point. The guilds would come in due course; the taxman, too.

Lamentable though the thought surely was, the bishop could not give it more than fleeting consideration. His mind was occupied with

283

the far more urgent matter of feeding his hungry people. The grain promised by Baron Neufmarché had not yet arrived, and Asaph had determined to go to Count de Braose and see what might be done. He had hoped his next audience with the count would be on more amiable terms, but the prospect of better dealings seemed always to remain just beyond his grasp.

He tightened the laces of his shoes, then made his way through the building site that had been his home—God's home—and walked out across the valley to Caer Cadarn. Upon presenting himself at the fortress gate, he was, as he had come to expect, made to tarry in the yard until the count deigned to see him. Here, the Bishop of Llanelli loitered in the sun like a friendless farmhand with muck on his feet, while the count sat at meat. He resented this treatment but tried not to take offence; he decided to recite a psalm instead.

284

Twenty psalms later, the count's seneschal finally came for him. At the door to the audience chamber, Asaph thanked Orval and composed himself, smoothing his robe and adjusting his belt. Stepping through the opened door, Bishop Asaph found the count hunched over a table laden with the half-empty plates of the meal just finished and squares of parchment on which were drawn plans for defensive fortifications.

"Forgive me, bishop, if I do not offer you refreshment," said the count distractedly. "I am otherwise occupied, as you see."

"I would not presume upon your attentions," said the bishop tartly. "You can be sure that I would not come here at all if need did not demand it."

Falkes glanced up sharply. "Pray, what are you prattling about now?"

"We were promised provisions," said the bishop.

"When?"

"Why, when Baron Neufmarché was here. It has been almost a month now, and the need grows ever—"

"Neufmarché promised grain, yes, I remember." Count de Braose returned to the drawings before him. "What of it?"

"My lord count," said the bishop, his palms growing wet with apprehension, "it has not arrived."

"Has it not?" sniffed the count. "Well, perhaps he has forgotten."

"The baron promised to send the supplies immediately upon his return to Hereford. It has been, as I say, almost a month now, and the need is greater than ever. The people are at the end of their resources—they faint with hunger; the children cry. In some settlements, they are already starving. If relief is not forthcoming, they will die."

"In that case," replied the count, picking up a scrap of parchment and holding it at arm's length before his face, "I suggest you take up the matter with the baron himself. It is his affair, not mine."

"But—"

"We are finished here," interrupted Count Falkes. "You may go."

Aghast and confounded, Bishop Asaph stood in silence for a moment. "My lord, do you mean to say that nothing has been sent?"

"Have you taken root?" inquired the count. "The matter is concluded. You are dismissed. Go."

The churchman turned and walked stiffly from the room. By the time he reached the monastery, some semblance of reason had returned, and he had determined that the count was right. The baron had made the promise and must be held to account. Therefore, he would go to the baron and demand a reckoning. If he left at once, he could be in Hereford in four or five days. He would obtain an audience; he would implore; he would plead; he would beg the baron to make good his vow and release the promised food and supplies without delay.

CHAPTER 29

It took the two aging priests of Llanelli more than a week to reach the Neufmarché stronghold in Hereford. Though Bishop Asaph fervently hoped to travel more swiftly, he could not go faster than doddering Brother Clyro could walk, nor could he bring himself to deny the needy who, upon seeing the passing monks, ran to beg them for prayers and blessings.

Weary and footsore, they reached Hereford toward evening of the eighth day and found their way to the Abbey of Saints James and John, where they took beds for the night. They were led by the porter to the guest lodge and provided with basins of water to wash and later joined the priests for prayers and a simple supper before going to sleep. After prime the next morning, the bishop left his companion at prayer and made his way to the baron's fortress. Set on a bluff overlooking the river Wye, the castle could be seen for miles in every direction: an impressive structure built of stone and enclosed by a deep, steep-sided ditch filled with water diverted from the river.

It was not the first fortress on this site; the previous one had been burned to the ground long ago during a battle with the English. The Ffreinc had rebuilt it, but in stone this time; larger, stronger, bristling with battlements, walls, and towers, it was built to last. Its latest inhabitant had extended the grounds around the stronghold to include common grazing lands, cattle pens, granaries, and barns.

The bishop paused before entering the castle gate. "Great of Might," he murmured, lifting a hand toward heaven, "you know our need. Let relief be swiftly granted. Amen." He then proceeded through the gate, where he was met by a gatekeeper in a short red tunic. "Pax vobiscum," said the bishop.

"God with you," answered the gateman, taking in the bishop's robe and tonsure. "What is your business here, father?"

"I seek audience with Baron Neufmarché, if you please. You may tell him that Bishop Asaph of Elfael is here on a matter of highest importance."

The servant nodded and led the cleric across a wooden bridge over the water ditch, through another gate, and into an inner yard, where he waited while the gatekeeper announced his presence to a page, who conveyed the request for an audience to the baron. While he awaited the baron's summons, Bishop Asaph watched the people around him as they went about their daily affairs. He found himself thinking about what a strange race they were, these Ffreinc, made up of many contradictions. Industrious and resourceful, they typically pursued their interests with firmness of purpose and an admirable ardour. Yet from what he had seen of the marchogi in Elfael, they could just as quickly abandon themselves to dejection and despondency when events betrayed them. Devout, stalwart, and reverent in the best of times, they also seemed inordinately subject to weird caprices and silly superstitions. A handsome people, hale and strong bodied, with long, straight limbs and clear eyes set in broad, open faces—they nevertheless seemed to suffer from a rare abundance of infirmities, maladies, and ailments.

All these things and arrogant, too. They were, the bishop concluded, fiercely ambitious. In appetite for acquisition: insatiable. In intensity for mastery: rapacious. In aspiration for achievement: merciless. In desire for domination: inexorable.

However, and he had always to remember this, they could be fairminded and loyal, and when it suited them, they displayed a laudable sense of justice—at least with their own. The English and Cymry were treated poorly for the most part, it was true; but the capacity for evenhanded tolerance was not entirely lacking. The bishop hoped he would encounter some of this fairness in his dealings with the baron today.

Presently, the page returned to announce that the baron would be pleased to see him at once, and Asaph was brought into a large, stone-flagged anteroom, where he was offered a cup of wine and some bread before making his way into the baron's audience chamber—an enormous oak-panelled room with a narrow arched window of leaded glass that kept out the wind but allowed the light to come streaming through.

"Bishop Asaph!" boomed the baron as the priest was announced. "Pax vobiscum!" He crossed the chamber in long, quick strides and held out his hand in the peculiar greeting of Ffreinc noblemen. "It is good to see you again." The bishop grasped the offered hand somewhat awkwardly. "You should have told me you were coming! I would have had a dinner prepared in your honour. But come! Come, sit with me. I will have some refreshment brought, and we will eat together."

The effusive greeting banished Bishop Asaph's worst fears. "Thank you, Baron Neufmarché, but your servant was kind enough to offer me bread and wine just now. I would not presume to keep you from your affairs a moment longer than necessary."

"So earnest," observed the baron lightly. "It is a most welcome interruption, bishop. You have an advocate in me. I hope you know that."

"You cannot imagine how it gratifies me to hear those words, Baron Neufmarché. You are very kind."

Neufmarché brushed aside the compliment. "It is nothing. However, I can see that you are troubled—and I think it must be something serious indeed to bring you from your beautiful valley." He gestured his guest to a chair beside his own. "Here, my friend; sit down and tell me what is distressing you."

"To be blunt, it is about the food supplies you promised to send."

"Yes? I trust they were put to good use. I assure you, the grain and meat were the finest I could lay hands to at short notice."

"I am certain they were," Bishop Asaph conceded. "But we never received them."

"Nothing? Nothing at all?" wondered the baron. Asaph shook his head slowly. "How is that possible?"

"That is what I have come to discover," replied the bishop, who then told of his conversation with Count Falkes. "In short," concluded the bishop, "the count gave me to know in no uncertain terms that the supplies had never been sent—or, if they had, they never arrived. He suggested I take up the matter with you"—the bishop spread his hands—"so here I am."

"I see." The baron pursed his lips in a frown of vexation and ran a broad hand through his long, dark hair. "This is most disturbing. I made arrangements for the supplies the same day I returned from Elfael, and was glad to do it. Why, the wagoners reported a successful delivery with no difficulties along the way."

"I do believe you, baron," the bishop assured him. "It can only be that de Braose has taken the food and kept it for himself."

"So it would seem," Baron Neufmarché concurred. Rising from

his chair, he crossed to the door in quick strides, opened it, and summoned the servant waiting outside. "Bring Remey here at once." The man hurried away, and the baron returned to his guest. "This will soon be put right."

"What do you intend—if I may be so bold?"

"I intend to send another consignment immediately," declared the baron. "What is more, I intend to make certain that it reaches you this time. I will give orders that the food is to be delivered to you and no one else."

"Baron Neufmarché," sighed Asaph, feeling the weight of care lift from his shoulders, "you have no idea how much this means to me. It is a blessing of the highest order."

"It is nothing of the kind," protested Neufmarché. "If I had been more diligent, this would not have happened, and you would not have had to undertake such an onerous errand. I am sorry." He paused. Then, his voice becoming grave, he said, "I can see now that we have no ally in Count de Braose. He is duplicitous and deceitful, and his word can no longer be trusted."

"Alas, it is true," confirmed Asaph readily.

"We must watch him closely, you and I," the baron continued. "I have received word of, shall we say, certain undertakings involving the count and his uncle." He offered a brief confidential smile. "But never fear, my friend; trust that I will do whatever I can to intercede for you."

Before the bishop could think what to say, the door opened and a thin man in a soft red hat entered the room. "Ah, there you are!" called the baron. "Remey, you will recall the supplies we sent to Count Falkes in Elfael, yes?"

"I do, my lord. Of course. I saw to it personally at your request."

"How many wagons did we send?"

The old servant placed a finger to his lips for a moment and then said, "Five, I believe. Three of grain, and two more loaded with meat and various other necessaries."

"That is correct, Remey," confirmed the baron. "I want you to ready another consignment of the same." He paused, glancing at the bishop, then added, "And double it this time."

"Ten wagons!" gasped Bishop Asaph. This went far beyond his most fervent hopes. "My lord baron, this is most generous—indeed, *more* than generous! Your largesse is as noble as it is needful."

"Think nothing of it," the baron replied grandly. "I am only too glad to be of some small service. Now then, perhaps I can persuade you to share a little sustenance with me before you return to Elfael. In fact, if you would consent to stay a day or so, you may depart with the first wagons."

"Nothing would please us more," replied the bishop, almost giddy with relief. "And tonight, Brother Clyro and I will hold vigil for you and extol your name before the Throne of Grace."

"You are too kind, bishop. I am certain I do not deserve such praise."

"On the contrary, I will spread word of your munificence from one end of Elfael to the other so that all our people will know who to thank for their provision." Tears started to his eyes, and he dabbed them with his hands, saying, "May God bless you richly, baron, for troubling yourself on our behalf. May God bless you well and richly."

Bran spent the day getting to know the people of *Cél Craidd*, the hidden heart of the greenwood. A few were folk of Elfael, but many were from other cantrefs—chiefly Morgannwg and Gwent, which had also fallen under Norman sway. All, for one reason or another, had been forced to abandon their homes and seek the refuge of the wood.

He talked to them and listened to their stories of loss and woe, and his heart went out to them.

That night he sat beside the hearth in Iwan's hut, and they talked of the Ffreinc and what could be done to reclaim their homeland. "We must raise a warband," Iwan declared, brash in his enthusiasm. "That is the first thing. Drive the devils out. Drive them so far and so hard they dare not come back again."

The three men faced one another across the small fire burning in the centre of the hut's single room. "We could get swords and armour," Siarles suggested. "And horses, to be sure. Good ones—trained to battle." The young man had been chief huntsman to the king of Gwent, but when the Ffreinc deposed his lord and took all hunting rights to themselves, Siarles had fled to the forest rather than serve a Ffreinc lord. He had assumed the position of Iwan's second. "De Braose has hundreds of horses. We'll raise a thousand," he said, exuberance getting the better of him. He considered this for a moment and then amended it, saying, "Not every warrior will need a horse, mind. To be sure, we must have footmen as well."

The mere thought of trying to find so many men and horses was laughable to Bran. Even if men in such numbers could somehow be found, arming and equipping a warband of that size could well take a year or more—and they must be housed and fed in the meantime. It was absurd, and Bran pitied his friends for their hopeless, pathetic dream; it might make the British heart beat faster, but it was doomed to failure. The Ffreinc were bred for battle; they were better armed, better trained, better horsed. Engaging them in open battle was certain disaster; every British death strengthened their hold on the land that much more and increased misery and oppression for everyone. To think otherwise was folly.

Listening to Iwan and Siarles, Bran grew more certain than ever

293

STEPHEN R.
LAWHEAD

that his future lay in the north amongst his mother's kinsmen. Elfael was lost—it had been so from the moment his father was cut down in the road—and there was nothing he could do to change that. Better to accept the grim reality and live than to die chasing a glorious delusion.

He looked sadly at the two men across from him, their faces eager in the firelight. They burned with zeal to drive the enemy from the valley and redeem their homeland. *Why stop there?* Bran thought. *They might as well hope to reclaim Cymru, England, and Scotland, too—for all the good it would do them.* Unable to endure the futile hope of those keen expressions, Bran rose suddenly and left the hut.

He stepped out into the moonlight and stood for a moment, feeling the cool night air wash over him. Gradually, he became aware that he was not alone. Angharad was sitting on a stump beside the door. "They have no one else," she said. "And nowhere else to go."

"What they want—," Bran began, then halted. Did anyone have even the slightest notion of the effort in time and money that it would take to raise a sufficiently large army to do what Iwan suggested? "It is impossible," he declared after a moment. "They are deluded."

"Then you must tell them. Tell them now. Explain why they are wrong to want what they want. Then you can leave knowing that, as their king, you did all you could."

Her words rankled. "What do you expect of me, Angharad?" He spoke softly so those inside would not overhear. "What they propose is madness—as you and I know."

"Perhaps," she conceded. "But they have nothing else. They have no kinsmen in the north waiting to take them in. Elfael is all they have. It is all they know. If their hope is mistaken, you must tell them."

"I will," said Bran, drawing himself up, "and let that be the end." He went back into the hut, taking his place at the fire once more.

"We could go to Lord Rhys in the south," Iwan was saying. "He has returned from Ireland with a large warband. If we convinced him to help us, he might loan us the troops we need."

"No," Bran said quietly. "There is no plunder to be had, and we have nothing to offer them. King Rhys ap Tewdwr will not get dragged into a war for nothing, and he has enough worries of his own."

"What do you suggest?" asked Iwan. "Is there someone else?"

Bran looked at his friend, the light still burning in his eyes; he could not bring himself to snuff out that fragile flame. Angharad was right: the people had no one to lead them and nowhere else to go. For Iwan, and for them all, it was Elfael or nothing.

Bran hesitated, wrestling with the decision. *God have mercy,* he thought, *I cannot abandon them.* In that instant, a new path opened before him, and Bran saw the way ahead. "We don't have to fight the Ffreinc," he declared abruptly.

"No?" wondered Iwan. "I think they won't surrender for asking—a pleasant thought even so."

"Have you forgotten, Iwan? We went to Lundein and spoke to the king's justiciar," Bran said. "Do you remember what he said?"

"Aye," conceded the big man, "I remember. What help is that to us now?"

"It is our very salvation!" Iwan and Siarles exchanged puzzled glances across the fire. Clearly, they did not see, so Bran explained, "The cardinal said he would annul Baron de Braose's grant for six hundred marks. So we will simply *buy* Elfael from the king."

"Six hundred marks!" muttered Siarles in dull amazement. "Have you ever seen that much?"

"Never," allowed Bran. "In truth, I don't know if there is that much silver to be had beyond the March. But the terms were laid down by William's own man. The cardinal said we could have Elfael for six hundred marks."

"Aye," mused Iwan, rubbing his chin doubtfully, "that is what he said—and it is just as impossible now as it was then."

"A high price, yes, but not impossible. Anyway, it is far less than what would be needed to raise and feed an army of a thousand men—not to mention weapons and armour. For that, we'd need ten times more than the cardinal is asking."

The two others fell silent gazing at him, calculating the enormity of the sums involved. Bran let his words work for a moment and then added, "That aside, I agree about the horses."

"You do?" wondered Siarles, much impressed.

"Yes, but not a thousand. Three or four will suffice."

"What can we do with three horses?" scoffed the young forester.

"We can begin raising the six hundred marks to redeem our homeland."

PART FOUR

THE
HAUNTING

Ten wagons laden with sacks of barley and rye, bags of dried beans and peas, and whole sides of beef and smoked pork trundled along the rising trackway through the forest. The supply van of Baron Neufmarché had spent all morning toiling up the winding incline of the ridge, and the crest was now in sight. Along with the wagons, the baron had sent an armed escort: five men-at-arms under the command of a knight, all of them in mail hauberks and armed with swords and lances, their shields and steel helmets slung behind their saddles. Their presence dared Count Falkes, or anyone else, to divert the consignment of supplies intended for the starving folk of Elfael.

The day had turned hazy and hot in the open places, the skies clear for the most part with but a smudgy suggestion of cloud to the west. The road, though deeply rutted and lumpy, was as dry as parchment. A drowsy hush lay over the rising woodland, as if the trees themselves dozed in the heat. The drivers did not press their teams too hard; the day was hot, the wagons were heavy, and they were loath to hurry. The food would arrive when it arrived, and that would be soon enough.

The six advance guards paused on the spine of the ridge and waited for the ox train to reach the top. From their high vantage point, the soldiers could see the Vale of Elfael spreading green and inviting to the north. "This is tedious work," muttered the knight leading the escort. Turning to one of his men, he said, "Richard, go down and tell them that we will ride on. There is a ford ahead—just there." He pointed down the descending slope to a place where a stream cut through the road as it pursued its switchback descent into the valley. "We will water the horses and wait for them there."

The man-at-arms gave a nod, put spurs to his horse, and trotted back down the slope. "This way," said the knight, and they rode down to the fording place, where they dismounted and stretched. After the animals had drunk their fill, the men drank, too, removing their round leather caps to lave cool water over their sweating heads. Kneeling in a sunny patch on the bank of the stream, the knight saw a shadow pass over him.

He watched the shade slowly engulf him, and thinking nothing more than that an errant cloud had passed over the sun, he ducked his head and continued cupping water to his mouth. Behind him, and a little way above, he heard the rustling of feathers and, still on his knees, craned his neck around to see a huge, dark, winglike shape disappear into the undergrowth—nothing more than a dull glimmering of black feathers, and then it was gone.

The sunlight returned, and the kneeling soldier was left with the strong sensation that something strange and unnatural had been watching him and, for all he knew, watched him still. The skin of his belly tightened beneath his chain mail tunic. Fear stretched both ways along his spine. The knight rose to his feet, replaced his leather cap, drew his sword, and prepared to fight. "To arms, men!" he cried. "To arms!"

Instantly, the soldiers unsheathed swords and levelled lances. They

300

drew together to form a protective line and waited for the anticipated onslaught. The moment stretched and passed. The attack did not come.

The knight advanced cautiously to the place in the brush where the dark shape had disappeared. Gesturing for his men to maintain silence, he summoned them to him, indicating that the enemy was hiding in the underbrush. They paused at the ready, and then, hearing nothing, seeing nothing, they started into the brushwood, where they discovered a narrow trail used by animals when passing to and from the stream. Stopping every few steps to listen, the five soldiers advanced cautiously along the trackway.

A hundred paces farther along, the trail divided. One way led into a deep-shaded game run; arched over by intertwining limbs, it was straight and narrow and dark as any underground tunnel. The other was more open and meandered amongst the trees, below which stunted saplings formed a scrubby underbrush where an enemy might hide.

It could have been his overwrought imagination, but the knight felt dank and chill air seeping along the darker path. It came spilling out from the entrance of the game run like a vapour, invisible to the eye; nevertheless, he could feel it curling and coiling around his feet and ankles, climbing his legs. He stopped in his tracks and motioned the others behind him to halt as well.

Loath to take the darker path, the knight was considering their position when he heard a far-off whinny. It seemed to come from behind them in the direction of the stream. "The horses!"

Turning as one, the warriors ran back the way they had come, stumbling in their haste as they emerged once again on the low banks of the stream to find that their horses had vanished.

"God in heaven!" cried the knight. "We have been tricked! Get up there," he shouted, pushing two men along the upstream bank. "Find them!"

301

STEPHEN R.
LAWHEAD

He sent his other two men-at-arms to search downstream and then ran to the road and hurried back to the ridgetop to see the ox-drawn wagons still some way off, creeping slowly up the last rise.

He returned to the fording place and sat down on a rock with his sword across his knees. Eventually, the two who had gone upstream returned to say they had found not so much as a hoofprint on the muddy bank. One of the guards who had been searching downstream returned with the same report—neither hide nor hair of any horse did he see.

"Where is Laurent?" asked the knight. "He was with you; what happened to him?"

"I thought he came back here," replied the soldier, glancing around quickly. "Did he not?"

"He did not," retorted the knight angrily. "As you can well see, he did not!"

"But he was just behind me," insisted the man-at-arms. Looking back along the bank, he said, "He must have turned aside to relieve himself."

Assuming this to be the case, they waited for a time to see if their missing comrade would reappear. When he failed to show up, the knight and his men walked back along the downstream bank. They shouted and called his name and listened for sounds of the absent soldier thrashing through the brush. The surrounding wood remained deathly still and quiet.

The five guardsmen were still shouting when the rider sent with the message for the wagons appeared. The knight turned on him. "Have you seen him?"

"Who, my lord?"

"Laurent—he's disappeared. Did you see anything amiss on the road?"

302

Catching the wild cast of the knight's eyes and frantic tone, he replied with studied caution. "Nothing amiss, my lord. All is well. The wagons will be here soon."

"All is *not* well, by heaven!" roared the knight. "Our horses have vanished, too."

"Vanished?"

"Spirited away!"

The rider's bald brow furrowed, and tiny creases formed at the corners of his eyes. "But I—are you certain, sire?"

"We watered the horses and knelt down to get a mouthful ourselves," explained one of the men-at-arms, pushing forward. "When we looked up"—he glanced around to gather the assent of his companions—"the horses had disappeared."

"One moment there, and the next gone?" wondered the rider. "And you saw nothing?"

"If we had, would we waste breath talking to you?" the knight charged angrily. Still gripping the hilt of his sword, he scanned the forest round about, a great, green, all-embracing wall. "Mark me, there is some witchery hereabouts. I can feel it."

They waited at the ford, armed and ready for whatever might happen next, however uncanny, but nothing more sinister than clouds of flies gathering about their heads had befallen them by the time the first of the ox-drawn wagons reached them. The driver stopped to allow his team to rest before continuing the descent into the Vale of Elfael. While they waited, the knight questioned the lead wagoner closely, and then all the rest in turn as they drew up to water their animals, but none of the drivers had seen or heard anything strange or disturbing on the road.

When the oxen had rested, the wagon van of supplies resumed its journey to the monastery at Llanelli. While they were still some little way off, the wagons were seen by the guards at the count's fortress.

Hoping for a way to ingratiate himself with the baron—and to distance himself from any whiff of thievery or misuse of this second shipment—Count Falkes sent his own contingent of soldiers down to help convey the much-needed food supplies the short remaining distance to the monastery.

The baron's guards grudgingly tolerated the count's men-at-arms, and the party continued on to Llanelli to supervise the unloading of the wagons at what remained of the monastery. While they watched the cargo being carried into the chapel, the soldiers began to talk and were soon relating the unchancy events that had just befallen them in the forest. Thus, word of the visiting soldiers' strange experience quickly reached Count de Braose, who summoned the baron's knight to his fortress.

"What do you mean the horses vanished?" inquired the count when he had heard what the knight had to say.

"Count de Braose," conceded the knight reluctantly, "we also lost a man."

"Men and horses do not simply dissolve into the air."

"As you say, sire," replied the knight, growing petulant. "Even so, I know what I saw."

"But you said you saw *nothing*," insisted Count Falkes.

"And I stand by it," the knight maintained stolidly. "I am no liar."

"Nor do I so accuse you," replied the count, his voice rising. "I am merely attempting to learn what it was that you saw—if anything."

"I saw," began the knight cautiously, "a shadow. As I knelt to drink, a shadow fell over me, and when I looked up, I saw . . ." He hesitated.

"Yes? Yes?" urged the count, impatience making him sharp.

Drawing a bracing breath, the knight replied, "I saw a great dark shape—very like that of a bird."

"A dark shape, you say. Like a bird," repeated Falkes.

"But larger—far larger than any bird ever seen before. Black as the devil himself, and a wingspread wide as your arms."

"Are you suggesting to me that this *bird* carried off your man and all the horses?" scoffed the count. "By heaven, it must have been a very Colossus amongst birds!"

The knight shut his mouth and stared at the count, his face growing hot with humiliation.

"Well? Go on; I would hear the rest of this fantastic yarn."

"We gave chase, sire," the knight said in a low, disgruntled voice. "We pursued the thing into the brushwood and found a deer track which we followed, but we neither saw nor heard anything again. When we returned to the stream, our horses were gone." He nodded for emphasis. "Vanished."

"You looked for them, I presume?" inquired the count.

"We searched both ways along the stream, and that is when Laurent disappeared."

"And again, I suppose no one saw or heard anything?"

"Nothing at all. The forest was uncannily quiet. If there had been so much as a mayfly to see or hear, that we would have. One moment Laurent was there, and the next he was gone."

Growing tired of the murky vagueness of the report, the count cut the interview short. "If there is nothing else, you may go. But do not for a single moment think to lay any of this at *my* feet. By the Holy Name, I swear I had nothing to do with it."

"I accuse no one," muttered the knight.

"Then you are dismissed. Take some refreshment for yourself and your men, and then you may return to the baron. God knows what he will make of the tale." When the knight made no move to leave, Count Falkes added, "I said, your service is completed. The supplies have been delivered, I believe? You may go."

"We have no horses, sire."

"And what do you imagine I should do about that?"

"I am certain Baron Neufmarché would deem it a boon of honour if you lent us some worthy mounts," the knight suggested.

The count glared at the man before him. "You want me to lend you horses?" He made it sound as if it was the most outlandish thing he had heard so far. "And what? Watch you make *my* animals disappear along with the others? I'll have none of it. You can ride back in the empty wagons. It would serve you right."

The knight stiffened under the count's sarcasm but held his ground. "The baron would be indebted to you, I daresay."

"Yes, I *daresay* he would," agreed the count. He regarded the knight; there was something in what he suggested. To have the baron beholden to him might prove a useful thing in future dealings. "Oh, very well, take some refreshment, and I will arrange it. You can leave tomorrow morning."

"Thank you, sire," said the knight. "We are most grateful."

When the knight had gone, Count Falkes put the matter out of his mind. Soldiers were a superstitious lot, all told, forever seeing signs and wonders where there were none. Even the most solid-seeming needed little prompting—a shadow in the woods, was that it?—to embark on a flight of delirious fancy and set tongues wagging everywhere. Probably the slack-witted guards, having ranged far ahead of the wagons, had emptied a skinful of wine between them and, in their drunken stupor, allowed their untethered horses to wander off.

Later that evening, however, as twilight deepened across the valley, the count was given opportunity to reappraise his hasty opinion when the missing soldier, Laurent, stumbled out of the forest and appeared at the gate of his stronghold. Half out of his head with fear, the fellow was gibbering about demons and ghosts and a weird phantom bird, and insisting that the ancient wood was haunted.

Before the count could interview the man in person, word had flashed throughout the caer that some sort of unworldly creature—a giant bird with a beak as long as a man's arm, wings a double span wide, and glowing red eyes—had arisen in the forest, called forth by means both mysterious and infernal to instil terror in the hearts of the Ffreinc intruders. This last appeared only too likely, the count considered, watching his men fall over themselves in their haste to hear the lunatic. This time tomorrow, the tale would spread from one end of the valley to the other.

Whatever it was that had frightened the stricken soldier, it would take more than some cockeyed tale involving an oversized bird and the dubious misplacement of a few horses to make Count Falkes tremble in his boots. Nothing short of a midnight shower of fire and brimstone and the appearance of Lucifer himself could drive a de Braose from his throne once he had got his rump on it. And that was that.

For Mérian, the invitation to attend the baron's festivities came as a command to undertake an onerous obligation. "Must we go?" she demanded when her mother informed her. "Must I?"

She had heard how the Ffreinc lived: how the men worshipped their ladies and showered them with expensive baubles; how the noble houses were steeped in lavish displays of wealth—fine clothes, sumptuous food, imported wine, furniture made by artisans across the sea; how the Ffreinc prized beauty and held a high respect for ritual, indulging many extraordinary and extravagant courtesies.

All this and more she had heard from one gossip or another over the years, and it had never swayed her from her opinion that the Ffreinc were little more than belligerent swine, scrubbed up and dressed in satin and lace, perhaps, but born to the stockyard nonetheless. The mere thought of attending one of their festive celebrations produced in her a dread akin to the sweating queasiness some people feel aboard ship in uneasy seas.

"It is an honour to be asked," Queen Anora told her.

"Then that is honour enough for me," she replied crisply.

"Your father has already accepted the invitation."

"He accepted without my permission," Mérian pointed out. "Let him go without me."

This was not the last word on the subject—far from it. In the end, however, she knew she must accept her father's decision; she would pretend the dutiful daughter and go, like a martyr, to her fate.

Galled as she was to think of attending the event, she worried that she would not be properly dressed, that she would not know how to comport herself correctly, that her speech would betray her for a brutish Briton, that her family would embarrass her with their backward ways, and on and on. Just as there were a thousand objections to consorting with the Ffreinc, there was, she discovered, no end of hazards to fear.

As the baron's castle at Hereford loomed into sight, rising in the deepening blue of a twilight summer sky above the thatched rooftops of the busy town, Mérian was overcome by an apprehension so powerful she almost swooned. Her brother, Garran, saw her sway and grasped her elbow to keep her from toppling from her saddle. "Steady there, Sister," he said, grinning at her discomfort. "You don't want to greet all those highborn Ffreinc ladies covered with muck from the road. They'll think you a stable hand."

"Let them think what they will," she replied, trying to sound imperious and aloof. "I care not."

"You do," he asserted. "Twitching like a sparrow with salt on its tail at the mention of the baron's name. Do you think I haven't seen?"

"Oh? And would it do you any harm to stand a little closer to the washbasin, brother mine? I doubt highborn Ffreinc ladies look kindly on men who smell of the sty."

"Listen to that!" Garran hooted. "Your concern is as touching as it is sincere," he chortled, "but your counsel is misdirected, dear Sister. It is yourself you should worry about."

And worry she did. Mérian had enough anxiety for the whole travelling party, and it twisted her stomach like a wet rag. By the time they reached the foot of the drawbridge spanning the outer ditch of the Neufmarché stronghold, she could scarcely breathe. And then they were riding through the enormous timber gates and reining up in the spacious yard, where they were greeted by none other than the baron himself.

Accompanied by two servants in crimson tunics, each bearing a large silver tray, the baron—his smooth-shaven face gleaming with goodwill—strode to meet them. "Greetings, *mes amis!*" bellowed the baron with bluff bonhomie. "I am glad you are here. I trust your journey was uneventful."

"Pax vobiscum," replied King Cadwgan, climbing down from his saddle and passing the reins to one of the grooms who came running to meet them. "Yes, we have travelled well, praise God."

"Good!" The baron summoned his servants with a wave of his hand. They stepped forward with their trays, which contained cups filled to the brim with wine. "Here, some refreshment," he said, handing the cups around. "Drink, and may it well become you," he said, raising his cup. He sipped his wine and announced, "The celebration begins tomorrow."

Mérian, having dismounted with the others and accepted the welcome cup, raised the wine to her lips; it was watered and cool and went down with undignified haste. When all had finished their cups, the new arrivals were conducted into the castle. Mérian, marching with the wooden stoicism of the condemned, followed her mother to a set of chambers specially prepared for them. There were two rooms behind a single wooden door; inside each was a single large bed with a mattress of goose down; two chairs and a table with a silver candleholder graced the otherwise bare apartment.

Food was brought to them, the candles lit, and a fire set in the hearth, for though it was a warm summer night, the castle walls were thick and constructed entirely of stone, making the interior rooms autumnal. Having seen to the needs of the baron's guests, the servants departed, leaving the women to themselves. Mérian went to the window and pushed open the shutter to look out and down upon the massive outer wall. By leaning out from the casement, she could glimpse part of the town beyond the castle.

"Come to the table and eat something," her mother bade her.

"I'm not hungry."

"The feast is not until tomorrow," her mother told her wearily. "Eat something, for heaven's sake, before you faint."

But it was no use. Mérian refused to taste a morsel of the baron's food. She endured a mostly sleepless night and rose early, before her mother or anyone else, and drawn by morbid curiosity, she crept out to see what she could discover of the castle and the way its inhabitants lived. She moved silently along one darkened corridor after another, passing chamber after chamber until she lost count, and came unexpectedly to a large anteroom that contained nothing more than a large stone fireplace and a hanging tapestry depicting a great hunt: fierce dogs and men on horseback chasing stags, hares, wild boars, bears, and even lions, all of which ran leaping through a woodland race. Drawn to the tapestry, she was marvelling at the prodigious size and the tremendous amount of needlework required for such a grand piece when she felt eyes on her back.

Turning quickly, she found that she herself was the object of scrutiny. "Your pardon, Lady Mérian," said her observer, emerging from the shadowed doorway across the room. Dressed entirely in black—tunic, breeches, boots, and belt—save for a short crimson cloak neatly folded across his shoulders and fixed with a large brooch of fine yellow gold almost the same colour as his long, flowing hair, he wore a short sword at his side, sheathed in a black leather scabbard.

"Baron Neufmarché," she said, suddenly abashed. "Forgive me. I did not mean to trespass."

"Nonsense," he said, smiling, "I fear it is *I* who am trespassing—on your enjoyment. I do beg your pardon." He moved to join her at the tapestry. She gazed at the wall hanging, and he gazed at her. "It is fine, is it not?"

"It is very beautiful," she said politely. "I've never seen the like."

"A mere trifle compared to you, my lady."

Blushing at this unexpected compliment, Mérian lowered her head demurely. "Here now!" said the baron. Placing a finger beneath her chin, he raised her face so that he could look into her eyes. "I see I have made you uncomfortable. Again, I must beg your pardon." He smiled and released her. "That is twice already today, and I have not yet broken fast. Indeed," he said, as if just thinking of it for the first time, "I was just on my way to the table. Will you join me?"

"Pray excuse me, my lord," said Mérian quickly, "but my mother will have risen and is no doubt looking for me."

"Then I must content myself to wait until the feast," said the baron. "However, before I let you go, you must promise me a dance."

"My lord, I know nothing of Ffreinc dancing," she blurted. "I only know the normal kind."

Neufmarché put back his head and laughed. "Then for you, I will instruct the musicians to play only the *musique normale*."

Unwilling to embarrass herself further, Mérian gave a small curtsy. "My lord," she said, backing away, "I give you good day."

"And good day to you, my lady," said the baron, smiling as he watched her go.

Mérian ducked her head, turned, and fled back down the corridor the way she had come, pausing at her chamber door to draw a breath and compose herself. She touched the back of her hand to her cheek to see if she could still feel the heat there, but it had gone, so she silently opened the door and entered the room. Her mother was awake and dressed in her gown. "Peace and joy to you this day, Mother," she said, hurrying to give her mother a kiss on the cheek.

"And to you, my lovely," replied her mother. "But you are awake early. Where have you been?"

"Oh," she said absently, "just for a walk to see what I might learn of the castle."

"Was your father or brother about?"

"No, but I saw the baron. He was going to break his fast."

"Did you see his wife, the baroness?"

"She was not with him." Mérian walked to the table and sat down. "Are they really so different from us?"

Her mother paused and considered the question. "I do not know," she said at last. "Perhaps not. But you must be on your best behaviour, Mérian," her mother warned, "and on your guard."

"Mother?"

The queen made no reply but simply raised an eyebrow suggestively.

"Whatever do you mean?" persisted Mérian.

"I mean," said her mother with exaggerated patience, "these Ffreinc noblemen, Mérian. They are rapacious and grasping, ever seeking to advance themselves at the expense of the Britons by any means possible—and that includes marriage."

"Mother!"

"It is true, Daughter. And do not pretend the thought of such a thing has never crossed your mind." Lady Anora gave her daughter a glance of shrewd appraisal and added, "More than one young woman has had her heart turned by a handsome nobleman—Ffreinc, English, Irish, or whatever."

"I would kill myself first," Mérian stated firmly. "Of that you can be certain."

"Nevertheless," her mother said.

Nevertheless, indeed.

And yet here they were, attending a feast-day celebration in the castle of a wealthy and powerful Ffreinc lord. Her mother was right, she knew, but she still resented such an untoward intrusion into what she considered the affairs of her own secret heart. She might not have the remotest intention of encouraging a dalliance with a loathsome Ffreincman, but she did not like having anyone, much less her mother, insinuating that she lacked the wits to govern her private affairs. And anyway, Baron Neufmarché was married and almost twice her age at least! What on earth was her mother thinking?

"Just you keep yourself to yourself, Mérian," her mother was saying.

"Mother, please!" she complained in a pained voice.

"Some of these noblemen need little enough encouragement— that is all I will say."

"And here was I," fumed Mérian, "thinking you had said too much already!"

On the same day that Baron Neufmarché's supply wagons departed, the second dispatch of Baron William de Braose's wagons arrived. As the heavy-laden vehicles trundled out across the valley floor, the sun dimmed in the west, leaving behind a copper glow that faded to the colour of an angry bruise. Nine wagons piled high with sacks of lime, rope, rolls of lead, and other supplies brought from Normandie were met by Orval, the count's seneschal, who instructed them to make camp below the caer. "Food will be brought to you here," he told them. "Stay with your teams tonight, and tomorrow you will be escorted to the building works."

The drivers passed a peaceful night at the foot of the hill beneath the fortress, moving on the next day to the three castle mounds now emerging on Elfael's borders. The farthest, a place newly dubbed *Vallon Verte*, took all of a long day to reach, and it was already growing dark by the time the wagoners began unhitching the oxen and leading them to the ox pen. Only when their animals were fed, watered, and put to rest for the night did the drivers join the masons and labourers gathered around their evening fire.

The workers camped a little distance away from the ditch beyond which rose the bailey mound where they had been working that day. Cups of ale and loaves of bread were passed from hand to hand as whole chickens, splayed on green elm branches, were turned slowly in the flames.

Men talked easily and watched the stars gather in the sky overhead as they waited for their supper. When they had eaten, they spread their bedrolls in the emptied wagon beds and lay down to pass a peaceful night amongst the heaps of stone and stockpiled timbers of the building site. It was not until one of the drivers went to yoke his team the next morning in preparation for the return journey that he noticed half of the oxen had disappeared. Of the twelve beasts to have entered the pen the night before, only six remained. Three of his own animals were missing, half of a second team, and one of a third.

He quickly called the other drivers to him, but other than standing and staring at the half-empty pen, no one had any explanation for the disappearance. They called the master, but he could offer nothing better than, "The Welsh are a thieving kind, as God knows. It's their nature. I say, find the nearest farmer and you'll find your oxen, like as not."

When asked, however, the master refused to spare any of his men from the building work to search for the missing beasts. They were still arguing over who should go to the fortress to request a party to track down the purloined animals when the count himself appeared. He had come with a small force to make a circuit of the construction works. Now that the long-awaited supplies had arrived, he wanted to make certain that nothing prevented the workmen from making good and speedy progress.

"Thieves, you say?" wondered Falkes when the drivers had explained the predicament. "How many?"

"Difficult to say, my lord," replied the driver. "No one saw them."

"No one saw anything?"

"No, my lord. We only discovered the theft a short while ago. It must have happened during the night."

"And the ox pens are not guarded, I suppose?"

"No, my lord."

"Why not?"

"No one steals oxen, my lord."

"I think," retorted the count, "you will find that they *do*. The Welsh will steal anything they can lay hands to."

"So it would appear."

"Indeed," replied the count sharply. "You will find them, or go back without them."

"We dare not go back without them," the driver said.

"Why not? The wagons are empty," Falkes pointed out. "You can get more oxen in Lundein."

"My lord," replied the driver gravely, "matched teams are scarce as bird hair just now. You won't find any for sale between here and Paris."

"Be that as it may," rejoined the count, "what do you expect *me* to do about it?"

"We thought—begging your pardon, sire—that his lordship might lend us some soldiers to find the thieves, my lord."

Unwillingness tugged the edges of the count's lips into a frown. First the missing horses, and now this. Was it really so difficult to keep animals from wandering off? "You want my men to search for oxen?"

"Five or six men-at-arms should be enough." Seeing the count's hesitation, the wagoner added, "The sooner we find the missing team, the sooner we can be on our way to fetch more supplies for the masons." When the count still failed to reply, he continued, "Now that the season is full on, the baron will not take kindly to any delays." As a last resort, he added, "Also, the workers will be wanting their pay."

Count Falkes regarded the empty wagons and the drivers standing idle. "Yes, yes, you have made your point," he said at last. "Ready your wagons and prepare to leave. We will find the stolen beasts. Oxen are slow; they cannot have gone far."

"Right you are, my lord," said the driver, hurrying away before the count changed his mind.

Turning to the soldiers who had accompanied him to the site, de Braose called the foremost knight to him. "Guiscard! Come here; a problem has arisen."

The knight attended his lord and listened to his instructions carefully. "Consider it done," he replied. "And the thieves, sire? What shall we do with them?"

"This land is now governed by the Custom of the March. You know what we do with thieves, do you not?"

A slow smile spread across the knight's smooth face. "Yes, I believe I recall."

"Then do it," ordered the count. "Show no mercy."

The knight bent his head in acknowledgement of his orders, then turned and started away. He had taken only a few paces when the count called after him, "On second thought, Guiscard, keep one or two alive, and bring them to me. We will draw and quarter them in the new town square and let their well-deserved deaths serve as a warning to anyone else who makes bold to steal from Baron de Braose."

"It will be done, sire." The knight mounted the saddle and called three men-at-arms to attend him.

"See you make some haste," the count shouted as they rode off. "The wagons must be on their way without further delay."

The day could not pass quickly enough for Mérian. In her impatience, she forgot her displeasure at her mother's meddling and her abhorrence of all things Ffreinc, and instead fell to fretting about clothes. She stood gazing with mounting chagrin at the gown spread out on her bed. Why, oh why, had she chosen that one? What had possessed her?

As much as she loathed the idea of consorting with Norman nobility, she did not want to give any of them the satisfaction of dismissing her as an ignorant British churl. When the time came to dress for the feast, she had worked herself into such a nervous state that she felt as if someone had opened a cage of sparrows inside her, and the poor birds were all aflutter to get out.

Trying her best to maintain her fragile composure, she forced herself to wash slowly and carefully in the small basin of cool water. She put on a fresh chemise of costly bleached linen and allowed her mother to brush her hair until it shone. Her long, dark tresses were gathered and braided into a thick and intricate plait, the end of which was adorned with a clasp of gold. Mérian then drew on her best gown of pale blue and, over it, a short, silk-embroidered mantle of fine cream-coloured linen. The gown and mantle were gathered at the waist by a wide kirtle of yellow satin, the beaded tassels of which almost brushed her toes. When she was ready, Queen Anora approved her daughter's choices and said, "But there is something missing . . ."

Suddenly stricken, Mérian gasped, "What? What have I forgotten?"

"Calm yourself, child," cooed her mother, bending to a small wooden casket that had travelled with them from Eiwas. Raising the lid, she produced a gossamer-thin veil of white samite hemmed with gold thread. She arranged the long rectangle of rare cloth with the point of one corner between Mérian's dark brows and the rest trailing down her back to cover, yet reveal, the young woman's braided hair.

"Mother, your best veil," breathed Mérian.

"You shall wear it tonight, my lovely," replied her mother. Bending to the casket once more, she brought out a thin silver circlet, which she placed on her daughter's head to secure the veil, then stepped back to observe her handiwork. "Exquisite," her mother pronounced. "A jewel to brighten any celebration. Let the Norman ladies gnaw their hearts with envy."

Mérian thanked her mother with a kiss. "I will be happy if I can survive the evening without falling over."

"Off with you now," said Anora, sending her away with a pat on the cheek. "Put on your shoes. The chamberlain will be here any moment."

Stepping into new soft leather slippers, never worn, Mérian tied the slender laces above her ankles, and as the knock sounded on the chamber door, she straightened, drew a deep, calming breath, and prepared to take her place amongst the highborn guests assembling in the baron's hall.

Though it was daylight still, the banqueting room was lit by rows of torches aflame in sconces on the walls. The immense oak doors were opened wide to allow the baron's guests to come and go as they pleased; iron candletrees in each corner and a bright fire in the hearth at the far end of the room banished the shadows and gloom like uninvited guests.

Boards had been set on trestles to form rows of tables down the length of the hall, at one end of which another table had been established on a riser so that it overlooked all the others. The room was aswarm with people—both guests in their courtly finery and servants in crimson tunics and mantles, bearing trays of sweetmeats and dainties to sharpen the appetite. Up in a small balcony in one corner of the hall, five musicians played music that sounded to Mérian like birds twittering in the trailing branches of a willow while water splashed in a crystal pool. It was so beautiful, she could not understand how it was that no one seemed to be listening to them at all. She had time enough to spare them only a fleeting glance before being drawn to observe the arrival of the baron and his lady wife.

"All hail the Lord of the Feast!" cried Remey, the baron's seneschal, as the couple appeared in the doorway. "Presenting my lord and lady, the Baron and Baroness Neufmarché. All hail!"

"Hail!" replied the guests with fervour. "Hail the Lord of the Feast!"

Baron Neufmarché, tall and regal in his black tunic and short red cloak, with his long, fair hair brushed back, the gold at his throat and on his tunic gleaming, stood on the threshold and passed a beneficent gaze over the glittering assembly. He carried a small jewelled knife on his wide black belt and wore a cross of gold on a gold chain around his neck. Beside him, slender as a willow wand, stood the baroness, Lady Agnes. She wore a pale gown of silvery samite that glistened like water in the torchlight; on her head was a small,

323

square-cornered caplet beaded with tiny pearls. A double circlet of tiny pearls adorned each slender wrist. Oh, but she was thin. The outlines of her hip bones could be seen through the fine material of her dress, and the bones at the base of her throat stood out like twin arrow points. Her cheeks were hollow. Only when she smiled, stretching her tight lips across her teeth, did a scrap of vitality steal into her features.

Neufmarché and his wife were attended by a dark-haired young woman—their daughter, Lady Sybil—whom Mérian judged to be a few years younger than herself. The girl wore a bored and aloof expression that declared to the world a lively disdain for the gathering and, no doubt, her forced attendance. Behind the imperious young lady marched a bevy of courtiers and servants carrying trays heaped with tiny loaves of bread made with pure white flour. Other servants in crimson livery followed pulling a tun of wine on a small wagon; still others brought casks of ale. Two kitchen servants followed bearing an enormous wooden trencher on poles; in the centre of the trencher was a great wheel of soft white cheese surrounded by brined onions and olives from the south of France.

The servants proceeded to make a slow circuit of the room so that the guests might help themselves to the cheese and olives, and Mérian turned her attention to the other guests. There were several young ladies near her own age, all Ffreinc. As far as she could tell, there were no other Britons. The young women were gathered in tight little gaggles and cast snide glances over their shoulders; none deigned to notice her. Mérian had resigned herself to having her mother's company for the evening when two young women approached.

"Peace and joy to you this day," one of the young women offered. Slightly the elder of the two, she had an oval face and a slender, swan-like neck; her hair was long, so pale as to be almost white, and straight and fine as silken thread. She wore a simple gown of glistening green material Mérian had never seen before.

"Blessings on you both," replied Mérian nicely.

"Pray, allow me to make your acquaintance," said the young woman in heavily accented Latin. "I am Cécile, and"—half-turning, she indicated the dark-haired girl beside her—"this is my sister, Thérese."

"I am Mérian," she responded in turn. "I give you good greeting. Have you been long in England?"

"*Non*," answered the young woman. "We have just arrived from Beauvais with our family. My father has been brought to lead the baron's warhost."

"How do you find it here?" asked Mérian.

"It is pleasant," said the elder girl. "Very pleasant indeed."

"And not as wet as we feared," added Thérese. She was as dark as her sister was fair, with large hazel eyes and a small pink mouth; she was shorter than her sister and had a pleasant, apple-cheeked face. "They told us it never stopped raining in England, but that is not true. It has rained only once since we arrived." Her gown was of the same shiny cloth, but a watery aquamarine colour, and like her sister's, her veil was yellow lace.

"Do you live in Hereford?" asked Cécile.

"No, my father is Lord Cadwgan of Eiwas."

The two young strangers looked at each other. Neither knew where that might be.

"It is just beyond the Marches," Mérian explained. "A small cantref north and west of here—near the place the English call Ercing, and the Ffreinc call Archenfield."

"You are Welsh!" exclaimed the elder girl. The two sisters exchanged an excited glance. "We have never met a Welsh."

325

Mérian bristled at the word but ignored the slight. "British," she corrected lightly.

"*Les Marchés,*" said Thérese; she had a lilting, almost wispy voice that Mérian found inexplicably appealing. "These Marches are beyond the great forest, *oui?*"

"That is so," affirmed Mérian. "Caer Rhodl—my father's stronghold—is five days' journey from here, and a part of the way passes through the forest."

"But then you have heard of the—" She broke off, searching for the proper word.

"*L'hanter?*" inquired the elder of the two.

"*Oui, l'hanter.*"

"The haunting," confirmed Cécile. "Everyone is talking about it."

"It is all *anyone* speaks of," affirmed Thérese with a solemn nod.

"What do they say?" asked Mérian.

"You do not know?" wondered Cécile, almost quivering with delight at having someone new to tell. "You have not heard?"

"I assure you I know nothing of it," Mérian replied. "What is this haunting?"

Before the young woman could reply, the baron's seneschal called the celebrants to find places at the board. "Let us sit together," suggested Cécile nicely.

"Oh, do please sit with us," cooed her sister. "We will tell you all about the haunting."

Mérian was about to accept the invitation when her mother turned to her and said, "Come along, Daughter. We have been invited to join the baron at the high table."

"Must I?" asked Mérian.

"*Certainement,*" gushed Cécile. "You must. It is a very great *honneur.*"

"Precisely," her mother replied.

"But these ladies have kindly asked me to sit with them," Mérian countered.

"How thoughtful." Lady Anora regarded the young women with a prim smile. "Perhaps, in the circumstance, they will understand. You may join them later, if you wish."

Mérian muttered a hasty apology to her new friends and followed her mother to the high table where her father and brother were already taking their places at the board. There were other noblemen—all of them Ffreinc, with their resplendently jewelled ladies—but her father was given the place at the baron's right hand. Her mother sat beside her father, and Mérian was given the place beside the baroness, at her husband's left hand. To Mérian's relief, Lady Sybil was far down at the end of the table with young Ffreinc nobles on either side, both of whom appeared more than eager to engage the aloof young lady.

As soon as all the remaining guests had found places at the lower tables, the baron raised his silver goblet and, in a loud voice, declared, "Lords and ladies all! Peace and joy to you this day of celebration in honour of my lady wife's safe return from her sojourn in Normandie. Welcome, everyone! Let the feast begin!"

The feast commenced in earnest with the appearance of the first of scores of platters piled high with roast meat and others with bread and bowls of stewed vegetables. Servants appeared with jars and began filling goblets and chalices with wine.

"I do not believe we have met," said the baroness, raising a goblet to be filled. In her gown of glistening silver samite, she seemed a creature carved of ice; her smile was just as cold. "I am Baroness Agnes."

"Peace and joy to you, my lady. I am called Mérian."

The woman's gaze sharpened to unnerving severity. "King Cadwgan's daughter, yes, of course. I am glad you and your family could join us today. Are you enjoying your stay?"

"Oh, yes, baroness, very much."

"This cannot be your first visit to England, I think?"

"But it is," answered Mérian. "I have never been to Hereford before. I have never been south of the March."

"I hope you find it agreeable?" The baroness awaited her answer, regarding her with keen, almost malicious intensity.

"Wonderfully so," replied Mérian, growing increasingly uncomfortable under the woman's unrelenting scrutiny.

"*Bon*," answered the baroness. She seemed suddenly to lose interest in the young woman. "That is splendid."

Two kitchen servants arrived with a trencher of roast meat just then and placed it on the table before the baron. Another servant appeared with shallow wooden bowls which he set before each guest. The men at the table drew the knives from their belts and began stabbing into the meat. The women waited patiently until a servant brought knives to those who did not already have them.

More trenchers were brought to the table, and still more, as well as platters of bread and tureens of steaming buttered greens and dishes that Mérian had never seen before. "What is this?" she wondered aloud, regarding what appeared to be a compote of dried apples, honey, almonds, eggs, and milk, baked and served bubbling in a pottery crock. "It is called a *muse*," Lady Agnes informed her without turning her head. "Equally good with apricots, peaches, or pears."

Whatever apricots or peaches might be, Mérian did not know, but guessed they were more or less like apples. Also arriving on the board were plates of steamed fish and something called *frose*, which turned out to be pounded pork and beef cooked with eggs . . . and several more dishes the contents of which Mérian could only guess. Delighted at the extraordinary variety before her, she determined to try them all before the night was over.

As for the baroness, sitting straight as a lance shaft beside her, she took a bite of meat, chewed it thoughtfully, and swallowed. She tore a bit of bread from a loaf and sopped it in the meat sauce, ate it, and then, dabbing her mouth politely with the back of her hand, rose from her place. "I hope we can speak together again before you leave," she said to Mérian. "Now I must beg your pardon, for I am still very tired from my travels. I will wish you *bonsoir*."

The baroness offered her husband a brisk smile and whispered something into his ear as she stepped from the table. Her sudden absence left a void at Mérian's right hand, and the baron was deep in conversation with her father, so she turned to the guest on her left, a young man a year or two older than her brother. "You are a stranger, I think," he said, watching her from the corner of his eye.

"Verily," she replied.

"So are we both," he said, and Mérian noticed his eyes were the colour of the sea in deep winter. His features were fine—almost feminine, except for his jaw, which was wide and angular. His lips curled up at the corners when he spoke. "I have come from Rainault. Do you know where that is?"

"I confess I do not," answered Mérian, remembering her mother's caution and trying to discourage him with an indifferent tone.

"It is across the narrows in Normandie," he said, "but my family is not Norman."

"No?"

He shook his head. "We are Angevin." A flicker of pride touched this simple affirmation. "An ancient and noble family."

"Still Ffreinc, though," Mérian observed, unimpressed.

"Where is your home?" he asked.

"My father is King Cadwgan ap Gruffydd—of an ancient and noble family. Our lands are in Eiwas."

"In Wallia?" scoffed the young man. "You are a Welsh!"

"British," said Mérian stiffly.

He shrugged. "What's the difference?"

"*Welsh*," she said with elaborate disdain, "is what ignorant Saxons call anyone who lives beyond the March. Everyone else knows better."

"I have heard of this March," he said, unperturbed. "I have heard about your haunted forest."

Mérian stared at the young man, agitation knitting her brows as curiosity battled her reluctance to encourage any Ffreinc affinity. Curiosity won. "This is the second time this evening someone has mentioned the haunting." Searching the lower tables, she found the two girls she had spoken to earlier. "Those two—there." She indicated the sisters sitting together. "They spoke of it also."

"They would," muttered the young man, obviously irritated that his important news had been spoiled.

"Do you know them?"

"My sisters," he said, as if the word pained his mouth. "What did they say?"

"Nothing at all. The baron was seated, and we had to come to table, so I learned nothing more about it."

"Well then, I will tell you," said the young man, recovering something of his former good humour as he went on to explain how the forest was haunted by a rare phantom in the form of an enormous preying bird.

"How strange," said Mérian, wondering why she had heard nothing of this.

"This bird is bigger than a man—two men! It can appear and disappear at will and swoop out of the sky to snatch horses and cattle from the field."

"Truly?"

He nodded with dread assurance. Apparently, the thing was black from head to tail and twice the height of the tallest man, possessing glowing red eyes and a beak as sharp as a sword. He smiled grimly, enjoying the effect his words were having on the young woman beside him. "It can devour a human being whole with one snatch of its beak, and also outrun the fastest horse."

"I thought you said it swooped from the sky," Mérian pointed out, dashing cold water on his fevered assertions. "Is it a bird or a beast?"

"A bird," the young man insisted. "That is, it has the wings and head of a bird, but the body of a man, only bigger. Much bigger. And it does not only fly, but hides in the forest and waits to attack its prey."

"How do you know this?" asked Mérian. "How does anyone know?"

Bending near, he put his head next to hers and said, "It was seen by soldiers—not so many days ago."

"Where?"

"In the forest of the March!" he replied confidently. "Some of the baron's own knights and men-at-arms were attacked. They fought the creature off, of course, but they lost their horses anyway."

The tale was so strange that Mérian could not decide what to make of it. "They lost their horses," she repeated, a sceptical note edging into her tone. "All of them?"

The young man nodded solemnly. "*And* one of the knights."

"What?" It was a cry of disbelief.

"It is true," he insisted hurriedly. "The knight was missing for three days but was at last able to fight free of the thing and escaped unharmed—except that he cannot remember what happened to him or where he was. Some are saying that the phantom is from the Otherworld, and everyone knows that any mortal who goes there cannot remember the way back—unless, of course, he eats of the food of the dead, and then he is doomed to stay there and can never return."

Speechless, Mérian could but shake her head in wonder.

"All the baron's court have been talking about nothing else," said the young man. "I have seen the man that was taken, but he will speak of it no more."

"Why not?"

"For fear that the creature has left its mark on him and will return to claim his soul."

"Can such a thing happen?"

"Bien sûr!" The young man nodded again. "It has been known. The priests at the cathedral have forbidden anyone to make sacrifice to the phantom. They say the creature is from the pit and has been sent by the devil to sift us."

An exquisite thrill rippled through Mérian's frame—half fear, half morbid fascination.

"You live beyond *les Marchés*," her companion said, "and yet you have no knowledge of the phantom bird?"

"None," replied Mérian. "I once heard of a great serpent that haunted one of the lakes up in the hills—Llyntalin, it was. The creature possessed the head of a snake and the slimy skin of an eel, but legs like those of a lizard, with long claws on its toes. It came out at night to steal cattle and drag them down into the bottom of the lake to drown."

"A wyrm," the young man informed her knowingly. "I, too, have heard of such things."

"But that was a long time ago—before my father was born. My grandfather told me. They killed it when he was a boy. He said it stank so bad that three men fell sick and one man died when they tried to bury it. In the end they burnt it where it lay."

"I would like to have seen that," the young man said appreciatively. Smiling suddenly, he said, "My name is Roubert. What is yours?"

"I am Mérian," she replied.

"Peace and joy to you, Lady Mérian," he said, "this night and all nights."

"And to you, Roubert," she smiled, liking this young man more and more. "Have you ever seen a wyrm?"

"No," he conceded. "But in a village not far from our castle in Normandie, there was a child born with the head of a dog. By this, the father knew his wife was a witch, for she had had unnatural relations with a black hound that had been seen outside the village."

"What happened?"

"The villagers hunted down the dog and killed it. When they returned home, they found the woman and the baby were also dead with the same wounds as those inflicted on the dog."

"Here now!" interrupted a voice next to Mérian. She turned to see Baron Neufmarché leaning across the empty place toward her. Glancing down the table, she saw that her father was deep in conversation with the Ffreinc nobleman next to him. "What is this nonsense you are telling our guest?"

"Nothing of importance, sire," answered the young man, retreating rapidly.

"We were speaking of the phantom in the Marches forest," volunteered Mérian. "Have you heard of this, sire?"

"Hmph!" puffed the baron. "Phantom or no, it cost me five horses."

"The creature ate your horses?" wondered Mérian in amazement.

"I did not say that," replied the baron. Smiling, he slid closer to her on the bench. "I lost the horses, it is true. But I am more inclined to the view that, one way or another, the soldiers were careless."

"What about the missing footman?" asked the young man.

"As to that," replied the baron, "I expect drink or too much sun will account for his tale." He paused to reconsider. "Still, I grant that he was a solid enough fellow. Whatever the explanation, the incident has much altered his mind."

Mérian shivered at the thought of something wild and freakish arising in the forest—the very forest she and her family had passed through on the way to Hereford.

"But come, my lady," said the baron with a smile, "I see I have upset you. We will not speak of such abhorrent things anymore. Here!" He reached for a bowl containing a pale purple substance. "Have you ever tasted *frumenty*?"

"No, never."

"Then you must. I insist," said the baron, handing her his own silver spoon. He pushed the bowl toward her. "I think you will like it."

Mérian dipped the tip of the spoon into the mushy substance and touched it to her tongue. The taste was cool and sweet and creamy. "It is very good," she said, handing back the spoon.

"Keep it," said the baron, closing his hand over hers. "A little gift," he said, "for gracing this celebration with your, ah, *présence lumineuse—* your radiant presence."

Mérian, feeling the heat of his touch on her skin, thanked him and tried to withdraw her hand. But he held it more tightly. Leaning closer, he put his mouth to her ear and whispered, "There is so much more I would give you, my lady."

CHAPTER 33

The knight called Guiscard, in command of eight doughty men-at-arms, ordered his troops to follow the tracks made by the missing oxen. Most of the hoofprints, as expected, led back toward the valley in the direction the wagons had come. A few, however, led out from the pen and down the hill to the nearby stream. "Here, men! To me!" shouted Guiscard as soon as he was alerted to this discovery. "We have them!"

When the searchers had assembled once more, they mounted their horses and set off together on the trail of the missing oxen, pursuing the track as it followed the stream, passing down around the foot of the castle work and behind the shoulder of the next hill. Once out of sight of the builders' camp, the trail turned inland, heading straight up over the hill and toward the forest a short distance to the northeast.

The searchers mounted the brow of the hill and started out across the wide grassy hilltop toward the leaf-dark woodland, blue in the distance and shimmering in the heat haze of summer. The tracks were easy to follow, and the soldiers loped easily through the long grass, slowing only as they approached the beeches, elms, and finger-thin fir trees that formed a protective bulwark at the edge of the forest.

Passing between the trunks of two large elms, the trail of the missing oxen entered the wood as through a timber gate. The light was somewhat poorer inside, but the beasts left good, well-shaped prints in the soft earth—and, occasionally, soft splats of droppings—which allowed the knight and his men to proceed without difficulty. A few hundred paces inside the wood, the ox trail joined a deer run, and the hoofprints of the four heavy-footed beasts mingled with those of their swift-running cousins.

The path traced the undulating hillside, rising and falling with the rock escarpment beneath it, until it descended into a deep-riven glen with a brook at the bottom. Here the trail turned to follow the trickle of water as it flowed out from the forest interior, eventually joining the stream that passed by the foot of the castle. They pushed on, and after a time, the banks became steeper and rock lined as the brook sank lower into the folded earth, dwindling to little more than a blue-black rivulet at the bottom of a ravine of shattered grey shale.

The searchers moved deeper into the forest, where the trees were older and bigger and the undergrowth denser. Sunlight came in dappled fits and starts, striking green glints from every leafy surface. When the search party came to the top of a ridge, Guiscard halted his men and paused a moment to survey the path ahead. The air was still and humid, the trail dark and close grown. The knight ordered his companions to dismount and proceed on foot. "The thieves cannot have gone much farther," Guiscard told his men. "The only grazing is behind us now. They will not want to stray too far from it."

"Who says the thieves intend to graze them?" wondered one of the men-at-arms.

"Valuable beasts like those?" scoffed the knight. "What else would they do with them?"

The man shrugged, then spat. "Eat them."

Guiscard glowered at the soldier and said, "Move on."

The trail pursued its way down the slope of the ridge beneath trees of ever-increasing size and age. The upper branches grew higher from the ground, lifting the roof of foliage and dimming the sunlight with a heavy canopy of glowing green leaves. On and on they went, and when the knight stopped again, the wood had become dark and silent as an empty church. The only sound to be heard was the rustling and chirping of small birds, unseen in the upper branches high above.

Thorny shrubs—blackberry and bilberry—grew man high on each hand; a few hundred paces farther along, the trail pinched down to a constricted corridor before disappearing into a tangled and impenetrable bank of brambles. As they neared the wall of thorns, they saw that the narrow trail turned sharply to the left. The oxen had passed between two overlapping hedges; the animals had been led single file in order to squeeze through, and there were tufts of tawny hair caught on some of the lower thorns. The silence of the forest had given way to the noisy chafe and chatter of crows emanating from the other side of the bramble bank. Easing cautiously through the thorny hedge, the searchers entered a clearing. The racket of the birds had risen to a piercing cacophony.

Gripping their lances, the soldiers crept out from the thorn hedge and into a small, sunlit meadow ringed about with birch and rowan trees. In the centre of the clearing was a roiling, boiling black mound of birds: hundreds of them. Crows, ravens, choughs, jays, and others were fighting over something on the ground, and still more were circling and diving in the air above this squirming, living heap of feathers, wings, and beaks.

The air was loud with their shrieks and heavy with a sweet, turgid stink.

"Drive them off," Guiscard ordered, and four of the men-at-arms rushed the mound of birds, swinging their lances before them and yelling as they ran.

The birds took flight at the sudden appearance of the men and fled squawking and screeching into the sky; most settled again in the branches of the surrounding trees, where they continued to shriek their outrage at being driven from their repast.

The birds gone for the moment, the knight and the rest of the men approached the mound where their four comrades were now standing still as stones, enthralled by the heap before them.

"Out of the way," ordered Guiscard, striding up. The footman stepped aside, and the knight took one look at the mound before him and almost vomited.

Before him were what appeared to be the entrails and viscera of the missing oxen—artfully heaped into a single, glistening purple mound of rotting slime. Rising from the centre of this putrefying mass was a long wooden stake, and on the stake was the severed head of an ox. The skin and most of the flesh had been ripped from the skull to reveal the bloody bone beneath. Two of the hapless animal's hooves were stuffed in its hanging mouth, and its tail protruded absurdly from one of its ears, and jutting from the naked eyeballs of the freshly flensed skull were four long, black raven feathers.

The weird sight caused these battle-hardened men to blanch and brought the gorge rising to their throats. One of the soldiers cursed, and two others crossed themselves, glancing around the clearing nervously. *"Sacre bleu!"* grunted a soldier, prodding a lopped-off hoof with the blade of his lance. "This is the work of witches."

"What?" said the knight, recovering some of his nerve. "Have you never seen a slaughtered beast?"

"Slaughtered," muttered one of the men scornfully. "If they were slaughtered, where are the carcasses?" Another said, "Aye, and where's the blood and hide and bones?"

"Carried away by them that slaughtered the beasts," replied another of the soldiers, growing angry. "It's just a pile of guts." With that, he shoved his spear into the curdling bulk, striking an unseen bladder, which erupted with a long, low hiss and released a noxious stench into the already fetid air.

"Stop that!" shouted the man beside him, shoving the offender, who pushed back.

"Enough!" shouted the knight. Quickly scanning the surrounding trees for any sign that they were being watched, he said, "The thieves may still be close by. Make a circuit of the clearing, and give a shout when you find their trail."

Only too glad to turn away from the grisly mound in the centre of the glade, the soldiers walked to different parts of the perimeter and, bending low, began to look for the footprints of the thieves. One complete circuit failed to turn up anything resembling a human footprint, so the knight ordered them to do it again, more slowly this time and with better care and attention.

They were all working their way around the circle when a strange sound halted them in midstep. It started as an agonised cry—as if someone, or something, was in mortal anguish—and then rose steadily in pitch and volume to a wild ululation that raised the short hairs on the napes of the warriors' necks.

The crows in the treetops stopped their chatter, and a dread hush descended over the clearing. The unnatural calm seemed to spread into the surrounding forest like tendrils of a stealthy vine, like a fog when it searches along the ground, coiling, moving, flowing amongst the hidden pathways until all is shrouded with its vapours.

The searchers waited, hardly daring to breathe. After a moment, the eerie sound rose again, closer this time, growing in force, rising and rising—and then suddenly trailing away as if stifled by its own strength.

The carrion birds in the high branches took flight all at once.

The soldiers, holding tight to their weapons, gazed fearfully at the sky and at the wood around them. The trees seemed to have moved closer, squeezing the ring tighter, forming a sinister circle around them.

"Christ have mercy!" cried a footman. He flung out a hand and pointed across the clearing.

The soldiers turned as one to see an indistinct shape moving in the shadows beneath the trees at the edge of the glade. Straining into the darkness, they saw a form emerge from the forest gloom—as if the shadow itself was thickening, gathering darkness and congealing into the shape of a monstrous creature: big as a man, but with the head and wings of a bird, and a round skull-like face that ended in an extravagantly long, pointed black beak.

Like a fallen angel risen from the pit, this baleful presence stood watching them from across the clearing.

"Steady, men," said the knight, holding his sword before him. "Close ranks."

No one moved.

"Close ranks!" shouted Guiscard. "Now!"

The soldiers, shaken to action, moved to obey. They drew together, shoulder to shoulder, weapons ready. Even as they formed the battle line, the phantom melted away, disappearing before their eyes as the shadows reclaimed it.

The soldiers waited, bloodless hands gripping their weapons, staring fearfully at the place where they had last seen the creature. When a cloud passed over the sun, leeching warmth from the air, the terrified men bolted and ran.

"Stand!" cried the knight, to no avail. He watched his men deserting him, thrashing through the brush in their blind haste to escape the horror encircling them. With a last glance around the tainted meadow, brave Guiscard joined his men in flight.

Back at the builders' camp, the breathless searchers told what they had found in the forest and how they had been attacked by the forest phantom—a creature so hideous as to defy description—and only narrowly escaped with their lives. As for the missing oxen, they had been completely devoured by the creature.

"Except for the vitals," one of the men-at-arms explained to his astonished audience. "The devil thing devoured everything but the guts," he said. The soldier next to him took up the tale. "The bowels it vomited in the meadow. We must have startled it at its feeding," he surmised. Another soldier nodded, adding, "*C'est vrai*. No doubt that was why it attacked us."

But the soldiers were wrong. It was not the phantom that fed on the stolen oxen. That very evening, in British huts and holdings all along the valley, a score of hungry families dined on unexpected gifts of good fresh meat that had been discovered lying on the stone threshold of the house. Each gift had been delivered the same way: wrapped in green oak leaves, one of which was pinned to the parcel by a long, black wing feather of a raven.

341

CHAPTER 34

Brother Aethelfrith paused on the road to drag a damp sleeve across his sweating face. The Norman merchants with whom he had been travelling had long since outpaced him; his short legs were no match for their mules and high-wheeled carts, and none of the four traders or their retainers had consented to allow him to ride in back of one of the wagons. To a man, all had made obscene gestures and pinched their nostrils at him.

"Stink? Stink, do I?" muttered the mendicant under his breath. He was a most fragrant friar, to be sure, but the day was sweltering, and sweat was honest reward for labours spent. "Normans," he grumbled, mopping his face, "God rot them all!"

What a peculiar people they were: big, lumpy lunks with faces like horses and feet like boats. Vain and arrogant, untroubled by any notions so basic as tolerance, fairness, equality. Always wanting everything their own way, never giving in, they reckoned any disagreement as disloyal, dishonest, or deceitful, while judging their own actions, however outrageously unfair, as lawful God-given rights. Did the Ruler of heaven really intend for such a greedy, grasping, gluttonous race of knaves and rascals to supplant Good King Harold?

"Blesséd Jesus," he muttered, watching the last of the wagons recede into the distance, "give the whole filthy lot flaming carbuncles to remind them how fortunate they are."

Then, chuckling to himself over the image of the entire occupying population hopping around clutching painfully swollen backsides, he moved on. Upon cresting the next hill, he saw a stream and a fording place where the road met the valley. Several of the carts had paused to allow the animals to drink. "God be praised!" he cried and hurried to join them. Perhaps they would take pity on him yet.

Arriving at the ford, he called a polite greeting, but the merchants roundly ignored him, so he walked a little way upstream until he came to a shady place, where, drawing his long brown robe between his legs, he tucked the ends into his belt and waded out into the stream. "Ahh," he sighed, luxuriating in the cool water, "a very blessing on a hot summer day. Thank you, Jesus. Much obliged."

When the merchants moved off a short while later, he remained behind, content to dabble in the stream a little longer. By all accounts, Llanelli was a mere quarter day's walk from the ford. No one was expecting him, so he could take all the time he needed; and if he reached the monastery by nightfall, he would count himself fortunate.

The fat friar padded in the stream, watching the small, darting fish. He hummed to himself, enjoying the day as if it were a meal of meat and ale spread before him with lavish abundance. Upon reflection, he had no right to be so happy. His errand, God knew, was sin itself.

How he had come to the idea, he still could not say. An overheard conversation—a marketplace rumour, an errant word, perhaps, spoken by a stranger in passing—had worked away in him, sending its black roots deep, growing unseen until it burst forth like a noxious flower in full bloom. One moment, he had been standing before the butcher's stall, haggling over the price of a rind of bacon, and the next his bandy legs were scuttling him back to his oratory to pray forgiveness for the thoroughly immoral idea that had so forcefully awakened in his ever-scheming brain.

"Oh my soul," he sighed, shaking his head at the mystery of it. "The heart of man is deceitful above all things, and desperately wicked. Who can know it?"

Although he had spent the night on his knees, begging both forgiveness and direction, as dawn came up bright in the east, that heavenly guidance was no more in evidence than the pope's pardon. "If you have qualms, Lord," he sighed, "stop me now. Otherwise, I go."

Since nothing materialised to prevent him, he rose, washed his face and hands, strapped on his sandals, and hastened to consummate his scheme. It was *not*—and he was fiercely adamant about this part—for his own enrichment, nor did he desire any gain but justice. This was the heart of the matter. Justice. For, as his old abbot had often said, "When iniquity sits in the judgement seat, good men must take their appeals to a higher court."

Aethelfrith did not know how that appeal to justice might come about, but trusted that his information would give Bran all the inspiration he required to at least set the wheels in motion.

The shadows lengthened over the valley, and the road was not shrinking; with grudging reluctance, Aethelfrith stepped from the water, dried his feet on the hem of his robe, and continued on his way. The merchants' van was well ahead of him now, but he dismissed the rude company from his thoughts. His destination was almost within sight. The Vale of Elfael stretched before him, its green fields spotted with slow-shifting cloud shadows. He doubted a more peaceful and serene dale could be found anywhere.

Buoyed by the beauty of the place, Brother Aethelfrith opened his mouth wide and began to sing aloud, letting his voice resound and echo out across the valley as he made his way down the long slope that would eventually bring him to Llanelli.

He was sweating again, long before reaching the valley floor. In the near distance he saw the old fortress, Caer Cadarn, rising on its hump of rock overlooking the road. "May your walls keep you safe as Jericho," Aethelfrith muttered, then crossed himself and hurried by.

The sun was touching the far western hills when he reached Llanelli—or what was left of it. The low wall of the enclosure had been taken down and most of the interior buildings either destroyed or converted to other uses. The yard had been enlarged to make a market square, and new structures—unfinished, their bare timbers rising from the builders' rubble—stood at each corner. All that remained of the original monastery was a single row of monks' cells and the chapel, which was only slightly larger than his own oratory. There seemed to be no one around, so he strode to the door of the chapel and walked in.

Two priests knelt before the altar, on which burned a single thick tallow candle that sent a black, oily thread of smoke into the close air. He stood in the doorway for a moment, then cleared his throat to announce his presence and said, "Forgive me, friends. I see I am interrupting your prayers."

The nearer of the two priests looked around and then nudged the other, who quickly finished his prayer, crossed himself, and rose to greet the newcomer. "God be good to you, brother," said the priest, taking in his visitor's robe and tonsure. "I am Bishop Asaph. How can I be of service?"

"Greetings in Christ and all his glorious saints!" declared the mendicant. "Brother Aethelfrith, I am, come on an errand of some . . .

ah"—he hesitated, not wishing to say too much about his illicit chore—"delicacy and importance."

"Peace and welcome, brother," the bishop said. "As you can see, we have little left to call our own, but we will help you in any way we can."

"It is easily done and will cost you nothing," the friar assured him. "I am looking for Bran ap Brychan—I have a message for him. I was hoping someone here could tell me where to find him."

At this, a shadow passed over the bishop's face. His smile of welcome wilted, and his eyes grew sad. "Ah," he sighed. "I would that you had asked anything but that. Alas, you will not find the man you seek amongst the living." He shook his head with weary regret. "Our young Prince Bran is dead."

"Dead! Oh, dear God, how?" Aethelfrith gasped. "When did this happen?"

"Last autumn, it was," replied the bishop. "As to how it happened—there was a fight, and he was cruelly cut down when trying to escape Count de Braose's knights." The English monk staggered backwards and collapsed on a bench against the wall. "Here; rest a moment," said Asaph. "Brother Clyro, fetch our guest some water."

Clyro hobbled away, and the bishop sat down beside his guest. "I am sorry, my friend," he said. "Your question caught me off guard, or I might have softened the blow for you."

"Where is he buried? I will go and offer a prayer for his soul."

"You knew our Bran?"

"Met him once. He stayed the night with me—he and that tall tree of a fellow—what was his name? John! They had a priest with them. Good man, I think. One of yours?"

"Iwan, yes. And Ffreol, perhaps?"

"The very fellows!" Aethelfrith nodded. "They were on their way to Lundein to see the king. I went with them in the end. Sorely

347

disappointed they were. But I could have told them. The Ffreinc are bastards."

"From what we have been able to learn," Asaph said, "our Bran was captured on his way home. He was killed a few days later trying to escape." He regarded his visitor with soft-eyed sadness. "It pains me the more," he continued, "but Iwan and Brother Ffreol also fell afoul of Count de Braose."

"Dead, too? All of them?" asked Aethelfrith.

Bishop Asaph bent his head in sorrowful assent.

"Filthy Norman scum," growled the friar. "Kill first and repent later. That is all they know. Worse than Danes!"

"There was nothing to be done," Asaph said. "We said a Mass for him, of course. But"—he lifted his hands helplessly—"there it is."

"So now you have no king," observed Aethelfrith.

"Bran was the last of his line," affirmed the bishop. "We must be content now to simply survive and endure this unjust reign as best we can. And now"—his voice quivered slightly—"another blow has been dealt us. The monastery has been taken over for a market town."

"Scabby thieves, the lot of 'em!" muttered Aethelfrith. "Nay, worse than that. Even the lowest thief wouldn't rob God of his home."

"Baron de Braose has determined to install his own churchmen in this place. They are to arrive any day—indeed, when you came to the door, we thought it might be the new abbot come to drive us from our chapel."

"Where will you go?"

"We are not without friends. The monastery of Saint Dyfrig in the north is sister to Llanelli, or once was. We will go to them . . . and from there?" The bishop offered a forlorn smile. "It is in God's hands."

"Then I am doubly sorry," said Aethelfrith. "This world is full of trouble, God knows, and he spares not his own servants." Brother

Clyro returned with a bowl of water, which he offered to their guest. Aethelfrith accepted the bowl and drank deeply.

"Why did you want to see our Bran?" asked the bishop when he had finished.

"I had a notion to help him," replied the friar. "But now that I see how events have fallen out, I warrant it a poor idea. In any event, it is of no consequence now."

"I see," replied the bishop. He did not press the matter. "Have you travelled far?"

"From Hereford. I keep an oratory there—Saint Ennion's. Have you heard of it?"

"Of course, yes," replied the bishop. "One of our own dear saints from long ago."

"To be sure," conceded Aethelfrith. "But it is home to me now."

"Then it is too far to come and return all at once. You must stay with us a few days"—the bishop lifted a hand in a gesture of helplessness—"or until the Ffreinc come to drive us all away."

Friar Aethelfrith spent the next day helping Asaph and Clyro pack their belongings. They wrapped the bound parchment copies of the Psalms and the book of Saint Matthew, as well as the small golden bowl used for the Eucharist on high holy days. These things had to be disguised and secreted amongst the other bundles of clerical implements and utensils, for fear that the Ffreinc would confiscate them if their value was known.

They finished their work and enjoyed a simple supper of stewed beans with a little sliced leek and burdock. The next morning, Brother Aethelfrith bade his friends farewell and started back to his oratory. The merchants he had followed to Elfael had also concluded their business, and as he passed Castle Truan—what the Normans were now calling Caer Cadarn—he saw five mule-drawn carts turn out onto the road and thought, now that the wagons were empty of goods, he might beg bold and ask for a ride.

So he quickened his pace and by midmorning had caught up with the wagon van when it paused to water the animals at the valley stream before starting up the long slope of the forested ridge. He came within hailing distance and gave a shout, which was not returned. "I see they still have some manners to learn," he muttered. "But no matter. They will have to be hard-hearted indeed to refuse my request."

As he neared the fording place, he saw that the traders were standing together in a clump, motionless, with their backs to him; they seemed to be staring at something on the far side of the stream.

He hurried to join them, calling, "Pax vobiscum!"

One of the traders turned on him. "Keep your voice down!" he whispered savagely.

Mystified, the friar shut his mouth with a click of his teeth. Taking his place beside the men, he stared across the fording place and into the wood. The mules, impassive creatures ordinarily, seemed restless and uneasy; they jigged in their traces and tossed their heads. And yet the wood beyond the stream seemed quiet enough. Brother Aethelfrith could see no one on the road; all seemed calm and tranquil.

"Forgive my curiosity, friend," he whispered to the man next to him, "but what is everyone looking at?"

"Gerald thought he saw the *thing*—the creature," the merchant whispered back, his voice tense in the unnatural silence. "The only sound to be heard was the lazy, liquid gurgle of the water as it slipped around and over the stones.

"What creature?" wondered the priest. Nothing moved amongst the lush green foliage of the trees and lower brushwood.

"The phantom," the man explained. He turned his face to the bowlegged friar. "Do you not know?"

"I know nothing of any phantom," replied Aethelfrith. "What sort of phantom is it presumed to be?"

"Why," replied the merchant, "it takes the form of a great giant of a bird. Men hereabouts call it King Raven."

"Do they indeed?" wondered the friar, much intrigued. "What does it look like—this giant bird?"

The merchant stared at him in disbelief. "By the rood, man! Are you dim? It looks like a thumping great *raven*."

"Shut up!" hissed one of the others just then. "You will have the demon down on us!"

Before anyone could reply to this, one of the other traders threw out his hand and shouted, "There it is!"

Friar Aethelfrith glimpsed a flash of blue-black feathers glinting in the sun and the suggestion of a massive black wing as the creature emerged from the brushwood on the opposite bank a few score paces downstream. Two of the merchants gave out shouts of terrified surprise, and two others fell to their knees, clasping their hands and crying aloud to God and Saint Michael to save them. The rest fled back down the road to the safety of Castle Truan, leaving their carts behind.

"Christ have mercy!" gasped one of the remaining merchants as the creature's head came into view. Its face was an oval of smooth black bone, devoid of feathers, with two round pits where its eyes should have been. Save for the wickedly long pointed beak, its head most resembled a charred human skull.

Lifting its swordlike beak, the thing uttered a piercing shriek that resounded in the deathly silence of the wood. Even as the cry hung in the air, the phantom turned and simply melted back into the shadow of the wood.

The terror-stricken merchants leapt to their feet and ran for their wagons, lashed their mules to motion, and fled back into the valley. Of all those at the stream, only Aethelfrith was left to give chase—which he promptly did.

Gathering up his robe, Aethelfrith strode boldly across the stream and started after the phantom. Upon reaching the far side of the stream, he paused and, finding nothing, proceeded into the brushwood, where the thing had vanished. There was no sign of the creature, and after a few paces he stopped to reconsider. He could hear the traders clattering away into the distance as their wagons bumped over the rutted road. Then, even as he was wondering whether to continue the chase or resume his journey, he saw the faint glimmer of glistening black feathers—just a quick flash before it disappeared into a hedge bank a few hundred paces down the trail. He hurried on.

The ground rose toward the ridge, and he eventually reached the top. Sweating and out of breath, he stumbled upon a game trail that led along the ridgetop. It was old and well established, overarched by the huge limbs of plane trees, elms, and oaks that formed a vault overhead and allowed only intermittent shafts of sunlight to strike down through the leaf canopy and illuminate the path. It was dark as a cellar, but since it was easier than pushing his way through the heavy underbrush, he decided to follow the run and soon realised just how quickly it allowed a man on foot to move about the forest.

The heat had been mounting steadily as the sun arced toward midday, and Aethelfrith was glad for the shade beneath the hanging boughs. He walked along, listening to the thrushes singing in the upper branches and, lower down, the click and chirrup of insects working the dead leaf matter that rotted along the trail. At any moment, he told himself, he would turn back—but the path was soft underfoot, so he continued.

After a time, the trail branched off; the left-hand side continued along the ridgetop, and the right-hand side descended the slope to a rocky hollow. Here the priest stopped to consider which path, if either, to take. The day was speeding from him, and he decided to resume his homeward journey. He turned around and started back, but he had not gone far when he heard voices: murmured only, light as thistledown on the dead-still air, there and gone again, and so faint as to be easily dismissed as the invention of his own imagining.

But years of living alone in his oratory with no company save his own inner musings had made his hearing keen. He held his breath and listened for the sound to come again. His vigilance was rewarded with another feather-soft murmur, followed by the unmistakable sound of laughter.

Frail as a wisp of cobweb adrift on the breeze, it nonetheless gave him a direction to follow. He took the right-hand trail leading down the back of the ridge. The path fell away steeply as it entered the hollow below, and Aethelfrith, his short legs unable to keep up with his bulk, plunged down the hill.

He entered the hollow in a rush, tripped over a root, and fell,

354

landing with a mighty grunt at the feet of the great black phantom raven. He slowly raised his fearful gaze to see the ominous black head regarding him with malevolent curiosity. The fantastic wings spread wide, and the thing swooped.

The priest rolled on his belly and tried to avoid the assault, but he was too slow, and he felt his arm seized in a steely grip as he squirmed on the ground. "God save me!" he cried.

"Shout louder," hissed the creature. "God may hear you yet."

"Let be!" he cried in English, wriggling like an eel to get free. "Let me go!"

"Do you want to kill him, or should I?"

Aethelfrith twisted his head around and saw a tall, brawny man step forward. He wore a long, hooded cloak into which were woven a multitude of small tatters of green cloth; twigs and branches and leaves of all kinds had also been attached to the curious garment. Regarding the priest with a frown, he drew a knife from his belt. "I'll do it."

"Wait a little," spoke the raven with a human voice. "We'll not kill him yet. Time enough for that later." To the friar, he said, "You were at the ford. Did anyone else follow?"

Struggling in the creature's unforgiving clutch, it took the priest a moment to realise that the thing had spoken to him. Turning his eyes to his captor once more, he saw not the bone-thin shanks of a bird, but the well-booted feet and legs of a man: a man wearing a long cloak covered entirely with black feathers. The face staring down at him was an expressionless death's head, but deep in the empty eye sockets, Aethelfrith caught the glimmer of a living eye.

"I ask for the last time," the black-cloaked man said. "Did anyone follow you?"

"No, sire," replied the priest. "I came alone. God have mercy, can we not talk this out? I am a priest, am I not?"

355

"That you are, Aethelfrith!" said the creature, releasing him at once.

"Pax vobiscum!" cried the priest, scrambling to his feet. "I mean no harm. I only thought to—"

"Tuck!" exclaimed the man in the leafy cloak.

Reaching up a black-gloved hand, the creature took hold of the sharp raven beak and lifted it to reveal a man's face beneath.

"Blesséd Jesus," gasped the astonished friar. "Is it Bran?"

"Greetings, Tuck," laughed Bran. "What brings you to our wood?"

"You are dead!"

"Not as dead as some might wish," he said, removing the high-crested hood from his head. "Tell us quickly now—how did you come to be here?"

"A hood!" cried the friar, relief bubbling over into exultation. "It is just a hood!"

"A hood, nothing more," admitted Bran. "Why are you here?"

"I came to find *you*, did I not?" The friar stared at the strangely costumed man in amazement. "And here you are. Sweet Peter's beard, but you do not half frighten a body!"

"Friar Tuck!" called Iwan, stepping close. He gave the priest a thump on the back. "You held your life in your hands just then. What of the others—the men at the ford—did they see you?"

"Nay, John. They all ran away clutching their bowels." He smiled at the memory. "You put the fear of the devil in them, no mistake."

Bran smiled. "Good." To Iwan he said, "Bring the horses. We will meet Siarles as planned."

"Tuck, too?" wondered Iwan.

"Of course." Bran turned and started away.

"Wait," called the cleric. "I came to Elfael to find you. I have something important to say."

"Later," Bran told him. "We must be miles from here before

midday. Our day's work has only begun. Come along," he said, beck-oning the priest to follow. "Watch and learn."

The game run was narrow, and the horses were fast, pounding along the ridgetop track as the outreaching hazel branches whipped past. Bran, following Iwan's lead, slashed his mount across the withers with his reins, careering through the forest. The trail continued to climb as the ridge rose, bending around to the north; upon reaching the summit, they abandoned the run and struck off along another trail, moving west toward the edge of the forest. The riders might have travelled more quickly but for the extra weight behind Bran, clinging on for dear life.

The trail dropped sharply into a rocky defile. The pathway became rough under hoof, and the riders slowed. Stones the size of houses rose abruptly on each hand, forming a winding and shadowed corridor through which they had to pick their way carefully. When the path grew too narrow, they abandoned their mounts, tying them to a small pine tree growing in a crevice, and then proceeded on foot.

Silently, they stalked along a stone gallery so close they could have touched both sides with arms outstretched. This trail ended, and they stepped out into a small clearing, where they were met by another man—also dressed in a long, hooded cloak of green tatters. "Where have you been?" he whispered sharply. He saw the bandy-legged priest toiling along in Bran's wake and asked, "Where did you find that?"

Ignoring the question, Bran asked, "Are they here?"

"Aye," answered the man, "but they will soon be moving on—if they are not already gone." He darted away. "Hurry!"

Bran turned to his visitor and said, "You must swear a sacred oath to hold your tongue and keep silent."

357

"Why? What is going to happen?" asked Aethelfrith.

"Swear it!" insisted Bran. "Whatever happens, you must swear."

"On my naked soul, I swear silence," the friar replied. "May all the saints bear witness."

"Now stay out of sight." To Iwan, looking on, he said, "Take up your position. You know what to do."

All three moved off at a fast trot. Brother Aethelfrith stood for a moment, catching his breath, and then hurried after them. Soon the surrounding wood began to thin somewhat, and they came to a dell with huge boulders strewn amongst the standing trees like miniature mountains. At the far end of the dell, the forest ended, and the Vale of Elfael opened before them.

Beneath a great spreading beech tree at the forest's edge, three swine-herds were taking their midday meal—two men and a boy, eating from a tuck bag they passed between them. All around them their scattered herd—thirty or more large grey-and-black-spotted swine—grubbed and rooted for last year's acorns and beech mast beneath the trees.

Without a word, Bran and his two companions left the trail, quickly melting into the shadowed greenwood. Aethelfrith knelt down on the path to catch his breath and wait to see what would happen.

Nothing happened.

His attention had begun to drift when he heard a shout from the swineherds. Turning his eyes back to the trio of herdsmen, the friar saw that all three were on their feet and staring into the wood. He could not see what had drawn their attention, but he could guess.

The three remained stock-still, unable or unwilling to move, rigid with fear. Then Aethelfrith saw what they had seen: the elusive black shape moving slowly in and out of the shadows amongst the trees. At the same time, two figures in green emerged from the wood behind the watching herdsmen. Keeping the low-hanging beech between the swineherds and the black shape that held their attention, the two green-cloaked men, using nothing more than short staves, quickly culled eight pigs from the herd and led them away into the wood.

Wonder of wonders, the swine followed the strange herdsmen willingly and without a sound. In less time than it would have taken Aethelfrith to tell, the livestock had been removed from the dell. Just as the animals disappeared into the forest, there arose a ghastly unnatural shriek from the surrounding wood. It was the same screech the priest had heard at the ford, only now he knew what it signified.

The swineherds, terrified by the inhuman cry, threw themselves to the ground and covered their heads with their mantles. They were still cowering there, not daring to move, when Iwan appeared and, with a gesture only, summoned Tuck to follow him. They returned to the horses then and waited for Bran, who soon joined them. "You can have Siarles's horse," Bran told the priest. "He is bringing the pigs."

The three retreated back down the narrow defile, retracing their steps until they reached a wider way, and then rode north into the heart of the forest. Unaccustomed to riding, it was all Aethelfrith could do to remain in the saddle, let alone guide his mount. He soon lost all sense of distance and direction and contented himself with merely keeping up as he pressed deeper and ever deeper into the dark heart of the ancient wood.

Eventually, they slowed their horses and, after splashing across a brook and gaining a long, low rise, arrived at the great black trunk of a lightning-blasted oak. Here Bran stopped and dismounted. Aethelfrith, grateful for the chance to quit the saddle, climbed down and stood looking around. The trees were giants of the forest, their limbs huge and majestic, their crowns lofty. Their great girth meant that their trunks were far apart from one another and little grew in the shadows beneath them. Younger trees struggled up, straight and thin as arrows, to reach the sun; most failed. Unable to sustain their own weight, they fell back to earth—but slowly, slanting down at unnatural angles.

"This way," said Bran, motioning his guest to follow. He stepped through the split in the trunk of the blighted oak as through an open door. The friar followed, emerging on the other side into a wide, sunlit hollow large enough to contain a most curious settlement, a veritable village of hovels and huts made from branches and bark and—could it be?—the horns, bones, and skins of deer, oxen, and other beasts. On the far side of the glade were small fields, where a number of settlement dwellers were at work amongst the furrowed rows of beans, peas, and leeks.

"Passing strange," murmured Aethelfrith, oddly delighted with the place.

"This is Cél Craidd," Bran told him. "My stronghold. You are welcome here, Tuck, my friend. The freedom of my home is yours."

The cleric made a polite bow. "I accept your hospitality."

"Come along, then," said Bran, leading the way into the peculiar settlement, "there is someone else I would have you meet before we sit down to hear your news."

Bran, his cloak of black feathers gleaming blue and silver in the bright daylight, led the way to one of the hovels in the centre of the settlement. As they approached, an old woman emerged, pushing aside the deer hide that served as her door. She regarded the newcomer with a keen dark eye and then touched the back of her hand to her forehead.

"This is Angharad," said Bran. "She is our banfáith." Seeing that the priest did not understand the word, he added, "It is like a bard. Angharad is Chief Bard of Elfael."

To the old woman, he said, "And this is Brother Aethelfrith—he helped us in Lundein." Clapping a hand to the friar's shoulder, Bran continued, "He has come with news he deems so important that he has travelled all the way from Hereford."

"Then let us hear it," said Angharad. Stepping back, she pulled aside the deerskin and indicated that her guests should enter. The single large room had a bare earth floor; packed hard and swept clean, it was covered by an array of animal skins and handwoven coverings. More skins encircled a round firepit in the centre of the room, where a small fire flickered amongst the embers. There was a sleeping pallet on one side and a row of woven grass baskets.

Bran untied the leather laces at the neck of his feathered cloak and hung it on the tine of a protruding antler above one of the baskets; above the cloak, he hung the high-crested hood with its weird mask, then removed the black leather gauntlets and put them in the basket. He knelt over a basin on the floor to splash water on his face and drew his hands through his black hair. Shaking off the excess moisture, he arched his back and then suddenly slumped and sighed, and his body quivered as if with cold. The tremor passed, and Bran straightened. When he turned, he had changed slightly; he was more the Bran whom Aethelfrith remembered.

Angharad invited her guests to sit and stepped out to a barrel beside the door; she dipped out a bowl, which she brought to the priest. "Peace, friend, and welcome," she said, offering him the cup. "May God be good to thee all thy days, and strengthen thee to every virtue."

The priest bowed his head. "May his peace and joy forever increase," he replied, "and may you reap the rich harvest of his blessing."

"It is water only," Bran explained. "We don't have enough grain to make ale just now."

"Water is the elixir of life," declared the priest, raising the bowl to his lips. "I never tire of drinking it." He sucked down a healthy draught and passed the bowl to Bran, who also drank and passed it to

361

Iwan. When the big man finished, he returned the bowl to Angharad, who set it aside and took her place at the fire ring with the men.

"I trust all is well in Hereford," said Bran, easing into the reason for the friar's journey to Elfael.

"Better than here," replied Aethelfrith. "But that could change." Leaning forward in anticipation of the effect his words would have, he said, "What if I told you a flood of silver was coming your way?"

"If you told me that," replied Bran, "I would say we will all need very big buckets."

"Aye," agreed the priest, "and tubs and vats and casks and tuns and barrels and cisterns large and small. And I say you had best find them quickly, because the flood is on the rise."

Bran eyed the stout priest, whose plump cheeks were bunched in a self-satisfied grin. "Tell us," he said. "I would hear more of this sil-ver flood."

CHAPTER 36 ⚕

The rider appeared unannounced in the yard at Caer
Rhodl. The horse was exhausted: hide wet with lather, spume pink
with blood, hooves cracked. Lord Cadwgan took one look at the suffering animal and its dead-eyed rider and commanded his grooms to
take the poor beast to the stables and tend it. To the rider, he said,
"Friend, your news must be grievous indeed to drive a good horse this
way. Speak it out, and quickly—there will be ale and warm meat waiting for you."

"Lord Cadwgan," said the rider, swaying on his feet, "the words I
have are bitter ashes in my mouth."

"Then spit them out and be done, man! They will grow no sweeter
for sucking on them."

Drawing himself up, the messenger nodded once and announced,
"King Rhys ap Tewdwr is dead—killed in battle this time yesterday."

Lord Cadwgan felt the ground shift beneath his feet. Only months
ago, Rhys, King of Deheubarth—and the man most Britons considered the last best hope of the Cymry to turn back the tide of the

Ffreinc invaders—had returned from exile in Ireland, where he had spent the last few years ingratiating himself with Irish kings, slowly eliciting support for the British cause against the Ffreinc. Word had gone out that Rhys had returned with a massive warhost and was preparing to make a bid for the English throne while William the Red was preoccupied in Normandie. Such was the strength of King Rhys ap Tewdwr's name that even men like Cadwgan—who had long ago bent the knee to the Ffreinc king—allowed themselves to hope that the yoke of the hated overlords might yet be thrown off.

"How can this be?" Cadwgan wondered aloud. "By whose hand? Was it an accident?" Before the messenger could answer, the lord collected himself and said, "Wait. Say nothing." He raised his hand to prevent the reply. "We will not stand in the yard like market gossips. Come to my chambers and tell me how this tragedy has come about."

On his way through the hall, King Cadwgan ordered drink to be brought to his room at once, then summoned his steward. With Queen Anora and Prince Garran in attendance, he sat the messenger down in a chair and commanded him to tell all he knew of the affair.

"Word came to our king that Ffreinc marchogi had crossed our borders and set fire to some of our settlements," the messenger began after taking a long pull on the ale cup. "Thinking it was only a few raiders, Lord Rhys sent a warband to put a stop to it. When none of the warriors returned, the alarm was raised and the warhost assembled. We found the Ffreinc encamped in a valley inside our lands, where they were building one of those stone caers they glory in so greatly."

"And this inside the Marches, you say?" asked Cadwgan.

The messenger nodded. "Inside the very borders of Deheubarth itself."

"What did Lord Rhys say to that?"

"Our king sent word to the commander of the foreigners,

demanding their departure and payment for the burned settlements on pain of death."

"Good," said Cadwgan, nodding his approval.

"The Ffreinc refused," continued the messenger. "They cut off the noses of the messengers and sent the bloodied men back to tell the king that the Ffreinc would leave only with the head of Rhys ap Tewdwr as their prize." The messenger lifted his cup and drank again. "By this we knew that they had come to do battle with our lord and kill him if they could."

"They left him no choice," observed Garran, quick to refill the cup. "They wanted a fight."

"They did," agreed the rider sadly, raising the cup to his lips once more. "Though the Ffreinc force was smaller than our own—fewer than fifty knights, and maybe two hundred footmen—we were wary of some treachery. God knows, we were right to be so. The moment we assembled the battle line, more marchogi appeared from the south and west—six hundred at least, two hundred mounted, and twice that on foot. They had taken ship and come in behind us." The messenger paused. "They had marched through Morgannwg and Ceredigion, and no one lifted a hand to stop them, nor to warn us."

"What of Brycheiniog?" demanded Cadwgan. "Did they not send the battle host?"

"They did not, my lord," replied the man curtly. "Neither blade nor shield of Brycheiniog was seen on the field."

Speechless with shock, King Cadwgan stared at the man before him. Prince Garran muttered an oath beneath his breath and was silenced by his mother, who said, "Pray continue, sir. What of the battle?"

"We fought for our lives," said the messenger, "and sold them dear. At the end of the first day, Rhys raised the battle call and sent to the cantrefs close about, but none answered. We were alone." He passed a hand before his eyes as if to wipe the memory from his sight. "Even so," he continued, "the fighting continued until the evening of the second day. When Lord Rhys saw that we could not win, he gathered the remnant of the warhost to him, and we drew lots—six men to ride with word to our kinsmen, and the rest to remain and seek glory with their comrades." The messenger paused, gazing emptily down. "I was one of the six," he said in a low voice, "and here I am to tell you—Deheubarth is no more."

King Cadwgan let out a long breath. "This is bad," he said solemnly. "There is no getting around it." *First Brychan at Elfael,* he thought, *and now Rhys at Deheubarth.* The Ffreinc, it seemed, would not be content with England. They meant to have all of Wales, too.

"If Deheubarth is fallen," said Prince Garran, looking to his father, "then Brycheiniog cannot be far behind."

"Who has done this?" asked Queen Anora. "The Ffreinc—whose warriors were they?"

"Baron Neufmarché," answered the messenger.

"You know this?" demanded Cadwgan quickly. "You know this for a truth?"

The messenger gave a sharp jerk of his chin sideways. "Not for a truth, no. The leaders amongst them wore a strange livery—one we have not seen before. But some of the wounded we captured spoke that name before they died."

"Did you see the end?" asked Anora, clasping her hands beneath her chin in anticipation of the answer.

"Aye, my lady. Myself and the other riders—we watched it from the top of the hill. When the standard fell, we scattered with the news."

"Where will you go now?" she enquired.

"I ride to Gwynedd, to inform the northern kingdoms," replied the messenger. "God willing, and my horse survives."

"That horse has run as far as it will go today and for many days, I fear," replied the king. "I will give you another, and you will rest and refresh yourself here while it is readied."

"You should stay here tonight," Anora told the messenger. "Continue on your way tomorrow."

"My thanks to you, my lady, but I cannot. The northern kings were raising warriors to join us. They must hear that they can no longer look to the south for help."

The king commanded his steward to bring food and make ready provisions the messenger could take with him. "I will see to the horse," said Garran.

"My lord king, I am much obliged." Having discharged his duty, the messenger slumped, grey faced, into the chair.

"We will leave you to your rest now," said the queen, leading her husband out.

Once out of hearing of the chamber, the king turned to his wife. "There it is," he concluded gloomily. "The end has begun. So long as the south remained free, it was possible to think that one day the Cymry might yet shake off the Ffreinc. There will be nothing to stop the greedy dogs now."

Queen Anora said, "You are client to Neufmarché. He will not move against us."

"Client I may be," spat the king bitterly. "But I am Cymry first, last, and always. If I pay tribute and rents to the baron, it is only to keep him far away from here. Now it seems he will not be satisfied with anything less than taking all of Cymru and driving us into the sea."

He shook his head as the implications of the catastrophe rolled over him. "Neufmarché will keep us only so long as it pleases him to do so. Just now he needs someone to hold the land and work it, but when the time comes to repay a favour, or provide some relative with an estate, or reward some service rendered—*then*," intoned Cadwgan ominously, "then all we have will be taken from us, and we will be driven out."

"What can we do?" asked Anora, bunching her mantle in her fists. "Who is left that can stand against them?"

"God knows," replied Cadwgan. "Only God knows."

Baron Neufmarché received the news of his resounding victory with a restrained, almost solemn demeanour. After accepting a report on the casualties suffered by his forces, he thanked his commanders for carrying out his orders so well and so completely, awarding two of them lands in the newly conquered territory, and another an advancement in rank to a lordship and the command of the unfinished castle that had so readily lured King Rhys ap Tewdwr to his doom. "We will speak more of this tonight at table. Go now; rest yourselves. You have done me good service, and I am pleased."

When the knights had gone, he went to his chapel to pray.

The simple room built within the stone walls of the castle was cool in the warmth of the day. The baron liked the air of calm quiet of the place. Approaching the simple wooden altar with its gilt cross and candle, he went down on one knee and bowed his head.

"Great God," he began after a moment, "I thank you for delivering the victory into my hand. May your glory increase. I beg you, almighty Lord, have mercy on those whose lives were given in this campaign. Forgive their sins, account their valour to their merit, and welcome them to your eternal rest. Heal the wounded, Lord Christ, and send them a swift recovery. In all ways comfort those who have suffered the pains of battle."

He remained in the chapel and was still enjoying the serenity when Father Gervais appeared. Aging now, though still vigorous, the cleric had been a member of the baron's court since coming to Beauvais as a newly shorn priest to serve Bernard's father.

"Ah, it is you, my lord," said the priest when the baron turned. "I thought I might find you here." The grey-robed priest came to stand beside his lord and master. "You are not celebrating the victory with your men?"

"God grant you peace, father," said Bernard. "Celebrating? No, not yet. Later this evening, perhaps."

The priest regarded him for a moment. "Is anything the matter, my son?"

Crossing himself, Neufmarché rose and, taking the priest by the arm, turned him and led him from the chapel, saying, "Walk with me, father. There is something I would ask you."

They climbed to the rampart and began making a slow circuit of the castle wall. "Earl Harold swore a sacred oath to Duke William, did he not?" said the baron after walking awhile. The sun was lowering, touching everything with gold. The summer air was warm and heavy and alive with the click and buzz of insects amongst the reeds and bulrushes of the nearby marshland below the east wall.

"An oath sworn on holy relics in the presence of the Bishop of Caen," replied Father Gervais. "It was written and signed. There is no doubt about it whatsoever." Glancing at the baron, he said, "But you know this. Why do you ask?"

"The oath," said Bernard, "confirmed the promise made to William that he was to follow Edward as rightful King of England."

"D'une certitude."

"And the matter received the blessing of the pope," said Bernard, "who is God's vicar on earth."

"Again, that is so," agreed the priest. He glanced at the baron, who continued walking, his eyes on the stone paving at his feet. "My lord, are you fretting over the divine right again?"

The baron's head turned quickly. "Fretting? No, father." He turned away again. "Perhaps. A little." He sighed. "It just seems too easy . . ." Unable to find the words, he sighed again. "All this."

"And what do you expect? God is on our side. It is so ordained. William has been chosen of God to be king, and thus any enterprise that supports and increases his kingdom will rightly be blessed of God."

Bernard nodded, his eyes still downcast.

The priest was silent for a moment, then declared, "Ah! I have it. You worry that your support of Duke Robert will be held against you. That you will be called to reckoning, and the price will be too heavy to bear. That is what is troubling you, *n'est ce pas?*"

370

"It has occurred to me," the baron confessed. "I sided with Robert against Rufus. The king has not forgotten, and neither will God, I think. There is an accounting to be rendered. Payment is due; I can feel it."

"But you were upholding the law," protested the priest. "You will remember that at the time, Robert *was* the rightful heir. He had to be supported, even against the claims of his own brother. You were right to do so."

"And yet," replied the baron, "Robert did not become king."

"In his heavenly wisdom, God saw fit to bestow the kingship on his brother William," said Father Gervais. "How were you to know?"

"How *was* I to know?" repeated Bernard, wondering aloud.

"*Précisément!*" declared the priest. "You could not know, for God had not yet revealed his choice. And I believe that is why Rufus did not punish those who went against him. He understood that you were only acting in good faith according to holy law, and so he forgave you. He returned you to his grace and favour, as was only just and fair."

The priest spread his hands as if presenting an object so obvious that it needed no further description. "Our king forgave you. *Voilà!* God has forgiven you."

In the clear light of the elderly priest's unfaltering certainty, Bernard felt his melancholy dissipating. "There is yet one more matter," he said.

"Let me hear it," said the priest. "Unburden your soul and obtain absolution."

"I promised to send food to Elfael," the baron confessed. "But I did not."

"But you did," countered the priest. "I saw the men readying the supplies. I saw the wagons leave. Where did they go, if not to the relief of the Welsh?"

"Before, I mean. I let the Welsh priest think that Count de Braose had stolen the first delivery, because it suited my purposes."

"I see." Father Gervais tapped his chin with an ink-stained finger. "But you made good your original vow."

"Oh yes—doubled it, in fact."

"Well then," replied the priest, "you have overturned the wrong and provided your own penance. You are absolved."

"And you are certain that my attainment of lands in Wallia is ordained by heaven?"

"*Deus vult!*" the priest confirmed. "God wills it." He raised his hand to the baron's arm and gave it a fatherly squeeze. "You can believe that. Your endeavours prosper because God has so decreed. You are his instrument. Rejoice and be grateful."

Bernard de Neufmarché smiled, doubts routed and faith restored. "Thank you, father," he said, his countenance lightening. "As always, your counsel has done me good service."

The priest returned his smile. "I am glad. But if you wish to continue in favour with the Almighty, then build him a church in your new territories."

"One church only?" said the baron, his spirits rising once more. "I will build ten!"

CHAPTER 37

You cannot save Elfael one pig at a time," Brother Aethelfrith was saying.

"Have you *seen* our pigs?" Bran quipped. "They are mighty pigs."

Iwan chuckled, and Siarles smirked.

"Laugh if you must," said the friar, growing peevish. "But you will wish soon enough you had listened to me."

"The people are hungry," Siarles put in. "They welcome whatever we can give them."

"Then give them back their land!" cried Aethelfrith. "God love you, man; do you not see it yet?"

"And is this not the very thing we are doing?" Bran said. "Calm yourself, Tuck. We are already making plans to do exactly what you suggest."

The friar shook his tonsured head. "Are you deaf as well as blind?"

"Why do you think we watch the road?" asked Iwan.

"Watch it all you like," snipped the priest. "It will avail you nothing if you are not prepared for the flood I'm talking about."

The others frowned as one. "Tell us, then," said Bran. "What is it that we lack?"

"Sufficient greed," replied the cleric. "By the rood and Jehoshaphat's nose, you think too small!"

"Enlighten us, O Head of Wisdom," remarked Iwan dryly.

"See here." Tuck licked his lips and leaned forward. "Baron de Braose is building three castles on the northern and western borders of Elfael, is he not? He has a hundred—maybe two hundred—masons, not to mention all those workers toiling away. Workmen must be paid. Sooner or later, they *will* be paid—every last man—hundreds of them." Aethelfrith smiled as he watched the light come up in his listeners' eyes. "Ah! You see it now, do you not?"

"Hundreds of workers paid in silver," said Bran, hardly daring to voice the thought. "A river of silver."

"A *flood* of silver," corrected Aethelfrith. "Is this not what I am saying? Even now the baron is preparing to send his wagons with strongboxes full of good English pennies to pay all those workers. All the money you need will soon be flooding into the valley, and it is ripe for the taking."

"Well done, Tuck!" cried Bran, and he jumped to his feet and began pacing around the fire ring. "Did you hear, banfáith?" he asked, turning suddenly to Angharad sitting hunched on her three-legged stool beside the door. "Here is the very chance we need to drive the foreigners from our land."

"Aye, could be." She nodded in cautious agreement. "Mind, the Ffreinc will not send their silver through the land unprotected. There will be marchogi, and in plenty."

Bran thanked her for her word of warning, then turned to his champion. "Iwan?"

He frowned, sucking his teeth thoughtfully before answering. "We have—what?—maybe six men amongst us who have ever held more than a spade. We cannot go against a body of battle-trained knights on horseback."

"Yet the silver will not leap into our hands of its own accord, I think," offered Siarles.

Angharad, frowning on her stool, spoke again. "If thou wouldst obtain justice, thou must thyself be just."

The others turned questioning glances toward Bran, who explained, "I think she means we cannot attack them without provocation."

The group fell silent in the face of such a challenge. "Truly," Bran said at last. Raising his head, he gazed across the fire ring, dark eyes glinting with merry mischief. "We cannot take on knights on horse-back, but King Raven can."

Brother Tuck remained unmoved. "It will take more than a big black bird to frighten battle-hardened knights, will it not?"

"Well then," Bran concluded. His smile was slow, dark, and fiendish. "We will give them something more to fear."

A bbot Hugo de Rainault was used to better things. He had served in the courts of Angevin kings; princes had pranced to his whim; dukes and barons had run to his beck and bidding. Hugo had been to Rome— twice!—and had met the pope both times: Gregory and Urban had each granted him audience in their turn, and both had sent him away with gifts of jewel-encased relics and precious manuscripts. He had been extolled for an archbishopric and, in due time, perhaps even a papal legacy. He had governed his own abbey, controlled immense estates, held dominion over the lives of countless men and women, and enjoyed a splendour even the kings of England and France could sincerely envy.

Alas, all that was before the rot set in.

He had done what he could to prevent the debacle once the tide of fortune began to turn against him—benefactions and indulgences; costly gifts of horses, falcons, and hunting hounds to courtiers in high places; favourable endorsements for those in a position to speak a good word on his behalf. The reach of kings is long, however, and their memories for insults even longer. When William the Red cut up rough over the throne of England, Hugo had done what any right-thinking churchman would have done—the *only* thing he could have done. What choice did he have? Robert Curthose, the Conqueror's eldest, was the legitimate heir to his father's throne. Everyone knew it; most of the barons agreed and supported Robert's claim. Who could have known the deceitful William would move so swiftly and with such devastating accuracy? He cut the legs out from under his poor deluded brother with such uncanny ease, one had to wonder whether the hand of God was not in it after all.

Be that as it may, the whole sorry affair was the beginning of a long decline for Hugo, who had seen his own fortunes steadily wane since the day William the Red snatched away the crown. Now, at long last, the abbot was reduced to this: exile in a dreary backwater province full of hostile natives, to be bootlicker to a half-baked nobody of a count.

Hugo supposed he should be grateful, even for this little, but gratitude was not a quality he had cultivated. Instead, he cursed the rapacious Rufus; he cursed the blighted wilderness of a country he had come to; and he cursed the monstrous fate that had brought him so very low.

Low, he may be. Shattered, perhaps. Even devastated. But not destroyed. And never, ever finished.

He would, like Lazarus, rise again from this dismal hinterland tomb. He would use this opportunity, weak and slender though it was, to haul himself up out of the muck of his disgrace and reclaim his former stature. The de Braoses' new church might be an unlikely place to start, but stranger things had happened. That Baron William de Braose was a favourite of Red William was the single bright light in the whole cavalcade of misery he now endured. The road to the successful restoration of the abbot's wealth and power ran through the baron, and if Hugo had to wet-nurse his lordship's snotty-nosed nephew to ingratiate himself, so be it.

Time was against him, he knew. He was no longer a young man. The years had not mellowed him, however; if anything, they had made him leaner, harder, and subtler. Outwardly serene and benevolent, with a charitable smile—when it suited his interests—his scheming, devious soul never slept. Though his hair had gone white, he had lost none of it, nor any teeth. His body was still resilient and sturdy, with a peasant's enduring strength. What is more, he retained all the ruthless cunning and insatiable ambition of his younger years. Allied to that was the sagacity of age and the sly wisdom that had kept him alive through travails that would have consumed lesser men.

He paused in the saddle and gazed out over the Vale of Elfael: his new and, he fervently hoped, temporary home. It was not much to look at, although it was not without, he grudgingly admitted, a certain bucolic charm. The air was good and the ground fertile. Obviously, there was water enough for any purpose. There were worse places, he considered, to begin the reconquest.

Attending the abbot were two of Baron de Braose's knights. They rode with him for protection. The rest of his entourage and belongings would come in a week or so—three wagons filled with the few books and treasures left to him, and a smattering of more practical ecclesiastical accoutrements, such as robes, stoles, his mitre, crook, staff, standard, and other oddments. There would be five attendants: two priests, one to say Mass and another to carry out the details of

administration, and three lay brothers—cook, chamberer, and porter.
With these, chosen for their loyalty and unfaltering obedience, Abbot
Hugo would begin afresh.

Once officially installed in his new church, Hugo would commence building his new empire. De Braose wanted a church; Hugo
would give him an abbey entire. First would come a stone-built minster worthy of the name, and with it, a hospital—both inn for passing dignitaries and healing centre for those wealthy enough to pay for
their care. There would be a great tithe barn and stable, and a kennel
to raise hunting hounds to sell to the nobility. Then, when these were
firmly established, a monastery school—the better to draw in the sons
of the region's noblemen and worthies and reap fat grants of land and
favours from appreciative parents.

With these thoughts, he lifted the reins and urged his brown palfrey on once more, following his escort to the count's fortress, where he
would spend the night, continuing on to the church the next morning.

Within sight of their destination now, the riders picked up the
pace. At the foot of the hill, they turned off the track and rode up
to the fortress, passing over the narrow bridge and through the newly
erected gate tower, where they were met by the snivelling nephew
himself.

"Greetings, Abbot Hugo," called Count Falkes, hurrying to meet
him. "I hope you have had a pleasant journey."

"Pax vobiscum," replied the cleric. "God be praised, yes. The journey was blissfully tranquil." He extended his hand for the young count
to kiss his ring.

Count Falkes, unused to this courtesy, was taken aback. After a
brief but awkward hesitation, he remembered his manners and pressed
his lips to the abbot's ruby ring. Hugo, having made his point, now
raised the hand over the young count in blessing. *"Benedictus, omni patri,"*

he intoned, then smiled. "I imagine it must be easy to forget when one is unaccustomed to such decorum."

"Your Grace," replied the count dutifully. "I assure you, I meant no disrespect."

"It is already forgotten," the abbot replied. "I suppose there is little place for such ceremony here in the Marches." He turned to take in the hall, stables, and yard with a sweep of his keen eyes. "You have done well in a short time."

"Most of what you see was here already," the count conceded. "Aside from a few necessary improvements, I have not had time to construct anything better."

"Now that you say it," intoned the abbot, "I thought it possessed a certain quaint charm not altogether fitting the tastes of your uncle, the baron."

"We have plans to enlarge this fortress in due course," the count assured him. "The town and church are of more immediate concern, however. I have ordered those to be finished first."

"A wise course, to be sure. Make no mistake, I am most eager to see it all—especially the church. That is the solid cornerstone of any earthly dominion. There can be no true prosperity or governance without it." Abbot Hugo raised his hands and waved off any reply the count might make. "But, no, here I am, preaching to my host when the welcome cup awaits. Forgive me."

"Please, Your Grace, come this way," said Falkes, leading the way to his hall. "I have prepared a special meal in your honour—and tonight we have wine from Anjou, selected especially for this occasion by the baron himself."

"Do you indeed? Good!" replied Hugo with genuine appreciation. "It has been a long time since I held a cup of that quality. It is a delicacy I will enjoy."

Count Falkes, relieved to have pleased his demanding guest, turned to greet the churchman's escort; he charged Orval, the seneschal, with the care of the knights and then led the abbot into the hall, where they could speak in private before supper.

The hall had been renovated. A fresh layer of clay and gypsum had been applied to the rough timber walls, and after being painstakingly smoothed and dried, the whole was whitewashed. The small window in the upper east wall was now closed with a square of oiled sheepskin. A new table sat a short distance from the hearth, with a tall iron candletree at each end. A fire cracked smartly on the big hearth, more for light than heat, and two chairs were drawn up on each side, with a jar and two silver goblets on the table between them.

The count filled the cups and passed one to his guest, and they settled themselves in their chairs to enjoy the wine and gain the measure of each other. "Health to you, Lord Abbot," said Falkes. "May you prosper in your new home."

Hugo thanked him courteously and said, "Truth told, a churchman has but one home, and it is not of this world. We sojourn here or there awhile, until it pleases God to move us along."

"In any event," replied the count, "I pray your sojourn amongst us is long and prosperous. There is great need hereabouts for a strong hand at the church plough—if you know what I mean."

"The former abbot incompetent, eh?" Raising his cup to his nose, he sniffed the wine, then sipped.

"Not altogether, no," said Falkes. "Bishop Asaph is capable enough in his way—but Welsh. And you know how contrary they can be."

"Little better than pagans," offered Hugo with a sniff, "by all accounts."

"Oh, it is true," confirmed the count. "They are an ill-mannered race—coarse, unlettered, easily inflamed, and contentious as the day is long."

"And are they really as backward as they appear?"

"Difficult to say," answered Falkes. "Hardheaded and stiff-necked, yes. They resist all refinement and delight in ostentation of every kind."

"Like children, then," remarked the abbot. "I also have heard this."

"You would not believe the fuss they make over a good tale, which they will stretch and twist until any truth is bent out of all recognition to the plain facts of the matter. For example," said the count, pouring more wine, "the locals will have it that a phantom has arisen in the forest round about."

"A phantom?"

"Truly," insisted the count, leaning forward in his eagerness to have something of interest with which to regale his eminent guest. "Apparently, this unnatural thing takes the form of a great bird—a giant raven or eagle or some such—and they have it that this queer creature feeds on cattle and livestock, even human flesh come to that, and the tale is frightening the more timorous."

"Do you believe this story?"

"I do not," replied the count firmly. "But such is their insistence that it has begun disturbing my workmen. Wagoners swear they lost oxen to it, and lately some pigs have gone missing."

"Simple theft would account for it, surely," observed the abbot. "Or carelessness."

"I agree," insisted the count, "and would agree more heartily if not for the fact that the swineherds contend that they actually saw the creature swoop down and snatch the hogs from under their noses."

"They saw this?" marvelled the abbot.

"In full light of day," confirmed the count. "Even so, I would not put much store by it save they are not the only ones to make such a claim. Some of my own knights have seen it—or seen *something*, at least—and these are sturdy, trustworthy men. Indeed, one of my men-at-arms was taken by the creature and narrowly escaped with his life."

"Mon Dieu, non!"

"Oh yes, it is true," affirmed the count, taking another sip from his cup. "The men I sent to track down the missing oxen found the animals—or the little left of them. The thing had eaten the wretched beasts, leaving nothing behind but a pile of entrails, some hooves, and a single skull."

"What do you think it can be?" wondered the abbot, savouring the extraordinary peculiarity of the tale.

"These hills are known to be home to many odd happenings," suggested Falkes. "Who is to say?"

"Who indeed?" echoed Abbot Hugo. He drank from his cup for a moment, then mused, "Pigs snatched away in midair, whole oxen gorged, men captured . . . It passes belief."

"To be sure," conceded the count. He drained his cup in a long swallow, then admitted, "Yet—and I do not say this lightly—the affair has reached such a state that I almost hazard to think something supernatural does indeed haunt the forest."

All through the night, Bran sat hunched beside the hearth, arms around his knees, staring into the shimmering flames. Iwan, Aethelfrith, and Siarles had long ago crawled off to sleep, but Angharad sat with him still. Every now and then she would pose a question to sharpen his thinking; otherwise, the hudolion's hut remained steeped in a seething silence—the hush of intense and turbulent thought—as Bran forged the perfect weapon in the glowing fires of his mind.

He was not tired and could not have slept anyway, with his thoughts burning bright. As dawn began to invade the darkness in the east, the fires began to cool, and the shape of his cunning craftwork was revealed.

"That is everything, I think," he said, raising his head to regard the old woman across the smouldering fire ring. "Have I forgotten anything?"

He was rewarded with one of her wrinkled smiles. "You have done well, Master Bran." Raising her hand, palm outward, above her head, she said, "This night you have become a shield to your people. But now, in the time-between-times, you are also a sword."

Bran took that as high approval. He stood, easing out the kinks in his cramped muscles. "Well then," he said, "let us wake the others and get started. There is much to do, and no time to lose."

Angharad lifted her hand to the men slumped across the room. "Patience. Let them sleep. There will be little enough time for that in the days to come." Indicating his own empty sleeping place, she said, "It would be no bad thing if you closed your eyes while you have the chance."

"I could not sleep now for all of the baron's riches," he told her.

"Nor could I," she said, rising slowly. "Since that is the way of it, let us greet the dawn and ask the King of Hosts to bless our battle plan and the hands that must work to make it succeed." She stepped to the door and pushed aside the ox hide, beckoning him to follow.

They stood for a moment in the early light and listened to the forest awaken around them as the dawn chorus of birds filled the treetops. Bran looked out at the pitiful clutch of humble dwellings, but felt himself a king of a vast domain. "The day begins," he said after a moment. "I want to get started."

"In a little while," she suggested. "Let us enjoy the peace of the moment."

"No, now," he countered. "Bring me my hood and cloak; then wake everyone and assemble them. They should remember this day."

"Why this day above any other?"

"Because," explained Bran, "from this day on, they are no longer fugitives and outcasts. Today they become King Raven's faithful flock."

"The *Grellon*," suggested Angharad—an old word, it meant both "flock" and "following."

"Grellon," repeated Bran as the banfáith moved off to strike the iron and rouse Cél Craidd. He turned his face to the warm red glow of the rising sun. "This day," he declared, speaking softly to himself, "the deliverance of Elfael begins."

It is a very great honour," said Queen Anora. "I would have thought you would be pleased."

"How should I be pleased?"

"Relations are strained just now, it is true," her mother granted. "But your father thought that perhaps—"

"My father, the king, has made his views quite clear," Mérian insisted. "Don't tell me he has changed his opinion just because an invitation has come."

"This may be the baron's way of making amends," her mother countered. It was a weak argument, and Mérian regarded her mother with a frown of haughty disdain. "The baron knows he has done wrong and wishes to restore the peace."

"Oh, so now the baron repents, and the king dances dizzy with gratitude?" said Mérian.

"Mérian!" reprimanded her mother sharply. "That will do, girl. You will respect your father and abide by his decision."

"What?" demanded Mérian. "And is there nothing to be said?"

"You have said quite enough." Her mother, stiff backed, turned in her chair to face her. "You will obey."

"But I do not understand," insisted the young woman. "It makes no sense."

"Your father has his reasons," replied the queen simply. "And we must respect them."

"Even if he is wrong?" countered Mérian. "That is most unfair, Mother."

Queen Anora observed her daughter's distraught expression—brows knit, mouth pressed hard, eyes narrowed—and remembered her as an infant demanding to be let down to walk in the grass on the riverbank and being told that she could not because it was too dangerous so close to the water. "It is only an invitation to join the court for a summer," her mother said, trying to lighten the mood. "The time will pass quickly."

"Pass as it may," Mérian declared loftily, "it will pass without me!" She rose and fled her mother's chamber, stalking down the narrow corridor to her own room, where she went to the window and shoved open the shutters with a crash. The early evening air was soft and warm, the fading light like honey on the yard outside her window, but she was not in a mood to take in such things, much less enjoy them. Her father's decision seemed to her arbitrary and unfair. She should, she felt, have a say in it since it was she who must comply.

The baron's courier had arrived earlier in the day with a message asking if Mérian might come to Hereford to spend the remainder of the summer with his lordship's daughter, Sybil. He was hoping Mérian would help teach the young lady something of British customs and speech. Sybil would, of course, gladly reciprocate. Baron Neufmarché was certain the two ladies would become fast friends.

Lord Cadwgan had listened to the message, thanked the courier, and dismissed him in the same breath, saying, "I am much obliged to the baron. Please tell my lord that Mérian would be delighted to accept his invitation."

So that, apparently, was that: a decision that trod heavily on some of her most deeply held convictions, and Mérian was to have nothing to say about it. Since the downfall of Deheubarth, her father had been writhing like a frog in cinders, desperate to distance himself from the reach of Neufmarché. And now, all of a sudden, he seemed just as eager to court the baron's good favour. Why? It made no sense.

The very thought of spending the summer in a castle full of foreigners sent waves of disgust coursing through her slender frame. Her aversion, natural and genuine, was also an evasion.

For what Mérian refused to admit, even to herself, was that she had enjoyed the baron's feast immensely. Truth be told, she had glimpsed an attractive alternative to life in a crumbling caer on the Marches border. She did not allow herself to so much as imagine that she might acquire this life for herself—God forbid! But somewhere in her deepest heart lurked the hunger for the charm and grandeur she had experienced that glittering night, and, heaven help her, it all danced around the person of Baron Neufmarché himself.

For his part, he had made it abundantly clear that he found her beautiful and even desirable. The mere notion awakened feelings Mérian considered so unholy that she tried to suffocate the fledgling thought by depriving it of all rational consideration. On her return to Caer Rhodl after the feast in Hereford, she had considered herself safely out of harm's way and beyond the reach of the temptation the baron's court represented. And now, without so much as an "If you please, Mérian," she was to be sent away to the baron's castle like so much baggage.

She pushed away from the window and flopped back on her bed. The thought that her father was simply using her to appease Neufmarché and further himself with the baron was too depressing to contemplate. All the same, that was the only explanation that made sense of the situation. If anyone else had suggested such a thing, she would have been the first to shout him down—all the while knowing it was her lot precisely.

In any event, the matter was closed to all appeal. Lord Cadwgan had made his decision and, regardless of anything Mérian or anyone else might say, would not reverse it. For the next few days, Mérian sulked and let everyone know exactly how she felt, delivering herself of long, soulful sighs and dark, moody glances until even Garran, her oblivious brother, complained about the damp chill in the air every time she passed by. But the evil day would not be held off. Her father commanded her to pack her belongings for her stay and had begun to make arrangements to take her to Hereford when Mérian received what she considered a reprieve. It came in the form of a summons for all the baron's nobles to attend him in council. The gathering was to be held at Talgarth in the baron's newly conquered territory, and all client kings and landed lords, along with their families and principal retainers, must attend. It was not an invitation that could be refused. Under feudal law, the unfortunate who failed to attend a formal council faced heavy fines and loss of lands, title, or in extreme cases, even limbs.

Baron Neufmarché did not hold councils often; the last had been five years ago when he had moved his chief residence to Hereford Castle. Then he had served notice that he meant to remain in England and expected his nobles to be ready and forthcoming with their support—chiefly in rents and services, but also in advice.

Lord Cadwgan took a cloudy view of the summons to Deheubarth—the scene of the late King Rhys ap Tewdwr's recent downfall and demise—considering it an insult to the Cymry and a none-too-subtle reminder of Ffreinc supremacy and ascendancy. The rest of the family felt likewise. Perversely, only Mérian welcomed the council, looking upon it as a pardon from the onerous duty that had been forced upon her. Now, instead of Mérian going alone into the enemy camp, the whole family would have to go with her.

"You need not look so pleased," her mother told her. "A little less gloating would better become you."

"I do not gloat," Mérian replied smugly. "But milk for the kit is milk for the cat—is that not what you always say, Mother?"

Three days of preparation followed, and the ordinarily sedate fortress shook life into itself in order to make ready the lord's departure. On the fourth day after receiving the summons, the entourage set out. All rode, save the steward, cook, and groom, who travelled in a horse-drawn wagon piled high with food supplies and equipment. The servants had dusted off and repaired the old leather tents Lord Cadwgan used for campaigns and extended hunting trips—of which there had been few in the last seven or eight years—in anticipation of making camp along the way and at the appointed meeting place.

"How long will the council last?" asked Mérian as she and her father rode along. It was early on the second day of travel, the sun was high and bright, and Mérian was in good spirits—all the more since her father's mood also showed signs of improving.

"How long?" repeated Cadwgan. "Why, as long as Neufmarché fancies." He thought about it for a moment and said, "There is no way to tell. It depends on the business to be decided. Once, I remember, Old William—the Conqueror, mind, not the red-bearded brat—held a council that lasted four months. Think of that, Mérian. Four whole months!"

Mérian considered that if the baron's council lasted four months, then summer would be over and she would not have to go to Hereford. She asked, "Why so long?"

"I was not there," her father explained. "We were not yet under the thumb of the foreigners and had our own affairs to keep us occupied. As I recall, it was said the king wanted everyone to agree on the levy of taxes for land and chattels."

"Agree with him, you mean."

"Yes," said her father, "but there was more to it than that. The Conqueror wanted as much as he could get, to be sure, but he also knew that most people refuse to pay an unjust tax. He wanted all his earls, barons, and princes to agree—and to *see* one another agree—so that there could be no complaint later."

"Clever."

"Aye, he was a fox, that one," her father continued, and Mérian, after their stormy relations of late, was happy to hear him speak and to listen. "The real reason the council lasted so long came down to the Forest Law."

Mérian had heard of this and knew all right-thinking Britons, as well as Saxons and Danes, resented it bitterly. The reason was simple: the decree transformed all forested lands in England into one vast royal hunting preserve owned by the king. Even to enter a forest without permission of the warrant holder became a punishable offence. This edict, hated as it was from the beginning, made outlaws of all those who, for generations, had made their living out of the woodlands in one way or another—which was nearly everyone.

"So that was when it began?" mused Mérian.

"That it was," Cadwgan confirmed, "and the council twisted and turned like cats on a roasting spit. They refused three times to honour the king's wishes, and each time he sent them back to think about the cost of their refusal."

"What happened?"

"When it became clear that no one would be allowed to return home until the matter was settled, and that the king was unbending, the council had no choice but to assent to the Conqueror's wishes."

"What a spineless bunch of lickspits," observed Mérian.

"Do not judge them too harshly," her father said. "It was either agree or risk being hung as traitors if they openly rebelled. Meanwhile, they watched their estates and holdings slowly descending into ruin through neglect. So with harvest hard upon them, they granted the king the right to his precious hunting runs and went home to explain the new law to their people." Cadwgan paused. "Thank God, the Conqueror did not include the lands beyond the Marches. When I think what the Cymry would have done had *that* been forced on us . . ." He shook his head. "Well, it does not bear thinking about."

PART FIVE

THE
GRELLON

Despite Count Falkes's repeated offer to accompany him, Abbot Hugo insisted on visiting his new church alone. "But the work is barely begun," the count pointed out. "Allow me to bring the architect's drawings so you can see what it will look like when it is finished."

"You are too kind," Hugo had told him. "However, I know your duties weigh heavily enough, and I would not add to them. I am perfectly capable of looking around for myself, and happy to do so. I would not presume to burden you with my whims."

He rode out from the caer on his brown palfrey and arrived at Llanelli just as the labourers were starting their work for the day. The old church, with its stone cross beside the door, still stood on one side of the new town square. It was a rude wood-and-wattle structure, little more than a cow byre in Hugo's opinion; the sooner demolished, the better.

The abbot turned from the sight and cast his critical gaze across the square at a jumbled heap of timber atop a foundation of rammed earth. What? By the rod of Moses!—was *that* the new church?

He strode closer for a better look. A carpenter appeared with a coiled plumb line and a chunk of chalk. "You there!" the abbot shouted. "Come here."

The man glanced around, saw the priestly robes, and hurried over, offering a bow of deference. "You wish to speak to me, Your Grace?"

"What is this?" He flipped a hand at the partially built structure.

"It is to be a church, father," replied the carpenter.

"No," the abbot told him. "No, I do not think that likely."

"Yes," replied the workman. "I do believe it is."

"I am the abbot here," Hugo informed him, "and I say that"—he flapped a dismissive hand at the roughly framed building—"*that* is a tithe barn."

The carpenter cocked his head to one side and regarded the priest with a quizzical expression. "A tithe barn, Your Grace?"

"*My* church will be made of stone," Abbot Hugo told the carpenter, "and it will be of my design and raised on a site of my choosing. I will not have my church fronting the town square like a butcher's stall."

"But, father, see here—"

"Do you doubt me?"

"Not at all. But the count—"

"This is to be *my* church, not the count's. I am in authority here, *compris?*"

"Indeed, Your Grace," answered the confused carpenter. "What am I to tell the master?"

"Tell him I will have the plans ready for him in three days," declared the abbot, starting away. "Tell him to come to me for his new instructions."

With that, the abbot marched to the old chapel, paused outside, and then pushed open the door. He was greeted by two priests; from the look of it, they had slept in the sanctuary amidst their bundled belongings.

"Who is in authority here?" demanded the abbot.

"Greetings in Christ, brother abbot," said the bishop, stepping forward. "I am Asaph, Bishop of Llanelli. We would have made a better welcome, but as you can see, this is all that is left of the monastery, and the monks have all been pressed to labour for the count."

"Be that as it may . . . ," sniffed Hugo, glancing around the darkened chapel. It smelled old and musty and made him sneeze. "I see you are ready to depart. I shall not keep you."

"We were waiting to pass the reins to you, as it were," replied Asaph.

"That will not be necessary."

"No? We thought you might like to know something about your new flock."

"Your presumption has led you astray, bishop. It is the flock that must get to know and heed the shepherd." Hugo sneezed again and turned to leave. "God speed you on your way."

"Abbot, see here," said the bishop, starting after him. "There is much we would tell you about Elfael and its people."

"You presume to *teach* me?" Abbot Hugo turned on him. "All I need to know, I learned from the saddle of my horse on the way here." He glanced balefully at the rude structure and the two lorn priests. "Your tenure here is over, bishop. God in his wisdom has decreed a new day for this valley. The old must make way for the new. Again, I wish you God's speed. I do not expect we will meet again."

The abbot returned to his horse across the square, passing the carpenter, who was now sitting on a stack of lumber with a saw across his lap. "What about this?" called the carpenter, indicating the unfinished jumble of timber behind him. "What am I to do with this?"

"It is a tithe barn," replied the abbot. "It will need a wider door."

ou, Tuck, have the most important duty," Bran had told him as he boosted the priest into the saddle. "The success of our plan rests on you."

"Aye," he had replied, "you can count on me!" Borne on waves of hope and optimism, he had departed Cél Craidd with cheers and glad farewells still ringing in his ears.

Oh, but the fiery blush of enthusiasm for his part in Bran's grand scheme had faded to dull, muddy pessimism by the time Aethelfrith reached his little oratory on the Hereford road. *How, by the beards of the apostles, am I to discover the movements of the de Braose treasure train?*

As if that were not difficult enough, he must acquire the knowledge far enough in advance to give Bran and his Grellon enough time to prepare. To that end, he had been given the best of the horses so that he might return with the news at utmost speed.

"Impossible," Aethelfrith muttered to himself. With or without a horse. Impossible. "Never should have agreed to such a lack-brain scheme."

Then again, the idea had originated with himself, after all. "Tuck, old son," he murmured, "you've gone and put both feet in the brown pie this time."

As he approached the oratory, he was relieved to see that no one was waiting for him. People had visited in his absence; small gifts of eggs, lumps of cheese, and beeswax candles had been placed neatly beside his door. After tethering his mount in the long grass around back, he filled a bucket from the well and left it for the animal. He gathered up the offerings from his doorstep and went in to light the fire, eat a bite of supper, and contemplate his precarious future. He fell asleep praying for divine inspiration to attend his dreams.

As the morning sun rose to dispel the mist along the Wye, so it brought a partial solution to Tuck's problem. Rising in his undershirt, he went out to the well to wash. Drawing his arms through the sleeves, he pushed the shirt down around his waist and splashed water over himself. The cold stung his senses and made him splutter. He dried himself on a scrap of linen cloth and stood for a moment, savouring the sweet air and calm of the little glade surrounding his cell. He watched the mist curling along the river, and it came to him that whatever else they did, the wagons would have to use the bridge at Hereford. It only remained to find out when. He could simply wait until the wagons passed his oratory on their way to Elfael; then he could saddle the horse and race to Bran with the warning and hope it gave him time enough. Bran had said they would need three days at least. "Four would be better," Bran had told him. "Give us but four days, Tuck, and we have a fighting chance."

He hurried back inside to pull on his robe and lace up his shoes. Taking his staff, he walked down to the bridge and into town. It was market day in Hereford, but there seemed to be fewer people around than usual—especially for a clear, fine day in summer. He wondered about this as he watched the farmers and merchants setting out their goods and opening their stalls.

As he loitered amongst the vendors, idly wandering here and there, he heard a cloth merchant complaining to another about the lack of custom. "Poor dealings today, Michael, m'lad," he was saying. "Might have stayed home and saved shoe leather."

"'Twill be no better next market week," replied the merchant named Michael, a dealer in knives, pruning hooks, and other bladed utensils.

"Aye," agreed the other with a sigh, "too right you are. Too right."

"Won't get better till the baron returns."

"Good fellows," said Aethelfrith, speaking up, "forgive me—I heard you speaking just now and would ask a question."

"Brother Aethelfrith! Mornin' to you," said the one named Michael. "God be good to you."

"And to you, my son," replied the friar. "Can you tell me why there are so few people at market today? Where has everyone gone?"

"Well," replied the cloth dealer, "sure as Sunday, it's the council, ent it?"

"The council?" wondered Aethelfrith. "I have been away on a little business and only just returned. The king has called a Great Council?"

"Nay, brother," replied the clothier, "not a king's council—only a local one. Neufmarché has convoked an assembly of all his nobles—"

"*And* their families," said Michael the cutler. "Off beyond the Marches somewhere. We'd ha' done better to follow the lot of them there."

"Indeed?" mused the priest. "I have heard nothing about this."

The two merchants, with no customers and time on their hands, were only too glad to oblige Aethelfrith of the news he had missed: the fierce battle and resounding defeat of the Welsh King Rhys ap Tewdwr, and the swift conquest of Deheubarth by the baron's troops. The cutler finished, saying, "Neufmarché called council to square things away, y'see?"

The squat friar nodded, thanked them, and asked, "When did they leave? Do you know? When did the council begin?"

The clothier shrugged. "I couldn't say, brother."

"Why, if I be not mistaken," said Michael, "it ent rightly begun as yet."

"No?"

"Don't see how it could." Michael picked up a small kitchen knife and tried its blade with his thumb. "The baron and his people rode out but yesterday—morning, it was, very early. I reckon 'twill take them two days at least to reach the moot—them and the other lords.

The council would seem to begin a day or two after that. So make that three days—four, to be safe. Five, maybe six, at most."

"Too right," agreed the clothier. "And all that means we lose custom next week—and maybe the week after as well."

"Blessings upon you, friends!" called Aethelfrith, already darting away. He fled back across the bridge, his soft shoes slapping the worn timbers, and steamed up the hill to his oratory. He wasted not a moment, but threw a few provisions into a bag, saddled the horse, and rode out again.

He knew exactly when Baron de Braose's money train would roll.

s Baron Bernard de Neufmarché gazed out upon the upturned faces of his subject lords gathered at Talgarth in the south of Wales, the treasure train of his rival Baron de Braose was approaching the bridge below his castle back in Hereford: three wagons with an escort of seven knights and fifteen men-at-arms under the command of a marshal and a sergeant. All the soldiers were mounted, and their weapons gleamed hard in the bright summer sun.

Hidden beneath food supplies and furnishings for Abbot Hugo's new church were three sealed strongboxes, iron-banded and bolted to the wagon beds. With ranks of soldiers leading the way and more riders guarding the rear, the train passed unhindered through Hereford. If any of Neufmarché's soldiers saw the train passing beneath the castle walls, they made no move to prevent it.

Thus, in accordance with Baron de Braose's plan, the wagon train rumbled across the bridge, through the town, and out into the bright, sunlit meadows of the wide Wye valley. It would take the slow ox train four days to pass through Neufmarché lands and the great forest of the March. But once past Hereford, there would be no stopping the wagons, and the knights could breathe a little easier knowing that nothing stood between them and the completion of their duty.

The leader of this party was a marshal named Guy, one of Baron de Braose's youngest commanders, a man whose father stood on the battlefield with the Conqueror and had been rewarded with the lands of a deposed earl in the North Ridings: a sizeable estate that included the old Saxon market town of Ghigesburgh—or Gysburne, as the Normans preferred it.

Young Guy had grown up in the bleak moorlands of the north, and there he might have stayed, but thinking that life held more for him than overseeing the collection of rents on his father's estate, he had come south to take service in the court of an ambitious baron who could provide him with the opportunities a young knight needed to secure wealth and fame. Inflamed with dreams of grandeur, he yearned for glory far beyond any that might be acquired grappling with dour English farmwives over rents paid in geese and sheep.

Guy's energy and skill at arms had won him a place amongst the teeming swarm of knights employed by William de Braose; his solid, dependable, levelheaded northern practicality raised him above the ranks of the brash and impulsive fortune seekers who thronged the southern courts. Two years in the baron's service, Guy had waited for a chance to prove himself, and it had finally come. Certainly, marshalling the guard for some money chests was not the same as leading a flying wing of cavalry into pitched battle, but it was a start. This was the first significant task the baron had entrusted to him, and though it fell far short of taxing his considerable skills as a warrior, he was determined to acquit himself well. Mounted on a fine grey destrier, he remained vigilant and pursued a steady, unhurried pace. To better safe-

404

guard the silver, no advance warning had been given; not even Count de Braose knew when the money would arrive.

Day's end found them camped beside the road on a bend in the river. High wooded bluffs sheltered them to the east, and the bow of the river formed an effective perimeter barrier on the other three sides. Any would-be thieves thinking to liberate the treasure would have to come at them on the road, and Guy positioned sentries in each direction, changed through the night, to prevent intruders from disturbing their peace.

They passed an uneventful night and the next morning moved on. Around midday they stopped to eat and to feed and rest the animals before beginning the long, winding ascent up out of the Vale of Wye. The first wagon gained the heights a little before sunset, and Guy ordered camp to be made in a grove of beech trees near an English farming settlement. Other than a herdsman leading a few muddy brown cows home to be milked, no one else was seen on the road, and the second night passed beneath a fair, star-seeded sky with serenity undisturbed.

The third day passed much the same as the previous day. Before climbing into their saddles on the fourth day, Guy assembled the men and addressed them, saying, "Today we enter the forest of the March. We will be wary. If thieves try to attack us, they will do so here, *compris*? Everyone is to remain alert for any sign of an ambush." He gazed at the ring of faces gathered around him: as solemn, earnest, and determined as he was himself. "If there are no questions, then—"

"What of the phantom?"

"Ah," replied Guy, "yes." He had anticipated such a question and was ready with an answer. "Many of you will have heard some gossip of this phantom, *non*?" He paused, trying to appear severe and dauntless for his men. "It is but a tale to frighten infants, nothing more. We are men, not children, so we will give this rumour the contempt it deserves." He offered a grimace of ridicule to show his scorn, adding, "It would take a whole forest full of phantoms to daunt Baron de Braose's soldiers, *n'est ce pas?*"

He commanded the treasure train to move out. The soldiers took their mounts and fell into line: a rank of knights, three abreast to lead the train, followed by men-at-arms alongside and between each of the wagons, with four knights serving as outriders patrolling the road ahead and behind on each side. At the head of this impressive procession rode Guy himself on his fine grey stallion; directly behind him rode his sergeant to relay any commands to those behind.

By morning's end the money train had reached the forest edge. The road was wide, though rutted, and the wagon drivers were forced to slow their pace to keep from jolting the wheels to pieces. The soldiers clopped along, passing through patches of sunlight and shadow, alert to the smallest movement around them. It was cool in the shade of the trees, and the air was thick with birdsong and the sounds of insects. All remained peaceful and serene, and they met no one else on the road.

A little past midday, however, they came to a place where the road dipped low into a dell, at the bottom of which trickled a sluggish rill. Despite the fine dry weather, the shallow fording place was a churned mass of mud and muck. Apparently, herders using the road had allowed their animals to use it for a watering hole, and the beasts had transformed the road into a wallow.

Stuck in the middle of the ford was a wagon full of manure sunk up to its axles. A ragged farmer was snapping the reins of his two-ox team, and the creatures were bawling as they strained against the yoke, but to no avail. The farmer's wife stood off to one side, hands on hips, shouting at the man, who appeared to be taking no heed of her. Both the man and his wife were filthy to their knees.

The road narrowed at the ford, and the surrounding ground was so soft and chewed up that Guy could see there would be no going around. Wary, senses prickling to danger, Guy halted the train. He rode ahead alone to see what had happened. "Pax vobiscum," he said, reining up behind the wagon. "What goes here?"

The farmer ceased swatting his team and turned to address the knight. "Good day, sire," the man said in rough Latin, removing his shapeless straw hat. "You see how it is." He gestured vaguely at the wagon. "I am stuck."

"I told him to put down planks," the farmwife called in shrill defiance. "But he wouldn't listen."

"Shut up, woman!" shouted the farmer to his wife. Turning back to the knight, he said, "We'll soon have it out, never fear." Eyeing the waiting train behind them, he said, "Maybe if some of your fellows could help—"

"No," Guy told him. "Just you get on with it."

"At once, m'lord." He turned back to the task of coaxing, threatening, and bullying the struggling team once more.

Guy rode back to the waiting train. "We will rest here and move on when they have cleared the ford. Water the horses."

The horses were watered and rested and the sun was beginning its long, slow descent when the farmer finally ceased shouting and slapping his team. Guy, thinking the wagon was finally free, hurried back down into the dell only to find the farmer lying on the grassy slope above the ford, his wagon as firmly stuck as ever.

"You! What in God's name are you doing?" demanded Guy.

"Sire?" replied the farmer, sitting up quickly.

"The wagon remains stuck."

"Aye, sire, it is that," agreed the farmer ruefully. "I have tried everything, but it won't budge for gold nor goose fat."

Glancing around quickly, the knight said, "Where's the woman?"

"I sent her ahead to see if there might be anyone coming the other way that could maybe lend a hand, sire," replied the farmer. "Seeing as how you and your men are busylike . . ." He left the rest of the thought unspoken.

"Get up!" shouted Guy. "Get back to your team. You have delayed us long enough."

"As you say, sire," replied the farmer. He rose and shambled back to the wagon.

Guy returned to the waiting train and ordered five men-at-arms to dismount and help pull the wagon free. These first five were soon as muddy as the farmer, and with just as little to show for it. So, with increasing impatience, Guy ordered five more men-at-arms and three knights on horseback to help, too. Soon, the muddy wallow was heaving with men and horses. The knights attached ropes to the wagon, and with three or four men at each wheel and horses pulling, they succeeded in hauling the overloaded vehicle up out of the hole into which it had sunk.

With a creak and a groan, the cart started up the greasy bank. The soldiers cheered. And then just as the wheels came free, there came a loud crack as the rear axle snapped. The hind wheels buckled and the cart subsided once more; men and horses, still attached to the ropes, were dragged down with it. The oxen could not keep their feet and fell, sprawling over each other. Caught in their yoke, they thrashed in the mud, kicking and bellowing.

Guy saw his hopes of a swift resolution to his problem sinking into the mire and loosed a spate of Ffreinc abuse on the head of the luckless farmer. "Loose those animals!" he ordered his men. "Then drag that cart out of the way."

Seven men-at-arms leapt to obey. Working quickly, they unyoked the oxen and led them from the wallow. Once free, the farmer led them aside and stood with them while the soldiers emptied his wagon, pitching the manure over the sides and then, slowly and with great effort, dragging the broken vehicle up the slippery bank and off the road.

"Thank you, sire!" called the farmer, regarding the wreck of his wagon with the dubious air of a man who knows he should be grateful but realises he is ruined.

"Idiot!" muttered Guy. Satisfied that his wagon train could now pass through, Guy rode back up the slope and signalled the drivers to come ahead.

When the first of the three teams had descended into the dell—which now resembled a well-stirred bog—Guy, taking no chances, ordered branches to be cut and laid down and ropes to be attached so riders could help pull the fully laden vehicle through the morass. Like a boat dragged across a tide-abandoned bay, the first wagon slid recklessly across. The laborious process was repeated for each of the two remaining wagons in turn.

Guy waited impatiently while the soldiers paused to clean the mud and ordure off themselves as best they could. His sergeant, a veteran named Jeremias, approached and said, "The sun is soon down, sire. Do you want to make camp now and journey on at daybreak tomorrow?"

"No," Guy growled, glancing at the miserable swamp now reeking with manure. "We've wasted enough time here today. I want to put this place behind us. We push on." Raising himself in the stirrups, he shouted, "Be mounted!"

A few moments later, all had regained the saddle. Guy waited until they had fallen into line and reformed the ranks, then called, *"Marcher sur!"* and the money train resumed its journey.

Once over the rim of the dell, the forest closed around them once more. The setting sun thickened the shadows beneath the overarching limbs, giving the riders the sensation of entering a dim green tunnel.

409

Darkness crept in, closing silently around them. Guy was soon wishing he had not been so hasty in rebutting the sergeant's suggestion and decided that they would make camp at the next glade or meadow; but the underbrush crowded close on each side of the road, the tree trunks so close that the wagon wheels bumped over exposed roots, forcing the drivers to slow the pace even more. All the while, the last of the daylight steadily faded to a murky twilight, and the evening hush descended on the forest.

It was only then, in the quiet of the wood, that Marshal Guy de Gysburne began to wonder why it was that two bedraggled English farmers should speak such ready Latin. The thought had little time to take root in his awareness when the soldiers saw the first of the hanging corpses.

CHAPTER 41

Marshal Guy heard the low, tight-mouthed cursing of the soldiers behind him and knew that something was amiss. Without stopping, he turned in the saddle and looked back along the trailing ranks. He saw his sergeant and motioned him forward. "Jeremias," he said as the sergeant reined in beside him, "the men are muttering."

"They are, sire," confirmed the sergeant.

"Why is this?"

"Methinks it is the mice, sire."

"The mice, sergeant," repeated Guy, casting a sideways glance at the man beside him. He appeared to be earnest. "Pray explain."

With a tilt of his head, the sergeant indicated a branch at the side of the road a few paces away. Guy squinted at the overhanging branch, which looked no different from a thousand others seen that day— entirely unremarkable, except . . . except: hanging from the branch was a dead mouse.

The tiny corpse was suspended by a long hair from the tail of a horse, its sun-shrivelled body turning slowly in the light evening breeze.

The marshal leaned from the saddle for a closer look and poked it with his finger as he passed. The little dead thing swung on its slender thread. Guy turned his face away and made a show of ignoring what he took to be a harmless, if somewhat sinister, prank.

The attitude was admirable but became increasingly hard to maintain. Try as he might to keep his eyes on the road before him, he could not prevent himself from glimpsing more of the things, and once he began to see them, he saw them everywhere. Swinging on their horsehair nooses from bushes and twigs, dangling from overhanging limbs and branches, high and low, on each side of the road, dead mice hung like grotesque fruit in an orchard of death.

The wagon train continued on into the gloaming, and the farther they went, the more of the weird little corpses they saw—and not mice only. Now, here and there amongst the hanging dead, were the bodies of larger creatures. He saw a vole first, and then another; then moles, shrews, and rats. Like the mice, the moles and rats were strung up with horsetail hair and left to twist gently in the breeze.

Soon, the soldiers were seeing dead rats everywhere—some shrivelled and desiccated as if dried in their skins, others that appeared freshly killed. But all, whether mummified or fresh, were hung by their necks, legs flat to their sides, tails stiff and straight.

Guy, glancing right and left, took them in with a shiver of disgust and, refusing to be cowed by the unnatural spectacle, rode on.

Then came the birds. Small ones first—sparrows, for the most part, but also wrens and nuthatches—scattered in amongst the rodents. The birds were dry husks of the creatures that had been—as if the avian essence had been sucked from them, along with all their vital juices—all of them suspended by their necks, wings folded tight against their bodies, beaks pointing skyward.

A few hundred paces down this weird gallery of death, the soldiers

412

began seeing faces leering from the leaf-bordered shadows. They were not human faces, but effigies of twigs and bark and straw tied together with bits of leather and bone: heads, large and small, their eyes of stone and shell gazing sightlessly from the wood at the passing riders.

The muttering of the men became a low rumble. Everywhere a knight or soldier looked, another disembodied face met his increasingly unsteady gaze—as if the wood were populated with Greene Men, come to menace the intruders. Some of the larger ones had straw mouths lined with animal teeth, bared as if in the frozen rictus of death. These effigies mocked the riders. They seemed to laugh at the living, their mute voices shrill with the unspoken words: *As we are, soon you shall be.*

The soldiers proceeded along this eerie corridor in silence, eyes wide, shoulders hunched with apprehension. The farther they went, the more uncanny it became. The feeling of dread deepened moment by moment, as if each step brought them closer to a doom unknown and deeply to be feared.

Guy, resolute but anxious, was no less affected than his men; the weird sights around them seemed both purposeful and malevolent; yet the meaning of the macabre display—if meaning there was—escaped him.

Then, all at once . . .

"Yeux de Dieu!" swore Guy, jerking back the reins involuntarily. The big grey halted in the road.

Affixed to a tree beside the road was what appeared to be the figure of a man with huge hands and an enormous misshapen head, drenched in blood, his arms stretched as if to welcome passersby with a grisly embrace.

A second glance revealed that it was not a man at all, but a statue of cloth and straw affixed to a scaffold of tree limbs and topped with

413

the head of a boar. The hideous thing had been drenched in blood and was covered with flies. *"Merde,"* Guy spat, urging his mount forward once more. "Pagans."

The heavy wagons rolled slowly past this grisly herald. Knights and men loosed curses even as they signed themselves with the cross.

The road descended gently into a shallow trough between the crests of two low hills. The forest pressed close, ominously silent. Guy, riding ahead, reached the bottom of the dell and, in the last light of day fading to the shadowy gloom of twilight, saw something lying across the road. Closer inspection revealed that a tree had fallen, its trunk spanning the road from side to side. There was no going around it.

Guy, now fully alert to danger, wheeled his mount. "Halt!" he shouted, his voice cracking loud in the deep forest hush. "Jeremias!" he said, indicating the tree behind him. "Remove it. Form a troop. Get it cleared away."

"At once, sire," replied the sergeant. Turning in the saddle, he called to the knights and men behind him. "First four ranks dismount!" he shouted. "The rest remain on guard."

Before the knights and men-at-arms could climb down from their saddles, there came a crashing from the surrounding wood— something huge and clumsy crashing through the tangled undergrowth toward the road. The soldiers drew their weapons as the unknown entity lumbered closer.

The bushes beside the road began quaking and thrashing from side to side. Guy's hand found his sword hilt and drew it. The sword was halfway out of the scabbard when, with the mewling, inarticulate squeal of a host of lost and tortured souls, the branches parted, and out from the vine-covered thicket to his left burst a herd of wild pigs.

Half-mad with fear, the animals tumbled through the opening and into the road. Whatever was driving the pigs terrified them more than

414

the men on horseback, for the squealing, squalling animals, seeing their only path of escape blocked by the fallen tree, swirled around once, then lowered their heads and charged into the halted ranks of soldiers.

The hapless creatures—four sows with perhaps twenty or more piglets—darted in amongst the legs of the horses, instantly throwing the ordered ranks into rearing, kicking chaos. Some of the soldiers tried to ward off the pigs by stabbing at them with their swords, which only increased the confusion.

"Hold!" cried Guy, trying to make himself heard above the frantic neighing of the horses. "Hold the ranks! Let them pass!"

Catching a movement out of the corner of his eye, he turned and saw something alight on the trunk of the fallen tree. It seemed to simply materialise out of the darkness—a shadow taking substance, darkness contracting to itself and coalescing into the shape of a gigantic birdlike creature with the wings and high-domed head of a raven and the torso and legs of a man. The face of the phantom was a smooth, black skull with an absurdly long, pointed beak.

Guy gaped at the unearthly creature. His shouted orders clotted on his tongue. He swallowed and found his mouth had gone dry.

The phantom perched on the massive trunk of the fallen tree, spread its great wings wide, and in a voice that seemed torn from the very forest round about, shrieked out a cry of raw animal rage that resounded through the forest, echoing amongst the treetops. Soldiers threw their hands over their ears to keep out the sound.

At once, the scent of smoke filled the air, and before Guy could draw breath to shout a warning to his men, twin curtains of flame leapt up on each side of the road along the length of the wagon train, which was now a confused mass of frightened men, pigs, and thrashing horses.

The phantom shrieked again. Lord Guy's grey destrier reared, its eyes rolling in terror. When Guy turned to look, the enormous raven had vanished. "Fall back!" cried the knight marshal. "Retreat!" His command was lost in the cacophony of pigs squealing, men shouting, and oxen bawling. "Turn around! Go back!"

As if in reply, the forest answered with a low groan and the shuddering creak of tree trunks cracking. The soldiers shouted—some pointing left, some right—as two huge oaks gave way on each side of the road, crashing to earth in a juddering mass of limbs and leaves. Knights on horseback scattered as the heavy pillars toppled, one atop the other, directly behind the last wagon in the train. The startled ox team surged forward, smashing into the stationary ranks directly ahead, overturning two horses and unseating their riders.

Trapped now in a corridor of flame and oily, pungent smoke, the wagons could neither turn around nor move off the road. The soldiers, still contending with the remaining pigs, strove to regain control of their mounts.

In the tumult and confusion, no one saw two furtive figures in deerskin cloaks rise from the bracken with pots of flaming pitch suspended from leather cords. Standing just beyond the shimmering sheet of fire, the skin-clad figures swung the pots in tight, looping arcs and let fly. The clay pots smashed into flaming shards, splattering hot, burning pitch over the sideboards of the nearest wagon.

The frightened oxen bolted, driving into the men and horses who could not get out of the way swiftly enough.

"Hold!" cried Guy. "Drivers, hold your teams!"

But there was no holding the terrified animals. They surged forward, heads down, driving into anything in their path. Knights and men-at-arms scattered, desperate to get out of the way of the wildly scything horns.

Some of the soldiers braved the wall of flames. Turning their mounts, they jumped the burning logs and struggled into the bramble-bound undergrowth. Those in the rearward ranks, seeing the flames and chaos ahead, abandoned their uncontrollable mounts and scrambled through the branches and over the fallen tree trunks blocking their retreat.

In the chaos of the moment, no one gave a thought to their trapped comrades; thoughts ran only to survival, and each man looked after himself. Once free, the men-at-arms took to their feet, running back down the road the way they had come.

The wagons were burning fiercely now, driving the horses and oxen wild with terror. There was no holding them. Everywhere, men were abandoning their saddles to flee the panic-stricken horses and flaming wagons.

Marshal Guy, his voice raw from shouting, tried to order his scattered retinue. With sword held high, he repeatedly called his men to rally to him. But the preternatural attack had overwhelmed them to a man, and Guy could not make himself heard above the clamour of beasts and men lost in the frenzy of escape.

In the end, he had no choice but to desert his own mount and follow his retreating men as they fled into the night. Working his way back along the riotous commotion of his flailing, devastated soldiers, Guy reached the rear of the treasure train and climbed onto the bole of one of the toppled oaks. There he took up the call to retreat. "Fall back! To me! Fall back!"

Those nearest swarmed over the fallen trunks, tumbling into the road and pulling the stragglers after them. When finally the last man had cleared the fiery corridor, Guy allowed himself to be pulled away from the wreckage by his sergeant. "Come, sire," said Jeremias, tugging him by the arm. "Let it go."

Still, Guy hesitated. He cast a last look over his shoulder at the inferno the road had become. Terrified horses still reared and plunged, hurling themselves headlong into the flames; the oxen lay dead—most had been killed by the knights in order to keep from being gored or trampled; discarded weapons and armour were strewn the length of the corridor. The rout was complete.

"It is over," said Jeremias. "You must rally the men and regain command. Come away."

Marshal Guy de Gysburne nodded once and turned away. A moment later, he was running into the flame-shattered darkness of a strange and hostile night.

The sound of frightened, mail-clad soldiers in headlong retreat dwindled away, and soon all that could be heard was the hiss and crackle of the burning brush and wagons. For a moment, the forest seemed to watch and wait with breath abated, and then the scouring of the king's road began.

Seven men carrying spears leapt over the burning logs and into the fiery corridor. Clad in green cloaks, the hooded men made quick work dispatching any wounded animals. They then signalled the rest of their band, and within the space of six heartbeats, twenty more men and women crept out from hiding in the surrounding wood. Likewise dressed in long green cloaks with leaves and twigs and bits of rag sewn onto them, they were the Grellon: King Raven's faithful flock.

Quickly removing their cloaks and hoods, the Grellon set about quenching the flames of the burning wagons and surrounding vegetation—using hides that had been soaked in the stream. As soon as the fires were out, torches were lit and sentries posted, and the flock fell to their appointed tasks with silent and urgent efficiency. While some of the band butchered the horses and oxen where they lay, others led the living animals away into the forest. Once the animals had been cared for, the workers unloaded the still-smouldering wagons, carefully examining the cargo. Much had been damaged by the flames, of course, but much remained unharmed; everything was carried off to be hidden in the wood for later use.

Once the vehicles had been unburdened of their baggage, the iron-bound strongboxes were prised from the planks before the wagons themselves were broken apart and hauled into the forest. The useable parts—wheels, harness, yokes, and iron fittings—would find their way back into service, and the rest would be scattered, hidden, and left to rot.

While the wagons were being dismantled, the discarded bits of armour and weapons, saddles and tack—as well as anything else of value—were heaped together in a single pile that was then sorted into bundles and carried off. Meanwhile, the leavings of the butchered animals were placed in a ready-dug pit near the road, which was then filled in and covered with bracken and moss, freshly dug elsewhere and transplanted. When everything of value had been salvaged, the tree trunks blocking the road were removed—an arduous task made more difficult by the necessity of having to work in darkness—and the pitch-bearing logs were rolled back into the underbrush; any scorched branches were carefully trimmed back to green growth.

Their work finished, the forest dwellers gathered up the meat of the slaughtered beasts and crept away, melting back into the darkness from which they had sprung.

When the sun rose upon the forest the next day, there was little to mark the odd, one-sided battle that had been fought in that place—saving only some singed tree limbs that could not be reached, broken earth, and a few damp, dark patches where the blood of an ox or a horse stained the road.

Loss of all goods and chattels under your care, loss of horses and livestock, loss of church property and sacred relics—not to mention loss of the treasure you were sworn to protect," Abbot Hugo de Rainault intoned solemnly as he stared out the window of the former chapter house he had commandeered for his own use. "Your failure is as ignominious as it is complete."

"I lost no men," Marshal Gysburne pointed out.

"Mon Dieu!" growled Hugo. "Do you think Baron de Braose will care about that?" He levelled a virulent stare at the knight. "Do you *think* at all?"

Guy de Gysburne held his tongue and waited for the storm to pass. Of the two men before him, the abbot was the more outraged and possessed far greater ability to make his anger felt. Next to the fiery Hugo's scathing excoriations, the irate Count Falkes seemed placid and reasonable, if perturbed.

"At the very least, Gysburne, you will be imprisoned," said Count Falkes, breaking in.

"At worst, you face execution for malfeasance and gross neglect of duty," said the abbot, concluding the thought in his own way.

"We were ambushed. I did my duty."

"Did you? Did you?" demanded Hugo. "No doubt that will be of great comfort when your head is on the block."

"Execute a knight in service?" scoffed Guy; the bravado was thin and unconvincing.

"Do not imagine such a fate unlikely. The baron may think it worthwhile to make an example of you."

Guy, standing at attention with his hands clasped behind him as he bore the brunt of their anger, now turned in appeal to the count. "Lord Falkes," he said, "you saw the place of ambush; you saw how—"

"I saw very little indeed," Falkes replied with cool disdain. "A few bloodstains and some withered foliage. What is that?"

"It is my point exactly," insisted Guy, his voice rising with frustration. "Someone removed the wagons and oxen—removed *everything!*"

"Yes, yes, no doubt it was this creature—this phantom."

"I did not say that," muttered Guy.

"Phantom?" asked Abbot Hugo, raising one eyebrow with interest.

Falkes gave the priest a superior smile and explained about the birdlike creature haunting the forest of the March. "The folk of Elfael call it the Hud," he said. Waving his hand dismissively, he added, "I am sick of hearing about it."

"Hood?" questioned the abbot. "Is that what you said?"

"Hud," corrected Falkes. "It means sorcerer, enchanter, or some such. It is a tale to frighten children."

"*Something* attacked us in the forest," the marshal said. "It commanded wild pigs, killed oxen, and burned our wagons."

"Yes, yes," replied Falkes impatiently, "and then carried everything away, leaving nothing behind."

"What do you want of me?" demanded Guy, tiring of the interrogation.

"I want the baron's money back!" roared Falkes. Guy lowered his head, and Falkes let out a sigh of exasperation. "*Mon Dieu!* This is hopeless." Looking to the abbot, he said, "Do what you will with him. I am finished here." With a last condemning glance at the miserable Guy de Gysburne, he paid the abbot a chilly farewell and strode from the room.

In a moment, they heard the clump of hooves in the yard as the count rode away. "A man in your precarious position, Gysburne," said the abbot quietly, "might rather ask what *I* can do for you." Clasping his hands before him, he regarded the dishevelled knight with a pitying expression. "I do not know what happened out there," Hugo continued in a more sympathetic tone, "but I see that it has shaken you and your men."

Gysburne clenched his jaw and looked away.

"There will be hell to pay, of course," resumed the abbot. "Yet I can ensure that the brunt of this catastrophe does not fall solely on your shoulders."

"Why should you help me?" asked the knight without looking up.

"Is not clemency an attribute of the Holy Church?" Abbot Hugo smiled. Guy's gaze remained firmly fixed on the floor at his feet. "If further explanation is needed, let us just say that I have particular reasons of my own."

The abbot crossed to the table on which cups and a jar were waiting. He placed his hands flat on the table. "You will, of course, return to face the wrath of Baron de Braose," he said. "However, I propose to send you with a letter informing the baron of certain mitigating facts which should be taken into consideration, facts which will ultimately exculpate you. Furthermore, I am prepared to argue, not for imprisonment or dismissal, but for your reassignment. In short, I might be persuaded to ask the baron to assign you to me here. I would then be willing to take full responsibility for you and your actions."

At this, the knight raised his eyes.

The abbot, pacing slowly around the small room of the former chapter house, continued, "After the debacle in the forest last night, de Braose will not refuse me. Far from it. He will think it a most salubrious suggestion—all the more when I offer to make up the pay for the workers out of my own treasury."

"You would do this?" wondered Guy.

"This and more," the cleric assured him. "I will request troops to be placed under my command. You, my friend, shall lead them."

423

Abbot Hugo paused again to regard the unlucky knight. He might have chosen someone older and more experienced for what he had in mind, but Gysburne had dropped into his lap, so to speak, and another opportunity might be a long time coming. All things considered, Sir Guy was not such a bad choice. "I trust this meets with your approval?"

"What about the count?"

"Count Falkes will have nothing to say about it one way or the other," the abbot assured him. "Well?"

"Your Grace, I hardly know what to say."

"Swear fealty to me as God's agent by authority of the Holy Church, and it is done."

"I swear it! On my life, I do so swear."

"Splendid." Hugo returned to the table and poured a cup of wine for his guest. "Please," he said, offering the goblet to the knight. Guy accepted the cup, almost expecting it to burn his hand. Even if it had been offered by the devil himself, he would still be bound to receive it. The calamity in the forest had left him with no better choice.

The abbot smiled again. Distressing as the loss of his property was, the strange turn of events had nevertheless provided him a welcome means of increasing his authority. With his own private army, he would be the most powerful prelate in all Wallia. "As you will appreciate, I lost a very great deal last night. The *church* lost treasure of significant value. That cannot be allowed to happen again." He poured wine into the second cup. "That *will not* happen again."

"No, Your Grace," agreed Guy. He raised his cup and wet his lips. Although greatly relieved not to have to return to Baron de Braose empty-handed, the knight had yet to obtain the measure of the abbot: less a saint, he thought, than a merchant prince in priestly robes. Job's bones, he had met more holy-minded pickpockets!

Guy took another sip of wine, and his thoughts returned to the events of that morning.

As soon as he had regrouped his men—who were still exhausted and shaken by the unnatural events in the haunted wood—he had started out by dawn's first light to bring the count and abbot the bad news. "It was most uncanny beginning to end," he had reported. "On my life, it seems the very stuff of nightmares." He then went on to explain, to an increasingly outraged and disbelieving audience, all that had transpired in the forest.

"Fool!" the abbot had roared when he finished. "Am I to believe that you think there is more to this affair than the rapacious larceny of the reprobate and faithless rabble that inhabit this godforsaken country?"

At those words, the unearthly spell surrounding the entire incident had relinquished some of its power over him. Guy de Gysburne stood blinking in the sunlight of the abbot's reception room. It was the first time he had stopped to consider that the attack had been perpetrated by mere mortals only—cunning mortals, perhaps, but flesh-and-blood humans nonetheless. "No, my lord," he had answered, feeling instantly very embarrassed and overwhelmingly absurd.

Obviously, it had all been an elaborate trap—from the dead creatures strung up along the roadside, to the flames and falling trees that had cut off any chance of escape . . .

But no.

Now that he thought about it, the ambush had begun well before that—probably with the broken wagon axle earlier in the day: the hapless farmer and his shrewish wife, loud and overbearing, impossible to ignore as they stood arguing over the spilled load, standing in mud where no mud should have been . . .

Yes, he was certain of it. The deception had begun far in advance of the actual attack. Moreover, the individual elements of the weird

425

assault had taken a considerable amount of time to prepare—perhaps many days—which meant that someone had known when the treasure train would pass through the forest of the March. Someone had known. Was there a spy in the baron's ranks? Was it one of the soldiers or someone else who had passed along the information?

As Guy sat clutching his cup, his heart burned for revenge. The offer of a new position with the abbot notwithstanding, he vowed to find whoever had ruined his position with the baron and make them pay dearly.

"Mark me, lord marshal, these pagan filth will learn respect for the holy offices. They will learn reverence for the mother church. Their heinous and high-handed deeds will not go unpunished." Though the abbot spoke softly, there was no mistaking the steel-hard edge to his words. "You, Marshal Gysburne, will be the instrument of God's judgement. You will be the weapon in my hand."

Sir Guy could not agree more.

The abbot poured another cup and lifted it in salute. "Let us drink to the prompt recovery of the stolen treasure and to your own swift advancement."

The marshal raised his cup to the abbot's, and both men drank. They then put their heads together to compose the letter to be delivered to the baron. Before the wax was dry on the parchment, Guy was already scheming how to find the stolen treasure, expose the traitor in their midst, and exact revenge on those who had disgraced him and robbed the abbot.

Under the keen watch of sentries hidden in the brush along the road, the Grellon walked hidden pathways. Moving with the stealth of forest creatures, men, women, and children ferried the plunder back to their greenwood glen on litters made of woven leather straps stretched between pine poles. It took most of the day to retrieve the spoils of their wild night's work and store it safely away. Thus, the sun was low in the sky when Bran, Iwan, Tuck, Siarles, and Angharad finally gathered to open the iron-banded caskets.

Iwan and Siarles set to work, hacking at the charred wood and metal bands of the first two strongboxes. The others looked on, speculating on what they would find. Under the onslaught of an axe and pick, Iwan's box gave way first; three quick blows splintered the sides, and three more released a gleaming cascade of silver onto the hearth-side floor. Tuck scooped up the coins with a bowl and poured them into his robe, as Siarles, meanwhile, chopped at the top of the chest before him and presently succeeded in breaking open the ruined lock.

He threw open the lid. The interior was filled with cloth bags—

each one tied by a cord that was sealed in wax with the baron's crest. At a nod from Bran, he lifted one out and untied the string, breaking the seal, and poured the contents into Brother Tuck's bowl: forty-eight English pennies, newly minted, bright as tiny moons.

"There must be over two hundred pounds here," Siarles estimated. "More, even."

Iwan turned his attention to the third box. Smaller than the other two, it had suffered less damage and proved more difficult to break open. With battering blows, Iwan smashed at the lock and wooden sides of the chest. The iron-banded box resisted his efforts until Siarles fetched a hammer and chisel and began working at the rivets, loosening a few of the bands to allow Iwan's pick to gain purchase. Eventually, the two succeeded in worrying the lid from its hinges; tossing it aside, they upended the box, and out rolled plump leather bags—smaller than the baron's black bags, but heavier. When hefted, they gave a dull chink.

"Open them," Bran commanded. He sat on his haunches, watching the proceedings with dazzled amazement.

Plucking a bag from the chest, Iwan untied the string and shook the contents into Bran's open hand. The gleam of gold flashed in the firelight as a score of thick coins plopped into his palm.

"Upon my vow," gasped Aethelfrith in awe, "they're filled with flaming *byzants!*"

Raising one of the coins, Bran turned it between his fingers, watching the lustrous shimmer dance in the light. He felt the exquisite weight and warmth of the fine metal. He had never seen genuine Byzantine gold *solidi* before. "What are they worth?"

"Well now," the priest answered, snatching up a coin from the floor. "Let me see. There are twelve pennies in a shilling, and twenty shillings in a pound—so a pound is worth two hundred and forty pennies." Tapping his finger on his palm as if counting invisible coins, the mendicant priest continued, amazing his onlookers with his thorough understanding of worldly wealth. "Now then, a mark, as we all know, is worth thirteen shillings and four pence, or one hundred sixty pennies—which means that there are one and a half marks in one pound sterling."

"So how much for a byzant?" asked Siarles.

"Give me time," said Tuck. "I'm getting to that."

"This will take all night," complained Siarles.

"It *will* if you keep interrupting, boyo," replied the priest testily. "These are delicate calculations." He gave Siarles a sour look and resumed, "Where was I? Right—so that's . . ." He paused to reckon the total. "That's over five pounds." He frowned. "No, make that six—more."

"A bag?" asked Bran.

"Each," replied the priest, handing the byzant back to him.

"You mean to say *this*," said Bran, holding the gold coin to the light, "is worth ten marks?"

"They are as valuable as they are scarce."

"Sire," said Iwan, dazzled by the extent of their haul, "this is far better than we hoped." Reaching into another of the leather bags, he drew out more of the fat gold coins. "This is a . . . a miracle."

"The Good Lord helps them who help themselves," Friar Tuck said, pouring coins from the fold of his gathered robe into the bowl on the floor before him. "Blessèd be the name of the Lord!"

"How much is there altogether?" wondered Bran, gazing at the treasure hoard.

"Several hundred marks at least," suggested Siarles.

"It is more than enough to pay the workers," observed Angharad from her stool. "Much more." She rose and gathered a deerskin from her sleeping place. Spreading it on the floor beside the kneeling priest, she instructed, "Count it onto this."

"And count it out loud so we can all hear," added Siarles.

"Help me," said the priest. "Put them into piles of twelve."

The two fell to arranging the silver coins into little heaps to represent a shilling, and then Brother Tuck began telling out the number, shilling by shilling. Siarles, using a bit of charred wood, kept a running tally on a hearthstone, announcing the reckoning every fourth or fifth stack, and calling out the total at each mark: one hundred . . . one hundred seventy-five . . . two hundred . . .

The women of Cél Craidd brought food—a haunch of roast meat from one of the slaughtered oxen and some fresh barley cakes made from the supplies intended for Abbot Hugo. Bran and the others ate while the counting continued.

After a while, they heard voices outside the hut. "Your flock grows curious," Angharad said. "They have been patient long enough. You should speak to them, Bran."

Rising, Bran stepped to the door and pushed aside the ox-hide covering. Stepping out into the soft night air, he saw the entire population of the settlement—forty-three souls in all—ranged on the ground around the door of the hut. Wrapped in their cloaks, they were talking quietly amongst themselves. A fire had been lit and some of the children were running barefoot around it.

"We are still counting the money," he told them simply. "I will bring word when we have finished."

"It is taking a fair sweet time," suggested one of the men.

"There is a lot to count."

"God be praised," said another. "How much?"

"More than we hoped," replied Bran. "Your patience will be rewarded, never fear."

He returned to Angharad's hearth and the counting. "Three hundred fifty . . . ," droned Siarles, making another mark on the stone, ". . . four hundred . . ."

"Four hundred marks!" gasped Iwan. "Why were they carrying so much money?"

"Something is happening that we have neither heard nor foreseen," Angharad replied, "and this is the proof."

Tuck, still counting, gave a cough to silence them. And the total continued to grow.

When the last silver penny had been accounted, the total stood at four hundred and fifty marks. Then, turning his attention to the leather bags in the last casket, the friar began to count out the gold coins to the value of ten marks each. The others looked on breathlessly as the friar arranged the golden byzants in neat little towers of ten.

When he finished, Tuck raised his head and, in a voice filled with quiet wonder, announced, "Seven hundred and fifty marks. That makes five hundred pounds sterling."

"Do I believe what I am hearing?" breathed Iwan, overwhelmed by the enormity of the plunder. "Five hundred *pounds* . . ." He turned his eyes to Bran and then to Angharad. "What have we done?"

"We have ransomed Elfael from the stinking Ffreinc," declared Bran. "Using their own money, too. Rough justice, that."

Turning on his heel, he moved to the door and stepped out to deliver the news to those waiting outside. Angharad went with him and, raising her hands, said, "Silence. Rhi Bran would speak."

When the murmuring died down, Bran said, "Through our efforts we have won five hundred pounds—more than enough to pay the redemption price Red William has set. We have redeemed our land!"

The sudden outcry of acclamation took Bran by surprise. Hearing the cheers and seeing the glad faces in the moonlight took him back to another place and time. For a moment, Bran was a child in the yard at Caer Cadarn, listening to the revelry of the warriors returning from a hunt. His mother was still alive, and as Queen of the Hunt, she led the women of the valley, singing and dancing in celebration of the hunters' success, her long, dark hair streaming loose as she spun and turned in the rising glow of a full moon.

Nothing could ever bring her back or replace the warmth he had known in the presence of that loving soul. But this he could do: he could reclaim the caer and, under his rule, return the court of Elfael to something approaching its former glory.

Angharad had once asked him what it was he desired. He had suspected even then that there was more to the question than he knew. Now, suddenly, he beheld the shape of his deepest desire. More than anything in the world, he wanted the joy he had known as a child to reign in Elfael once more.

Angharad, standing at his side, felt the surge of emotion through him as a torrent through a dry streambed, and knew he had made up his mind at last. "Yes," she whispered. "This night, whatever you desire will bend to your will. Choose well, my king."

Raising his eyes, he saw the radiant disc of the moon as it cleared the sheltering trees, filling the forest hollow with a soft, spectral light. "My people, my Grellon," Bran said, his voice breaking with emotion, "tonight we celebrate our victory over the Ffreinc. Tomorrow we reclaim our homeland."

Mérian had determined to endure the baron's council with grace and forbearance. Spared the greater evil of having to spend the summer in the baron's castle in Hereford, she could afford to be charitable toward her enemies. Therefore, she vowed to utter no complaint and to maintain a respectful courtesy to one and all in what she had imagined would be a condition little better than captivity.

As the days went by, however, her energetic dislike for the Ffreinc began to flag; it was simply too difficult to maintain against the onslaught of courtesy and charm with which she was treated. Thus, to her own great amazement—and no little annoyance—she found herself actually enjoying the proceedings despite the fact that the one hope she had entertained for the council—that she might renew her acquaintance with Cécile and Thérèse—was denied her: they were not in attendance.

Their brother, Roubert, cheerfully informed her that his sisters had been sent back to Normandie for the summer and would not return until autumn, or perhaps not even until next spring. "It is good for them to acquire some of the finer graces," he confided, adopting a superior tone.

What these graces might be, he did not say, and Mérian did not ask, lest she prove herself a backward hill-country churl in need of those same finer graces. She welcomed Roubert's company but felt awkward in his presence. Although he always appeared eager to see her, she sensed a natural haughtiness in him and a veiled disdain for all things foreign—which was nearly everything in fair Britain's island realm, including herself.

Aside from Roubert, the only other person near her own age was the baron's dour daughter, Sybil. Mérian and the young lady had been introduced on the first day by Neufmarché himself, with the implied directive that they should become friends. For her part, Mérian was willing enough—there was little to do anyway with the council in session most of the day—but so far had received scant encouragement from the young noblewoman.

Lady Sybil appeared worn down by the heat of the summer sun and the innate discomforts of camp. Her fine dark hair hung in limp hanks, and dark shadows gathered beneath her large brown eyes. She appeared so listless and unhappy that Mérian, at first annoyed by the young woman's affected swanning, eventually came to pity her. The young Ffreinc noblewoman languished in the shade of a canopy erected outside the baron's massive tent, cooling herself with a fan made of kidskin stretched over a willow frame.

"*Mère de Dieu*," sighed the young woman wistfully when Mérian came to visit her one day, "I am not . . . um"—she paused, searching for a word she could not find—"*accoutumé* so much this heated air."

Mérian smiled at her broken English. "Yes," she agreed sympathetically, "it is very hot."

"It is always so, *non?*"

"Oh no," Mérian quickly assured her. "It is not. Usually, the weather is fine. But this summer is different." A cloud of bafflement passed over Lady Sybil's face. "Hotter," Mérian finished lamely.

The two gazed at each other across the ditch of language gaping between them.

"There you are!" They turned to see Baron Neufmarché striding toward them, flanked by two severe-looking knights dressed in the long, drab tunics and trousers of Saxon nobility. "My lords," declared the baron in English, "have you ever seen two more beautiful ladies in all of England?"

"Never, sire," replied the two noblemen in unison.

"It is pleasant to see you again, Lady Mérian," said the baron. Smiling into her eyes, he grasped her hand and lifted it to his lips. Turning quickly, he kissed his daughter on the forehead and rested his hand on her shoulder. "I see you are finding pleasure in one another's company at last."

"We are trying," Mérian said. She offered Sybil a hopeful smile. Clearly, the young woman had no idea what her father was saying.

"I hope that when the council is over, you still plan to attend us in Hereford," the baron said.

"Well, I . . . ," Mérian faltered, unable to untangle her mixed emotions so quickly. After all, when originally mooted, the proposition had been greeted with such hostility on her part that now she hardly knew *what* she felt about the idea.

Neufmarché smiled and waved aside any excuse she might make. "We would make you most welcome, to be sure." He stroked his daughter's hair. "In fact, now that you know each other better, perhaps you might accompany Sybil to our estates in Normandie when she returns this autumn. It could be easily arranged."

Uncertain what to say, Mérian bit her lip.

"Come, my lady," coaxed the baron. He saw her hesitancy and offered her a subtle reminder of her place, "We have already made arrangements, and your father has consented."

"I would be honoured, sire," she said, "seeing my father has consented."

"Good!" He smiled again and offered Mérian a little bow of courtesy. "You have made my daughter very happy."

A third soldier came rushing up just then, and the baron excused himself and turned to greet the newcomer. "Ah, de Lacy! You have word?"

"*Oui, mon baron de seigneur,*" blurted the man, red-faced from rushing in the heat. The baron raised his hand and commanded him to speak English for the benefit of the two knights with him. The messenger gulped air and dragged a sleeve across his sweating face. Beginning again, he said, "It is true, my lord. Baron de Braose did dispatch wagons and men through your lands. They passed through

Hereford on the day the council convened and returned but yester-day." The man faltered, licking his lips.

"Yes? Speak it out, man!" Calling toward the tent, the baron shouted, "Remey! Bring water at once." In a moment, the seneschal appeared with a jar and cup. He poured and offered the cup to the baron, who passed it to the soldier. "Drink," Bernard ordered, "and let us hear this from the beginning—and slowly, if you please."

The messenger downed the water in three greedy draughts. Taking back the cup, the baron held it out to be refilled, then drank a little himself. "See here," he said, passing the vessel to the nobles with him, "de Braose's men passed through my lands without permission—did you mark?" The nobles nodded grimly. "This is not the first time they have trespassed with impunity. How many this time?"

"Seven knights and fifteen men-at-arms, not counting ox herds and attendants for three wagons. As I say, they returned but yesterday, only—most were afoot, and there were no wagons."

"Indeed?"

"There is rumour of an attack in the forest. Given that some of the men were seen to be wounded, it seems likely."

"Do they say who perpetrated the attack?"

"Sire, there is talk . . . rumours only." The soldier glanced at the two noblemen standing nearby and hesitated.

"Well?" demanded the baron. "If you know, say it."

"They say the train was attacked by the phantom of the forest."

"Mon Dieu!" exclaimed Remey, unable to stifle his surprise.

The baron glanced hastily over his shoulder to see the two young women following the conversation. "Pray excuse us, ladies. This was not for your ears." To the men, he said, "Come; we will discuss the matter in private." He led his party into the tent, leaving Mérian and Lady Sybil to themselves once more.

"Le fantôme!" whispered Sybil, eyes wide at what she heard. "I have heard of this. It is a creature *gigantesque*? *Oui*?"

"Yes, a very great, enormous creature," said Mérian, drawing Sybil closer to share this delicious secret. "The people call him King Raven, and he haunts the forest of the March."

"Incroyable!" gasped Sybil. "The priests say this is very impossibility, *n'est ce pas*?"

"Oh no. It is true." Mérian gave her a nod of solemn assurance. "The Cymry believe King Raven has arisen to defend the land beyond the Marches. He protects Cymru, and nothing can defeat him—not soldiers, not armies, not even King William the Red himself."

CHAPTER 44

Dressed as humble wool merchants, Bran, Iwan, Aethelfrith, and Siarles swiftly crossed the Marches and entered England. Strange merchants these: avoiding towns entirely, travelling only by night, they progressed through the countryside—four men mounted on sturdy Welsh horses, each leading a packhorse laden with provisions and their wares, which consisted of three overstuffed wool sacks. Laying up in sheltered groves and glades and hidden glens along the way, they slept through the day with one of their number on watch at all times.

They arrived in Lundein well before the city gates were open and waited impatiently until sleepy-eyed guards, yawning and muttering, drew the crossbeams and gave them leave to enter. They went first to the Abbey of Saint Mary the Virgin, where, after a cold-water bath, the travellers changed into clean clothes and broke fast with the monks. Then, groomed and refreshed, they led their packhorses through the narrow streets of the city to the tower fortress. At the outer wall of the tower, they inquired of the porter and begged audience with Cardinal Ranulf of Bayeux, Chief Justiciar of England.

"He is not here," the porter informed them. "He is away on king's business."

"If you please, friend," said Aethelfrith, "could you tell us where we might find him? It is of utmost importance."

"Winchester," replied the porter. "Seek him there."

Bran and Iwan exchanged a puzzled glance. "Where?"

"Caer Wintan—the king's hunting lodge," the friar explained for the benefit of the Welsh speakers. "It is not far—maybe two days' ride."

The four resumed their journey, pausing long enough to provision themselves from the farmers' stalls along the river before crossing the King's Bridge. Once out of the city, they turned onto the West Road and headed for the royal residence at Winchester. Riding until long after dark, rising early, and resting little along the way, the travellers reached the ancient Roman garrison town two days later. Upon asking at the city gate, they were directed to King William's hunting lodge: a sprawling half-timbered edifice built by a long-forgotten local worthy, and carelessly enlarged over generations to serve the needs of various royal inhabitants. The great house was the one place in all England the Red King called home.

Unlike the White Tower of Lundein, the Royal Lodge boasted no keep or protective stone walls; two wings of the lodge enclosed a bare yard in front of the central hall. A low wooden palisade formed the fourth side of the open square, in the centre of which was a gate and a small wooden hut for the porter. As before, the travellers presented themselves to the porter and were promptly relieved of their weapons before being allowed into the beaten-earth yard, where knights, bare to the waist, practised with wooden swords and padded lances. They tied their horses to the ringed post at the far end of the yard and proceeded to the hall. They were made to wait in an antechamber, where they watched Norman courtiers and clerks enter and leave the hall, some clutching bundles of parchment, others bearing small wooden chests or bags of coins. Bran, unable to sit still for long, rose often and returned to the yard to see that all was well with Iwan and Siarles, who waited with the horses, keeping an eye on their precious cargo. Brother Aethelfrith, meanwhile, occupied himself with prayers and psalms that he mumbled in a low continuous murmur as he passed the knots of his rope cincture through his pudgy hands.

The morning stretched and dwindled away. Midday came and went, and the sun began its long, slow descent. Bran had gone to see if Iwan had watered the horses when Aethelfrith called him back inside. "Bran! Hurry! The cardinal has summoned us!"

Bran rejoined Tuck, who was waiting for him at the door. "Mind your manners now," the friar warned, taking him by the arm. "We need not make this more difficult than it is already. Agreed?"

Bran nodded, and the two were conducted into Ranulf of Bayeux's chamber. A whole year and more had passed, and yet the same two brown-robed clerics sat at much the same table piled high with rolled and folded parchments, still scratching away with their quill pens. Between them in a high-backed chair sat the cardinal, wearing a red satin skullcap and heavy gold chain. His red hair was cut short; it had been curled with hot irons and dressed with oil so that it glimmered in the light from the high window. Three rings adorned the fingers of his pale hands, which were folded on the table before him. Eyes closed, Cardinal Ranulf rested his head against the back of his chair, apparently asleep.

"My lord cardinal," announced the porter, "I bring before you the Welsh lord and his priest."

"And his *English* priest," added Aethelfrith with a smile. "Don't you be forgetting."

"Cardinal," said Bran, not waiting to be addressed, "we have come about the de Braose grant."

The chief justiciar slowly opened his eyes. "Have I seen you before?" he asked, passing a lazy glance over the two men standing before him at the table.

"Yes, sire," replied the friar respectfully. "Last year it was. Allow me to present Lord Bran of Elfael. We discussed the king's grant of Elfael to Baron William de Braose."

Recognition seemed to come drifting back to the cardinal then. Presently he nodded, regarding the slim young man before him. "Just so." The Welsh lord appeared different somehow—leaner, harder, with an air of conviction about him. "Do you speak French?" inquired the cardinal.

"No, my lord," answered Aethelfrith. "He does not."

"Pity," sniffed Bayeux. Changing to Latin, he asked, "What is your business?"

"I have come to reclaim my lands," replied Bran. "You will recall that you said the grant made to Baron de Braose could be rescinded for a fee—"

"Yes, yes," replied the cardinal as if the memory somehow pained him, "I remember."

"I have brought the money, my lord cardinal," answered Bran. He raised a hand to Tuck, who hurried to the door and gave a whistle to the two waiting outside. A moment later, Iwan appeared, lugging a large leather provision bag. Approaching the cardinal, the champion hoisted the bundle onto the table, opened it, and allowed some of the smaller bags of silver to spill out.

"Six hundred marks," said Bran. "As agreed." He put his hand to the sack. "Here is two hundred. The rest is ready to hand."

Ranulf reached for one of the bags and weighed it in his palm as he raised his eyes to study Bran once more. "That is as it may be," he allowed slowly. "I regret to inform you, however, six hundred marks was last year's price."

"My lord?"

"If you had redeemed the grant when offered," continued the cardinal, "you could have had it for six hundred marks. You waited too long. The price has gone up."

"Gone up?" Bran felt the heat of anger rising to his face.

"Events move on apace. Time and tide, as they say," intoned the cardinal with lofty sufferance. "It is the same with the affairs of court."

"Pray spare me the lesson, my lord," muttered Bran through clenched teeth. "How much is required now?"

"Two thousand marks."

"You stinking bandit!" Bran spat. "We agreed on six hundred, and I have brought it."

The cardinal's eyes narrowed dangerously. "Careful, my hotheaded prince. If it were not for the king's need to raise money for his troops in Normandie, your petition would not be considered at all." He reached a hand toward one of the money sacks. "As it is, we will accept this six hundred in partial payment of the two thousand—"

"You want money?" cried Bran. He saw the cardinal, officious and smug in his sumptuous robes as he reached for the coins; his vision dimmed as the blood rage came upon him. "Here is your money!"

Reaching across the table, he seized the cardinal by the front of the robe, pulled him up out of his chair, and thrust him down on the table, crushing his face against the coins spilled there. Ranulf let out a strangled cry, and his two scribes jumped up. As the nearest one bent to his master's aid, Bran took up an ink pot and dashed the contents into his face. Instantly blinded, the clerk fell back, bawling, shaking black ink everywhere. The other started for the door. "Stay!" shouted Bran, his knife in his hand.

Iwan, uncertain what was happening, glanced nervously at his lord. Tightening his grip on the money sack, he backed toward the door.

Cardinal Ranulf, squirming under his grasp, pulled free, falling back in his chair. Bran leapt onto the table and kicked the pile of parchments, scattering letters, deeds, and royal writs across the room. He kicked another pile and then jumped down, seizing the cardinal once more. "Does the king know what you do in his name?" asked Bran.

The cardinal spat at him, and Bran slammed his head down on the table. "Answer me, pig!"

"Bran!" Iwan put a hand to his lord's shoulder to pull him away. "Bran, enough!"

Shaking off Iwan's hand, Bran pulled the cardinal up, wielding the knife in his face and shouting, "Does the king know what you do in his name?"

"What do you think?" sneered the cardinal. "I act with William's authority and blessing. Release me at once, or I will see you dance on the gibbet before the day is out."

"Pray forgive him, Your Eminence," said Tuck, pushing in beside Bran. "He is overwrought and emotional." Taking Bran's hand in both of his own, it took all his considerable strength to wrest the knife from his grasp and pull him away. "If you please, sire, accept this six hundred marks in part payment for the whole. We will bring you the rest when we have it."

He looked to Bran, indicating that an answer was required. "Not so?"

Bran took a step back from the table. "They get nothing from me—not a penny."

"Bran, think of your people," pleaded Aethelfrith.

But Bran was already walking away. He signalled Iwan and Siarles, still holding the leather bags. "Bring the money," he told them. The two scooped the loose coins and money bags back into the sacks and then hurried to follow their lord.

"I will have you in chains!" shouted the cardinal. "You cannot treat the royal justiciar this way!"

"Again I beg your indulgence, Your Eminence," said Friar Tuck, "but my lord has decided to take his appeal to a higher court."

"Fool, this is the king's court!" the cardinal roared. "There is none higher."

"I think," replied Tuck, hurrying away, "you will find that there is one."

Tuck rejoined the others in the yard. Bran was already mounted and ready to ride. Iwan and Siarles were securing the money sacks when from the hall entrance burst Cardinal Ranulf, shouting, *"Saivez-les! Aux armes!"*

Some of the knights still lingering in the yard heard the summons and turned to see the cardinal. Red-faced and angry, his robes splotched with black ink, hands outthrust, he was pointing wildly at the departing Britons.

"Aux armes! Gardes!" bawled the cardinal. "To arms! Seize them!"

"Iwan! Siarles!" shouted Bran. Slapping the reins across his mount's withers, he started for the gate. "To me!"

The porter, hearing this commotion, stepped from his hut just in time to see Bran bearing down on him. He flung himself out of the way as Bran slid from his still-galloping horse and dove into the hut, appearing three heartbeats later with the weapons that had been given over on his arrival. Raising his longbow and nocking an arrow to the string, he loosed one shaft at a bare-chested knight who was readying a lance for Iwan's unprotected back. The arrow sang across the yard with blazing speed, striking the knight high in the chest. He dropped to the ground, clutching his shoulder, writhing and screaming.

Iwan finished tying the money sack and swung into the saddle. Siarles followed an instant behind, and both rode for the open gate.

Tuck's horse, skittish with the sudden commotion, reared and shied, unwilling to be mounted. The friar held tight to the reins and tried to calm the frightened animal.

Meanwhile, the porter, having regained his feet and his wits, threw himself at Bran and received a jab in the stomach with the end of the bow. He crumpled to his knees, and Bran, returning to the business at hand, raised the bow, drew, and buried a second shaft in the doorpost a bare handsbreadth from the cardinal's head. Ranulf yelped and stumbled back into the hall. The porter struggled to his knees again—just in time to receive a sidelong kick to the jaw, which took him from the fight. "If you want to live," said Bran, "stay down."

Iwan reached the porter's hut, and Bran, darting inside again, retrieved the champion's bow and sword. "Ride on ahead!" shouted Bran, handing the champion his weapons; he galloped away, leading the packhorse. "Wait for me at the bridge!"

Siarles followed, holding tight to the reins of the second packhorse. He paused at the porter's hut long enough to snatch his bow and a sheaf of arrows from Bran's grasp. "Go with Iwan."

"My lord, I won't leave you behind."

"Keep the money safe," Bran shouted. "I'll bring Tuck. Wait for us at the bridge."

"But, my lord—," objected Siarles.

"Just go!" Bran waved him away as he darted back into the yard.

The friar had his hands full now; he was surrounded on three sides by Ffreinc knights—two holding the padded lances they had been using when the fight began, and one wielding a wooden practise sword. One of the knights made a lunge with his lance, striking the priest on the back of the neck. Tuck fell, still clinging to the reins of his rearing mount, and was dragged backwards.

Bran, running to the middle of the yard, loosed a shaft as the knight drove in to crush Tuck's skull with the butt of the lance. The arrow struck just above the hip, throwing the knight sideways; his lance spun from his hand. "Pick it up!" shouted Bran. Out of the corner of his eye, he saw the dull glint of metal as two helmeted heads appeared in the doorway of the hall. He sent another arrow into the doorway to keep them back and shouted for Tuck to release the horse. "The spear, Tuck!" he cried, pointing to the weapon on the ground. "Use it!"

Understanding came to him at last. The friar let go of the reins and snatched up the practise weapon just as the knight with the wooden sword closed on him. Spinning the shaft like a quarterstaff, Tuck dealt the man a solid blow on the forearm as the wooden blade swung down. The sword slipped from his grasp. As the soldier grabbed his broken arm, Tuck swung hard at the man's knee; the soldier's leg buckled, and he went down. Meanwhile, Tuck, spinning on his toes, whirled around to face his last assailant. He neatly parried one swipe of the padded lance and dodged another before landing a double-handed blow on top of the knight's unprotected head. The lance pole bounced and split with a resounding *crack!* as the knight dropped senseless to the ground.

"Away, Tuck!" cried Bran. Seizing the reins of the friar's skittish horse, he held the animal until the priest gained the saddle and, with a slap on the beast's rump, sent him off. "Fly!"

Bran turned around to face the next assault, only to find himself alone in the yard. There were other soldiers in hiding close by, he guessed, but none brave enough to face his bow until they could better protect themselves. He walked to the soldier squirming in the dirt with an arrow in his hip. "If you're finished with this, I'll be having it back," Bran told him. Placing a foot on the wounded man's side, he gave a hefty yank and pulled the arrow free; the knight screamed in

447

agony and promptly passed out. Bran set the bloody arrow on the string and, watching for anyone bold enough to challenge him, backed toward the gate and his own waiting mount.

Upon reaching his horse, he cast a last look at the hall, where a knight's red-painted shield was just then edging cautiously into view from the open doorway. He drew and loosed. The arrow blazed across the distance and struck the shield just above the centre boss. The oak shaft of the arrow shattered, and the shield split. Bran heard a yowl of pain as the splintered shield disappeared. Smiling to himself, he climbed into the saddle, wheeled his horse, and rode to join his swiftly fleeing band.

CHAPTER 45

The fields and groves of Winchester fell away behind the steady hoofbeats of the horses. Bran pushed a relentless pace, and the others followed, keeping up as best they could. When Bran finally paused to rest his mount, the sun was a golden glow behind the western hills. The first stars could be seen in patches of clear sky to the east, and the king's town was but a dull, smoke-coloured smudge on the southern horizon.

"Do you know what this means?" demanded Tuck. Out of breath and sweating from the exertion, he reined in beside Bran and gave vent to his anger.

"I suppose it means we won't be asked to join the king's Christmas hunt," replied Bran.

"It means," cried Tuck, "that a worse fate has befallen Elfael than any since Good King Harold quit the battle with an arrow in his eye. Christ and all his saints! Attacking the cardinal like that—you could have got us all killed—or worse! What were you thinking?"

"Me? You blame me?" shouted Bran. "You cannot trust these

people, Tuck. The Ffreinc are two-faced liars and cheats, every last one—beginning with that red-haired maggot king of theirs!"

"Well, boyo, you showed *them*," the friar growled. "This time tomorrow there will be a price on your head—on *all* our heads, thanks to you."

"Good! Let Red William count the cost of cheating Bran ap Brychan."

"For the love of God, Bran," Tuck pleaded, "all you had to do was swallow a fair-sized chunk of that blasted Welsh pride and you could have had Elfael for two thousand marks."

"Yesterday it was six hundred marks, and today two thousand," Bran spat. "It'll be ten thousand tomorrow, and twenty the day after! It is always more, Tuck, and still more. There is not enough silver in all England to satisfy them. They'll never let us have Elfael."

"Not now," Tuck snapped. "You made fair certain of that, did you not?"

Bran, glaring at the fat priest, turned his face away.

Iwan and Siarles, leading the packhorses, reined up then. "Sire," said Iwan, "what about the money? What are we going to do now?"

"Why ask me?" Bran replied, not taking his eyes from the far horizon. "I had one idea and risked everything to make it work—we all did—but it failed. I failed. I have nothing else."

"But you will think of something," said Siarles. "You can always come up with something."

"Aye, and it had better be quick," Friar Tuck pointed out. "After what happened back there, the Ffreinc will be fast on our trail. We cannot stand here in the middle of the road. What are we going to do?"

Can't you see? thought Bran. *We tried and failed. It is over. Finished. The Ffreinc rule now, and they are too powerful. The best we can do is take the money* and divide it out amongst the people. They can use it to start new lives somewhere else. For myself, I will go to Gwynedd and forget all about Elfael.

"Bran?" said Iwan quietly. "You know we will follow you anywhere. Just tell us what you want to do."

Bran turned to his friends. He saw the need in their eyes. It was as Angharad had said: they had no one else and nowhere else to go. For better or worse, beleaguered Elfael was their home, and he was all the king they had.

Well, he was a sorry excuse for a king—and no better than his father. King Brychan had cared little enough for his people, pursuing his own way all his life. "You are not your father," Angharad had told him. "You could be twice the king he was—and ten times the man—if you so desired."

Yet here he was, set to follow in his father's footsteps and go his own way. Was this his fate? Or was there another way? Competing thoughts roiled in his mind until one finally won out: He was *not* his father; it was not too late; he could still choose a better way.

God in heaven, thought Bran, *I cannot leave them. What am I to do?*

"What are you thinking, Bran?" asked Aethelfrith.

"I was just thinking that the enemy of my enemy is my friend," said Bran as the words came to him.

"Indeed?" Tuck wondered, regarding him askance. "And who is this dubious friend of yours?"

"Neufmarché," said Bran. "You said the baron had called a council of his vassals and liege men—"

"Yes, but—"

"The place where they are meeting, could you find it?"

"It would not be difficult, but—"

"Then lead me to him."

"See here, Bran," Tuck remonstrated, "let us talk this over."

451

"You said the Ffreinc will be searching for us," he countered. "They will not think to look for us in the baron's camp."

"But, Bran, what have we to do with the baron?"

"There is no justice to be had of England's king," Bran answered, his voice cutting. "Therefore, we must make our appeal wherever we find a ready ear."

Turning in the saddle, the priest appealed to Iwan. "Talk to him, John. I've grown fond of this splendid neck of mine, and before I risk it riding into the enemy's camp, I would know the reason."

"He has a fair point, Bran," said the champion. "What have we to do with Neufmarché?"

Bran turned his horse around to address them. "The king weighs heavily on de Braose's side," he said, his face aglow in the golden light of the setting sun. "With the two of them joined against us, we need a powerful ally to even the balance." Regarding Tuck, he said, "You have said yourself that Neufmarché and de Braose are rivals—"

"Rivals, yes," agreed Tuck, "who would carve up Cymru between them—and then squabble over which one had the most." He shook his head solemnly. "Neufmarché may hate de Braose every mite and morsel as much as we do, but he is no friend to us."

"If we make alliance with him," said Bran, "he will be obliged to help us. He has the power and means to rid us of de Braose."

"Tuck is right," said Iwan. "Besides, how can we persuade him to ally with us? We have nothing to offer him that he wants."

"Even so," said Siarles, "would Neufmarché make such a bargain?"

"Aye, and if he did," added Tuck, "would he keep it?"

Bran paused in silent reflection. Could Neufmarché be trusted? There was no way to tell. "Lord Cadwgan in Eiwas holds him trustworthy and just. He and his people have been treated fairly. But whether the baron honours his word or not," Bran said, the words like stones in his mouth, "we will be no worse off than we are now."

"This is a remedy of last resort," Tuck argued. "Let us exhaust all other possibilities first."

"We have done that, my friend. We have. All that is left us now is to watch the Ffreinc grow from strength to strength at our expense. Baron de Braose and the Red King mean us nothing but harm. As for Neufmarché? We have nothing to lose." Bran offered a bitter smile. "If we must sleep with the devil, let us do it and be done. This is nothing more than what my father should have done long ago. If Brychan had sworn allegiance to the Ffreinc when he had the chance, we would not be in this predicament now."

The others, unable to gainsay this argument, reluctantly agreed.

Bran, brightening at last, said, "Lead the way, Tuck, and pray with every breath that we find the friend we seek."

Baron Bernard de Neufmarché had dismissed the last of the day's petitioners and returned to his tent, where, after summoning Remey to bring him refreshment, he removed his short cloak and eased himself into his chair. It had been a long day but, in balance, a good one and a fitting conclusion to a council that had, in the end, satisfied his every demand. Convening at Talgarth—the scene of vaunted Lord Rhys ap Tewdwr's recent demise—had been the masterstroke, providing a strong and present reminder to all under his rule that he was not afraid to deal harshly with those who failed to serve him faithfully. The point had been made and accepted. Tomorrow the council would formally end, and he would send his vassals home—some to better fates than they had hoped, others to worse—and he would return to

Hereford to oversee the harvest and begin readying the castle for the influx of fresh troops in the spring.

"Your wine, sire." Remey placed a pewter goblet on the table beside the baron's chair. "I have ordered sausages to be prepared, and there is fresh bread soon. Would you like anything else while you wait?"

"The wine will suffice for now," the baron replied, easing off his boots and stretching his legs. "Bring the rest when it is ready—and some of those *fraises*, if there are any left."

"Of course, sire," replied the seneschal. "The sessions went well today, I assume?"

"They went very well indeed, Remey. I am content." Baron Neufmarché raised his cup and allowed himself a long, satisfying sip, savouring the fine, tart edge of the wine. Councils always brought demands, and this one more than most—owing to the prolonged absence of the king. Royal dispatch fresh from Normandie indicated that the conflict between Red William and his brother, Duke Robert, had bogged down; with summer dwindling away, there would be no further advances at least until after harvest, if then. Meanwhile, the king would repair to Rouen to lick his wounds and restock his castles.

Thus, the king's throne in England appeared likely to remain vacant into the foreseeable future. An absent king forced the lesser lords to look for other sources of protection and redress. This, Neufmarché reflected, created problems and opportunities for the greater lords like himself, whose influence and interests rivalled the king's. A baron who remained wary and alert could make the most of the opportunities that came his way.

He was just congratulating himself on the several exceptional opportunities that he had already seized this day when one of the squires who served as sentry for the camp appeared outside the tent. Bernard saw him hovering at the door flap and called, "Yes? What is it?"

"Someone requests audience, sire."

"Affairs are concluded for the day," Neufmarché replied. "Tell them they are too late."

There was a short silence, and then a small cough at the door flap.

"What? Did you not hear what I said? The council is over."

"I have told them, sire," the squire replied. "But they insist."

"Do they!" shouted the baron. Rising from his chair, he stumped to the doorway in his stocking feet and threw back the hanging flap. "I am at rest, *idiot!*"

The squire jumped back, almost colliding with the two strangers behind him—Welshmen from the look of them: a young one, dark and slender, with a puckered scar along his cheek, and an older one, broad and bandy-legged, who, despite his outgrown tonsure, appeared to be a priest of some kind. Both men were dusty from the road and stank of the saddle.

"Well?" demanded the baron, glaring at the strangers who had disturbed his peace. "What is it? Be quick!"

"Pax vobiscum," said the fat priest. "We have come on a matter we think will be of special interest to you."

"The only thing that interests me right now," snarled the baron, "is a cup of wine and the comfort of my chair—which I possessed until your unseemly interruption."

"William de Braose," said the young man quietly.

Neufmarché turned a withering gaze upon the lithe stranger. "What about him?"

"His star ascends in the king's court while yours declines." The young man smiled, the scar twisting his expression into a fierce grimace.

"I would have thought the humiliation of that would be a constant embarrassment to a man like you. Am I wrong?"

"Impudent knave!" spat Neufmarché, thrusting forward. "Who are you to speak to me like this?"

The stranger did not flinch but replied with quiet assurance. "I am the man who offers you a way to reverse your sorry fate."

Baron Neufmarché succumbed to his own curiosity. "Come inside," he decided. "I will listen to what you have to say." Holding the flap aside, he invited the strangers to enter and dismissed the squire. "I would ask you to sit," the baron said, returning to his camp chair, "but I doubt you will be here that long. For I warn you, the moment I lose interest in your speech, I will have you thrashed and thrown out of this camp."

"As you say," replied the young man.

Taking up his cup once more, the baron said, "You have until this cup is drained." He drank deeply and said, "Less now. I would speak quickly if I were you."

"De Braose is a tyrant," the young man said, "with little understanding of the land he has taken, and none at all of the people under his rule. Most of them have fled, and those that remain are made to perform slave labour at the cost of their own fields and holdings. If they were allowed to return to their homes, to work the land and tend their herds, Elfael would enjoy prosperity unequalled by any other cantref. All that is required is someone who can guide the will of the people—someone the Cymry will follow, who can deliver them to you."

The baron sipped again, more slowly this time, and considered what he had heard. "You can do this?"

"I can." There was no hint of hesitation or doubt in the young man.

"Your offer is tempting, to be sure," allowed the baron cautiously. Putting the cup aside, he said, "But who are you to make such an offer?"

At this, the bowlegged friar spoke up. "Before you stands Bran ap Brychan, the rightful heir to Elfael. And I am Aethelfrith, at your service."

Neufmarché gazed at the young man before him. It never ceased to amaze him how very often events beyond his reckoning conspired to bring his plans to bountiful fruition. Here, he had not lifted a hand, and the prize plum had simply dropped into his lap. "The rightful heir is dead," he said, feigning indifference. "At least, that is what I heard."

"To my great relief," replied Bran, "it remains a rumour only. Still, it serves a useful purpose."

"When the time is right," put Aethelfrith, "we will make his presence known, and his people will rally to him and overthrow the de Braose usurpers."

"In exchange for your promise to restore me to the throne," Bran said, "I would pledge fealty to you. Elfael would then abide in peace."

Now the baron smiled. "What you have said has roused my interest—and more than you know." He rose and walked to the rear of the tent. "Will you take some wine?"

"It would be an honour," replied Tuck. "There is much to discuss."

"A moment, please," said the baron. "I will order cups to be brought." With that, he disappeared through the rear flap into the room used by his servants for preparing food for the baron and his guests. "Remey!" Neufmarché called aloud. "Wine for my visitors." The servant, just returning from the kitchen tent with a trencher of sausages, appeared at his summons. Stepping quickly to meet him, the baron raised a finger to his lips for silence, leaned close, and whispered, "Fetch me four knights—armed and ready to fight. Bring them here at once."

Remey's brow wrinkled in confusion. "Sire? Is something amiss?"

"No time to explain—but the two Welshmen are to be taken cap-

457

tive. Indeed, they will not leave this place alive. Understand?" The aging seneschal inclined his head in a compliant nod. "Go," said Neufmarché, taking the trencher from his hands. "I will keep them occupied until you return."

Remey turned on his heel and padded away. The baron returned to his audience room with the sausages, which he placed on the table, inviting his guests to help themselves. "Sit you down, please. Enjoy!" he said with expansive warmth. "The wine will come in a moment. In the meantime, I would hear more about how you plan to bring about de Braose's defeat."

CHAPTER 46

The last day of the baron's council found Mérian in a pensive mood. Having resigned herself to the fact that she would leave the council and return, not to Caer Rhodl, but to Castle Neufmarché in Hereford, she was nevertheless apprehensive. A sojourn amongst the Ffreinc in the baron's household? Secretly she was fascinated by the thought—even regarding the prospect of a winter spent in Normandie in a kindly light. Even so, she could not deny the feeling that she was behaving as something of a traitor. A traitor to what? Her family? Her country? Her own ideas about who and what the Ffreinc were?

She could not decide.

Her father had as much as commanded her to go. Her own mother had told her, "It is important that you do well in the baron's court, Mérian. He likes you, and we need his friendship just now." Although she did not say it outright, her mother had given her to know that by currying favour with the baron, she was helping her family survive. In short, she was little more than a hostage to the baron's good pleasure.

She told herself that Cymru would be the same whether she was

attached to the baron's court or not. She told herself that in all likelihood, her poor opinion of the Ffreinc was based on hearsay and
ignorance and that this was a chance to discover the truth. Of course,
she still considered the Ffreinc enemies, but was not a Christian
required to love her enemy? From the time she was old enough to
stand beside her mother in church, she had been instructed to love her
enemies and do good to those who persecuted her. So if not the
Ffreinc, then who? She told herself that any young woman in her
position would welcome the chance to advance herself in this way,
and that she should be grateful.

She told herself all these things and more. Yet the feeling of
betrayal would not go away.

It was with these thoughts turning over in her mind that she made
her way amongst the untidy sprawl of tents to the baroness's pavilion
in the centre of the camp. Mérian had been sent to find Sybil and
inform her friend that she had said her good-byes to her parents and
that her things were packed and awaiting collection by the baron's servants. As she passed the baron's tent, however, a shout brought her up
short. She stopped.

It sounded like an argument had broken out. There was a crash, as
if a table had been overturned, and suddenly, out of the tent burst
four marchogi dragging two men between them. At the sight of the
young noblewoman standing directly in their path, the soldiers halted.
The foremost prisoner raised his head. Even with the blood streaming
from a cut above his eye, even though she never thought to see him
again amongst the living, she knew him.

"Bran!" She blurted the name in startled amazement. "Is it you?"

"Mérian," gasped Bran, no less astonished to see her.

"Step aside, lady," said one of the knights, jerking Bran to his feet.

Without thinking, Mérian held up her hand. "Stop!" she said, and the soldiers paused. She stepped nearer. "I thought you died—everyone said so."

"Wishful thinking."

"You know this man?" The voice was Neufmarché's. He stepped from the tent and came to stand beside Mérian.

"I did once," Mérian replied, turning to the baron. "I—until this moment, I thought him dead! Why are you treating him so? What has he done?"

"He claims to be the heir of Elfael," the baron replied. "Is this true?"

"It is," Mérian granted.

"That is all I need to know." The baron, sword in hand, waved the soldiers on. "Take them away."

"I am sorry you had to see that, my dear—," the baron began. He did not finish the thought, for as the knights, still distracted by Mérian, stepped past her, Bran twisted in their grasp and shook himself free. Snatching a dagger from the belt of his nearest captor, he spun on his heel, grabbed Mérian, and pulled her roughly to him. Neufmarché made a clumsy attempt to snatch her from Bran's grasp, and almost lost his hand.

"Stay back!" Bran shouted, raising the naked blade to Mérian's slender neck.

"Bran, no—," Mérian gasped.

One of the knights made a sudden lunge toward him. Bran evaded the move, pressing the knife to Mérian's throat and drawing a frightened scream from the young woman. "If you have any care for her at all," he snarled, "you will stand aside."

"Stand easy, men," the baron told his soldiers. To Bran he said, "Do you imagine this will aid you in any way?"

"That we will soon discover," he said. Turning to the soldiers holding Tuck, he commanded, "Release the priest."

The knights looked to the baron. He saw the sharp blade pressed against the soft white flesh—flesh he coveted—and could not bear to see it harmed. Neufmarché surrendered with a nod. "Do it," he said dully. "Let him go."

"Tuck," called Bran, "bring the horses!"

The English friar shook free of his captors, giving one a pointed kick, saying, "That is for laying unclean hands on one of God's humble servants." He hurried to where the horses had been left on the nearby picket line.

"Bran, let me go," pleaded Mérian, her fear quickly melting into anger. "This is not meet."

"I asked you to come with me once," he said, his mouth close to her ear. "You refused. Now it seems you are to join me whether you will or no."

Tuck hurried back, leading the horses. He passed one pair of reins to Bran and scrambled into the saddle. Bran, stepping gingerly backwards to the horse, pulled Mérian with him. "Climb up and be quick," he told her, maintaining his grip on the knife. Gathering her skirts, she put her foot to the stirrup, and Bran, with a sudden movement, boosted her onto the horse and, quick as a cat, vaulted up behind her.

"Farewell, baron," said Bran, shaking out the reins. "Had you been true, you would have enjoyed the spectacle of your rival's downfall. Now you will have to content yourself with the knowledge that this day you sealed your own."

"I will track you down like an animal," said Neufmarché. "When I find you, I will gut you and hang your carcass for the birds."

"You must catch me first, Neufmarché," said Bran. "And if we are followed from this place, Mérian's lovely corpse will be all you find on the trail."

"Don't waste your breath on them," said Tuck. "Let us hie from this vipers' den."

"Away, Tuck!" With that, Bran slapped the reins across the shoulders of his mount, and the horse leapt ahead. The fat priest followed, and the two riders disappeared with their hostage, passing between the close-set tents and out of sight. The soldiers watched in flat-footed amazement.

"After them!" shouted the baron. "Mérian is not to be harmed."

"What about the other two?" asked one of the knights.

"Once the lady is safe—and only then," the baron cautioned, "kill them. If anything happens to her, your lives are forfeit."

The four knights ran for their horses and clattered off in pursuit of the fugitives. Baron Neufmarché watched until they were out of camp and then returned to his tent, his spirits soaring with jubilation. By the time his knights returned with Mérian, the last heir to the throne of Elfael really would be dead, his unwanted presence a fast-fading memory. The troops promised by his father, the duke, would arrive with the first ships in the spring, and in the council just concluded, he had—through bargaining, wheedling, threatening, and cajoling over many days—finally obtained the support of his vassal lords for his threefold plan.

The unexpected appearance of Elfael's prince might have swiftly undone all his hard work over the last many days, but fortunately, that problem would be swiftly resolved when the knights returned with his head in a sack. Thus, no sooner than it had arisen, the unforeseen impediment had been cleared. The conquest of Wales could begin.

463

Friar Tuck was first to reach the little dell where the four had made camp—not far from the fields where the council was meeting, but hidden in a fold between two hills. "Iwan! Siarles!" he shouted, thundering down the hillside to the stand of beech trees where they had camped. "To arms! The Ffreinc are coming!"

The two men appeared, drawing their swords as they ran. Iwan took in the situation at a glance, thrust his sword into the turf, and raced back for his longbow. Tuck reached the shelter of the trees and threw himself from the saddle as Iwan appeared, clutching two bow staves in one hand and a sheaf of arrows in the other. "There are four of them!" cried Tuck. "Bran has a woman with him and cannot out-pace them much longer. We had but a few yards' start on them."

"Four only?" said Iwan, tossing a bow to Siarles. "The way you were shouting, I thought all the Normans in England were on your tail—and their hounds as well."

"What woman?" wondered Siarles, bracing the bow against his leg to string it.

"Our escape required a hostage," Tuck explained. "For God's sake, hurry!"

A cry arose from the rim of the dell. They turned to see Bran pounding down the gentle slope, encumbered by a squirming, scream-ing female. His mount was tired and clearly labouring. Even as they watched, he was overtaken by the two Ffreinc knights sweeping up behind him with swords raised.

"For the love of God!" cried Tuck. "Hurry!"

"All in good time, brother," said Iwan, passing a handful of arrows to Siarles. "It does not do to hurry an archer. It makes him miss."

With quick downward jabs, the two stuck the arrows point first in the turf and, plucking one each, nocked it to the string.

"Left!" said Iwan.

"Right!" answered Siarles, and with almost languid motion, the two pressed the longbows forward as if trying to step through them. There was a single dull thrum and fizzing hiss as the arrows flew. The knight on the left, standing in his stirrups, his arm raised high, ready to begin the fatal downward slash with his blade, was struck in the centre of the chest. Already unbalanced, the impact slammed him backwards over the rump of his horse, dead when he hit the ground. The rider on the right had time but to glance once at the suddenly empty saddle of his companion before Siarles's arrow buried itself in his chest. The sword spun from his hand, and he clutched the arrow, fighting to turn his galloping mount—a fight he lost when Siarles's second arrow struck just below the first and knocked him from the saddle.

Bran galloped on. The two remaining knights appeared on the rim of the dell and started down. "Left!" said Iwan again and loosed. The arrow, a blurred streak in the air, seemed to lift the soldier up ever so slightly as the horse ran out from under him.

The sole remaining knight must have seen the two riderless horses breaking off to the side, for he tried to halt his headlong pursuit. With a cry of dismay, he jerked the reins back hard. The horse's churning hooves slipped in the long grass, and the animal slid. The knight, occupied with his stumbling mount, did not see the arrow that flung him from the saddle. He landed heavily on his side, rolled over, and did not move again.

"Get their horses!" shouted Bran to Siarles as he reined his lathered mount to a halt. "Tuck! Iwan! Break camp. It will not be long before Neufmarché realises his knights are not coming back—and then he will come in force." The two hurried off to gather the water and provisions and saddle the horses.

"Let me go!" shouted Mérian, scratching at Bran's hands. He released his hold and let her fall. She landed in an awkward sprawl, her mantle sliding up over bare legs. Her shoes had come loose and been lost in the mad dash from the baron's camp. "You did that on purpose!" she raged, pulling down her mantle and scrambling to her feet. Bran slid down from the saddle. Livid with rage, dark eyes ablaze,

Mérian flew at him with her fists. "How dare you! I am not a sack of grain to be picked up and thrown over your shoulder. I demand—"

"Enough!" Bran snapped, grabbing both of her wrists in one strong hand.

"Take me back at once."

"So your friend the baron can carve my head from my shoulders?" he said. "No, I think I would rather live a little longer."

"My father will do the same unless you let me go. Whatever trouble you're in will not be helped by taking me. I am certain that it can be cleared up if we all just—"

"Mérian!" Bran's hand flicked out and connected with her cheek in a resounding slap. "Do you understand what just happened here?" He pointed to the dead knights on the hillside. "Look out there, Mérian. This is no misunderstanding. The baron means to kill me, and I do not intend to give him another chance."

"You hit me!" she said darkly. "Never do that again."

"Then do not give me cause."

Siarles returned, leading three horses. "One got away," he said.

"Go help Iwan and Tuck," Bran told him, taking the reins. "Three is enough."

"What are you going to do?" asked Mérian, her voice shaking with anger.

"Get as far away from here as possible," he replied, examining the horses. There was blood on one of the saddles, and the horse that had stumbled had a ragged gash in a foreleg. Bran released the animal and, selecting one for Mérian, pulled her around to the side and held out the stirrup for her. "Mount up."

"No."

"You are acting like a child."

"And you are acting like a brigand," she said. Raising both hands, she pushed him over backward, turned, and started running—gaining only a few paces before she felt his arms around her waist, lifting her from her feet.

"I *am* a brigand," he said. Lugging her back to the horse, he heaved her clumsily into the saddle and proceeded to tie her feet to the stirrups with the straps used to secure a lance. "Do not try me again, Mérian, or I might forget I ever loved you."

"You flatter yourself," she snarled. "But you were ever a flatterer and a liar."

Iwan, Tuck, and Siarles emerged from the beech grove just then, leading two horses. "Ready!" called Iwan.

"Ride out," Bran said. Holding tight to the reins of Mérian's mount, he swung up into the saddle. "Come, my lady," he said, his voice cold and cutting. "Let us hope that, along with your loyalty and good sense, you have not also forgotten how to ride."

"Where are you taking me?"

"To Cél Craidd," he replied. "Our fortress may not be as fine and rich as Castle Neufmarché, but it is blessedly free of Ffreinc, and you will receive a better welcome there than I received at the baron's hands."

"They will find me, you know," she said, trying to sound brave and unconcerned. "And you will pay dearly for what you've done."

"They will find you when I choose to let them find you, and *they* are the ones who will count the cost."

Turning his eyes to the line of advancing twilight away to the east, Bran gazed at the gathering darkness and embraced it like a friend. He lifted his head, squared his shoulders, and drew the evening air deep into his lungs. When he glanced again to Mérian, his eyes were veiled with the night, and she realised Bran was no longer the boy she had once known. "But now," he said, his words falling like a shadow between them, "it is time for this raven to fly."

467

⊰ EPILOGUE ⊱

Nine days after the searchers returned to Castle Neufmarché in Hereford with the sorry news that they had failed to turn up any sign of the Welsh outlaws' trail, a solitary rider appeared at the door of the Abbey of Saint Dyfrig—the principal monastery of Elfael in the north of the cantref near Glascwm. "I am looking for a certain priest," the rider announced to the brother who met him at the gate. Wearing a dark green hooded cloak and a wide-brimmed leather hat pulled low over his face, he spoke the Cymry of a trueborn Briton. "I was told I might find him here."

"Who is it you seek?" asked the monk. "I will help you if I can."

"One called Asaph, a bishop of the church."

"Then God has rewarded your journey, friend," the monk told him. "He is here."

"Fetch him, please. My time is short."

"This way, sir, if you please."

The brother led the visitor to the guest lodge, where he was given a cup of wine, a bowl of soup, and some bread to refresh himself while he waited. Lifting the bowl to his lips, he drank down the broth and used the bread to sop up the last drops. He then turned his attention to the wine. Sipping from his cup, he leaned on the doorpost and gazed out into the yard at the monks hurrying to and fro on their business. Presently, the doorkeeper appeared, leading a white-robed priest across the yard.

"Bishop Asaph," said the monk, delivering his charge, "this man has come asking for you."

The priest smiled, his pale eyes crinkling at the corners. "I am Asaph," he said. "How may I serve you?"

"I have a message for you," said the stranger. Reaching into a pouch at his belt, he brought out a piece of folded parchment, which he passed to the bishop.

"How very formal," remarked the bishop. He received the parcel, untied the leather binding, and unfolded it. "Excuse me; my eyes are not what they were," he said, stepping back into the light of the yard so that he could see what was written there.

He scanned the letter quickly and then looked up sharply. "Do you know what this letter contains?" The rider nodded his assent, and the bishop read the message again, saying, ". . . and a sum of money to be used for the building of a new monastery on lands which have been purchased for this purpose the better to serve the people of Elfael should you accept this condition." Raising his face to the stranger, he asked, "Do you have the money with you?"

"I do," replied the rider.

"And the condition—what is it?"

"It is this," the messenger informed him. "That you are to preside over a daily Mass and pray for the souls of the people of Elfael in their struggle and for their rightful king and his court, each day without fail, and twice on high holy days." The rider regarded the bishop impassively. "Do you accept the condition?"

"Gladly and with all my heart," answered the bishop. "God knows, nothing would please me more than to undertake this mission."

"So be it." Reaching into his pouch, the messenger brought out a leather bag and passed it to the senior churchman. "This is for you."

With trembling hands the bishop opened the curiously heavy

bag and peered in. The yellow gleam of gold byzants met his wondering gaze.

"Two hundred marks," the rider informed him.

"Two *hundred*, did you say?" gasped the bishop, stunned by the amount.

"Begin with that. There is more if you need it."

"But how?" asked Asaph, shaking his head in amazement. "Who has sent this?"

"It has not been given for me to say," answered the rider. He stepped to the bench and retrieved his hat. "It may please my lord to reveal himself to you in due time." He moved past the bishop into the yard. "For now, it is his pleasure that you use the money in the service of God's kingdom for the relief of the folk of Elfael."

The bishop, holding the bag of money in one hand and the sealed parchment in the other, watched the mysterious messenger depart. "What is your name?" asked Asaph as the rider took up the reins and climbed into the saddle.

"Call me Silidons, for such I am," replied the rider. "I give you good day, bishop."

"God with you, my son!" he called after him. "And God with your master, whoever he may be!"

Later, as the monks of Saint Dyfrig's gathered at vespers for evening prayers, Bishop Asaph recalled the condition the messenger had made: that he perform a Mass each day for the people of Elfael and the king. Lord Brychan of Elfael was dead, sadly enough. If any soul ever needed prayer, his surely did—but who amongst the living cared enough to build an entire monastery where prayers could be offered for the relief of that suffering soul?

But no . . . no, the messenger did not name Brychan. He had said *"the people in their struggle and for their rightful king and his court . . ."*

Sadly, the king and heir were dead—so who *was* the rightful ruler of Elfael?

Bishop Asaph could not say.

Later that night, the faithful priest led the remnant of Elfael's monks, the handful of loyal brothers who had entered exile with him, in the first of many prayers for the cantref, its people, and his mysterious benefactor. "And if it please you, heavenly Father," he whispered privately as the prayers of the monks swirled around him on clouds of incense, "may I live to see the day a true king takes the throne in Elfael once more."

⊰ ROBIN HOOD IN WALES? ⊱

It will seem strange to many readers, and perhaps even perverse, to take Robin Hood out of Sherwood Forest and relocate him in Wales; worse still to remove all trace of Englishness, set his story in the eleventh century, and recast the honourable outlaw as an early British freedom fighter. My contention is that although in Nottingham, the Robin Hood legends found good soil in which to grow, they must surely have originated elsewhere.

The first written references to the character we now know as Robin Hood can be traced as far back as the early 1260s. By 1350, the Robin Hood legends were well-known, if somewhat various, consisting of a loose aggregation of poems and songs plied by the troubadours and minstrels of the day. These poems and songs bore little relation to one another and carried titles such as "Robin Hood and the Potter," "Robin Hood's Chase," "Robin Hood and the Bishop of Hereford," "The Jolly Pinder of Wakefield," "The Noble Fisherman," "Robin Whood Turned Hermit," "Robin Hood Rescuing Three Squires," and "Little John a'Begging."

As the minstrels wandered around Britain with their lutes and lyres, crooning to high and low alike, they spread the fame of the beloved rogue far and wide, often supplying local place-names to foster a closer identification with their subject and give their stories more immediacy. Thus, the songs do not agree on a single setting, nor do they agree on the protagonist's name. Some will have it Robert Hood, or Whoode, and others Robin Hod, Robyn Hode, Robinet, or even Roger. Other contenders include Robynhod, Rabunhod, Robehod, and, interestingly, Hobbehod. And although these popular tales were committed to paper, or parchment, by about 1400, still no attempt was made to stitch the stories together to form a whole cloth.

In the earliest stories, Robin was no honourable Errol Flynn-esque hero. He was a coarse and vulgar oaf much given to crudeness and violence. He was a thief from the beginning, to be sure, but the now-famous creed of "robbing from the rich to give to the poor" was a few hundred years removed from his rough highwayman origins. The early Robin robbed from the rich, to be sure—and kept every silver English penny for himself.

As time went on, the threadbare tales acquired new and better clothes—until they possessed a whole wardrobe full of rich, colourful, sumptuous medieval regalia in the form of characters, places, incidents, and adventures. Characters such as Little John, Friar Tuck, Will Scarlet, and Sir Guy of Gisbourne joined the ranks one by one in various times and places as different composers and writers spun out the old tales and made up new ones. The Sheriff of Nottingham was an early addition and, contrary to popular opinion, was not always the villain of the piece. The beautiful, plucky Maid Marian was actually one of the last characters to arrive on the scene, making her debut sometime around the beginning of the sixteenth century.

Others are notable by their absence. In the early tales there is no evil King John and no good King Richard—no king at all. And the only monarch who receives so much as a mention is "Edward, our comely king," though which of the many Edwards this might be is never made clear.

So we have an amorphous body of popular songs and poems about a lovable rascal whose name was uncertain and who lived someplace on the island of Britain at some unknown time in the past. Of all the possibilities to choose from in locating the legend in place and time, why choose Wales?

Several small but telling clues serve to locate the original source of the legend in the area of Britain now called Wales in the generation following the Norman invasion and conquest of 1066. First and foremost is the general character of the people themselves, the Welsh (from the Saxon *wealas*, or "foreigners"), or as they would have thought of themselves, the Britons.

In AD 1100, Gerald of Wales, a highborn nobleman whose mother was a Welsh princess, wrote of his people: "The Welsh are extreme in all they do, so that if you never meet anyone worse than a bad Welshman, you will never meet anyone better than a good one." He went on to describe them as extremely hardy, extremely generous, and extremely witty. They were also, he cautioned, extremely treacherous, extremely vengeful, and extremely greedy for land. "Above all," he writes, "they are passionately devoted to liberty, and almost excessively warlike."

Gerald painted a picture of the Cymry as a whole nation of warriors in arms. Unlike the Normans, who were sharply divided between the military aristocracy and a mass of peasants, every single Welshman was ready for battle at a moment's notice; women, too, bore arms and knew how to use them.

Within two months of the Battle of Hastings (1066), William the Conqueror and his barons, the new Norman overlords, had subdued 80 percent of England. Within two years, they had it all under their rule. However—and I think this is significant—it took them over two *hundred* years of almost continual conflict to make any lasting impression on Wales, and by that late date it becomes a question of whether Wales was really ever conquered at all.

In fact, William the Conqueror, recognising an implacable foe and unwilling to spend the rest of his life bogged down in a war he could never win, wisely left the Welsh alone. He established a baronial buffer zone between England and the warlike Britons. This was the territory known as the March. Later, this sensible no-go area and its policy of tolerance would be violated by the Conqueror's brutish son William II, who sought to fill his tax coffers to pay for his spendthrift ways and expensive wars in France. Wales and its great swathes of undeveloped territory seemed a plum ripe for the plucking, and it is in this historical context (in the year AD 1093) that I have chosen to set *Hood*.

A Welsh location is also suggested by the nature and landscape of the region. Wales of the March borderland was primeval forest. While the forests of England had long since become well-managed business property where each woodland was a veritable factory, Wales still had enormous stretches of virgin wood, untouched except for hunting and hiding. The forest of the March was a fearsome wilderness when the woods of England resembled well-kept garden preserves. It would have been exceedingly difficult for Robin and his outlaw band to actually hide in England's ever-dwindling Sherwood, but he could have lived for years in the forests of the March and never been seen or heard.

This entry from the Welsh chronicle of the times known as *Brenhinedd Y Saesson*, or *The Kings of the Saxons*, makes the situation very clear:

Anno Domini MLXXXXV (1095). In that year King William Rufus mustered a host past number against the Cymry. But the

Cymry trusted in God with their prayers and fastings and alms and penances and placed their hope in God. *And they harassed their foes so that the Ffreinc dared not go into the woods or the wild places, but they traversed the open lands sorely fatigued, and thence returned home empty-handed. And thus the Cymry boldly defended their land with joy.* (emphasis mine)

That, I think, is the Robin Hood legend in seed form. The plucky Britons, disadvantaged in the open field, took to the forest and from there conducted a guerrilla war, striking the Normans at will from the relative safety of the woods—an ongoing tactic that would endure with considerable success for whole generations. That is the kernel from which the great durable oak of legend eventually grew.

Finally, we have the Briton expertise with the warbow, or longbow as it is most often called. While one can read reams of accounts about the English talent for archery, it is seldom recognized—but well documented—that the Angles and Saxons actually learned the weapon and its use from the Welsh. No doubt, the invaders learned fear and respect for the longbow the hard way before acquiring its remarkable potential for themselves.

As military historian Robert Hardy has observed, "The Welsh were the first people on the British Isles to have and use longbows. The Welsh became experts in the use of the longbow, and used the longbow very effectively in battles against the invading English." The Welsh repelled Ralph, Earl of Hereford, in 1055 using the longbow. There is a story about Welsh longbowmen penetrating a four-inch-thick, solid oak door with their arrows at the siege of Abergavenny Castle. Hardy goes on to say,

"Like the Welsh, the English learned an important lesson by fighting against the longbow. That lesson being that the longbow is a formidable weapon when used correctly. With the eventual defeat of the Welsh, and 'alliance' of the English and Welsh, the English employed Welsh longbowmen in its own army. During this time, the English began a campaign to train their own long-bowmen as well."

In his book *Famous Welsh Battles*, British historian Philip Warner writes:

"There were no easy victories over the Welsh. They were greatly esteemed and widely feared, whether fighting as mercenaries in the Middle Ages or engaging in guerrilla combat. From south Wales came a new weapon, the longbow, as terrifying as modern weapons of mass murder. Some 6 feet long and discharging an arrow 3 feet in length, averaging 12 arrows a minute, they blanketed a target like a dark, vengeful cloud. In the next moment all would be groans, screams and confusion."

Taken altogether, then, these clues of time, place, and weaponry indicate the germinal soil out of which Robin Hood sprang. As for the English Robin Hood with whom we are all so familiar . . . just as Arthur, a Briton, was later Anglicised—made into the quintessential English king and hero by the same enemy Saxons he fought against—a similar makeover must have happened to Robin. The British resistance leader, outlawed to the primeval forests of the March, eventually emerged in the popular imagination as an aristocratic Englishman, fighting to right the wrongs of England and curb the powers of an overbearing monarchy. It is a tale that has worn well throughout the years. However, the real story, I think, must be far more interesting.

And so, in an attempt to centre the tales of this British hero in the time and place where I think they originated—*not* where they eventually ended up—I have put a British Rhi Bran, and all his merry band of friends and enemies, in Wales.

—Stephen Lawhead

⊰ ACKNOWLEDGMENTS ⊱

The author gratefully acknowledges the assistance of Mieczysław Piotrowski and the cooperation of Józef Popiel, Director of Białowieski National Park, Poland, who kindly allowed me to roam freely in the last primeval forest in Europe.

Scarlet

KING RAVEN: BOOK II

To the dedicated
men and women at
UWMC and SCCA,
without whom . . .

CHAPTER **I**

So, now. One day soon they hang me for a rogue. Fair enough. I have earned it a hundred times over, I reckon, and that's leaving a lot of acreage unexplored. The jest of it is, the crime for which I swing is the one offence I never did do. The sheriff will have it that I raised rebellion against the king.

I didn't.

Oh, there's much I've done that some would as soon count treason. For a fact, I et more of the king's venison than the king has et bread, and good men have lost their heads to royal pikes for far less; but in all my frolics I never breathed a disloyal word against the crown, nor tried to convince any man, boy, horse, or dog to match his deeds to mine. Ah, but dainties such as these are of no concern when princes have their tender feelings ruffled. It is a traitor they want to punish, not a thief. The eatin' o' Red William's game is a matter too trifling—more insult than crime—and it's a red-handed rebel they need. Too much has happened in the forests of the March and too much princely pride hangs in the balance to be mincing fair about a rascal poaching a few soft-eyed deer.

Until that ill-fated night, Will Scarlet ran with King Raven and his band of merry thieves. Ran fast and far, I did, let me tell you. Faster and farther than all the rest, and that's saying something. Here's the gist: it's the Raven Hood they want and cannot get. So, ol' Will is for the jump.

Poor luck, that. No less, no more.

They caught me crest and colours. My own bloody fault. There's none to blame but the hunter when he's caught in his own snare. I ask no pardon. A willing soul, I flew field and forest with King Raven and his flock. Fine fun it was, too, until they nabbed me in the pinch. Even so, if it hadn't a' been for a spear through my leg bone they would not a' got me either.

So, here we sit, my leg and me, in a dank pit beneath Count de Braose's keep. I have a cell—four walls of stone and a damp dirt floor covered with rotting straw and rancid rushes. I have a warden named Guibert, or Gulbert or some such, who brings me food and water when he can be bothered to remember, and unchains me from time to time so I can stretch the cramps a bit and wash my wound. I also have my very own priest, a young laggard of a scribe who comes to catch my wild tales and pin them to the pages of a book to doom us all.

We talk and talk. God knows we've got time to kill before the killing time. It pleases me now to think on the dizzy chase we led. I was taken in the most daring and outrageous scheme to come out of the forest yet. It was a plan as desperate as death, but light and larksome as a maiden's flirting glance. At a blow, we aimed to douse the sheriff's ardour and kindle a little righteous wrath in lorn Britannia. We aimed to cock a snook at the crown, sure, and mayhap draw the king's attention to our sore plight, embarrass his sheriff, and show him and his mutton-headed soldiers for fools on parade—all in one

fell swoop. Sweet it was and, save for my piddling difficulties, flawless as a flower until the walls of the world came crashing down around
our ears.

Truth is, I can't help thinking that if we only knew what it was
that had fallen plump into our fists, none of this would have happened
and I would not be here now with a leg on fire and fit to kill me if the
sheriff don't. Oh, but that is ranging too far afield, and there is ground
closer to home needs ploughing first.

Ah, but see the monk here! Asleep with his nose in his inkhorn.

"Odo, you dunce! Wake up! You're dozing again. It ill becomes
you to catch a wink on a dying man's last words. Prick up your ears,
priest. Pare your quill, and tell me the last you remember."

"Sorry, Will," he says. He's always ever so sorry, rubbing sleep
from his dreamy brown eyes. And it is sorry he should be—sorry for
himself and all his dreary ilk, but not for Will.

"Never feel sorry for Will, lad," I tell him. "Will en't sorry for
nothing."

Brother Odo is my scribe, decent enough for a Norman in his simpering, damp-handed way. He does not wish me harm. I think he does
not even know why he has been sent down here amongst the gallows
birds to listen to the ramblings of a dangerous scofflaw like myself.
Why should he?

Abbot Hugo is behind this wheeze to scribble down all my doings.
To what purpose? Plain as daylight in Dunholme, he means to scry
out a way to catch King Raven. Hugo imagines languishing in the
shadow of the noose for a spell will sober me enough to grow a tongue
of truth in my head and sing like a bird for freedom.

So, I sing and sing, if only to keep Jack o'Ladder at arm's length

485

a little longer. Our larcenous abbot will learn summat to his profit, as may be, but more to his regret. He'll learn much of that mysterious phantom of the greenwood, to be sure. But for all his listening he'll hear naught from me to catch so much as a mayfly. He'll not get the bolt he desires to bring King Raven down.

"So, now," I say, "pick up your pen, Brother Odo. We'll begin again. What was the last you remember?"

Odo scans his chicken tracks a moment, scratches his shaved pate and says, "When Thane Aelred's lands were confiscated for his part in the Uprising, I was thrown onto my own resources . . ."

Odo speaks his English with the strange flat tongue of the Frank outlanders. That he speaks English at all is a wonder, I suppose, and the reason why Hugo chose him. Poor Odo is a pudgy pudding of a man, young enough, and earnest in faith and practice, but pale and only too ready to retire, claiming cramp or cold or fatigue. He is always fatigued, and for no good reason it seems to me. He makes as if chasing a leaking nib across fresh-scraped vellum is as mighty a labour as toting the carcass of a fat hind through the greenwood on your back with the sheriff's men on your tail.

All saints bear witness! If pushing a pen across parchment taxes a man as much as Odo claims, we should honour as heroes all who ply the quill, amen.

I am of the opinion that unless he grows a backbone, and right soon, Brother Odo will be nothing more in this life than another weak-eyed scribbler squinting down his long French nose at the un-diluted drivel his hand has perpetrated. By Blessed Cuthbert's thumb, I swear I would rather end my days in Baron de Braose's pit than face eternity with a blot like that on my soul.

Perhaps, in God's dark plan, friend Will is here to instruct this indolent youth in a better lesson, thinks I. Well, we will do what can be done to save him.

When Thane Aelred's lands were confiscated for his part in the Uprising, I was thrown onto my own resources, and like to have died they were that thin."

This I tell him, repeating the words to buy a little time while I cast my net into streams gone by to catch another gleaming memory for our proud abbot's feast. May he choke on the bones! With this blessing between my teeth, I rumble on . . .

Thane Aelred was as fair-minded as the Tyne is wide, and solid as the three-hundred-year-old oak that grew beside his barn. A bull-necked man with the shaggy brown mane of a lion and a roar to match as may be, but he treated his people right and well. Never one to come all high and mighty with his minions, he was always ready enough to put hand to plough or scythe. Bless the man, he never shirked the shearing or slaughtering, and all the grunt and sweat that work requires. For though we have lived a thousand years and more since Our Sweet Jesus came and went, it is a sad, sad truth that sheep will still not shear themselves, nor hogs make hams.

There's the pity. Toss a coin and decide which of the two is the filthier chore.

Under Aelred, God rest him, there was always a jar or three to ease our aching bones when the day's work was done. All of us tenants and vassals who owed him service—a day or two here, a week there—were treated like blood kin whenever we set foot on the steading to honour our pledge of work. In return, he gave neither man nor maid worse than he'd accept for himself or his house, and that's a right rare thane, that is. Show me another as decent and honest, and I'll drink a health to him here and now.

Not like these Norman vermin—call them what you like: Franks, Ffreinc, or Normans, they're all the same. Lords of the Earth, they trow. Lords of Perdition, more like. Hold themselves precious as stardust and fine as diamonds. Dressed in their gold-crusted rags, they flounce about the land, their bloody minds scheming mischief all the while. From the moment a Norman noble opens his eye on the day until that same eye closes at night, the highborn Frankish man is, in Aelred's words, "a walking *scittesturm*" for anyone unlucky enough to cross his path.

A Norman knight lives only for hunting and whoring, preening and warring. And their toad-licking priests are just as bad. Even the best of their clerics are no better than they should be. I wouldn't spare the contents of my nose on a rainy day to save the lot of them . . .

Sorry, Odo, but that is God's own truth, groan as you will to hear it. Write it down all the same.

"If it please you, what is scittesturm?" Odo wants to know.

"Ask a Saxon," I tell him. "If bloody Baron de Braose hasn't killed them all yet, you'll learn quick enough."

But there we are. Aelred is gone now. He had the great misfortune to believe the land his father had given him—land owned and worked by his father's father, and the father's father before that—belonged to him and his forever. A dangerous delusion, as it turns out.

For when William the Conqueror snatched the throne of England

and made himself the Law of the Land, he set to work uprooting the deep-grown offices and traditions that time and the stump-solid Saxons had planted and maintained since their arrival on these fair shores—offices and traditions which bound lord and vassal in a lock-step dance of loyalty and service, sure, but also kept the high and mighty above from devouring the weak and poorly below. This was the bedrock of Saxon law, just and good, enforcing fairness for all who sheltered under it. Like the strong timber roof of Great Alfred's hall, we all found shelter under it however hard the gales of power and privilege might blow.

The thanes—freeholders mostly, men who were neither entirely noble nor completely common . . . Willy Conqueror did not understand them at all. Never did, nor bothered to. See now, a Norman knows only two kinds of men: nobles and serfs. To a Norman, a man is either a king or a peasant, nothing else. There is black and there is white, and there is the end of it. Consequently, there is no one to stand between the two to keep them from each other's throats.

The Welshmen laugh at both camps, I know. The British have their nobility, too, but British kings and princes share the same life as the people they rule. A lord might be more esteemed by virtue of his deeds or other merits, real or imagined, but a true British prince is not too lofty to feel the pinch when drought makes a harvest thin, or a hard winter gnaws through all the provisions double-quick.

The British king will gladly drink from the same clay cup as the least of his folk, and can recite the names of each and every one of his tribesmen to the third or fourth generation. In this, King Raven was no less than the best example of his kind, and I'll wager Baron de Braose has never laid eyes on most of the wretches whose sweat and blood keep him in hunting hawks and satin breeches.

Like all Norman barons, de Braose surveys his lands from the back of a great destrier—a giant with four hooves that eats more in a day than any ten of his serfs can scrape together for the week. His knights and *vavasors*—hateful word—spill more in a night's roister than any hovel-dweller on his estate will see from Christmas Eve to Easter morn, and that's if they're lucky to see a drop o' anything cheerful at all.

Well, de Braose may never have shaken hands with one of his serfs, but he knows how much the man owes in taxes to the nearest ha'penny. That's a kind of talent, I suppose, give him that.

I give him also his shrewd, calculating mind and a farsighted sense of self-preservation. He could see, or maybe smell, the right way to jump a long way off. The old goat rarely put a foot wrong where his own vital interests were concerned. The king liked him, too, though I can't think why. Still and all, royal favour never hurts a'body while it lasts. Making it last: aye, there's the grit in the loaf.

So, when William the Conquering Bastard got himself killed in a little foray in France—took an arrow, they say, just like poor King Harold—*that* upset the apple cart, no mistake. And Thane Aelred was one of those ruddy English pippins as got bounced from the box.

Aye, heads rolled everywhere before the dust settled on that one. Stout Aelred's lands were confiscated, and the good man himself banished from the realm. All of us vassals were turned out, thrown off the land by the king's stinking sheriff and his bailiffs; our village was burned to the last house and pigsty. Aelred's holding was returned to forest and placed under Forest Law, devil's work.

Most of us, myself included, lingered in the area awhile. We had nowhere else to go, and no provision made for us. For, like the others in Aelred's keep, I was born on his lands, and my father served his father as I served him. The Scatlockes have been vassals ever and always, never lords . . .

492

"es, Odo, that is my real name—William Scatlocke," I pause to explain. "Y'see, it's just some folk have it hard with such a ragged scrap between their teeth, and *Scarlet* has a finer sound."

"I agree," says he.

"Splendid," I tell him. "I will sleep so much better for knowing that. Now, where was I?"

Odo scans what he has written, and says, ". . . you were telling about Forest Law. You called it the devil's work."

ye, and so it is. Forest Law—two perfectly honest and upright words as ever was, but placed together they make a mad raving monster. See now, under Forest Law the crown takes a piece of land useful and needful for all folk in common and at a stroke turns it into a private hunting park forever closed to common folk for any purpose whatsoever. Forest Law turns any land into king's land, to be used by royals only, them and their fortune-favoured friends. The keep of these so-called parks is given to agents of the crown known as sheriffs, who rule with a noose in one hand and a flamin' hot castration iron in the other for anyone who might happen to trespass however lightly on the royal preserve.

Truly, merely setting foot in a royal forest can get you maimed or blinded. Taking a single deer or pig to feed your starving children can get you hung at the crossroads alongside evil outlaws who have burned entire villages and slaughtered whole families in their sleep. A petty thing, hardly worth a morning's sweat, as it may be. Yes, that dark-eyed deer with the fine brown pelt and tasty haunches is worth more than any fifty or a hundred vassals, be they serfs or freemen, and there's a fact.

Forest Law is what happened to Thane Aelred's lands—hall, barn, sty, granary, milkhouse, and mill all burned to the last stick and stake, and the ashes ploughed under. The age-old boundary stones were pulled up, and the hides taken off the registry books, and the whole great lot joined up to the lands of other English estates to be declared king's forest. Aelred himself was hauled away in chains, leaving his poor lady wife to make her way as best she could. I heard later he and his were dumped aboard a ship bound for Daneland with other miserable exiles, but I never really knew for sure. The rest of his folk were turned out that same day and herded off the property at the point of long Norman spears.

Those of us without friends or relations we might flee to for aid and comfort took to the greenwood. We aimed to live off the land in spite of the threat of death hanging over us if we were caught. As one of Aelred's foresters this was no great hardship for me, but others who were not used to such stark conditions suffered mightily. Cold and fever took a heavy toll, and the sheriff's men took more. They killed us whenever they could, and chased us always.

494

It was no kind of life, Odo lad, let me tell you." He glances up with his big dreamy eyes, his soft mouth caught in a half smile. "You would not last above three days."

"I might be stronger than I look," says he.

"And looks are ever deceiving," I reply, and we go on . . .

Eventually, with winter coming on and the sheriff and his men growing wise to our ways, the few of us that had survived those many months broke company and drifted off to other parts. Some went north where the Harrowing had desolated the land; in those empty parts it was said honest folk might begin again. Trouble there was that too many dishonest folk had gathered up there, too, and it was fast becoming a killing ground of another kind.

Me, I decided to go west, to Wales—to Wallia, land of my mother's birth.

I'd always wanted to see it, mind, but there was more to it than whim. For I had heard a tale that stirred my blood. A man, they said, had risen in defiance of the Norman overlords, a man who flew in the face of certain death to challenge King William himself, a man they called King Raven.

CHAPTER 3

Lundein

Cardinal Ranulf de Bayeux stepped from the small, flat-bottomed boat onto the landing stone set into the soft shore of the River Thames. The rank brown water was awash in dung and garbage, awaiting the estuary tide to rise and bear it away. Pressing the cloth of his wide sleeve against his nose, he motioned impatiently to his companions as they clambered from the boat.

Two men-at-arms had travelled down to Lundein with the cardinal and they followed his lead, remaining a few paces behind, the red pennants atop their spears fluttering in the breeze. Clutching the skirts of his scarlet satin robe to avoid the mud, Ranulf tiptoed up the embankment to the wooden walkway that led to the city street and passed the walls of the White Tower. The new stone of that magnificent fortress glowed in the full light of a warm sun, a blazing milky brilliance against the yellow leaves and dazzling blue autumn sky.

King William had returned from Normandie two days previous and had summoned his chief advisor straightaway—no doubt to review the accounts which Ranulf carried in a velvet pouch beneath his arm. It had been a good year, all things considered. The treasury was showing a small surplus, for a change, so Ranulf was to be congratulated. Thanks to his tirelessly inventive mind, the king would have money to pay his bribes and his troops, with a little more besides.

Oh, but it was becoming ever more difficult. The people were taxed to the teeth, the nobles likewise, and the chorus of grumbling was becoming a deafening din from some quarters, which is why Ranulf—a man of the cloth, after all—could no longer travel about the land alone, but went with an armed escort to protect him from any who felt themselves particularly aggrieved by his efforts on the king's behalf.

William, of course, was ultimately to blame for the resentment festering throughout his realm. It was not that the king was a spendthrift. Common opinion to the contrary, William the Red was no more wastrel than his father—a man who lived well, to be sure, although far less so than many of his barons—but war was a costly business: much expenditure for piddling little gain. Even when William won the conflict, which he usually did, he almost always came away the poorer for it. And the warring was incessant. If it wasn't the Scots, it was the Bretons; and if not foreign troublemakers it was his own brothers, Prince Henry and Duke Robert, fomenting rebellion.

Yet today, if only for today, the news from the treasury would please the king, and Ranulf was eager to share this good news and advance another step towards reaping a substantial reward for himself—the lucrative bishopric of Duresme, perhaps, which was empty now owing to the death of the previous incumbent.

Cardinal de Bayeux and his escort passed through the wide and handsome gate with but a nod to the porter. They quickly crossed the yard where the king's baggage train still waited to be unloaded. Ranulf dismissed his soldiers and commanded them to remain ready outside, then entered the tower and climbed the stairs to the antechamber above, where he was admitted by the steward and informed that the king was at table and awaiting his arrival.

Entering silently, Ranulf took one look at his royal patron and read the king's disposition instantly. "His Majesty is displeased," declared Cardinal Ranulf from the doorway. He made a small bow and smoothed the front of his satin robe.

"Displeased?" wondered William, beckoning him in with a wave of his hand. "Why would you say displeased? Hmm?" Rising from his chair, the king began to pace along the length of the table where he had lately enjoyed a repast with his vavasours. The king's companions had gone, or been sent away, and William was alone.

"Why, indeed?" said the king, without waiting for Ranulf's reply. "My dear brother, Robert, threatens war if I do not capitulate to his ridiculous whims . . . my barons find ever more brazen excuses to reduce their tributes and taxes . . . my subjects are increasingly rebellious to my rule and rude to my person!"

The king turned on his chief counsellor and waved a parchment like a flag. "And now this!"

"Ill tidings, *mon roi?*"

"By the holy face of Lucca!" William shouted. "Is there no end to this man's demands?"

"Which man, Sire, if you please?" Ranulf moved a few paces into the room.

"This jackanapes of a pope!" roared the king. "This Urban—he says Canterbury has been vacant too long and insists we invest an archbishop at once."

"Ignore him, Sire," suggested Ranulf.

"Oh, but that is not the end of his impudence," continued the king without pausing to draw breath. "Far from it! He demands not

499

only my seal on a letter of endorsement, but a public demonstration of my support as well."

"Which, as we have often discussed, you are understandably loath to give," sympathised the cardinal, stifling a yawn.

"Blast his eyes! I am loath to give him so much as the contents of my bowels." William, his ruddy cheeks blushing hot with anger, threw a finger in his counsellor's face. "God help me if I ever suffer one of his lick-spit legates to set foot in my kingdom. I'll boil the beggar in his own blood, and if Urban persists in these demands, I will throw my support to Clement—I swear I will."

"Tell him so," suggested Ranulf simply. "That is what the Conqueror would have done—and did, often enough."

"There! There you say it, by Judas!" crowed William. "My father had no illusions about who should rule the church in his kingdom. He would not suffer any priest to stick his nose into royal affairs."

It was true. William's father, the Conqueror, had ruled the church like he ruled everything else on his adopted island. Not content to allow such a wealthy and powerful institution to look to its own affairs, he continually meddled in everything from appointing clerics to the collection of tithes—ever and always to his own advantage. Ranulf knew that the son, William the Red, was peeved because, try as he might, he could not command the same respect and obedience from the church that his father had taken as his due.

"Mark me, Bayeux, I'll not swear out my throne to Urban no matter how many legates and emissaries he sends to bedevil me."

"Tell His Eminence that his continued attempts to leech authority from the throne make this most sacred display of loyalty a mockery." Cardinal Ranulf of Bayeux moved to a place across the table from his pacing king. "Tell him to stuff the Fisherman's Ring up his sanctimonious—"

"Ha!" cried William. "If I told him that, he would excommunicate me without a second thought."

"Do you care?" countered Ranulf smoothly. "Your Majesty holds Rome in contempt in any of a hundred ways already."

"You go too far! My faith, or lack of it, is my own affair. I'll not be chastised by the likes of you, Bayeux."

Ranulf bowed his head as if to accept the reprimand and said, "Methinks you misunderstand me, Sire. I meant that the king of England need spare no thought for Pope Urban's tender feelings. As you suggest, it is a simple enough matter to offer support to his rival, Clement."

William allowed himself to be calmed by the gentle and shrewd assertions of his justiciar. "It is that," sneered William. The king of England surveyed the remains of his midday meal as if the table were a battlefield and he was searching for survivors. "I much prefer Clement anyway."

"You see?" Ranulf smiled, pleased with the way he had steered the king to his point of view. "God continues to grace your reign, Sire. In his wisdom, he has provided a timely alternative. Let it be known and voiced abroad that you support Clement, and we'll soon see how the worm writhes."

"If Urban suspected I was inclined to pledge loyalty to Clement, he might cease badgering me." William spied a nearby goblet on the table; there was still some wine in it, so he gulped it down. "He might even try to woo me back into his camp instead. Is that what you mean?"

"He might," confirmed Ranulf in a way that suggested this was the very least William might expect.

"He might do more," William ventured. "How much more?"

"The king's goodwill has a certain value to the church just now. It is the pope who needs the king, not the other way around. Perhaps

501

this goodwill might be bartered for something of more substantial and lasting value."

William stopped pacing and drew his hand through his thinning red hair. "The pope has nothing I want," he decided at last. He turned and stumped back to his chair. "He is a prisoner in his own palace. Why, he cannot even show his face in Rome." William looked into another cup, but it was empty so he resumed his search. "The man can do little enough for himself; he can do nothing for me."

"Nothing?" asked the cardinal pointedly. "Nothing at all?"

"Nothing I can think of," maintained William stubbornly. "If you know something, Bayeux, tell me now or leave me alone. I grow weary of your insinuations."

"Given Urban's precarious position—a position made all the more uncertain by the king's brother . . ."

"Robert?" said William. "My brother may be an ass, but he has no love for Rome."

"I was thinking of Henry, Sire," said the cardinal. "Seeing that Henry is courting Clement, it seems to me that Urban, with the proper inducement, might be willing to recognize the English crown's right to appoint clergy in exchange for your support," suggested the cardinal. "What is that worth, do you think?"

William stared at his chief justiciar. "The wheels of government grind slowly, as you well and truly know," he said, his pale blue eyes narrowing as he considered the implications of his counsellor's suggestion. "You are paid to see that they do."

"Yes, and every day a pulpit stands empty, the crown collects the tithe, as *you* well and truly know."

"A tithe which would otherwise go to the church," said William. "Ultimately to Rome."

"Indirectly, perhaps," agreed Ranulf. He buffed his fingernails against the sleek satin of his robe. "Urban contests this right, of course. But if the pope were to formally relinquish all such claims in favour of the crown . . ."

"I would become head of the church in England," said William, following the argument to its conclusion.

"I would not go so far, Sire," allowed Ranulf. "Rome would never allow secular authority to stand above the church. Urban's power ebbs by the day, to be sure, but you will never pry that from his miser's grasp."

"Well," grumped the king, "it would amount to the same thing. England would be a realm unto itself, and its church an island in the papal sea."

"Even so," granted Ranulf gallantly. "Your Majesty would effectively free the throne of England from the interference of Rome for good and forever. That would be worth something."

"How much?" said William. He leaned across the table on his fists. "How much would it be worth?"

"Who can say? Tithes, lands—the sale of benefices alone could run to—"

William might not understand the finer points of the papal dispute that had inadvertently thrown up two rival claimants to Saint Peter's golden chair, but he knew men and money. And clerics were the same as most men in wanting to ease the way for their offspring in the world. A payment to the church to secure a position for an heir was money well spent. "Thousands of marks a year," mused William.

"Pounds, Sire. Thousands, yes—thousands of pounds straight into your treasury. It would only take a letter."

William looked at the empty goblet in his hand, and then threw it the length of the room. It struck the far wall and tumbled down the tapestry. "By the Blesséd Virgin, Flambard, you are a rascal! I like it!"

503

Returning to his chair, William resumed his place at the table. "Wine!" he shouted to an unseen servant lurking behind the door. "Sit," he said to Ranulf. "Tell me more about this letter."

The cardinal tossed the black velvet bag onto the bench and sat down; he cleared a place among the crumbs and bones with the side of his hand. Choosing a goblet from those on the table before him, he emptied it and waited for the servant to appear with a jar. When the cups were filled once more, the king and his chief advisor drank and discussed how to make best use of the pope and his predicament.

CHAPTER 4

Brother Odo is dozing over his quill again. Much as I like to see him jump, I won't wake him just yet. It gives me time. The longer I stretch this tale, the more time I have before the tale stretches me, so to speak. Besides, I need a little space to think.

What I think on now is the day I first set eyes on King Raven. A pleasant day it was, too, in all its parts. Crisp, bright autumn was descending over the March. I had been months a-wandering, poking here and there as fancy took me, moving ever and always in the direction of the setting sun. I had no plan other than to learn more of this King Raven, and find him if I could. A fellow of the forest, such as myself, might make himself useful to a man like that. If I did, I reckoned, he might be persuaded to take me under his wing.

I kept my ears sharp for any word of King Raven, and asked after him whenever I happened on a settlement or holding. I worked for food and a bed of straw in barn or byre, and talked to those who were bold enough to speak about the abuses of the crown and events in the land. Many of those I spoke to had heard the name—as well they might, for Baron de Braose, Lord of Bramber, had set aside a right hand-some reward for his capture. Some of the folk had a tale or two of how this Raven fella had outwitted the baron or abbot, or some such; but none knew more than I did of this elusive blackbird or his whereabouts.

The further west I wended, however, the pickings got better in one respect, but worse in another. More had heard of King Raven, to be sure, and some were happy enough to talk. But those who knew of him held that this Raven was not a real man at all. Rather, they had it that he was a phantom sent up from the lowest infernal realm to bedevil the Normans. They said the creature took the form of a giant, high-crested bird, with wings to span a ten-foot pike, and a wicked long beak. Deadly as plague to the Normans, they said, and black as Satan's pit whence he sprung, he was a creature bred and born of deviltry—although one alewife told me that he had given some kinfolk of hers aid in food and good money when they were that desperate for it, so he couldn't be all that bad.

As green spring gave way to summer, I settled for a spell with a swineherd and his gap-toothed wife on their small farm hard by Hereford, where Baron Neufmarché keeps his great stone heap of a castle. Although Wales is only a few days' saunter up the road, I was in no hurry just then. I wanted to learn more, if more was to be learned, and so I lay low, biding my time and listening to the locals when they had cause to speak of matters that interested me.

When the day's work was finished, I'd hie up to town to spend a fair summer evening at the Cross Keys, an inn of questionable repute. The innkeeper was a rascal, no mistake—it's him they should be hang-ing, not Will—but he served a worthy jar and thick chops so tender and juicy your teeth could have a rest. I came to know many of the local folk who called at the Keys, and they came to trust me with their more private thoughts.

Always, I tried to steer the talk towards happenings in the March, hoping for a word or two of King Raven. Thus, it fell out one night that I met a freeman farmer who traded at Hereford on market days. He had come up to sell a bit of bacon and summer sausage and, seeing me cooling my heels, came to sit down beside me on the low wall that fronted the inn. "Well," said I, raising my jar, "here's hail to the king."

"Hail to the king, devil take him when he will."

"Oh? Red William gone out of favour with you?" I ask.

"Aye," says the farmer, "and I don't care who knows it." All the same, he glanced around guiltily to see who might be overhearing. No one was paying any mind to a couple of tongue-wags like ourselves, so he took a deep draught of his ale and reclined on his elbow against the wall. "I pray for his downfall every day."

"What has the king done to you to earn such ire?"

"What hasn't he done? Before Rufus I had a wife and a strapping big son to help me with the chores."

"And now?"

"Wife got croup and died, and son was caught in the greenwood setting rabbit snares. Lost his good right hand to the sheriff's blade. Now he can't do more'n herd the stock."

"You blame the king for that?"

"I do. If I had my way King Raven would pluck out his eyes and eat his right royal liver."

"That would be a sight," I told him. "If that feathered fella was more than a story to tell on a summer night."

"Oh! He is," the farmer insisted. "He is, right enough."

My vengeful friend went on then to relate how the dread bird had swooped down on a passel of Norman knights as they passed through the March on the King's Road one fine night.

507

"King Raven fell out of the sky like a venging angel and slew a whole army o' the baron's rogues before they could turn and run," the farmer said. "He left only one terrified sot alive to warn the baron to leave off killin' Brits."

"This creature—how did he kill the knights?" I wondered.

The farmer looked me in the eye and said, "With fire and arrows."

"Fair enough," says I. "But if it was with fire and arrows, how do they know it was the phantom bird who did it, and not just some peevish Welshman? You know how contrary they can be when riled."

"Oh, aye," agreed the farmer. "I know that right enough. But it was the King Raven, no mistake." He shook his head with unwavering assurance. "That I know."

"Because?" I prodded lightly.

"Because," says he with a slow smile, "the arrows was black. Stone tip to feather, they was black as Beelzebub's tongue."

This bit of news thrilled me more than anything I'd heard yet. Black arrows, mind! Just the kind of thing ol' Will Scarlet might think up if he was about such business as spreading fear and havoc among the rascal brigade. In this tetchy farmer's tale, I saw the shape of a man, and not a phantom. A man that much like myself it gave me the first solid hope to be getting on with.

I lingered on the holding through harvesttime to help out, and then, as the leaves began to fall and the wind freshened from the north, I took my leave and, one bright day, took to the road once more. I walked from settlement to settlement, pausing wherever I could to seek word of King Raven.

Autumn had come to the land, as I say, and I eventually arrived at the edge of the March and entered the forest. Easy in my own company, I remained alert to all around me. I travelled slow and with purpose, camping by the road each night. On those clean, clear mornings

I rose early and made for a high place, the better to watch and listen and learn what I could of the woodland 'round about.

See now, the Forest of the March is an ancient wood, old when Adam was a lad. A wild place not like any forest I'd known in England. Denser, darker, more tangled and woolly, it clutched tight to its secrets and held them close. Mind you, I am a man used to forest ways and byways, and as the bright days chased one another off toward winter, I began to get the measure of it.

One morning, just as the weather turned, I woke to a chill mist and the sound of voices on the King's Road. I had seen wolf scat on the trail before sunset and decided a prudent man might do well to sleep out of reach of those rangy, long-toothed hunters. So, having spent the night in the rough crook of a stout oak within sight of the King's Road—a stiff cradling, to be sure—I stirred as the daylight broke soft on a grey and gusty day, and heard the sound of men talking on the trail below. Their voices were quiet and low, the easy rhythmic tones familiar, even as the words were strange. It took me a moment to shake the sleep out of my ears and realise they were speaking Welsh. My mother's tongue it was, and I had enough of it from my barefoot days to make myself understood.

I heard the words *Rhi Bran y Hud* and knew I was close to finding what I was looking for, so . . .

Yes, Odo, what is it?" My scribe rouses himself from his snooze and rubs his dream-dulled eyes.

"These words *Riban Hood*," he asks, yawning wide. "What do they mean?"

"If you would let a fella get on wi' the tellin', God knows you'd find out soon enough," I say. "But, see here now, it en't *Riban Hood*, as you will have it. It is *Rhi Bran*—that part means "King Raven." And *Hud* means . . . well, it means "Enchanter." It is what the British folk call the phantom lord of the Marchlands."

"Ree Bran a Hood," he says, dutifully writing it down. "A good name."

"Aye, a good name, that," I agree, and we rumble on.

ell, I shinnied down to join those fellas on the road and see what they could tell me of this mysterious bird.

"Here now," I called, dropping lightly from the last branch onto the bank above the road. "Can you fellas spare a traveller a word or two?"

You would have thought I'd dropped down from the moon to see the look on those two faces. Two men, one big as a house and the other slighter, but muscled and tough as a hickory root. They were dressed in odd hooded cloaks with greenery and rags sewn on, and both carried sturdy longbows with a quiver of arrows at their belts. "What!" cried the big one, spinning around quicker than you'd have thought possible for so large a lump of humanity.

This one has spent a fair bit of time in the greenwood, thinks I, his knife is in his hand that quick. "I mean no harm, friend," I said. "And full sorry I am if I startled you. I heard you talkin' and was hopin' for a little chin music, is all."

"You lurking devil," growled the slight one, thrusting forward, "we'll not be singing for you." He looked to the big one, who nodded slowly. "Not until we know more about you."

"Well, I've got time now if you do," said I. "Where would you like me to begin?"

"A name if you have one," said he. "That will do for a beginning."

"My name's William Scatlocke," I told them. "Think what you like, but there's some as tug a forelock when they hear that name." I give him a smile and a wink. "But a doff o' the hat will do nicely just now."

"I am Iwan," replied the big one, warming up a little. "This here is Siarles."

"Scatlocke's a Saxon name," observed the slight one with a frown. "But William, now that's Ffreinc." He seemed ready to spit to show me what he thought of Normans.

"Saxon and Ffreinc, aye," I agreed politely. "My mother, bless her dear, sweet, well-meaning soul, thought a Frankish William would make my life that little mite easier seeing as our land was overrun by the vermin. With a William to go before me, they might mistake me for one of their own, see, and give me an easier ride."

"Do they?" he asked, suspicion making his voice a threat.

"Not as I've noticed," I said. "Then again, it en't as if I'd been named Siarles. Now, there's a name just begging for trouble, if ever I heard one."

The slight one bristled and bunched up his face, but the big one chuckled aloud, his voice like thunder over green hills. "You are a bold one, give you that," said he. "But you're in the March now, friend. What causes you to be dropping from our good Welsh trees, Bold William?"

"Friendly folk call me Will Scarlet," I answered. "Forester by trade, I am—just like my father before me. I see you two know your way around leafland yourselves."

"That we do, Will," Iwan said. "Are you running from someone, then?"

"Running to, more like."

Well, they wanted to hear more, so I went on to explain about Thane Aelred getting banished and his lands taken in Forest Law and all that ruck. I told about taking to the greenwood, and all my travels since then. They listened, and I could feel them relaxing their distrust as I described hiding from the sheriff and his men on land that used to belong to my good thane, and poaching the king's precious deer to survive. Pretty soon, they began nodding and agreeing, siding with me in my plight. "Thing is, since then I've been on the move all summer looking for this fella they call King Raven. Naturally, when I heard you mention Rhi Bran, my ears pricked right up."

"You speak Cymru?" asked Siarles then.

"Learned it on my dear mum's knee," I told him. "Same mum, in fact, that named me William. I also bothered myself to learn a little Frank so I'd know what those buggers were up to."

"Why do you want to see King Raven?" asked Iwan. "If you don't mind my asking."

"To offer my services," I replied, "and I'd be much obliged for any help you could give me in that direction."

"Might we know the nature of these services?" asked Siarles, looking me up and down. He was softening a bit, but still a little brittle for my taste.

"Seems to me that if he is even half the man I think he is, he'll be needing a strong and fearless hand like Will Scarlet here."

"What do you know of him?"

"I know he en't a phantom, as some would have it. I know Baron de Braose is offering fifty pounds of pure English silver for his fine feathered head on a pike."

"Truly?" Siarles asked, much impressed.

"Aye," I assured him, "did you not know that?"

"We maybe heard something about it," he muttered. Then a new thought occurred to him. "And just how do we know you don't want to claim all that money for yourself?"

"Good question," I allowed. "And it deserves a good answer."

"Well?" he said, suspicion leaping up lively as ever. Siarles, bless him; his grey eyes are quick and they are keen, but he distrusts most of what he sees. Half of it is living in the wildwood, I reckon, where your eyes and wits are your best and truest friends; but the other half is just his own leery nature.

"As soon as I think up an answer good enough, I'll tell you," I said. This brought a growl from young Siarles, who wanted to run me off then and there.

Iwan only laughed. He had already made up his mind about me. "Peace, Siarles," he said. "He doesn't want the money."

"How can you be so sure?"

"Any man after the reward money would have thought of a better answer than that. Why, he'd have a whole story worked out and like as not say too much and get himself all tangled in the telling. Will, here, didn't do that."

"Maybe he's just that stupid."

"Nay, he isn't stupid," replied Iwan. I liked him better and better by the moment. "I'll wager my good word against anything in your purse that claiming the reward money never crossed his mind."

"You would win that bet, friend," I replied. "In truth, it never did." Seeing as how Iwan had made such a fine argument for me, I asked, "Am I to be thinking that you know this Rhi Bran?"

Siarles, still suspicious, frowned as Iwan said, "Know him, aye, we do."

"Would you kindly tell me where he can be found?" I asked, nice as please and thank you.

"Better than that," said Iwan, "we'll take you to meet him."

"Iwan!" snapped Siarles. He was tenacious as a rat dog, give him that. "What are you saying? We don't know this Saxon, or anything about him. We can't be taking him to Bran. Why, he might be any-body—maybe even a spy for the abbot!"

513

"If he's Hugo's spy we can't be leaving him here," countered Iwan. "I say we take him with us and leave it to Bran to decide who and what he is—aye, and what is to be done with him." Turning to me, he said, "If we take you with us, do you swear on your life's blood to abide by our lord's decision whatsoever it may be?"

Ordinarily, I do not like swearing my life away on the whims of persons unknown, but seeing as he was only granting me the chance I'd been seeking all summer, I readily agreed. "On my life's blood, I swear to abide by your lord's decision."

"Good enough for me," said Iwan. "Follow us."

"And see you keep quiet," added Siarles for good measure.

"I'll be as quiet as you were when you woke me from my treetop perch just now," I told him.

Iwan gave out a laugh and, in two quick strides, disappeared up over the bank and into the brushwood beside the road. "After you," said Siarles, prodding me with the tip of his bow. "I'll come last, and don't you put a foot wrong, 'cause I'll be watching you."

"There's relief, to be sure," I replied. Stepping into the forest, I was led a merry chase to meet the man I'd crossed half the country to see. God save me, but I never imagined him the way he first appeared.

CHAPTER 5

The trail went on and on. My guides maintained a curious wolf-trot pace: three steps quick walk alternating with four steps slow running. It took a bit of getting used to, but, once I got the knack, I soon understood that it allowed a body to move quickly over long distances and still have breath enough and strength to do what you came to do when you reached your destination. I had never seen this neat trick before, and was glad to add it to my own tidy store of forest craft . . .

You should try it, Odo," I tell my bleary-eyed scribe. He raises his pudding face to see if I jest. "It would do you good."

"I will take you at your word," he says, stifling a yawn. He dips his quill in the horn, and the wet nib hovers over the parchment. "Where did they take you, these hooded strangers?"

"Where did they take me? Pay attention, and you'll learn soon enough. Now then, where was I?"

"Running through the greenwood to meet the Raven King."

"Not the Raven King," I tell him. "It is King Raven—there is a difference, monk. Get it right."

Odo gives an indifferent shrug, and I resume my tale . . .

Well, we ran miles that morning, and I am firmly persuaded most of it was just to confuse me so as to prevent me leading anyone else to their forest hideaway.

For the most part, it worked well enough. On a fella less firmly rooted in woodland lore, it would have been well-nigh confounding. As for myself, it produced only mild befuddlement, as Iwan probably guessed after a while. For we came to a place where a little clear water stream issued from beneath a natural rock wall, and after we'd got a few good mouthfuls, the big man produced a scrap of cloth from his quiver. "Sorry, William," he said, handing me the cloth. "You must bind your eyes now."

"If it makes you and yours feel better, I'm happy to do it," I said. "I'll even let Siarles here tie the knot."

"Right, you will," said Siarles, stepping behind me as I wound the cloth around my head. He tied the loose ends, gave them a sharp tug, and then we were away again, more slowly—this time Iwan leading, and me stumbling along with my hand on his shoulder, tripping over roots and stones and trying to keep up with his long-legged strides. It was more difficult than I would have thought—try it yourself in rough wood and see how you go. After a time I sensed the ground beginning to rise. The slope was gradual at first, but grew steeper as we went along. I heard birdsong high up, scattered and far off—the trees were getting bigger and farther apart.

Gaining the top of the ridge, we came to a stony ledge and

stopped again. "Here now," said Iwan, taking me by the shoulders and turning me around a few times, "not far to go. A few more steps is all."

He spun me around some more, and then Siarles spun me the other way for good measure. "Mind your step," said Siarles, his mouth close to my ear. "Keep your head low, or you'll get a knock." He pressed my head down until I was bent double, and then led me through a gap between two trees and, almost immediately, down a steep incline.

"Cél Craidd," said Iwan. "I pray it goes well with you here."

"You better pray so, too," added Siarles in tone far less friendly. He had taken against me, I don't know why—maybe it was that jibe about his name. Or maybe it was the cut of my cloth, but whatever it was, he gave me to know that he held me of small regard. "Play us false, and it will be the last place you ever see."

"Now, now," I replied, "no need to be nasty. I've sworn to abide, and abide I will, come what may."

Siarles untied the binding cloth, and I opened my eyes on the strangest place I have ever seen: a village made of skins and bones, branches and stones. There were low hovels roofed with ferns and moss, and others properly thatched with rushes; some had wattle-and-daub walls, and some were made of woven willow withies so that the hut seemed to have been knitted whole out of twigs, and the chinks stuffed with dried grass, giving the place an odd, fuzzy appearance as if it wore a pelt in moulting. If a few of the hovels in the centre of the settlement were larger and constructed of more substantial stuff— split timber and the like—they also had roofs of grassy turf, and wore antlers or skull bones of deer or oxen at the corners and above their hide-covered doorways, which gave them the look of something grown up out of the forest floor.

If a tribe of Greenmen had bodged together a settlement out of bark and brake and cast-off woodland ruck, it would look exactly like

517

this, I thought. Indeed, it was a fit roost for King Raven—just the sort of place the Lord of the Forest might choose.

Nested in a shallow bowl of a glade snugged about by the stout timbers of oak and lime and ash and elm, Cél Craidd was not only protected, but well hidden. The circling arm of the ridge formed a wall of sorts on three sides which rose above the low huts. A fella would have to be standing on the ridgetop and looking down into the bowl of the glade to see it. But this concealment came at a price, and the people there were paying the toll with their lives.

Our arrival was noticed by a few of the small fry, who ran to fetch a welcome party. They were—beneath the soot and dirt and ragged clothes—ordinary children, and not the offspring of a Greenwife. They skittered away with the swift grace of creatures birthed and brought up in the wildwood. Chirping and whooping, they flew to an antler-decked hut in the centre of the settlement, and pounded on the doorpost. In a few moments, there emerged what is possibly the ugliest old woman I ever set eyes to. Mother Mary, but she was a sight, with her skin wrinkled like a dried plum and blackened by years of sitting in the smoke of a cooking fire, and a wiry, wayward grizzled fringe of dark hair—dark where it should have been bleached white by age, she was that old. She hobbled up to look me over, and though her step might have been shambling there was nothing wrong with the eyes in her head. People talk of eyes that pierce flesh and bone for brightness, and I always thought it mere fancy. Not so! She looked me over, and I felt my skin flayed back and my soul laid bare before a gaze keen as a fresh-stropped razor.

"This is Angharad, Banfáith of Britain," Iwan declared, pride swelling his voice.

At this the old woman bent her head. "I give thee good greeting, friend. Peace and joy be thine this day," she said in a voice that creaked like a dry bellows. "May thy sojourn here well become thee."

She spoke in an old-fashioned way that, oddly enough, suited her so well I soon forgot to remark on it at all.

"Peace, Banfáith," I replied. I'd heard and seen my mother's folk greeting the old ones from time to time, using a gesture of respect. This I did for her, touching the back of my hand to my forehead and hoping the sight of an ungainly half-Saxon offering this honour would not offend overmuch.

I was rewarded with a broad and cheerful smile that creased her wrinkled face anew, albeit pleasantly enough. "You have the learning, I ween," she said. "How came you by it?"

"My blesséd mother taught her son the manners of the Cymry," I replied. "Though it is seldom enough I've had the chance to employ them these last many years. I fear my plough has grown rusty from neglect."

She chuckled at this. "Then we will burnish it up bright as new soon enough," she said. Turning to Iwan, she said, "How came you to find him?"

"He dropped out of a tree not ten steps from us," he answered. "Fell onto the road like an overgrown apple."

"Did he now?" she wondered. To me, she said, "Pray, why would you be hiding in the branches?"

"I saw the sign of a wolf on the road the night before and thought better to sleep with the birds."

"Prudent," she allowed. "Know you the wolves?"

"Enough to know it is best to stay out of reach of those long-legged rascals."

"He says he is searching for our Bran," put in Siarles. Impatient, he did not care to wait for the pleasant talk to come round to its destination as is the way with the Cymry. "He says he wants to offer his services."

519

"Does he now?" said Angharad. "Well, then, summon our lord and let us see how this cast falls out."

Siarles hurried away to one of the larger huts in the centre of the holding. By this time, the children had been spreading the word that a stranger had come, and folk were starting to gather. They were not, I observed, an altogether comely group: thin, frayed and worn, smudged around the edges as might be expected of people eking out a precarious life in deep forest. Few had shoes, and none had clothes that were not patched and patched again. At least two fellas in the crowd had lost a hand to Norman justice; one had lost his eyes.

A more hungry, haunted lot I never saw, nor hope to see—like the beggars that clot the doorways of the churches in the towns. But where beggars are hopeless in their desperation, these folk exuded the grim defiance of a people who exist on determination alone. And all of them had the look I'd already noticed on the young ones: an aspect of wary, almost skittish curiosity, as if, drawn to the sight of the stranger in their midst, they nevertheless were ready to flee at a word. One quick move on my part, and they'd bolt like deer, or take wing like a flock of sparrows.

"If your search be true," the old woman told me, "you have naught to fear."

I thanked her for her reassurance and stood to my fate. Presently, Siarles returned from the house accompanied by a young man, tall and slender as a rod, but with a fair span of shoulders and good strong arms. He wore a simple tunic of dark cloth, trousers of the same stuff, and long black riding boots. His hair was so black the sun glinted blue in his wayward locks. A cruel scar puckered the skin on the left side of his face, lifting his lip in what first appeared to be a haughty sneer—an impression only, belied by the ready wit that darted from eyes black as the bottom of a well on a moonless night.

There was no doubt that he was their leader, Bran—the man I had come to find. If the right and ready homage of the ragged forest folk failed to make that clear, you had only to take in the regal ease with which he surveyed all around him to know that here was a man well used to command. His very presence demanded attention, and he claimed mine without effort to the extent that at first I failed to see the young woman trailing behind him: a fine, dark-haired lady of such elegance and grace that, though she was dressed in the same humble drab as the starvelings around her, she held herself with such an imperious bearing that I took her to be the queen.

"I present Rhi Bran, Lord of Elfael," said Iwan, speaking loud enough for all gathered round to hear.

"*Pax vobiscum*," said the tall young man, looking me up and down with a sweep of a quick, intelligent eye.

"God's peace, my lord," I replied in Cymric, offering him the courtesy of a bow. "I am William Scatlocke, former forester to Thane Aelred of Nottingham."

"He's come to offer his services," Siarles informed his lordship with a mocking tone to let his master know what he thought of the idea.

Bran looked me over once again and finding no fault, I think, replied, "What kind of services do you propose, William Scatlocke?"

"Anything you require," I said. "From slaughtering hogs to thatching roofs, sawing timber to pollarding hazel, there's not much I haven't done."

"You said you were a forester," mused Bran, and I saw the glint of interest in his glance.

"Aye, I was—and a good one, if I say it myself."

"Why did you quit?"

"Thane Aelred, God bless him, lost his lands in the succession dispute and was banished to Daneland. All his vassals were turned

521

out by Red William to fend for themselves, most like to starve, it was
that grim."

The dark-haired young woman, who had been peering from
behind Bran's shoulder, spoke up just then. "No wife, or children?"

"Nay, my lady," I replied. "As you see, I'm a young man yet, and
hope burns bright. Still, young or old, a man needs a bit of wherewithal to keep even one small wife." I smiled and gave her a wink to
let her know I meant it lightly. Unamused, she pressed her lips together
primly. "Ah, well, I was just scraping some of that wherewithal together
when the troubles began. Most lost more than I did, to be sure, but I
lost all the little I had."

"I am sorry to hear it," said Bran. "But we are hard-pressed here,
too, what with the care of ourselves and the folk of Elfael as well. Any
man who would join us must earn his way and then some if he wants
to stay." Then, as if he'd just thought of it, he said, "A good forester
would know how to use a longbow. Do you draw, William?"

"I know which end of the arrow goes where," I replied.

"Splendid! We will draw against one another," he declared. "Win
and you stay."

"If I should lose?"

His grin was sly and dark and full of mischief. "If you would stay,
then I advise you not to lose," he said. "Well? What is it to be? Will
you draw against me?"

There seemed to be no way around it, so I agreed. "That I will,"
I said, and found myself carried along in the sudden rush—the people
to the contest, and myself to my fate.

CHAPTER 6

"Obviously, you won the contest," says Odo, raising his sleepy head from his close-nipped pen.

"You think so, do you?" I reply.

"Of course," he assures me smugly. "Otherwise, you would not be here in Count De Braose's pit waiting to be hung for a traitor and an outlaw."

Brother Odo is feisty. He must have got up on the wrong side of his Hail Marys this morning. "Now, monk," I tell him, "just you try to keep your eyes open a little while longer, and we'll get to the end of this and then see how good you are at guessing." I settle myself on my mat of mildewed rushes and push the candle a little closer to my scribe. "Read back the last thing I said. Quick now before I forget."

"Siarles? Iwan? Your bows," says Odo, in rough imitation of my voice.

"Oh, right." And I resume . . .

The two foresters, Iwan and Siarles, handed Rhi Bran their long-bows and, taking one in either hand, he held them out to me. "Choose the one you will use."

"My thanks," I said, trying first one and then the other, bending them with my weight. There was not a spit of difference between them, but I fancied winning with Siarles's bow and chose that one.

"This way, everyone!" called Bran, already striding off towards the far side of the settlement. We came to the head of a miserable patch of barley. They were about growing a few pecks of grain for them-selves, but it was a poor, sad field, shadowed and soggy as it was. The people ranged themselves in a wide double rank behind us, and by now there were upwards of sixty folk—most all of the forest dwellers, I reckoned, saving a few of the women and smaller children. The grain had been harvested and only stubble remained, along with the straw man set up at the far edge of the clearing to keep the birds away. The figure was fixed to a pole some eighty or a hundred paces from where we stood—far enough to make the contest interesting.

"Three arrows. The scarecrow will be our mark," Bran explained as Iwan passed arrows to us both. "Hit it if you can."

"It's been that long since I last drew—" I began.

"No excuses," said Siarles quickly. "Just do your best. No shame in that."

"I was not about making excuses," I replied, nocking the arrow to the string. "I was going to say it's been that long since I last drew, I almost forgot how good a yew bow feels in my hand." This brought a chuckle or two from those gathered around. Turning to Rhi Bran, I said, "Where would you like this first arrow to go, my lord?"

"Head or heart, either will do," Bran replied.

The arrow was on its way the instant the words left his mouth. My

524

first shaft struck the bunched tuft of straw that formed the scarecrow's head, with a satisfying *swish!* as it passed through on its way to the far end of the field.

A murmur of polite approval rippled through the crowd.

"I can see you've drawn a longbow before," said Bran.

"Once or twice."

Lord Bran drew and loosed, sending his first shaft after mine, and close enough to the same place that it made no matter. The people cheered their lord with loud and lusty cries.

"My lord," I said, "I think you have drawn a bow once or twice yourself."

"The heart this time?" he suggested, as we accepted our second arrows from Iwan.

"If straw men have hearts," I said, drawing and taking good aim, "his has thumped its last." This time I sent the shaft up at a slight arc so that it dropped neatly through the centre of the scarecrow and stuck in the dirt behind it.

"Your luck is with you today," sniffed Siarles as polite applause spattered among the onlookers.

"Not a bit of it," I told him, grinning. "That was so the lads wouldn't have to run so far to retrieve my arrow."

"Then I shall do likewise," said Bran, and again, drew and aimed and loosed so quickly that each separate motion flowed into the next and became one. His arrow struck the scarecrow in the upper middle and stuck in the ground right beside mine. Again, the people cheered heartily for their young king.

"Head and heart," I said. "We've done for your man out there. What else is left?"

"The pole on which he hangs," said Iwan, handing over the last arrow.

525

"The pole then?" asked Bran, raising an eyebrow.

"The pole," I confirmed.

Well, now. The day was misty and grey, as I say, and the little light we had was swiftly failing now. I had to squint a bit to even see the blasted pole, jutting up like a wee nubbin just over the peak of the scarecrow's straw head. It showed maybe the size of a lady's fist, and that gave me an idea. Turning to Bran's dark-haired lady, I said, "My queen, will you bless this arrow with a kiss?"

"Queen?" she said, recoiling. "I am not his queen, thank you very much."

This was said with considerable vehemence . . .

Yes, vehemence, Odo." My scribe has wrinkled his nose like he's smelled a rotten egg, as he does whenever I say a word he doesn't understand. "It means, well, it means fire, you know—passion, grit, and brimstone."

"I thought you said she was the queen?" objects Odo.

"That is because I thought she was the queen."

"Well, was she or wasn't she?" he complains, lifting his pen as if threatening to quit unless all is explained to his satisfaction forthwith. "And who is she anyway?"

"Hold your water, monk, I'm coming to that," I tell him. And we go on . . .

This time we draw together," said Bran. "On my count."

"Ready." I press the bow forward and bring the string to my cheek, my eyes straining to the mark.

"One . . . two . . . three . . ."

I loosed the shaft on his "three" and felt the string lash my wrist with the sting of a wasp. The arrow sliced through the air and struck the pole a little to one side. My aim was off, and the point did nothing more than graze the side of the pole. The arrow glanced off to the left and careered into the brush beyond the tiny field.

Bran, however, continued the count. "Four!" he said, and loosed just a beat after me—enough, I think, so that he saw where my shaft would strike. And then, believe it or not, he matched it. Just as my arrow had grazed the left side of the scarecrow's pole, so Bran's sheared the right. He saw me miss, and then missed himself by the same margin, mind. Proud bowman that I was, I could but stand humbled in the presence of an archer of unequalled skill.

Turning to me with a cheery grin, he said, "Sorry, William, I should have told you it was four, not three." He put a friendly hand on my shoulder. "Do you want to try again?"

"Three or four, it makes no matter," I told him. Indicating the straw man, I said, "It seems our weedy friend has survived the ordeal."

"Arrows, Gwion Bach!" called Bran, and an eager young fella leapt to his command; two other lads followed on his heels, and the three raced off to retrieve the shafts.

Iwan walked out to examine the scarecrow pole. He pulled it up and brought it back to where we were waiting, and he and Angharad the banfáith scrutinized the top of the pole, with Siarles, not to be left out, pressing in between them.

"Judging by the notches made by the passing arrows," announced the old woman after her inspection, "Iwan and I say the one on the right has trimmed the most from the pole. Therefore, we declare Rhi Bran the winner."

The people cheered and clapped their hands for their king. And, suddenly disheartened as the meaning of their words broke upon me,

527

I choked down my disappointment, fastened a smile to my face, and prepared to take my leave.

"You know what this means," said Bran, solemn as the grave.

I nodded. "The contest was fair—all it wanted was a better day." I lifted my eyes to his, hoping to see some compassion there. But where the moment before they had been alive with light and mirth, his eyes were flat and cold. Could he change his demeanour so quickly?

"You deserved better," said the dark-haired lady.

"I make no complaint," I said.

"It is a hard thing," Bran observed, glancing at the young woman beside him, "but we do not always get what we want or deserve in this life."

"Sadly true, my lord," I agreed. "Who should know that better than Will Scarlet?"

528

I lowered my head and prepared to accept my defeat, and as I did so I saw that he was not looking at me, but at the young woman. She was glaring at him—why, I cannot say—seeming to take strenuous exception to the drift of our little talk.

"But, sometimes, William," the forest king announced, "we get better than we deserve." I looked up quickly, and I saw a little of the warmth ebbing back into him. "I have decided you can stay."

It was said so quick I did not credit what I had heard. "My lord, did you say . . . I can *stay*?"

He nodded. "Providing you swear allegiance to me to take me as your lord and share my fortunes to the aid of my *Grellon*, and the oppressed folk of Elfael."

"That I will do gladly," I told him. "Let me kneel and I will swear my oath here and now."

"Did you hear that, everyone?" His smile was suddenly broad and welcoming. To me, he said, "I would I had a hundred hardy men as right ready as yourself—the Ffreinc would be fleeing back to their ships and reckoning themselves lucky to escape with their miserable hides." With that Iwan—

Beg pardon?" says Odo, interrupting again.

"Are we never to get this told?" I say with a sigh of resignation, although I do not mind his questions as much as I let on, for it lengthens the time that much more.

"That word *Grellon*—what does it mean?"

"It is Britspeak, monk," I tell him. "It means *flock*—like birds, you know. It is what the people of Coed Cadw—and that means, well that's a little more difficult. It means something like *Guarding Wood*, as if the forest was a fortress, which in a way, it is."

"Grellon," murmurs Odo as he writes the word, sounding out the letters one by one. "Coed Cadw."

"As I was saying, Grellon is what Rhi Bran's people call themselves, right? Can we move on?" At Brother Odo's nod, I continue . . .

So now, Iwan sent someone to fetch Bran's sword; and I was made to kneel in the barley stubble; and as the first drops of rain begin to fall upon my head, I plighted my troth to a new lord, the exiled king of Elfael. No matter that he was an outlaw hunted even then by every Norman in the territory, no matter that he had less in his purse than a wandering piper, no matter that a fella could pace the length and breadth of his entire realm while singing "Hey-Nonny-Nonny," and finish before the song was done. No matter any of it, nor that to follow him meant I took my life in my own two hands by joining an outlaw band. I knew in my heart that it was right to do, if only to annoy

529

the rough and overbearing Normans and all their heavy-handed bar-
barian ways.

Oh, but it was more than that. It felt right in my soul. It seemed
to me even as I repeated the words that would bind my life and fortunes to his that I had come home at last. And when he touched my
shoulder with his sword and raised me to my feet, a tear came to my
eye. Though I had never seen him or that forest settlement before, and
knew nothing of the people gathered close around, it felt as if I was
being welcomed into the fellowship of my own tribe and family. And
nothing that has happened since then in all our scraps and scrapes has
moved me from that stand.

The rain began coming harder then, and we all returned to the village. "Your skill is laudable, William," said Bran as we walked back
together.

"Almost as good as your own," said the lady, falling into step
beside him. "You may as well admit it, Bran, your man William is as
good with a bow as you are yourself."

"Just Will, if you please," I told them. "William Rufus has disgraced our common name in my eyes."

"Rufus!" Bran laughed. "I have never heard him called that before."

"It is common enough in England," I replied. Willy Conqueror's
second son—the rakehell William, now king over us—was often
called Rufus behind his back, on account of his flaming torch of red
hair and scalding hot temper. His worthless brother, Duke Robert, is
called Curthose owing to his penchant for wearing short tunics.

Thinking of those two ne'er-do-well nobles made me that sorry
for Thane Aelred who, like all right-thinking men of his kind, had
thrown in his lot with Robert, the lawful heir to the throne. Alas,
Robby Shortshift turned out to be unreliable as a weathercock, forever
turning this way and that at the slightest breath of a favourable wind

from each and any quarter. That poor numbskull never could make up his mind, and would never fully commit himself to any course, nor stay one once decided. He was a flighty sparrow, but imagined himself a gilded eagle. The shame of it is that he led so many good men to ruination.

Aye, the only time he really ever led.

Of course, Red William held tight to the throne he'd stolen from his brother, and used the confusion over the succession—confusion he himself caused, mind—to further strengthen his grip. After he seized the royal money mintery, he had himself crowned king, sat himself on the throne, and decreed that what was in truth little more than a family disagreement had actually been a rebellious uprising, and all those who supported sad brother Robert were made out to be dangerous traitors. Lands were seized, lives lost. Good men were banished and estates forfeited to the crown. Only a small handful of fortune-kissed *aristos* came away scapegrace clean.

Turning to the lady, I said, "Speaking of names, now that I've given mine . . ."

"This is Lady Mérian," Bran said. "She is our . . ." He hesitated.

"Hostage," she put in quickly. The way she mouthed the word with such contempt, I could tell it was a sore point between them.

"Guest," Bran corrected lightly. "We are to endure the pleasure of her company for a little while longer, it seems."

"Ransom me," she said crisply, "or release me and your trial will be over, my lord."

He ignored the jibe. "Lady Mérian is the daughter of King Cadwgan of Eiwas, the next cantref to the south."

"Bran keeps me against my will," she added, "and refuses to set a price for my release even though he knows my father would pay good silver, and God knows the people here could use it."

"We get by," replied Bran amiably.

"Forgive my curiosity," I said, plunging in, "but if her father is only over in the next cantref, why does he not send a host to take her back by force?" I lifted a hand to the patched-together little village we were entering just then. "I mean, it would not take much to overwhelm this stronghold, redoubtable as it is."

"My father doesn't know where I am," Mérian informed me. "And anyway, it is all the baron's fault. I wouldn't be here if he had not tried to kill Bran."

"Is that Baron de Braose?" I asked.

"No." She shook her head, making her long curls bounce. "Baron Neufmarché—he is my father's overlord. Bran took me captive when the baron turned traitor against him."

"It is somewhat complicated," offered Bran with a rueful smile.

"No," contradicted Mérian, "it is simplicity itself. All you need do is send a message to my father and the silver is yours."

"When the time is right, Mérian, I will. Be sure of it. I will."

"That's what you always say," she snipped. To me she confided, "He always says that—it's been a year and more, and he's still saying it."

The way they talked a fella'd thought they were a married couple airing a grudge nursed through long seasons of living together. There was little hostility in it, and instead I sensed a certain restraint and even a sort of backwards respect. They'd had this discussion so often, I suppose, that the heat had gone out of it long ago and they were left with the familiar warmth of genuine affection.

"Forgive my asking, but why was the baron trying to kill you, my lord?"

"Because he wants Elfael," said Iwan, coming up behind me. "No Ffreinc usurper can ever sit secure on the throne while Bran is alive."

"Elfael is a good place to stand if you're trying to conquer all

Cymru," Bran explained. "Elfael may be small, but it is a prize both de Braose and Neufmarché want to possess for their own. De Braose has it now, but that could change."

"Aye," said Iwan firmly, "it will and one day soon."

In this, I began to see the shape of the desperate necessity that had driven them into hiding. As in England, so in Wales. The Welsh now faced what Saxon England had suffered a generation ago. The difference was that now the Normans were far more numerous, far better supplied, and far more deeply entrenched in land and power than ever before. Restless, industrious, and determined as the day is long, the Norman overlords had stretched their long, greedy fingers into every nook and cranny of life in the Island of the Mighty. They are relentless, constantly searching out and seizing whatever they want and, often as not, destroying the rest. And now they had turned their attention to the hill-fast lands beyond the March.

I would not have given an empty egg for Wales' chances of surviving the onslaught. England in its strength, with its massed war host and bold King Harry leading the best warriors the land ever saw, could not resist the terrible Norman war machine. What hope in hell did proud little Wales ever have?

So now. Fool that I am, I had joined my fate to theirs, exchanging the freedom of the road and the life of a wandering odd-jobber for certain death in a fight we could never win.

Well, that's Will Scarlet for you—doomed beginning and end. Oh, but shed him no tears—he had himself a grand time between.

CHAPTER 7

Castle Truan

A little more than a year had passed since Baron William de Braose decreed that a market town would be built within the borders of his newly seized lands in Elfael. In that short time, the place had grown to respectable size. Already it was larger than Glascwm, the only other settlement worthy of a name in the region. True, the inhabitants had been moved in from the baron's other estates—some from Bramber and lands beyond the March and some from the baron's lands in France—for, unfortunately, the local Welsh shunned the place and refused to reside there. That, however, did not detract from the pride that Count Falkes felt in what he reckoned a considerable achievement by any measure: creating a town with a busy little market from a run-down, worthless monastery housing a few doughty old monks.

One day, thought Falkes as he surveyed the tidy market square, this town, his town, would rival Monmouth or perhaps even Hereford. One day, if he could just maintain order in the cantref and keep his uncle off his back. Baron de Braose might have many good qualities, but patience, like a lame hound, was lagging far to the rear of the pack.

Falkes was only too aware that his uncle chafed at what he considered his nephew's slow progress. In the baron's view, the conquest of Wales should have concluded long since. "It has been almost two years," he had said last time Falkes had visited him at Bramber.

It was at the first of summer that the baron had invited him, along with his cousin and closest friend, the baron's son, Philip, on a hunting foray in the south of England. The sunny, open countryside of his uncle's estate made a welcome change from grey, damp Wales. Falkes was enjoying the ride and basking in the warmth of a splendid summer day, if not in his uncle's good opinion.

"Two years!" said William de Braose as they paused beneath an elm tree to rest the horses. "Two years and what have we to show for it?"

"We have a town, Uncle," Falkes had pointed out. "A very fine town. And, if I may be so bold to suggest, it has not been two years, but only a little more than one since work began."

"A town." William de Braose turned a cold eye on his nephew. "A single town."

"And an abbey," added Falkes helpfully, casting Philip a sideways glance. "The new church is almost finished. Indeed, Abbot Hugo is hoping you will attend the consecration ceremony."

His uncle had allowed that while that was all well and good, he had far grander plans than this solitary town. Elfael was still the only cantref he had conquered in the new territories, and it was costing him more than he liked. "Taxes are low," he observed. "The money collected hardly pays the supply of the abbey."

"The British are poor, Sire."

"They are lazy."

"No, my lord, it may be true they work less than the English," granted Falkes, who was beginning to suspect his uncle entertained a faulty understanding of the Britons, "but their needs are less. They are a simple folk, after all."

"You should be more stern with them. Teach them to fear the steel in your hand."

"It would not help," replied Falkes calmly. "Killing them only makes them more stubborn."

As Falkes had learned to his regret, the slaughter of the ruling Welsh king and his entire warband—while offering an immediate solution to the problem of conquering Elfael—had so thoroughly embittered the people against him that it made his position as ruler of the cantref exceedingly difficult and tenuous.

"Impose your will," the baron insisted. "Make them bend to your bidding. If they refuse, then do what I do—knock some heads, seize lands and property."

"They own little enough as it is," Falkes pointed out. "Most of them hold land in common, and few of them recognise property rights of any kind. Money is little use to them; they barter for what they need. Whenever I tax a man, I am far more likely to be paid in eggs than silver."

"Eggs!" sneered his uncle. "I speak of taxes and you talk eggs."

"It happens more often than you know," declared Falkes, beginning to exhaust his own small store of patience.

"What about this creature of yours—this phantom of the forest? What do they call it?"

"*Rhi Bran y Hud,*" replied Falkes. "It means King Raven the Enchanter."

"The devil, you say! Have you caught the rascal yet?"

"Not yet," confessed Falkes. "Sheriff de Glanville is hopeful. It is only a matter of time."

"Time!" roared the baron. "It has been two years, man! How much more time do you need?"

"Father," said Earl Philip, speaking up just then, "may I suggest a visit to the commot? See it for yourself. You will quickly get the measure of Elfael. And you will see what Falkes is making of the place."

"A worthy suggestion, Philip," the baron had replied, curling the leather reins around his gloved fist as around the neck of an enemy, "but you know that is impossible. I am away to Rouen within the month. If all goes well, I should return before Christmas."

"I will speak to Abbot Hugo," said Falkes, "and we will hold the consecration at Christmas."

"Rouen is where Duke Robert is encamped," mused Philip, concern wrinkling his smooth brow. "What takes you there, Father?"

Then, while the hounds and their handlers spread out across the field before them, Baron de Braose had confided his plans to meet in secret with a few like-minded noblemen who were anxious to do something about the incessant fighting between the king and his brothers. "Their silly squabble is costing us money that would be better spent on the expansion of our estates and the conquest of Wales," the baron fumed, wiping sweat from his plump round face. "Whenever one of them thumbs his nose at the other, I have to raise an army and sail off to Normandie or Angevin to help the king slap down the knave. I've had a bellyful of their feuding and fighting. Something must be done."

"Dangerous words, Father," cautioned Philip. "I would be careful about repeating any of that anywhere. You never know who is listening."

"Phaw!" scoffed the baron. "I would tell Rufus to his face if he were here. The king must know how his noblemen feel. No, the situation is intolerable, and something must be done. Something will be done, by heaven."

Philip and Falkes exchanged a worried glance. Speech like this was dangerously close to treason. King William, who knew better than anyone else how little his nobles and subjects esteemed him, viewed even the slightest wavering of support as disloyalty; open disagreement was considered outright betrayal.

"If the king learns of this secret *société*, he will not be best pleased," Philip pointed out. "You will all be condemned as traitors."

"The king will not learn of it," the baron boasted. He drew off a glove and swatted at a fly buzzing before his face, then dragged his blue linen sleeve across his forehead. "Special measures have been taken. We have appealed to the archbishop of Rouen, who has agreed to summon a council of noblemen concerning the papal succession."

"The archbishop has recognised Urban as pope," declared Philip, unimpressed with this revelation, "as everyone knows."

"Yes," granted his father, "but Urban's position is faltering just now. He is increasingly out of favour, and Clement occupies Rome. It would not take much to swing the balance his way."

"Is this what you propose to do? Throw the weight of the nobles behind Clement?"

"For certain concessions," the baron replied. "A papal ban on this continual family warring would be a good beginning."

"The king would ignore any declaration the pope might make— just as his father always did," scoffed Philip. *"Comme le père, donc le fils."*

The baron frowned and looked to Falkes. "What say you, Count? Do you agree with my upstart son?"

"It is not my place to agree or disagree, Sire."

"Hmph!" snorted the baron in derision. "What good is that?"

"But if I might offer a suggestion," continued Falkes, choosing his words carefully, "it seems to me that while it is true the king is likely to ignore any censure by the church, were you to establish Clement firmly on the throne of Saint Peter, Clement would be in a position to offer William certain benefits in exchange for a signed treaty of peace between the king and his brothers."

"Precisely," agreed the baron. "Is this not what I was saying?"

"To make good Clement's claim," said Philip, "you must first depose Urban for good. Blood would flow."

"It may not come to that," replied the baron.

"If it did?"

"*Qué será*," answered his father. A drum began beating just then, and Baron de Braose gazed out across the field to a clump of beech trees where the handlers were waiting. "If all goes well, you will receive a sign before Christmas. I will send it with the winter supplies." With that, he put spurs to his mount and galloped away.

Earl Philip watched his father's broad back, his frown a scowl of displeasure. "A word beyond this field and we are dead men," he muttered.

"Count Falkes!" The baron called back to him. "When you catch this phantom raven of yours, let me know. I think I'd like to see him hang."

Well, thought Falkes de Braose as he rode into the town square, *we would all like to see King Raven hang*. And hang he would, there was no doubt about that. But there were other, more pressing matters on his mind than chasing down elusive thieves. And anyway, Elfael had been quiet lately—not an incident in many months. Most likely, the black bird and his band of thieves had been frightened away by the sheriff, and was now raiding elsewhere—someplace where the purses were fatter and the pickings easier.

Count Falkes paused outside Abbot Hugo's stone-built church. It was a handsome building. The abbot had spared no expense, commanding the finest materials available and gathering the best masons, and it showed.

The count had no great love for his abbot, a haughty, high-handed cleric who connived and conspired to get his way in everything—from the cloth of gold for the altar to the lead roof gleaming dully in the sun. That very roof Falkes paused to admire just now. Ordinary thatch was not good enough for Hugo; it had to be lead, cast in heavy sheets in Paris and shipped at great expense across the channel. And then there was the stonework—only the most skilled stonecutters were allowed to work on the archway carvings, producing the finest decoration money could buy. At the church entrance, Falkes stopped to examine a few of the finished sculptures—some of the last to be finished: a dragon with wings, chasing its tail for eternity; a centaur brandishing a sword; a lion and horse intertwined in mortal combat; Aquarius, the water man, with his bucket and ladle; an angel driving Adam and Eve from the Garden; a winged ox; a mermaid rising from the waves clutching an anchor; and more, all of them contained in dozens of small stone plaques around the arch and on the pillars.

Falkes traced the shapely outline of the mermaid with his finger. He had to admit that the work was extraordinary, but then, so was the cost—and increasingly difficult to bear. It meant, among other things, that he required constant support; he was still far too dependent for his survival on regular supplies from his uncle. True, the largest part of the problem was the baron himself, and his unquenchable zeal for conquest. If Baron de Braose was prepared to build slowly, to develop the land and settle the people, Count Falkes had no doubt that Elfael and the territories west could eventually be made to yield untold wealth. But the baron was not willing to wait, and Falkes had to bear the brunt of his uncle's impatience—just as he had to endure the umbrage of the abbot, whose spendthrift ways could well ruin them all.

Falkes entered the church. Cool and dim inside, it breathed an air of quiet serenity despite the steady chink of chisel on stone. He stood for a moment and watched the two masons on the wooden scaffold dressing the capitals of one of the pillars. One of them was carving what looked like a bear, and the other a bird.

"You there!" shouted Falkes, his voice loud in the quiet of the sanctuary. "What is your name?"

541

The masons stopped their work and turned to look down at the count, striding down the centre of the nave. "Me, Sire? I am Ethelric."

"What is that you are carving, Ethelric?"

"A raven, Sire," replied the sculptor, pointing to the leafy bough issuing from the face carved into the top of the pillar. "You can tell by the beak, Sire."

"Remove it."

"Sire?" asked the mason, bewilderment wrinkling his brow.

"Remove it at once. I do not wish to see any such images in this church."

The second stone-carver on the scaffold spoke up. "Begging your pardon, Sire, but the abbot has approved of all the work we are doing here."

"I do not care if the king himself has approved it. I am paying for it, and I do not want it. Remove the hideous thing at once."

"There you are, Count Falkes!" exclaimed Abbot Hugo, moving up the nave to take his place beside the count. His white hair was neatly curled beneath a fine cloth cap, and his robe was glistening white satin. "I saw your horse outside and wondered where you had gone." Glancing at the two stone-carvers on the scaffold, he nodded to them to get back to work and, taking the count by the arm, led Falkes down the aisle. "We'll let these men get on with their work, shall we?"

"But see here," protested the count.

"Come, there is something I wish to show you," said the abbot, surging ahead. "The work is going well. We have years of construction still before us, of course, but the building will soon be service-able. I'm contemplating a consecration ceremony on the eve of All Souls. What do you think of that?"

"I suppose," agreed Falkes diffidently, "although Baron de Braose will not be likely to attend. But see here, that carving in there . . ."

The abbot opened the door and stepped out. "Why not?" he asked, turning back. He looped his arm through the count's and walked him into the market square. "I would very much like the baron to attend. In fact, I insist. He must see what we have achieved here. It is his triumph as much as my own. He must attend."

"I agree, of course," said Falkes. "However, the baron is away in France and not expected to return much before Christmas."

"Pity," sniffed the abbot, none too distraught. "Then we will simply wait. It will give us time to finish more of the corbels and capitals."

"That is what I wanted to speak to you about, Abbot," said Falkes, who went on to explain that his treasury was all but depleted and there would be no more funds to pay the workers. "I sent a letter to the baron—and it, like everything else, awaits his return from France."

Abbot Hugo stopped walking. "What am I to do until then? The men must be paid. They cannot wait until Christmas. The work must continue. The work must go on if we are ever to see the end of it."

"That is as may be," granted the count, "but there is no money to pay them until the baron returns."

"Can you not borrow from somewhere?"

"Do you really need cloth of gold to dress the altar?"

The abbot pursed his lips in a frown.

"You said you wished to show me something," said Falkes.

"This way," said the abbot. They walked across the empty market square to what was left of the former monastery of Llanelli, on whose ruins the town was being raised. The modest chapter house had been enlarged to provide adequate space for the abbot's needs—which, so it appeared to Falkes, were greater than his own, though he had a score of knights to house. Inside, what had been the refectory was now the abbot's private living quarters.

"I have drawn plans for the abbey garden and fields," the abbot said, placing a rolled parchment in the count's hands. "Some wine?"

"You are too kind," said Falkes. Unrolling the skin, he carried it to the room's single window and held it to the light. The outline of the town was a simple square, and the fields, indicated by long narrow parallel lines, seemed to be some distance from the town and almost twice as large as Llanelli itself. "What are you thinking of growing?"

"Flax mostly," replied the abbot, "and barley, of course. We will use what we need and sell the surplus."

"With such a great extent of fields," said the count, "you will surely have a surplus. But I am wondering who will work these fields for you?"

"The monks." Abbot Hugo handed him a cup of wine.

"How many monks do you reckon you will need?"

"As to that," replied the abbot with a smile, "I estimate that I can make do with no fewer than seventy-five, to begin."

"Seventy-five!" cried Falkes. "By the Virgin! If you had said thirty I would have thought that was fifteen too many. Why do you need so many?"

"To carry on the work of Saint Martin." Falkes turned an incredulous gaze upon the abbot who, still smiling, sipped his wine and continued, "It is ambitious, I confess, but we must begin somewhere."

"Saint Martin's?"

"You cannot imagine," said the abbot, "that we would continue to call our new Norman abbey by its old heathen Welsh name. In fact, I have prepared a letter to the pope requesting a charter to be drawn up in the name L'Abbaye de Martin de Saint dans les Champs."

At the mention of the pope, Falkes rolled up the parchment and handed it back to the abbot, saying, "You would be well advised to hold onto that letter a little longer, Abbot."

CHAPTER 8

King Raven's greenwood refuge served in most respects as a village for those forced to call it home. Deep in the forest, King Raven's flock had carved out a clearing below the protecting arm of a stony ridge. At great effort, they had extended the natural glade to include a pitiful little field for barley, a sorry bean patch, and one for turnips. They had dragged together bits of this and that for their huts and crude shelters, and the pens for their few scrawny animals. There was a patched-together tun which served as a granary for storing a scant supply of grain, and a seeping pool at the foot of the rock scarp that served them for a well.

In the days following the archery contest, I came to see the place in a little better light than had greeted me on first sight, but that en't saying much. For it did seem that a lorn and lonely air hung over the place—the vapour of suffering produced by the folk whose lives were bound to this perilous perch. No one was here who had hope of a better life elsewhere—saving, maybe, only myself. Now, a right fair forester like myself might find living in such a place no great hardship for a few weeks, or even months. But even I would be screaming to get free long before a year had come round. And these poor folk had endured it for more than a year—a tribute, I suppose, to Lord Bran and his ability to keep the flame of hope burning in their hearts.

I greatly wondered how they could keep such a place hidden, all the more since there was a bounty on Rhi Bran's head. The baron's reward had been set at a price, and it kept on creeping up, higher and higher as King Raven's deeds became more outrageous and damaging to the de Braose interests. The reward was enough to make me wonder how far some poor fella's loyalty might stretch before it snapped like a rotten rope. I also wondered how long it would be before one of the sheriff's search parties stumbled upon Cél Craidd.

Yet as I settled in amongst my new friends, I soon learned that the location was well chosen to confound discovery; to find it would take a canny and determined forester well trained to the March, which the baron did not possess. Beyond that, the folk worked hard to keep their home secret. They contrived everything from confusing the trails to sowing rumours specially concocted for Norman ears and sending spies among the folk of Elfael and Castle Truan. They kept perpetual watch on the King's Road and the forest approaches 'round about, marking the movements of all who came and went through the March.

Also call me tetched if you will—I came to believe there was something supernatural in it, too. Like in the old legends where the weary traveller comes upon a village hidden among the rocks on the seacoast. He sups there with the local folk and lays him down to sleep in a fine feather bed only to wake raw the next morn with sand in his eyes and seaweed in his hair, and the village vanished never to be found again . . . until it pleases its protectors to show itself to the next footsore wanderer.

I arrived at this odd belief after several curious encounters with Banfáith Angharad. They called her *hudolion* . . .

It means *enchantress*, Odo, thank you for interrupting."

"Ah, it is the same as *hud*, no?" he says, the glint of understanding briefly lighting up his dull eyes. "Enchant."

"Yes, from the same word," I tell him. "And it is pronounced *hood*, so see you set it down aright."

My leg is on fire again today. It pains me ferocious, and I am in no mind to suffer Odo's irritating ways. I watch as he bends his nose to the scrap of parchment and scratches away for a moment. "So now," I say, "while we're about it, his name is not Robin, as you would have it. His name is Rhi Bran—that is, King Bran, to you."

"*Rhi* is the word for *king*, yes, you told me already," he intones wearily. "And Bran—it is the same as Raven, no?"

"Yes, the word is the same. Rhi Bran—King Raven, see? It is the same. I will have you speaking like a Welshman yet, Odo, my lad." I give him a pain-sharp smile. "Just like a true-born son of the Black Country."

Odo frowns and dips his pen. "You were telling me about Angharad," he says, and we resume our meandering march . . .

Indeed. Angharad was wise in ways beyond measure. Accomplished in many arts—some now all but lost—she could read signs and portents, and, as easily as a child tastes rain on the wind, she could foretell the shape of things to come long before they arrived. Old? She was ancient. Wreathed in wrinkles and bent low beneath the weight of years, she appeared to the unsuspecting eye merely one more old soul awaiting Elijah's chariot.

But the eyes in her head were bright as baubles. Her mind was quick and keen, restless as a wave on the strand and deep as that self-same sea. If she sometimes shuffled in her shapeless dress, her mind leapt light-footed and deerlike. Yet she never rushed, never strove, was never seen to be straining after anything. Whatever she needed seemed to come to her of its own accord. And if, betimes, their elders grew uncomfortable in her presence, the children always found peace and comfort in those stout arms.

She was, as I say, adept in all manner of curious arts. And it is through one of these or another that I suspect she purposed to keep Cél Craidd concealed from all intruders. How she did it, I have never yet discovered. But I know the old ones put great store in what they called the *caim*—a saining charm, you might say, useful for protection against many dangers, threats, and ills. Something like this must pro-tect King Raven's roost. Then again, it may be I that am that big a fool and there is no such thing.

I soon came to regard our banfáith not as a doddering, spindle-shanked hag, but as the very life and spirit of Cél Craidd. Her soul was deep and gentle and blessed, her wisdom true as the arrow from Bran's unerring bow, her will resilient as heartwood and stronger than iron. From the flutter of the first dove of morning to the hushed feather-sweep of the midnight owl, nothing eluded her notice. The reach of her restless, searching senses ranged over her forest strong-hold and far, far beyond. At times, I do believe, they reached right into the very castles of the Norman barons.

One particular occasion taught me to respect her judgement, how-ever queer that judgement might seem at first blush. Well, a fine dry winter had set in. I had been some weeks with the forest tribe, learn-ing their ways and getting to know the folk right well. I helped in the fields to gather in the paltry root crop; I chopped firewood by the

wagonload; I helped slaughter two of the three pigs, and salt and smoke
the meat to keep over the winter. I also turned my hand at building two
new huts—one for a family that had come a week or so earlier than
myself, and one for a young widow and her wee daughter rescued from
Count Falkes's marauders and their hounds.

Mostly, however, I went hunting with Iwan, Siarles, and one or
two of the other men. Occasionally, Bran would join us; more often,
Iwan led the party. Siarles, whose skills as a forester were greater even
than my own, always served as guide since he knew the greenwood
well: where the deer would be found, around which bend the pigs
would appear, or when the birds would flock or fly. A good and worthy huntsman, uncanny in his own way, he made sure we rarely
returned empty-handed from the chase. To be sure, it was desperate
hunting—we brought back game or we went hungry.

In all these things, I was tested in small ways, and never openly.
Still, through a word or gesture, or a glance exchanged, I soon came to
understand that, while they accepted my presence among them, they
did not wholly trust me yet. They were testing both my abilities and
mettle, as well as my honour. This was only natural, I know, for a
folk whose lives depended on remaining out of sight. The baron's
spies were everywhere, and the abbot was a wily, relentless foe. King
Raven lived or died on the loyalty of his flock, even as they lived or
died with him.

So, they watched and they tested. Far from begrudging them their
doubt, I welcomed every opportunity to prove myself.

"What's that, Odo? Strayed from the point, you say?" Lately, our
Odo has taken to interrupting me whenever he thinks I have wandered
too far afield and may not be able to make it back to the place of my

departure. So he checks me with a word or two. "Perhaps," I allow, "but it is all of a piece, you see."

"That is as may be," he says, rubbing his bald priest patch. "But you were speaking of an incident that, ah"—he scans his scribbled scrip—"taught you to trust Angharad's wisdom."

"Right you are, Odo, lad. So I was. Well, then . . . where was I?"

"The days were growing dimmer and a fine dry winter had set in."

He resumes writing, and we go on . . .

One morning a few days before Christmas, I heard the call of a raven, but thought nothing of it until I saw people hurrying to the bare circle of earth beneath the tree they called Council Oak. "Will! Come, join us," called Iwan. "It is the summons!"

Angharad was there, wrapped head to foot in her cloak, although the day was mild enough for that time of year and the sun, low in the southern sky, was bright. Standing beside her was a small boy; I'd seen him before darting here and there about the place, always moving, never still. He seemed a clever, curious child, and a favourite of Bran's among the youngsters.

"Gwion Bach has news from Elfael," she announced when Bran had taken his place. "Count Falkes is expecting winter supplies from his uncle, the baron. The wagons are to arrive any day."

"Is it known what is coming?" asked Bran.

"Grain and wine, cloth and such," she replied, glancing at the boy, who gave a slight nod. "And some things for the abbot's new church."

"Any day," mused Bran. "Not much time."

"None to lose," agreed the hudolion.

"Then we must hurry if we are to make ready a warm welcome for them." Bran was already moving towards his hut. "Iwan! Siarles! To me!" He paused in midstep, turned, and regarded me as if weighing the prudence of taking an untried hound a-hunting with the pack.

I sensed his reluctance and guessed what he was thinking. "My lord, I stand ready to lend both hand and heart to whatever command you give me." Indicating young Gwion Bach, who was following in his lord's footsteps, I said, "But if even children serve you in this fight, then perhaps you would not deny a willing elder to aid you in your purpose."

He nodded once, deciding it then and there. "Come along, Will. Join us."

"Rhi Bran!" Angharad called after him. "One thing more—something else comes with the wagons."

"Yes?"

"There will be snow," she said, gathering her robe around her more tightly.

Bran accepted this without hesitation, but I had not yet learned to honour these utterances with unquestioning belief. Unable to help myself, I glanced up at the sky, bright and fine, and not the least smudge of a cloud to be seen anywhere. The amused expression on my face must have given me away, for as I stood looking on, Bran called to me. "What, Will? Could it be that you doubt our good ban-fáith's word?"

"Nay, Lord," I replied, softening his accusation. "Let us rather say that it will be the first time I've seen snow from a clear blue sky."

"Hmph!" sniffed Angharad, muttering as she stumped away, "These old bones know snow when they feel it."

I followed Bran to his hut and took my place alongside the other two. Iwan seemed comfortable enough with my presence, but Siarles did not appear to prize it much. Even so, I was there at the king's pleasure, so there was nothing to be said or done. "It seems the baron

551

in his boundless generosity is sending us a Christmas blessing," Bran said. "We must make ready to receive it with all good grace."

The other two grinned at the thought, and all three began planning how best to greet the supply wagons when they passed through the forest on their way to Castle Truan. I listened to their talk, keeping my own counsel—as I was yet a little uncertain what manner of outlawry I had fallen into. Every now and then, the name *King Raven* arose in their discussion. It was the first time I had heard the name used among them in just this way. It was Bran himself they meant, and yet all three spoke of him as if it were someone else.

Finally, after this had gone on awhile, I asked, "Pardon my ignorance, Lord, but are you not King Raven?"

"Of course," replied Bran, "as you already know."

"To be sure," I said, "but why when you speak the name do you say, 'he will go . . .' or, '. . . when he calls . . .' and the like, if it is yourself you mean?"

Bran laughed.

Iwan answered, "It is Bran and not Bran. See?"

"Again, I must beg pardon. But that makes no sense to this dull head at all."

"Bran is King Raven," Siarles explained, giving me a superior smile, "but King Raven is not Bran."

"Sorry." I shook my head. "I may be slow of wit, God knows, but it still seems nonsense to me."

Bran said, "Then you'll just have to wait and see."

Well, we spent most of the day planning the welcome for the baron's supply train. While they talked about all they would do, I still had little real idea what to expect save for my part in the proceedings, which amounted to little more than watching the road and being ready with a bow in case events did not fall out as predicted.

Scarlet

A few of the Grellon were involved, but not many, and none of them was given duty at the sharp end. Bran, Siarles, and Iwan assumed the greatest risk and made particular efforts to keep the people both out of sight and out of danger as much as possible.

Oh, but it would be dangerous. There was no avoiding that.

565

CHAPTER 9

It was an odd thing: everyone scurrying around like ants in the rain—the children dragging wood into heaps near the door of each hut, and the women bundling foodstuffs, and the men drawing water and snugging the shelters—all labouring under a clear, bright sky to prepare for snow, the only hint of which was a twinge in an old woman's bones.

While the rest of us were taking such measures against the coming storm, Iwan and Siarles went to spy out the best place for the welcome. We did not know how many soldiers would come with the wagons, nor how many wagons there might be. But Iwan and Siarles knew the road and knew where an ambush might succeed.

They were gone all that short winter's day, returning at dusk. Upon arrival, they went directly to our lord's hut. Tired from the day's work, I settled by the common fire where a stew pot was bubbling, to warm myself and wait for the food to be served. "You were busy all day," observed a woman nearby.

"I was that." I turned to see Mérian, bundled in her cloak, taking her place on the log beside me. "My lady, I give you good greeting."

"You didn't go with the others," she observed.

"No, there was enough to be done here. They only went to see where the wagons might pass."

"To see where the wagons might be attacked," she corrected. "That is what you mean."

"Yes, I suppose that is my meaning." She made a small tut of disapproval. "You do not agree with the king in this?"

"Whether I agree or not makes no difference," she replied crisply. "The point is that Bran will never achieve peace with the baron if he insists on raiding and thieving. It only angers the baron and provokes him and the count to ever more cruel reprisals."

"You are right, of course," I agreed. "But from where I stand, I don't see Rhi Bran making peace with the baron or the count, either one. He wants to punish them."

"He wants the return of his throne," she corrected crisply, "and he will not achieve it by plundering a few supply wagons."

"No, perhaps not."

"There!" she said, as if she had won a victory herself. "You agree. You see what must be done."

"My lady?"

"You must talk to Bran and persuade him to change his mind about the raid."

"Me?" I said. "I cannot. I dare not."

"Why?" she said, turning her large dark eyes on me.

"It is not my place."

"I would have thought it the place of any right-thinking man to help his lord whenever he can. Certainly, if you saw him sticking his hand in a nest of vipers you would warn him."

I regarded her closely before answering. "My lady, please," I said. "I cannot do as you ask. Iwan might, and I daresay Siarles would risk it. But Will here cannot. I do beg your pardon."

She lifted one slender shoulder and sighed. "Oh, very well. It was worth a try. Do not think poorly of me, Will Scarlet. It is just that . . ." She paused to find the right word. "I get so vexed with him sometimes. He will not listen to me, and I don't know what else to do."

I accepted this in silence, stretching my hands towards the flames.

"I know he will get himself killed one day," she continued after a time. "If the sheriff catches him, or one of the baron's men, Bran is as good as dead before the sun sets."

"You worry about him."

"Truly, I do so worry," she confided. "I do not think I could bear losing him again."

"Again?"

She nodded, growing pensive. "It was just after the Ffreinc came to Elfael. The king—Bran's father, Lord Brychan—had been killed and all the warband with him. Only Iwan survived." She went on to describe how Bran had been seized and taken hostage by Count Falkes, and how he had fled the cantref. "He might have made good his escape, but he stopped to help a farmer and his wife who were being attacked by the count's rogues. He fought them off, but others came and gave chase. They caught him, and he was wounded and left for dead." She paused, adding in a softer voice, "Word went out that he had been killed . . . and so I thought. Everyone thought he had been killed. I only learned the truth very much later."

She drew breath as if there was more she would say, but thought better of it just then, for she fell silent instead.

"How did Bran survive?" I asked after a moment.

"Angharad found him," she explained, "and brought him back to life. He has lived in the forest ever since."

I considered this. It explained the curious bond I sensed between the old woman and the young man, and the way in which he honoured her. I thought on this for a time, content in the silence and the warmth of the flames.

"He won't always live in the forest," I said, more to have something to say and so prolong our time together.

"No?" she replied, glancing sideways at me. She was kneading her fingers before the fire, and the flames made her eyes shine bright.

"Why, he intends to win back his throne. You said so yourself just now. When that happens, I expect we will all bid the forest a fond fare-thee-well."

"But that will never happen," she insisted. "Does no one see? The baron is too strong, his wealth too great. He will never let Elfael go. Am I the only one who sees the truth?" She shook her head sadly. "What Bran wants is impossible."

"Well," I said, "I wouldn't be too sure. I have seen the lone canny fox outwit the hunter often enough to know that it matters little how many horses and men you have. All the wealth and weapons in the world will not catch the fox that refuses to be caught."

She smiled at that, which surprised me. "Do you really think so?"

"God's truth, my lady. That is exactly what I think."

"Thank you for that." She smiled again and laid her hand on my arm. "I am glad you are here, Will."

Just then, the first fresh flakes of snow arrived. One brushed her forehead and caught on her dark eyelashes. She blinked and looked up as the snow began to fall gently all around. God help me, I did not look at the snow. I saw only Mérian.

s she?" Odo wants to know. His question brings me out of a reverie, and I realise I've drifted off for some moments.

"Is she what, lad?" I ask.

"Is she very beautiful—as beautiful as they say?"

"Oh, lad, she is all that and more. It is not her face or hair or fine noble bearing—it is all these things and more. She is a right fair figure of a woman, and I will trounce the man who slanders her good name. She was born to be a queen—and if there is a God in heaven, that is what she will be."

"Pity," sniffs Odo. "With men like you to protect her, I wouldn't give a rat's whisker for her chances. Most likely, she'll share the noose with your Rhi Bran."

Oh, this makes me angry. "Listen, you little pus pot of a priest," I say, my voice low and tight. "This en't finished yet, not by a long walk. So, if you have any other clever ideas like this, keep 'em under your skirt." Tired of him, of my confinement, sick of the pain that burns in my wounded leg, I lean back on my filthy pallet and turn my face away.

Odo is silent a moment, as well he should be, then says, "Sorry, Will, I did not mean to offend you. I only meant—"

"It makes no matter," I tell him. "Read back where we left off."

He does, and we go on.

he snow fell through the night. We awoke to a thick layer of white fluff over the forest. Branches dragged down and saplings bent low beneath the weight of cold, wet snow. Our little village of low-roofed huts lay almost hidden beneath this shroud. Early yet, the sun was just rising as we gathered our gear and made our final preparations. After a quick meal of black bread, curds, and apples, we gathered to receive our marching orders.

"Here," said Siarles, handing me what appeared to be a bundle of rags covered with bark and twigs and leaf wrack, "put this on."

Taking the bundle, I shook it out and held it up before me. "A cloak?" I asked, none too certain of my guess. Long, ragged, dun-coloured things with all manner of forest ruck sewn on, they looked like the pelt of some fantastical woodland creature born of tree and fern.

"We wear these when moving about the forest," he said, pulling a similar garment around his shoulders. "Good protection."

Folk—whether two-legged or four—are difficult enough to see in dense wood. This, any forester will tell you for nothing. Wearing these cloaks, a fella would be well-nigh impossible to see even for eyes trained in tracking game along tangled pathways through dense brush in the dim or faulty light that is the forest. Nevertheless, bless me for a dunce, I saw a flaw in the plan. "It has snowed," I said.

"You noticed," replied Siarles. "Oh, you're a shrewd one, no mistake." He indicated a basket into which the others were digging. "Get busy."

The basket was filled with scrags of sheep's wool, birch bark, and scraps of bleached linen and such which we fixed to the distinctive hooded cloaks of the Grellon, quickly adapting them for use in the snow.

One of the men, Tomas—a slender, light-footed little Welshman—helped me with mine, then set it on my shoulders just right and adjusted the hood as I drew the laces tight. I did the same for him, and Iwan passed among us with bow staves, strings, and bags of arrows. I tucked the strings into the leather pouch at my belt and slung the bag upon my back. At Bran's signal, we fell in behind Iwan and tried our best to keep up with his great, ground-covering stride; no easy chore in the best of times, it was made more difficult still by the snow.

After a while we came to a place beneath the great overhanging limbs of oak and ash and hornbeam where the path was wide and still mostly dry. I found myself walking beside Tomas. "Once in Hereford, a man told me a tale about Abbot Hugo losing his gold candlesticks to King Raven," I said, opening a question that had been rumbling around in my skull for some time now. "Is it true at all?"

"Aye, 'tis true," Tomas assured me. "Mostly."

"Which part? Pardon my asking."

"What did you hear?" he countered.

"There were twenty wagons full of gold and silver church treasure, they said—and all of it under guard of a hundred mounted knights and men-at-arms. They say King Raven swooped down, killed the soldiers with his fiery breath, and snatched away the gold candlesticks to use in unholy devil rites," I told him. "That's what I heard."

"We did stop the wagons and help lighten the load," replied the Welshman. "And there was some gold, yes, and the candlesticks— that's true enough. But there were never a hundred knights."

"Twenty, more like," put in Siarles, who had overheard us talking.

"Aye, only twenty," confirmed Iwan, joining in. "And there weren't but three oxcarts. Still, we got more than seven hundred marks in that one raid, not counting the candlesticks."

"And how much since then?" I asked, thinking I had come into a most gainful employment.

"A little here and there," said Siarles. "Nothing much."

"Only some pigs and a cow or two now and then," put in Iwan.

"Aye, any that wander too close to the forest," said Tomas. "Them's ours."

"But the way people talk you'd think the raids were ten-a-day."

"You can't help the way people talk," Iwan said. "We might stop the odd wagon betimes to remind folk to respect King Raven's wood, but there was only the one big raid."

"What did you do with all the money?"

"We gave it away," said Tomas, a note of pride in his voice. "Gave it to Bishop Asaph to build a new monastery."

"All of it?"

"Most of it," agreed Iwan placidly. "We still have a little kept by."

"Thing is," said Siarles, "silver coin isn't all that useful in the forest."

"We give out what is needful to the folk of Elfael to help keep body and soul together."

I had heard this part of the tale, too, but imagined it merely wishful thinking on the part of those telling the story. It seemed, however, the generosity of Rhi Bran the Hud was true even if the greater extent of his notorious activities was not.

"Just the one big raid? Why so?"

"Two good reasons," Iwan replied.

"It is flamin' dangerous," put in Siarles.

"To be sure," said Iwan. "It does no one any good if we are caught or killed in a needless fight. Neither did we want the Ffreinc to become so wary they would make the escorts too large to easily defeat . . ."

"Or change the route the wagons followed," Siarles said. The slight edge to his tone suggested that he did not altogether agree with the caution of his betters.

"As a result," continued Iwan, "the Ffreinc have grown lax of late. Because they have passed through the forest without trouble these many months, they think they can come and go at will now. Today, we will remind them who allows them this right."

Such prudence, I thought. They would not spend themselves except for great and certain gain, nor kill the goose that laid the silver eggs. Meanwhile, they watched and waited for those chances worthy of their interest.

"Am I to take it that today's supply train is of sufficient value to make a raid worth the risk?"

"That is what we shall soon discover." Iwan surged on ahead, and it was all we could do to keep up with him.

Finally, as the unseen sun stretched toward midday, we came in sight of the King's Road. Here we stopped, and Bran addressed us and delivered his final instructions. My own part was neither demanding nor all that dangerous so long as things went according to plan. I was to work my way along the road to a position a little south of the others, there to lie in wait for the supply train. I was to keep out of sight and be ready with my bow if anything went amiss.

Just before he sent us to our places, Bran said, "Let no one think we do this for ourselves alone. We do it for Elfael and its long-suffering folk, and may God have mercy on our souls. Amen."

CHAPTER 10

men!" We pledged our lives with our king's, and then stood for a moment, listening to the hush of a woodland subdued beneath the falling snow. And there was that much to goad a fella to reflection. Some or all of us might be dead before the day's journey had run, and there's a thought to make a man think twice.

"You heard him, lads. Be about your work," said Iwan, and we all scattered into the forest.

I moved a few dozen paces along the roadside and found a place behind the rotting bole of a fallen pine. It lay atop the slight rise of a bank overlooking the road below with a clear view ahead to the place where our rude welcome would commence. Trying not to disturb the snow too much, I cleared me a place and heaped up some dry leaves and pine branches, and lay my bowstave lengthwise along the underside of the pine trunk, where it would be somewhat protected from the snow and ready to hand. Then I hunkered down amongst the boughs and bracken. I need not have worried about leaving too many telltale signs, for the snow kept falling, gradually becoming heavier as the morning wore on. By midday the tracks we'd made had been filled in, removing any traces of disturbance. All the world lay beneath a clean, unbroken breast of glimmering white.

I sat and watched the flakes spin down, snow on snow, and still it fell. The day passed in silence, and aside from a few birds and squirrels, I saw no movement anywhere near the road. All remained so quiet I began to think that the soldiers guarding the supply train had thought better of continuing their journey and decided to lay up somewhere until the snow stopped and travel became easier. Maybe little Gwion Bach had it wrong and the wagons were not coming at all.

The daylight, never bright, began to falter as the snow fell thicker and faster. Warm as a cock in a dovecot under my cloak, I dozed a little the way a hunter will, alert though his eyes are closed, and passed the time in my half-sheltered nook . . .

. . . and awakened to the smell of smoke.

I looked around. Nothing had changed. The road was still empty. There was no sign of anyone passing or having passed; the snow was still falling in soft, clumping flakes. The light was dimmer now, the winter day fading quickly into an early gloom.

And then I heard it: the light jingle of a horse's tack.

I fished a dry string from my pouch and was rigging the bow before the sound came again. I shook the snow off from the bag of arrows and opened it. Bless me, there were nine black arrows inside— black from crow feather to iron tip. I placed four of them upright along the trunk of the tree in front of me, and blew gently on my hands to steady and warm them.

Oh, a fella can get a bit cramped waiting in the snow. I tried to loosen my stiff limbs a little without making too much commotion.

The sound came again and, again, the faint whiff of smoke. I had no time to wonder at this, for at that same instant two riders appeared.

The snow softened all sound but the jingle of the tack as they rode, and the hooves of their horses breaking a path in the snow. Big men—knights—they loomed larger still in their padded leather jerkins and long winter cloaks which covered their mail shirts. Helmeted and gauntleted, their shields were on their backs and their lances were tucked into the saddle carriers; their swords were sheathed.

They passed quietly up the road and out of sight. I counted slow beats until those following them should arrive. But none came after.

I waited.

After a time, the first two returned, hastening back the way they had come. When they reached a place just below my overlook, one of the riders stopped and sent the other on ahead while he tarried there.

Scouts, I thought. Wary, they were, and right prudent to be so.

The soldier below me was so close, I could smell the damp horse-hair scent of his mount and see the steam puff from the animal's nostrils and rise from its warm, sodden rump. I kept my head low and remained dead still the while, as would a hunter in the deer blind. In a moment, I heard the jingle of horse's tack once more and the second rider reappeared. This time, eight mounted soldiers followed in his wake. All of them joined the first knight, who ordered the lot to take up positions along either side of the road.

So now! These were not complacent fools. They had identified the hollow as potentially dangerous and were doing what they could to pare that danger to a nub. As the last soldier took his place, the first wagon hove into view. A high-sided wain, like that used to carry hay and grain, it was pulled by a double team of oxen, its tall wheels sunk deep in the snow-covered ruts of the King's Road. And though the wagon bed was covered against the snow, it was plain to a blind man by the way the animals strained against the yoke that the load was heavy indeed. Within moments of the first wain passing, a second followed.

567

The oxen plodded slowly along, their warm breath fogging in the chill air, the falling snow settling on their broad backs and on their patient heads between wide-swept horns.

No more appeared.

The ox-wains trundled slowly down between the double ranks of mounted knights, and that hint of smoke tickled my nostrils again— nor was I the only one this time, no mistake. The soldiers' horses caught the scent too, and came over all jittery-skittery. They tossed their fine big heads and whinnied, chafing the snow with hooves the size of bleeding-bowls.

The soldiers were not slow to notice the fuss their mounts were making; the knights looked this way and that, but nothing had changed in the forest 'round about. No danger loomed.

As the first wain reached the far end of the corridor, I caught a flicker of yellow through the trees. A glimmering wink o' light. Just that quick and gone again. With it, there came a searing, screeching whine, like the sound an arrow-struck eagle might make as it falls from the sky.

The short hairs on my arms and neck stood up to hear it, and I looked around. In that selfsame moment, one of the scouts' horses screamed, and broke ranks. The stricken animal reared and plunged, its legs kicking out every direction at once. The rider was thrown from the saddle, and as he scrambled to regain control of his mount, the animal reared again and went over, falling onto its side.

The other knights watched, but held firm and made no move to help the fella. They were watching still when there came another keening shriek and another horse reared—this one on the other side of the long double rank. As with the first animal, the second leapt and plunged and tried to bolt, but the rider held it fast.

As the poor beast whirled and screamed, I chanced to see what none of the soldiers had yet seen: sticking from the horse's flank low behind the saddle was the feathered stub of a black arrow.

The knight yelled something to the soldier nearest him. My little bit of the Frankish tongue serves me well enough most times, but I could not catch hold of what he said. He flung out a beseeching hand as the horse beneath him collapsed. Another soldier in the line gave out a cry—and all at once his horse likewise began to rear and scream, kicking its hind legs as if to smite the very devil and his unseen legions.

Before a'body could say "Saint Gerald's jowls," three more horses—two on the far side of the road and one on the near side—heaved up and joined in that dire and dreadful dance. The terrified animals crashed into one another, bucking and lashing, throwing their riders. One of the beasts bolted into the wood; the others fell thrashing in the snow.

It was then one of the knights caught sight of what was causing all this fret and flurry: an arrow sticking out from the belly of a downed horse. With a loud cry, he drew his sword and called upon his fellows to up shields and hunker down. His shouts went unheeded, for the other knights were suddenly fighting their own mounts. The poor brutes, already frightened by the scent of smoke and blood and the sight of the other animals flailing around, broke and ran.

The soldiers could no longer hold their terrified mounts.

The wagon drivers, fearful and shaking in their cloaks, had long since halted their teams. The commander of the guard—one of the two fellas I had first seen—spurred his mount into the middle of the road and began shouting at his men. Black arrows cut his horse from under him just that quick, and he had to throw himself from the saddle to avoid being crushed.

Dragging himself to his feet, he shouted to his men once more, trying to rally them to his side. Then, over and above the shouts and

569

confusion, there arose a cry from the wood the like of which I had never heard before: the tortured shriek of a creature enraged and in terrible agony, and it echoed through the trees so that no one could tell whence it came.

The sound faded into a tense and uneasy silence. The Norman soldiers put hands to their weapons, turning this way and that, ready to defend themselves against whatever might come.

The screech rang out again, closer this time—devilishly close— and, if possible, even louder and angrier.

Three more horses went down, and the last followed in turn. Now all the knights were afoot, their mounts dead or dying. Oh, but it was a sorrowful sight—those proud destriers flailing away in the bloodred snow. It fair brought a sorry tear to the eye to see such fine animals slaughtered, I can tell you.

The commander of the knights summoned his soldiers to him. They seized their lances and hastened to join their commander. Back-to-back, weapons drawn, they formed a tight circle and waited behind their long, pointed shields for the next flight of cursed black arrows.

For a moment, all was quiet save for the quick breathing of the men and the neighing of the wounded horses. And then . . .

I saw a clump of snow fall from an elm branch overhead, sending a glistening curtain of down upon the road. When the frozen dust settled, there he was: King Raven. Black as Satan's tongue from the crown of his head to booted feet, and covered all over with feathers, great wings outspread with long, curving claws on the ends. But the thing which gave him the look of the pit was the absolutely smooth, round skull-like face with its wide hollow eyes and unnaturally long sword of a beak.

King Raven—it could be none other.

The knights saw this phantom creature and shrank back at the sight. I forgave them their fright. I felt it, too. Indeed, it seemed as if the day, already cold and dim, grew cold and dark as the grave in the moment of his appearing.

That dread beak rose slowly until it pointed straight up toward the dense webwork of snow-laden branches and boughs. The creature loosed another of its horrific cries. As if in reply, I saw a bright flicker in the air, and a flaming brand landed in the snow midway between King Raven and the cowering knights. Another joined the first—more or less the same distance from the knights, but behind them. Then a third fell behind the second—to the left of the huddled body of knights this time. A fourth fell among the others, on the opposite side of the third. I saw it arc high through the surrounding trees, and before it had even touched the ground, three more were in the air.

The knights, stunned and lifeless with disbelief, were ringed about with fire. The torches sputtered in the snow, sending thick black smoke boiling up through the down-drifting flakes.

So far, all had fallen out as planned, and I imagined we would escape clean away with the goods. But bad luck has a knack for catching a fella when he least can abide it. Even as our numb fingers reached for victory, ill fortune arrived in the person of Abbot Hugo. Dressed in a white satin robe with white leather boots and a woollen cloak of rich dark purple, he appeared more king than cleric as he came galloping into the clearing. With him was Marshal Guy de Gysburne, commanding a small company of oafish louts spoiling for a fight.

Truth be told, at the time I did not know who these men might be, though I would be learning soon enough. All I knew was that they had come to the banquet as guests uninvited, and had to be driven off before one or another of our folk got hurt.

Well, they burst into the clearing, weapons drawn, ready to start lopping heads and making corpses. Eight soldiers not counting the

571

abbot broke into the ring of torches. Guy, all in mail and leather, greaves and gorget, charged ahead on a pale grey destrier. He took one look at the black-feathered phantom, reared up in the saddle, and let fly with his lance.

King Raven darted lightly to the side as the spear sailed past, easily evading the throw, even as I nocked one of the black arrows onto the string and, holding my breath, drew and aimed at the marshal.

Someone else had the same idea.

Out from the brushwood beside the trail streaked an arrow. It blazed across the clearing, struck Guy, and slammed him backwards in the saddle as he reached to draw his sword.

That reaching saved his life, I think. The arrow pierced the steel rings of his hauberk at the fleshy part of his upper arm and stuck there. If he had been more upright in the saddle, he'd have had it in his bonnet. As it was, he dropped the sword and called his men to shield themselves as the arrows began falling thick and fast.

Three men went down before they could unsling their shields, and a fourth took an arrow in the back the instant he swung it around to protect his chest. They fell like stones dropped in a well.

Abbot Hugo, shouting in Ffreinc, drove into the clearing, heedless of the missiles flying around him. Well, I suppose killing a priest is serious business—Norman or no—and Hugo maybe felt safe even with men falling all around him. Or, it may be he is that brave or stupid. Even so, he was urging the knights and men-at-arms to throw off their fear and attack, but that showed no understanding of the nature of the assault. A fella afoot cannot strike what he cannot see, and a warrior on a horse cannot charge into the brush and brake if he hopes to live out the day.

The soldiers on foot drew together, trying to form a shield ring to give them protection from the whistling death all around. I loosed two, and made good account of myself so that, by now, any soldier still in the saddle threw himself to the ground even as his horse was slaughtered beneath him. Those who somehow escaped being skewered with an oaken shaft scuttled on hands and knees to join the others as arrow after arrow slammed into the shield wall, splintering the wood, ripping the leather-covered panels apart, striking with the force of heavy hammers. I sent two more arrows to join those of the others.

The commander of the knights showed heart, if not brains. He struggled to his feet and, shield thrown high to protect his head, broke ranks, charging off in the direction of the main attack. He made but four steps from the ring before an arrow found him. There was a thin whisper as it cut through the snow-clotted air. I caught the dull glimmer of the metal head—and then the knight was lifted off his feet and thrown back a pace by the shock of the oaken missile driving into his chest.

He was dead before his heels came to rest in the snow.

Marshal Guy, clutching his arm with the slender shaft sticking out both sides of the wound, gave his thumping great warhorse his head, and the animal charged the black-cloaked phantom standing in the trail at the far end of the clearing.

King Raven stood motionless for a moment, allowing the beast and wounded rider to come nearer, lifting his long, narrow beak to the sky as if taunting them. As the horse closed the distance between them, Guy released his bloody arm and drew the dagger from his belt, making a clumsy swipe with his left hand.

The phantom ducked under the stroke. As the big horse sped by, he gave a last wild shriek and turned, wings spread wide, retreating not into the wood, as anyone might expect, but straight down the centre of the road—the way the wagons had come.

Abbot Hugo, seeing his adversary on the run, reined up and

screamed for the soldiers to give chase, but they remained cowering behind their shields. Crying down heaven on their craven heads, the abbot threatened strong punishment for any and all who disobeyed. The soldiers looked around, and when they saw King Raven fly, they did what Norman soldiers always do when an enemy retreats: they followed.

The soldiers, weighed down by their long mail shirts and shields and heavy cloaks and what have you, lurched through the snow after King Raven, who was swift and nimble as a bird. The abbot and marshal charged after them, guarding the rear. That soon, all of them disappeared from my view; I waited, wondering what would happen next. The drivers must have wondered, too, for they stood on the wagon benches and gazed into the murk after the departing soldiers. One of them shouted for the guardsmen, calling them back; but no reply was returned.

He did not shout again. Before he could draw breath, four cloaked figures swarmed out of the forest and onto the wain; I saw Tomas and Siarles leading the flock, two men to each wagon. While one of the Grellon threw a cloak over the head of the driver and pulled him off his bench, the other took up the ox goad and began driving the team.

The two wagons were taken up the road a little way to a place where the track dipped into a dell. Upon reaching the dingle, wonder of wonders, the wall of bush and brush beside the road parted and the oxen were led off the track and into the wood. As the second wagon followed the first into the brake, four more of the Grellon appeared and began smoothing out the tracks in the snow with pine branches.

The two drivers were bound in their cloaks, dragged to the side of the road, and each one left beside a dead horse where, I suppose, they might stay a mite warmer for a while. Frightened out of their wits, they lay still as dead men, offering only the occasional soft whimper to show the world they were still alive.

New snow was carried in reed baskets and spread lightly over any remaining tracks, and then the Grellon departed, flitting away into the gloaming, vanishing as quickly and quietly as they had appeared.

I waited for a time, listening, but heard only the whispering hush of falling snow. I did not know what would happen next, and wondered if the attack was over and I should now begin making my way back to Cél Craidd. The wood was growing dark, and if I did not leave soon it would be a lonely slog on a frozen night for old Will.

Nothing moved in the forest or on the ground, save the lone wounded man who had taken the arrow in his back. He lay with the dead, moaning and trying now and then to rise, but lacking the strength. I felt that sorry for the fella, I thought that if someone did not come back for him soon, I might risk putting him out of his misery. But my orders were to watch and wait, so that is what I would do until told otherwise. I kept my eyes sharp and bided my time.

Winter twilight deepened the shadows, and the snow had been steadily melting into my cloak; the icy damp was spreading across my shoulders. As night came on, I knew I would have to leave my post soon or freeze there with the corpses on the trail.

As I was pondering this, I heard someone approaching on the road from the dingle where the wagons had disappeared in the direction of Elfael. In a moment, a man on horseback emerged from the gathering gloom. Not a tall man, he sat his saddle straight as a rod, his head high. Across his legs was folded a deerskin robe; his hat had a thin, folded brim which was pointed in front like the sharp prow of a seagoing ship. Heavily swaddled against the winter storm, he wore a monk's cloak of brown coarse-woven cloth secured at the throat with a thick brooch of heavy silver. Even from a distance in the failing light, I could tell he was more devil than monk: something about that narrow hatchet-shaped nose and jutting chin, the cruel slant of those close-set eyes, gave me to know that Richard de Glanville was happier with a noose in his hand than a rosary.

He reined up at the carcase of the first dead horse, regarded it, and then slowly swept his eyes across to one of the dead knights. He observed the arrows jutting rudely from the corpses and, after due contemplation, let out a shrill whistle. I've heard the same when falconers call their hawks to roost and, quick enough, four riders emerged from the gloaming to join him on the road . . .

V es, Odo, this was the first time I laid eyes on the sheriff," I tell him. My monkish friend knows well of whom I speak. Our sheriff is a right sharp thorn of a man and that nasty—a man who thinks frailty a fatal contagion, and considers mercy the way most folk view the Black Death.

"If it was the first time," says my scribe, "how did you know it was the sheriff?"

"Well," says I with a scratch of my head, "the authority of the man could not be mistaken."

"Even in a snowstorm?" asks Brother Odo with the smarmy smile he uses when he thinks he has caught me decorating the truth a little too extravagantly for his taste.

"Even in a snowstorm, monk," I tell him. "Anyway, it was the same with Abbot Hugo and Marshal Guy—if I did not know their names right off the first I saw them, I knew them well enough before the day was over. More's the pity, Odo, my friend. More's the pity."

Odo grunts in begrudging agreement, and we stumble on . . .

The sheriff's men quickly dismounted and began searching among the dead men and horses for survivors. De Glanville remained in the saddle; he did not deign to get his fine boots wet, I reckon.

Well, they found the bundled-up wagon drivers, untied them, and brought them to stand before the sheriff. The drivers were still quaking from fright and gawking around as if they expected to be swooped upon by the phantom bird again. Under the sheriff's stern questioning, however, they soon lost their fear of the great preying bird. The sheriff had them now, and he was flesh-and-blood fiercer than any phantom or host of unseen archers.

I could tell from the way the ox handlers were gesturing and squawking that they were filling the sheriff's ears with their weird and wonderful tale. Oh, yes! And I could tell by the way the sheriff's scowl deepened by the moment that he was having none of it. He listened to them prate a while, and then cut off their mewling with a shout that travelled through the silent wood like a clap. Wheeling his mount, he cantered down the King's Road in the direction the abbot and soldiers had gone, passing so close to my perch I could have reached down and plucked that absurd hat from his pointy head.

He rode on, leaving his men and the ox drivers behind. Meanwhile, I studied hard to see what they might find, but was relieved to see that the snow had mostly filled in the tracks of men and beasts and wagon wheels; the only disturbance now to be seen was that left by the sheriff and his men themselves.

Soon enough, de Glanville returned. Close on his heels came Abbot Hugo and the marshal and the surviving soldiers. The fighting men were that weary and out of breath, they could hardly hold their weapons upright. King Raven had led them a wild chase right enough. Their snow-caked feet dragged, and their hair was stringy wet beneath their steel caps; they looked as cold and damp and limp as their own soggy cloaks.

They assembled in the road, gawking at the dead horses and knights, casting many a sideways glance into the wood lest the phantom catch them unawares. After a brief word with the sheriff, Marshal Guy sent his knights and the remaining soldiers and wagon drivers down the road. It would be a long, frozen walk to Count de Braose's castle, and I did not envy them the welcome they would likely receive. The wounded soldier, clinging to life, was taken up behind one of the sheriff's men, and they all clattered off with a rattle of tack and weapons.

Thoughts of home fires and welcomes put me in mind of a nice steaming bowl of something hot, and I was that close to quitting my post and finding my way back home . . . but glanced back to see that the sheriff had not yet departed. He simply sat there on his horse, alone, in the middle of the road, waiting. I could in no wise leave before he did, so I stayed put.

Good thing, too.

For as winter twilight settled over the forest, out from the undergrowth stumbled a man with two fat hares slung on a snare line over his neck, and another in his hand. I did not recognise the fella and supposed he was from Elfael—a farmer, out to get a little meat for his table.

"You there!" shouted the sheriff, his voice loud in the quiet glade. Startling as it was, it took a moment before I realised old rat face was speaking English. "Stand where you are!"

The poor man was so surprised he dropped the hare in hand and turned to run. The sheriff was that quick; he spurred his mount forward to catch the poacher. The fleeing man lunged for the brush at the side of the road, but was caught and hauled back by the hood of his cloak.

The fella gave out a yelp and tried to struggle free of the cloak. The sheriff, well used to catching folk this way, pulled him off his feet. He hung there at the side of the sheriff's saddle, feet dangling off the ground, swinging his fists, and yelling to be released. When the sheriff drew his knife and put it to his squirming captive's neck, I reckoned the affair had gone far enough. Easing myself from my place, I tucked three arrows in my belt, put another on the string, and moved down onto the road as quickly and quietly as stiff muscles would allow.

Creeping like a shadow, I came up behind the sheriff's horse and, with an arrow already on the string, drew and took aim. "Let him go," I said, in my best English. "Or wear this arrow to your wake."

The sheriff's head spun around so fast I thought his neck would snap. He gaped at me and at the bow in my hand, opened his mouth, then thought better and closed it.

"You might be thinking your little knife will save you," I said, "but I think it won't. If you want to find out, just you hold on to that Welshman."

De Glanville recovered himself then, and said, "I am sheriff of the March. This thief is caught poaching in the king's forest, and unless you want a share of what is coming to him, turn aside and go your way."

"Bold words, Sheriff," I replied. "But it is myself who holds the bow, and my fingers on this string are getting tired."

I gave my arm a jiggle to sharpen my point, as it were, whereupon the sheriff dropped our man. "Pick up the hare," I told the farmer, "and light out." He scrambled to his feet, snatched up his prize, and dived into the wood.

"You cannot hope to gain anything by this," the sheriff informed me. "I have marked you for a felon. You will not escape the king's justice."

"The king's justice!" I hooted. "Sir, the king's justice is rough, to be sure, but it is fickle and inconstant as a flirty milkmaid. I will gladly take my chances."

"Fool!" cried the sheriff, suddenly angry. Heedless of the arrow, he spurred his horse at me so as to run me down. I stepped lightly aside, and he made a wild, looping slash at me with his small blade as he passed.

He wheeled the horse at once. A beast well trained to war, it turned so fast the sheriff's long cloak flung out behind him. I saw it flying like a dull flag against the dark bulwark of an oak bole as he made to drive me down, and loosed the shaft.

The arrow whined through the air, catching the heavy cloak and pinning it to the oak as he passed. The cloak snapped taut, the horse charged on, and de Glanville was jerked clean from the saddle.

The sound of ripping fabric cut sharp in the little glade, but the cloth and arrow held fast. Sheriff de Glanville was strung up like a ham in a chimney to dangle with his feet a few inches from the snowy ground. Oh, he squirmed and wriggled and cursed me up one side and down t'other. But I was not ready to let him go so easy, so I sent two more arrows into the trunk to better nail my captive to the tree.

Red-faced and foamin' with rage, if that fella coulda spit poison, he would have. No mistake. Instead, he swung there, ripening the air with his rage. I calmly trained an arrow at the centre of his chest.

I was this close to loosing the shaft when I felt a hand on my shoulder. "Put up," said a familiar voice in my ear. "The sheriff's men are returning. It is time to fly."

"I have him," I insisted. "I can take him and save the world a load of trouble."

"It may bring more trouble than it saves. Another day. We have what we came for—and now we must fly."

With that, Bran pulled me into the brushwood at the side of the road and we were away.

No sooner in the wood and on the path than we heard the sheriff shouting behind us, "After them! Through there! Ten marks to the man who brings them back!"

Immediately, we heard the crack and snap of branches as the soldiers searched for our trail. In less time than it takes to tell, they found it and were onto us.

So now, here was a bother: fleeing through the woods over snow-covered pathways and no way to cover our tracks. Those fellas would have no difficulty at all seeing where we went. The first clearing we came to, I stopped to make a stand. "We can take them here, my lord," I said. "I'll drop the first one, you take the second."

"I don't have a bow, Will," said Bran. "So, tonight, we let them live."

"They will not pay us the same coin if they catch us," I replied. "That is a fair certainty."

"True enough," Bran allowed. Gone was the feathered cloak and the long-beaked headpiece; dressed in his customary black tunic and trousers, he shivered slightly with the cold. "Consider it just one of the many things that makes us better men than they are."

Our pursuers could be heard thrashing through the wood, coming closer with every heartbeat.

Bran smiled and winked his eye, his face a disembodied shape floating in the gloom. "But that does not mean we cannot have a little fun at their expense." Turning lightly on his heel, he said, "Come, Will, let's give them something to talk about when they join their comrades at Castle de Braose."

With that, he flitted away. I glanced over my shoulder, then followed him into the forest. I caught up with him a few dozen paces down the path, where he had stopped beside an ancient oak and was tugging on a bit of ivy vine. "This is where we start," he said, as the end of a rope snaked down from a branch above. "Stand where you are and make no more tracks," he instructed.

I did as I was told. Bran wound the end of the rope around one wrist and gave it a tug. The rope snapped taut. He tugged again and the end of a rope ladder dropped from the limb overhead.

"Up you go, Will," he said, passing the ladder to me. "I will hold it for you, but be quick."

Slinging my bow, I grasped the highest rung I could reach and swung myself up, climbing the ladder with no little difficulty as it twisted and turned like an angry serpent under my weight. I gritted my teeth and hung on. After some tricksy rope climbing, I gained the limb of the oak at last. "Pull up the ladder!" hissed Bran in an urgent whisper. The sheriff's men were that close he could not speak more loudly or risk being overheard.

"There is time," I whispered back. "Take hold and I'll pull you up." But he was already gone.

I hauled up the ladder as fast as I could and crouched in the crux of the largest bough to wait. Within five heartbeats the sheriff's men burst into the clearing we had just left. A few more steps along our trail carried them to the base of the oak, where our tracks became slightly confused. Although I could no longer see the path below, and was not fool enough to risk looking down, I could well imagine what they were seeing: the well-formed footprints of two flee-ing men set in deep, undisturbed snow, and then . . . one set of foot-prints vanishing.

Only a solitary track continued along the path, and they were not slow to mark this.

They paused to catch a breath beneath my hiding place. I could hear them puffing hard as they stood below, searching, trying to find where the second pair of tracks had gone. One of them muttered some-thing in French—something about the futility of catching anything in this accursed forest. And then another voice called from the trail, and they moved on. From my perch, I caught a fleeting glimpse of three soldiers in dark cloaks barely visible in the winter twilight.

No doubt they were loath to return to the sheriff empty-handed, and seeing only a single set of footprints leading away, they had no choice but to follow them. So, panting and cursing, off they went to continue the pursuit. When they had gone, I settled myself more securely on the branch to wait for whatever would happen next. The night was not getting any warmer, nor my cloak any drier; folding my arms across my chest to keep warm, I prayed to Saint Christopher that they would not be pulling my frozen corpse from the oak come Christmas.

Twilight deepened to night and the wind sharpened, kicking up gusts to drive the snow. I wrapped myself tight in my cloak and had just closed my eyes beneath my hood when I heard the creak and clatter of tree limbs nearby as if something big was moving among the branches. My first thought was that all the fuss and fury had awakened a bear or wildcat asleep in its treetop bower. Peering around, Lord bless me, but I saw a great dark shape walking toward me along the very bough I had chosen.

The thing came closer. "Get back!" I hissed, fumbling beneath my damp cloak for my knife.

"Hush!" came the whisper. "You'll bring them back."

"Bran?"

"Who else?" He laughed lightly. "Heavens, Will, you look like you were ready to take wing."

"I thought you were a bear," I told him.

"Follow me," he said, already turning away. "They will be coming back this way soon, and it is best we are not here."

Teetering on the bough, I edged after him, sliding one cautious, slippery foot at a time while clinging to a branch overhead. The bough narrowed as it went out from the trunk but, at the place where it would have begun to bend under our weight, I discovered another stout limb had been lashed into place to make a bridge, of sorts, on which to cross the gap between trees. This makeshift bridge spanned the trail below, linking two big oaks together.

And this was not all! No fewer than four trees were likewise linked in a mad squirrel-run through the treetops. We worked our way along this odd walkway until we came to another rope ladder, and so at last climbed down to a completely different forest track.

"You knew we would be chased," I said the moment I set foot on solid ground once more.

"Aye," he replied, "King Raven can see the shapes of all things present and yet to come," he told me.

"Peter and Paul on a donkey, Bran!" I gasped. "Then you must have seen the sheriff and—"

"Peace, Will," he said, chuckling at his jest. "Angharad might be blessed with such a gift on occasion, but I am not."

"No?" I said, none too certain.

"Listen to you," he said. "It does not take the Second Sight to know that any time you take arms against a company of Norman knights you might soon be running for your life."

"True," I allowed, feeling stupid for being taken in so easily. "That's a fact, right enough. Still and all, it was a canny piece of luck they chased you the way you wanted to go."

"Not at all," he said, moving lightly away. "I led them. This way or another it makes no difference. We have worked all summer to prepare such deceptions. There are ladders and treewalks scattered all over the forest, and especially along the King's Road."

"Treewalk," I said, enjoying the word. I hurried after him.

"Ladders and limbs and such," he said. "It makes for easier escape if you can move from tree to tree."

587

"I agree. But do the Normans never see them?"

"The Ffreinc only ever view the world from the back of a horse," Bran declared. "They rarely dismount, even in dense forest, and almost never look up." He shook his head again. "I should have told you about all that, but I confess I did so want to see your face the first time we used it."

This revelation stopped me in my tracks. "I hope it gave you enjoyment, my lord," I said, the complaint sharp in my voice. "I live to provide amusement for my betters."

"Oh, do not take on, Will. No harm done."

"I thought you were a bear, I did."

He laughed. "Come. Iwan and Siarles will be wondering what has become of us."

He hurried off along the darkened path, and it was all I could do to keep up with him. His long legs carried him by fast strides—and his sight, even in the dark, led him unerringly along a path that could no longer be seen. I struggled along, slipping and sliding in his footsteps, trying to avoid the branches and twigs that whipped back in my face. After a time, Bran slowed his pace; the trees were closer here, the wood more dense and the snow less deep on the path. We moved along at a much improved pace until we arrived at a place far from the road and where we had last seen the sheriff's men.

Bran paused and put his hand back to halt me. He hesitated, and then I heard Iwan's voice murmur something, and Bran stepped from the trail and into a small, snug clearing that had been hewn from the dense undergrowth beside the trail. A fire burned brightly in the centre of this bower and, aside from Iwan and Siarles, there were five of the Grellon huddled close around the flames. They all rose when Bran stepped through the brush, and welcomed him. They made room for us by the fire, but before Bran sat down, he spoke to each one personally, telling them how pleased he was of their accomplishments this day.

Aside from the men, there were two women from Cél Craidd. They had prepared barley cakes and a little mulled ale to help draw the chill from our bones, so while Bran spoke to the others, I sat down and soon had my frozen fingers wrapped around a steaming jar. "We were getting worried," said Siarles, settling down beside me. "I might have known there would be trouble."

"A little," I confessed. "The sheriff turned up and took it into his head to have us give some of his men a run through the wood."

"The sheriff? Are you certain?"

"Oh, aye, it was himself. I challenged him, and he tried to talk me into giving myself up for a hanging." I sipped my hot ale. "Tempting as it was, I declined the offer and made one of my own. I decorated his fine cloak with arrow points."

Siarles regarded me in the firelight with a look approaching appreciation. "Did you kill him, then?"

"I drew on him, but did not loose."

"Weeping Judas, why not?"

"King Raven prevented me," I replied. "He appeared just as I was about to let fly, and we've been running ever since. And now that I think of it, why did no one tell me about the treewalks and ladders?"

Siarles grinned readily. "Oh, that—well, it's a secret we like to keep to ourselves as much as possible. A man's life could depend on it."

"As my own did this selfsame night. It would have cheered me no end to know I wasn't about to end my days with a Norman spear in my back."

"So, now you know."

"Now I know," I agreed. "One of these days, I'll thank you to show me which of the other trails have been prepared this way and which trees."

"Oaks," replied Siarles, taking the jar from me and helping himself to a sip.

"Oaks," I repeated, taking the cup back.

"It's always oak trees," Iwan confirmed. "Look for a dangling vine. As for the trails, we'll show you next time we come out. But that won't be for a while now. We will let the trail grow cold."

"It is plenty cold now," I said, quaffing down a hearty gulp. "If the snow keeps up, by morning you won't be able to tell anyone passed this way at all."

Iwan nodded and stood abruptly. "Nóinina!" he called. "A dry cloak for our man here."

One of the women turned away from the fire and withdrew a bundle from a wicker basket they had brought. She came around the ring to where I sat, untied the bundle, and shook out a clean, dry cloak. "Oooh," she cooed gently, "let me get that cold wet thing off you before you take a death."

Leaning over me, she deftly untied the laces and lifted off the wet garment; the cold air hit my damp clothes and I shivered. She spread the dry cloak over my shoulders and rubbed my back with her hands so as to warm me. "There now," she said, "you'll be warm and dry that soon."

"Many thanks," I said, craning my head around to see her better. It was the woman who had come to Cél Craidd after being rescued from the Ffreinc. As it happens, I had helped build a hut for her and her wee daughter. "Nóinina, is it?" I asked, though I knew well and good that it was.

"Aye, that's me." She gave me a fine smile, and I realized that she was a right fetching woman. Now, it might have been the heat of the fire after a long, cold day, or then again, it might have been something else, but I felt a certain warmth spread through me just then. "You're called Will."

"That I am."

She lingered close, gazing down at me as I sat with my cup on my knees. "I helped build the hut for you and the little 'un," I told her.

"I know." She smiled again and moved off. "And for that I'll give you a barley cake."

She was back a few moments later with a jug of warm ale and a barley cake fresh from the griddle stone. "Get that into you and see if you don't warm up."

"I'm feeling better already," I told her. "Much better."

It didn't last long. As soon as we all had a bite and drained our cups, Iwan put out the fire and we were away. Oh, but it was a long, slow trek back to the settlement through deep-drifting snow. We tried to walk in one another's footsteps as much as possible so as not to disturb the snow overmuch, but that was tedious and taxing. We were fair exhausted by the time we reached Cél Craidd, and the night was far gone. Even so, our folk had built up a big, bright fire and were waiting for us with hot food and drink. They let out a great cheer when first we tumbled through the hedgewall and slid down the bank.

Well, our trials were forgotten just that quick, and we all gathered round the fire to celebrate our victory. There was still a thing or two needin' done—the oxen and wagons had been secured for the night, but the wagons would have to be unburdened and the oxen would require attention before another day had run. Our work was far from finished. Even so, the cares of tomorrow could fend for themselves a little while; this night we could celebrate.

The mood was high. We had fought the Ffreinc and delivered a blow they would not soon forget. As soon as we took our places at the fire, cups were pressed into our hands and meat set to roast on skewers. We drank the first of many healths to one and all, and I was that surprised to find myself standing beside the widow woman once more.

"Hello again, Nóinina," I said, my clumsy half-Saxon tongue attempting the lilt she had given it. "It's a good night that ends well even with the snow."

"Call me Nóin," she said. Indicating my cup with a quick nod of her head, she said, "Your jar big enough for two?"

"Just big enough," I replied, and passed it to her.

She raised it to her lips and drank deep, wiping her mouth with the back of her hand as she returned the jar. "Ah, now, that is as it should be—hale and hearty and strong, with a fine handsome head." She leaned near, and her lips curved with sweet mischief as she added, "Just like our man here himself."

Oh, my stars! It had been long since any woman had spoken to me with such invitation in her voice. My heart near leapt out of my throat, and I had to look at her a second time to make sure it was ol' Will Scarlet she was talking about. She gave me a wink with the smile, and I knew my fortunes had just improved beyond all reason. "Do not be leaving just yet," she said, and skipped away.

"I'll keep a place for you right here," I called after her.

She returned with another jar and two skewers of meat for us to roast at the fire. We settled back to share a stump and a cup, and watch the snow drift down as the meat cooked. Sweet Peter's beard, but the flames that warmed my face were nothing compared to the warmth of that fine young woman beside me. An unexpected happiness caught me up, and my heart took wing and soared through a winter sky ablaze with stars.

I was on the point of asking her how she came to be in the forest when Lord Bran raised his cup and called for silence around the fire ring. "Here's a health to King Raven and his mighty Grellon, who this night have plucked a tail feather from that stuffed goose de Braose!"

"To King Raven and the Grellon," we all cried, lofting our cups, "mighty all!"

When we had drunk and recharged our cups, Bran called again, "Here's a health to the men whose valour and hardihood has the sheriff and his men gnashing their teeth in rage tonight!"

We hailed that and drank accordingly, swallowing down a hearty draught at the happy thought of the sheriff and count smarting from the wallop we'd given them.

"Hear now!" Bran called when we had finished. "This health is for our good Will Scarlet who, heedless of the danger to himself, snatched a poor man from the sheriff's grasp. Thanks to Will, that man's family will eat tonight and him with them." Raising his cup, he cried, "To Will, a man after King Raven's heart!"

The shout went up, "To Will!" And everyone raised their jars to me. Ah, it was a grand thing to be hailed like that. And just to make the moment that much more memorable to me, as the king and all his folk drank my health, I felt Nóin slip her hand into mine and give it a squeeze—only lightly, mind, but I felt the tingle down to my toes.

CHAPTER 13

Eiwas

The journey to Wales seemed endless somehow. Although only a few days from his castle in England's settled heart, Bernard Neufmarché, Baron of Hereford and Gloucester, always felt as if he had travelled half a world away by the time he reached the lands of his vassal, Lord Cadwgan, in the Welsh cantref of Eiwas. The country was darker and strangely uninviting, with shadowy wooded keeps, secret pools, and lonely rivers. The baron thought the close-set hills and hidden valleys of Wales mysterious and more than a little forbidding—all the more so in winter.

It wasn't only the landscape he found threatening. Since his defeat of Rhys ap Tewdwr, a well-loved king and the able leader of the southern Welsh resistance, the land beyond the March had grown decidedly unfriendly to him. Former friends were now hostile, and former enemies implacable. So be it. If that was the price of progress, Neufmarché was willing to pay. Now, however, the baron made his circuits more rarely and, where once he might have enjoyed an untroubled ride to visit his vassal lords, these days he never put foot to stirrup in the region unless accompanied by a bodyguard of knights and men-at-arms.

Thus, he was surrounded by a strong, well-armed force. Not that he expected trouble from Cadwgan—despite their differences, the two had always got along well enough—but reports of wandering rebels stirring up trouble meant that even old friends must be treated with caution.

"Evereux!" called the baron as they came in sight of Caer Rhodl perched on the summit of a low rock crag. "Halt the men just there." He pointed to a stony outcrop beside the trail, a short distance from the wooden palisade of Cadwgan's fortress. "You and I will ride on together."

The marshal relayed the baron's command to the troops and, upon reaching the place, the soldiers paused and dismounted. The baron continued to the fortress gate—where, as expected, he was admitted with prompt, if cold, courtesy.

"My lord will be informed of your arrival," said the steward. "Please wait in the hall."

"But of course," replied the baron. "My greetings to your lord."

The Welsh king's house was not large, and Neufmarché had been there many times; he proceeded to the hall, where he and his marshal were kept waiting longer than the baron deemed hospitable. "This is an insult," observed Evereux. "Do you want me to go find the old fool and drag him here by the nose?"

"We came unannounced," the baron replied calmly, although he was also feeling the slight. "We will wait."

They remained in the hall, alone, frustration mounting by the moment, until eventually there came a shuffle in the doorway. It took a moment for the baron to realise that Lord Cadwgan had indeed appeared. Gaunt and hollow-cheeked, a ghastly shadow fell across his face; his clothes hung on his once-robust form as upon a rack of sticks. His skin had an unhealthy pallor that told the baron his vassal lord had not ventured outdoors for weeks, or maybe even months.

"My lord baron," said Cadwgan in the soft, listless voice of the sickroom. "Good of you to come."

His manner seemed to suggest that he imagined it was he who had summoned the baron to his hall. Neufmarché disregarded the inapt remark, even as he ignored the sharp decline evidenced in Cadwgan's appearance. "A fine day!" the baron declared, his voice a little forced and overloud. "I thought we might make a circuit of your lands."

"Of course," agreed Cadwgan. "Perhaps once we have had some refreshment, my son could accompany you."

"I thought you might ride with me," replied the baron. "It has been a long time since we rode together."

"I fear I would not be the best of company," said Cadwgan. "I will tell Garran to saddle a horse."

Unwilling to press the matter further, the baron said, "How is your lady wife?" When the king failed to take his meaning, he said, "Queen Anora—is she well?"

"Aye, yes, well enough." Cadwgan looked around the empty room as if he might find her sitting in one of the corners. "Shall I send someone to fetch her?"

"Let it wait. There is no need to disturb her just now."

"Of course, Sire." The Welsh king fell silent, gazing at the baron and then at Evereux. Finally, he said, "Was there something else?"

"You were going to summon your son, I think?" Neufmarché replied.

"Was I? Very well, if you wish to see him."

Without another word the king turned and padded softly away.

"The man is ill," observed the marshal. "That, or senile."

"Obviously," replied the baron. "But he has been a useful ally, and we will treat him with respect."

"As you say," allowed Evereux. "All the same, a thought about the succession would not be amiss. Is the son loyal?"

"Loyal enough," replied the baron. "He is a young and supple reed, and we can bend him to our purpose."

A few moments later, they were joined by the young prince himself who, with icy compliance, agreed to ride with the baron on a circuit of Eiwas. The baron spoke genially of one thing and another as they rode out, receiving nothing but the minimum required for civility in return. Upon reaching a stream at the bottom of the valley, the baron reined up sharply. "Know you, we need not be enemies," he said. "From what I have seen of your father today, it seems to me that you will soon be swearing vassalage to me. Let us resolve to be friends from the beginning."

Garran wheeled his horse and came back across the stream. "What do you want from me, Neufmarché? Is it not enough that you hold our land? Must you own our souls as well?"

"Guard your tongue, my lord prince," snarled Evereux. "It ill becomes a future king to speak to his liege lord in such a churlish manner."

The prince opened his mouth as if he would challenge this remark, but thought better of it and glared at the marshal instead.

"Your father is not well," the baron said simply. "Have you sent for a physician?"

Garran frowned and looked away. "Such as we have."

"I will send mine to you," offered the baron.

"My thanks, Baron," replied the prince stiffly, "but it will be to no purpose. He pines for Mérian."

"Mérian," murmured the baron, as if searching his memory for a face to go with the name. Oh, but not a day had passed from the moment he first met her until now that he did not think of her with longing, and stinging regret. Fairest Mérian, stolen away from his very grasp. How he wished that he could call back the command that had sealed her fate. A clumsy and ill-advised attempt to capture the Welsh renegade Bran ap Brychan had resulted in the young hellion taking the lady captive to make good his escape from the baron's camp. Neufmarché had lost her along with any chance he might have had of loving her.

Mistaking the baron's pensive silence, Prince Garran said, "The king thinks her dead. And I suppose she is, or we would have had some word of her by now."

"There has been nothing? No demand for ransom? Nothing?" asked the baron. His own efforts to find her had been singularly unsuccessful.

"Not a word," confirmed Garran. "We always knew Bran for a rogue, but this makes no sense. If he only wanted money, he could have had it long since. My father would have met any demand—as well he knows." The young man shook his head. "I suppose my father is right; she must be dead. I only hope that Bran ap Brychan is maggot-food, too. "

Following Mérian's kidnapping, the baron had sorrowfully informed Mérian's family of the incident, laying the blame entirely at Bran's feet while failing to mention his own considerable part in the affair. All they knew was what the baron had told them at the time: that a man, thought to be Bran ap Brychan, had come riding into the camp, demanding to speak to the baron, who was in council with two of his English vassals. When the Welshman's demands were denied, he had grown violent and attacked the baron's knights, who fought him off. To avoid being killed, the cowardly rebel had seized the young woman and carried her away. The baron's men had given chase; there was a battle in which several of his knights lost their lives. In all likelihood, the fugitives had been wounded in the skirmish, but their fate was unknown, for they escaped into the hills, taking Lady Mérian with them.

"Her loss has made my father sick at heart," Garran concluded gloomily. "I think he will not last the winter."

"Then," said the baron, a tone of genuine sympathy edging into his voice, "I suggest we begin making plans for your succession to your father's throne. Will there be any opposition, do you think?"

Garran shook his head. "There is no one else."

"Good," replied Neufmarché with satisfaction. "We must now look to the future of Eiwas and its people."

CHAPTER 14

O do wants to know why I have never mentioned Nóin before. "Some things are sacred," I tell him. "What kind of priest are you that you don't know this?"

"Sacred?" He blinks at me like a mole just popped from the ground and dazzled by a little daylight. "A sacred memory?"

"Nóin is more than a memory, monk. She's a part of me forever."

"Is she dead, then?"

"I'll not be telling the likes of you," I say. I am peeved with him now, and he knows it. Nóin may be a memory, but even so she is a splendid pearl and not to be tossed to any Ffreinc swine.

Odo pouts.

"I meant no disrespect," he says, rubbing his bald spot. "Neither to you, nor the lady. I just wanted to know."

"So you can run off and tell the blasted abbot?" I shake my head. "I may be crow food tomorrow, but I en't a dunce today."

My scribe does not understand this, and as I look at him it occurs to me that I don't rightly understand it, either. I protect her however I may, I suppose. "So now!" I slide down the rough stone wall and assume my place once more. "Where was I?"

"Returned to Cél Craidd," he says, dipping his pen reluctantly. "It is the night after the raid and it is snowing."

"Snowing, yes. It was snowing," I say, and we press on . . .

It snowed all night, and most of the next day, clearing a little around sunset. Owing to Angharad's timely warning, we were well prepared and weathered the storm in comfort—sleeping, eating, taking our ease. To us, it was a holy day, a feast day; we celebrated our victory and rare good fortune.

Around midday, after we'd had a good warm sleep and a little something to break our fast, Lord Bran and those of us who had helped in the raid crowded into his hut to view the spoils. In amongst the bags of grain and beans, sides of smoked meat, casks of wine, and bundles of cloth that made up the greater part of the take, the Grellon had found two small chests. The heavier goods had been hidden in the wood not far from the road, to be retrieved later when the weather was better and the sheriff far away.

The wooden boxes, however, had been toted back to our snuggery. With a nod from Angharad, standing nearby to oversee the proceedings, Bran said, "Open them. Let's see what our generous baron has sent us."

Siarles, waiting with an axe in his hand, stepped forward and gave the oak chest a few solid chops. The lid splintered. A few more blows and the box lay open to reveal a quantity of small leather bags that were quickly untied and dumped on a skin beside the hearth around which we all stood. The bags were full of silver pennies, which was more or less to be expected.

"Again," said Bran, and Siarles wielded the axe once more and the second chest gave way. In it were more leather bags full of coins, but also three other items of interest: a pair of fine white leather calfskin gloves, richly embroidered on the back with holy crosses and other symbols in gold braid; a thick square of parchment, folded, bound with a blue cord, and sealed with wax; and, in its own calfskin bag, a massive gold ring.

"A fine bauble, that," said Siarles, holding up the ring. He handed it to Bran, who bounced it on his palm to judge the weight of gold before passing it on to Angharad.

"Very fine work," she observed, holding the ring to her squint. She passed it along, saying, "Much too grand for a mere count."

Indeed, the ring looked like something I imagined an emperor might wear. The flat central stone was engraved with a coat of arms such as might be used by kings or other notables for imprinting their seal on important documents. Around the carved stone was a double row of glittering rubies—tiny, but bright as bird's eyes, and each glowing like a small crimson sun.

"A most expensive trinket," replied Bran. Leaning close, he examined the engraving. "Whose arms, I wonder? Have you ever seen them, Iwan?"

The big man bent his head close and then shook it slowly. "Not English, I think. Probably belong to a Ffreinc nobleman—a baron, I'd say. Or a king."

"I doubt if anyone in all Britain has ever worn the like," said Siarles. "Where do you think de Braose got it?"

"And why send it here?" asked Iwan.

"These are questions that will require some thought," replied Angharad as Bran slipped the ring onto his finger. It was far too big, so he put it on his thumb, and even then it did not fit; so he took a bowstring, looped it through the ring, and tied it around his neck. "It will be safe enough there," he said, "until we find out more."

We counted up the silver, and it came to fifty marks—a splendid haul.

"The gloves might be worth twenty or thirty marks all by themselves," Mérian pointed out. She had come in during the counting and stayed to see the result. Stroking the gauntlets against her cheek, she remarked that they were the sort of thing a high-placed cleric might wear on festal days.

"What about the ring?" wondered Iwan aloud. "What would that be worth?"

No one knew. Various sums were suggested—all of them fancies. We had no more idea how much that lump of gold and rubies might be worth than the king of Denmark's hunting hound. Some said it must be worth a castle, a cantref, maybe even a kingdom. Our ignorant speculation ran amok until Angharad silenced us, saying, "You would do better to ask why it is here."

"Why indeed," said Bran, his fingers caressing the bauble.

604

We fell silent gazing at the thing, as at a piece of the moon dropped from the sky. Why had it been sent to Elfael in the bottom of a supply wagon?

"Oh, aye," said Angharad, her voice cracking like dry twigs, "a treasure like this will bring swarms of searchers on its trail." She tapped it with a bony finger. "It might be as well to give it back."

This dropped us in the pickle pot, I can tell you. With these words, the realisation of what we'd done began to break over us, and our triumph turned to ashes in our mouths. We each crept away to our beds that night full of foreboding. I hardly closed my eyes at all, I was that restless with it. God knows, it may be deepest sin to steal, and in ordinary times I would never take so much as a bean from a bag that was not mine. But this was different.

This was a fight for survival.

Rule of law . . . king's justice . . . these words are worth less to the

Ffreinc than the air it takes to breathe them out. If we steal from those who seek ever to destroy us, may the Good Lord forgive us, but we en't about to stop and we en't about to start giving things back. It does irritate the baron and his nephew no end, I can say. And the sheriff, it upsets him most of all on account of the fact that he's the one who is meant to prevent our raiding and thieving.

Shed no tears for Richard de Glanville. He is a twisted piece of rope if ever there was one. It is said he killed his wife for burning his Sunday pork chop in the pan—strangled her with his own bare hands.

Personally, I do not believe this. Not a word. In the first place, it means our Richard Rat-face would have had to get someone to marry him, and I heartily doubt there is a woman born yet who would agree to that. Even granting a marriage, impossible as it seems, it would mean that he had taken matters into his own hands—another fair impossibility right there. You might better claim the sun spends the night in your barn and get more people to believe you than that the sheriff of the March ever sullied his lily-whites with anything so black. See, de Glanville never lifts a finger himself; he pays his men to do all his dirty deeds for him.

To the last man, the sheriff's toadies are as cruel and vengeful as the day is long; a more rancorous covey of plume-proud pigeons you never want to meet. God bless me, it is true.

The folk of Derby still talk of the time when Sheriff de Glanville and three of his men cornered a poor tinker who had found his way into mischief. The tale as I heard it was that one bright day in April, a farmwife went out to feed the geese and found them all but one dead and that one not looking any too hearty. Who would do a mean and hateful thing like that? Well, it came to her then that there'd been a tinker come to the settlement a day or two before hoping to sell a new pot or get some patchwork on an old one. Sharp-tongued daughter of Eve that she was, she'd sent him off with both ears burnin' for his troub¹

Now then, wasn't that just like a rascal of a tinker to skulk around behind her back and kill her prize geese the moment she wasn't looking? She went about the market with this news, and it soon spread all over town. Everyone was looking for this tinker, who wasn't hard to find because he wasn't hiding. They caught him down by the river washing his clothes, and they hauled him half-naked to the sheriff to decide what to do with the goose-killer.

As it happened, some other townsfolk had rustled about and found a serf who'd broken faith with his Norman lord from somewhere up north. He'd passed through the town a day or so before, and the fella was discovered hiding in a cow byre on a settlement just down the road. They bound the poor fella and dragged him to town, where the sheriff had already set up his judgement seat outside the guildhall in the market square. De Glanville was halfway to hanging the tinker when the second crowd tumbles into town with the serf.

So now. What to do? Both men are swearing their innocence and screaming for mercy. They are raising a ruck and crying foul to beat the devil. Well, the sheriff can't tell who is guilty of this heinous crime, nor can anyone else. But that en't no matter. Up he stands and says, "You call on heaven to help you? So be it! Hang them both, and let God decide which one shall go to hell."

So his men fix another noose on the end of the first rope, and it's up over the roof beam of the guildhall. He hangs both men in the market square with the same rope—one wretch on one end, and one on t'other. And that is Richard bloody de Glanville for you beginning and end . . .

What's that, monk?" I say. "You think it unlikely?"

Odo sniffs and wrinkles his nose in disbelief. "If you please, which ¬ killed the geese?"

"Which one? I'd a thought that would be obvious to a smart fella like you, Odo. So now, you tell me, which one did the deed?"

"The tinker—for spite, because the farmwife refused to buy his pots or give him work."

"Oh, Odo," I sigh, shaking my head and tutting his ignorance. "It wasn't the tinker. No, never him."

"The serf then, because he . . ." He scratches his head. "Hungry? I don't know."

"It wasn't the serf, either."

"Then who?"

"It was a sneak-thief fox, of course. See, Odo, a man can't kill a goose but that the whole world knows about it. First you gotta catch the bloody bird, and that raises the most fearsome squawk you ever heard, and that gets all the others squawking, too. By Adam's axe, it's enough to wake the dead, it is. But a fox, now a fox is nimble as a shadow and just as silent. A fox works quick and so frightens the flock that none of them lets out a peep. With a fox in the barn, no one knows the deed is done till you walk in and find 'em all in a heap of blood and feathers."

Odo bristles at this. "Are you saying the sheriff hanged two innocent men?"

"I don't know that they were innocent, mind, but de Glanville hanged two men for the same crime that neither could have done."

Odo shakes his head. "Hearsay," he decides. "Hearsay and slander and lies."

"That's right," I say. "You just keep telling yourself that, priest. Keep on a-saying it until they find a reason to tighten the rope around your fine plump neck, and then we'll see how you sing."

CHAPTER 15

The snow continued through the night and over the next days, covering all, drifting deep on field and forest, hilltop and valley throughout Elfael. As soon as the hard weather eased up a little, we fetched the captured spoils back to Cél Craidd, along with the four oxen kept in a pen not far from the road, trusting to the windblown snow to remove any traces of our passing. We kept a right keen watch for the sheriff and his scabby men, but saw neither hank nor hair of them, and so hurried about our chores. The wagons we dismantled where they stood, keeping only the wheels and iron fittings; the animals were more useful, to be sure. One we kept to pull the plough in the spring; the others would be given to farmers in the area to replace those lost in one way or another to the Ffreinc.

It was the same with the money. Bran did not keep what he got from the raid, but shared it out among the folk of his realm, helping those who were most in need of it—and there were plenty of them, I can tell you. For the Normans had been in Elfael going on two years by then, and however bad it was in the beginning it was much worse now. Always worse with that hell crew, never better. So, the money was given out, and those who received it blessed King Raven and his men.

Oh, but that great gold ring began to weigh heavy on the slender strap around Bran's princely neck. Worth a king's ransom it was, and we all stoked a secret fear that one day the Red King himself would come after it with an army. We were all atwist over this when Friar Tuck showed up.

I had heard his name by then, and some few things about him—how he had helped Bran in his dealings with the king and cardinal. But whatever I had heard did nothing to prepare me for the man himself. Part imp, part oaf, part angel—that is Friar Tuck.

His arrival was announced in the usual way: one of the sentries gave out the shrill whistle of a crake. This warned the Grellon that someone was coming and that this visitor was welcome. An intruder would have demanded a very different call. For those few who were allowed to come and go, however, there was a simple rising whistle. Well, we heard the signal, and folk stopped whatever they were doing and turned towards the blasted oak to see who would appear through the hedge. A few moments later, a fat little dumpling rolled down the bank, red face shining with a sheen of sweat despite the chill in the air, the hem of his robe hiked up and stuffed in his belt to keep it from dragging through the snow.

"Happy Christ-tide!" he called when he saw all the folk hurrying to greet him. "It is good to see you, Iwan! Siarles! Gaenor, Teleri, Henwydd!" He called out the names of folk he knew. "Good to see you! Peace to one and all!"

"Tuck!" shouted Siarles, hurrying to greet him. "Hail and welcome! With all this snow, we did not think to see you again until the spring."

"And where should I be at Christ-tide, but with my own dear friends?"

"No bag this time?"

"Bag? I've brought half of Hereford with me!" He gestured vaguely toward the trail. "There's a pack mule coming along. Rhoddi met me on the trail and sent me on ahead."

Bran and Mérian appeared then, and Angharad was not far behind. The little friar was welcomed with laughter and true affection; I glimpsed in this something of the respect and high regard this simple monk enjoyed amongst the Grellon. The king of England might receive similar adulation on his travels, I'll warrant, but little of the fondness.

"God with you, Friar," said Mérian, stepping forward to bless our visitor. "May your sojourn here well become you." She smiled and bent at the waist to bestow a kiss on his cheek. Then, taking that same round red cheek between finger and thumb, she gave it a pinch. "That is for leaving without wishing me farewell the last time!"

"A mistake I'll not be making twice," replied Tuck, rubbing his cheek. He turned as Angharad pushed forward to greet him. "Bless my soul, Angharad, you look even younger than the last time I saw you."

Wise and powerful she may be, but Angharad was still lady enough to smile at the shameless compliment. "Peace attend thee, friend friar," she said, her wrinkled face alight.

"Brother Tuck!" cried Iwan, and instantly gathered the sturdy friar in a rib-cracking embrace. "It is that good to see you."

"And you, Wee John," retorted the priest, giving the warrior a clip 'round the ear. "I've missed you and all." Iwan set him down, and the priest gazed at the ring of happy faces around him. "Well, Bran, and I see you and your flock have fared well enough without me." Adjusting his robe to cover his cold bare legs once more, he then raised his hands in a priestly benediction. "God's peace and mercy on us all, and may our Kind Redeemer send the comfort of this blessèd season to cheer our hearts and heal our careworn souls."

611

Everyone cried "Amen!" to that, and when Tuck turned back to Bran, he said, "Some new faces, I see."

"One or two," confirmed Bran. He grasped the priest's hands in his own, then presented the newcomers; I found myself last among them. "And this one here," he said, pulling me forward, "is the newest member of our growing flock and as handy with a bow as King Raven himself."

"That's saying something, that is," remarked Tuck.

"Will Scatlocke, at your service," I said, thrusting out my hand to him.

He took it in both his own and shook it heartily. "Our Lord's abundant peace to you, Will Scatlocke."

"And to you, Friar. See now, two Saxons fallen among Welshmen," I said in English.

He cast a shrewd eye over me. "Is that the north country I hear in your voice?"

"Oh, aye," I confessed. "Deny it, I'll not. Your ear is sharp as Queen Meg's needle, Friar."

"Born within sight of York Minster, was I not? But tell me, how did you come to take roost among these strange birds?"

"Lost my living to William Rufus—may God bless his backside with boils!—and so I came west," I told him, and explained quickly how, after many months of living rough and wandering, Bran had taken me in.

"Enough!" cried Bran. "There is time for all that later. We have Christmas tomorrow and a celebration to prepare!"

Ah, Christmas . . . how long had it been since I had celebrated the feast day of Our Sweet Saviour in proper style? Years, at least—not since I had sat at table in Thane Aelred's hall with a bowl of hot punch between my hands and a huge pig a-roasting on the spit over red-hot coals in the hearth. Glad times. I have always enjoyed the Feast of Christ—the food and song and games . . . everything taken together, it is the best of all the holy days, and that is how it should be.

I did not know how the Cymry hereabouts celebrated the Christ Mass, and nursed the strong suspicion that if Friar Tuck had not arrived when he did, King Bran's pitiable flock would have had little with which to make their cheer. But when his pack mule arrived a short while later, it was clear that the friar had brought Christmas with him.

Within moments, he seemed to be everywhere at once, kindling the banked coals of the forest-dwellers' hearts—a word of greeting here, a song there, a laugh or a story to lift the spirits of our down-cast tribe. Bless him, he fanned the cold embers of joy into a cracking fine blaze.

Although they have adopted some of the more common Saxon practices, the Britons appeared not to observe the trimming of pine boughs, so it fell to Tuck and me to arrange this part of the festivities. The day had cleared somewhat, with bright blue showing through the clouds, so the two of us walked into the nearby wood to cut some suitable branches and bring them back. This we did, talking as we worked, and learning to know one another better.

"What we need now," declared Tuck when we had cut enough greenery to satisfy tradition, "is a little holly."

"As good as got," I told him, and asked why he thought it needful.

"Why? It is a most potent symbol, and that is reason enough," the priest replied. "See here, prickly leaves remind us of the thorns our dear Lamb of God suffered with silent fortitude, and the red berries remind us of the drops of healing blood he shed for us. The tree remains green all the year round, and the leaves never die—which shows us the way of eternal life for those who love the Saviour."

"Then, by all means," I said, "let us bring back some holly, too."

Shouldering our cut boughs of spruce and pine, we made our way back to the village, pausing to collect a few of the prickly green branches on the way. "And will we have a Yule log?" I asked as we resumed our walk.

"I have no objection," the friar allowed. "A harmless enough observance, quite pleasant in its own way. Yes, why not?"

Why not, indeed! Of all the odd bits that go to make up this age-old fest, I hold the Yule log chief among them and was glad our friar offered no objection. The way some clerics have it, a fella'd think it was Lucifer himself dragged into the hall on Christmas day. For all, it's just a log—a big one, mind, but a log all the same.

As Thane Aelred's forester, it always fell to me to find the log. We'd walk out together, lord and vassal, of a Christmas morn—along with one of the thane's sons or daughters astride a big ox—and drag the log back to the hall, where it would be pulled through the door and its trimmed end set in a hearth already ablaze. Then, as the end burned, we'd feed that great hulk of wood inch by inch into the flame. Green as apples, that log would sputter and crack and sizzle as the sap touched the flame, filling the hall with its strong scent. We always chose a timber too green to burn any other time for the simple reason that, so long as that log was a-roast, none of the servants had to lift a finger beyond the simple necessities required to keep the celebration going.

A good Yule log could last a fortnight. I suspect it was the idleness of the vassals that got up so many priest's noses. They do so hate to see anyone taking his ease. Then again, there was the ashes. See, when the feasting was over and the log reduced to cold embers, those selfsame ashes were gathered up to be used in various ways: we sprinkled some on cattle to ensure health and hearty offspring; we scattered some in the fields to encourage abundant crops; and, of course, sheep had their fleece dusted to improve the quality of their wool. A little was mixed with the first brewing of ale for the year to aid in warding off sickness and ill temper, and so on. In all, the ashes of a Yule log provided a useful and necessary commodity.

Over time, a good few of the Britons took up the Yule log tradition, just like many of the Saxons succumbed to the ancient and honourable Celtic rite of eating gammon on Christ's day. To be sure, a Saxon never requires much encouragement where the eating of pigs is at issue, less yet if there is also to be drinking ale. So, naturally, a great many priests try to stamp out the practice of burning Yule trees.

"Well now," said Tuck, when I remarked on his obvious charity towards a custom most of his ilk found offensive, "they have their reasons, do they not? But I tell the folk who ask me that the fire provided is the flame of faith, which burns brightest through the darkest nights of the year, feeding on the log—which is the holy, sustaining word of God, ever new and renewed, day by day, year by year. The ashes, then, are the dust of death, the residue of our sins when all has been cleansed in the Refiner's fire."

"Well said, Brother."

"You seem a thoughtful sort of man, Will," the cheerful cleric observed.

"I hope I am," I replied.

"And dependable?"

"It would please me if folk considered me so."

"And are you a loyal man, Will?"

I stopped walking and looked at him. "On my life, I am."

"Good. Bran has need of men he can trust."

"As do we all, Friar. As do we all."

He nodded and we resumed our walk. The light was fading as the short winter day dwindled down.

615

"You said you lost your living," he said after a moment. "I would hear that tale now, if nothing prevents you."

"Nothing to tell you haven't heard before, I'll warrant," I replied, and explained how I had been in service to Thane Aelred, who ran afoul of King William the Red during the accession struggle. "As punishment, the king burned the village and claimed the lands under Forest Law." I went on to describe how I had wandered about, working for bread and bed and, hearing about King Raven, decided to try to find him if I could. "I found Iwan and Siarles first, and they brought me to Cél Craidd, where Bran took pity on me. What about you, Tuck? How did an upright priest like yourself come to have a place in this odd flock?"

"They came to me," he replied. "On their way to Lundein, they were, and stopped for a night under the roof of my oratory." He lifted a palm upward. "God did the rest."

By the time we returned to the settlement, the first stars were peeking through the clouds in the east. A great fire blazed in the ring outside Bran's hut, and there was a fine fat pig a-sizzle on a spit. A huge kettle of spiced ale was steaming in the coals; the cauldron was surrounded by spatchcocks splayed on willow stakes, and the savory scent brought the water to my mouth.

With the help of some of the children, Tuck and I placed pine branches over the doors of the huts and around the edge of the fire ring itself. At Bran's hut and those of Angharad and Mérian, and Iwan and Siarles, we also fixed a sprig or two of the holly we had cut. A few of the smaller girls begged sprigs for themselves and plaited them into their hair.

As soon as the ale was ready, everyone rushed to the fire ring with their cups and bowls to raise the first of a fair many healths to each other and to the day. As wives and husbands pledged their cups to one another, I lofted my cup to Brother Tuck. *"Was hale!"* I cried.

Ruddy face beaming, he gave out a hearty, "Drink hale!" And we drank to one another.

Bran and Mérian, I noticed, shared a most cordial sip between them, and the way those two regarded one another over the rim of the cup sent a pang of longing through me, sharp and swift as if straight from the bow. I think I was not the only one sensing this particular lack, for as I turned around I glimpsed Nóin standing a little off to one side, watching the couples with a wistful expression on her face.

"A health to you, fair lady," I called, raising my cup to her across the fire.

Smiling brightly, she stepped around the ring to touch the rim of her cup to mine. "Health and strength to you, Will Scarlet," she said, her voice dusky and low.

We drank together, and she moved closer and, wrapping an arm around my waist, hooked a finger in my belt. "God's blessing on you this day, and through all the year to come."

"And to you and yours," I replied. Glancing around, I asked, "Where is the little 'un?"

"Playing with the other tads. Why?"

"There will be no keeping them abed tonight," I suggested, watching the excited youngsters kicking up the snow in their games.

"Nor, perhaps, their elders," Nóin said, offering me a smile that was both shy and seasoned. Oh, she knew the road and where it led; she had travelled it, but was a mite uncertain of her footing just then. It opened a place in my heart, so.

Well, we talked a little, and I remembered all over again how easy she was to be near, and how the firelight flecked her long, dark hair with red, like tiny sparks. She was the kind of woman a man would find comfortable to have around day in, day out, if he should be so fortunate.

I was on the point of asking her to join me at table for the feast when Friar Tuck raised his voice and declared, "Friends! Gather around, everyone! Come, little and large! Come fill your cups. It is time to raise a health to the founder of the feast, our dear Blésséd Saviour—who on this night was born into our midst as a helpless infant so that he might win through this world to the next and, by his striving, open the gates of heaven so that all who love him might go in." Lofting his cup, Tuck shouted, "To our Lord and Eternal Master of the Feast, Jesus!"

"To Jesus!" came the resounding reply.

Thus, the Feast of Christ began.

The devil, however, is busy always. Observing neither feast nor fest, our infernal tormentor is a harsh taskmaster to his willing servants. The moment we dared lift cup and heart to enjoy a little cheer, that moment the devil's disciples struck.

And they struck hard.

CHAPTER 16

The first sign of something amiss came as our forest tribe gathered to share the festal meal. We drank the abbot's wine and savoured the aromas of roasting meat and fresh bread, and then Friar Tuck led us in the Christ Mass, offering comfort and solace to our exiled souls. We prayed with our good priest and felt God's pleasure in our prayers.

It was as we were singing a last hymn the wind shifted, coming around to the west and bringing with it the scent of smoke.

Yes, Odo." I sigh at his interruption. "It is not in any way unusual to smell smoke in a forest. In most forests there are always people burning things: branches and twigs to make charcoal, or render lard, clear land . . . what have you. But the Forest of the March is different from any other forest I've ever known, and that's a fact."

My monkish friend cannot understand what I am saying. To him, a forest is a forest. One stand of trees is that much like another. "See here," I say, "Coed Cadw is ancient and it is wild—dark and danger-ous as a cave filled with vipers. The Forest of the March has never been conquered, much less tamed."

"You would call a forest tame?" He wonders at this, scratching the side of his nose with his quill.

"Oh, aye! Most forests in the land have been subdued in one way or another, mastered long ago by men—cleared for farmsteads, har-vested for timber, and husbanded for game. But Coed Cadw is still untouched, see. Why, there are trees that were old when King Arthur rallied the clans to the dragon flag, and pools that have not seen sun-light since Joseph the Tin planted his church on this island. It's true!"

I can see he doesn't believe me.

"Odo, lad," I vouch in my most solemn voice, "there are places in that forest so dark and doomful even wolves fear to tread—believe that, or don't."

"I don't, but I begin to see what you mean," he says, and we move on . . .

Well, as I say, we are all of us in fine festive fettle and about to sit down to a feast provided, mostly, at Abbot's Hugo's expense, when one of the women remarks that something has caught fire. For a moment, she's the only one who can smell it, and then a few more joined her, and before we knew it, we all had the stink of heavy tim-ber smoke in our nostrils. Soon enough, smoke began to drift into the glade from the surrounding wood.

In grey, snaking ropes it came, feeling its way around the boles of trees, flowing over roots and rocks, searching like ghost fingers, touch-ing and moving on. Those of us seated at the table rose as one and looked to the west, where we saw a great mass of slate-black smoke churning up into the winter sky. Even as we stood gaping at the sight, ash and cinders began raining down upon us.

Someone gave out a cry, and Bran climbed onto the board. He stood with hands upraised, commanding silence. "Peace!" he said. "Remain calm. We will not fear until there is cause to fear, and then we will bind courage to our hearts and resist." Turning to the men, he said, "Iwan, Siarles, fetch the bows. Will, Tomas, Rhoddi, follow me. We will go see what mischief is taking place." To the others he said, "Those who remain behind, gather supplies and make ready to leave in case we must flee Cél Craidd."

"Be careful, Will," said Nóin, biting her lip.

"A little work before dinner," I replied, trying to make my voice sound light and confident although the smoke thickening and ash raining down on our heads filled me with dread. "I'll be back before you know it."

Iwan and Siarles returned and passed out the bows and bundles of arrows. I slung the strung bow over my chest and tied a sheaf of arrows to my belt. Leaving the folk in the care of Angharad and the friar, we departed on the run. We followed the drift of the smoke as the wind carried it from the blaze, and with every step the darkness grew as the smoke clouds thickened. Before long, we had to stop and wet the edges of our cloaks and pull them fast around our faces to keep from breathing the choking stuff.

We pressed on through the weird twilight and soon began to see the flicker of orange and yellow flames through the trees ahead. The fire produced a wind that gusted sharply, and we felt the heat lapping at our hands and faces. The roar of the blaze, like the surge of waves hurled onto the shore, drowned out all other sound.

"This way!" urged Bran, veering off the track at an angle towards the wall of fire.

Working quickly and quietly, we came around to a place where the fire had already burned. And there, standing on the charred, still-smouldering earth stood a body of Ffreinc soldiers—eight of them, loitering beside a wagon pulled by two mules and heaped with casks of oil. Some of them carried torches. The rest held lances and shields. All were dressed for battle, with round steel helmets and swords strapped to their belts; their shields leaned against the wagon bed.

We dropped to the ground and wormed back out of sight behind the screen of smoke and flames.

"Sheriff's men," spat Siarles.

"Trying to burn us out," observed Tomas, "and on Christmas day, the sots. Not very friendly, I'd say."

"Shall we take them, Bran?" asked Rhoddi.

"Not yet," Bran decided. "Not until we know how many more are with them." Turning to me and Rhoddi, he said, "You two go with Iwan. Siarles and Tomas come with me. Go all the way to the end and take a good look"—he pointed off into the wood where the wall of flame burned brightest—"and then come back here. We will do the same."

Rhoddi and I fell into step behind Iwan, and the three of us made our way along the inside of the fiery wall, as it were, until, after a few hundred paces, we reached the end. Keeping low, to better stay out of the smoke, we crawled on hands and knees to peer around the edge of the flames. Ten Ffreinc soldiers were working this end of the blaze—two with torches and three with casks of oil they were sprinkling on the damp underbrush. Five more stood guard with weapons ready.

Iwan pointed out the one who seemed to be the leader of the company, and we withdrew, hurrying back to the meeting place. Bran and Iwan spoke briefly together. "We will take the first group here and now," Bran told us, unslinging his bow. "Then we will take the others."

Iwan drew three arrows from the cloth bag. "Fan out," he told us, indicating the spread with three jerks of his hand, "and loose on my signal."

We all drew three shafts and crept into position, halting at the edge of the flame wall. The Ffreinc were still watching the fire, their faces bright. When I saw Iwan fit an arrow to the string, I did likewise. When he stood, I stood. He drew, and so did I . . .

"Now!" he said, his voice low but distinct.

Six shafts streaked out from the wood, crossing the burned clearing in a wink. Four soldiers dropped to the ground.

The two remaining men-at-arms had no time to wonder what had happened to the other fellas. Before they could raise their shields or look around, winged death caught them, lifted them off their feet, and put them on their backs—pierced through with two shafts each.

Then it was a fleet-footed race to the further end of the flame wall. The fire was burning hotter as more of the underbrush and wood took light, drawing wind to itself and spitting it out in fluttering gusts. The smoke was heavy. We clutched our cloaks to our faces and made our way as best we could, stumbling half-blind through the murk to take up new positions.

The flames were now between us and the Ffreinc. We could see the soldiers moving as through a shimmering curtain. Imagine their surprise when out from this selfsame curtain flew not frightened partridges to grace the Christmas board, but six sizzling shafts tipped with stinging death.

Four of the arrows found their marks, and three Marchogi toppled into the snow. A fifth shaft ripped through a soldier's arm and into the cask in the hands of the fella behind him. The amazed soldier dropped

623

the cask, dragging down his companion, who was now securely nailed to the top of the cask.

"Ready . . . ," said Iwan, placing another arrow on the string and leaning into the bow as he drew and took aim. "Now!"

Six more arrows sped through the high-leaping flames, and four more Ffreinc joined the first four on the ground. The remaining two, however, reacting quickly, threw themselves down, pulling their shields over them, thinking to protect themselves this way. But Iwan and Siarles, pressing forward as far as the flames would allow, each sent a shaft pelting into the centre of the shields; one glanced off, taking the edge of the shield with it. The other shaft struck just above the boss and penetrated all the way through and into the neck of the soldier cowering beneath it.

The last fella, crouching behind his shield, tried to back away. Bran knelt quickly and, holding the bow sideways, loosed a shaft that flashed out of the flames, speeding low over the ground. It caught the retreating soldier beneath the bottom edge of the shield, pinning the man's ankles together. He fell screaming to the snow and lay there moaning and whimpering.

We held our breath and waited.

When no more soldiers appeared, we began to imagine it safe to leave.

"What are we to do about the fire?" I asked.

"We cannot fight it," Siarles replied. "We'll have to let it go and hope for the best."

"We will watch it," Iwan said. "If it spreads or changes direction, we should know."

Bran looked back through the curtain of flame towards the fallen soldiers. "I did not see the sheriff." Turning to us, he said, "Did anyone see the sheriff?"

Scarlet

No one had seen him, of course, for just as the question had been spoken there came a shout and, from the night-dark wood behind us, mounted knights appeared, lances couched, crashing up out of the brush where they had been hidden.

CHAPTER 17

I saw the spearheads gleam sharp in the firelight and the fire glow red on the helmets of the knights and chamfers of the horses as they clattered up out of the brake. I tried to count and made it eight or ten of them, closing fast.

They were that near we had time but to pull once and loose.

In less time than it takes to catch a breath, our arrows streaked out, the stinging whine followed by a slap and crack like that of a whip as steel heads met padded leather jerkin and then ring mail, piercing both. The force of the blow lifted two hard-charging riders from the saddle and sent a third backwards over the rump of his horse.

Before the onrushing knights could check their mounts, we each had another shaft on the string. Iwan took the foremost knight, and I took the one behind him. Bran changed his aim at the last instant and sent a shaft into the breast of a charger that had already lost its rider. The oncoming horse's legs tangled and it stumbled, taking down the two horses behind it as well. The knights tried to quit the saddle before their steeds rolled on them, but only one avoided the crush. The other was lost in a heap of horseflesh and churning hooves.

I pulled another arrow from my sheaf and nocked it, but did not have time to aim. I threw myself to the ground as a lance blade swept the place lately occupied by my head. As I scrambled to my feet, a trumpet sounded. I looked to the sound as at least eight more knights came bounding from the wood with Marshal Gysburne leading the charge.

Slow cart that I am, it was only then that I understood we had been caught in a neatly spread net and the ends were about to close on us.

Bran had already seen it. "Fall back!" he shouted.

But there was nowhere to flee.

Behind us was a wall of burning trees and brush, ahead a swarm of angry soldiers—each one in a blood-rage to take our heads.

The trumpet sounded again, and there he was: Sir Richard de Glanville, the devil himself, looking powerfully pleased with his surprise. He swept out of the darkness flanked by two knights holding torches, and I do believe he imagined that at the very sight of him the fight would go out of us. For as he emerged from the dark wood he called out in English.

The others looked to me. "He says we must surrender, but that quarter will be given."

Siarles spat and put an arrow on the string. Iwan said, "We ask no quarter."

Raising his bow, Siarles said, "Shall I make reply, Lord?"

Bran nodded. "Give him our answer."

Before Bran had even finished speaking, the shaft was on its way. The sheriff, anticipating such a response, was ready.

Having faced a Welsh bowman before, he had provided himself with a small round shield clad in iron plate. As Siarles' arrow seared

628

across the flame-shot distance, de Glanville threw his heavy round shield before him, taking the blow on the iron boss. There was a spark as metal struck metal, and the sturdy oak shaft shattered from the impact.

There was no time for a second flight, for at that moment a second body of knights charged in on the flank. I could not count them. I saw only a rush out of the darkness as the horses appeared.

We all loosed arrows at will, sending as fast as we could draw. Three knights were despatched that quick, and two more followed before the first were clear of the saddle. Then, with the horses on top of us, it was time to flee.

"This way!" cried Bran, edging back and back towards the burning trees and brush—a place even the best-trained Norman horses would not willingly go. "Through there," said Bran, already starting towards a gap between two burning elm trees. Pulling his cloak over his head, he darted through the narrow, fire-filled space as through a flaming arch.

Siarles and Rhoddi followed. Iwan, Tomas, and I made good their escape, sending another shaft each into the mounted soldiers as they wheeled and turned to get a good run at us. Then it was our turn to face the fire.

Pulling my cloak over my head, I bent low and ran for the flames, diving headlong between the two elms. I felt the heat lick out, scorching the cloth of my cloak, and then I was through to the other side. Tomas was not so fortunate. He got a little too close and his cloak caught fire. He came through in a rush, shouting and crying that he was burning alive. I grabbed him and threw him down on the ground, rolling him until the flames were out. He was singed, and his cloak was blackened a little along the hem in the back, but he was unharmed.

"To me!" shouted Bran. Through the flames, he had seen the Marchogi regrouping. As I took my place beside him, I could hear the sheriff rallying his men on the other side of the flame wall. "Take the horses!"

With that, he sent a shaft through the shimmering flames into the indistinct shapes that were the Ffreinc knights and their horses. The arrow found a target, for at once a knight gave out a cry. Soon we were all at it, braving the heat and smoke, to stand and deliver death and havoc from out of the flames. Again and again, I drew and loosed, working in rhythm with the others.

We made good account of ourselves, I think—though it was hard to be sure as we could not always see where our shafts went. But by the time the soldiers had regrouped and come charging around the end of the flame wall, there were far fewer than there had been just moments before.

"Away!" shouted Bran, pointing to the wood behind us. Siarles was already disappearing into the scrub at the edge of the clearing. Bran followed on his heels.

"Time to run for it," said Iwan. Loosing one last shaft, he turned and fled.

I slung my bow and pushed Tomas ahead of me, saying, "Go! Run! Don't lose them!"

We crossed the smouldering ground, leaping over the bodies of the soldiers we had killed before the sheriff had tipped his hand. While Tomas dived into the underbrush, I cast a glance over my shoulder as the knights came pounding into the clearing.

By the time Sheriff de Glanville took command of the field, he found it occupied only by his own dead men-at-arms, lying where they'd fallen in the melted snow. His voice sounded sharp in the cold night air. I fancied I could hear the disappointment and frustration as he began calling for his men to start searching the area for our tracks.

That much I got, anyway. The luck of Cain to 'em, I thought. The ground was that chewed up—what with the soldiers setting fires and all—I did not think they'd be able to find our trail in a month of Christmases, but we did not wait to find out. From the cover of the wood, we sent some more arrows into them, killing some, wounding others. The sheriff, realising the battle was now beyond winning, called the retreat. They fled back the way they had come and, since our arrows were mostly spent, we let them go.

"They might return," Bran said, and ordered us all to scatter and work our way around the blaze. "Confuse your trail and make certain you are not followed. Then fly like ravens for the roost."

I put my head down and lit out through the dark winter wood. Keeping the blaze on my left, I worked my way slowly and carefully around until I'd coursed half the circle, then faded back along a deer run that took me near to the bottom of the ridge protecting Cél Craidd. After a time picking my way carefully through a hedge of brambles and hawthorn, I reached the foot of the ridge and paused to listen, kneeling beside a rock to rest a moment before continuing.

I heard nothing but the night wind freshening the tops of the larches and pines. The fire still stained the night sky, tinting the smoke a dull rusty red, but it was less fierce now; already the blaze was dying out. Overhead, there were patches of winter sky showing through the clouds, and stars glimmering bright as needle pricks. The air was cold and crisp. As I started up the snow-covered slope it came to me that this attack signalled a change in our fortunes. We had beaten the sheriff this time, but it was just the beginning. Next time he would come with more men, and still more. There would be no stopping him now.

631

CHAPTER 18

In the bleak heart of midwinter, with the snow deep and white, the air cold and still, it seemed as if the greenwood awaited the coming of the new year with breath abated. We of the Raven Flock held our breath, too, waiting and watching through the night and all the next day. Bran doubled the number of watchers on the road, and set others in a surrounding ring around Coed Cadw. But the sheriff and his men did not return.

The evening of the day after the attack, Lord Bran summoned his advisors to his hut. Wary and uncertain still, we gathered. Iwan, Siarles, Mérian, Tuck, and myself took our places around the small hearth in the centre of his hut. "We have rattled the hornets in their nest," Iwan pointed out as we settled to discuss what had happened the night before and what it might mean.

"That much is plain as your big feet," replied Siarles.

"Where is Angharad?" wondered Mérian. "She should be with us."

"So she should," agreed Bran. "But she has begged leave to absent herself."

"Not like her," observed Iwan. "Not like her at all."

"Is she well?" asked Tuck. "I could go see her."

"She is well," replied Bran, adding, "but the raid last night has disturbed her mightily. She did not foresee it."

"Nor did any of us," pointed out Tuck.

"No, but our *budolion* feels she should have sensed it. She is going to her cave to learn the reason and"—he lifted the ring on its string around his neck—"to learn more of this lovely trinket." The gold shone with a fine lustre, and the jewels gleamed even in the dim light of the hut.

Tuck took one look at the heavy gold bauble and cried, "Lord have mercy! Where did you get that?"

Bran explained about the raid on the supply train. Tuck sucked his teeth, shaking his head all the while. "I do not wonder Angharad is distressed. You have called down the wrath of Baron de Braose upon your silly heads, my friends." Tapping the ring with a finger to watch it swing, he added, "He wants it back, and now you have made it worth his while to find you."

"This wasn't all," said Iwan. "Show him the rest."

Mérian fetched a small box, which she opened, drawing out the richly embroidered gloves and passing them to the friar.

"Well, well, lookee here," chirped the priest, "what a fine pair of mittens." Seizing them, he pulled them tightly over his chubby hands and held them up for all to see. "Goatskin, if I'm not mistaken," he said, "and made in France, I shouldn't wonder." He withdrew his hands and stroked the leather flat again. "Someone will be missing these sorely."

"Aye, but who?" asked Bran. "Abbot Hugo?"

"For him?" wondered Tuck. "Possibly. It would not surprise me that he holds himself so highly. But see here—" he indicated the cross on the right hand and, on the left glove, a curious symbol shaped something like a cross, but with two extra arms and a closed loop at its head. "That is the Chi Rho," he told us, "and most often seen on the vestments of high priests of one kind or another." He passed the gloves back to Mérian. "If you asked me, I'd say these were made for a prince among priests—an archbishop or cardinal, at least."

"Then what are they doing here?" asked Iwan.

"Perhaps our humble abbot has more exalted ambitions," replied Bran.

"Was there ever any doubt?" quipped Tuck. His smooth brow wrinkled with thought. "Ring and gauntlets," he mused. "It must mean something. But for the love of Peter, I cannot think what it might be."

"We were hoping you would have an idea," sighed Mérian.

"Nay, lass," replied the friar. "You will have to find a better and wiser man than the one that sits before you to get an answer."

"There is one other thing," said Bran. Reaching into the box, he brought out the square of parchment and passed that to the priest.

In the hurly-burly of the feast and later attack, I had mostly forgotten all about that thick folded square of lambskin. I looked at it now—I think we all did—as the very thing needed to explain the mystery to us.

"Why didn't you say you had this?" said Tuck. He turned it over in his hands. "You haven't opened it."

"No," answered Bran. "You may have the honour."

We all edged close as the friar's stubby fingers fumbled with the blue cord. When he had untied it, he laid it in his lap and looked around at the circle of faces hovering above him. "If we break this," he said, fingering the wax seal, "there is no going back."

"Break it," commanded Bran. "It has already cost the lives of a score of men or more. We will see what it is that the abbot and sheriff value at such a high price."

Drawing a breath, Tuck cracked the heavy wax seal and carefully unfolded the parchment, spreading it before him on the rush-strewn floor of the hut.

"What is it?" asked Iwan.

"What does it say?" said Siarles.

"Shh!" hissed Mérian. "Give the man a chance." To Tuck she said, "Take your time." Then, when he appeared to do just that, she added, "Well, what does it say?"

Lifting his face, he shook his head.

"Bad news?" wondered Bran.

"I don't know," replied the priest slowly.

Bran leaned close. "What then?"

"God knows," Tuck lifted the parchment to pass around. "It is written fair enough, but not in Latin. I cannot read the bloody thing."

"Are you certain?"

"I think so. I read little enough Latin, to be sure. But I cannot make out a word of that." He shook his round head. "I don't know what it is."

We passed the parchment hand to hand, and as it came to me, I saw the entire surface covered with a fine, flowing script in dark brown ink. As I had never acquired the knack of reading—not English, nor Latin either—I had nothing to say about it. But it seemed to me that the words were well formed, the letters long and graceful—it put me in mind of ivy and how it loops and curls around all it touches. The skin was fine-grained and well prepared; there were hardly any grease smudges or ink spatters at all.

"I think it is Ffreinc," Mérian decided, holding it up to the light and bending her head close. "I can speak it well enough, but I have only seen it written once or twice, mind." She concluded, "It looks very like Ffreinc to me."

"Yes, well, that would make sense," mused Tuck, taking back the parchment. The two of them proceeded to examine it closely, tracing various letters with their fingers and muttering over it. "See, here that is a *D*," said Tuck, "and that an *I* followed by *E* and *U*." He paused to string together what he'd found. "Dee-a-oo," he said.

"God!" exclaimed Mérian. "*Dieu* means God." She put her finger on a letter. "What is that?"

Tuck peered hard at the script. "I think it might be an *S*," he said. "With an *A* . . . *F* . . . ah, no that might be an *L* . . . *U* . . . *T* . . ." He continued picking out letters one by one and uttered the word as he did so. I followed some of this, but my small store of Ffreinc was of the more rough and ready sort spoken in the market, not the court or church, and it soon left me trailing far behind.

"*Salutations!*" said Mérian before he finished. "'Greetings!'" She beamed happily. "*Salutations dans Dieu,*" she said. "'Greetings in God'— that must be it."

Tuck agreed. "I think so."

"That would be expected," said Iwan. "What else?"

The two continued, trying to scry out the letters and make words of them that Mérian knew. And though they succeeded in guessing several more, they fell far short of the mark and were forced to give up in the end, leaving us little the wiser for the effort. "We know it is Ffreinc, at least," said Bran. "That is something."

"Well, whatever is in that letter," said Tuck, tapping the sheepskin with his finger, "you can be sure the baron will be missing it. I think de Braose wants his treasures back."

"Oh, aye," affirmed Iwan, "and he's willing to risk good men to get them."

Tuck nodded thoughtfully. "Mark me, there is a dread mystery here. You would be wise to return these things as soon as possible," he concluded, "before any more blood is shed."

"That I will not do," declared Bran. "At least, not until I know what it is we have found. If de Braose considers it worth an army to recover"—he smiled suddenly—"perhaps it is worth more."

"A castle!" suggested Siarles.

"Perhaps," allowed Bran. "Maybe even a kingdom."

And, no, Odo," I say with a sigh, "I cannot read. Not even my own name when it is writ. Then again, Thane Aelred couldn't read a whit, either, nor any of his vassals, saving the monks at the abbey, and he was a towering oak of a man, bless him."

"Oh," smirks he, "but there is nothing to it once you have the learning. I could teach you," he says, hopeful as a puppy.

"Well then, Odo, me lad," I tell him, "one day when I have the leisure of a cleric, as you most certainly do, I shall let you teach me to read. Now, where was I?"

"Bran considered the ring of great value," replies Odo. I lick my lips and rumble on . . .

The next day, when Angharad learned what Tuck had revealed about the parchment, she thanked Bran for telling her, gave him a few words of advice, and took her leave. Pulling on her cloak, she bunged a few leftovers from our truncated feast into a leather bag slung on her back, took up her staff, and departed Cél Craidd then and there.

Some of us saw her leave. "Is she angry?" Tomas asked. "She seems fair put out with the world."

"I don't know," I replied. "Maybe."

"Where is she going?"

"She has a cave somewhere in the greenwood," said Huw, one of the elder Grellon. "She goes there of a time to think."

Well, the sheriff's attack had cast a shadow of gloom over our none-too-happy home, I can tell you. As soon as Angharad left, Bran hived himself in his hut with Iwan and Tuck to decide what to do next.

"God with you, Will," said Mérian, coming to stand beside me.

"And with you, my lady," I answered.

She rubbed her hands to warm them. "I wonder what they will decide."

"Difficult to say. Weighty decisions require patience and pondering aplenty."

"Do you think it dangerous, this ring?"

"I think it valuable, and that is usually danger enough." I nodded towards the hut. "I think Tuck is right when he says there is a dread mystery in the thing."

As we were talking, I caught sight of someone out of the corner of my eye. I looked across the clearing to see Nóinina disappearing between two huts; she cast a last look over her shoulder as she moved from view. Something about her expression as she passed out of sight gave me to think she had been watching Mérian and me and did not approve, not one tiny little scrap.

It was just the merest glimmer of a glance, to be sure. Still, it gave me a curious warmth that lasted throughout the day.

The king and his advisors emerged a short time later. "What was decided?" I asked Iwan as he came out to join us.

"We will take the treasure to Saint Tewdrig's for safekeeping as Angharad has advised," he told me. "We will also show the letter to Bishop Asaph. Perhaps he or one of his monks can read it and tell us something about how and why this ring has come to Elfael."

"That sounds a sensible plan," Mérian remarked.

I nodded my agreement. "Good," I said.

"I'm glad you approve, Scarlet," he answered, turning on his heel and walking backwards a step or two. "Because it's you that's going."

CHAPTER 19

In less time than it takes a fella to lace up his boots, I was on my way. I suppose others reckoned that, as a half-Saxon with a snip of Ffreinc under my belt, I could more easily pass among the Normans as a wandering labourer—which is what I was until joining King Raven's flock.

This decision did not sit well with at least one member of our band. Siarles got it into his thick head that I was more affliction than remedy and asked to be allowed to accompany me. After a brief discussion, it was agreed that Siarles, who had been to the monastery before and knew the way, would go with me to act as guide. We were given a deerskin bundle containing the ring and gloves, and the parchment in its wrap, which we were to take to the bishop at Saint Tewdrig's and learn whatever we could from the monks—they, being men of learning, might know how to read the letter and could be trusted to hold their peace about whatever there was that might be gleaned. The rest of the treasure was to be placed with them for safekeeping.

"If the sheriff or any of his men catch you with these things," Bran warned, the flat of his hand on the parcel as he handed it to Siarles, "they will hang you for thieves—and that is the least they will do. Stay sharp, and hurry back with all speed."

"My lord," I replied, "this skin of mine may be poor quality as some would judge, but it is my own and I have grown to love it. Rest assured, I will not risk it foolishly." I might have added that Nóin also had a definite interest in seeing me return hale and whole.

"There is yet one thing more," said Tuck. He had been standing beside Bran, listening to the instructions. "Hear me, if you will. Hear me, everyone."

"Silence!" called Bran. "Friar Tuck will speak."

When all had quieted, he said, "The ring has value and therefore power, does it not? It may be that God has given it to us to aid in the redemption of Elfael. Brothers and sisters all, we must hold tight to this hope and guard it with a mighty strength of purpose. Therefore, know that this is a solemn charge that has been laid upon you, Will and Siarles." He regarded Siarles and me with a commanding stare. "You take our lives in your hands when you leave this place. See you do nothing that would endanger them, or there will be hell to pay. Is this understood?"

We nodded our assent, but he would have more. "Say it," he insisted. "Pledge it on your honour."

This we did, and Tuck declared himself satisfied. He turned to Bran and said, "We have done what we can do. Now, it is for God to do as he will do." Raising his hands high, he said, "I pray the Lord of Hosts to send an army of angels to guard you every step of the way, to smooth your path in the rough world and bring you safely home. Amen and God with you."

"Amen!"

Nóin and I shared a kiss of farewell. She clutched me tight, and whispered, "Come back to me, Will Scarlet. I have grown that fond of you."

"I will come back, Nóin, never fear."

With that, we took leave of our king and rode out, taking a path that was only rarely used by the Grellon. The trail, which was tangled and overgrown in many places, would lead us north a fair distance where, once well away from Cél Craidd, we would double back to the Norman lands of the south and east. It was decided that we should stay off the King's Road so as to avoid any travellers, especially Norman soldiers. For two days we made our slow way through the winterland and shivered in a frosty silence as we moved through a world bleached white by the snow and cold—the stark, bloodred berries of holly and the deep green strands of ivy twining round boles of elm and oak the only hues that met our colour-starved eyes.

The Forest of the March seemed to slumber beneath its thick mantle, although here and there we saw the tracks of deer and pigs, sometimes those of wolves and other creatures—the long slashing strides of the hare, and the light skittery tracings of mice and squirrels. Overhead we heard the creak and crack of cold boughs and branches, and the occasional twit and chirp of birds interested in our passing. But these were the only things to relieve the dull sameness of the slumbering greenwood.

Nor was Siarles the easiest companion a man might choose. Short-tempered and quick to judge; easily stirred to anger or despair; in character, steadfast; in mood as changeable as water—he is Cymry through and through, Siarles is. Poor fella, he is one of God's creatures that is happiest when most miserable. And should he lack sufficient cause for misery, an imaginary source is all too easily conjured. For some reason he had taken against me from that first day I dropped out of the tree.

043

By day's end, I reckoned I had endured enough of his rudeness. "Siarles, my friend, there is a boil of contention between us as wants lancing."

"So you say."

"I do say it. You act like a fella with bees in his breeches every time we meet. For the life of me, I cannot think why that should be. Nevertheless, I know an unhappy man when I see one, and here I have one in my eye."

"I am not unhappy," he said, his whole face puckered in a petulant scowl.

"I think you are. Or, if not unhappy, then displeased. Tell me what you've got caught in your craw, and I will do my best to help you."

He glared at me, then turned away. "Finish saddling your horse. It is time we were on our way."

"No," I replied. "Not until you tell me what is wrong with you."

He turned on me with sudden anger. "With me?" he said, almost shouting. "You find fault with me when it is yourself you should be chiding."

"Me! What have I done?"

He made a sound like the growl of a frustrated dog and turned away again.

"Well, this is going to be a long day a-standin' here," I told him. "I'm not moving until I know your mind." He glared at me balefully, and I thought he would not speak.

"Well? What is it to be? Either we make peace between us, or stand here and glower at one another like two stubborn roosters in a yard."

He snarled again, his frustration boundless, and I could not help but laugh at the hopelessness of the situation. "See here, Siarles, my contrary friend. You're going to have to give me something more than grunts and growls if we are to get to the meat of the matter. So you might as well tell me and get it done."

"I don't like Englishmen," he grimaced through gritted teeth. "Never have. Never will."

"Half an Englishman only," I corrected. "My mother was a Briton, mind. As was your own if you had one."

"You know what I mean. Bran had no business taking you in."

"No? It seems to me that a lord can take a vassal of any fella willing to swear fealty to him. I bent the knee to Bran right gladly, and my word holds fast through fair or foul," I declared. "You wanted to come along because you don't trust me. You thought I'd steal the ring and fly away as soon as I got out of sight."

He glowered at me, and I could see I'd hit near the mark. "You don't know what I think," he muttered at last.

"Yes, I do," I told him. "You had a cosy little nest in the greenwood and then along comes this big ol' Englishman, Will Scarlet, stomping all over your tidy garden with his great boots, and you're afraid he's going to squash you like a bug." Siarles frowned and climbed into the saddle. "But, see here, I en't about squashing you or anybody else, nor usurping 'em from their rightful place. Neither am I leaving my sworn liege lord just because you don't like the cut of my cloth. Lord Bran's dealings are his own, and if that sticks in your gizzard, then talk to him. Don't punish me."

He turned his mount and rode away. I followed a few paces behind, giving him space and time, hoping he would come 'round to a better humour sooner or later. But though I tried my best to cheer him along and show him I bore no ill feelings over his churlishness, his mood did not improve. I resolved to ignore his sour disposition and get on with the chore at hand.

Saint Tewdrig's in the north is but a short distance beyond the border of Elfael—a new monastery tucked in the curving arm of a valley across the river close on the border of the cantref. I counted five

645

buildings, including a small church, all of timber arranged in a loose square and surrounded by a low whitewashed wall. Small fields—flat squares of snow with barley stubble showing through like an unshaved chin—flanked the monastery. We crossed one of these and arrived at the gate and pulled the braided bell cord hanging at the gatepost. A light, clinking ring sounded in the chill air, and presently a small door opened within the larger. "*Pax vobiscum.* How can I help you?" asked the porter. He looked blandly at me, and then at Siarles, and his eyes lit with recognition. "Silidons! Welcome! Come in. Come in! I will tell Father Asaph you are here." He turned and hurried off across the yard, leaving us to stand outside with our mounts, which could not pass through the small door.

"Silidons?" I said. "What is that?"

"It was Bran's idea," he said. "He thought it would be better for the monks if they did not know our real names."

True enough, I reckoned, for if the Normans suspected the monks knew anything to help them find us, they would be in danger deep and dire. "Nor can they sell us out," I considered.

"Not likely, that."

"You must have a high opinion of priests. I've known one or two that would not spare a moment's thought to trade their mothers to the Danes for a jug of ale and two silver pennies."

"The priests you know may be rogues," he said, "but the brothers here can be trusted."

"How do you know they won't go running to the sheriff behind our backs?"

"Lord Bran built this monastery," he explained simply. "That is, our Bran gave the money so that it could be built. Asaph was the bishop of Llanelli, the monastery at Caer Cadarn before the Ffreinc took it and drove the monks out and turned the place into a market town. Asaph accepts the patronage without asking who gives it."

I was not really concerned, but if I'd had any fear of betrayal, meeting Bishop Asaph removed even the most niggly qualm. The man was like one of those saints of old who have churches named after them. White haired and wispy as a willow wand, the old man pranced like a goat as he swept us into the holy precinct of the monastery, arms a-fly, bare heels flashing beneath his long robe, welcoming us even as he berated the porter for leaving us loitering at the gate.

"God's peace, my friends. All grace and mercy upon you. Silidons! It is good to see you again. Brother Ifor, how could you leave our guests standing outside the gate? You should always insist they wait inside. Come in! Come in!"

"Bishop Asaph," said Siarles, "I present to you a friend of mine"— he hesitated a moment, and then said—"by the name of . . . Goredd."

O do has stopped to scratch his head. He is confused. "Yes," I tell him, "Siarles and Silidons are one and the same. The monks know him as Silidons, see? They know me now as Goredd. Can we get on?"

"Just one question, Will . . ."

"One?"

"Another question, then. This monastery you speak of in Saint Tewdrigs? Where would that lie, specifically?"

"Why, it lies exactly on the spot where it stands, not a foot's breadth to the north nor to the south."

Odo frowns. "I mean to say it sounds a pagan name. Would you know the French?"

I let my temper flare at him. "No—I would not! If the Ffreinc will insist on renaming every village and settlement willy-nilly, it is unreasonable of them to expect honest men such as myself to commit them all to memory and recite them at the drop of a hat! If your good abbot wishes to visit the place, I suggest that he begin further enquiries in hell!"

Odo listens to this with a hurt, doglike expression. As I finish, his hurt gives way to wryness. "Honest men such as you?" he asks.

"There is more honesty in me than there is in a gaggle of Norman noblemen, let us not be mistaken."

Odo shrugs and dips his quill. After allowing me to cool for a moment, he repeats the last line written, and we trudge on . . .

Long robes flapping around his spindly shanks, the old bishop led us across the yard. For all his joy at seeing us, a doleful mood seemed to rest heavy on the place, and I wondered about it.

The brother stabler took our horses away to be fed and watered, and the bishop himself prepared our rooms, which, I believe, had never been used. They were spare and smelled of whitewash, and the beds were piled with thick new fleeces. "I see they don't get many visitors," I observed to Siarles when Asaph had gone.

"The monastery is new still," he allowed, "and since the Ffreinc came to Elfael not many people travel this way anymore."

One of the brothers brought a basin of water and some soap for us to wash away the last few days of travel. Siarles and I took turns splashing our faces and rinsing our hands in the basin before joining the bishop for refreshment in his quarters above the building they called a refectory.

"We eat a meal after evening prayers," Asaph informed us, "but travel is hungry work." He stretched a hand towards the table that had been prepared for us. "So please, my friends, take a little something to keep body and soul together until then."

We thanked him and filled our wooden bowls from the fare on offer: boiled eggs and sliced sheep's cheese and cold mutton. There was some thin ale—no doubt the best they had—and fresh buttermilk. We sat down to eat, and the bishop drew his chair near the table. "You must tell me the news," he said, his tone almost pitiful. "How does our benefactor fare?"

"Never better," Siarles answered. "He looks forward to the day when he can visit you himself. And he sends me with this token of his earnest goodwill for your work here." With that, Siarles produced a small leather bag of coins from his purse, and placed it on the table before the cleric.

The bishop smiled and, thanking God and us both, opened the bag and poured out a handful of silver pennies. "Tell your lord that this will go far towards easing the burden of the poor hereabouts. The Ffreinc press everyone so very hard . . ." Here he faltered and looked away.

"Father?" I said. "You look like a fella who has just bit his tongue rather than speak his mind. Why not tell us what is wrong?"

"Things are bad just now—worse than ever before."

"Indeed?" asked Siarles. "What has happened?"

Asaph tried to talk, but could not. Siarles passed him a cup of the watery ale, and said, "Drink some of that down and maybe it will help loosen the words."

He drank and placed the cup carefully on the table before him as if he was afraid it might shatter. "I do not know how it came about," he said when he had found his voice again, "but something of great value to the count has gone missing. They are saying it was stolen by the creature called King Raven."

"We have heard of this," I told him, to encourage him and keep him talking now that he had begun. "What has the count done?"

"He has taken prisoners—men and boys—pulling them out of their beds in the dead of night. A decree has gone out. He says he will start hanging them on Twelfth Night . . ."

"The great steaming pile!" exclaimed Siarles.

The bishop turned large, sad eyes on us. "One man or boy each day at sunset until what was stolen is returned. That is what Count de Braose has said. How this will end, God only knows."

So that was it. When their attempt to burn us out failed, the cowardly Ffreinc turned to those unable to defend themselves. "How many?" I asked. "How many has he taken?"

"I don't know," said the bishop. "Fifty or sixty, they say." The ageing cleric drew both hands down his face and shook his head in despair. "God help us," he murmured.

"You know what they say," Siarles told him. "King Raven only takes back what was stolen in the first place. No doubt it is the same with whatever was taken this time . . ."

hat is that, Odo? Did the old bishop know that King Raven was his mysterious benefactor?" I give him a fishy smile. "Do I look such a fool that you think you can trap me so easily? Think again, my scribbling friend. Will cannot be drawn." I regard him with his smooth-shaved pate and his ink-stained fingers. "What do you think?"

"I think he must have known," Odo says. "A man knows whose largess keeps him."

"Does he now?" I crow. "Do you know who keeps you, monk?"

"God keeps me," replies the monk, his sanctimony nigh insufferable.

"Ha! It's Abbot Hugo keeps you, priest—and you're as much a

captive as Will Scarlet ever was. Hugo owns you as much as he owns the food you put in your mouth and the bed you sleep in at night—don't think he doesn't. See here, our Bishop Asaph is not a stupid man. Only a right fool would pry into things that could bring ruin if all was known."

"Then he is a sinner," concludes Odo loftily.

"A sinner," I repeat. "How so?"

"Receiving the benefit of money acquired by theft makes a thief of any who accept it."

"Is that right?" I say. "Is that what they teach in the monkery?"

"It is." Oh, he is so smug in his righteousness, sometimes I want to throttle him with the belt around his sagging middle.

"Well," I allow, "you may be right. But tell me which is the greater theft—stealing a man's purse, or his homeland?"

"Stealing is stealing," he replies smoothly. "It is all the same in God's eyes."

"God's eyes! I will give you God's eyes, Odo! Get out! We are finished. I will speak no more today." He looks at me with a hurt expression. "Out with you," I roar. "Leave me."

He rises slowly and blows on the parchment and rolls it. "You take offence where none was offered," he sniffs. "I merely point out the church's position in the matter of theft, which—as we all know, is a mortal sin."

"Well and good, but this is war, you scurvy toad. And war makes thieves of all good men who would oppose the cruel invader."

"There is no war," declares my weak-eyed scribe. His sanctimony is boundless. "There is only rebellion to the established rule."

"Out!" I cry, and pick up a handful of mouldy straw from the damp floor of my cell. I fling the clump at him. "Out! And do not come back."

651

He turns to go, showing as much haste as I have ever seen in him. But at the door he hesitates. "If I do not return, the hangman comes the sooner."

"Let him come!" I shout. "I welcome him. I would rather listen to him raising his gibbet than you telling me about the established rule. For the love of the Holy Virgin, Odo! It is a rule established in blood on a stolen throne. So now! Who is the saint and who the sinner?"

He ducks his head as he steps through the ironclad door of my cell and slinks away into the darkness. I lie back and close my eyes. *Sweet Lord Jesus*, I pray, *let my enemies kill me, or set me free!*

CHAPTER 20

Odo has not come today, and I begin to think that he has taken me at my word. Perhaps he has gone to our false abbot with my rantings and Hugo has decided to be done with me at last. If Odo does not come tomorrow, I will send for him and make my shrift. A lame piece of priesthood he may be, but in truth I do not trust anyone else in this nest of vipers to hear my confession. Odo can do that, at least, and though he riles me no end, I know he will see me right.

I hear from my keeper, Gulbert—or is it Gibbert?—that the wet weather has passed and the sun has returned. This is good news. It may be that my damp pit will dry out a little—not that ol' Will plans to wear out the world much longer. Even without my bone-headed outburst, the abbot's patience must be growing thin as his mercy. From all accounts, he was never a fella to suffer long to begin with.

So now, my execution day must be drawing nigh.

But, what is this?

There is a muffled scrabbling in the corridor beyond my cell . . . hushed voices . . . and then the familiar slow, shuffling footfall.

"Good day, Will Scarlet," says Odo as he appears at the door. "God with you." His voice is that much strained as if addressing a stroppy stranger.

"This day is almost done, my friend," I say to put him at ease. Well, he is the closest thing to a friend I have in this forsaken place. "I'll say good evening and God bless."

He makes no move to open the door, but stands in the narrow stone corridor. "Are you coming in, then?" I ask.

"No, it will be dark soon, and I could not get any candles."

"I see."

"The abbot does not know I am here. He has forbidden me to listen to you."

"He has had enough of my ravings and ramblings, I suppose."

"Oh, no," Odo is quick to assure me, "it is that he has gone and does not want me talking to you while he is away."

"Gone? Where has he gone?"

"I am not to say," Odo replied, but continued anyway. "There is an envoy from Rome visiting some of the towns hereabouts—a Spaniard, a Father Dominic. Abbot wishes him to visit, so he has ridden out to find him."

"I see." I suck my teeth and give him a shrug to show I will not try to pry any more out of him. "Well, then . . ."

Odo bites his lip. He has something more to tell me, but cannot yet trust himself to speak. So I fish a little and see if I can tickle him into my net. "How long will the abbot be away?"

"I cannot say, my lord," says Odo, and I smile. He does not know what he has said yet. Give him time.

He blushes as it comes to him. "Will, I mean . . ."

I chuckle at his small mistake. He has begun to think of me as a nobleman, and his superior. "No harm, monk," I tell him.

"It is just that there are a few things I do not understand."

"Only a few?" I laugh. "Then you are a better man than I."

"In your story, I mean."

"It is not a story, Odo," I tell him. "It is a man's life—I'm telling my life. And we both know how it's going to end. See you remember that."

He looks at me, blinking his big, soft eyes. "Well, the abbot has said we are not to pursue our tale any further just now."

"Ah, I see."

"So, I should be on my way." He stands flat-footed and hunched in the cramped corridor.

He says he cannot stay, and yet he will not leave. Something holds him here.

"Well, perhaps," I suggest lightly, "the abbot would not mind if you spent a little time stalking the understanding that eludes you. It is for the abbot's benefit, after all."

Odo brightens at once. "Do you think so?"

"Oh, aye. Who else cares about the ravings of a wild outlaw?"

"This is exactly what I was thinking," says he. "It would do no harm to clarify a few of the details—clear up any misunderstandings for the abbot's benefit."

"For the abbot's benefit, of course."

Odo nods, making a firm decision for once in his soft pudding of a life. "Good. I will come tomorrow." Then he smiles; pleased with himself and revelling in this milk-mild defiance. He turns to go, but lingers. "God's peace this night, Will."

"And also with you," I reply as off he scuttles.

There may be hope for Odo yet, please God.

Although the ending is in sight, there is, of course, much more of this tale, this life, to be told. How I came to be in this pinch, for one— but I will not tell this to Odo. Not yet. Distraction may be my best weapon just now—indeed, my only weapon. I must distract our ambitious abbot as long as I can to buy King Raven time to work and achieve his purpose. And it is all to do with that blasted ring and infernal letter.

Job's bones! I would not be here now if not for that stupid, bloody treasure. It will be the death of me, beyond a doubt. Truth be told, I fear it will be the death of many before this dreadful tale is done.

Vale of Elfael

Marshal Guy de Gysburne leaned against the freshly daubed wall of Saint Martin's new tax house, and took in his first sight of the latest arrivals sparring at the edge of the square. Seven soldiers—three knights and four men-at-arms—they were the first muster of Abbot Hugo's personal army. Arguing that no abbot worthy of the name could long exist without a bodyguard to protect him as he performed his sacred office in a blighted wilderness full of hostile and bloodthirsty barbarians, Abbot Hugo had prevailed upon Baron de Braose to send troops for his protection and, Gysburne had no doubt, prestige. Indeed, the abbot seemed determined to create his own fiefdom within Elfael, right under de Braose's long, aristocratic nose.

Having arrived while Gysburne was away visiting his father in the north country, the seven newcomers had spent the last few days practising and idling in the town's market square. As Sir Guy watched them now, he found little to dislike. Though they were young men, judging from the way each deftly lunged and parried all were skilled in their weapons. Guy supposed that they had received their training in

Aquitaine or Angevin before being recruited to join the baron's forces. Indeed, they reminded him of himself only a few short years ago: keen as the steel in their hands for a chance to prove themselves and win advancement in the baron's favour, not to mention increased fortune for themselves.

All the same, it would have surprised Guy if any of the newcomers had ever drawn human blood with their painstakingly oiled and sharpened blades, much less fought in a battle.

God willing, that would come. Just now, however, it was time to make the acquaintance of his new army. On a whim, Guy decided to take them hunting; a day in the saddle would give him a chance to see what manner of men they were, and it would do the fresh soldiers good to learn something of the territory that was their new home.

He walked out to meet his men in the square.

"To me!" he called, using the rally cry of the commander in the field. The soldiers stopped their practice and turned to see the lanky, fair-haired marshal striding across the square.

"Lord Gysburne!" shouted one of the knights to his fellows. "Put up! Lord Gysburne has returned."

The others stopped their swordplay and drew together to meet their commander. "At your service, Lord," said the foremost knight, a bull-necked, broad-shouldered youth who, like the others, had the thick wrists and slightly bowed legs of one who has spent most of his short life on the back of a horse, with a sword in his hand. The others, Guy noted, seemed to defer to him as leader of the band and spokesman.

"The sergeant said you were away," the young knight explained. "I thought best to keep our blades busy until you returned." He smiled, the sun lighting his blue eyes. "Jocelin de Turquétil at your service."

"My best regards, Jocelin," replied Guy. "And to you all," he said, turning to the others. "Welcome to Elfael. Now then, if any of the rest of you have names, let's hear them."

They proceeded to introduce themselves around the ring: Alard, Osbert, Warin, Ernald, Baldwin, and Hamo. They spoke with the easy exuberance of men for whom the day held only possibilities, never disappointment. As Guy had surmised, two came from Angevin and three from the baron's lands in Aquitaine; the others had been born in England, but raised in Normandie. This was their first sojourn in Wallia, but all had heard of the ferocity of the native Britons and were eager to try their strength at arms against them.

Sergeant Jeremias appeared in the yard just then and, seeing the marshal, hurried to greet him. "God be good to you, my lord. We've been expecting you these last days. I trust you had a peaceful journey."

"Entirely uneventful," replied Guy.

"And your father is well?"

"He thrives." Regarding the soldiers gathered around him, he said, "It seems our ranks have grown in my absence."

"As you see, Lord Marshal," agreed Jeremias. "And, if I may say so, they are second to none. The abbot is well pleased."

"Then who am I to disagree with the abbot?" remarked Guy, and ordered his new cohort to saddle their horses and prepare for a day's hunting. The soldiers hurried off to ready their mounts, leaving the marshal and sergeant in the yard.

"See all is ready," instructed Guy. "I must go inform the abbot that I have returned."

"Ah," said the sergeant, "no need. He is away and not expected back before Saint Vincent's Day."

"Well, then, we will just have to struggle on as best we can," said Guy, his heart lifting at the thought of not having to pay court to the abbot for a spell. Truth be told, he did not care much for Abbot

Hugo—Guy respected him, and obeyed him, and had vowed to serve him to the best of his ability . . . but he did not like the arrogance, vanity, and ever-more-insistent demands that were becoming a burden.

He owed Hugo a great deal for taking his part and saving him following that first disastrous encounter with King Raven—as the abbot was ever swift to point out. The baron would have had the young marshal horsewhipped and driven from his ranks if not for Hugo's intervention. Guy knew it was not out of sympathy or compassion for himself that the power-grasping cleric had acted but, as with the newly acquired soldiers, it was all part of a carefully devised scheme to gain a force of men who answered to no one but Abbot Hugo alone.

Guy, the abbot's commander, was liking the circumstances of his service less and less. In fact, the reason for braving the cold journey to the North Riding was to see if there might be some place for him in his father's retinue. Sadly, the state of affairs that had sent him south and forced him to link his fortunes with Baron de Braose remained unaltered. There was no living to be had in the north and, as he had long ago discovered, it was too far away from the dance of power and influence attending the king and his court—which was the only hope of the landless lord for advancement, or even a living.

Marshal Guy de Gysburne still needed the abbot because he still needed the baron and ultimately the king. But he was determined that when a better situation presented itself, he would not hesitate to seize it. For now, however, the prospect of commanding a new company of men was an agreeable development and one he determined to bend to his own advantage.

After taking a few mouthfuls of wine and some bread, the knights mounted their horses and rode out, striking north from the town towards the shaggy hills and great encircling arms of the forest. The day was brisk and the sky speckled with grey-edged clouds which passed as shadows over the smooth green snow-spattered hillsides before them. The soldiers, glad for a chance to explore the unfamiliar territory of their new home, galloped through the long grass, exulting in the strength of the horses beneath them.

They reached the edge of the forest, found the entrance to a game run, and entered the long, dim, tree-lined tunnel. The path was wide and they rode easily along, each with a spear ready in case they caught a glimpse of a stag or doe, or some other creature to give them a good chase. But, though they followed the trail as it coursed deeper into the heart of the greenwood, the would-be hunters found nothing worthy of their sport, and as the day began to wane, Guy signalled to Jocelin, riding ahead, that it was time to turn toward home.

Loath to come away without bloodying his spear, Jocelin suggested, "My lord, let us ride on to the top of the ridge just there. If we haven't found any fresh tracks by then, we will turn back."

"The trail is cold today," Guy replied, "and I am getting hungry. Leave it," he said, turning his mount to begin the ride back, "and save a stag or two for another day."

The soldiers followed reluctantly, and as soon as they had quit the forest once more, the ride became a race. Letting their horses have their heads, they flew over the low hills towards the low-sinking sun. Guy, unwilling to restrain their high spirits any longer, let them go.

"Shall I call them back?" asked Jeremias, reining in beside the marshal as the last of the soldiers disappeared over the crest of the hill.

"No, Sergeant, it would serve no purpose," Guy answered. "They will have their ride and feel better for it."

The two proceeded at an easy trot until, reaching the place where they had seen the last rider, they heard shouts and cries echoing up from the valley below. Little more than a crease between two slopes, the valley angled away towards the south and east, broadening slightly before ending in a rocky outcrop. There, in the centre of this close-set defile, was a Welsh herdsman with his cattle.

The soldiers had the man and his few forlorn beasts surrounded and were attempting to separate them from each other. Darting this way and that, their horses wheeling and plunging, they charged and charged again as the frantic Welshman tried to keep his frightened cows together.

As Marshal Guy and his sergeant watched, one of the terrified animals broke from the herd and ran bawling along the valley floor. Jocelin gave out a wild whoop and set out after the beast. He quickly closed on his quarry and, with a quick thrust of his lance, drove the spearhead into the cow's side. The poor creature bellowed the more as the soldier speared it again, and yet again.

The cow crashed to its knees and, still bawling, rolled onto its side as the soldier galloped past. Wheeling his mount, the knight returned to deliver the killing blow with a quick thrust between the dying cow's ribs and into its heart.

Seeing this was all the fun to be had, the other knights followed their comrade's example. Ignoring the shouts and cries of the herdsman, the Ffreinc soldiers quickly cut another cow from the herd and drove it screaming down the valley to its eventual slaughter. The third, a young bullock, gave a good account of itself, turning on its attacker and raking its horns along the pursuing horse's flanks and causing the soldier to abandon the saddle before being killed where it stood by the uninjured but angry knight.

"I shall stop this, my lord, before it goes too far," said Jeremias as a fourth cow was cut out and just as swiftly slaughtered. He lifted the reins and made to ride on.

"Hold," said Guy, putting out a hand to restrain him. "There is little enough harm in it, and they are almost finished. It is the only sport they've had since they came out here."

The herdsman, beside himself at what was happening to his cattle, happened to glimpse the marshal and sergeant watching from the hilltop and decided to take his appeal to them. He started up the slope, shouting and waving his arms to be recognized. One of the Ffreinc knights saw the farmer starting away and rode him down. The Welshman tried to evade his pursuer, but the knight was quicker. Turning his spear butt first, he struck the fleeing herdsman from behind, knocking him to the ground, where he squirmed in pain until the knight gave him a solid thump on the head and he lay still.

When the last animal had been slaughtered, Lord Guy rode down to join his troops. *"Bon chance,"* he said, regarding the carnage: seven head of cattle lay dead on the valley floor, along with a stunned herdsman who was holding his head and moaning gently. "It would seem our hunt has provisioned a feast after all. Jeremias, you and the men gut that young bullock and we'll take it back with us." He pointed to another young animal, "And that heifer as well. I'll ride ahead and tell the cook to prepare the roasting pit. We will eat good Welsh beef tonight."

Jeremias looked around at the dead cattle and their wounded herdsman. "What about the Welshman, my lord?"

"What about him?"

"He might make trouble."

"He is in no condition to make trouble."

"That never seems to stop them, my lord."

"If he persists, then I am certain you will deal with him accordingly." Marshal Guy turned and rode back up the hillside, leaving his sergeant and men to their work.

Later, Gysburne sat on a stump behind the abbey cookhouse watching the bullock turn slowly on the spit while the cook and kitchener's boy basted the roasting meat with juices from the basin nestled in the glowing embers below the carcass. The smell of the meat filled the air and made his mouth water. He lifted his jar and drank down another healthy draught of new ale. Yes, he thought, at times like this he could almost forget that he was stranded in a backward no-account province awaiting the pleasure of the abbot to advance or deny him.

Although it might have been the ale making him feel benevolent and expansive, Guy considered that, despite his frustration and disappointment, perhaps life in the March was not so bad after all.

At that moment, if only then—as the blue winter twilight deepened across the Vale of Elfael and the voices of the knights chorused rough laughter beneath the glow of a rising moon—that was true.

I am explaining about Bishop Asaph and our visit to Saint Tewdrig's monastery and here is Odo, frowning. It is the ring he wants to hear about, only the ring.

"What's wrong now, monk?" I ask him, sweet and innocent as a milkmaid's smile. "You look like a fella that mistook a bolt of vinegar for ale."

"I am certain that this bishop of yours is every bit as kind and holy as you claim," he complains in that irritating whine that he uses when he thinks he is being long-suffering.

"Well then?"

"How did the bishop know about the stolen ring?"

"How did he know?" I say. "Odo, you dullard, the good bishop did not know the first thing about it."

"Then why did you go to see him?"

"We went to find out what he knew," I say, "and to show him the letter, and give him the stolen goods for safekeeping." I spread my hands wide. "In the end, he knew nothing about the ring, he could not read the letter, and would not agree to keep the treasure for us."

"Then you discovered exactly nothing," concludes Odo. "A wasted journey."

"God's mill grinds slowly, my monkish friend, but it grinds exceedingly fine. Our ways are not his ways, and there's a rare fact."

Odo makes a sour face. "Then why tell—"

"All will come 'round in good time," I say, squashing his objection in the egg.

Brother Scribe sighs like a broken bellows, and we trudge on . . .

Well, as we were alone in the bishop's private quarters, we soon got down to showing the churchman the letter. He confirmed that it was indeed written in Ffreinc.

"Can you tell us what it says?" asked Siarles hopefully.

"I am sorry, my friend," said the cleric with a thin smile. "That skill has defied this old head, I'm afraid."

"Can you make nothing of it?" I said, annoyed and more than a little disappointed at having risked so much to come so far for no purpose.

The old man bent his head to the square of parchment and studied it once more, his nose almost touching the surface. "Ah, yes! Here," he said, stabbing at a word in the middle of the page, "that is *carpe diem*."

"Latin?" I said.

Asaph nodded. "It means 'seize the day'—you might say an exhortation to be about your work, perhaps, or to make the most of your present opportunity." He shrugged. "Something like that, anyway."

So, aside from another scrap or two of Latin, we were no better off for our trouble save in one respect only: we knew that Count de Braose was that anxious for the return of his stolen goods that he would dare to hang the population of Elfael to get it.

"Is there nothing else you can tell us?" asked Siarles.

"I am sorry," replied the old man as the bell sounded for evening prayers. "No one here can read Ffreinc, either." He brightened with a thought. "Perhaps one of the monks at Saint Dyfrig's could help you."

But, having learned about de Braose's cruel plans for the men and boys of Elfael, Siarles and I were loath to waste even so much as a day extending a chase that might not succeed. "We must move on at once," my companion told him. "Could you take it, Father?"

The old man did not like the idea. Who could blame him? It was a cold and dangerous errand we were asking. But he was too much in his benefactor's debt to say no outright. His pale eyes pleaded to be excused, and my heart went out to the old fella. Yet there was no other way. Even if we'd had the time to spare, neither of us knew anyone at Saint Dyfrig's, nor which of them might be trusted. Bishop Asaph saw this too, I think, for in the end he allowed himself to be persuaded to take the letter for us. But, having agreed to that, he would not in any wise agree to hold the rest of the treasure in safekeeping at the monastery.

This he had decided, even though we had not yet shown him the parcel containing the ring and gloves. It made no difference; the old man would not be moved. "I don't know what you have, or whence it came." Siarles opened his mouth to tell him, but Asaph held up his hand to prevent him speaking. "Nor do I wish to know. But if something happened and any of those things were found here, my monks and those few forlorn souls under my care would suffer for it." He shook his head, his mouth firm. "As shepherd of my flock, I cannot in good conscience allow it."

That was that.

So we ate a hearty supper and took a little nap, resting ourselves as well as our horses. We were awake again at midnight and lit out under a cold winter moon for Cél Craidd. The Twelfth Night observance was six days away. We had only that much time and no more before the hangings began.

The sun was already down and a freezing mist was rising with the moon in the east by the time we reached our forest hideaway at Cél Craidd. We had pushed the horses hard all the way, and they were almost spent. Yet the Welsh breed a hardy little beast, as everyone knows, and they lifted their dragging feet once we came in sight of the greenwood, because they knew they were almost home.

The Grellon greeted our return with keen interest, assembling before the Council Oak as we rode into the glade. I swung down from the saddle, searching for the face I suddenly wanted to see above all others and, before I could find it, was taken by the shoulder and spun around.

"Nóin, I—" was all I got out before I was immediately folded into a sweetly robust embrace.

She kissed me once, very hard, and then again. "I have missed you, Will Scarlet." She put her cheek against mine as she held me close. I could feel her shivering beneath her cloak, and thought it was not merely from the cold. "I was afraid something might happen to you."

"Ah, now, nothing that a good night's sleep won't cure," I replied lightly, clutching her tight to me.

"Siarles! Will!" Bran cried, striding across the clearing to greet us. Tuck, Iwan, and Mérian followed, slipping in the well-trodden snow. "What news?"

Without wasting a breath, Siarles told Bran and all the others about the hangings. "Fifty or sixty stand to forfeit their lives if we do not act quickly. It is for us to save them."

This caused an outcry among the Grellon, who raised a clamour to be allowed to march on Castle Truan and free the prisoners. "That we will not do," Bran said, raising his voice above the shouting. He called his council to attend him and for food and drink to be brought to help revive the travellers, and we all trooped off to join him in his hut.

670

This began a lengthy session of rumination about what we had learned, what it might mean, and what might be done about it. "Asaph refused to accept the ring and gloves for safekeeping," Siarles explained, returning the leather-wrapped bundle to Bran. "Nor could he read the letter."

"But we prevailed upon him to take the parchment to the abbey to see if someone there might help us," I offered. "We would have taken it ourselves, but seeing as the abbot means to start hanging half of Elfael, we thought best to hightail it home."

"You did well," Bran said. "It is, no doubt, what I would have done."

Iwan and the others agreed, and they began to discuss the hangings and what could be done to prevent them. I endured as long as I could, but soon the warmth of the hearth and the food combined to club me over the head and pull me down. Bran noticed my yawning and, thanking me for my diligence in bringing the news so quickly, ordered me to go and get some rest.

Creeping from Bran's hearth, I went to Nóin and found her waiting at her own small fire in her hut. Little Nia was asleep on her mat in the corner, and Nóin was idly feeding twigs into the flames. She turned and smiled as I entered. "They kept you long," she said.

"They did, but I am here now." I settled on the roebuck hide beside her. "Ah," I sighed, "there is nothing like a warm fire and a roof over your head at the end of the day."

"And you a brave forester," she chided lightly, lifting a warm hand to my face. "Well, rest yourself, Will Scarlet." She paused and smiled. "You need not stir until tomorrow's light if that is what you wish."

We kissed then and she nestled in my arms. We talked a little then—but, try as I might, I could not keep my eyes open. I fell asleep with Nóin in my embrace.

I awoke the next morning wrapped in her cloak. When I sat up who should be watching me but little Nia, her pixie face shining with some sort of happiness known only to herself. "Hello, blossom," I said, rolling up onto my elbow. "Where has your mam gone?"

The little darling giggled and pointed to the door. "Come here, sprite," I said, holding my arms out to her. She needed no coaxing. Up she jumped and dashed into my arms, her bare feet slapping the beaten earth. I gave her a hug and settled her in my lap. We sat together and broke branches and bits of bark into the coals on the hearth to build up the fire again. By the time we had a small blaze going, Nóin returned with freshly baked loaves of barley bread, a knob of new butter, and a jar of honey. She planted a kiss on my rough cheek, then busied herself preparing the food to break our fast.

"I must have fallen asleep," I said as she spread a cloth on the floor next to the hearth, "but I don't remember."

"I'm not surprised," she replied. "You were already halfway gone when you sat down. It did not take much to send you on your way."

"I'm sorry."

"How so? You were near worn through from your journey." Nóin smiled, more to herself than to me. "I have no cause to blame you, Will, nor do I."

That was good enough for me. She broke open a steaming loaf, slathered it with butter, and dribbled honey over it. "You know," I said, trying to sound as if I had just thought of it, "you are a right fine woman who needs a man, and I am a fella without a wife. If we got married that would fell two birds with a single stone."

"Oh, would it now?" she said, turning to regard me with a look I could not quite read. She folded her hands in her lap. "What makes you think I care to get married?"

"Well, I . . . I don't know. Do you?"

She said nothing, but tore off a bit of the prepared half loaf and passed it to Nia, handing the remaining portion to me.

"Nóin, I'm asking you to be my wife if . . . if you'll have me, that is."

"Shush! Will I have you? Do you have to ask?" She smiled and began buttering the second half of the warm loaf. "Was I not thinking the same thing the moment I laid eyes on you?"

This was news to me. "Were you?"

"If you're a man of your word, Will Scarlet, our friar could marry us tomorrow."

"He could," I agreed, my head swimming a little at the turn this conversation had taken.

"I've already spoken to him. We talked while you were gone."

"And?" I asked, thinking this was all happening far faster than I could have imagined.

"He said he could not do it," she replied just like that. "He said that he would give up Holy Orders before he allowed the likes of you to tie the knot."

"What? He said that?" I started up, climbing to my feet. "He has no cause to—"

"Oh, sit down, you big ox." She laughed. "What do you think he said?"

"Well, knowing him," I conceded, "it might be anything."

"He said he would be honoured to do it. We have but to name the day and it is good as done." She handed me the bread. "So? What day shall we tell him?"

"Tomorrow it is," I said.

"Tomorrow," said Nóin, and now the doubt crept into her voice. "Are you certain that is what you want?"

"No, of course not. Today! That is better still."

"William!" she cried. "It can't be today."

"Why not?" I reached for her and pulled her close. "The sooner the better, I say."

"There are things to be done!" she exclaimed, pushing me away. "Eat your bread and stop talking nonsense."

"Tomorrow, then." I reached down and cupped Nia's face in my hand. "What do you say, snowdrop? Shall your mam and me get married tomorrow?"

The little mite laughed and hid behind her mother's shoulder.

"See? She likes the idea. I'm going to go hunt the biggest stag in the forest for our wedding supper—and a boar or two, as well."

"Listen to you," Nóin said, beaming with pleasure at my bold talk. "Eat." She pushed a chunk of honeyed bread into my mouth and kissed the sweetness on my lips.

"One day more, then," I murmured, drawing her close, "and we will be together always."

Oh! Would that I had said anything but that, for the bread and honey was still warm in my mouth when Iwan appeared at the door. "Will Scarlet? Are you in there, Will?"

673

"Aye, I am," I called in reply. "Come in if you can. We have bread and honey if you're hungry."

He opened the narrow plank door and put his head into the hut. I don't know what he expected to find. "Oh," he said when he saw Nóin, "beg pardon, I—" He lowered his eyes with embarrassment. "I must pull Will away. Lord Bran has summoned a council of war."

"That sounds right dire," said I, taking another bit of bread as I rose to follow him. "Soldiers never rest," I sighed, and bent to steal another kiss.

"Go," she said, sending me on my way with a quick peck, "the sooner to return."

Outside, I fell into step beside Iwan. "A handsome woman there," he said thoughtfully. "You're that much a lucky man, Will."

"And I know it. Pray God, I never forget."

"There's some as would have plucked that flower for themselves."

"Aye," I allowed, "Siarles for one, I think. But do you mean you would have done likewise?"

"The thought occurred to me," he confessed. "But, no, no . . . ," he sighed. "I am too old."

"Too old?" I scoffed. "Job's bones! Where did you ever pick up a two-headed notion like that? Have you been listening to Siarles?"

"Something like that."

"Well, it is a wicked falsehood, Iwan, my friend. Stop up your ears to such odious blather; it will fair addle what little is left of the brain God gave you."

The others were already gathered in Bran's hut by the time we arrived, and we entered to take our places around the hearth. Angharad had not returned from her sojourn in the cave, but Tuck took her place on Bran's right hand, with Mérian at his left. I found a place beside the door and waited to see what the others would decide.

674

When we were all settled, Bran nodded to Tuck, and he began a long invocation.

Tilting his round face towards the unseen heavens, he said, "Eternal Encompasser, Fair Redeemer, Holy Friend the All-Wise Three in One, hear our prayer! Our enemies are many, and their strength is mighty. Bless our deliberations on this fairest of mornings that we may search your will for us in the days to come, and searching, find, and finding, make fast. Protect us from the foul deceptions of the evil one, and from the weapons of all who wish us harm. Be our fortress and our shield in the hour of our sorest trial . . ." His lips moved a moment longer, but his voice could no longer be heard.

In the silence of the moment, Bran said, "By the power just bespoken, we seek justice for our people and freedom from the usurper and all who would oppress. We ask the Almighty Lord, who is ever swift to aid his children, to guide us in the task before us and grant us assurance of victory."

We all added our *amens* to that. And then Bran smiled.

Oh, he could change quick as water! That smile was dark as the fearsome gleam in his eye. He was steeped in mischief as any imp, and itching to begin spreading discord and disorder among our enemies. He was that keen, I felt my own blood warm to the chase just the same as if we'd been out tramping the forest runs and spotted a fine, big stag to bring home.

"There is much we do not know about this," he said, pulling up the loop on which the ring hung around his neck, "but I am persuaded that we will not learn more by keeping it here in the forest. It has already caused death and destruction; I will not stand by and let it harm the people of Elfael more than it has already."

"Hear him! Hear him!" boomed Iwan heartily. No doubt, it had chafed him to remain behind while Siarles and I were away,

675

and disappointed as we were that our journey had been for naught.
Now that there was a prospect of something to be done, he was for it,
every British scrap of him.

"Well and good," affirmed Tuck. "And what do you propose to do?"

"We will give back the treasures taken in the raid."

"Give 'em back!" cried Siarles. "My lord, think what you are saying!"

Bran silenced him with a glance. "I propose to return them before
the sheriff hangs anyone." Siarles huffed and rolled his eyes, but Bran's
smile deepened. "See here, we still have five days until Twelfth Night—
five days before we give up the treasure," he said. "Five days to learn why
the Ffreinc place such high value on it."

"Good," said Mérian. "That is the most sensible thing I have heard
since Christmas. But if anyone thinks the sheriff will just let you walk
into the castle and hand it over, you best think again." She regarded us
with a high and haughty glance. "Well, does anyone have any idea how
to give back what was stolen without getting hung for a thief? Does
anyone have a plan?"

Bran heard the iron in her tone and said, "You are right to remind
us of the danger, my lady. And have you conceived such a plan?"

"As it happens," she answered, her satisfaction manifest, "I have."

"And will you yet tell us this plan?"

"Gladly," she answered, lowering her shapely head a little in deference to him. Turning again to those of us gathered around the king's
hearth, she added, "However, I am certain that once you have heard
what I have to say, you will contrive an even better banquet on the bare
boards I lay before you . . ."

What did she say?" asks Odo. He raises his head and rubs the
side of his nose in anticipation.

"That," I say with a great, gaping yawn, "must wait until tomorrow."

"Oh!" he whines. "You did that deliberately to spite me."

"We have talked long, brother monk, and I am tired," I reply, drawing a hand down my face. "Leave me to my rest."

"You are a mean and spiteful man, Will Scarlet," grumps Odo as he gathers up his inkpot and parchment.

I roll onto my side and face the damp stone wall. "Close the door behind you," I tell him as if already half asleep. "It does get cold down here of a night."

He hesitates at the door and says, "God with you this night, Will." He shuffles off and I listen until his slow footfall has died away. Then I am alone in the dark with my thoughts once more.

"What did she say?" demands Brother Odo as he bustles breathless into my cell. He is that much like an overgrown puppy—all feet and foolish fervour—it makes me smile.

It seems to me that my dull but amiable scribe is as much a prisoner of Abbot Hugo's devices as Will Scarlet ever was. Here he sits most days, scribbling away in this dim, dank pit with its mud and mildew, the reek of piss and stagnant water in his nostrils, dutifully fulfilling his office, never complaining. What an odd friendship has grown between us. I wonder what it can hold, yes, and how much it can bear.

"God with you this morning, Odo," I reply.

He settles himself in his place, the short plank balanced on his knees, and begins paring a new quill. "What did she say?"

"Who?"

"Mérian!" he shrieks, impatience making his soft voice shrill as an old fishwife's. "You remember—do not pretend otherwise. We were talking about King Raven's council."

"Soup and sausages," I sigh, shaking my head in weary dismay. "Are you certain that's what we were talking about? I must have slept the memory right out of my head. I have no recollection of it at all."

"I remember!" he cries. "Lord Bran called a council, and Mérian volunteered a plan she had devised."

"Yes? Go on," I urge him. "What next?"

"But that's all I know," he cries. He is that close to throwing his inkhorn at me. "That is where you stopped. You must remember what happened next."

"Peace, Odo," I say, trying to placate him. "All is not lost. Remind me of what you have written, and we'll see soon enough if that stirs the pot."

Odo busies himself with unrolling his scrap of parchment and unstopping his inkhorn.

"Read it out," I say, as he smoothes the sheepskin beneath his podgy palms. "Perhaps that will help me remember."

He begins, and I hear once again how he nips and crimps my words, giving them all a monkish cast. He bleeds them dry, and makes them all grey and damp like the greenwood in the grip of November. Still and all, he gets the gist of it, and renders my ramblings rather more agreeable than many would find them.

What his high-nosed infernal majesty Abbot Hugo makes of all this, I cannot say.

". . . the captive Lady Mérian begged leave to reveal a plan she had made. The rebels fell silent to hear what she would say . . ." He stops here and looks up expectantly. "That is where we ended for the night."

"If you say," I tell him, shaking my head slowly. It is all I can do to keep from laughing. "But my head is a cup scoured clean this morning."

Odo makes a face and grinds his teeth in frustration. "Well, then, what *do* you remember?"

"I remember something . . ." I pause and reflect a little. Ah, yes, how well I remember. "See now, monk, when the council finished I returned to Nóin's hut," I tell him, and we go on . . .

Nóin was not in her hut when I returned, nor was Nia. The council had taken the whole of the morning, and they had gone out to do some chores; so I went along to find them and lend a hand. The snow still lay deep over our ragtag little settlement, and the day, though bright, was cold. Many of King Raven's rag-feathered flock were at work chopping and splitting wood for the many hearth fires needed to keep warm. I could hear their voices sharp in the crisp air, chirping like birds as they toiled to fill their baskets and drag bundles of cut wood back to their huts. I saw this now, as I had seen such work countless times since coming to Cél Craidd, but this time something had changed.

Maybe it was only ol' Will Scarlet himself, but I did see the place in a different way, and did not much like what I saw. It put me in an edgy, uneasy mood, and I did not know why. Perhaps it was only to do with the bad news I had just now to deliver.

Oh, it was that, to be sure, but perhaps there was something else as well.

Even so, thinking to make the bitter draught a little easier to swallow, I put a big smile on my face and tried to take cheer in the sight of my beloved. But my heart was weighty and cold as a stone in a mountain stream. I saw Nóin bending low to pick up a split branch, and thought how I would love nothing more than to carry her away this instant to leave this place and its demands and duties, to flee far away from the bastard Normans and their overbearing ways. Alas, there was no longer such a place in all Britain. It made me sad and angry and disappointed and frustrated all at the same time, because I did not know what to do about it and feared nothing could be done.

I gathered my thoughts and, swallowing my disappointment, strode to where Nóin was working. "Here, my love," I said, "let me carry that basket for you. Heap it high now, so you won't have to fetch any more today."

She stood and turned with a smile. "Ah, Will," she began, then saw something in my face I was not able to hide. "What is it, love?"

She looked at me with such tender concern, how could I tell her?

"The council has decided . . . ," I said, hearing my voice as from the bottom of a well. "We have come to a decision."

Nóin's smile faded; she grew sombre. "Well, what is it, Will? Speak it out."

I bent my head. "I have to leave again."

"Is that all?" She fairly shouted with relief. "Mother Mary, I was afraid it was serious."

"I thought you would be unhappy."

"Oh, I am right enough," she replied, balling her fist on her hip. "But I would be more unhappy if I thought you had changed your mind about marrying."

"But I do want to marry you, Nóin. I do."

"Then all is well between us." She turned as if to go back to her work, but paused. "When do you go?"

"As soon as all can be made ready," I said.

"Go, then and help them see it through. We will fare as best we can while you are away," she said, lifting a hand to my face, "and count the days until your return."

"I will bring our friar back with me if I have to carry him on my back, and we will be wed the day I return." This I told her, kissing the palm of her hand. We talked about our wedding day and the plans I had to build her a new house on my return—with a big bed, a table, and two chairs.

So it was, the five of us were set to leave the next morning: Friar Tuck and myself; Bran, of course; Iwan, because we could use another pair of hands and eyes on the road; Mérian because the plan was her idea entire, and she would in no wise stay behind in any event.

However, this notion was not without difficulties of its own and, though I was loath to do it, the chore fell to me to point this out. "Forgive me, my lord, if I speak above myself," I began, "but is it wise for a hostage—begging your pardon, my lady—to . . . well, to be allowed to enter into affairs of such delicacy?"

"You doubt my loyalty?" challenged Mérian, dark eyes all akindle with quick anger. "I thought I knew you better, William Scatlocke."

"I do heartily beg your pardon, Lady," I said, raising my hands as if to fend off blows of her fists. "I only meant—"

"Here's the pot calling the kettle black!" she fumed. "That is rich indeed, my friend!"

Siarles smiled to see me handed my head so skilfully. But Bran waded into the clash. "Mérian, peace. Will is right."

"Right!" she snapped. "He is a fool, and so are you if you believe for even one heartbeat that I would ever do anything to endanger—"

"Peace, woman!" Bran said, shouting down her objection. "If you would listen for a moment, you would consider that Will has raised a fair point."

"It is not," she sniffed. "It is silly and insulting—I don't know which the more."

"No, it is neither." Bran shook his head. "It goes to the heart of things between us. The time has come for you to decide, Mérian Fair."

"Decide what?" she asked, her eyes narrowing with suspicion.

"Are you a hostage, or are you one of us?"

She frowned. "You tell me, Bran ap Brychan. What am I to you?"

"You know that right well. I would call you queen if you would but hear it."

Her frown deepened, and a crease appeared between her brows. She was caught on the thorns this time, no mistake—and she knew it. "See here!" she snapped. "Do not think to make this about that."

"Say what you will, my lady. It comes 'round to the same place in the end—either you stand with us, join us in heart and spirit or . . ."

"Or?" she replied, haughty in her indignation. "Or what will you do?"

"Or you must stay here like a good little hostage," Bran replied, "while we enact your plan."

"That I will not do," she snipped.

"Then?"

Those of us who stood 'round about found other places to look just then, so as not to be drawn into what had become the latest clash in a royal battle of tempers and wills.

Mérian glared at Bran. She did not like having her loyalty questioned, but even she could see the problem now.

"What will you do?" Bran pressed. "We are waiting."

"Oh, very well!" she fumed, giving in. "I will forswear my captivity and pledge fealty to you, Bran ap Brychan—but I'll not marry you." She smiled with sour sweetness at the rest of us. "There! Are we all happy now?"

"I accept your pledge," replied Bran, "and release you from your captivity."

"Then I can go with you?" inquired Mérian, just to make sure.

"My lady, you are a free woman," granted Bran gently, and I could see how much the words cost him. "You can go with us, or you can simply go. Should you choose to stay, you will be in danger—as you already know."

"I am not afraid," she declared. "It is my plan, remember, and I will not have any clod-footed men mucking it up."

She was not finished yet, for as we gathered to depart, Mérian spied a woman named Cinnia, a slender, dark-eyed young widow a few years older than herself, Mérian's favourite amongst the forest dwellers— another of the Norman-widowed brides of which there were so many. My lady asked Cinnia to join us. She would serve as a companion for Mérian, who explained, "A woman of rank would never travel alone in the company of men. The Ffreinc understand this. Cinnia will be my handmaid."

We loaded our supplies and weapons—longbows and sheaves of arrows rolled in deer hides—onto two packhorses. When we were at last ready to depart, Tuck said a prayer for the success of our journey, although he could have no idea what he was praying. Thus blessed, we took our leave. Angharad was still gone, so Tomas and Rhoddi were charged with keeping watch over Cél Craidd and Elfael while Lord Bran was away, and to reach us with a warning if the sheriff got up to anything nasty.

Thus, on a splendid winter's day, we rode out to beard the sleeping lion in his den.

685

hat is that, Odo? I have not told what we planned to do?" My weak-eyed scribe thinks I have skipped too lightly over this important detail. "All in good time," I tell him. "Patience is also a virtue, impetuous monk. You should try it."

He moans and sighs, rolls his eyes and dips his pen, and we go on . . .

CHAPTER 25

Coed Cadw

Richard de Glanville watched the forest rising before him like the rampart of a vast green fortress, the colours muted and misty in the pale winter light. Just ahead lay the stream that ran along the valley floor at the foot of the rise leading to the forest. He raised his hand and summoned the man riding behind him to his side. "We will stop to water the horses, Bailiff," he said. "Tell the men to remain alert."

"Of course," replied the bailiff in a voice that suggested he had heard the command a thousand times and it did not bear repeating.

The man's tone of dry irritation piqued his superior's attention. "Tell me, Antoin," said the sheriff, "do you think we will catch the phantom today?"

"No, Sheriff," replied the bailiff. "I do not think it likely."

"Then why did you come on this sortie?"

"I came because I was ordered thus, my lord."

"But of course," allowed Sheriff de Glanville. "Even so, you think it a fool's errand. Is that so?"

"I did not say that," replied the soldier. He was used to the sheriff's dark and unpredictable moods, and rightly cautious of them. "I say merely that the Forest of the March is a very big place. I expect the phantom has moved on."

The sheriff considered this suggestion. "There is no phantom, Bailiff. There are only a devil's clutch of Welsh rebels."

"However that may be," replied Antoin blandly, "I have no doubt your persistence and vigilance has driven them away."

De Glanville regarded his bailiff with benign disdain. "As always, Antoin, your insights are invaluable."

"King Raven will be caught one day, God willing."

"But not today—is that what you think?"

"No, Sheriff, not today," confessed the soldier. "Still, it is a good day for a ride in the greenwood."

"To be sure," agreed the sheriff, reining up as they reached the fording place. The water was low, and ice coated the stones and banks of the slow-moving stream. Sir Richard did not dismount, but remained in the saddle, swathed in his riding cloak and leather gauntlets, his eyes on the natural wall of bare timber rising on the slope of the ridge before him. Coed Cadw, the locals called it; the name meant "Guardian Wood," or "Sheltering Forest," or some such thing he had never really discovered for certain. Whatever it was called, the forest was a stronghold, a bastion as mighty and impenetrable as any made of stone. Perhaps Antoin was right. Perhaps King Raven had flown to better pickings elsewhere.

When the horses had finished drinking and his soldiers had taken their saddles once more, the sheriff lifted the reins and urged his mount across the ford and up the long slope. In a little while, he and the four knights with him passed beneath the bare, snow-covered boughs of elm trees on either side of the road and entered the greenwood as through an arched doorway.

The quiet hush of the snowbound forest fell upon him, and the winter light dimmed. As he proceeded along the deep-shadowed track into the wood, the sheriff's senses pricked, wary to a presence unseen; his sight became keen, his hearing more acute. He could smell the faint whiff of sour earth that told him a red deer stag had passed a short while earlier, or was lying in a hidden den somewhere nearby.

After a fair distance, they came to a place where a narrow animal trail crossed their own. Here the sheriff paused. He sat for a moment, looking both ways along the ground. The tracks of pigs and deer lay intertwined in the snow and, here and there, the spoor of wolves— and all were old. Just as he was about to move along, his eye caught the sign that had no doubt caused him to stop in the first place: the slender double hoofprint of a deer and, behind and a little to one side, a slight half-moon depression. Without a word, he climbed down from the saddle and knelt for a better look. The half-moon print was followed by another a short stride length away.

"You have found something, Sire?" asked Bailiff Antoin after a moment.

"It seems our ride is to be rewarded today," replied de Glanville.

"Deer?"

"Poacher."

Antoin raised his eyes and peered down the tunnel formed by the overhanging branches. "Better still," he replied.

The sheriff resumed his saddle and, with a gesture to silence the chattering soldiers, turned onto the narrow trail and began following his quarry. The trail led up a low rise and then down into a dell with a little rock-bound rill trickling along the bottom. There in the soft mud were a half dozen depressions—including the mark of a knee where a man had knelt to drink.

De Glanville raised a gauntlet to halt those coming from behind.

He caught the sheen of a damp glimmer where water had splashed onto a rock. "He was here not long ago," observed the sheriff. Turning in the saddle, he singled out two of his men. "Stay here and be ready should he double back before we catch him."

He lifted the reins and urged his mount across the brook, up the opposite bank, and into a thicket of elder that formed a rough hedge along the streambed. Once beyond the hedge, the trail opened slightly, allowing the sun to penetrate the dense tangle overhead. Shafts of weak winter light slanted down through the naked branches above. A few hundred paces further along, the sheriff could see that the track entered a snow-covered glade. He reined up and, pointing to the clearing ahead, motioned Antoin and the remaining knights to dismount and circle around on foot. When they had gone from sight, Sir Richard proceeded on alone, pausing again as he entered the clearing. There, across the snowy space, kneeling beside the sleek, ruddy stag he had just brought down, was a swarthy Welshman. Knife in hand, he stooped to begin butchering his kill. In a glance the sheriff saw the hunter, the knife, and the longbow leaning against the trunk of a fallen birch a few paces from the crouching man.

Drawing his sword silently from its sheath with his left hand, de Glanville unslung his shield with his right. Tightening his grip on the pommel of his sword, he drew a deep breath and called across the glade, "In the name of the king!"

The shout rang clear in the chilly air, shattering the quiet of the glade.

The startled Welshman lurched and spun. "Throw down your weapons!" shouted de Glanville. The hunter dived for his bow. In the time it took the sheriff to swing his shield into place, the hunter had an arrow on the string. "Halt!" cried the sheriff as the poacher drew and loosed.

The arrow struck home with a jolt that rocked the sheriff in his high-cantled saddle. The arrow point pierced the solid ashwood planking that formed the body of the shield, the iron point protruding a finger's width below the sheriff's eye.

The man's quickness was impressive, but ultimately futile. Before he could nock another arrow, two knights rushed into the clearing from either side. The hunter whirled and loosed at the nearest of the two, but the arrow merely grazed the top of the soldier's shield and careered away. Desperate, the Welshman swung the bow at the second knight and turned to flee. The two soldiers captured him in a bound, subduing him with a few skull-crushing blows before dragging him to where Sheriff de Glanville sat watching from his horse.

"Poaching deer in the king's forest," the sheriff said, his voice loud in the sanctuary of the glade, "is an offence punishable by death. Do you have anything to say before you are hanged?"

The hunter, who clearly did not understand the language of the Ffreinc, nevertheless knew the fate he faced just then. He gave out a cry and, with a mighty heave, tried to shake off the two soldiers clinging to him. They hung on, however, and showered blows upon his head until he subsided once more.

"Bailiff Antoin," said the sheriff, "you profess some proficiency in the tongue of these brutes. Ask him if he has anything to say."

The bailiff, clinging to the man's right arm, informed him of the charge against him. The Welshman struggled and shouted, pleading and cursing as he flailed helplessly in the grasp of his captors until he was silenced with blows to the head and stomach. "It appears he has no defence," Bailiff Antoin declared.

"No, I wouldn't think so," remarked the sheriff. The three remaining knights burst into the glade just then. "The rope, Bailiff," de Glanville ordered, and Antoin reached into the bag behind the sheriff's saddle and drew out a coiled length of braided leather.

The Welshman saw the rope and began shouting and struggling again. The sheriff ordered his knights to haul the man to the nearest tree. The rope was lofted over a stout bough and the quickly fashioned noose pulled tight around the wretch's neck.

"By order of His Majesty, King William of England, in whose authority I am sworn, I sentence you to death for the crime of poaching the king's deer," said the sheriff, his voice low and languid, as if pronouncing such judgement was a dreary commonplace of his occupation. He directed Bailiff Antoin to repeat his words in Welsh. The bailiff struggled, lapsing now and again into French, and finished with a shrug of indifference.

The sheriff, satisfied that all had been done in proper order, said, "Carry out the sentence."

The knight holding the end of the rope was joined by two others and the three began pulling. The leather stretched and creaked as the victim's weight was lifted from the ground. The poor Welshman scrabbled with his hands as the noose tightened around his neck and his dancing feet swung free, toes kicking up clods of snow.

Then, as the suffocated choking began, the sheriff seemed to reconsider. "Hold!" he said. "Let him down."

Instantly the rope slackened, and the man's feet touched ground once more. The wretch collapsed onto his knees, and his hands tore at the constricting leather band around his neck, his breath coming in great, grunting gasps.

When the colour had returned to the Welshman's face, the sheriff said, "Inform the prisoner that I will give him one more chance to live."

Antoin, standing over the gasping man, relayed the sheriff's words. The unfortunate looked up, eyes full of hope, and grasped the bailiff's leg as might a beggar beseeching a would-be benefactor.

"Tell him," continued de Glanville, "that I will let him go if he will but tell me where King Raven can be found."

The bailiff duly repeated the offer, whereupon the Welshman rose to his feet. Speaking slowly and with care, aware of the dire consequence of his reply, the hunter folded his hands in supplication to the sheriff and delivered himself of an impassioned speech.

"What did he say?" asked the sheriff when the hunter finished.

"I cannot be certain," began the bailiff, "but it seems that he is a poor man with hungry children—five in number. His wife is dead—no, ill, she is ill. He says his cattle were killed by soldiers of the marshal. They have nothing."

"That is no excuse," replied de Glanville. "Does he know that? Ask him."

The bailiff repeated the sheriff's observation, and the Welshman retorted with an impassioned plea.

"He says," offered Antoin, "that they are starving. The loss of his cattle has driven him to take the deer. This, he grieves, ah, no, regrets— but always when hunger drove him to the wood, he could take a deer with his lord's blessing."

The sheriff considered this, and then said, "The law is the law. What about King Raven? Make him understand that he can walk free, and take the deer with him, if he tells me where to find that rebel and thief."

This was told to the prisoner, who replied in the same impassioned voice. The bailiff listened, then answered, "The poacher says, if it is a crime to be hungry, then a guilty man stands before you. But if there be a thing such as mercy under heaven, then he pleads to you before God to let him go for the sake of mercy. He calls upon Christ to be his witness, for he knows nothing of King Raven or where he might be found."

The sheriff listened to this, impressed as he occasionally was with the Welsh facility with expression. If talking could save them, they had nothing to fear. Alas, words were but empty things, devoid of power and all too easily broken, discarded, and forgotten. "I will ask one last time," said the sheriff. "Tell me what I want to know."

When the sheriff's words had been translated, the captive Briton drew himself up full height and gave his answer, saying, "Release me, for the sake of Christ before whom we all must stand one day. But know this, if it lay in my power to know the wiles and ways of the creature you call King Raven, I would not spare so much as a breath to tell you."

"Then save your breath for dying," replied the sheriff when the captive's reply had been relayed. "Hang him!"

The three knights began hauling on the end of the rope. The Welshman's feet were soon kicking and his hands clawing at the noose once more. His strangled cries were swiftly choked off, and his face, now purple and swollen, glared his dying hatred for the sheriff and all Ffreinc invaders.

In a few moments, the victim's struggles ceased and his hands fell limp to his sides, first one and then the other. The sheriff leaned on the pommel of his saddle, watching the poacher's body as it swung, twisting gently from side to side. After a time, the bailiff said, "He is dead, Sire. What do you want us to do with the body?"

"Let it swing," said the sheriff. "It will be a warning to others of his kind."

With that, he turned his mount and started from the clearing, mildly satisfied with the day's work. True, he was no closer to finding King Raven, but hanging a poacher was always a good way to demonstrate his authority and power over the local serfs. A small thing, perhaps, as some would reckon, but it was, after all, in the exercise of vigilance and attention to such small details that power was maintained and multiplied.

Richard de Glanville, Sheriff of the March, knew very well the ways and uses of power. He would find the rebel known as King Raven one day, and on that day all Elfael would see how traitors to the crown were punished. Justice might be delayed, but it could not be escaped. King Raven would be caught, and his death would make that of the hanged poacher seem like a child's game. He would not merely punish the rebel, he would destroy him and snuff out his name forever. That, he considered, would be a delight to savour.

We rode hard for Glascwm and passed through the gates of Saint Dyfrig's as a wet winter storm closed over the valleys. Rain, stinging cold, spattered into the hard-packed yard as the monks scurried to pull the horses into the stable and bundle us soggy travellers into the refectory where they could spoon hot soup into us. They did not yet know who it was they entertained—not that it would have made a difference, I reckon, for the abbey yard was already full of local folk who, having fled the Ffreinc, sought sanctuary within the walls of the abbey.

Wet and wretched, battered and beaten down, they stood slump-shouldered in the rain before the low huts they had built in the yard, watching us with the mute, dull-eyed curiosity of cattle as we trotted through the gate. Forlorn and past caring, they huddled before their hovels, shivering as the rain puddled in the mud at their bare feet. The monks had made a fire in the middle of the yard to warm them, but the damp fuel ensured that it produced more smoke than heat. Most were thin, half-starved farmers by the look of them; and more than a few bore the signs of Norman justice: here a missing hand, or chopped-off foot, there an eye burned out by a red-hot poker.

Oh, the Ffreinc love lopping bits off the poor folk. They are tireless at it. And when a Norman noble cannot find good excuse to maim some unfortunate who wanders across his path . . . why, he'll concoct a reason out of spit and spider silk.

As soon as we dismounted, the ladies were taken to the guest lodge where they could dry their clothes, but the rest of us foreswore that comfort for a hot meal instead. The abbot, a stiff old stick with a face like a wild pig's rump, huffed and puffed when he saw our lord and his rough companions puddling up his dining hall. "Bran ap Brychan!" he cried, bursting into the long, low-beamed room. "They told me you were killed dead a year ago or more."

"I am as you see me, Father," replied Bran, standing to receive Abbot Daffyd's blessing. "I hope we find you well."

"Well enough. If the Ffreinc would leave off harrowing the valleys and driving decent folk from their homes, we would fare that much better. I hope you do not plan on staying—we are stretched tight as a drum head with caring for those we have already."

"We will not trouble you any longer than necessary," Bran assured him.

"Good." The old man did not waste words. His forthright manner made me smile. Here was a fella who would listen to reason, and give back the same. "I'm glad you're not dead. What are you doing here?"

"And here I was thinking you would never ask," replied Bran. Iwan and Siarles chuckled, but Bran silenced them with a stern glance. "A few days ago, a letter was brought to you by Bishop Asaph."

"That is so," answered the abbot, folding his hands over his chest.

His frown suggested he suspected grave mischief, and he was not wrong. "What is that to you, my son—if I may be so bold?"

"Be as bold as you like," answered Bran. "Only tell me that you have that letter."

"I do."

"And have you read it, Father?"

"I have not," said Daffyd. "But another has."

"I hope he is a trustworthy man."

"If he was not, I would not have given him the task."

"Come, then." He put a hand to the abbot's shoulder and turned him around. "We will hear it together."

"You're soaking wet!" remarked the abbot, shrugging off Bran's hand. "I'll not have you shaking water all over my abbey. Stay here and finish your soup. I will bring the letter here."

I began to appreciate the abbot right well. He was a bluff old dog whose bark concealed the fact that he would never bite. Bran returned to his place on the bench with a rueful smile. "He knew me as a boy," he explained, "when he was under Asaph at Llanelli."

The abbot returned as we were finishing our soup and bread. He brought the folded square of parchment clutched tight in both hands, as if he thought it might try to wriggle free; with him was a dark-haired, slender monk of middling years with a long face, prominent nose, and skin the colour of good brown ale.

"This is Brother Jago," announced the abbot. "He was born in Genoa and raised in Marseilles. He speaks Ffreinc far better than any-one here in the abbey. He has read the letter."

The slender monk dipped his head in acknowledgement of his superior's wishes. "I am happy to serve," he said, and I discerned in his speech a lightly lisping quality I'd never heard before. He turned to the

699

abbot, who still stood holding the parchment bundle. "Father?" he said, extending his hand.

Abbot Daffyd gazed at the letter and then at Bran. "Are you certain you wish to proceed with this?"

Bran nodded.

The abbot frowned. "I will not be a party to this. You will excuse me."

"I understand, Abbot," replied Bran. "No doubt, it is for the best."

Placing the bundle in Brother Jago's hands, the abbot turned and left the room. When the door had closed again, Bran nodded to the monk. "Begin."

Jago untied the blue cord and carefully unfolded the prepared skin. He stood for a moment, gazing at it, then placed it on the board in front of him and, leaning stiff-armed on his hands, began to read in a slow, confident voice.

"I, William, by the grace of God, Baron of Bramber and Lord of Brienze, to the greatly esteemed and reverend Guibert of Ravenna. Greetings in God, may the peace of Christ, Our Eternal Saviour, remain with you always. Pressed—" Jago paused. "Ah, no, rather . . . urged by faith, we are obliged to believe and to maintain that the Church is one: Holy, Catholic, and also Apostolic. We believe in Her firmly and we confess with simplicity that outside of Her there is neither Salvation nor the remission of Sins, and She represents one sole mystical Body whose Head is Christ and the Head of Christ is God."

Although we understood little enough of what he said, the musical quality of his speech drew us near; as he continued to read, we gathered around to hear him better.

"In all our Realms and whatsoever lands exist under our rule, granted by God, we venerate this Church as one. Therefore, of the one and only Church there is one Body and one Head, not two heads like a monster; that is, Christ and the Vicar of Christ, Peter and the successor of Peter, since the Lord speaking to Peter Himself said: 'Feed my sheep,' meaning, my sheep in general, not these, nor those in particular, whence we understand that He entrusted all to this same Peter, entrusting to him and him alone, the Keys of the Kingdom . . ."

Well, I never would have believed it—that Bloody Baron de Braose should preach so about the nature of the church and whatnot—well, it passed understanding.

". . . Therefore, if anyone should say that they are not belonging—" Jago broke off, read to himself for a moment, then raised his head and said, "I am sorry. It has been some time since I read French like this."

"You are doing well," Bran said. "Pray, continue."

"Ah . . . that they are not *under the authority* of Peter and his successors, they must confess not being the Sheep of Christ, since Our Lord says in the Gospel of John 'there is one sheepfold and one Shepherd.' Therefore, whoever resists this power thus ordained by God, resists the ordinance of God, unless he invent like Manicheus two beginnings, which is false and judged by us heretical, since according to the testimony of Moses, it is not 'in the beginnings' but 'in the beginning' that God created Heaven and Earth. Furthermore, we declare, we proclaim, we define that it is absolutely necessary for Salvation that every human creature be subject to the Roman Pontiff . . ."

When Jago broke off once more to collect himself, Iwan said, "What is the old rascal talking about?"

"Shh!" hissed Tuck. "Let him read on and we will see."

Jago resumed his reading. ". . . Be it known to all sons of our Holy Church present and future that we have heard the Spirit's admonition to seize the day of Peace, and have ordained this concord to be made between William and Guibert, formerly Archbishop of Ravenna . . ."

Mérian and Cinnia, given dry robes by the monks, entered just

701

then. "You started without us!" Mérian said, her voice sharp with disapproval.

"Shh!" said Bran. "You have missed little enough." He gestured to Jago. "Go on."

". . . attendant with very Sacred vows to uphold His Holiness, the Pope, and bind our Powers to the Throne of Saint Peter and the One Church Universal, recognizing him as Pontiff and Holy Father, forsaking all other Powers, henceforth holding only to the Authority invested in His Holiness, the Patriarch of Rome. May the Divinity preserve you for many years, most Holy and Blessed Father.

"Given at Rouen on the third day of September, before these witnesses: Roger, Bishop of Rheims; Reginald des Roches, Bishop of Cotillon; Robert, Duke of Normandy; Henry Beauclerc; Joscelin, Bishop of Véxin; Hubert de Burgh, Justiciar of King Philip; Gilbert de Clare, Count of Burgundy and Argenton; Ralph fitzNicholas, our seneschal; Henry de Capella, Baron of Aquitaine; and others in most Solemn and August Assembly."

Jago glanced up quickly and, seeing all eyes on him, concluded. "Written by the hand of his servant Girandeau, scribe to Teobaldo, Archbishop of Milan."

Well, I won't say I gleaned the full meaning of that letter just then. Then again, no one did. Indeed, we all sat looking a little perplexed at what we'd heard. Iwan spoke for us all, I think, when he said, "That was worth a man's life on Christmas day?"

"There is something in it we cannot yet see," replied Bran.

"If we only knew where to look," sighed Tuck. "For all its folderol, it is only a simple offer of support for the pope. I confess, I make nothing of it."

Jago straightened and turned a thoughtful gaze to Bran. "Pray, how did you come by this, my lord?" he asked, his voice quiet in the silence.

702

"It was with some other items taken in a raid," Bran said simply.

Jago nodded, accepting this without comment. "These other items—may I see them?"

Bran considered for a moment, then turned to Tuck. "Show him."

Tuck rose and turned his back to one and all and, from a hidden pocket in his robe, produced a roll of cloth tied with a horsehair string. He untied the string and unrolled the cloth on the table to reveal the ruby-studded ring and the finely embroidered gloves.

Jago took one look at the ring and picked it up; he held it between thumb and forefinger, turning it this way and that so that the light glinted on the gold and ring of tiny rubies. "Do you know whose crest this is?"

"That of a Ffreinc nobleman," replied Iwan.

"Beyond that?" said Bran. "We know nothing."

Jago nodded again. Replacing the ring, he picked up the gloves, lifting them to his nose to take in the scent of the fine leather. Almost reverently, he traced the heavy gold thread of the cross and the looped whorl of the Chi Rho with a respectful fingertip. "I have seen gloves like this only once in my life—but once seen, it is never forgotten." He smiled, as if recalling the memory even then. "They were on the hands of Pope Gregory. I saw him as a boy when he passed through the village where I was born.

"But," he said, replacing the gloves, "I fear this does little to help you. I am sorry I could not be of better service." He placed the palm of his hand on the parchment. "I agree with the friar. There is something in the letter that the baron does not wish known to a wider world."

Well, you could have knocked us down with a wren feather. We all looked at each other, the mystery deeper now than when we had begun.

Lady Mérian found her voice first. "Nevertheless, it goes back. Whether we discover what it means or not," she declared, "it must be returned—all of it—as we agreed."

"What do you want me to do?" asked the abbot, when, after Jago had been dismissed, he returned to see if we would like to join the monks for vespers.

Bran pressed the folded parchment into Daffyd's hands. "Make a copy of this," he commanded. "Letter for letter, word for word. Make it exactly the same as this one."

"I cannot!" gasped the abbot, aghast at the very suggestion.

"You can," Bran assured him. "You will."

"Leave it to me," said Tuck, stepping boldly forward. "This is an abbey, is it not?" He took the abbot by the elbow, turned him, and led him to the door. "Then let us go to your scriptorium and see what can be done."

Odo is frowning again. He does not approve of our King Bran's high-handed ways. My scribe has put down his quill and folded his hands across his round chest. "Copying a stolen letter—you had no right."

This makes me laugh out loud. "Hell's bells, Odo! That is the least of the things we have done since this whole sorry affair began, and it en't over yet."

"You should not have done that," he mutters. "It is a sin against the church."

"Well, I suppose you could hold to that if you like," I tell him, "but your friend Abbot Hugo was willing to burn defenceless folk in their beds to get that letter. He sent men to their deaths to reclaim it, and was only too willing to send more. Seems to me that if we start totting up sins, his would still outweigh the lot."

In his indignation, my podgy scribe has forgotten this. He makes his sour face and pokes out his lower lip. "Copying a stolen letter," he says at last. "It's still a sin."

"Perhaps."

"Undoubtedly."

"Very well," I concede. "I suppose you have never stood on a battle-ground naked and alone while the enemy swarms around you like killing wasps with poison in their stings."

"No!" he snorts. "And neither have you."

I grant him that. "Maybe not. But we are sorely outmanned in this fight. The enemy has all the knights and weapons, and he has already seized the high ground. Whatever small advantage comes our way, we take it and thank God for it, too."

"You stole the letter!" he complains.

Oh, Odo, my misguided friend, takes what refuge can be found in dull insistence. Well, it is better than facing the truth, I suppose. But that truth is out now, and it is working away in him. I leave it there, and we roll on . . .

There were but four days remaining before Twelfth Night, when the hangings would commence. At Bran's insistence, and with Tuck's patient cajoling, the monks of Saint Dyfrig's abbey prepared a parchment the same size and shape as that of the baron's letter; they then proceeded to copy the letter out exact, matching pen stroke to pen stroke. If they had been archers, I'd have said they hit the mark nine times for ten and the tenth a near miss—which is right fair, considering they didn't know what they were scribing. True, they were not able to use the same colour brown ink as the original; the ink they made for their use at the abbey had a more ruddy appearance when it dried. Still, we reasoned that since none of the Ffreinc in Elfael had ever seen the original, they would not know the difference.

While the monks toiled away, Bran and Iwan undertook to carve a seal of sorts out of a bit of ox bone. Working with various tools gathered from around the abbey—everything from knife points to needles—they endeavoured to copy the stamp that made the seal that was affixed to the letter. And, while they laboured at this, Mérian and Cinnia made a binding cord, weaving strands of white satin which they then dyed using some of the ruddy ink and other stuff supplied by the abbey.

It took two days to finish our forgery, and a fine and handsome thing it was, too. When it was done, we placed the letters side by side and looked at them. It was that difficult to tell them apart, and I knew which was which. No one who had not seen the genuine letter would be able to tell the difference, I reckoned, and anyone who did not know, would never guess.

Abbot Daffyd held a special Mass of absolution for the monks

707

who had worked on the parchment and for the monastery itself for its complicity in this misdeed; he sought the forgiveness of the High Judge of the world for the low crimes of his followers. I held no such qualms about any of this myself, considering it a right fair exchange for the lives of those who awaited death in the count's hostage pit.

When the service was finished, Bran ordered everyone to make ready to ride to Castle Truan to return the stolen goods to the count. "And just how do you intend to do that?" asked Daffyd; if his voice had been a bodkin, it could not have been more pointed. I suppose he imagined he had caught Bran in a mistake that would sink the plan like a millstone in a rowboat. "If you are caught with any of this, the sheriff will hang you instead."

"Good abbot," replied Bran, "your concern touches me deeply. I do believe you are right. Yet, since we have no interest in providing fresh meat for the hangman, we must make other arrangements."

Warned by the devious smile on Bran's face, Daffyd said, "Yes? And those would be?"

"*You* shall return the treasures to the count."

"Me!" cried the abbot, his face going crimson in the instant. "But see here! I will do no such thing."

"Yes," Bran assured him, "I think you will. You must."

Well, the abbot was the only real choice. When all was said and done, he was the only one who could come and go among the Ffreinc as neatly as he pleased without rousing undue suspicion.

"This will not do at all," the abbot fumed.

"It will," countered Bran. "If you listen well and do exactly as I say, they will hail you as a champion and drink your health." Bran then explained how the stolen goods would be returned. "Tomorrow you will awaken and go to the chapel for your morning prayers. And there, on the altar, you will find a bag containing a box. When you open the box you will find the letter and the ring and the gloves. You will recognize them as the very items Count de Braose is missing, and you will take them to him, telling him precisely how you found them."

"It hardly serves the purpose if they hang me instead," Daffyd pointed out.

"If you can contrive to have the sheriff and abbot present when you hand over the goods," continued Bran, "that would be better still. De Glanville was there. He knows you could not have been involved in the theft; therefore you will remain above suspicion. And since you did not see who left the bundle on the altar, they cannot use you to get at us."

The abbot nodded. "It would all be true," he mused.

"You would not have to lie to them."

"But it would pare the truth very narrowly, my lord," humphed Abbot Daffyd.

"Narrow is the gate," chuckled Tuck, "and strait is the way. Do as Rhi Bran says, and they will sing your praises."

"And I will give you silver enough to feed the hungry in your yard."

The abbot twisted and turned like a worm on a griddle, but even he had to admit that it was the only way. He agreed to do it.

"Stay long enough to see the prisoners released," added Bran. "Once the abbot and count have received the goods, they should set the captives free as promised."

"I am not an imbecile," sniffed the abbot. "I fully appreciate why we're going to all this trouble."

"As you say," replied Bran. "Please do not take offence, Abbot; I just wanted to make sure we were all working to the same end. It is the lives of those men and boys we are saving. Lest anyone forget."

While the others worked on preparing the forged letter, I had not been idle. I had been gathering bits of this and that from the abbey's

709

stores and supplies. Tuck, Mérian, and the others had helped, too, when they could, and on the Eve of Twelfth Night all was nearly ready.

We slept little that night, and dawn was a mere rumour in the east when we departed the abbey. There was no one about in the yard, and I do not think we were observed. But if any of the poor asleep in their miserable hovels had looked out, they would have observed a far different group of travellers leaving than that which arrived.

CHAPTER 28

Saint Martin's

Richard de Glanville sat at table with a knife in one hand and a falcon on the other. With the knife he hacked off chunks of meat from the carcase before him, which he fed to the fledgling gyrfalcon—one of two birds the sheriff kept. He had heard from Abbot Hugo that falconry was much admired in the French court now that King Philip owned birds. De Glanville had decided, in the interest of his own advancement, to involve himself in this sport as well. It suited him. There was much in his nature like a preying bird; he imagined he understood the hawks, and they understood him.

The day, newly begun, held great promise. The miserable wet weather of the week gone had blown away at last, leaving the sky clean scoured and fresh. A most impressive gallows had been erected in the town square in front of the stable, and since there had been no communication on the part of the thieves who had stolen the abbot's goods, all things considered it was a fine day for a hanging.

He flipped a piece of mutton to the young bird and thought, not for the first time in the last few days, how to direct the executions for best effect. He had made up his mind that he would begin with three. Since it was a holy day there was a symbolic symmetry in the number three and, anyway, more than that would certainly draw the disapproval of the church. Count Falkes De Braose insisted on waiting until sundown rather than sunrise, as the sheriff would have preferred, but that was a mere trifle. The count clung doggedly to the belief that the threat of the hangings would yet bring results; he wanted to give the thieves as much time as possible to return the stolen treasure. In this, the sheriff and count differed. The sheriff held no such delusions that the thieves would give up the goods. Even so, just on the wild chance that the rogues were foolish enough to appear with the treasure, he had arranged a special reception for them. If they came—and somewhere in the sheriff's dark heart he half hoped they would ride into Saint Martin's with the treasure—none of them would leave the square alive.

When he finished feeding the hawk, he replaced it on its perch and, drawing on his riding boots, threw a cloak over his shoulder and went out to visit his prisoners. Though the stink of the pit had long since become nauseating, he still performed this little daily ritual. To be sure, he wanted the wretches in the pit to know well who it was that held their lives in his hands. But the visits had another, more practical purpose. If, as the death day lurched ever nearer, any of the prisoners suddenly remembered the whereabouts of the outlaw known as King Raven, Sheriff de Glanville wanted to be there to hear it.

He hurried across the near-empty square. It was early yet, and few people were about to greet the blustery dawn. He let himself into the guardhouse and paused at the entrance to the underground gaol where, after waking the drowsy keeper, he poured a little water on the hem of his cloak. Holding that to his nose, he descended the few steps and proceeded along the single narrow corridor to the end, pausing only to see if anyone had died in either of the two smaller cells he passed along the way. The largest cell of the three lay at the end of the low corridor, and though it had been constructed to hold as many as a dozen men, it now held more than thirty. There was not enough room to lie down to sleep, so the prisoners took turns through the day and night; some, it was said, had learned to sleep on their feet, like horses.

At first sight of the sheriff, one of the Welsh prisoners let out a shout and instantly raised a great commotion, as every man and boy began crying for release. The sheriff stood in the dank corridor, the edge of his cloak pressed to his face, and patiently waited until they had exhausted their outcry. When the hubbub had died down once more—it took less time each day—the sheriff addressed them, using the few words of Welsh that he knew. "Rhi Bran y Hud," he said, speaking slowly so that they would understand. "Who knows him? Tell me and walk free."

It was the same small speech he made every day, and each time produced the same result: a tense and resentful silence. When the sheriff finally tired of waiting, he turned and walked away to a renewed chorus of shouting and wailing the moment his back was turned.

They were a stubborn crowd, but de Glanville thought he could detect a slight wearing down of their resolve. Soon, he believed, one of his captives would break ranks with the others and would tell him what he wanted to know. After a few of them had hanged, the rest would find it increasingly difficult to hold their tongues.

It was, he considered, only a matter of time.

The sheriff did not care a whit about retrieving Abbot Hugo's stolen goods, despite what Hugo told him about the importance of the letter. It was the capture of King Raven he desired, and nothing short of King Raven would satisfy.

After his morning visit to the gaol, the sheriff returned to the upper rooms of the guardhouse to visit the soldiers and speak with

713

the marshal to make certain that all was in order for the executions. It was Twelfth Night and a festal day, and the town would be lively with trade and celebration. Sheriff de Glanville had not risen to his position by leaving details to chance.

He found Guy de Gysburne drinking wine with his sergeant. "De Glanville!" called Guy as the sheriff strolled into the guardhouse. A fire burned low in the grate, and several soldiers lolled half-asleep on the benches where they had spent the night. Empty cups lined the table and lay on the floor. *"Une santé vous, Shérif!"* Gysburne cried, raising his cup. "Join us!"

As the sheriff took a seat on the bench, the marshal poured wine into an empty cup and pressed it into de Glanville's hands. They drank, and the sheriff replaced his cup after only a mouthful, saying, "I will expect you and your men to be battle-sharp today."

"But of course," replied Guy carelessly. "You cannot think there will be any trouble?" When the sheriff did not reply, he adopted a cajoling tone. "Come, de Glanville, the rogues would never dare show their faces in town."

"I bow to your superior wisdom, Lord Marshal," he replied, his voice dripping honey. "I myself find it difficult to forget that a little less than a fortnight ago we lost an entire company of good men to these outlaws."

Guy frowned. "Nor have I forgotten, Sheriff," he said stiffly. "I merely see nothing to be gained by wallowing in the memory. Then again," he added, taking another swig of wine, "if it was my plan that had failed so miserably, perhaps I would be wallowing, too."

"Bâtard," muttered de Glanville. "You're rotten drunk." He glared at the marshal and then at the sergeant. "You have until sundown to get sober. When you do, I will look for your apology."

Marshal Guy mouthed a curse and took another drink. The sheriff rose, turned on his heel, and strode from the room. "There was never but one *bâtard* in this room, Jeremias," he muttered, "and he is gone now, thank God."

"I thought I smelled something foul," remarked Sergeant Jeremias, and both men fell into a fit of laughter.

In truth, however, the sheriff was right: they were very drunk. They had been drinking most nights since that disastrous Christmas raid. Most nights they, along with the rest of the soldiers in the abbot's private force, succeeded in submerging themselves in a wine-soaked stupor to forget the horror of that dreadful Christmas night. Alas, it was a doomed effort, for with the dawn the dead came back to haunt them afresh.

Upon leaving the guardhouse, the bell in the church tower rang to announce the beginning of Mass. The sheriff walked across the square to the church, pushed open the door, and entered the dim, damp darkness of the sanctuary. A few half-burnt candles fluttered in sconces on the walls and pillars, and fog drifted over the mist-slick stones underfoot. De Glanville made his way down the empty aisle to take his place before the altar with the scant handful of worshippers. As he expected, one of the monks was performing the holy service, his voice droning in the hollow silence of the near-empty cave of the church; the abbot was nowhere to be seen.

He watched as the Mass moved through its measured paces to its ordained finish and, with the priest's benediction ringing in his ears, left the church feeling calm and pleasantly disposed towards the world. There were more people about now. A few merchants were erecting their stalls, and some of the villagers carried wood for the bonfire which would be lit in the centre of the square. He stood for a moment, watching the town begin to fill up, then looked to the sky. The sun was bright, but there were dark clouds forming in the west.

There was nothing he could do about that, so he hurried on, pausing now and again to receive the best regards of the townsfolk as he progressed across the muddy expanse, visiting some of the stalls along the way. There were a few provisions he needed to procure for his own Twelfth Night celebration. Odd: he was always ravenously hungry following a public execution.

He spent the rest of the morning going over the preparations with his men. There were but four of them now—the others had been killed in the raid—and de Glanville was concerned about the survivors falling into melancholy. They had been caught off guard in the forest, for which the sheriff took the blame; he had not anticipated the speed with which the outlaws had struck, nor the devastating power of their primitive weapons. Tonight's executions would provide some redress, he was sure, and remove some of the lingering pain from the beating they had taken.

When he had determined that all was in order, the sheriff returned to his quarters for a meal and a nap. He ate and slept well, if lightly, and rose again late in the day to find that the sun had begun its descent in the west and the threatened storm was advancing apace. It would be a snowy Twelfth Night. He buckled his sword belt, drew on his cloak and gloves, and returned to the town square, which was now filled with people. Torches were being lit, and the bonfire was already ablaze. Judging from the sound alone, most had already begun their celebrations. Spirits were high, with song and the stink of singed hair in the air; someone had thrown a dead dog onto the bonfire, he noted with distaste. It was an old superstition, and one he particularly disliked.

He proceeded across the crowded square to the guardhouse to deliver final instructions to the marshal and his men. Out of the corner of his eye, he noticed a group of travelling merchants setting out their wares. The fools! The feast about to begin and here they were, arriving when everyone else was finishing for the day and making ready to celebrate. Two women he had never seen before lingered nearby, attracted, no doubt, by the possibility of a bargain from traders desperate to make at least one sale before the hangings began.

At the guardhouse, he delivered his message to the sergeant, who seemed sober enough now. That done, he proceeded to the abbot's quarters to share a cup of wine while waiting for the evening's festivities to begin. "So!" said Abbot Hugo as de Glanville stepped into the room. "Gysburne came to see me. He doesn't like you very much."

"No," conceded the sheriff, "but if he would learn to follow simple commands, we might yet achieve a modicum of mutual accord."

"Mutual accord—ha!" Abbot Hugo snorted. "You don't like him, either." He splashed wine into a pewter goblet and pushed it across the board towards de Glanville. "Personally, I do not care how you two get on, but you might at least accord me the respect of asking my permission before you begin ordering around my soldiers as if they were your own."

"You are right, of course, Abbot. I do beg your pardon. However, I would merely remind you that I am aiding your purpose, not the other way around—and with the king's authority. I require things to be done properly, and the marshal has been lax of late."

"Tut!" The abbot fanned the air in front of his face, and frowned as if he smelled something rancid. "You pretty birds get your feathers ruffled and pretend you have been ill used. Drink your wine, de Glanville, and put these petty differences behind you."

They began to discuss the evening's arrangements when the porter interrupted to announce the arrival of Count Falkes, who appeared a moment later wrapped head to heel in a cloak of double thickness, thin face red after the ride from his castle, his pale hair in wind-tossed

717

disarray. In all, he gave the impression of a lost and anxious child. The abbot greeted his guest and poured him a cup of wine, saying, "The sheriff and I were just speaking about the special entertainment."

An expression of resigned disappointment flitted across Count Falkes's narrow features. "Then you think there is no hope?"

"That the stolen items will be returned?" countered the sheriff. "Oh, there is hope, yes. But I think we must stretch a few British necks first. Once they learn that we are in deadly earnest, they will be only too eager to return the goods." The sheriff smiled cannily and sipped his wine. "I still do not know what was in those stolen chests that is so important to you."

Abbot Hugo saw Falkes open his mouth to reply, and hastily explained, "That, I think, is for the baron to answer. The count and I have been sworn to secrecy."

The sheriff pursed his lips, thinking. "Something the baron would prefer to remain hidden—a matter of life and death, perhaps."

"Trust that it is so," offered the count. "Even if it were not at first, it is now. We have *you* to thank for that."

The sheriff, quick to discern disapproval, stiffened. "I did what I thought necessary under the circumstances. In fact, if I had not anticipated the wagons, we would not have had any chance of catching King Raven at all."

"You still maintain that it was the phantom."

"He is no phantom," declared the sheriff. "He is flesh and blood, whatever else he may be. Once word reaches him that we have hung three of his countrymen, he'll be only too eager to return the baron's treasure."

"Three?" wondered the count. "Did you say three? I thought we had agreed to execute only one each day."

"Yes, well," answered de Glanville with a haughty and dismissive flick of his head, "I thought better to start with three tonight—it will instil a greater urgency."

"Now, see here!" objected the count. "I must rule these people. It is difficult enough without you—"

"Me! We would not be in this quagmire if you had—"

"Peace! There is enough blame for all to enjoy a healthy share," said the abbot, breaking in. Holding the wine jar, he refreshed the cups. "I, for one, find this continual acrimony as tiresome as it is futile." Turning to Falkes, he said, "Sheriff de Glanville has responsibility for controlling the forest outlaws. Why not trust him to effect the return of our goods in his own way?"

The count finished his wine in a gulp and took his leave. "I must see to my men," he said.

"A good idea, Count," said Abbot Hugo. Turning to the sheriff, he said, "You must also have much to do. I have kept you from your business long enough."

In the square outside, Gulbert, the gaoler, had assembled the prisoners—sixty men and boys in all—at the foot of the gallows. They were chained together and stood in the cold, most of them without cloaks or even shoes, their heads bowed—some in prayer, some in despair. Marshal Guy de Gysburne, leading his company of soldiers, established a cordon line to surround the miserable group and keep any from escaping—as if that were possible—but also to keep townspeople from interfering with the proceedings in any way. A few of the wives and mothers of the Cymry captives had come to plead for the release of their sons or husbands, and Sheriff de Glanville had given orders that no one was to have even so much as a word with any of the prisoners. Guy, nursing a bad headache, wanted no trouble this night.

To a man, the Ffreinc knights were helmed and dressed in mail; each carried a shield and either a lance or naked sword; and though none were expecting any resistance, all were ready to fight. Count Falkes had brought a dozen men-at-arms, and these all carried torches; additional torches had been given to the townsfolk, and two large iron braziers set up on either side of the gallows—along with the bonfire—bathed the square in a lurid light.

The mostly Ffreinc population of Saint Martin's had gathered for the Twelfth Night spectacle, along with the residents of Castle Truan and the merchants who had traded in town that day. Abbot Hugo appeared, dazzling in his white satin robe and scarlet cloak; two monks walked before him—one carrying a crosier, the other a gilt cross on a pole. Fifteen monks followed, each carrying a torch. The crowd shifted to accommodate the clerics.

Richard de Glanville, Sheriff of the March, stepped up onto the raised platform of the gallows. An expectant hush swept through the crowd. "In accordance with the Rule of the March, and under authority of King William of England," he called, his voice loud in the silence of fluttering torches, "we are come to witness this lawful execution. Let it be known to one and all, here and henceforth, that refusal to aid in the capture of the outlaw known as King Raven and his company of thieves will be considered treason towards the crown, for which the punishment is death."

The sheriff glanced up as the wind gusted, bringing the first frigid splash of the promised rain. He took a last look around the square—at the bonfire, the torches, the soldiers armed and ready, the close-gathered crowd. It occurred to him to wonder what had become of those late-arriving merchants, who seemed to have disappeared. Finally, satisfied that all was as it should be, de Glanville gave the order to proceed. Stepping to the edge of the platform, he turned his gaze upon the cringing victims. None dared raise their heads or glance up to meet his eye, for fear of being the one singled out.

He raised his hand and pointed to an old man who stood shivering in a thin shirt. Two soldiers seized the man and, as they were removing the wretch's shackles, the sheriff's finger came to rest over another. "Him, too," said the sheriff.

This victim, shocked that he should have been chosen as well, gave out a shout and began struggling with the soldiers as they removed his chains. The man was quickly beaten into submission and dragged to the platform.

One more. From among the younger captives, de Glanville chose a boy of ten or twelve years. "Bring him." The youngster, dazed by his captivity, was too brutalized to put up a fight, but some of the men nearest him began pleading with their captors, offering to take the lad's place. Their desperate protests went unheeded by soldiers who did not speak Welsh, and did not care anyway.

Excitement fluttered through the crowd as the captives were dragged onto the platform and the spectators realized they would be feted to three hangings this night.

Ropes were produced and the ends snaked over the strong beam of the gallows arm; sturdy nooses were looped around the necks of the three Cymry—one old, one young, and one in his prime—whose only real crime under heaven was having been captured by the Normans.

As the nooses were being tightened, there came a shout from the crowd. "Wait! Stop the execution!"

Those gathered in the square, Ffreinc and Welsh alike, heard the cry in priestly Latin and, upon turning towards the commotion, saw a company of monks in dull grey robes pushing their way through the throng to the front of the gallows. "Stop! Release these men!"

The sheriff, his interest piqued, called for the crowd to let them through. "Dare you interrupt the execution of the law?" he asked as they came to stand before him. "Who are you?"

721

"I am Abbot Daffyd of Saint Dyfrig's near Glascwm!" he called in a loud voice. "And I have brought the ransom you require."

The sheriff cast a quick glance at Abbot Hugo, whose plump round face showed, for once, plain wide-eyed astonishment. On the ground, Count Falkes shoved his way towards the newly arrived monks. "Where is it?" he demanded. "Let us see it."

"It is here, Lord Count," said Daffyd, his face glistening with sweat from the frantic scramble to reach the town. "Praise Jesu, we have come in time." He turned to one of the priests behind him and took possession of a small wooden box, which he passed to the count. "Inside this casket, you will find the items which were stolen from you."

"Here! Here!" cried Abbot Hugo. "Make way!" He pushed through the crowd to the count's side. "Let me see that."

Seizing the chest from the count's hands, he opened the lid and peered inside. "God in heaven!" he gasped, withdrawing the gloves. He took out the leather bag and, shoving the casket into the count's hands, fumbled at the strings of the bag, opened it, and shook the heavy gold ring into his hand. "I don't believe it."

"The ring!" said the count. Looking up sharply, he said, "Where did you get this?"

"These are the things that were stolen in the forest raid at Christ-tide, yes?" Daffyd asked.

"They are," confirmed Count Falkes. "I ask again, where did you get them?"

"With God and the whole Assembly of Heaven bearing witness, I went to the chapel for prayers this morning, and the box was on the altar. When it was left there, no one knows. We saw no one." Raising his arm, the Welsh abbot pointed to the gallows. "Seeing that the goods have been returned and accepted, I beg the release of all prisoners."

For the benefit of the Cymry hovering at the edges of the crowd, he repeated his request in Gaelic; this brought a cheer from those brave enough to risk being identified by the count and sheriff as potential troublemakers.

Abbot Hugo, still examining the contents of the box, withdrew the carefully folded bundle of parchment. "Here it is—the letter," he said, holding it up so he could see it in the torchlight. "It is still sealed." Looking to the count, he said, "It is all here—everything."

"Excellent," Falkes replied. "My thanks to you, Abbot. We will now release the prisoners."

"Not so fast, my lord," said Hugo. "I think there are still questions to be answered." He turned with sudden savagery on the Welsh abbot. "Who gave these things to you? Who are you protecting?"

"My lord abbot," began Daffyd, somewhat taken aback by his fellow churchman's abrupt challenge. "I do not th—"

"Come now, you don't expect us to believe that you know nothing about this affair? I demand a full explanation, and I will have it, by heaven, or else these men will hang."

Daffyd, indignant now, puffed out his chest. "I resent your insinuation. I have acted in good faith, believing that box was given to me so that I might secure the release of the condemned men—doomed, I would add, through no fault of their own. It would seem that your threat reached the ears of those who stole these things and they contrived to leave the box where it would be found so that I might do precisely what I have done."

The abbot frowned and fumed, unwilling to accept a word of it. Count Falkes, on the other hand, appeared pleased and relieved; he replied, "For my part, I believe you have acted in good faith, Abbot." Turning towards the gallows, where everyone stood looking on in almost breathless anticipation, he shouted, *"Relâcher les prisonniers!"*

Marshal Guy turned to the gaoler and relayed the command to

723

release the prisoners. As Gulbert proceeded to unlock the shackles that would free the chain, Sheriff de Glanville rushed to the edge of the platform. "What are you doing?"

"Letting them go," replied Gysburne. "The stolen goods have been returned. The count has commanded their release." He gave de Glanville a sour smile. "It would appear your little diversion is ruined."

"Oh, is it?" he said, his voice dripping venom. "The count and abbot may be taken in by these rogues, but I am not. These three will hang as planned."

"I wouldn't—"

"No? That is the difference between us, Gysburne. I very much would." He turned and called to his men. "Proceed with the hanging!"

"You're insane," growled the marshal. "You kill these men for no reason."

"The murder of my soldiers in the forest is all the reason I need. These barbarians will learn to fear the king's justice."

"This isn't justice," Guy answered, "it is revenge. What happened in the forest was your fault, and these men had nothing to do with it. Where is the justice in that?"

The sheriff signalled the hangman, who, with the help of three other soldiers, proceeded to haul on the rope attached to the old man's neck. There came a strangled choking sound as the elderly captive's feet left the rough planking of the platform.

"It is the only law these brute British know, Marshal," remarked the sheriff as he turned to watch the first man kick and swing. "They cannot protect their rebel king and thumb the nose at us. We will not be played for fools."

He was still speaking when the arrow sliced the air over his shoulder and knocked the hangman backwards off his feet and over the edge of the platform. Two more arrows followed the first so quickly that

724

they seemed to strike as one, and two of the three soldiers hauling on the noose rope simply dropped off the platform. The third soldier suddenly found himself alone on the scaffold. Unable to hold the weight of the struggling prisoner, he released the rope. The old man scrambled away, and the soldier threw his hands into the air to show that he was no longer a threat.

The sheriff, his face a rictus of rage, spun around, searching the crowd for the source of the attack as an uncanny quiet settled over the aston-ished and terrified crowd. No one moved.

For an instant, the only sound to be heard was the crack of the bon-fire and the rippling flutter of the torches. And then, into the flame-flickering silence there arose a horrendous, teeth-clenching, bone-grating shriek—as if all the demons of hell were tormenting a doomed soul. The sound seemed to hang in the cold night air; and as if chilled by the awful cry, the rain, which had been pattering down fitfully till now, turned to snow.

De Glanville caught a movement in the shadows behind the church. "There!" he cried. "There they go! Take them!"

Marshal Gysburne drew his sword and flourished it in the air. He called to his men to follow him and started pushing through the crowd towards the church. They had almost reached the bonfire when out from its flaming centre—as if spat from the red heat of the fire itself—leapt the black feathered phantom: King Raven.

One look at that smooth black, skull-like head with its high feath-ered crest and the improbably long, cruelly pointed beak, and the Cymry cried out, "Rhi Bran!"

The soldiers halted as the creature spread its wings and raised its beak to the black sky above and loosed a tremendous shriek that seemed to shake the ground.

Out from behind the curtain of flame streaked an arrow. Guy, in the fore rank of his men, caught the movement and instinctively raised his shield; the arrow slammed into it with the blow of a mason's hammer, knocking the ironclad rim against his face and opening a cut across his nose and cheek. Gysburne went down.

"Rhi Bran y Hud!" shouted the Cymry, their faces hopeful in the flickering light of the Twelfth Night bonfire. "Rhi Bran y Hud!"

"Kill him! Kill him!" screamed the sheriff. "Do not let him escape! Kill him!"

The shout was still hanging in the air as two arrows flew out from the flames, streaking towards the sheriff, who was commanding the gallows platform as if it was the deck of a ship and he the captain. The missiles hissed as they ripped through the slow-falling snow. One struck the gallows upright; the other caught de Glanville high in the shoulder as he dived to abandon his post.

Suddenly, the air was alive with singing arrows. They seemed to strike everywhere at once, blurred streaks nearly invisible in the dim and flickering light. Fizzing and hissing through the snow-filled air, they came—each one taking a Ffreinc soldier down with it. Three flaming shafts arose from the bonfire, describing lazy arcs in the darkness. The fire arrows fell on the gallows, kindling the post and now-empty platform.

Count Falkes, transfixed by the sight of the phantom, stood as arrows whirred like angry wasps around him. He had heard so much about this creature, whom he had so often dismissed as the fevered imaginings of weak and superstitious minds. Yet here he was—strange and terrible and, God help us all, magnificent in his killing wrath.

The last thing Falkes de Braose saw was Sheriff de Glanville, eyes glazed, clutching the shaft of the arrow that had pierced his shoulder, passed through, and protruded out his back. The sheriff, staggering like a drunk, lurched forward, dagger in his hand, struggling to reach the phantom of the wood.

Count Falkes turned and started after the sheriff to drag him back away and out of danger. He took but two steps and called out to de Glanville. The word ended in a sudden, sickening gush as an arrow struck him squarely in the chest and threw him down on his back. He felt the cold wet mud against the back of his head and then . . . nothing.

See now, Odo," I tell my dull if dutiful scribe, "we did not plan to attack the sheriff and his men—we were sorely outmanned, as you well know—but we came ready to lend muscle to Abbot Daffyd's demand to stop the hangings."

"But you killed four men and wounded seven," Odo points out. "You must have known it would come to a fight."

"Bran suspected the sheriff would betray himself, and he wanted to be there to prevent the executions if it came to that. As it happens, he was right. So, if you're looking for someone to blame for the Twelfth Night slaughter, you need look no further than Richard de Glanville's door."

Odo accepts this without further question, and we resume our slow dance towards my own appointment with the hangman.

Bran was angry. Furious. I'd never seen him so enraged—not even in the heat of battle. When fighting, an icy calm descended over him.

With swift but studied motion, he bent the belly of the bow and sent shaft after shaft of winged death to bite deep into enemy flesh. He did not exult; neither did he rage. But this! This was something different—a black, impenetrable fury had swept him up, and he shook with it as he stalked around the fire ring in his hut, his face twisted into a rictus of ferocity. Like a terrible, monstrous beast, anger had consumed him completely.

Seeing him now, a body would not have known him as the same man from the night before. For as we stood in the town square on Twelfth Night and the realisation broke upon us that Sheriff Bloody de Glanville would hang those three men even after recovering the treasure, Bran simply turned to us as we gathered close about and said in a low voice, "String your bows."

Then he calmly set about the destruction of our enemies.

As I said to Odo, it was no great surprise that the vile sheriff would betray his own promise. Truth be told, we fairly expected it. That is why we had hurried from the abbey to the town ahead of Abbot Daffyd to ensure that the sheriff would release the captives once the stolen goods were returned. I reckon that each of us, in some corner of our hearts, knew it was all too likely de Glanville would show his true colours that grim night.

Now that it was over, however, Bran had stewed and fretted and worked himself into a towering rampage. "The man is a craven butcher," spat Bran, pacing around the hearth. Fleeing the town, we had ridden all night to reach Cél Craidd; none of us had slept, nor could we. Though exhaustion heaved heavy rollers upon us, we sat around the low-flickering fire and listened to our lord give voice to his anger.

In the time I had been among the Grellon, I had picked up hints and suggestions that our Lord Bran sometimes suffered from black, unreasoning rages. But I had never seen it for myself . . . until now.

"He must be stopped," snarled Bran, smashing his fist against his thigh with each word. "God as my witness, he will be stopped!"

"De Glanville had no intention of keeping his word," Iwan pointed out. "He meant to kill as many as he could from the start. I'd like to see him dance on the end of that leather rope."

"It may be too late for that," said Tuck quietly. As everyone turned toward him, he yawned hugely and said, "He may be dead already. I saw him struck, did I not?"

"It's true," I affirmed. "I saw it, too."

"He took an arrow maybe," allowed our incensed lord. "But I won't rest until I've seen his head on a pole."

"For a certainty," Tuck insisted, "I saw him go down."

"He might have been struck, but was he killed?" Bran glared around at us as if we were a troop of enemy soldiers sprung up to surround him. "Was he killed?" Bran demanded, his voice aquiver with passion. "Is he dead?"

There was no way for any of us to know that beyond a doubt; when the time came to flee, we had all cleared off like smoke. We had done what we could do, the few of us, and were in danger of overstaying our welcome. So with the confusion at its height, we used the chaos in the town square to cover our retreat.

"I was not counting bodies," remarked Iwan; he glanced around, somewhat defiantly. "Nor did I see anyone else with a tally stick."

"De Glanville must have been killed," said Mérian. "If he took an arrow, he must be dead by now. Bran, calm yourself. It is over and done. You saved those men, and the Ffreinc have been dealt a blow. Be satisfied with that."

Bran regarded her with a look of cruel disdain, but he held his tongue. When he could trust himself to speak again, he said, "Dead or alive, we must know beyond a doubt. One way or the other, we must find out."

731

"We'll know soon enough," pointed out Tuck. "Word will spread."

"Aye, but late in coming here," suggested Siarles.

"Unless someone went to Llanelli to find out," said Bran, using the Welsh name for the place. Like all true sons of Elfael, our Bran refused to dignify the Norman name of Saint Martin's by uttering it aloud.

"None of us can go," Iwan said. "They know us now. We'd be caught and strung up on sight."

"Someone who has never been there, then," said Tuck, thinking aloud.

"Or," added Bran, glancing up quickly, "someone who goes there all the time . . ." Turning to Siarles, he said, "Fetch Gwion Bach. We have a chore for him."

Well, before anyone could gainsay the plan, the boy was found and brought to sit with the council. A quick, intelligent lad, he is, as I say, a mute and such a furtive little sneak that he easily flits from place to place with no one the wiser, and so quiet folk don't often know he's around. The townsfolk had long since grown used to seeing him here and there, and it is a fair bet that no one thought anything of it when he appeared the evening following what the alarmed citizens of Saint Martin's are now calling the Twelfth Night Massacre.

Iwan and I walked him to the edge of the forest and beyond as far as we dared go, then left him to hurry on his way into town. It was long past dark by the time we returned. Gwion stayed in town overnight, God knows where, and returned to Cél Craidd late the next day. The winter sun was almost down when he appeared, red-cheeked from his run through the frosty air. Bran had food and drink ready and waiting for him, but the boy would not sit down, less yet touch a bite, until he had delivered his charge. He fairly danced with excitement at being included in the plans of his elders.

732

"Good lad, good," said Bran, kneeling down in front of him. "Did you learn what we want to know?"

Gwion nodded so hard, I thought his head might fall off.

"Is the sheriff alive?" asked Iwan, unable to restrain himself.

Bran gave the big man a perturbed glance, and said, "Is he alive, Gwion? Is the sheriff still alive?"

The boy nodded again with undimmed enthusiasm.

"And the count?" asked Tuck. "He was hit, too? Did the count survive?"

The boy turned wide eyes towards the friar and lifted his shoulder in an elegant shrug. "You don't know?" asked Mérian.

The boy shook his head. He did not know how the count fared, but the sheriff, it seemed, had indeed survived.

Bran thanked the boy with a hug, and dismissed him to his sup-per with a pat on the head and chuck under the chin. "So now!" he said, when Gwion had gone. "It seems the sheriff lives. I think we must invite him to Cél Craidd and arrange a suitable welcome for him when he arrives."

733

The anger, which I had allowed myself to imagine had burned itself out between times, leapt up—renewed, refreshed, and just as poisonous as before—all in that blinding instant. I saw the darkness draw a veil across his eyes and his grin become malicious, frightening. "Hear me now," he said, his voice a smothered whisper, "this is what we are going to do . . ."

When he had delivered his demands to us, we were allowed to go rest and eat, and prepare ourselves for the fight ahead. I walked by Nóin's hut, and although it was early yet, could discern no light from a welcome fire in the hearth. I reckoned she had given up waiting for me and gone to sleep. I was that tired myself that I left her and the mite to their rest and took myself off to my own cold bed.

Thus, I did not see Nóin until the next day. She had heard all about the Twelfth Night battle, of course, and was that heartily glad we had freed the captives and lived to tell the tale. She was not best pleased, however, to learn that we could not be wed just yet on account of Lord Bran's plan to host a visit by the sheriff.

"And how do you imagine the sheriff will agree to come?" she asked in all innocence.

"I do not imagine for one moment that old Richard Rat-face will agree to anything we say or do," I replied.

"Then how—," she protested.

"Shh!" I laid a fingertip to her lips, and then kissed them. "Enough questions now. I cannot tell you any more than I have."

"But—"

"It is a secret until all is in order. I've said too much already," I whispered. "Let us talk of something else."

"Very well," she agreed with grudging reluctance, "let us talk of our wedding. Tuck is here now, and I've been thinking that—"

She must have seen my face fall just then, for she said, "Now what is the matter? What have I said?"

"Nothing," I replied. "All is well, truly, love. It is just that we cannot be married yet."

"And why not?" Nóin frowned dangerously, warning me that my explanation had better be good enough to save a hiding.

In the end, since I could not tell her what Bran was planning, I simply replied, "It seems I must go away again."

"Go?" she asked. "Where this time?"

"Not far," I said. "And it will only take a day or so—but we are leaving at once."

She sighed and tried to smile. "Ah, well, I suppose I should be grateful you bothered to come back at all."

Before I could think what to say to that, she rose. "Come back to me when you can stay, Will Scarlet," she said. I saw the sheen of tears in her eyes as she turned away.

"Nóin, please don't."

But she was already gone.

Iwan found me a short time later. "Ready, Will?"

"It makes no matter," I grumbled.

"Then let us be about our work."

Our work was to reassemble the wagons we had taken apart in the Christmas raid. Bran's plan was simple, but required a little preparation. While Iwan, Tomas, Siarles, and I carried our tools and fittings into the wood and set about putting the wains back together, some of the other Grellon gathered the other items we would need in order to make Bran's plan succeed.

In all, it took most of the day to make the wagons serviceable once more and fortify the woodland alongside the road. When we finished, Bran inspected the work and declared that all was ready. Early the next morning, as the others made their way to the wagons leading the oxen, I enjoyed a warm dip-bath and a change of clothes—I was to pass as the servant of a Saxon merchant—and then, armed with only a knife in my belt, I lit out for Saint Martin's.

After a brisk ride, I approached the town on the King's Road and entered the square as the bell in the church began tolling. At first I imagined it was some kind of alarm, and braced myself to ride away again in retreat. But it was only the summons to midday prayers; it drew few worshippers and no soldiers at all. Plucking up my courage, I dismounted, walked to the guardhouse, and knocked on the door.

After a few moments standing in the cold, the door opened and a young soldier looked out. Seeing no one but a rough Saxon standing before him, he said, *"Quel est? Que voulez-vous, mendiant?"*

735

This was spoken rudely, as one would speak to a bothersome dog. I do not think he even expected an answer, for before I could make a reply, he began to shut the door. *"Arrêter, s'il vous plaît! Un moment."*

Hearing his own language spat back at him like that, he paused and opened the door once more. "Please, Sire," I said, feeling the French words strange in my mouth, "I was told I would find the sheriff here."

"You were told wrong," he said, then pointed to a large house across the square. "He lives there."

I thanked the soldier for his trouble and walked across the town square. So far, the plan was holding together. Now that I knew where the sheriff could be found and that I could trust myself in marketplace Ffreinc it was time to get down to business. I knocked on the door that opened onto the street. "A word, if you please," I said to the man who answered. He appeared to be a servant only—whoever he was, I knew it was not the sheriff. "I have come to see the sheriff on an urgent matter."

"What would that be?" inquired the fella.

"It is a matter for His Honour, the sheriff, himself alone," I said. "Are you Sheriff de Glanville?"

"No, I am his bailiff." Without another word, he opened the door wider and indicated that I was to come inside. "This way," he said. Closing the door behind him, he led me up stone steps to the single large room which occupied the upper floor. A fire burned in a stone fireplace and, near it, a heavy table had been set up. Richard de Glanville sat in a big, thronelike chair facing the fire, his legs and feet covered by a deerskin robe. There was a young gyrfalcon perched on a wooden stand next to him.

"What?" he said without taking his gaze from the fire. "I told you I was not to be disturbed, Antoin." I noticed his voice was thick in his throat.

"Please, my lord sheriff," I said, "I have come from Hereford with a message from my master."

"I do not care if you have come from hell with a message from the devil," he snarled with unexpected savagery. "Go away. Leave me."

The bailiff called Antoin gave me a half shrug. "As you see, he is not feeling well. Come back another time, maybe."

"Is he injured?" I asked, trying to determine if, in fact, he had been wounded in the skirmish as Tuck believed.

"No," replied Antoin. "Not that way."

"Bailiff!" growled the sheriff from his chair. "I said to leave me alone!" He did not turn from staring at the fire.

"It would be best to come back another time," Antoin said, turning me toward the door once more.

"This is not possible," I said. "You see, my master is a gold merchant. He and some other merchants are on the way to Saint Martin's today. He has sent me to beg soldiers to help us through the forest." I lowered my voice and added, "We have been hearing worrisome tales about a, ah, phantom of the wood, this King Raven, no? We beg protection, and we can pay."

Antoin frowned. I could see him wavering.

"My master has said he will gladly pay anything you ask," I told him. "Anything reasonable."

"Where is your master now?"

"They were already entering the forest when I left them on the road."

"How many?"

"Four only," I answered, "and two wagons."

He considered this a moment, tapping his chin with his finger. Then he said, "A moment, please."

Leaving me by the door, he walked to where the sheriff was seated and knelt beside the chair. They exchanged a brief word, and Antoin

737

rose quickly and returned to me. "He has agreed to provide you with an escort. See to your horse and wait for me in the square outside. I will summon the men and meet you there."

"Very well, Sire," I said, ducking my head like a dutiful vassal. "Thank you."

I returned to the square and watered my mount in a stone trough outside the guardhouse, then waited for the sheriff and his soldiers to appear. While I waited, I observed the square, searching for any signs of the battle that had taken place only a few nights before.

There were none.

Aside from a few hoofprints in the churned-up mud and, here and there, a darker stain which might have been made by blood, there was nothing at all to suggest anything more than a Twelfth Night revel had taken place. Even what was left of the gallows had been removed.

I wondered about this. Why take away the gibbet? Was it merely that it was not needed now that the captives would not be executed? Or was there more to it—an end to the sheriff's hanging ways, perhaps?

I determined to find out if I could. When Bailiff Antoin appeared a short time later, I found my chance. Quickly scanning the double rank of knights, I did not see the one man I wanted. "Where is Sheriff de Glanville?" I asked.

"He has asked me to lead the escort," said Antoin.

Just like that our deception was dashed to pieces.

"Will he come later?" I asked, climbing into the saddle. Mind whirling like a millwheel in the race, I tried my best to think how to rescue our shattered plan.

"No," replied the bailiff, "he will remain here and await our return. Ride on; lead the way."

That is how I came to be leading a company of six knights, a bailiff, and three men-at-arms into the forest—and myself to my doom.

CHAPTER 30

Ogof Angharad

It had taken far longer to reach the cave than she hoped. The deep snow underfoot made for slow going, and now, as Angharad toiled up the long steep track leading to the rock cave, she wished she had left Cél Craidd earlier. Already, there were stars peeping between the clouds to the east; it would be dark before she could get a fire going. Exhausted, she paused and sat on the cracked bole of a fallen tree to rest for a moment and catch her breath for the final climb up to the cave entrance.

She listened to the silence of the forest, keen ears straining for wayward sounds. All she heard was the tick of branches settling in the evening air and, far off, the rasping call of a rook coming in to roost. The distant, lonely sound moved her unexpectedly. She loved the winter and the night. She loved the forest, and all its wonders—just one of innumerable gifts bestowed by a wildly benevolent Creator.

"Before Thee, may I be forever bowing, Kindly King of All Creation," sighed Angharad, the prayer rising gently upward with the visible mist of her breath. And then, leaning on her staff, much more heavily than before, she continued on her way.

Upon reaching the small level clearing halfway up the hill, she paused again to catch her breath. The day would come when she would no longer have the strength to climb up to her *ogof*, her cave house.

The snow lay undisturbed, deep and crisp and white before the open black entrance. All was as it should be, so she moved quickly inside, throwing off her tuck bag and cloak at the threshold. Then, gathering the dry kindling from its place by the cave mouth, she carried it to the fire ring. Working in utter darkness, her deft fingers found the steel and flint and wisps of birch bark, and soon the rosy bloom of a fire was spreading up through the mass of broken twigs. With patience born of long practice, Angharad shepherded the flames, slowly feeding in larger branches until the fire spread its rosy glow over the interior of the cave.

Rising from her knees, she removed her shoes and her wet, cold robe and drew the undershift over her head, then hung the damp garments from hooks set in the rock walls of the cave so that they could dry. She unrolled her favourite bearskin nearer the still-growing fire and lay down. Closing her eyes, she luxuriated in the blесséd warmth seeping into her ancient bones.

After a time, she roused herself, and, wrapping herself in a dry cloak she kept in a basket in the cave, she began to prepare a simple meal, singing as she worked. She sang:

O Wise Head, Rock and Redeemer,
In my deeds, in my words, in my wishes,
In my reason, and in the fulfilling of my desires, be Thou.
In my sleep, in my dreams, in my repose,

In my thoughts, in my heart and soul always, be Thou.
And may the promised Son of Princely Peace dwell,
Aye! in my heart and soul always.
May the long-awaited Son of Glory dwell in me.

Taking the stone lid from a jar, she placed a double handful of barley meal into a wooden bowl, adding a splash of water from the stoup and a bit of lard from the leather tuck bag she had brought with her. She kneaded the dough and set it aside to rest while she filled her kettle and put it on the fire to boil. Next she formed the dough into small cakes and set them on the rounded stones of the fire ring.

Then, while waiting for the water to boil and the cakes to bake, she resumed her song . . .

In my sleep, in my dreams, in my repose,
In my thoughts, in my heart and soul always, be Thou.
Thou, a bright flame before me be,
Thou, a guiding star above me be,
Thou, a smooth path below me be,
And Thou a stout shield behind me be,
Today, tonight, and ever more.
This day, this night, and forever more
Come I to Thee, Jesu—
Jesu, my Druid and my Peace.

She rested, listening to the fire as the flames devoured the fuel and the water bubbled in the kettle. When the water reached the boil, she roused herself and turned the cakes. Then she rose and, taking a handful of dried herbs and roots from another of her many jars and baskets, she cast the stuff into the steaming bath, removing the kettle from the fire to allow the mixture to steep and cool.

When it was ready, she poured some of the potion into a wooden bowl and drank it, savouring the mellow, calming effect of the brew as it eased the stiffness in her old muscles. She ate a few of the cakes, and felt her strength returning. The warmth of the fire and food, combined with the exertions of the last days, made her drowsy.

Yawning, she rose and carried some more wood to the hearth so that it would be close to hand. Then, banking the fire for the night, she lay down to sleep. She stretched out on the bearskin, and pulled her cloak over her and along with it a covering made from the downy pelt of a young fallow deer. There was no special significance to these but, like the wise women of old who esteemed the hides of the red ox for qualities friendly to dreams and visions, Angharad had always had good luck with this particular combination.

At once, exhaustion from her long walk overwhelmed her and dragged her down into the depths of unknowing. She fell asleep with the words of her song still echoing through her mind and heart . . .

In my sleep, in my dreams, in my repose,
In my thoughts, in my heart and soul always, be Thou.
Thou, a bright flame before me be,
Thou, a guiding star above me be,
Thou, a smooth path below me be,
And Thou a stout shield behind me be,
Today, tonight, and ever more.

She had come to her cave to dream. She had come to think, and to spend time alone, away from Bran and the others, in order to discern the possible paths opening before them into the future. Following the last raid, the feeling had come upon her that Bran stood at a crossing of the ways.

It may have been the appearance of the baron's odd gifts—the gold ring and embroidered gloves and mysterious letter—which filled her with sick apprehension. But the count's swift retaliation in burning the forest indicated that the theft was far more damaging than any of them had yet suspected.

This did seem to be the case. Whatever value those particular objects possessed was far beyond silver or gold; it was measured in life and death. This is what concerned Angharad most of all. Not since the coming of King Raven to the greenwood had anything like this happened; she did not know what it meant, and not knowing made her uneasy. So she had come to her snug ogof to seek an answer.

All along the way, as she trudged through the deep-drifted snow, she had turned this over in her mind. As her aged body stumped along, her agile mind ranged far and wide through time and realms of ancient lore, searching out the more obscure pathways of knowledge and knowing, means now largely forgotten.

As a child, sitting at the feet of Delyth, her people's wise hudolion, little Angharad had seen how the old woman had cast a pinch of dry herb powder into the flames as she stirred her porridge. Taking a deep breath, she had announced that the hunting party that had been away for three days was returning.

"Go, Bee." That was her nickname for young Angharad. "Go tell the queen to fill the ale vat and fire the roasting pit, for her husband will soon arrive." Angharad knew better than to question her banfáith, so she jumped up and darted off to deliver the message. "Three pigs and four stags," Delyth called as the youngster scampered away. "Tell her we will be entertaining strangers as well."

Before the sun had quartered the sky, the hunting party rode into the settlement leading pack animals bearing the dressed carcases of three big boars and four red deer stags. With them, as the banfáith had said, were strangers: three men and two boys from Penllyn, a cantref to the north, who were to be their guests.

That was not the first or last time she had witnessed such foretelling of events, but it was the time she asked how the banfáith gained this knowledge. "Knowledge is easy," the old woman told her. "Wisdom is hard."

"But how did you know?" she persisted. "Was it in the smoke?"

Banfáith Delyth smiled and shook her head. "When something happens, little one, it is like casting a rock into a pool—it sends ripples through the subtle currents of time and being." Her fingers lightly bounced as if tracing such ripples. "If you know how, you can follow all the rings back to where they began and see the rock that made them."

"Can you teach me?" she had said, blissfully ignorant of what she was asking.

Banfáith Delyth had cupped her small face in her wrinkled hand and gazed deep into her eyes for a long time. "Aye, yes, little Bee. I think I can." In that moment, Angharad's life and destiny had been decided.

The cave had been Delyth's ogof, and that of the hudolion before her, and so on. Now, a lifetime or two later, she was about to call on those same skills she had first learned from her wise teacher so many, many years ago.

It would take all her considerable skill and experience to succeed. Events which had happened so far away were much more difficult to discern; their ripples—she still thought of it that way—were faint and diffused by the time they reached Angharad's cave in the forest. She would have to be on her best mettle to learn anything useful at all. But if she was right in thinking that the appearance of the baron's curious gifts signalled an event of great significance, the ripples cast in the pool of time and being would be more violent, and she still might be able to learn something about what, and who, had caused them.

She slept and rose early, but rested. The herbal tincture had done its restorative work, and she felt clearheaded and ready to proceed. She built up the fire from coals smoored the night before, and set about making some porridge on which to break her fast. It was dark outside yet; the sun would be late rising. So she lit a few of the clay candle pots she had scattered around the cave, and soon the dark interior was glowing with soft, flickering light. She had brought a bit of cooked meat with her, and decided to warm it up, too. If all went well, she would need a little flesh to carry her through until she could eat again.

After she had eaten, Angharad went outside, knelt in the snow, and as a pale pink sun broke in the east, she lifted her hands in a morning prayer of thanksgiving, guidance, and protection. When she finished, she walked to an alcove deeper in the cave and took up the hide-wrapped bundle there—her harp. Returning to the hearth, she settled herself on her three-legged stool and began to play, stroking the strings, tuning them as needed, limbering up fingers that were no longer as supple as they had once been.

After a time, the music began to work its ancient magic. She could feel her body relax as her mind began to drift on the music, as a leaf drifts on the river's flow. She felt all around her the dip and swirl of time, like the tiny flutters of butterfly wings causing minute eddies in the air. She imagined herself standing to her thighs in a wide, slow-flowing stream and resting her fingertips lightly on the surface of the water so as to feel each tiny wave and ripple as it passed. Each of these, she knew, was some small happening in Elfael or beyond.

It was always the same picture in her mind: the broad easy-moving water, dense with the myriad particles of random happenstance, glowing

745

like pale gold beneath a sky of sunset bronze in the time-between-times.
She moved deeper into the warm wash and felt the water surge around
her, gently tugging against legs and gown as she stood there—head held
to one side as if listening, her face intent, but calm—touching the
sliding skin of the river as it flowed.

After a time, her hands fell from the harp strings and found their
way to a small jar she had placed beside her stool. She withdrew a
pinch of a pungent herb and dropped it into the flames, just as Delyth
had done so long ago. The smoke rose instantly—a clean, dry, aromatic
scent that seemed to sharpen her inner sight and touch. She imagined
she could feel the ripples more easily now as her fingers played among
them.

There were so many, so very many. She shrank within herself to
see how many there were and each one connected in some way to another
and to many others. It was impossible to know which of all those flowing ripples bore significance for her. She lifted her fingers to the strings
and began strumming the harp once more, holding in her mind an
image of the ring and the gloves, demanding of the flowing stream to
bring her only those waves and ripples where the ring and gloves could
be felt.

It took monumental patience, and ferocious concentration, but at
last the river seemed to change course slightly—as when the tide, which
has been rising all the while, suddenly begins to ebb. This it does
between one wave and the next and, while there is nothing to signal the
change, it is definite, inexorable, and profound. The flow of time and
being changed just as surely as the tide, and she felt the inescapable pull
of events flowing around her—some definite and fixed, others half-
formed and malleable, and still others whose potential was long since
exhausted. For not everything that happened in the world was fixed
and certain; some events lingered long as potentialities, influencing

all around them, and others were more transient, mere flits of raw possibility.

As a child might dangle its fingers in the water to attract the tiny fish, Angharad trailed her fingers through the tideflow of all that was, and is, and is yet to be. She imagined herself strolling through the water, feeling the smooth rocks beneath her bare feet, the shore moving and changing as she walked until she came to a familiar bend. She had dabbled here before. Taking a deep breath, she stretched out her hands, tingling with the pulse of possibility.

There!

She felt a glancing touch like the nibble of a fish that struck and darted away. An image took shape in her mind: A host of knights past numbering, all on the march, swarming over the land, burning as they advanced, crushing and killing any who stood in their way. Black smoke billowed to the sky where they had passed. At the head of this army she saw a banner—bloodred, with two golden lions crouching, their claws extended—and carrying the banner, a man astride a great warhorse. The man was broad of shoulder and gripped the pole of the banner in one hand and a bloody sword with the other; he bestrode his battle horse like a champion among men. But he was not a mere man, for he had flames for hair and empty pits where his eyes should be. The vast army arrayed behind this dread, implacable lord carried lances upraised—a forest of slender shafts, the steel heads catching the livid glimmer of a dying sun's rays.

Inwardly, she shrank from this dread vision, and half turned away. Instantly, another image sprang into her mind: a broad-beamed ship tossed high on stormy waves, and a rain-battered coastline of a low, dark country away to the east. There were British horses aboard the ship, and they tossed their heads in terror at the wildly rocking deck. This image faded in its turn and was replaced by another: Bran, bow

in hand, fleeing to the wood on the back of a stolen horse. She could
feel his rage and fear; it seared across the distance like a flame. He had
killed; there was blood behind him and a swiftly closing darkness she
could not penetrate—but it had a vague, animal shape, and she sensed
a towering, primitive, and savage exultation.

The image so shocked her that she opened her eyes.

The cave was dark. The fire had burned out. She turned towards
the cave entrance to see that it was dark outside. The whole day had
passed, maybe more than one day. She rose and began pulling on her
dry clothes, dressing to go out. She wished she had thought to prepare
something to eat; but she had rested somewhat, and that would have
to keep her until she reached Cél Craidd.

If she left at once and walked through the night, she could be
there before nightfall tomorrow. Knowing she was already too late to
prevent whatever had taken place—something terrible, she could feel
it like a knife in her gut—she nevertheless had to go now, if only to
tend the wounded and gather up the broken pieces.

Well, here I was twixt hammer and anvil, no mistake. I had little choice but to carry on as best I could, hoping all the while that when we reached the meeting place in the forest I might alert Bran to the disaster before the trap was sprung. Our plan to capture the sheriff when he arrived to escort the merchant's wagons depended wholly on de Glanville's eagerness to catch King Raven. Not one of us had foreseen the possibility that he would choose to stay home.

As I led those knights and soldiers into the wood on that clear bright day, I felt as if I was leading them to my own funeral . . .

Odo thinks this is funny. He stifles a chuckle, but I see his sly smirk. "Tell me, monk," says I, "since you know so much—which is funnier, a man about to die speaking of funerals? Or a priest laughing at death while the devil tugs at his elbow?"

"Sorry, my lor—" He catches himself again, and amends his words. "Sorry, Will, I didn't mean anything. I thought it amusing, is all."

"Well, we live to entertain our betters," I tell him. "The condemned must be a constant source of pleasure for you and your bloody Abbot Hugo."

"Hugo is not my abbot." This he says in stark defiance of the plain facts. "He is a disgrace to the cloth."

How now! There is a small wound a-festering, and I poke it a little, hoping to open it more.

"Odo," I say, shaking my head, "is that any way to talk about your spiritual superior?"

"Abbot Hugo is not my spiritual superior," he sniffs. "Even the lowest dog in the pack is superior to him."

This is the first time I'd ever heard him dishonour the abbot, and I cannot help but wonder what has happened to turn this dutiful pup against his master. Was it something I said?

"I do believe you are peevish, my friend," I say. "What has happened to set your teeth on edge?"

Odo sighs and rolls his eyes. "It is nothing," he grunts, and refuses to say more. I coax but, stubborn stump that he is, Odo will not budge. So, we go on . . .

We followed the King's Road up from the Vale of Elfael and into the bare winter wood. Bailiff Antoin was more than wary. He was not a fool, mind. He knew only too well what awaited him if King Raven should appear out of the shadows. Yet, give him his due, he showed courage and good humour riding into the forest to offer protection to the merchants. All the soldiers did, mind, and most were eager to take arms against the phantom.

I was the Judas goat leading these trusting sheep to the slaughter. True, I did not know what Bran would do when he saw that the sheriff was not with us. The bailiff noticed my fretful manner and tried to reassure me. "You're worrying for nothing," he said. "The raven creature will not attack in daylight. He only comes out at night."

Where he had picked up this notion, I have no idea. "You would know best, Sire," I replied, trying to smile.

The road rose up the long slope into the wood, eventually following the crest a short distance before beginning the long descent into the Valley of the Wye. The soldiers maintained an admirable wariness; they talked little and kept their eyes moving. They were learning: if not to fear the wood and its black phantom, then at least to show a crumb of respect.

The road is old and descends below deep banks for much of the way; here and there it crosses streams and brooks that come tumbling out of the greenwood. Little humps of snow still occupied the shadows and places untouched by the sun. The going is slow at the best of times, and on that winter day, with the weak sunlight spattered and splayed through bare branches, little puffs of mist rising from the rocks or roots warmed by the sun, eternity seemed to pass with every dragging step. The men grew more quiet the deeper into the wood we went. I was thinking that we must be near to meeting the wagons when I heard the low bellow of an ox and the creaking of wooden wheels. I raised myself in the saddle to listen.

A moment later, the first wagon hove into view. I saw Iwan walking beside the lead ox, holding a long goad. In his merchant's clothing—a long wool cloak, tall boots, and a broad belt to which a fat purse was attached—he seemed only slightly more tame than usual. He was shaved, and his hair had been trimmed to make him appear more like a merchant, or the guard of a travelling trader. The other wagon was some distance behind, and I could only just make it out as it lumbered toward us, bumping along the rutted road.

I did not wait for Bailiff Antoin to make the first move. "There they are!" I called. "This way!"

With a slap of the reins, I rode on ahead, leaving the Ffreinc to come on at their own pace. I wanted a word with Bran before they arrived.

Rhi Bran was sitting in the second wagon, which was being led by Siarles. I rode directly to Bran. He smiled when he saw me and raised his hand in greeting, but the smile quickly faded. "Trouble?"

"De Glanville is not with us," I said. "He would not come, and sent his bailiff instead."

Bran's eyes narrowed as his mind began to work on the problem. Iwan joined us just then, and I explained what I had just told Bran. "Do you think he suspected a trap?"

I shook my head. "He is sick, I think—maybe from the wound he took on Twelfth Night. He would not leave his chamber."

Iwan cast a glance at the advancing soldiers. We had but a moment more before a decision would be needed.

Siarles said, "We cannot send them back, I suppose."

Said I, "Maybe you could go explain to them that they are no longer needed." Siarles frowned and gave a snort of derision, then turned to Bran to see what he would say.

We were all looking at Bran by then. It was time to decide.

"Well, my lord?" I asked. "What will you do?"

"We will go on." Bran smiled and raised his hand as the bailiff came riding up. "Come back and speak to me when we reach the town."

"All is well," I told Antoin in my broken French. "They say there has been no sign of the phantom of the wood."

"We will not see that black coward today," the bailiff declared, but I noticed he cast a hasty glance 'round about just to make certain he had not spoken too soon. He called a command for some of his men to fall in behind the last wagon and guard the rear. "If you are ready," he said, wheeling his horse, "we will move along. We must hurry if we are to reach Saint Martin's by nightfall."

"Lead the way, my lord," I said, and accompanied him to the front of the train.

"Only two wagons?" asked Antoin as we began the return journey.

"Only two," I confirmed. "Why do you ask?"

He shrugged. "I thought it would be more. Where are they from?" he asked.

"From the north country," I told him. The southern Ffreinc knew little about anything beyond the Great Ouse. "It is a hard winter up there. Trading is easier in the south this time of year."

Antoin nodded as if this were well known, and we made our way up the slope to the crest of the ridge once more, the wagons rumbling slowly behind us. Every now and then the bailiff would ride off to one side and look back to reassure himself that all was as it should be. As we started down into the Vale of Elfael, I wondered what Bran was thinking, and how we would make good the deception. We might have posed as the traders we professed to be, but we had no goods to trade; we had a few pelts and some other odds and ends, but that was only for show. Once we reached the market square, we would be discovered for the rascals we were.

Now and again I found a chance to look back, but Bran was too far behind and I could not see him. I tried slowing down so as to drop back to speak to him, but the bailiff kept everyone moving, saying, "Step up! Step up! Don't fall behind. We want to reach the town before dark."

Indeed, the sun was well down by the time we left the forest. Clouds were drifting in from the west, and the wind was picking up— a wild night in the offing. We came to the fording place where the road crossed the stream that cuts through the floor of the valley. "The animals need water," I called. Before the bailiff could say otherwise, I slid down from the saddle and gave my horse to drink. One by one, the others joined us at the ford. While the oxen drank, I sidled over to where Bran was standing.

"What are we to do?" I asked, smiling and nodding as though we talked of nothing more consequential than the weather.

"It will be almost dark by the time we reach the square," he said. "So much the better. Tell the bailiff we mean to make camp for the night behind the church, and that we will set out our wares in the morning. I'll explain the rest when they've left us alone."

I nodded to show I understood, and then felt his hand on my shoulder. "Nothing to fear, Will," he said. "We'll just have a little further to ride when we snatch de Glanville—nothing more. All will be well."

I nodded again, and then walked back to my mount.

Bailiff Antoin called to his men to move the wagons on, and we were soon rolling again: down and down, into the valley, leaving the protection of the forest behind. The clouds thickened and the wind sharpened. The sun set as the first wagon passed Castle Truan, the old caer, Bran's former home. Though we were that close we could almost reach out and touch the wooden palisade, Bran gave no sign that he knew the place. As we passed, one of Count De Braose's men came out to meet us on the road, and I feared he might make trouble. He and Antoin exchanged a brief word and he rode back up to the fortress; we continued on to the town, which we could see in the near distance.

The wind fell away as we rounded the foot of the fortress mount. A silvery pall of smoke hung over the town. Folk were expecting a cold night and had already built their fires high. I could well imagine the warmth of those flames burning brightly on the hearth and longed to stretch my cold bones beneath a tight roof. The soldiers, seeing we were within sight of the town and there were no bandits lurking on the hilltops, asked to be relieved of duty. The bailiff turned to me and said, "The town is just there. You are safe now."

I thanked him for his good care and said, "We will make camp behind the church and offer trade tomorrow. Pray, do not trouble yourself any longer on our account."

"Then I will bid you good night," said Antoin. He made no move to leave until I dipped my fingers into the leather purse at my belt and drew out some silver. I dropped the coins into his palm and his fist closed over them. Without a word, he signalled to the others; his men put spurs to their mounts and they all galloped for home.

I wheeled my mount and hurried back to the second wagon. "They're away home," I told Iwan in the first wagon as I passed him. "Keep moving." Reining in beside Bran, I said, "They've gone on ahead to town. I thanked them and explained that we'd make camp behind the church. I don't think they suspect anything."

"Good," said Bran. "We should have some time to work." Rising in his seat, he turned and looked back the way we'd come. I thought he was looking at the fortress, but he said, "Now where did those other soldiers get to?"

"Other soldiers?" I asked. "They all returned to Saint Martin's."

"All but three," said Bran. "There were five behind us, and only two rode on."

Now I looked back along the trail to see if I might catch sight of the missing three. I saw nothing but a dull grey mist rising with the oncoming night. "I don't see anyone."

"It would be good to know what happened to them."

"Could they have stopped at the caer?" I wondered.

Bran shrugged. "More likely stopped to pee." He turned around again, and said, "Lead on, Will. Let's get to the church."

It was well and truly dark by the time we reached the little town square. No one was about. The mud underfoot had hardened with the cold and crunched under the heavy wagon wheels. A single torch burned outside the guardhouse, and it fluttered in the rising wind. Of our escort of soldiers, there was no sign. No doubt, they had already stabled their horses and gone in to their supper. The thought of a hot meal brought the water to my mouth and made my stomach gurgle.

As we passed the stone keep of the guardhouse, a burst of laughter escaped into the square. It was the sound of soldiers at their drink—a fella has only to hear that once to know it whenever he hears it again. Crossing the square, we passed the church and made our way to the little grove behind. We put the wagons in the grove, unhitched the oxen, and led them to the wall of the church, where they might get some shelter from the wind. We tethered them so they might graze, and left them. "Gather round," said Bran, and we formed a tight circle around him as he explained how we were to proceed. "But before we go any further, we must get some horses," he concluded.

"Leave that to me," said Iwan. "Siarles and I will get them."

Bran nodded. "Then Will—you and I will fetch the sheriff. Tomas," he said, turning to the young Welshman, "you wait here and ready our weapons. Pray, all of you, that we don't need them."

We all crept to the corner of the church and looked across to the stables. "God with you," said Bran.

"And you," said Iwan; then he and Siarles moved out into the square. They walked quickly, but without seeming to hurry.

A half-moon sailed high overhead, shining down through rents in the low clouds. They reached the stables and let themselves in. Bran turned to me, his smile dark and sinister. "Ready, Will?"

I nodded, and told him what to expect inside the sheriff's house. "Maybe I should lead the way."

We hurried along the wall of the church and then passed in front of the entrance. I thought I could hear the monks praying inside as we moved off towards the sheriff's house. We paused at the door, and as I put my hand to the latch, Bran eased the sword from where it had been hidden beneath his cloak. "Sick or not, I do expect de Glanville to come along quietly," he said. "But I would prefer not to kill him."

"It may come to that," I said. Pushing open the door, we began to climb the stairs to the upper floor as quietly as we could. Even so, de Glanville heard us. *"Cela vous, Antoin?"* he called out in Ffreinc, his words slurred in his mouth.

I hesitated and glanced at Bran. "Answer him," he whispered.

"Antoin?" the sheriff called again.

"Oui, c'est," I replied, speaking low, trying to make my voice sound as much like the bailiff's as I could—easier to do, I discovered, in Ffreinc than Saxon.

"Venir," he said, *"le vin de boisson avec moi."*

"Un moment," I called. To Bran, I whispered, "I think he wants us to come drink with him."

"Right friendly of him," whispered Bran. "Let us not keep him waiting."

We started up the stairs; I let my feet fall heavily on the wooden treads to cover the sound of Bran's lighter steps behind me.

We entered together, pausing in the doorway to take in the room, which was deep in shadow; the only light came from the fire in the hearth, which had burned low. The sheriff was still sitting wrapped in his deerskin robe before the hearth; the remains of a meal lay scattered over the nearby table.

"Remettre votre manteau, Antoin," said de Glanville, *"et dessiner une chaise près du feu."*

"Take him now!" whispered Bran in my ear. I felt his hand on my back urging me forward as he sprang past me into the room.

De Glanville sensed the sudden surge towards him, but made no move to prevent us or call out. He simply turned his head as we rushed to his chair, Bran on one side and myself on the other. He did not seem especially surprised to see us, but when he languidly raised his hand as if to fend us off with backward flick of his wrist, I saw that he understood something of the danger descending upon him.

"Drunk as a bishop," I said. "He's probably been sucking the bottle all day."

A lazy smile spread across the sheriff's narrow rat face. *"Vous n'êtes pas Antoin,"* he said, the wine rank on his breath. *"Où est Antoin?"*

"Look at him," I said, shaking my head with disgust. "Doesn't even know who we are."

"Good," replied Bran. "It makes our chore that much easier." Taking de Glanville's arm, he pulled the sheriff to his feet, where he stood swaying like a willow wand in a gale.

"He can't walk," I said. "We'll have to carry him."

"Take his feet." Bran allowed the sheriff to topple gently backwards and caught him under the arms. Stooping, I grabbed his ankles, and together we slung him between us and started hauling him down the stairs and out the door. De Glanville, unresisting, allowed himself to be rough handled all the way to the bottom. He revived somewhat as we stepped outside and the cold air hit him. He moaned and rolled his head from side to side.

We started out across the square and, as we passed in front of the church, the door opened and out came a gaggle of monks carrying torches. Prayers finished, I suppose they were returning to the abbey and were brought up short by the sight of two men makin' off with a third.

"Tell them he's drunk and we're taking him home," Bran said. "Quick, Will, tell them!"

I did as he commanded, and that might have succeeded—as indeed we thought for a fleeting moment that it had—but for the knights that appeared out of the night. We heard the sound of hooves and turned to see the three missing soldiers pounding into the square.

There we were, Bran and Will Scarlet with Sheriff de Glanville slung between us like a bag of wet corn—thieves caught with the plunder in hand.

"*Arrêt! Vous, arrêtez là-bas!*" shouted the foremost knight.

"He says we are to halt," I told Bran.

"I got that. Keep going," urged Bran. "We'll lose them when we get to the horses."

"*Ils ont tué le shérif!*" shouted another.

I might have misunderstood, but that brought me up short. "They've recognised the sheriff," I gasped. "They think we've killed him."

"Tell them they're wrong," said Bran. "Tell them he's a friend of ours fallen drunk. But for God's sake, keep moving!"

I shouted back as Bran commanded, but the knights came on regardless. As they drew nearer, I saw that one of them carried a bulky bundle across the back of his horse. As the knight passed into the torchlight, I saw a dark head of hair and small arms hanging limply down and knew at once what they had captured.

"Bran!" I hissed, dropping the sheriff's heels. "They've got Gwion Bach!"

The knights rode on, drawing their weapons as they came. One of them shouted for us to halt. *"Arrêt! Arrêt!"* Bran released the sheriff's shoulders. De Glanville landed heavily on the frozen ground, which seemed to revive the fella somewhat. He grunted and rolled over.

We streaked down the side of the church, shouting to Iwan and Siarles that we were attacked. We rounded the corner to discover that those two had not yet returned from the stables. But Tomas was there, waiting with longbows strung and swords unsheathed. We each grabbed a bow and a handful of arrows and spread out, keeping the wall of the church behind us.

The soldiers did not stop to help the sheriff—no doubt they thought him dead already—but came pounding around the corner of the church and into a sharp hail of arrows. We loosed at will. One rider was struck high in the chest and thrown over the rump of his mount.

The two remaining knights tried to swerve out of the way, but horses are far from the nimblest creatures afoot. As they slowed to turn, we drew and loosed again. A second knight went down, and the third—the one with Gwion bound to his saddle—threw his hands high in surrender.

"Get the horses!" shouted Bran. Tomas and I ran to catch the two riderless mounts, and Bran took care of the third. He gestured with a strung arrow for the knight to dismount and lay down flat on the ground, then ever so gently lifted the head of the boy. "Gwion? Gwion, wake up."

The lad opened his eyes, saw Bran, and began to cry. Bran untied him double quick, lifted him down from the horse, and began rubbing the warmth back into the little 'un's hands and feet. "Will!" he shouted as I came running back. "Go see what has happened to Iwan and Siarles."

I skittered down the side of the church towards the square. The sheriff still lay where we had dropped him, sound asleep again in his drunken stupor. The square was empty; the monks had disappeared— either back into the church or, more likely, they'd scurried off to the abbey. I ran to the stables and quietly pulled open the door. First to meet my eye were three Ffreinc grooms lying on the floor of the stable, dead or unconscious, I could not tell. Iwan and Siarles were cinching the saddle straps of the last two mounts.

"Hsst!" I said, putting my head through the gap in the door. "What is taking so long?"

Iwan glanced around as he pulled the strap tight. "We had to put some fellas to sleep," he said. "We're ready now."

"Then hurry!" I said. "We've been attacked."

"How many?" asked Siarles, gathering the reins of two fresh horses.

"Three knights," I said. "Two are down and the other surrendered. Hurry!"

I pulled open the stable doors, allowing Iwan and Siarles to lead the saddled horses out; they headed down the short ramp and into the quiet square. All was silent and dark.

Just as we started across to the church, however, the door to the guardhouse opened and out swarmed six knights or more. "Bloody blazes!" I said. "The monks must have told them. Fly!"

The Ffreinc saw us with the horses and cried for us to stop. Iwan leapt into the saddle of his mount and lit out for the church across the square, with Siarles right behind. I paused to loose an arrow at the soldiers, thinking to take at least one down. I missed the mark, but the arrow buried itself in the door frame. One fella, who was still inside, slammed the door hard, which briefly prevented any more Ffreinc from spilling out.

That was the last of my arrows, so I turned and hightailed it after the others. I ran but a half dozen strides and my leg buckled under me and I fell. In the same instant, a pain like no other ripped through the meaty part of my thigh. Reaching down, I felt the shaft of a lance. The spear had hit the ground and caught me as it bounced up. Even as I lay clutching the wound, with blood streaming through my fingers, I thought, *That was lucky. I could have been killed.* Hard on the heels of this thought came the next: *Will, you bloody fool! Get up or they'll be carving your dull head from your shoulders.*

I got to my feet and staggered forward; my injured leg felt like a lump of wood on fire, but I limped on. Bran and Iwan, mounted now, came charging from around the back of the church, bows in hand. Both loosed arrows at my pursuers, and two soldiers fell, screaming and rolling on the hard winter ground. Siarles, cradling Gwion in the saddle before him and holding the reins of one of the big Ffreinc horses, rode out to meet me. "Time to go," he said, tossing the reins to me.

I caught the traces and tried to haul my foot to the stirrup, but

765

could not lift my leg. I tried once and missed. The Ffreinc were almost upon us. "Go on! Ride!" I said. "I'm right behind you."

Siarles wheeled his mount and galloped away without a backward glance as I tried once more to get my clumsy foot into the stirrup. I did catch the bar with my toe, but the horse, frightened by the noise and confusion, jigged sideways. My hands, slippery with blood, could not hold, and the reins slipped from my grasp. Unbalanced on one leg, I fell on my back, squirming on the frozen ground. I was still trying to get my feet under me when the Ffreinc rushed up and laid hold of me.

I glimpsed a swift motion above me, and the butt of a spear crashed down on my poor head . . .

So that, Odo, is how they caught me," I tell him. He lifts his ink-stained hand from the page and looks at me with his soft, sad eyes. I shrug. "All the rest you know."

"The others got away," he says, and the resignation in his voice is that thick you could stuff it in your shoe.

"They did. Got clean away," I reply. "Fortunate for me that the sheriff was sleeping like the drunken lump he was, or I would have been strung high long since. By the time he woke up, Abbot Hugo already had me bound hand and foot and was determined to have his wicked way with me."

Odo scratches the side of his nose with the feathered end of his quill. He is trying to think of something, or has thought of something and is trying to think how to say it. I can see him straining at the thought. But as I have all the time God sends me, I do not begrudge him the time it takes to spit it out.

"About that night," he says at last. "Did Siarles leave you behind on purpose?"

"Well, I've asked myself the same thing once and again. Truth is, I don't know. Could he have helped me get away? He did bring the horse, mind. Could he have helped me more than he did? Yes. But remember, he had Gwion Bach with him, and any help he could have offered me would have risked all three of us. Could he have told Iwan or Bran to come back for me? Yes, he could have done that. For all I know, maybe he did. But then again, the Ffreinc were on me that quick, I don't think anyone could save me getting captured." I spread my hands and give him a shrug. "He did, more or less, what I would have done, I suppose."

"You would have made sure he got away, Will," Odo asserts.

"Why, Odo, what a thing to say," I reply. "A fella'd think you cared what happened to ol' Will here."

He makes a worm face and looks down at his scrap of parchment.

"You have to remember that it was dark and cold, and everything was happening very fast," I say. "I doubt anyone could have done more than they did. It was bad luck, is all. Bad luck from the beginning if you ask me." I pause to reflect on that night. "No," I conclude, "the only regret I have is that we didn't kill the sheriff when we had the chance."

"Why didn't you kill him?"

"We had some idea of holding him to justice," I say, and shake my head. "I suspect Bran wanted to make him answer before the king. God knows how we would have brought that about. Bran had a way, I guess. He has a way for most things."

Odo nods. He is thinking. I can see the tiny wheels turning in his head. "What about the ring and the letter?" he wants to know.

"What about them?"

"Well," says he, "who were they for?"

"Now, I've thought about that, too. The letter was addressed to the pope, so I suppose they were for him."

"Which pope?"

I stare at him. "The pope—head of the Mother Church."

"Will, there are two popes."

Dunce that he is, some of the most fuddling things come out of his mouth. "There are *not* two popes," I tell him.

"There are."

He seems quite certain of this.

I hold up two fingers—my bowstring fingers—and repeat, "Two popes? I'll wager a whole ham on the hoof that you didn't mean that just now. It cannot happen."

"It can," he assures me. "It happens all the time."

"See now, Odo, have you been staring at the sun again?" I shake my head slowly. "Two popes! Whoever heard of such a thing? Next you'll be tellin' me the moon is a bowl of curds and whey."

Odo favours me with one of his smug and superior smirks. "I do not know about the moon, but it happens from time to time that the church must choose between two popes. So it is now. I do not wonder that, living in the forest as you do, you might not have heard about this."

"How in the name of Holy Peter, James, and John has it come about?"

I have him now. A wrinkle appears on Odo's smooth brow. "I do not know precisely what has happened."

"Aha! You see! You think to play me for a fool, monk, but I won't be played."

"No, no," he insists, "there are two popes right enough." It is, he contends, merely that the facts of such an event taking place so far away are difficult to obtain, and more difficult still to credit. All that can be said for certain is that there has been some kind of disagreement among the powers governing the Holy Church. "Papal succession came under question," he tells me. "How it fell out this time, I cannot say. But kings and emperors always try to influence the decision."

"Now that I can believe, at least." Indeed, this last did not surprise me overmuch. It is all the same with kings of every stripe; nothing they get up to amazes me anymore. But as Odo spoke, I began to discern the glimmering of suspicion that this strange event and the appearance of the ring and letter in Elfael might in some way share a common origin, or a common end. Find the truth of one, and I might well discover the truth of the other.

"No doubt this is what has caused the rift this time."

"Go on," I tell him. "I'm listening."

"However it came about, the disagreement has resulted in a dispute in which the two opposing camps have each chosen their own successor who claims to be the rightful pontiff."

"Two popes," I mutter. "Will wonders never cease?"

Odo has been toying with the scrap of parchment before him. "This is what made me think of it," he says, and holds up the ragged little shred. There, in one corner of the scrap, someone has drawn a coat of arms. I glance at it and make to hand it back. My hand stops midway, and I jerk back the parchment. "Wait!"

I study the drawing more closely. "I've seen this before," I tell him. "It is on the ring. Odo, do you know whose arms these are?"

"The arms of Pope Clement," he says. "At least, that is what the abbot has said."

"Abbot Hugo told you that?"

Odo nods.

I regard him with an excitement I have not felt for months. Odo has never lied to me. That is, perhaps, his singular virtue. I think about what he has said before speaking again. "But see here," I say slowly, "it is not Clement we recognise as head of the church. It is Urban."

"This is the difficulty," he replies. "Some hold with Urban, others with Clement."

"Yes, as you say. Now, Odo, my faithful scribe, tell me the truth."

"Always, Will."

"Which Pope does Baron de Braose support?"

He answers without hesitation, his tone flat, almost mocking. "Clement, of course."

I hear that in his tone which strikes a tiny spark of hope in my empty heart. "The way you say it, a fella'd think you didn't entirely approve."

"It is not for me to approve or disapprove," he counters.

"Perhaps not," I allow slowly, desperate to keep alive that wee spark. "Perhaps not, as you say. Probably it is better to let the kings and nobles fight it out amongst themselves. No doubt they know best."

Odo yawns and stretches. He gathers his inkhorn and his penknife, stands, and shuffles to the door of my cell, where he hesitates. "God with you, Will," he says, almost embarrassed, it seems.

"God with you, Odo," I reply. When he has gone I lie awake listening to the dogs bark, and thinking that there is something very important in all this two popes business . . . if this dull head of mine could only get a grip on what it might be.

CHAPTER 33

Coed Cadw

The damage was done. In a single ill-advised, ignorant stroke, Bran had dashed Angharad's carefully considered design for defeating the Ffreinc invaders and driving them from Elfael. In a mad, impulsive rush he had destroyed months of subtle labour and, she could well imagine, stirred the ire of the enemy to white-hot vengeance. For this and much else, the hudolion blamed Bran—but, more, she blamed herself. Angharad had allowed herself to believe that she had weaned Bran away from that unreasoning rage that he had possessed when she first met him, that she had at long last extinguished the all-consuming fire of an anger that, like the *awen* of the legendary champions of old, caused the lord of Elfael to forget himself, plunging him into the bloodred flames of battle madness—a worthy attribute for a warrior, perhaps, but unhelpful in a king. No mistake, it was a king she wanted for Elfael, not merely another warrior.

Alas, there was nothing for it now but to pick up the pieces and see if anything could be salvaged from the wreckage of that disastrous attempt to capture the sheriff.

What she had seen in the cave while testing the onrushing stream of time and events had caused her to return to Cél Craidd with as much haste as she could command. Her old bones could not move with anything near their former speed, and she had arrived too late to prevent Bran from acting on his ludicrous scheme. The small warband had already departed for Saint Martin's, and the die was cast.

The wise hudolion was waiting when the raiders returned. Dressed in her Bird Spirit cloak, she stood beneath the Council Oak and greeted them when they returned. "All hail, Great King," she crowed, "the people of Elfael can enjoy their peace this night because you have gained for them a mighty victory over the Ffreinc." As the rest of the forest tribe gathered, she said, "I see a riderless horse. Where is Will Scarlet?"

"Captured," Bran muttered. There was a stifled cry from the crowd, and Nóin rushed away from the gathering.

"Captured, is he?" the hudolion cooed. "Oh, that is a fine thing indeed. Was that in your plan, Wise King?"

Heartsick over his failure, he knew full well that he had made a grave and terrible mistake and was not of a mood to endure her mockery—deserved as it might be. "Silence, woman! I will not hear it. We will speak of this tomorrow."

"Yes," she croaked, "the rising sun will make all things new, and the deeds done in darkness will vanish like the shadows."

"You go too far!" Bran growled. Weary, and grieving the loss of Will, he wanted nothing more than to slink away to his hut and, like the beaten hound he was, lick his wounds. "See here," he said, pointing to Gwion Bach as Siarles eased the lad down from his mount. "We rescued the boy from the Ffreinc. They would have killed him."

"Oh? Indeed?" she queried, her eyes alight with anger. "Has it not yet occurred to you that the boy was caught only because he was following you?"

Bran drew breath to reply but, realizing she was right, closed his mouth again and turned away from her scorn.

When Bran did not answer, the old woman said, "Too late you show wisdom, O King. Too late for Will Scarlet. Go now to your rest, and before you sleep, pray for the man whose trust you have betrayed this night. Pray God to keep him and uphold him in the midst of his enemies."

That is exactly what Bran did. Miserable in his failure, he prayed the comfort of Christ for Will Scarlet, that the All-sustaining Spirit would keep his friend safe until he could be rescued or redeemed.

The next morning, Lord Bran gathered the Grellon and formally confessed his failure: they had not succeeded in taking the sheriff, and Will Scarlet had been captured instead. Nóin, who already knew the worst, did not join the others, but remained in her hut taking consolation with Mérian. Bran went to her to beg forgiveness and offer reassurance. "We will not rest until we have secured Will's release," he promised.

Angharad soon learned of the vow and cautioned, "The sentiment is noble, but word and deed are not one. It will be long ere this vow is fulfilled."

"Why?" he asked. "What do you know?"

"Only that wishing does not make doing easier, my impetuous lord. If our Will is to be rescued, then you must become wiser than the wisest serpent."

"What does that mean?"

By way of reply, Angharad simply said, "I will tell you tonight. When the sun begins to set, summon the Grellon to council."

So as twilight claimed the forest stronghold, the men stoked the fire in the fire ring, and the people of Cél Craidd gathered once more to hear what their wise banfáith had to say.

As Angharad took up her harp, the children crowded close around her feet, but their elders, apprehensive and fearful now, did not join them in their youthful eagerness. Will's fate cast a pall over everyone old enough to understand the likely outcome of his capture, and every thought was on the captive this night.

Looking out upon her audience, Angharad saw the faces grim in the reflected fire glow; and they seemed to her in this moment not faces at all, but empty vessels into which she would pour the elixir of the song which was more than a song. They would hear and, God willing, the story would work in their hearts and minds to produce its rare healing fruit.

As silence descended over the beleaguered group, she began to strum the harp strings, letting the notes linger and shimmer in the air, casting lines of sound into the gathering darkness—lines by which she would ensnare the souls of her listeners and draw them into the story realm where they could be shaped and changed. When at last she judged the fortuitous moment had arrived, she began.

"After the Battle of the Cauldron, when the men of Britain conquered the men of Ireland," she began, her voice quavering slightly, but gathering strength as she sang, "the head of Bran the Blesséd was carried back to the Island of the Mighty and safely buried on the White Hill, facing east, to protect forever his beloved Albion."

Recognition flickered among some of the older forest dwellers as the familiar names of long ago tugged at the chords of memory. Angharad smiled and, closing her eyes, began the tale known as "Manawyddan's Revenge."

As the warriors made their farewells and departed for their homes, Manawyddan, chief of battle, gazed down from the hill upon the muddy village of Lundein, and at his companions, and gave a sigh of deepest regret. "Woe is me," said he. "Woe upon woe."

"My lord," said Pryderi, a youth who was his closest companion, "why do you sigh so?"

"Since you ask, I will tell you," replied Manawyddan. "The reason is this: every man has a place of his own tonight except one only— and that one happens to be me."

"Pray do not be unhappy," answered Pryderi. "Remember, your cousin is king of the Island of the Mighty, and although he may do you wrong, you have never asked him for anything, though well you might."

"Aye," agreed the chieftain, "though that man is my kinsman, I find it somewhat sad to see anyone in the place of our dead comrade, and I could never be happy sharing so much as a pigsty with him."

"Then will you allow me to suggest another plan?" asked Pryderi.

"If you have another plan," answered Manawyddan, "I will gladly hear it."

"As it happens, the seven cantrefs of Dyfed have been left to me," said young Pryderi. "It may please you to know that Dyfed is the most pleasant corner of our many-coloured realm. My mother, Rhiannon, lives there and is awaiting my return."

"Then why do we linger here, feeling sorry for ourselves, when we could be in Dyfed?"

"Wait but a little and hear the rest. My mother has been a widow for seven years now, and grows lonely," explained the youth. "I will commend you to her if you would only woo her; and wooing, win her; and winning her, wed her. For the day you wed my mother, the sovereignty of Dyfed will be yours. And though you may never possess more domains than those seven cantrefs, there are no cantrefs in all of Britain any better. Indeed, if you had the choice of any realm in all the world, you would surely have chosen those same seven cantrefs for your own."

"I do not desire anything more," replied Manawyddan, inspired by the generosity of his friend. "I will come with you to see Rhiannon and this realm of which you boast so highly. Moreover, I will trust God to repay your kindness. As for myself, the best friendship I can offer will be yours, if you wish it."

"I wish nothing more, my friend," Pryderi said. And the next morning, as the red sun peeped above the rim of the sea, they set off. They had not travelled far when Manawyddan asked his friend to tell him more about his mother.

"Well, it may be the love of a son speaking here," said the young warrior, "but I believe you have never yet met a woman more companionable than she. When she was in her prime, no woman was as lovely as Queen Rhiannon; and even now you will not be disappointed with her beauty."

So they continued on their way, and however long it was that they were on the road, they eventually reached Dyfed. Behold! There was a feast ready for them in Arberth, where Cigfa, Pryderi's own dear wife, was awaiting his return. Pryderi greeted his wife and mother, then introduced them to his sword brother, the great Manawyddan. And was it not as Pryderi had said? For, in the battle chief's eyes, the youth had only told the half: Rhiannon was far more beautiful than he had allowed himself to imagine—more beautiful, in fact, than any woman he had seen in seven years, with long dark hair and a high, noble forehead, lips that curved readily in a smile, and eyes the colour of the sky after a rain.

During the feast, Manawyddan and Rhiannon sat down together and began to talk, and from that conversation the chieftain's heart and mind warmed to her, and he felt certain that he had never known a woman better endowed with beauty and intelligence than she. "Pryderi," he said, leaning near his friend, "you were right in everything you said, but you only told me the half."

774

Rhiannon overheard them talking. "And what was it that you said, my son?" she asked.

"Lady," said Pryderi, "if it pleases you, I would see you married to my dear friend Manawyddan, son of Llyr, an incomparable champion and most loyal of friends."

"I like what I see of him," she answered, blushing to admit it, "and if your friend feels but the smallest part of what I feel right now, I will take your suggestion to heart."

The feast continued for three days, and before it had ended the two were pledged to one another. Before another three days had passed, they were wed. Three days after the wedding, they began a circuit of the seven cantrefs of Dyfed, taking their pleasure along the way.

As they wandered throughout the land, Manawyddan saw that the realm was exceedingly hospitable, with hunting second to none, and fertile fields bountiful with honey, and rivers full of fish. When the wedding circuit was finished, they returned to Arberth to tell Pryderi and Cigfa all they had seen. They sat down to enjoy a meal together and had just dipped their flesh forks into the cauldron when suddenly there was a clap of thunder, and before anyone could speak, a fall of mist descended upon the entire realm so that no one could see his hand before his face, much less anyone else.

After the mist, the heavens were filled with shining light of white and gold. And when they looked around they found that where before there were flocks and herds and dwellings, now they could see nothing at all: neither house, nor livestock, nor kinfolk, nor dwellings. They saw nothing at all except the empty ruins of the court, broken and deserted and abandoned. Gone were the people of the realm, gone the sheep and cattle. There was no one left in all Dyfed except the four of them, and Pryderi's pack of hunting dogs, which had been lying at their feet in the hall.

"What is this?" said Manawyddan. "I greatly fear some terrible tribulation has befallen us. Let us go and see what may be done."

Though they searched the hall, the sleeping nooks, the mead cellar, the kitchens, the stables and storehouses and granaries, nothing remained of any inhabitants, and of the rest of the realm they discovered only desolation and dense wilderness inhabited by ferocious beasts. Then those four bereft survivors began wandering the land; they hunted to survive and banked the fire high each night to fend off the wild beasts. As day gave way to day, the four friends grew more and more lonely for their countrymen, and more and more desperate.

"God as my witness," announced Manawyddan one day, "we cannot go on like this much longer."

"Yet unless we lie down in our graves and pull the dirt over our own heads," pointed out Pryderi, "I think we must endure it yet a while."

The next morning Pryderi and Manawyddan got up to hunt as before; they broke fast, prepared their dogs, took up their spears, and went outside. Almost at once, the leader of the pack picked up the scent and ran ahead, directly to a small copse of rowan trees. As soon as the hunters reached the grove, the dogs came yelping back, all bristling and fearful and whimpering as if they had been beaten.

"There is something strange here," said Pryderi. "Let us see what hides within that copse."

They crept close to the rowan grove, one trembling step at a time, until they reached the border of the trees. Suddenly, out from the cover of the rowans there burst a shining white boar with ears of deepest red. The dogs, with strong encouragement from the men, rushed after it. The boar ran a short distance away, then took a stand against the dogs, head lowered, tusks raking the ground, until the men came near. When the hunters closed in, the strange beast broke away, retreating once more.

After the boar they went, chasing it, cornering it, then chasing it again until they left the familiar fields and came to an unknown part of the realm, where they saw, rising on a great hill of a mound in the distance, a towering caer, all newly made, in a place they had seen neither stone nor building before. The boar was running swiftly up the ramp to the fortress with the dogs close behind it.

Once the boar and the dogs had disappeared through the entrance of the caer, Pryderi and Manawyddan pursued them. From the top of the fortress mound the two hunters watched and listened for their dogs. However long they were there, they heard neither another bark, nor whine, nor so much as a whimper from any of their dogs. Of any sign of them, there was none.

"My lord and friend," said bold Pryderi, "I am going into that caer, to recover our dogs. You and I both know we cannot survive without them."

"Forgive me, friend," said Manawyddan, leaning on his spear to catch his breath, "but your counsel is not wise. Consider, we have never seen this place before and know nothing about it. Whoever has placed our realm under this enchantment has surely made this fortress appear also. We would be fools to go in."

"It may be as you say," answered Pryderi, "but I will not easily give up my dogs for anything—they are helping to keep us alive these many days."

Nothing Manawyddan could say would divert Pryderi from this plan. The young warrior headed straight for the strange fortress and, reaching it, looked around quickly. He could see neither man, nor beast, nor the white boar, nor his good hunting dogs; neither were there houses, or dwellings, or even a hall inside the caer. The only thing he saw in the middle of the wide, empty courtyard was a fountain with marble stonework around it. Beside the fountain was a golden bowl of exquisite design, attached by four chains so that it hung above the marble slab; but the chains reached up into the air, and he could not see the end of them.

Astonished by the remarkable beauty of the bowl, he strode to the fountain and reached out to touch its lustrous surface. As soon as his fingers met the gleaming gold, however, his hands stuck to the bowl and his two feet to the slab on which he was standing. He made to shout, but the power of speech failed him so he could not utter a single word. And thus he stood, unable to move or cry out.

Manawyddan, meanwhile, waited for his friend outside the entrance to the caer, but refused to go inside. Late in the afternoon, when he was certain he would get no tidings of Pryderi or his dogs, he turned and, with a doleful heart, stumbled back to camp. When he came shambling in, head down, dragging his spear, Rhiannon stared at him. "Where is my son?" she asked. "Come to that, where are the dogs?"

"Alas," he answered, "all is not well. I do not know what happened to Pryderi, and to heap woe on woe, the dogs have disappeared, too." And he told her about the strange fortress and Pryderi's determination to go inside.

"Truly," said Rhiannon, "you have shown yourself a sorry friend, and fine is the friend you have lost."

With that word she wrapped her cloak around her shoulders and set off for the caer, intending to rescue her son. She reached the place just as the moon rose, and saw that the gate of the fortress was wide open, just as Manawyddan had said; furthermore, the place was unprotected. In through the gate she walked, and as soon as she had entered the yard she caught sight of Pryderi standing there, his feet firmly planted to the marble slab, his hands stuck fast to the bowl. She hastened to his aid.

"Oh, my son! Whatever are you doing here?" she exclaimed.

Without thinking, she put her hand to his and tried to free him. The instant she touched the bowl, however, her two hands stuck tight and her feet as well. Queen Rhiannon was caught, too, nor could she utter a single cry for help. And as they stood there, night fell upon the caer. Lo! There was a mighty peal of thunder, and a fall of shining mist so thick that the caer disappeared from sight.

When Rhiannon and Pryderi failed to return, Cigfa, daughter of Gwyn Gloyw and wife of young Pryderi, demanded to know what had happened. Reluctantly, Manawyddan related the whole sorry tale, whereupon Cigfa grieved for her husband and lamented that her life to her was no better than death. "I wish I had been taken away with him."

Manawyddan gazed at her in dumb disbelief. "You are wrong to want your death, my lady. As God is my witness, I vow to protect you to my last breath for the sake of Pryderi and my own dear wife. Do not be afraid." He continued, "Between me and God, I will care for you as much as I am able, as long as God shall wish us to remain in this wretched state of misery."

And the young woman was reassured by that. "I will take you at your word, Father. What are we to do?"

"As to that, I have been thinking," said Manawyddan, "and as much as I might wish otherwise, I think this is no longer a suitable place for us to stay. We have lost our dogs, and without them to help in the hunt we cannot long survive, however hard we might try. Though it grieves me to say it, I think we must abandon Dyfed and go to England. Perhaps we can find a way to support ourselves there."

"If that is what you think best, so be it," Cigfa replied through her tears; for she was loath to leave the place where she and Pryderi had been so happily married. "I will follow you."

So they left the comely valleys and travelled to England to find a way to sustain themselves. On the way, they talked. "Lord Manawyddan," said Cigfa, "it may be necessary while among the English to labour for our living. If that be so, what trade would you take?"

"Our two heads are thinking as one," replied Manawyddan. "I have been contemplating this very thing. It seems to me that shoe-making would be as good a trade as any, and better than some."

"Lord," the young woman protested, "think of your rank. You are a king in your own country! Shoe-making may be very well for some, and as good a trade as others no doubt deserve, but it is far too lowly for a man of your rank and skill."

"Your indignation favours me," replied Manawyddan ap Llyr. "Nevertheless, I have grown that fond of eating that it does me injury to go without meat and ale one day to the next. I suspect it is the same with you."

Lady Cigfa nodded, but said nothing.

"Therefore, I have set my sights on the trade of making shoes," he said, "and you can help by finding honest folk to buy the shoes I shall make."

"If that is what you wish," said the young woman, "that is what I will do."

The two travelled here and there, and came at last to a town where they felt they might settle for a spell. Manawyddan took up his craft and, though it was harder than he had imagined, he persevered—at first making serviceable shoes, then good shoes and, after much diligence and hard labour, fashioning the finest shoes anyone in England had ever seen. He made buckle shoes with gilt leather and golden fittings, and boots of red-dyed leather, and sandals of green with blue laces. He made such wonderful shoes that the work of most other cobblers seemed crude and shabby when compared to his. It was soon voiced aloud through all England that as long as either a shoe or boot could be got from Manawyddan the Welshman, no others were worth having. With lovely Cigfa to sell his wares, the nobles of the realm were soon refusing to buy from anybody else.

Thus, the two exiles spent one year and another in this way, until the shoemakers of England grew first envious and then resentful of their success. The English cobblers met together and decided to issue a warning for the Welshman to leave the realm or face certain death, for he was no longer welcome among them.

"Lord and father," said Cigfa, "is this to be endured from these ill-mannered louts?"

"Not the least part of it," Manawyddan replied. "Indeed, I think it is time to return to Dyfed. It may be that things are better there now."

The two wayfarers set off for Dyfed with a horse and cart, and three good milk cows. Manawyddan had also supplied himself with a bushel of barley, and tools for sowing, planting, and harvesting. He made for Arberth and settled there, for there was nothing more pleasant to him than living in Arberth and the territory where he used to hunt: himself and Pryderi, and Rhiannon and Cigfa with them.

Through the winter, he fished in the streams and lakes, and despite the lack of dogs, was able to hunt wild deer in their woodland lairs. When spring rolled around, he began tilling the deep, rich soil, and after that he planted one field, and a second, and a third. The barley that grew up that summer was the best in the world, and the three additional fields were just as good, producing grain more bountiful than any seen in Dyfed from that day to this.

Manawyddan and Cigfa peacefully occupied themselves through the seasons of the year. When harvest time came upon them, they went out to the first hide and behold, the stalks were so heavy with grain they bowed down almost to breaking. "We shall begin reaping tomorrow," said Manawyddan.

He hurried back to Arberth and honed the scythe. The following day, in the green light of dawn, he went out to begin the harvest. When he arrived at the field he discovered, to his shock and dismay, nothing but naked stalks. Each and every stalk had been broken off and the ear of grain nipped clean away, leaving just the bare stem.

It fair broke his heart to see it. "Who could have done this?" he wailed, thinking it must have been English raiders because there were no countrymen near, and no one else around who could have accomplished such a feat in one night. Even as he was thinking this, he hurried on to examine the second field; and behold, it was fully grown and ready to harvest.

"God willing," said he, "I will reap this tomorrow."

As before, he honed the scythe and went out the next morning. But upon reaching the field, he found nothing except stubble.

"O, Lord God," he cried in anguish, "am I to be ruined? Who could do such a thing?" He thought and thought, but reached only this conclusion: "Whoever began my downfall is the one who is completing it," he said. "My enemy has destroyed my country with me!"

Then he hurried to examine the third field. When he got there, he was certain no one had ever seen finer wheat fully grown and bending to the scythe. "Shame on me," he said, "if I do not keep guard tonight, lest whoever stripped the other fields will come to carry off this one, too. Whatever befalls, I will protect the grain."

He hurried home and gathered his weapons, then went out and began guarding the field. The sun went down and he grew weary, but he did not cease from walking around the borders of the grain field.

Around midnight, the mighty lord of Dyfed was on watch when all of a sudden there arose a terrific commotion. He looked around, and lo, there was a horde of mice—and not just a horde, but a horde of hordes! So many mice it was not possible to count or reckon them, though you had a year and a day to do it.

Before Manawyddan could move, the mice descended upon the field, and every one of them was climbing to the tip of a barley stalk, nipping off the ear, and bearing it away. In less time than it takes to tell, there was no stalk untouched. Then, as quickly as they had come, the mice scurried off, carrying the ears of grain with them.

A mighty rage gripped the warrior. He lunged out at the fleeing mice. But he could no more catch them than he could catch the birds in the air—except for one that was so fat and heavy Manawyddan was able to spring upon it and snatch it up by the tail. This he did and dropped it inside his glove; then he tied the end of the glove with a string. Tucking the glove in his belt, he turned and started back to where Cigfa was waiting with a meal for the hungry guardsman.

Manawyddan returned to the simple hut where he lived with Cigfa, and hung the glove on a peg by the door. "What have you there, my lord?" asked Cigfa, brightening the fire.

"A marauding thief," replied mighty Manawyddan, almost choking on the words. "I caught him stealing the food from our mouths."

"Dear Father," wondered Cigfa, "what sort of thief can you put in your glove?"

"Since you ask," sighed Manawyddan, "here is the whole sad story." And he told her how the last field had also been destroyed and the harvest ruined by the mice that had stripped it bare, even as he was standing guard.

"That mouse was very fat," he said, pointing to the glove, "so I was able to catch it, and heaven and all the saints bear witness, I will surely hang that rascal tomorrow. Upon my oath, if I had caught any more of the thieves I would hang them all."

"You may do as you please, for you are lord of this land and well within your rights," replied the young woman. "However, it is unseemly for a king of your high rank and nobility to be exterminating vermin like that. It can avail you little to trouble yourself with such a creature. Perhaps you might better serve your honour by letting it go."

"Your words are wise counsel, to be sure," answered Manawyddan. "But shame on me if it should become known that I caught any of those thieving rascals only to let them go."

"And how would this become known?" wondered Cigfa. "Is there anyone else, save me, to know or care?"

"I will not argue with you, my daughter," answered Manawyddan. "But I made a vow, and since I only caught this one, I will hang it as I have promised."

"That is your right, Lord," she replied. "You know, I hope that I have no earthly reason to defend this creature, and would not deign to do so except to avoid humiliation for you. There, I've said it. You are the lord of this realm; you do what you will."

"That was well said," granted Manawyddan. "I am content with my decision."

The next morning, the lord of Dyfed made for Gorsedd Arberth, taking the glove with the mouse inside. He quickly dug two holes in the highest place on the great mound of earth, into which he planted two forked branches cut from a nearby wood. While he was working, he saw a bard coming towards him, wearing an old garment, threadbare and thin. The sight surprised him, so he stood and stared.

"God's peace," said the bard. "I give you the best of the day."

"May God bless you richly!" called Manawyddan from the mound. "Forgive me for asking, but where have you come from, bard?"

"Great lord and king, I have been singing in England and other places. Why do you ask?"

"It is just that I haven't seen a single person here except my dear daughter-in-law, Cigfa, for several years," explained the king.

"That is a wonder," said the bard. "As for myself, I am passing through this realm on my way to the north country. I saw you working up there and wondered what kind of work you might be doing."

"Since you ask," replied Manawyddan, "I am about to hang a thief I caught stealing the very food from my mouth."

"What kind of thief, Lord, if you don't mind my asking?" the bard wondered. "The creature I see squirming in your hand looks very like a mouse."

"And so it is."

"Permit me to say that it poorly becomes a man of such exalted station to handle such a lowly creature as that. Thief or no, let it go."

"I will not let it go," declared Manawyddan, bristling at the suggestion. "I caught this rascal stealing, and I will execute the punishment for a thief upon it—which, as we all know, is hanging."

"Do as you think best, Lord," replied the bard. "But rather than watching a man of your rank stooping to such sordid work, I will give you three silver pennies that I earned with song if you will only pardon that mouse and release it."

"I will not let it go—neither will I sell it for three pennies."

"As you wish, mighty lord," said the bard. And taking his leave, he went away.

Manawyddan returned to his work. As he was busy putting the crossbeam between the two gallows posts, he heard a whinny and looked down from the mound to see a brown-robed priest riding towards him on a fine grey horse.

"Pax vobiscum!" called the priest. "May our Great Redeemer richly bless you."

"Peace to you," replied Manawyddan, wondering that another human being should appear so soon. "May the All Wise give you your heart's desire."

"Forgive my asking," said the priest, "but time moves on and I cannot tarry. Pray, what kind of work occupies you this day?"

"Since you ask," replied Manawyddan, "I am hanging a thief that I caught stealing the means of my sustenance."

"What kind of thief might that be, my lord?" asked the cleric.

"A low thief in the shape of a mouse," explained the lord of Dyfed. "The same who, with his innumerable comrades, has committed a great crime against me—so great that I have now no hope of survival at all. Though it be my last earthly act, I mean to exact punishment upon this criminal."

"My lord, rather than stand by and watch you demean yourself by dealing so with that vile creature, I will redeem it. Name your price and I will have it."

"By my confession to God, I will neither sell it nor let it go."

"It may be true, Lord, that a thief's life is worthless. Still, I insist you must not defile yourself and drag your exalted name through the mud of dishonour. Therefore, I will give you three pounds in good silver to let that mouse go."

"Between me and you and God," Manawyddan answered, "though it is a princely sum, the money is no good to me. I want no payment, except what this thief is due: its right and proper hanging."

"If that is your final word."

"It is."

"Then you do as you please." Picking up the reins, the priest rode on.

Manawyddan, lord of Dyfed, resumed his work. Taking a bit of string, he fashioned a small noose and tied the noose around the neck of the mouse. As he was busy with this, behold, he heard the sound of a pipe and drum. Looking down from the *gorsedd* mound, he saw the retinue of a bishop, with his sumpters and his host, and the bishop himself striding towards him. He stopped his work. "Lord Bishop," he called, "your blessings if you please."

"May God bless you abundantly, friend," said the satin-robed bishop. "If I may be so bold, what kind of work are you doing up there on your mound?"

"Well," replied Manawyddan, growing slightly irritated at having to explain his every move, "since you ask, and if it concerns you at all—which it does not—know that I am hanging a dirty thief which I caught stealing the last of my grain, the very grain which I was counting on to keep myself and my dear daughter-in-law alive through the coming winter."

"I am sorry to hear it," answered the bishop. "But, my lord, is that not a mouse I see in your hand?"

"Oh, aye," confirmed Manawyddan, "and a rank thief it is."

"Now see here," said the bishop, "it may be God's own luck that I have come upon the destruction of that creature. I will redeem it from its well-deserved fate. Please accept the thirty pounds I will give you for its life. For, by the beard of Saint Joseph, rather than see a lordly man as yourself destroying wretched vermin, I will give that much and more gladly. Release it and retain your dignity."

"Nay, Lord Bishop, I will not."

"Since you will not let it go for that, I will give you sixty pounds of fine silver. Man, I beg you to let it go."

"I will not release it, by my confession to God, for the same amount again and more besides. Money is no use to me in the grave to which I am going since the destruction of my fields."

"If you free the mouse," said the satin-robed one, "I will give you all the horses on the plain, and the seven sumpters that are here, and the seven horses that carry them."

"I do not want for horses. Between you and me and God," Manawyddan replied, "I could not feed them if I had them."

"Since you do not want that, name your price."

"You press me hard for a churchman," said the lord of Dyfed. "But since you ask, I want, more than anything under heaven, the return of my own dear wife, Rhiannon, and my good friend and companion, Pryderi."

"As I live and breathe, and with God alone as my witness, they will appear the moment you release that mouse."

"Did I say I was finished?" asked Manawyddan.

"Speak up, man. What else do you want?"

"I want swift and certain deliverance from the magic and enchantment that rests so heavily upon the seven cantrefs of Dyfed."

"That you will have also," promised the bishop, "if you release the mouse at once and do it no harm."

"You must think me slow of thought and speech," countered Manawyddan, his suspicions fully roused. "I am far from finished."

"What else do you require?"

"I want to know what this mouse is to you, that you should take such an interest in its fate."

"I will tell you," said the bishop, "though you will not believe me."

"Try me."

"Will you believe me if I tell you that the mouse you hold is really my own dear wife? And were that not so, we would not be freeing her."

"Right you are, friend," agreed Manawyddan. "I do not believe you."

"It is true nonetheless."

"Then tell me, by what means did she come to me in this form?"

"To plunder this realm of its possessions," the bishop answered, "for I am none other than Llwyd Cil Coed, and I confess that it was I who put the enchantment on the seven cantrefs of Dyfed. This was done to avenge my brother Gwawl, who was killed by you and Pryderi in the Battle of the Cauldron. After hearing that you had returned to settle in the land," the false bishop continued, "I turned my lord's war-band into mice so they might destroy your barley without your knowledge. On the first night of destruction the warband came alone and carried away the grain. On the second night they came too, and destroyed the second field. On the third night my wife and the women of the court came to me and asked me to transform them as well. I did as they asked, though my dear wife was pregnant. Had she not been pregnant, I doubt you would have caught her."

"She was the only one I caught, to be sure," replied Manawyddan thoughtfully.

"But, alas, since she was caught, I will give you Pryderi and Rhiannon, and remove the magic and enchantment from Dyfed." Llwyd the Hud folded his arms across his chest and, gazing up to the top of the mound at Manawyddan, he said, "There! I have told you everything—now let her go."

"I will not let her go so easily."

"Now what do you want?" demanded the enchanter.

"Behold," the mighty champion replied, "there is yet one more thing required: that there may never be any more magic or enchantment placed upon the seven cantrefs of Dyfed, nor on my kinfolk or any other people beneath my care."

"Upon my oath, you will have that," the Llwyd said, "now, for the love of God, let her go."

"Not so fast, enchanter," warned Manawyddan, still gripping the mouse tightly in his fist.

"What now?" Llwyd moaned.

"This," he said, "is what I want: there must be no revenge against Pryderi, Rhiannon, Cigfa, or myself, ever, from this day henceforth, forever."

"All that I promise and have promised, you shall get. And, God knows, that last was a canny thought," the enchanter allowed, "for if you had not spoken thus, all of the grief you have had till now would be as nothing compared to that which would have soon fallen upon your unthinking head. So if we are agreed, I pray you, wise lord, release my wife and return her to me."

"I will," promised Manawyddan, "in the same moment that I see Pryderi and Rhiannon standing hale and hearty in front of me."

"Look then, and see them coming!" said Llwyd the Hud.

Thereupon, Pryderi and Rhiannon, together with the missing hounds, appeared at the foot of the gorsedd mound. Manawyddan, beside himself with joy, hailed them and welcomed them.

"Lord and king, now free my wife, for you have certainly obtained all of what you asked for."

"I will free her gladly," Manawyddan said, lowering his hand and opening the glove so the mouse could jump free. Llwyd the Enchanter took out his staff and touched the mouse, and she changed into a charming and lovely woman once more—albeit a woman great with child.

"Look around you at the land," cried Llwyd the Hud to the lord of Dyfed, "and you will see all the homesteads and the settlements as they were at their best."

Instantly, the whole of the country was inhabited and as prosperous as it had ever been. Manawyddan and Rhiannon and Pryderi and Cigfa were reunited, and, to celebrate the end of the dire enchantment, they made a circuit of all the land, dispensing the great wealth Rhi Manawyddan had obtained in his bargain with the enchanter. Everywhere they went, they ate and drank and feasted the people, and no one was as well loved as the lord of Dyfed and his lovely queen. Pryderi and Cigfa were blessed with a son the next year, and he became, if possible, even more beloved than his grandfather.

ere, Angharad stopped; she let the last notes of the harp fade into the night, then added, "But that is a tale for another time." Setting aside the harp, she stood and spread her hands over the heads of her listeners. "Go now," she said softly, as a mother speaking to a sleep-heavy child. "Say nothing, but go to your sleep and to your dreams. Let the song work its power within you, my children."

Bran, no less than the others, felt as if his soul had been cast adrift—all around him washed a vast and restless sea that he must navigate in a too-small boat with neither sail nor oars. For him, at least, the feeling was more familiar. This was how he always felt after hearing one of Angharad's tales. Nevertheless, he obeyed her instruction and did not speak to anyone, but went to his rest, where the song would continue speaking through the night and through the days to come. And although part of him wanted nothing more than to ride at once to Llanelli, storm the gaol, and rescue the captive by force, he had learned his lesson and resisted any such rash action. Instead, Bran bided his time and let the story do its work.

All through the winter and into the spring, the story sowed and tended its potent seeds; the meaning of the tale grew to fruition deep in Bran's soul until, one morning in early summer, he awoke to the clear and certain knowledge of what the tale signified. More, he knew what he must do to rescue Will Scarlet.

791

I wake in the night all a-fever with the odd conviction that I know what it all means. The letter, the ring, the gloves—I know what this strange treasure signifies, and why it has come to Elfael. For the first time, I am afraid. If I am right, then I have discovered a way to save Elfael, and I fear I may not live to pass on this saving knowledge to those who can use it. Oh, Bléssed Virgin, Peter, and Paul, I pray I am not too late.

I sit in the cold dark and damp of my cell, waiting for daylight and hoping against hope that Odo will come early, and I pray to God that my scribe has true compassion in his heart.

I pray and wait, and pray some more, as it makes the waiting easier.

I am at this a long time when at last I see the dim morning light straggling along the narrow corridor to my cell. I hear Gulbert the jailer stumbling around as he strikes up a small fire to heat his room. I content myself with the sorry fact that our jailer lives only a little better than his prisoners. He is as much a captive of the abbot as I am, if not the more. At least I will leave this rank rat hole one day and he, poor fella, will remain.

Odo is long in coming. I shout for Gulbert, asking if the scribe has been seen, but my keeper does not answer me. He rarely does, and I remain a tightly wrapped bundle of worry until I hear the murmur of voices and then the scrape of an iron door against the stone flags of the corridor. In a moment, I hear the familiar shuffling footfall, and my heart leaps in my chest.

Easy now, Will me lad, I tell myself, *you don't want to scare the scribe; he's skittery enough as it is without you gettin' him up all nervous.* So to make it look like I have been doing anything but waiting for him, I lie back on my musty mat and close my eyes.

I hear the jingle of a key, and the door to my cell creaks open. "Will? Are you asleep?"

I open one eye and look around. "Oh, it is you, Odo. I thought it might be the king of England bringing my pardon."

Odo smiles and shakes his head. "No luck today, I fear."

"Don't be too sure, my friend." I sit up. "What if I told you I knew a secret that could save our sovereign king from black treachery and murder, or worse."

Odo shakes his head. "I know I should be well accustomed to your japes by now . . ." The look in my eye brings him up short. "I do begin to believe you are in earnest."

"Aye, that I am, lad."

I am pleased to see that he is in a mood to humour me this morning. He settles heavily into his accustomed place. "How will you save King William?"

"I will tell you, my friend, but you must promise me a right solemn oath on everything you hold most sacred in the world—promise me that what I tell you will not pass your lips. You cannot write it down, nor in any other way repeat what I say to another living soul."

He glances up quickly. "I cannot."

"You will, or I will not say another word."

"Please, Will, you do not understand what you're asking."

"See here, Odo, I am asking you to pledge your life with mine—no more, no less." He would look away, but I hold him with the strength of my conviction. "Hear me now," I continue after a moment, "if I am wrong, nothing will happen. But if I am right, then a great treachery will be prevented and hundreds, perhaps thousands of lives will be saved."

He searches my face for a way out of this unexpected dilemma. All his natural timidity comes flooding to the fore. I can see him swimming in it, trying to avoid being swept away.

Fight it, Odo, boy. It is time to become a man.

"Abbot Hugo . . . ," he begins, then quits. "I could never . . . he would find out anything you said . . . he would know."

"Has he the ears of the devil now? Unless you told him, he would never know."

"He would find out."

"How?" I counter. Here is where the battle will be fought. Is his desire to do right stronger than his fear of the black abbot?

After a moment, I say, "Only the two of us will know. If you say nothing to him, then I fail to see how Hugo will ever know what I mean to tell you."

He looks at me, his round face a tight-pinched knot of pain.

"It is life and death, Odo," I tell him quietly. He is that close to fleeing. "Life and death in your hands."

He stands abruptly, scattering pen and parchment and spilling his inkhorn. "I cannot!" he says, and bolts from the cell.

I hear his feet slapping the stones in the corridor; he calls Gulbert to let him out, and then he's gone.

Well, it was a risk doomed from the start. I should have known

795

better than to think he could help. Now escape is my only hope, and it is such a starved and wretched thing it brings sad tears to my eyes. I tug at the chain on my leg and feel the lump in my throat as frustration bites. To hold the solitary answer to the riddle of the baron's treasure—to be entrusted with the key to free Elfael and to be unable to use it—that fair makes the eye-water roll down my whiskered cheeks.

I lie on my filthy bed and think how to get word to Bran, and my head—dull from these weeks and months of captivity—feels like a lump of useless timber. I think and think . . . and it always comes out at the same place. I can do nothing alone. I must have help.

Oh, God, if it is true that you delight in a heartfelt prayer, then hear this one, and please send Odo back.

Odo returns, and so quickly that I am surprised. He has not shown such clear and ready resolve before. There is something on his mind—a blind man could see it—and he has come back with all the bluster of a fella who has made up his mind to embark on a dangerous journey, or a long-neglected chore that will get him mucked up from heel to crown. I do greatly wonder at the wild glint in his soft brown eyes. This is not the Odo I have come to know.

So, here is Odo, standing outside the door of my cell, like a faithful hound returning to a harsh master he would rather forgive than leave. I see he has his parchment and goose feather in one hand and inkhorn in the other as always; but the sharpness in his aspect gives me to know this is not like all the other times.

"Are you coming in, Odo?" I say. He has made no move to join me.

"I have to know something," he says, glancing down the corridor as if he fears we might be overheard. Gulbert, if he hears anything from the cells at all, is long past caring. "I have to know beyond all doubt that you will not betray me."

"Odo," I reply, "have we known each other so long that you ask me that?"

"Swear it," he insists. I hear in his voice what I have not often heard— a little bone and muscle, a little bit of iron. "Swear it on your soul that you will not betray me."

"As God is my witness, I swear on my everlasting soul that I will not betray you."

This seems to satisfy him; he opens the door to my cell and takes his customary place. I see by the firm set of his soft mouth that he is chewing on something too big to swallow, so I let him take his time with it.

"It is the abbot," he says at last.

"It usually is," I reply. "What has he done now?"

"He has been lying to me," remarks Odo. "Lying from the very beginning. I have caught him time and again, but said nothing."

"I understand."

"No, Will," replies my scribe, "you do not. I have been lying to him, too."

I stare at him. "Odo, you do amaze me."

"That is why I rushed away. If I am to do as you ask, I had to make confession. If I am killed, I want to go to God with clean hands and a clean heart."

"As do we all, Odo. But tell me more about this deception."

He nods. "I knew you would not give up Bran—not even to save yourself."

"Truly, I never would."

"When I saw that you were a man of honour, I decided to spin the abbot a tale that would keep us talking, but would tell him little."

Astonished at this turn, I do not know what to say. It seems best to just let him talk as he will. "Oh?"

798

"That is what I did. Some of what you said, I used, but most I made up." He shrugs. "It is easy for me. The abbot knows nothing of Mérian, or Iwan, Siarles, or Tuck, and what he knows of Bran is mostly fancy." He allows himself a sly smile. "The more you told me of the real Bran, the less I told the abbot."

"Well, you have me, Odo. I don't know what to say."

But Odo is not listening.

"Abbot Hugo has been lying to me from the beginning. Nothing he says can be trusted. He thinks I am stupid, that I cannot see through his veil of lies, but I have from the start." He pauses to draw breath. I can see that he is working himself up to do the thing he has come to do. "Like the letter Bran stole—abbot says it was nothing, a simple letter of introduction only. But if that was true then why was he so desperate to get it back?"

"And they were that desperate, I can tell you," I said, recalling the Christmas raid. "A good many men died that night to recover it. I think you can fair be sure it was far more than a letter of introduction."

"What you said about treachery against the crown . . ." His voice falls to a creaky whisper. "Knowing the abbot, I do not doubt it. Still, I cannot think what it might be."

"Nor could I, Odo, nor could I—not for the longest time," I tell him. "But the answer was starin' me in the face all along. Blind dog that I am, I could not see it until you showed me where to look."

"I showed you?" he says, and smiles.

"Oh, aye," I tell him, and then explain how I tumbled to what the Bloody Baron and Black Abbot were up to at last. He listens, nodding in solemn agreement as I conclude, "Fortunately, we are not without some tricks of our own."

"Yes?" He nods and licks his lips, eager now to hear what I propose.

"But as you made me swear on my solitary soul, so must I hear

799

your pledge, my friend. We are in this together now, and you can tell no one—not even your confessor." This I tell him in a tone as bleak as the tomb which will certainly claim us both if he fails to keep his vow.

Odo hesitates; he knows full well the consequence of what I am about to ask him. Then, squaring his round shoulders, he nods.

"Say it, Odo," I say gently. "I must hear the words."

"On my eternal soul, I will do exactly as you say and breathe a word to no one."

"Good lad. You have done the right thing," I tell him. "It is not easy to go against your superior, but it is the right thing."

"What do you want me to do?" he says, as if anxious now to get the deed done.

"We must get a message to Bran," I say. "We must let him know what is about to happen so he can move against it."

Odo agrees. He unstops the inkhorn and pares his quill. I watch him as he spreads the curled edge of parchment beneath his pudgy hands— I have seen this countless times, yet this time I watch with my heart in my mouth. *Do not let us down, monk.*

He dips the pen and holds it poised above the parchment. "What shall I write?"

"Not so fast," I say. "It is no use writing in Ffreinc, as no one in Cél Craidd can read it. Can you write in Saxon?"

"Latin," he says. "French and Latin." He shrugs. "That's all."

"Then Latin will have to do," I say, and we begin.

In the end, it is a simple message we devise, and when we finish I have him read it back to me to see if we've left anything out. "See now, we must think what word to add to let Bran know that this has come from me, and no one else. It must be something Bran will trust."

It takes me a moment to think of a word or two—something only Bran and I would know . . . about Tuck, or one of the others? . . . Then it comes to me. "Odo, my fine scribe, at the end of the message add this: 'The straw man was shaved twice that day: once by error, and once by craft. Will's the error, Bran's the craft. Yet Will took the prize.' This Bran knows to be true."

Odo regards me with a curious look.

"Write it," I tell him.

He dips his quill and leans low over the parchment scrap, now all but covered with his tight script. "What does it mean?"

"It is something known between Bran and myself, that is all."

"Very well," says Odo. He bends to the task and then raises his head. "It is done."

"Good," I say. "Now tuck that up your skirt, priest, and keep it well out of sight."

"It is my head if I fail," he says, and frowns. "But how am I to find Rhi Bran?"

I smile at his use of the name. "It is more likely that he will find you, I expect. All you have to do is start down the King's Road, and, if you do what I tell you, he'll find you soon enough." I begin to tell him how to attract the attention of the Grellon, but he makes a face and I stop. "Now what?"

"I am watched day and night," he points out. "I can't go wandering around in the forest. The abbot would catch me before I was out of sight of the town."

He has a point. "So, then . . ." I stare at him and it comes to me. "Then we will look for someone in town—a Welshman. Despite everything, they must come to the market still."

"Sometimes," Odo allows. "Would you trust a Welshman? Someone from Elfael?"

"Would and do," I reply. "All the more if the fella knew it was to serve King Raven and Elfael."

"Tomorrow is a market day," Odo announces, "and with the snows gone now there will likely be traders from Hereford and beyond. That always seems to bring a few of the local folk into town. They don't stay long, but if I was able to keep close watch, I might entrust the message to someone who could pass it along."

Bless me, Mother Mary, there are more things wrong with this plan than right. But in the end, we are left face-to-face with the plain ugly fact that we can do no better. I reluctantly agree, and tell Odo he is a good fella for thinkin' of it. This small praise seems to hearten him, and he hides the scrap of parchment in his robes and then stands to leave. "I should like to pray before I go, Will," he says.

"Another fine idea," I tell him. "Pray away."

Odo bows his head and folds his hands and, standing in the middle of the cell, begins to pray. He prays in Latin, like all priests, and I can follow only a little of it. His soft voice fills the cell like a gentle rain and, if only for a moment, I sense a warming presence—and sweet peace comes over me. For the first time in a long time, I am content.

CHAPTER 36

I make it five days since Odo took the message out of the cell. He has not come back, and I fear he has been caught. A weak choice to begin with, true, but if the poor fella'd got even a thimble's worth o' luck he might have got a fair chop at it. I guess even that little was too much to hope for.

No doubt he did his best with the scant handful he was given, but Odo was not born to the outlaw life, like ol' Will, here. I do not hold him to blame.

Blame, now. There is a nasty black bog if ever there was one. If I think about it long enough I come 'round to the conclusion that if blame must be spooned out to anyone at all the Good Lord himself must take the swallow for making it so fiendishly easy for the strong and powerful to crush down the weak and powerless. Would that he had foreseen the host of problems arising from that little error. Oh, but that en't the world we got. I suppose we don't deserve a better one.

I close my eyes on that bitter thought and feel myself begin to drift off when . . . what's this, now? I hear the door open at the far end of the corridor. I guess it is Gulbert bringing me some sour water and the scrag end of a mutton bone to gnaw on.

I roll over and look up as he comes to my cell and . . . it's Odo!

He's back, but one look at his pasty face and doleful eyes tells me all is not cream and cakes in the abbey.

"I feared they'd caught you, monk. I reckoned we'd be soon enough sharing this cell. Ah, but look at you now. A face like the one you're a-wearin' could bring clouds to a clear blue sky."

"Oh, Will . . . ," he sighs and his round shoulders slump even further. "I am so sorry."

"They found the message," I guess. "Well, I thought as much. At least they didn't lock you up."

Odo is shaking his head. "It's not that."

"Then?"

"It's something else," he moans, "and it's bad."

"Well, tell me, lad. Ol' Will is a brave fella; he can take the worst you got to give him."

"They're going to hang you, Will."

"That much I know already," I say, giving him a smile to jolly him along a bit. "If that's all, then we're no worse off than before."

Odo will not look at me. He stands there drooping like a beaten dog. "It's today, Will," he breathes, unable to rise above a whisper.

"What?"

"They mean to hang you today."

A dozen thoughts spin through my poor head at once, and it fair steals the warm breath from my mouth. "Well, now," I say when I have hold of myself once more, "that is something new, I do confess."

Odo lets loose another sigh and snivels a little. Bless him, he feels that bad for me.

"Why not tell me what's happened?" I say, for I would rather

804

hear him talk than dwell on my predicament. "But first, I have to know—did you get the message out? That is the most important thing anyway."

He nods. "It was not difficult," he says, brightening a little as he remembers. "The first Welshman I found was brother to one of those the sheriff meant to hang on Twelfth Night. He was only too happy to take the message for you." The ghost of a smile brushes his lips. "The farmer said we were not to worry. He said he'd get the message to Rhi Bran without fail."

"Good," I say, feeling a little of my ruffled peace returning. "All is well then." Another thought occurs to me. "But that was five days ago, as I make it. Why did you not come to tell me sooner?"

"The abbot has returned and said I could not come here anymore. But the day before yesterday some important visitors arrived, and the whole town has gone giddy. Everyone is busy preparing a special reception and feast."

Who, I wonder, could have come? Instead, I ask him, "Then why did they let you come today?"

"I begged the abbot to be the one to tell you," he says, and adds, ever so softly, "and to shrive you."

So now, my death is to be for the entertainment of important guests. Well, that is the Normans first and last. The devils can think of nothing better than a good hanging to impress their betters. The notion makes me right angry, it does.

"So, there it is," I say. Odo cannot find his voice. He just stands there, suddenly miserable once more.

Aye, there it is. I could have wished it had all turned out better. I could have wished Nóin and me had got married, that I'd had the chance to love that good woman as she deserves, that little Nia had known a doting father, and on and on . . . but then a man can wish all he likes his whole life through and it's like flinging a raindrop into the raging sea, and just as much use.

"When is it to be?"

"Before the feast," he says, and still will not look at me. "At midday."

Well, that takes some of the wind out of my sails, to be sure. "At least," I say, trying to swallow around the lump in my throat, "I will not have long to think on it." I offer a smile, but it is a thin, simpering thing. "Sitting here dwellin' on a thing like that—why, a fella might lose heart."

Odo smiles. As quickly as it comes, it is gone again. "They will come soon. We should begin."

"Will you come in and sit with me?"

"I was told not to," he says.

"Odo, please," I say, "after all the days we've spent together. At least let us sit together one last time . . . as friends."

He doesn't have it in him to disagree. He opens the door and steps in, but this time, judging by his mournful expression, it is as if he is entering a tomb. In a way, I suppose he is.

"I know I grumbled and growled like a bear with a sore head most days," I tell him. "But I did enjoy our talks. I did."

"You did all the talking," Odo points out.

"True," I agree. "I reckon a fella never knows what he's got stored up in his purse until it comes time to pay the tax man."

He smiles again. "Tax man?"

"We all owe a debt to nature, Odo, never forget. Pay we must."

He nods sadly. I can see his feelings are running on a razor's edge. He's fighting to keep from melting into a puddle of grief on the floor.

"Shrive me, Odo. I don't want to go to meet our Maker filthy in sin and stinkin' of brimstone. Let's get it done so I can go in peace."

He brings out a little roll he has tucked into his sleeve. It contains the proper words for a man's last rites. This makes me happier than I could have imagined. I knew I could trust him to see me right. I know our Black Abbot would never have troubled himself as much, and that's a fact. If left to him, I'd be knockin' at heaven's gates one dirty, naked sinner instead of standing in the clean white robe of a saint. Odo has ensured that will not happen now, and for that I am forever grateful.

Aye, and I am that close to forever.

Odo bends his round head and offers a prayer. His voice is gentle and humble as a priest's should be. Although he speaks to God in Latin, I hear that in it that puts me at ease. When he finishes, he says in English, "God our Father, long-suffering, full of grace and truth, you create us from nothing and give us life. Man born of woman has but a short time to live. We have our fill of sorrow. We blossom like the lowly flowers of the field and wither away. We slip away like a shadow and do not stay. In the midst of life we are in death. Where can we turn for help? Only to you, Lord, who are justly angered by our sins.

"Though we are weak and easily led astray, you do not turn your face from us, nor cast us aside. When we confess, you are right glad to forgive. Hear, Loving God, the final confession of William Scatlocke . . ." He glances up and says, "Repeat the words as I say them."

I nod, and we go on.

"Almighty and most merciful Father, maker of all things, judge of all people, like a poor lost sheep, I have wandered from your ways. I have followed too much my own will and ways. I have offended against your holy laws . . ."

Odo pauses at each hurdle—and I climb over after him. The words are simple and sincere, not like those most priests use, and I know he is trying his best to do right by me.

"We have left undone those things that we ought to have done; and we have done those things that we ought not to have done; and

807

there is no righteousness in us," he says, and I notice that he is including himself in my prayer now, and it makes me smile.

"We confess that we have sinned against you and our brothers. We acknowledge and confess the wickedness which so often ensnares us. O Lord, have mercy upon us sinners. You spare those who confess their faults. We earnestly repent, and are deeply sorry for all our wrongdoings, great and small. Eternal and merciful judge, both in life and when we come to die, let us not fall away from you. Do not abandon us to the darkness and pain of death everlasting.

"Have mercy upon us, Gracious Redeemer. Restore us as you have promised, and grant, O Merciful Father, that we may enter your peace. Hear us for the sake of your Son, and bring us to heavenly joy, in the name of Jesus Christ our Lord. Amen."

I add my "Amen" as he has directed, and then we sit in silence a moment. I feel the thing was squarely done. There is no more to be said, nor need be. I am content.

From down the corridor, I hear the grating whine of the iron door opening and know that my time has run its course. They are coming for me. My heart lurches at the thought, and I draw a deep breath to steady myself.

I have thought about this day every day since I was dragged into Black Hugo's keep. Truth to tell, I thought it would be different somehow, that I would meet the evil hour with a smile and a tip o' my hat. Instead, my bowels squirm and ache, and I feel death's cold hand resting heavy on my shoulder.

There was so much I meant to do, and now the end has come. It is all done but the dyin', and that's a true fact.

CHAPTER 37

Saint Martin's: The Pavilion

"Look! Here he comes," cried Count de Braose, his voice fluttering high with excitement as the shambling heap of a man appeared at the door of the guardhouse.

The count's visitors turned to see a number of Ffreinc soldiers spilling out of the keep. Armed with lances and led by Marshal Guy, they started across the market square, dragging a ragged wreck between them. The man's hands were bound and his legs were unsteady; he kept listing to one side as if the ground were constantly shifting beneath his feet.

"Oh, he is a rogue!" continued Count Falkes. "You can tell that simply by looking at him."

The count's words were directed to the visiting dignitaries, whose arrival two days before had surprised and thrilled the entire population of the emerging town of Saint Martin's. The count's words were translated and conveyed to the others by a priest named Brother Alfonso—a tall, sallow, somewhat sombre and officious monk in a new brown robe. While Count Falkes looked on, smiling, his guests exchanged a brief word amongst themselves. Being Spanish, they were strangers to England and to the rough ways of the March. Most of them bore the swarthy complexion of their countrymen, and the black hair and dark, inquisitive eyes. They professed to find everything fascinating and, in the brief time they had been with him, had shown themselves to be enthusiastic and appreciative guests. Then again, one might expect no less from the personal envoy of none other than Pope Clement himself.

The ambassador, Father Dominic, was far younger than the count would have imagined for one in such an important, nay exalted, position. Dark and slender in his impeccable black robes, he held himself with a solemn, almost melancholy reserve, as if the thoughts inside him bore on body and soul alike and he sagged a little beneath their weight. Though there was dignity and reverence in his glance, his natural expression was the pensive reflection of a man who, despite his youth, had seen and suffered much at the hands of an unrepentant world. His black hair was trimmed short and his tonsure newly shaved. He moved with deliberation, his steps measured and sure as he dispensed priestly blessings to those who looked on.

Attending Father Dominic were two servants—most likely lay brothers but of a hardy sort. Tall and strong and none too genteel, they had no doubt been chosen to protect the envoy on his journey. Besides the interpreter, Brother Alfonso, there were two young women: a young highborn woman of unmistakable nobility, and her maidservant. The lady was quiet, well-spoken, gracious, and possessed of a warm and winsome manner, but also, alas, undeniably plain, with poor skin, dull hair, and discoloured teeth. "Drab as a farmyard drudge," was Guy of Gysburne's assessment. "I prefer her maid." The sheriff had expressed a similar judgment, if in less kindly terms. Even so, Count Falkes found himself attracted to her despite her plainness and the difficulty imposed by the language divide. He even allowed himself to fancy that she regarded him with something more than passing affection.

"Oh!" gasped Lady Ghisella, averting her eyes at the sight of the condemned man. Her maid followed the lady's example.

"Never fear, my lady," offered the count, mistaking her reaction. "He cannot escape. You may rest assured, this one will soon trouble the world no longer."

Unexpected visitors, their abrupt arrival had initially roused the count's suspicions. On second thought, however, it was more than reasonable given the circumstances: a small party travelling together without an extensive entourage of servants and courtiers might more easily pass unmolested through the countryside and, considering who they represented, would more easily elude the notice of the king. Such a group would not likely draw the unwanted attentions of rival factions and potential adversaries.

Abbot Hugo, who had been south with Count Falkes's uncle, Baron de Braose, at Bramber, had returned to find the dignitaries already established in his abbey. "All well and good," he had complained to Falkes, "but we should have received word of their coming. This is awkward, to say the least."

"It is nothing of the sort," the count reassured him. "You worry too much, Hugo."

"And you not enough."

"I suspect it is merely Clement's way of judging the faith and loyalty of those who have pledged to him, before . . . you know . . ." He let the rest remain unspoken.

Abbot Hugo fixed him with an ominous stare. "No," he replied stiffly, "I do not know."

"Before the fighting begins," said the count. "Must I shout it from the rooftop? Think, man. The king will have spies everywhere. It is open rebellion we are talking about."

The abbot's frown deepened, but he held his tongue.

"See here," offered Count Falkes, adopting a lighter tone, "the envoy and his people will only be here another day or two. We will simply entertain them with good grace, reassure them of our intentions, and send them on their way. Where's the harm in that?"

"Why are they here?" demanded the abbot. "That's what I want to know. His Holiness has given no indication of sending an envoy to England."

"And does the pope now confide his every private thought to you, Abbot?" Falkes gave an airily dismissive wave of his hand; the movement caused a twinge of pain in his chest—a lingering reminder of the arrow wound that had nearly taken his life. "All will be well. I propose that we host a feast in their honour and send them on their way."

"A feast," murmured Hugo. "Yes, I think we might do just that. We could also hang that tiresome rogue for them—that should give them something to talk about."

"Hang the rebel?" wondered Falkes. "Are you finished with him, then?"

"Long since," answered the abbot. "It was folly to hope he would tell us anything worth hearing. It's all a morass of confusion and lies, and so tedious it makes my teeth ache."

"Well, it cost us little enough to find out," Falkes countered. "In any event, it hurts nothing to try."

"I suppose," allowed the abbot. "I should hang him twice over for wasting my time."

"Well, you would have hanged him anyway in the end," concluded Falkes. "De Glanville and I had our disagreements over the Twelfth Night executions, God knows. But I cannot say I will be sorry to see this one dangle. The sooner we rid ourselves of these bandits, the better."

Now, with the feast about to begin, they were all seated in a hastily erected pavilion facing the open ground behind the church, where some of Marshal Guy's knights and a few of the sheriff's men were performing mock battle manoeuvres. In a show of military might, the great, galloping destriers' hooves threw clots of turf high, churning up the soft earth. The glint of sword blade and lance head blazed like lightning strokes in the bright sunlight; the resounding crack of oak lance shafts, the clank of heavy steel, and the shouts of the soldiers lent excitement to an otherwise ordinary display. The feast-day crowd swarmed the square behind the canopy-covered platform, their voices filling the air with loud, if somewhat forced, levity as they bellowed rude songs and screamed with laughter at the antics of the wandering troupe of tumblers, minstrels, and storytellers the count and abbot had procured especially for the occasion.

At the entrance to Saint Martin's churchyard, a new gibbet had been erected from which to hang the criminal, whose execution was now to mark the occasion of the papal envoy's visit. One sight of the captive as he was escorted from the guardhouse sent the crowd scampering for places from which to view the spectacle. Some cheered, others blew their noses, and still others threw rotten apples and eggs at the bearded, dishevelled prisoner as he was hauled across the square on the arms of his guards.

As the wretch neared the pavilion, Father Dominic summoned his interpreter and whispered something into his ear. Brother Alfonso leaned close, nodded, then turned to the count and said, "My Lord Count, the envoy says that he is most interested in this case. He would like to know what crime this unfortunate has committed."

"Pray, tell His Eminence that he is a traitor to the crown," the count explained. "He, along with other desperate rebels, has sought to pervert the course of the king's justice, and has on numerous occasions attacked the king's men and prevented them from engaging in their lawful duties. He has incited rebellion against the crown. This, of course, is treason."

"A very grave crime, indeed," observed the envoy through his interpreter. "Is that not so?"

"Indeed," agreed the sheriff, intruding into the conversation. "But if that was not enough, this criminal is also a thief. He has stolen money and other valuables from travellers passing through the forest."

"A very rogue," agreed the envoy.

"That and more," said Count Falkes. "We have good reason to believe that he was part of a gang of outlaws that have plagued this commot since we established our rule in this lawless region. Indeed, we have it from his own lips that he has violated Forest Law by killing the king's deer—also a capital offence."

As these words were delivered to the envoy, the sheriff added, "These murderers have been responsible for the deaths of many good men. They answer to one known as King Raven, who styles himself a phantom of the greenwood."

At this, the special ambassador of Pope Clement turned suddenly, clapped his hands, and exclaimed, "Rhi Bran y Hud!"

Both count and sheriff were taken aback by this unexpected outburst and regarded the priest with alarm. After a quick word with the ambassador, Alfonso, the interpreter, confided, "His Eminence says that word of this phantom has reached him."

"Truly?" wondered Count Falkes, greatly amazed.

"It must be the same," said Father Dominic through his interpreter. "There cannot be more than one, surely."

"Surely not," confirmed the sheriff. "But never fear, Your Eminence.

814

These outlaws cannot elude us much longer. We will bring them to justice. They will all hang before another year is out."

The condemned man was brought to stand before the nobles and dignitaries in the pavilion. He stared dull-eyed, his expression slack, hair and beard matted and filthy. The sheriff, splendid in his green velvet cloak and belt of gold discs, rose and held up a gloved hand for silence from the swiftly gathering crowd. "Be it known," he called out, his voice cutting through the chatter, "that on this day, in accordance with the rule of law, the criminal William Scatlocke, also known as Scarlet, is put to death for crimes against the crown—namely treachery, rebellion, robbery, and the abuse of the king's sheriff, Richard de Glanville." The sheriff's eyes narrowed. "None other than myself."

He paused to allow these words to be translated for the foreigners, then continued, saying, "The hour of your death is upon you, thief and murderer. Have you anything to say before justice is served?"

The outlaw known as Will Scarlet glowered at the sheriff and spat. "Do your worst, de Glanville," he growled, his voice low. "We all know who the real rogues are."

With a disinterested flick of his hand, the sheriff said, "Take him away."

"It is said that the Welshmen are cunning archers," observed Father Dominic as the prisoner was dragged away to the gibbet.

"So they would have their ignorant countrymen believe," sneered the sheriff. "Believe me, they are nothing more than a rabble—unruly as they are untrained."

"Even so, I have heard a Welsh archer can put an arrow into the eye of a blackbird in flight."

"Tales for children," said Falkes, with a small, hollow laugh. "Although, I daresay the Welsh appear to believe it themselves."

"I understand," replied the envoy through his interpreter. "As it happens, I myself am an archer."

"Indeed, my lord?" said Falkes, feigning interest.

"Oh, yes!" said the envoy, his enthusiasm plain, even through the remove of a translator. "I count the days spent with a bow in my hand blessed. It helps ease the burden of my office, you see."

"Well, I suppose," granted the count, "it must be pleasant for you."

"It is the one secular pursuit I allow myself," continued the envoy, confiding his observations to Alfonso, who dutifully passed them along. "As a child, I myself often enjoyed hunting with a bow on my father's estate in Spain. I know well enough what such a weapon can do in the hands of one well schooled in its use. You are right to fear the rebels."

"We do not fear them," insisted the sheriff. "It is merely that . . ." Unable to finish this assertion in a convincing way, he paused, then concluded lamely, "They do not fight fairly."

The prisoner was brought to stand beneath the gallows, and the rope was knotted and thrown over the short stout gibbet arm. The soldiers began tying the victim's legs with short bands of cloth.

"I see," replied Father Dominic when the sheriff's words had been made clear to him. He shrugged, then smiled, turned to Lady Ghisella beside him and exchanged a brief word, whereupon the envoy suddenly announced, "My cousin would like to see the Welshman ply the bow."

"What!" asked the sheriff, looking around suddenly. The request caught him off guard.

"But that is not possible, Your Eminence," said Count de Braose. "A man like that"—he flung his hand towards the group at the gallows—"must not be given a deadly weapon under any circumstances."

"Ah, I understand," said Father Dominic through his translator. "It is that you fear him too greatly. I understand. Perhaps there is something in this children's tale you speak of after all, no?"

"No!" said Abbot Hugo, at the count's silent urging, "Pray do not misunderstand. It is not that we fear him, but merely that it would be unwise to allow him to lay hands to the very weapon he has used to kill and maim our soldiers. He is a condemned man and must be executed according to the law."

At this the papal envoy's ordinarily woeful features arranged themselves in a wide grin of pleasure. Brother Alfonso turned and announced, "His Eminence wishes to assure you that he is looking forward to the execution as much as anyone, but suggests that there is good sport to be had before it takes place. These affairs are, after all, very short-lived, shall we say." The sallow monk smiled at his wordplay. "It is a commonplace in Italy and elsewhere, that wagers are placed on such things as how many kicks the condemned will produce, how long he will swing before he succumbs, or whether he will piss himself, things like this. A good wager heightens the enjoyment of the occasion, yes?"

"I see," replied the count coolly. "What sort of wager does your master think appropriate here?"

After a quick consultation, Brother Alfonso replied, "His Eminence suggests that a demonstration of some sort would be amusing."

"Perhaps," granted the count. "What sort of demonstration?"

"As an archer himself, Father Dominic is especially keen to see this prisoner's skill."

"Well, I suppose something might be arranged," Count Falkes conceded at last. "If it is what our guest wants, I see no good reason to deny him."

"No. Wager or no, it is impossible," declared the sheriff. "Out of the question."

But the discussion had already moved on. "His Eminence suggests that as his own skill with the bow is exceptional, he begs the boon of participating in an archery contest with the condemned, and that in

817

accordance with the best tradition the prisoner be allowed to draw for his freedom."

"What?" wondered the sheriff in slack-jawed dismay at the insane proposal.

Brother Alfonso continued, "His Eminence says that the contest can have no meaning or excitement without consequences, and of course the only prize to rouse the poor wretch's interest would be the chance to draw for his life."

"If His Eminence should fail, a dangerous criminal—one who has attacked me personally, mind!—would be spared the consequences of his crimes. Justice would be made a laughingstock."

"The man has been in your dungeons for how long?"

"Five months or so," replied the sheriff. "Why?"

"Five months is a very great punishment in itself," observed Brother Alfonso. "Aside from that, Father Dominic will no doubt hold the advantage over the prisoner and wishes to assure you that the wretch will hang this day. Nevertheless, there must be a prize at stake—otherwise the sport is meaningless."

It took a moment for the emissary's meaning to become absolutely clear. "An archery contest," considered Count Falkes carefully, "with freedom of the prisoner as the prize."

"It is what the pope's ambassador wants," answered Brother Alfonso. "Lady Ghisella would be much amused as well. They are certain to carry back a good report to His Holiness."

Both sheriff and count appealed to Abbot Hugo, who had suddenly become very quiet and thoughtful. "Well? Speak up!" hissed the sheriff. "Tell His Eminence it is impossible. The rogue hangs here and now, and that is that."

"But it is not," whispered the abbot sharply in reply. "Our guest seems determined to have his way, and Baron de Braose would not be pleased to hear that we refused the envoy any simple request it was in our power to grant."

"Any simple request!" muttered the sheriff in a strangled voice. "We cannot risk setting that rogue free."

"Nor will we," Hugo assured him. "Let the pope's fool have his contest. All we need do is make certain the Welshman does not win."

"He is right," concluded Falkes. "My uncle would not look kindly on anything that threatened his good favour with Clement. We must find a way to please His Eminence, however strange the request. Need I remind you that we are not in favour with the baron just now? Letting the legate have this ridiculous contest might be just what we need to return ourselves to the baron's good graces."

The sheriff gazed at the other two as at men bereft of their reason.

"Find a bow, and let the contest begin," commanded the count. "Meanwhile, de Glanville, I think you should go"—he paused so the sheriff would not mistake his meaning—"and *prepare* the prisoner."

"Yes," added the abbot. "See to it nothing is left to chance."

"Very well," answered the sheriff, catching their meaning at last. "I will attend the prisoner personally."

Turning to his guests, Count Falkes adopted a grand and gracious air and announced, "Please convey to His Eminence and his entourage that I am pleased to grant his request. I have therefore arranged for the contest to take place. However, I fear it may not be as entertaining as His Grace might wish. As we shall see, these bandits are not as skilled as they make out."

"My thanks to you, Lord Count," said the envoy, and immediately climbed down from the pavilion and began making his way across the grounds towards the gibbet.

"Wait! Your Eminence, a moment, if you please!" cried the count, hurrying after him. "You must allow us to ready the contest."

The papal envoy was led back to his place in the pavilion to be entertained by Abbot Hugo; meanwhile, the count hurried on to order a target to be made up, and a bow and arrows to be found and brought to the field.

"This is absurd!" growled Marshal Guy when Falkes explained what was going to take place. "Is he insane?"

"No doubt," remarked the count, "but he has Pope Clement's ear and goodwill. We dare not upset him or give him cause to complain of his reception while he was here."

The marshal glanced at the pavilion across the greensward. "What do you want me to do?"

"Just make it look like a reasonable competition between two archers. The sheriff is taking measures to make certain our prisoner is in no way able to win this contest," said the count, stepping away. "Do your best to make it look fair, and all will be well."

Guy de Gysburne looked across to the bound captive with the rope around his neck as he stood waiting beneath the gallows. "Knowing the sheriff, the contest is well in hand."

CHAPTER 38

Saint Martin's: The Green

To Will Scarlet, it seemed as if all of Elfael had turned out to see him swing. A bright and festive air hung over the little town, which was alight with flags and the coloured banners of a wandering troupe—the same that was performing tricks in the square to the bawdy laughter of the crowd. Of all those in attendance, only Will himself failed to rise to the full mirth of the occasion. He had other things on his mind as the soldiers half walked, half dragged him out of the guardhouse and across the thronging square. Only a few of the town's citizens left off their merrymaking to watch the condemned man hauled to his doom, and these few were Welshmen who dared come into town, braving the scorn and ridicule of the townsfolk, to witness the death of one of those who had risked his life to prevent the Twelfth Night hangings of their countrymen.

Will Scarlet did not notice the silent Britons looking on from the margins of the celebration. He did notice how very bright the sunlight was and how soft and impossibly fresh the breeze that bathed his shaggy features. How sad, really, that his last moments should be lived out on such a fine, hopeful day in direct opposition to the black gloom that filled his soul. Just his luck, he thought unhappily, to go down to the grave while all the rest of the world was awash in singing and dancing and the glad feast a-roast on the fire. Not to taste a lick of that handsome fare, nor a drop of the ale that would be served up in cups overflowing—now there was real pity.

As the rough procession passed along the side of the stone church, he saw that a platform had been set up for the visiting dignitaries, a pavilion with a splendid blue canopy from which the nobles and their guests could watch him kick his last as the cruel rope choked out his life. The idea of providing sport for these highborn scum roused a fleeting flame of anger he thought might sustain him in his last moments. Alas, this was not to be. For the moment the cold length of braided leather touched his neck and the soldiers began lashing his legs together, anger fled and was replaced by a stark, empty, bottomless fear. *Lord have mercy,* he thought, looking up at the gibbet arm and the clear blue boundless sky beyond. *Christ have mercy on my soul.*

This swift prayer had no sooner winged through his mind than Sheriff de Glanville was standing before him, his sharp features set in a malicious sneer. "Untie him," he commanded the soldiers. "It seems we are to have a little sport before he hangs."

Will, whose French stretched at least this far, understood from what the sheriff said that death had been delayed a little, and was grateful for even that little. He drew a deep breath as the noose was removed and the bands loosed. From behind the sheriff he saw two dark figures approaching—a tall, slender priest in long black robes, and another, a monk in brown, beside him. Behind these two came the count, hurrying to keep up with the black-robed priest's long, eager strides.

"This is your lucky day, traitor," de Glanville told him in a low, menacing voice. "Our guest desires an archery contest. Your life is the prize." The sheriff eyed him closely. "Do you understand?"

It took Will a moment to work out what the sheriff had said. There was to be a contest for his life. He nodded. "I understand," he replied in Ffreinc.

"Good," said the sheriff. Taking Will's bound hands in his gauntleted fist, he seized the fingers of his right hand and began to squeeze.

"Just so there will be no mistake," de Glanville added. Before Will knew what was happening, the sheriff gave his fingers a sudden, vicious twist. There was a pop and crack like that of dried twigs as his finger bones snapped. "We will make certain you understand who is to win this contest."

Pain streaked up his arm and erupted in a fiery blast that stole Will's breath away. Tears instantly welled up in his eyes, distorting his vision. He sank to his knees, whimpering with agony and struggling to remain conscious.

"There," said de Glanville with a satisfied nod. "Now there will be no surprises."

The condemned man glowered up at the sheriff, mouthing a silent curse as he cradled his ruined fingers to his chest, tears streaming from his eyes.

He was jerked to his feet again and marched between two knights out onto the centre of the green. There he stood upright as best he could, shaking with the effort. He struggled to keep from weeping from the humiliation of being so easily bettered by his enemies—as much as from the physical pain itself.

While Will was trying to regain some small part of his composure, Marshal Guy of Gysburne appeared with a longbow and bag of arrows. The sight of the bow cast Will into a dismal, all-embracing

823

despair. Here was the instrument of his salvation, now useless to him because of the sheriff's wicked ploy. He could no more draw a bow with broken fingers than he could have walked across the sea to Ireland.

But, what was this? Guy was handing the bow to the tall, dark priest.

Forcing the pain from his mind, Will brought all his concentration to bear on what was being said. Because the marshal's instructions had to be repeated for the visiting priest, Will could just about work out what was happening. They were each to loose three arrows in turn, and the closest to the mark would be declared the winner. The priest gave a sign that he understood and accepted the terms of the contest; no one asked Will if he understood, or accepted, anything.

Then, while a hastily constructed straw man was set up a hundred paces or so down the greensward, the two contestants walked out to take their places, followed by a large, excited crowd of onlookers. Two soldiers stood at Will's elbow, watching his every move. Guy, who was supervising the contest, handed the bow to the priest, saying, "You will each use the same bow, Your Eminence. Here is the weapon."

The young priest took the offered bow and tried the string, bending the bow tentatively: back stiff, elbows awry. The action, while not entirely awkward, lacked something of the confidence of great skill. Will, even in his agony, was not slow to see it, and the gesture kindled a flicker of hope in his woeful heart.

That hope leapt up the higher when the priest turned to him and offered the bow, indicating that he should try it as well. "My thanks," muttered Will through teeth clenched against the pain in his throbbing fingers.

Although it had been some time since he had held a bow, Will found the instrument balanced well enough; but the draw, when tested with his thumb, was far too loose. Clearly, this was a toy the Ffreinc had either made themselves or found somewhere; it was not the warbow of a Welshman. Still, it might serve for a simple contest; if both of them were to use it, there could be no advantage to either party.

Will made to pass the bow back to his smiling adversary, who waved him off and, taking an arrow from Guy, handed it to the captive and then stepped back to allow him the honour of loosing first.

Sweating now, his jaw clenched so hard he thought his teeth would shatter, Will tried to nock the arrow onto the string. But the injured fingers would not obey, and the arrow slipped from his grasp and fell at his feet. The priest was there in an instant to retrieve it for him. With a flourish of his hand and a smile to the sheriff and Marshal Guy, who stood looking on with unmitigated malice, the envoy indicated that he would allow the condemned man another chance to draw.

Will, with great difficulty and much fumbling, at last fitted the arrow to the string and held it there with his left hand while attempting to hook his swollen, mangled fingers into some semblance of an archer's grip. Sweating and shaking with the effort, he did not so much draw back the string as simply hold it and press the bow forward. The arrow flew from the string with little conviction and described a lacklustre curve to plant its point in the turf a good many yards short of the straw target.

The injured criminal passed the bow to the priest and bent down, arms on his knees, gasping, trying to remain conscious as the pain coursed up through his arm like a fire-spitting snake. Meanwhile, his black-robed rival took up the bow and with far more aplomb nocked the arrow to the string. Marshal Guy gave de Glanville a knowing nudge with his elbow and smiled as the visiting dignitary pulled back and loosed his first arrow. Somehow, what seemed an easy draw suddenly went wildly wrong: the missile flew not out as it should have but almost straight up, spinning sideways in a loopy spiral to land behind the onlookers on the green.

Some of the townspeople gathered around laughed. The priest, still smiling, shrugged and held out his hand for another arrow. Marshal Guy gave him another arrow with the admonition to take his time and aim. Nodding, the priest made a gesture of dismissal and handed the bow and arrow back to his opponent.

Will, his face white and beaded with sweat, took up the bow once more and strained with every nerve, the target swimming before his eyes as he strove to pinch the string between thumb and forefinger. When he could hold the string no longer, he released it and sent the arrow forward in a low arc to skid along the grass, almost reaching the foot of the target.

Full of confidence and beaming with bravado, the priest took the bow and received an arrow from Guy, who repeated his counsel to take time, draw, and aim properly. The priest made a reply, which the translator passed along, saying, "His Eminence is aware of the problem and will adjust his stance accordingly."

Taking the arrow, he placed it on the string and, gazing hard at the target, narrowed his eyes and drew the string to his cheek, holding the bow straight and strong in front of him. He released after the briefest pause, and the crowd's eyes followed the path of the arrow as it seemed to streak towards the target. But, wonder of wonders, the arrow did not arrive. A second glance confirmed that it had not, in fact, left the string at all, but there remained dangling, caught somehow, one of its feathered flights ripped off and sent halfway across the green. The arrow fell at the embarrassed priest's feet, its iron point in the ground.

More people laughed now.

"The idiot!" grumbled the sheriff. "This is no contest. Neither one of them can draw worth a fart."

"I will draw for the priest," suggested Marshal Guy. "I can do no worse than he has done."

The sheriff stared at him. "Don't be stupid. The contest has begun," he grumbled. "We cannot change now; it would not be seemly."

"Why not?" demanded the marshal. "You broke that wretch's fingers—that was not seemly. How did you ever agree to such a thing anyway?"

"He said he could draw!" replied the sheriff. He forced a sour smile and nodded at the envoy.

"He is hopeless," insisted Guy once more. "Let me take his place."

"Too late," answered the sheriff. "Everyone is watching now. We cannot be seen to force the outcome." Scanning the pavilion, he caught sight of Count Falkes and Abbot Hugo frowning furiously at the disaster slowly unfolding before them. "One more arrow," he said. "Make certain the envoy understands what is at stake here."

Taking the last arrow, Guy of Gysburne handed it to Brother Alfonso, saying, "This is his last chance to win the contest. Make him understand."

Brother Alfonso made a bow and turned to confer with the papal emissary, who frowned and snatched the offered arrow with a gesture of haughty impatience. As before, the papal cleric stepped close and passed the bow and arrow to Will Scarlet, who drew a long breath as he took the weapon.

"One more, Will," whispered the priest. "It is almost over. I will not let you fail."

It was all Scarlet could do to catch himself shouting, "Bran?" For the first time he looked into the face of the man he had been drawing against and recognized his lord and friend.

"Shh!" said the priest with a wink.

"Bloody de Glanville broke my fingers!" whispered Will, his voice tight and quivering with pain.

"Do your best, Will," Bran whispered. "Try a left-handed pull."

The condemned man took the bow and, with a groan and gritting of teeth, wrapped his discoloured fingers around the belly of the bow this time and took the strain against the cradle of his palm and thumb. Then, even as the pain sent flags of ragged black misery fluttering before his eyes, he drew with his left hand, steadied the trembling weapon, and loosed. The arrow slanted up, flashing into the air higher and higher; it seemed to hang momentarily before falling, spent, to the ground at the straw man's feet.

This brought a murmur from the crowd, most of whom had by now worked out what was unfolding before their eyes.

The priest, still gracious, took the bow and waited for the final arrow to be passed to him along with the marshal's stern caution to take care and aim properly this time. Nodding, he nocked an arrow to the string and, even as he bent the bow, Guy stepped in behind him and placed his hands over the priest's, steadying his aim as the priest let fly.

The envoy, shocked at this bold intrusion, gave out a yelp and jerked back. But the arrow was already on its way. This time it flew true, but the distance was woefully misjudged, for the missile sang over the straw man's head and flew on, swiftly disappearing into the long grass far beyond the greensward. The condemned man saw it, knew that he had won the contest, and sank to his knees, tears of relief and agony rolling down his bewhiskered cheeks.

Before anyone could intervene, the black-robed envoy summoned his aide, Brother Alfonso, to take the injured criminal under his care. "Stupid!" roared the sheriff at Guy. "What did you do?"

"I was only trying to help," said the marshal. "It would have worked, too, if he hadn't pulled so hard."

The black priest accepted his failure with good grace. Beaming with pleasure, he offered his hand to the condemned man, raising him to his feet. Placing his arm around the criminal's shoulders, the slender priest proclaimed in a loud voice so all could hear, "I declare the contest was fair and the results are conclusive. This man is the winner!" He paused so that Brother Alfonso could relay his words to the gathering. "I do not know what he has done to merit his punishment, but let his example teach us the humility of forgiveness and redemption. For all men stand in need of salvation. Therefore, as our Lord's vicar on earth, I stand ready to absolve him of guilt and lead him into the paths of righteousness. I accept full responsibility for his life and will do all in my power to redeem him from his reprobate ways."

As the startled Ffreinc looked on aghast at what had just taken place, he whispered, "Never fear, Will, I have you now and will not let you go."

Will Scarlet, dabbing at his eyes with the back of his hand, clung to the black-robed envoy as to a kinsman long lost. "God bless you, my lord," he murmured. "God bless you right well."

CHAPTER 39

Hamtun Docks

Mérian gently tied the ends of the rag binding Will Scarlet's wounded hand and tucked the ends under. "If Angharad was here," she apologized, "she would know better what to do for you." She had carefully straightened his swollen and discoloured fingers and bound each one to a bit of hazel twig Iwan had cut and shaped to serve for splints. She surveyed her work with a hopeful smile. "Does it hurt much?"

"Not much," Will replied, grimacing even as he said it. "I am that glad to be feeling anything at all just now. It reminds me I am alive."

"And back with those who love you," she said, brushing his finger-tips with her lips as she released him.

"I do thank you, my lady," he said, his voice thick with sudden emotion. He raised his hand and regarded his bandaged fingers, amazed that something so small could hurt so much. Despite the throbbing insistence of the pain, however, he remained overawed at his rescue, and his friends' continued deception. They had risked all for him, and his gratitude could not be contained. "My heart has no words to say thanks enough."

"I only wish we could have come sooner," said Siarles, who had been hovering at Mérian's shoulder.

"And thanks to you, Siarles," replied Will, acknowledging the forester's presence. "It does a body good to see you again. God's truth, I did not recognise any of you. "'Course, I had other things on my mind just then."

"When Bran said what we were to do," replied Siarles, "I told him it would never work—we could never dupe the sharp-eyed sheriff." He chuckled. "But Bran would not be moved. He was determined to steal you away and right from under their long Ffreinc noses. We collected Brother Jago from Saint Dyfrig's, and we all dressed up like priests and such and"—he smiled again—"here we are."

Iwan, who had been standing watch on the little bower, hurried to rejoin them. "They're coming back," he announced. "Be on your best guard. We are not safe home yet."

Following the archery contest, Father Dominic had thanked the count and abbot for their inestimable hospitality and announced his desire to resume his journey. In taking their leave of the count the next morning, the papal envoy was surprised to learn that the count had decided to send an escort of knights and men-at-arms to see them safely to their ship at Hamtun Docks. Despite the envoy's protestations that this was in no way necessary, the count—his own resolve bolstered by the insistence of an increasingly suspicious sheriff—would not allow his guests to depart on their own. "It is the least I can do for our Mother Church," he insisted. "If anything should happen to you on the road—may heaven forbid it!—I would never be forgiven, especially since it is so easily prevented."

"Bloody meddler," muttered Iwan, when he learned of the plan. "There is no ship waiting for us. We've never been anywhere near Hamtun Docks."

"They don't know that," Bran replied. "We will go on as we've begun and look for the first opportunity to send them on their way."

"And if we don't find such an opportunity?" demanded Iwan. "What then?"

"We can always disappear into the wood," Bran told him. "Leave it to me. You keep your eyes on the soldiers and remain alert. If anything goes wrong, I want you ready to break some heads."

"Oh, aye," agreed Iwan grimly, "if it comes to that. I'll be ready right enough."

They had set off with Count de Braose, Sheriff de Glanville, and ten Norman soldiers—four knights and six men-at-arms—to provide protection from King Raven and his outlaw minions, who haunted the greenwood and preyed on unwary travellers. The papal envoy and his small entourage—the Lady Ghisella and her maidservant, Brother Alfonso the interpreter, and the two lay brothers surrounded by heavily armed Ffreinc men, kept to themselves for the most part. Outwardly, they behaved much as before—cheerful, if quiet, and appreciative of the largess lavished on them by their ever-watchful hosts.

"I do not trust that priest," the sheriff had said as the travelling party prepared to set off. "He is no more an ambassador of Pope Clement than my horse. Mark me, there is some deception playing out here, and we are fools if we let them get away with it."

"You may be right," conceded Count de Braose. "But we dare not risk a confrontation until we are more than certain. This way, at least, we can keep a close watch on them."

"Be sure of it," growled the sheriff. "The first time any one of them looks sideways, I'll have him."

"You are not to antagonise them," Falkes warned. "If word of any mistreatment were to reach my uncle—not to mention Pope Clement—we'd be peeled and boiled in our own blood."

"Never fear, my lord," replied the sheriff. "I will be nothing but courtesy itself to our esteemed guests. But I will watch them—by the rood, I will."

Thus, a forced and wary pleasantness settled over the travellers. Because of the small coach in which Lady Ghisella and her maid rode, and which carried the tents used by the envoy and his company, they could not travel as quickly as the Normans might have wished. At night they made camp separately, each side watching the other, wary and suspicious, across the distance. The only time the foreigners were able to confer openly with one another was when the Ffreinc were occupied with picketing the horses and establishing the guard for the night.

It was during one of these times that Bran moved among the members of his disguised flock, speaking words of encouragement and hope. He also apologized to Will and begged the forester's forgiveness. "I am sorry, Will. It was my fault you were taken, and I grieve that you suffered because of it."

"I suffered a little, true," Will granted. "But Gwion Bach would have suffered more, I reckon. Still, I forgive you free and fair. I won't say I didn't think ill of that night, all the same." He smiled. "But you've more than made up for it by saving my scrawny neck from that hide noose. And for that I truly thank you, my lord."

"We're not out of danger yet," Bran said. "So you might want to wait until we say farewell to our nosey friends before thanking me."

"Whatever happens," replied Will, "we're square, my lord, and no hard feelings."

The party endured four more days of anxious watching, until at last coming in sight of the bluffs overlooking the river estuary at Hamtun.

"What if there is no ship?" Iwan wondered. "What will we do then?"

"You should pray there is no ship," Siarles observed. "Then we can at least say they have gone to get supplies, or some such thing. The Ffreinc are not about to wait around many days to see us away."

"But what if there is a ship?" demanded Iwan, plainly worried.

"We will take it," concluded Bran. "Either way, it could not be simpler."

Simple as the choices may have been, the doing was only slightly more difficult. When, the next day, as they followed the road over the bluff and started down into the river valley, they caught sight of the docks on the waterfront below the town, the travellers could see there was, indeed, a ship waiting there—a sturdy, broad-beamed vessel built for hauling men and horses across the sea. To all appearances, it was just the sort of vessel that the patriarch of Rome might provide for his personal ambassador.

"Well, there is your boat," muttered Iwan. "Now what?"

Bran glanced around. The sun was low, and the wind freshening out of the west. The count and sheriff had picked up the pace and were drawing closer, expressions of keen anticipation lighting their watchful eyes. "Ride to the ship and secure it. Take Siarles and Jago with you. Go now before the Ffreinc prevent you."

"And what do you suggest I tell them when I take their ship?"

"Tell them the pope's ambassador needs it," replied Bran. "Tell them we will buy our passage. Tell them anything, but just secure it and keep the sailors out of sight when we get there."

Scowling with determination, Iwan signalled to Siarles and Jago, and all three galloped away. Bran, turning to Will, Mérian, and Cinnia, quickly explained that they were to continue on in the wagon and, upon reaching the ship, they were to go aboard as if that was what had been intended from the start. "Whatever happens," he said hurriedly, "the two of you get down below deck and stay there. Mérian," he said, dismounting and helping her down from the wagon, "you come with me."

Will, from his seat in the wagon, cast a last backward glance at the sheriff, then turned and set his face towards the river and the freedom waiting there.

Seeing the monks gallop off, Count Falkes and the sheriff rode directly to Father Dominic for an explanation. "Where are they going?" demanded de Glanville suspiciously.

"Qué?" replied the envoy with a smile of incomprehension. He gestured towards the ship, waving and nodding as if to indicate that they had arrived at last and all was well. Lady Ghisella, who possessed a smattering of French, tried to explain. "They go to make ready the sailing," she said.

"You mean to leave tonight?" asked the count.

"But of course," replied the lady pleasantly. "It is the wish of His Eminence to leave at once."

The sheriff, unable to think of any reason why this should not be perfectly reasonable, looked to the count to mount an objection. "Are you certain?" Falkes said lamely. "It will be getting dark soon."

"It is the wish of His Eminence," the lady repeated, as if this was all the explanation required.

"Well," said the sheriff, "we will attend you to see that nothing is amiss." He lifted the reins and started down the road once more.

"Please, Lord Count," said Lady Ghisella, "you must not trouble yourself."

"But it is no trouble at all, my lady," replied the count. "If anything should happen to you while you remained in our care . . ." He allowed the thought to go unfinished. "Never fear," he said with a stiff, somewhat condescending laugh, "we will see you safely aboard and properly under sail. We could do no less for the pope's personal confidant."

"That is a relief, to be sure," replied Ghisella crisply. "I will tell His Eminence."

Although it made her uncomfortable to speak to the Ffreinc, her reticent, regal manner went a long way towards easing the count's suspicions. His attraction to her despite her undeniable plainness made him more willing to overlook his doubts. She relayed the count's sentiments to Father Dominic, who gave a nod of approval. "What are we to do now?" she asked, keeping her voice low to avoid being overheard.

"We see it through," Bran told her, "and hope for the best. Thank them, and walk on."

She smiled, revealing her unfortunate, off-colour teeth. "His Eminence is delighted with your diligence and care. He will speak of it to His Holiness."

"The delight is ours alone, my lady," replied the count.

"They are getting away, and we sit here trading pleasantries," muttered the sheriff. "I don't like this."

"I cannot forbid their departure; they have done nothing wrong."

"This whole affair is wrong!" grumbled the sheriff.

"Then find a way to stop them if you can," said Count Falkes. "But unless you discover something very soon, they will be away on the tide."

The travellers moved on, descending the narrow road into the valley, passing quickly through the town and its low-built, dark houses and single muddy street to the large timber wharf on the river where the ship was moored. All seemed quiet aboard the vessel—no screams or shouting, no evidence of a struggle or fight—although there was no sign of Iwan or any of the others. Bran, his stomach tightening with every step, prayed that they might yet make good their escape. As they drew near the dock, there appeared on deck a man in a red cap and brown tunic which reached past his knees. He was barefoot and carried a knotted rope in his hand. He scanned the wharf quickly and then hurried to greet the new arrivals. "*Mes seigneurs! Ma dame! J'offre vous accueille. Etre bienvenu ici. S'il vous plaît, venir à bord et être à l'aise. Tout est prêt!*"

At this, the French speakers fell silent, dumbstruck. Lady Ghisella gave a little gasp of pleasure.

"Saints and angels!" whispered Bran tensely. "What did he say?"

"We are welcome to come aboard," Mérian told him. "He says everything is ready for us."

"Peter and Paul on a donkey!" exclaimed Bran. "How did they accomplish that?" Before she could answer, he said, "Hurry now. Get on board. Send Jago back to help me get rid of our friends here, and tell Iwan and Siarles to make ready to cast off." When Mérian hesitated, he said, "Quickly! Before something goes wrong."

Bran, alone now, turned to his obliging, if suspicious, hosts and, summoning up his little store of Latin, attempted to sever the last ties and bid them farewell. *"Vicis pro sententia Deus volo est hic, vae. Gratias ago vos vobis hospitium quod ignarus. Caveo, ut tunc nos opportunus."*

This might have lacked the polish of a senior churchman, but it was more than either Sheriff de Glanville or Count Falkes possessed, at any rate. The two Frenchmen stared at him, unable to comprehend what had just passed.

"His Eminence says the time has come to bid you farewell," explained the one known as Brother Alfonso, hastening to join Father Dominic on the dock just then. "His Grace thanks you for your hospitality—a debt he can never repay—and wishes you a most wonderfully pleasant and uneventful journey home. Be assured that, owing to your kind and attentive service, your praises will ring in the pope's ears."

The man in the red hat, who, it turned out, was master of the ship, hurried to greet the papal emissary. He knelt to receive a blessing, which was deftly delivered, then rose, saying, "My apologies, Your Grace, but if we are to take the tide, we must hurry. The horses must be secured and the ship made ready to cast off."

"Now see here," protested the sheriff, still unwilling to see the suspicious foreigners slip away so easily.

"Was there something?" inquired the ship's master.

"No," said the count. "Be about your business." To the sheriff, he said, "Come, de Glanville, there is no more to be done here."

When this was translated for His Eminence, Father Dominic gave his Norman hosts a blessing and, with a last promise to mention their care and attention to the pope, released them from their duty of guarding him and his entourage. He walked onto the ship and went below deck. A moment later, the two lay brothers appeared and helped the ship's master lead the horses on deck and secure them for the voyage. When this was done, they helped the master cast off and, using stout poles, pushed the craft away from the dock and out into the river, where it drifted for a little while before finding the current. Then, as they entered the stream, Father Dominic, Lady Ghisella, and Will Scarlet came back onto the deck and waved farewell to the Normans, who, although they could not be sure, thought they heard the sound of laughter carried on the wind as the ship entered the centre of the channel and was carried along by the slowly building tide-flow, and away.

CHAPTER 40

Rouen

King William Rufus, wet and miserable in the driving
rain, rode at the head of a company of his best and most loyal knights.
The royal ranks were followed by sixty men-at-arms grimly slogging
through the sticky mud. Water streamed down from a low sky of seamless grey from horizon to horizon, falling in steady rivulets from helmet,
shield, and lance blade, puddling deep in the wheel-rutted road. The
farms and villages flung out around the low, squat city of Rouen appeared
just as cheerless and desolate as the king and his dreary entourage.

Curse his fool of a stiff-necked brother, he thought. It should be
Duke Robert—not himself, the king of England—who was saddle
sore and catching his death in the rain. Blast the imbecile and his infernal scheming! Why could Robert not accept his divinely appointed lot
and be happy ruling the family's ancestral lands? William told himself
that if that had been his own particular fate, he would have embraced
it and worked to make something of his portion and not be forever
wasting his substance fomenting rebellion and inflaming the rapacious
ambitions of France's endless supply of muttering malcontents.

These thoughts put the already irritated king in a simmering rage. And when he contemplated the time and money wasted on keeping his idiot brother appeased and under control, his thin blue blood began to boil.

Thus, William arrived in the yard of the archbishop's palace at Rouen already angry and spoiling for a fight. The palace, a solid square of cut stone three floors high and studded with wood-shuttered windows, occupied the top of a prominent hill a mile or so beyond the city wherein stood the cathedral. William's cool and indifferent welcome by the current incumbent of the palace did little to mollify the king, or sweeten his disposition.

"Ah, William," intoned Archbishop Bonne-Âme, "good of you to come." Heavily robed and leaning on his bishop's staff, the old man puffed, out of breath from his short walk across the vestibule. An honour guard of six knights and two earls entered with the king, the water from their cloaks dripping on the polished stone floor, which sent a bevy of clerical servants scampering for rags to mop up the mess.

"My pleasure," grumbled William, shedding his sopping cloak and tossing it to a waiting servant. "Where is he? What's it to be this time? Come, let's get to it."

The archbishop's pale hand fluttered up like an agitated bird. "Oh, my lord king, this is to be a most serious conclave. I hope you understand the gravity of the moment."

"I understand that my brother is as worthless," quipped William, "as is anyone who sides with him. Beyond that, there is only the money it will take to buy him off."

The archbishop stiffened and lowered his head in a bow. "This way, Your Majesty."

The archbishop turned and started away with King William a step or two behind; the king's men threw off their wet cloaks and assembled in a double rank behind him. And as servants rushed to pick up the sodden garments, the ageing archbishop led them down a lofty corridor to a large audience room where the king found assembled a few minor lords standing around the blazing hearth at one end of the room. They looked around guiltily as the king of England and his men entered. Duke Robert was not among them, nor anyone William recognised.

"Where is he?" demanded the king. "I have ridden hard for three days in the rain. I am not playing at games."

"This is what I wanted to tell you, Majesty," explained the archbishop. "Duke Robert is not here. Indeed, few of those summoned to attend have arrived. It's the weather, you see . . . but we expect them at any moment."

"Do we!" snapped the angry king. "Do we indeed, sir!"

"We do, Majesty," the old cleric assured him. "I have ordered chambers to be prepared for you. If you would like to rest a little before the proceedings, I will have refreshment sent to you."

843

William gave a last scowl around the near-empty room and allowed himself to be persuaded. "Very well," he said. "Have wine brought to me in my chambers." To one of his men, he said, "Leicester, fetch me dry clothes. I'll change out of these blasted wet things."

"Of course, Sire. At once," replied the Earl of Leicester. With a nod and flick of his hand, he sent one of his men to carry out the errand. "Will there be anything else?"

"No," said the king, feeling a great weariness settling upon him. He started after the archbishop, saying, "You and Warwick will attend me. The others are to see to the horses, then take food and rest for themselves."

"At once, Sire." The earl gave quick instructions to the rest of the king's guard and sent them away. He and the Earl of Warwick accompanied the king to the apartment that had been prepared for him—a

large room with a bed and a square oak table with four chairs. Archbishop Bonne-Âme pushed open the heavy door and stepped into the
room, glancing around to assure himself that all was in order for his
tetchy guest.

A fire burned in the small hearth, and on the table sat a jug of
wine with four cups and, beside these, a platter with loaves of bread
and soft cheese wrapped in grape leaves.

William walked to the table and poured wine into three of the
cups. "Thank you, Archbishop," he said, offering a cup to the nearest
earl, "we are well satisfied with our arrangements. You may go."

Bonne-Âme bowed his old white head and retreated, closing the
door. "I leave you to your rest."

"My brother is planning mischief," observed the king, his nose in
his cup as he gulped down a healthy draught. "I can feel it in my bones."

844

"Do you know le Bellay?" asked the Earl of Leicester.

"I know my brother," replied William.

"If there is to be bloodshed . . . ," began young Lord Warwick.

The king cut him off with an impatient wave of his hand. "It
won't come to that, I think," William said, handing him a cup. "At
least not yet." He drank again and said, "I wish I knew what he and
his sycophants were up to, though."

"Those men down there," said Leicester. "Who were they?"

"God knows," answered the king. "Never seen the rascals before.
You?"

"I might have met one or another. Difficult to say." He replaced his
cup on the board and said, "I think I might just go and see if I can
find out."

"Never mind," said the king. Drawing out a chair, he dropped
heavily into it, then shoved a second chair towards the earl. "Here. Sit.
You must be as tired as I am. Sit. We'll drink and rest."

"With respect, Sire, I would rest easier if I knew who those men are and what they're doing here."

The king shrugged. "Go then, but hurry back. And tell the chamberlain we need some meat to go with this bread and cheese."

"Of course, my lord," said the Earl of Leicester, moving quickly towards the door. He hoped to catch the archbishop for a private word before the old man disappeared into the cavern of his palace.

"And more wine!" called the king after him.

William leaned back in the chair and closed his eyes. "Sire?" said the Earl of Warwick, setting aside his cup. He came to stand before the king. "If you would allow me," he offered, indicating the monarch's feet, "I think we might dry those boots a little."

William nodded, and with a sigh raised his foot so that the young man might pull off the sodden shoe. He guzzled down another draught as the young nobleman attended to the other boot.

"There, now," said Warwick, when he had finished. "Better, no?"

"Mmmm," murmured William into the cup. "Much."

The earl carried the wet boots to the hearth and put them on the warm stones to dry, then returned to the table and sat down. He and the king sipped their wine in silence for a time, feeling the tensions of the road begin to ease beneath application of the sweet, dark liquid.

"This is all my father's fault," mused William after a time. "If he had not promised my ninny of a brother the throne of England, all would be well. He roused Robert's hopes and, fool that he is, the duke has set the value too high—thinks it worth more than it is." He drained the cup and then filled it again. "Truth is," he continued, "the blasted island costs more than you can ever get out of it."

"It was ever thus," Warwick suggested. "King Harold never had two pennies to rub together one day to the next, as my father used to

845

say. And Aelfred was in debt from the day he took the crown till the day they took it off him in the grave."

"This is supposed to cheer me, Warwick?" grumbled the king.

"I merely suggest that your condition is neither more nor less than that which all English rulers have endured. God knows, it is difficult enough even for an earl, much less a duke or a king."

"Duke Robert does right well," William pointed out. He took up a loaf of bread, broke it, and stuffed half into his mouth. He chewed heavily for a moment. "To be sure, most of what he has he got from me."

"Cut him off, Sire," suggested Warwick. "Or make him sign a settlement treaty in exchange for his promise never to raise rebellion again. Get him to put his name to it."

"Robert would have nothing if it wasn't for me propping him up," growled William, the bread half-eaten in his mouth. "No more! No more, hear? This is the end."

"With your permission, Sire, I'll have a treaty drawn up at once," the earl suggested, raising his cup. "We'll get Robert to sign it and be done with him once and for all."

"If he thinks I'll buy him off again, he's woefully mistaken," said William. "If he demands another penny from me, I'll march on him, curse the devil, I will! I swear it."

"Well," replied Warwick judiciously, trying to calm the agitated monarch, "perhaps he will listen to reason this time. Would you like me to arrange for a treaty?"

Lord Leicester returned with another jug of wine and, behind him, a servant bearing a platter of cold roast duck and chicken. "His Grace the archbishop says that he is retiring for the night. He wishes you a good night's rest and sleep. He will conduct a Mass in the morning and break fast after."

"And my brother? When is he expected?"

"The archbishop could not say, Sire. Tomorrow, I expect."

"Well, then," decided William, "we could do worse than make a night of it. Here, bring that platter! I'm famished."

They ate and drank, talking long into the night. Both Lord Leicester and his brother, Warwick, remained with the king, sleeping in chairs beside the hearth while William snored in his feather bed. As dawn cracked the damp grey sky in the east, the chapel bell sounded, calling the faithful to Mass. William and his noblemen stirred at the sound, then went back to sleep, awaking again when they heard a clatter in the courtyard below. Warwick got up and walked to the narrow window, pushed open the wooden shutter and looked out. He could see seven men on horseback, or perhaps five men and two women. On closer inspection, at least two of them appeared to be priests. Although the day was still new, their mounts appeared fresh and fairly unsoiled by the mud on the rain-soaked roads. They had not travelled far, the earl surmised. He watched for a moment, scanning the group, but failed to recognise anyone—in any event, they were certainly not Duke Robert and his entourage. Turning from the window, he went to the king's bed and gave a polite cough. When this failed to rouse His Majesty, he took hold of the royal shoulder and gave it a shake.

847

"Sire," he said, "I think the vultures are gathering. We should be ready for them."

William opened his eyes and tried to raise his head. The effort was too much and he lay back with a groan. "Who has come? Is my brother finally here?"

"I do not know, my lord. I did not see him," replied Warwick. "A priest or two have arrived, but unless the duke travels in the company of priests now, he is not yet here."

"Oh," sighed William, struggling upright. "Why did you let me drink so much?"

"It is a fault of mine, Majesty," the Earl of Warwick assured him. "I must try to do better. Then again, the archbishop's wine is very good."

"It is," agreed William, swinging his short, stout legs off the bed. "Is there any left, do you think?"

Henry walked to the table and began examining the jugs and cups.

"Where is Leicester?" asked the king, stretching his back and yawning.

"He has gone to Mass," Warwick reported. "I expect him to return soon. Shall I have someone fetch him for you?"

"No, no," decided the king. "Let him be." Heaving his bulk up onto unsteady legs, he tottered to the table and the cup which Lord Warwick now held out to him. The king took a sip, tasted it, then drained the cup. "Ah, that's better."

The young earl disappeared momentarily to summon a servant lurking in the corridor to prepare a basin of water for the king, and commanded another to bring the king's chest to the room. Presently, the servant appeared with a basin of hot water, and while William washed, Warwick supervised the cleaning of the king's boots. "Get all that muck off there and brush them well," he ordered, so that His Majesty would not look like a common farmhand before the other noblemen. The chamberlain meanwhile appeared with the king's chest and a message that some people had come and were seeking audience on a most urgent matter.

"What do they want?" asked William, raising the hem of his tunic and drawing it over his head. Warwick opened the chest and withdrew a clean, white tunic.

"They did not say, Your Majesty," replied the chamberlain. "I was told only that it was of utmost importance that they speak to you at once, and before you speak to anyone else today."

"Impertinent lot," observed William, pulling the tunic over his head. The garment, though handsomely wrought, was made for a slightly smaller frame; the fine fabric stretched over his expansive gut. "Warwick," he said, "go see who it is and find out what they want. I have not broken fast yet, and I'm not in a humour to brook any silliness."

"To be sure, Sire," replied the young earl.

William nodded, picked up a scrap of bread from the remains of last night's supper, sniffed it, and took a bite. Seeing the servant still stood staring at him, he threw the rind of dried bread crust at him. "Bring me my food!" The servant ducked the missile and darted for the door. "And be quick about it," William called after him. "Important people have come. We must not keep them waiting."

CHAPTER 41

S'truth, I'd never make a sailor. Even the smallest stretch o' water seen from the deck of a ship brings me out in a sweat. If a wave should rock the boat, it's me there hanging onto the rail and spilling my supper into the briny deep. Oh, and I had cause enough. Even the master of the ship said it was the worst storm in many a year o' sailing. And he should know—he's crossed that narrow sea more times than a rooster with a henhouse across the road. Our own small voyage might not have been so bad, and indeed I had allowed myself to imagine that the worst was over when we entered the wide estuary of the Thames and sallied slowly upriver to the White Tower of Lundein to pay our ruddy King William a visit.

Alas, the king was not in residence.

Gone to Rouen, they told us—gone to parley with his brother, not to return till Saint Matthew's Day, maybe not till Christmas.

Never mind, said Bran, we've come this far, what's a little further? "Master Ruprecht!" he called, and I can still hear those fateful words: "Cast off and make sail for France!"

*A*s it had turned out, our man Ruprecht, the ship's owner and master, was Flanders born and raised, and could speak both French and English into the bargain. His ship was a stout ploughhorse of a vessel, and he was kept right busy fetching and carrying Ffreinc noblemen and their knights back and forth to England from various ports on the coast of Normandie. Thus, he knew the coasts of both lands as well as any and far better than most. Seizing his ship had been easier than rolling off a stump. We lifted nary a finger, nor ruffled a hair—we simply bought his services.

This easy conquest was not without its moment of uncertainty, however. For as we came in sight of the docks at Hamtun that day and Bran gave Iwan, Siarles, and Jago the command to secure the ship, those three hastened down to the wharf. Cinnia and I arrived close behind and scrambled onto the dock hard on their heels. "Let me talk to them first," offered Brother Jago, as they dismounted. "Do nothing until we see how things stand."

"Hurry then," Iwan said. "We do not have much time before the others get here."

"What will you tell them?" asked Siarles, swinging down from the saddle. "Maybe it would be better to take them by surprise."

"Force is the first resort of the coward," suggested Jago lightly. "Peace, Brother. We have enjoyed great success with our disguises until now. We can trust them a little further, I think."

"Go then," Iwan told him. "See if they will talk to you."

"Whatever you do, make it quick," said I, urging them on.

"All the same, we will be ready to stifle any objections with our fists," Siarles called after him.

I myself could not have stifled so much as a sneeze with my fists, weak and miserable as I was just then. My months of captivity had left me exhausted, and the last few days of travel had all but killed me. It took my last strength to clamber down from the wagon and, on Cinnia's tender arm, hobble onto the dock and make my slow, aching way aboard the waiting vessel where, if it had not happened, I would not have believed it: the ship's master himself welcomed us with open arms.

"Greetings, friends!" he called, leaping lightly to the rail to help me aboard. "My ship and myself are at your service. I am Master Ruprecht, and this is the *Dame Havik*." His English was flat and toneless, but clear, and the ruddy face beneath his floppy red hat was friendly as it was wind-burned. "The good brother has told me of your urgent mission. Never fear, I will see you safely to your destination." He paused to wave at the approaching Ffreinc, and to Father Dominic.

What Jago had told him, in the first part, was that Father Dominic was a papal legate, which was no more than de Braose and his lot already believed. Jago merely added that we were all on a secret embassy to England bearing a message of utmost importance for the king. As it happens, this last part was true enough. Bran did indeed bear an important message for the king—the one I had sent him through Odo from my prison cell concerning the letter we had stolen in the Christmas raid. Now, as a result of his sojourn with Count Falkes and Abbot Hugo, our King Raven knew better what that letter meant. The importance of reaching King William might have been overstated somewhat. But in light of the mounting suspicions of Falkes and the sheriff, it was simple good sense to make the captain think our errand urgent. Even so, that excuse was closer to the truth than any of us could have guessed, and it was to be the saving of us.

The *Dame Havik*'s master had only one small impediment towards our leaving straightaway—he had no crew. He had come to England shorthanded, and with a cargo of fine cloth, which he had sold days before; he had put in at Hamtun to pick up more sailors and a load of hides and wool. "We will have to wait until I can find some more hands to help with the sails and such. I hope you understand. It should not take long," he hastened to add, "no more than three or four days maybe."

"Even that is too long," Jago, as Brother Alfonso, informed him. "Perhaps you would allow my fellow monks and me to serve as your crew at least as far as Lundein. If you tell us what to do, we will do it. And," he added, "the king will reward you well when we tell him how you have helped us."

Ruprecht of Flanders pulled on his chin and cast a weather eye at the sky, then to the river. "The tide is beginning to run, and the wind is in a favourable quarter." He made up his mind with a snap of his fingers. "Well, why not? As soon as His Eminence is aboard, we will cast off. Here! I will show you what to do. Step to the music, friends!"

And just like that, Iwan and Siarles were no longer lay brothers, but sailors. Under Ruprecht's direction, they hauled on the ropes and picked up the poles and, in as much time as it takes to tell it, we were away, leaving the Ffreinc standing on the shore, mouths agape, eyes a-boggle at the swiftness of our departure. The ship, light of its load, spun out into the deeper channel; the tide lifted her and carried her off. We saw the dock and Hamtun town growing small behind us and laughed out loud. We were so relieved to have done with those treacherous Ffreinc, we laughed until the tears streamed down our cheeks.

We made for Lundein, sailing along the coast and up the wide Thames until we came in sight of the White Tower—a splendid thing it is, too, all gleaming pale and tall like an enormous horn rising from the bank of the muddy river. But we had no sooner made anchor and summoned a tender alongside to carry us to shore than we learned that the king was not in England. "Gone to France," said the tenderman. He counted the days on his fingers. "A week or more ago, give or take."

"Are you certain?" asked Jago.

"Show him this," said Bran, handing Jago a silver penny. "Give it to him if he answers well."

Jago questioned the man closely, and at the end declared himself satisfied that the man was telling the truth; he tossed the boatman the coin. "What is your wish, my lord?"

"We have no choice," Bran replied. I saw the keen glint in his eye and knew he'd already decided.

Mérian saw it, too. "You mean . . . ? We can't!"

"Why not?" said Bran. "I've been thinking, and the sooner we get this out in the open, the sooner we can reclaim Elfael."

"What are you talking about?" said Iwan.

Bran turned and called: "Master Ruprecht! Cast off and make sail for France."

"France!" scoffed the big warrior. "I wouldn't set foot beyond the high tide mark on the word of an Englishman."

"Careful, friend," I warned, smiling as I said it. "Some of us English-men are that touchy when our honour is called into question."

Iwan pawed the air at me with his hand. "You know what I mean."

"He has a point," Siarles put in. "France is a fair size, so I'm told."

"And full of Ffreincmen," I added.

"We might want to know where we're going if we aim to meet up with Red William."

Bran agreed and, with Brother Jago for company, ordered Ruprecht to hire the men to crew the ship and get whatever provisions might be necessary for a voyage to France, and then climbed down into the wait-ing tender boat. Rhi Bran and Jago went ashore to learn what they could of the king's whereabouts, and we were soon occupied with securing provisions and fodder for the horses, and hauling water aboard. Seeing as how his passengers were ambassadors of the pope, the ship's master

855

also bought a cask of wine and two of ale, and a barrel of smoked herrings, two bags of apples, four live chickens, two ducks, and a basket of eggs. These he bought from the merchant boats plying the wide river, bartering for a price and then hauling the various casks, crates, and cages up over the rail. He then went in search of sailors to make the voyage with us. While he was gone, we stowed all of the cargo away in the little rooms below deck and then waited for Bran and Jago to return.

We waited long, watching the river sink lower and lower as the tide ebbed out. The bare mud of the upper bank was showing and the sun had disappeared below the horizon and Iwan was almost ready to swim ashore to storm the tower, he was that sure Bran and Jago had been taken captive, when Mérian called out, "Here they are! They're coming now."

Indeed, they were already in a boat and making their way out to where *Dame Havik* rode at anchor. Moments later, we were pulling them aboard. We all gathered around to hear what they had learned ashore.

"The king has gone to attend a council at Rouen," Bran said. "He left with sixty men ten days ago. I know not where Rouen may be, but I mean to go there and lay before him all that we know and suspect."

"I know Rouen," volunteered Ruprecht when he returned a short while later leading four Flemish sailors to crew the ship. "Ten days, you say?" He tapped his chin thoughtfully. "If they were travelling overland on horseback, we may still be able to catch them before they arrive."

"Truly?" wondered Iwan. "How is that possible?"

"My ship draws lightly," he said. "We can easily go upriver as far as the bridge. It is but a short ride from there to the town."

The tide was on the rise, so we had to wait until it had begun to ebb again. We settled down to a good meal which the ship's master and

Jago prepared for us, then slept a little, rising again when the tide began to flow. As a dim half-moon soared overhead, we upped anchor and set out once more.

Dawn found us skirting the high white cliffs of the southern coast, and as the sun rose, the clouds gathered and the wind began to blow. At first it wasn't so bad that a fella couldn't stand up to it, but by midday, the waves were dashing against the hull and splashing over the rail. Ruprecht allowed that we were in for some rough water, but assured us that we would come to no harm. "A summer storm, nothing more," he called cheerfully. "Do not fret yourselves, Brothers. See to the horses—there are ropes to lash them down so they cannot hurt themselves."

Throughout the day, the storm grew. Wind howled around the bare mast—they'd long since taken down the sails—and the waves tossed the ship like thistledown: now up, now down, now tail over top. It was all I could do to hold on for dear life and keep my poor bandaged fingers from smashing against the hull as I tried to keep from getting battered bloody.

As evening fell on that wild day, our ship's master was the only one still cheerful. Ruprecht alone maintained his usual good humour in the teeth of the storm. Moreover, he was the only one still standing. The rest of us—his sailors included—were hunkered down below the deck, clinging to the stout ribs of the ship as she bucked and heaved in the rowdy waves.

More than once, my innards tried to leave the wretched confines of their piteous prison—and I without strength or will to stop them. My stomach heaved with every wave that rolled and tried to sink our vessel. Along with my miserable companions, I shut my eyes against the dizzying pitch and twist, and stopped my ears against the shriek of the wind and the angry sea's bellowing roar.

857

This seagoing calamity continued for an eternity, so it seemed. When at last we dared lift our heads and unclasp our limbs and venture onto the deck, we saw the clouds torn and flying away to the east and rays of sunlight streaming through, all bright gold and glowing like the firmament of heaven. "Have we died then?" asked Siarles, grey-faced with the sickness we all shared. The front of his robe was damp from his throwing up, and his hair was slick and matted with sweat.

"No such luck," groaned Iwan; his appearance likewise had not improved with the ordeal. "I can still feel the beast bucking under me. In heaven there will be no storms."

"And no ships, either," muttered Mérian. Pale and shaky, she tottered off to find water to wash her face and hands. Bran was least affected by the storm, but even he strode unsteadily to where Ruprecht stood smiling and humming at the tiller; summoning Jago to him, Bran said, "Ask him how many days we have lost."

"Only one, Your Grace," came the reply. "The storm blew itself out overnight. The sea has been running high, but it is calming now. Och! That was a bad one—as bad as any I've seen in a month of years."

"Are we still on course?" asked Bran.

"More or less," affirmed the master. "More or less. But we will be able to raise the sails soon. Until then, have your men see to the horses. Unbind them and give the poor beasts a little food and water."

While Iwan and Siarles saw to that chore, two of the sailors began preparing a meal for us. Bran and I watched this activity as we leaned heavily on the rail, neither of us feeling very bold or hearty just then. "What a night," Bran sighed. "How is the hand?"

"Not so bad," I lied. "Hardly feel it at all." Looking out at the still-rumpled sea, I asked, "What will happen when we get to Rouen, if we should be so fortunate?"

"I mean to get an audience with Red William."

"As Lord Bran," I wondered, "or Father Dominic?"

He showed me his lopsided smile. "Whichever one the king will agree to see. It is the message that is important here, not the messenger."

"Leaving that aside," I said, "I'm beginning to think we're mad for risking our necks aboard this mad ship and storm-stirred sea to save a king we neither love nor honour."

He regarded me curiously. "Is that you talking, Will? It was you who put us onto it, after all."

"Yes, but, I didn't think—"

"If you're right, then it is well worth the risk of a kingdom," Bran said.

"Whose kingdom, my lord?" I wondered. "William's . . . or yours?"

We talked until Cinnia called us to our food which, following a little good-natured teasing by the sailors, we were able to get down. After we had eaten, Ruprecht gave orders to his crew for the sail to be run up. Once this was done, the ship began to run more smoothly. We had no more trouble with the ever-contrary weather and reached the French mainland that evening. We dropped anchor until morning, then proceeded up the coast until reaching the estuary of a wide inland river at a place called Honfleur. Although some of our provisions had been damaged by seawater in the storm, we did not stop to take on more provisions because Ruprecht assured us that Rouen was only a day or so upriver and we could get all we needed there at half the cost of the harbour merchants.

So, we sailed on. The storm we had endured at sea had gone before us and was now settled over the land. Through a haze of rain we watched the low hills of Normandie slowly slide by the rail. Although we could not escape the rain, the river remained calm, and it was good to see land within easy reach on either side of the ship. I confess, it did feel strange to go into the enemy's land. And I did marvel that no one tried to apprehend us or attack us in any way. But no one did, and we spent the night anchored in the middle of the stream, resuming our slow way at sunrise the next day. As promised, we reached the city of Rouen while it was still morning and made fast at the wharf that served the city. Iwan and Siarles readied the horses, and Bran meanwhile arranged with Ruprecht to provision the boat and wait for our return.

Then, pausing only to ask directions of one of the harbour hands, we set off once more beneath clearing skies on blesséd dry land. Oh! It was that good to be on solid ground again, and it was but a short ride to the palace of the archbishop where, it was said, the English king had arrived the previous day.

"Here is the way it will be," Bran said as we entered the palace yard. "To anyone who asks, we are still ambassadors of the pope with an urgent message for the king."

"Aye," agreed Iwan dryly, "but which pope?"

"Pray we do not have to explain beyond that," Bran told him. "At all events, do not any of you speak to anyone. Let Jago, here, do the talking for us." He put his hand on the priest's shoulder. "Brother Alfonso knows what to say."

"What if someone asks us something?" wondered Siarles, looking none too certain about this part of the enterprise.

"Just pretend you don't speak French," I told him.

The others laughed at this, but Siarles, bless him, was worried and did not catch my meaning. "But I don't speak a word of French," he insisted.

"Then pretending should be easy," Mérian chirped lightly. She patted her hair, working in the ashes that greyed it; then took out the small wooden teeth that were part of her disguise and slipped them into her mouth; they were an off colour and made her jaw jut slightly, giving her face an older, far less comely appearance.

Bran and the others straightened their monkish robes and prepared to look pious. I had no disguise, but since no one in France had ever seen me before it was not thought to matter very much. Then, standing in the rain-washed yard of the archbishop of Rouen's palace, Brother Jago led us in a prayer that the plan we set in motion would succeed, that bloodshed could be avoided, and that our actions would bring about the restoration of Elfael to its rightful rule.

When he finished, Bran looked at each of us in turn, head to toe, then, satisfied, said, "The downfall of Baron de Braose is begun, my friends. It is not something we have done, but something he has done to himself." He smiled. "Come, let us do all we can to hasten his demise."

CHAPTER 42

We were given a beggar's greeting by the archbishop's porter, who at first thought us English and then, despite his misgivings, was forced to take Bran at his word. For standing on his threshold was a legate of the pope and his attending servants and advisors. What else could he do but let us in?

Thus, we were admitted straightaway and shown to a small reception room and made to wait there until someone could be found who might more readily deal with us. There were no chairs in the room, and no fire in the hearth; the board against one wall was bare. Clearly, it was not a room used to receive expected, or welcome, visitors.

"Pax vobiscum," said a short, keen-eyed cleric in a white robe. *"Bona in sanctus nomen."*

"Pax vobiscum," replied Bran. He nodded to Brother Jago, who stepped forward and, with a little bow of respect, began to translate for Father Dominic and his companions.

The man, it turned out, was a fella named Canon Laurent, and he was the principal aid to Archbishop Bonne-Âme. "His Grace has asked me to express his regrets, as he is unable to welcome you personally.

Your arrival has caught us at a very busy and eventful time. Please accept our apologies if we cannot offer you the hospitality you are certainly due, and which it would be our pleasure to provide under more ordinary circumstances."

The priest was as slippery and smooth as an eel in oil, but beneath the mannered courtesy, I sensed a staunch and upright spirit. "How may I be of service to you?" he said, folding his hands and tucking them into the sleeves of his robe.

"We have come bearing an important message for King William from His Holiness, the pope."

"Indeed," the canon replied, raising his eyebrows. "Perhaps if I knew more about this message it would aid your purpose."

"Our message is for the king alone," explained Bran, through Jago. "Yet I have no doubt that His Majesty will explain all to you in the time and manner of his choosing. If you would inform him that we are waiting, we will be in your debt."

That was plain enough. The canon, unable to wheedle more from our Bran, conceded and promised to take our request to the king. "If you wish, I can arrange for you to wait somewhere more comfortable," he offered.

Jago thanked him and said, "That will not be necessary. But if you could have some food brought here, that would be a mercy."

"It will be done," replied the canon as he withdrew.

"That went well," Bran observed cheerfully.

"Job's bones, Bran," muttered Iwan. "You are a bold one. How can you think of food at a time like this?"

"I'm hungry," Bran said.

"I'm with Iwan," said Siarles. "Give me a fair fight any day. This skulking around the enemy camp fair gives me the pip."

"Steady on, boys," said Mérian, her voice altered by her wooden teeth. "All you need do is keep your eyes open and your mouths shut. Let Bran do the rest." Our lord smiled at her quick defence of him. "And you," she said to him, "see you get us out of here in the same condition we came in, and I might consider marrying you after all."

"Oh, if I thought that was possible, my love," he answered, taking her hand and kissing it, "then you would be amazed to see what I can do."

How this little dance might have continued we would never learn, for at that moment the door opened and three servants bearing platters of bread and sausage, and jars of watered wine entered the room, and hard on their heels none other than King William of England in the very solid flesh. We knew straightaway that it was Rufus: the fiery red hair; the high, ruddy complexion; the squat, slightly bowed legs; the spreading belly and beefy arms—all of which had been reported by anyone who'd met him. Well, who else could it be?

Attending the king were two noblemen, and our man Canon Laurent, who seemed unable to hold himself out of the proceedings.

The king of England was a younger man than I had imagined, but the life he led—the fighting and drinking and what all—was exacting a price. Still, he was formidable and with long, thick arms, heavy shoulders, and a deep chest, would have made a fearsome enemy on a battlefield. His short legs were slightly bent from a life in the saddle, as his father's were well reputed to have been, and like his father, his hair was red, but grizzled now and thinning. He looked like one of those fighting dogs I'd seen in market squares where their owners set them on bears or bulls for the wagering of a feast-day crowd.

Oh, he'd seen a few fights, had Bloody Red William, and won his share to be sure. As he stumped into the room, the glance from his beady, bloodshot eyes sweeping quickly left and right, he seemed as if he expected to meet an enemy army. Like that marketplace bulldog, he

865

appeared only too ready to take a bite out of whomever or whatever got in his way.

"*Quel est cette intrusion impolie?*" the king demanded, puffing himself up. He spoke quickly, and I had trouble understanding his somewhat pinched voice.

"*Pax vobiscum, meus senior rex regis,*" said Brother Alfonso, bowing nicely.

"Latin?" said the king, which even I could understand. "Latin? Mary and Joseph, someone tell him to speak French."

"*Paix, mon roi de seigneur,*" offered Brother Alfonso smoothly, and went on to introduce the king to his visitor.

"When you learn why we have come," said Bran, taking his place before the king as Jago translated his words for the French-speaking monarch, "you will forgive the intrusion."

"Will I, by the rood?" growled the king. "Try me, then. But I warn you, I rarely forgive much, and fools who waste my time—never!"

"If it be foolish to try to save your throne," Bran replied, his voice taking an edge the king did not mistake, "then fool I am. I have been called worse."

"Who are you?" demanded the king. "Leicester? Warwick? Do you know this man?"

"No, my lord," answered the younger of the two knights. "I have never seen him before."

"Nor I," answered the elder. "Any of them."

"Save my throne, eh?" said the king. I could see that, despite his bluster, he was intrigued. "My throne is not in danger."

"Is it not?" countered Bran. "I have good reason to believe otherwise. Your brother Duke Robert is raising rebellion against you."

"Tell me something I do not know," snorted the king. "If this is your message, you are the very fool I thought."

"This time, Lord King," replied Bran quickly, "he has the aid and support of Pope Clement and your brother Henry Beauclerc, and many others. It is my belief that they mean to force your abdication in favour of Duke Robert, or face excommunication."

This stole the swagger from the English monarch's tail, I can tell you. "I knew it!" he growled. To his knights, he said, "I told you they were scheming against me." Then, just as quick, he turned to Bran and demanded, "You have proof of this?"

"I do, Lord King," said Bran. "A document has come into my possession which has been signed by those making conspiracy against you."

"You have this document, do you?" said the king.

"I do, Sire," replied Bran.

William thrust out a broad, calloused hand. "Give it to me."

Bran put his hand inside his robe and brought out the folded parchment which had been so painstakingly copied by the monks at Saint Dyfrig's abbey. It was wrapped in its cloth, and Bran clutched it firmly in both hands. "Before I deliver it to you," he said, "I ask a boon."

"Ha!" sneered the king. "I might have guessed that was coming. You priests are always looking to your own interests. Well, what is it you want? Reward—is that what you want? Money?"

"No, Sire," said Bran, still holding out the document. "I want—"

"Yes?" said the king, impatience making him sharp. "What! Speak, man!"

"Justice," said Bran quietly. "I want justice."

Jago gave our lord's reply, to which William shouted, "You shall have it!" as he snatched the document away. Unwrapping the thick, folded square, he opened it out and stared at it long and hard. Glancing at Canon Laurent hovering nearby, he lifted a hand to the cleric and said, "This should be spoken in the presence of witnesses."

Some have said he never learned to read—at least, he could not

867

read French. "As it lays, pray you," he said, thrusting the letter into the cleric's hands. "Spare us nothing."

The canon took a moment to study the document, collected himself, cleared his throat, and began to read it out in a clear, strong voice. *"Moi Guillaume par le pardon de Dieu, de Bramber et Seigneur et Brienze, qux trés estimer et reverend Guibert et Ravenna. Salutations dans Dieu mai les tranquillité de Christ, Notré Éternelle Sauveur, rester á vous toujours."*

It was the letter Jago had read to us that day in Saint Dyfrig's following the Christmas raid. That Laurent read it with far more authority could not be denied; still, though I could understand but little of what he read, I remembered that day we had gathered in Bran's greenwood hut to see what we had got from the Ffreinc. The memory sent a pang of longing through me for those who waited there still. Would I ever hold Nóin in my arms again?

Canon Laurent continued, and his voice filled the room. It seemed that I heard with new ears as I listened to him read the letter again. Adding what I'd learned from Odo to my own small store, the dual purposes behind the words became plain. Yet the thing still held the mystery I had first felt when kneeling in Bran's greenwood hut and staring in quiet wonder at that great gold ring, and the fine gloves, and that wrapped square of expensive parchment. If I failed to see the sense, I had only to look at King William's face hardening into a ferocious scowl to know that whatever he heard in the high-flown words, he liked it not at all.

By the time Laurent reached the letter's conclusion and began reading out the names at the end, William was fair grinding his teeth to nubbins.

"Blood and thunder!" he shouted as the cleric finished. "Do they think to cast me aside like a gnawed bone?" Turning, he glared at the two knights with him. "This is treason, mark me! I will not abide it. By the Virgin, I will not!"

Bran, who had been closely watching Red William's reaction to the letter, glanced at Mérian, who gave him a secret smile. Straight and tall in the black robe of a priest, hands folded before him as he awaited the king's judgement, he appeared just then more lordly than the ruddy-faced English monarch by a long walk. The king continued to fume and foam awhile, and then, as is natural to a fella like him, he swiftly fell to despatching his enemies. "How came you by this letter?" he said, retrieving the parchment from the cleric's hands. "Where did you get it?"

Bran, calm and unruffled as a dove in a cote, simply replied, "I stole it, Sire."

"Stole it!" cried William, when Bran's words were translated for him. "Ha! I like that! Stole it, by the rood!"

"Who did you steal it from?" asked one of the knights, stepping forward.

"It was found among items sent by Baron de Braose to his nephew, Count Falkes in Elfael. The letter, along with a pair of gloves and a papal ring, was taken in a raid on the wagons carrying provisions."

"You attacked the wagons and stole the provisions?" asked the knight, speaking through Jago.

"I did, yes. The other items were returned to de Braose, along with a careful copy of the letter just read. You have before you the original, and they are none the wiser."

The knight stared at Bran, mystified. "Thievery and you a priest. Yet, you stand here and admit it?"

"I am not as you see me," replied the dark Welshman. "I am Bran ap Brychan, rightful ruler of Elfael. I was cheated out of my lands by the deceit of Baron de Braose. On the day my father rode out to swear fealty to Your Majesty, the baron killed my father and slaughtered his entire warband. He established his nephew, Count Falkes de Braose, on our lands and continually supplies him with soldiers, money, and provisions in order to further his rule. Together they have made slaves of my people, and forced them to help build fortresses from which to further oppress them. They have driven me and my followers into the forest to live as outlaws in the land our people have owned since time beyond reckoning. All this has been possible through the collusion of Cardinal Ranulf of Bayeux, who acts with the blessing and authority of the crown, and in the king's own name." Bran paused to let this dagger strike home, then concluded, "I have come before you this day to trade that which bears the names of the traitors"—he pointed to the letter still clutched in the king's tight grasp—"for the return of my throne and the liberation of my people."

Into the silence that followed this bold assertion, Bran added, "A throne for a throne—English for Welsh. A fair trade, I think. And justice is served."

Oh, that was well done! Pride swelled in me like a rising sun, and I basked in its warmth and glory. It was that sweet to me just then.

"You shameless and impudent rogue!" snarled the elder of the two knights. "You stand in the presence of your king and insinuate—"

"Leicester!" shouted King William. "Leave off! This man has done me a service, and though the circumstances may well be questionable"—he turned again to Bran—"I will honour it in the same spirit in which it has been rendered."

At this, Mérian, who had been able to follow most of what was said, clasped her hands and gave out a little gasp of joy. "God be praised!" she sighed.

"See here, my lord," protested the one called Leicester. "You cannot intend—"

"Hold your peace," cautioned William. "I do not yet know what I intend. First, I must know what my roguish friend Bran ap Brychan presumes." To Bran, he said, "You have presumed so much already, what do you propose for these traitors?"

All eyes were on Bran as Jago conveyed the king's words and Bran answered, his voice steady, "I leave their punishment in your hands, Sire. For myself I ask only the return of my lands and the recognition of my right to rule my people in peace."

"You ask a very great deal, thief," observed the second nobleman.

"And yet it is no more than my due," Bran countered.

"How do we know this letter is even genuine?" demanded the young knight.

"Do not be an ass," the king growled. "The thing is genuine. The imbecile de Braose affixed his seal. I know it well enough. We must think now what is to be done, and that quick. We have a day, likely less, before the others arrive in force. We must work quickly if we are to save ourselves from the trap they have laid for us."

King William folded the parchment and tucked it under his arm, then stepped forward, extending his hand to Bran. "My thanks and my friendship. You and your men are forthwith pardoned from any wrong-doing in this matter. Come, friend, we will sit and break fast together and decide what is to be done with those who would steal my kingdom."

871

CHAPTER 43

$\int$uch palaver with the high and mighty was hard on this simple forester, I can tell you. Ol' Will has had his fill of Ffreinc enough to last him all his allotted days thrice over. If every last one of those horse-faced foreigners were to hop ship back to Normandie, this son of Britain would sing like a lark for joy till the crack o' doom. Nevertheless, here we were up to our neck bones in Normans of every kind, and most of them with sharp steel close to hand.

It fair made me wish for the solace of the greenwood, it did.

And I wasn't the only one with my teeth on edge. Poor Siarles was about as rattled as a tadpole in a barrel of eels. The fella could neither sit nor stand, but that he had to be jumping up every other breath to run to the door to see if any Ffreinc were lurking about ready to pounce on us. Still, though we could hear men moving about the palace, both inside and out, as more of the nobles arrived for their council, they left us to ourselves. The morning passed into midday, and the waiting began to wear on us.

For myself, the pain in my throbbing hand and the toils of the past few days rolled over me like a millstone, and I curled up in a corner and closed my eyes.

"We should go find out what is happening," I heard Mérian say, and Iwan agreed.

"Aye," replied the big man. "Bran might need our help."

The two had just about worked themselves up to go and see what they could discover, Siarles was fussing and fretting, and Cinnia—too frightened to know what to do—had come to sit beside me, when the door opened and Bran and Jago strolled into the room.

You'd be forgiven for thinkin' they'd been twice around the moon and back the way we ran to greet them. Before either one of them could speak, Iwan swooped in. "Well?" he demanded.

"What did the king say?" asked Mérian. "Will he help us?"

"Will he give back our lands?" said Siarles, joining the tight cluster around Bran. "When can we go?"

I roused myself, and Cinnia helped me to my feet and we joined the others.

"Come, tell us, Bran," said Iwan. "What did the king say?"

"He said a great many things," Bran replied, his voice a sigh of resignation. "Not all of them seemly, or even sensible."

To my weary eye, our Bran and Brother Jago seemed a little frazzled and frayed from their encounter with the English monarch. "King William keeps a close counsel," Jago added. "He gives away little and demands much. Yet I believe he has a mind to help us insofar as it helps him to do so. Beyond that, who can say?"

Who could say, indeed!

We had risked all to bring word of high treason to the king—and now that he had it, we were to be swept aside like the crumbs of yesterday's supper.

"He didn't give us back our lands?" whined Siarles.

"No, he did not," Bran confirmed. "At least, not yet. We are to wait here for his answer."

Siarles blew air through his nostrils. "To think that after all this we are beholden to that fat toad of a king!" he grumbled. "We should have supported Duke Robert instead!"

"No, we made the right choice." Bran was firm on that point. "Listen to me, all of you, and do not forget: we made the right choice. William is king, and only William has the power to give us back our lands. The king is justice for the people who must live beneath his rule. Our only hope is Red William."

"Duke Robert would have been king and returned our lands to us," Siarles insisted. "If we had supported him, he would have supported us in turn, and we'd have what is ours by rights."

Mérian gave Siarles a glance that could have cut timber. The rough forester glared back at her, but mumbled, "If I have spoken above myself, I am sorry, my lord, and I do beg your pardon. It just seems that for all our trouble we are no better off than before."

Bran clapped his hand to the back of Siarles' neck, drew him close, and said, "Siarles, my friend, if you truly think supporting Robert would avail us anything, you might as well join those traitors who are even now gathering to work their wiles." Bran spoke softly, but there was no mistaking his resolve. "But while you are thinking on it, remember that Baron de Braose is one of the chief rebels. It is his hand squeezing our throats and his arm supporting Robert. If Duke Robert were to become king of England, bloody de Braose would become more powerful still, and he would never surrender his grip on our lands."

"Bran is right," Iwan declared. "The only way to get rid of de Braose is to expose him to the king."

"We have warned Red William in good time, and now he can move to disarm the traitors," Bran explained, releasing Siarles. "I have put our case before the king, and we must hope he succeeds in punishing those who have conspired against him."

"Well," said Siarles, rubbing his neck. He was still not completely convinced. "It seems we have no other hope."

"It has been this way from the start," Bran said. "We have done all we can. It is in God's hands."

See now, Bran was right. Never doubt it. We had no other hope for redress in this world, save William and William alone. But Siarles, bless his thick head, was not wrong to raise the question. Truth to tell, it was something I wondered at first myself—and it was not until Odo told me about the two popes that I began to see my way through that tangled wood. Why would Baron de Braose write a letter like that? Who was it for? Then I remembered who had signed that letter, and although I could not recall all the names, I remembered Duke Robert right enough, and wondered why the king's brother and one of Red William's dearest barons should be makin' up a letter like that.

Oh, it was a right riddle to be sure. But the answer was there starin' us in the face all along. We just didn't see it.

Yet sitting there in that rank pit of a gaol, a fella begins to see lots of things in a different way, if you know what I mean. Ol' Will had time to think and little else.

Even so, when my monkish scribe let out there were two popes, God knows I didn't believe him. Odo was so convinced, his conviction carried me along in the end. I considered it a mite curious that Baron de Braose should take up with Clement when the whole of England, so far as I knew, answered to a pope named Urban. What could it mean?

Two popes. One throne. What else could it mean but that the men who signed the letter had bartered their support for Pope Clement in order to gain the throne of England for their favourite, Duke Robert? Outright rebellion had been tried and had failed; Robert could not be trusted to enter the fray even in his own interest, as many an upright Englishman discovered to his hurt—my old master Aelred included, God rest him. So this time, they meant to use the church somehow. Although I could not rightly say how they meant to force the abdication, the more I thought about it, the more certain I became that the men who had put their names to that letter had formed a conspiracy with the aim of plucking the crown from William's round grizzled head and placing it on luckless brother Robert's. This is why de Braose was so murderously desperate to get that letter back. More valuable by far than the big gold ring or fine leather gloves—mere fancies, after all—that sealed square of parchment exposed the traitors and, if I guessed aright, was well worth a throne.

"God's hands or no," Mérian was saying, "I could wish we knew what was happening now. To have come this far only to be shut out sits ill, so it does."

"Never fear," Brother Jago replied. "God's ways may be mystery past finding out, but he hears all who call upon his name. Therefore, be of good cheer! God alone is our rock and our fortress, our friend and very present help in times of trouble."

"That was a sermon entire, Brother," observed Iwan. He turned to Bran and asked, "How much longer are we to loiter here?"

Some little time, I reckoned. As the day wore on, though we heard men moving in the corridors and rooms 'round about the palace, no one darkened our doorway. One by one, we settled back to wait. I sat propped against the wall in one corner, and after a time, Bran joined me. "How are the fingers, Will?" he asked, sliding down into his place beside me.

"Not so bad," I told him. "The pain comes and goes, but not so much as before." I did not like dwelling on that, so I asked, "What do you think Red William will do?"

Bran was quick to reply. "I expect he'll give back our lands," he said, an edge to his voice. "Brother Jago was eloquent on our behalf, and I think we made him understand in the end. He promised justice, and we will hold him to it."

That, of course, was deeply to be hoped. "We owe you a debt, Will Scarlet," he said. "Your quick thinking gave us the chance we needed to save Elfael."

"Well, it took me long enough," I allowed, "but we got here in time. That is all that matters."

"There's still one thing I wonder," Bran said. "How did you work out the nature of the conspiracy?"

"Well, now," I said, running back over the events of the last days in my mind. "It was all those days talking to Odo and getting an idea how those Normans think—that's what started it. Then, when I learned about the two popes, it seemed to me that the letter was intended as a treaty of sorts—why else write it all down?"

"A treaty," mused Bran. "I never thought of that. You mean Duke Robert and Baron de Braose agreed to support Clement's claim to the throne of Peter, if the pope would support Robert's claim to the throne of England."

"Our William is not well loved," I added. "And, as I know from my old master Aelred, his barons almost succeeded in unseating the king last time they rebelled. I reckoned things have only got worse for them since then. I know William is no lover of the church."

"He uses it as his own treasure store," Bran said. "Helps himself whenever he can."

"Aye, he does—and that's the nub. Our William milks it like a cow, keeping all the cream for himself. But if that was to stop, his throne would begin to totter, if you see what I mean."

"With both the barons and the church against him, the king could not stand," observed Bran. "I got that much from your message."

"A bit o' blind luck, that," I told him, shaking my head at the remarkable string of events that small patch of parchment had set off. "I wasn't sure what you'd make of it, or what you'd be able to do about it. I didn't even dare hope that scrap would reach you. I had only Odo to depend on, mind. He's a Norman, but he gave good service in the end. I'd like to do something for him one day." I paused and looked around the bare room and at our unlikely company. "God's own truth, my lord, I never dreamed it would come to this—squattin' in the palace of the archbishop of Rouen and waitin' for the king of England to decide our fate."

"My lord!" said Siarles, speaking up from his place across the room. "Are we to be expected to sit here all day like moss on a log?"

As if to answer his question, there was a bustle in the corridor and the door to our chamber opened. Canon Laurent strode into the room with two clerics dressed in robes similar to his own; with them were three knights from King William's force. All wore solemn expressions. The knights carried swords at their belts, and two gripped lances. The canon held a scrap of parchment and carried it flat between his hands as if the ink was still wet on the surface of the page. "Peace and grace," said the canon, which I understood. "I have come directly from private council with King William, who expresses his highest regards, and sends this message to you."

Mérian stepped beside Bran and slid her hand into his. They stood side by side, an unlikely pair in their disguises. The rest of us drew near, too, taking our places beside our lord and his lady to receive the judgement of the king. Whatever the king's decision might be, whether for good or ill, we would take it standing together as one.

"Hear the king's words," said Laurent, raising the parchment. "Be it known that in gratitude for his good service to our crown and throne, William, by the grace of God, king of England, does hereby bestow the sum of thirty pounds in silver to be used to aid and assist Lord Bran ap Brychan and his company to return home by the way he has come . . ."

"What?" complained Iwan, when this much had been translated for us. "He's sending us home? What about the return of our lands?"

"Peace, Iwan." Bran held up his hand for silence. He nodded to Jago.

"Pray, continue," Jago said to the canon.

"Further," resumed Laurent, "His Majesty, King William, serves notice that you are commanded to attend him at the royal residence at Winchester on the third day after the Feast of the Archangels, known as Michaelmas. At that appointed place and time you will receive the king's judgement in the matters laid before him this day."

Here Laurent broke off. Looking up from the proclamation, he said, "Do you understand what I have read to you?"

When Jago had finished translating these words, Bran said, "With all respect to the king, we will stay here and await his judgement. It may be that we can help bear witness against the rebels."

"No," answered the cleric, "after today it will be too dangerous for you to remain here, and the king cannot ensure your safety. The king has commanded that you are to be escorted to your ship at once and you are to make your way home by the swiftest means possible. His Majesty the king wishes you a pleasant journey and may God speed you in all safety to your destination."

Steal breath from a baby, we were stunned.

We had come all this way prepared to bargain, plead, fight tooth and nail for the return of our lands only to be tossed lightly onto the midden heap like so much dung. It beggared belief, I can tell you. Though Bran tried to get the canon to see the thing as we did, and though the cleric sympathised in his way, Laurent could do nothing. The king had allowed him no room to wiggle; there was nothing for it but to take the money and go.

Red William is every inch as much a rogue as any of his bloody barons, no mistake. The king's knights escorted us to our horses and accompanied us back down the hill and through the town to the river wharf and our waiting ship. We rode in silence all the way, and my own heart was heavy until we came in sight of the *Dame Havik* at her mooring—and then I remembered Nóin. Suddenly, I cared no longer about the doings of the high and mighty. My sole aim and desire was to see my love and hold her in my arms—and each moment I was prevented from doing that was a moment that chafed and chapped me raw. From the instant I set foot on the deck of that ship to the day I stepped off it and onto solid English earth once more, I was a man with an itch I could not scratch.

When on that fine, sunny day we bade our friend Ruprecht farewell and took our leave a little lighter in the pocket, to be sure—for we paid that Flemish sailor well for his excellent and praiseworthy care— it was all I could do to keep from lashing my poor mount all the way back to Elfael. I counted the quarters of the days until I at last saw the greenwood rising in the distance on the slopes of the ridge beyond the Vale of Wye, and then I counted the steps as I watched that great shaggy pelt bristling beneath a sky of shining blue and my heart beat faster for the sight. S'truth, only the man who has journeyed to far distant lands and returned to his native earth after braving dangers, toil, and hardships aplenty can know how I felt just then. I was seized by joy and flown to dizzy heights of elation only to be dashed to the rocks again with the very next thought. For as glad as I was to be going

88]

home, I was that afraid something might yet prevent me reaching the one I loved. All saints bear witness, our little company could not move fast enough for me. I fair wore out the goodwill of my companions long before we reached the blasted oak at the entrance to Cél Craidd.

When I came in sight of that black stump, I threw myself from the saddle and was halfway to the lightning-riven oak as through heaven's own gate before I noticed someone standing there.

"Nóin?" I could scarce believe my eyes. She was there waiting for me!

"Is that you, Will Scarlet?" Her voice held a quiver. Surprise? Uncertainty? But she made no move toward me.

I stepped nearer, my heart beating high up in my throat, and put out a hand to her. "It is . . . ," I replied, unable to speak above a whisper just then. "It is Will come home."

She regarded me with an almost stern expression, her eyes dry. "Have you, Will? Have you come home at last?"

"That I have, my love." I stepped nearer. "Now that I see you, I know I am home at last."

As many times as I saw this glad reunion in my mind, I did not see it this way. She nodded. I saw her swallow then, and guessed something of what this confrontation—for such it was—cost her. But she did not back down. She held me with her uncompromising gaze. "I have to know, Will," she said, "if you've come back to stay. I cannot wait for you any longer. I have to know."

"Nóin, my love, with God as my witness, I will nevermore part from you."

"Don't!" she cried. "Don't you say that. You don't know."

"What do you want me to say?" I asked. "If it is a pledge you seek, tell me what pledge you will accept and I will give it gladly." As she considered this, I added, "I love you, Nóin. I loved you every blesséd day I lay in that dark hole, and if I could have come to you even a heartbeat sooner, I would have been back at your side long ere you knew I'd gone."

She bent her head then, and her long hair fell down around her face. I could see her lips trembling.

"Nóin," I said, moving closer. "If you no longer want me, you have only to say the word and I will leave you be. Is that what you want?"

She shook her head, but did not look at me.

I raised my arms and held them out to her. "Then come to me, my love. Let us return to the happiness we once knew. Or, if that be not possible anymore, let us begin a new and better joy."

When she raised her head this time, I saw the tears streaking her fair cheeks. "Oh, Will . . . ," she sobbed. "I've missed you so much . . . so much . . . I did not dare to hope . . ."

She came into my arms, and I crushed her to my chest with all the strength I did possess. I held her and felt the hardness in her melt away as she clung to me, her tears soaking into my shirt.

"Will dear, sweet Will, I'm so sorry," she said. "I had to be sure. I couldn't live thinking . . . forgive me."

"There is nothing to forgive. I am here now, and I love you more than ever I did the day I left."

"And will you yet wed me?" she asked, looking tearfully into my face.

The sight of those tears glistening on her cheeks melted any shreds of dignity I might have had left. I sank to my knees before her and clasped her around the waist. "Marry me, Nóin. I want you so bad it hurts my heart."

The words were still fresh on my lips when I felt her arms encircle my neck; she raised me to my feet, and her warm lips bathed my scruffy face in kisses. "Nóin . . . ," I gasped when I could breathe again. "Oh, Nóin, I will never leave you. I swear . . ."

"Shh," she hushed. "Don't speak, Will. Just hold me."

I was happy to do that, no mistake. We stood there in the heart of the greenwood clutching one another so tight we could hardly draw a breath between us. And we were clinging still when the others reached the riven oak where we stood. They dismounted, and Bran let out a wild, withering screech. Instantly, the Grellon began pouring up out of the bowl of Cél Craidd to greet the return of their king and kinsmen.

The next thing I knew, I was half pulled, half pushed through the oak and tumbled down the hillside into the bowl of our hidden settlement. At first glance, everything appeared just as I remembered it—only it was early summer now, and I had left in the dead of winter. Still, all was as it should be, I reckoned, until I began to tell the little differences. The forest folk were right glad to see us, but there was a hollow sound to their laughter, and their smiles, though genuine and heartfelt, held more pain than pleasure. The faces gathered 'round us were greyer than I remembered, the bodies thinner. Winter had been hard for them, yes, and spring no better, I reckoned. Many were gaunt, with skin pinched around their deep-set eyes; their clothes were that much more tattered and frayed; the dirt on their hands and faces was there for good and always.

My heart went out to them. I had endured captivity in the sheriff's odious hellhole, but they were no less captive here. The wildwood of Coed Cadw had become as much a prison as any that the vile de Glanville held key to. It was clear to me then, if never before: this sorry state could not be endured much longer. God willing, our bold King William would soon give us redress, and Bran and all us forest folk could move out into the light once more.

In amongst the young 'uns I saw little Nia's face poking out. I turned and scooped her up. She did not cry out, but twisted in my arms to see who held her. "Weo!" she squealed, grabbing my beard with both hands. "Wee-o!"

Bless her, she was trying to say my name. "It's me, dear heart. Ol' Will is here."

From among the flock gathering to greet our return, I glimpsed Angharad, hobbling forward on her long staff, her wrinkled face alight with pleasure. "I bid thee glad homecoming, William Scatlocke," she crowed, her old voice quavering slightly. "The Lord of Hosts is smiling on this day."

"Greetings, Wise Banfáith," I said, offering her a bow and touching the back of my hand to my forehead. "It is that good to see you again."

"And you, Will." She drew close and stood for a moment, smiling up at me. Then, closing her eyes, she raised her hand and touched two fingers lightly to my forehead. "All Wise and Loving Father, we thank you for redeeming the life of our friend, delivering him from his enemies, and bringing him back to us in answer to our prayers. Bless him and prosper him for your name's sake, and bless all who think well of him this day and all days henceforth."

As she prayed, I felt Nóin's hand squeeze my arm. I thanked our bard and then turned to the others who were crowding in to make good my welcome. "Here now! Here now!" came a shout, and I was enwrapped and lifted off my feet in a rib-cracking embrace.

"Tuck!" I said. "Are you here, too?"

"Where else should I be, but among my own dear flock on the day of your miraculous return? We've been waiting for this day with a greedy impatience, my friend," he said, his round face beaming. God bless him, there were tears in his eyes.

"Brother," I said, pulling Nóin close, "if you are not too busy, this lady and I are that keen to be married. If you have no objection, I want you to perform the ceremony today."

"Today!" replied Tuck. "Today, says he! Well!" To Nóin, he said, "Is this also your desire?"

"It is my deepest desire," she replied, her arm around my waist.

"Well, then," concluded Tuck, "I do not see any reason to delay." He glanced around. "What have you done with Bran and the others?"

Casting a glance behind me, I saw my travelling companions standing on the top of the low natural rampart that surrounded Cél Craidd. I called to them. "Why were you standing there?" I asked when they had joined us.

"We wanted you to have a proper greeting all to yourself," Iwan explained.

"And would you leave me standing here alone on my wedding day?" I said.

"Oh, Will! Nóin!" cried Mérian. She pressed Nóin's hands in hers, then kissed me lightly on the cheek. "This is such good news."

We then endured the good wishes of Bran, Iwan, and the others in turn, and I was pummelled good-naturedly by one and all. When the festive drubbing was finished, I turned to Tuck and said, "Friar, I'd be much obliged if you could perform the rites without delay." I glanced at Nóin and saw the desire in her dark eyes. "As soon as may be."

Tuck nodded and adopted a solemn air. "Is it your wish to be married to this man?" he asked.

"It is, Friar," she replied. "I would have done it long since, and there is no better day that I know than this, and I would mark it always in my heart as the day my man was given back to me."

"Then so be it!"

Turning to the Grellon crowding around, the little friar called, "Hear now! Will and Nóin have declared their desire to be married. Let us give them a wedding they will never forget!"

If I had any notion of simply saying a few words before the priest and carrying off my bride to a little greenwood bower in the manner of my English father, that idea was dashed to pieces quicker than it

886

takes a fella to spit and say "I do!" The forest folk fell to with a will. I suppose the safe and successful return of the rescue party was the best excuse any of them had had to celebrate anything in many a month, and the people were that eager to make a fair run at it. Nóin and I were immediately caught up in the preparations for this sudden celebration.

The cooking fire was built up; partridges and quail were pulled from the snares, then plucked and spitted along with half a young wild pig, and six coneys and a score of barley loaves set to bake. The children were sent into the thickets to gather raspberries and red currants, which were mixed with honey and made into a deep red compote; asparagus and wild mushrooms were likewise picked, chopped, and boiled into a stew with borage and herbs; the last of the walnuts which had been dried over the winter were shelled into a broth of milk and honey; and many another dish to make the heart glad. Whatever stores had been set aside against even leaner days were brought out for our wedding feast, and it did rightly make a humble man of me, I can tell you.

While the men constructed a bower of birch branches for us to enjoy our first night together, some of the women gathered flowers to strew our path and for Nóin to carry, and one or two of the younger ones helped dress the bride and make her even more lovely in my eyes.

As for myself, with little else to do, I set about trying to drag a razor through the tough tangle of my beard. I succeeded in cutting myself in such extravagant fashion that our good friar took the blade from my hand, sat me down and, expert barber that he was, shaved me clean as a newborn. He also combed and cut my hair so that I appeared almost a nobleman when my clothes were brushed and my shoes washed. He found a new belt for me and a clean cloak of handsome green. "There now!" he declared, like God regarding Adam with a critical eye. "I have made me a man."

I thanked him kindly for his attentions, and observed that my only regret was that I had no ring to give my bride. "A ring is a fine thing, is it not?" he agreed. "But it is by no means necessary. A coin will do; and some, I have heard, have a smith bend the coin to make a ring. You might easily do this."

This cheered me no end. "You are a wonder, no mistake," I told him. "I can get a coin." And, leaving the friar to his own preparations, I set off to do just that.

The first person I went to was Bran. "My lord," I said, "I do not think I have asked a boon of you since swearing the oath of fealty."

Lord Bran allowed that, as he could not think of any occasions, either.

"Then, if it please you, my lord," I continued, "I will make bold to request the small favour of a coin to give my bride." I quickly went on to explain that I had no ring, but that Tuck had said a coin would serve as a suitable token.

"Indeed?" wondered Bran. "Then leave it to me."

Well, we were soon caught up in countless small activities and the mood was high. Before I knew it, the sun had already begun its descent when our good friar declared that all was finally ready and we gathered beneath the Council Oak to speak our vows before our friends. Tuck, scrubbed until he gleamed, and beaming like a cherub fresh from the Radiant Presence, took his place before us and called all to solemn purpose. "This is a holy time," he said, "and a joyous celebration. Our Heavenly Father delights in love in all its wondrous forms. Especially dear to him is the love between a husband and wife. May such love increase!"

This brought a rousing chorus of agreement from the onlookers, and Tuck waited for silence before continuing. "Therefore," he said, "let us ask the Author and Sustainer of our love and life to bless the

888

union of these two dear people who have pledged life and love to one another."

With that he began to pray and prayed so long I feared we would not finish the ceremony until the sun had gone down, or possibly the next morning. Eventually, he ran out of words to say to bless and beseech, and moved on to the vows, which we spoke out as Tuck instructed. There in the greenwood, beneath that venerable oak, we pledged life to life, come what may, and I took Nóin to be my wife. When the time came to give my bride a token of honour, I turned to Bran and, taking my one good hand in both of his, he pressed a coin into my palm. "With greatest esteem and pleasure," he said.

I looked down and saw that he had given me a solid gold byzant, gleaming dull and heavy in my hand. I gazed at that rare coin as at a fortune entire. Truly, I had never had anything worth so much in all my life. That he should think so much of me made the tears come to my eyes. The long months of my captivity were somehow redeemed in that moment as I placed that matchless coin in the hand of my beloved, pledging to honour and keep her through all things forever more.

Then it was another prayer—this one for children aplenty to bless us and keep us in our old age—and we knelt together as Tuck placed a hand on each of our heads and proclaimed, "I present to you Master William Scatlocke and his wife, Nóinina. All praise to our Lord and Kind Creator for his wise provision!"

Of the feast, I remember little. I am told it was very good, and I must have tasted some of it. But my appetite was elsewhere by then, and I could not wait until Nóin and I could be together. We sat on the bench at the head of the board and received the good wishes of our friends. Mérian, with Lord Bran in tow, came by twice to say how much she had longed for this day on our behalf. Iwan and Siarles came to give us an old poem that they knew, full of words with double

meanings which soon had everyone screaming with laughter. The celebration was so light and full of joy that I clean forgot about my mangled fingers, and I cannot recall giving them a solitary thought all that
fine and happy day.

When the moon rose and the fire was banked high, Angharad
brought out her harp and began to sing. She sang a song unknown to
me, as to most of us, I suppose, about a beautiful maiden who conceived a love for a man she had seen passing by her window one day.
The young woman decided to follow the stranger, braving great hardship crossing mountain and moor in her quest to find him once more
and declare her love for him. She persevered through many terrors and
misfortunes and at last came into the valley where her love lived. He
saw her approaching—her beautiful gown begrimed and bedraggled,
her fine leather shoes worn through and wrapped in rags, her beautiful hair dull with dust from the road, her once-fair cheeks sunken with
hunger, her slender fingers worn, her full lips chapped and bleeding—
and ran to meet her. As she came near, however, she chanced to see her
own reflection in a puddle in the road, and horrified at what she saw,
she turned and ran away. The man pursued her and caught her, and
knowing what she had endured to find him, his heart swelled with love
for her. And in that moment, he saw her as she was, and the power of
his love transformed her broken form into one even more beautiful
than that which had been.

I confess, there might have been more, but I was only listening
with half an ear, for I was gazing at my own lovely bride and wishing
we could steal away to the birch bower in the wood. Bran must have
guessed what was in my mind, for as the song concluded and the
people called for another, he came up behind me and said, "Go now,
both of you. Mérian and I will take your places."

We did not need urging. That quick I was up and out of my seat and taking Nóin by the hand. We flitted off into the wood, leaving Bran and Mérian at the board. By the light of a summer moon, we made our way along the path to the bower, where candles were already lit and the mead in a jar warming by a small fire. Fleeces had been spread on a bed of fresh rushes. There was food beneath a cloth for us to break our fast in the morning. "Oh, Will!" said Nóin, when she saw it, "It is lovely—just as I always hoped it would be."

"And so, my lady, are you," I told her, and, pulling her close, kissed her with the first of countless kisses we would share that night.

As for the rest, I need not say more. If you have ever loved anyone, then you will know full well. If not, then nothing I can say will enlighten you.

CHAPTER 44

Caer Rhodl

Even though he had known this day was coming, the news caught Baron Neufmarché off his guard. He had just returned from a short trip to Lundein and afterward gone to his chapel to observe Mass and to offer a prayer of thanks for his safe return and a season of gainful commerce. Father Gervais was officiating, and the old priest who usually mumbled through the service in a low, unintelligible drone, perked up when the lord of Hereford appeared in the doorway of the small, stone church tucked inside the castle wall.

Priest and worshipper acknowledged one another with a glance and a nod, as the baron slipped into the enclosed wooden stall which served his family during their observances in the chapel. The priest moved through the various sequences of the daily office, lifting his voice and lingering over the scripture passages so that the baron, whose Latin he knew to be limited, could follow more easily. He chanted with his eyes closed, saying, "*Deus, qui omnipoténtiam tuam parcéndo maxime et miserando maniféstas,*" his old voice straining after the notes that once came so easily.

At those long familiar strains, Bernard felt himself relax; the toil of his recent journey overtook him, and he slumped back on the bench and rested his head against the high back of the stall. He was soon asleep, and remained happily so until some inner prompting woke him at the beginning of the dismissal. Upon hearing the words *"Dominus vobiscum,"* he roused himself and sat up.

Father Gervais was making the sign of the cross above the altar of the near-empty sanctuary. *"Benedicat vos omnipotens Deus Pater, et Filius, et Spiritus Sanctus,"* he intoned, his deep voice loud in the small, stone chapel; and Neufmarché joined him in saying, "Amen."

The service concluded, the elderly priest stepped down from the low platform to greet the baron. "Dear Bernard," he said, extending his hands in welcome, "you have returned safely. I trust your journey was profitable?"

"It was, Father," answered the baron. He stifled a yawn with the back of his hand. "Very profitable." The old man took his arm and the two walked out into the brilliant light of a glorious late-summer day. "And how are things with you, Father?" he said as they stepped into the shaded path between the castle rampart and the rising wall of the tower keep.

"About the same, my son. Oh, yes, well . . ." He paused a moment to collect his thoughts. "Ah, now then. But perhaps you haven't heard yet. I fear I may be the bearer of bad news, Bernard."

"Bad news, Father?" The baron had not heard anything on the road, nor in the town when he passed through. None of the household servants had hinted that anything was amiss; he had not seen Lady Agnes since his return, otherwise he would certainly have been informed. His wife delighted in ill tidings—the worse the better. He glanced at the old man beside him, but Father Gervais did not appear distraught in the least. "I have heard nothing."

"A rider arrived this morning from your foreign estates—what do you call them? Eye-ass?"

"Eiwas," the baron corrected gently. "It is a commot in Wales, Father, ruled by my client, Lord Cadwgan—a local nobleman enfeoffed to me."

"Ah, your liegeman, yes." The doddering priest nodded.

"The messenger, Father," prompted Neufmarché gently, "what did he say?"

"He said that the king has died," said the priest. "Would that be the same one, King Kad . . . Kadeuka . . . no, that can't be right."

"Cadwgan," corrected Neufmarché. "King Cadwgan is dead, you say?"

"I am sorry, Bernard, but yes. There is to be a funeral, and they are wanting to know if you would attend. I asked the fellow to wait for you, but we didn't know when you would return, so he went on his way."

"When is the funeral to be held?"

"Well." The priest smiled and patted his temple. "This old head may not work as swiftly as once it did, but I do not forget." He made a calculation, tapping his chin with his fingertips. "Two days from tomorrow, I believe. Yes, something like that."

"In three days!" exclaimed the baron.

"I think that's what he said, yes," agreed the priest affably. "Is it far, this Eye-as place?"

"Far enough," sighed the baron. He could reach Caer Rhodl in time for the funeral, but he would have to leave at once, with at least one night on the road. Having just spent six days travelling, the last thing he wanted was to sit another three days in the saddle.

A brief search led the baron to the one place he might have guessed his wife would be found. She was sitting in the warmest room of Castle Hereford—a small, square chamber above the great hall. It had no feature other than a wide, south-facing window which, during the long summer, admitted the sunlight the whole day through. Lady Agnes, dressed in a gauzy fluff of pale yellow linen, had set up her tapestry frame beside the wide-open window and was plying her needle with a fierce, almost vengeful concentration. She glanced up as he came in, needle poised to attack, saw who it was, and as if stabbing an enemy, plunged the long needle into the cloth before her. "You have returned, my lord," she observed, pulling the thread tight. "Pleasant journey?"

"Pleasant enough," said Neufmarché. "You have fared well in my absence, I trust."

"I make no complaint."

Her tone suggested that his absence was the cause of no end of tribulations, too tiresome to mention now that he was back. *Why did she always do that?* he wondered, and decided to ignore the comment and move straight to the meat of the matter at hand. "Cadwgan has died at last," he said. "I must go to the funeral."

"Of course," she agreed. "How long will you be away this time?"

"Six days at least," he answered. "Eight, more like. I'd hoped I'd seen the last of the saddle for a while."

"Then take a carriage," suggested Agnes, striking with the needle once more.

"A carriage." He stared at her as if he'd never heard the word before. "I will not be seen riding in a carriage like an invalid," he sniffed.

"You are a baron of the March," his wife pointed out. "You can do what you like. There is no shame in travelling in comfort with an entourage as befits a man of your rank and nobility. You could also travel at night, if need be."

The baron spied a table in the corner of the room and, on it, a silver platter with a jar and three goblets. He strode to the table and took up the jar to find that it contained sweet wine. He poured himself a cup, then poured one for his lady wife. "If I got a carriage, you could come to the funeral with me," he said, extending the goblet to her.

"Me?" What little colour she had drained from the baroness's thin face; the needle halted in midflight. "Go to Wales? Perish the thought. *C'est impossible!* No."

"It is not impossible," answered her husband, urging the cup on her. "I go there all the time, as you know."

She shook her head, pursing her thin lips into a frown. "I will not consort with barbarians."

"They are not barbarians," the baron told her, still holding out the cup of wine. "They are crude and uneducated, true, and given to strange customs, God knows. But they are intelligent in their own way, and capable of many of the higher virtues."

Lady Agnes folded her spindly arms across her narrow bosom. "That is as may be," she allowed coolly. "But they are a contentious and bloody race who love nothing more than carving Norman heads from Norman shoulders." She shivered violently and reached for the shawl that was perpetually close to hand. "You have said as much yourself."

"In the main, that may be true," the baron granted, warming to the idea of his wife's company as he contemplated the more subtle nuances of the situation. To arrive at the funeral on horseback leading a company of mounted knights and men-at-arms would certainly reinforce his position as lord and master of the cantref—but arriving with the baroness beside him in a carriage, accompanied by a domestic entourage, would firmly place his visit on a more social and personal footing. This, he was increasingly certain, was just the right note to strike with Cadwgan's family, kinsmen, countrymen, and heir. In short, he was convinced it was an opportunity not to be missed.

Placing the goblet firmly in her hand, he drank from his cup and

897

declared, "Ordinarily, I would agree with you. However, my Welsh fiefdom is an exception. We have been on productive and peaceful terms for many years, and your appearance at this time will commence a new entente between our two noble houses."

Lady Agnes frowned and glared into her cup as if it contained poison. She did not like the way this conversation was going, but saw no way to disarm the baron in his full-gallop charge. "May it please you, my lord," she said, shoving back her chair and rising to her feet, "I will send with you a letter of condolence for the women of the house and my sincere regret at not being able to offer such comforts in person."

She stepped around the tapestry frame to where the baron was standing, rose up on her toes, and kissed his forehead, then bade him good afternoon. Bernard watched his wife—head high, back stiff—as she walked to the door. Oh, she could be stubborn as a barnyard ass. In that, she was her father's daughter to the last drop of her Angevin blood.

She might balk, but she would do as she was told. He hurried to his chambers below and called for his seneschal. "Remey," he said when his chief servant appeared carrying a tray laden with cold meat, cheese, bread, and ale. "I need a carriage. Lady Agnes and I will attend the funeral of my Welsh client, Cadwgan. My lady's maidservants will attend her, and tell my sergeant to choose no fewer than eight knights and as many men-at-arms. Tell them to make ready to march before nightfall."

"It will be done, Sire," replied the seneschal, touching the rolled brim of his soft cap.

"Thank you," said Neufmarché with a gesture of dismissal. As the ageing servant reached the door, the baron called out, "And Remey! See to it that the carriage is good and stout. The roads are rock-lined ruts beyond the March. I want something that will get us there and back without breaking wheels and axles at every bump."

898

"To be sure, my lord," replied Remey. "Will you require anything else?"

"Spare no effort. I want it ready at once," the baron said. "We must leave before the day is out if we are to reach Caer Rhodl in time."

The seneschal withdrew, and the baron sat down to his meal in solitude, his thoughts already firmly enmeshed in grand schemes for his Welsh commot and his long-cherished desire for expansion in the territory. Prince Garran would take his father's place on the throne of Eiwas, and under the baron's tutelage would become the perfect tool in the baron's hand. Together they would carve a wide swathe through the fertile lowlands and grass-covered slopes of the Welsh hill country. The Britons possessed a special knack with cattle, it had to be admitted; when matched with the insatiable Norman appetite for beef, the fortune to be made might well exceed even the baron's more grandiose fancies.

The carriage Remey chose for the journey was surprisingly comfortable, muffling the judders and jolts of the deeply rutted roads and rocky trackways, making the journey almost agreeable. Accompanied by a force of sixteen knights and men-at-arms on horseback, and a train of seven pack mules with servants to attend them, they could not have been more secure. The baron noted that even Lady Agnes, once resigned to the fact that there was no escaping her fate, had perked up. After the second day, a little colour showed in her pale cheeks, and by the time the wooden fortress that was Caer Rhodl came into view, she had remarked no fewer than three times how good it was to get out of the perpetual chill of the castle. *"Merveilleux!"* she exclaimed as a view of the distant mountains hove into view. "Simply glorious."

"I am so glad you approve, my dear," remarked the baron dryly.

"I had no idea it could be like this," she confessed. "So wild so beautiful. And yet . . ."

"Yes?"

"And yet so, so very, very empty. It makes me sad somehow—the *mélancolie*, no? Do not tell me you do not feel it, my love."

"Oh, but I do," answered the baron, taking unexpected delight in his headstrong wife's rare reversal of opinion. "I do feel it. No matter how often I visit the lands beyond the March, I always sense a sorrow I cannot explain—as if the hills and valleys hold secrets it would break the heart to hear."

"Yes, perhaps," granted Agnes. "Quaint, yes, and perhaps a little mysterious. But not frightening. I thought it would be more frightening somehow."

"Well, as you see it today, with the sun pouring bright gold upon the fields, it does appear a more cheerful place. God knows, that is not always the way."

In due course, the travelling company was greeted on the road by riders sent out from the caer to welcome them and provide a proper escort into Cadwgan's stronghold. Upon entering the circular yard behind the timber palisade, they were met by Prince Garran and his three principal advisors—one of his own and two who had served his father for many years.

"Baron Neufmarché!" called Garran, striding forth with his arms outspread in welcome as his guests stepped down from the carriage. "*Pax vobiscum*, my lord. God be good to you."

"And to you," replied the baron. "I could wish this a happier time, but I think we all knew this day would come. Now that it is here, my sympathies are with you and your mother. You have suffered much, I think, the past two years."

"We struggle on," replied the prince.

"You do," agreed the baron, "and it does you credit." He turned to his wife and presented her to the young prince.

"Baroness Neufmarché," said Garran, accepting her hand. "Rest assured that we will do all in our power to make your stay as pleasant as possible."

"Lady Agnes, if you please," she replied, delighted at the prince's dark good looks and polite manner—not to mention his facility in her own language. The baroness thanked her handsome young host and was in turn presented to Cadwgan's widow, Queen Anora. "My lady, may God be gracious to you in your season of mourning," Agnes said, speaking in simple French though she suspected the queen did not fully comprehend. Prince Garran smoothly translated for his mother, who smiled sadly and received the baroness's condolences with austere grace.

"Please, come inside," said Garran, directing his guests towards the hall. "We have prepared a repast to refresh you from your journey. Tonight we will begin the feast of remembrance."

"And the funeral ceremony?" inquired the baron.

"That will take place later today at twilight. The feast follows the burial."

They were led to the hall, where a number of mourners were gathered. Lady Agnes, who had imagined the Welsh to be dressed in rough pelts, their faces tattooed in weird designs, and feathers in their hair and necklaces made from the bones of birds and small animals, was pleasantly impressed with not only the general appearance of the barbarians—most of whom were dressed neither better nor worse than the typical English or French serf of her limited acquaintance—but with their solemn, almost stoic dignity as well. The room was festooned with banners of various tribes and illumined by the light of countless beeswax candles, the warm scent of which mingled with that of the clean rushes bestrewing the floor. On trestles set up in the centre of the room, on a board covered with fresh juniper branches, lay

901

King Cadwgan himself, covered in his customary cloak, on which was placed a large white-painted wooden cross.

Lady Agnes blanched to see him, but no one else seemed to consider it odd that the deceased should reside in the hall surrounded, as in life, by his subjects and kinsmen. Indeed, every now and then, one of the mourners would come forward to stroke the head of the dead king, whose hair had been washed and brushed to form a wispy nimbus around his head. One by one, the new arrivals were introduced to the other notables in the room, and they were given shallow bowls of mead to drink. Kitchen servants and young girls circulated with trays of small parcels of spiced meat, nuts, and herbs wrapped in pastry, which they served to the funeral guests.

The baroness, although unable to understand anything that was said around her—or perhaps because of it—began watching these courtesies intently. What she saw was a people, whether highborn or low, who seemed to enjoy one another's company and, crude as they undeniably were, revelled in the occasion. A time of sadness, of course, yet the funereal room rang with almost continual laughter. In spite of any previous notions, she found herself drawn to the unabashed sincerity of these folk and was moved by their honest displays of kindness and fellowship.

Thus, the mourners occupied themselves until the sun began to set, at which time a body of priests and monks arrived. As if on signal the mourners began to sing, and though the words were strange and there were no musical instruments, Agnes thought she had never heard music so sweetly sad. After a lengthy stint of singing, a grey-robed priest who seemed to be in charge of the proceedings stepped to the bier and, bowing three times, stretched his hands over the corpse and began to pray. He prayed in Latin, which the baroness had not expected. The prayer, while curious in its expression, was more or less like any she might have heard in Angevin.

When the prayer was finished, the priest was given a crosier—by which Agnes was given to know that he was actually a bishop. Striking the crosier on the floor three times, he gestured to the board. Six men of the tribe stepped forward and, taking their places around the dead king, lifted the board from the trestles and carried it from the hall. The mourners all fell into place behind them, and in this way they were led out into the yard and down from the fortress mound into the valley, eventually arriving in the yard of a small wooden church, where a grave had been dug within the precinct of the low, stone-walled yard. The grave was lined with large flat flagstones, some of which had been roughly shaped for the purpose.

The mourners paused to remove their shoes before entering the churchyard, which Lady Agnes considered very odd; but entering the holy precinct barefoot stirred her soul more profoundly than anything which had happened thus far. When the body on its board was carefully lowered into the hole prepared to receive it by six barefoot men, her ever-watchful eyes grew a little moist at the corners. There were prayers over the grave, and still more when the earth was replaced in the hole, covering the dead king. Then, this part of the service concluded, the people began drifting away in small clumps of two or three.

It was simple, but genuine and heartfelt, and the sincerity of the people winsome. Agnes, more intensely affected by the experience than she could possibly have imagined, became very thoughtful and silent on the way back to the caer. And when, as they mounted the hill and saw the first stars beginning to shine, the mourners began singing, Lady Agnes, for whom life presented nothing more than a series of challenges and hardships to be overcome, felt something tight loosen in her heart, and the tears began to flow. She heard in the melody such indomitable spirit and courage that she was ashamed of her former disparagement of these fine and dignified people. She walked along, slippers in hand, listening to the voices as they mingled in the sweet summer air, tears of joy and sadness glistening on her cheeks.

The baron, walking with Prince Garran and his mother, did not see his wife, or he might well have been alarmed. Later, as they sat down to the first of several feasts in honour of the dead king, he did note that Lady Agnes seemed subdued, but pleasantly so, her smile unforced, her manner more calm and peaceable than he could recently remember. *No doubt,* he thought, *she is tired from the journey.* But as she smiled at him when she saw him regarding her from his place near the prince, he returned her smile and thought to himself that he had been right to insist she come.

The next days were given to preparations for the coronation of Prince Garran who, as the baron had long ago determined, should follow his father to the throne. This decision was roundly ratified by the people of Eiwas, so there was no awkwardness or difficulty regarding the succession, and the coronation took place in good order, with little ceremony but great celebration by those who, having laid to rest the old king, had stayed to welcome the new.

When Baron Neufmarché and his wife took their leave of King Garran two days later, they urged the new monarch to come to visit them in Hereford. "Come for Michaelmas," the baron said, his tone gently insistent. "We will hold a feast in your honour, and talk about our future together." As if in afterthought, he added, "You know, I think my daughter would like to know you better—you have not met Sybil, I think?" The young king shook his head. "No? Then it is arranged."

"You must come," added the baroness, pressing his hand as she stepped to the carriage, "and bring your mother, too. Do promise to bring her. I will send a carriage so she will travel more comfortably."

"My lady," replied the new-made king, unable to gainsay his lord's wife, "it will be my pleasure to attend you at Michaelmas."

Later, as the carriage climbed the first of many hills that would take the caer from view, Lady Agnes said, "King Garran and our Sybil, so? You have not mentioned this to me."

"Ah, um—" The baron hesitated, uncertain how to proceed now that his impromptu plan had been revealed. "I meant to tell you about that, but ah, well, the notion just came to me a day or so ago, and there wasn't time to—"

"I like it," she told him, cutting short his stuttering.

He stared at her as if he could not think he had heard her right. "You would approve of such a union?" wondered Bernard, greatly amazed at this change in his wife's ordinarily dour humour.

"It would be a good match," she affirmed. "Good for both of them, I should think. Yes, I do approve. I will speak to Sybil upon our return. See to it that you secure Garran's promise."

"It will be done," said the baron, still staring at his wife in slight disbelief. "Are you feeling well, my love?"

"Never better," she declared. She was silent a moment, musing to herself, then announced, "I think a Christmas wedding would be a splendid thing. It will give me time to make the necessary plans."

Baron Neufmarché, unable to think of anything to say in the presence of this extraordinary transformation of the woman he had known all these years, simply gazed at her with admiration.

905

Nóin and I spent the rest of the summer luxuriating in one another's love, and talking, talking, talking. Like two blackbirds sitting on a fence we filled the air morning to night with our chatter. She told me all the greenwood gossip—all the doings large and small that filled the days we were apart. I told her of my captivity and passing the time with Odo scribbling down my ramblings. "I should like to read that," Nóin said, then smiled. "That alone would make it worth learning to read."

"Odo tells me that reading is not so difficult," I explained, "but the only things written are either for lawyers or priests, and not at all of interest to plain folk like you and me."

"I should like it all the same," Nóin insisted.

As the days passed, I considered making good on my promise to build my wife and daughter a new house. I found a nice spot on a bit of higher ground at one end of Cél Craidd, and marked out the dimensions on the ground with sticks. I then went to our Lord Bran to beg his permission to clear the ground and cut a few limbs of stout oak for the roof beam, lintel, and corner posts.

"Why build a house?" he asked, holding his head to one side as if he couldn't understand. Before I could point out that I had promised it to my bride, and that her own small hut was a bit too snug for three or more he added, "We will be gone from here come Michaelmas."

"I know, but I promised Noín—" I began.

"Come hunting with us instead," Bran said. "We've missed you on the trails."

My broken fingers were slowly healing, but as my usefulness with a bow was still limited, I served mainly to beat the bushes for game. "Don't worry," Siarles told me after that first time we went out. "You'll be drawing like a champion again in no time. Rest those fingers while you can."

In this, he was a prophet, no mistake. I did not know it then, but would have cause to remember his words in times to come.

Thus, the summer slowly dwindled down and golden autumn arrived. I began counting the days to Michaelmas and the time of leaving we called the Day of Judgement. Bran and Angharad held close counsel and determined that we would go with as many of the Grellon as could be spared, leaving behind only those who could not make the journey and a few men to protect them. We would go to Caer Wintan—known to the English as Winchester—and receive the king's decision on the return of our lands. "The king must see the people who depend on his judgement for their lives," Angharad said. "We must travel together and stand before him together."

"What if he will not see us all in a herd?" wondered Iwan when he learned this.

"He will speak to all, or none," Bran replied, "for then he will judge what is right and for the good of all, and not for me only."

The next day, Bran sent Siarles with an extra horse to Saint Dyfrig's Abbey to fetch Brother Jago, and twelve days before the

Feast of Saint Michael, we set off. It is no easy thing to keep so many people moving, I can tell you. We were thirty folk in all, counting young ones. We went on foot, for the most part; the horses were used to carry provisions and supplies. None of us rode save Angharad, for whom the walk would have been far too demanding. Her old bones would not have lasted the journey, I believe, for it is a fair distance to Caer Wintan from Elfael.

The weather stayed good—warm days, nights cool and dry. We camped wherever we would; with that many people and enough of them bearing longbows, we had no great fear of being harassed by Englishmen or Normans either one. The only real danger was that we would not reach Caer Wintan in time, for as the days of travel drew on, the miles began to tell and the people grew weary and had to rest more often. We moved more slowly than Bran had reckoned. "Do not worry," counselled Friar Tuck. "You can always take a few with you and ride ahead, can you not? You will get there in time, never fear."

Bran rejected this notion outright. We would arrive together each and every last one, he said, or we would not arrive at all. It was for the people we were doing this, he said, so the king must look into the eyes of those for whom his judgement is life or death. There was nothing for it but that we would simply have to travel more quickly.

That night he gathered us all and told us again why we were going to see the king and what it meant. He explained how it was of vital importance that we should arrive in good time, saying, "King William must have no grievance against us, nor any cause to change his mind. We must endure the hardships of the road, my friends, for what we do we do not for ourselves alone, but for the sake of all those in Elfael who cannot join us. We do it for the farmers who have been driven from their fields, and families from their homes; for the widows who have lost their men, and those who stood in the shadow of the gallows.

909

We do it for all who have been made to labour on the baron's hateful strongholds and town, for those who have fled into bleak and friendless exile. We do it for those who will come after us to help shoulder the burden of reclaiming that which we have lost to the enemy. Yes, and for all who have gone before us we do this, theirs the sacrifice, ours the gain." He gazed at all of those clustered around him, holding their eyes with his. "We do not do this for ourselves alone, but for all who have suffered under the oppression of the Ffreinc."

Thus he braced our flagging spirits, speaking words of encouragement and hope. The next day, he became tireless in urging each and every one of us to hasten our steps; and when anyone was seen to be dragging behind, he hurried to help that one. Sometimes he seemed to be everywhere at once—now at the front of the long line of travellers, now at the rear among the stragglers. He did all this with endless good humour, telling one and all to think what it would be like to be free in our own lands and secure in our own homes once more.

The next day he did the same, and the next. He coaxed and cajoled until he grew hoarse, and then Friar Tuck took over, leading our footsore flock in songs. When we ran out of those, he started in on hymns, and little by little, all the urging and singing finally took hold. We walked easier and with lighter hearts. The miles fell behind us at a quicker pace until at last we reached the low, lumpy hills of the southlands.

Caer Wintan was a thriving market town, helped, no doubt, by the presence of the royal residence nearby. Not wishing to risk trouble, we skirted the town and did not draw attention to ourselves beyond sending Tuck and a few men to buy fresh provisions.

We arrived with a day to spare and camped within sight of the king's stronghold—an old English hunting lodge that had once belonged to an earl or duke, I suppose. It was the place where Red William spent those few days he was not racing here or there to shore up his sagging kingdom in one place or another. It reminded me of Aelred's manor, my old earl's house, but with two long wings enclosing a bare dirt yard in front of the black-and-white half-timbered hall. The only defence for the place was a wooden palisade with a porter's hut beside the timber gate.

With a day to spare, we spent it washing our clothes and bathing, ridding ourselves of the road and making ourselves ready to attend the king. At sunrise on the third day after Saint Michael's Day, we rose and broke fast; then, laundered and brushed, washed and combed, we walked to the king's house with Bran in the lead, followed by Angharad leaning on her staff and, beside her, Iwan, holding his bow and a sheaf of arrows at his belt. Siarles and Mérian came next, and then the rest of us in a long double rank. I carried Nia and walked with Nóin; as we passed through the gate, I felt her slip her hand into mine and give it a squeeze. "I am glad to be here today," she murmured. "I will remember it always."

"Me, too," I whispered. "It is a great day, this, and right worthy to be remembered."

We assembled in the king's yard, and Bran had just asked Brother Jago to inform the king's porter that we had come in answer to the king's summons as commanded and were awaiting his pleasure, when who should appear but Count Falkes de Braose and Abbot Hugo, accompanied by Marshal Guy de Gysburne and no fewer than fifteen knights. They swept in through the gates, heedless of our folk, who had to scatter to let them through.

One look at our straggled lot, and the Ffreinc drew their swords. Our own men set arrows on their strings and took a mark. We all stared at one another, eyes hard, faces grim, until Count Falkes broke the silence. "Bran ap Brychan," intoned the count in his high nasal voice, *"Et tous vos compatriotes foule. Qu'une surprise désagréable!"*

Brother Jago, taking his place at Bran's shoulder, whispered the count's greeting in our lord's ear. I needed no translation to know that he had insulted Bran by calling us all "filthy countrymen" and a "disagreeable surprise."

"Count Falkes, your arrival is as untimely as it is unwelcome," replied Bran lightly. "What are you doing here?"

"One could ask the same of you," countered Falkes. "I thought you were dead."

"I am as you see me," returned Bran. "But it would seem you still irk the earth with your presence. I asked why you have come."

Marshal Gysburne muttered an oath at this reply when Jago had delivered it, and several other knights spat at us. I saw a flicker of anger flit across the count's face, but his reply was restrained. "We are obeying the king's summons. I cannot think you are here by accident."

"We likewise have been summoned," returned Bran. "Therefore, let us resolve to hold the peace between us for at least as long as we must stand before the king."

With some reluctance, it seemed to me, Count Falkes agreed, although he really had no better choice. Starting a battle in the king's yard would have gained him little and cost him much. "Very well," he said at last. "We will keep the peace insofar as you keep your rabble subdued."

I could not tell how much the count knew about our Bran and his busy doings—very little, I guessed, for his remark about Bran having been killed seemed to signify that Falkes did not recognise Bran as Father Dominic, or as King Raven, either. I thought the whole contest would be over once he recognised me, though, but after bandying words with Bran, he feigned disinterest in us and turned his face away, as if we were beneath his regard. I suppose I appeared just a married man with a child in his arms and a wife by his side.

So now, an uneasy truce was established—but it was that thin, I can tell you, a single lance point or arrow tip could have pierced it anywhere along the line. We waited there in the yard, wary and watching one another. Nóin, bless her, stood with her head high and shoulders straight, returning the glare of the marshal and his hard-eyed knights, and little Nia found a pile of pebbles to keep her busy, moving them from one place to another and singing to them all the while.

When it seemed that we must all snap under the strain, the great oak-and-iron door of the king's royal residence opened and out stepped the king's man, accompanied by two other household servants. "His Majesty the king has been informed of your arrival," he announced in good English. "He begs the boon of your patience and will give audience as soon as may be." Taking in the horde of Welshmen standing with Bran in the yard, he added, "It will not be possible for all of you to enter. The hall is not large enough. You must choose representatives to attend you; the rest will wait here."

When Jago had relayed these words to our lord, Bran replied, "With respect, as the king's judgement will serve all my people, we will hear it together. Perhaps the king will not mind delivering his decision to us here as we wait so patiently."

The fella made no answer, but simply bent his head, turned on his heel, and scuttled back inside. "All stand together," sneered Count Falkes. "How very Welsh." The word was a slur in his mouth.

"All hang together, too," observed Abbot Hugo. His eye fell on me just then, and recognition came to him. His ruddy face froze. "You there!" he shouted. "Hold up your hands."

"Don't do it, Will," warned Bran, glancing quickly over his shoulder. "He may suspect, but we need not feed his suspicion."

I stood my ground, silently returning his gaze, but I kept my hands well out of the Black Abbot's sight. It was then I saw Odo, sitting most uncomfortably on the back of a brown mare. He saw me, too, knew me, and—bless him—held his tongue. He would not betray me to his masters.

"I say!" cried the abbot, growing angry. "Order your man to show me his hands."

"As he is my man," said Bran, "he is mine to command. I will make no such demand."

"By the Virgin, it *is* him," insisted the abbot.

"What are you talking about?" wondered Count Falkes.

"The prisoner!" cried Hugo, jabbing his finger at me. "Scatlocke—the one they called Scarlet. That is him, I tell you!"

Count Falkes turned his gaze my way and studied me for a moment. "No," he decided. "That is not the man." No doubt my haircut and shave, and change of clothes and fleshing out a little on my wife's good cooking, had changed me enough to make them just that little uncertain.

"It is him," put in Gysburne. He looked at Bran and concluded, "And the last time we saw that one, he gave his name as Father Dominic. I would swear to it." He gazed at the rest of us, his eyes passing back and forth along the ranks. "By the rood, they're *all* here!" He pointed at Iwan. "I know I've seen that one before. I know it."

"You are imagining things," remarked the count. "They all look alike anyway, these Welsh."

"Say nothing," advised Angharad, speaking mostly to Bran, but to the rest of us as well. "Let them think what they will—it no longer matters what they say. Let them rail. We will not stoop to satisfy their accusations."

So Bran ignored the Ffreinc taunts and finger-pointing which continued to be cast at him and some of the rest of us; instead, he and Angharad turned their faces to the ironbound door and waited. The sun rose slowly higher, and still we waited, growing warm beneath the bright autumn rays. Some of the Ffreinc grew tired of waiting in the saddle and, sheathing their weapons, climbed down from their horses. Others led their mounts away to water them. Most, however, remained to glare and frown and mutter curses at us. But that is the worst of what they did, and we braved it in silence without giving them cause for greater anger.

Then, as the sun climbed toward midday, the door to the royal residence opened once more and the king's man appeared with the two servants. "Hear! Hear!" he called. "His Majesty William, King of England!"

Out from the house came the Red King and five attendants: one of them a priest of some exalted kind, robed in red satin with a gold chain and cross around his neck, and another the young Lord Leicester we had met in Rouen; the rest were knights carrying lances. The king himself, surrounded by his bodyguard, seemed smaller than I remembered him; his stocky form was wrapped in a blue tunic that stretched tight across his bulging stomach; his short legs were stuffed into dark brown trousers and tall riding boots. His flame-coloured hair glowed with bright fire in the sunlight, but he seemed tired to me, almost haggard, and there were chapped patches on his cheeks. In his hand, he carried a rolled parchment.

"Which one is the king? Is it the one in red?" whispered Nóin, and I realised that, like most people, she'd never set eyes to the king of England before and had no idea how William or any other king might appear when not tricked out in their regal frippery.

"No, the fat one with orange hair," I told her. "That's our William Rufus."

This information was repeated down the ranks, along with other pungent observations. De Braose and his lot, seeking an advantage somehow, called out greetings to the king, who ran his eye quickly over them but did not respond to their bald attempt at flattery. After this had gone on for a time, the king gestured to his man, who cut short the speeches and called for silence.

With a somewhat distracted air, the king held the parchment roll out to the priest. "Cardinal Ranulf of Bayeux will read out the royal judgement proclamation at this time," he declared. Brother Jago relayed these words to the Welsh speakers.

The cardinal known as Flambard stepped forward and, with a short bow, received the scroll from William's hand. He took his time untying it and unrolling it. Holding it high, he stepped forward and began to read it out. It was Latin, of course, and I could make nothing of it. Fortunately, I was standing near enough to Brother Jago to catch most of what he said as he translated the words for Bran and Angharad. Tuck was close by to offer his understanding as well.

"I, William, by the grace of God, king of England, greets his subjects with all respect and honour according to their rank and station. Be it known that this day, the third day after the Feast of Saint Michael, this judgement was made public by the reading hereof in the presence of the same king and those persons summoned by the crown to attend him. Owing to the perfidious nature of certain noblemen known to the king, and because of dissensions and discords which have arisen between the king and the lord king's brother, Duke Robert of Normandie, and a company of rebellious barons of the kingdom concerning William's lawful right to occupy the throne and to rule unimpeded by the slanders and allegations of traitorous dissenters, this recognition has been made before the Chief Justiciar of England, and Henry, Earl of Warwick, and other great men of the kingdom, and has been signed and sealed in their presence."

Here the cardinal paused to allow the crowd to unravel the mean-

916

ing of this address. We were by no means the only ones struggling to keep up; the Ffreinc in Count de Braose's camp were having their own difficulties with all that high-flown Latin and were being aided by Abbot Hugo, who was interpreting for the count and others.

When Cardinal Flambard decided that all had caught up with him, he continued, "Accordingly, I, William, under authority of Heaven, do hereby set forth my disposition in the matters arising from the recent attempt by those rebellious subjects aforementioned to remove His Majesty from his throne and the rightful rule of his realm and subjects. Be it known that William de Braose, Baron of Bramber, for his part in the rebellion has forfeited his lands and title to the crown and is henceforth prohibited from returning to England under ban of condemnation for treason and the penalty thereof. Regarding his son, the Earl Philip de Braose, and his nephew the Count Falkes de Braose, being found to have no part in the wicked rebellion against their lawful king, but owing to their familial proximity to the traitors, it is deemed prudent to extend the ban to them and their households; therefore, they are to follow the baron into exile to whatever lands will receive them."

The Ffreinc moaned and gnashed their teeth at this, while at the same time it was all we could do to keep from cheering. Oh, it was all we'd hoped for—Baron de Braose was banished, and his noxious nephew exiled with him. The throne of Elfael was freed from the Normans, and victory was sweet in our mouths.

But, as the Good Lord giveth with his right hand, and taketh with his left—so with kings.

"Further," continued the cardinal, "it pleases His Majesty to assume those lands now vacated to be placed under Forest Law as a Protectorate of Royal Privilege, to be administered for the crown by a regent chosen to serve the interests of the crown, namely Abbot Hugo de Rainault.

As our regent and an officer of the crown, he will exercise all authority necessary to hold, maintain, and prosper those lands and estates, and with the aid of our sheriff, Richard de Glanville, to more firmly establish the realm in the fealty due its rightful monarch."

Here the cardinal broke off to allow the translators to catch up. While we were struggling to work out what had just happened, Cardinal Flambard concluded, saying, "All others professing grievance in this matter, having been rewarded according to their service, are herewith disposed. No further action in regard to this judgement shall be countenanced. Under the sign and seal of William, King of England."

Owing to the slight murkiness of courtly Latin, it took us a while to get to grips with the outrage that had just been revealed in our hearing. Tuck and Jago held close council with Bran and Angharad. Count Falkes de Braose, astonished beyond words, stared at the king as if at the devil's own manservant; Abbot Hugo and Marshal Guy put their heads together, already preparing to seed more mischief. In both camps, Ffreinc and British, there were dire mutterings and grumblings. Along with many another, I pressed forward to hear what the clerics among us were saying, and caught part of the discussion. "So, it comes to this," Tuck said, "Baron de Braose and all his kith and kin have been banished, never to return to English soil on pain of death—well and good . . ."

"But, see here," pointed out Jago, "Abbot Hugo is made regent and remains in possession of the lands granted to de Braose by the king."

"But the bloody abbot keeps Elfael!" growled Tuck dangerously.

A dull, damp sickness descended over me. Some of those around me swore and called down curses on the head of the English king. "What does it mean?" said Nóin, pressing close beside me.

"It means we have been used and cast aside," I spat. "It means that red-haired rogue has gutted us like rabbits and thrown us to the dogs."

"That cannot be," said Bran, already starting forth. "Heaven will not allow it!" He stepped forward three long paces and halted, calling upon the king to hear him. "My lord king," he said, with Jago's help, "am I to understand that you have allowed Abbot Hugo to keep our lands in Elfael?"

"The king has decreed that the abbot will serve as his regent," replied Cardinal Ranulf. His eyes narrowed as he gazed at Bran. "I remember you right well," he said, "and I warn you against trying any such foolishness as you attempted last time we met."

"Then pray remind the king that I was promised the return of our lands and the rule of our people," Bran countered, speaking through Jago. "This I was promised by the king himself in recognition of our part in exposing the traitors."

The king heard this, of course, but glanced away, a pained expression on his face.

"I cannot answer for any promises which might or might not have been made in the past," responded the cardinal, making it sound as if this had all taken place untold years ago and could have no part in the judgement now. "After a suitable season of reflection, the king has determined that it does not serve the interests of the crown to return Elfael to Welsh rule at this time."

"What is to become of us?" cried Bran, growing visibly angry. "That is our land—our home! We were promised justice."

"Justice," replied the silk-robed cardinal coolly, "you have received. Your king has decreed; his word is law."

Bran, holding tight to the reins of his rage, argued his case. "I would remind His Majesty that it was from within the abbot's own stronghold that we learned of the conspiracy against him! Your regent is as guilty of treason as those you have already condemned and punished."

"So you say," countered the cardinal smoothly. "There has been no proof of this, and therefore the right practice of justice decrees no guilt shall be laid at the abbot's feet."

"Call it what you will, my lord, but do not call it justice," said Bran, his voice shaking with fury. Sweet Jesus, I had never seen him so angry. His face was white, his eyes flashing quick fire. "This is an offence against heaven. The people of Elfael will not rest until we have gained the justice promised to us."

"You and your people will conform yourself to the regent's rule," Flambard declared. "As regent, Abbot Hugo is charged with your care and protection. Henceforth, he will provide you with the comfort and solace of the king's law."

"With all respect, Cardinal," Bran called, fighting to keep his rage from devouring his reason, "we cannot accept this judgement."

"The king has spoken," concluded Cardinal Bayeux. "The continued prosecution of this dispute has no merit. The matter is herewith concluded."

King William, impervious to our lord's anger, nodded once and turned away. He and his soldiers and confidants walked back to the house and went inside. The cardinal rolled up the parchment and turned to follow his monarch.

With that, our Day of Judgement was over.

As the door closed on the backs of the royal party, a wide double door opened at the far end of the yard, and soldiers who had been awaiting this moment streamed out to encircle us. Weapons ready, they formed a wall, shoulder-to-shoulder around the perimeter of the yard.

"We must leave here at once," said Angharad. "Bran!"

He was no longer listening. "We will not be denied!" he shouted, starting forth. "This is not the end. Do you hear?"

She pulled Bran's sleeve, restraining him. Shaking off her grasp, he started after the swiftly retreating cardinal. "Iwan! Siarles!" she snapped, "See to your lord!"

The two leapt forward and took hold of Bran, one on either side. "Come away, my lord," said Iwan. "Don't make things worse. They only want half a reason to attack us."

"You do well to drag him away," called Marshal Guy, laughing. "Drag the beaten dog away!"

Gysburne was the only one to find amusement in this disaster, mind—he and a few of the less astute-looking soldiers with him. The rest appeared suitably grim, realising that this was no good news for them, either. Count Falkes looked like a man who has had his bones removed, and it was all he could do to remain in the saddle. His pale countenance was more ghastly still, and his lips trembled, no doubt in contemplation of his ruin.

921

Iwan and Siarles were able to haul Bran back. Mérian rushed to his side to help calm him. Meanwhile, Tuck and Angharad, fearful of what the Ffreinc might do next, moved quickly to turn everyone and march them from the yard before bloodshed could turn the disaster into a catastrophe.

Obeying cooler heads, we turned and started slowly away under the narrowed eyes and naked weapons of the king's soldiers. As we passed Count de Braose's company, I looked up and saw Odo, his round, owlish face stricken. On impulse, I raised my hand and beckoned him to join us. "Come, monk," I told him. "If you would quit the devil and stand on the side of the angels, you are welcome here."

To my surprise, he lifted the reins and moved out from the Ffreinc ranks. Some of those around him tried to prevent him, but he pulled away from their grasp; the abbot, sneering down his long nose, told them to let the craven Judas go. "Let him leave if he will," said Marshal

Gysburne, snatching the bridle strap and halting Odo's mount, "but he goes without the horse."

So my dear dull scribe took his life in his hands, plucked up his small courage, and slid down from the saddle to take his place among the Grellon.

As we marched from the yard, the soldiers tightened the circle and drew in behind us to make certain we would depart without causing any trouble. Abbot Hugo called out one last threat. "Do not think to return to Elfael," he said, his voice ringing loud in the yard. "We have marked you, and we will kill you on sight should you or any of your rabble ever set foot in Elfael again."

When Jago translated the abbot's challenge for us, I saw Bran stiffen. Turning to address the abbot, he said in Latin, "Enjoy this day, vile priest—it is the last peace you will know. From this day hence, it is war."

Abbot Hugo shouted something in reply, and the Ffreinc soldiers made as if they might mount an attack. They drew swords and lowered their shields, preparing to charge. But Bran snatched up a bow, and quick as a blink, planted an arrow between the abbot's legs, pinning the hem of his robe to the hard ground. "The next arrow finds your black heart, Abbot," Bran called. "Tell the soldiers to put up their weapons." Hugo heeded the warning and wisely called for the king's men to hold and let us depart. Slowly, Bran lowered the bow, turned, and led his people from the king's stronghold.

Heads held high, we strode out through the gate and into our blood-tinged fate.

⇥ EPILOGUE ⇤

Are you sure he's the one?" asked Marshal Guy of
Gysburne.

"Absolutely certain," muttered Abbot Hugo. "There is no doubt.
Bran ap Brychan was heir to the throne of Elfael. That idiot de Braose
killed his father, and he himself was thought to be dead—but of course
that was bungled along with everything else the baron and his milksop
nephew touched."

"To think we had him in our grasp and didn't recognise him,"
Gysburne observed. "Curious."

Hugo took a deep breath and fixed his marshal with a steely gaze.
"King Raven, the so-called Phantom, and Bran are one and the same.
I'd stake my life on it."

"We should have taken him when we had the chance," remarked
Gysburne, still puzzling over the deception played upon them.

"A mistake," spat Hugo, "we will not repeat."

Count Falkes de Braose had been escorted from the yard by
knights of the king, to be taken to Lundein and there put on a ship
to Normandie. Abbot Hugo and his marshal were left to consider the
unexpected rise in their fortunes, and the threats to their rule. Their
first thoughts turned to Bran and his followers. They quickly decided
that so long as Bran and his men remained at large, they would never

enjoy complete control over the people and lands that King William had entrusted to their stewardship.

"I can take him now," said Guy.

"Not here," said Hugo. "Not in sight of the king and his court. That will not do. No, let the upstart and his rabble get down the road a pace, and follow them. They won't get far on foot. Wait until they make camp for the night, and then kill them all."

"There are women and children, and at least one priest," Guy pointed out. "What shall we do with them?"

"Spare no one," the abbot replied.

"But, my lord," objected Guy. He was a knight of the realm, and did not fancy himself a murderer. "We cannot slaughter them like cattle."

"Bran ap Brychan said it himself," countered the abbot. "It is war. His words, not mine, Gysburne. If it is war he wants, this is where it begins."

Before Marshal Guy could argue further, the abbot called his knights and men-at-arms—and as many of the count's men who wished to join his army—to gather in a corner of the yard. "On your knees, men," he said. "Bow your heads." With a clatter of armour, the knights under Guy Gysburne's command drew their swords and knelt in a circle around the abbot. Folding their hands over the hilts of their unsheathed swords, they bowed their heads. Raising his right hand, Hugo made the sign of the cross over the kneeling soldiers.

"Lord of Hosts," he prayed, "I send these men out to do battle in your name. Shield them with your hand, and protect them from the arrows of the enemy. Let their toil be accounted righteousness for your name's sake. Amen."

The soldiers raised their heads as the abbot said, "For any and all acts committed in carrying out the charge laid upon you this day, you are hereby absolved in heaven and on earth. Obey the will of your commander, who serves me even as I serve God Almighty. For the sake of God's anointed, King William, the holy church, and the Lord Jesus Christ himself, show no mercy to those who rebel against their rule, and do so with the full knowledge that all of your deeds will be accounted to your favour on the earth and in heaven, and that you bear no stain of guilt or sin for the shedding of blood this day."

With that, Guy and his men mounted their horses and silently rode from the yard in pursuit of King Raven and his flock.

KING RAVEN: BOOK III

Dedicated to
The Outlaw Tony Wales

⊰ PROLOGUE ⊱

Wintan Cestre
Saint Swithun's Day

King William stood scratching the back of his hand and watched as another bag of gold was emptied into the ironclad chest: one hundred solid gold byzants that, added to fifty pounds in silver and another fifty in letters of promise to be paid upon collection of his tribute from Normandie, brought the total to five hundred marks. "More money than God," muttered William under his breath. "What do they do with it all?"

"Sire?" asked one of the clerks of the justiciar's office, glancing up from the wax tablet on which he kept a running tally.

"Nothing," grumbled the king. Parting with money always made him itch, and this time there was no relief. In vain, he scratched the other hand. "Are we finished here?"

Having counted the money, the clerks began locking and sealing the strongbox. The king shook his head at the sight of all that gold and silver disappearing from sight. *These blasted monks will bleed me dry,* he thought. A kingdom was a voracious beast that devoured money and was never, ever satisfied. It took money for soldiers, money for horses and weapons, money for fortresses, money for supplies to feed the troops, and as now, even more money to wipe away the sins of war. The gold and silver in the chest was for the abbey at Wintan Cestre to pay the monks so that his father would not have to spend eternity in purgatory or, worse, frying in hell.

"All is in order, Majesty," said the clerk. "Shall we proceed?"

William gave a curt nod.

Two knights of the king's bodyguard stepped forward, took up the box, and carried it from the room and out into the yard where the monks of Saint Swithun's were already gathered and waiting for the ceremony to begin. The king, a most reluctant participant, followed.

In the yard of the Red Palace—the name given to the king's sprawling lodge outside the city walls—a silken canopy on silver poles had been erected. Beneath the canopy stood Bishop Walkelin with his hands pressed together in an attitude of patient prayer. Behind the bishop stood a monk bearing the gilded cross of their namesake saint, while all around them knelt monks and acolytes chanting psalms and hymns. The king and his attendants—his two favourite earls, a canon, and a bevy of assorted clerks, scribes, courtiers, and officials both sacred and secular—marched out to meet the bishop. The company paused while the king's chair was brought and set up beneath the canopy where Bishop Walkelin knelt.

"In the Holy Name," intoned the bishop when William Rufus had taken his place in the chair, "all blessing and honour be upon you and upon your house and upon your descendants and upon the people of your realm."

"Yes, yes, of course," said William irritably. "Get on with it."

"God save you, Sire," replied Walkelin. "On this Holy Day we have come to receive the *Beneficium Ecclesiasticus Sanctus Swithinius* as is our right under the Grant of Privilege created and bestowed by your father King William, for the establishment and maintenance of an office of penitence, perpetual prayer, and the pardon of sins."

"So you say," remarked the king.

Bishop Walkelin bowed again, and summoned two of his monks to receive the heavy strongbox from the king's men in what had become an annual event of increasing ceremony in honour of Saint Swithun, on whose day the monks determined to suck the lifeblood from the crown, and William Rufus resented it. But what could he do? The payment was for the prayers of the monks for the remission of sins on the part of William Conqueror, prayers which brought about the much-needed cleansing of his besmirched soul. For each and every man that William had killed in battle, the king could expect to spend a specified amount of time in purgatory: eleven years for a lord or knight, seven years for a man-at-arms, five for a commoner, and one for a serf. By means of some obscure and complicated formula William had never understood, the monks determined a monetary amount which somehow accorded to the number of days a monk spent on his knees praying. As William had been a very great war leader, his purgatorial obligation amounted to well over a thousand years—and that was only counting the fatalities of the landed nobility. No one knew the number of commoners and serfs he had killed, either directly or indirectly, in his lifetime—but the number was thought to be quite high. Still, a wealthy king with dutiful heirs need not actually spend so much time in purgatory—so long as there were monks willing to ease the burden of his debt through prayer. All it took was money.

931

Thus, the Benefice of Saint Swithun, necessary though it might be, was a burden the Conqueror's son had grown to loathe with a passion. That he himself would have need of this selfsame service was a fact that he could neither deny nor escape. And while he told himself that paying monks to pray souls from hell was a luxury he could ill afford, deep in his heart of hearts he knew only too well that—owing to the debauched life he led—it was also a necessity he could ill afford to neglect much longer.

Even so, paying over good silver for the ongoing service of a passel of mumbling clerics rubbed Rufus raw—especially as that silver became each year more difficult to find. His taxes already crushed the poor and had caused at least two riots and a rebellion by his noblemen. Little wonder, then, that the forever needy king dreaded the annual approach of Saint Swithun's day and the parting with so much of his precious treasury.

The ceremony rumbled on to its conclusion and, following an especially long-winded prayer, adjourned to a feast in honour of the worthy saint. The feast was the sole redeeming feature of the entire day. That it must be spent in the company of churchmen dampened William's enthusiasm somewhat, but did not destroy it altogether. The Red King had surrounded himself with enough of his willing courtiers and sycophants to ensure a rousing good time no matter how many disapproving monks he fed at his table.

This year, the revel reached such a height of dissipation that Bishop Walkelin quailed and excused himself, claiming that he had pressing business that required his attention back at the cathedral. William, forcing himself to be gracious, wished the churchmen well and offered to send a company of soldiers to accompany the monks back to the abbey with their money lest they fall among thieves.

Walkelin agreed to the proposal and, as he bestowed his blessing, leaned close to the king and said, "We must talk one day soon about establishing a benefice of your own, Your Majesty." He paused and then, like the flick of a knife, warned, "Death comes for us all, and none of us knows the day or time. I would be remiss if I did not offer to draw up a grant for you."

"We will discuss that," said William, "when the price is seen to fall rather than forever rise."

"You will have heard it said," replied Walkelin, "that where great sin abounds, great mercy must intercede. The continual observance and maintenance of that intercession is very expensive, my lord king."

"So is the keeping of a bishop," answered William tartly. "And bishops have been known to lose their bishoprics." He paused, regarding the cleric over the rim of his cup. "Heaven forbid that should happen. I know I would be heartily sorry to see you go, Walkelin."

"If my lord is displeased with his servant," began the bishop, "he has only to—"

"Something to consider, eh?"

Bishop Walkelin tried to adopt a philosophical air. "I am reminded that your father always—"

"No need to speak of it any more just now," said William smoothly. "Only think about what I have said."

"You may be sure," answered Walkelin. He bowed stiffly and took a slow step backwards. "Your servant, my lord."

The clerics departed, leaving the king and his courtiers to their revel. But the feast was ruined for William. Try as he might, he could not work himself into a festive humour because the bishop's rat of a thought had begun to gnaw at the back of his mind: his time was running out. To die without arranging for the necessary prayers would doom his soul to the lake of everlasting fire. However loudly he might rail against the expense—and condemn the greedy clerics who held his future for ransom—was he really prepared to test the alternative at the forfeit of his soul?

934

❦ PART ONE ❦

Come listen a while, you gentlefolk alle,
    That stand this bower within,
A tale of noble Rhiban the Hud,
    I purpose now to begin.

Young Rhiban was a princeling fayre,
    And a gladsome heart had he.
Delight took he in games and tricks,
    And guiling his fair ladye.

A bonny fine maide of noble degree,
    Mérian calléd by name,
This beauty soote was praised of alle men
    For she was a gallant dame.

Rhiban stole through the greenwoode one night
    To kiss his dear Mérian late.
But she boxed his head till his nose turn'd red
    And order'd him home full straight.

Though Rhiban indeed speeded home fayrlie rathe,
    That night he did not see his bed.
For in flames of fire from the rooftops' eaves,
    He saw all his kinsmen lay dead.

Ay, the sheriff's low men had visited there,
    When the household was slumbering deepe.
And from room to room they had quietly crept
    And murtheréd them all in their sleepe.

Rhiban cried out "wey-la-wey!"
    But those fiends still lingered close by.
So into the greenwoode he quickly slipt,
    For they had heard his cry.

Rhiban gave the hunters goode sport,
    Full lange, a swift chase he led.
But a spearman threw his shot full well
    And he fell as one that is dead.

CHAPTER I

Tuck shook the dust of Caer Wintan off his feet and prepared for the long walk back to the forest. It was a fine, warm day, and all too soon the friar was sweltering in his heavy robe. He paused now and then to wipe the sweat from his face, falling farther and farther behind his travelling companions. "These legs of mine are sturdy stumps," he sighed to himself, "but fast they en't."

He had just stopped to catch his breath a little when, on sudden impulse, he spun around quickly and caught a glimpse of movement on the road behind—a blur in the shimmering distance, and then gone. So quick he might have imagined it. Only it was not the first time since leaving the Royal Lodge that Tuck had entertained the queer feeling that someone or something was following them. He had it again now, and decided to alert the others and let them make of it what they would.

Squinting into the distance, he saw Bran far ahead of the Grellon, striding steadily, shoulders hunched against the sun and the gross injustice so lately suffered at the hands of the king in whom he had trusted. The main body of travellers, unable to keep up with their lord, was becoming an ever-lengthening line as heat and distance mounted. They trudged along in small clumps of two or three, heads down, talking in low, sombre voices. *How like sheep*, thought Tuck, *following their impetuous and headstrong shepherd.*

A more melancholy man might himself have succumbed to the oppressive gloom hanging low over the Cymry, dragging at their feet, pressing their spirits low. Though summer still blazed in meadow, field, and flower, it seemed to Tuck that they all walked in winter's drear and dismal shadows. Rhi Bran and his Grellon had marched into Caer Wintan full of hope—they had come singing, had they not?—eager to stand before King William to receive the judgement and reward that had been promised in Rouen all those months ago. Now, here they were, slinking back to the greenwood in doleful silence, mourning the bright hope that had been crushed and lost.

No, not lost. They would never let it out of their grasp, not for an instant. It had been stolen—snatched away by the same hand that had offered it in the first place: the grasping, deceitful hand of a most perfidious king.

Tuck felt no less wounded than the next man, but when he considered how Bran and the others had risked their lives to bring Red William word of the conspiracy against him, it fair made his priestly blood boil. The king had promised justice. The Grellon had every right to expect that Elfael's lawful king would be restored. Instead, William had merely banished Baron de Braose and his milksop nephew Count Falkes, sending them back to France to live in luxury on the baron's extensive estates. Elfael, that small bone of contention, had instead become property of the crown and placed under the protection of Abbot Hugo and Sheriff de Glanville. Well, *that* was putting wolves in charge of the fold, was it not?

Where was the justice? A throne for a throne, Bran had declared that day in Rouen. William's had been saved—at considerable cost and risk to the Cymry—but where was Bran's throne?

S'truth, thought Tuck, *wait upon a Norman to do the right thing and you'll be waiting until your hair grows white and your teeth fall out.*

"How long, O Lord? How long must your servants suffer?" he muttered. "And, Lord, does it have to be so blasted hot?"

He paused to wipe the sweat from his face. Running a hand over his round Saxon head, he felt the sun's fiery heat on the bare spot of his tonsure; sweat ran in rivulets down the sides of his neck and dripped from his jowls. Drawing a deep breath, he tightened his belt, hitched up the skirts of his robe, and started off again with quickened steps. Soon his shoes were slapping up the dust around his ankles, and he began to overtake the rearmost members of the group: thirty souls in all, women and children included, for Bran had determined that his entire forest clan—save for those left behind to guard the settlement and a few others for whom the long journey on foot would have been far too arduous—should be seen by the king to share in the glad day.

The friar picked up his pace and soon drew even with Siarles: slim as a willow wand, but hard and knotty as an old hickory root. The forester walked with his eyes downcast, chin outthrust, his mouth a tight, grim line. Every line of him bristled with fury like a riled porcupine. Tuck knew to leave well enough alone and hurried on without speaking.

Next, he passed Will Scatlocke—or Scarlet, as he preferred. The craggy forester limped along slightly as he carried his newly acquired

939

daughter, Nia. Against every expectation, Will had endured a spear wound, the abbot's prison, and the threat of the sheriff's rope . . . and survived. His pretty dark-eyed wife, Noín, walked resolutely beside him. The pair had made a good match, and it tore at his heart that the newly married couple should have to endure a dark hovel in the forest when the entire realm begged for just such a family to settle and sink solid roots deep into the land—another small outrage to be added to the ever-growing mountain of injustices weighing on Elfael.

A few more steps brought him up even with Odo, the Norman monk who had befriended Will Scarlet in prison. At Scarlet's bidding, the young scribe had abandoned Abbot Hugo to join them. Odo walked with his head down, his whole body drooping—whether with heat or the awful realization of what he had done, Tuck could not tell.

A few steps more and he came up even with Iwan—the great, hulking warrior would crawl on hands and knees through fire for his lord. It was from Iwan that the friar had received his current christening when the effort of wrapping his untrained tongue around the simple Saxon name Aethelfrith proved beyond him. "Fat little bag of vittles that he is, I will call him Tuck," the champion had said. "Friar Tuck to you, boyo," the priest had responded, and the name had stuck. *God bless you, Little John,* thought Tuck, *and keep your arm strong, and your heart stronger.*

Next to Iwan strode Mérian, just as fierce in her devotion to Bran as the champion beside her. Oh, but shrewd with it; she was smarter than the others and more cunning—which always came as something of a shock to anyone who did not know better, because one rarely expected it from a lady so fair of face and form. But the impression of innocence beguiled. In the time Tuck had come to know her, she had shown herself to be every inch as canny and capable as any monarch who ever claimed an English crown.

Mérian held lightly to the bridle strap of the horse that carried their wise hudolion, who was, so far as Tuck could tell, surely the last Banfáith of Britain: Angharad, ancient and ageless. There was no telling how old she was, yet despite her age, whatever it might be, she sat her saddle smartly and with the ease of a practiced rider. Her quick dark eyes were trained on the road ahead, but Tuck could tell that her sight was turned inward, her mind wrapped in a veil of deepest thought. Her wrinkled face might have been carved of dark Welsh slate for all it revealed of her contemplations.

Mérian glanced around as the priest passed, and called out, but the friar had Bran in his eye, and he hurried on until he was within hailing distance. "My lord, wait!" he shouted. "I must speak to you!"

Bran gave no sign that he had heard. He strode on, eyes fixed on the road and distance ahead.

"For the love of Jesu, Bran. Wait for me!"

Bran took two more steps and then halted abruptly. He straightened and turned, his face a smouldering scowl, dark eyes darker still under lowered brows. His shock of black hair seemed to rise in feathered spikes.

"Thank the Good Lord," gasped the friar, scrambling up the dry, rutted track. "I thought I'd never catch you. We . . . there is something . . ." He gulped down air, wiped his face, and shook the sweat from his hand into the dust of the road.

"Well?" demanded Bran impatiently.

"I think we must get off this road," Tuck said, dabbing at his face with the sleeve of his robe. "Truly, as I think on it now, I like not the look that Abbot Hugo gave me when we left the king's yard. I fear he may try something nasty."

Bran lifted his chin. The jagged scar on his cheek, livid now, twisted his lip into a sneer. "Within sight of the king's house?" he scoffed, his voice tight. "He wouldn't dare."

"Would he not?"

"Dare what?" said Iwan, striding up. Siarles came toiling along in the big man's wake.

"Our friar here," replied Bran, "thinks we should abandon the road. He thinks Abbot Hugo is bent on making trouble."

Iwan glanced back the way they had come. "Oh, aye," agreed Iwan, "that would be his way." To Tuck, he said, "Have you seen anything?"

"What's this then?" inquired Siarles as he joined the group. "Why have you stopped?"

"Tuck thinks the abbot is on our tail," Iwan explained.

"I maybe saw something back there, and not for the first time," Tuck explained. "I don't say it for a certainty, but I think someone is following us."

"It makes sense." Siarles looked to the frowning Bran. "What do you reckon?"

"I reckon I am surrounded by a covey of quail frightened of their own shadows," Bran replied. "We move on."

He turned to go, but Iwan spoke up. "My lord, look around you. There is little enough cover hereabouts. If we were to be taken by surprise, the slaughter would be over before we could put shaft to string."

Mérian joined them then, having heard a little of what had passed. "The little ones are growing weary," she pointed out. "They cannot continue on this way much longer without rest and water. We will have to stop soon in any event. Why not do as Tuck suggests and leave the road now—just to be safe?"

"So be it," Bran said, relenting at last. He glanced around and then pointed to a grove of oak and beech rising atop the next hill up the road. "We will make for that wood. Iwan—you and Siarles pass the word along, then take up the rear guard." He turned to Tuck and said, "You and Mérian stay here and keep everyone moving. Tell them they can rest as soon as they reach the grove, but not before."

He turned on his heel and started off again. Iwan stood looking after his lord and friend. "It's the vile king's treachery," he observed. "That's put the black dog on his back, no mistake."

Siarles, as always, took a different tone. "That's as may be, but there's no need to bite off *our* heads. We en't the ones who cheated him out of his throne." He paused and spat. "Stupid bloody king."

"And stupid bloody cardinal, all high and mighty," continued Iwan. "Priest of the church, my arse. Give me a good sharp blade and I'd soon have him saying prayers he never said before." He cast a hasty glance at Tuck. "Sorry, Friar."

"I'd do the same," Tuck said. "Now, off you go. If I am right, we must get these people to safety, and that fast."

The two ran back down the line, urging everyone to make haste for the wood on the next hill. "Follow Bran!" they shouted. "Pick up your feet. We are in danger here. Hurry!"

"There is safety in the wood," Mérian assured them as they passed, and Tuck did likewise. "Follow Bran. He'll lead you to shelter."

It took a little time for the urgency of their cries to sink in, but soon the forest-dwellers were moving at a quicker pace up to the wood at the top of the next rise. The first to arrive found Bran waiting at the edge of the grove beneath a large oak tree, his strung bow across his shoulder.

"Keep moving," he told them. "You'll find a hollow just beyond that fallen tree." He pointed through the wood. "Hide yourselves and wait for the others there."

The first travellers had reached the shelter of the trees, and Tuck was urging another group to speed and showing them where to go when he heard someone shouting up from the valley. He could not make out the words, but as he gazed around the sound came again and he saw Iwan furiously gesturing towards the far hilltop. He looked where the big man was pointing and saw two mounted knights poised on the crest of the hill.

The soldiers were watching the fleeing procession and, for the moment, seemed content to observe. Then one of the knights wheeled his mount and disappeared back down the far side of the hill.

Bran had seen it too, and began shouting. "Run!" he cried, racing down the road. "To the grove!" he told Mérian and Tuck. "The Ffreinc are going to attack!"

He flew to meet Iwan and Siarles at the bottom of the hill.

"I'd best go see if I can help," Tuck said, and leaving Mérian to hurry the people along, he fell into step behind Bran.

"Just the two of them?" Bran asked as he came running to meet Siarles and Iwan.

"So far," replied the champion. "No doubt the one's gone to alert the rest. Siarles and I will take a stand here," he said, bending the long ashwood bow to string it. "That will give you and Tuck time to get the rest of the folk safely hidden in the woods."

Bran shook his head. "It may come to that one day, but not today." His tone allowed no dissent. "We have a little time yet. Get everyone into the wood—carry them if you have to. We'll dig ourselves into the grove and make Gysburne and his hounds come in after us."

"I make it six bows against thirty knights," Siarles pointed out. "Good odds, that."

Bran gave a quick jerk of his chin. "Good as any," he agreed. "Fetch along the stragglers and follow me."

Iwan and Siarles darted away and were soon rushing the last of the lagging Grellon up the hill to the grove. "What do you want *me* to do?" Tuck shouted.

"Pray," answered Bran, pulling an arrow from the sheaf at his belt and fitting it to the string. "Pray God our aim is true and each arrow finds its mark."

Bran moved off, calling for the straggling Grellon to find shelter in the wood. Tuck watched him go. *Pray?* he thought. *Aye, to be sure— the Good Lord will hear from me. But I will do more, will I not?* Then he scuttled up the hill and into the wood in search of a good stout stick to break some heads.

945

$\mathcal{S}$wift and furtive as wild things, the women and children disappeared into the deep-shadowed grove. Bran called all the men together at the edge of the wood. "We have six bows," he said. "Iwan, Siarles, Tomas, Rhoddi . . ." He paused, eyeing the men gathered around him, assessing their abilities. His gaze lit on one of the eager young men who had joined the Grellon following the loss of his family's home to the Ffreinc. "You, Owain, will join me. I want a guard with each bowman to watch his back and retrieve any arrows that fall within easy reach. So now, archers and guards come with me. The rest of you go with Tuck and help protect the others."

"We want to fight too," said one of the men, speaking up.

"If any of the Ffreinc get in behind us," Bran told him, "you'll have your hands full right enough. Tuck will tell you what to do."

As Bran turned to lead his small group of archers to their places at the edge of the grove, a hand reached out and halted him. "Lend me a bow. I can draw."

Bran turned and shook his head. "I know, Will—when you're healed and practiced."

"Even crippled as I am I'd wager I can still draw better than anyone here—saving only yourself, my lord."

"No doubt," Bran allowed, placing a hand on the man's shoulder. "But let be today, Will." Bran's eyes slid past Will to Noín and Nia, and the young, round-shouldered, whey-faced Ffreinc monk hovering a few steps away. "Look after your family and your friend here—and take care of Angharad. See that none of them come to harm. That will be help enough."

Bran hurried away to join the archers, and Will turned to the worried young monk behind him. "Come along, Odo," he said. "Follow Noín and help her see to the old woman and her horse, and look sharp, unless you want Abbot Hugo to get his hands on you again."

They hurried to join the others in the hollow, and Tuck gathered the rest. "This way!" he called, and led his crew of seven unarmed warriors to a small glade midway between the archers and the hollow where the rest of the Grellon had found their hiding places. "We will stand here," he told them. Then, raising his stubby oak branch lengthwise, he held it high, saying, "Get one of these to hand quick as you can, and hurry back. We'll make ourselves scarce behind the trees there, and there"—he pointed out the nearby boles of massive oaks—"and over there. If any Ffreinc get past Bran and the others we'll do for 'em."

The last words were still hanging in the air when there came a cry from the edge of the wood where Bran and the bowmen were waiting. As the shout echoed through the grove, they heard the fizzing whir of an arrow as it sped from the string. Almost instantly, there followed a short, sharp scream and a crash. A heartbeat later, a riderless horse careered into the wood.

948

"Bless me," remarked Tuck. Turning to his company, he said, "Get some wood in your hands, lads, and make a good account of yourselves. Go!"

As the forest-dwellers scattered, two knights burst into the grove in full gallop. One of them had an arrow sticking out of his shield, and the other had a shaft buried deep in his thigh. Both turned their horses and prepared to attack the archers from behind. But even as the great steeds slowed and came around, the soldiers seemed to crumple upon themselves; their weapons fell from slack hands, and both plunged from the saddle with arrows jutting from their backs like feathered quills.

Tuck heard a call from beyond the grove, and suddenly the attack was finished. They waited a few moments, and when no other riders appeared, the Grellon darted out to retrieve the arrows, pulling them from the dead knights.

"Here," said Tuck, gathering the shafts, "I'll take those. The rest of you get back out of sight."

The friar quickly made his way to the edge of the grove, where the archers were hidden amongst the trees. He hurried to the first one he saw.

"Siarles," he called softly. "What's happened? Have we turned them away?"

"No, Brother," replied the forester. "They're down the valley." He pointed down the slope, where a body of knights was milling about on horseback. "They're just regrouping. They'll charge again when they get their courage banked up." He cast a glance behind him into the grove. "The two that broke through—what of them?"

"Dead, I think. Or as good as." He handed over the retrieved arrows.

"That makes three, then," said Siarles, sticking the shafts in the soft earth at his feet.

"God with you," Tuck said, "and with your bow." He made a hasty sign of the cross and hurried back to his place behind the tree to await the next attack. In a little while he heard the hard drumming of horses' hooves. The sound grew, and when it seemed the riders must be on top of them, he heard the thin, singing whine of arrows streaking to their marks—followed by the awful clatter of horses and heavily armoured men crashing to earth.

The second attack faltered and broke off as quickly as the first, and for a moment all was quiet in the grove again, save for the agonized whinny of a dying horse. Again, Tuck waited a little space, and when nothing else seemed about to happen, out he crept and ran to speak to Siarles.

950

"Is that the last of them?"

"Maybe." Siarles gestured with his bow toward the valley. "They've gone away again, but I can't see what they're up to this time."

"Pray they've had enough and decided to go home and lick their wounds." Tuck peered around the trunk of the tree to the near hillside, taking in the corpses of four more horses and men lying in the grass. But for the arrows sticking out of their bodies, they might have been napping in the sun. The guards of the archers were already at work pulling arrows from the bodies. "Looks like they've gone," the friar concluded.

"Just to be sure, you and yours best stay hid until Bran says it's safe to come out."

The friar returned to his crew of defenders to find that they had stripped the weapons from the fallen knights. One of the Grellon offered him a sword. "Thanks, but no," he replied. "You keep it. I'm at my best with a staff in my hand. I wouldn't know what to do with an awkward long blade like that. Now get back to your places and stay alert."

The third attack was long in coming, but when it came the Ffreinc struck as before, charging straight for the grove—and as before, the arrows sang and horses screamed. But this time three knights succeeded in getting past the archers. Arrows sprouting from shield and hauberk, they pounded into the grove swivelling this way and that, looking for something to slash with their swords.

The Ffreinc charge carried them past the tree where Tuck was hiding. Gripping his branch, he lunged out as the nearest horse passed, thrusting the sturdy length of oak in amongst its churning hooves. The resulting jolt nearly yanked his arm from his shoulder. The makeshift staff was torn from his grip and went spinning across the ground. But his aim succeeded, for the horse stumbled to its knees, pitching its rider over its broad neck as it went down.

The knight landed with a grunt on the soft earth, arms flailing, weapons scattering. Tuck ran for his staff and snatched it up. The unhorsed knight made to rise, but the stalwart priest gave him a sharp rap on the back of the skull which sent his pot-shaped metal hat rolling. A second tap put him to sleep.

Two of the Grellon were on the unconscious knight instantly. They rolled him over; one relieved the soldier of his sword and belt, and the other took his dagger and shield. They pulled his mail shirt up over his head and tied it there, then quick-footed it back to the shelter of the trees.

"God have mercy," breathed Tuck, and looked around to see what had become of the other two knights. One had quit his saddle owing to the wounds he had received and was lying on his side on the ground wheezing like a broken bellows; the other was in the grip of three Cymry who were taking turns bashing him with their clubs while he slashed wildly with his sword. The nimble Welshmen dodged the strokes and succeeded in hauling the knight from the saddle. While one of the Cymry seized the reins of the horse, the other two pounded the enemy into dazed submission. One of them wrested his sword from an unresisting hand and, with a swift downward stroke, dispatched the Ffreinc with it.

Three more knights appeared—charging in hard from the wood to the right. Their sudden appearance so surprised the Grellon that they were thrown into a momentary confusion. But as the foremost knight passed beneath the low-hanging branch of an oak one of the Grellon dropped onto the rear of the horse as it passed beneath him. Throwing his arms around the soldier's neck, the forest-dweller hurled himself from the horse, dragging his enemy with him. The horse careened on, and as the knight squirmed in the grasp of the Welshman, two more of the Grellon rushed to help subdue the armoured soldier.

Before the two remaining knights could rally to the aid of their fallen comrade, they too were under assault by screaming, sword-wielding Cymry. More horses were crashing through the wood— they had circled around and were attacking through the grove. Tuck, cursing the duplicity of the Norman race, ran to find Bran.

"Rhi Bran!" he shouted, making for the edge of the grove. "Rhi Bran!"

"Here, Tuck!" came the reply, and Bran appeared from behind a tree a few hundred paces away. "Over here!"

The priest scrambled to him fast as he could, his short legs stumbling over the uneven ground. "We're attacked!" he shouted, pointing with his staff. "They've come round to take us from behind."

"The devils!" shouted Bran, already running to head off the assault. "Iwan! Siarles! To me! The rest of you stay where you are and keep them busy. Make every arrow count!"

The three archers reached the glade to find five mounted knights in a deadly clash with four Grellon. The knights were stabbing with spears and slashing with swords, and the Cymry danced just out of reach, darting in quickly to deliver clout after clout with their makeshift staffs.

"Iwan—the two on the left," ordered Bran, nocking an arrow to the string. "Siarles—the one on the right. I'll take the two in the centre." He grasped the string in his two-fingered grip, pressing the belly of the longbow forward until it bent full and round. "Now!"

The word was hardly spoken when it was overtaken by a buzzing whine as Bran's arrow streaked across the shadow-dappled distance. Before it had reached its mark, two more arrows were sizzling through the air. There was a sound like cloth ripping in the wind, and the knight in the centre of the swarm was thrown back over the cantle of his saddle and off the rear of his mount. Two more knights followed the first to the ground, and as the two remaining Ffreinc soldiers swerved to meet this new threat, they were set upon by the Cymry, who pulled them down from their horses and slew them with their own weapons.

More knights were pounding into the glade now, charging in force. They came crashing through the underbrush in twos and threes. Tuck held his breath and tightened his grip on his staff. It seemed that Bran and the others must surely be overwhelmed. But the three bows sang as one, sending flight after flight of arrows streaking through the glade. Horses screamed and reared, throwing their riders, who were then set upon by the Grellon. Other soldiers, pierced by multiple shafts, simply dropped from the saddle, dead before they reached the ground.

Four knights just coming into the grove were met by three others fleeing the slaughter. The four newcomers glimpsed the carnage, then wheeled their mounts and joined their comrades in quick retreat.

"Get the weapons!" shouted Bran, already racing back to rejoin those at the front line. "Iwan, stay here and give a shout if any come back."

But the Ffreinc did not return to the attack.

One long moment passed, and then another. No more knights entered the glade from behind, and none dared challenge the archers on the front line again. The lowering sun deepened the shadows in the grove and began to fill up the valleys, and still the attack did not come. The Grellon watched and waited, and asked themselves if they had beaten the enemy back. Finally, when it appeared the assault had foundered, Tuck joined Iwan and the two ran to find Bran at the edge of the grove.

"What do you reckon, my lord?" asked Iwan. "Have we turned them aside?"

"So it would appear," Bran concluded.

"I dearly hope so," sighed Tuck. "All this rushing about is hard on an old fat man like me."

"But they may be waiting for us to show ourselves," Bran suggested.

"Or for nightfall," Iwan said, "so they can take us under cover of darkness."

"Either way," said Bran, making up his mind, "they will not find us here. Get everyone up and ready to move on."

The Grellon assembled once more and, like ghosts drifting away on the vapours of night, faded silently into the depths of the wood.

Tuck

The men had stripped the weapons from the enemy soldiers—swords and lances mostly, but also daggers, helmets, belts, and shields. Arrows were retrieved, and three uninjured horses led away, leaving the heavy saddles and tack behind.

By the time the setting sun had turned the sky the colour of burnished bronze, the grove was abandoned to the dead, who lay still and quiet in the soft green grass.

"May God have mercy on their vile and wretched souls," Tuck whispered, hastening away, "and grant them the peace they have denied to others." Thinking better of this crabbed prayer, he added, "Welcome them into Your eternal kingdom—but not for my sake, Good Lord, no—but for the sake of Your own dear Son who always remembered to forgive His enemies. Amen."

955

CHAPTER 3

Hereford

Baron Bernard Neufmarché unexpectedly found himself in complete agreement with Lady Agnes, who was determined to make the wedding of her daughter Sybil splendid in every way possible. Much to his amazement and delight—for the baron had long ago resigned himself to a wife he considered little more than a frail ghost of a woman—the baroness was now a creature transformed. Gone were the headaches, vapours, and peculiar lingering maladies she had endured since coming to Britain. She was energetic and enthusiastic, tireless in her work at organizing the wedding. Major military campaigns received less attention, in his experience. What is more, the too-slender Agnes had gained weight; her previously skeletal figure had begun filling out to a more robust shape, and a wholesome glow of ruddy good health had replaced her customary sickly pallor.

This change in the woman he had known fully half his life was as surprising as it was welcome. He had never before seen anyone altered so utterly, and he revelled in it. Indeed, the renewal of his wife affected him far more deeply than he could have imagined. His own outlook had altered as well. Something like gratitude had come over him; he looked at the world around him with a warm and pleasant feeling of contentment. For the first time in a very long time he was happy.

For all this, and more, he had his Welsh minions to thank.

On reflection, the baron thought he knew almost to the precise moment when the change—no, the *transformation*—of Agnes began. It was in the churchyard of the little Welsh church where they had laid to rest the body of his vassal, King Cadwgan of Eiwas. Something had touched his wife at the funeral, and when the three days of observance drew to a close, the rebirth had begun.

Perhaps nowhere was the change more evident than in her view of the Welsh themselves. Where before Lady Agnes had considered them subhuman savages, a nation of brutish barbarians at best, now she viewed them more as unfortunates, as children who had survived an infancy of deprivation and neglect—which she was now intent on redressing.

Sybil's wedding was just the beginning; once she and Prince Garran—no, the young man was king now, it must be remembered—once the two young people were married, Lady Agnes planned nothing less than the rehabilitation of the entire realm and all its people. "They only want a town or two and markets," Agnes had informed him a few weeks ago, "some proper churches—good stone, mind—and a monastery, of course. Yes, and a better road. Then farms would flourish. I do believe it would be one of the finest cantrefs in the land."

"They are cattle herders, mostly," the baron had pointed out as he skimmed through a list of provisions he was amassing for the wedding.

"That, I suspect, is because they know little else," she concluded. "We shall show them how to husband the land."

"Teach them to farm?"

"*Bien sûr*," she replied lightly. "Why not? Then they will have things to trade in the markets. With the money that brings, they can begin making something of themselves."

In Agnes's view, the pitiful Welsh holdings were to be built up and made productive, the wasteland tilled and the wildwood managed— as in her father's prosperous estates in Normandie. With the considerable aid and support of the Neufmarché nobility, Eiwas would become a dazzling jewel, a bright and shining star leading all of Wales into a glorious new day of abundance and prosperity.

This was in the future, thank heaven—just thinking about the work involved made the baron tired. Nevertheless, he had to admit that he liked this new, industrious, spirited, far-thinking wife much better than the frail, sharp-tongued, sickly old one. And, truth be told, her plans for the cantref were not so very different from his own. Now that she was of similar mind, accomplishing his will in Eiwas and establishing himself more firmly in Wales would be that much easier. Yes, forging a lasting alliance through the marriage of his daughter to a Welsh king was a match that made good sense in more ways than one.

For his part, Bernard had assembled all the necessary supplies for a feast the like of which he was sure no one beyond the March had ever seen. It was his intention that the occasion should be spoken of in awed tones by his Welsh vassals for years to come. He wanted to cow them with a spectacle of such stunning opulence that they

959

would fight one another to be next in line to receive such largess from his hand.

There was also the matter of a house. After all, as the doting father of the bride, he could not allow his precious daughter to live in the tumbledown wooden fortress that was Caer Rhodl. She would have a proper house of stone, with solid stone walls to keep her and his grandchildren—when they came along—safe from the buffeting winds of war and strife. Not that he expected trouble; since his defeat of King Rhys ap Tewdwr in the lightning conquest of Deheubarth things were much more peaceful in the region. He was, he felt, succeeding in winning over the inhabitants of that southern cantref just as he had won over the people of Eiwas.

Still, in Wales, one never knew what to expect. It was better to be ready for whatever martial crisis might arise—not to mention the fact that it would eventually become a convenient base from which to extend his power deeper into Wales. To that end, he had his master builder draw up plans for a castle with stout ramparts, a high donjon, garrison, stables, flagstone yard, and, surrounding all, a steep-sided moat. The house and its castle would be his wedding gift to the couple.

King Garran, proud Welshman that he was, would no doubt have rejected outright the suggestion that his stronghold was inadequate in any aspect. But if the fortress came as a wedding gift for himself and his new bride—well, the young king could hardly refuse it. Baron Neufmarché would have his way in the end.

Thus, as the days drew down toward the celebration, the baron put the finishing touches on his elaborate preparations. And on a bright summer day, he and the baroness and their daughter broke fast on a bit of bread and watered wine, and then walked out into the yard, where a covered carriage drawn by two chestnut horses awaited. As the ladies were helped up into the carriage, the baron issued final instructions to the servants who were staying behind, then climbed into the carriage himself.

They proceeded out through the castle gate and down into the town and out onto the King's Road. At the edge of Hereford they were met by a bodyguard of twenty knights and men-at-arms accompanied by nine wagons piled high with provisions, dishes and utensils, clothes and personal belongings; and four wagons filled with cooks, kitchen helpers, musicians, and sundry servants, all under the supervision of Remey, the baron's aged seneschal.

"God with you, Sire," said the baron's master-at-arms.

"God with you, Marshal Orval," returned the baron. "Is all well this morning?"

"All is well and in order, and awaiting your command," replied the marshal, making a small bow from the saddle. "If you will give the order, we will be on our way."

The baron glanced at the double rank of knights arrayed at the edge of the field beside the road. "Is this all you have mustered?" wondered the baron. "I thought there would be more."

"Indeed, Sire, yes," replied Marshal Orval, "there are as many more as you see here. I thought best to send the others on ahead to make certain the way is clear. We should encounter no trouble on the way."

"Very good, Marshal," agreed Neufmarché, satisfied at last. "Then you may give the signal and move out. We have a wedding to attend." With this last, he reached over and gave his daughter's hand a squeeze.

For her part, the young lady was suitably demure beneath a cap of pale blue silk with a veil that rested lightly over her long dark hair. In her lap she carried a posy of tiny white flowers bound in a bit of green cloth. She smiled at her father as the carriage lurched into motion, and said, "You have gone to far too much trouble—as I feared you might."

"Nonsense!" replied the baron. "Only what was necessary—nothing more."

"Nine wagons—necessary?" She laughed, not at all put out by her father's extravagance. "I'm not marrying the entire realm."

"*Au contraire, chérie,* but you are," insisted Bernard. "You will be queen and ruler of the realm—the woman all your male subjects will admire and all female subjects emulate."

"Your father is right," offered the baroness. "A future queen cannot be seen to hold herself too low, or she will lose the respect of those who must live beneath her rule."

"Nor would we care to be thought close-fisted on such an important occasion," continued the baron. "We must by all means demonstrate the prosperity we intend to cultivate in the realm. The people must see what it is that we intend for them."

"Not *all* the people, surely," said Sybil in mild derision. "I doubt I will have any dealings with the serfs."

"Do you not think so?" replied her mother. "Each and every one of your vassals will benefit from your rule—serfs as well as nobility. You must not allow yourself to become distant from those you rule. This is something that happens far too often in France, and I do not think it altogether a good thing."

This last pronouncement surprised the baron into silence. Coming from a bishop or cardinal such a sentiment would not seem out of place; but this—from the lips of a woman who, after fourteen years still did not know the names of the cook or any of the kitchen servants, and had yet to meet the porter, stabler, and grooms—it fair took his breath away.

Lady Agnes turned to him. *"Ce n'est pas, mon mari?"* she inquired with a lift of her eyebrow.

It took him a moment to realize she was speaking to him. "Oh! Indeed! Indeed, yes," he agreed hurriedly. "Sadly, it is much the way of things in France, but we have the opportunity to do better now." He smiled at the grave expression on his daughter's face. "But do not worry, *mon coeur*. It will soon be second nature to you." He glanced from his daughter to his wife, and added, "Why, you'll be surprised at how naturally it grows."

"And you will have your handmaids and servants to help—as well as a seneschal," Agnes continued. "A good seneschal is worth his weight in gold—and we shall make it a matter of some urgency to find one who knows what he's about. Your grandfather will have some ideas, I think; I will write to him and ask him to send two or three and you can choose the one that suits you best."

963

"A Welsh seneschal would be better, surely," ventured Sybil. "Because of the language . . ."

"Tch!" her mother countered. "That would never do. You would soon fall into the errors of their ways. As I said, it will be your duty—the duty of us all—to teach them."

They talked of this and other things, and the day passed with the countryside juddering slowly by. Because of all the wagons, they could not move with any speed, and as the sun dropped lower and ever lower in the west, Marshal Orval searched for and found a suitable place to make camp for the night. While the servants prepared a meal for all the entourage, the baron and baroness walked up to the top of the nearest hill to stretch their legs after riding in the carriage all day. In the distance they could see the dark, close-crowded hills of Wales, misty with the coming of night.

"What do you see?" asked Agnes.

The baron was thoughtful for a moment, then said, "I see wealth and power and a throne to rival England's." His naked declaration embarrassed him a little; he could feel Agnes's eyes on him, so he shrugged and added, "At least, it is closer now than it has ever been. The wedding will make a glorious beginning."

She returned his smile and took his hand. "That, *mon amour*, is exactly what I was thinking."

It was five days of anxious travel before Bran and the Grellon reached Coed Cadw. Footsore, weary, and disheartened beyond measure, they sought the safety of their forest keep. As they moved into the lush, green-shadowed solitude of the Guardian Wood, the heat of the day dropped away and they walked a little easier and lighter of step. There among the trees the weary, heart-sick band began to heal the wounded memories of the last days—the betrayal of the Ffreinc king, the treachery of the Black Abbot, the fierce and bloody battle, and their anxious flight.

Though they had escaped the battle without fatality—a few of the men suffered cuts and bruises, one a broken arm, and another a deep sword wound to the thigh—the carnage had exacted a toll that only became apparent in the days that followed. For most of the Grellon the panic and horror of that day was a plague that worked away on their souls, and they were infected with it.

Thus, soul-sick and exhausted they crept back into the solace of the greenwood to heal the raw, inflamed wounds of their memories, arriving at Cél Craidd to the great relief of those who had been left to look after the settlement in their absence.

The watchers had seen them on the road and hastened back to prepare a welcome: jars of cool water flavoured with elderflower blossoms and honey seed cakes to restore their strength. But the travellers were in no mood to rejoice, and their stark response to what should have been a glad homecoming soon dashed any notions of celebration. "Something is amiss, my lord," observed Henwydd delicately; an older man, he had been given the care of Cél Craidd in Bran's absence. "Forgive me if I speak in error, but the faces I see around me would be better suited to a funeral party, not a homecoming."

"How can it be otherwise?" said Bran, his voice thick with bitterness. "The black-hearted English king broke his promise. The realm belongs to the Ffreinc, and we are outlaws still."

"Sooner have milk from a stone," grumbled Iwan, following Bran, "than get satisfaction from a Norman."

Angharad arranged her wrinkled face into a sad smile. She thanked Henwydd and the others for their thoughtfulness and accepted a drink from the welcome cup. Then, taking her leave of Bran and the others, she shuffled slowly to her hut.

"Did Red William not redeem your throne?" asked another, pressing forward.

"He did not," answered Bran. "Count Falkes is banished to Normandie with his uncle the Baron de Braose, and Elfael is claimed by the king."

"Bloody Black Abbot Hugo and his gutless marshal, Gysburne, are placed over us for our *care* and *protection*," growled Siarles.

"Then we won't be going home," said Henwydd.

"No," Bran replied. "We stay here—for now, at least."

"Are we to remain in the forest forever?" asked Teleri, another who had remained behind. An older woman, she had lost all she had to the Ffreinc when the count took her house for the new church. There were tears in her eyes as the meaning of Bran's words broke upon her.

Mérian had come to stand beside Bran; she reached out and put her arm around the woman's shoulders to comfort her. "We have endured the forest this long," Mérian said, "what is another season or two?"

"Season or two?" said Henwydd, growing angry. "Why not ten or twenty?"

"If you have something to say," Bran replied sternly, "go on, say it. Speak your mind."

"We believed in you, my lord. We trusted you. I have suffered this outlaw life for the hope of the deliverance you promised. But I cannot abide another season scrabbling hand to mouth in the green-wood. It is no fit life, and I am too old."

Others, too, spoke out against the desperate life in the forest, with its darkness and dangers—exposure, privation, and the constant fear of discovery. If the Ffreinc didn't kill them, they said, the wolves would. They had followed Bran this far, but now that there was no hope of justice to be had from the Ffreinc, it was time to think what was best for themselves. "William the Red commands armies beyond number," one man said. "We cannot fight them all, and only a fool would try."

Bran glowered, but held his tongue.

"I am sorry, my lord," continued Henwydd, "but you see how it is. I beg leave to quit the forest. I have never asked anything of you, but I'm asking you now to grant me leave to depart."

967

"And where will you go?" asked Mérian.

"Well," considered the old man, "I have kinsmen still in Dyfed. It may be they will take me in. But whether they do or don't makes no matter, 'cause anywhere is better than here."

"There we have it," Bran said, eyes alight and voice cold. He turned and addressed the rest of the settlement. "Who else feels this way? Who else wants to leave the forest?" He swung around, his voice attacking. "Iwan? Will Scarlet? Siarles, what about you? Mérian— God knows you've wanted to leave often enough, why not go now?" He glared around at the ring of grim faces. None would meet his ferocious stare.

Mérian, standing beside Tuck, grasped the friar's hand. "Oh, no," she breathed, tears starting to her eyes. Tuck grasped her hand and gave it a squeeze.

"Who else is for leaving?" demanded Bran. "If you would go, speak up. All who wish to leave may go with my blessing. I do not force anyone to stay who would not do so gladly and of their own accord."

There was an instant commotion at this, and the forest-dwellers began arguing it over amongst themselves. Some were for leaving, others for staying, and all shouting to be heard and convince the rest. Bran let this continue until most had had a chance to speak out, then said, "Well? What say you? Anyone else want to go? Step up and take your place with Henwydd. For all saints bear witness, I do not care to stand with anyone who does not care to stand with me."

At first, no one moved, and then, one by one, others joined Henwydd until a group of seventeen men and women, some with children, stood together in a dismal clump.

"So, now," Bran, his face hard, addressed those who had chosen to leave. "Gather your things and make ready to depart—take whatever you need for your journey. If you would have my advice, wait until the sun goes down and make your way by night; you should avoid any Ffreinc and reach the borders of Elfael before sunrise tomorrow. I bid you God's speed, and may you all fare well."

With that, he turned and strode to his hut.

A shocked and dismayed Cél Craidd watched him go. Iwan and Siarles looked on aghast, and Scarlet and Mérian began to persuade those who had decided to leave that they were making a mistake—but thought better of it. The tight bond between King Raven and his proud Grellon was broken; the settlement was divided and there was nothing anyone could do.

Later, as twilight deepened the shadows in the wood, Friar Tuck called the people together for a prayer of thanks for their deliverance from the hands of the enemy and for a safe return, and for the future of the realm. He then led his discouraged flock in a hymn; he sang the first verses alone, but soon everyone joined in, lifting their voices and singing loudly as the moon rose in the pale blue sky. Neither Bran nor Angharad attended the prayer service, but the banfáith appeared after sundown when the first of those leaving the forest settlement were setting off. Gripping her staff, she offered blessings for the journey and safe arrivals for all who would travel that night.

The next morning after breaking fast, the remaining Grellon resumed their chores; there was more work now that a fair number of the most able-bodied had gone. As those who remained took stock of their numbers it was clear that others, unwilling to be seen by their friends, had departed silently during the night. Taking a silent tally, they soon realized that fewer than half their number remained.

With heavy hearts they set to and were just discussing how to divide the duties of the day and the days to come when Angharad called all Cél Craidd to gather at the Council Oak in the centre of the settlement. As the forest-dwellers assembled beneath the spreading boughs of the great, grey giant, they found Bran seated in his chair made of ash branches lashed together and covered by a bearskin. Bran looked like a Celtic king of old—an impression only strengthened by the long-beaked mask of King Raven that lay at his feet. Angharad stood behind her king, wearing the Bird Spirit cloak and holding a long, thin, rodlike staff in her right hand.

As soon as everyone had settled themselves close about this primitive throne, the banfáith raised the staff and said, "Heed the Head of Wisdom and attend her counsel. You are summoned here to uphold your king in his deliberations with strong consideration. Therefore, make keen your thoughts and carefully attend your words, for the course we determine here among us will be the life and death of many."

She paused, and Bran said, "If anyone here does not wish to bear this burden, you may leave now in peace. But if you stay, you will agree to abide by the decisions we shall make and pledge life, strength, and breath to fulfil them whatever they shall be."

Iwan, grim and deeply aggrieved, spoke for them all when he said, "Those who wanted to leave have gone, my lord, and God bless 'em. But those you see before you are with you to the end—and that end is to see you take your rightful throne and lead your people in peace and plenty."

"Hear him!" said Scarlet. "Hear him!"

"S'truth," added Siarles, and others shouted, "God wills it!"

Bran nodded to Angharad, who struck the bare earth three times with the end of her staff to silence the commotion. Then, raising her hand, palm outward, she tilted her face to the light slanting down through the leaf-laden branches. "Goodly Wise, Strong Upholder, Swift Sure Hand," she said in a queer chanting voice, "draw near to us; enter into our minds and hearts; be to us the voice that speaks the True Word. Be to us our rock and fortress, our shield and defender, our strength and courage. Go before us, Lord of Hosts, bare Your mighty arm, set Your face against our enemies, and as You destroyed the army of the wicked pharaoh in the sea, let fear swallow up those who raise their hands against us. These things we ask in the name of Blesséd Jesu, Our Hope and Redeemer, and Michael Militant the Terrible Sword of Your Righteousness." Her mouth moved silently for a moment longer; then she said, "Amen."

All gathered in the solemn assembly echoed. "Amen."

Bran turned his head and thanked his Wise Banfáith for her prayer. To the people gathered before him, he said, "We are here to decide how the war with the Ffreinc shall be pursued. On my most solemn vow, there will be an end to their rule in this realm . . . or there will be an end to me. For I will not tolerate their presence in the land of my fathers while there is yet a single breath in my body."

"I am with you, my lord!" cried Iwan, slapping his knee. "We will drive them from this realm—or die in the attempt."

Bran gave a downward jerk of his chin by way of acknowledgement of Iwan's pledge, and continued. "Let us speak freely now, holding nothing back. As we must stand together in the days to come, let us share our hearts and minds." He paused to let his listeners gather their thoughts. "So now." He spread his hands. "Who will begin?"

Tuck was first to find his voice. "To speak plain, I am grieved in heart, soul, and mind since the attack in the grove—and any man who said otherwise is a liar. Our King William has proven himself a greedy, grasping rogue and a stranger to all honour. If that was not a bitter enough brew to swallow, our Ffreinc overlords have shown us that they will attack with impunity, little respecting women and children—"

"Devil take them all," muttered Siarles.

"Nevertheless," the friar continued, raising a hand for silence, "I have bethought myself time and time again, and it seems to me that if our enemies have any tender feelings within reach of their cold hearts, it may be that they are even now sorely regretting that rash act."

"What are you saying, Tuck?" asked Bran softly.

"It would be well to send Abbot Hugo an offer of peace."

"Peace!" scoffed Bran. "On my father's grave, a moment's peace they will not have from me."

"I know! My lord, I know—they have earned damnation ten times over. Is there anyone here who does not know it? But, I pray you, do not dismiss the notion outright."

Tuck turned to appeal to those gathered beneath the oak boughs. "See here, it is not for our enemies that I make this plea—it is for *us* and for our good. The pursuit of war is a dire and terrible waste— of life and limb, blood and tears. It maims all it touches. Maybe we gain justice in the end, maybe not. No one knows how it will end. But, know you, we will lose much that we hold dear long 'ere we reach the end, and of that we can be more than certain."

"We have little to lose, it seems to me," remarked Iwan.

"True enough," Tuck allowed, "but it is always possible to lose even that little, is it not? Think you now—if war could be avoided, we might be spared that loss. By pursuing peace as readily as war, we might even gain the outcome we seek—and is that not a thing worth the risk of trying?"

Tuck's plea fell into silence even as he implored the others to at least consider what he had said. No one, so it appeared, shared his particular sentiment.

"Our priest is right to speak so," said Mérian, moving to stand beside the little cleric. "War with the Ffreinc will mean the deaths of many—maybe all of us. But if death and destruction can be avoided, we must by all means try—for the sake of those who will be hurt by what we decide today, we must make an offer of peace."

"Offer peace?" wondered Scarlet aloud. "That's begging for trouble with a dog and bowl."

"Aye, trouble and worse," growled Siarles. "If you have no stomach for the fight ahead, maybe you should both join Henwydd and his band of cowards. They're not so far ahead that you couldn't catch 'em up."

"Coward? Is that what you think?" asked Tuck, voicing the question to the whole gathering. "Is that what everyone thinks?"

"I don't say it is, I don't say it en't," replied Siarles. "But the shoe fits him who made it."

"Enough, both of you. Courage is not at issue here," Bran pointed out. "I was willing to swear fealty to William Rufus. Indeed, I encouraged my father to do so, and we would not be here now if he had listened to me and acted before it was too late . . ."

"Do you not see?" said Mérian. "You're in danger of becoming just like your father—too proud and stubborn for the good of your people. And, like your father, you will die at the end of a Norman spear." She put out a slender hand and softened her tone. "Red William is a false king; that is true. His decision was the ruin of all our hopes, and now everything has changed. Look around, my lord—only half of Cél Craidd remains. Even if we were mighty warriors, champions each and every one, we could not take back Elfael by force of arms alone."

Bran glared at her, his brow low and furrowed. Judging from the expressions on the faces around him, Mérian had won solid support for her opinion. "What do you suggest?" he said at last.

Mérian glanced at Tuck. "That is not for me to say, my lord."

"It seems to me you have said a great deal already, my lady. Why stop now?" He lifted his head to include the rest of the gathering. "Come, speak up, your lord is asking for your counsel. What do you advise?"

"If I may speak freely, my lord," began Tuck.

"I doubt anything in heaven or earth could prevent you," remarked Bran. "Speak, priest."

"Hardheaded Saxon that I am, I have always thought it a good thing that the clerics rule the church and kings rule the realm. That is the way God has ordained it, has He not? Render unto Caesar the things that are Caesar's, to be sure, but give to God the things that are God's. Like it or not, the Ffreinc—"

"Is there a point to this sermon, Friar?" interrupted Bran.

"Only that we must be prepared to compromise if we are to persuade the abbot and sheriff to accept the peace."

"Compromise," repeated Bran dully.

"What sort of compromise?" asked Siarles.

"That any Ffreinc who have settled should be allowed to remain in Elfael under your rule, and that Hugo will remain in charge of the spiritual concerns of the abbey."

"Let Hugo keep the abbey and I take the fortress—is that what you're saying?" said Bran.

"In a word, yes, my lord."

"Why in heaven's name would Hugo agree to that?"

"Because," suggested Tuck, "it would allow him to put his efforts into saving his abbey, which he will certainly lose if he continues to pursue this war. Lose the abbey and he has lost his place in the church—and I heartily doubt he'll ever get another one. Who'd have him?"

"Indeed," said Bran.

"You know what I mean," Tuck continued. "If he agrees to the peace, he will survive, and keep much that he will lose if the war continues."

"My lord, you would have to swear fealty to William," Will Scarlet pointed out.

"He has offered to do that already," Iwan reminded him. "Twice."

"What about the king? He has given the realm to Hugo."

"Then he can take it away again and give it back to its rightful ruler," said Tuck, adding, "of course, the abbot would have to agree to support you before the king."

"He'd never do it," said Siarles.

"Share my realm with that rank Ffreinc butcher?" wondered Bran, shaking his head. "My stomach churns at the very thought."

He glanced to Angharad for support, but the old woman admonished him, saying, "What the friar suggests has merit, Lord King. Think you: force has availed us nothing, nor has any other remedy offered a cure for this wasting blight. We hurt them in the grove, mind. Our enemies may be ready to listen to such an offer. It would be well to ponder the matter further."

"I bow to your judgment," allowed Bran grimly. Turning to the assembly, he said, "Let us suppose, for the moment, that we send an offer of peace to the abbot. What then?"

975

"Then it is for the Ffreinc to decide, is it not?" replied Tuck. "Either they accept and proceed according to your decree—"

"And if they don't?" wondered Siarles.

"We will be no worse off," suggested Mérian.

"But whatever happens will be on their heads," added Tuck. "At all events, it is our Christian duty to try for peace if it lays in our power."

Bran chewed his lip thoughtfully for a moment. Tuck thought he could see a chink of light shining in the darkness of Bran's bleak mood. "Lord Bran," the friar said, "I would like to take the message to Hugo myself and alone."

"Why alone?" said Bran.

"Priest to priest," replied Tuck. "That is how I mean to approach him—two men of God answerable to the Almighty. Blesséd are the peacemakers, are they not?"

"As Angharad suggests," put in Mérian, "the abbot may welcome the opportunity to be rid of this bloodshed."

"Hugo will welcome the opportunity to carve him like a Christmas ham," observed Scarlet. To Tuck, he said, "He'll roast your rump and feed it to his hounds."

"Nay," said Tuck. "He'll do no such thing. I am a brother cleric and a minister of the church. A rogue he may be, but he will receive me, as he must."

"While I do not expect the abbot to honour any offer we put before him," said Iwan, "I agree with our man Tuck—we should do what we can to avoid another bloodletting, as it may well be our blood next time instead of theirs. Try as I might, however, I can think of no other way to avoid it—our choices are that few. It is worth a try."

There was more talk then, as others added their voices to the discussion—some for the idea, others against. In the end, however, Tuck's proposition carried the day.

"Then it is decided," declared Bran when everyone had had their say. "In observance of our Christian duty, and for the sake of our people, we will make this offer of peace to Hugo and urge him by all means to accept it and to support me before King William."

"It is the right decision, my lord," said Mérian, pressing close. "If Hugo will listen to reason, then you'll have reclaimed what is rightfully yours without risking the lives of any more of your people."

"Right or wrong it makes no difference," Bran told her. "We are too weak to pursue the war further on our own." He declared the council at an end and said, "I will frame a message for Tuck to deliver to the abbot. If he accepts my offer, we will soon be out of the forest and back in our own lands."

"I'll believe it when it happens," grumbled Siarles.

977

"You're not alone there," Scarlet said. "Give 'em a year o' Sundays and a angel choir to show 'em the way, the bloody Ffreinc will never shift an English inch."

"Then pray God to change their hearts," Tuck said. "Do not think it impossible just because it has never happened."

The council concluded, and as everyone dispersed Tuck lingered in Angharad's presence a little longer. Close to her, he was aware once again of a curious sensation—like that of standing beneath one of the venerable giants of the forest, an oak or elm of untold age. It was, he decided, the awareness that he was near something so large and calm and rooted to depths he could scarcely imagine. With her face a web of wrinkles and her thinning hair a haze of wisp on her head, she seemed the very image of age, yet commanded all she beheld with the keen intelligence of her deep-set, dark eyes. "I hope I have served him wisely," he told the old woman.

"So hope we all," she replied.

"I am afraid Siarles is right—offering peace is just begging for trouble."

"Trouble have we in abundance," the banfáith pointed out. "It is a most hardy crop."

"Too true," the friar agreed.

"Hear me, friend priest," she said, holding him with her deep-set, dark eyes. "This war began long ago; we merely join it now. The trouble is not of our making, but it is our portion and ours to endure."

"That does not cheer me much," sighed Tuck.

"Regrets, have you?"

"No, never," he answered. "That is the duty of any Christian."

"Then trust God with it and that which is given you, do."

"You are right, of course," he said at last.

Angharad regarded the friar with a kindly expression. The little priest with his rotund, bandy-legged form, his shaggy tonsure, his stained and tattered robe—smelling of smoke and sweat and who knows what else—there was that much like a donkey about him. And like the humble beast of burden, he was loyal and long-suffering, able to bear the heavy load of responsibility placed upon him now. "As God is our lord and leader," she said, "it is our portion to obey and follow. We trust him to lead us aright. As with our Heavenly Lord, so with Bran. More we cannot do just now, but we must do that at least."

"Ah, but earthly vessels are all too fragile, are they not? We trust them at our peril."

The old woman smiled gently. "Yet it is all we have."

"Too true," Tuck agreed.

"So we trust and pray—never knowing which is the more needful."

Tuck accepted her counsel and made his way to the edge of the forest settlement, where he found Bran and Mérian sitting knee to knee on stumps facing one another as if in contest, while Will, Noín, and Odo stood looking on. "They *know* we will fight," Mérian was saying. "If ever there was the smallest doubt, we showed them in the grove. But you *must* give them some assurance that we will not seek revenge if they accept your offer."

Bran nodded, conceding the point.

"They have to know that they are not simply cutting their own throats," she insisted.

"I understand," Bran replied. "And I agree. Go on."

"It must be something they can trust," she continued, "even if they don't trust *you.*"

"Granted, Mérian," said Bran, exasperation edging into his voice. "What do you suggest?"

"Well"—she bit her lip—"I don't know."

"Maybe we could get the abbot at Saint Dyfrig's to oversee the truce," suggested Noín. "He is a good man, and they know him."

"After what happened in the square on Twelfth Night, I cannot think they would trust any of us any farther than they could spit a mouthful of nails," Scarlet said, shaking his head.

"It must be someone they know, someone they can rely on to be fair."

Mérian's face clenched in thought. "I know!" she said, glancing up quickly. "We could ask my father . . ."

"Your father—what possible reason could Hugo have for trusting him?"

"Because he is a loyal vassal of King William, as is the abbot himself . . ."

"No," said Bran, jumping up quickly. "This is absurd." He began stalking around the stump. "It won't work."

"Why—because *you* did not think of it?"

"Your father hates me," Bran said. "And that was *before* I abducted you! God alone knows what he thinks of me now. If that was not enough, Lord Cadwgan answers to Baron Neufmarché, his liege lord—and if the baron were to get wind of this there is no way we could keep him out of it."

"The Ffreinc would trust the baron," Mérian said.

"They might, but could *we?*" wondered Scarlet.

"Have you forgotten Neufmarché tried to kill me last time I went to him for help?" said Bran. "If it is all the same to you, I'd rather not give him another chance."

Mérian frowned. "That was unfortunate."

"Unfortunate!" cried Bran. "Woman, the man is a two-faced Judas. He betrayed me outright. Indeed, he betrayed us both. Your own life was none too secure, if you'll recall."

"What you say is true," she conceded. "I'll not argue. Still, he is a Ffreinc nobleman and if—together with my father, of course—we could convince him that it was in his own best interest to help us, I know he'd agree."

"Oh, he'd agree," Bran retorted, "agree to help empty Elfael of his rivals so he could have it all to himself. We'd just be exchanging one tyrant for an even bigger, more powerful tyrant." Bran gave a sharp chop of his hand, dismissing the suggestion. "No. If the Ffreinc require assurance that we will hold to our word, we will appeal to Abbot Daffyd to swear for us and they will have to accept that." He sat back down. "Now then, what do we want Tuck to tell them?"

They fell to discussing the substance of the message and soon hammered out a simple, straightforward appeal to meet and discuss the proposed offer of peace. By the time Siarles came to say that the horse was ready, the Ffreinc scribe, Odo, had schooled and corrected Tuck's creaky Latin so there would be no mistake. "I have some of the Norman tongue too," Tuck pointed out in French. "Picked up a fair bit in my years in Hereford."

"Not enough, God knows," snipped Odo.

"I understand far more than I can speak," said Tuck.

"Even so," allowed the scribe, "it is not what you understand that will lead you to difficulty, but what you are likely to *say*."

"Perhaps you should come with me, then," suggested Tuck. "To keep a poor friar from stumbling over the rocky places."

The colour drained from the already pasty face of the young cleric.

"I thought not," replied Tuck. "'Tis better I go alone."

"Ah!" said Odo. "I will write it down for you so the abbot can read it for himself if you go astray." He bustled off to find his writing utensils and a scrap of something to carry the ink.

"All is well?" asked Bran, seeing the scribe depart on the run.

"Right as rain in merry May," replied Tuck. "Odo is going to write it for me so if all else fails I have something to push under the abbot's nose."

"Scarlet is right—this is dangerous. Hugo could seize you and have you hung, or worse. You don't have to go. We can find another way to get a message through."

"The Lord is my shield and defender," replied Tuck. "Of whom shall I be afraid?"

"Well then," Bran concluded, "God with you, Tuck. Siarles and I will see you to the edge of the forest at least."

A short while later, the would-be peacemakers paused at the place where the King's Road crossed the ford and started down into the valley. Bran and Siarles were each armed with a bow and bag of arrows, and Tuck carried a new-made quarterstaff. In the distance they could see Caer Cadarn on its hump of rock, guarding the Vale of Elfael. "I do not expect the abbot will have let the fortress stand abandoned for long," Bran surmised. "He would have moved men into it as soon as Count Falkes had gone."

"If any should see me, they will only see a poor fat friar on a skinny horse making for town—nothing to alarm anyone."

"And if they should take exception and stop you?" asked Siarles.

"I will tell them I bring a word of greeting and hope to Abbot Hugo," replied Tuck. "And that is God's own truth."

"Then off with you," said Bran, "and hurry back. We'll wait for you here."

It took Tuck longer to reach the town than he had reckoned, and the sun was already beginning its descent as he entered the market square—all but empty, with only a few folk about and no soldiers that he could see. Always before there had been soldiers. Indeed, the town had a tired, deserted air about it. He tied his mount to an iron ring set in a wall, drew a deep breath, hitched up his robe, and strode boldly across the square to stand before the whitewashed walls of the abbey. He pounded on the timber door with the flat of his hand and waited. A few moments later, the door opened, and the white-haired old porter peered out.

"*Nous avons un message pour l'abbé,*" Tuck intoned politely. "*Je vous prie de l'amener à lui tout de suite.*"

Brother porter ducked his head respectfully and hurried away.

"Thank you, Lord," said Tuck, breathing a sigh of relief to have passed the first test.

Tuck waited, growing more and more uneasy with each passing

moment. Finally, the door in the abbey gate opened once more and the porter beckoned him to come inside, where he was led across the yard to the abbot's lodge. A few of the monks stopped to stare as he passed—perhaps, thought Tuck, recognizing him from their previous encounter in King William's yard not too many days ago.

Once inside, he was conducted through a dark corridor and brought to stand before a panelled door. The porter knocked and received the summons to enter. He pushed open the door and indicated that Tuck should go in.

The abbot was standing over a table on which was spread a simple supper. He was spearing a piece of cheese with a long fork as Tuck entered. Glancing up, Hugo stopped, his mouth agape. Then, collecting himself, he said in a low voice, *"Vous devez être fous, de venir ici de cette manière. Que voulez-vous?"*

Tuck understood this to mean that the abbot thought he must be insane to come there, and demanded to know what he wanted.

At this, Tuck, speaking in measured tones and with many haltings as he searched for the words, began his prepared speech. He appealed to Abbot Hugo as a brother in their common calling as priests of the church, and thanked the abbot for allowing him to speak. He then said that he had come with an offer of peace from the forest-dwellers. When words began to fail, he took out the little scrap of parchment Odo had prepared for him, listing the central stipulations of the plan. The abbot's face grew red as he listened, but he held his tongue. Tuck concluded, saying, "You have until midday tomorrow to give your answer. If you accept Bran's offer, you will ring the abbey bell nine times—three peals of three. Then, come to the edge of the forest, where you will be told what to do next. Do you understand?"

To which the abbot replied, "I do not know which offends me

the more—your uncouth speech or the crudeness of your appear-ance." He waved a hand in front of his nose. "You smell worse than a stable hound."

Tuck bore the insult with a smile. He'd not expected an easy ride through enemy territory. "But you understand what I am saying?"

"Oh, I understand," confirmed Hugo. "However, I fail to see why I should dignify this ridiculous idea of sharing the governance of Elfael with a vile outlaw and rebel."

"Bran ap Brychan is neither outlaw nor rebel," Tuck replied evenly, hoping he had got the words right. "In truth, his family has ruled this realm for a hundred years or more. If you agree, you would be sharing the dominion of the cantref with the rightful heir to the throne of Elfael, who—no fault of his own—has been deprived of his kingship."

"And if I do not agree?"

"Then there will be a bloody price to pay."

"Is that supposed to frighten me?" asked Hugo, arching an eye-brow. "If so, forgive me if I refuse to take this threat of retribution seriously. It seems to me that *if* your Lord Bran could take this town by force, he would have done so long ere now, no?"

"He is giving you one last chance," said Tuck.

"One last chance."

"Yes, Abbot—this is the last and best chance you will receive."

"So, I am supposed to simply abandon the town and fortress to the outlaws and imprison myself in the abbey here—is that it?"

"You would not be held captive," said Tuck, struggling to make himself understood. "Bran would rule the realm as a liegeman of the king, and you would support him in this and . . . ah, *confine* . . . your activities to the work of the abbey."

"Non!" roared the abbot, throwing down the long-handled fork. *"C'est impossible!* The king has given me Elfael to rule as I see fit. I will in no wise share the governance of this realm with a low brigand." Hugo leaned on the table with his fists, his anger mounting. "I may not have enough men to drive your King Raven from his forest perch, but if he has the might to defeat me, then let him try."

Tuck stared at the abbot, his mind whirling as he tried to decipher this last outburst. "But you will consider the offer?"

"I think our talk is finished." The abbot made a dismissive gesture with his hand. "You may go, but if you ever come here again I will have you arrested to stand trial as a traitor to the crown. You can tell your friends that if I ever catch you or any of them your lives are forfeit."

Tuck stiffened at the insult. "I came here in good faith, Abbot, as a Christian priest. Even so, I don't expect you'll see me again."

"Out!"

"I am going," Tuck said, stepping towards the door. "But I urge you to seriously consider the offer of peace—pray, discuss it with your marshal and the sheriff. You have until midday tomorrow to decide, and if you accept—"

"Porter!" shouted the abbot. "Take this man away!"

Outside once more, Tuck returned to his mount, untied it, and heaved himself up into the saddle. As he lifted the reins he cast a backward look at the abbey and saw a monk flitting along the front of the church towards the guard tower.

He did not linger, but departed quickly lest the abbot betray his word and arrest him. He urged his mount to a trot and left the town, hastening back to the forest with the curious sensation that he had been given a valuable prize but could not remember what it was—something Abbot Hugo had said . . . but what?

In any event, he was satisfied that, as a priest of the church, he had done his duty. "Blesséd are the peacemakers," he murmured to himself. "And the Good Lord help us all."

CHAPTER 6

Saint Martin's

"As long as those outlaws hold the King's Road," complained Marshal Guy, swirling the wine in his cup, "nothing enters or leaves the forest without their notice. We lost good men in that ill-advised attack at Winchester and—"

"You need not whip that dead horse any longer, Marshal," growled Abbot Hugo, slamming down the pewter jar. Wine splashed out and spattered the table linen, leaving a deep crimson stain. "I am only too aware of the price we are paying to maintain this accursed realm."

"My point, Abbot, was that without hope of raising any more soldiers, the cantref is lost already. Sooner or later, the rogues will discover how few men we have, and when they do, they will attack and we will not be able to repel them. That, or they will simply wear us down. Either way, they win."

"Possibly." Hugo shook the wine from his hand, raised his cup, and drank.

"Their Raven King has made us an offer of peace—take it, I say, and let us be done with this godforsaken realm. I wish to heaven I'd never heard of it."

"Be that as it may," Hugo said, staring into his cup, "King William has given the governance of the realm to me, and I will not suffer that ridiculous King Raven and his scabrous minions to hold sway over it. They will be defeated."

"Have you heard a single word I've said?"

"I heard, Marshal, but I do not think you understand the depth of my resolve. For I propose we root out King Raven and his brood for once and all."

"Then just you tell me how do you *propose* we do that?" Guy de Gysburne glared at the abbot, daring him to put up something that could not be knocked down with a single blow. "As many times as we have gone against them, we have been forced to retreat. Swords and spears are no use against those infernal longbows because we cannot get close enough to use them. Pitched battle is no good: they will not stand and fight. They hide in the woods where our horses cannot go. They know the land hereabouts far better than we do, so they can sit back and slaughter us at will."

Abbot Hugo was in no mood to listen to yet another litany of Guy's complaints. They never advanced the cause and always fell back on the tired observation that unless they found a powerful patron to supply men and weapons, and provisions, the realm would fall. The battle in the grove had cost them more than either one of them cared to contemplate—though Guy had not allowed anyone within hearing distance to forget it. Of the thirty-three knights and men-at-arms left to them after the departure of the exiled Baron de Braose, only twenty-one remained. And Elfael, nestled in its valley and surrounded by forest on three sides, was far too vulnerable to the predation of Bran and his outlaw band, who had proven time and again that they could come and go as they pleased.

"If we cannot get to them," replied Hugo, adopting a more conciliatory air, "then we will bring the so-called Raven and his flock to us."

"Easier said than done," muttered Guy. "Our Raven is a canny bird. Not easy to trick, not easy to catch."

"Nor am I an adversary easily defeated." Hugo raised his cup to his mouth and took a deep draught before continuing. "Simply put, we will entice them, draw them out into the open where they cannot attack us from behind trees and such. Their bows will be no good to them at close quarters."

Guy stared at the abbot in amazement and shook his head. "The forest is their fortress. They will not leave it—not for any enticement you might offer."

"But I need offer nothing," the abbot remarked. "Don't you see? They have outwitted themselves this time. Under pretence of accepting the peace, we will lure them into the open. Once they have shown themselves, we will slice them to ribbons."

"Just like that?" scoffed the marshal, shaking his head.

"If you have a better plan, let us hear it," snapped the abbot. Growing weary of arguing with Gysburne at every turn, he decided to end the discussion. "Count Falkes was no match for the Welsh, as we all know. He paid the price for his mistakes and he is gone. I rule here now, and our enemies will find in me a more ruthless and cunning adversary than that de Braose ninny."

Clearly, they had reached an impasse, and Marshal Guy could think of nothing more to say. So he simply dashed the wine from his cup and took his leave.

"If all goes well, Marshal," said the abbot as Guy reached the door, "we will have that viper's nest cleaned out in three days' time."

ow very optimistic," observed Sheriff de Glanville when the marshal told him what the abbot had said. "So far, in all our encounters with these brigands, we've always come off the worse—while *they* get away with neither scratch nor scrape."

"Putting more men in the field only gives them more targets for their accursed arrows," Guy pointed out.

"Precisely," granted the sheriff. He removed the leather hood from his falcon and blew gently on the bird's sleek head. With his free hand he picked up a gobbet of raw meat from a bowl on the table and flipped it to the keen-eyed bird on his glove. "Still, the abbot has a point—we might fare better if we could lure the outlaws from the wood. Have you any idea what the abbot has planned?"

"The outlaws have sent a message offering a truce of some kind."

"Have they indeed?"

"They have," confirmed Gysburne, "and the abbot thinks to use that to draw them out. He didn't say how it would be done."

The sheriff lifted a finger and gently stroked the falcon's head. "Well, I suppose there is no point in trying to guess what goes on in our devious abbot's mind. I have no doubt he'll tell us as soon as he is ready."

They did not have long to wait. At sundown, just after compline, the abbot summoned his two commanders to his private chambers, where he put forth his plan to rid the realm of King Raven and his flock.

"When the abbey bell goes," Abbot Hugo explained for the third time. "I want everyone in place. We don't know—"

"We don't know how many will come, so we must be ready for

anything," grumbled Marshal Gysburne irritably. "For the love of Peter, there is no need to hammer us over the head with it."

The abbot arched an eyebrow. "If I desire to lay stress upon the readiness—or lack of it—of your men," he replied tartly, "be assured that I think it necessary."

"The point is taken, Abbot," offered the sheriff, entering the fray, "and after what happened in the grove at Winchester I think a little prudence cannot go amiss."

Marshal Guy flinched at the insinuation. "You weren't there, Sheriff. Were you? Were you there?"

"You know very well that I was not."

"Then I will thank you to shut your stinking mouth. You don't know a thing about what happened that day."

"*Au contraire, mon ami,*" answered de Glanville with a cold, superior smile. "I know that you left eight good knights in that grove, and four more along the way. Twelve men died as a result, and we are no closer to ridding ourselves of these outlaws than we ever were."

The marshal regarded the sheriff from beneath lowered brows. "You smug swine," he muttered. "You dare sit in judgement of me?"

"Judge you?" inquired de Glanville innocently. "I merely state a fact. If that stings, then perhaps—"

"Enough!" said Abbot Hugo, slapping the arm of his chair with his palm. "Save your spite for the enemy."

Sheriff de Glanville gave the abbot a curt nod and said, "Forgive me, Abbot. As I was about to say, we will never have a better chance to take the enemy unawares. If the outlaws escape into the forest, it will be just like the massacre in the grove. We cannot allow that to happen. This is, I fear, our last best chance to take them. We must succeed this time, or all is lost."

"I agree, of course," replied the abbot. "That goes without saying."

"I beg your pardon, Abbot," remarked the sheriff, "but in matters of war, nothing *ever* goes without saying."

"Well then," sniffed Gysburne, "we have no worries there. You've seen to that—most abundantly."

"Get out of here—both of you," said the abbot. Rising abruptly, he flapped his hands at them as if driving away bothersome birds. "Go on. Just remember, I want you to have your men ready to attack the moment I draw the rogues out of hiding. And strike swiftly. I will not be made to stand waiting out there alone."

"You will not be alone, Abbot. Far from it," said de Glanville. "Gysburne and I will be hidden in the forest, and some of my men will be among your monks. We have thought of everything, I assure you."

"Just you match deed to word, Sheriff, and I will consider myself assured."

The two commanders left the abbey, each to look after his own preparations. Sometime later, when the moon was low and near to setting, but dawn was still a long way off, a company of soldiers departed Saint Martin's. Moving like slow shadows across the valley, ten mounted knights in two columns—their armour and horses' tack muffled with rags to prevent the slightest sound, their weapons dulled with sooted grease so that no glint or shine could betray them—rode in silence to the edge of the forest. Upon reaching the dark canopy of the trees, they dismounted and walked a short distance into the wood, hid their horses and themselves in the thick underbrush, then settled back to wait.

CHAPTER 7

Coed Cadw

With the approach of dawn, the forest awakened around the hidden soldiers—first with birdsong, and then with the furtive twitching and scratching of squirrels and mice and other small creatures. A light mist rose in the low places of the valley, pale and silvery in the early-morning light; it vanished as the sun warmed the ground, leaving a spray of glistening dew on the deep green grass. A family of wild pigs—a sow and six yearling piglets under the watchful eye of a hulking great boar—appeared at the margin of the trees to snuffle along the streambed and dig among the roots. The world began another day while the hidden soldiers dozed with their weapons in their hands. Slowly, the sun climbed higher in a cloud-ruffled sky.

And they waited.

Some little while before midday, there came a sound of movement further back in the forest—the rustling of leaves where there was no breeze, the slight creak of low branches, a sudden flight of sitting birds—and the soldiers who were awake clutched their weapons and nudged those still sleeping beside them. The ghosts of the greenwood were coming. King Raven would soon appear.

But the sounds died away. Nothing happened.

The sun continued its climb until it soared directly overhead. The soldiers, awake now and ready, strained their ears in the drowsy quiet of the wood as, above the whir and buzz of insects, the first faint chimes of a church bell sounded across the valley—far off, but distinct: three peals.

Then silence.

They listened, and they heard the signal repeated. After another lengthy pause, the sequence of three peals sounded for the third and last time.

After the second sequence had sounded, Marshal Gysburne, pressing himself to the ground, craned his neck from his hiding place behind an ash tree and looked down the long slope and into the bowl of the valley, where he saw a faint glimmering: Abbot Hugo and his white-robed monks making their way toward the forest. They came on, slow as snails it seemed to an increasingly impatient Gysburne, who like the other knights was sweating and stiff inside his armour. He inched back behind the tree and listened to the greenwood, hoping to catch any telltale sign of the outlaws' presence.

When at last the abbot's party came within arrow-flight of the edge of the wood, a call like that of a raven sounded from the upper branches of a massive elm tree. The party of white-robed monks surrounding the abbot heard it, too, and as if acting upon a previously agreed signal, stopped at once.

The raucous croak sounded twice more—not quite a bird's cry, Gysburne thought, but certainly not human, either. He scanned the upper branches for the source of the sound, and when he looked back, there, poised at the edge of the tree line, stood the slender young man known as Bran ap Brychan.

"Ah!" gasped Gysburne in surprise.

"Where the devil did he come from?" muttered Sergeant Jeremias from his place on the other side of the ash tree.

Dressed all in black, his dark hair lifting in the breeze, for an instant it seemed to the soldiers that he might indeed have been a raven dropped out of the sky to assume the form of a man. He stood motionless, clutching a longbow in his left hand; at his belt hung a bag of dark arrows.

"Had I one of those bows," Jeremias whispered, "I'd take him now, and save us all a load of bother."

"Shh!" hissed Gysburne in a tense whisper. "He'll hear you."

When the outlaw made no move to approach the group of monks, the abbot called out, *"Entendez-moi! Nous avons fait comme vous avez ordonné. Donc, on a fait ce que vous avez demandé, qu'est-ce qui arrive maintenant?"*

Marshal Gysburne heard this with a sinking heart. *You old fool!* he thought, *the outlaws don't speak French. He'll have no idea what you're saying.*

But to the marshal's surprise, the young man answered, *"Attendez! Un moment!"*

He turned and gestured toward the wood behind him, and there was a rustling of leaves in the brush like a bear waking up; and out from the greenwood stepped the slump-shouldered Norman scribe— the one called Odo.

The two advanced a few more paces into the open, and then halted. At a nod from Bran, the scribe called out, "Have you come to swear peace?"

"I have come as requested," replied Abbot Hugo, "to hear what this man has proposed." Regarding the young scribe, he said, "Greetings, Odo. I suppose I should not be surprised to see you here—traitors and thieves flock together, eh?"

Odo cringed at his former master's abuse, but turned and explained to Bran what the abbot had said, received his lord's answer, and replied, "The proposal is simple. Lord Bran says that you will agree to the terms put to you, or he will pursue the war he has begun."

"Even if I were to agree," replied the abbot, "we must still discuss how the rule of Elfael is to be divided, and how we are to conduct the peace. Come, let us sit down together and talk as men."

Odo and Bran exchanged a quick word, then Odo replied, "First, my lord would have you swear a truce. You must promise to cease all aggression against himself and his people. Then he will *parler* with you."

The abbot and his monks held a quick consultation, and the abbot replied, "Come closer, if you please. My throat grows raw shouting like this."

"I am close enough," Bran replied. "Swear to the truce."

Abbot Hugo took a step forward, spreading his arms wide. "Come," he said, "let us be reasonable. Let us sit down together like reasonable men and discuss how best to fulfil your demands."

"First you must swear to the truce," answered Bran through Odo. "There will be no peace unless you pledge a sacred vow to uphold the truce."

Frowning, the abbot drew himself up and said, "In the name of Our Lord, I swear to uphold the truce, ceasing all aggression against the people of Elfael from this day hence."

"Then it is done," said Bran through Odo. "You may come forward—alone. Your monks are to stay where they are."

"A moment, pray," called the abbot. "There is more . . . I wish to—"

Bran halted. One of the monks behind Hugo dropped his hand to his side, and Bran caught the movement and glimpsed a solid shape beneath the folds of the monk's robe. Grabbing Odo by the arm, Bran whispered something, and the two began backing away.

"He's onto them!" whispered Sergeant Jeremias from his hiding place among the roots.

"I see that!" spat Gysburne. "What do you expect me to do?"

"Stop him!" urged the sergeant. "Stop him now before he reaches the wood."

"Wait!" cried Abbot Hugo from the clearing. "We need safe conduct back to the village. Send some of your men to guard us."

When Odo had relayed these words to Bran, the young man called over his shoulder and said, "You came here under guard—you can leave the same way. There is no truce."

The two outlaws started for the wood again, and again Hugo called out, but Bran took no further notice of him.

"Blast his cursed bones!" muttered Gysburne.

"Stop him!" urged Jeremias with a nudge in the marshal's ribs.

With a growl between his teeth, Guy rose from his hiding place and, stepping out from behind the ash tree, called out, "Halt! We would speak to you!"

At the sudden appearance of the marshal, Bran shoved Odo toward the nearest tree. Dropping to one knee, he raised his bow, the arrow already on the string. Gysburne had time but to throw himself to the ground as the missile streaked toward him. In the same moment, the nine knights hidden since midnight in anticipation of this moment rose with a shout, charging up out of the undergrowth.

Odo gave out a yelp of fright and stumbled backwards to where Bran was drawing aim on the wriggling figure of Gysburne as he snaked through the grass toward the safety of the bracken.

Swinging away from the marshal, Bran drew and let fly at the soldiers just then bolting from the wood to his left. His single arrow was miraculously multiplied as five more joined his single shaft in flight. Hidden since dawn in the upper branches of the great oaks and elms, the Grellon took aim and released a rain of whistling death on the knights scrambling below. Shields before them, the Ffreinc soldiers tried to keep themselves protected from the falling shafts. One knight stumbled, momentarily dropping his guard. An arrow flashed and the knight slewed wildly sideways, as if swatted down by a giant, unseen hand. A second arrow found its mark before the wounded man stopped rolling on the ground.

1000

Three more knights were down just that quick, and the five remaining soldiers moved surprisingly fast in their mail and padded leather tunics. Ten running paces carried them across the open ground between the wood and the lone kneeling archer. Swords drawn, they roared their vengeance and fell upon him.

In the instant the soldiers raised their arms to strike, there came a sound like that of a hard slap of a gauntleted fist smashing into a leather saddle. Arrows streaked down from the upper branches of the surrounding trees, and the cracking thump was repeated so quickly the individual sounds merged to become one. The foremost knight seemed to rise and dangle on his tiptoes, as if jerked upright by a rope, only to crumple when his feet touched earth again. He collapsed in the grass, three arrows in his back.

A second knight threw his arms wide, his sword spinning from his grasp as he crashed to his knees and flopped face-first to the ground. A third knight paused in midstroke and glanced down at his chest, where he saw a rose-coloured stain spreading across his pale tunic; in the centre of the crimson stain, the steel tip of an arrowhead protruded. With a cry of pain and disbelief, he threw down his sword, grabbed at the lethal missile, and tried to pull it free even as he toppled.

The fourth knight took an arrow on his shield and was thrown onto his back as two more arrows ripped the autumn air, one of them striking the soldier a step or two ahead of him. The knight faltered, his legs tangling in midstep as the missile jolted into him, twisting his shoulders awkwardly. His shield banged against his knees, and he plunged onto his side at Bran's feet.

The sole remaining knight, still on the ground, covered his helmeted head with his shield and lay unmoving as the dead around him. Nocking another arrow to the string, Bran surveyed the battleground with a rapid sweep to the right and left. Several of the monks with Abbot Hugo had thrown off their robes to reveal mail shirts and swords, and others—five mounted soldiers including Sheriff Richard de Glanville—charged out from the nearest trees.

Stooping swiftly, Bran picked up Odo, dragging the frightened monk to his feet and driving him headlong into the safety of the greenwood. There came the sound of leaves rustling and branches thrashing in the forest nearby, and they were gone.

The mounted knights galloped to the edge of the wood and halted, listening.

All that could be heard were the groans of the wounded and dying. The marshal and Sergeant Jeremias ventured slowly out from behind their shields. "See to those men, Sergeant," ordered Gysburne. To the knight who lay unharmed among the bodies, he called, "Get up and find the horses."

1001

"Are we going after the outlaws, Sire?" inquired the knight.

"Why, by the bloody rood?" cried the marshal. "To let them continue to practice their cursed archery on us? Think, man! They're hiding in the trees!"

"But I thought the abbot said—" began the knight.

"Obey your orders, de Tourneau!" snapped the marshal irritably. "Forget what the abbot said. Just do as you're told—and take Racienne with you."

The two knights clumped off together, and Gysburne turned to see Sheriff de Glanville and his bailiff turning back from the edge of the wood. "Have no fear," called the marshal. "The outlaws have gone. You are safe now."

The sheriff stiffened at the insinuation. "It was not for fear that we held back."

"No," granted the marshal, "of course not. Why would I think that? You merely mislaid your sword, perhaps, or I am certain you would have been in the fore rank, leading the charge."

"Enough, Gysburne," snarled the sheriff. "The last time I looked, you were crawling on your hands and knees like a baby."

The abbot shouted from the clearing, cutting short what promised to be a lively discussion. "De Glanville! Gysburne! Did you get him? Is he dead?"

"No," answered the marshal, "he got away." He promptly amended this, adding, "They got away. It was a trap; they were waiting for us."

Abbot Hugo turned his gaze to the bodies lying in the long grass. His face darkened. "Are you telling me you've lost four men and the outlaws have escaped again?" He swung around to face the marshal. "How did this happen?" he shouted.

"You ask the wrong man, Abbot," replied Gysburne coolly. "We did our part. It was the sheriff who failed to attack."

"*You* were supposed to draw them from hiding, Abbot, remember?" said the sheriff darkly. "Since you *failed* in the first order, no good purpose would be served by pursuing the second." He pointed to the bodies on the ground. "You can see what that accomplished. If I had attacked, it would have been at the cost of more men, and more lives wasted."

"If you had attacked as planned," the marshal said, his voice rising, "we could have taken him and we'd not be standing here now heaping blame on each other."

"There is plenty of blame to go around, it seems to me," retorted de Glanville angrily. "But I'll not own more than my share. The plan was flawed from the beginning. We should have anticipated that they would not be drawn out so easily. And now they know we have no intention of accepting their ridiculous peace offer. We've gained nothing." Turning away from the other two, he shouted for his men to load the bodies of the dead onto the backs of their horses and return to Saint Martin's. He climbed into the saddle, then called, "Gysburne! I turn my duties over to you while I am away. Bailiff will assist you."

De Glanville wheeled his horse.

"Where are you going?" demanded the marshal.

"To Londein," came the answer. "I am the king's man, and I require soldiers and supplies to deal with these outlaws."

"We should discuss this," Gysburne objected.

"There is nothing to discuss. We need more soldiers, and I'm going to get them. I should return within the fortnight."

Marshal Guy looked to the abbot. "Let him go," said Hugo. "He is right."

"I would not linger here any longer if I were you," called the sheriff. "We are finished, and it is not safe." He snapped the reins, and the big horse bounded off.

"Do not underestimate me, Sheriff," muttered Abbot Hugo, watching him go. "I am far from finished . . . very far from finished."

Marshal Guy de Gysburne walked over to where a knight had been slain; there was blood in the grass. He picked up the dead man's sword and stuck it in his belt. "You can stay if you like, Abbot, but they are probably watching from the forest."

Casting a hasty glance over his shoulder, the abbot hurried to rejoin his bodyguard and scuttled back to the abbey in undignified retreat.

⊰ PART TWO ⊱

Came Little John through the forest that morn,
    And chanc'd upon poor Rhiban Hud,
So high on his back he carries him to
    A priest on the edge of the woode.

"God save you, Fryer Tuck," quod John.
    "A handsome fish I've here.
His length's as longe from snout to tail
    As any I've seen this yere."

"Then don't delay, friend John," quod Tuck,
    "But lay him here on the hearthe.
Let's get him skinned and then get him cleaned
    And warmed up quick and smart."

Young Rhiban quickly mended himself
    At Fryer Tuck's strong, healing hands.
And when he had sense, the two hearde account
    Of the change that had passed in those lands.

"For twenty long summers," quoth Rhiban, "by God,
 My arrows I here have let fly.
Methinks it quite strange, that within the march,
 A reeve has more power than I.

"This forest and vale I consider my own,
And these folk a king think of me;
I therefore declare—and so solemnly swear:
 I will live to see each of them free."

"By t'rood, this is a most noble sport,"
 John Little did him proclaim.
"I'll stand with thee and fight 'til death!"
 "And I," quod Tuck, "The same!"

"Then send you bold captains to head up our men
 And meet in the greenwoode hereon:
Mérian, Llech-ley, and Alan a'Dale,
 Thomas, and Much Miller's son."

Two riders picked their way carefully along the rock-lined riverbed, one in front of the other, silent, vigilant. Dressed in drab, faces hidden beneath wide-brimmed, shapeless hats, they might have been hunters hoping to raise some game along the river or, more likely, a party of merchants making for a distant market. Strange merchants, however—they shunned the nearby town, going out of their way to avoid it.

It was Bran's idea to appear as wayfarers simply passing through, in the hopes of attracting as little notice as possible. He watched the hilltops and ridgeways on either side of the valley, while Tuck remained alert to anyone approaching from the rear. Overhead, a brown buzzard soared through the empty air, its shadow rippling over the smooth, cloud-dappled slopes. Ahead the river forked into two branches: one wide and shallow, one little more than a rill snaking through a narrow, brush-choked defile. Upon reaching the place where the two streams divided, Bran paused.

"Which way?" Tuck said, reining in beside him. Odo halted a few paces behind.

"You ask me that?" replied Bran with a grin. "And still you call yourself a priest?"

"I am a priest," affirmed Tuck, "and I do ask you—for, all evidence to the contrary, I cannot read the minds of men, only their hearts." He regarded the two courses. "Which way do we go?"

"The narrow way, of course," answered Bran. "'Narrow is the way and hard the road that leads to salvation . . .' Isn't that the way it goes?"

"'Straight is the gate and narrow the way that leadeth to life, and there be few that find it,'" the friar corrected. "You should pay better attention when the Holy Script is read."

"We'll have to walk from here," Bran said, climbing down from the saddle. "But when we reach the end, we will be beyond the borders of Elfael and out of reach of de Glanville's soldiers." He glanced at Odo. The young priest had maintained a gloomy silence since climbing into the saddle. "Do either of you want to rest a little before we move on?"

"My thanks, but no—a chance to quit this saddle is all I need just now," Tuck said, easing himself down from the saddle. "Come, Odo. A change is as good as a rest, is it not?" He wiped the sweat from his face. "Although, to be sure, a jar of ale would not go amiss."

"When day is done," said Bran, starting into the gorge. "This way, you two."

Leading the horses, they resumed their trek, picking their way along the stream. It was slow going because rocks, brush, and nettles filled the defile, making each step a small ordeal. The bowlegged priest struggled to keep up with his long-legged companions, scrambling over the rocks and dodging thorny branches, all the while ruing the turn of events that had made this journey necessary.

They had left the forest before dawn, crossing the open ground to the south of the caer while it was still dark, quickly losing themselves in the seamed valleys of Elfael, keeping out of sight of the fortress and town until both were well behind them—and even then Bran continued with all caution. A chance encounter with a wayward Ffreinc party was to be avoided at all costs.

"We acted in good faith," Bran had declared in the council following the abbot's misguided ambush. "But Hugo sought to betray us—once again. It is only by God's favour that Odo and I escaped unharmed and none of our men were killed or wounded."

Bran and his archers had just returned from their encounter with the Ffreinc, and one glance at their scowling faces gave everyone to know that all was not well.

Tuck, with Mérian a close step behind, was there to meet the returning peace party. "God love you, Iwan, what happened?" Tuck asked, snagging hold of the big man's arm as he came through the blasted oak. "Did they fail to ring the bell?"

"Nay, Friar," answered the champion, shaking his head slowly. "They rang the bell for all to hear—but then attacked us anyway."

"They were lying in wait for us," said Siarles, joining them. "Hiding in the forest."

"Gysburne and his men showed themselves for the black devils they are," said Scarlet.

"Aye, and the sheriff too," added Siarles. "Dressed up as monks, some of 'em."

"Even so, we honoured our part," said Iwan. "We did not draw on them until they attacked Bran."

"Was anyone hurt?" Tuck glanced quickly at the other archers

1009

trooping into the settlement. There was no blood showing; all seemed to be in ruddy good health.

"No hurt to anyone but themselves," Scarlet pointed out. "A fella'd a thought they'd have learnt a little respect for a Welsh bowman by now. Seems they are a thick lot, these Ffreinc, say what you will."

The friar heard these words, and his heart fell like a stone dropped into a bottomless well. The slender hope that the abbot would accept the offered peace sank instantly, swallowed in the knowledge that Abbot Hugo would never be appeased. In light of this new outrage, he felt the fool for even imagining such a thing possible.

"You did what Christian duty required, and it will be accounted to your credit," Tuck assured them lamely. "God will yet reward you for remaining true to your part."

"No doubt, Friar," replied Siarles. "The same way he helps them who help themselves, methinks."

"I do not blame you for being disappointed," Tuck said, "but you should not place the failure at the Almighty's feet, when it—"

"Spare us, Tuck," snapped Bran. He and Odo, the last to arrive, passed the others as they stood talking. "I am not of a mind to hear it." Addressing the men, he said, "Get something to eat, all of you. Then I want my advisors to come to me and we will hold council again—this time it is a council of war."

The six archers moved off to find some food, leaving Tuck, Mérian, and the others looking on in dismay.

"I feared this might happen," said Mérian. "Still, we had to try." She looked to the friar for assurance. "We *did* have to try."

"We did," confirmed the priest. "And we were right." He glanced at the young woman beside him. How lovely she was; how noble of face and form. And how determined. A pang of regret pierced him to see her once-fine clothes now stained and growing threadbare from their hard use in the greenwood. She was made for finer things, to be sure, but had cast her lot with the outlaw band; and her fate, like all who called the forest home, was that of a fugitive.

"Ah, my soul," he sighed, feeling the weight of their failure settle upon him. "So much hardship and sadness could have been avoided if only that blasted abbot had agreed."

"I had my hopes, too, Friar," offered Mérian. "My father has ruled under Baron Neufmarché these many years—to the benefit of both, I think. It can be done—I know it can. But Hugo de Rainault is a wicked man, and there is no reasoning with him. He will never leave, never surrender an inch of ground until he is dead."

"Alas, I fear you've struck to the heart of it," confessed Tuck, shaking his head sadly. "No doubt that is where the trouble lies."

"Where, Friar?"

"In the hearts of ever-sinful men, my lady," he told her. "In the all-too-wicked human heart."

After the men had eaten, those who were counted among King Raven's advisors joined their lord in his hut. As they took their places around the fire ring, Bran said, "We need more men, and I am going to—"

More men, thought Tuck, and remembered what it was that he had learned from the abbot. "Good Lord!" he cried, starting up at the memory. "Forgive me," he said quickly as all eyes turned towards him, "but I have just remembered something that might be useful."

Bran regarded him, waiting for him to continue.

"It is just that—" Glancing around, he said to Iwan, "How many soldiers did you say the abbot and sheriff had with them?"

"No more'n twenty," replied the champion.

"At most," confirmed Siarles.

"Then that is all they have," said Tuck. "Twenty men—that is all that are left to them following the two attacks." He went on to explain about meeting with the abbot, and how Hugo had let slip that he no longer had enough men to defend the town. "So, unless I am much mistaken, those who attacked you are all that remain of the troops Baron de Braose left here."

"And there are fewer now," Siarles pointed out. "Maybe by four or five. He can have no more than fifteen or sixteen under his command." He turned wondering eyes towards Bran. "My lord, we can defeat them. We can drive them out."

"We can take back control of the cantref," echoed Iwan. "One more battle and it would be ours."

They fell to arguing how this might be accomplished, then, but arrived always at the same place where the discussion had begun.

"Gysburne may have only sixteen left," Bran pointed out. "But you can believe he won't be drawn into open battle with us. Nor can we take the town or the fortress, for all we are only six able-bodied bowmen. So, it comes to this: we need more men, and I am going to raise them." He paused. "First things first. Iwan, I want you and Owain and Rhoddi to watch the road—day and night. Nothing is to pass through the forest without our leave. All travellers are to be stopped. Any goods or weapons they carry will be taken from them."

"And if they refuse?" asked the champion.

"Use whatever force you deem necessary," Bran replied. "But only that and no more. All who comply willingly are to be sent on their way in peace."

"Nothing will get past us, my lord. I know what to do."

"Siarles," said Bran, "you and Tomas are to begin making arrows. We'll need as many as we can get—and we'll need bows too."

"And where will we be getting the wood for all these bows and arrows?" asked Siarles.

"Wood for bows, I know, and where to find it," Angharad said, speaking up from her place behind Bran's chair. "We will bring all you need, Gwion Bach and I."

Bran nodded. "The rest of the Grellon are to be trained to the longbow."

"Women too?" asked Mérian.

"Yes," confirmed Bran. "Women too." He turned to Will Scarlet. "Until your hand is healed, you will teach others what you know about the bow."

"That much is easily done," said Scarlet. "It's the trainin' that takes the time."

"Then start at once. Today."

Owain, one of the newer members of the council, asked, "You said you meant to raise more men. What is in your mind, my lord, if you don't mind my asking?"

"I have kinsmen among my mother's people in Gwynedd," replied Bran. "I mean to start there. Once the word spreads that we are gathering a force to overthrow the Ffreinc, I have no doubt we'll soon get all the warriors we need."

"There are warriors nearby that are yours for the asking," Mérian pointed out. "I have but to go to my father and—"

"No," said Bran firmly.

"The fact is, my father—"

"Your father is a vassal of Baron Neufmarché," Bran said in a pained tone, "a fact you seem determined to ignore."

1013

Mérian opened her mouth to object, but Bran cut her off, saying, "That is the end of it."

Mérian glared at him from under lowered brows, but gave in without another word.

"Well then," said Bran, declaring himself satisfied with the preparations. "Be about your work, everyone. If all goes well, Tuck and I will return with a war band large enough to conquer the Ffreinc and force their surrender." As the others shuffled out, Bran called Tuck to him. "I will see to the horses, and you take care of the provisions—enough for four days, I make it."

The friar spent the rest of the day assembling the necessary provisions for their journey. While he was scraping together the few items they would need for making camp, Scarlet came to him. "I am worried about Odo," he said, sitting down on a nearby stump. "That scrape this morning has pitched the poor fella into the stew."

"Oh? I am sorry to hear it," replied Tuck. "Has he said anything?"

"Not so much," said Will. "He wouldn't. But if there was ever a creature ill fashioned for the wildwood, that's Odo through and through."

Tuck paused, considering what Scarlet was telling him. "What do you think we should do?"

"Well, seeing as you are heading north, I was wondering if it might be best for everyone if you took Odo along."

"To Gwynedd?"

"Aye," said Scarlet, "but only as far as that monastery with the old bishop."

"Saint Tewdrig's."

"That's the one. I know he'd fare better there, and no doubt the way things are with the folk so hard-pressed everywhere hereabouts, he'd be a better help there than here, if you see what I mean."

"He's suffering, you say."

"I've seen whipped dogs more cheerful."

"Well then," said Tuck. "I'll speak to Bran and see what we can do." He paused, then asked, "Why did you bring this to me?"

"I deemed it a priest thing—like confession," replied Scarlet, rising. "And Odo would never be able to lift his head again if he thought Bran reckoned him a coward."

Tuck smiled. "You're a good friend, William Scatlocke. Consider it done, and Bran will think no ill of Brother Odo."

The travellers spent a last night in the forest, departing early enough to cross the Vale of Elfael before dawn.

Only Angharad was awake to see them off, which she did in her peculiar fashion. Raising her staff, she held it aloft, and blessed them with a prayer that put Tuck in mind of those he had heard as a child in the north country.

The three climbed into their saddles—Bran swinging up easily, Odo taking a bit more effort, and Tuck with the aid of a stump for a mounting block—and with a final farewell, quickly disappeared into the gloaming. By the time the sun was showing above the horizon, the riders had passed the Ffreinc-held Saint Martin's and were well on their way. Now, as the sun sailed high over head, they eked their way over bare rocks along the edge of the rill and, a little while later, passed beyond the borders of Elfael and into the neighbouring cantref of Builth.

It was well past midday when they came within sight of the monastery, and in a little while stood in the yard of Saint Tewdrig's introducing the young Ffreinc priest to Bishop Asaph, who professed himself overjoyed to receive an extra pair of hands. "As you see," he told them, "we are run off our feet day and night caring for the souls who come to us. We will put him to work straightaway, never fear." He fixed Bran with a look of deepest concern. "What is this I am hearing about you declaring war on Abbot Hugo?"

"It is true," Bran allowed, and explained how the English king had reneged on his promise to restore Bran's throne, appointing the abbot and sheriff as his regents instead. "We are on our way north to rally the tribes."

The ageing bishop shook his head sadly. "Is there no other way?"

"If there was," Bran conceded, "we are beyond recalling it now." He went on to tell how the Black Abbot had rebuffed his offer of peace. "That was Tuck's idea."

"We had to try," offered the friar. "For Jesus' sake we had to try."

"Indeed," sighed the bishop.

They stayed with the monks that night, and bidding Odo farewell, they departed early the next morning. They rode easily, passing the morning in a companionable silence until they came to a shady spot under a large outcrop of stone, where Bran decided to stop to rest and water the horses, and have a bite to eat before moving on once more. The going was slow, and the sun was disappearing beyond the hill line to the west when they at last began to search for a good place to make camp for the night—finding a secluded hollow beside a brook where an apple tree grew; the apples were green still, and tart, but hard to resist, and there was good water for the horses. While Bran gathered wood for the fire, Tuck tethered the animals so they could graze in the long grass around the tree, and then set about preparing a meal.

"We should reach Arwysteli tomorrow," Bran said, biting into a small green apple. The two had finished a supper of pork belly and beans, and were stretched out beneath the boughs bending with fruit. "And Powys the day after."

"Oh?" Tuck queried. "We are not stopping?"

"Perhaps on the way back," Bran said. "I am that keen to get on to Bangor. I know no one in these cantrefs, and it might be easier to get men if on our return we are accompanied by a sizeable host already."

This sounded reasonable to the friar. "How long has it been since you've seen your mother's people?" he asked.

Bran gnawed on his sour apple for a moment, then said, "Quite a long time—a year or two after my mother died, it must have been. My father wanted to return some of her things to her kinfolk, so we went up and I met them then."

"You were—what? Eight, nine years old?" Tuck ventured.

"Something like that," he allowed. "But it will make no difference. Once they have heard what we intend, they will join us, never fear."

They spent a quiet night and moved on at dawn, passing through Builth without seeing another living soul, and pressing quickly on into Arwysteli and Powys, where they stopped for the night in a settlement called Llanfawydden. Tuck was happy to see that the hamlet had a fine wooden church and a stone monk's cell set in a grove of beeches, though the village consisted of nothing more than a ring of wattle-and-mud houses encircling a common grazing area. After a brief word from the local priest, the chief of the village took them in and fed them at his table, and gave them a bed for the night. The chieftain and his wife and three sons slept on the floor beside the hearth.

The travellers found the family amiable enough. They fed them well, entertained them with news of local doings, and asked no questions about who their guests were, or what their business might be.

However, when they were preparing to leave the next morning, one of the younger lads—upon learning that they had travelled from Elfael—could not help asking whether they knew anything about King Raven.

"I might have heard a tale or two," Bran allowed, smiling.

The boy persisted in his questions despite the frowns from his mother and brothers. "Is it true what they say? Is he a very bad creature?"

"Bad for the Ffreinc, it would seem," Bran said. "By all accounts King Raven does seem a most mysterious bird. Do you know him hereabouts?"

"Nay," replied the middle lad, shaking his head sadly. "Only what folk say."

One of his older brothers spoke up. "We heard he has killed more'n two hundred Ffreinc—"

"Swoops on 'em from the sky and *spears* 'em with his beak," added the one who had raised the subject in the first place.

"Boys!" said the mother, embarrassed by her sons' forthright enthusiasm. "You have said enough."

"No harm," chuckled Bran, much amused by this. "I don't know about spearing knights with his beak, but at least the Ffreinc are afraid of him—and that's good enough for me."

"They say he helps the Cymry," continued the younger one. "Gives 'em all the treasure."

"That he does," Tuck agreed. "Or, so I've heard."

The travellers took their leave of their hosts shortly after that, resuming their journey northward. The day was bright and fair, the breeze warm out of the south, and the track good. Bran and Tuck rode easily along, talking of this and that.

"Your fame is spreading," Tuck observed. "If they know King Raven here, they'll soon enough know him everywhere."

Bran dismissed the comment with a shrug. "Children are readily persuaded."

"Not at all," the friar insisted. "Where do children hear these things except from their elders? People know about King Raven. They are talking about him."

"For all the good it does," Bran pointed out. "King Raven may be better liked than William the Red, but it is the Red King's foot on our neck all the same. The Ffreinc may be wary of the Phantom of the Wood, but it hasn't changed a blessed thing."

"Perhaps not," Tuck granted, "but I was not thinking of the Ffreinc just now. I was thinking of the Cymry."

Bran gave an indifferent shrug.

"King Raven has given them hope," insisted Tuck. "He has shown them that the invaders can be resisted. You must be proud of your feathered creation."

"He had his uses," Bran admitted. "But, like all things, that usefulness has reached its end."

"Truly?"

"King Raven has done what he can do. Now it is time to take up bows and strap on swords, and join battle with the enemy openly, in the clear light of day."

"Perhaps," Tuck granted, "but do not think to hang up your feathered cloak and long-beaked mask just yet."

"There will be no more skulking around the greenwood like a ghost," Bran declared. "That is over."

"Certain of that, are you?" Tuck said. "Just you mark my words, Bran ap Brychan, King Raven will fly again before our cause is won."

Long before Rome turned its eyes toward the Isle of the Mighty, Bangor, in the far north of Gwynedd, was an ancient and revered capital of kings. There, among the heavy overhanging boughs of venerable oaks, the druids taught their varied and subtle arts, establishing the first schools in the west. That was long ago. The druids were gone, but the schools remained; and now those aged trees sheltered one of the oldest monasteries in Britain, and for all anyone knew, all of Christendom. Indeed, the proud tribes of Gwynedd had sent a bishop and some priests to Emperor Constantine's great council half a world away in Nicea—as the inhabitants of north Wales never tired of boasting.

When Bran's father—Brychan ap Tewdwr, a prince of the south—found himself in want of a wife, it was to Gwynedd that he had come looking. And in Bangor he had discovered his queen: Rhian, a much-loved princess of her tribe. While she had lived, ties between the two kingdoms north and south had remained strong.

Thus, Bran expected to find a hearty welcome among his mother's kinsmen.

After three days on the road, the two travellers drew near the town and the pathways multiplied and diverged. So they stopped to ask directions from the first person they met—a squint-eyed shepherd sitting under a beech tree at the foot of a grassy hill.

"You'll be wanting to see your folk, I expect," observed the shepherd.

"It is the reason we came," Bran told him, a hint of exasperation colouring his tone. Having already explained that his mother had been the daughter of a local chieftain, he had asked if the fellow knew where any of her people might be found.

"Well," replied the shepherd. He craned his neck around to observe his sheep grazing on the hillside behind him, "you won't find any of 'em in town yonder."

"No?" wondered Bran. "Why not?"

"They en't there!" hooted the man, whistling through his few snaggled teeth.

"And why would that be?" wondered Bran. "If you know, perhaps I could persuade you to tell me."

"No mystery there, Brother," replied the shepherd. "They've all gone over to Aberffraw, en't they."

"Have they indeed," said Bran. "And why is that?"

"It's all to do with that Ffreinc earl, 'n' tryin' to stay out o' his reach, d'ye ken?"

"I think so," replied Bran doubtfully. "And where might this Aberffraw be?"

"Might be anywhere," the shepherd replied. His tanned, weather-beaten face cracked into a smile as he tapped his nose knowingly.

"Just what I was thinking," remarked Bran. "Even so, I'll wager that *you* know, and could tell me if you had a mind to."

"You'd win that wager, Brother, I do declare."

"And will you yet tell me?"

The shepherd became sly. "How much would you have wagered?"

"A penny."

"Then I'll be havin' o' that," the man replied.

Bran dug in his purse and brought out a silver coin. He held it up. "This for the benefit of your wide and extensive knowledge."

"Done!" cried the shepherd, delighted with his bargain. He snatched the coin from Bran's fingertips and said, "Aberffraw is on the Holy Isle, en't it. Just across the narrows there and hidden round t'other side o' the headland. You won't see it this side, for it is all hidden away neat-like."

Bran thanked the shepherd and wished him good fortune, but Tuck was not yet satisfied. "When was the last time you went to church, my friend?"

The shepherd scratched his grizzled jaw. "Well now, difficult to say, that."

"Difficult, no doubt, because it has been so long you don't remember," ventured Tuck. Without waiting for a reply, he said, "No matter. Kneel down and bow your head. Quickly now; I'll not spend all day at it."

The shamefaced shepherd complied readily enough, and Tuck said a prayer for him, blessed his flock, and rode on with the stern admonition for the herdsman to get himself to church next holy day without fail.

At Bangor, they stopped to rest and eat and gather what information they could about the state of affairs in the region. There was no tavern in the town, much less an inn, and Tuck was losing hope of finding a soothing libation when he glimpsed a clay jar hanging from a cord over the door of a house a few steps off the square. "There!" he cried, to his great relief, and made for the place, which turned out to be the house of a widowed alewife who served the little town a passing fair brew and simple fare. Tuck threw himself from his saddle and ducked inside, returning a moment later with generous bowls of bubbly brown ale in each hand and a round loaf of bread under his arm. "God is good," he said, passing a bowl to Bran. "Amen!"

The two travellers established themselves on the bench outside the door. Too early for the alewife's roast leg of lamb, they dulled their appetites with a few lumps of soft cheese fried in a pan with onions, into which they dipped their bread. While they ate and drank, they talked to some of the curious townsfolk who came along to greet the visitors—quickly informing them that they'd arrived at a bad time, owing to the overbearing presence of the Earl of Cestre, a Ffreinc nobleman by the name of Hugh d'Avranches.

"Wolf Hugh is a rough pile," said the ironsmith from the smithy across the square. He had seen the travellers ride in and had come to inquire if their horses needed shoeing or any tack needed mending.

"That he is," agreed his neighbour.

"You call him Wolf," observed Tuck. "How did he come by that?"

"You ever see a wolf that wasn't hungry?" said the smith. "Ravening beast like that'll devour everything in sight—same as the earl."

"He's a rough one, right enough," agreed his friend solemnly. "A rogue through and through."

"As you say," replied Bran. "Here's to hoping we don't meet up with him." He offered his bowl to the smith.

The smith nodded and raised the bowl. "Here's to hoping." He took a hearty draught and passed the bowl to his friend, who drained it.

When they had finished, Bran and Tuck made their way down to the small harbour below the town. A fair-sized stretch of timber and planking, the wharf was big enough to serve seagoing ships and boats plying the coastal waters between the mainland and Ynys Môn, known as Holy Island, just across the narrow channel. They found a boatman who agreed to ferry them and their horses to the island. It was no great distance, and they were soon on dry land and mounted again. They followed the rising path that led up behind the promontory, over the headland, and down to a very pleasant little valley on the other side: Aberffraw and, tucked into a fold between the encircling hills, the settlement of Celyn Garth.

Less a town than a large estate consisting of an enormous timber fortress and half a dozen houses—along with barns, cattle pens, granaries, and all surrounded by apple orchards and bean, turnip, and barley fields scraped from the ever-encroaching forest which blanketed the hills and headlands—it had become the royal seat of the northern Welsh and was, as the shepherd had suggested, perfectly suited to keeping out of the voracious earl's sight.

Bran and Tuck rode directly to the fortress and made themselves known to the short, thick-necked old man who appeared to serve the royal household as gateman and porter. With a voice like dry gravel, he invited them to enter the yard and asked them to wait while he informed his lord of their arrival.

Whatever life the kings of North Wales had known in earlier times, it was clear that it was much reduced now. As in England, the arrival of the Normans meant hardship and misery in draughts too great to swallow. The Cymry of the noble houses suffered along with the rest of the country, and Celyn Garth was proof of this. The yard was lumpy, rutted, and weedy; the roof of the king's hall sagged, its thatch ratty and mildewed; the gates and every other door on the nearly derelict outbuildings stood in need of hingeing and rehanging.

"I hope we find the king well," said Bran doubtfully.

"I hope we find him at his supper," said Tuck.

What they found was Llewelyn ap Owain, a swarthy, nimble Welshman who received them graciously and prevailed upon them to stay the night. But he was not the king.

"It's Gruffydd you're looking for, is it?" he said. "Aye, who else? It pains me, friend, to inform you that our king is a captive." Llewelyn explained over a hot supper of roast pork shanks and baked apples. They were seated at the hearth end of the near-empty hall. Their host sat at table with his guests, while his wife and daughters served the meal. "He's held prisoner by Earl Hugh, may God rot his teeth."

"Wolf Hugh?" asked Bran. "Is that the man?"

"Aye, Cousin, that's the fellow—Hugh d'Avranches, Earl of Cestre—devious as the devil, and cruel as Cain with a toothache. He's a miserable old spoiler, is our Hugh, with a heart full of torment for each and all he meets."

"How long has Gruffydd been captive?" wondered Tuck.

Llewelyn tapped his teeth as he reckoned the tally. "Must be eight years or more, I guess," he said. "Maybe nine already."

"Has anyone seen him since he was taken prisoner?" Tuck asked.

"Oh, aye," replied Llewelyn. "We send a priest most high holy days. The earl allows our Gruffydd to receive food and clothing and such since it whittles down the cost of keeping an expensive captive. We use those visits for what benefit we can get."

Bran nodded; he and Tuck shared a glance, and each could sense the sharp disappointment of the other. "Who's ruling in Gruffydd's place?" asked Bran, swallowing his frustration.

Llewelyn paused to consider.

It was a simple enough question, and Tuck wondered at their host's hesitation. "You must be looking at him, I reckon," Llewelyn confessed at last. "Although I make no claim myself, you understand." He spread his hands as if to express his innocence. "I merely keep the boards warm for Gruffydd, so to speak. I am loyal to my lord, while he lives, and would never usurp his authority."

"Which is why the Ffreinc keep him alive, no doubt," observed Bran. As long as Gruffydd drew breath, no one else could occupy his empty throne, much less gather his broken tribe.

1027

"But people do come to me for counsel and guidance," Llewelyn offered, "and I see it my duty to oblige however I can."

"I understand," said Bran. He fell silent, contemplating the depth of his difficulty. The kingdom of Gwynedd, leaderless and adrift, was in no shape to supply a war host to help fight a war beyond its borders. He realized with increasing despair that he had come all this way for nothing.

"So then, I'll be sending for your relations," said Llewelyn, breaking the silence. "They'll be that glad to see you."

"And I them," replied Bran, and complimented his host on his thoughtfulness. "Thank you, Llewelyn; I am in your debt."

They finished supper, and the guests were given their own quarters so they would not have to share with the rest of Llewelyn's household, who mostly slept on benches and reed mats in the hall.

The next morning—on the counsel and guidance of their host—Bran and Tuck rode out to get the measure of the land and people of the northern part of Gwynedd, and to speak frankly without being overheard.

"This is going to be more difficult than I thought," Bran admitted when, after riding for a goodly time, they stopped to water the horses at a stream flowing down a rocky, gorse-covered hill and into Môr Iwerddon, the Sea of Ireland, gleaming blue under a fine early autumn sky.

"Raising an army of king's men with the king in an enemy prison?" Tuck queried. "What is difficult about that?"

"I don't think he even *has* an army."

"Well, that would make it slightly more tricky, I suppose," remarked Tuck.

"Yes," mused Bran. "Tricky." He walked a few paces away, then back. Glancing up suddenly, he grinned that twisted, roguish smile that Tuck knew meant trouble. More than that, however, it was the first time in many, many days that Tuck had seen him smile, and the friar had almost forgotten the magic of that lopsided grin—truly, it was as if a slumbering spirit had awakened in that instant to reanimate a young man only half-alive until now. He was once again himself, Rhi Bran y Hud, alive with mischief and alert to possibility. "That's it, friend friar—a trick!"

"Eh?"

"To raise a king's army from a king who is in prison."

Tuck caught his meaning at once.

Gathering up the reins, Bran stepped quickly to his horse, raised his foot to the stirrup, and swung up into the saddle. "Come, Tuck, why are you dragging your feet?"

Tuck

Why, indeed? Tuck walked stiffly to his horse and, after leading it to a nearby rock big enough to serve as a mounting block, struggled into the saddle. "You'll get us killed, you know," the priest complained. "Me most of all."

Bran laughed. "A little more faith would become you, Friar."

"I have faith enough for any three—and I'll thump the man who says me nay. But you go jumping into a bear trap with both feet, and it'll not be faith you feel chomping on your leg bones!"

Grabbing up the reins, he raised his eyes towards heaven. "Is there no rest for the weary?" he sighed. By the time he regained the path, Bran was already racing away.

On their return to Celyn Garth, Bran secluded himself in his quarters and set Tuck to finding certain items that he needed. When they had assembled everything necessary, Bran went to work and the change was swiftly effected. It was nearly time for the evening meal when he emerged, and Tuck accompanied him to the hall where Llewelyn was waiting with some of Bran's relations he had invited especially to meet their long-lost kinsman. There were seven of them: three young men in the blue-and-red checked tunics of the north country; three of middling age in tall boots and leather jackets over their linen shirts; and one old man, bald as a bean, in a pale robe of undyed wool.

"Lead the way, Tuck," Bran murmured. "And remember, I speak no Cymry."

"Oh, I'll remember," Tuck retorted. "It's yourself you should be reminding."

Stepping into the hall, the little friar approached the long table where the men were already gathered over their welcome cups. Llewelyn took one look at the cleric and his companion and rose quickly.

"Friar Aethelfrith," he said, "I did not know you brought a guest. Come, sit down." To the unexpected visitor, he said, "Be welcome in this house. Pray, sit and share a cup with us."

Tuck kept his eyes on Llewelyn, who seemed to recognize something familiar in the young man beside him. But if the long black robes did not fully disguise him, then the sallow, sombre expression, the slightly hunched shoulders and inwardly bending frame, the close-shorn hair and gleaming white scalp of his tonsure, the large sad eyes, hesitant step, and almost timid way he held his head—taken all together, the appearance was so unlike Bran ap Brychan that Llewelyn did not trust his first impression and withheld judgement on the newcomer's identity.

For his part, Bran inclined his head in humble acceptance and offered, as it seemed to those looking on, a somewhat melancholy smile—as if the slender young man carried some secret grief within and it weighed heavily on his heart. He turned to Tuck, and the others also looked to the priest as for an explanation.

"My lords," said Tuck, "allow me to present to you my dear friend, Father Dominic."

Speaking with the humble, yet confident authority that one would expect of a papal envoy, the slender young man introduced as Father Dominic charmed his listeners with tales of his travels in the service of the Holy Father and his dealings with kings and cardinals. It fell to Tuck, of course, to translate his stories for the benefit of his listeners since Bran spoke in the curious, chiefly meaningless jibber-jabber of broken Latin that passed for the language of the Italian nobility among folk who had never heard it. Tuck was able to keep one step ahead of his listeners by his many sudden consultations—to clarify some word or thought—where Bran, as Father Dominic, would then whisper the bare bones of what his struggling translator was to say next. Such was Father Dominic's winsome manner that Tuck found himself almost believing in the charming lies, even knowing them to be spun of purest nonsense and embellished by his own ready tongue.

Father Dominic revealed that he was on a mission from Rome,

and explained that he had come to the region to make acquaintance with churchmen among the tribes of Britain who remained outside Norman influence. This was announced in a casual way, but the subtlety was not lost on his listeners. Father Dominic, speaking through Tuck, told them that because of the delicate nature of his inquiry, he was pleased to travel without his usual large entourage to enable him to go where he would, unnoticed and unannounced. The Mother Church was reaching out to all her children in Britain, he said, the silent and suffering as well their noisier, more overbearing, and belligerent brothers.

All the while, their distracted host would glance towards the empty doorway. Finally, when Bran's absence could no longer be comfortably ignored, Llewelyn spoke up. "Forgive me for asking, Friar Aethelfrith, but I begin to worry about our cousin. Is he well? Perhaps he has fallen ill and requires attention."

Bran ap Brychan's kinsmen had done him the honour of travelling a considerable distance to greet their cousin from the south, and although beguiled by the unexpected arrival of a genuine emissary of the pope in Rome, they could not help but wonder about their cousin's puzzling absence. Father Dominic heard Llewelyn's question, too, and without giving any indication that he knew what had been said, he smiled, raised his hands in blessing to those who sat at the table with him, then begged to be excused, as he was feeling somewhat tired from his journey.

"Certainly, we understand," said Llewelyn, jumping to his feet. "I will have quarters prepared for you at once. If you will kindly wait but a moment—"

Father Dominic waved off his host, saying, through Tuck, "Pray do not trouble yourself. I shall find my own way."

With that he turned and, despite Llewelyn's continued protests, walked to the door of the hall, where he paused with his hand on the latch. He stood there for a moment. Then, with the others looking on, stepped back from the door, shook himself around and—wonder of wonders—seemed to grow both larger and stronger before the startled eyes of his audience. When he turned around it was no longer Father Dominic who stood before them, but Bran himself once more—albeit berobed as a priest, and with a shorn and shaven pate.

Llewelyn was speechless, and all around the board stared in astonishment at the deception so skilfully executed under their very noses. They looked at one another in baffled bemusement. When Llewelyn finally recovered his tongue, he contrived to sound angry— though his tone fell short by a long throw. "How now, Cousin? What is this devilment?"

"Forgive me if I have caused offence," said Bran, finding his own true voice at last, "but I knew no better way to convince you all."

"Convince?" wondered Llewelyn. "And what, pray, are we to be convinced of, Cousin?"

Bran shrugged off the black robe, resumed his place at the board, and poured himself a cup of ale, saying, "That I will tell, and gladly." Smiling broadly, he raised his cup to the men around the board. "First, I would know these kinsmen of mine a little better."

"As soon said as done," replied Llewelyn, some of his former goodwill returning. Indicating the elder man sitting beside him, he said, "This is Hywel Hen, Bishop of Bangor, and the granduncle of young Brocmael beside him; Hywel was brother to your mother's father. Next is Cynwrig, from Aberffraw, and his son Ifor. Then we have Trahaern, Meurig, and Llygad from Ynys Môn. Meurig is married to your mother's younger cousin, Myfanwy."

"God with you all," said Bran. "I know your names, and I see my dear mother in your faces. I am pleased to meet you all."

"We've met before, my boy," said Hywel Hen, "though I don't expect you to remember. You were but a bare-bottomed infant in your mother's arms at the time. I well remember your mother, of course— and your father. Fares the king well, does he?"

"If it lay in my power to bring you greetings from Lord Brychan, trust that nothing would please me more," replied Bran. "But such would come to you from beyond the grave."

The others took this in silence.

"My father is dead," Bran continued, "and all his war band with him. Killed by the Ffreinc who have invaded our lands in Elfael."

"Then it is true," said Meurig. "We heard that the Ffreinc are moving into the southlands." He shook his head. "I am sorry to hear of King Brychan's death."

"As are we all," said Trahaern, whose dark hair rippled across his head like the waves of a well-ordered sea. "As are we all. But tell us, young Bran, why did you put on the robes of a priest just now?"

"I cannot think it was for amusement," offered Meurig. "But if it was, let me assure you that I am not amused."

"Nor I," said Cynwrig. "Your jest failed, my friend."

"In truth, my lords, it was no jest," replied Bran. "I wanted you to see how easily men defer to a priest's robe and welcome him that wears it."

"You said it was to *convince* us," Llewelyn reminded him.

"Indeed." Hands on the table, Bran leaned forward. "If I had come to you saying that I intended to fetch King Gruffydd from Earl Hugh's prison, what would you have said?"

"That you were softheaded," chuckled Trahaern. "Or howling mad."

"Our king is held behind locked doors in a great rock of a fortress guarded by Wolf Hugh's own war band," declared Llygad, a thickset man with the ruddy face of one who likes his ale as much as it likes him. "It cannot be done."

"Not by Bran ap Brychan, perhaps," granted Bran amiably. "But Father Dominic—who you have just seen and welcomed at this very table—has been known to prise open doors barred to all others."

He looked to Tuck for confirmation of this fact. "It is true," the friar avowed with a solemn shaking of his round head. "I have seen it with my own eyes, have I not?"

"Why should you want to see our Rhi Gruffydd freed from prison?" asked Hywel, fingering the gold bishop's cross upon his chest. "What is that to you?"

Despite the bluntness of the question, the others looked to Bran for an answer, and the success of King Raven's northern venture seemed to balance on a knife edge.

"What is it to me?" repeated Bran, his tone half-mocking. "In truth, it is *everything* to me. I came here to ask your king to raise his war band and return with me to help lead them in the fight. Unless, of course, *you* would care to take the throne in his absence . . . ?" He regarded Hywel pointedly and then turned his gaze to the others around the board. No one volunteered to usurp the king's authority, prisoner though he was.

"I thought not," continued Bran. "It is true that I came here to ask your king to aid me in driving the Ffreinc from our homeland and freeing Elfael from the tyranny of their rule. But now that I know that my best hope lies rotting in a Ffreinc prison—for all he is my kinsman, too—I will not rest until I have freed him."

Bran's kinsmen stared at him in silence that was finally broken by Trahaern's sudden bark of laughter.

"You dream big," the dark Welshman laughed, slapping the table with the flat of his hand. "I like you."

The tension eased at once, and Tuck realized he had been holding his breath—nor was he the only one. The two younger Cymry, silent but watchful, sighed with relief and relaxed in their elders' pleasure.

"It will take more than a priest's robe to fetch Gruffydd from Wolf Hugh's prison," Meurig observed. "God knows, if that was all it took he'd be a free man long since."

The others nodded knowingly, and looked to Bran for his response.

"You have no idea," replied Bran, that slow, dangerous smile sliding across his scarred lips, "how much more there is to me than that."

CHAPTER II

Caer Rhodl

The wedding was all Baroness Neufmarché hoped it would be, conducted in regal pomp and elegance by Father Gervais, who had performed the marriage ceremony for herself and the baron all those years ago. Lady Sybil—resplendent in a satin gown of eggshell blue, her long brown hair plaited with tiny white flowers—made a lovely bride. And King Garran, his broad shoulders swathed in a long-sleeved, grey tunic falling to the knees and a golden belt around his lean waist, looked every inch a king worthy of the name. It was to Agnes's mind a fine match; they made a handsome couple, and seemed unusually happy in one another's company. Garran's French was not good, though better than Sybil's Welsh, but neither seemed to care; they communicated with smiling glances and flitting touches of fingers and hands.

The final prayer caught Lady Agnes somewhat by surprise.

When Sybil's attendants—several of the groom's young female cousins—stepped forward to hold the *carr* over the couple kneeling before Father Gervais, Agnes felt tears welling up in her eyes. The simple white square of cloth was the same one that had been stretched above her head the day she married the baron and which had swaddled the infant Sybil at her baptism. Now it sheltered her daughter on her wedding day, and would, please God, wrap Sybil's baby in turn. This potent reminder of the continuity of life and the rich depth of family and tradition touched the baroness's heart and moved her unexpectedly. She stifled a sob.

"My love," whispered the baron beside her, "are you well?"

Unable to speak, she simply nodded.

"Never mind," he said. "It is soon over."

No, she thought, *it is only beginning. It all begins again.*

1038

After the service in the rush-strewn hall, the wedding feast began. Trestles and boards, tables, chairs, and benches filled the courtyard where a pit had been dug to roast a dozen each of spring lambs and suckling pigs; vats of ale sat upon stumps, and tuns of wine nestled in cradles; the aroma of baking bread mingled with that of the roasting meat in the warm, sun-washed air. As the newly wedded couple emerged from the hall, the musicians began to play. The bride and groom were led by their attendants in stately procession around the perimeter of the yard, walking slowly in opposite directions, pausing to distribute silver coins among the guests, who waved hazel branches at the royal pair.

After the third circuit of the yard, Garran and Sybil were brought to the high table and enthroned beneath a red-and-blue striped canopy where they began receiving gifts from their subjects: special loaves of bread or jars of mead from humbler households; and from the more well-to-do households, items of furniture, artfully woven cloth, and a matched pair of colts. Visitors who had made the journey from the baron's holdings in France brought more exotic gifts: crystal bowls, engraved pewter platters, a gilded cross, soft leather shoes and gloves, and jeweled rings with golden bands. Having given their gifts, the celebrants took their places at the long tables. When everyone was seated, the servants filled the cups and bowls with wine, and the first of many healths were raised to the married couple, often accompanied by a word or two in Welsh that none of the Ffreinc understood, but which brought bursts of laughter from all the Britons.

Then, as the servants began carrying platters of food to the tables, some of the groom's men seized the instruments from the minstrels and, with great enthusiasm, began playing and singing as loudly as they could. Their zeal, though commendable, was far in excess of their abilities, Lady Agnes considered; however, they were soon joined by others of the wedding party, and before a bite of food was touched the entire Welsh gathering was up on their feet dancing. Some of the groom's men hoisted the bride in her chair and carried it around the yard, and three of the bride's maids descended on the groom and pulled him into the dance. The servants attempting to bring food to the tables quickly abandoned the task since it was all but impossible to carry fully laden trenchers and platters through the gyrating crowd.

Lady Agnes, at first appalled by the display, quickly found herself enjoying the spectacle. "Have you ever seen the like?" asked the baron, smiling and shaking his head.

"Never," confessed the baroness, tapping her foot in time to the music. "Is it not . . ."

"Outrageous?" suggested the baron, supplying the word for her.

"Glorious!" she corrected. Rising from her place, she held out her hands to her husband. "Come, *mon chéri*, it is a long time since we shared a dance together."

Baron Neufmarché, incredulous at his wife's eagerness to embrace the raucous proceedings, regarded her with a baffled amazement she mistook for reluctance. "Bernard," said Lady Agnes, seizing his hand, "if you cannot dance at a wedding, when will you dance?"

The baron allowed himself to be pulled from his chair and into the melee and was very soon enjoying himself with enormous great pleasure, just one of the many revellers lost in the celebration. Amidst the gleeful clatter, he became aware that his wife was speaking to him. "There it is again," she said.

"What?" he asked, looking around. "Where?"

"There!" she said, pointing at his face. "That smile."

"My dear?" he said, puzzled.

She laughed, and it was such a thrilling sound to his ears that he wondered how he had lived without it for so long. "I haven't seen that smile for many years," she declared. "I had all but forgotten it."

The music stopped and the dance ended.

"Has it been all that rare?" Bernard asked, falling breathless back into his chair.

"As rare, perhaps, as my own," replied the baroness.

He suddenly felt a little giddy, although he had only had a mouthful or two of wine. "Then we shall have to do something about that," he said, and reaching out, pulled his wife to him and gave her a kiss on the cheek.

"Tonight, *mon cher*," she whispered, her lips next to his ear, "we shall discover what else we have forgotten."

The feast resumed in earnest then, and the happy celebrants sat down to their meal, and the day stretched long into the twilight. As the shadows began to deepen across the yard and the first pale stars winked on in the sky, torches were lit and the ale vats and wine tuns replenished. There was more singing and dancing, and one of King Garran's lords rose to great acclaim to tell a long and, judging from the laughter of his listeners, boisterously entertaining story. Lady Agnes laughed too, although she had not the slightest idea what the story might have been about; it did not matter. Her laughter was merely the overflowing of an uncontainable abundance of joy from a truly happy heart.

As the festivities continued into the night, Lady Agnes noticed that some of the groom's men had taken up places by the gate— three on each side—and as the musicians began another lively dance, she saw two more of the groom's men creeping along the far wall. She stiffened to a tingle of fear in the knowledge that something was about to happen—treachery of some kind? Perhaps an ambush?

She nudged the baron with her elbow; he was leaning back in his chair, nodding, tapping his hands on the armrests in time to the music. "Bernard!" she hissed, and nodded towards the gate. The two groom's men had reached the gate. "Something is happening."

He looked where she indicated and saw the gathered men. He could make out the forms of horses standing ready just outside the gate. He glanced hurriedly around for his knights. All that he could see were either dancing or drinking, and some had coaxed Welsh girls onto their laps.

Before he could summon them, one of the men at the gate raised a horn and blew a sharp blast. Instantly, a hush fell upon the revellers. "My cymbrogi!" the man called. "Kinsmen and countrymen all!"

"Wait! That's Garran," said Baron Bernard.

"Shh! What's he saying?"

He spoke in Welsh first, and then again in French, saying, "I thank you for your attendance this day, and pray let the celebration continue. My wife and I will join you again tomorrow. You have had the day, but the night belongs to us. Farewell!"

The second groom's man turned, and Agnes saw her daughter—with a man's dull cloak pulled over her glistening gown—raise her hand and fling a great handful of silver coins into the crowd. With a shout, the people dashed for the coins, and the newly wedded couple darted through the doorway towards the waiting horses. The groom's men shut the gate with a resounding thump and took up places before it so that no one could give chase; the music resumed and the festivity commenced once more.

1042

"Extraordinary," remarked Baron Neufmarché with a laugh. "I wish I had thought of that on my wedding day. It would have saved all that commotion."

"You *loved* the commotion, as I recall," his wife pointed out.

"I loved *you*," he said, raising her hand to his lips. "Then—as I love you now."

Perhaps it was the wine and song making him feel especially expansive, or the music and contagious spirit of the celebration; but it was the first time in many years that Bernard had said those words to his wife. Yet, even as he spoke them he knew them to be true. He *did* love Agnes. And he wondered why he had allowed so many other concerns—and women—to intrude upon his love for her, to wither it and debase it. Now, in this moment, all else faded in importance, growing dim and inconsequential beside his life with Agnes. In that moment, he vowed within himself to make up for those years of waste and the pain his neglect and infidelity must have caused her.

The baron stood. "Come, my dear, the revelry will continue, but I grow weary of the throng. Let us go to our rest." He held out his hand to his wife; she took it and he pulled her to her feet. The celebration did continue far into the night, the revellers pausing to rest only when dawnlight pearled the sky in the east.

For three days the wedding festivities continued. On the fourth day people began taking their leave of the bride and groom, paying homage to both as their king and queen before departing for home. Baron Neufmarché, well satisfied that he had done all he could to strengthen his client king and provide for his daughter, turned his thoughts to Hereford and the many pressing concerns waiting for him there.

"My dear," he announced on the morning of the fifth day after the wedding, "it is time we were away. I have ordered the horses to be saddled and the wagon made ready. We can depart as soon as we have paid our respects to the dowager queen, and said our farewells."

Lady Agnes nodded absently. "I suppose . . ." she said mildly.

The baron caught the hesitancy in her tone. "Yes? What are you thinking?"

"I am thinking of staying," she said.

"Stay here?"

"Where else?"

"In Wales?"

"Why not?" she countered. "I am happy here, and I can help Sybil begin her reign. She still has much to learn, you know. You could stay, too, *mon chéri*." She reached for his hand and squeezed it. "We could be together."

The baron frowned.

"Oh, Bernard," she said, taking his arm, "I am happy for the first time in many years—truly happy. Do not take that away from me, I beg you."

"No," he said, "you need not beg. You can stay, of course—if that is what you want. I only wish I could stay with you. I'd like nothing more than to see the building work on the new castle properly begun. Alas, I am needed back in Hereford. I must go."

Agnes sympathized. "But of course, *mon chéri.* You go and tend to your affairs. I will remain here and do what I can to help. When you have finished, you can return." She smiled and kissed him on the cheek. "Perhaps we will winter here."

"I would like that." He leaned close and kissed her gently. "I shall return as soon as may be."

So, that was that. Lady Agnes stayed at Caer Rhodl, and the baron returned to Hereford, leaving behind his wife and daughter and, to his own great surprise, a piece of his heart.

While Bran continued to court the confidence of Llewelyn and the lords of Gwynedd, slowly converting them to his scheme, Tuck was given the chore of gleaning all the information and gossip he could discover about Earl Hugh d'Avranches. He begged a ride across the strait in one of the local fishing boats to the busy dockyards at Bangor, where he spent a goodly while talking to the seamen of various stripes; all had strong opinions, but were weak on actual facts. When he reckoned he had gleaned all that could be learned on the docks, he moved on to the market square and strolled among the stalls, listening to the merchants and their customers, and stumping up the cost of a jar or two to share when he found someone whose opinions seemed worth his while to hear. As the day began to fade toward evening, he took shelter at the monastery, sat with the monks at table, and talked to the porter, kitchener, and secnab.

In this way, Tuck had collected a tidy heap of tittle-tattle and, after sifting everything well and wisely, it came to this: Hugh d'Avranches had come to England with the invading forces of the Duke of Normandy—William the Conqueror to some, Willy Bastard to others, father of the present King of England, William Rufus. And although Hugh did not actually fight at Hastings against Good King Harold, the Norman nobleman was nevertheless granted generous swathes of land in the north of England as a reward for his loyalty and support. Why was this? He had ships.

It was said that if not for Hugh d'Avranches' ships, the invasion of England would never have taken place. The master of upwards of sixty seaworthy vessels, he lent them to Duke William to carry the Ffreinc army across the Narrow Sea to Britain's green and pleasant shores, thereby earning himself an earldom. Most of the Cymry knew Earl Hugh as a fierce adversary well deserving of his wolfish nickname; more extreme views considered him little more than a boot-licking toady to his bloat-gut royal master, and called him Hw Fras, or Hugh the Fat. In either case, the Cymry of the region had long since come to know and loathe him as a ruler who made life a torrent of misery for all who lived within his reach, and a very long reach it was.

From his sprawling fortress at Caer Cestre on the northern border between England and Wales, Earl Hugh harrowed the land: raiding, thieving, spoiling, feuding, burning, and wreaking whatever havoc he might on any and all beyond the borders of his realm. Forever a thorn in the side of the local Cymry, he pricked them painfully whenever he got the chance.

It went without saying that it fell to King Gruffydd of Gwynedd to make a stand against this rapacious tyrant. Time and again Gruffydd's warriors and the earl's—or those of the earl's blood-lusting kinsman, Robert of Rhuddlan—tangled and fought. Some-

times the Cymry bloodied the Norman noses, but more often it
went the other way. On one disastrous day, however, King Gruffydd
ap Cynan had been captured. Earl Robert had bound his prize in
chains and hauled him to Caer Cestre, where Gruffydd was cast into
Fat Hugh's hostage pit. That was eight years ago, and he was still
there, kept alive at Hugh's pleasure to torment and torture as whim
moved him. It was thought that the Welsh king would rot in captivity. Hugh had no intention of releasing him and had refused to
set either a ransom or a day of execution, but the earl did allow the
Welsh king's kinsmen to pay their respects on high holy days, when
a selected few were admitted to the danksome keep with carefully
inspected parcels of food, clothing, candles, and other necessaries
for their captive king.

The earl's fortress at Caer Cestre was a squat square lump of
ruddy stone with thick walls and towers at each corner and over the
gate, and the whole surrounded by a swampy, stinking ditch. It had
been constructed on the remains of a stout Saxon stronghold which
was itself built on foundations the Romans had erected on the banks
of the River Dee. The town was also walled, and those walls made
of stone the Roman masons cut from the red cliffs along the river.
The caer, it was said, could not be conquered by force.

These and other things Tuck learned and reported it all to Bran.

"He likes his whoring and hunting, our Hugh," he reported.
They were sitting in the courtyard of Llewelyn's house, sharing a jug
of cool brown ale. A golden afternoon sun was slanting down, warming the little yard agreeably, and the air was soft and drowsy with the
buzz of bees from the hives on the other side of the wall. "They say
he likes his mistresses better than his money box, his falcons better
than his mistresses, and his hounds better than his falcons."

"Thinks himself a mighty hunter, does he?" mused Bran with his nose in the jar. He took a sip and passed it to Tuck.

"That he does," the friar affirmed. "He spends more on his dogs and birds than he does on himself—and he's never been known to spare a penny there, either."

"Does he owe anyone money?" wondered Bran.

"That I cannot say," Tuck told him. "But it seems he spends it as fast as he gets it. Musicians, jugglers, horses, hounds, clothes from Spain and Italy, wine from France—he demands and gets the best of whatever he wants. The way people talk, a fella'd think Fat Hugh was one enormous appetite got up in satin trousers."

Bran chuckled. He took back the jar and raised it. "A man who is slave to his appetites," he said, taking another drink, "has a brute for a master."

"Aye, truly. That he has," the friar agreed cheerfully. "Here now! Save a bit o' that for me!"

Bran passed the jar to the friar, who upended it and drained it in a gulp, froth pouring down his chin, which he wiped on a ready sleeve.

When Tuck handed the empty jar back, Bran peered inside and declared, somewhat cryptically, "It is the master we shall woo, not the slave."

What he meant by this, Tuck was not to discover for several days. But Bran set himself to preparing his plan and acquiring the goods he needed, and also pressed his two young cousins, Brocmael and Ifor, into his service. He spent an entire day instructing the pair in how to comport themselves as members of his company. Of course, Tuck was given a prime part in the grand scheme as well, so the bowlegged little friar was arrayed accordingly in some of Bishop Hywel Hen's best Holy Day vestments borrowed for the purpose.

Tuck

At last, Bran declared himself satisfied with all his preparations. The company gathered in Llewelyn's hall to eat and drink and partake of their host's hospitality before the fire-bright hearth. Llewelyn's wife and her maids tended table, and two men from the tribe regaled the visitors and their host with song, playing music on the harp and pipes while Llewelyn's daughters danced with each other and anyone else they could coax from their places at the board. Some of the noblemen had brought their families, too, swelling the ranks of the gathering and making the company's last night a glad and festive time.

The next morning, after breaking fast on a little bread soaked in milk, Bran repeated his instructions to Llewelyn, Trahaern, and Cynwrig. Then, mounting their horses, the four set off for the docks in search of a boat heading north. Caer Cestre sat happily on the Afon Dyfrdwy, which Tuck knew as the River Dee. All told, Earl Hugh's castle was no great distance—it seemed to Tuck that they could have reached it easily in three easy days of riding—but Bran did not wish to slope unnoticed into town like a fox slinking into the dove cote. He would have it no other way but that they would arrive by ship and make as big an occasion of their landing as could be. When Bran came to Caer Cestre, he wanted everyone from the stablehand to the seneschal to know it.

Lord love us," said Tuck, a little breathless from his ride to the caer, "It's an Iberian trading vessel on its way to Caer Cestre. The ship's master has agreed to take us on board, but they are leaving on the tide flow."

"Tuck, my friend, I do believe things are going our way at last," declared Bran happily. "Fetch young Ifor and Brocmael. I'll give Llewelyn our regards and meet you at the dock. Just you get yourself on board and make sure they don't leave without us."

The travelling party arrived wharfside just as the tide was beginning to turn and got themselves to the ship with little time to spare. As the last horse was brought aboard and secured under the keen gaze of the ship's master—a short, swarthy man with a face burned by wind and sun until it was creased and brown as Spanish leather—Captain Armando gave the order to up anchor and push away from the dock. A good-natured fellow, Armando contented himself with the money Bran paid him for their passage, asking no questions and treating his passengers like the nobility they purported to be. The ship itself was broad abeam and shallow drafted, built for coasting and river travel. It carried a cargo of olive oil and wine in an assortment of barrels and casks; bags of dried beans and black pepper, rolls of copper and tin, and jars of coloured glass. And for the noblemen of England and France: swords, daggers, and helmets of good Spanish steel; and also rich garments of the finest cloth, including silks and satins from the Andalus, and wool from the famous Spanish merinos. The four travellers ate well on board, and their quarters, though cramped—"a body cannot turn around for tripping over his own feet," complained Tuck—were nevertheless clean enough. At all events it was but a short voyage and easily endured. Mostly, the passengers just leaned on the rail and watched shoreline and riverbank slide slowly by, now and again so close they could almost snatch leaves from the passing branches.

On the third day, having skirted the north coast of Wales and then proceeded inland by way of the River Dee, the ship and its passengers and cargo reached the wharf at Caer Cestre. After changing their clothes for the finery bought at some expense in Bangor, the four prepared to disembark.

All during the voyage, Bran had laboured over the tale they were to tell, and all knew well what was expected of them. "Not a cleric this time," Bran had decided on the morning of the second day out. He had been observing the ship's master and was in thrall of a new and, he considered, better idea.

"God love you, man," sighed Tuck. "Changing horses in the middle of the stream—is this a good idea, I ask myself?"

"From what you say, Friar," replied Bran, "Wolf Hugh is no respecter of the church. Good Father Dominic may not receive the welcome he so rightly deserves."

Tuck

"Who would fare better?" wondered Tuck.

"Count Rexindo!" announced Bran, taking the name of a Spanish nobleman mentioned by the ship's master.

Tuck moaned. "All very well for you, my lord. You can change like water as mood and whim and fits of fancy take you. God knows you enjoy it."

"I confess I do," agreed Bran, his twisted smile widening even more.

"I, on the other hand, am a very big fish out of water. For all, I am a poor, humble mendicant whom God has seen fit to bless with a stooped back, a face that frightens young 'uns, and knees that have never had fellowship one with the other. I am not used to such high-flown japes, and it makes me that uneasy—strutting about in some-one else's robes, making airs like a blue-feathered popinjay."

"No one would think you a popinjay," countered Bran. "You worry too much, Tuck."

"And you not enough, Rhi Bran."

"All will be well. You'll see."

Now, as they waited for the horses to be taken off, Bran gathered his crew close. "Look at you—if a fella knew no better," he said, "he'd think you had just sailed in from Spain. Is everyone ready?" Receiving the nodded affirmation from each in turn, he declared, "Good. Let the chase begin."

"And may God have mercy on us all," Tuck added and, bidding their captain and crew farewell, turned and led the landing party down the gangplank. Bran came on a step or two behind, and the two young Welshmen, doing their best to look sombre and unimpressed with their surroundings, came along behind, leading the horses.

Their time aboard the Spanish ship had served Bran well, it had to be admitted. The moment his feet touched the timber planks on the landing dock, Bran was a man transformed. Dressed in his finery—improved by garments he'd purchased from the trading stock Captain Armando carried—he appeared every inch the Spanish nobleman. Tuck marvelled to see him, as did the two young noblemen who were inspired to adopt some of Bran's lofty ways so that to the unsuspecting folk of Caer Cestre, they did appear to be a company of foreign noblemen. They were marked accordingly and soon drew a veritable crowd of volunteers eager to offer their services as guides for a price.

"French!" called Tuck above the clamour. "Anyone here speak French?"

No one did, it seemed; despite the years of Norman domination, Caer Cestre remained an English-speaking town. The disappointed crowd began to thin as people fell away.

"We'll probably have better luck in the town," said Bran. "But offer a penny or two."

So they proceeded up the steep street leading to the town square, and Tuck amended his cry accordingly. "A penny! A penny to anyone who speaks French," he called at the top of his voice. "A penny for a French speaker! A penny!"

At the end of the street stood two great stone pillars, ancient things that at one time had belonged to a basilica or some such edifice but now served as the entrance to the market square. Though it was not market day, there were still many people around, most paying visits to the butcher or baker or ironmonger who kept stalls on the square. A tired old dog lay beside the butcher's hut, and two plough horses stood with drooping heads outside a blacksmith's forge at the far end of the square, giving the place a deceptively sleepy air.

Tuck strode boldly out into the open square, offering silver for

1054

service, and his cry was finally answered. "Here! Here, now! What are you on about?"

Looking around, he saw a man in a tattered green cloak, much faded and bedraggled with mud and muck; he was sitting on the ground with his back against the far side of the butcher hut and his cap in his hands as if he would beg a coin from those who passed by. At Tuck's call, he jumped up and hurried towards the strangers. "Here! What for ye need a Frankish man?"

Tuck regarded him with a dubious frown. The fellow's hair was a mass of filthy tangles hanging down in his face, and his straggling beard looked as if mice had been at it. The eyes that peered out from under the ropy mass were watery and red from too much strong drink the night before, and he reeked of piss and vomit. Unshorn and unkempt he was, Tuck considered—not the sort of person they had in mind for this special chore. "We have business in this town," Tuck explained brusquely, "and we do not speak French."

"I does," the beggar boasted. "Anglish and Frenchy, both alike. What's yer sayin' of a penny, then?"

"We have a penny for anyone who agrees to bear a message of introduction for us," Tuck replied.

"I'm t'man fer ye," the beggar chirped, holding out a filthy hand to receive his pay.

"All in good time, friend," Tuck told him. "I've heard you speak English, but how do I know you can speak French?"

"Speaks it like t'were me ine mither tongue," he replied, still holding out his hand. "*Naturellement, je parle français,* ye ken?"

"Well?" said Bran, stepping up beside them. "What's he say?"

Tuck hesitated. "This fellow says he'll help us, but if his French is as poor as his English, then I expect we're better off asking the butcher's dog over there."

Bran looked around. Seeing as no one else had come forward, and the day was getting on, he said, "Had we a better choice . . . but"—Bran shrugged—"he will have to serve. All the same, tell him we'll give him an extra penny if he will wash and brush before we go."

Tuck told the scruffy fellow what Bran had said, and he readily agreed. "Go then," Tuck ordered. "And be quick about it. Don't make us wait too long, or I'll find someone else."

The beggar dipped his head and scampered off to find a trough in which to bathe himself. Tuck watched him go, still nursing deep misgivings about their rough guide; but since they only needed someone to make introduction, he let the matter rest.

While they waited for the beggar to return, Bran rehearsed once again the next portion of his plan with the two young noblemen so they might keep in mind what to expect and how to comport themselves. "Ifor, you know some Ffreinc."

"A little," admitted Ifor. A slender young man with dark hair and wary eyes beneath a smooth, low brow, he was that much like Bran anyone could well see the family resemblance, however distant it might have been. Blood tells, thought Tuck, so it does. "Not as much as Brocmael, though."

"We hear it at the market in Bangor sometimes," Brocmael explained. Slightly older than Ifor, he had much about him of a good badger dog.

"You may find it difficult to pretend otherwise," Bran told them, "but you must not let on. Keep it to yourselves. The Ffreinc will not be expecting you to understand them, and so you may well hear things to our advantage from time to time." He smiled at their dour expressions. "Don't worry. It's easy—just keep remembering who you are."

The two nodded solemnly. Neither one shared Bran's easy confidence, and both were nearly overwhelmed by their arrival in a Norman town and the deception they meant to work—not to say frightened by the prospect of delivering themselves into their chief enemy's hands. Truth be told, Tuck felt much the same way. The sun climbed a little higher, and the day grew warmer accordingly. Bran decided that they should get a bite to eat, and Tuck, never one to forego a meal if it could be helped, readily agreed. "Unless my nose mistakes me," he said, "the baker is taking out fresh pies as we speak."

"Just what I was thinking," said Bran. Turning to his young attendants, he said, "Here is a good time to test your mettle. Remember who we are." He pulled a leather bag from his belt and handed it to Ifor. "Get us some pies—one for each and one for our guide, too, when he returns. He looks like he could use a meal."

"And, lads, see if there is any beer," Tuck added. "A jug or two would be most welcome. This old throat is dry as Moses' in the wilderness."

They accepted the purse, turned, and with the air of men mounting to the gibbet, moved off to the baker's stall. "They'll be all right," observed Bran, more in hope than conviction.

"Oh, aye," Tuck agreed with equal misgiving. "Right as a miller's scale."

The presence of wealthy foreign strangers in the square was attracting some interest. A few of the idlers who had been standing at the well across the square were staring at them now and nodding in their direction. "You wanted to be noticed," Tuck said, smiling through his teeth. "But I don't think those fellas like what they're seeing."

1057

"You surprise me, Tuck. This is just what we want. If word of our arrival reaches the earl before we do, so much the better. See there?" He indicated two of the men just then hurrying away. "The news is on its way. Be at ease, and remember—as highborn Spanish noblemen it is beneath us to pay them heed."

"*You* may be the king of Spain for all Caer Cestre knows," Tuck declared, "but these rich clothes fit me ill, for all I am a simple Saxon monk."

"A simple Saxon worrier it seems to me," Bran corrected. "There is nothing to fear, I tell you."

Brocmael and Ifor returned a short while later with pies and ale for all. Their errand had settled them somewhat and raised their confidence a rung or two. The four ate in the shade of the pillar at the side of the square and were just finishing when three of the idlers approached from the well.

"Here's trouble," muttered Tuck. "Keep your wits about you, lads."

But before any of them could speak, the beggar returned. He came charging across the square and accosted the men in blunt English. Bran and the others watched in amazement as the idlers halted, hesitated, then returned to their places at the well.

"A man after my own heart," said Tuck. He looked their reprobate guide up and down. "Here now, I hardly know you."

Not only had he washed himself head to toe, but he had cleaned his clothes with a bristle brush, cut his hair, and trimmed his beard. He had even found a feather to stick in his threadbare hat. Beaming with somewhat bleary good pleasure, he strode to where Bran was standing and with a low bow swept his cap from his head and proclaimed in the accent of an English nobleman, "Alan a'Dale at your service, my lord. May God bless you right well."

"Well, Tuck," remarked Bran, much impressed, "he's brushed up a treat. Tell him that I mean no offence when I say that I'd not mark him for the same man."

The man laughed, the sound full and easy. "The Alan you see is the Alan that is," he said. "Take 'im or leave 'im, friend, 'cause there en't no ither, ye ken?"

When Tuck had translated, Bran smiled and said, "We'll take you at your word, Alan." To Tuck, he said, "Give him his pennies and tell him what we want him to do."

"That is for the wash," said Tuck, placing a silver penny in Alan's pink-scrubbed palm, "and this is for leading us to Earl Hugh's castle. Now, sir, when we get there we want you to send for the earl's seneschal and tell him to announce us to the earl. Do that, and do it well—there's another penny for you when you're finished."

"Too kind, you are, my friend," said Alan, closing his fist over the coins and whisking them out of sight.

"And here's a pie for you," Tuck told him. The pie was still warm, its golden crust clean and unbroken.

"For me?" Alan was genuinely mystified by this small courtesy. He looked from Tuck to Bran and then at the younger members of their party. His hand was shaking as he reached out to take the pie. "For me?" he said again, as one who could not quite believe his good fortune. It seemed to mean more to him than the silver he had just been given.

"All for you, and we saved a little ale too," Tuck told him. "Eat now, and we will go as soon as you've finished."

"Bless you, Father," he said, grabbing Tuck's hand and raising it to his lips. "May the Good Lord repay your kindness a thousand times."

It happened so fast the little friar had no time to snatch his hand away again before the teary-eyed fellow had kissed it. "Here now! Stop that!"

"Bless you, good gents all," he said, lapsing into the accents of the street once more. "Alan a'Dale en't one to fergit a good turn."

He sat down on the ground at the base of the pillar and began to eat, stuffing his mouth hungrily and smacking his lips with each bite. Bran sent Ifor and Brocmael to water the horses while they waited, and then asked Tuck to find out what he could from their hungry guide. "Tell him who we are, Tuck, and let's see how he takes it."

"My lord wants you to know that you are in the service of an esteemed and wealthy foreign nobleman in need of your aid. Perform your service well and you will be amply rewarded. He gives you good greeting."

At this, Alan carefully laid his pie aside, rose to his knees, swiped off his hat, and bowed his head. "You honour your servant, m'lord. May God be good to you."

"Give him our thanks," Bran said, "and ask him how long he's been in the town, and what news of the earl and his court."

Turning to Alan, Tuck relayed Bran's question. "My lord thanks you and wishes to know how long you have sojourned in this place."

Alan raised his eyes heavenward, his lips moving as he made his calculations. "In all, three year—give or take. No more than four."

"And how do you find the lord here—Earl Hugh?" Tuck asked, then added, "Please, finish your meal. We will talk while you eat."

"Aye, that's him," replied their guide, settling himself against the pillar once more. He picked up the pie and bit into it. "Fat Hugh, they call him—aye, and well-named, he. There's one hog wants the whole wallow all to himself, if ye ken."

"A greedy man?"

"Greedy?" he mused, taking another bite and chewing thought-fully. "If a pig be greedy, then he's the Emperor o' Swine."

"Is he now?" Tuck replied, and translated his words for the Cymry speakers, who chuckled at the thought.

"That tallies with what we've heard already," replied Bran. "Ask him if he knows the castle—has he ever been inside it?"

"Aye," nodded Alan when Tuck finished. "I ken the bloody heap right well. Lord have mercy, I been up there a few times." He crinkled up his eyes and asked, "Why would a bunch o' God fearin' folk like yerselves want to go up there anyway?"

"We have a little business with the earl," explained Tuck.

"Bad business, then," observed Alan. "Still, I don't suppose you can be blamed for not knowing what goes on hereabouts . . ." He tut-ted to himself. "Mark me, you'd be better off forgetting you ever heard of Wolf d'Avranches."

"If it's as bad as all that," Tuck ventured, "then why did you agree to take us there so quickly?"

"I didn't ken ye was God-fearin' gents right off, did I?" he said. "I maybe thought you were like his nibs up there, an' ye'd give as good as get, ye ken?"

"And now?"

"Now I ken different-like. Ye en't like them rascals up t'castle. Devil take 'em, but even Ol' Scratch won't have 'em, I daresay." Alan gazed at the strangers with pleading eyes. "Ye sure ye want to go up there?"

"We thank you for the warning. If we had any other choice, no doubt we'd take your advice," Tuck told him. "But circumstances force us to go, and go we must."

"Well, don't ye worry," said Alan, brushing crumbs from his clothes as he climbed to his feet. "I'll still see ye right, no matter. An' what's more, I'll say a prayer for yer safe return."

"Thank you, Alan," Tuck said. "That's most thoughtful."

"Hold tight to yer thanks," he replied. "For ye might soon be a'thinkin' otherwise."

With that subtle warning still hanging in the air, the visitors and their rascal of a guide set off.

❧ PART THREE ❧

"But where is Will Scadlocke?" quod Rhiban to John,
    When he had rallied them all to the forest,
"One of these ten score is missing who should
    Be stood at the fore with the best."

"Of Scadlocke," spoke young Much, "sad tidings I give,
    For I ween now in prison he lay;
The sherif's men fowle have set him a trap,
    And now taken the rascal away.

"Ay, and to-morrow he hangéd must be,
    As soon as ere it comes day.
But before the sheriff this victory could get,
    Four men did Will Scadlocke slay!"

When Rhiban heard this loathly report,
    O, he was grievéd full sore!
He marshalled up his fine merrye men
    Who one and together all swore:

That William Scadlocke rescued should be,
    And brought in safe once again;
Or else should many a fayre gallant wight
    For his sake there would be slain.

"Our mantles and cloaks, of deep Lincoln green,
    Shall we behind us here leave;
We'll dress us six up as mendicant monks—
    And I whist they'll not Rhiban perceive."

So donned they each one of them habits of black,
    Like masse-priests as such are from Spayne.
And thus it fell out unknowingly, that,
    Rhiban the reeve entertain'd.

To the sherif bold Rhiban proposéd a sport,
    For full confidence he had achiev'd.
If Will could outshoot monk Rhiban, disguised,
    The prisoner should earn a reprieve.

This sheriff was loath but at length did agree
    For a trick on the prisoner he planned.
Before William Scadlocke had taken his turn,
    The sheriff had twisted Will's hand.

Earl Hugh's castle was built on the ancient foundations of the old Roman fort, partly of timber and partly of the same bloodred stone the Roman masons carved from the bluffs above the river so long ago. It loomed over the town like a livid, unsightly blemish: inflamed and angry, asquat its low hilltop.

For all the brightness of the day, the place seemed to breathe a dark and doomful air, and Tuck shivered with a sudden chill as they passed through the gate—as if the frost of bitter winter clung to the old stone, refusing to warm beneath the autumn sun. And although it was but a short distance from the town which carried its name, Caer Cestre remained as remote behind its walls as any Ffreinc stronghold across the sea.

This impression was due in part to the unseemly number of Ffreinc soldiers loitering in the courtyard—some in padded armour with wooden practice weapons, others standing about in clumps looking on, and still others sitting or reclining in the sun. There must have been twenty or more men in all, and a good few women too; and from the way they minced about the perimeter of the yard, smirking and winking at each and all, Tuck did not imagine they were wives of the soldiers. A heap of sleeping hounds lay in one corner of the yard, dozing in the sun, while nearby a group of stablehands worked at grooming four large chestnut-coloured hunting horses—big, raw-boned heavy-footed beasts of the kind much favoured by the Ffreinc.

Striding along after the porter who conducted them to the hall, the small procession consisting of two young foreigners, a rotund priest, their noble leader, and a local guide caused nary a ripple of interest from anyone they passed. Upon entering the vestibule, they were shortly brought to stand before the seneschal. Alan a'Dale, despite his many shortcomings, performed the service of interpreter surprisingly well, and they were admitted into the hall without the slightest difficulty whatever. Tuck breathed a prayer as they entered Wolf Hugh's den: a noisy and noisome room filled with rough board benches and tables at which men and women, and even a few children, appeared to be entering the final progressions of a night's debauch—even though the sun had yet to quarter the sky. The roil of eating and drinking, dicing and dancing, flirting and fighting amidst gales of coarse laughter and musicians doggedly trying to make themselves heard above the revellers greeted the visitors like the roll and heave of a storm-fretted sea. In one corner, dirty-faced boys tormented a cat; in another, an amorous couple fumbled; here, a man already deep in his cups shouted for more wine; there, a fellow poked at a performing juggler with a fire iron. Hounds stalked among the benches and beneath the tables, quarrelling over bones and scraps of meat. There was even a young pig,

1066

garlanded and beribboned, wandering about with its snout in the rushes underfoot.

Crossing the threshold, Bran paused to take in the tumult, collected himself, and then waded into the maelstrom. Here Bran's special genius was revealed, for he strode into the great, loud room with the look of a man for whom all that passed beneath his gaze in this riotous place was but dreary commonplace. His arrival did not go unnoticed, and when he judged he had gathered enough attention, he paused, his dark eyes scanning the ungainly crowd, as if to discern which of the roisterers before him might be the earl.

"By Peter's beard," muttered Tuck, unable to believe that anyone entering the castle could experience so much as a fleeting doubt about which of the men at table was Fat Hugh. *Only look for the biggest, loudest, most slovenly and uncouth brigand in the place,* he thought, *and that's the man. And yet . . . here's our Bran, standing straight and tall and searching each and every as if he could not see what was plain before his nose. Oh, this shows a bit of sass, does it not?*

What is more, Tuck could tell from the curious look on the earl's face that Hugh was more than a little taken aback at the tall dark figure standing before him. For there he was, a very king in his own kingdom, the infamous Wolf d'Avranches renowned and feared throughout his realm, and who was this that did not know him? And here was Bran without so much as a word or gesture, taking the overbearing lord down a peg or two, showing him that he was nothing more than a wobble-jowled ruffian who could not be distinguished from one of his own stablehands.

Oh, our canny King Raven is that shrewd, Tuck considered, a little courage seeping back into his own step. He glanced at Ifor and Brocmael and saw from the frozen expressions on their faces that the two Cymry, appalled by what they saw, were nevertheless struggling to maintain any semblance of calm and dignified detachment. "Steady on, lads," Tuck whispered.

Alan a'Dale, however, seemed at ease, comfortable even, walking easily beside Tuck, smiling even. At the friar's wondering glance, he said, "Been here before, ye ken."

"Often?"

"Once or twice. I sing here of a time."

"You sing, Alan?"

"Oh, aye."

Bran silenced them with a look and turned to address the onlooking crowd. *"Qua est vir?"* Bran announced in that curious broken Latin that passed for Spanish among folk who knew no better. *"Qua est ut accersitus Señor Hugh?"*

The seneschal, not understanding him, looked to Alan for explanation. He conferred with Tuck, then replied, "My lord wishes to know where is he that is called Earl Hugh?"

"But he is *there*," answered the chief servant as if that should be every whit as obvious as it was. He indicated the high table where, surrounded by perhaps six or eight ladies of the sort already glimpsed in the courtyard, sat a huge man with a broad, flat face and hanging dewlaps like a barnyard boar. Swathed in pale sea-green satin so well filled one could see the wavelike ripples of flesh beneath the tight-stretched fabric, he occupied the full breadth of a thronelike chair which was draped in red satin lined with ermine. Dull brown hair hung in long, ropy curls around his head, and a lumpy, misshapen wart besmirched one cheek. He held a drinking horn half raised, his wide, full-lipped mouth agape as he stared at the strange visitors with small, inquisitive eyes.

"I present my Lord Hugh d'Avranches," proclaimed the seneschal, his voice striving above the commotion of the great room.

Alan passed this along to Bran, who made a sour face as if he suddenly smelled something foul. *"Et? Et?"* he said. *That?*

Even the seneschal understood him then. "Of course," he said, stiffly. "Who else?"

Without another word, Bran approached the table where the earl sat drinking with his women. A strained silence fell at his approach as attention turned to the newcomers. Bran inclined his head in the slightest of bows and waved both Tuck and Alan to his side. *"Adveho, sto hic. Dico lo quis ego detto,"* he said grandly, and Tuck relayed his words to Alan, who offered: "His estimable lord Count Rexindo greets you in the name of his father, Ranemiro, Duke of Navarre, who wishes you well."

"Mon Dieu!" exclaimed the earl, his astonishment manifest.

Bran, looking every inch a Spanish nobleman, made another slight bow and spoke again. When he finished, he nodded at Tuck, who said, speaking through Alan, "Count Rexindo wants you to know that word of your fame has reached him in his travels, and he requests the honour of a private audience with you."

"Duke of Navarre, eh?" said Earl Hugh. "Never heard of him. Where is that?"

"It is a province in Spain, my lord," explained Alan politely. "The duke is brother to King Carlos, who is—"

"I know who King Carlos is, by the rood," interrupted the earl. "Heard of him." He passed an appraising eye over the tall man before him, then at his companions, evidently finding them acceptable. "Nephew of the king of Spain, eh? However did you find your way to a godforsaken wilderness like this?"

Tuck and Count Rexindo conferred, whereupon Alan replied, "The count has been visiting the royal court, and heard about the hunting here in the north."

"Eh? Hunting?" grunted the earl. He seemed to remember that he held a cup in his hand and finished raising it to his mouth. He guzzled down a long draught, then wiped his lips on the sleeve of his green satin shirt.

As if this was the signal the room had been awaiting, the hall lurched into boisterous life once more. The earl slapped his hand on the board before him, rattling the empty jars. "Here! Clear him a place." He began shoving his cups and companions aside to make room for his new guests. "Sit! All of you! We'll share a drink—you and your men—and you can tell me about this hunting, eh?"

By Saint Mewan's toe, thought Tuck, *he's done it! Our Bran has done it!*

Earl Hugh filled some empty cups from a jar and sent one of the women to fetch bread and meat for his new guests. Turning to regard his visitors from across the table, he observed, "Spaniard, eh? You're a long way from home."

Bran gazed placidly back at him as Alan, translating Tuck's hurried whispers, relayed his words.

"That is so, may it please God," replied Count Rexindo. Even speaking through two interpreters his highborn courtesy was clear to see. "We have heard that the hunting in England is considered the best in the world. This, I had to see for myself." He smiled and spread his hands. "So, here I am."

The count drank from his cup while his words were translated for the earl, smiling, looking for all the world like a man at utter ease with himself and his fellows. The women at the board seemed to find his dark looks attractive; they vied for his notice with winks and none-too-subtle smiles. When Alan finished, Count Rexindo indicated his companions and conferred with his interpreter, who said, "Pray allow me to introduce the count's companions. I present to you Father Balthus, Bishop of Pamplona," he said, and Tuck dipped his head in modest acknowledgement. "Also, I give you Lord Galindo of Tolosa"—and here he indicated Ifor—"and next to him is Lord Ramiero of Petilla." Brocmael, solemn as the tomb, inclined his head. "They are favourites among the count's many cousins."

If Alan suspected that he was part of a cunning deception, he did not let it show in the slightest. On the contrary, the further into the tale he delved, the more comfortable he became, and the more his admiration for the dark-haired young nobleman grew. Bran, as Count Rexindo, was a very marvel: his manner, his air, his being—everything about him had changed since entering that den of rogues; even his voice had taken on a subtle quality of refinement and restraint.

Tuck, too, was impressed, for when Bran spoke his made-up Spanish, it was with the light, soft lisping tone of Hibernia that Tuck recalled in their friend from Saint Dyfrig's, the stately Brother Jago. Slow boat that he was, it finally occurred to the friar that this was where Bran had got the names and titles and all the rest for them all. All that time spent travelling together last spring, Bran had had plenty of time to learn all that and more besides from the Spanish monk.

"You like to hunt, eh?" mused Earl Hugh into his cup. "So do I, by the bloody rood! So do I."

A brief conference between Tuck, Alan, and Bran set the course for the next part of the plan. "Give him to know that in Spain I am renowned as a great hunter, and that my father keeps a stable of the best horses in the realm. There is nothing I have not hunted." Bran nodded. "Make a good tale of it, Tuck, but be sure to remember what you have said so you can tell me after."

Tuck relayed to Alan what Bran had said, and added his own warning, "And don't over-egg the pudding, boyo," he said. "I'll be listening, mind, so keep it pure and simple."

"Never fear," replied Alan, who then turned to Earl Hugh and said, "My apologies, Lord. The count is embarrassed by his lack of French. But he wishes you to know that in his home country, he is a very champion among hunters and has ridden to the hunt throughout Spain. His father, the duke, keeps a stable of the finest horses to be found anywhere in the realm."

The earl listened, his interest piqued. "No finer horses than mine, I'll warrant," he suggested when Alan finished. "I'd like to see them. Did you bring any with you?"

"Alas no, Lord," answered Alan, without waiting to consult his master. "They are very valuable animals, as you must imagine, and could not be allowed to make a voyage, however short."

"A pity," replied Hugh. "I should like to have seen them in the flesh. My own horses have been praised by those who know a good animal when they see one. I'll show them to you, eh?"

Alan turned his head to receive the count's decision, then said, "My lord would like nothing more than to have the pleasure of viewing your excellent animals."

"Then let's be at it!" said Hugh, hoisting himself from his chair with the aid of the board before him. Calling for his seneschal, he motioned his visitors to follow and bowled from the hall with a lurching, unsteady gait.

"We're well on our way, men," Bran whispered. To Ifor and Brocmael, he said, "This next part will be in your hands. Are you ready?" Both young men nodded. "Good." To Tuck, he added, "Tell Alan—"

"My lord," said Alan, with a fishy grin at Tuck, "it is not necessary, as I speak a fair bit of Cymry, too, ye ken?"

"You do amaze me," Bran confessed. "I begin to believe you were born to this."

"Just where *did* you learn to speak like that?" Tuck wondered. "I mean no offence, but you spoke like a roadside beggar before we passed through these gates."

Alan lifted one shoulder in a halfhearted shrug. "It is useful for the earnin' o' a penny or two," he said, putting on the rough speech again as easily as a man putting on a hat. "A wanderin' musician is a pitiful lump without his harp."

"Wandering musician," echoed Tuck. "A minstrel?"

"If ye like," said Alan.

"How did you lose your harp?" the friar asked.

"Let's just say some lords appreciate a jest more'n others, ye ken?"

Bran laughed and clapped him on the shoulder. "I want you to stay with us while we're here—will you do that? I'll reward you well. Perhaps when this is over we can even find you a harp."

"I am honoured, Sire," the beggar answered.

"Here now!" called Earl Hugh from a doorway across the way. "This way to the stables."

"Let the hunt begin," said Bran, and the four Spanish noblemen and their interpreter hurried to join their host.

CHAPTER 15

Cél Craidd

Mérian held the long smooth length of ash between her fingers and carefully wrapped the thin rawhide strap in a tight spiral around the end, placing the clipped halves of stripped feathers from a goose's wing just so as she slowly turned the rounded shaft. Half her mind was on her task—fletching arrows required patience and dexterity, but consumed little thought—and the other half of her mind was on the worrying news that had reached them the night before.

The news had come after nightfall. Mérian and Noín and two of the other women were tending to the evening meal, and the rest of Cél Craidd was still at work: some trimming and shaping branches of ash and yew for war bows, or assisting Siarles in splitting narrow lengths of oak for arrows; two of the women were weaving hemp and linen for strings, and Tomas was helping Angharad affix the steel points. Scarlet and his small host of warriors—two of the younger women and three of the older children—were hard at work training to the longbow—they would practice until it was too dark to see. And any who were not busy with either bows or arrows were tending the bean field. The forest round about was sinking into a peaceful and pleasant autumn twilight.

And then they heard the long, low whistle that signalled the return of the scouts—those who had been away all day watching the King's Road. A few moments later, Rhoddi and Owain tumbled breathless down the bank and into the settlement bearing the news: Sheriff de Glanville had returned with upwards of fifty knights.

"They came quick and they came quiet," Rhoddi said when he had swallowed a few mouthfuls of water and splashed a cup over his head. "It was already getting dark, and they were on us before we knew it or we would have prepared a welcome for them."

"Where's Iwan?" asked Siarles, already halfway to flying off to his aid.

"He stayed to watch and see if any more came along," explained Owain. "He sent us on ahead." Catching Siarles's disapproving glance, the young warrior added, "There was nothing we could do. There were just too many, and we didn't have men or arrows enough to take 'em on."

"We thought better to let be this once," offered Rhoddi.

"Rhi Bran would have fought 'em," said Siarles.

"Given men enough and clear warning to get set in place, aye," agreed Rhoddi, "King Raven would have taken 'em on and no doubt won the day. But we en't Bran, and we didn't have men enough or time."

Iwan had returned a little while later to confirm what the others had said. "So now, Bloody Hugo has fifty more knights to throw at us. I hope Bran and Tuck fare well on their errand—we'll need all the help we can get. I just wish there was some way to get word to them."

Now, as the sun beat down brightly upon their wildwood settlement, Mérian looked around at the quiet industry around her, Iwan's words circling in her mind like restless birds. *I might not be able to get word to Bran,* she thought, *but I can do better than that—I can raise troops myself.* In that moment, she knew what she had to do: she would go to her father and persuade him to join Bran in the battle to drive the Ffreinc out of Elfael. Her father could command thirty, perhaps forty men, and each one trained to the longbow. Experienced archers would be more than welcome and, added to however many men Bran was able to raise, would form the beginnings of a fair army. She knew Bran's feelings about involving her father, but he was wrong. She'd tried to persuade him otherwise and met with a stubborn— nay, prideful—resistance. But in this matter of life and death, she considered, the outcome was just too important to allow such petty concerns to cloud good judgement. They needed troops, her father had them, and that was that.

Bran, she knew, would forgive her when he saw the men she would bring. Moreover, if she left at once, she could be back in Cél Craidd with the promise of warriors or better, the warriors themselves, before Bran returned.

Having made up her mind, the urge to go reared up like a wild horse and she was borne along like a helpless rider clinging to its neck. She made short work of the arrow she was fletching, set it aside, and rose, brushing bits of feather from her lap. *I can't be wearing this home to meet my family,* she decided, looking down at her stained and threadbare gown. Hurrying to her hut, she went inside and drew a bundle down from the rafters, untied it, and shook out the gown she had worn as an Italian noblewoman when accompanying Bran on the mission to rescue Will Scarlet. Though of the finest quality, the material was dark and heavy and made her look like an old woman; nevertheless, it was all she had and it would have to do. As she changed into the gown, she thought about what she would say to the family she had not seen for . . . how long had it been? Two years? Three? Too long, to be sure.

She brushed her hair and washed her face, and then hurried off to prepare a little something to eat on the way, and to ready a horse. Caer Rhodl was no great distance. It was still early; if she left at once and did not stop on the way, she could be there before nightfall.

"Are you certain, my lady?" said Noín with a frown when Mérian explained why she was saddling a horse while wearing her Italian gown. "Perhaps you should wait and speak to Iwan. Tell him what you plan."

"I am only going to visit my family," replied Mérian lightly. "Nothing ill can come of it."

"Then tell Angharad. She should—" Mérian was already shaking her head. "But you must tell *someone*."

"I am," said Mérian. "I'm telling *you*, Noín. But I want you to promise me you won't tell anyone else until this evening when I'm sure to be missed. Promise me."

"Not even Will?"

"No," said Mérian, "not a word to anyone—even Will. I should be at Caer Rhodl by the time anyone thinks to come looking for me, and by then there will be no need."

"Take someone with you, at least," suggested Noín, her voice taking on a note of pleading. "We could tell Will, and he could go with you."

"He is needed here," answered Mérian, brushing aside the offer. "Besides, I will be safe home before anyone knows it."

Noín's frown deepened; a crease appeared between her lowered brows. "There are dangerous folk about," she protested weakly.

"I shouldn't worry," replied Mérian, a smile curving her lips. "The only dangerous folk here about are *us*." She took the other woman's hand and pressed it firmly. "I'll be fine."

With that, she took up her small cloth bag, mounted quickly into the saddle, and was gone.

She struck off along a familiar path—it seemed as if she had lived a lifetime in this forest; were there any paths she didn't know?—and with swift, certain strides soon reached the King's Road. There she paused to take a drink of water from her stoppered jar and listen for anyone moving in the greenwood. Satisfied there was no one else about, she crossed the road, flitting quickly as a bird darting from one leafy shelter to another, and rode quickly on.

Just after midday, the trail divided and she took the southern turning, which, if she remembered correctly, would lead to her father's lands in Eiwas. The day was warm now, and she was sweating through her clothes; she drank some more water and moved along once more, riding a little slower now; she was well away from Cél Craidd, and there had been no sign of anyone following her. Except for a few stands of nettles and some brambles to be avoided, the path was clear and bright and easy underfoot. When she grew hungry, she ate from the bag slung under her arm, but she did not stop until finally reaching the forest's southwestern border.

Here, at the edge of the great wood that formed the boundary

1079

of the March, the land fell away to the south in gentle, sloping runs of low, grassy hills and wooded valleys—the land of her home. As she gazed out upon it now, Mérian was lifted up and swept away on wave after wave of guilt: it was so close! And all this time it had been awaiting her return—her *family* had been awaiting her return.

Stepping from the forest, she started down the broad face of a long hill towards the small, winding track she knew would lead her home—the same track Bran had used so often in the past when he came calling, usually in the dead of night. The thought sent another pang through her. Why, oh why, had she never tried to get home sooner?

It was no good telling herself that she had been taken prisoner and held against her will. That had been true for only the first few moments of her captivity. Events had proven Bran right: Baron Neufmarché was a sly, deceitful enemy, and no friend of hers or her family's. He had shown neither qualm nor hesitation in sending men to kill them following their escape. Once she understood that, she had stopped trying to get away. In fact, she had been more than content to remain at Bran's side in his struggle to save Elfael. And after that first season, the greenwood had become her home, and truth be told, she had rarely spared a passing thought for Eiwas or her family since.

The reason was, she decided, because in her heart of hearts she knew there was nothing waiting for her at Caer Rhodl except marriage—most likely to an insufferable Ffreinc nobleman of her father's choosing in order to advance her family's fortunes and keep the cantref safe. As true as that may have been, it was still only part of the tale. Partly, too, her lack of interest in returning home was due to the fact that in the months following her abduction she had

1080

become a trusted member of King Raven's council. In Cél Craidd she was honoured and her presence esteemed by all, and not merely some chattel to be packed off to the first Norman with a title that her father deemed advantageous to befriend. Mérian did not mean to condemn her father, but in the precarious world her family inhabited that was the way things were.

In short, with Bran she had a place—a place where she was needed, valued, and loved, a place she did not have without him. And that, more than anything else, had prevented her from leaving.

Now Bran needed her more than ever, if he only knew it. Stubborn as an old plough horse, Bran had refused to even consider asking her father for aid. They needed warriors; Lord Cadwgan had them. The solution was simple, and Mérian was not so childish as to allow anything so inconsequential as stubbornness or pride or a misplaced sense of honour to stand in the way of obtaining the aid her people so desperately needed.

Oh, there was a question: when, exactly, had she begun thinking of them as *her people?*

Mérian continued along the well-trod trail, her mind ranging far and wide as her mount carried her unerringly home. Once she passed a farmer and his wife working in a turnip field; they exchanged greetings, but she did not turn aside to talk to them. In fact, she stopped only once for a short rest in a little shady nook beside the road; she watered the horse, then drank some herself, and splashed some water on her face before moving on again. The sun quartered the sky, eventually beginning its long descent.

The sun was well down and the first stars were alight in the east when Mérian came in sight of Caer Rhodl. The old fortress with its timber walls stood tall and upright on the hill, the little wooden church quiet in the valley below. The place breathed an air of peace and contentment. In fact, nothing about the settlement had changed that she could see. Everything was still just the same as she remembered it.

This thought gave her heart a lift as she hurried on, reaching the long ramp leading to the gate, which stood open as if awaiting her arrival. A few more quick steps brought her through the gate and into the yard, where Mérian paused to look around.

Across the way, two grooms were leading horses to the stables; the horses were lathered, lately ridden—and at some distance and speed. Odd, she had not seen them on the road.

And then she saw Garran, her brother. Mérian had only the briefest glimpse of him as he disappeared through the entrance to the hall, but she thought he was in the company of a young woman. With a shout, she called his name and started across the yard. Three men and several women stood talking near the kitchen; they turned at Mérian's cry and saw a dark-haired young woman in a long dark gown flitting across the yard.

"Here! You!" shouted one of the men, moving forward. "Stop!"

When Mérian gave no sign that she had heard him, he cried out again, and moved to catch her before she reached the hall.

"Here, now!" he called, stepping into her path. "Where might you be going, young miss?"

So intent was she that it was not until the man took hold of her arm that she noticed him. "What?" she said. Feeling the man's hand tighten around her arm, she tried to pull away. "Let me go!" Looking towards the door to the hall, she cried, "Garran! Garran, it's me!"

"Be still," said the man, pulling her back. "You just stop that now. We're going to have a talk."

"Let me go!" She turned to face her captor, and recognized him as one of her father's men. "Luc?"

"Here, now," he said, his eyes narrowing in suspicion. "How do you know my name?"

"Luc, it's Mérian," she said. "*Mérian*—do you not know me?"

A figure appeared in the doorway behind Luc. "What's this?"

Mérian's gaze shifted to the hall entrance. "Garran!"

"I warned you," said her father's man, pulling her away. "Come along. You're going to—"

"Release me!" Mérian wriggled in his grasp.

"Mérian?"

She turned to find herself looking into the face of her very astonished brother.

"Saints and angels, Mérian," he gasped, "is it really you?"

"Oh, Garran—thank God, you're here. I—I . . ." she began, and suddenly could not speak for the lump in her throat.

"Lady Mérian," said Luc, "forgive me. On my word I didn't recognize you." He turned and called to the others who stood looking on. "El! Rhys! It's Lady Mérian come home!"

The others surged forward, clamouring all at once. Garran silenced them with a wave of his hand. "Look at you," he said, lifting her face with a thumb and finger. "Where have you been all this time?"

"Father and Mother—are they here? Of course they are," she said, finding her voice again. She started towards the hall. "I'm longing to see them. Come, Garran, you can present me to the king." When her brother did not move, she turned to him again. The solemn look on his face stopped her. "Why? What is it?"

"Father is dead, Mérian."

She heard what he said, but did not credit the words. "Where?" she asked. "Come along, I'm certain they—"

"Mérian, no," said Garran firmly. "Listen to me. Father is dead."

"He was sick for a very long time, my lady," offered Luc. "My lord Cadwgan died last spring."

"Father . . . dead?" Her stomach tightened into a knot, and her breath came in a gasp as the full weight of this new reality broke upon her. "It can't be . . ."

Garran nodded. "I'm the king now."

"And mother?" she asked, fearing the answer.

"She is well," replied Garran. "Although, when she sees you . . ."

Some of the others who had gathered around spoke up. "Where have you been?" they asked. "We were told you had been killed. We thought you dead long ago."

"I was taken captive," Mérian explained. "I was not harmed."

"Who did this to you?" demanded Luc. "Tell us and we will avenge you, my lady. This outrage cannot be allowed to stand—"

"Peace, Luc," Garran interrupted. "That is enough. We will discuss this later. Now I want to take my sister inside and let her get washed. You and Rhys spread the news. Tell everyone that Lady Mérian has come home."

"Gladly, Sire," replied Rhys, who hurried off to tell the women standing a little way off.

Rhi Garran led the way into the hall, and Mérian followed, walking across the near-empty hall on stiff legs. She was brought to her father's chamber at the far end of the hall and paused to smooth her clothes and hair with her fingers before allowing Garran to open the door. She gave him a nod, whereupon he knocked on the door, lifted the latch, and pushed it open.

1084

The dowager queen sat alone in a chair with an embroidery frame on a stand before her. With a needle in one hand and the other resting on the taut surface of the stretched fabric, she hummed to herself as she bent over her work.

"Mother?" said Mérian, stepping slowly into the room as if entering a dream where anything might happen.

"Dear God in heaven!" shrieked Queen Anora, glancing up to see who it was that had entered the room.

"Mother, I—"

"Mérian!" Anora cried, leaping up so quickly she overturned the embroidery frame. She stretched out her arms to the daughter she had never hoped to see again. "Oh, Mérian. Come here, child."

Mérian stepped hesitantly at first, then ran, and was gathered into her mother's embrace. "Oh, oh, I—" she began, and found she could not speak. Tears welled in her eyes and began to run down her cheeks. She felt her mother's hands on her face and her lips on her cheek.

"There now, dear heart," her mother said soothingly. "All is well now you're home."

"Oh, Mother, I-I'm so sorry," she sobbed, burying her face in the hollow of her mother's throat. "There are so many times I would have come to you—so many times I *should* have come . . ."

"Hush, dearest one," whispered Queen Anora, stroking her daughter's hair. "You are here now and nothing else matters." She held Mérian for a time without speaking, then said, "I only wish your father could have seen this day."

Mérian, overcome with grief and guilt, wept all the more. "I'm so sorry," she murmured again. "So very sorry."

"Never mind," Anora sighed after a moment. "You're home now.

Nothing else matters." She held her daughter at arm's length and cast her eyes over her, as if at a gown or tunic she had just finished sewing. "You're half starved. Look at you, Mérian: you're thin as a wraith."

Mérian stepped back a little and looked down the length of her body, smoothing her bedraggled clothing with her hands. "We have many mouths to feed, and there is not always enough," she began.

There was a movement behind her, and a voice said, *"Qu'est-ce que c'est?"*

Mérian's shock at hearing the news of her father's death was only slightly greater than that of seeing the women who had entered the room. "Sybil!" gasped Mérian. "Baroness Neufmarché!"

At the sight of Mérian, Lady Agnes Neufmarché put her hands to her face in amazement. *"Mon Dieu!"*

"Mérianne," said Sybil, echoing her mother's astonishment.

Prince Garran stood to one side, a half smile on his face, enjoying the women's surprise at seeing one another again so unexpectedly.

Mérian saw his smile and instantly turned on him. "What are *they* doing here?" she hissed.

The baroness crossed quickly to her. *"Ma chérie,"* she cooed, placing a hand on her shoulder. "How you must have suffered, *non?"*

Mérian reacted as if she had been burned by the touch. She gave a start and shook off Lady Agnes's hand. "You!" she snarled. "Don't touch me!"

"Mérian!" said Garran. "Have you gone mad?"

"Why are they here?" demanded Mérian, her voice quivering with pent rage. "Tell me why they're here!"

Lady Agnes stepped back, her expression at once worried and offended.

"Darling, what do you mean?" asked her mother. "They are living here."

Mérian shook her head. "No," she said, backing away a step. "That cannot be . . . it can't."

"Listen to you," replied the queen gently. "Why ever not? Garran is married now. Sybil is his queen. The baroness is spending the winter here helping Sybil settle in and begin her reign."

Mérian's horrified gaze swung from the baroness to the slender young queen standing mute and concerned beside her. Garran moved to take Sybil's hand, and she leaned toward him. "It is true, Mérian," said Garran. "We were married four months ago. I'm sorry if we failed to seek your approval," he added, sarcasm dripping from his voice.

"My lord," said Anora, her tone sharp. "That was not worthy of you."

"Forgive me, Mother," Garran said, inclining his head. "I think the excitement of this meeting has put us all a little out of humour. Come, Mérian, you are distraught. Be at peace, you are among friends now."

"Friends, is it?" scoffed Mérian. "Some friends. The last time we met they tried to kill me!"

On your mettle, my lords," said Alan a'Dale, glancing over Bran's shoulder across the yard, where the earl of Cestre had just appeared at the stable door.

"Everyone ready?" asked Bran. Ifor and Brocmael nodded, their brows lowered with the weight of responsibility that had been laid upon them. "When we get into the forest," Bran continued, "find your place and mark it well. If we should become separated, go back to the head of the run and wait for us there. Whatever happens, don't linger in the run waiting for one of Hugh's men to see you."

"We know what to do," said Ifor, speaking up for the first time since entering the Ffreinc stronghold.

"Count on us," added Brocmael, finding his voice at last. "We won't fail."

"Just you and Alan keep the earl busy, my lord," the friar said. "Let Tuck and his young friends here worry about the rest. If any of the earl's men come looking for us, I'll make sure they don't twig to the lads' doings here, never fear."

Bran nodded and drew a deep breath. He arranged his features into the curiously empty-eyed, slightly bored guise of Count Rexindo, then turned to greet the earl with his customary short bow and, *"Pax vobiscum."*

Earl Hugh, waddling like a barnyard sow, came puffing up already red faced and sweating with the exertion of walking across the courtyard. Accompanying him were two of his men: rough fellows in once-fine tunics spattered with wine stains and grease spots, each with a large dagger thrust into his leather belt—nasty brutes by both look and smell. Behind these two trailed three more stout Ffreinc in leather jerkins and short trows with high leather leggings; they wore soft leather caps on their heads and leather gauntlets on their hands with which they grasped the leashes of three hunting hounds. The dogs were grey, long-legged beasts with narrow heads and chests and powerful haunches; each looked fully capable of bringing down a stag or boar all on its own strength.

"Pax! Pax!" said Hugh as Bran stepped to meet him. "Good day for a chase, eh?"

"Indeed," replied Bran, speaking directly through Alan now. "I am keen to see if the trails of England can match those of Spain."

"Ho!" cried the earl in joyous derision. "My hunting runs are second to none—better even than Angevin, which are renowned the world over."

Count Rexindo sniffed, unimpressed when the earl's boast was relayed to him. He turned his attention to the dogs, walking to the animals and wading in amongst them, his hands outstretched to let them get his scent. It did not hurt that he had rubbed his palms and fingers with the meat he had filched from the supper platter the previous night. The hounds nuzzled his hands with ravenous enthusiasm, licking his fingers and jostling one another to get a taste. Bran smiled and stroked their sleek heads and silken muzzles, letting the animals mark and befriend him.

"Very unusual, these dogs," he said through Alan. "What breed are they?"

"Ah, yes," said Hugh, rubbing his plump palms together. "These are my boys—a breed of my own devising," he declared proudly. "There are none like them in all England. Not even King William has hounds as fine as these."

This required a small conference, whereupon the count replied through his translator. "No doubt your king must spare a thought for more important matters," allowed Count Rexindo with a lazy smile. "But never fear, my lord earl. If your dogs are even half as good as you say, I will not hold your boast against you."

The earl flinched at the slight. "You will not be disappointed, Count," replied Hugh. He called for the horses to be brought out— large, well-muscled beasts, heavy through the chest and haunches. Hugh's own mount was a veritable mountain of horseflesh, with a powerful neck and thick, solid legs. With the help of a specially made mounting stool and the ready arms of his two noblemen, Fat Hugh hefted himself into the saddle. But when the earl saw Bishop Balthus likewise struggling to mount, he called out in Ffreinc, "You there! Priest." Tuck paused and regarded him with benign curiosity. "This hunt is not for you. You stay here."

Although Tuck understood well enough what was said, he appealed to Alan, giving himself time to think and alerting Bran to the problem. Once it was explained to him, Bran reacted quickly.

"My lord Balthus rides today, or I do not," he informed the earl through Alan; he tossed aside the reins and made as if preparing to dismount.

Alan softened this blunt declaration by adding, "Pray allow me to explain, my lord."

The earl, frowning mightily now, gave his permission with an irritated flick of his hand.

"You see," Alan continued, "it seems Count Rexindo's father required Bishop Balthus to make a sacred vow never to allow the count out of his sight during his sojourn in England."

"Eh?" wondered the earl at this odd revelation.

"Truly, my lord," confessed Alan. He leaned forward in the saddle and confided, "I think my lord the duke believes his son a little too . . . ah, *spirited* for his own good. He is the duke's only heir, you understand. It is the bishop's head if anything ill should befall the count."

Earl Hugh's glower lightened somewhat as he considered the implications of what he had just been told. "Let him come, then," said the earl, changing his mind. "So long as he can keep his saddle— the same as goes for anyone who rides with me."

Alan explained this to Count Rexindo, who picked up the reins once more. *"Gracias, señor,"* he said.

The dog handlers departed from the castle first, and after a few rounds of the saddle cup, the riders followed. Hugh and Count Rexindo led the way, followed by the earl's two knights; the two young Spanish lords, Ramiero and Galindo, followed them, and Bishop Balthus fell into line behind the others, thinking that if he was last from the start no one would mark him dawdling along behind. "Wish us God's speed, Alan," he said as he kicked his mount to life.

Tuck

"Godspeed you, my lord," replied Alan, raising his hand in farewell, "and send you his own good luck."

Out through the castle's rear gate they rode. A fair number of the earl's vassals were at work in his fields, and from his vantage point at the rear of the procession, Tuck could not help noticing the looks they got from the folk they passed: some glared and others spat; one or two thumbed the nose or made other rude gestures behind the backs of the earl and his men. It was sobering to see the naked hostility flickering in those pinched faces, and Tuck, mindful of his bishop's robes, smiled and raised his hand, blessing those few who seemed to expect it.

Once beyond the castle fields, the hunting party entered a rough countryside of small holdings and grazing lands, hedged about by dense woodland through which wide trails had been clear cut—Earl Hugh's vaunted hunting runs. Wide enough to let a horse run at full gallop without getting slapped by branches either side, they pursued a lazy curving pattern into the close-grown wood; a few hundred paces inside the entrance the dense foliage closed in, cutting off all sight and sound of the wider world. This, Tuck considered, would serve their purpose right fair—*if* Ifor and Brocmael could keep their wits about them in the tangle of bramble thickets and scrub wood brush that cloaked the edges of the run.

The party rode deeper into the wood, and Tuck listened to the soft plod of the horses' hooves on the damp turf and breathed the warm air deep. As the sun rose and the greenwood warmed, he began to sweat in his heavy robes. He allowed himself to drop a little farther behind the others, and noticed that the two young Welshmen had likewise fallen behind the leaders.

The search has begun, thought Tuck.

Soon the others were some distance ahead. Tuck picked up a little speed and drew up even with the Welshmen. "Be about your business, lads," he said as he passed by them. "I'll go ahead and keep watch and give a shout if Hugh or his men come back this way."

Ifor and Brocmael stopped then, and Tuck rode on, still taking his time, keeping his eye on Bran and Earl Hugh and the others now fading into the dappled shadow of the trail far ahead. When he had put enough distance between himself and the two behind him, the friar reined his mount to a stop and waited, listening. He heard only the light flutter of the breeze lifting the leaves of the upper branches and the tiny tick and click of beetles in the long grass.

He had almost decided that Hugh and the others had forgotten about them when he heard the sound of returning hoofbeats. In a moment, he saw two horses emerge from the shadowed pathway ahead. The earl had sent his knights back to see what had happened to the stragglers.

Glancing quickly behind him, Tuck searched for a sign of his two young comrades, but saw nothing. "Hurry, lads," he muttered between his teeth. "The wolf's pups are nosing about."

Then, as the two Ffreinc knights neared, Tuck squirmed ungracefully from the saddle and, stooping to the right foreleg of his mount, lifted the animal's leg and began examining the hoof. There was nothing wrong with it, of course, but he made as if the beast might have picked up a stone or a thorn. As the two hailed him in French, he let them see him digging at the underside of the hoof with his fingers. One of the knights directed a question at him as much as to say, "What goes here?"

"*Mon cheval est* . . ." Tuck began. He pretended not to know the word for *lame*, or *limping* either, so just shrugged and indicated the hoof. The two exchanged a word, and then the second knight dismounted and crossed to where he stood. He bent and raised the hoof to examine it. Tuck stole a quick glance behind; the two tardy Welshmen were nowhere in sight. Sending up a prayer for them to hurry, he cleared his throat and laid his finger to the hoof in the huntsman's hand, pointing to a place where he had been digging with his finger. *"Une pierre,"* he said. That the animal had picked up a pebble was perhaps the most likely explanation, and the knight seemed happy with that.

"Boiteux?" he asked.

Tuck shrugged and smiled his incomprehension. The knight released the hoof and took hold of the bridle, and walked the animal in a circle around him, studying the leg all the while. Finally, satisfied that whatever had been wrong was no longer troubling the beast, he handed the reins back to Tuck, saying, *"On y va!"*

Tuck took his time gathering his bishop's skirts and, with the help of the knight to boost him, fought his way back onto the high horse. Taking up the reins once more, he heard the sound of hoofbeats thudding on the trail behind. He turned in the saddle to see Ifor and Brocmael trotting towards them. Tuck hailed them and, satisfied now that the stragglers were all together once more, the Ffreinc knights led them up the game run to rejoin the others.

They soon came to a small clearing where Count Rexindo and Earl Hugh were waiting. At that moment, the hounds gave voice. *"La chasse commence!"* cried the earl and, lashing his horse, galloped away, followed by his knights.

Bran wheeled his mount but lingered a moment to ask, "Success?"

"Just as we planned, my lord," replied Ifor.

Brocmael made a furtive gesture, indicating the empty lance holder attached to his saddle, and said, "Never fear; we were not seen."

"Well done," said Bran. "Now we hunt, and pray we sight the game before our beefy host. Nothing would please me more than to steal the prize from under Hugh's long Ffreinc nose."

Three days of hunting from earliest daylight to evening dusk, and each day Bran, having taken a great interest in the earl's hounds, greeted the dogs with morsels of food he had saved from the previous night's supper board—gobbets of meat he kept in a little bag. Tuck watched the process with fascination and admiring approval as Earl Hugh swallowed the bait in a manner not at all unlike his hounds: and all because Count Rexindo let it be known that he wanted to buy three or four of the animals to take back to Spain as a gift for his father, the duke. The ever-greedy earl welcomed the sale, of course, fixing the price at a princely thirty marks— a price that made Tuck's eyes water. He could never have brought himself to buy three smelly hounds when he might have built an entire church—altar to steeple and everything in between—and had money left over.

Having favoured the hounds, they mounted their horses and all rode out to spend the day working the runs—to be followed by a night's drinking and roister in the hall. By the fourth day, Earl Hugh's nightly feasting began to tell on them all—everyone except Bran. Somehow Bran seemed to bear up under the strain of these all-night revels, awaking the next morning none the worse for his excesses. Indeed, Tuck began to think him blessed with the fortitude of Samson himself until he noticed the trick. Friar Tuck—himself an enthusiastic consumer of the earl's good wine and fortifying meat—happened to discover Bran's secret the second night. Bran quaffed as readily as the next man; however, the instant their host's attention wandered elsewhere, quick as a blink Bran's cup dipped below the board and the contents were dashed onto the soiled rushes under their feet. Thereafter, he drank from an empty vessel until it was filled again, and the process was repeated.

From then on, Tuck did the same himself even though it pained him to throw away good drink.

Wolf Hugh himself was ragged and mean of a morning, sore-headed, stinking of stale wine and urine, his eyes red and his nose running as he shuffled from his chambers bellowing for food and drink to drive the demons from head and belly. Still he seemed to possess unusual powers of recovery, and by the time the sun had breached the castle walls, the earl was ready to ride to his hounds once more, steady as a stone and keen for the chase. On the third day, Tuck freely complained that the nightly debauch was too much for him, and begged Bran to let him observe the hunt from the rails of his bed; but Bran insisted that they must go on as they had started. Ifor and Brocmael had youth on their side, and tolerated the revelry, but were increasingly reticent participants. Alan a'Dale fared less well and was laid low of a morning.

On the fourth day, the earl decided to rest the horses and

hounds. He had business to attend to with some of his nobles, leaving his guests free to take their ease and amuse themselves as they would. Bran let it be known that he wanted to go into the town and attend the market, and so they did. A hundred paces beyond sight of the castle gate, he gathered his crew around him and said, "You are doing very well, lads. I beg but a little more patience and we are done. We will not abide here much longer."

"How much longer?" asked Alan a'Dale.

"Next time we ride."

"That might be tomorrow," Brocmael pointed out.

Bran nodded. "Then we best make certain everything is ready today."

The two young men glanced at one another. "Do you think the earl will tumble?" Ifor wondered.

"Why not?" replied Bran. "He suspects nothing. If all goes well, we should be far away from here before he learns what has happened . . ." Regarding the solemn expressions on the faces of his two young comrades, he gave them his slightly twisted smile. ". . . if he ever learns—and I strongly suspect he never will."

Bran resumed his stroll into the town with Alan at his side, leaving Tuck and the two young lords to reckon what had just been said. "Don't you worry, lads," Tuck said, trying to bank their courage a little higher. "By tomorrow night we'll be well on our way back to Wales with our prize, and beyond the claws and teeth of Wolf d'Avranches."

A short while later they entered a fair-sized market in full cry; merchants shouting for custom, animals bawling, dogs barking. Bran paused and surveyed the comely chaos for a moment. "Good," he said, "there are enough people about that we should not draw undue attention to ourselves. You all know what to do?"

Brocmael and Ifor nodded grimly. Bran opened his purse and fished out a few pennies. "This should be enough," he told them. "We are not clothing him for his coronation, mind."

"We know what to do," said Ifor.

"Then off you go. Return here when you are finished and wait for us."

When they had gone, Bran, Tuck, and Alan commenced their own particular quest. "Have you given any thought to my idea?" asked Bran as they began to stroll among the stalls and booths of the busy market.

"That I have," Tuck replied.

"And?"

"Oh, I think it should work—although I am no dog-handler. It seems a simple enough matter, does it not? We will require a little oil and perhaps an herb or two to mix with it—something strong, but not too offensive. No doubt if Angharad were here she would know better."

"But she is not here, so we look to you now," Bran said. "What do you suggest?"

"Essence of angelica for the oil," Tuck answered after a moment's consideration. "It is light, yet easily stains a cloth. Get it on your skin and it lingers long, even after you wash."

"Excellent! Just the thing," said Bran. He gazed around at the seething crowd of people and animals. "What do you say, Alan? Will we find what we need here?"

"I expect so, my lord. I know of a 'pothecary who comes to market most days."

"And the herbs?" he asked. "What are we looking for?"

"There are several—any one of which will suffice," Tuck mused aloud. "Lavender is strong, but not unpleasant. It is distinctive and not to be mistaken for anything else. There is also thyme, marjoram, or sage. Any of those, I think. Or all of them, come to that."

Bran commended his cleric happily. "Splendid! One day Alan here will laud your native Saxon cunning from one end of this island to the other."

"Lord help us, I don't want to be lauded," Tuck told him. "I'd as soon settle for a month of peace and quiet in my own snug oratory with nary a king or earl in sight." He paused, considering. "I think about that, do I not?" He caught Bran's expression and said, "I do! Sometimes."

Bran shook his head. "Ah, Tuck, my man, you were born for greater things."

"So you say. The world and his wife says different, methinks."

The three waded into the busy square and made short work of purchasing the items required. Alan prevailed upon the apothecary to mix the lavender and angelica oil for them, and add in the herbs. This made a fairly sticky concoction with a strong odour which seemed right for the purpose. They also bought a stout hemp bag with a good leather cord to close it, and then wound their way back to meet their two young companions and see how they had fared.

"We bought these," said Brocmael, offering up the bundle of goods they had purchased. "Not new, mind, but good quality." Still looking doubtful, he added, "I would wear them."

"It cost but a penny," Ifor explained. "So we bought a cloak as well." He shook out a hooded cloak and held it up. It was heavy wool of a tight weave, dyed green. It had once been a handsome thing, made perhaps for a nobleman. It was slightly faded now and patched in several places, but well-mended and clean. "No doubt he'd choose a better one," Ifor admitted, looking to Bran for approval, "but needs must, and this is better for hiding."

"He will be glad of it," Bran assured him. "You've done well— both of you. So now"—he looked around with the air of a man about to depart for territories unknown—"I think we are ready at last."

With that, the party began making their way back to the castle. The day had turned fair and bright; the breeze coming inland from the sea was warm and lightly scented with the salt-and-seaweed smell of the bay. They walked along in silence as thoughts turned to the danger of what lay ahead. All at once, Bran stopped and said, "We should not go on this way."

"Which way should we go?" Alan said. "This is the shortest way back to the castle."

"I mean," Bran explained, "it will not do to rouse the wolf in his den."

Tuck puzzled over this a moment, and said, "Dunce that I am, your meaning eludes me, I fear."

"If we return to the caer like this—all long-faced and fretful— it might put the earl on edge. Tonight of all nights we need the wolf to sleep soundly while we work."

"I agree, of course," Tuck replied. "So, pray, what is in your mind?"

"A drink with my friends," Bran said. "Come, Alan, I daresay you know an inn or public house where we can sit together over a jar or two."

"Right you are there, m'lord. I'm the man fer ye!" he declared, lapsing once more into that curious beggar cant he adopted from time to time. "Fret ye not whit nor tiddle, there's ale aplenty in Caer Cestre. Jist pick up yer feet an' follow Alan."

He turned and led the little group back down the street towards the centre of the town. It is a commonplace among settlements of a

1102

certain size that the better alehouses will be found fronting the square so as to attract and serve the buyers and sellers on market days. And although the Normans ruled the town of late, it was still Saxon at heart, which meant, if nothing else, that there would be ale and pies.

Alan pointed out two acceptable alehouses, and they decided on the one that had a few little tables and stools set up outside in the sun. There were barrels stacked up to one side of the doorway, forming a low wall to separate the tables from the bustle of the square. They sat down and soon had jars of sweet dark ale in their fists and a plate of pies to share amongst them.

"I would not insult you by repeating your instructions yet again," Bran said, setting his jar aside. "You all know what to do and need no reminding how important it is." He looked each in the eye as he spoke, one after the other as if to see if there might be a weakening of will to be glimpsed there. "But if any of you have any questions about what is to come, ask them now. It will be the last time we are together until we cross the river."

Bran, mindful of the trust he was placing on such young and untried shoulders, wanted to give the two Welshmen a last opportunity to ease their minds of any burdens they might be carrying. But each returned his gaze with studied determination, and it was clear the group was of one accord and each one ready to play his part to the last. Nor did anyone have any questions . . . save only their guide and interpreter.

"There is something I've been thinking these last few days, m'lord," Alan said after a slight hesitation, "and maybe now is a good time to ask."

"As good a time as any," agreed Bran. "What is in your mind, Alan?"

"It is this," he said, lowering his eyes to the table as if suddenly embarrassed to speak, "when you leave this place, will you take me with you?"

Bran was silent, watching the man across the table from him. He broke off a bit of crust from a pie and popped it into his mouth. "You want to come with us?" Bran said, keeping his voice light.

"That I do," Alan said. "I know I'm not a fighting man, and of no great account by any books—"

"Who would say a thing like that?" teased Bran.

"I know what I know," insisted Alan seriously. "But I can read and write, and I know good French and English, some Welsh, and a little Latin. I can make myself useful—as I think I've been useful to you till now. I may not be all—"

"If that is what you want," said Bran, breaking into Alan's carefully prepared speech. "You've served us well, Alan, and we could not have come this far without you. If we succeed, we will have you to thank." Bran reached out his hand. "Yes, we'll take you with us when we leave."

Alan stared at Bran's offered hand for a moment, then seized it in his own and shook it vigorously. "You will not be sorry, m'lord. I am your man."

So, the five sat for a while in peace, enjoying the ale and the warmth of the day, talking of this and that—but not another word of what was to come. When they rose a little later to resume their walk back to Castle d'Avranches, it was with lighter hearts than when they had sat down.

They slipped back into the castle and went to their separate quarters to prepare for the next day's activities. That night at supper, Bran baited and set the snare to catch Wolf Hugh.

"Ah, there you are!" cried Earl Hugh as his Spanish guests trooped into the hall. With him at the table were several of his courtiers, six or seven of the women he kept, and, new to the proceedings, five Ffreinc noblemen the others had not seen before— large looming, well-fleshed Normans of dour demeanour. Judging from the cut and weave of their short red woollen cloaks, white linen tunics and fine leather boots, curled hair and clean-shaven faces, they were more than likely fresh off the boat from France. Their smiles were tight—almost grimaces—and their eyes kept roaming around the hall as if they could not quite credit their surroundings. Indeed, they gave every appearance of men who had awakened from a pleasant dream to find themselves not in paradise, but in perdition.

"Here's trouble," whispered Bran through his smile. "Not one Norman to fleece, but five more as well. We may have to hold off for tonight."

"No doubt you know best," Tuck said softly; and even as he

spoke, an idea sprang full-bloomed into his round Saxon head. "Yet, here may be a godsend staring us dead in the eye."

"What do you see?" Bran said, still smiling at the Ffreinc, who were watching from their places at the board. He motioned Alan and the others to continue on, saying, "Keep your wits about you, every-one—especially you, Alan. Remember, this is why we came." Turning once more to Tuck, he said, "Speak it out, and be quick. What is it?"

"It just came to me that this is like John the Baptiser in Herod's pit."

Bran's mouth turned down in an expression of exasperated incomprehension. "We don't have time for a sermon just now, Friar. If you have something to say—"

"King Gruffydd is John," Tuck whispered. "And Earl Hugh is Herod."

1106

"And who am I, then?"

"It is obvious, is it not?"

"Not to me," Bran muttered. He gestured to the earl as if to beg a moment's grace so that he might confer a little longer.

"Lord bless you." Tuck sighed. "Do you never pay attention when the Holy Writ is read out? Still, I'd have thought some smat-tering of the tale would have stuck by you."

"Tuck! Tell me quick or shut up," Bran rasped in a strained whis-per. "We're being watched."

"You're Solomé, of course."

"Refresh my memory."

"The dancing girl!"

Bran gave him a frustrated glare and turned away once more. "Just you be on your guard."

The two approached the board where the earl and his noble

visitors were waiting. Alan, standing ready, smiled broadly for the Normans and made an elaborate bow. "My lords, I give you greetings in the name of Count Rexindo of Spain"—he paused so that Bran might make his own gesture of greeting to the assembled lords— "and with him, Lord Galindo and Lord Ramiero"—he paused again as the two young Welshmen bowed—"and Father Balthus, Bishop of Pamplona." Tuck stepped forward and, thinking it appropriate, made the sign of the cross over the table.

"Welcome, friends!" bellowed Earl Hugh, already deeply into his cups. "Sit! Sit and drink with us. Tonight, we are celebrating my good fortune! My lords here"—he gestured vaguely at the five newcomers— "bring word from Normandie, that my brother has died and his estates have passed to me. I am to be a baron. Baron d'Avranches— think of that, eh!"

"My sympathies for the loss of your brother," replied the count.

"He was a rascal and won't be missed or mourned," sniffed the earl. "But he leaves me the family estates, for which I am grateful."

"A fine excuse for a drink, then," remarked Count Rexindo through his able interpreter. "I can think of none better than sudden and unexpected wealth." Bran sent up a silent prayer that none of the earl's new guests could speak Spanish and took his place on the nearest bench; the rest of his company filled in around him. Two of the women—one of whom had been openly preening for the count's attention ever since he stepped across the threshold—brought a jar and some cups. She placed these before Bran, and then bent near to fill them—bending lower and nearer than strictly necessary. The count smiled at her obvious attentions, and gave her a wink for her effort. Such blatant flirtation was shameless as it was bold. But then, Tuck reflected, shame was certainly an oddity in Earl Hugh d'Avranches's court, and quite possibly unknown. Nevertheless, as Bishop Balthus, Tuck felt he should give the brazen woman a stiff frown to show his clerical displeasure; he did so and marked that it did nothing to chasten her. Nor did it prevent her from insinuating herself between him and the handsome count. *Oh well*, thought Tuck as he slid aside to make room for her, *with a toothsome prize in sight folk are blind to all they should beware of—and that has been true since Adam first tasted apple juice.*

The jars went round and round, filling cups and bowls and goblets, and then filling them again. Earl Hugh, in a high and happy mood, called a feast to be laid for this impromptu celebration of his windfall of good fortune. His musicians were summoned, and as the kitchen servants began laying a meal of roast venison on the haunch, loaves of bread, rounds of cheese, and bowls of boiled greens, a gang of rowdy minstrels entered the hall and commenced perpetrating the most awful screech and clatter, pushing an already boisterous gathering into a barely restrained chaos. Tuck viewed the convivial tumult as a very godsend, for it offered a mighty distraction to lull suspicious minds. He glanced around the board at his nearest companions: Alan seemed to be watching the roister in an agony of want as jar after jar passed him by. Yet, Lord bless him, he resisted the temptation to down as many as might be poured, and contented himself with coddling his one small cup; Ifor and Brocmael, true to their duty, resisted the temptation to indulge and passed the jars along without adding anything to their cups.

Bran, as Count Rexindo, on the other hand became more expansive and jolly as the evening drew on. He not only filled his own cup liberally, but was seen to fill others' as well—including those of the earl and the hovering women. Engaging the visiting Norman lords in loud conversation about hunting and fighting and the like—with the aid of Alan's ready tongue—he drew them out of their stony shells and coaxed a laugh a time or two. Therefore, no one was the least surprised when he rose from his seat and hoisted his cup high and announced, again through Alan, "I drink to our esteemed and honoured host! Who is with me?"

Of course, everyone stood with him then—as who would not?—and raised their cups, shouting, *"Bravo!"*

The Spanish count tipped down a great draught of wine, wiped his mouth, and said, speaking loudly and with some little passion, "My friends and I have enjoyed our sojourn here in your realm, my lord earl. Your hospitality is as expansive as your girth—"

The earl looked puzzled as this was spoken, and Alan quickly corrected the count's meaning, saying, "—generosity . . . as expansive as your generosity, my lord. Please excuse my poor translation. He means your hospitality is as great as your generosity."

"It is nothing," replied Earl Hugh grandly. "Nothing at all!"

"I must beg your pardon, my good earl," replied Count Rexindo a little blearily, "but it is *not* nothing to me. In Spain, where all the virtues are accorded great regard, none sits higher in our esteem than the welcome given to kin and countrymen, and the strangers in our midst." His words came across a little slurred through the wine, though Alan cleaned them up. "As one who knows something of this, I can say with all confidence that your hospitality is worthy of its great renown." He lifted his cup once more. "I drink to you, most worthy and esti . . . estimable lord."

"To Earl Hugh!" came the chorused acclaim.

All drank, and everyone sat down again and made to resume the meal, but Count Rexindo was not finished yet. "Alas, the time has come for us to leave. Tomorrow's hunt will be my last, but it will be memorable . . ." He paused to allow these words to penetrate the haze of drink and food befogging his listeners' heads. "Indeed, all the more if our exalted earl will allow me to suggest a certain refinement to tomorrow's ride."

"Of course! Of course!" cried the earl, his spirits lofty, goodwill overflowing like the wine sloshing over the rim of his cup. "Anything you desire," he said with an airy wave of his hand. "Anything at all." He smiled, his ruddy face beaming with pride at the way he'd been feted and flattered by the young count in the presence of his visiting noblemen.

"How very gracious of you, my lord. In truth, I expected nothing less from one whose largesse is legendary," Count Rexindo replied, beaming happily.

"Come, man!" bellowed the earl, thumping the table with his hand. "What is it that you want? Name it and it is done."

Count Rexindo, all smiles and benevolence, gave a little bow and said, "In my country, when a lord wishes to make a special hunt in honour of his guests he releases a prisoner into the wild. I can assure you that it is sport second to none."

Ah, there it is, thought Tuck. *Our Bran has remembered his Bible story at last.*

It took a moment for the earl and the others to work out what had just been suggested. "Hunt a *man?*" said the earl, his smile growing stiff.

"Yes, my lord," agreed the count, still standing, still commanding the proceedings. "A criminal or some other prisoner—someone of no account. It makes for a very good chase."

"But . . ." began the earl, glancing around the table quickly. He saw his other guests looking to him expectantly. Tuck saw the hesitation and, instantly, the distress that followed, and knew the earl was well and truly caught in Bran's trap. "Surely, that is unworthy of your attention," Hugh replied lamely. "Why not choose something else?"

"I see I have overreached myself," the count said, sitting down at last. "I understand if you have no appetite for such rich sport . . ."

"No, no," Earl Hugh said quickly, seeing the frowns appear on the faces of his gathered noblemen. Having accepted the count's effusive praise for his untethered largesse, how could he now refuse to grant Rexindo's wish? He had no wish to appear tightfisted and mean before his noblemen. So, like a ferret trapped in a snare, squirm though he might he could not get free without gnawing off one of his own legs. "Did I say no? I am intrigued by your suggestion," he offered, "and would be eager to try it myself. It is just that I keep no criminals here. As it is, I have only one captive in my keep . . ."

"And he is too valuable," concluded Count Rexindo, his disappointment barely contained. "I understand."

The earl glanced around at his noblemen as if to explain, saw their frowns growing and his own reputation diminishing in their eyes, and hastily reconsidered. "However, it seems to me that this prisoner would be well worthy of our sport—a king in his own country who has enjoyed my hospitality far too long already."

"*Splendido!*" cried the count. Through Alan, he continued, "It will give me a chance to try the hounds I am buying."

Again, a slight hint of a grimace crossed the earl's face. He did not like the idea of using valuable dogs for such dangerous sport—especially, considered Tuck, dogs that had not yet been purchased. But, rising to the bait, the earl shrugged off his misgivings. "Why not?" he roared, stirring the feast to life once more. "Why not, I say! Here! Let us drink to the count, and to tomorrow's sport!"

Thus, the trap was set and sprung, and the prey neatly captured. Tuck waited until the festivity slowly resumed, and when the music and drink were once again in full spate, he rose. Bowing to their host, who had recovered his good cheer, he approached the earl's chair and, with Alan's help, declared, "This game you propose sits ill with me, I do confess, my lord."

"Does it?" he replied lazily. "Does it indeed? How so, pray?"

"The hunting of men is an abomination before the throne of God." Before the earl could reply, he added, "True, it is a custom long honoured in Spain and elsewhere, but one that the church does not endorse."

This rocked the old wolf back a step or two. He frowned and swirled the wine in his cup. "If I told you that this rogue of a prisoner has earned his death ten times over, would that make it sit more comfortably with you?"

"Perhaps," Tuck allowed. "Though I would still wish to give the wretch the benefit of absolution. By your leave, Earl, I will hear his confession and shrive him now. Then he will be ready to face his ordeal with a clear mind and clean soul."

Seeing that Bishop Balthus was determined, and he equally anxious to maintain his top-lofty dignity in the eyes of his guests, Earl Hugh agreed. "Then do so," he said, as if it had been his own idea all along. He put his nose in his cup once more. "Do so by all means, if it pleases you. One of my men will take you down to him."

Tuck thanked him, begged his dinner companions to excuse his absence, and then departed. In the company of the earl's seneschal, who was standing at the door, the friar made his way down and down into the low-vaulted under-castle, to the hostage pit, to see for the first time the man they had come to free. Leaving the hall and its uproar behind, they passed along a dark, narrow corridor to an even darker, more narrow passage through the castle inner wall to a round chamber below what must have been the guardhouse. *"Attendez ici, s'il vous plaît,"* said the seneschal, who disappeared up the steps to the room above, returning a few moments later with a dishevelled man who had very obviously been drug from his bed. Yawning, the guard applied a key to an iron grate that covered a hole in the floor, unlocked it, and pulled back the grate. He took up a torch from a basket on the floor, lit it from the candle in the seneschal's hand, and beckoned Bishop Balthus to follow. A short flight of spiral steps led them to another passage, at the end of which stood another iron grate which formed the door of a cell. Upon reaching the door, the guard thrust his torch closer, and in the fitful light of it Tuck saw the prisoner slumped against the wall with his head down, legs splayed before him, hands limp at his sides, palms upward. With his thick and matted tangle of hair and beard, he looked more like a bear dressed up in filthy rags than a man.

Once again, the guard plied the key, and after a few moments huffing and puffing, the lock gave and the door swung open, squealing on its rusted hinges like a tortured rat. The prisoner started at the sound, then looked around slowly, hardly raising his head. But he made no other move or sound.

Stepping past the gaoler, Tuck pushed the door open farther and, relieving the porter of his torch, entered the cell. It was a small, square room of unfinished stone with a wooden stool, a three-legged table, and a pile of rancid rushes in one corner for a bed. Although it stank of the slop bucket standing open beside the door, and vermin

1113

crawled in the mildewed rushes, the room was dry enough. Two bars of solid iron covered a square window near the top of one wall, and an iron ring was set into the opposite wall. To this ring was attached a heavy chain which was, in turn, clamped to the prisoner's leg.

"I will shrive him now," Tuck said to the guard.

The fellow settled himself to wait, leaning against the corridor wall. He picked his teeth and waited for the bishop to begin.

"You are welcome to stay, of course," said Tuck, speaking as the bishop. "Kneel down. I will shrive you too."

Understanding came slowly to the guard, but when it did he opened his mouth to protest.

"Come!" insisted the smiling bishop. "We all need shriving from time to time. Kneel down," he directed. "Or leave us in peace."

The gaoler regarded the prisoner, shrugged, and departed, taking the key with him. Tuck waited, and when he could no longer hear the man's footsteps on the stairs outside, he knelt down before the prisoner and declared in a loud voice, sure to be overheard, *"Pax vobiscum."*

The prisoner made no reply, nor gave any sign that he had heard.

"Lord Gruffydd, can you hear me? Are you well?" Tuck asked, his voice hushed.

At the sound of these words spoken in his own language by a priest, the king raised his head a little and, in a voice grown creaky from disuse, asked, "Who are you?"

"Friar Aethelfrith," Tuck replied softly. "I am with some others, and we have come to free you."

Gruffydd stared at him as if he could not make sense of what he had been told. "Free me?"

"Yes."

Tuck

The captive king pondered this a moment, then asked, "How many are with you?"

"Three," Tuck said.

"It cannot be done," Gruffydd replied. His head sank down again. "Not with three hundred, much less three."

"Take heart," Tuck told him. "Do as I say and you will soon gain your freedom. Rouse yourself, and pay me heed now. I must tell you what to do, and we do not have much time."

1115

Count Rexindo and his entourage assembled in the yard to await the appearance of the earl and his men. The stable-hands and idlers in the yard—many who had been in the hall the night before—watched them with an interest they had not shown in several days. Word of the day's unusual sport had spread throughout the castle, and those who could had come to observe the spectacle for themselves. Under the gaze of the earl's court, Bran gathered his company at a mounting block near the stables and traced out the steps of his plan one last time. All listened intently, keenly aware of the grave importance of what lay before them. When he finished, Bran asked, "You gave Lord Gruffydd the oil, Tuck?"

"I did," the friar answered, "and Brocmael here has the clothes we bought."

Bran glanced at the young man, who patted a bulge beneath his cloak.

"Alan, you know what to say?" he asked, placing his hand on the fellow's shoulder and searching his face with his eyes.

"That I do, my lord. Come what may, I am ready. Never let it be said Alan a'Dale was ever at a loss for words."

"Well then," Bran said, gazing around the ring of faces. "It's going to be a long and dangerous day, God knows. But with the Good Lord's help we'll come through it none the worse."

"And the hounds?" asked Ifor.

"Leave them to me," answered Bran. There was a noise in the yard as the earl and his company—including the five Ffreinc noblemen they had feasted with the previous night—emerged from the doorway across the yard. He gave Brocmael and Ifor an encouraging slap on the back and sent them on their way. "To the horses, lads. See you keep your wits about you and all will be well."

As the two young Welshmen moved off to fetch their mounts, Bran composed himself as Count Rexindo; then, straightening himself, he turned, smiled, and offered a good-natured salute to Earl Hugh. Out of the side of his mouth, he said, "Pray for all you're worth, good friar. I would have God's aid and comfort on this day."

"Hey now," Tuck replied, "it's potent prayers I'm praying since first light this morning, am I not? Trust in the Lord. Our cause is just and we cannot fail."

The earl and his company came into earshot then, and the count, piping up, said, *"Pax vobiscum, mes amis."* Alan added his greeting and gave the earl a low bow he did not in any way deserve.

"Pax," said Hugh. He rubbed his fat hands and glanced quickly around the yard, looking for his hounds and handlers. The lately arrived Ffreinc noblemen stood a little apart, stiff-legged and yawning; with faces unshaven and eyes rimmed red, they appeared ill-

rested and queasy in the soft morning light. Clearly, they were not accustomed to the roister and revel such as took place in Castle Cestre of an evening. The earl shouted across the empty yard, his voice echoing off the stone walls. In response to his call, a narrow door opened at the far end of the stable block and the porter entered the yard, pulling a very reluctant prisoner at the end of a chain behind him. "Here! Here!" said Hugh.

A moment later, from a door at the other end of the stables, the hounds and their handlers entered the yard. The hounds, seeing the horses and men assembled and waiting, began yapping with eager anticipation of the trail as hounds will. Count Rexindo, however, took one look at the chained captive and began shaking his head gravely.

"This is very bad," he said, speaking through Alan, who made a sour face as he spoke—so as to emphasize the count's displeasure. "No good at all."

In truth, it *was* very bad. Years of captivity had reduced the Welsh king to little more than a rank sack of hair and bone. His limbs, wasted through disuse, were but spindles, and his skin dull and grey with the pallor of the prison cell. The bright morning light made him squint, and his eyes watered. Although he was so hunched he could hardly hold himself erect, Gruffydd nevertheless attempted to display what scraps of dignity he still possessed. This served only to make him appear all the more pathetic.

"My lord the count says that this prisoner will not serve," Alan informed the earl.

"Why not?" wondered Hugh. "What is wrong with him?"

The Spanish count flicked a dismissive hand at the shambling, ragged baggage before him and conferred with his interpreter, who

1119

said, "This man is in such wretched condition, the count fears it will be poor sport for us. The hunt will be over before it has begun." The count shook his head haughtily. "Please, get another prisoner."

"But this is the only one I have, God love you!" retorted the earl, although he too peered at the captive doubtfully.

Tuck wondered wonder how long it had been since the earl had last laid eyes on the Welsh lord—several months at least, he reckoned, perhaps years.

"I say he will serve," Hugh said stiffly. "In any event, he must, for there is no other."

Alan and Count Rexindo held a short consultation, whereupon Alan turned and said, "Begging your pardon, Lord Earl, but the man is clearly unwell. If he cannot give good chase there is little point in pursuing him. We regret that the hunt must be abandoned. With your permission, we will bid you farewell and prepare instead to take our leave."

The earl frowned mightily. He was that unused to having his will thwarted that he became all the more adamant that the hunt should take place as planned. He argued with such vehemence it soon became clear to the others that the earl and his visiting noblemen had wagered on the outcome of the day's hunt—or, more likely, which among them would draw first blood. Having set such great store by his prowess, he was now loath to see that particular prize elude him.

"The hunt will go ahead," he declared flatly, and motioned for the porter to remove the chains from the prisoner. "This was *your* idea, after all, Count. We will make what sport of it we can."

Count Rexindo accepted the earl's decision with good grace. He seemed to brighten then and said something to Alan, who translated, "Let it be as you say, Lord Earl. As it happens, the count has thought of a way to make a better game of it. We will not use the dogs, and this will give our quarry a fighting chance."

"Not use the dogs?" scoffed the earl. "But, see here, I thought you wished to try them one last time before the purchase."

Alan and the count held a brief discussion, and Alan replied, "It is not done this way in Spain," he explained. "However, the count allows that you know your realm best. Might he suggest using just one hound? If you agree, the count would like to use one of the dogs he will buy. Moreover, he is prepared to wager that he will make the kill today."

"How much will he wager?" wondered Hugh, his pig eyes brightening at the thought.

"Whatever you like," answered Alan. "It makes no difference to the count."

"One hundred marks," answered the earl quickly.

Alan relayed this to Rexindo, who nodded appreciatively.

"Done!" shouted the earl. Turning to Bishop Balthus, he said, "You! Priest! Mark this. You are a witness to the wager—one hundred marks silver to the one who makes the kill."

Tuck gave him a nod of acceptance, wondering where on God's green earth Bran imagined he would find such a princely sum *if*—heaven forbid it!—he should lose the wager.

Meanwhile, Bran, ignoring the stare of the captive king who stood shivering but a few paces away, instead approached the hounds and walked in amongst them, holding out his hands, as he was wont to do, allowing the dogs to lick his fingers and palms. He chose one from among those he had marked to buy—a big, sleek, shaggy grey creature—and rubbed the animal's muzzle affectionately. Reaching into the pouch at his belt, he brought out a morsel he'd filched from last night's meal and fed it to the hound, rubbing the dog's nose and muzzle all the while. "This one," he said through Alan. "Let us take this one with us and leave the others."

The earl, happy with the choice—all the more so since it meant he would not risk his other hounds developing a taste for this unusual game—agreed readily. Count Rexindo then gestured to his two young attendants and directed them to take charge of the prisoner. *"Relâchez le captif,"* Alan said to the gaoler, who began fumbling at his belt for the key to the shackles.

The earl frowned again as the chains fell away, and it appeared he might have second thoughts about disposing of such a valuable prisoner in this way. The hound was given to sniff the captive's clothing, and as the two young nobles began marching the prisoner away, he protested, "Here now! What goes?"

Alan explained. "The count has ordered his men to take the wretch to the head of the hunting run and release him. They are to ride back here and tell us as soon as it is done, and then the chase will begin." He paused, regarding the Ffreinc noblemen, then added, "With this many hunters there will surely be no sport unless the prey is given a fair start."

"Go then," directed Earl Hugh, "and hurry back all the sooner." Spying one of the servants just then creeping across the yard, he shouted, "Tremar! Bring us a saddle cup!" The man seized up like a thief caught with his hand in the satchel, then spun about and ran for the hall entrance. "Two of them!" roared Hugh as the man disappeared. To his noblemen, he added, "Hunting is such thirsty business."

When Count Rexindo finished with the hounds, he turned and walked back to where Bishop Balthus stood, and the cleric saw the count slip his fingers back into the pouch at his belt, replacing the rag that had been liberally doused with herb oil, and with which he had smeared his palm—the same that had stroked the dog's nose and muzzle.

"Do you think it will work?" Tuck whispered as the grooms brought out the horses. "Or are we mad?"

"We can but pray. Still, if Gruffydd has followed your instruction," he said, "we have a chance at least—*if* he can endure the hunt." He motioned Alan to him and said, "You had best come with us today; we may need you. Tell the earl that Count Rexindo requires the aid of his servant and to bring a horse for you. Can you ride?"

"I can keep a saddle, my lord," he answered.

"Good man."

As Alan arranged for himself to accompany the hunt, a servant appeared with two saddle cups overflowing, and these were passed hand to hand around the ring of gathered hunters. The Ffreinc noblemen revived somewhat with the application of a little wine, and were soon showing themselves as keen as the earl to begin the day's amusement.

"Watch them," muttered Bran as he passed the cup to Tuck and Alan once more. "We have the measure of Hugh, but as for these— we don't know them and cannot tell how they will behave once we're on the trail. They may be trouble."

"I will keep my eye on them, never fear," Tuck told him.

The grooms brought the horses then, and to pass the time the hunters examined the tack and weapons. It had been decided that each would have two spears and a knife: ample weapons to bring down a defenceless prey. By the time the count's two young attendants returned from their errand, the earl was in a fever to begin the pursuit. Despite any lingering misgivings about losing a valuable captive, the idea of hunting a man had begun to work a spell in him, and like the hounds he cherished so much, waiting chafed him raw. At the earl's cry, the company took to their saddles and clattered from the yard. Earl Hugh sang out for Count Rexindo to ride with him—which, of course, Bran was only too happy to do—and they were off.

At first, Ifor and Brocmael and Tuck pretended to be as eager for the pursuit as those around them. They kept pace, staying only a little behind the earl, who was leading the chase; the Ffreinc noblemen thundered along behind—so close that Tuck could have sworn he could hear the bloodlust drumming in their veins.

They reached the head of the game run at the gallop and entered the long, leafy avenue in full flight. Rather than wait for the hound and handler to catch up, Earl Hugh proceeded headlong down the run with Count Rexindo right beside. After a few hundred yards or so, the count swerved to the right as if to begin searching that side of the run. Two of the Ffreinc noblemen went with him, and the rest followed the earl. However, no one turned up a trail, so the party slowed, eventually coming to a halt. There was nothing for it but to return to the head of the run and await the hound, which was not long in coming.

Nor was the animal slow in raising the scent of the fugitive. Only a few hundred paces into the run, the great grey beast gave out with a loud baying yelp and leapt ahead, straining at the leash—and the party was away once more. This time, they were led directly to the tree where Ifor and Brocmael had hidden Brocmael's spear a few days earlier, the hound bawling and barking all the way. Upon arrival, the hunters discovered a heap of filthy rags—the prisoner's ratty clothes, now cast aside.

The dog handler picked up the heap of rags and showed it to the earl, whose eyes narrowed. "He is smart, this one," he said with grudging appreciation. "But it will take more than that to throw one of my dogs off the scent." To the handler, he said, "Give him to mark."

The handler shoved the bundle against the dog's muzzle to renew the scent, and the hound began circling the tree to raise the trail. Once, and again, and then three more times—but each time the beast stopped in the place where the clothes had lain, confusing himself the more and frustrating his handler.

"We must raise another scent, my lord," reported the handler at last. "This trail is tainted."

"Tainted!" growled Hugh. "The man shed his clothes is all. Give the hound his head and he will yet raise the trail."

The handler loosed the hound from the leash and urged it to search a wider area around the tree. This time the dutiful hound came to stand before Count Rexindo, who gazed placidly down from his saddle as the dog bayed at him. *"Lontano!"* said the count, waving the dog away.

The handler pulled the animal off, but time and again, the fuddled dog ran between the heap of clothing on the ground and Count Rexindo on his horse. Finally, the handler picked up some of the rags and gave them a sniff himself. Then, approaching the earl, he handed up the rags. "There is some mischief here, Sire," he said. "As you will see."

The earl gave the scraps a sniff and straightened in the saddle. "What?" He sniffed again. "What is that?"

"Lavender, methinks," replied the handler. "Tainted, as I said."

The earl looked around suspiciously. "How in the devil's name . . . ?"

Count Rexindo, impatient and keen to be off, spoke up, and Alan offered, "The count says that clearly the dog is useless. Our prey cannot be far away. He suggests we spread out and raise the trail ourselves."

"Yes, yes," replied Earl Hugh. "You heard him, eh?" he said to the Ffreinc noblemen. "Go to it—and give a shout when you find the trail."

So all scattered, each a separate way. The count led the search farther down the run, and several of the Ffreinc followed that way. Bishop Balthus led lords Galindo and Ramiero to the opposite side of the run and began searching there—all of them knowing full well that Gruffydd would not be found.

CHAPTER 20

Caer Rhodl

Mérian's fingernails dug deep grooves in her palm, and she fought to control the rage she felt roiling inside her. She did not expect the ladies Neufmarché to understand, much less accept the least part of what she had to tell them. They would refuse to listen, call her liar, heap scorn upon her. So be it.

Her mother and brother, however, could be counted on to support her. Once she had explained what had happened the day she was abducted—as well as all that had happened since—she knew they would rally to her aid without question. She drew a calming breath and organized her thoughts, deciding how she would relate the events of the past two years in the greenwood. Then, raising her head, she squared her shoulders and put her hand to the latch. She pushed open the door to the hall and stepped inside. They were all assembled to hear her: Lady Agnes beside her daughter, Queen Sybil, and in the next seat, her brother, Garran; beside him sat her mother, the dowager Queen Anora. The two Ffreinc women sat erect, grim-faced, clearly unhappy; they had heard the accusations Mérian had laid at their feet. Her brother, the king, appeared no happier; drawn and somewhat haggard, he was torn between his own family and that of his new bride. Only her mother looked at all sympathetic, offering her a sad smile, and saying, "Do come along, Mérian. We have been waiting for you."

"Pray forgive me," she said, moving farther into the room. She saw there was no chair for herself. Very well, she would stand; it was better this way. Taking her place before them, she folded her hands and glanced at each in turn. "I see you have been discussing the problem of Mérian already."

"You're not a problem to be solved, my dear," her mother replied. "But we thought it wise to talk a little among ourselves before seeing you again. You will appreciate how awkward—"

"Some of the things you have said," said Lady Agnes. "These *allégations*—"

"If it please you, my lady," interrupted Garran, "we will yet come to that. First," he declared, turning to face his sister, "I want you to know that these are grave charges you have made, and we are taking them very seriously."

"Naturally," replied Mérian, feeling more and more like a criminal with each passing moment. She rankled against the feeling. "Be assured, Brother, I would not have declared them if they were not true."

"We do not doubt you, Mérian," her mother put in quickly. "But you must see how difficult this has become—"

"Difficult?" Mérian snapped, her voice instantly sharp. "Mother, you have no idea. Living in the greenwood with the dispossessed who have been driven from their homes and lands, whose hands have been cut off or eyes gouged out for petty offences and imaginary crimes, is difficult. Living in a hovel made of sticks and mud and covered with animal skins in deep forest where the sun cannot penetrate and stifling every stray sound for fear of discovery is difficult. Creeping place to place, careful to stay out of sight lest the Ffreinc soldiers see you is difficult. Hiding day on day from a sheriff who slaughters any unfortunate who happens to cross his path—*that* is difficult. Grubbing in the dirt for roots and berries to feed—"

"Enough, Mérian!" snapped her brother, his tone matching hers. "We know you've suffered, but you are home now and safe. There is no one in this room who wishes you harm. Mind your tongue and we will all fare the better for it."

"Your brother is right, *ma chère*," said Agnes Neufmarché, controlling her tone. Her Welsh was fair, if simple; that she was able to speak it at all Mérian considered a revelation. "We are your family now. We seek nothing but your good."

"How kind," Mérian retorted. "And was it for *my good* that your husband the baron pursued me and tried to kill me?"

"Of course, you have endured the ordeal terrible," Agnes granted loftily. "Yet, knowing my husband as I do, I cannot . . . *accepter?* . . . accept this as the truth."

Mérian stiffened. She had been expecting this. "You would call me liar?"

"*Pas de tout!*" said the baroness. "I suggest only that perhaps in your fear you mistook the baron's, ah . . . *action* as the *assaut* . . ."

She glanced to her daughter, who supplied the proper word. "As an attack," said Sybil.

"Is that what you think?" challenged Mérian. "You were there that day, Sybil. You saw what happened. Is that what you think? Bran was forced to flee for his life. He took me with him, yes—at first I thought he meant to abduct me for ransom, but it was to save me. He saw the danger I was in before I did, and he acted. When the baron discovered our escape he sent men to kill us both."

"Very well!" said Garran irritably. "Granting what you say is true, what can be done about it now?" He stared at his sister, his lips bent in a frown of deep dissatisfaction. "It's been two years, Mérian. Things have changed. What do you want me to do?"

There it was: the question she had been anticipating, her sole reason for coming. "I want," she replied, taking time to choose her words carefully, "I want you to join with us. I want you to raise a war band and come help us recover Elfael."

"Us?" wondered Garran. It was not a response Mérian had anticipated. "Have you lived so long among the outlaws that you no longer know where your true loyalties lie?"

"*My* loyalties?" She blinked at him in confusion. "I don't understand."

"What your brother is saying," offered Anora, "is that the affairs of Elfael are nothing to do with us. You are safe now. You are home. What is past is past."

"But the fate of Elfael *is* my worry, Mother—as it is for all Cymry who would live free in their own country." She turned to her brother, the king, and his nervous young queen beside him. "*That* is where my loyalties lie, Brother—and where yours should lie too. Unless that bit of French fluff beside you has addled your mind, you would know this."

Her brother bristled. "Careful, Mérian dear, you will go too far."

"I am sorry," she said, changing her tone from haughty self-righteousness to appeal. She smoothed the front of her gown beneath her hands and began again. "I truly do not mean to offend. But if I cannot speak my mind here in this room among those who know me best, then perhaps I do not belong here anymore. In any event, the urgency of my errand leaves me little choice." She licked her lips. "Baron de Braose has been banished from his lands and holdings in England and Wales, as you may have heard by now. Elfael is in the hands of Abbot Hugo de Rainault and the king's sheriff, Richard de Glanville. Without the baron to back them up, they are weak. This is the best chance we've had in many years to drive the invaders from our land—but we must strike soon. The sheriff has brought more men, and we must act quickly if we are to keep our advantage. If you were to—"

"We know all this," her brother interrupted. "Elfael belongs to the king now. I should not have to remind you that to go against Red William is treason. To raise rebellion against him will get you drawn and quartered at the White Tower and your pretty head fixed to a pike above the gates."

"De Braose *stole* the land from Bran and his people. King William promised justice, but betrayed Bran and kept the land for himself."

"He is the king," countered Garran. "It is his right to do with it what pleases him."

"Oh? Truly?" said Mérian, growing angry again. "Is that what you think? You would sing a different song if the king's greedy eye was on *your* throne, brother mine. Or has Baron Neufmarché already bought your throne for the price of a wife?"

"Mérian!" warned her mother. "That is beneath you."

"*Non! S'il vous plaît,*" put in the baroness. "Do not tax her so. She has had the . . . *traumatisme*, yes? She is not herself. In time she will see that the *famille* Neufmarché means only good for the people of this realm."

"Thank you, Lady Agnes," said Garran. "As always your judgement is most welcome." To Mérian, he said, "Bran's affairs are nothing to do with us. He has become an outlaw and a rebel and will pay with his life for his crimes. Of that I have no doubt."

"Do not speak to me of crimes," Mérian said, her face flushing hot. "Abbot Hugo and the sheriff rule with blood and terror. They hang the innocent and subject the Cymry living beneath their rule to all manner of torment and starvation. They are the real criminals, and chief among them is King William himself." She tried one last desperate appeal. "Listen to me, please. Bran and his people are preparing for war. They mean to take the fight to the invaders, and there is every chance they can succeed, but they need help." Glancing at Queen Sybil, whose face appeared unnaturally white and pinched with worry, she said, "Join us. Help us overthrow this wicked throne and restore the rightful king to Elfael."

"No," said her brother. "We will speak no more about it."

"Then there is nothing more to say." Mérian turned on her heel and prepared to walk from the hall and out through the gates. Stunned by her brother's outright rejection, the only thing she could think was returning to Cél Craidd, and that if she hurried, she might make it back before the night had passed.

"Where do you think to go, Mérian?" King Garran called after her.

"To the greenwood," she said. "I am needed there. It is plain to me now that I have no place here."

"You will not leave the caer," Garran informed her.

She spun around and stormed back to confront her brother. "Who are you to tell me where I will or will not go?"

"Father is dead," Garran replied. "Until you are wed and have a husband, I am your guardian. Moreover I am king and you are a member of my household. You will obey me in this."

"My guardian! When did you ever lift a finger to help me, dear brother?" demanded Mérian. Her defiance gave her a terrible aspect, but Garran stood his ground. "I am a lady in my own right, and I will not submit to your ridiculous rule."

"You will never see those outlaws again," Garran told her with icy calm. "Never. You will remain here for your own protection."

The audacity of the command stole the warm breath from her body. "How dare you!"

"It is for your own good, Mérian," said her mother, trying to soften the blow. "You will see."

"I see very clearly already, Mother," Mérian retorted. "I see I was wrong to come here. I see that you have all made your bed with the enemy. Where once there was a family, I see only strangers. Mark me, you will yet curse this day."

"You are much mistaken, Sister," Garran said.

"Oh, indeed," agreed Mérian. She began backing away. "Thinking my own flesh and blood would understand and want to help—that was my mistake." She turned once more toward the door. "But do not worry, dear hearts. It is not a mistake I will make again."

She pulled open the heavy door, stepped through, and slammed it shut behind her with a resounding crack. She marched out into the yard, her heart roiling with anger at the unfeeling hardness of her own nearest kin. How could they fail to see the need and refuse her plea for help? Their intimate contact with the Ffreinc had corrupted them, poisoned their judgement and tainted their reason. That was the only explanation. Mérian shuddered. She, too, had come very close to succumbing to that same corruption once. If Bran had not rescued her

1133

she would be like her brother now—perhaps married off to some odious Norman nobleman or other. She would rather be dead.

Mérian strode to the stable, brought out her horse, and led it to the gate—only to find it closed. "Open it, please," she said to the gateman, a young man with a bad limp.

"Forgive me, my lady—" he began.

"Spare me!" she snapped. "Open the gate at once. I am leaving."

"Lord help me, I cannot."

"Why?" she demanded. "Why not?"

"My lord King Garran said I was to keep it locked and let no one in or out until he told me otherwise."

"Oh, he did?" she said. "Well, I am sure he did not mean me. Open the gate at once."

"Sorry, my lady. He mentioned you especially—said it was more than my life was worth to let you pass." The young man crossed his arms across his chest and stood his ground.

Mérian stepped around him and moved to the gate. At that moment there came a call from across the yard, and three men-at-arms issued from the hall and ran to apprehend her. "Now, now, Lady Mérian, come away from there," said the first to reach her. "You are to follow us—king's orders."

"And if I should refuse?"

The warrior made no reply, but simply wrapped his arms around her waist and hoisted her off her feet. She shrieked her outrage and kicked at his legs. The remaining two warriors joined the first, and all three laid hold; Mérian was hauled back to the hall in a spitting rage and thrown into her room.

No sooner had the door been shut than she began hammering on it with her fists, shouting to be let out.

Tuck

"Scream all you like; it will avail you nothing," came the voice of her brother through the planking of the door.

"Let me out!" she cried.

"When you are prepared to listen to reason," he replied blandly, "and pledge to rejoin your true family."

"To the devil with you!"

Her only reply was the sound of the heavy iron bar dropping into place outside, and her brother's retreating footsteps.

CHAPTER *21*

When a painstaking search of the hunting run and woodland surrounding the tree where the captive's cast-off clothing had been found failed to turn up any trace of their human prey, the hunters moved down the run and deeper into the forest. Owing greatly to Count Rexindo's many wrongheaded interventions, the company was subtly led farther and farther away from any path Gruffydd might have taken, thus spending the entire day without discovering their quarry or raising even so much as a whiff of his trail. As twilight began to glaze the trails with shadow, the frustrated company was forced to conclude that the captive king had miraculously eluded their pursuit. It appeared that Bran's audacious plan had worked; all that remained was to suffer the wrath of a very angry earl and then they, too, would be free.

The Spanish visitors endured an extremely acrimonious ride back to the fortress, the earl fretting and fuming all the way, cursing everything that came to mind—most especially, Count Rexindo's ineptitude and the incompetence of Spaniards in general, as well as his own misguided complicity in a fool-bait scheme which had not only cost him a very valuable prisoner, but also had returned a powerful enemy to the battlefield. "Courage, men," counselled Bran as they paused before the doors of the hall. "It is soon over." To Ifor and Brocmael, he said, "Are the horses ready?"

The young men nodded.

"Good. Whatever happens, be ready to depart on my signal. We may have to bolt."

They entered a hall much subdued from the previous night; where before the walls had reverberated with song and laughter, this night's supper was taken in sullen silence and bitter resentment. Count Rexindo and his retinue braved the blast of ill-will with stoic silence as they listened to Hugh d'Avranches alternately berating one and all for their gross failure and bemoaning the loss of his captive. As the drink took hold of him, the livid, simmering anger gave way to morose distemper, with the earl declaring loudly for all to hear that he wished he had never laid eyes on Count Rexindo and his miserable company. This, then, was the signal for the visitors to make their farewells and remove themselves from the castle.

The count, having been seen to bear the earl's complaints and abuse with the good grace of one who could not grasp the more subtle nuances of insult in a foreign tongue, rose from his seat and with the aid of his able interpreter, said, "No one is more sorry than I that we have failed today. Still, it is in the nature of things that the hunter is sometimes outwitted by his prey and must return to his hearth empty-handed." He gave a slight shrug. "I, myself, blame no one. It happens. We live to hunt another day. But a man would be a fool to remain where his friendship is no longer welcome or valued.

Therefore, I thank you for your hospitality, my lord, and bid you farewell."

Oh, well done, thought Tuck, rising at Bran's gesture. As bishop, he gave the earl a small, benedictory flourish and, turning, followed the count from the hall.

"What about the hounds?" cried Hugh after the departing count. Too late he remembered the money he hoped to make on the sale of his expensive animals.

Alan, taking the count's elbow, restrained him and whispered into his ear. Rexindo shook his head, gave a final gesture of farewell, and stepped through the door. "I am sorry, my lord," Alan said, standing with his hand on the latch, "but the count says that he could not possibly consider buying such ill-trained and ungovernable beasts as the one he witnessed today. He has withdrawn his offer. You may keep your dogs."

With that, Alan disappeared, following Bishop Balthus, Lord Galindo, and Lord Ramiero across the threshold and into the corridor beyond. As soon as the heavy door shut behind them, they fairly flew to the stable and relieved the grooms of the care of their horses. Rexindo, true to his noble Spanish character, paid the grooms a few silver pennies each—as much to buy their aid as for their unwitting diligence—and with kind words and praise, bade them farewell. The chief groomsman, pleased and charmed by the count's noble treatment, led the company from the yard and opened the gate for them himself.

As they mounted their horses, Bran reached down a hand to Alan. "If you still want to come with me," he said. Without hesitation, Alan a'Dale grabbed the offered hand, and Bran pulled him up to sit behind him.

1139

At last, having successfully skinned the wolf in his den, the short ride to Caer Cestre became a jubilant race. In the fading evening light, the company came clattering into a nearly deserted town square, where they dismounted and quickly made their way to the docks to meet King Gruffydd. When a cursory search failed to find him, they split up and, each taking a separate street, began combing the town. This, too, failed. "Perhaps he is waiting at one of the inns," suggested Alan.

Bran commended the idea and said, "You and Tuck go look there. Ifor, Brocmael, and I will wait for you at the wharf in case he should come there."

The two hurried off and were soon approaching the first of the river town's three inns—a place called the Crown and Keys. Despite the somewhat lofty ambitions of its name, it was a low place, smuggy with smoke from a faulty chimney and poorly lit. A cushion of damp reeds carpeted the uneven floor upon which rested one long table down the centre of the room with benches on either side. Four men sat at the table, and the brewmistress stood nearby to fetch the necessaries for her patrons. One glance into the room told them they must pursue their search elsewhere.

The next inn—The Star—was the place where they'd sat outside in the sun and enjoyed a jar on a day that now seemed years ago. Inside, the single large room was full of travellers and townsfolk; pipers had taken up residence beside the great hearth, and the skirl of pipes lent a festive atmosphere to the room. It took them longer here to look among the tables and investigate all the corners. Alan asked the alewife if anyone answering Gruffydd's description had been seen in or about the place that day. "Nay—no one like that. It's been a quiet day all told," she said, shouting over the pipers. "Not being a market day, ye ken?"

They had another look around the room and then moved on to the last of the town's inns—a mean place only a rung or two up from a cattle stall; with a few small tables and a few nooks with benches, it had little to recommend it but its ready supply of ale, which many of the boat trade seemed to prefer, judging from the number of seafarers in the place. Again, they quickly gleaned that not only was King Gruffydd not in the room, but no one answering his description had been seen that day or any other. Tuck thanked the owner, and he and Alan hurried back to rejoin Bran and the others at the dock.

"What now?" asked Ifor when Alan finished his report. "We've looked everywhere."

"I told him where to go," said Tuck. "I made certain he understood."

"Maybe he's hiding in a barn or byre somewhere," suggested Alan.

"When you took him out to the hunting run," said Bran, "what did you tell him?"

"To come to the dock in town and wait for us there," said Ifor. "He said he would."

"Then, I think we must assume he is not in the town at all," suggested Bran. "Otherwise he'd be here."

Tuck considered this. "He never made it, you mean?"

"Either that," confirmed Bran, "or he took matters into his own hands and fled elsewhere."

"You think he didn't trust us to get him away safely?" said Brocmael.

Ifor countered this, saying, "He knew we were kinsmen, and he was keen as the blade in my belt to be leaving Caer Cestre at last. He said he'd reward us right well for helping him."

"Did he say anything else?" asked Tuck.

"He kept asking about Lord Bran—about why he would risk so much to free him."

"What did you tell him?" Bran asked.

"We told him he would have to speak to you, my lord. Your reasons were your own."

"It does not seem as if he feared to trust us," remarked Tuck. "Something ill must have befallen him."

"What now?" asked Alan again.

"It's back to foul Hugh's hunting run," Bran decided. "We must try to raise Gruffydd's trail and track him down—this time in earnest. We'll get what rest we can tonight and ride as soon as it is light enough to see the trail beneath our feet." He hesitated, then added, "In any event, finding Gruffydd might be the least of our worries . . ."

"Why?" said Tuck. "What else?"

"The ship is gone."

Only then did it occur to Tuck to look among the vessels at anchor along the dock and in the central stream of the river. It was true; the Iberian boat that had brought them was no longer to be seen. "I thought he said he'd wait for us."

"He said his business would take him no more than a week," Bran corrected. "Maybe he finished sooner than he expected."

"Or, it's taken longer," Alan pointed out.

The two young noblemen shared a worried glance, and Tuck sighed, "Bless me, when it rains, it pours."

"Never mind," said Bran. "So long as we stay out of sight of the earl, we'll make good our escape. The Welsh border is only a day and a half away. We can always ride if need be."

They found a dry place on the dock among piles of casks and rope, and settled down for a restless night. It was warm enough, but as night drew on, clouds drifted in, bringing rain with the approach of dawn. Tuck awoke when his face grew wet and then could not get back to sleep, so contented himself with saying the Psalms until the others rose and they departed once more, leaving Alan a'Dale behind in case the Iberian ship should return.

Skirting the earl's stronghold, they made for the hunting run. By the time they reached the place where Gruffydd had shed his prison rags for those supplied by his rescuers, the sky was light enough and they could begin making out marks on the trail. Ifor and Brocmael dismounted and, on hands and knees, began searching the soft earth in the undergrowth around the tree where the clothes had been hidden. Ifor found a mark which he thought could have been made by the butt of a spear being used as a staff, and before Bran and Tuck could see it for themselves, Brocmael, working a little farther on, called out that he had found a half-print of a shoe.

1143

Bran and Tuck dismounted and hurried to where the dark-haired young nobleman was waiting. "It is a footprint, no doubt," agreed Tuck when he saw it. "But is it our man? Or one of the Ffreinc handlers? That is the question, is it not?"

"Follow it," instructed Bran. "See if you can find out where it leads."

The trail was slight and difficult to follow, which made the going slow. Meanwhile, the sky flamed to sunrise in the east. By the time they had determined that the tracks they were finding did indeed belong to King Gruffydd, the sun was up and casting shadows across the many-stranded pathways of the wood.

"This is not good," observed Bran, gazing upwards at the cloud-swept heavens.

"My lord?" said Tuck, following his glance. "What do you see?"

"He's going the wrong way," Bran pointed out. "We're being led deeper into the wood and away from the town."

So they were. But there was nothing for it. They had to follow the trail wherever it led, and eventually arrived at a sizeable clearing on the south-facing slope of a hill, in the centre of which was a small house made of mud and wattles; brush and beech saplings and small elm trees were growing up around the hovel, and the grass was long. Clearly, the steading had been abandoned some few years ago—no doubt when the earl became its nearest neighbour. The surrounding wood was actively reclaiming the clearing and had long since begun to encroach on what once had been fine, well-drained fields. The grass still bore the faint trace of a path: someone had walked through the place not long ago.

At the edge of the clearing, the searchers paused to observe the house. "Do you think he's down there, my lord?" asked Ifor.

"He is," affirmed Bran, "or was. Let's find out." He lifted the reins and proceeded into the old field. The house was decrepit—two of the four walls were in slow, dissolving collapse—but the upright posts still stood strong, and stout crossbeams supported what was left of the roof. "Go and see," he told Ifor. "The rest of us will wait here so that we don't make more of a trail than is here already."

The young man hurried off, and the others watched his progress across the field until he disappeared around the far side of the house. They waited, and Ifor reappeared a moment later, signalling them to come on ahead. By the time the others reached the house, they found a very groggy King Gruffydd sitting on a stump outside the ruined doorway and Ifor sprawled on the ground clutching his head.

Tuck

"I nearly did for your man, here," said Gruffydd, looking up as Bran, swiftly dismounting, came to stand over him. "He woke me up and I thought he was a Ffreinc come to take me back."

"You hit him?" said Tuck, kneeling beside the injured Ifor.

"Aye," admitted the king, "I did, and for that I am heartily sorry."

Tuck jostled the young man's shoulder. "Are you well, Ifor?"

Ifor groaned. "Well enough," he grunted between clenched teeth. "I think he broke my skull."

"I said I was sorry, lad," offered Gruffydd somewhat testily. "Have you brought anything to eat?"

"What are you doing here?" Bran asked. "We waited for you in the town. Why didn't you come?"

The grizzled king frowned as he watched Tuck gently probing the young man's head. "I got lost."

Bran stared at the man, unable to think of anything to say.

"It's eight years since I was beyond the walls of that vile place," Gruffydd explained. "I must have got muddled and turned around. And the air made me tired."

"The air," repeated Bran dully.

"I expect that's so," offered Tuck. "Considering his lordship hasn't been out of that cramped cell in a good long while, his endurance might have suffered in that time. It makes sense."

"I apologize, my lord," said Bran then. "It never occurred to me that your strength would be impaired."

"I'm *not* impaired, curse your lying tongue," growled the king. "I was just a little tired is all." He made to stand and tottered as he came to his feet. He swayed so much Tuck put out a hand to steady him, then thought better of it and pulled it away again. "Have you brought me a horse?"

1145

"We had no time to get you one," Bran replied. "But it isn't far—you can share with one of us."

"I will not ride behind anyone!" the king asserted stiffly.

"You can have my horse, Sire," volunteered Brocmael. "Ifor and I will share. For all it's only back to town."

Bran nodded. "We best be on our way. I want to be as far from here as possible when Wolf Hugh realizes what has been done to him—if he hasn't guessed already."

Dismounting quickly, Brocmael gave over the reins of his horse and helped his king into the saddle; then he vaulted up behind Ifor and the party set off.

The fastest way to the town was along one of the hunting runs towards the castle. As the morning was still fresh, Bran decided the need for a speedy retreat outweighed the concern of being seen, so they made their way to the nearest hunting run and headed back the way they had come. They passed along the slightly undulating green-walled corridor, eyes searching the way ahead, alert to the barest hint of danger.

Even so, danger took them unawares. They had just rounded a blind bend, and as the leaf-bounded tunnel of the run came straight they saw, in the near distance, a hunting party riding towards them. Without a word, the four fugitives urged their mounts into the brake and were soon concealed in the heavier undergrowth amongst the trees. "Do you think they saw us?" asked Ifor, drawing up beside Bran.

"Impossible to say," replied Bran. Dismounting, he darted back toward the run. "Stay here, everyone, and keep the horses quiet."

"Do as he says," instructed Tuck, sliding from the saddle. He followed Bran, and found him crouched in the bracken, peering out from beneath low-hanging yew branches onto the run.

"Any sign of them?" he said, creeping up beside Bran.

"Not yet," whispered Bran, laying a finger to his lips.

In a moment, they heard the light jingling of the Ffreinc horses' tack and the faint thump of hooves on the soft earth as they came. Bran flattened himself to the ground, and Tuck likewise. They waited, holding their breath.

The first of the riders passed—one of the visiting Ffreinc noblemen who had ridden with them the previous day—scouting ahead of the others. At that moment, there was a rustling of brush behind them and King Gruffydd appeared.

"Is it him?" demanded Gruffydd. "Is it Wolf d'Avranches?"

"Shh!" Bran hissed. "Get down."

Just then the main body of hunters passed: four knights and Earl Hugh, riding easily in the early morning. "There he is!" said Gruffydd, starting up again.

"Quiet!" said Bran.

"That vile gut-bucket—I'll have him!" growled Gruffydd, charging out of the brake. Bran made a grab for the king, caught him by the leg and pulled. Gruffydd kicked out, shaking Bran off, and stumbled out onto the run. The riders were but a hundred paces down the run when the Welsh king appeared out on the open track behind them. He gave a shout, and one of the riders turned, saw him, and jerked hard on the reins. *"Ici! Arrêtez!"* he cried, wheeling his horse.

"He's insane!" snarled Bran. Out from the wood he leaped, snagged the king by the neck of his cloak, and yanked him back under the bough of the yew tree.

"Release me!" shouted the king, wrestling in his grasp.

"You'll get us all killed!" growled Bran, dragging him farther into the wood.

"Let them come!" sneered Gruffydd, shrugging off Bran's hands. "I'm not afraid."

"Jesu forgive," said Tuck to himself. Stepping quickly behind the king, he tapped him on the shoulder. Gruffydd turned, and the friar brought the thick end of a stout stick down on the top of his head with a crack. The king staggered back a step, then lurched forward, hands grasping for the priest. Tuck gave him another smart tap, and the king's eyes fluttered back in his head and he fell to his knees.

"Good work, Tuck," said Bran, catching Gruffydd as he toppled to the ground. From the hunting run there came a sound that set their hearts beating all the faster: hounds. The first dog gave voice, followed by two others. "Hurry! Get back to the horses."

Dragging the half-conscious king between them, they fought through the bracken and tangled vines of ivy to where Ifor and Brocmael were waiting with the horses. "Get his clothes off him," directed Bran, pointing to Gruffydd. As Brocmael and Ifor began stripping off the Welsh king's clothing, Bran laid out his plan. "Fly back to town and make for the docks. Find Alan and have him get any ship that's going." Bran began shucking off his boots. "I'll keep them busy while you make good your escape."

The baying of the hounds seemed to fill the forest now, drawing ever nearer.

"What are you going to do?" said Tuck, watching Bran pull off his tunic and trousers.

"Give those to me." He took Gruffydd's tunic and cloak from Ifor. "Get his trousers."

There was shouting from the hunting run; the hunters had found their trail. As the others hefted an unresisting Gruffydd into the saddle, Bran pulled on the Welsh king's trousers and stuffed his feet into his boots.

"I'll stay with you," said Tuck.

"No," said Bran. "Go with them. Take care of Gruffydd. If I don't find you before you reach the town, see you get yourselves on the first ship sailing anywhere. Leave the horses if you have to—just see you get clear of the town with all haste."

"God with you," said Tuck as Bran disappeared into the forest, racing towards the sound of the barking dogs.

"We should stay and help him," Ifor said.

"He can take care of himself," replied the priest, struggling into the saddle. "Believe me, no one knows how to work the greenwood like Rhi Bran."

"I'm staying," Ifor declared, drawing his sword.

"Put that away, lad," Tuck told him. "There's been enough disobedience for one day. We'll do as we're told."

With a grimace of frustration, the young Welshman thrust his blade back into the scabbard and the three took to flight, leading Bran's horse with the wounded king slung sideways across his mount like a bag of grain.

They worked deeper into the wood and heard, briefly, shouts echoing from the direction of the hunting run, and horses thrashing into the close-grown bushes and branches. There was a crash—as if a horse or its rider had fallen into a hedge—and then a cry of alarm, followed by other shouts and the frenzied barking of the hounds sighting their quarry. Then, slowly, the sounds of the chase began to dwindle as the pursuit moved off in another direction.

The riders continued on, eventually working back to the head of the hunting run. By this time Gruffydd was able to sit up in the

1149

saddle, so they lashed their horses to speed and made quick work of the remaining distance, keeping out of sight of the castle until they reached the track leading to Caer Cestre. Alan was there on the wharf, waiting where they'd left him. He waved as Tuck and the others came in sight—a quick, furtive flick of his hand. Tuck then saw why Alan was trying to warn them. His heart sank. For between Alan and the dock stood two of the Ffreinc noblemen they had been hunting with the day before, and there was no ship in sight.

Leaping, ducking, dodging through the thick-grown woodland tangle like a wild bird, Bran flew towards the sound of the baying hounds. In a little while, he reached the edge of the hunting run and burst out onto open ground—not more than a few hundred paces from the hunting party: four men on horseback, lances ready. They were standing at the edge of the run, watching the wood and waiting for the dogs and their handler to flush the quarry into the open so they could ride it down.

It was their usual way of hunting. Only, this time, their quarry was Bran.

Without a moment's hesitation, Bran put his head down and ran for the opposite side of the wide grassy corridor. He had made it but halfway across when there arose a shout behind him. *"Arrêt! Arrêt!"*

He ran even faster and reached the far side of the hunting run and flashed into the undergrowth with the riders right behind. There was more shouting behind him and the sound of ringing steel as the four knights began hacking their way into the wood. Bran found a big elm tree and paused to catch his breath. He waited until he heard the hounds again and then darted off once more, this time working his way back through the woods in the direction of the earl's castle.

The chase was breathless and frantic. The hounds were quick on his scent, and as fast as Bran hurtled through the brake, the dogs were faster still. It was only a matter of time before he would be caught and brought to bay. He ran on, trying his best to put some distance between himself and the hunters. He heard the slavering growls as the beasts closed on him. He was searching for a heavy branch to wield as a club when the first hound finally reached him.

The dog bounded over a fallen limb, and Bran turned meet it. The animal—a great, long-legged rangy grey beast—howled once and leaped for him. Bran, standing still in the path, made no move to flee. Instead, he held out his hands. "Here! Come, old friend. Come to Count Rexindo."

The dog, confused now, hesitated. Then, identifying the man who had fed him and befriended him, it gave a yelp of recognition and ran to Bran, put his paws on his chest, and began licking Bran's face. "Good fella," said Bran. "That's right, we're friends. Here, come with me. Let's run."

Bran started off again with the dog loping easily beside him. They were joined by a second dog and, within another dozen running steps, the third hound came alongside. The four of them, dogs and man, flowed through the forest with the ease and grace of creatures born to the greenwood, quickly outdistancing the handler and the hunters still sitting on their horses in the hunting run.

They came onto a path lying roughly parallel to the hunting run; a few flying steps farther and it began sloping down towards a stream which would, Bran guessed, lead to the river and the river to the town. "This way, boys," called Bran, hurtling down towards the water. They splashed into the stream and continued on at a slower pace. After a time, Bran paused to listen.

He heard nothing—no crack and swish of branches, no shouts of hunters keen on the trail, no sounds of pursuit at all. He had out-stripped the chase, and without the constant howling of the dogs to lead them, the hunters were floundering far, far behind and likely on a different path altogether.

He paused in the stream, then stooped and cupped water to his mouth and swallowed down a few gulps. Then stood, sunlight splash-ing down from a gap in the branches overhead, and drew the moist air deep into his lungs. The sky was clear and blue, the day stretching out fine before him. "Come on, lads," said Bran. "Let's go home."

They resumed their long walk, splashing downstream, sometimes in it, more often on the wide, muddy bank. The dogs did not follow so much as accompany him—now running ahead, now lagging behind as they sniffed the air for scent of errant game. Bran kept up a steady pace, pausing to listen every now and then, but heard noth-ing save the sounds of the forest. Some little time later, the wood-land began to thin and he glimpsed cultivated fields through the trees. He stepped out to find himself at the edge of a settlement— a few low houses, a barn, and a scattering of outbuildings with a small pen for pigs. He watched the place for a moment, but saw no one about, so quickly moved on, working his way towards the track he knew he would find eventually—the path that connected the settle-ment to the town.

Once on the road, he made good time. Reaching Caer Cestre after midday, he hurried down the narrow streets and proceeded directly to the wharf, alert to any threat of discovery. At the lower town, he made for the dockyard and was still a little way off when he saw the mast of a moored ship: a small coast-crawling cog with a single low central mast and broad tiller. Closer, he saw a clump of men standing on the dock, and picked out the plump form of Tuck and, with him, four of Earl Hugh's soldiers. They seemed to be arguing.

He halted, thinking what to do.

There was no sign of the other Welshmen, so Bran resumed his walk down to the dock, picking up his speed as he went until, with a sudden furious rush, he closed on the group of men. He was on them before they knew he was there. Seizing the nearest soldier by the arm, he marched the surprised knight to the edge of the jetty and, with a mighty heave, vaulted him into the river. The body hit with a loud thwack, and the resulting splash showered the dock with water.

Bran dropped lightly down into a small fishing boat moored to the pier below and, seizing an oar from the oarlock, fended off the flailing knight. The soldier's companions stared in slack-jawed astonishment at this audacious attack. One of them dashed to the end of the dock and extended his hand to his comrade. Bran dropped the oar, grabbed the hand, and pulled for all he was worth. The knight gave out a whoop as he toppled over the edge and into the water as well.

The two remaining knights backed away from the edge of the dock and drew their swords. One of them raised the point of his blade to Tuck's throat, while the other waved his weapon impotently at Bran, who remained out of reach in the boat. Both were shouting in French and gesturing for the two Welshmen to surrender. "Tuck!" cried Bran, lofting the other oar. "Catch!"

Up came the oar. The friar snatched it from the air and, gathering his strength behind it, drove the blade into the soldier's chest, propelling him backward and over the edge of the dock to join his two companions in the water. The last knight standing swung towards Tuck, his blade a bright arc in the air.

Tuck was quicker than he knew. Sliding his hands along the shaft of the oar, he deftly spun it up into the man's face. The knight stumbled backwards, retreating step by step. Bran, meanwhile, scrambled back onto the dock. "Now, Tuck!"

Tuck drove forward with the oar, and the knight fell back a step, tripping over Bran's outstretched foot. The knight lurched awkwardly, trying to keep his feet under him. He swung the blade wildly at Tuck, who easily parried the stroke, knocking it wide. Another thrust with the oar sent the soldier sprawling onto his backside, and before he could recover, Bran had grabbed his legs, pulled them up over his head, and pitched the knight heels first off the dock and into the river.

Bran and Tuck paused to look at their handiwork: four soldiers thrashing in the water and crying for help. Owing to the weight of their padded jerkins and mail shirts, they were unable to clamber out of the river; it was all they could do to keep their heads above water. Their cries had begun to draw would-be rescuers to the waterfront.

"Where are Gruffydd and the others?" asked Bran.

"They're hiding across the way," Tuck said, waving vaguely behind him. "I told Alan to keep them out of sight until the ship was ready. It has only just arrived."

Bran glanced around. Two boys stood on deck, laughing at the spectacle played out on the dock. Their shipmates had gone ashore, leaving the youngest crew members to watch the vessel. "Go get them," ordered Bran. "Get everyone aboard the ship and cast off!"

1155

"But the captain and crew are not here," replied Tuck. "They've gone up to the town."

"Just go," Bran urged, picking up the oar. "I'll keep the soldiers busy."

Tuck dashed away, returning as fast as his stubby legs allowed with Alan, Gruffydd, and the two young Welshmen trailing in his wake. They arrived on the dock to find Bran swinging the oar and shouting, keeping the water-logged Ffreinc in the water and the gathering crowd of onlookers at bay. Truth be told, Bran found preventing the rescue far easier than he imagined. Most of the townsfolk seemed to be enjoying the spectacle of the earl's thugs at such an embarrassing disadvantage. Several boys were throwing stones at the knights, who singed the air with curses and obscenities.

"Get aboard!" cried Bran. "Cast off!"

Tuck turned on the others. "You heard him! Get aboard and cast off."

While Ifor and Brocmael untied the mooring ropes, Alan picked up two long poles that were lying on the dock and tossed them onto the deck of the ship. The boat's two young guardians protested, but were powerless to prevent their vessel from being boarded. They stood by helplessly as Tuck and Gruffydd set the plank on the rail and climbed aboard. "Ready!" Tuck called.

"Push away!" shouted Bran, wielding the oar over his sputtering charges.

Using the poles, Alan and Brocmael began easing the cog away from the dock. As the ship floated free, Ifor grabbed the tiller and tried to steer the vessel into deeper water in the centre of the stream. The ship began to move. "Bran!" shouted Tuck. "Now!"

Bran gave a last thrust with the oar and threw it into the water.

Then, with a running jump, he leapt from the dock onto the deck of the ship. He was no sooner aboard than a howling arose from the wharf; he turned to see the three hounds pacing along the edge of the dock and barking.

"Come!" called Bran, slapping the side of the vessel. "Come on, lads! Jump!"

The dogs needed no further encouragement. They put their heads down and ran for the ship, bounded across the widening gap, and fell onto the deck in a tangle of legs and tails. Bran laughed and dived in among them. They licked his hands and face, and he returned their affection, giving them each a chuck around the ears and telling them what good, brave dogs they were.

"You've stolen the earl's hounds," Brocmael said, amazed at Bran's audacity—considering the high price Wolf Hugh set on his prize animals.

"Hounds?" said Ifor. "We've stolen a whole ship entire!"

"The ship will be returned," Bran told them, still patting the nearest dog. "But the hounds we keep—they'll help us to remember our pleasant days hunting with the earl. Anyway, we've left him our horses—a fair enough trade, I reckon."

"Does anyone know how to sail a ship of this size?" wondered Alan.

"Maybe the lads there can help us," Tuck said, regarding the boys—who were thoroughly amazed at what had taken place and were enjoying it in spite of themselves. "Maybe they know how to sail it."

"We don't have to sail it," Bran countered. "We'll let the tideflow carry us downriver as far as the next settlement and try to pick up a pilot there. Until then, Ifor, you and your two young friends will man the tiller and see you keep us in the stream flow and off the bank. Can you do that?"

"I've seen it done," replied the young man.

"Then take us home," said Bran. Ifor called the two young crewmen to him and, with an assortment of signs and gestures, showed them what they were to do. Bran crossed to where Gruffydd was sitting against the side of the ship, knees up and his head resting on his arms.

"Are you well, my lord?" Bran said, squatting down beside him.

"My blasted head hurts," he complained. "Did you have to hit me so hard?"

"Perhaps not," Bran allowed. "But then, you did not give us much choice."

The king offered a grunt of derision and lowered his head once more. "You will feel better soon," Bran told him, rising once more. "And when we cross over into Wales you'll begin to see things in a better light."

Gruffydd made no reply, so Bran left him alone to nurse his aching head. Meanwhile, Tuck and Brocmael had begun searching the hold of the ship to see what it carried by way of provisions. "We have cheese, dried meat, and a little ale."

"We'll pick up more when we stop. Until then, fill the cups, Tuck! I feel a thirst coming on."

⇥ PART FOUR ⇤

"O cowardly dastard!" Will Scadlocke exclaim'd.
    "Thou faint-hearted, sow-mothered reeve!
If ever my master doth deign thee to meet,
    Thou shalt thy full paiment receive!"

Then Rhiban Hud, setting his horn to his mouth,
    A blast he merrily blows;
His yeomen from bushes and treetops appeared,
    A hundred, with trusty longbows.

And Little John came at the head of them all,
    Cloath'd in a rich mantle, green;
And likewise the others were fancif'ly drest,
    A wonderous sight to be seen.

Forth from the greenwoode about they are come,
    With hearts that are firm and e'er stout,
Pledging them all with the sheriff's yeomen
    To give them a full hearty bout.

And Rhiban the Hud has removéd his cloak,
    And the sheriff has uttered an oath,
And William now smites him on top of his pate
    and swift exit is now made by both.

"Little I thought," quod Scadlocke eft-soon,
    "When I first came to this place,
For to have met with dear Little John,
    Or again see my master's fine face."

"It is a grand day, my lord Bran," Llewelyn proclaimed, grinning blearily through a haze of brown ale. "A grand and glorious day. Though it shames me to admit it, I never hoped to see our Gruffydd on his throne again. No, I never did. Yet, here he is—all thanks to you. Here he is."

Two days of riotous celebration had followed the rescuers' triumphant return to Aberffraw with their newly freed captive. King Gruffydd's homecoming was heralded as a miracle on the order of Lazarus walking out of his tomb; and Bran, Tuck, Ifor, Brocmael, and Alan were lauded as champions and made to recount their exploits time and again to rapturous listeners until they grew hoarse for speaking. The revel was entering its third day before Bran and Tuck finally found the opportunity to speak to Gruffydd and Llewelyn in private.

"Here are men after my own heart!" declared Gruffydd, closing the door on the celebration to join them in his chamber. Bathed and shaved, his matted, moth-eaten locks shorn to his scalp, arrayed in a new wool cloak and fine red linen shirt, the king of the Northern Cymry finally resembled something worthy of the name. "You should have seen them, Llewelyn," he bellowed. "They were mighty giants doing battle for me. It's true!" Swaying unsteadily, he draped an arm across Bran's shoulders. "I am forever in your debt, my friend. Hear me, Bran ap Brychan, may God blind me if I should ever forget."

"That would be most uncomfortable for you," allowed Bran with a smile, "but, never fear. I have a way to help you."

"Then speak it out, man, and see how quickly it is accomplished," said Gruffydd. Reeling slightly, he looked around for his cup, saw one in Llewelyn's hand, and took it.

Bran hesitated, uncertain whether to take advantage of the king's ale-induced generosity or wait until Gruffydd was sober once more— which might mean a wait of several more days.

"Speak, man, and if it is in my power to grant, you shall have it before the sun has set on another day," boasted Gruffydd. He drained the cup and wiped the foam from his moustache. "What will you have?"

"Your friendship," said Bran.

"That you have in abundance already," replied Gruffydd grandly. He waved his hand airily.

"What else?" prompted Llewelyn, well aware of Bran's true desire.

Bran looked to Tuck, who urged him with a glance to ask for the help he had come north to seek. "As I have aided the return of your king to his lands and people," replied Bran, speaking slowly and deliberately, "I ask the king's pledge to aid me in the return of my lands and people."

A shadow passed over Gruffydd's square face just then. The smile remained firmly fixed, but his eyes narrowed. "Then receive my pledge," Gruffydd said. "How can I help you?"

"With men and weapons," Bran said. "Raise the tribes of Gwynedd and the north and ride with me. Together we can wrest Elfael from the Ffreinc and drive them from our lands."

Gruffydd frowned. He looked into the empty cup as if it had offended him, then thrust it back at Llewelyn. "If that lay within my power," he said, his voice falling, "you would have it this very night. Alas, I cannot grant such a request."

Bran's face tightened. Staring at the king, he said, "You will not help?"

"I cannot," replied Gruffydd, who seemed to have sobered in the matter of a moment. "You must understand," he continued, half turning away, "I have been absent from my realm eight years! For eight years my people have been without a king—"

"They've had Llewelyn," Bran pointed out.

"True enough," granted Gruffydd, "and I am the first to say he has served faithfully and well. But you and I both know that it is not the same thing at all."

"Then you will not help me," Bran said, his voice tight.

"I wish you had asked anything but that," the king replied. "My first duty is to my people and my realm. I cannot resume my reign by running off again as soon as I am home. Much less can I mark my return by forcing my people into a war that does not concern them. If you were in my place, you would see that."

"My friends and I risked all to save you—"

"And for that you have my friendship and gratitude to my dying breath," Lord Gruffydd replied.

"It is not your gratitude I want," Bran said, his tone taking on an edge. "It is your aid in arms."

"That," said Gruffydd carelessly, "is the one thing you cannot have."

Bran made to step closer. Gruffydd held his ground.

"My lord," said Tuck, insinuating his bulk between Gruffydd and an increasingly angry Bran, "if you knew the precarious hold the Ffreinc possessed, you would see our request in a different light."

"How so?" asked Llewelyn, doing what he could to help.

"The Ffreinc forces are few in number," Tuck said, still holding himself between the increasingly angry lords, "and poorly supplied. We have seen to that, have we not? For though we are few in number, living rough in the greenwood on pitiful fare, with families and little 'uns to keep—even so, we have pressed them hard these last two years and more, and they are bent that near to breaking. All it needs is some stout warriors, a few fresh fighters, a last battle or two—a final push over the edge and the thing is done."

"How long would you need the use of the men?" asked Llewelyn.

1164

"A month perhaps," said Bran quickly. "The Ffreinc do not have enough soldiers to make a lengthy campaign. It would be finished in a month—no more. That is little enough, it seems to me."

"Alas," rued Gruffydd, unmoved, "even that little is too much. I wish I could help."

"My lord, I urge you to reconsider," pleaded Llewelyn. "A month, mind you. Surely, it is not beyond our ability to aid them in this—"

His entreaty was cut short by a curt gesture from his king. "I have spoken." Gruffydd turned and stepped towards the door. "My friends," he said, adopting a stiffly formal air even as he clutched the doorpost to steady himself, "you are most welcome to remain with me as long as you like. I am happy for your company. Nevertheless, we will not speak of this again."

With that, the king returned to the celebration.

"Come, Tuck," said Bran, watching Gruffydd through the open

door as the king moved among his kinsmen and friends, embracing some, sharing the cup with others. "We will not remain here a moment longer than it takes to scrape the dung of this miserable place off our feet."

"My lord," said Llewelyn, deeply embarrassed by his king's behaviour, "do not be overhasty. Stay a little longer—a few days only—and we will yet change his mind. I will summon the lords to council with the king, and he will be persuaded. On my word, you will yet have your just reward."

"If only you were king, Llewelyn," replied Bran darkly. Then, remembering himself, he softened his tone and said, "You have shown me honour and respect, and I thank you for that. Nor do I hold Gruffydd's ingratitude against you. But I see now that I was wrong to come here, wrong to ask, wrong to think the fate of Elfael meant anything to my family in the north."

Llewelyn opened his mouth to protest this last assertion, but a warning glance from Tuck prevented him. Instead, he moved quietly to the door, and there he paused and regarded Bran sadly. "I'm sorry," he said, then stepped back into the hall, leaving Tuck and Bran alone.

"And God with you, too, Cousins," muttered Bran to men who were no longer there. "Bring the horses, Tuck," he said after a moment, "and find Alan. We're leaving."

They left the hall and moved out into the yard. It was after midday, and the clouds were low and dark, threatening rain. Tuck thought to argue for staying at least one day longer to allow Gruffydd the chance to change his mind and so they would not have to ride in the rain, but he knew Bran would not hear it. As the cinch belts were being tightened on the saddles, Ifor and Brocmael came into the stables.

1165

"We were looking for you," said Brocmael. "You're leaving?"

"So soon?" said Ifor.

Both young men appeared so crestfallen that Tuck tried to put a better face on it. "We have finished here, and anyway we are needed back home. But, God willing, we'll come back one day," he told them, then added, patting the fresh mount beside him, "Do thank your father for the gift of these fine horses."

"It is the least we could do," said Ifor, "after all you've done for us."

"What about the troops?" wondered Brocmael.

"Your king does not see fit to raise any," Bran told him.

"That's why you're leaving," said Ifor.

"Aye," confessed Bran. "That is why."

"We'll come with you," Ifor offered. He nudged Brocmael, who agreed. "We can fight."

"Your place is here," said Bran. "Your king will not give you leave to go. He has made it very clear he does not think Elfael worth saving." Reaching out a hand, he gave each of their arms a squeeze by way of farewell. "Nevertheless, you have been brave and loyal companions these past days. You have done yourselves and your families proud. No one could have served me better. But here is where it ends."

The two young warriors exchanged an unhappy glance. "What about Earl Hugh's hounds?" asked Brocmael. "Shall I fetch them for you?"

"No, I want you and Ifor to have them," answered Bran. "Consider them a small gesture of thanks for your help."

"We cannot, my lord," protested Ifor. "They are worth a very fortune."

"It is too much," agreed Brocmael. "They are far too valuable."

"No more valuable than the help you gave me when asked," Bran replied. "They are yours, my friends. Make your fortune with them."

Tuck, Alan, and Bran left Aberffraw as soon as the horses were ready. Bran did not speak the rest of the day, but fumed and fretted, working himself into such a dark and threatening gloom that Tuck began to fear for the havoc unleashed when the gathering storm finally broke. He had seen Bran like this before—once in Londein when they had gone to redeem the lands from the crown at the enormous price of six hundred marks, only to have Cardinal Flambard cheat him by raising the price to two thousand. Tuck and Iwan had pulled him off the scoundrel churchman or in all likelihood none of them would have lived out the day. Angharad knew best how to ease Rhi Bran's murderous moods, but she was in faraway Elfael.

"Alan," Tuck had said, "if you know any songs that would put our Bran in a better mood, I pray you sing one now."

"As it happens," replied Alan a'Dale, "I have been thinking of a song he might enjoy. It isn't finished yet—I need a rhyme for Count Rexindo, d'ye ken?"

"Sing it anyway," Tuck told him.

So Alan sang them on their way.

Four days later, he was still singing, as from time to time Bran's dark and dangerous mood threatened to swallow them all. Alan, it seemed, was full of unexpected talents, and ever ready to cheer his lord along with a quip or a joke or a song. Of the latter, most of his ditties were English drinking songs and ballads more appreciated by Friar Tuck than by Bran, who from time to time slipped back into his moody darkness. The French and Welsh songs had lilting melodies—some glad, some mournful to suit their solemn

1167

humour—but the best songs were those Alan had made up himself: including the new one that extolled the exploits of Count Rexindo and his merry band, who deceived the wicked earl and won the freedom of the captive king of Gwynedd. Tuck found this highly amusing, but Bran was not so sure he wanted his doings voiced about the countryside like so much scattered seed.

Still, the singing and stories told under the clear, open sky worked their wonders, and by the time the travellers came within sight of the towering green wall of the great forest of Coed Cadw, Bran's temper had cooled to the point where Tuck thought he might risk venturing a thought or two of his own regarding their predicament as it now stood. "Perhaps," he suggested, "it might be well to heed Mérian's advice and go see her father."

Bran considered this only as long as it took to purse his lips and shake his head. "God knows that man is no friend of mine. Even if Cadwgan did not hate me when this began, I will not have risen any higher in his esteem by holding his daughter captive."

"At the first, maybe," granted Tuck. "But she stayed on of her own free will. When given the choice, she stayed."

"Even if he was inclined to help," countered Bran, "he is a vassal of Baron Neufmarché. As it runs against his interests, the baron would never allow it. No," said Bran, shaking his head again, this time with resignation, "we will get no help from Lord Cadwgan."

They skirted Saint Martin's, the abbot's town, and entered the sheltering forest just as the sky of lowering clouds sent rain streaming down the wind. It would be a wet night in the greenwood, but the rain did little to dampen the welcome the travellers received at their homecoming. The Grellon gathered to greet them, and Bran roused himself from his grim melancholy to say that he was glad to be home once more. But as he scanned the faces gathered around, the one looked-for face did not appear.

"Where's Mérian?" Bran asked.

An uneasy hush drew across the forest dwellers, and Iwan stepped forward. "Welcome, my lord," he said, his voice booming in the quiet. "It is good to have you back safely. I trust your journey was successful."

"Your trust is misplaced," snapped Bran. "We failed." Still searching among the Grellon, he said, "Mérian . . . where is she, Iwan?"

The big warrior paused, looking thoughtful. "Mérian is not here," he said at last. "She left and went back to Eiwas."

Before Bran could ask more, the champion gestured to someone in the crowd of onlookers, and Noín stepped forward. "Tell him what happened," Iwan instructed.

Noínina made a small bow of greeting to her king and said, "It is true, my lord. Mérian went home." She folded her hands into the apron at her waist. "It was in her mind to go and ask her father to send men to aid us in the fight against the Ffreinc."

"I see," Bran replied coldly. "When did she leave?"

"Two days after you departed for the north."

"Who went with her?"

"My lord," said Noín, a note of anxiety rising in her voice, "she went alone."

"Alone!" Turning on Iwan, he demanded, "You let her go alone?" When the big man made no reply, Bran glanced around at the others. "Did no one think to go with her?"

"We did not know she was going," Iwan explained. "I would have prevented her, of course. But she told no one of her intentions and left before anyone knew she was gone."

"*Someone* knew, by the rood," Bran observed, indicating the worried Noín before him.

"Forgive me, my lord, but she made me promise not to say anything until after she had gone," Noín said, looking down at her feet. "I did try to persuade her otherwise, but she would not hear it."

"I was halfway down the trail for going after her," said Will Scarlet, pushing forward to stand beside his wife. "Would'a gone, too, but by the time we found out, it was too late. Mérian was already home, and if anything was going to happen to her . . ." He paused. "Well, I reckoned it already did."

Bran took this in, his fists clenching and unclenching at his side. "I leave you in charge, Iwan," he snarled. "And this is how my trust is repaid? I am—"

"Peace!" said Angharad, speaking from a few steps behind him. Pushing through the gathered throng of welcomers, the Wise Banfáith planted herself in front of him. "This is not seemly, my lord. Your people have given you good greeting and the same would receive from their king." She fixed him with a commanding stare until Bran remembered himself and, in a somewhat stilted fashion, thanked his champion and others for keeping Cél Craidd in his absence.

Tuck, drawing near, gave Bran a nudge with his elbow and indicated Alan a'Dale standing a short distance apart from the group, ignored and unremarked. So Bran introduced the Grellon to Alan a'Dale and instructed his flock to make the newcomer feel at home among them. Having satisfied courtesy, Bran retreated to his hut, saying he wished to be left in peace to rest after his journey.

"Rest you will have," said Angharad, following him into the hut.

"But not from you, I see."

"Not from me—and *not* until you learn that berating those who have given good service is beneath one who would account himself a worthy king. Angry with Mérian you may be—"

"She disobeyed me—"

"She must have had good reason, think you?"

"We discussed it and I told her not to go," Bran complained, throwing himself into his hide-and-antler chair. "Yet the moment my back is turned, what does she do?"

"Your Lady Mérian is a woman of great determination and resourcefulness; she is not one to be easily dominated by others." Angharad gazed at him, her eyes alight within their wreath of familiar wrinkles. "It is her own mind she has followed—"

"She has disobeyed me," Bran said.

"This it is that tears at you?" replied the banfáith. "Or is it that she might have been right to go?" Before Bran could answer, she said, "It matters not, for now there is nothing to be done about it."

Bran glared at her but knew that pursuing this argument any further would avail him nothing.

"Too late you show the wisdom of silence," Angharad observed. "So now, if you would put away childish things, tell me what happened in the north."

Bran frowned and passed a hand over his face as if trying to wipe away the memory. He gave a brief account of finding the king of Gwynedd a captive to Earl Hugh and riding into Caer Cestre to free him. "The long and short of it," he continued, "is that we failed to persuade King Gruffydd to rally the tribes to our support. We cannot count on them for any men."

The old woman considered this, nodded, but said nothing.

"Not one," said Bran. "We are worse off than when we began," he concluded gloomily.

Into the fraught and fretted silence of the hut there drifted a soft, lilting melody sung by a clear and steady voice—a sound not unfamiliar in Cél Craidd, but this one was different. Angharad went to the door of the hut, opened it, and stepped outside. Bran followed and felt his anger and disappointment begin to melt away in the refrains of the tune. There, surrounded by the forest-dwellers, his head lifted high and with a voice to set the glade shimmering, Alan was singing his song about Rhi Bran and the Wolf of Cestre.

When Bran learned that Sheriff de Glanville had returned to Saint Martin's with a force of fifty soldiers, he said nothing, but took his bow and went alone into the greenwood. Siarles was all for going after him, but Angharad advised against it, saying, "Think yourself a king to bear a king's burden? His own counsel he must keep, if his own mind he would know." And, to be sure, Rhi Bran returned that evening with a yearling buck and a battle plan.

First, he determined to do what he could to even the odds against him. The fine, dry summer had given way to a blessedly mild autumn, and the harvest in the valleys had been good. Most of the crops would be gathered in now against the lean seasons to follow. The granaries and storehouses would be bulging. Bran decided to help his people and, at the same time, hit the Ffreinc where it would hurt the most. He would attack in the dead heart of the darkest night of the month.

The moon had been on the wane for several days, and tonight

there would be a new one; the darkness would be heavy and would aid his design. Early in the morning, Bran sent spies into the town to see what could be learned of the disposition of the sheriff's troops. Noín and Alan had been chosen—much to Will's displeasure. "I have no objection," Scarlet complained, "so long as I go along."

"They know you too well," Bran reminded him. "I don't want to see you end up in that pit again—or worse. One glimpse is all the sheriff would need to put your head on a spike."

"But you don't mind if my Noín's sweet face ends up decorating that bloody spike," he griped.

"Scarlet!" The sound was sharp as a slap. "You go too far." Angharad shuffled forth, wagging a bony finger. "A proper respect for your king would well become you."

Will glared at her, his jaw set.

"Now, William Scatlocke!"

"Forgive me, Sire," offered Will, striving to sound suitably contrite. "If I have spoken above myself, I do most humbly beg your pardon."

"Pardon granted, Will," Bran told him. "A man would have a heart of stone who did not care for his wife. But the raids I have in mind succeed or fail on what we learn. We need to know how things sit in the town before we go rushing down there."

Will nodded and glanced to Noín, who pressed his hand. "I have gone to market before, you know. That's all it is—just two folk going to market."

"You had best leave now," said Bran. "Stay only as long as it takes to find out what we need and then hurry back. We will wait for you at the ford."

"There and back and no one the wiser, m'lord," Alan volunteered. "Alan a'Dale will see to it." To Scarlet, he said, "They've never seen me before, and I can talk the legs off a donkey if I have to. We'll be back safe and sound before you know it."

Bran commended them to their task, and Angharad spoke a brief blessing of protection over them and the two departed. The rest of the Grellon began preparing for the night's activities: weapons and ropes were readied, and five riders were sent to the holdings and farms in the valley to warn the folk about King Raven's plans and to enlist any aid they could find. In the end, there were so many willing volunteers that they chose only the most hale and hearty to help and told them where to go, and when.

Tuck decided that he would best be served by a new staff, so took himself into the wood to find a sturdy branch of ash which he cut to length and then shaped. As he worked, he found great satisfaction in reciting a few of the Psalms that the young Israelite warrior David composed when seeking deliverance from his many enemies.

By the time the sun began its long, slow plunge into the western sea, all was ready. The raiders, eight in all, departed for the ford to meet the spies. Alan and Noín were already waiting at the forest's edge when they arrived. Will Scarlet was the first to see them and ran to where the two sat beside the stream near the ford. "Is all well?" he asked, and received a brushing kiss by way of answer from his wife.

"No one paid us any heed at all," Alan told them. "Why would they? We were just two humble folk attending the market, ye ken?"

"Well and good," said Bran. "So now, what did you discover?"

"It is true the town is full of Ffreinc," began Alan, "but they trust their numbers a little too much, it seems to me." He went on to explain that the soldiers were everywhere to be seen—at the entrance to the town square, before the abbey gate, clustered around the guardhouse tower—but almost to a man they appeared bored and lax. "You can see those fellas idling here and there, dicin' and drinkin' and what-all. They swagger around like little emperors all, and most of them don't carry weapons—maybe a dagger only."

"No doubt they know where to find a ready blade smart enough when pressed to it," observed Iwan.

"Oh, no doubt," agreed Alan readily. "But I'm just saying what I saw."

"What about the sheriff?" asked Will. "Did you see that rat-faced spoiler?"

"I did not," answered Alan. "Neither hide nor hair. Plenty of soldiers though, as I say."

"You found where they keep the supplies?" asked Bran.

"We did, Lord," answered Alan. Looking to Noín, he nodded. "Noín here did that easy as please and be thanked."

"I went to the church when they rang the bell for the midday mass," Noín reported. "There were but a few townsfolk and a merchant or two, so I knelt in the back and waited for the service to finish. Then I followed the monks to the abbey, pretending that I was hungry and in need of food for myself and my poor starving children three."

"You told them that?" said Scarlet, chagrined at the barest suggestion that he was no fit provider for his family.

"It was only pretence," she said lightly. "But I have been pared near enough to the bone to know how it feels. To their credit the priests took pity on me and let me inside the abbey walls. I was made to wait in the yard while they fetched a few provisions."

"And you saw where these were kept?" said Siarles.

"Oh, aye—made sure of it. There is a granary behind the bishop's house. It looks new to me—wattled and thatched like a barn, but smaller."

"They brought you food from these stores?" asked Tuck. "You saw this?"

"Aye, they did—brought me some grain and a rind of salt pork," Noín told him, "and a handful of dried beans. There was plenty more whence that came, believe me."

"There must be," mused Iwan, "if they are about giving away food to needy Cymry."

"At least," suggested Siarles, "they are not over-worried about running out of provisions anytime soon."

"They will be running out sooner than they know," said Bran. "What else?"

The raiding party listened to all that Alan and Noín had to say about the troops and stores. When they finished, Bran praised their good service and sent them on their way back to Cél Craidd, saying, "Tell the others we're going ahead with the raid. If all goes well, we will return before dawn."

So Alan and Noín continued on their way, and the raiding party settled down to wait, watching a pale blue velvet dusk settle over the Vale of Elfael below. The stars winked on one by one, and the raiders sat and talked, their voices a low murmur barely audible above the liquid splash of the nearby stream.

It is so beautiful, thought Tuck, so peaceful. *"Ach, fy enaid,"* he sighed.

"Second thoughts, Friar?" asked Siarles, sliding down beside him.

"Never that, boyo," replied Tuck. "But it does seem a very shame to violate such tranquillity, does it not?"

"Perhaps, but it will be far more tranquil when the Ffreinc are gone, Friar," answered Siarles. "Think of that."

"I pray that it is so." Tuck sighed again. "It is a beautiful valley, though."

They talked a little while, and then Tuck closed his eyes and drifted off to sleep, to be awakened sometime later by Siarles jostling his shoulder. "Time to be about the devil's business, Friar."

Regaining their saddles, the party rode down into the vale, circling around to the north of the town and the abbey fields. They came to the edge of a bean field which lay just beyond the stone walls of the monastery Abbot Hugo had erected. "If I heard it right, the abbot's storehouse is just the other side of that wall," Iwan pointed out. The wall, like the abbey and town behind it, was an indistinct mass, black against the deeper, featureless blackness of a moonless night.

1178

"Owain and Rhoddi," said Bran, "go and rouse the others. Bring them here—and for the love of God and all the angels, tell everyone to keep quiet." The two warriors turned and rode for the forest's edge north of town. As soon as they had gone, Bran said, "Tuck, you will stay with the horses and keep order outside the walls. Tomas and Scarlet—go with Iwan. Siarles, you come with me. Once over the wall, meet at the storehouse." The old sly smile played on his lips as he said, "Time for Rhi Bran y Hud to fly."

The raiders urged their mounts forward across the leafy field, now black beneath the hooves of their horses. A few paces from the wall, they stopped and dismounted. "God with you," whispered Tuck as they hefted first one man and then the next up onto the top of the abbey wall. When the last raider disappeared, the friar turned to look for Rhoddi and Owain, but could see nothing in the darkness.

He waited, gazing wide-eyed into the darkness and listening for any stray sounds from the other side of the wall, but saw nothing and heard only the sound of the horses breathing and, once in a while, chafing the ground with an idle hoof. After a time, there came a whispered hiss from somewhere above his head. "Ssssst!" Once, and then again. "Ssssst!"

"Here!" whispered Tuck. "This way—to your right."

"Get ready," said the voice. It was Siarles kneeling atop the wall. "We'll send over the grain sacks first. Ready?"

"I'm the only one here," Tuck told him.

"Where is everyone?"

"They're here," came the reply as Rhoddi appeared silent as a ghost out of the darkness. To his unseen companions, he said, "Owain, line 'em up behind me. Keep out of the way, and stay alert."

"How many are with you?" Siarles called down softly.

"Ten," answered Owain "We're ready, so heave away."

A moment later another figure joined Siarles on the wall. There was a dry scraping sound followed by a thick thud as the first sack hit the ground at the base of the wall. Three more followed in quick succession. "Get 'em up," whispered Siarles.

Fumbling in the darkness, the Cymry from the surrounding settlements jostled the bulging sacks of grain onto the shoulders of three of their number, who disappeared into the darkness. "Ready," Rhoddi called quietly.

There followed a pause, and then, without warning, a large, weighty object thudded to the ground. "What was that?" wondered Tuck, mostly to himself. Four more objects were sent over the wall in quick succession, followed by numerous smaller bundles dropped over the wall to form a growing heap on the ground.

"Clear it out," whispered Siarles.

"You heard him, men," said Owain. Again, the waiting Cymry leapt forward and fell upon the bundles, sacks, and casks that had been tossed over the wall. The process was repeated two more times, and each time there were fewer Cymry left to carry the supplies away. Finally, Siarles reappeared atop the wall and said, "There's people stirring in the abbey. I'm coming over." Squatting down, he turned, grabbed an edge, and lowered himself lengthwise down the face of the wall.

"The others are clean away," Tuck told him. "I've got the horses ready."

"We best stir ourselves and get this lot loaded, too," Siarles said. "Bring 'em up, and let's have at it."

The two of them began piling the goods onto the carriers attached to the saddles of the horses. One by one, the remaining raiders joined Tuck and Siarles outside the wall; Bran and Iwan were the last, and all made short work of toting the bundles and casks to the waiting horses. The back-and-forth continued until from somewhere beyond the wall a bell sounded and the raiders halted. The bell tolled three times. "It's *Lauds*," said Tuck. "They'll be going to the chapel for prayer."

"That's it, lads," said Bran. "Time to fly." He glanced away towards the east, where a dull glow could be seen above the dark line of treetops. "Look, now! It's beginning to get light, and all this thieving has made me hungry."

"Luckily, there's ale for our troubles," Scarlet said, picking up a cask and shaking it so it sloshed. "And wine, too, if I'm not mistaken."

The last of the goods were packed and tied into place, and as each horse was ready one of the riders led it away. Bran and Tuck were last to leave, following the others across the broad black expanse of the bean field to the forest edge, where they met with the Cymry who had helped; and a rough division of the spoils was made then and there. "Spread it around to those who need it most," Bran told them. "But mind to keep it well hid in case any of the Ffreinc come sniffing around after it."

The rest of the way back to the forest was a long, slow amble through the night-dark vale and up the rise into the greenwood. They moved with the mist along cool forest pathways and arrived back at Cél Craidd as the sun broke fair on another sparkling, crisp autumn day—but a day that Abbot Hugo would remember as dismal indeed, the day his troubles began in earnest.

King Raven visited the abbey stores again the next night, despite the watch the sheriff and abbot had placed on the gate and storehouse. This time, however, instead of carrying off the supplies, the black-hooded creature destroyed them. Iwan and Tuck rode with him to the edge of the forest and, as they had done the previous night, waited for night to deepen the darkness. The moon would rise late, but it would be only a pale sliver in the sky. In any event, Bran planned to be back in the forest before his trail could be followed.

When he judged the time was right, he donned his feathered cloak and the high-crested beak mask, and climbed into the saddle. "I could go with you," Iwan said.

"There's no need," Bran demurred. "And it will be easier to elude them on my own."

"We'll wait for you here, then," replied the champion. He handed Bran his bow and six black arrows, three of which had been specially prepared.

"Go with God," Tuck said, and passed Bran the chain from which was suspended a small iron canister—a covered dish of coals. "Oh, it's a sorry waste," he sighed as Bran rode away. His dark form was swiftly swallowed by the darkness.

"Aye," agreed Iwan, "but needful. Taking food from the mouth of an enemy is almost as good as eating it yourself."

Tuck considered this for a moment. "No," he decided, "it is not."

The two settled back to watch and wait. They listened to the night sounds of the forest and the easy rustling of the leaves in the upper boughs of the trees as the breeze came up. Tuck was nodding off to sleep when Iwan said, "There he is."

Tuck came awake with a start at the sound. He looked around, but saw nothing. "Where?"

"Just there," said Iwan, stretching out his hand towards the darkness, "low to the ground and a little to your left."

Tuck looked where Iwan indicated and saw a tiny yellow glow moving along the ground. Then, even as he watched, the glow floated up into the air, where it hung for a moment.

"He's on the wall," said Iwan.

The glowing spark seemed to brighten and burst into flame. In the same instant the flame flared and disappeared and all was darkness again.

They waited.

In a moment, the glow fluttered to life once more in midair. It flared to life and disappeared just as quickly.

"That's two," said Iwan. "One more."

They waited.

This time the glow did not reappear at once. When it did, it was some distance farther along the wall. As before, the faint firefly glow brightened, then flared to brilliant life and disappeared in a smear of sparks and fire. Darkness reclaimed the night, and they waited. A long moment passed, then another, and they heard the hoofbeats of a swiftly approaching horse, and at almost the same time a line of light appeared low in the sky. The light grew in intensity until they could see the form of a dark rider galloping toward them. All at once, the light bloomed in the sky, erupting in a shower of orange and red flames.

"To your horses," shouted Bran as he came pounding up. "They'll be wanting our heads for this. I fired the storehouse and granary both."

"Did anyone see you?" wondered Iwan as he swung up into the saddle.

"It's possible," Bran said. "But they'll have their hands full for a little while, at least."

"Tsk," clucked Tuck with mild disapproval. "Such a sad waste."

"But necessary," offered Iwan. "Anything that weakens them, helps us."

"And anything that helps us, helps Elfael and its people," concluded Bran. "It was necessary."

"A holy waste, then," replied Tuck. He raised himself to a fallen limb and squirmed into the saddle. By the time he had the reins in his fist, his companions were already riding along the edge of the field up the long rising slope towards Coed Cadw, a dark mass rising like a wall against a sky alive with stars.

As the news about what had happened spread throughout the Vale of Elfael, everyone who heard about the theft and fire of the previous nights knew what it meant: King Raven's war with the Ffreinc

had entered a new, more desperate stage. Burning the abbey's storehouse and granary would provoke Abbot Hugo and the sheriff to a
swift and terrible reaction. If an army cannot eat, it cannot fight, and
the abbot's army had just lost its supper.

"Sheriff de Glanville won't be dainty about taking what he needs
from the poor Cymry round about," Scarlet pointed out after hearing an account of the previous night's raid. "He'll make a right fuss,
no mistake."

"I expect he will," Bran agreed. "I'd be disappointed otherwise."

"Will's got a fair point," Siarles affirmed. "De Glanville will steal
from the farm folk. It's always them he turns to."

"Yes, and when he does, he'll find King Raven waiting for him,"
said Bran.

Bran's reply stunned his listeners—not what he said—the words
themselves were reasonable enough. It was the way he said them;
there was a coldness in his tone that chilled all who heard it. There
wasn't a man among them who did not recognize that something had
changed in their king since his return from the north. If he had been
determined before, he was that much more determined now. But it
was more than simple purpose—there was a dark, implacable hardness to it, as if somehow his customary resolve had been chastened
and hardened in a forge. There was an edge to it, keen and lethal as
stropped steel. Scarlet put it best when he said, "God bless me,
Brother Tuck, but talking to Rhi Bran now is like talking to the blade
of a spear." He turned wondering eyes on the little priest. "Just what
did you two get up to in the north that's made him so?"

"It's never the north that's made him this way," replied the friar,
"although that maybe tipped the load into the muck. But it's coming back home and seeing how things are here—all this time passing,

1186

and the abbot is ruling the roost and the sheriff cutting up rough and all. The Ffreinc are still here and nothing's changed—nothing for the better, at least."

Scarlet nodded in commiseration. "It may be as you say, Friar, but *I* say that little jaunt up north changed him," he insisted. "I'll bet my back teeth on't."

"Perhaps," allowed Tuck. "Oh, you should have seen him, Scarlet. The way he peeled that hard-boiled earl—it was a gladsome sight." The friar went on to describe the elaborate deception he'd witnessed and in which he'd taken part—the clothes, the hunting, Alan's tireless translating, the young Welshmen and their willing and industrious participation, the breathless escape, and all the rest. "We were Count Rexindo and his merry band, as Alan says—albeit, his song makes it sound like a frolic of larks, but it was grim dire, I can tell you. We were tiptoeing in the wolf's den with fresh meat in our hands, but Bran never put a foot wrong. Why, it would have made you proud, it truly would."

"And yet it all came to nothing in the end."

"Saints bear witness, Scarlet, that's the naked bleeding heart of it, is it not? We dared much and risked more to save King Gruffydd's worthless neck," Tuck said, his voice rising with the force of his indignation. "And we succeeded! Beyond all hope of success, we succeeded. But that selfish sot refused to help. After we saved his life, by Peter's beard, that rascal of a king would not lend so much as a single sausage to our aid." He shook his head in weary commiseration. "Poor Bran . . . that his own kinsman would use him so ill—it's a wicked betrayal, that's what it is."

"Raw as a wound from a rusty blade." He considered this for a moment. "So that's the grit in his gizzard—our Bran knows we're on

1187

our own now," concluded Scarlet gloomily. "Aye, we're alone in this, and that's shame and pity enough to make man, woman, horse, or dog weep."

"Never say it," Tuck rebuked gently. "We are *not* alone—for the Lord of Hosts is on our side and stretches out His mighty arm against our enemies." The little friar smiled, his round face beaming simple good pleasure at the thought. "If the Almighty stands with us, who can stand against us, aye?" Tuck prodded Scarlet in the chest with a stubby finger. "Just you answer me that, boyo. Who can stand against us?"

The friar had a point, Scarlet confessed, that no one could stand against God—then added, "But there does seem no end o' folk that'll try."

1188

The Grellon resumed the task of accumulating what provisions they could—meat from the hunt, grain and beans from the raid, tending the turnips in the field, making cheese from the milk of their two cows—preserving all they could and storing it up against the days of want that were surely coming.

Bran turned his attention to the other matter weighing on his mind. With everyone else already occupied, he called Scarlet and Tuck to him and announced, "Put on your riding boots. We're going to find Mérian—and while we're at it, we'll see if we can convince King Cadwgan to lend some of his men to aid us."

"This is what Mérian has been arguing all this while," Tuck pointed out.

"Aye, it is," Bran conceded. "I was against it at first, I confess, but our feet are in the flame now and we have no other choice.

Tuck

Maybe Mérian is right—maybe her family will help where mine would not. Lord Cadwgan holds no kindly feelings towards me, God knows, but she's had a few days with him; I have to know whether she's been able to soften her father's opinion and persuade him. Pray she has, friends—it's our last hope." He spun on his heel and started away at once. "Ready the horses," he called over his shoulder. "We have only this day."

"It seems his disappointment has passed," said Scarlet. "And we're for a ride through lands filled with vengeful Ffreinc."

"Lord have mercy." Tuck sighed. "The last thing I need is to spend more time jouncing around on horseback. Still, if we can convince Cadwgan to help us, it will be worth another saddle sore."

"So now, if the Ffreinc catch us rambling abroad in plain daylight," warned Scarlet, "saddle sores will be least of all your earthly worries, friend friar."

1189

Arriving just after midday, the three riders paused to observe King Cadwgan's stronghold from a distance. All appeared peaceable and quiet on the low hill and surrounding countryside. There were folk working in the fields to the west and south of the fortress, and a few men and dogs moving cattle to another pasture for grazing. "Seems friendly enough from here," remarked Scarlet. "Any Ffreinc around, d'you reckon?"

"Possibly," answered Bran. "You never can tell—Cadwgan is client king to Baron Neufmarché."

"Same as tried to kill you?" wondered Scarlet.

"One and the same. I made the mistake of asking Neufmarché for help, and thought he might behave honourably," replied Bran. "It is not a mistake I shall make a second time."

"A bad business, that," mused Tuck. "It is a very miracle Cadwgan has survived this long under the baron's heavy thumb."

"You know him?" asked Scarlet.

"Aye, I do—we're not the best of friends, mind, but I know him when I see him—for all I've lived in the shadow of Hereford castle for many years."

"That is why I am sending you on ahead," said Bran.

"Me!"

"I dare not show my face within those walls until you have seen how things sit with the king."

"You want me to go in there alone?" Tuck said.

"Who better to spy out the lay of the land?" said Bran. "No one up there has ever seen you," he pointed out. "To the good folk of Caer Rhodl you will simply be who you are—a wandering mendicant priest. You've nothing to fear."

"Then why do I feel like Daniel sent into the lions' lair?"

He made to urge his mount forward, but Bran took hold of the

bridle strap and pulled him up. "On foot."

"I have to walk?"

"Wandering mendicant priests do not ride fine horses."

"Fine horses, my fat arse." Tuck rolled his eyes and puffed out his cheeks. "You call these plodders we ride 'fine'?" Complaining, he squirmed down from his mount, landing hard on the path below.

"That grove of beeches," said Bran, pointing a little way down the track the way they had come. "We'll wait for you there."

"What do you want me to tell Cadwgan?" Tuck asked, untying the loop that held his staff alongside the saddle.

"Tell him anything you like," said Bran. "Only find out if it is safe for me to come up there and speak to him. And find out what has become of Mérian."

Tuck beetled off on his bowed legs while Bran and Will rode back to wait in the grove. Upon reaching the foot of the fortress mound, Tuck worked his way along the rising, switchback path towards the entrance. The thought—the fervent hope—of cool dark ale awaiting him in a welcome cup sprang up, bringing the water to his thirsty mouth. By the time he reached the gate atop the long ramp, he was panting with anticipation. A word with the gatekeeper brought the desired result, and he was quickly admitted and directed to the cookhouse.

"Bless you, my son," said Tuck. "May God be good to you."

At the cookhouse, he begged a bite to eat and a cup of something to drink, and found the kitchener most obliging. "Come in, Friar, and be welcome," said the woman who served the king and his household as master cook. "Sit you down, and I'll soon set a dish or two before you."

"And if you have a little ale," suggested Tuck lightly, "I would dearly love to wash the dust of the road from my mouth."

"That you shall have," replied the cook—so amiably that Tuck remembered all over again how well he was so often received in the houses of the great lords. For however high and mighty the lord might be—with his own priests or those nearby to attend him as he pleased—his vassals and servants were usually more than glad to receive a priest of their own class. She busied herself in the next room and returned with a leather cannikin dripping with foam. "Here," she said, passing the vessel to Tuck, "get some of this inside you and slay the nasty dragon o' thirst."

Tuck seized the container with both hands and brought it to his face. He drank deep, savouring the cool, sweet liquid as it filled his mouth and flowed over his tongue and down his chin. "Bless you," he sighed, wiping his mouth with his sleeve. "I was that parched."

"Now, then," said the master cook, "just enjoy your cup. I won't be a moment."

The cook left the kitchen for the larder, and Tuck sat on his stool, elbows on the board, sipping the good dark ale. In a moment, a young woman came in with a wedge of cheese on a wooden plate. "Cook said to give you this while you wait," said the serving maid.

"Thank you, my child," replied Tuck, taking the plate from her hand.

"If you please, Friar," she said, "I have a sore foot." She looked at him doubtfully. "Would you know of a cure or blessing?"

"Let me see," he said, glancing down at her feet. "Which foot is it?"

She slipped off her shoe—a wooden clog with a leather top— and held the foot up slightly. Tuck saw a red welt at the base of her big toe that looked to him like the beginning of a bunion.

"Ah, yes," he said. "I have seen this before." He gently lifted the young woman's foot and touched the raw, red bulge. "I think you are fortunate to catch this before it has become incurable."

She winced, drawing in her breath sharply. "Can you fix it?"

"I think so. Can you get a little mayweed hereabouts?"

"For a certainty," she replied. "We use it all the time."

"Then you'll know how to make a tisane, do you not?"

The girl nodded.

"Good—make one and drink it down. Then take the wet leaves from the bowl and apply them to the sore. Do this three times a day, every day for five days, and you'll soon feel better. Oh, yes, put off your shoes for a few days."

The girl made a sour face. "My lady does not like us to go barefoot," she said. "Leastwise, not in the house."

"Not to worry," said Tuck. "When you go in the house, just put some willow bark shavings in your shoe. But take off your shoes whenever you can. Oh, yes—find some larger shoes if you can. The ones you are wearing are too small for you, and that, no doubt, is what has caused this ailment." He laid a finger to his lips. "Now, then, I think Saint Birinius is the one to seek on this one," he said. "Bow your head, child."

The young woman did as she was told, and Tuck held his hand over her and sought the blessing of Birinius, whose feet were held in the fire by one of the old Mercian kings as a test of his faith and thus was one who knew the pain associated with various foot ailments. The young lady thanked the friar and left—only to be replaced by another woman bringing a small woollen cloak she had just finished making. "If it is not too much trouble, Friar," she said politely, "I would ask a blessing for this cloak, as I've made it for my sister's baby that's due to come any day now."

"May God be good to you for your thoughtfulness," said Tuck. "It is no trouble at all." And he blessed the soft square of delicate cloth.

When he finished, the cook returned and began placing bowls of minted beans and new greens and a plate of cold duck before him. The woman with the infant's cloak thanked him and said, "My man is outside with a horse he'd like you to see when you've finished your meal."

"Tell him I will attend directly," replied Tuck, reaching for a wooden spoon. He ate and drank and worked out what he wanted to say to Lord Cadwgan. When the cook returned to see how he fared, Tuck asked, "The lord of this place—is he well?"

"Oh, indeed, Friar. Never better."

"Good," replied Tuck. "I am glad to hear it."

"How could it be otherwise? A new-married man and his bride—why, birds in a nest, those two."

This caught Tuck on the hop. "Lord Cadwgan . . . newly married, you say?"

"Lord have mercy, no!" laughed the cook. "It's Garran I'm talking about. He's king now, and lord of this place."

"Oh, is he? But that must mean—"

The cook was already nodding in reply. "The old king died last year, and Garran has taken his father's place on the throne, may God keep him."

"Of course," replied Tuck. He finished his meal wondering whether this revelation made his task easier or more difficult. Knowing little about Cadwgan, and nothing at all about Garran, there was no way to tell, he decided, until he met the young king in the flesh. He finished his meal and thanked the cook for extending the hospitality of her lord to him, then went out into the yard to see the horse. The stablehand was waiting patiently, and Tuck greeted him and asked what he could do. "The mare's with foal," the man told him, "as you can see. I would have a blessing on her that the birth will be easy and the young 'un healthy."

"Consider it done," replied the friar. Placing his hand on the broad forehead of the animal, Tuck said a prayer and blessed the beast, asking for the aid of Saint Eligius for the animal and, for good measure, Saint Monica as well. While he was praying he became aware that there were others looking on. On concluding, he turned to see that he was being watched by a young man who, despite his fair hair, looked that much like Mérian—the same large dark eyes, the same full mouth and high, noble forehead—that

Tuck decided the fellow had to be her brother. "I do beg your pardon, my lord," Tuck said, offering a slight bow, "but mightn't you be Rhi Garran?"

"God be good to you, Friar, I might be and, as it happens, I am," replied the young man with a smile. "And who, so long as we're asking, are you to be blessing my horses?"

"I am as you see me," replied Tuck, "a humble friar. Brother Aethelfrith is my name."

"A Saxon, then."

"I am, and that proud of it."

"Now I know you must be a Christian," replied Garran lightly, "for you speak the language of heaven right well. How is that, if you don't mind my asking? For I've never known a Saxon to bother himself overmuch with learning the Cymry tongue."

"That is easily told," answered Tuck, and explained that as a boy in Lincolnshire he had been captured in a raid and sold into slavery in the copper mines of Powys; when he grew old enough and bold enough, he had made good his escape and was received by the monks of Llandewi, where he lived until taking his vows and, some little time later, becoming a mendicant.

The young king nodded, the same amiable smile playing on his lips the while. "Well, I hope they have fed you in the kitchen, friend friar. You are welcome to stay as long as you like—Nefi, here, will give you a corner of the stable for a bed, and I am certain my people will make you feel at home."

"Your generosity does you credit, Sire," Tuck said, "but it is you I have come to see—on a matter of some urgency."

The young man hesitated. He made a dismissive gesture. "Then I commend you to my seneschal. I am certain he will be best able to help." Again, he turned to go, giving Tuck the impression that he was intruding on the busy life of this young monarch.

"If you please, my lord," said Tuck, starting after him, "it is about a friend of yours and mine—and of your sister Mérian's."

At this last name, the young king halted and turned around again. "You know my sister?"

"I do, my lord, and that right well, do I not?"

"How do you know her?" The king's tone became wary, suspicious.

"I have lately come from the place where she has been living."

Garran tensed and drew himself up. "Then you must be one of those outlaws of the greenwood we have been hearing about." Before Tuck could reply, he said, "You are no longer welcome here. I suggest you leave before I have you whipped and thrown out."

"So that is the way of it," concluded Tuck.

"I have nothing more to say to you." Garran turned on his heel and started away.

"God love you, man," said Tuck, stepping after him. "It can do no harm to talk—"

"Did you not hear me?" snarled Garran, turning on the little friar. "I can have you beaten and cast out like the filth you are. Get you from my sight, or heaven help me, I will whip you myself."

"Then do so," Tuck replied, squaring himself for a fight. "For I will not leave until I have said what I came here to say."

Garran glared at him, but said, "Go on, then. If it will get your repulsive carcase out of my sight the sooner, speak."

"You seem to think that we harmed Mérian in some way," Tuck began. "We did no such thing. Indeed, Mérian was not held against her will. She stayed in the greenwood, *lived* with us in the greenwood, because she believes in the cause that we pursue—the same cause that brings me here to ask your aid."

"What cause?"

"Justice, pure and simple. King William has erred and fomented a great injustice against the rightful lord and people of Elfael, who are most cruelly used and oppressed. A most grievous wrong has been committed, and we seek to put it right. To speak plainly, we mean to drive out the wicked usurpers and reclaim the throne of Elfael. Your sister, Mérian, has been helping us do just that. She has been a most ardent and enthusiastic member of our little band. Let us go ask her," Tuck suggested, "and you can hear this from her own lips."

Garran was already shaking his head. "You're not going anywhere near her," he said. "Mérian is home now—back among her family where she belongs. You will no longer twist her to your treason."

"Twist her?" wondered Tuck. "She has been more than willing. Mérian is a leader among the forest folk. She is—"

"Whatever she *was* to you," sneered Garran, "she is no more. Be gone!"

"Please, you must—"

"Must? Know you, Baron Neufmarché is my liege lord, as William is his. We are loyal to the crown in this house. If you persist in speaking of this, I will report you for treason against the throne of England—as is my sworn duty."

"I beg you, Sire, do not—"

"Daffyd! Awstin!" the king shouted, calling for his men, who appeared on the run from the stables. Thrusting a finger at the friar, he said, "Throw him out and bar the gate behind him. If he does not leave, whip him, and drag him to the border of Eiwas—for I will not suffer him to remain in my sight or on my land another moment."

"I will go, and gladly," Tuck said. "But let me speak to Mérian—"

Garran's face clenched like a fist. "Mention her name again and, priest or no, I will cut out your tongue." He gave a nod to the two stablehands, who stepped forward and roughly took hold of Tuck.

The friar was hauled from the yard and pushed out through the gate. "Sorry, Friar," said one as he closed the gate.

"Bless you, friend," replied Tuck with a sigh, "I do not hold it against you." He took a moment to shake the dust from his feet, and then started the long walk back to where Bran and Scarlet were waiting for a better word than he had to give them.

Nor was Bran any better pleased than Tuck imagined he would be. He listened to all that Tuck had to say about what had taken place up at the caer, and then walked a few paces apart and stood looking at the fortress mound in the near distance. He stood there so long that Scarlet eventually approached him and said, "My lord? What is your pleasure?"

When Bran failed to respond, he said, "If we hurry, we can be back in Cél Craidd before dark."

Without turning, Bran replied, "I am not leaving until I have spoken to Mérian."

"How?" wondered Tuck. "He will hardly allow any of us inside the caer again."

Bran turned and flashed his crooked smile. "Tuck, old friend, I have been in and out of that fortress without anyone the wiser more times than you've et hot soup." He looked around for a soft spot in the shade. "It's going to be a long night; I suggest we rest until it gets dark."

They tethered the horses so that they might graze among the trees, and then settled back to nap and wait for night and the cover of darkness. The day passed quietly, and night came on. When Bran reckoned that all in the fortress would be in bed asleep, he roused the other two. Tuck rose, yawned, shook out his robe, and clambered back into the saddle, thinking that he would be heartily glad when all this to-ing and fro-ing was over and peace reigned in the land once more. They rode in silence around the base of the hill on which the fortress sat, Bran picking his way with practiced assurance along a path none of the others could see in the darkness. They came to a place below the wall where a small ditch or ravine caused the wall to dip slightly. Here, Bran halted and dismounted. "We are behind the kitchen," he explained. "Mérian's chamber used to be just the other side of the wall. Pray it is so now."

"And is this why Lord Cadwgan took such umbrage against you?" wondered Scarlet.

"Now that you mention it," Bran allowed, his grin a white glint in the dark, "that could have had something to do with it—not that any other reason was needed." He started up the steep hillside. "Let's be at it."

Quick and silent as a shadow, Bran was up the slope and over the wall, leaving Scarlet and Tuck to struggle over as best they could. By the time Tuck eased himself over the rough timber palisade and into the yard, Bran was already clinging onto the sill below a small glass window—one of only three in the entire fortress. Bran lightly tapped twice on the small round panes . . . paused, and tapped three more times.

When nothing happened, he repeated the same series of raps.

"D'you think she's there?" asked Scarlet.

Bran hissed him to silence and repeated his signal yet again. This time there was a tap from the other side, and a moment later the window swung inward on its hinges and Mérian's face appeared where the glass had been. "Bran! Saints and angels, it *is* you!"

"Mérian, are you well?"

"I thought you would never get here," she said. "I have been praying you would come—and listening for you each night."

"Are you well, Mérian?"

"I am very well—for all I am made prisoner in my own house," she said tartly. "But I am not mistreated. They think you took me hostage—"

"I did."

"—and held me against my will. They seem to think that if I am given a little time I will come to see how I was tricked into siding with you against the Ffreinc. Until I repent of my folly, I am to remain locked in this room."

"We'll have you out of there soon enough," said Bran. He glanced across to the shuttered window of the kitchen. "Give me a moment and I'll come through there. Is there likely to be anyone awake in the kitchen?"

"Bran, no—wait," said Mérian. "Listen to me—I've been thinking. I should stay here a little longer."

"But, you just said—"

"I know, but I think I can persuade Garran to send men to aid us."

"Tuck tried to ask him already. He asked to see you, too, and Garran refused. He wouldn't hear anything we had to say."

"You talked to him? When?"

"Today. Tuck came up, but Garran had him thrown out of the caer. It's no use; your brother will not go against Baron Neufmarché in any case."

"He has good reason," Mérian said. "He's married to the baron's daughter."

"What?"

"Lady Sybil Neufmarché—they were wed in the spring." She explained about her father's death and funeral, and the match the baron had proposed. "They are living here—Lady Agnes and Sybil, I mean."

Bran dropped lightly to the ground. "They won't let you go. And no matter what you say, you'll never persuade them to join us." He gestured behind him. "Scarlet, Tuck, come here."

"What are you going to do?"

"Free you."

"Please, Bran, not like this. If I stay here I might yet be able to convince them to join us. If I leave now, it will enrage them—and then you will have Garran and his men against you, too. We cannot risk making enemies of those who should be our friends."

"Come with me, Mérian. I need you."

"Bran, I pray you, think what this means."

Bran paused and looked up at her. "I remember once, not so long ago, when I stood where I'm standing now and asked you to come with me," he said. "Do you remember?"

"I remember," she said.

"You refused to come with me then too."

"Oh, Bran." Her voice became plaintive. "This is not like that. I *will* come—as soon as I can. Until then, I will work to bring Garran around to our side. I can do this; you'll see."

Bran started away, fading into the night-shadowed darkness.

"It is for the best," Mérian insisted. "You will see."

"Farewell, Mérian." Bran called over his shoulder. "Come," he said to Scarlet and Tuck, "we are finished. There is nothing for us here."

1203

CHAPTER 27

Saint Martin's

The small steading lay amidst fields of barley in a narrow crook of a finger of the Vale of Elfael north of Saint Martin's—not the largest holding in Elfael, nor the closest to the caer, but one that Gysburne had marked before as a prosperous place and well worth keeping an eye on. Captain Aloin, commander of the knights that had been sent to help the abbot and sheriff maintain order in the cantref, surveyed the quiet farm from the back of his horse.

"Are you certain this is the place?" asked the captain, casting his gaze right and left for any sign of trouble. "It seems peaceful enough."

"The calm can be misleading," replied Marshal Gysburne. "These Welsh are sly devils every one. You must be prepared to fight for your life at any moment."

The sheriff and abbot had determined to begin retaliation for the most recent predations of King Raven and his thieving flock. The sack of the Welsh farms and confiscation of all supplies, stock,

and provisions would serve as a warning to the folk of the cantref—
especially those who benefited from the thievery. To this end, a large
body of knights—fully half of the entire force, accompanied by men-
at-arms and four empty hay wains—had been dispatched to the
holding with orders to strip it of all possessions and kill anyone bold
enough to resist.

"And when we've finished here?" Captain Aloin asked.

"We continue on to the next farm, and the next, until the wagons are full. Or until King Raven and his foul flock appear."

"How do you know he will come?" asked Captain Aloin as he
and Gysburne rode out from the caer, each at the head of a company
of soldiers.

"He will appear, without a doubt," replied Marshal Guy. "If not
today, then tomorrow. Attacking one of his beloved settlements raises
his ire—killing a few Cymry is sure to bring him out of hiding."

"If that is so," surmised Aloin. "Then why have you not done
this before? Why have you waited so long and put up with his thievery and treasons all this time?"

"Because Count Falkes de Braose—the ruler of Elfael before he
was driven into exile—had no stomach for such tactics. He thought
it important to gain the trust and goodwill of the people, or some
such nonsense. He said he could not rule if all hands were against
him at every turn."

"And now?"

Gysburne smiled to himself. "Now things have changed. Abbot
Hugo is not so delicate as the count."

"And Sheriff de Glanville?"

"What about him?"

"Where does he stand in this matter? It was de Glanville who begged our services from the king. I would have thought he would ride out with us today."

"But he *has*," replied Gysburne. "He most certainly has—as you shall see." The marshal lifted the reins. "Walk on," he said.

Captain Aloin raised his fist in the air and gave the signal to move out, and the double column of soldiers on horseback continued on. Upon reaching the farmstead, the knights quickly arrayed themselves for battle. While half of the company under the command of Gysburne rode into the yard and took over the holding, Aloin's division fanned out to form a shield wall to prevent any approach to the property and discourage anyone who might be minded to take an interest in the affair.

Sitting on his great warhorse in the centre of the yard, Gysburne gave the command to begin.

Knights and men-at-arms swarmed into the house and dragged out the farmer, his wife and daughter, and three grown sons. There were several others as well, hauled out into the early-morning light to stand in the yard surrounded by enemy soldiers and watch while all their possessions, provisions, and supplies were bundled into wagons. None of the Welshmen made even the slightest attempt to interfere with the sack of their home. The farmer and his sons stood in stiff-legged defiance, glowering with pent rage at all those around them, but said nothing and did not lift a hand to prevent the pillage— which Gysburne put down to their display of overwhelming military might. For once, the superior Ffreinc forces had cowed the indomitable Welsh spirit.

The ransacking of the house and barn and outbuildings was swiftly accomplished. The fact that the soldiers had not had to subdue the hostile natives and the piteous lack of possessions meant that the raid was finished almost as soon as it began. "It is done," reported Sergeant Jeremias as the last grain sacks were tossed into a waiting wagon. "What is your command?"

"Burn it, Sergeant."

"But Sire—Sheriff de Glanville said—"

"Never mind what de Glanville said. Burn it."

"Everything?"

"To the ground."

The sight of torches being lit brought the farmer and his sons out of their belligerent stupor. They began shouting and cursing and shaking their fists at the Ffreinc soldiers. One of the younger boys made as if to rush at one of the knights as he passed with a torch. But the farmer grabbed his son back and held him fast. They all watched as the flames took hold, rising skyward on the soft morning air. The farmwife held her head in her hands, tears streaming down her face. Still, none of the Cymry stirred from where they stood.

When it was certain that the flames could not be extinguished, Marshal Guy gave the order for the knights to be mounted, and the company moved off.

"That went well," observed Aloin when the last of the wagons and soldiers had cleared the yard. "Better than I expected—from what you said about the Welshies' love of fighting."

"Yes," agreed the marshal slowly, "in truth I expected more of a fight. Just see you keep your sword ready. We cannot count on the next one being so peaceful."

But, in fact, the Cymry at the second farm were no more inclined to take arms and resist the pillagers than the first lot. Like those at the previous settlement, the second clan put up no struggle at all,

1208

bearing the assault with a grave and baleful silence. If they did not voice their fury outright, their doomful expressions were nevertheless most eloquent. Again, Marshal Guy could not quite credit the odd docility of the natives when faced with the destruction of their homes. But there it was. In spite of this conundrum, he decided to burn the second farm, too—the better to provoke King Raven to show himself.

"What now?" asked Captain Aloin as the smoke rolled skyward. "The wagons are almost full."

"Almost full is not enough," replied Guy. "We go on."

"And if this King of the Ravens does not appear? What then?"

"Then we'll take the wagons back to the caer and raid again tomorrow. We keep at it until he comes."

"You're sure about that, *oui?*"

"Oh, yes, he'll come. He always does."

The third farmstead lay almost within sight of the walls of Caer Cadarn. It was small and, owing to its nearness to the town and stronghold, it had suffered plundering by Ffreinc troops before, and Guy remembered it. The farm was quiet as the soldiers surrounded the property. No one came out to meet the soldiers as they entered the yard, so Gysburne ordered Sergeant Jeremias to go in and bring the farmer and his family out.

The sergeant returned a moment later. "There is no one here, my lord."

"They must have gone into hiding," concluded the marshal.

"They knew we were coming?" asked Captain Aloin. "How so?"

"The Welsh are uncanny this way," explained Gysburne. "I don't know how they know, but word travels on the air in these valleys. They seem to know everything that happens." Turning back to the sergeant, he said, "Ransack the barn and granary. They will not have had time to carry anything away."

Jeremias hurried off. "Strip it!" he called. "Take everything."

The soldiers dismounted and, while the wagons were driven into position, they moved off to the buildings. The first man-at-arms to reach the barn threw open the doors and started in—to be met by the angry wasp-buzz of arrows streaking out of the dark interior. He and two other soldiers dropped dead to the ground; three more staggered back clutching their chests and staring in horror at the oaken shafts that had so suddenly appeared there.

Marshal Guy saw the arrows flash and realized they were under attack. He turned to the soldiers who were just then about to enter the house. "Halt!" he shouted. "Don't go in there!"

But the knight's hand was on the door and he had already pushed it open.

With a sound like that of a whip snapping against naked flesh, the first flight of arrows struck home. Four knights fell as one. An errant arrow glanced off a soldier's helmet and careered off at an angle, striking a horse standing in the yard. The animal reared and began bucking in a forlorn effort to relieve the lethal sting in its side.

Then all was chaos, as everywhere knights and men-at-arms were stumbling back, colliding with one another, fleeing the deadly and unseen assault. With desperate shouts and screams of agony they shrank from the arrows that continued to stream into the yard, seemingly from every direction at once. There was no escaping them. With each flight more soldiers dropped—by twos and threes they fell, pierced by the lethal missiles.

"To arms! To arms!" cried Captain Aloin, trying to rally his troops. "Seal the barn! Seal the barn and burn it!"

1210

Tuck

In answer to the command, three well-armoured knights leapt to obey. Through the deadly onslaught they ran, their shields high before them as shaft after shaft hammered into the splintering wood. One of the knights reached the right-hand door of the barn and flung it closed. He put his back against it to hold it shut while his two comrades flung the left-hand door closed.

"The torches! Get the torches!" shouted the first knight, still bracing the door shut. He drew breath to shout once more and shrieked in agony instead as, with the sound of a branch breaking in a storm, the steel point of an arrow slammed through the planking and poked through the centre of his chest. He gave out a strangled yelp and slumped down, his body snagged and caught by the strong oaken shaft of the arrow.

His two companions holding the left-hand barn door heard the sharp cracking sound and watched aghast as three more arrows penetrated the stout timber doors to half their length. Had their backs been to the door they would have suffered the same fate as their unfortunate comrade.

Meanwhile, arrows continued to fly from the house—from the door and the two small windows facing the yard, which had become a tumult of plunging horses and frightened men scrambling over the bodies of corpses. The wagon drivers, defenceless in the centre of the yard, threw themselves from their carts and ran for safety beyond range of the whistling shafts. This left the oxen to fend for themselves; confused and terrified by the violent turmoil, the beasts strained at their yokes and tried to break their traces. Unable to escape, they stood in wild-eyed terror and bawled.

When the barn doors burst open once more, a tall slender figure appeared in the gap: a man's form from shoulders to the tips of his tall black boots, but bearing the head of an enormous bird with a weird skull-like black face and a wickedly long, narrow beak. In its hand, the creature clutched a longbow with an arrow nocked to the string. The smooth, expressionless face surveyed the churning turmoil with a quick sweep of its head, picked out Gysburne, and directed an arrow at him. The marshal, who was already wheeling his horse, took the arrow on his shield as three more archers joined the creature and proceeded to loose shaft after shaft at will into the melee.

"Retreat!" cried Gysburne, trying to make himself heard above the commotion. "Retreat!"

Arrows singing around his ears, Guy put his head down and raced from the yard. Those soldiers still in the saddle, and those yet able to walk or run, followed. Five more met their deaths before the last of the knights had cleared the yard.

The Ffreinc raiding party continued to a place beyond arrow's reach and halted to regroup.

"What was *that*?" shouted Captain Aloin as he came galloping in beside the marshal. "What in the holy name *was* that?"

"That was King Raven," replied Guy, pulling an arrow from his shield, and another from the cantle of his saddle. "That was the fiend at his worst."

"By the blood," breathed the captain. "How many were with him?"

"I don't know. It doesn't matter."

"Doesn't matter!" Captain Aloin cried in stunned disbelief. Gazing quickly around him, he counted those who had escaped the massacre. "Are you insane? We've lost more than half our men in a one-sided slaughter and you say it doesn't matter?"

1212

Tuck

"Six or sixty," muttered Guy. "What does it matter? We were beaten by those God-cursed arrows."

"This is an outrage," growled the captain of the king's men. "Mark me, by heaven, someone will pay for this."

"I daresay they will," agreed Guy, looking away towards the forest, where he imagined he saw the glint of sunlight off a steel blade.

"What are we to do now?" demanded Aloin. "Are we to retreat and let the bastards get away with it?"

"We run, but they won't get away," said Guy. "Sheriff de Glanville will see to that."

1213

CHAPTER 28 ⚖

"Are they gone?" asked Owain, his fingers tight around the arrow nocked to his bowstring.

"Shhh," said Iwan gently. "Stay sharp. We'll wait just a little and then take a look round." He turned to Siarles, crouched low behind the doorpost of the farmhouse. "See to it, Siarles, but keep an eye out for the wounded. There might be some fight in one or two yet."

Siarles nodded and continued to watch the yard from one of the small windows. Nothing moved outside. The three archers waited a few moments more, alert, arrows on string, listening for any sound of returning horses—but, save for a low, whimpering moan from one of the fallen soldiers, all seemed quiet enough. Siarles rose and stepped lightly through the door, paused and looked around, then disappeared into the yard at a run. He was back a few moments later saying, "They've gone. It's safe to come out."

As they stepped from the house, Bran, Tomas, and Rhoddi emerged from the barn. "To me, men!" Bran called, pulling off the hooded raven mask. When everyone had gathered, he said, "Strip the dead of anything useful. Throw it in the wagons and let's fly home. Scarlet and the others will be tired of waiting."

"Aren't we going to give back all the supplies they've stolen?" asked Owain.

"Aye, lad," replied Iwan, "but not now, not today."

"Your concern does you credit, Owain," Bran told him. "But the enemy will return to the caer and muster the rest of the soldiers to come and retrieve their dead. Unless we hurry, we'll meet them again, and this time we'll not own the advantage."

"Too many Ffreinc around for the few of us," Iwan told him. "We'll return the supplies when it's a mite safer."

"There's eighteen fewer Ffreinc now than there were a while ago," announced Siarles, who had been making a count. "And four more that will likely join 'em before the sun is over the barn."

"Twenty-two!" gasped Rhoddi. "God help us, that must be near half their force—destroyed in one battle."

"There will be hell to pay," muttered Tomas as the realization of the enormity of their success came over him.

"Too right, there will," agreed Bran. "But we must make very sure it is the abbot who pays. Come, men, let's be about our business before the marshal comes back."

So while Siarles kept watch, the other five archers stripped the dead and dying, tossing the various articles into the wagons the soldiers had abandoned in their retreat. Then, leading the oxen from the yard, they departed—not by the road which led away to the fortress and town—but by the field track that led up through the valley towards Coed Cadw, the Guardian Wood.

Owing to the weight of the wagons and the slowness of the

oxen, they could not travel as swiftly as the demands of the situation warranted; even so, they reached the edge of the forest in due course without any sign of pursuing Ffreinc. As they drew in towards the line of trees, however, the leaves of the nearby hawthorn bushes quivered, rattling an alarm.

Bran, in the lead, glanced up in time to see the round gleaming top of a Norman helmet rising from the brush.

The spear was in the air before Bran could shout a warning. He dodged to the side, and the missile caught Owain a few steps behind him. The young man gave out a yelp and fell back. Bran had an arrow in the air before Owain's body came to rest in the grass.

The stone point struck the helmet and shattered, scattering shards into the attacker's eyes. He screamed and sank out of sight. Instantly, another soldier was there in his place, and others were appearing in a ragged rank all along the forest line.

"Ambush!" shouted Bran, loosing an arrow at the nearest head to appear.

"Fall back!" shouted Iwan. Stooping low, he scooped up the wounded Owain, put him over his shoulder as lightly as a sheaf of wheat, and ran to the nearest wagon, ducking behind it as the spears began to fall.

The four archers joined the champion behind the wagon, and all looked to Bran for a way out of their predicament.

"How many are there?" asked Siarles. "Anybody see?"

"Plenty for each of us," Iwan said. "Never you fear."

"Owain?" said Bran. "Owain, look at me. How bad are you?"

"It hurts," groaned the young man through gritted teeth. He held his side above his hip; blood seeped through his fingers. "I'm lying if I say otherwise, but get my feet under me and I can walk."

"We can't stay here," Iwan told them. "They'll charge soon and cut us down in the open like this."

"Right," said Bran. "Everyone nock an arrow and be ready to move. They can't run and throw at the same time, so as soon as they mount the charge, we go for the greenwood."

"Go into them?" said Tomas.

"Aye," replied Iwan. "Headfirst into the charge."

"Smack 'em hard in the teeth," said Siarles, glancing up as a spear head chipped through the side of the wagon above his head. "It'll be the only thing they're not expecting."

"Once we're in the trees we have a chance," Bran said. Reaching over the side of the wagon, he pulled down a Norman shield and handed it to Owain, then took the young man's bag of arrows and passed them around to the others.

"Did anyone see which manjack is leadin' 'em?" asked Siarles as he peered around the back of the wagon towards the tree line.

The question went unanswered, as there came a rising cry from the forest and Ffreinc soldiers rushed up out of the brush towards the wagons. "Ready!" shouted Bran. "Now! Fly!"

Out from behind the wagon he darted. Raising his bow, he drew on the foremost knight just then charging up out of the bush. The bowstring slapped, and the arrow blurred across the distance, lifting the onrushing soldier off his feet and throwing him onto his back. The sudden absence of the soldier created a hole in the line, and Iwan, running hard behind his lord, opened it a little wider by taking out the soldier to the left of the first.

Spears sailed in deadly arcs, slicing through the sun-drenched air, sprouting like leafless saplings in turf. The archers dodged those that sprang up in their path, loosing arrows as they ran. The gap which

Iwan and Bran had opened narrowed as more knights, screaming and cursing, drove in, desperate to close on the fleeing outlaws before they could reach the wood.

Bran loosed the last of his arrows, put his head down, and ran. Two heavily armoured knights lurched into the gap, low behind their spears. The nearest lunged, making a wide swipe with the spear blade, and the second let fly. The throw was low and skidded along the ground. Bran leapt over it easily; but Iwan, coming two steps behind, was not so lucky. The sliding shaft snaked through the grass, gliding between his feet; he tripped and fell onto his left side.

The knight was on him instantly, sword drawn. With a shout of triumph, he swung the blade high and prepared to deliver the killing stroke. Iwan, defenceless on his back, saw the blade flash as it swung up, and threw his hands before him to ward off the blow. But the knight's cry of triumph stuck in his throat, and he seemed to strain against the blade that had become inextricably caught in the air.

The knight, sword still high, crashed to his knees, his eyes wide in shock and disbelief. Iwan had just time enough to roll aside as the knight's body jolted forward with the force of the second arrow, which drove him facedown into the ground.

As Iwan scrambled to his feet, he saw twin shafts protruding from the knight's mail hauberk.

"Here! Iwan!"

The champion looked to the shout and saw Scarlet, bow in hand, waving him forward.

The first knight, still gripping his spear, made a second swipe at Bran, who grabbed hold of the spear shaft with his free hand, pulling the soldier towards him. As the knight fell forward, Bran swung his longbow like a club into the man's face. The knight lowered his head and let his helmet take the blow, then thrust again with the spear. Bran lashed out with his foot, catching the knight on the chin; his jaw snapped shut with a teeth-shattering crack, and his head flew back. Bran swung the body of the longbow down hard, and the mail-clad knight went down. As he sprawled on the ground, Bran, light as a deer in flight, took a running step, planted a foot in the middle of the man's back, and vaulted over him.

He reached the shelter of the trees to find Scarlet waiting for him. "Here, my lord," said the forester, thrusting a handful of arrows at him. "You'll be needing these, I think."

"Thanks, Will," said Bran, breathing hard.

"This way." Scarlet led him along the tree line, and together they loosed arrow after arrow into the Ffreinc from behind until the remaining archers had reached the wood.

Now King Raven and his men occupied the wood, and the Ffreinc were exposed on open ground. As the lethal oaken shafts struck again and again, some of the knights sought shelter behind the wagons. Others crawled back into the wood.

Bran and Scarlet gathered the archers. "How many arrows have you got left?" Bran asked as the men gathered under cover of a bramble thicket. "Two," said Siarles; Tomas and Scarlet each had two as well. None of the others had any.

"Then this fight is over," said Bran.

"Just leave?" objected Siarles. "We can end it now."

"With but six arrows? No, Siarles," Bran told him. "We live to fight another day. It's time to go home."

"Where's Tuck got to?" wondered Iwan.

"He should be nearby," Scarlet replied. "He was right beside me before the charge. Do you want me to go look for him?"

1220

Tuck

"We can't be leaving him behind for the Ffreinc to capture," said Iwan.

"Scarlet and I will find him," Bran said. "The rest of you start back to Cél Craidd." He held out his hand. "Give us the arrows." He took the remaining arrows and urged them away. "Go. We'll join you on the way."

The others disappeared into the bush. "Where were you when this started?" Bran asked, passing three arrows to Scarlet. "Show me."

"This way," Will told him, starting back along the tree line to the place he and Tuck had been hiding when the attack began.

No sooner had they skirted a large bramble thicket than they heard someone call out. "Scarlet! Here, boyo!"

"I think it came from over there somewhere," said Scarlet. Both men turned and started for the spot. They quickly came to a dense wall of elder and halted. "Tuck! Sing out, Brother. Where are you?"

"Here!" came the voice once more. "This way! Hurry!"

The two pushed through the elder hedge to find the little priest holding a sturdy quarterstaff in one hand and a sword in the other as he stood astraddle an inert figure on the ground. The figure groaned and made to rise, and the friar gave him a sharp rap between the shoulder blades that pushed him back down.

"Thank the Good Lord you're here," breathed Tuck. "I was halfway to wishing I'd never a'caught this one. He's getting to be a handful."

"Here now," said Bran, taking the sword. "Stand aside and let's see who you've got."

Tuck moved away, but kept the staff at the ready.

Bran took hold of the prostrate man's hair and lifted his head from the ground. "Richard de Glanville!" he exclaimed, his surprise genuine. Glancing around to the friar, he said, "Well done, Tuck.

You are a very wonder." He released his handful of hair, and the groggy head thumped back onto the earth. "With a little luck and Providence on our side, we may reclaim the throne of Elfael far sooner than we ever dared hope."

"Truly?"

"Aye," declared Bran, "with the sheriff's valuable assistance, of course. But we must act quickly. We cannot give Gysburne and Hugo time to think."

1222

W ell, here's a prize we never thought to get," remarked Iwan. He put a hand to the sheriff's shoulder and rolled him over onto his back. The sheriff moaned, his eyelids fluttering as he struggled for consciousness, but he made no effort to rise.

Bran had quickly recalled his men, and they gathered once more to receive new instructions. As Bran began to explain what he had in mind, their prisoner regained his senses. *"C'est vous! J'ai pensé qu'il y'avait une odeur de merde,"* groaned the sheriff in a voice thick and slurred.

"What did he say?" asked Bran.

"Nothing nice," replied Tuck. He gave the sheriff a kick with the toe of his shoe and warned him to speak respectfully or keep his mouth shut.

"Achevez-moi, et finissez l'affaire."

"He wants us to kill him now and be done with it," offered the friar.

"Kill a valuable prisoner like you?" said Bran. Squatting down, he patted the sheriff's clothes and felt along his belt before withdrawing a dagger, which he took and handed to Scarlet. "I suppose you'd prefer death just now, but you'll have to become accustomed to disappointment." To Tuck, he added, "Tell him what I said."

Tuck relayed Bran's words to de Glanville, who groaned and put his face to the ground once more.

"What is in your mind, my lord?" asked Iwan.

"Bind him," Bran directed, "and get him on his feet. Gysburne and his men will be recovering their courage, and any moment they might take it into their heads to come after us. Siarles, Tomas—see how many arrows you can get from the field, and hurry back."

The two hurried off, returning a short while later with eight shafts collected in fair condition from dead soldiers, which added to the six they already possessed brought the total to fourteen. "I would there were more, but these will have to do," Bran said. "Pray it is enough." He gave arrows to each of the archers, save the wounded Owain and himself. Instead, he shouldered his bow and took the sheriff's sword, and instructed Tuck to ask de Glanville where the Ffreinc had hidden their horses.

Tuck did so, and received a terse reply—to which Tuck responded with another sharp rap of his staff against the sheriff's shins. De Glanville let out a yelp of pain and spat a string of words. "He says they're behind the rocks," reported Tuck, pointing a short distance away to a heap of boulders half covered in ivy and bracken.

While Siarles and Rhoddi collected the horses, Bran turned to Owain. "Do you think you can ride?"

His face was white and he was sweating, but his voice was steady as he replied, "I can ride, my lord."

"Very well." Bran nodded. He turned to Tomas. "I'm sending

you and Owain back to Cél Craidd. Tell Angharad and the others what has happened, and to see to Owain's wound. Then get Alan and bring him. The two of you meet us on the road—the place near the stream where the willows grow."

Tomas nodded. "I know the place."

"Then go. Ride like the devil himself was on your tail." To the others Bran said, "Find us something to drink and be ready to ride as soon as Siarles and Rhoddi return with the horses."

"What about the wagons?" asked Iwan.

"Leave them," said Bran. "If all goes well, we will own not only the wagons but all the rest of Elfael before nightfall."

The graves had been dug outside the abbey walls and the first bodies were being laid to rest under the solemn gaze of Captain Aloin and the chanting of Psalms from some of Saint Martin's monks when one of the gravediggers glanced up and saw, in the crimson light of a fading sunset, a body of men on horseback riding towards them from the direction of the forest. At first thought, he assumed it must be Sheriff de Glanville and his men returning at last from their part in the day's events, so he said nothing. But as the riders came closer, a trickle of doubt began to erode his assumption.

Captain Aloin, bruised and battered by his first encounter with King Raven and the lethal Welsh longbows, had determined to raise the issue of what he considered Marshal Guy's murderous incompetence with both the abbot and the sheriff at first opportunity. Clearly, Gysburne had to go. Aloin was thinking how best to put his case before the abbot and did not hear the monk speaking to him. He felt a touch on his arm and glanced up.

"Mon seigneur, regardez . . . " said the monk.

Aloin shifted his eyes from the corpse being lowered into the grave and looked where the monk was pointing. The approaching horsemen were near enough now to make out their faces, and what he saw was not the sheriff and his men, but strangers riding Ffreinc horses. *"Qui diable!"*

"C'est lui . . ."

"Qui?"

"The one they call King Raven," said the monk.

"Blind them! They have Sheriff de Glanville!"

Instantly terrified, the monks and soldiers scattered, running for the safety of the abbey walls. Within moments, the abbey bells were signalling alarm. The few remaining knights who were not seriously wounded scurried to arm themselves and meet the attack. What they met instead were seven outlaws surrounding a red-faced, sullen Sheriff Richard de Glanville bound with his own belt.

The town square had been given over to the wounded from the day's earlier skirmishes; they had been laid on pallets in the open air to have their injuries tended by the monks, who moved among the rows of pallets, bathing and bandaging the injuries and offering what comfort they could to the dying. The outlaws rode to the entrance of the square, and one of them—in good plain French—called aloud for Abbot Hugo. The abbot, heeding the warning of King Raven's approach, had hidden himself in the guard tower to be defended by the eight knights still able to fight. These had arrayed themselves before the tower, weapons levelled, ready for the attack.

When the abbot failed to present himself, the French-speaking outlaw called, "Marshal Guy de Gysburne! Show yourself!"

There was a movement at the foot of the tower. "I am Guy," said the marshal, shoving through the knot of men. "What is this?"

"This," replied Alan, putting out a hand to the sheriff, "is all that is left of the company sent out to plunder the countryside this morning. The battle is over, and we have come to negotiate the terms of surrender."

"Surrender!" scoffed Gysburne. "*Your* surrender, I expect."

"No, my lord," replied Alan a'Dale. "The surrender of Abbot Hugo and yourself, and those of your men still alive. You will bring the abbot now so that we can begin."

A knight moved to take his place beside the marshal. "You must be insane," he charged, "coming here like this." He flung an accusing finger at the outlaw band. "Come down off your horses, you filthy dogs. We will settle this here and now!"

Bran leaned near his interpreter and spoke a few words, which Alan passed on, speaking to Gysburne. "Who is this man? My lord wishes to know."

"I am Captain Aloin, by the blood! Come down here and—"

"Hear me, Marshal Gysburne," interrupted Alan, "you will tell your man to hold his tongue. We have nothing to say to him."

"You arrogant dog!" sneered Guy. He spat on the ground in a show of contempt. "There will be no talk of surrender."

Alan paused to confer with Bran, then nodded and continued, "Rhi Bran urges you to take a good, long look around you, Marshal," he said. "Unless you wish to join your men here in the square—or out in the ground behind the abbey—you will do well to reconsider."

Gysburne and Aloin exchanged a word, and the marshal replied, "We hold this realm by order of King William—"

"You have gone against my lord's longbows twice today and have been beaten both times. Do you truly wish to try again? If so, be assured that you and the sheriff will be the first to die—and then what is left of your men will join you." Alan paused to allow this to sink in among all those listening. Then, in a plaintive tone, he added, "Think, man. There has been enough killing today. Bring the abbot and let him surrender and put an end to the bloodshed."

Bran lifted the sword in his hand and, from their saddles, the archers on either flank bent the bellies of their longbows.

Guy hesitated a moment more, then called out, "Sergeant Jeremias, do as he says. Fetch the abbot."

"Prudence is a virtue," Tuck muttered under his breath as he watched the sergeant dart up the stone steps of the tower, "and wisdom is gained through trials of many kinds."

"Most always too late," added Scarlet.

There followed a tense and uneasy interval in which both sides glared across the square at one another. Captain Aloin, seeing that there were but six Cymry archers, one ragged monk, and an unarmed translator, was for rushing them on the chance that his few healthy knights might overwhelm them. "We can take them," Aloin whispered. "At most they'll only get an arrow or two off before we cut them down."

"Yes, and it's the first arrow that kills you," replied Marshal Guy. "Have you already forgotten what happened at the farm?"

"It is madness to deal with them."

"That is as may be," granted Gysburne. "But do you really want to add another slaughter to your tally today? It is the abbot they want. So, we let him decide."

At last the abbot appeared, and owing to the look of stunned horror on his face he hardly seemed the same man. Clearly, the last thing he expected of this day was to find his enemy standing in the town square delivering demands of capitulation. But that was how things stood.

"*Bouchers!*" he snarled as he came striding up, trying to rouse his innate defiance. "*Les meutriers!*"

"*Silence!*" shouted Bran across the yard. "Your life and those of your men is in our hands. Be quiet and listen if you want that life to continue another breath longer."

Alan relayed these words to the abbot, who subsided. "Ask him what he wants—my head on a silver platter, I suppose?"

Bran smiled when he heard this, and replied, "No, Abbot. Your head is worth less than the trouble it would take to carve it from your scabby shoulders. But here is what I want: you are to lay down your arms and leave Elfael—you and all your men, and any of the townsfolk who choose to go with you."

Alan translated Bran's demand, and the abbot's face darkened. "See here!" he protested. "You have no ri—"

"You sent soldiers against me today, and the issue has been decided. I claim the victor's right to the spoils. If you would keep your life, you must leave this place and never return."

"Allow me a moment to confer with my commander," said the abbot when Alan had finished. Without waiting for a reply, he turned to Marshal Gysburne. "Idiot, do something—you just stand there. Attack! Kill them."

"The first man to advance against them is dead where he stands, my lord abbot," replied Guy. "So, please, by all means lead the way."

"But they cannot get away with this—just like that."

"Just like that? They've killed nearly forty of our men today already, priest!" Gysburne's voice was an ugly growl. "Are you blind as well as stupid? Look around you. The soldiers you see on their feet are *all* we have left. How many more must die to satisfy your insane ambitions?"

The abbot gazed around at his sorely beaten troops, as if seeing them for the first time. "This is all we have left?"

"Every last one," replied Gysburne.

"Where are the rest?"

"Either dead or dying—and I'm not joining them. Not like this. Not today."

"The marshal is right, Abbot," conceded Captain Aloin at last. "Make the best bargain you can, and we'll go back to the king and raise a force large enough to vanquish these bandits for once and all. We were beaten today, but the war is not over. We live to fight again."

Bran, having permitted them to speak freely, signalled Alan to bring the discussion to an end. "Enough!" he called. "What is it to be? Lord Bran says you must give your answer now."

Abbot Hugo drew himself up to full height. He lifted his head, some of the old defiance returning. "I agree to nothing," he announced, "until you accept our conditions."

"What conditions?" Bran asked, when Alan informed him of the abbot's reply. "Perhaps you will accept the same conditions you offered those farm families this morning?"

The abbot's lip curled into a silent snarl.

"I thought not," continued Bran, speaking through Alan. "Here are the conditions I offer: you are to depart now, taking nothing with you but the clothes on your back."

This reply occasioned a long and impassioned plea from the abbot.

"What did he say?" Bran asked.

"The coward is afraid you mean to slaughter them all the moment their backs are turned. He wants safe conduct to the border of Elfael."

"Tell him he can have that, and gladly," agreed Bran. "Also, tell him that as long as he abides by the terms of surrender, no one will be killed."

When this was relayed to the abbot, the cleric made another impassioned speech.

"Now what does he want?" said Bran, losing his patience.

"He says he needs time to gather his things—his papers and such," said Alan.

"I wouldn't trust him further than I could spit," muttered Tuck. "Look at him—the old devil. He probably means to empty the treasury before he goes."

"I know I would," added Scarlet.

"Do not let them out of your sight," said Iwan. "There's no telling what he might get up to."

"They have to leave *now*," insisted Siarles. "With nothing but the clothes on their backs."

Bran lifted the reins and urged his mount a few steps closer. "Hear me, Abbot. That you live to draw breath when so many who served you are dead this day is insult to heaven above and God's creatures below. You will go now, taking only what you have hidden in your robes. Your men are to lay down their arms now. When that is done, you will all be escorted from Elfael—never to return on pain of death."

"What about the wounded?" said Gysburne. "They cannot travel."

Bran held a quick consultation with Tuck and Iwan, and Alan relayed the decision. "They will continue to be cared for by the monks of the abbey until they are well enough to leave." He pointed to the sheriff, who sat slumped in the saddle with his head down, miserable in defeat. "When the last is fit to travel, all will be sent along with the monks in the care of the sheriff. To ensure that this agreement is upheld, de Glanville will remain a hostage until that time. His life is forfeit if you fail to honour your part."

"You mean to kill them all anyway as soon as we're gone," said Gysburne.

As Alan relayed the marshal's words, Bran gazed at his adversary with an expression so hard it might have been carved of stone. "Tell him," he replied, "that if I meant to kill them, they would be dead already."

"How do we know you'll keep your word?" demanded Aloin when the translator finished.

"You will all die here and now if the surrender is not agreed," said Alan. "My lord Bran says that if his word is not acceptable, then you are free to take your wounded with you now."

The abbot did not like this last proviso, and made to dispute it, but Bran would not relent. In the end, Gysburne sealed the bargain by turning the sword in his hand and throwing it down in the dirt halfway between himself and Bran.

"God in heaven be praised!" said Tuck. "I do believe they're going to surrender. You've done it, Bran. You beautiful man, you've done it!"

"Steady on, Friar," replied Bran. "This is not finished yet by a long throw. We are dancing on a knife edge here; pray we don't yet slip." He cast his gaze around the square. "I greatly fear a fall now would prove fatal."

"All of you," said Iwan, pointing to the sword on the ground.

One by one, the soldiers added their weapons to the marshal's; Captain Aloin was the last to disarm.

Tuck

"What now?" said Siarles.

"Gather round, everyone," said Bran, and explained how they were to shepherd the Ffreinc through the forest. "We'll see them to the Vale of Wye and release them at the border of the March. Then, they are on their own."

"It will be dark soon," Tuck pointed out.

"Then we had best get started," Bran replied. "All saints and angels bear witness, on my life they will not spend another night in my realm."

CHAPTER 30

Castle Neufmarché

Four long days on the road brought the weary abbot and his footsore company—six soldiers, three monks, and two dejected commanders—to the busy market town of Hereford, the principal seat of Baron Neufmarché. Very possibly, the baron may have been the closest thing to an ally that Abbot Hugo possessed just then. Exhausted, begrimed from his journey, and aching from sleeping in rude beds appropriated from settlements alongside the road, Hugo lifted his sweaty face to the solid stone walls of the castle on the hill above the town and felt what it must be like for weary pilgrims to behold the promised land.

Here, at last, he would be given a welcome worthy of his rank. Moreover, if he sharpened his appeal with hints of clerical patronage—offers of perpetual prayer and special indulgences excusing the baron from certain past sins—Hugo imagined he might enlist the baron's aid to help him recover his abbey and reclaim Elfael from the hands of that blasted King Raven and his troop of outlaws. "Captain

Aloin," he called, climbing down from a swaybacked horse—the only one they had been able to commandeer from the first Norman town they had come to after leaving the March. "You and your men will rest and wait for us in the town. Go to the monastery and get some food and drink—my monks will take you there."

"Where are you going, Abbot?"

"Marshal Guy and I will go to the baron and see if he is of a mood to receive us. If all goes well, I will send for you as soon as suitable arrangements can be made."

The captain, who had risked life and limb in the abbot's service, and whose troops bore the brunt of the failure to roust King Raven from his roost, was not best pleased to be shut out of the proceedings now. But Aloin was too tired to argue, so agreed—if only that he might find a cool place to sit down that much sooner. He waved the marshal and abbot away, ordered his men to go with the monks and fetch food and drink from the abbey and bring some back for him; and then, sitting himself down in the shade of the stone archway leading into the town square, he pulled off his boots and closed his eyes. Before he drifted off to sleep, it occurred to him that this was likely the last he would see of the abbot. This caused him fleeting concern. Yet, close on this first thought was another: if he never saw that grasping, arrogant, conniving churchman again . . . well, all things considered, that was fine too.

Meanwhile, Bernard Neufmarché, Lord of Hereford and Gloucester, was sitting in his private courtyard gazing up at the sky for no other reason than that he thought a shadow had passed over him and he felt a sudden chill. He glanced up to see if an errant cloud had obscured the sun for a moment, but there were no clouds, and the sun shone as brightly as ever. The baron was not a man for

1236

omens or portents, but it did seem to him that lately—at least, ever since his lady wife had become smitten with all things Welsh—he often had odd feelings and sudden urges to do things he had never done before, such as sit quietly alone with his thoughts in his pleasant courtyard. Moreover, he often entertained the notion that strange forces were swirling around him, moving him towards destinations and destinies unknown.

He smiled at his own superstitious nature—something else he never did.

When Remey, his red-capped seneschal, appeared in the doorway to tell him that he had visitors, he felt the intrusion like a clammy dampness in the small of his back. Odd, that. "Who is it?" he asked, and before Remey could reply, he added, "Send them away. I do not wish to see anyone today."

"Of course, my lord baron," replied the seneschal smoothly, "but you may wish to reconsider when I tell you that Abbot Hugo de Rainault and Marshal Guy de Gysburne have arrived on foot, alone, and wish to speak to you most urgently."

"Indeed?" wondered the baron, intrigued now. "Very well." He sighed, rising from his warm bench. "Give them something to drink, and I will join them in the hall. I want to speak to Father Gervais first."

"Very wise, my lord." Remey withdrew to find the steward and order some refreshments for the baron's unexpected guests.

When his servant had gone, the baron walked slowly across the courtyard to an opposite doorway which led onto the porch of the little chapel, where he found the family's elderly priest sitting in a pool of light from the courtyard and nodding over a small parchment chapbook in his lap. The baron picked up the book; it was the

1237

Gospel of Saint Matthew in Latin. He was able to pick out a few words here and there, and the thought came to him that perhaps it was time he learned to read properly—not like a barnyard chicken pecking seeds willy-nilly.

The old priest awoke with a start. "Oh! Bless me, I must have dozed off. Good day to you, my son, and God's rich blessing."

"Very well, Father," replied the baron, and thanked the priest. "I would not disturb your meditations, but we have visitors—Abbot Hugo de Rainault and his marshal, Guy of some such. I believe you know the abbot?"

"I had dealings with him now and then," replied the priest, "but that was a long time ago. I would not say I knew him."

The baron considered this and turned another page of the book in his hand. "There must be trouble in Elfael," mused the baron idly. "I can think of no other reason de Rainault would turn up at my door."

The priest considered this. "Yes," he agreed slowly, "no doubt you are right about that. Then again, it has been very quiet of late. We would have heard about any trouble, I think."

"Perhaps not," countered the baron. "The outlaws own the King's Road through the forest. Nothing moves in or out of Wales that they do not allow—which is why I expect this visit means trouble."

"You know best, Bernard."

"Well, in any event we'll soon find out," said the baron with a sigh. "I'm going to see them now, but I wanted to ask if you would come with me to greet them. I'd like to have you there, Father."

"Certainly, my son. I'd be delighted."

The baron held out his hand to the elder man and helped him to his feet.

"These old bones get slower every day," said the priest, rising heavily.

"Nonsense, Father," replied Baron Neufmarché. "The years touch you but lightly."

"Bah! *Now* who is speaking nonsense?"

They strolled amiably to the baron's great hall, where, at a table near the wide double door leading to the castle's main yard, a very dusty Gysburne and travel-soiled abbot were finishing their wine and cheese. "My lord baron!" declared Gysburne, standing quickly and brushing crumbs from his tunic. "God be good to you, Sire. My thanks for your inestimable hospitality."

"God with you, Marshal," replied the baron, "and with you, Abbot de Rainault. Greetings and welcome. I hope you are well?"

Abbot Hugo extended his hand to be reverenced. "God with you, Baron. I fear you find me not at all well."

"Oh? I am sorry to hear it." The baron turned to his companion, and they exchanged a knowing glance. "May I present my dear friend, Father Gervais. I think you may know one another."

The abbot glanced at the elderly cleric. "No, I don't think so. I would remember. God with you, Father." He gave the old man a nod and dismissed him with a slighting smile. "It will save us all some bother if I come to the point, my lord."

"I am all for it," replied the baron. "Please, continue."

"There has been a wicked uprising in Elfael. Soldiers under the command of Marshal Guy, here, were slaughtered in an unprovoked attack and the fortress taken. In short, we have been driven from our lands by an uprising of Welsh rebels. I say rebels, and so they style themselves. In truth, they are little more than thieves and outlaws, every last one."

1259

"I see." Baron Bernard frowned thoughtfully. "That is not good news."

"What is more, they have killed a regiment of king's men under the command of one Captain Aloin. The few survivors have been driven into exile with me."

"Hmmm . . ." said the baron, shaking his head.

"These rebels, Lord Abbot," said Father Gervais, "would they be the same that control the King's Road through the forest? We have heard about them."

"The same, since you ask. Yes, the same. Their strength in arms and numbers has grown in these last months, and they have become ever more bold in their raiding and thieving. We had hoped that the arrival of the king's soldiers would have been sufficient to discourage them. Alas, they respect no authority and live only to shed innocent blood."

"How many men did the king lend you?" wondered the baron, summoning a steward with a gesture. "A chair for Father Gervais," he said. "And one for myself. Bring us wine too."

The steward brought the chairs, and another produced a small table for the wine; while the cups were filled, the abbot continued. "How many king's men did I have? Too few, by the rood. If we had received numbers sufficient to the task—and which I specifically requested, mind you—I am certain this disaster could have been averted. It is only through my most stringent endeavours at persuasion that any of us have survived at all."

Marshal Guy stared at the abbot, whose lies he almost believed himself.

"The attack was vicious and unprovoked, as I say," concluded the abbot. "They struck without warning and showed no mercy. Though we mounted a vigorous defence, we were at last overwhelmed. We were fortunate to escape with our lives."

"Yes, no doubt," mused the baron thoughtfully. "You said they were with you, the soldiers who survived the attack—where are they now?"

"In the town," replied Guy. "We've been on the road for four days without horses. We are all of us exhausted."

"Of course," replied the baron.

Guy could not fail to notice that the baron did not offer to send for the troops and bring them to the castle to be fed. In fact, the baron seemed more than content to let the matter rest where it lay. The abbot, however, was not so inclined; he had the spoon in his fist and meant to stir the pot with it.

"My lord baron," said Hugo, offering up his cup to be refilled. "How many men have you under your command?"

The baron waited while the wine was poured. "Not as many as I should like," he answered, raising his cup to his lips, "times being what they are." He drank a sip to give himself a little time to think. "No doubt, King William would be able to raise as many as required." He smiled. "But I am no king."

"No, of course not," replied the abbot. He placed his cup carefully on the table and looked the baron full in the face. "Even so, I would like to ask you to consider lending me some of your soldiers. Now"—he raised his hand as if to forestall an objection he saw coming—"think carefully before you answer. You would be aiding the church in its ongoing affairs, and that would place me in a position to pass along certain indulgences . . ." He watched the baron for his reaction. "Certain, shall we say, very *valuable* indulgences. The perpetual prayers of an abbey can guarantee salvation on the Day of

Judgement, as we know—which is ordinarily obtained only at great expense."

The baron, still smiling, said nothing.

"You could of course lead your men," continued Hugo. "I would not presume to usurp your place on the field. Indeed, I have no doubt that under your able command Elfael would be rid of the outlaws within two or three days—a week at most."

Baron Neufmarché placed his cup very deliberately on the table and leaned forward. "Your confidence in me is most gratifying, Lord Abbot. And of course, I wish I were in a position to help. Unfortunately, what you suggest is difficult just now—not to say impossible. I am truly sorry."

The abbot's face froze. His white hair wild on his head, his pristine satin robe stained from the toil of his flight, he appeared haggard and old as he gazed at the baron, trying to find a way over the stone wall so deftly thrown into his path. "Ah, well," he said at last, "I find it never hurts to ask."

"You have not because you ask not," declared Father Gervais suddenly. "Saint James . . . I believe."

"Precisely," murmured the abbot, thinking furiously how to rescue his stranded request.

"What plans have you made?" inquired the baron, looking to Gysburne.

"We will go to the king," answered Guy. "His men would return in any case, and we—"

"The king, yes," interrupted the abbot, rousing himself to life again. "It is *his* cantref, after all, and his to defend."

"My thoughts exactly," concurred the baron—as if the point had been under dispute but was now successfully resolved to the sat-

1242

isfaction of all. "It goes without saying that I *would* ask you to stay here and rest a few days, but I can see that the urgency of your journey requires you to reach Londein without delay. I only wish it was possible to lend you horses for the remainder of your journey"—he spread his hands helplessly—"but, alas, such is not the case."

"Your thoughtfulness is commendable," intoned the abbot. He slumped wearily in his chair, looking more and more like an old bone that had been gnawed close and tossed onto the midden heap.

"No, no," countered the baron, "it is nothing. Please, you will stay and eat something before you go. I insist. Then, my commander will escort you to rejoin your men in the town and see you on your way. You've come this far without incident; we don't wish to see anything ill befall you now, do we?"

And that was that.

A cold supper was brought to the chamber, and while the abbot and marshal ate, two mules were loaded with provisions to be led by a driver who would accompany them and bring the animals back upon their arrival in Londein.

As the abbot and marshal were preparing to leave, the baron and several of his men joined them in the yard to bid the visitors farewell. "God speed you, my friends," he said cheerily. "At least you have good weather for your journey."

"At the very least," agreed the abbot sourly.

"Ah," said the baron, as if thinking of it for the first time, "There was a sheriff, I believe, in Elfael. You didn't say what became of him. Killed, I suppose, in the battle?"

"Not at all," answered Gysburne. "Sheriff de Glanville was leading a division of men who were butchered by the rebels. All were murdered, save the sheriff, who was taken prisoner and is being held hostage. They promise to release him once our wounded soldiers are well enough to travel. Although, what is to become of him, I cannot say."

"I see," said Baron Neufmarché gravely. "A bad business all around. Well, I bid you *adieu* and wish you safe travels." He turned and summoned his commander to his side. "See here, Ormand," he said, "my friends are travelling to Londein on an errand of some urgency. I want you to escort them through the town and see them safely to the borders of my realm. Let nothing untoward happen to them while they are with you."

"To be sure, Sire." Ormand, a capable and levelheaded knight who served as the baron's marshal, put out a hand to his new charges. "Shall we proceed, my lords? After you."

The baron, standing at the topmost gate, waved his unwanted guests away; he waited until they were lost to sight in the narrow street leading down from the castle. Then, hurrying to his chambers, he called for a pen and parchment to send a message to the baroness in Wales informing her of the uprising and instructing her to tell King Garran to gather his soldiers and be ready to step in should the revolt show signs of spreading.

"Remey!" he called, waving the small square of parchment in the air to dry the ink. "I need a messenger at once—and see that he has the fastest horse in the stable. I want this delivered to Lady Agnes this time tomorrow and no later."

1244

CHAPTER 31

Londein

Cardinal Flambard pulled up the hem of his robe and stepped over the low rail of the boat and onto the dock. He dipped into his purse for a coin and flipped it to the ferryman, then turned and strolled up the dock, avoiding the gulls fighting over piles of fish guts some unthinking oaf had left to swelter in the sun. He raised his eyes to the Billings Gate and started his climb up the steep bank, stifling an inward sigh. It was his lot ever to run to the king's least whim and answer His Majesty's flimsiest fancy. Like two men sharing a prison cell, they were chained to one another until one of them died. Such was the price of standing so near the throne.

Standing? Ranulf Flambard occupied that gilded seat as often as ever the king sat there—considering that Red William remained in perpetual motion, flitting here and there and everywhere . . . stamping out rebellion, squabbling with his disgruntled brothers, resisting the constant incursions by the Mother Church into what he considered his private affairs. And when the king wasn't doing that, he was hunting. In fact, that was William: always at the sharp end of any conflict going or, failing that, causing one.

And the dutiful Ranulf Flambard, Chief Justiciar of England, was there at his side to pick up the pieces.

It was to William's side that he was summoned now, and he laboured up from the stinking jetty with a scented cloth pressed to his nose. The riverside at the rank end of summer was a very cesspool—when was it not? Proceeding through the narrow streets lining the great city's wharf he allowed himself to think what life might be like as a bishop in a remote, upcountry see. As attractive as the notion seemed at the moment, would all that serenity soon pall? It was not likely he would ever find out. Turning from that, he wondered what fresh debacle awaited him this time.

At the gate to the White Tower he was admitted without delay and personally conducted by the porter to the entrance to the king's private apartment, where his presence was announced by the chamberlain. Following a short interval, he was admitted.

"Oh, Flambard, it's you," said William, glancing up. He was stuffing the voluminous tail of his shirt into his too-tight breeches. Finishing the chore, he started towards the door. "At last."

"I came as soon as I received your summons, Majesty. Forgive me for not anticipating your call."

"Eh? Yes, well . . ." Red William looked at his chief advisor and tried to work out whether Flambard was mocking him. He could not tell, so let it go. "You're here now and there's work to do."

"A pleasure, Sire." He made a tight little bow that, perfected over years of service, had become little more than a slight nod of the head with a barely discernible bend at the waist. "Am I to know what has occasioned this summons, my lord?"

1246

Tuck

"It is all to do with that business in Elvile," William said, pushing past the justiciar and bowling down the corridor which led to his audience rooms. "Remember all that ruck?"

"I seem to have a recollection, Sire. There was some trouble with one of the barons—de Braose, if I recall the incident correctly. You banished the baron and took the cantref under your authority—placed it in the care of some abbot or other, and a sheriff somebody."

"You remember, good," decided the king. "Then you can talk to him."

"Talk to whom, Majesty, if I may ask?"

"That blasted abbot—he's here. Been driven off his perch by bandits, apparently. Demanding an audience. Screaming the roof down." The king stopped walking so abruptly that the cardinal almost collided with his squat, solid form. "Give him whatever he wants. No—whatever it takes to make him go away. I'm off to Normandie in a fortnight, and I cannot spare even a moment."

"I understand, Highness," replied the cardinal judiciously. "I will see what can be done."

They continued on to the audience chamber, discussing the king's proposed journey to Normandie, where he planned to meet with King Philip to challenge the French monarch's increasingly flagrant incursions beyond the borders of the Vexin. "Philip is a low, craven ass. His trespasses will not be tolerated, hear?" said William as he pushed open the chamber door. "Ah! There you are." This was spoken as if the king had spent the better part of the day in a harried search for the petitioner.

"My lord and majesty," said the abbot, once again resplendent in a simple white satin robe and purple stole. "You honour your servant with your presence."

William waved aside the flattery. "What is it you want? I was told it was a matter of some urgency. Speak, man, let's get it done."

"My lord," said Abbot Hugo, "I fear I bring unhappy tidings. The—"

"Who are you?" asked the king, turning to the young man standing a few steps behind the abbot. "Well? Step up. Let me know you."

"I am Marshal Guy de Gysburne at your service, Sire," replied the knight.

"Gysburne, eh? I think I know your father—up north somewhere, isn't it?"

"Indeed, Majesty."

"Are you the sheriff?"

"Majesty?"

"The sheriff I appointed to Elvile—or whatever the miserable place is called."

"No, Majesty," replied Guy, "I am the abbot's marshal. Sheriff de Glanville is—"

"De Glanville—yes! That's the fellow," said the king as the memory came back to him. "Came to me begging the use of some soldiers. Where is he? Why isn't he here?"

"That is what we've come to speak to you about, Highness," said the abbot, resuming his tale of woe. "It pains me to inform you that the realm of Elfael is in open rebellion against your rule. The rebels have slaughtered most of the men you sent to aid in the protection of your loyal subjects."

Abbot Hugo then proceeded to describe a realm under siege and a population captive to chaos and terror. He spoke passionately and in some detail—so much so that even Gysburne felt himself moved to outrage at the accumulated atrocities, though the abbot's description had parted company with the truth after the first few words. "If that was not enough," concluded Hugo, "the outlaws have seized the throne and taken your sheriff hostage."

"They have, eh? By the rood, I'll have their eyes on my belt! I'll hang the—"

"Your Majesty," interrupted Cardinal Flambard, "perhaps it would be best if I were to sit down with the abbot here and see what can be done?"

"No need, Flambard," retorted the king. "A blind man can see what needs to be done. Rebellion must be snuffed out swiftly and mercilessly, lest it spreads out of hand. These Welsh must be taught a lesson. I've too long been over-lenient with them—too generous, by the blood, and they've used me for a fool."

"Sire," ventured Cardinal Flambard gently, "I do not think this present circumstance is quite as simple as it might seem at first blush. I think I remember this outlaw fellow from Elfael, Sire. Was he not the same who came to you at Rouen with word of Duke Robert's treason? He uncovered the plot against you—that was why Baron de Braose was exiled, if you will recall."

1249

"Yes? What of it?"

"Well, it would seem that the fellow sought restitution of his lands in exchange for his service to your throne."

Abbot Hugo's expression grew grim. He had carefully avoided any mention of the circumstances leading up to the insurrection—lest his own part in the baron's conspiracy against William should inadvertently come to light.

"Ah, yes. Good hunting land, Elvile, I believe."

"The best, Sire," encouraged Hugo.

"What is your point, Flambard? We settled with Duke Robert and his schemers. That is over and done."

"Quite so, Sire," offered Hugo.

"If I may," continued the justiciar, undeterred, "I would suggest that inasmuch as this Welshman did not receive the reward he was looking for at the time, it would seem that he has taken matters into his own hands."

"I am to blame for this?" said William. "Is that what you're suggesting? *I* am to blame for this rebellion?"

"By no means, Sire. Far from it. I merely point out that the two matters are related. Perhaps in light of the present circumstance it would be most expedient simply to allow the Welshman to claim the throne. I believe he offered to swear fealty to you once. If you were to allow him his due this time, I have no doubt he could be persuaded to make good his previous offer."

William the Red stared at his chief counsellor in disbelief. "Give him what he wants—is that what you said?"

"In a word, Majesty, yes."

"By the bloody rood, Flambard, that I *will not* do! If we were to allow these rogues to murder my troops and then take whatever they want with our blessing, the kingdom would soon descend into anarchy! No, sir! Not while I sit on the throne of England. All such insurrections will be crushed. This rogue will be captured and brought to the tower in chains. He will be tried for treason against the crown, and he will be hung before the city gate. That is how we deal with rebels while William sits the throne!"

"Very wise, Your Majesty," intoned the abbot. "It goes without saying that you shall have my entire support—and that of my marshal."

William glanced at the abbot and gave a short blast through his nostrils. "Huff." Turning swiftly on the cardinal, he said, "Summon the barons. I want them to—" He stopped, did a rapid calculation in his head, and then said, "No, send to them and command them to raise their men and attend me at Hereford . . . Who's that?"

"Neufmarché, Highness," volunteered the abbot, with smug satisfaction at the thought that the baron would be forced to help in the end.

"All are to meet me at Hereford Castle with their troops. We will march on Elfael from there and take these rebels. I want sufficient force to quash the rebellion in the egg. It shouldn't take long." He looked to the marshal for agreement.

"A few days, Sire," said Gysburne, speaking up. "There are not so many that they cannot be brought to justice in a day or two of fighting—a week at most."

"There! You see? A week and the thing is done, the rebels brought to heel, and I can go to Normandie."

Cardinal Flambard pursed his lips doubtfully.

"Well?" demanded the king accusingly. "You're sulking, priest. Out with it."

"With all respect, Highness, I still believe an embassy to this nobleman, outlaw as he may be, would achieve the same end with far less cost—and then there is the bloodshed to think about."

"Nonsense," snorted William. "Hang the cost and bloodshed. The rest of Wales will see and understand by this that our sovereign rule will not be violated. Treason will not be tolerated. And *that* will save blood and silver in days to come."

"You can always invade Wales as a last resort, my liege," suggested Cardinal Flambard. "Should the embassy fail, that is, which I doubt . . ."

But William the Red was no longer listening. He had turned his back and was striding for the door. "Send to the barons, Cardinal," he called over his shoulder. "All are to meet me in Hereford ready to fight in six days' time."

1252

⊰ PART FIVE ⊱

For nine seasons long they lived in the woode
    The sheriff, they vexed, and his men.
The regent's reeve bent but did not yet break,
    and Rhiban was angered with him.

"I must regayne my land and my rights,
    My people needs all must be free.
Let's go with our bows to the true king's keep,
    And there with our points make our plea."

"I rede that not," said Mérian fayre,
    "Belovéd, repent of your haste.
Let's all of us, yeomen and women alike,
    Go with you to argue your case."

So soon they are gone up to greate Lundein Town,
    Wives, maids, and warriors same.
But when city folk 'round there them saw,
    They thought that besiegers there came.

The ploughman he leaves his plough in the fields,
 The smithy has fled from his shop;
And beggars who only a'creeping could go,
 Over their crutches did hop.

The king is informed of the forth-marching host
 And assembles his armies at speed.
He swings-to the gates and he marshals his men,
 Their progress he means to impede.

With Fryer Tuck, Rhiban approaches the king
 Under the true sign of peace.
The king gives him entrance, for he is full wise
 And wishes hostility cease.

"God save the king," quod Rhiban to he,
 "And them that wish him full well;
And he that does his true sovereign deny,
 I wish him with Satan to dwell."

Iwan awoke in the hall of the fortress where he had been born, raised, and grown to manhood. As a young warrior, he had become champion to Brychan ap Tewdwr, Bran's father—a hard man, fair but uncompromising, easily angered and stony as flint—and until the arrival of the Ffreinc invaders Caer Cadarn, the Iron Stronghold, had been his home. God willing, it would be again.

He sat up and looked around at the scores of bodies asleep on the floor around him, then rose and quietly made his way to the entrance, pushed open the heavy oaken door, and stepped out into the quiet dawn of a fresh day. He turned his face to the new-risen sun and drew the soft morning air deep into his lungs, exhaling slowly. From somewhere high above a lark poured out its heart in praise of a glorious day. "It should be like this always," he murmured.

Surveying the yard and surrounding buildings, he noted the alterations made to the old fortress during the Ffreinc occupation of the last four years—mostly for the better, he had to admit. The timber palisade had been shored up all around, and weak timbers replaced and strengthened; a covered guard station had been erected above the entrance gate; the roof of the hall had been replaced with new thatch and given stout new doors; there were new storehouses, a granary, and the kitchen and cookhouse had both been enlarged. There were other changes he would notice in the days to come, to be sure.

Still, it felt like home to him. The thought brought a rare smile to his lips. He had come home.

What the day held, he could not say, but if it was anything like the last it would be busy. Since the capture of the sheriff and the departure of Hugo and his retinue from Saint Martin's, Cymry had been streaming to the caer bringing provisions and livestock; men and women brought their families for protection and to help defend the caer against the retaliation all knew was surely coming. For now, they were housed mostly in the hall and outbuildings of the fortress—with a few, here and there, sleeping on the ramparts.

He washed his face in the big, iron basin beside the door and then walked across the deserted yard to an empty storehouse behind the stables. Outside the small, square wooden building he found Alan a'Dale sitting slumped against a nearby post, his head on his knees.

"God with you, Alan," said Iwan, nudging the minstrel with his foot.

Alan jolted awake and jumped to his feet. "Oh, Iwan—it's you. Here, I must have nodded off for a few winks just then."

"Never mind," said Iwan. "No harm done. Has our captive made any trouble?"

"Quiet as a lamb," replied Alan. He yawned, rubbing the sleep from his eyes. "Quieter, even. Maybe he has resigned himself to his fate."

"Not likely," replied Iwan. "Open the door, and let's have a look at him."

Alan untied the braided leather rope used to secure the storehouse and pulled open the rough plank door. There, huddled in his cloak on the beaten dirt floor, sat Richard de Glanville, Sheriff of Elfael, chained at the wrists and ankles, red-eyed from lack of sleep, his hair wild on his head as if he had been beating his skull against the walls of his prison. He spat and began cursing as soon as he saw who had come to observe him.

Iwan regarded the enraged prisoner for a moment, then said, "You would think a man so eager for the captivity of others would endure his own with a little more dignity. What is he saying?"

Alan listened to the sheriff's onrushing gush of abuse, then said, "Nothing worth hearing. Suffice it to say that he holds himself ill-used."

"No doubt," Iwan agreed, then addressed the prisoner. "If you think yourself mistreated now, Sheriff, try escaping and whole new realms of woe will open before you." To Alan he added, "Tell him what I said."

Alan did as commanded, which loosed another tirade in snarled French from the captive. *"Tuez-moi maintenant, ou relâchez-moi—je l'exige!"* shouted Sheriff de Glanville. *"Espèces de cochons! Vous m'entendez? Je l'exige!"*

"What did he say?" asked Iwan. "Something about pigs?"

"Aye, swine came into it," replied Alan. "More to the point, he says he wants us to kill him now or set him free."

"If it was left to me," replied the champion, "he would have had his wish long since. But our Lord Bran thinks he may be of some value yet."

1257

"Je suis désolé, Monsieur le Shérif, mais c'est impossible," said Alan to the sheriff, who spat by way of reply.

Iwan said, "I'll send someone to relieve your watch very soon. But before you go, see his water bowl is filled and get him some bread and a little meat if there is any."

"As good as done," replied Alan.

"And tell our hostage that he is going to be with us for a few more days at least, so he must try to endure his captivity with better grace than he has shown till now."

This was passed along to the prisoner, who spat again and turned his face to the wall. Alan retied the rope securing the door, and he and Iwan walked across the yard to the hall. "He is a right rogue, that one," Alan observed. "As black-souled a brute as ever strode the earth on two legs. What if King William will not bargain for his life?"

"Oh, he'll bargain, never fear," Iwan assured him. "For all his faults, de Glanville is a Ffreinc nobleman. And if I've learned anything these last years, it is that the noble Ffreinc look out for their own. William may not like de Glanville very much—no blame there, God knows—but he will bargain. All we need do is make sure the ransom is not so high that the king will refuse to pay."

1258

Following the eviction of the Ffreinc from the cantref, Bran had swiftly moved to occupy not only the fortress of Caer Cadarn, but the nearby town as well, reclaiming them for the Cymry. To that end, he had summoned the venerable Bishop Asaph to return and take charge of the abbey at Saint Martin's. Before being forced into exile by Abbot Hugo, the elderly cleric had been the head of Llanelli, the monastery Count Falkes de Braose had pulled down and rebuilt, and around which he had constructed his new town. As soon as Asaph, along with a goodly body of monks, was firmly installed and keeping watch over the town and its inhabitants—both the remaining Ffreinc townsfolk and the wounded knights, all of whom had been left behind by the abbot and his troops—Bran then moved to regain control of the fortress. This was swiftly done, since the Ffreinc had abandoned the stronghold before the last battle; they had never worried that King Raven would attack it in any case, and only ever kept a token occupation in place. Bran gave the defence of the caer and the valley round about to Iwan, with Siarles and Alan to help. He sent Tomas and Rhoddi on fast horses to ride throughout Elfael and to settlements in the nearest cantrefs and spread the news that King Raven had driven out the Ffreinc invaders and taken Caer Cadarn: all who could were to gather weapons and supplies and come occupy the caer—for safety, for defence, and so that Elfael's ancient stronghold would not be abandoned.

1259

With these measures in place, Bran had returned to Cél Craidd; and now, two days after escorting Abbot Hugo and Marshal Gysburne and their few remaining troops to the borders of the March, he planned his defence of his realm. He had spent the day at the caer working with Iwan on the fortifications there, returning at sundown. And now, while the rest of the forest dwellers slept, Bran sat in council with his closest advisors: Angharad, his Wise Banfáith, Friar Tuck, Will Scarlet, and Owain. Mérian's absence was a pang felt by them all.

"Forgive me, Rhi Bran, but I thought—" Owain gave a shrug. "What is the point of driving out the enemy if we still must skulk around in the greenwood like outlaws?"

"We have not seen the last of the Ffreinc," Bran told him. "Iwan and Siarles can direct the defence of the caer, but we need Cél Craidd as well."

"How long, then?" Owain asked.

"Until William the Red recognizes my claim," Bran replied.

"Surely, that cannot be long in coming," Owain said. "The king must recognize your kingship now. We've defeated his lackeys."

"Nothing of the kind, lad," Scarlet told him. "We've bloodied their noses a bit, is all. They'll come back—"

"In force," added Tuck. "You can bet your last ha'penny on that."

Two days of jubilation following the Ffreinc defeat had given way to more sober reflection. It was, Tuck thought, as if the farm dog that chased every passing wagon had, against every sane expectation, finally caught one. Now the forest dwellers were faced with the awful realization that there would be reprisals, and they were woefully outmanned. How could they hope to protect their gains? That was the question in the forefront of their minds, and it leached the joy from their hearts.

"The point is," Bran continued, "we will never be secure in Elfael until we have King William's seal on a treaty of peace and protection. I do not expect Red William to grant that without a fight—which is why we're still skulking around in the greenwood like outlaws." He broke another stick and tossed the ends into the fire, then declared the council at an end.

Scarlet rose and shuffled off to join Noín and Nia in their hut; Owain, whose wound, though still painful, was healing quickly, went to his rest. Tuck and Angharad were left to sit with Bran a little while longer. "You are right to prepare for war, of course," Tuck began.

"Did you think we would gain Elfael without one?"

"But perhaps King William's appetite for this war is no match for your own," the friar ventured, watching the firelight and shadows flicker over Bran's sharp features. "Perhaps even now he is searching for a way to avoid a fight."

"Perhaps," Bran allowed. "What are you suggesting?"

"We might send an emissary to the king with an offer of peace."

Bran regarded the little priest thoughtfully.

"Peace, that is," Tuck clarified, "in exchange for fealty."

"If William recognizes my throne, I agree to swear fealty—and the war is over."

"Over before it has begun."

Bran looked to Angharad sitting quietly beside the fire on her three-legged stool. "What do you see?" he asked.

"The friar is right to suggest an offer of peace," observed Angharad. "It is close to God's heart always." She rose stiffly and pulled the edges of her Bird Spirit cloak closed. "But unless God moves in the Red King's heart, peace we will not have."

The old woman made a little stirring motion with her hands in the smoke from the fire, then lifted her palms upward as if raising the fragrance towards the night-dark sky above. Tilting her face heaven-ward, her small, dark eyes lost in the creases of her wrinkled face, she stood very still for a long moment.

Bran and Tuck found themselves holding their breath in anticipation. At last, she sighed.

"What do you see, Mother?" asked Bran gently, his voice barely audible above the crackle of the flames.

"I see . . ." she began, drawing a deep breath and letting it out slowly as she searched the tangled pathways of the future. ". . . I see a trail of blood that leads from this place and spreads throughout the land. Where it ends, God knows." She opened her eyes, and her face crinkled in a sad smile. "What we sow here will be reaped not by our children, but by our children's children—or those who after them come. But sow we must; another course we have not."

"Yet, there is hope?" asked the friar.

"There is always hope, Aethelfrith," replied the old woman. "In hope we do abide. As children of the Swift Sure Hand, hope is our true home. You, a priest, must understand this."

Tuck smiled at the gentle rebuke. "I bow to your teaching, Banfáith. And you are right, of course. I used to know a bishop who said much the same thing. Hope is the treasure of our souls, he would say."

"It is an end worth fighting for," mused Bran. "It may be for others to complete what we've begun, but there must be a beginning. And we will carry this fight as far as we can before passing it on to those who come after."

The three of them sat in silence, watching the flames and listening to the crack and hiss of the wood as it burned. From somewhere in the forest an owl called to its mate. It was a sound Tuck had heard countless times since throwing in his lot with the forest folk, but tonight it filled him with an almost unbearable sadness. He rose from his place and bade the other two a good night. "God rest you right well, friends, and grant you His peace."

"Tuck," said Bran as the friar stepped from the hearth, "the Ffreinc are grasping, devious devils—false-hearted as the sea is wide. Even so, I am willing to swear fealty to Red William if it means we can draw a living breath without their foot on our neck. If you can find a way to speak peace to William, I stand ready to do my part. I want you to know that."

That night the friar did not sleep. Though cool and damp, the sky was clear and ablaze with stars; he found a place among the roots of one of the giant oaks and settled down in the dry bracken to pray for Elfael and its people, and all those who would not be able to avoid the war that was coming. He was praying still when the watchers rose, silently saddled their horses, and departed Cél Craidd to take up their posts on the King's Road.

CHAPTER 33

Hereford

"Spare me the excuses, Marshal," said King William, cutting off the lengthy beggings of pardon as read out by Guy of Gysburne. Following his eviction from Elfael, his fortunes had risen beyond anything he might have dared to hope. Owing to his intimate knowledge of the Cymry and the lands beyond the March, the young marshal had become an aide-de-camp to William Rufus for the purpose of what the king now referred to as the Harrowing of Wales. "Tell it to me plain—who has come?"

Gysburne allowed his gaze to drop down the parchment roll prepared for him by the court scribes in attendance. "Besides Huntingdon, Buckingham, and Surrey, who marched out with you, there is Bellême of Shrewsbury and de Reviers of Devon. Salisbury arrived a short while ago," he read on. "FitzRobert of Cornwall has sent word ahead and should arrive before nightfall. Earl Hugh of Chester—accompanied by Rhuddlan—will join us tomorrow or the day after. Le Noir of Richmond is on the road; he begs pardon, but the distance is too great and the time too short . . ."

"Yes, yes," interrupted the king irritably. "Go on."

"There is de Mowbray of Northumberland, who also sends regrets and apologies, albeit he is en route and will join you as soon as travel permits." Guy looked up from the roll. "As for the rest, we must presume they are either on their way, or sending petitions of pardon."

The king nodded. "There is one notable absence."

"Sire?"

"Neufmarché, of course. This is his castle, by the bloody rood! He should be here to receive us. Where is he?"

"I have spoken to his seneschal, Sire, who will say only that the baron is away visiting his lands in Wales. The summons was sent on, but it is not at all certain that it reached him, since the messenger has not yet returned."

1266

"I swear upon my father's grave, if Neufmarché does not appear in two days' time, it would be better for him not to appear at all."

"Sire?"

"The baron is a devious, two-faced schemer, Marshal. I snubbed him once to put him in his place—summoned him to attend me and then kept him wearing out the waiting bench for three days . . . and this is how he repays the insult. He should have learned humility."

"So one would think, Majesty."

William began pacing, his short, bowed legs making quick steps from one side of the chamber to the other. "On the martyrs' blood, I will not have it. Mark me, Gysburne, the king will not have it! I will make an example of this vexsome baron for once and all. God help me, I will. If Neufmarché does not appear with his men by the time we leave this place, he is banished and his estates in England fall forfeit to the crown. I vow it."

Gysburne nodded. Clearly, there was some deeper grievance between the two that had caused this rift between the baron and his sovereign lord. Whatever it was, Neufmarché was now in very grave danger of losing everything.

"How far away is Mowbray?" asked William, returning to the business at hand.

Guy glanced once more to the parchment roll in his hand. "The messenger indicated that unless he encounters some difficulty Mowbray will reach the March in three days' time. It will be the same with Richmond, I would expect—three or four days."

"The incursion will be over by then," fumed the king. He spun on his heel and started pacing again. "From what you have said, the Welsh have few horses, no knights, and only a handful of archers."

Gysburne nodded.

"Well then. Two days," decided William. "One day of fighting, and one to sluice down the abattoir floor, as it were. Two days at most."

"That is greatly to be hoped, Sire," answered Gysburne, all the while thinking that it was manifestly imprudent to underestimate the amount of havoc that could be wreaked by a single Welsh bowman. No one knew that better than did Guy himself, but he kept his mouth shut before the king.

"Ha!" said William. "I hope Neufmarché misses the battle entirely. Then I can banish him for good and sell all this." He looked around at the interior of the chamber as if considering how much it might bring in the marketplace. "How many men do we have now?"

"With the arrival of Salisbury's sixty-eight we have three hundred ten knights and five hundred forty men-at-arms at present. All are encamped in the fields outside the town." Anticipating the king's next question, Guy added, "Counting those en route should almost double that number, I believe."

"That, friend marshal, is counting eggs, not chickens," cautioned a voice from the doorway.

Both men turned to see a haggard young man in boots and gauntlets, his green cloak and long dark hair grey with dust. The fellow took one step into the room and went down on one knee. "Forgive my tardiness, Sire," he said, "I was on my way to Londein when I received your summons, but came as soon as I could assemble my men."

"All is forgiven now you're here," said the king, smiling for the first time that day. "Rise, Leicester, and let's have a look at you." The king crossed to the young lord and clapped him in a warm embrace. "Heaven bless you, Robert, I am right glad to see you. It has been too long."

1268

The king called over his shoulder to Marshal Guy, "You can go now, Gysburne. But bring me word if anyone else should arrive this evening." Taking the Earl of Leicester by the arm, he steered the young man to a nearby table and drew out a chair. "What news from your brother?"

"I had word this morning, Sire. Henry is well and has raised two hundred. He hopes to join us tomorrow."

"Two hundred! Splendid! Here, have some wine. You must be parched," said the king. He picked up the jar, but the younger man took it from him.

"Allow me, Majesty," he said, pouring out the wine. He handed the cup to his king. "It would not do for anyone to think that the king served a lowly earl by his own hand."

"Hang what they think," said William recklessly. He took the cup and raised it. "Let us drink to a swift campaign," he said.

"And successful," said the earl.

"Swift and successful!" echoed the king. "This time next week, we shall be on our way to France."

"To be sure," affirmed Leicester lightly. "God willing."

"The Almighty has nothing to do with it," declared William, his nose in his cup. He swallowed down a bolt, then said, "This uprising will be crushed in the egg. We need not invoke heaven's help to apprehend a few scofflaw rogues and rebels."

hy this *agonie?* I do not see that you have any choice, *mon chéri,*" said Lady Agnes Neufmarché. "You must go. You must attend the king."

"I know! I know!" snapped the baron. "But this king will be the ruin of us all. He is an idiot. What is more, he is an idiot with a stick and a hornet's nest."

"Perhaps it will not be as bad as you fear," counselled his wife. "And if you were there, *mon coeur,* you could see that our interests were well defended."

Bernard was not listening. "He has no idea of the hell he is about to loose on the land. No idea at all."

"You could warn him," suggested Agnes.

"Too late for that," the baron replied. "I know William. He's just like his father. Once he has his sword drawn, he will not see reason—only blood." The baron shook his head gravely. "There will be plenty of blood . . . on both sides."

"All the more reason to go and see what can be done to prevent it."

Bernard shook his head again and looked at the scrap of parchment on the table. He had received many royal summonses over the years and had always responded—to do anything else invited royal wrath at the very least or, at worst, banishment or hanging. There was no way around it; this summons had come at a most inopportune time: just when the baron was winning over the devotion of his Welsh vassals and preparing to expand his interests in the region, the king declared war. Neufmarché stood to lose years of patient work and hard-won goodwill to the unthinking ire of a flighty king who would tramp around the hills and valleys for a few days and then beetle off back to Londein or Normandie, as the whim took him.

Pretending he had not received the king's summons had bought him enough time to assemble his men and flee Hereford before the king arrived; not the wisest course, he would be the first to agree, but in his mind the only one open to him just now.

"There is something else," Agnes said.

Her tone made him abandon his ruminations on the problems posed by the king's untimely summons. He glanced at his wife to see the pucker of concern between her brows. "And that is?"

"Mérian," she said simply.

"Mérian," he repeated. His heart quickened at the name, but he stifled any sign of recognition. "What of her?"

"She is here," said the baroness.

"Alive—you mean . . ."

"Yes, alive and well—and *here* in this castle. She returned a few weeks ago—escaped from her captors, it seems. Although she does not admit to being held so. She—"

"Mérian . . . here," said the baron, as if trying to understand a complex calculation.

1270

"Oh, yes," said Agnes. "And the curious thing about it is that Garran has locked her in her chamber—for her own safety, of course. Given the chance, there is no doubt she would run straight back to the brigands who took her captive in the first place."

"How extraordinary," mused the baron.

"You should know, husband," continued Agnes, "that she has been saying some very disturbing things about you."

"About *me*?"

"Yes, *mon chéri*, about you. It seems that through her ordeal she has come to believe that you tried to kill her. And this is why she fled her home and family for the forest."

"*Mon Dieu*," breathed Bernard. Recalling his bungled attack on Bran that day, his heart beat faster still. "She thinks *I* tried to kill her? Has the poor girl lost all reason then?"

"Oh, no," his wife assured him quickly, "she seems as sane as anyone. But she does cling to this absurd belief—perhaps it was a way for her to keep her sanity while captive. I only tell you about this so that when you see her you will not be taken by surprise at anything she says."

"I see, yes." Bernard nodded thoughtfully, considering the implications of what he had just been told. "I will speak to her, of course, but not just yet, I think. Perhaps when I have decided what to do about the king's summons."

"Well, do see her before you leave," advised the baroness. "If we were able to make her understand just how ridiculous is this notion of hers, then perhaps she might be trusted to obey and we could release her." Lady Agnes smiled. "It is a very cruelty to keep her captive in her own home after the torment she has endured, wouldn't you agree?"

"Oh, indeed," replied the baron, his mind racing to how this meeting might be put off. He was not of a mood to deal with angry, contrary, and likely vengeful women just now, and perhaps not for a very long time. "A very cruelty, as you say."

CHAPTER 34

They're coming!"

At the shout, Tuck sat up and rubbed his face. He had been trimming the end of his staff and had fallen asleep in the warm sunlight. Now, he rose and, taking up the sturdy length of ashwood, gave it a swing once around his head, offering a grunt of satisfaction at the comforting heft of the simple weapon. He then turned around in time to see the messenger slide down the grassy bank and into the bowl of Cél Craidd. It was Prebyn, the son of one of the farmers whose house and barn had been burned by the Ffreinc when they ransacked their settlement a few days before. "They're coming! The Ffreinc are coming!"

Bran and Tuck hurried to meet the young man. "My lord Rhi Bran! Rhi Bran! They're coming," announced Prebyn, red faced and breathless from his run. "The Ffreinc . . . King William . . . they're on the road . . . they'll be here any moment." He gulped air. "There's thousands of them . . . thousands . . ."

"Steady on, Prebyn," said Bran. "Draw breath." He put his hand on the farmer's broad back. "Calm yourself."

The young man bent over and rested his hands on his knees, blowing air through his mouth. When he was able to speak again, Bran said, "Now, then. Tell me, what did Rhoddi say?"

"My lord Rhi Bran, he said I was to tell you that Red William's soldiers have been sighted on the road at the bottom of the long ridge—where the stream crosses—"

"I know the place," Bran said. "Rhoddi has given us fair warning. We have a little time yet." He sent the youth away with instructions to get something to drink, saddle a horse, and hurry back for new orders. "Well, my friend, we're in it now," he said when the messenger had gone. "I'll send Prebyn to the caer to alert Iwan and Siarles."

"God have mercy," breathed Tuck.

Bran turned and called out across Cél Craidd, "Scarlet! Owain! To me! Tomas—my weapons. To me, lads! The Ffreinc have been sighted."

This call roused the sleepy settlement, and soon the few remaining inhabitants were running here and there to help the warriors on their way. Out from a nearby dwelling, Angharad emerged. Bran hurried to meet her. "It begins," he said.

"So it does." She unfolded a bit of soft leather and handed Bran three coiled bowstrings. "God with you, Rhi Bran," she said. "These I made especially for this day." Her face froze then, and she drew a breath as if to speak, but thought better of it.

"I thank you, Wise Banfáith," he replied, placing the bowstrings in a pouch at his belt. "Was there something else you wanted to say?"

The old woman stared at him, her dark eyes peering as through a mist. Bran could sense her struggling . . . to find the words? To reach him in some way? Finally, she relaxed. Her face softened and she smiled, her wrinkled face smoothing somewhat in simple pleasure. "All that needs saying have I said." Reaching out, she covered his hands with hers and gripped them tight. "Now it is for us to remember."

"Then we will do the work of remembering," replied Bran.

The old woman lifted her hand to his face; then, rising on tiptoes, she brushed his cheek with her dry lips. "I am proud of you, my king. Do remember that."

Prebyn returned then and received orders to tell Iwan and those in the valley fortress that the king's army was on its way. "Come back as soon as you've delivered your message," Bran told him. "There may be Ffreinc outriders around, and you do not want to be caught." Then, turning to the rest of the Grellon, he said, "You all know what to do." There were murmurs of assent all around, and some voices called out encouragements, which the king acknowledged. Then, addressing Angharad one last time, he said, "Pray for us, all of you, and let your prayers strengthen our courage and sharpen our aim."

"I will uphold you in battle with psalms and prayers and songs of power as befits a bard of Britain," Angharad said. Raising her staff, she held it crosswise in her hands and lifted it high. "Kneel before the High King of Heaven," she instructed.

Bran knelt before his Wise Banfáith, to receive her blessing. "Fear nothing, O King," she said, placing one withered hand on his head. "The Almighty and His angelic battlehost go before you. Fight well and behold the glory of the Lord."

Bran thanked his bard and commended his people to her care. Tomas passed him his longbow, and Scarlet handed him a sheaf of arrows which he tied to his belt. "Come, friends. Let's be about the day's business."

Shouldering a thick bundle of arrows each from their sizeable stockpile of begged, bought, and Grellon-made shafts, they climbed the rim of Cél Craidd's encircling rampart and started off along one of the many pathways leading into the forest. Bran had taken but half a dozen steps when he heard a heavy tread on the trail behind him. "What are you doing, Tuck? I thought we agreed you would stay here and help Angharad."

"I seem to recall that we discussed something of the sort, yes," allowed the friar. "But *agreed*? No, I think not."

"Tuck—"

"You leave your flock in safe hands, my lord. Angharad needs no help from me, and I will be more aid to you on the battle line." The priest patted the satchel at his side. "I am bringing cloths and such for wounds. I can serve you better at the sharp end, can I not?"

"Come, then," Bran said, shifting the bundle of arrows on his hip. "It would not do to keep King William waiting."

They marched at a steady pace, moving silently as shadows through the thick-grown trees and heavy undergrowth of bracken and tangled ivy vines and bramble canes, guided by an intimate knowledge of the greenwood's myriad trackways—many of which would be invisible to anyone who had not spent years in the wild woodlands of the March. They changed direction often, abandoning one trail for another, always working south, however, towards the King's Road.

"Do you think William Rufus himself has come?" asked Tuck.

"Perhaps," allowed Scarlet a few paces behind him. "Where you find king's men, you sometimes find a king leading them. Red William is said to like a fight."

"It would be good if he has come," Tuck observed. "Then when we sue for peace he will be ready to hand."

"Sue for peace," said Bran. "I have no intention of suing for peace."

"I was not thinking of *you*, my lord," replied the friar. "I was think-ing of the Ffreinc. After a few days, I would not be surprised if we see a flag of truce from William's camp."

"A few days?" wondered Bran. "Tuck, bless you, we have but ten men! If we make it to the end of this day with body and soul knit together, I will count it a triumph."

"Oh, ye of little faith!" the priest scoffed, and on they went.

The land rose steadily beneath to form the long slope of the ridge that was the southern border of Elfael. At the place where the old road crested the ridge—dropping low as it passed between two steep banks of stone like a river flowing through a gorge—Bran had chosen to engage the enemy. They dropped their bundles at the foot of a high rock stack shielding them from view of the road below. While Scarlet and the others took a moment's rest, Tuck and Bran climbed the stack. On a flat rock jutting out above the road, they found Rhoddi lying on his stomach and gazing down the long southern slope towards the foot of the ridge.

"Thank God," said the warrior, squirming upright as Bran crawled up on hands and knees to join him. "Here I was thinking Prebyn had lost his way."

"Where are they?" asked Bran, squatting beside Rhoddi.

"Just there." He pointed down the slope towards a stand of oaks that grew beside the deep-rutted road. "They seem to have stopped. They've been there for a while, but they should come in sight any time now."

Tuck scrambled up at last and, lying on his belly, turned his eyes to the dark stretch of road far down the slope where the intertwin-ing limbs still overhung the deep-sunk path. The Grellon had cleared

1277

the trees for a dozen yards on either side of the defile to give themselves a clear and unobstructed view from above.

"How many do you think there are?" asked the friar.

"I don't know," replied Rhoddi. "A fair few, I reckon."

Bran returned to where the others were waiting. "Scarlet, you and
Tomas will command the other side. Llwyd and Beli," he said, refer-
ring to the two newcomers, both farmers' sons who had been added
to their number following the abbot's disastrous raid, "go with
Scarlet. He'll show you what to do. You'd better hurry. We don't
want the Ffreinc to see you."

The four left on the run, and Bran and Owain took up an armful of bundled arrows and scrambled back up to the lookout post.
"I see them!" said Tuck, pointing down the long incline. "That spot
of red, there. It's moving."

"It's one of the scouts," Rhoddi told him. "They advance and
fall back. They're plenty wary."

"They know we will attack," said Bran. "Trying to tempt us into
showing ourselves."

"Brave men," Tuck murmured to himself.

"Brave fools," amended Owain.

"Is this the main body?" asked Bran.

"I made it three divisions," Rhoddi replied, and explained how
he had worked his way down to the bottom of the ridge to see what
could be learned of the king's army from that vantage. "Most are
mounted, but there are a number on foot as well. And those I saw
appeared but lightly armed."

"They know they will not be facing knights on horseback," surmised Bran, "so they need not overburden themselves or their animals."

Tuck backed slowly down the rocks and into a little sunny patch nearby; hitching up his robe, he knelt in the long grass and, crossing his hands over his chest, he lifted his face to the clear blue sky above and began to pray, saying, "Commander of the Heavenly Host, You are no stranger to war and fighting. I know You'd rather have peace, and I'd have it, too, if it was left to me. But You know that sometimes that en't possible, and if peace was in William's mind I don't reckon he'd be marching against us now. So, I'm asking You to think back to Your man, Moses, and how You supported him in all his wrangles with the Pharaoh-Who-Knew-Not-Joseph. Great of Might, I'm asking You to support Bran and his men today—and like You did with the Hebrew slaves when Pharaoh chased them out of Egypt, I'm asking You to drown the armies of the enemy in their own bloodlust. Last but not least, I'm asking You to ease the suffering of the wounded and, above all, to treat kindly the souls of those who will be coming to stand before You in a little while. Grant them eternal rest in Your wide kingdom for the sake of Your most Merciful Son, Our Lord Jesus."

Tuck was roused from his prayers by the sound of a trumpet—small but bright as a needle point in the quiet forest. "Amen, so be it," he whispered and, crossing himself, he picked up his staff and hauled himself back up the rocks to where Bran, Owain, and Rhoddi were waiting.

The trumpet sounded again: a single long, unwavering note.

"What is the meaning of that?" wondered Owain. "Vanity?"

"Maybe they think to frighten us," suggested Tuck.

"Take more than a pip on the horn to send a shiver up my spine," said Rhoddi. He nocked an arrow to the string, but Bran put a hand on his arm and pulled it down.

"They're still trying to get us to show ourselves so they can mark

1279

our positions," said Bran, "perhaps get some idea how large a force they will face. If they only knew how few . . ." He let the rest of the thought go.

The trumpet called once more, and this time the trumpeter himself rode into view. Behind him came two knights bearing banners: a blue square with three long tails of green and a cross of gold in the centre surrounded by small green crosslets. Behind them could be seen the first ranks of knights; some of these also carried banners of red and blue, some with yellow lions, some with crosses of white and red.

"Owain," said Bran, "find yourself a good position somewhere just there"—he pointed a little farther along the rock wall—"and be ready to loose on my signal." As the young warrior departed, Bran turned to the friar. "Tuck," he said, placing a bundle of arrows upright at his feet, "I want you to see that we do not run out of arrows in this first skirmish. Keep us supplied and let us know how many we have left if supplies run low."

"Good as done," said Tuck. He scuttled back down the rocks and arranged the bundles in stacks of three which he then hauled up to a place just below the archers to keep them within easy reach. By the time he rejoined Rhoddi and Bran, the Ffreinc were much closer. Tuck could make out individual faces beneath the round helmets of the knights. They rode boldly on, scanning the rocks for the first sign of attack. Some were sweating beneath their heavy mail, the water glistening in the sunlight as it dripped down their necks and into their padded leather tunics.

Both Bran and Rhoddi had arrows nocked and ready. "We'll wait until they come directly below us," Bran was saying. "The first to fall will—"

1280

Tuck

Even as he was speaking there came the whining shriek of an arrow, followed by the hard slap of an iron head striking home. In the same instant, one of the knights was thrown so far back in the saddle he toppled over the rump of his horse.

"No!" muttered Bran between clenched teeth. "Not yet. Who did that?" he demanded, looking around furiously. "Rhoddi, Tuck—did you see? Who did that?"

"There!" said Tuck. "It came from up there."

He pointed to a place where the road crested the ridge and there, four men could be seen kneeling in the middle of the road.

The Ffreinc knights saw them, too, and those in the fore rank lowered their spears, put spurs to their horses, and charged.

"Take them!" cried Bran, and before the words had left his mouth two arrows were streaking towards the attacking knights. The missiles struck sharp and fast, dropping the foemen as they passed beneath the rocky outcrop. Two more knights appeared and joined the first two in the dust of the King's Road.

The archers on the road seemed unconcerned by the commotion their appearance had caused. They calmly loosed arrow after arrow into the body of knights now halted in the road still some distance away from the place Bran had set for the ambush.

"Tuck!" said Bran, furious that his plan had been spoiled—so needlessly and so early. "Get down there and stop them. Hurry!"

While Bran and Rhoddi worked to keep the knights pinned down, Tuck scrambled back into the forest and, tearing through the undergrowth and bracken, made for the top of the ridge where the unknown archers had placed themselves.

"Hold!" he shouted, tumbling into the road. "Put up!"

"Friar Tuck!"

Tuck recognized the voice. "Brocmael! God love you, man, get out of here!"

"We saw some Ffreinc down there and thought to put the fear of God into them, Friar."

"There's a battle on," the friar told him. He glanced at the young man's companions. "Follow me before the whole Ffreinc army falls on your foolish heads."

"Greetings, Bishop Balthus," said the man nearest him.

"Ifor! Bless your unthinking head, that's King William the Red's army you've attacked, and they'll be on us like bees on honeycomb."

By the time the newcomers reached the rocks, Bran and Rhoddi were slinging arrows down into the road as fast as they could draw. Shouts and screams of men and horses crashing and thrashing echoed along the rock walls of the defile. Already, the bodies were thick on the ground. Brocmael and his companions took one look at the chaos below and joined in.

"*Cenau* Brocmael," said Bran as the young man came to stand beside him, "as good as it is to see you, I could have wished you'd held your water a little while longer."

"Forgive me, my lord. I did not know you were lurking here-abouts. Have we spoiled the hunt for you?"

"A little," Bran admitted, sending feathered death into the churning mass of soldiers below. "Would you have taken on the king's army by yourself?"

"I thought it was just a few knights out for a jaunt in the forest." He paused to consider. "Is it really the king's army, then?"

"The king and his many minions, yes," put in Tuck, "along with a right handsome multitude of knights and men-at-arms so they won't be lonely."

1282

"Another sheaf, Tuck!" called Bran, loosing the last arrow from his bag.

Tuck hurried to the pile and, taking a bundle under each arm, climbed up to the archers. He opened one bundle for Bran and placed one nearby for Rhoddi, then took two more to Owain. Across the road, the arrows streaked through the sun-bright air as Scarlet and Tomas and their two farm lads loosed and loosed again in deadly rhythm. Many of the knights had quit their saddles and were trying to scale the rocks. Weighed down by their heavy mail coats, they moved slowly and were not difficult to pick off, but more and more soldiers were streaming up the hill to the fight.

"How many are with you?" Bran asked the young lord, drawing and loosing in the same breath.

"Besides Ifor—only Geronwy and Idris," answered Brocmael, "good bowmen both. I would like to have brought more, but we had to sneak away as it was."

"I expect . . ." Bran began, drawing and loosing again. The arrow sang from his bow into the heaving chaos below. ". . . that your uncle will not be best pleased."

"Then he must accustom himself to displeasure," replied the young nobleman. "It is the right and honourable thing to do."

"And now, gentlemen all," said Rhoddi, picking up his bundle of arrows, "the right and honourable thing for us to do is to leg it into the greenwood."

He started away, and Tuck risked a look down into the chasm. The dust-dry road, where it could be seen, was taking on a ruddy hue and was now made impassable by the corpses of men and horses piled upon one another. The knights and soldiers coming up from the rear were scaling the rocks in a courageous effort to get at the

1283

archers above. Even as he looked over the cliff, a spear glanced off a nearby rock, throwing sparks and chips of stone into the air before sliding back down into the road. Duly warned, Tuck scuttled back from the edge.

Bran gave out a loud, shrieking whistle and waved with his bow to Scarlet and the others on the high bank across the road in a signal to abandon the attack. And then they were running for their lives into the deep-shadowed safety of the greenwood.

A mad scramble through the forest brought them to a tiny clearing where Bran and his men paused to regroup. "We had the devils trapped and trussed," Brocmael said, breathing hard from his run. "We could have defeated them."

"There are too many," Rhoddi countered. "We dare not stay in one place very long or they'll surround us and drag us under."

"Like crossing a mud flat," said Tuck, hands on knees, his lungs burning. "The longer you stand . . . the deeper you sink." He shook his head. "Ah, bless me, I am too old and fat for this."

"Will they come in after us, do you think?" wondered Geronwy, leaning on his longbow.

"Oh, aye," answered Rhoddi. "Count on it."

There was a clatter in the wood behind them just then, and Scarlet, followed by Llwyd and Beli, tumbled into the clearing. The two farm lads were looking hollow-eyed and a little green. Clearly, for all their skill with the bow, they had never killed before—at least, thought Tuck, not living men. While Bran and the others exchanged battle reports, Tuck undertook to gentle the skittish newcomers. Putting a hand on each of their shoulders, he said, "Defending your people against the cruel invader is a good and laudable thing, my friends. This is not a war of your making, God knows—does He not?"

The two glanced at one another, and one of them, Llwyd, found his voice. "We never killed before."

"Not like that," added Beli.

"If there is sin in it," Tuck told them, "then there is also grace enough to cover it. You have done well this day. See you remember your countrymen whose lives depend on you and let your souls be at peace."

Overhearing this, Bran turned to address the newest members of his tiny war band. "To me, everyone," he said. "Believe me when I say that I wish no one had to learn this cruel craft within the borders of my realm. But the world is not of our choosing. We have many battles to fight before this war is through, and your lives may be required long since." He spoke softly, but in grim earnest. "You are men now. Warriors. And part of my Grellon. So grasp your courage and bind it to your hearts with bands of steel." His twisted smile flashed with sudden warmth. "And I will pray with every shaft I loose that all will yet be well and you will live to see Elfael at peace."

"My lord," said Llwyd, bending his head.

Beli went one better and bent the knee as well. "Your servant," he said.

Then Bran addressed those who had come with Brocmael. "Greetings, friends, and if you've come to stay, then welcome. But if now that you've had a taste of this fight and find it bitter in your mouth, then I bid you farewell and God go with you."

1286

"We came to help you fight the Ffreinc, my lord," said Brocmael. "As you know me, know my cousins. This is Geronwy." He put out a hand to a slender, sandy-haired youth holding a fine bow of polished red rowan.

"My lord Rhi Bran," said Geronwy, "we have heard how you bested Earl Hugh and would pledge our aid to such a king as could humble that mangy old badger in his den."

The other, not waiting to be presented, spoke up, saying, "I am Idris, and I am glad to lend my bow to your cause, my lord. It seems to me that either we fight the Ffreinc with you here and now—or we will fight them by ourselves later." A stocky lad with a thick, tight-knit frame, he seemed rough-carved of the same yew as the sturdy bow in his hand.

Scarlet, listening to the sounds echoing up from the road and forest behind them, called, "We must fly if we are to stay ahead of the chase. This way!"

1287

"Our horses are back there." Brocmael jerked a thumb in the direction of the road.

"Leave them," Bran said, hurrying after Scarlet. "Horses are a hindrance in the forest. Anyway, it isn't far."

The archers started away again, disappearing into the close-grown trees and bramble and hawthorn undergrowth. It soon became clear that Bran was leading them along a stony trail up the long slope of the ridge where, in no more than a few hundred paces, the path suddenly erupted in outsized stones and boulders big as houses, all tumbled together to form a sizeable cairn—a natural fortress of stone. In the gaps and crevices between the rocks grew holly and briar, into which had been driven stakes of ash whose ends were sharpened to narrow spear points.

"Find a place to hide and wait for my signal," called Bran, disappearing into a holly hedge at the base of the cairn.

"Up we go, lads," called Scarlet. "Get snugged in good. There are arrow sheaves in the hidey-holes. Keep 'em close to hand."

Brocmael glanced at his cousins, gave a shrug, and followed the others up into the storied heap of rocks. They picked their way carefully among the thorns and stakes to find that, in amongst the spaces between rocks, small wooden platforms had been prepared where the archers could stand. The warriors found bundles of arrows tied to the timber supports and stuffed into crevices within easy reach. "I told you Rhi Bran was cunning clever," Brocmael declared to his kinsmen. "And here is the proof."

"Did we ever doubt you?" said Idris.

"Shh!" hissed Scarlet, taking his place on a nearby stand. "Sharp and quiet, lads. They'll likely try to come by stealth, so be ready for the signal."

"What *is* the signal?" wondered Brocmael aloud.

"You'll know it when you hear it," answered Scarlet, "for you've never heard the like in your whole sweet life entire."

"And when you hear it," said Tuck, squirming up onto one of the lower platforms, "be sure you take no fright, for it is only our Bran distracting our foemen from the task at hand."

"If they're about thinking they can run us to ground," added Rhoddi, "they'll soon be thinking twice about chasing blind through the phantom's wood."

"The phantom," said Geronwy. "*Rhi Bran y Hud*—is that who you mean?"

"One and the same," replied Scarlet. "You've heard of him?"

"*Everyone* has heard of him," answered the young warrior. "Are you saying he is real?"

"Brace yourself, boyo," said Tuck, "you're about to see for yourself."

Fitting arrows to strings, the Cymry settled down to wait. The sounds of the chase grew louder as the Ffreinc drew nearer until, with a thrashing of branches and bushes, the first wave of armour-clad foot soldiers reached the base of the rock wall. There they paused to determine which way to go and in that briefest of hesitations were doomed. For as they stood looking at the boulders in their path, there arose a thin, bloodless cry—like that of the wind when it moans in the high tree branches, but no kindly breeze lifted the leaves.

The soldiers glanced around furiously, trying to discover the source of the sound. The cry became a shriek, gathering strength, filling the surrounding woodland with a call at once unnatural and unnerving, full of all the mystery of the greenwood—as if the forest itself had taken voice to shout its outrage at the presence of the Ffreinc.

They were still looking for the source of this fearsome cry when there appeared, near the top of the wall of stones, a strange, dark shape that in the green half-light of the forest seemed far more shadow than substance: a great, bird-shaped creature with the body of a man and the wings of a raven, with a naked, round, skull-like head and a long, wickedly sharp beak. This phantom moved with uncanny grace among the rocks, pausing now and again to utter its scream as a challenge to the wary, half-frightened soldiers on the ground.

One of the knights took up the challenge and, rearing back, loosed his spear, lofting it with a mighty heave up at the strange creature sliding among the rocks. The bravely launched spear struck the smooth face of a boulder, and the iron tip sparked. At the same moment, a black arrow sang out from the dark recess of the stones, struck the knight, and with a sound like the crack of a whip, threw him onto his back, dead before his body came to rest in the bracken.

It took a moment for the rest of the knights to realize what had happened, and by then it was too late. Three more arrows sped to their marks with lethal accuracy, dropping the enemy in their tracks.

The phantom of the greenwood gave out a last, triumphant scream and disappeared once more as the arrows began to fly thick and fast, filling the air with their hateful hiss. The Ffreinc fell back and back again, stumbling over one another, over themselves, over the corpses of the dead to escape the feathered death assailing them from the rocks. Those still coming up from behind choked off the escape, holding their unlucky comrades in place, thus sealing their fate.

And then it was over. The last soldier, an arrow in his thigh, pulled himself into the undergrowth, and all that could be heard was the clatter of the Ffreinc knights in full-tilt retreat . . . and then only the distant croak of gathering crows and the soft, whimpering moans of the dying.

1290

CHAPTER 36

Coed Cadw

The war between Bran ap Brychan and King William for the throne of Elfael continued as it began—with short, sharp skirmishes in which the Grellon unleashed a whirlwind of stinging death before disappearing into the deep-shadowed wood. These small battles were fought down in the leafy trenches of greenwood trails, down amongst roots and boles of close-grown trees and the thick-tangled undergrowth where Ffreinc warhorses could not go and swords were difficult to swing. The Welsh rebels struck fast and silently; sometimes it seemed to the beleaguered knights that the Cymry materialized out of the redolent forest air. The first warning they had was the fizzing whine of an arrow and the crack of the shaft striking leather and breaking bone.

And although there was never any telling when or where the dreaded attack would come, the result was always the same: arrow-pierced dead, and wounded Norman soldiers lurching dazed along the narrow trackways of the greenwood.

After a few disastrous running battles, the Ffreinc knights, whose fighting lives were spent on horseback, quickly lost all interest in facing King Raven and his men in the dense forest and on foot. In this, Coed Cadw lived up to its name—the Guardian Wood—providing the rebels with an immense and all-but impenetrable defensive bulwark against an enemy whose numbers far exceeded their own many times over.

Without the use of their horses, and forced to traverse unknown and difficult terrain, the knights' supreme effectiveness as a weapon of war became nothing more than a blunt and broken stub of a blade. They might thrash and hack along the borders of the wood but could do little real damage, and the elusive King Raven remained beyond their reach.

1292

Still, the king of England was determined to bring this rebel Welsh cantref to heel. He insisted that his commanders pursue the fight wherever they could. Even so, rather than send yet more men to certain death in the forest, they made endless sorties along the road and told themselves that at least they controlled the supply route and enforced the peace for travellers. King Raven was more than happy to grant William the rule of the road, since it allowed his archers time to rest and the Grellon to make more arrows and increase their stockpile.

As it became clear that there would be no easy victory over King Raven in the forest, King William moved to take the Vale of Elfael. The Ffreinc army set up encampment in the valley between the forest and Saint Martin's, laying siege to the Welsh fortress at Caer Cadarn. William invaded the town of Saint Martin's with a force of five hundred knights and men-at arms with himself in the lead. There was no resistance. The invaders, discovering only monks there—most of them French, under the authority of an ageing Bishop Asaph—

and a few wounded soldiers and frightened townsfolk with little enough food to supply those already there, simply declared the town conquered and effectively reclaimed for the king's domains.

Caer Cadarn was not so easily defeated. The occupying Ffreinc troops quickly learned that they could not approach nearer than three hundred paces of the timber walls without suffering a hail of killing arrows. But as the old fortress itself seemed to offer no aid or support to King Raven and the rebels in the wood, William decided to leave it alone, and trust to a rigorous siege to bring the stronghold into submission.

Day gave way to day, and sensing a cold, wet winter on the near horizon, with no advancement in his fortunes and the time for his departure for France looming ever closer, the king decided to force the issue. He called his commanders to him. "Our time grows short. Autumn is at an end, and winter is soon upon us," William announced. Standing in the centre of his round tent with his earls and barons ranged around him, he looked like a bear at a baiting, surrounded by wolves with extravagant appetites. "We must leave for Normandie within the fortnight or forfeit our tribute, and we will have this rebellion crushed before we go."

1293

Hands on hips, he glared at the grim faces of his battle chiefs, daring them to disagree. "Well? We will have your council, my lords, and that quick."

One of the barons stepped forward. "My lord and king," he said, "may I speak boldly?"

"Speak any way you wish, Lord Bellême," replied William. A thick-skinned warhorse himself, he was not squeamish about any criticisms his vassals or subjects might make. "We do solicit your forthright opinion."

"With all respect, Majesty," began Bellême, "it does seem we have allowed these rebels to run roughshod over our troops." The Earl of Shrewsbury could be counted on to point out the obvious. "What is needed here is a show of strength to bring the Welsh to their knees." He made a half turn to appeal to his brother noblemen. "The savage Welshman respects only blunt force."

"And yours would be blunter than most," remarked a voice from the rear of the tent.

"Mock me if you will," sniffed Bellême. "But I speak as one who has some experience with these Welsh brigands. A show of force— *that* will turn the tide in our favour."

"Perhaps," suggested Earl de Reviers of Devon, stepping forward, "you might tell us how this might be accomplished when the enemy will not engage? They strike out of the mists and disappear again just as swiftly. My men half believe the local superstition that the forest is haunted by this King Raven and we fight ghosts."

"Bah!" barked Earl Shrewsbury. "Your men are a bunch of old women to believe such tales."

"And yet," replied Devon, "how is this show of strength to be performed against an enemy who is not there?" He offered the craggy Shrewsbury a thin half smile. "No doubt this is something your vast experience has taught you."

Shrewsbury gave a muttered growl and stepped back.

"The rebels refuse to stand and fight," put in Le Noir of Richmond. "That is a fact. Until we can draw them out into the open we will continue to fail, and our superior numbers will count for nothing."

"To be sure," agreed the king, "and meanwhile our superior numbers are eating through all our supplies. We're already running out of meat and grain. More will have to be brought in, and that takes time. Time we do not have to spare." William's voice had been rising as he began to vent his rage. "My lords, we want this ended now! We want to see that rebel's head on a pike tomorrow!"

"Your Majesty," ventured another of the king's notables, "I would speak."

William recognized his old friend, the Earl of Cestre. "Lord Hugh," he said, "if you see a way out of this dilemma, we welcome your wisdom."

"Hardly wisdom, Sire," answered Hugh. "More an observation. When facing a particularly cunning stag, you must sometimes divide your party in order to come at the beast from unexpected quarters."

"Meaning?" inquired William, who was in no mood for hunting lessons.

"Only this, my lord: that unless these rebels are truly spirits, they cannot be in two places at once. Sending a single large force into the wood is no use—as we have seen. So, send three, four, five or more smaller ones. Come at them from every direction."

"He's right," affirmed Lord Rhuddlan. "They cannot defend all sides at once. We can cut them down before they can escape again."

"We never know where they are," complained another lord. "How can we muster troops on the flanks and rear if we cannot tell where they will attack?"

"We must create a lure to draw them into battle," suggested Earl Hugh, "and when the bastards take the bait, we're ready to sally in from the rear and flanks and slice them up a treat."

There was more discussion then, about how this might be best accomplished, but the plan was generally accepted and agreed: the king's army would adopt a new tactic. They would abandon their normal course of moving into the forest in a single large force, and would instead advance in smaller groups towards a single destination using a body on horseback as a lure to draw the rebels into a fight, whereupon the individual parties would rally to the fight and, sweeping in from the flanks, quickly surround them, cutting off any escape.

The king, satisfied that this plan offered a better way forward, gave his blessing to the scheme and ordered all to be made ready for it to be implemented the following morning. Then, in a far better mood than he had enjoyed since his arrival in Elfael, he ordered a good supper for himself and Earl Hugh and a few others, to celebrate their impending victory.

At dawn the next day, six separate hunting parties rode out with a seventh, larger body of knights and men-at-arms to serve as the lure to draw the rebels into the trap. Upon reaching the forest's edge, they dismounted and proceeded on foot; the six smaller bodies fanned out around the main group and proceeded with all stealth.

It was slow and arduous work, hacking through the vines and branches, searching out pathways and game trails through the dense woodland. But just after midday, their determination was rewarded when the main body of knights encountered the Welsh rebels.

They had been stalking through a rock-lined rill, following the stream, when suddenly the canopy of branches seemed to open and begin raining arrows down upon them. The soldiers took shelter where they could, pressing themselves against the rocks and stones, all the while sounding blast after blast on the trumpets some of them were carrying. The attack continued much as previous assaults, but faltered when there arose a great shout and a second body of Ffreinc knights entered the battle from behind the rebel position. This was quickly followed by the appearance of a third body of knights that drew in from the left flank and mounted a fierce resistance to the killing shafts.

The battle lasted only moments and ended as abruptly as it had begun. There was a rustling in the branches overhead—as if a flock of nesting rooks had just taken flight—and the arrows stopped.

As the king's men reassembled to gather up their wounded and reckon their losses, they found a longbow lying among the rocks in the streambed—one of the rebels' weapons. What is more, it had blood on it. And there was no Ffreinc body in sight.

After the ruinous ventures of the previous encounters, this was deemed a triumph. It shrank in significance, however, when the victorious troops returned to their camp in the Vale of Elfael to learn that the other three search parties had become lost in the forest and unable to join the battle as planned. In their confusion, they had stumbled upon a hidden settlement—a cluster of crude huts and hovels made of sticks and skin around a great oak tree and a stone-lined well, together with a few storehouses and a pitiful field. Caught unawares, the inhabitants scattered. But the knights did manage to kill one of them as they fled—an old woman who seemed to be in some way guarding the place with only a wooden staff.

Tuck half carried, half dragged the wounded Tomas through the wood, pausing now and then to rest and listen for sounds of pursuit. He heard only the nattering of squirrels and birds, and the rapid beating of his own heart. The spear, so far as he could tell, had been hurled in blind desperation up into the branches where the soldier had marked the arrow that killed the man beside him. By chance, the missile had caught Tomas in the soft place below the ribs on his left side. Tuck had been hiding in a crevice behind the tree and saw Tomas fall.

The archer landed hard among the roots of the tree, and Tuck heard the bone-rattling thump. Without a moment's hesitation, Tuck rushed to the warrior's aid and, with a shout to alert the others, hefted Tomas up onto his shoulders and started for home. He paused at the nearest stream to get some water and to assess the injury.

The spearhead had gone in straight and clean and, by the look of it, not too deep. There was plenty of blood, however, and Tuck wet one of the cloths he carried in his satchel and pressed it to Tomas's side. "Can you hold that?" he asked.

Tomas, his face ashen, nodded. "How bad is it?" he asked between clenched teeth.

"Not so bad," Tuck replied, "for all I can see. Angharad will be able to put it right. Is there much pain?"

Tomas shook his head. "I just feel sick."

"Yes, well, that is to be expected, is it not?" replied the friar. He offered the archer another drink. "Get a little more water down you and we'll move along."

Tomas drank what he could, and Tuck hefted him onto his feet once more. Draping the injured man's arm across his own round shoulders so as to bear him up, they continued on. The way was farther than he remembered, but Tuck kept up a ready pace, his short, sturdy legs churning steadily. As he walked, he said the Our Father over and over again, as much for himself as for the comfort of the man he carried.

After two more brief pauses to catch his breath, Tuck approached Cél Craidd. He could see the lightning-blasted oak that formed an archway through the hawthorn hedge which helped to hide the settlement. "Almost there," Tuck said. "A few more steps and we can rest."

There was a rush and rustle behind him. "Tuck! How is he?"

The friar half turned, bent low beneath the warrior whose weight he bore. "Iwan, thank God you're here." He glanced quickly around. "Is anyone else hurt?"

"No," he replied. "Only Tomas here." Tossing aside his bow, he helped ease the weight of the wounded man to the ground. Tomas, now only half-conscious, groaned gently as they stretched him out. "Let's have a look."

"I lost my bow," moaned the injured warrior.

"No matter, Tomas," replied Iwan. "We'll get you another. Lie still while we have a look at you."

Tuck loosened the young man's belt and pulled up his shirt. The wound was a simple gash in the fleshy part of his side, no more than a thumb's length. Blood oozed from the cut, and it ran clean. "Not too bad," Iwan concluded. "You'll be chasing Ffreinc again before you know it." To Tuck, he said, "Let's get him to a hut and have Angharad see to him."

As the two lifted Tomas between them, the rest of the war band appeared. "We're clean away," reported Rhoddi, breathing hard from his run. "No one gave chase."

Scarlet, Owain, and Bran were the last to arrive. Bran glanced around quickly, counting his men. "Was anyone else injured?"

"Only Tomas here," said Iwan, "but he—"

Before the words were out of his mouth there arose a piercing shriek—the voice of a woman—from the settlement beyond the concealing hedge. The cry came again: a high-pitched, desperate wail.

"Noín!" shouted Scarlet, darting forward. He dived through the archway of the riven oak and disappeared down the path leading into Cél Craidd.

The men scrambled after him, flying down into the bowl of a valley that cradled their forest home. At first glance all appeared to be just as they had left it earlier that morning . . . but there were no people, none to greet their return as on all the other days when they had gone out to do battle with the Ffreinc.

"Where are they?" wondered Owain.

The shuddering wail came again.

"This way!" Scarlet raced off along one of the many pathways radiating out into Coed Cadw.

Only a few steps down the path he found his wife standing in the path, bent almost double, her shoulders shaking with the violence of her sobs.

"Noín!" Scarlet rushed to her side. "Noín, are you hurt?"

She turned, her face stricken and crumpled with pain, although she appeared to be unharmed. And then Will looked at the bundle she cradled in her arms. It was little Nia, her arms and legs limp and still. The child appeared to be asleep, eyes closed, her features composed. There was a dark, ugly purple bruise on her throat.

Will Scarlet put his ear to the little one's face. "She's not breathing."

"Oh, Will . . ." sobbed Noín as Scarlet gathered them both in his arms.

1302

"Bran!" shouted Rhoddi. "Over here!"

A few dozen steps farther along the path lay another, larger bundle—a shapeless mass of bloody rags, as if a sack of meat had been rolled and crushed beneath a millstone. Beside what was left of this body lay the banfáith's staff. Bran halted in midstep, staring, his face frozen.

"Angharad!" he cried, rushing swiftly to the body. He sank to his knees beside the pathetic heap of rag and bone and gathered it into his arms. He knelt there, rocking back and forth, cradling the corpse of his beloved teacher and advisor, his confidante, his best and dearest friend.

After a time, Bran collected himself somewhat; he lowered the body to the ground and gently smoothed the hair from the old woman's face and then cupped her wrinkled cheek in his hand. "Farewell,

Mother," he whispered, gazing at the wizened features he had come to know so well. He placed the tips of his fingers to her eyes and drew her eyelids shut, then bent his head in sorrow as his tears flowed freely.

Owain and the others raced off to make a search of the path and surrounding wood. Bran gathered up the broken body of the Wise Banfáith in his strong arms and returned to Cél Craidd; Scarlet and Noín came after, bearing their beloved daughter. Tuck, ministering to Tomas's wound, looked up as Bran and Scarlet returned with the little girl and the old woman. He rose and ran to them as they laid the corpses beneath the spreading boughs of the Council Oak. "Who is it? Who—?" he said and stopped in his tracks. "Lord have mercy," he sighed when he saw who had been killed. "Christ have mercy."

Turning to Noín and Scarlet, he gathered them in a gentle embrace and prayed for them then and there, that the Lord of Life would give them strength to bear their loss. He did the same for Bran and, seeing as there was nothing more to be done just then, he returned to tending the wounded Tomas.

Bran was kneeling by the still body of Angharad when Owain came to him. "We found no one else injured, Rhi Bran. I think—I hope—everyone got away."

He was silent for a moment, watching Bran straighten the old woman's battered limbs. "Do you think they knew it was King Raven's home they attacked?"

"Those knights weren't looking for this place, but they found it anyway."

"But do they know what they found?" asked Owain.

"Perhaps not," allowed Bran. "But if they do come back, they'll come in force, and we will not be able to defend it. We will stay here

1303

tonight and abandon Cél Craidd in the morning—and pray we have at least that much time." He folded one of the old woman's wrinkled hands over the other. "Tell everyone to prepare to leave. We'll take only what we can carry easily. Bundle up all the arrows and extra bows—get Brocmael and Ifor to help you secure all the weapons. Tell Siarles to set sentries in the usual places. Go. We must be ready to move at first light tomorrow."

Owain nodded. "Where will we go, my lord?"

"It is a big forest," he said, brushing a wispy strand of hair away from Angharad's face. "We'll find someplace to camp."

It was early evening, and the sun had tinged the sky with a crimson hue when Noín finally brought herself to speak about what had happened, which was that after the war band had departed, the Grellon went about their daily chores. She and Cia had gone to gather blackberries in the wood; she had taken Nia with her, and the three of them had spent the morning picking. When they had filled their bowls, they started back. "Nia was so excited," Noín said, "she'd gathered more and bigger berries than ever before, and she wanted to show Angharad. So she went ahead of us . . . I tried to call her back . . ." Noín paused, choking back the tears. "But she didn't hear me, and anyway she knew the path. I let her go . . ." Her voice faltered. Scarlet, grim with grief, put his arm around her shoulders and pulled her close.

Bran offered her a cup of water. After she had swallowed a little, she continued. "We started back. Cia and I were talking . . . Then we heard shouts and voices . . . scared . . . We met some of the Grellon on the path, running away. Cél Craidd had been discovered, they said; the Ffreinc had found us. Everyone had scattered, and everyone had got away. 'What about Nia? Did anyone see my little girl?'"

Noín shook her head, her lips trembling. "No one had seen her. I started running toward the settlement. But it was all over." She shook her head in bewilderment. "The Ffreinc were gone. There was no one around. I began calling for Nia, but there was no answer. I started looking for her, calling her . . . I thought, I hoped—maybe one of the others picked her up in the confusion, someone had taken her to safety. I searched one path and then another until . . ." She let out a wrenching sob and lowered her face into her hands. "I found her on the path—just before you came. I think she got trampled by a horse . . . one of the hooves struck her head . . ." She turned eyes full of tears to the others. "How could anyone do that to a little child? How could they?"

Bran and Tuck left Noín and Scarlet to their grief then and went to see what could be done for Tomas. The wounded warrior had been laid out on a bed of rushes covered with a cloak.

"He is sleeping," Rhoddi told them. "I did as you said, Friar—I put a clean cloth and some dry moss on the cut. It seems to have stopped bleeding."

"That's a good sign, I think," said Tuck.

Bran nodded. He raised his eyes; the tops of the tallest trees were fading into the twilight. "We must bury Nia and Angharad soon. I will dig the graves."

"Allow me, my lord," said Rhoddi.

Bran nodded. "We'll do it together."

"I want to help," said Tuck.

"Is it wise to leave him alone?" said Rhoddi, with a nod towards Tomas.

Tuck glanced at the sleeping warrior beside him. "We'll hear him if he wakes," he said. So the three went off to begin the bleak task of digging the graves: one pitifully small for Nia, and another for Angharad. Iwan and Scarlet came to help, too, and all took their turn with the shovel. While they were at their work, some of the Grellon who had fled the settlement began coming back—one by one, and then in knots of two or three—and they gave their own account of what had happened.

The settlement had been discovered by a body of Ffreinc knights on horseback—eight or ten, maybe more—who then attacked. The forest-dwellers fled, with the knights in pursuit. They would have been caught, all of them, but Angharad turned and blocked the trail. They had last seen her facing the enemy with her staff raised high, a cry of challenge on her lips; and though it cost her life, the enemy did not follow them into the forest. The returning Grellon were shocked to find their good bard had been killed, and dear little Nia as well. The tears and weeping began all over again.

The women attended Noín, helping her wash and dress little Nia in her best clothes. They combed her hair and plaited flowers in the braids, and laid her on a bed of fresh green rushes. They washed the blood from Angharad's body and dressed her in a clean gown and brought her staff to lay beside her. Bran made a cross for the graves using arrows which he bound together with bowstring. Meanwhile, Tuck moved here and there, comforting his forest flock, giving them such solace as he possessed. He tried to instil some hope in the hearts of the grieving, and show a way to a better day ahead. But his own heart was not in it, and his words sounded hollow even to himself.

When the graves were ready, Scarlet came and, taking Noín by the hand, said, "It is time, my heart." Noín nodded silently. He knelt and gathered up his daughter and carried her to the new-dug grave; Noín walked beside him, her eyes on the bundle in her husband's arms.

Iwan and Owain bent to Angharad, but Bran said, "Wait. Bring her Bird Spirit cloak and put it on her. And her staff. We will bury her as befits the last True Bard of Britain."

Owain fetched the black-feathered cloak and helped Bran wrap it around the old woman, and the two bodies were laid to rest in the soft earth. Iwan brought Angharad's harp to place in the grave, but Bran prevented him. "No," he said, taking the harp. "This I will keep." As he cradled the harp to his shoulder, his mind flashed with the memory of one of their last partings. *All that needs saying have I said,* his Wise Banfáith had told him. *Now it is for us to remember.*

He held the harp, and his mind returned to the time of their first meeting—in the old woman's winter cave hidden deep in the forest. There, she had healed his body with her art, and healed his soul with her songs. "A raven you are, and a raven you shall remain—until the day you fulfil your vow," Bran murmured, remembering the words of the old story. He turned his eyes one last time to the face of his friend—a face he had once considered almost unutterably ugly: the wide, downturned mouth and jutting chin; the bulbous nose; the small, keen eyes burning out from a countenance so wrinkled it seemed to be nothing but creases, lines, and folds. Death had not improved her appearance, but Bran had long ago ceased to regard her looks, seeing instead only the bright-burning radiance of a soul alight with wisdom. "She called me a king."

"My lord?" said Iwan. "Did you say something?"

"She had never done that before, you see? Not until now."

Darkness deepened in the greenwood. The Grellon lit pitch torches at the head of each body and began a service for the dead which Tuck led, praying softly through the Psalms and the special prayers for those recently deceased. It was a service he had performed

1307

as many times as christenings and weddings combined, and he knew
it by heart.

The mourners held vigil through the night. Bran, Scarlet, and
Noín kept watch while others came and went silently, or with a few
words of comfort and condolence. Twice in the night, Bran was heard
to groan, his shoulders heaving with silent sobs. The tie that had
bound him and Angharad together was strong, and it had been cruelly severed, the wound deep and raw.

Then, at sunrise, the Grellon gathered at the graveside. Tuck said
another prayer for the dead and for those who must resume life without them. Noín and Will wept as the dirt was replaced and heaped over
the mounds. Bran pressed the small wooden crosses he had made into
the graves and then knelt, solemn but dry-eyed, and said a last, silent
farewell to the woman who had saved his life. Then, while the rest of
the forest-dwellers prepared to abandon Cél Craidd, Tuck went to look
in on Tomas. Bran joined him a little later to ask after his injured archer.
"My lord," said Tuck softly, "I fear we have lost a good warrior."

"No . . ." sighed Bran.

"His wounds were greater than we knew," the friar explained. "I
think he must have died in the night. I am sorry." He looked sadly
at the still body beside him. "If my skill had been greater, I might
have saved him."

"And if there had been no battle and he had not been wounded . . ."
Bran shook his head and let the rest go unsaid. He pressed a hand to
Tomas's chest and thanked the dead warrior for his good service, and
released him to his rest. Then, bidding Tuck to have the body prepared for burial, he rose and went to dig another grave.

1308

CHAPTER 38

Caer Rhodl

"When were you going to tell me that Friar Tuck had been here?" asked Mérian, her tone deceptively sweet. "Or did you plan to tell me at all, brother mine?"

"I did not think it any of your concern," answered Garran dismissively. He leaned back in his chair and regarded his sister with suspicion. And then the thought struck him. "But how did *you* know they had come here?"

Mérian offered Garran a superior smile. "Bran has been a visitor to these halls more often than you know. Did you really think he would leave without seeing me?"

The king of Eiwas remained unmoved. "You said you wanted to speak to me. I hope it was not merely to berate me. If so, you are wasting your breath."

"I did not come to berate you, but to tell you that there is no need to keep me locked up. I will not try to escape, or leave Caer Rhodl without your permission and blessing."

"Coming to your senses at last, dear sister?" intoned Garran. "May I ask what has brought about this change of heart?"

"I have come to see that there is no point in leaving here without you and your war band to accompany me." Garran opened his mouth to reject that possibility outright, but Mérian did not give him the chance. "Bran and his people are fighting for their lives in Elfael. We must help them. We must ride at once—"

Garran held up his hand. "We have had this discussion before," he said, "and I have not changed my mind. Even if I was so inclined to raise the war band for them, the time for that is past, I fear."

"Past?" inquired Mérian. "Why past?"

"King William has raised his entire army and now occupies Elfael himself. It is said he has more than a thousand knights and men-at-arms encamped in the valley."

"What of Bran and his people? Is there any word?"

"Only that they fight on—foolishly, it seems to me, since no one has come to their aid."

"Then that is all the more reason to raise the war band," Mérian insisted. Clasping her hands before her, she stepped nearer her recalcitrant brother. "You must see that, Garran. We have to help them."

"Ride against King William and his army?" laughed Garran. "There is no force in all Britain that could defeat him now."

There came a knock on the door of the king's chamber, and Luc, the king's seneschal, entered. "Forgive me, Sire, but Baron Neufmarché has come and would see you most urgently. He says—"

Before the servant could finish, Baron Bernard himself pushed past him and stepped into the room. One glance at Mérian brought him up short. He stared at her as if at a ghost, then collected himself. "I see I am intruding," he said. "I am sorry. I will come back in—"

"Pray, do not leave, Baron," said Garran. Mérian noticed her brother's French had become quite fluent—as had her own since returning to Caer Rhodl. "Stay. This concerns you, too, I think. Mérian here is urging us to raise an army and ride to the defence of Elfael. She thinks we should take arms against the king of England's forces for the sake of Bran ap Brychan and his pitiful band of rebels."

The baron raised his eyebrows, but did not condemn the notion. "Does she indeed?" he said, stepping farther into the room. "I would like to hear her reasons." He made a stiffly formal bow to the young woman. "Please, speak freely, my lady. I assure you no harm will come of it."

Garran was quick to protest. "With all respect, Baron, my sister's fancies cannot be seriously entertained."

"Fancies!" snapped Mérian.

"Please," replied Neufmarché. He appealed to Mérian. "If you would kindly explain, I would like to hear your reasons."

Fearing some kind of trap was being laid for her, she replied, "Baron, you have the advantage here. Sending our war band to aid Bran against the king is treason, and if I were to argue such a course before one of the king's noblemen, it would be to my death—if such a thing were to be reported. In any event, aiding Elfael would go against your own interests, and I cannot think you, or anyone else, would willingly choose such a course."

"Exactly!" crowed Garran.

"Do not be so hasty," cautioned the baron. "As it happens, aiding Elfael may sit with my interests very nicely."

Garran stared at his father-in-law and patron, momentarily lost for words.

"Does this surprise you?" wondered the baron. "So long as we are speaking freely, the king is not always right, you know. William Rufus is not the man his father was. He makes mistakes. One of his early mistakes was to cross the Neufmarchés—but that is not at issue here."

He began pacing before the young king's chair, to Mérian's mind the very image of a man wrestling with an intractable problem. She watched him, hardly daring to hope that something good might come from what he was about to say.

"It comes to this—the king has ordered me to attend him and support him in this war against the rebel cantref. To aid the king is to undo all I have worked for in Wales for the last ten years or more. This I will not do—especially since my own grandchildren, when they arrive, will be Welsh. And yet"—he raised a finger—"to fail to respond to a royal summons is considered treason, and my life and lands are forfeit if I do not ride to the aid of the king."

1312

The baron regarded Mérian as he concluded. "The king has left me with a very difficult choice, but a clear one."

Garran did not see it, but Mérian did.

"Which would be?" asked the young king.

"You know it, my lady," said Neufmarché, holding her in his gaze. "I suspect you've known it for some time."

Mérian nodded. "You must march against the king."

"Surely not," complained Garran. "We cannot hope to achieve anything against William and all his men."

"Perhaps not," replied Bernard, "but that is my—that is *our*—only choice. If we hope to hold onto what we have, we must defeat the king—or at least hold him off until peace can be reached."

"A peace," volunteered Mérian, "that will include justice for Elfael and pardon for all those who have fought for what is right."

"*Amnistie royale, oui,*" replied the baron.

"But we risk everything," Garran pointed out.

"Our only hope of keeping what we have is to risk it all," agreed Neufmarché.

Garran fell silent, contemplating the enormous jolt his life and reign as king had just taken.

"And that, I suspect," continued the baron after a moment, "is why the Welsh noblemen have come."

"Cymry noblemen?" said Mérian. "Here?"

"*Mais oui,*" Neufmarché assured her, "it is the reason I intruded just now. A number of Welsh noblemen have arrived, and are seeking audience with the king. I asked Luc to bid them wait a little because I wanted to speak with my son-in-law first." He smiled. "So, you see, *c'est fortuit.*"

"*Non,*" corrected Mérian, "*c'est la providence.*" She turned to her brother, freshening her appeal in Welsh. "Don't you see, Garran? Riding to the aid of Elfael *is* the only way. And with the baron's help we cannot fail."

The young king was far from convinced, but as client to the baron, he knew he must do whatever his overlord commanded. Still, he sought to put off his consent a little longer. "Perhaps," he suggested, "before going any further, we should see who has come, and hear what they have to say."

"They have been brought to the hall," said Baron Bernard, "and the serving maids instructed to give them refreshment." He held out his arm to Mérian who, after a slight hesitation, took it. Garran went ahead of them, and the baron followed with Mérian on his arm. As soon as Garran had left the room, the baron turned to her and whispered, "Lady Mérian," he said, "hear me—we have not much time.

I do most humbly beg your pardon, for I have not always had your best interest at heart. I pray your forgiveness, my lady, and vow that in the days ahead I will make every effort to find a way to make up for my past mistakes."

"You are forgiven, my lord baron," replied Mérian nicely. "What is more, your determination to aid Bran and Elfael absolves a great many trespasses. I pray now that we are not too late."

"So pray we all," replied the baron.

They followed King Garran and his seneschal into the hall, where they found the benches full of strangers. Some of the king's men had already gathered to host the visitors, and all rose to their feet when the young king appeared.

"My lord king," said one of the visitors, stepping forward at once, "in the name of Our Saviour Jesus Christ, I give you good greeting. I am Lord Llewelyn of Aberffraw at your service." He gave a small bow of deference. "I present to you, my lord, King Gruffydd of Gwynedd"—a tall, lean man stepped forward—"and with him, my lord, King Dafydd ap Owain, lord of Snowdon"—a stern-faced battle chief stepped forward and, putting a hand to the hilt of his sword, gave a nod of his head—"and Iestyn ap Gwrgan, king of Gwent." The last of the great Welsh noblemen stepped forward and made his obeisance to the young king.

"Peace, and welcome to you all," said Garran, deeply impressed that such renowned men should have come to beg audience with him. "You honour me with your presence, my lords. Please, be seated again, and fill the cups. I am eager to hear what has brought you to Eiwas and to my hall."

"Lord Garran, if it please you," said the lanky nobleman called Gruffydd, "I speak for all of us when I say that we are grateful for your friendship and would like nothing more than to sit with you and drink your health and that of your people." His eyes shifted to the baron and he hesitated for a moment, then continued, "Unfortunately, we cannot partake of that estimable luxury. Time presses. Do not think me rude, therefore, if I decline your hospitality. We are passing through your lands on our way to Elfael."

"Elfael," remarked Garran with a glance at his sister, who was quietly translating for Baron Neufmarché. "It does seem to be a busy place of late."

"I will be brief," said Gruffydd. "We go to join forces with Bran ap Brychan to aid him in his fight to reclaim the throne of Elfael from the Ffreinc. As God is my witness, Lord Bran has done me a very great service which I can never hope to repay in full. But I go to do what I can. Moreover, it has been borne upon me with some considerable force"—here he glanced at Lord Llewelyn—"that if any of us would be free in our own land, we must all be free. To that end, I have persuaded these lords to join me." He put out a hand to his august companions and their commanders, who filled the benches at the board. He stepped before Garran to address him more directly. "I would persuade you, too, my lord." He regarded the young king steadily. "Join us, Rhi Garran. Help us right a great wrong and win justice for Elfael, and all who call Cymru home, against the Ffreinc and their overreaching king."

One of the lords stepped near to Gruffydd just then and whispered something in his ear. The king of Gwynedd squared himself, turned, and gazed boldly at the baron. "It seems I have spoken too freely," Gruffydd said. "I am informed that we have a Ffreinc baron among us. Had I known that he was here—"

"Truly," said Garran, "there is no harm done." He turned and

1315

beckoned the baron and his sister nearer. "My lords, I present Baron Neufmarché, my liege lord, and with him, my sister Lady Mérian."

"My lord baron," said Gruffydd in stiff acknowledgement of Neufmarché. His hand went to the sword at his side and stayed there.

"As the baron is my overlord," Garran continued, "it is well that he has heard your intentions for himself."

"How so?" said Gruffydd suspiciously.

"For the fact that this was the very course he himself was urging only moments before we joined you here."

"*Mes seigneurs et mes rois,*" said the baron. "*C'est vrai.*" Mérian translated for the Welsh kings, and explained that the baron had defied Red William's summons and had come to Eiwas instead, and that he and Garran had just been discussing the need to aid the rebels of Elfael in their struggle against the crown. After a quick consultation with Bernard, she concluded, "Baron Neufmarché wishes you to know that he stands willing to pledge his men to the aid of Elfael, and asks only to be taken at his word."

This provoked a hasty and heated discussion among the Welsh noblemen. Mérian watched as the debate seemed to roll back and forth. It was swiftly over, and the Welsh lords turned to face the baron with their answer. Gruffydd said, "We have argued your offer, Lord Baron, and it is most unexpected, to be sure—but no less welcome for that. We will accept your pledge and thank you for it."

The baron expressed his gratitude to the Welsh kings for placing their trust in him, and then, through Mérian, asked, "How soon can you be ready to march?"

"We are already on the march," replied Gruffydd. "Our men are on their way to Elfael even now."

1316

"Then," replied the baron, when he had received Gruffydd's answer, "we must make haste to overtake them. Among my people, it is counted a very great shame for a commander to lead from the rear."

Rhoddi scrambled through the upper branches of the greenwood canopy, skittering along the hidden path of the sky way, to drop deftly into the little clearing where the Grellon had set up camp after abandoning Cél Craidd the day before. He searched among the sleeping bodies huddled in their cloaks on the ground for the one he sought, and hastened to kneel beside it. "Bran!" he said, leaning close. "Owain says to come at once."

Bran sat up. It was early still, the feeble grey light barely penetrating the heavy foliage of oak and elm round about. Reaching instinctively for his bow, he rose to his feet. "Trouble?"

Rhoddi shook his head. "There's something moving on the King's Road," he said quietly, "something you should see."

"Will," called Bran softly, rousing the forester, "begin waking the others and get everyone ready to move. I'll send word back." To Rhoddi, he said, "Lead the way."

The two climbed up the rope ladder onto the interconnected

arrangement of limbs and boughs, planks and platforms that the Grellon maintained to move easily and quickly to and from the King's Road overlook. A swift and precarious dash brought them to the place where Owain was perched high up among the rocks on the bank of the cliff overlooking the road. "What is it?" asked Bran, climbing up beside him. "More troops?"

"Aye," replied Owain, "it is more troops, Sire. But there is something odd about these ones." He pointed down the road to where a column of knights was just coming into view. "A scouting party passed just a little while ago. I think this is the main body just coming now."

"Ffreinc, yes," said Bran. "I see them. What is so odd about them?"

"The scouts were Cymry," said Owain.

"Cymry!" said Bran. "Are you sure?"

"As sure as I can be. They were Welsh-born, I swear on Job's bones—and all of them carried longbows same as us."

"Not good," muttered Bran. "Our own countrymen going to join King William—not good at all." Before his companion could offer a reply, Bran grabbed his arm. "Look!" He pointed down to the second rank of mounted soldiers riding behind a double row of men-at-arms on foot. "I know that man—I know his standard . . . Saints in heaven!"

"Who is it?"

"Wait . . ." said Bran, straining forward. "Let them come a little closer . . ." He slapped the rock with his hand. "Yes!"

"Do you recognize someone, my lord?"

"It is Baron Neufmarché—or I am the archbishop of Canterbury," said Bran, still squinting down into the road, "and, God help us, that is Mérian beside him."

1320

"Are you sure?"

Bran squirmed around on the rock and called down to Rhoddi waiting below. "Go get Scarlet! Tell him to bring every man who can draw a bow. Tell him I want them to be ready to fight when they get here. We'll have to take them on the fly. Hurry, man! Go!"

In the road below, the soldiers came on, slowing as they neared the place where the road narrowed beneath the overhanging rocks. "Do you think they know we're here?" wondered Owain.

"Perhaps," replied Bran, withdrawing an arrow from the bundle and nocking it to the string. "Come closer, proud baron," he whispered, pressing the belly of the bow forward. "Just a little closer and you're mine."

But when the riders resumed their march, it was not Neufmarché who advanced—it was Mérian, and another, riding beside her. The two advanced together.

"Who is that with her?" said Owain.

Bran stared hard at the mounted warrior beside Mérian.

After a moment, Owain observed, "He doesn't look like a Ffreinc."

"He isn't," concluded Bran. "He is Cymry."

"Do you know him?"

Bran lowered the bow and eased the string. "That is Gruffydd, Lord of Gwynedd. Though what he is doing here in the company of Baron Neufmarché is a very mystery."

"Maybe Neufmarché has taken them captive," suggested Owain.

By way of reply, Bran drew and loosed an arrow into the road. It struck the dirt a few paces ahead of the two oncoming riders. Mérian reined up. She lifted her face to the rock walls rising to either side of the road and then, placing a hand to her mouth, called, "Rhi

Bran! Are you here?" She waited a moment, then said, "Bran if you are here, show yourself. We have come to talk to you."

Owain and Bran exchanged a puzzled glance. Bran moved to rise, but Owain put a hand on his arm. "Don't do it, my lord. It might be a trick."

"From anyone but Mérian," replied Bran. "I will talk to them— keep an arrow on the string just in case."

Bran stood on the rock. He lofted the bow and called down to the riders in the road. "Here I am."

"Bran!" cried Mérian. "Thank God—"

"Are you well, Mérian? Have they hurt you?"

"I am well, Bran," she called, beaming up at him. "I have brought help." She twisted in the saddle and indicated the ordered ranks of troops behind her. "We have come to help you."

"And Neufmarché," said Bran. "What is he doing here?"

"He has joined us," said Gruffydd, speaking up. "Greetings, Rhi Bran."

"Greetings, Gruffydd. I never thought to see you again."

"For that I am full sorry," replied the lord of Gwynedd. "But I beg the chance to make it up to you. I have brought friends—and, yes, Baron Neufmarché is one of them."

"You will forgive me if I am not wholly persuaded," remarked Bran.

"Could you come down, do you think?" asked Gruffydd. "I grow hoarse and stiff-necked shouting up at you like this."

Slinging his bow across his chest, Bran prepared to meet them on the road. "Keep an eye on them," he said to Owain. "When Scarlet and the others get here, position the men on the rocks there and there"—he pointed along the rocky outcropping—"and tell them to be ready to let fly if things are not what they seem."

"God with you, my lord," said Owain, putting an arrow on the string. "We'll wait for your signal."

Bran lowered himself quickly down the rocks, dropping from ledge to ledge and lighting on the edge of the road a hundred paces or so from where Mérian and Gruffydd were waiting. Behind them stood the ranks of the baron's knights and men-at-arms, and Bran was relieved to see that none of them had moved and seemed content merely to stand looking on. Unslinging his bow, he put an arrow on the string and advanced cautiously, keeping an eye on the troops for any sign of movement.

He had walked but a few dozen paces when Mérian spurred her horse forward and galloped to him, throwing herself from the saddle and into his embrace. Her mouth found his, and she kissed him hard and with all the pent-up passion of their weeks apart. "Oh, Bran, I have missed you. I'm sorry I could not come sooner."

"Mérian, I—"

"But, look!" she said, kissing him again. "I've brought an army." She flung out a hand to those behind her. "They've come to help save Elfael."

"Truly," replied Bran, still not entirely trusting this turn of fortune. "How many are with you?"

"I don't know—over five hundred, I think. Baron Neufmarché has come in on our side, and Rhi Gruffydd is here, and Garran and—"

"*Votre dame est très persuasive,*" said Neufmarché, reining up just then. King Garran rode beside him.

"It is true," said Garran. "My sister can be very persuasive. She would not rest until we agreed to come help you."

King Gruffydd rode up and took his place beside the baron. Seeing Gruffydd and Neufmarché side by side seemed so unnatural,

1323

Bran could hardly credit what he saw, and his native suspicion returned full force. Instinctively, he stepped in front of Mérian.

"That is close enough, Baron," said Bran, raising his bow.

"*Aros, Rhi Bran,*" said Gruffydd. "You are among friends—more than you know. The baron has pledged his forces to your aid." Indicating the troops amassed behind him with a wide sweep of his hand, he said, "We have come to confront King William and his army, and would be much obliged if you would lead us to them."

"If you have truly come to fight the Ffreinc," said Bran, "you will not go home disappointed. I can show you all you care to see."

King Gruffydd climbed slowly down from the saddle. He walked to where Bran stood and then, in full sight of everyone there, went down on one knee before him. "My lord and friend," he said, bending his head, "I pledge my life to you and to this cause. My men and I will see you on the throne of Elfael, or gladly embrace our graves. One or the other will prevail before we relinquish the fight. This is my vow." Drawing his sword, he laid it at Bran's feet. "From this day, my sword is yours to command."

"Rise, my lord, I—" began Bran, but his throat closed over the words, and overcome with a sudden, heady swirl of emotions, he found he could not speak. In all that had happened in the last days and weeks, he had never foreseen anything like this: the help he had so long and so desperately needed had come at last, and the realization of what it meant fair whelmed him over.

Gruffydd rose, smiling. "I owe you my life and throne and more. Blind fool that I am, it took me a little time to see that." Taking Bran by the arm, he pulled him away. "But come, Llewelyn is here—he has been most persuasive, too—and I've brought some others who are anxious to meet the renowned Rhi Bran y Hud."

Tuck

The next thing Bran knew he was surrounded by knights and noblemen—both Cymry and Ffreinc—all of them pledging their swords to him. He greeted all in turn, his thoughts churning, emotion running high as he tried to comprehend the magnitude of the good that had just befallen him. Baron Neufmarché remained a little apart, looking on from his saddle; he motioned Mérian to him and had a brief word. She hurried to Bran and said, "No one is happier than I am for this glad meeting, but the baron wishes me to say that it would not be the wisest course to be caught on the road just now. He asks if you might lead us to your camp, where the commanders can discuss the ordering of the troops and prepare the battle plan."

"The baron is right," allowed Gruffydd. "Is it far, your camp?"

"My settlement was destroyed—"

"Oh, Bran, no," said Mérian. "Was anyone . . . ?"

"I am sorry, Mérian." Bran put a hand to her shoulder to steady her for the blow. "Angharad was killed protecting Cél Craidd, and little Nia by accident. It happened when we were on a raid. Tomas is dead, too—from a Ffreinc spear."

Mérian's face crumpled. Bran slid his arm around her shoulders. "Later, my love," he whispered, his mouth close to her ear, "we will grieve them properly later. I need your strength just now."

Nodding, she lifted her head and rubbed the tears from her eyes. "What would you have me do?"

"Tell the baron there is a place farther on along the road where we can gather." He shook his head. "The troops will have to spread out into the forest and find places to camp of their own. My men can lead them."

Bran raised his bow and loosed a shrill whistle that pierced the forest quiet and resounded among the rocks. From every side appeared

1325

his fighting men: Scarlet, Tuck, Rhoddi, Owain, Ifor, Brocmael, Idris, Geronwy, and Beli and Llwyd. They clambered down the rocks to join the company on the road and receive the good news. Moments later, Bran's new army was on the move with Bran himself leading them—through the gorge and beyond it to a place where the land flattened out once more. The forest thinned somewhat around a stand of great oaks and elms, and here Bran gave orders for Rhoddi and Owain to lead the army into the wood round about and let them rest. "Tuck," he said, snatching the friar by the sleeve as he greeted Mérian, "stay with me—and you, too, Scarlet. We are going to hold council to plan the battle."

While men and horses and wagons trundled into a glen in the wood, there to establish a rude camp, the kings and noblemen sat down with Bran to learn the state of affairs in Elfael, and the strength and position of King William's troops. Thus the council began, and it was long before each of the great lords had their say and all points of view had been taken into account. The sun was a dull copper glow low in the west, and the first stars were beginning to light up the sky, when a plan of battle that all agreed upon began to emerge.

Bran was, by turns, impressed with the expertise of his new battle chiefs and irked at the necessity of biding his time while they hammered out details he would have settled long ago. But, all in all, as the last light of day faded, he declared himself pleased with the plan and confident in his commanders. The scouts would go out at dawn and make a final assessment of the enemy position ahead of the battle. Then the rebel forces would take the field against the king's army, led by the Cymry archers, supported and guarded on the flanks by Baron Neufmarché and his knights.

As soon as the council concluded, the lords went to find food

1326

Tuck

and drink with their men. Bran sent Scarlet and Tuck to tell his own war band what had happened, and then sought Mérian. "It is the answer to prayer long in coming," he told her. She stepped easily into his embrace. Feeling the living warmth of her in his arms, he confessed, his voice faltering slightly, "I never hoped to see you again. I thought we had parted for good."

"Shhh," she said. "I will never leave you again." She gave him a lingering kiss and then said, "Tell me all that has happened while I've been away."

They talked then, and the twilight deepened around them. They were still talking when Tuck came upon them. Unwilling to intrude on their intimate moment, he settled himself on the root of a tree to wait, thinking what a strange and wonderful day it had been. And here were Bran and Mérian, such a good match. There would be a wedding soon if he had anything to say about it . . . and, he thought, *if* they were all still alive this time tomorrow.

Leaning back against the rough bole of the old elm, he closed his eyes. From the depths of misery over the recent loss of Angharad, Tomas, and Nia, who could have foreseen that their fortunes would rise to such heights so quickly? Even so, the victory was not yet won—far from it. There were battles to be fought, and the lives of many swung in the balance. Death and destruction would be great indeed. *Oh, Merciful Lord,* he sighed inwardly, *if that could somehow be prevented . . .* "Let this cup pass from us," he prayed softly.

"Ah, Tuck," said Bran, interrupting the friar's meditation, "you're here—good." Still holding Mérian, he turned to the little friar. "I have a job for you."

1327

CHAPTER 40

Dawn was still but a whisper in the pale eastern sky when Tuck finally reached Saint Martin's. He paused below the brow of a hill a short distance from the little town and dismounted. He trudged wearily up to the top of the hill and there stood for a time to observe. The moon, bright still, illuminated the hills and filled the valleys with soft shadows. Nothing moved anywhere.

He yawned and rubbed his face with his hands. "This friar is getting too old for these midnight rambles." His empty stomach growled. "Too right," he muttered.

At Bran's behest, Tuck had ridden all night, making a wide, careful circuit of the valley to avoid being seen by any Ffreinc sentries or watchmen posted on the outer perimeter of King William's sprawling encampment, which lay between the forest and Elfael's fortress, Caer Cadarn. Now, coming upon the town from the north, he paused to make certain he could continue to the completion of his mission. Having come this far, it would not do to be caught now.

There did not seem to be any Ffreinc troops around; he could not see anyone moving about the low walls. The town was quiet, asleep. "Well, Tuck, my man, time to beard the lion in his den."

Struggling back into the saddle, he resumed his errand, descending the hill and starting up the gentle slope to the town, keeping his eyes open for any sign of discovery at his approach. But there was no one about, and he entered the town alone and, for all he could tell, unobserved. He dismounted and tethered the horse to an iron ring set in the wall of the guardhouse, then quickly and quietly started across the deserted market square towards the abbey.

The abbey gates were closed, but he rapped gently on the door and eventually managed to rouse the porter. "I have a matter of utmost urgency for the bishop," he announced to the priest who unlatched the door. "Take me to him at once."

The young monk, yawning, shook his head. It was then Tuck recognized him. "Odo! Wake up, boyo. It's me, Tuck. I have to see Bishop Asaph without delay."

"God with you, Friar," said Odo, rubbing his eyes. "The bishop will be asleep."

"There is no time," said Tuck, pressing himself through the gap. "It is life and death, Odo. We'll have to wake him."

Tuck took the young monk's elbow, spun him around, and started walking towards the palatial lodge Abbot Hugo had built for himself. "Never fear, Brother, I would not disturb the good bishop's rest if it was not of highest importance."

"This way, then," said Odo, and led Tuck not to the main entrance, but around the side to a small room where the secnab had lodged. "He prefers a less ostentatious cell," explained the young scribe, knocking on the door.

There came a sleepy voice asking them to wait, and in a moment the door opened. There stood the wizened, elderly priest, barefoot, his haze of white hair a wispy nimbus on his head. One look at Tuck and he said, "How may I serve you, Brother?"

"Bishop Asaph," said Tuck, "it is Brother Aethelfrith—do you remember me?"

The old priest studied his face in the moonlight. Then, recognition flooded into the pale eyes. "Bran's friend! Yes, I remember you. But, tell me, has something happened? Is he well?"

"All is well, Father," replied Tuck. "Or soon will be. I have come—"

Asaph shivered. "Come in, Brother Aethelfrith, and let us sit by the fire." Tuck thanked Odo and stepped inside; the old priest showed him to a stool by a tiny fire in the hearth. "These old bones are hard to keep warm," explained the bishop. "My advice, Brother, do not get old—and if you do, see you keep a little fire going in the corner. It works miracles."

"I'll remember that," replied Tuck.

"Now then," said Asaph, "what has kept you from your bed this night?"

"Bran has sent me with a message," replied the friar, and went on to explain about the miraculous arrival of Gruffydd and the Cymry kings. "And that is not all—far from it!" he remarked. "Baron Neufmarché has joined the rebellion. He is lending the full force of his troops to the cause. It is, I think, the only way he can hope to hold on to his estates."

Bishop Asaph gasped with a sharp intake of breath. "Lord Almighty!" His eyes grew round. "Then it is soon over, praise be to God."

"One way or another, yes," replied Tuck, "and perhaps sooner than you know. The Cymry mean to attack tomorrow. We have not the supplies and such for a prolonged clash. The troops are ready, and the weather is good. We will have the higher ground . . ." He paused. "In short, there is no point in waiting. That is what I came to tell you. The battle attack will come in the morning, when the sun has risen above the trees so that it will be in the eyes of the Ffreinc troops."

"God have mercy." Asaph shook his head. "I will make ready to receive the wounded, of course."

"Yes," agreed Tuck, "and one other thing—we must get word to Iwan and Siarles at the fortress. They must know so they can be ready to strike from the rear if and when the opportunity arises." He paused. "Bran has asked if you will take the message to them."

"Me?" blustered Asaph. "Well, of course, but—"

"Have the king's men made any trouble for you?"

"No, no," replied the bishop quickly. "It has been very quiet. They come here for prayer and confession—and to ensure the wounded are receiving good care. But they leave us alone."

"Well then," concluded Tuck. "Perhaps you might take two or three brothers with you and go to the caer. Take a bell and ring it as you go so the Ffreinc will know you're on holy business."

Asaph nodded slowly. "What if they make bold to stop us?"

"Simply tell them that you are going up to shrive the Cymry in the stronghold, yes? You can do that, too, once you've delivered the message, can you not?"

The old churchman considered this for a moment, then, making up his mind, he said, "If there is to be a battle, soldiers must be shriven. Men facing their eternal destiny have no wish to die with sins unconfessed dragging their souls into perdition. The Ffreinc understand this."

"Thank you, Father," said Tuck. They talked a little more then, and Tuck gave the bishop a lengthy account of all that had taken place in the last days—the running battle with King William's troops in the forest, leading up to the unexpected return of Mérian bringing King Gruffydd and the baron. They talked of the difficulties looming in the days ahead—caring for the injured and wounded in the aftermath of battle, finding food for the survivors, and rebuilding lives and livelihoods destroyed by the war.

Finally, Tuck rose and, with great weariness of body and spirit, made his farewells and moved to the door.

"God with you, Brother Aethelfrith," said Asaph with deepest sincerity.

"And also with you, Father," replied Tuck. "May the Good Lord keep you in the hollow of His hand."

"Amen," said Asaph. "I will leave you to make your own way out. I want to pray for a while before we go up to the caer."

Tuck left the monastery without bothering Odo again. He slipped out of the abbey gate and started across the deserted square of the still-sleeping town. As he was passing the church, he heard the sound of horses approaching and turned just as four or five riders entered the square. Ffreinc soldiers. He was caught like a ferret in a coop.

Instinctively, he dived for the door of the church. It was dark and cool inside, as he knew it would be. A single candle burned on the altar, and the interior was filled with the sweet stale odour of spent incense and beeswax. The baptismal font stood before him, square and solid, the cover locked with an iron hasp. That was vile Hugo—

locking the font lest any poor soul be tempted to steal a drop of holy water.

Gazing quickly around the empty space for a place to hide, he saw—could it be? Yes! In the far corner of the nave stood a strange, curtained booth. Oh, these Normans—chasing every new whim that whispers down the road: a confessional. Tuck had heard of them, but had never seen one. They were, it was said, becoming very fashionable in the new stone churches the Ffreinc built. The notion that a body could confess without looking his priest in the eye all the while seemed faintly ludicrous to Tuck. Nevertheless, he was grateful for this particular whim just now. He crossed quickly to the booth. It was an open stall with a pierced screen down the centre: on one hand was a chair for the priest; on the other a little low bench for the kneeling penitent. A curtain hung between the two, and another hid the priest from view.

1334

Tuck could not help clucking his tongue over such unwonted luxury. Not for the Norman cleric a humble stool; no, nothing would do but that Hugo's priests must have an armchair throne with a down-filled cushion. "Bless 'em," said Tuck. Pulling aside the curtain, he stepped in and closed the curtain again, then settled himself in the chair, thanking the Good Lord for his thoughtful provision.

No sooner had he leaned back in his chair than the door of the church opened and the soldiers entered.

Tuck remained absolutely still, hardly daring to breathe.

The footsteps came nearer.

They were coming towards the confessional. One of the knights was standing directly in front of the booth now, and Tuck braced himself for discovery. The soldier put a hand on the curtain and pulled it aside. The soldier saw Tuck, and Tuck saw the soldier—only it was no ordinary knight. The squat, thick body, the powerful chest and slightly bowed legs from a life on horseback, the shock of flaming red hair: it was none other than King William Rufus in the flesh.

Tuck pressed his eyes closed, expecting the worst.

But the king turned away without the slightest hint of recognition in his pale blue eyes and called over his shoulder to the two with him. *"Le prêtre est ici,"* he said. *"Retire-toi."*

The priest is here, thought Tuck, translating the words in his head. *God help me, he thinks I am the priest to hear his confession.*

King William dropped the curtain and settled himself on the kneeling bench. *"Père, confessez-moi,"* he said wearily.

Knowing he would have to speak now—and that his French was not up to the challenge—he said, *"Mon seigneur et mon roi, en anglais, s'il vous plaît."*

There came a heavy sigh from the other side of the curtain, and then the king of England replied, *"Oui*—of course, I understand. My *anglais* is not so good, forgive *moi,* eh?"

"God hears the heart, my lord," offered Tuck. "It makes no difference to him what language we use. Would you like me to shrive you now?"

"Oui, père, that is why I have come." The king paused, and then said, "Forgive me, Father, a sinner. Today I ride into battle, and I cannot pay for the souls of those who will be slain. The blood-price is heavy, and I am without the silver to pay, eh?"

It took Tuck a moment to work out what William was talking about, and he was glad the king could not see him behind the curtain. "I see," he said, and then it came to him that William Rufus was talking about the peculiar Norman belief that a soldier owed a blood debt for the souls of those he had slain in battle. Since one could never know whether the man he had just killed had been properly shriven, the souls of the combat dead became the survivor's responsibility, so to speak—he was obligated to pray for the remission of their sins so that they might enter heaven and stand blameless before the judgement seat of God.

"Oh, yes," intoned Tuck as understanding broke upon him. The king, like many great lords, was paying priests to pray for the souls of men he had slain in battle, praying them out of purgatory and into heaven.

"By the Virgin, the cost is heavy!" muttered William. "*Intolérable,* eh? It is all I can do to pay my father's debt, and I have not yet begun to pay my own."

"A very great pity, yes," Tuck allowed.

"*Oui, c'est dommage,*" sighed William, "*c'est bien dommage.*"

"Begging your pardon, *mon roi,*" said Tuck. "I am but a lowly priest, but it seems to me that the way out of your predicament is not more money, but fewer souls."

"Eh?" said William, only half paying attention. "Fewer souls?"

"Do not kill any more soldiers."

The king laughed outright. "You know little about warring, priest! *Un innocent!* I like you. Soldiers get killed in battle; that is the whole point."

"So I am told," replied Tuck. "But is there no other way?"

"It could all be settled tomorrow—*Sang de Dieu,* today!—if the blasted Welsh would only lay down their weapons. But they have raised rebellion against me, and that I will not have!"

"A great dilemma for you," conceded Tuck. "I see that."

Before he could say more, William continued. "This cantref *infortuné* has already cost me more than it will ever return. And if I do not collect my tribute in Normandie in six days' time, I will lose those too. Philip will see to that."

Tuck seized on this. "All the more reason to make peace with these rebels. If they agreed to lay down their arms and swear fealty to you—"

"*Et payer le tribut royal,*" added William quickly.

"Yes, and pay the royal tribute, to be sure," agreed Tuck. "Your Majesty would not have to feed an army or pay for the souls of the dead. Also you could go to Normandie and collect the tribute that is due—all this would save the royal treasury a very great load of silver, would it not?"

"*Par la Vierge!* Save a great load of silver, yes."

Tuck, hardly daring to believe that he was not in a dream, but unwilling to wake up just yet, decided to press his luck as far as it would go. "Again, forgive me, *mon roi,* but why not ask for terms of peace? This rebel—King Raven, I believe they call him—has said that all he wants is to rule his realm in peace. Even now, I believe he could be convinced to swear fealty to you in exchange for reclaiming his throne."

There was a long and, Tuck imagined, baleful silence on the other side of the curtain. He feared the king was deciding how to slice him up and into how many pieces.

Finally, William said, "I think you are a man of great faith." The wistful longing in that voice cut at Tuck's heart. "If I could believe this . . ."

"Believe it, Sire," said Tuck. "For it is true."

"If I am seen to allow rebellion, every hand will be raised against me."

"Perhaps," granted Tuck. "But if you are seen to practice mercy, it would inspire others to greater loyalty, would it not?" He paused. "The sword is always close to hand."

"*Hélas, c'est vrai*," granted the king.

"Alas, yes, it is too true."

There was silence again then. Tuck could not tell what was happening beyond the curtain. He prayed William was seriously considering the idea of suing for peace.

When he spoke again, the king said, "Will you yet shrive me?"

"That is why I am here. Bow your head, my son, and we begin," replied Tuck, and proceeded with the ritual. When at last the king rose to depart, he thanked his priest and walked from the church without another word.

Tuck waited until he heard the sound of horses in the square, and then crept to the door. King William and his knights were riding away in the grey dawn of a new day. He waited until they were out of sight and then ran to his own horse and flew to the greenwood as if all the hounds of hell were at his heels.

1338

The sun was well up and climbing towards the tops of the higher trees by the time Tuck reached the safety of the greenwood. The combined armies of Cymry rebels were already amassing at the edge of the forest. Hampered by the trees and undergrowth, Tuck worked his way along the battle line, searching for Bran. By the time he found him, the sun was that much higher and the assault that much nearer.

"Bran!" cried Tuck. "Thank God, I've found you in time." He slid from the saddle and ran to where Bran was waiting with Scarlet, Owain, and his own small war band, engulfed and surrounded by King Gruffydd's troops and those of the northern lords. "I bring word—"

"Be quick about it," Bran told him. "I am just about to give the command—"

"No!" said Tuck, almost frantic. "Forgive me, my lord, but do nothing until you've heard what I have to say."

"Very well," Bran agreed. He called across to Gruffydd and Llewelyn, who were standing a little apart. "Stand ready to march as soon as I have returned." To Tuck, he said, "Come with me."

He led them a little way into the wood, to a place where they would not be overheard. "Well? Is the bishop able to get a message to the caer?"

It took a moment for the priest to recall his original errand. "Oh, that, yes." Tuck licked his lips and swallowed. "I have seen the king."

"The king . . . Red William?"

"The same," replied the friar, and explained what had happened in the town—how he had been surprised by Ffreinc riders and hid himself in the church, how William had mistaken him for one of the abbey priests and asked to be shriven, and their talk about the rebellion.

"Did you shrive him?"

"I did, yes, but—"

"So that means they intend to attack today," concluded Bran. "Well done, Tuck; it confirms us in our plan. We will strike without delay." He started away.

"That is not all," said Tuck. "The king was distraught about the cost of this war. It weighs heavily with him. He stands to lose his tribute money from Normandie."

"Good."

"Above all else he desires a swift end to this conflict," Tuck explained. "I believe he would be moved towards peace."

"That he will not have," declared Bran. "And you are certain Bishop Asaph will warn Iwan and Siarles at the fortress?"

"He will."

1340

"Then all is ready." He commended Tuck for his diligence, and returned to the battle line, where he gave a nod to Gruffydd, Llewelyn, and the others. "God with you today, my lords, and with us all," he called, and raising his warbow, he gave the signal to move out.

The massed armies of Cymry archers and Ffreinc soldiers under the command of Baron Neufmarché slowly moved out from the shelter of Coed Cadw; the knights on horseback and the Cymry on foot, they marched down the slope and into the Vale of Elfael. Their appearance threw William's troops into a chaos of frantic activity as the alarms were sounded through the various camps. The knights, men-at-arms, and footmen were well trained, however, and hastily mustered for battle. As the Cymry drew nearer, the Ffreinc moved to meet them, first one division and then another until the gaps in the line were filled and they had formed a single, dense body of soldiers—the knights in the centre, flanked by the footmen.

Tuck, with his staff, taking his place behind Bran and Scarlet, found himself walking beside Owain. "Whatever happens today," said the young warrior, "I would have you say a prayer for me, Friar."

"And here I have been praying for us all since first light, have I not?"

"Then," said Owain, "I will pray for you, Friar Tuck."

"Do that, boyo," agreed Tuck. "You do that."

The Cymry moved slowly down from the forest, spreading out along the rim of the valley a little north of the King's Road so that when they attacked the sun would be at their backs and in the eyes of the enemy. They came to the steepest part of the slope and stopped so that William's troops would have to toil uphill to engage them, while they could rain arrows down into the ranks of advancing knights as well as those behind.

King William's barons and earls, each in command of his own men, formed the battle line, filling in the gaps between the separate bodies until the knights rode shoulder to shoulder and shield to shield, spears raised and ready to swing down into position when the order was given to charge. The footmen scrambled into ranks behind the knights and prepared to deliver the second assault when the knights broke the enemy line.

Up on the slopes across the valley, the Cymry archers took handfuls of arrows and thrust them point-first into the turf before them, ready to hand when the order came to loose havoc on the advancing Ffreinc. Baron Neufmarché, at the head of his troops, drew into position to the northwest—ready to swoop down upon the unprotected flanks of William's army the moment the charge faltered under the hail of shafts. If, however, the knights survived the charge and carried the attack forward, he would come in hard to protect the archers' retreat.

"Come on, you ugly frog-faced knaves . . ." muttered Scarlet. He stretched and flexed the stiffness from his injured hand, then plucked a shaft from the ground and nocked it to the string. ". . . a little closer and you're mine."

Other men were speaking now—some in prayer, and others in derision of the enemy, banking courage in themselves and those around them. Bran stood silent, watching the slow, steady advance of the Ffreinc line. He suddenly found himself wishing Angharad were alive to see this day. He missed her and the knowledge that she was upholding him in her mysterious and powerful way. Closing his eyes, he prayed that she was gazing down on him and would intercede with the angels of war on his behalf and sustain him in the battle.

He was still occupied with this thought when he heard Gruffydd say, "Here, now! What's this?"

Bran opened his eyes to see that the Ffreinc had halted just out of easy arrow flight. The early sun glinted off the polished surfaces of their shields and weapons. There was a movement from the centre, and the line broke, parting to the left and right as a small body of knights rode forward. Two of the riders carried banners—one bearing the royal standard of King William: a many-tailed flag with a red cross on a white field and a strip of ermine across the bottom separating the body from the green, blue, and yellow tails. The other knight bore the standard of England: the Cross of Jerusalem in gold surrounded by smaller crosslets of blue; its tails were green, gold and blue, each tail ending in small gold tassels.

These banners preceded a single knight, riding between them. Two more knights followed the lone rider, and all advanced to a point halfway between the two armies, and there they halted.

"Saints and angels," said Gruffydd, "what's the old devil about?"

"I think Bloody William wants to talk," replied Llewelyn.

"I say we give him an arrow in the eye and let that do our talking for us," declared Gruffydd. He nudged Llewelyn beside him. "Your aim is true, Cousin; let fly and we'll see that rascal off right smart."

"No!" said Tuck, pressing forward. "Begging your pardon, my lords, I do believe he wants to beg terms of peace."

"Peace!" scoffed Gruffydd. "Never! The old buzzard wants to sneak us into a trap, more like. I say give him an arrow or two and teach him to keep his head down."

"My lord," pleaded Tuck, "if it is peace he wants, it would be the saving of many lives."

Bran gazed across the distance at the king, sitting on his fine horse, his newly burnished armour glinting in the golden light of a brilliant new day. "If he *does* want to talk," Bran decided at last, "it will cost us nothing to hear what he has to say. We can attack as soon as the discussion is concluded." He turned to Gruffydd. "I will talk to him. You and Llewelyn be ready to lead the assault if things go badly." He motioned to Will Scarlet, saying, "Come with me, Will. And you, too, Tuck—your French is better than mine."

"Baron Neufmarché speaks French better than any of us," Tuck pointed out. "Send for him."

"Maybe later," allowed Bran. "We'll see if there's anything worth talking about first."

Together the three of them walked down the grassy slope to where the king of England had established himself between his billowing standards.

"Perhaps the friar is right," suggested Will Scarlet. "It would not hurt to have Neufmarché with us."

"We will call him if we need him," allowed Bran.

"William speaks English," Tuck told them.

"Does he indeed?" said Bran.

"A little, anyway—more than he'll admit to."

"Then we will insist," Bran decided. "That way we can all be very careful about what we say to one another."

They came to within fifty paces of the knights on horseback. *"Mon roi,"* said Bran, with a glancing nod of respect. *"Parlerez-vous?"*

"Oui," replied King William. *"Je veux vous parler de la paix."*

"He wants to talk to you about making peace," said Tuck.

"Bon," said Bran. To Tuck, he said, "Tell him that we will speak in English and that you will relay my words to him."

1344

Tuck did as he was commanded, and a strange expression passed over the king's face. *"You,"* he said. "Have I seen you before?"

"You've seen us *all* before, you mule-headed varlet," muttered Scarlet in Welsh.

"Steady on, Scarlet," said Bran. "We're here to listen."

"Oh, indeed, yes, Sire," replied Tuck. "We met first in Rouen last year—when my Lord Bran came to warn you of the plot by your brother against your throne."

William nodded. "Somewhere else, I think."

"Yes," said Tuck. "I was at Wintan Cestre when you gave your judgement against Baron de Braose and Count Falkes, and delivered this cantref into the care of Abbot Hugo Rainault and Sheriff de Glanville."

William squinted his eyes and regarded the little friar with a suspicious look—as if trying to decide if the priest was mocking him in some subtle way. "No . . . somewhere else." Realization came to him, and his eyebrows raised. *"Sang de la Vierge!* You were that priest in the church this morning."

"True, Majesty," answered Tuck. "That is a fact I cannot deny."

"Good Lord, Tuck," whispered Scarlet, "you've been a busy fella."

The king frowned, then said, *"C'est la vie*—I am glad you are here." Turning his attention to the task at hand he said to Bran, "Good day for a battle, eh?"

"None better," replied Bran, through Tuck.

"What is this about you, ah . . . *désirer* the throne of this godforsaken cantref? You have caused me the very devil of trouble, my lord."

"With respect, Sire," answered Bran, "I want only what is rightfully mine—the throne my family has occupied for two hundred years."

"Hmph!" sniffed William, unimpressed. "That is finished. Britain is a Norman country now. I made my decision. Can you not accept it?"

Tuck and Bran conferred, and the friar said, "Again, with respect, Sire, my Lord Bran would remind you that the two of you made a bargain in Rouen—a throne for a throne. That is what you said. Bran helped you save your throne; now he wants the one he was promised."

King William frowned. He took off his helmet and rubbed a gloved hand through his thinning red hair. After a moment, he said, "Your priest here," he jabbed a stubby finger at Tuck, "says you will swear fealty to me. Is that true?"

"*Oui,*" said Bran. "Yes."

"If I restore you to the throne," William said, "you will cease this rebellion—is that so?"

1346

Again, Bran and Tuck conferred. "That is what I intended from the first."

"This miserable little cantref has already cost me more than I will ever see out of it," grumbled William. "What you want with it, God knows. But you are welcome to it."

"Your Majesty!" gasped one of the barons attending William. "I fear you are making a grave mistake."

The knight moved up beside the king, and the forest-dwellers recognized him for the first time. "You had your say long ago, Gysburne," Tuck told him. "*Tais-toi.*"

"You cannot just give it back to them," insisted Marshal Gysburne, "not after what they've done."

"Can I not?" growled the king. "Who are you, sir, to tell me what I can do? The priest is right—shut your mouth." Turning to Bran, he said, "It grows hot and I am thirsty. Can we discuss this somewhere out of the sun? I have wine in my tent. Come, let us talk together."

"I would like nothing more," replied Bran when Tuck had told him what the king said. "However, I would like to choose the place of discussion."

"Where, then?"

"The fortress is just there," said Bran, pointing down the slope to the caer on its mound in the near distance. "We will talk there."

"But the stronghold is full of your warriors," the king pointed out.

"Some warriors, yes," allowed Bran. "But farmers and herders, too—the people who have suffered under de Braose, Abbot Hugo, and Sheriff de Glanville these last years."

"Am I to go into this den of wolves alone?" said the king.

"Bring as many of your knights as you wish," Bran told him. "The more who see us swear peace with one another, the better it will be for everyone."

1347

When King William and his knights rode into the fortress yard at midday, Bran and his people were ready to receive them. Bran, with Mérian on one hand and Tuck on the other, was flanked by Iwan and Siarles on the right, and Will Scarlet and Alan a'Dale on the left. Behind him were other members of the Grellon—Noín, Owain, Brocmael, and Ifor, and most of the forest-dwellers. Baron Bernard Neufmarché stood a little apart, with two of his knights holding Sheriff Richard de Glanville, bound at the wrists, between them. Beside the knights stood Bishop Asaph gripping the oaken shaft of his brass-topped crosier, and Odo clutching a big Bible.

The king of England was accompanied by a dozen knights, Marshal Guy of Gysburne amongst them. Around the perimeter of the yard stood the people of Elfael. Outside the walls of the fortress, the army was drawn up and waiting. Beyond them, on the heights above the valley, the Cymry kings and their archers kept watch on the proceedings. If William's army moved to attack, they would move to prevent it.

William Rufus rode to the centre of the yard, where his personal canopy had been set up. He dismounted and was greeted by Bran. Mérian and Baron Neufmarché joined them to make certain that no misunderstandings arose because of a simple lack of language on either side. A small table had been set up beneath the canopy, and two chairs. On the table was a jar and a single bowl.

"Your Majesty," said Bran, "if it please you, sit with me. We will drink together."

"I would like nothing better," said the king. Seeing Neufmarché, he stopped and turned to his wayward vassal. "Baron, do not think that your part in this will be ignored."

The baron inclined his head in acceptance of the king's charge, but replied, "What I have done I did for the greater good."

"Ha!" scoffed the king. "Your own good most of all, I do not doubt. By the Virgin, man, how could you turn against me?"

"It was not so much turning against you, Sire," replied the baron, "but protecting myself. Even so, it is fortunate that we did not have to try one another in battle."

"Fortunate, eh?" said the king. "We will talk of this another time." He moved to take his place beneath the brightly coloured canopy. Bran joined him and sat down, with Mérian on one side and Tuck on the other. The baron stood to one side between the two kings and, acting as steward, poured wine into the bowl. He handed the bowl to Bran, who took it up, drank a draught, and then offered it to William.

Red William accepted the bowl and drank, then returned it to Bran. The back-and-forth continued until the bowl was drained, whereupon Baron Neufmarché refilled it and placed it on the table between them.

"God with you, Your Majesty," said Bran, who between Mérian and the baron was able to make his thoughts known. "And though we might both wish that the occasion was otherwise, I do bid you welcome to Caer Cadarn and Elfael. It is my hope that we rise from this table better friends than when we sat down."

"Let us cut to the bone," replied the king in English. "What are your terms?"

Bran smiled. "I want only what I have always wanted—"

"Your precious throne, yes," answered the king. "You shall have it. What else?"

"Full pardon for myself and my Grellon, and any who have aided me in returning the realm to my rule," said Bran. "And that will include Baron Neufmarché."

The king frowned at this last part when it was explained to him, but gave a grudging nod of assent. "What else?"

"Nothing more," said Bran. "Only your seal on a treaty of peace between our kingdoms."

William gave a bark of disbelief when Neufmarché translated Bran's last remarks. "Nothing else? No reparations? No silver to pay your soldiers?"

"My warriors are mine to repay," said Bran. "We Cymry take care of our own."

1349

"I wish every fiefdom took care of itself, by the blood," replied William. He leaned back in his chair and gave every appearance of beginning to enjoy himself. "If you have nothing else, then hear my terms. I require your oath of fealty and a tribute to be paid each year on . . ." He tapped his chin as he thought, then caught a glimpse of Tuck and said, "You, there, priest—if you *are* a priest—what is the nearest holy day to this one?"

Tuck moved a step forward. "That would be *Gwyl Iwan y Coed*," he replied. "The Feast of Saint John the Baptist, in plain English."

"*John le Baptiste, oui*," said Neufmarché, passing this along to the king.

"Henceforth, on the Feast of Saint John the Baptist, a tribute of . . ." He looked around at the rude fortress and the mean, common dress of the half-starved inhabitants and the grim determination he saw on their faces and made his decision. "A tribute of one good longbow and a sheaf of arrows to be presented to the Royal Court at Londein and given over to the care of the Chief Justiciar."

Mérian gasped with joy, and Tuck, who caught most of what was said, chuckled and told the others standing round about.

"Oh, Bran," breathed Mérian, giving Bran's shoulder a squeeze. Tuck relayed the terms to the Grellon and all those looking on. "The king has decided to be generous."

Baron Neufmarché and the king exchanged a brief word, and the baron said, "King William will accept the release of his sheriff now." He summoned the knights forward, and de Glanville was marched to the table.

"As a token of the peace we have sworn between us, I release him to your authority," said Bran. He motioned to his champion, standing behind Friar Tuck. "Iwan, cut him loose."

1350

The big warrior stepped forward and, grinning with good pleasure at the astonishing turn events had taken, drew the knife from his belt and began cutting through the bonds at the sheriff's wrists. The rawhide straps fell away, and with a sweep of his hand, Iwan indicated that the prisoner was free to go.

As Iwan replaced the knife and made to step back, de Glanville snatched the dagger from his belt and leaped forward. In the same swift movement, he drew back his hand and prepared to plunge the dagger into Bran's unprotected neck. The naked blade flashed forward and down. Tuck saw the arcing glint hard in the bright sunlight and gave out a yelp of warning. Iwan, startled, put out his hand.

But it was too late.

The knife slashed down a killing stroke.

Then, even as the cruel blade descended to its mark, the sheriff's hand faltered and appeared to seize in its forward sweep. Halted, it hovered in midstroke. The knife point quivered, then fell to the ground.

It happened so fast that almost no one saw what had arrested the knife until Sheriff de Glanville let out a shriek of agony and crumpled to his knees. Only slowly, as if in a dream, did the stunned onlookers discover Will Scarlet standing over the sheriff, his own hand clamped tight over de Glanville's. He gave the captured hand a squeeze, and there was a meaty crunch and pop as the sheriff's fingers gave way.

De Glanville gave out a roar of pain and anger and swung at Scarlet with his free hand. Tuck, snatching the crosier from Bishop Asaph's hand, grasped it like a quarterstaff and swung it once around his head and brought it down with a solid thump on the top of the sheriff's head; de Glanville crumpled to the ground, where he lay on his side, whimpering and cradling his broken fingers.

"Stand him up!" commanded William with an airy wave of his hand. Turning to Bran he spoke with some sincerity. "His Majesty offers heartfelt apologies," Neufmarché translated. "He asks what you would like him to do with the rogue."

"I will leave that to Scarlet," replied Bran, looking to Will for an answer.

"Broken fingers are a long and painful reminder of a man's failure," replied the forester. "As I should know. I am satisfied if he takes that away with him—so long as we never have to see him again."

"That's a far sight more mercy than he deserves," said Bran. "And more than he ever showed you, Will."

"And is my husband not the better man?" said Noín, taking Will's arm.

Bran's decision was delivered to King William, who merely grunted. "This man is no longer one of my sheriffs. Remove him from our sight." Then, rising, he held out his hand to one of his knights. "Your sword," he said.

The knight drew his blade and handed it to the king, who turned to Bran. He spoke and indicated a place on the ground before him.

"His Majesty is saying that he must leave now if he is to reach Normandie in time to collect his tribute," Baron Neufmarché explained. "He says there is but one more thing he must do before he goes."

"Sire?" said Bran.

Again the king spoke and indicated the place on the ground at his feet.

"He says you are to kneel and swear your fealty to him," said Neufmarché.

Bran called Bishop Asaph to him. "Father, will you see that it is done properly?"

"Of course, Rhi Bran," said the old man. "It will be an honour."

As the bishop took his place beside King William, Bran knelt and stretched out his hand to grasp the king's foot. William, holding the sword upright in both hands, directed his newest vassal in the age-old ceremony which bound man to lord, and lord to king. Bishop Asaph lofted his crosier and offered a prayer to seal the vow, and the simple rite was concluded.

William touched the edge of the sword to the back of Bran's neck and told him to rise. "You are now my liegeman, and I am your liege lord," the king told him, and Mérian, standing near, interpreted. "Rule your realm in peace as God gives you strength."

"In the strength of God," replied Bran, "I will." As he said those words, he felt Mérian slip her hand into his, and then he was caught up in the tremendous sea wave of acclamation that rose up from the long-suffering folk of Elfael, whose joy at seeing their king triumphant could not be contained.

King William called for his horse to be brought and his men to depart. "We will meet again, no doubt," he said.

"On the Feast of Saint John the Baptist," replied Bran.

"Rule well and wisely," said the king in English. He searched the crowd for a face, and found it. "And see you keep this man close to your throne," he said, pulling Tuck forward. "He has done you good service. If not for him, there would be no peace to celebrate this day."

"In truth, Your Majesty," said Bran. "I will keep him with me always."

That night Rhi Bran ap Brychan celebrated his return to the

throne with the first of what would become many days of feasting, song, and merriment, and went to sleep in his own bed. And though in the days ahead he would often return to the greenwood to visit Angharad's grave and tell his Wise Banfáith how his kingdom fared, he never spent another night in the forest so long as he lived.

1354

⫷ EPILOGUE ⫸

Nottingham, 1210

Rumour had it that King John had come north to hunt in the royal forest at Sherwood. His Majesty was lodged with High Sheriff Wendeval in the old castle on the mound overlooking the river. Thomas a'Dale, following the royal progress, had come to Nottingham hoping for a chance to perform for the king and add a royal endorsement to his name—*and* a handsome fee to his slack purse.

As he walked along the dirt track, humming to himself, he recalled the last time he had been here; it was with his father, when he was a boy learning the family trade. As he remembered, he had juggled while his father played the psaltery and sang the songs that made his family a fair living. Thomas remembered Nottingham as a good-sized city with a lively market and plenty of people from whom to draw the crowds a minstrel required. Passing quickly through the town now, he saw that the market was just opening and merchants beginning to set out their wares, including a pie man who carried his steaming gold treasures on a long plank from the bakery oven to his stall. The aroma brought the water to Thomas's mouth, and he felt the pinch in his empty stomach.

Still, hungry as he was, he did not dally. He marched straight-away to the castle and presented himself at the gate. "God bless you right well, sir," he addressed the gateman. "Is the lord of the manor at home?"

"He is," replied the grizzled veteran controlling the castle entrance, a man with one eye and one hand: both lost in some nameless battle or other. "Not that it is any business of your'n."

"Oh," replied Thomas lightly, "that is where you mistake me, sir. I am a minstrel, Thomas a'Dale by name. I've performed before the crowned heads of many a land, and now I've come to entertain the lord high sheriff and the king."

"What makes you think the king is here?" queried the gateman, sizing up the wanderer with a long, one-eyed appraisal.

1356

"That is all the talk of the countryside," answered Thomas. "You can hear it anywhere."

"Do you believe ever'thing you hear?"

"And do *you* believe everything you see?" countered Thomas. Producing a silver penny from his purse he held it up between thumb and finger for a moment before placing it on his eye. Squinting to hold the coin in place, he showed both hands empty, palms out. Then with a shout, he clapped his hands and the coin vanished.

The gateman gave a snort of mild amusement and said, "Where's it gone, then?"

By way of reply, Thomas opened his mouth and showed the silver penny on his tongue.

"That's a good'un, that," the old man chuckled. "You have more o' those japes, sim'lar?"

"As many as you like," said Thomas. "And more of *these*, too," he added, offering the man the penny, "for a fella who speaks a good word of me to his lordship's steward tonight."

"I reckon I'm that fella," answered the porter, plucking the penny from the young man's fingers. "You come back at e'ensong bell, and you'll find a welcome."

"Good man. Until then," replied Thomas. "God be good to you, sir."

Having secured his employment, he returned to the town square and found a place to sit while he watched the market folk. When the first rush of activity was over—the wives and maids of wealthier house-holds, first in line to buy the best on offer—the market assumed a more placid, easygoing air. People took time to exchange news and gossip, to quench their thirst at the tavern keeper's ale vat, and to more casually examine the contents of the various booths and stalls lining the square.

Thomas pulled his psaltery from its bag on his back and began tuning the strings, humming to himself to get his voice limbered and ready. Then, slinging the strap around his neck, he strolled among the market-goers, plucking the strings and singing snatches of the most fashionable tunes. One by one, folk stopped to listen, and when he had gathered enough of an audience, he cried, "Who would like to hear 'The Tale of Wizard Merlyn and the Dragon King'?"

A clamour went up from the throng. "I sing all the better with the sweet clink of silver in my ear."

He placed his hat on the ground before him and strummed the psaltery. In a moment, the chink of coins did ring out as people pitched bits of pennies and even whole coins into the minstrel's hat. When he reckoned he had got all there was to get, he began the song: a spirited and very broad tale with many humorous and unflattering allusions to the present reign thinly disguised as the antics of King Arthur's court.

When he finished, he thanked his patrons, scooped up his hat, and made his way to a quiet place to count his takings. He had managed three pence—enough for a pie or two, which he bought; leaving the market, he strolled down to the river to find a shady spot to eat and rest. He took from his bag an apple he had found in the ditch, and ate that along with his pork pie. Having slept badly in the hedge beside the road the night before, he napped through the warm afternoon, waiting for the long summer day to fade.

At the appointed time, Thomas roused himself, washed in the river, gave his clothes a good brushing, combed his hair, and proceeded up the track to the castle once more, where he was admitted and led to the great hall. The meal was already in progress, but it would be a while yet before the crowd was ready to be entertained. He found a quiet corner and settled back to wait, snatching bits of bread and cheese, meat and sweets from the platters that went past him. He ate and tried to get the measure of his audience.

In the centre of the high table, resplendent in blue silk, sat King John, called Lackland by his subjects—not well liked, but then, truth be told, few monarchs ever were while still alive. John's chief misfortune seemed to be that he was not his brother, Richard, called Coeur de Lion. The lionhearted king was better regarded—perhaps because he had hardly ever set foot in England during his entire reign. And where Richard was remembered as tall and robust, John was a squat, thick-necked man with heavy shoulders and a spreading paunch beneath his tight-stretched silks. His best years were behind him, to be sure; there was silver showing among the long dark locks that his shapeless hat could not hide.

1358

Tuck

The High Sheriff, Lord William Wendeval, was a bluff old champion who was said to rule his patch with an authority even the king himself could not claim. He was a tall, rangy fellow with long limbs and a narrow, horsy face, and short grey curls beneath his hat of soft green velvet. The king and his sheriff had been drinking some time, it would seem, for both men wore the rosy blush of the vine across cheeks and nose. And both laughed louder and longer than any of the revellers around them.

Slowly, the meal progressed. As the many dishes and platters circulated around the tables, musicians trooped into the hall and sent a fine commotion coursing among the throng at table. This Thomas considered a good sign, as players always gave an evening's roister a more festive air. When men enjoyed themselves, the money flowed more easily, and never more easily than when they were in a celebratory mood.

He watched and waited, listening to the happy clatter around him and idly tuning the strings of his instrument; and when he judged the time to be right, he rose and walked to the high table.

"My lords and ladies all!" he cried aloud to make himself heard above the raucous revel. "A songster! A songster!"

"Hear!" shouted the high sheriff, rising from his chair and pounding on the board with the pommel of his knife. "Hear him! Hear him! We have a minstrel in our midst!"

When the hall had sufficiently quieted, Thomas faced the high table and, with a wide sweep of his hat, bowed low, his nose almost touching his knee. "My lord high sheriff, my best regards," he said. He bowed again, lower still, and said, "Your Majesty, I beg the honour of your attention on this splendid festal evening." Turning to the rest of the company, he waved his arm. "My lords and ladies, gentlefolk all, it is my good pleasure to sing for your amusement."

"What will you sing?" called the sheriff, resuming his seat.

"Tonight, I have prepared a special surprise right worthy of this splendid occasion—but more of that anon. I will begin with a tune that is sure to please Your Majesty." He began strumming, and soon the hall was ringing to the strains of a song called "The Knight and the Elf Queen's Daughter." It was an old song, and most minstrels knew it. Though not the most taxing on a songster's abilities, it had a soothing effect on a restive audience and made a good prelude to better things.

The song concluded, and the last strains were still lingering in the air when Thomas began the lay known as "The Wooing of Ygrain"—also a firm favourite among the nobility, what with its themes of flirtation and forbidden love.

He sang two more short songs, and then, pausing to retune his psaltery, he announced, "Majesty, Lord Sheriff, distinguished lords and ladies, hearken to me now! Tonight in your hearing for the first time anywhere, I give you a song of my own composing—a stirring epic of adventure and intrigue, of kingdoms lost and won, and love most fair and wondrous. I give you 'The Ballad of Brave Rhiban Hud'!"

In fact it was not, strictly speaking, the first time he had sung this song. He had laboured over its verses, true, but in the main it remained much as it had been composed by his grandfather and sung by his father. Indeed, the song had earned his family's reputation and never failed to find favour with an audience so long as the singer took care to adapt it to his listeners: dropping in names of the local worthies, the places nearby that local folk knew, any particular features of the countryside and its people—it all helped to create a sense of instant recognition for those he entertained, and flattered his patrons.

1300

Tuck

Thomas strummed the opening notes of the song and then, lifting his head, sang:

> Come listen a while, you gentlefolk alle,
>> That stand here this bower within,
> A tale of brave Rhiban the Hud,
>> I purpose now to begin!

The song began well and proceeded through its measured course, pulling the audience into the tale. Very soon the listeners were deep in the singer's thrall, the various lines drawing, by turns, cheers and cries of outrage as events unfolded.

Thomas, knowing full well that he had captured them, proceeded to bind his audience with the strong cadences of the song. For tonight's performance, the tale was set in Nottingham and the forest was Sherwood. William Rufus and the Welsh March and Richard de Glanville never received a mention. Tonight, the king of the tale was John, and the sheriff none other than Sheriff Wendeval himself. It was a risky change of cast—noble hosts had been known to take umbrage at a minstrel's liberties—but Thomas perceived the mood was light, and everyone thrilled to the daring of it.

> "God save the king," quod Rhiban to he,
>> "And them that wish him full well;
> And he that does his true sovereign deny,
>> I wish him with Satan to dwell."

> Quod the king: "Thine own tongue hast cursèd thyself,
>> For I know what thou verily art.

Thou brigand and thief, by those treasonous words,
　　I swear that thou lyest in heart."

"No ill have I done thee," quod Rhiban to king,
　　"In thought or in word or in deed,
Better I've served than the abbot's foule men,
　　Who robbéd from them in sore need.

"And never I yet have any man hurt
　　That honest is and true;
Only those that their honour give up
　　To live on another man's due.

"I never harmed the husbandman,
　　That works to till the ground;
Nor robbed from those that range the wood
　　And hunt with hawk or hound.

"But the folk you appointed to rule my stead,
　　The clergymen, shire reeves, and knights,
Have stolen our homes and impoverish'd our kin
　　And deny'd us what's ours by full rights."

The good king withdrew to consider the case
　　And did with his counsellors sit,
In very short time they had come to agree
　　On a ruling all saw justlie fit:

"King Bran, thenceforward, full pardon shall have,
　　By order of royal decree.

And the lands that his fathers and grandsires kept,
   Have no other ruler than he."

Quod Rhiban: "Praise Christ! This suits me full goode,
   And well it becomes of us both.
For kings must be e'er protecting their folk
   So hereby we swear you our troth.

"And vow we this day, to the end of the earth,
   shall grief ne'er come 'tween us twain."
And the glory of Rhiban Hud, eke his king,
   i'this worldsrealm always shall reign.

Thomas led the crowd a merry chase through the greenwood and the exploits of the noble rogue Rhiban and his struggle to regain his birthright. Justice denied and at last redeemed was a theme that always swayed an English crowd, and it seemed now as if he played upon the very heartstrings of his audience as blithely as he plucked the psaltery. Both king and sheriff listened with rapt expressions; there were occasional sighs from the ladies, and grunts of approval from the men. Deeper and deeper did the spell become, recounting those days long ago—times all but forgotten now, but kept alive in his song. Inevitably, stanza gave way to stanza and the song moved to its end, and Thomas, singing for his king as he had rarely sung before, delivered the final lines:

1363

The seasons pass quickly in the realm of King Bran—
   As seasons of joye always do.
John and Will Scadlocke many children now owne
   And each have another past due.

Strong sons and fayre daughters to them and their wyves
    The Good Lord upon them has blest.
But the fairest and strongest and smartest who is,
    None of them e'er has guess'd.

And Rhiban the Hud now feasts in his hall,
    For marriéd now has he beene.
And summer has settled in clear, peaceful lands,
    For Mérian reigns as his queene.

But we see not the fryer who wedded them two,
    What has become him his luck?
Lo, newly installed in the bishopric there,
    Is one: Bishop Fryer Tuck.

1364

Good gentlefolk all, we have finished our laye—
    A song of brave Rhi Bran the Hud;
Taking only from others what never was theirs,
    He restoréd his land to the good.

But one final ride has our Rhiban to make,
    Before his and our paths shall part.
See, he has outlived his queene and his friends
    And bears he within a sadde heart.

He rides on his steede with a bow by his side,
    Much as he has done of olde.
His long hair is white and his eyesight is weak
    But he calls in a voice strong and bold:

Tuck

"Once again, O, my fine merrye men,
　　We shall in the greenwood meet,
And there we'll make our bowstrings twang—
　　A music for us, very sweet."

It is the ultimate QUEST
for the ultimate TREASURE.
Chasing a MAP tattooed on human SKIN,
across an OMNIVERSE of
intersecting realities, to unravel
the future of the FUTURE.

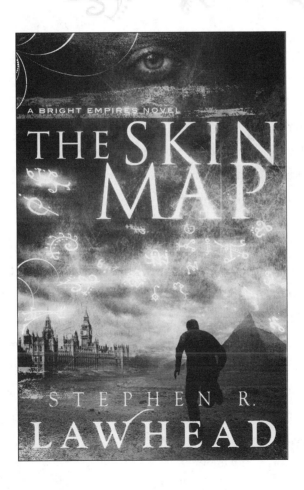

A BRIGHT EMPIRES NOVEL

THE SKIN MAP

STEPHEN R. LAWHEAD

EXCERPT FROM *THE SKIN MAP*,
BOOK I: THE BRIGHT EMPIRE SERIES

1308

Had he but known that before the day was over he would discover the hidden dimensions of the universe, Kit might have been better prepared. At least, he would have brought an umbrella.

Like most Londoners, Kit was a martyr to the daily travails of navigating a city whose complexities were legendary. He knew well the dangers even the most inconsequential foray could involve. Venturing out into the world beyond his doorstep was the urban equivalent of trial by combat and he armed himself as best he could. He had long ago learned his small patch of the great metropolitan sprawl; he knew where the things most needful for survival were to be found and how to get to them. He kept in his head a ready-reference library of street maps, bus routes, and time schedules. He had memorised the pertinent sections of the London Underground tube schematic; he knew the quickest ways to work, and from work to his favourite pubs, the grocers, the cinema, the park where he jogged.

Sadly, it was rarely enough.

This morning was a perfect case in point. Only minutes before, he had stepped out the door of his flat in Holloway on a jaunt to accompany his girlfriend on a long-promised shopping trip. Oblivious to the fact that he had already embarked on a journey of no return, he proceeded to the nearest tube station, flapped his Oyster card at the gate, stormed down the stairs as the train came rattling to the platform, and leapt aboard as the beeping doors began to close. He counted off the first two of the four stops to his destination and was just allowing himself to imagine that all was running according to plan when he was informed at the third stop that the line was closed ahead for routine maintenance.

"All passengers must change," crackled a voice through tinny loudspeakers. "This train is terminated."

Joining the grumbling pack, Kit found his way once again to street level, where a special bus had been provided for tube users to continue their journey—but which was artfully hidden at the far side of King's Cross station. The fact that it was Sunday, and that Tottenham Hotspur was playing Arsenal, had completely slipped his mind until he glimpsed the waiting bus and the queue of Tottenham fans stretching halfway down Euston Road. Unwilling to wait, he quickly devised an alternative plan for meeting Wilhelmina: just nip across the road and take the Northern Line from King's Cross to Moorgate, then take the train to Liverpool Street, change to the Central Line, and get off at Bethnal Green; from there it would be a quick bus ride up to Grove Road. A brisk walk through Victoria Park would bring him to Wilhelmina's place on Rutland Road. Easy peasy, he thought as he dived back into the Underground.

Once again, Kit fished his Oyster card from his pocket and waved it at the turnstile. This time, instead of the green arrow, the light on the pad flashed red. Aware of the foot traffic already piling into him from behind, he tapped the card against the sensor again and was awarded with the dreaded "Seek Assistance" display. Terrific. He sighed inwardly and began backing through the queue to the scorn and muttered abuse of his fellow travellers, most of whom were dressed in football jerseys of one kind or another. "Sorry," he grumbled, fighting his way through the press. "Excuse me. Terribly sorry."

He dashed for the nearest ticket booth and, after negotiating an obstacle course of barriers and railings, arrived to discover there was no one around. He rapped on the window and when that failed ran on to the next window where, after a vigorous pounding, he managed to rouse the attendant. "My Oyster card doesn't work," Kit explained.

"It's probably out of money," replied the agent.

"But I just topped it up a couple days ago. Can't you check it?"

The agent took the card and looked at it. He swiped it through a terminal beside the window. "Sorry, mate." He pushed the card back through the slot. "The computer is down."

"Okay, never mind," Kit relented. He started digging in his pockets. "I'll put five pounds on it."

"You can do it online," the agent informed him.

"But I'm here now," Kit pointed out, "in person."

"It's cheaper online."

"That is as may be," Kit agreed. "But I have to travel now—today."

"You can pay at a machine."

"Right," said Kit. Down on the platform below, he could hear the train clattering in and he hurried to the nearest ticket machine—which, after repeated attempts, refused to accept his five-pound note, spitting out the limp bill each time. The next machine along was for credit cards only, and the last of three was out of service. Kit ran back to the booth. "The ticket machine won't take my money," he said, sliding the fiver through the gap in the window. "Can you give me coin? Or another bill?"

The attendant regarded the crumpled bill. "Sorry."

"Sorry what?"

"Computer's down."

"But I can see the money there," Kit said, frustration mounting. He pointed through the window to a change machine cartridge stacked with rows of coins waiting to be dispensed. "Can't you just reach over and get some money?"

"We're not allowed to take money out of the machine."

"Why not?"

"It's automatic, and the comp—"

"I know, I know," grumped Kit, "the computer's down."

"Try one of the other windows."

"But there's nobody at the other windows."

The attendant gazed at him pityingly. "It's Sunday."

"Yeah, so?"

"Reduced service on Sunday."

"No kidding!" cried Kit. "Why do you even bother coming to work?"

The attendant shrugged. Directing his gaze past Kit, he called, "Next!"—although there was no one in line.

Accepting temporary defeat, Kit made his way back up to the street. There were numerous shops where he might have changed a five-pound note—if not for the fact that it was Sunday and all were either observing weekend hours or closed for the day. "Typical," sniffed Kit, and decided that it would be easier, and no doubt faster, just to walk the three or so miles to Wilhelmina's. With this thought in mind, he sailed off, dodging traffic and Sunday-morning pedestrians in the sincere belief that he could still reach Mina's on time. He proceeded along Pentonville Road, mapping out a route in his head as he went. He had gone but a few hundred paces when he began to experience the sinking feeling that he had become completely disoriented and was going the wrong way—something that had happened to him before around the no-man's-land of King's Cross. Realizing that he had to head north and west, he turned left onto Grafton Street, tooled along avoiding a barrage of roadwork, and quickly reached the next street north—an odd little lane called Stane Way.

So far, so good, he thought as he charged down the narrow walkway—really, nothing more than an alley providing service access for the shops on the parallel streets. After walking for two minutes, he started looking for the crossing street at the end. Two more minutes passed . . . He should have reached the end by now, shouldn't he?

Then it started to rain.

Kit picked up his speed as the rain poured into the alley from low, swirling clouds overhead. He hunched his shoulders, put his head down, and ran. A wind rose out of nowhere and whipped down the length of the blank brick canyon, driving the rain into his eyes.

He stopped.

Pulling his phone from his pocket, he flipped open the screen. No signal.

"Bloody useless," he muttered.

Drenched to the skin, water dripping from the ends of his hair and tip of his nose, he shoved the phone back into his pocket. Enough of this, he decided. Abort mission. He made a swift about-face and, shoes squelching with every step, headed back the way he had come.

Good news: the wind ceased almost at once and the rain dwindled away; the storm diminished as quickly as it had arisen.

Dodging one oily puddle after another, he jogged along and had almost regained the alley entrance at Grafton Street when he heard someone calling him—at least, he thought that is what he had heard. But with the spatter of rain from the eaves of the buildings round about, he could not be sure.

He slowed momentarily, and a few steps later he heard the call again—unmistakable this time: "Hello!" came the cry. "Wait!"

Keep moving, said the voice inside his head. As a general rule it kept him from getting tangled in the craziness of London's vagrant community. He glanced over his shoulder to see a white-haired man stumbling toward him out of the damp urban canyon. Where had he come from? Most likely a drunk who had been sleeping it off in a doorway. Roused by the storm, he had seen Kit and recognized an easy mark. Such was life; he prepared to be accosted.

"Sorry, mate," Kit called back over his shoulder as he turned away. "I'm skint."

"No! Wait!"

"No change. Sorry. Got to run."

"Cosimo, please."

That was all the vagrant said, but it welded Kit to the spot.

He turned and looked again at the beggar. Tall, and with a full head of thick silvery hair and a neatly trimmed goatee, he was dressed in charity-shop chic: simple white shirt, dark twill trousers, both sturdy, but well-worn. The fact that he stuffed the cuffs of his trousers into his high-top shoes and wore one of those old-timey greatcoats that had a little cape attached to the shoulders made him look like a character out of Sherlock Holmes.

"Look, do I know you?" asked Kit as the fellow hastened nearer.

"I should hope so, my boy," replied the stranger. "One would think a fellow would know his own great-grandfather."

Kit backed away a step.

"Sorry I'm late," continued the old man. "I had to make certain I wasn't followed. It took rather longer than I anticipated. I was beginning to fear I'd missed you altogether."

"Excuse me?"

"So, here we are. All's well that ends well, what?"

"Listen, mate," protested Kit. "I think you've got the wrong guy."

"What a joy it is to meet you at long last, my son," replied the old gentleman, offering his hand. "Pure joy. But of course, we haven't properly met. May I introduce myself? I am Cosimo Livingstone." He made a very slight bow.

1374

"Okay, so what's the joke?" demanded Kit.

"Oh, it is no joke," the old man assured him. "It's quite true."

"No—you're mistaken. I am Cosimo Livingstone," he insisted. "And anyway, how do you know my name?"

"Would you mind very much if we discussed this walking? We really should be moving along."

"This is nuts. I'm not going anywhere with you."

"Ah, well, I think you'll find that you don't have much choice."

"Not true."

"Sorry?"

"Listen, mate, I don't know how you got hold of my name, but you must have me mixed up with someone else," Kit said, hoping to sound far more composed than he actually felt at the moment. "I don't mean to be rude, but I don't know you and I'm not going anywhere with you."

"Fair enough," replied the stranger. "What would it take to change your mind?"

"Forget it," said Kit, turning away. "I'm out of here."

"What sort of proof would you like? Names, birth dates, family connections—that sort of thing?"

He started off. "I'm not listening."

"Your father is John. Your mother is Harriet. You were born in Weston-super-Mare, but your family soon moved to Manchester, where your father worked as a managerial something or other in the insurance trade and your mother was a school administrator. When you were twelve, your family upped sticks again and resettled in London. . . ."

Kit halted. He stood in the middle of the alley, wrestling with the twin sensations of alarm and disbelief. He turned around slowly.

The old man stood smiling at him. "How am I doing so far?"

Even in the uncertain light of the alley, the family resemblance was unmistakable—the strong nose, the heavy jaw and broad brow, the hair that rippled like waves from the forehead, the broad lips and dark eyes, just like his father's and obnoxious Uncle Leonard's. It was all of a basic design that Kit had seen repeated with greater or lesser variation in family members his entire life.

"Since university—Manchester, Media Studies, whatever that is—you have been working here and there, doing nothing of any real value—"

"Who are you?" demanded Kit. "How do you know these things?"

"But I've already told you," chuckled the old gentleman. "I am your great-grandfather."

"Oh, yeah? Would this be the great-grandfather who went down to the shops for a loaf of bread one morning and never came back?

1375

The same who abandoned a wife and three kids in Marylebone in 1893?"

"Dear me, you know about that, do you? Well, lamentably, yes. But it wasn't a loaf of bread; it was milk and sausages." The old man's gaze grew keen. "Tell me, what did *you* go out for this morning?"

Kit's mouth went dry.

"Hmm?" replied the stranger. "What was it? Tin of beans? Daily paper? This is how it always happens, don't you see?"

"No . . ." said Kit, feeling more unhinged by the second.

"It's a family proclivity, you might say. A talent." The older man took a step nearer. "Come with me."

"Why, in the name of everything that's holy, would I go anywhere with you?"

"Because, my dear boy, you are a lonely twenty-seven-year-old bachelor with a worthless education, a boring no-hope job, a stalled love life, and very few prospects for the improvement of your sad lot."

"How dare you! You don't know anything about me."

"But I know *everything* about you, old chap." The old man took another step closer. "I thought we had already established that."

"Yeah? What else?"

The elder gentleman sighed. "I know that you are an overworked drone in a soul-destroying cube farm where you have been passed over for promotion two times in the last nine months. The last time you don't know about because they didn't even bother telling you."

"I don't believe this."

"You spend too much time alone, too much time watching television, and too little time cultivating the inner man. You live in a squalid little flat in what is referred to as a no-go zone from which your friends, of whom you see less and less, have all fled for the suburbs long ago with wives and sprogs in tow. You are exceedingly unlucky in love, having invested years in a romantic relationship which, as you know only too well, is neither romantic nor much of a relationship. In short, you have all the social prospects of a garden gnome."

Kit had to admit that except for the low crack about his love life, the old geezer was remarkably close to the mark.

"Is that enough?"

"Who are you?"

"I'm the man who has come to rescue you from a life of quiet desperation and regret." He smiled again. "Come, my boy. Let's sit down over a cup of coffee and discuss the matter like gentlemen. I've gone to a very great deal of trouble to find you. At the very least, you could spare me a few minutes out of your busy life."

Kit hesitated.

"Cup of coffee—thirty minutes. What could it hurt?"

Trepidation and curiosity wrestled one another for a moment. Curiosity won. "Okay," he relented. "Twenty minutes."

The two started walking toward the street. "I've got to call my girlfriend and tell her I'll be a little late," Kit said, pulling out his phone. He flipped it open and pressed the speed-dial key for Mina's number. When nothing happened, he glanced at the screen to see the "Network Not Connected" message blinking at him. He waved the phone in the air, then looked again. Still no tiny bars indicating a signal.

"Not working?" asked the older man, watching him with a bemused expression.

"Must be the buildings," mumbled Kit, indicating the close brick walls on either hand. "Blocking the signal."

"No doubt."

They continued on, and upon approaching the end of the alley, Kit

1377

thought he heard a sound at once so familiar, and yet so strange, it took him a full two seconds to place it. Children laughing? No, not children. Seagulls.

He had little time to wonder about this, for at that moment they stepped from the dim alleyway and into the most dazzling and unusual landscape Kit had ever seen.

Coming September 2011

A Bright Empires Novel
Quest the Second

THE
BONE HOUSE

the dragon king trilogy

Stephen R. Lawhead's best-selling trilogy—relaunched for a new generation of young adult readers.

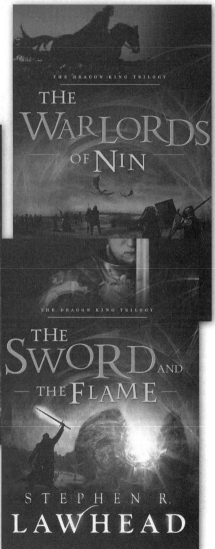

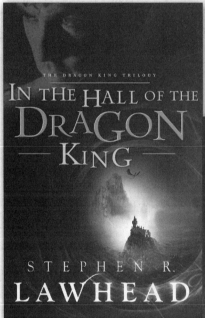

THE SONG OF ALBION TRILOGY

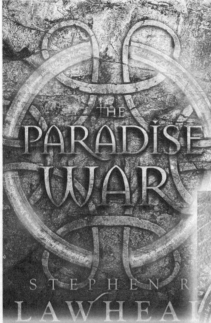

Picture a world intricately entwined with our own yet separate, pulsing with the raw energy and vivid color of Celtic myth come to life.

❧ ABOUT THE AUTHOR ❧

STEPHEN R. LAWHEAD is an internationally acclaimed author of mythic history and imaginative fiction. His novels include the King Raven trilogy, the Song of Albion trilogy, the Dragon King trilogy, and the Pendragon Cycle series. Lawhead makes his home in Oxford, England, with his wife.

visit StephenLawhead.com